CLAUDE DUVAL,

THE

DASHING HIGHWAYMAN

No. 1.

CHAPTER I.

THE MARRIAGE FEAST.—THE UNBIDDEN GUEST.—THE JEWELS.—A DANCE ON
THE GREEN.—AN UNEXPECTED ARRIVAL.

"THE harvest moon! How bright and beautiful it gilds yon distant vale; and see, the little streamlet, in the hollow, is a sheet of molten gold. There's not a tree—a flower—a blade of grass, that is not tinctured by the wondrous beauty of the radiant orb. More wine! more wine. We can look at the moon and watch the wedding party, and drink a health to the bright-eyed bride yet, before the bells peal out the news of the——"

Before the speaker could complete the sentence, a burst of melody from the bells of old Hampton Church made the air vocal with gleesome sounds. The scene was in good truth a joyous one. He who had spoken so bravely and enthusiastically of the harvest moon, was one of a group of some twenty persons of both sexes, who stood upon a raised terrace at the back of one of those pleasure taverns which are so popular in the neighbourhood of London. Behind them was a house that rather merited the name of a mansion, although, amid all its magnificence, the style of architecture was decidedly cottage. The turrets—pinnacles—deep embayed windows, and general aspect of one portion of the building, bespoke the Gothic taste. Indeed, to look at the incongruous pile, it would seem as though some half-score of cottages of gentility had been by some process suddenly engrafted up on an old baronial hall. The apartment immediately behind the speakers, the windows of which all opened wide on to the terrace we have mentioned, was one of a size and appointments rarely to be met with. A feast! a marriage feast! was spread in this hall, for a hall it was, rich in all the emblazonry of Gothic taste. The ceiling was festooned with flowers. The mirrors were nearly hidden by the rich floral gifts of a glorious autumn. The fruits of all ages and of all climes were piled up on the table in receptacles of massive silver. Richly embossed covers yet kept the curious eye from the secrets of the rare and dainty dishes that were beneath them. Wine! nothing as yet but wine, had begun to flow freely at that festive board upon the occasion of the marriage of the owner of all the taste and of all the wealth that met the eye on every hand. But if at the back of that terrace, with its slim marble balustrades, and its statues, and its vases, and its flowers, there were much of art to attract the attention and to fill the imagination with agreeable associations, in what language shall we paint the glorious space of hill and vale that nature had spread out in front of it? By successions of marble steps you might descend from the terrace to the gardens, and from the gardens you might wander into the meadows—from the meadows to the pleasant hills, and to the little village of Hampton, from the spire of whose humble and unpretending little church came that gush of melody which had so quickly interrupted the speaker, who, from the style of his discourse, appeared to enter so heart and soul into the scene. And all this beauty of nature and of art was lighted by the sweet harvest moon, that slowly topped a hill and looked down upon the green earth, as though there had never been upon its surface aught but love and virtue.

"Truly," cried another of the throng upon the balcony, which consisted for the most part of young men. "Truly, the old bells make a merry din. Upon my faith I did not think there was so much life in them."

"A toast—a toast!" cried another.

"Have with you then," cried the whole party. "Have with you, and let it be a bumper, whatever it is."

"Ay, a bumper! a bumper! Now, friends all; let us drink to many a jovial meeting beneath this roof, even though Sir Felix Moffat be going to give it a young mistress."

"A young mistress is better than an old one," cried another of the somewhat disorderly assemblage. "She will not object to a little harmless merriment, I'll be bound, and so that we keep the flavour of our cigars from the drawing-room, there will be no fault found."

"Ha! ha! ha!"

"The toast! the toast! Let us have the toast! Every glass is charged."

"Then, here's health, long life, and toleration to Lady Felix Moffat."

"Hold!" cried a voice.

There was something in the tone and manner of the pronunciation of the word that suspended every man's uplifted glass, and all eyes were directed to one of the open windows, in the centre of which stood a tall figure, that in the dim and dusky twilight, particularly as its back was towards the bright and glowing moon, could only be so far distinguished as to be seen to be the form of a man. During the stillness that prevailed, for a space of time that might have been sufficient for one to count six in, slowly the church bells rang clearly and distinctly, and then came a sudden jarring sound, and the gay strain abruptly ceased.

"Lights! lights!" cried one.

The sound of that one voice seemed to have a magic in its tones, for it at once awakened to animation every person there present, and the cry for lights came from every throat. The stranger who had cried "hold" still preseved his same attitude in the window, where he looked like some dim portrait set in as dim a frame.

"Lights! lights!"

The cry was raised again, and in the course of a few moments a pair of folding doors opened at the farther extremity of the room, and several servants appeared, bearing silver candelabra, in which there were wax lights.

"The bells have stopped," said a voice.

"Ay," cried another, "one of them has broken down, and spoiled the whole set. I thought the old belfry would not stand such a peal."

"It's ominous!" said a third.

"Very!" said the stranger at the window, who, now that the lights, having recovered from the flaring occasioned by their passage to the room, began to cast a steady glare around them, advanced into the centre of the apartment. All eyes were naturally bent upon him. The stranger could well bear that scrutiny. Tall, and slim of figure, with remarkably small feet, and the most feminine-looking hands that could at all look manly, he stood in an attitude that a sculptor might have sighed in vain to animate his marble with—so fine, so airy, and so graceful was it. His eyes were of the dark and sparkling hazel which is so rarely to be met with, and his long silken lashes might have been a proud appendage for a court beauty. His coal black hair, instead of being, according to the barbarous fashion of the time, confined in a peruke, flowed down his back and shoulders in massive folds rather than curls. His dress was a rich one, and might well have graced a wedding guest. At his side hung a sword, with a jewelled hilt, but the sparkle of its gems was nothing to be compared to the brilliancy of the rings that adorned his fingers, and the diamond that held together the folds of a long laced cravat. The age of this apparition, for such to the bewildered guests he almost seemed to be, of manly grace, did not appear to be above twenty-two.

"Gentlemen,' he said, slightly bowing, "accept my apologies for being rather late at these festivities."

No one could help returning the salute.

"The fact is," said the stranger, in the most fascinating manner possible, "a little affair on the road detained me."

He took from his pocket a richly-chased gold repeater, and made it strike the hour.

"Seven!—Really, gentlemen, you will hardly forgive me for being a whole hour behind my time. But business must be attended to."

The idea of the elegant and sumptuously-dressed personage before them having anything to do with business, was too out-of-the-way, and raised a smile upon the lips of some of the party. One only had the boldness to say—

" Sir, I regret I have not the pleasure of knowing you."

" And so do I, sir, from my soul," said the stranger.

This was a sort of answer, coming from such a personage, too, that it was by no means an easy matter to make a rejoinder to. The young man who had spoken only bit his lip and was silent.

" A fragrant and delightful evening," said the stranger, taking from his pocket a snuff-box set with brilliants, and slightly smelling it.

" That may be, sir," said he whose toast and sentiment had been so singularly interrupted. " That may be, sir; but perhaps you will allow me, for my own private satisfaction, to ask you who you are?"

" Certainly, sir, certainly."

" Well, sir ?"

" Extremely well, I thank you. I never felt better in all my life."

The stranger, with an easy grace, reclined upon one of the gorgeous couches with which the apartment was amply provided. A general titter ran through the room at the expense of the discomfited toast-proposer, who had evidently met with one by far his superior in badinage, and in the science of repartee.

" Sir," he said " this shall not suffice; I am as fond of a joke as any man, but you interrupted my toast, and for that I insist upon a reason."

" Insist! My dear sir, you shall have one without the necessity of insisting at all upon it. What was your toast, now ?"

" The health of Lady Felix Moffat."

" Ah, there it is. There is no Lady Moffat. Allow me to put a question or two to you, sir, in all courtesy ?"

" Say on, sir."

" Well, is it not true that Sir Felix Moffat is a Catholic?"

" Quite true, sir."

" Then, sir, is not Mary Dundas, whom he is about to do the high honour of calling his, a Protestant ?"

" It is so."

" Very well. If my information respecting these espousals be correct, the parties, in order to satisfy the scruples upon both sides, are to be married according to the forms of both churches. At the little church yonder, by the Protestant minister, and at the Catholic chapel attached to this house, by the Catholic priest."

" You are right, sir."

" 'Tis well. I hope, then, before we talk of Lady Moffat, we can afford to wait till both the ceremonies are performed, which appear to be thought necessary to make her such."

" Oh, a mere quibble."

" Indeed, sir!—there's many a slip between the cup and lip."

" Well, sir, we will not quarrel about such a trifle. Let the toast be deferred until the ceremony is over. Then will you pledge it ?"

" With all my heart, sir."

" Agreed."

" And as you wished to know how I came here, I can only inform you that I am here upon the urgent request of him who has most right to be present at the nuptials of Mary Dundas."

" That is sufficient, sir. Of course you mean the bridegroom ?"

" Of course I do, sir."

A loud hurrah! now proclaimed the arrival of the wedding party within the gates of the Oaks, as the little estate was called, which could boast of a mansion of such beauty and character.

" They come !" cried every voice. " They come !"

At this moment an individual made his appearance up the steps from the garden to the terrace, and thence into the room. This was no other than the parish beadle of Hampton, who, in full official costume, had run on before, and the moment he reached one of the windows, he cried—

"Gentlemen and ladies—leastways, ladies and gentlemen, Sir Felix has giv'd me a guinea to run and denounce to you all—Oh—oh—only wait till I catches my breath, and I'll denounce it."

"What's the matter?—What's the matter?" cried everybody.

"Ladies and gentlemen, Sir Muffin—no—no I don't mean that, Sir Felix has giv'd me a guinea."

"You said that before, stupid," said one.

The beadle's cheeks inflated, and he looked from one to the other in surprise and wrath, as he cried—

"Stupid!—stupid! Me stupid! Oh—oh, and after what's here!"

He tapped his head significantly to intimate that the quantity of brains therein contained ought at once to refute the allegation.

"Stupid! Well arter that, gentlemen, I can only say, I wonder all the candles don't burn blue."

"Never mind," said another, "you tell us what you came to announce."

"Denounce, if you please, sir. Mind your pernunciwation. What I come to say is, that the Rev. Mr. Nicholas Flumerly didn't come to the church, and that the wedding ain't a wedding."

"Not a wedding? Why, we heard the bells."

"Very true, but the ringers ringed 'em without being told—then one on 'em breaks down; but as to the wedding not being a wedding, that ain't neither here nor there, for the ceremony in the Catholic sort of way is to be done first, and then when the Rev. Mr. Nicholas Flumerly does come, they will go back to the church and finish off, you see, gentlemen; but what Sir Felix wanted me all for to say to you all was, not to make no remarks to the wirgin bride about it."

"Oh, certainly not—certainly not."

This communication, with its caution, was not made a whit too soon, if it were intended to be effective, for the bridal was seen approaching the terrace at the moment that the beadle ceased to speak. The first couple that put in an appearance in the room, and came within the full blaze of its numerous wax-lights, consisted of a superannuated old beau, whose attire was a ludicrous burlesque upon the fashion of the day, and a female of the most awful dimensions. The female—we wish we could call her lady—was one blaze of satins and jewels, and the turban upon her head was a most triumphant structure indeed. This was no other than Mrs. Dundas, the mother of Mary, who was to be the bride of Sir Felix. The elderly beau, upon whose arm she leant, was a certain Major Lumbley, of whom more anon. Mrs. Dundas was speaking loudly and rapidly, partly addressing her discourse to those who followed her, and who consisted of some ladies and gentlemen, of no particular mark or likelihood, and partly to the occupants of the large room, towards which the whole of the party seemed to be making its way as quickly as possible.

"It's not the least consequence," cried Mrs. Dundas. "Of course everything will go on in a comfortable, easy way, and it will be quite time enough when Dr. Flumerly does come to go back to the church, and do that part of the wedding There's no harm done."

All this was intended to polish over the flaw in the proceedings contingent upon the non-arrival of the Protestant divine at the little church, and everybody understood it as such. Almost immediately, now, all eyes were fixed upon the bride and bridegroom as they entered the room together. A more remarkable contrast than they presented could not have been found. Sir Felix Moffat was a man about fifty years of age, but a long life of dissipation had left its traces upon his form and face. He looked, in fact, just what he was, an old debauchee. He was attired in a splendid suit of blue velvet, and upon his shrivelled fingers he wore jewels that would have bought a German principality. And now let us glance upon the fair young creature by his side, whose arm hung, rather than clasped his. This was Mary Dundas. Her age was sixteen only, and yet, by the intrigues of one who should have been her next friend under God, she was brought to the sacrifice—to be the victim of such a man as Sir Felix. The beauty of

Mary was of that character which can scarcely be described; it was rather the beauty of expression than of features, and yet a more fascinating creature was never fashioned. Her hair was a glossy auburn, her eyes blue, her complexion purity itself. She shuddered as she entered the room, in which now about forty people were collected.

"All's right," said Mrs. Dundas. "The first marriage can take place here, and by then, no doubt, the Rev. Dr. Flumerly will have arrived. How are you, my chick?"

"Sir Felix," said a servant, "the Catholic priest, Father Loftus, has not come yet."

CHAPTER II.

THE FIGHT.—A CHANGE OF HANDS.—OFF AND AWAY.—THE HIGHWAYMAN'S BRIDE.—LOVE AND DESPAIR.

SIR FELIX MOFFAT dropped the fair hand that he had been holding in his own, and drew himself bolt upright, and cried—

"What is the meaning of all this? Can we get no clergyman, Catholic or Protestant, to do his duty?"

There was a slight inclination to laugh upon the part of the younger portion of the company. The released Mary sunk upon a chair, the deep arms and high back of which shielded her from most of the company, and wept alone.

"One would think," added Sir Felix, speaking with bitterness. "One would think, that if one was not aware that that Claude Duval had been shot through the head by a gentleman last night, that he had stopped both the Reverend gentlemen."

"Claude Duval shot?" said several.

"Yes," added Sir Felix. "He has kept the neighbourhood in terror for some time, but I have been credibly informed to-day that last night he was shot by one whom he tried to stop."

"Did he die easy, sir?" said the stranger, who had before excited the curiosity of Sir Felix's guests.

"Sir?" said Sir Felix, grandly.

"I ask, did he die easy?"

"Sir, I neither know nor care whether highwaymen die easy or uneasy. I only know that I have been uncommonly uneasy since he robbed me of my gold repeater, and my snuff-box set with brilliants, only last week, in my own park. Yes, in my own park, sir!"

"Uncommonly impudent that," said the stranger.

"Yes, sir, and I can truly say that I have not been so vexed since by anything as by the non-appearance of the two clergymen, whose good offices were required to unite me to the loveliest and most amiable of her sex."

The old *roue* leered offensively upon Mary, and then he muttered to himself—

"I suppose this puppy has been invited by Mrs. Dundas, my troublesome mother-in-law that is to be."

Mrs. Dundas looked at the stranger through her eye-glass, and muttered—

"I wonder at Sir Felix asking so young and good-looking a man here to-day."

Mrs. Dundas then took Sir Felix aside, and, laying her hand upon his arm, she said—

"My dear Sir Felix, be assured that all will be well, and that the less you show any sort of disappointment, the better. Only recollect the trouble I have had in breaking down the spirit of that girl."

She pointed to Mary.

"Never mind, madam," said Sir Felix, coarsely and sarcastically. "You shall have your thousand pounds a year for the job."

Mrs. Dundas bit her lip, and then said—

"Well, well, make as much bustle as you can and get your dinner over. The wedding can be done after that, when both the parsons will, I dare say, be in the way."

During this brief dialogue, the mysterious stranger sauntered up to the chair in which Mary sat, and as he passed it, he dropped a small ring in her lap. The moment her eyes fell upon it, she uttered a piercing shriek, and then she cried—

"Not dead—not dead!"

There was a general scene of confusion in the banqueting room; on the instant Mrs. Dundas made her way to Mary, and with angry gestures, cried—

"What is this—what is the meaning of this childness?"

"Not dead! Not dead!" was all that Mary replied, as she clutched the ring tightly. "Not dead—not dead!"

"What does she mean?" said Sir Felix.

"Seize that man," said one of the guests. It was the one who had been interrupted in his toast by the stranger, and who had from that time kept an observant eye upon him. "Seize that man; I saw him make some communication to the bride."

"Did you, sir?" said the stranger, stepping a pace back.

"Ay, did I. Do you know him, Sir Felix?"

"Not I."

"Nor you, Mrs. Dundas?"

"Gracious Heaven, no!"

"Then he is an intruder here. Perhaps a—

"Beware!" said the stranger, as he stepped nearer to the window at which he had entered. "Beware, sir, how you finish a sentence with a word you may find it best to swallow again, and yet necessary to do so. I know I am an unbidden guest. I never avowed myself aught else."

"Speak to *me*," cried Mary, rising, "Speak to *me*, be you whom you may, and tell me he is not dead."

"He lives!"

"Oh, joy, joy! Then I say to all here, that I am sold to this man, whom I abhor, and to whom, although presented by my mother, and assured of the death of one I truly loved, I believed I never should have found strength in the presence of God to pledge my faith to."

"This is madness!" said Sir Felix.

"It is villany!" said the mother; and then pointing to the stranger, she added,

"Look, girl, if you have eyes. Yon man is a head taller than the drowned sailor you fancied loved you."

"Yes, yes," added Mary, as though answering her own thoughts rather than anything another said to her. "Yes, I am strong now. They told me he was dead—that the ring and he to whom I gave it as a token of my love, had gone together to the depths of the ocean; but it is not so."

"It is not so!" cried the stranger, with a voice that sounded through the apartment like the sound of a trumpet. "It is not so."

"My heart told me it was not; but my mother wrung from me a slow consent to give my life, for my life it would have been, that she might pass her remaining years in luxury. It was a cheat. He lives! he lives!"

"Yes," said the stranger. "He lives and loves as he ever loved. I know him, and a better—a truer heart never yet beat in human bosom than in that of Gilbert Rushton."

"Yes," shrieked Mary, with hysterical joy. "That is his name!" and then, as if to deprecate any scorn at the mention of it in such a place, she drew herself up proudly, and added—"I love him!"

By this time several of Sir Felix Moffat's dissolute guests, finding that the stranger was the cause of the breaking up of the feast to which they had looked forward with so much satisfaction, drew their swords, and made a rush in a body towards him, to make him prisoner. That individual, however, was not so easily to be thrown off his guard. The bright blade he wore by his side performed a circle round him like a flash of light, and two of his foes shrank back bleeding.

"Down with him! Down with him!" cried those who were in the back ground. Ladies fainted. Mrs. Dundas screamed and clung to Sir Felix, as though her amnesty were compromised in the grasp by which she held him. Some of the rich ornaments of the room were upset and broken, and by the din of voices it would seem as if every one had something to say.

It was in the midst of this tumult that Mary rushed between the swords of the combatants, and clung to the stranger's left arm, exclaiming—

"Take me to him! You tell me that he lives, and I will trust to you. Take me to him. Let us go—oh, let us go at once. What arm will dare to stay us? He lives, you say, my Gilbert?"

"I swear it, lady, by the God above us."

"Now for it!" cried one of the stranger's opponents, and as he spoke he made a rush forward. At the same instant Mary cried—

"They attack you from the terrace! Turn and save yourself."

The stranger plunged his hand into his breast, and drew forth a pistol, and handed it to Mary, saying—

"Dare you frighten them with this?"

"Oh, yes—yes."

Still upon her knees and grasping the arm of her defender, she presented the weapon at two lackeys who had been ordered to go round and seize the stranger from behind. They shrank back aghast. The swordsman who had sought to profit by the opportunity of the attack from the rear had dashed forward, and the blades of the weapons borne by him and the stranger clashed together.

"Beware," said the latter. "Tamper with me another moment, and your death be on your own head.

"Yield, robber, for I take you to be no better."

At this moment he made a furious thrust at the breast of the stranger, who easily parried it, but by so doing, the sword's point touched Mary on the arm, inflicting a slight wound. She uttered a cry, and before the echo of it could die away, there leapt through the open window a young man in a slight undress naval uniform. He had a cutlass in his hand, and with one blow he sent the aggressor of the stranger and of Mary senseless and bleeding to the floor.

"Well done, Gilbert," said the stranger. "Are the horses quite ready?"

"Quite."

"Gilbert—my Gilbert!" screamed Mary, and in another moment she was in his arms.

"Flee," said the stranger, "I will follow."

"No—no," said Mary. "Come with us—they will kill you! Come with u now."

"Fear nothing," he replied in a voice that sounded like a strain of music "Fear nothing, all will be well. I will follow directly. Flee, Gilbert, flee, for well I know there are those here who would take your life."

The young sailor caught Mary in his arms, and as though her weight were nothing, he dashed down the steps of the terrace into the garden; in his right hand he still waved his cutlass, crying—

"Let any one who may be weary of his life stop me and mine!"

"Who are you? Fiend! monster! speak! Give me a name that I may append my maledictions to," cried Sir Felix, still writhing in the grasp of Mrs. Dundas. "I will have you prosecuted—transported—hanged. I will spend thousands upon you, but I will have my revenge upon you. Speak, who are you? Will none seize him?"

No one seemed exactly disposed to risk a personal encounter with a man who possessed such prowess, but a pistol was fired at him. All looked to see the effect;

but there he stood as before, one foot on the terrace, and one upon the window-lead.

"A bad shot," he said. "I shall not forget who fired it; and now, Sir Felix Moffat, you want to know who I am?"

"I do—I do, villain!"

"Hold, Sir Felix. I am no friend of yours, so do not call me villain. First let me explain to you the unavoidable absence of your two clergymen. You know the little wood called Oak Copse close at hand? In that wood are two gigantic elms. The protestant divine is tied to one, and the catholic divine to the other."

"Irreverent man!"

"Ha! ha! 'tis well for the hoary reprobate, who would sacrifice to his base, decaying passions, youth and innocence and beauty, such as Mary's, to talk of reverence. Sir Felix, I wish you and all your goodly company good-night."

"Who are you?" cried a dozen voices.

"Who am I? Who should I be but Claude Duval? Ha! ha! ha! A prize for him who can catch me. Ladies, I am your very humble servant. I admire and salute all, and would marry you all if there were not an absurd law against bigamy. Adieu! Off and away!"

A rush was made in the direction of the terrace, but the only effect it had was to upset the table upon which all the lights were placed, and the consequence was, that in the darkness most of the guests sprawled amid the fragments of the marriage feast. In the confusion, nothing could be easier than the escape of the renowned Claude Duval. Hastily descending the terrace-steps, he looked anxiously about him by the light of the harvest moon for his young friends, but he could not see them, and he was constrained to call upon them aloud.

"Gilbert—Gilbert!"

"It is our friend," he heard a voice say, and he knew the voice to belong to the fair Mary.

"Yes," said Gilbert. "This way—this way."

Both Gilbert and Mary emerged from the shelter of a little copse of laurels, leading three horses, and they testified the greatest pleasure at the sight of Claude Duval.

"Oh, how shall I thank you?" said Mary.

"By mounting and fleeing from this spot at once. Remember, at your age, that your mother has a legal power over you, which she will not fail to exert, if once she can find an opportunity. A panic just now possesses those who would pursue you; but that will pass away."

"It will," said Gilbert, "and the pirates are too many for us. Come, my Mary, let us be off."

They all three mounted, and Claude, casting only one glance behind him, then took the lead, and, at a canter, went through the gardens. So sudden—so full of daring and hardihood had been the whole of the proceeding, that the guests in the large hall were too thunderstricken to take the advantage one would have supposed they might and ought to have taken of their numbers. And when they did recover from that stun, as it were, of the intellect, of what avail was a pursuit of three persons mounted upon three of the fleetest steeds England could produce? We may leave Sir Felix Moffat to settle his own affairs with Mrs. Dundas, and to make such excuses as he may think tangible to his friends and guests whom he had gathered together to be witnesses to a very different scene than the one that had evidently taken place within his lordly residence. Rage, mortification, revenge, disappointment, all were struggling in his heart for mastery, and finally, unable to control or gratify his feelings, he fell into a partial swoon upon the gorgeous carpet of that banqueting-room, which exhibited now such a scene of confusion. This was probably the only circumstance that could very well have freed him from the importunities of Mrs. Dundas, who stuck to him with a pertinacity that could only belong to the delicate nerves of a fat old lady who would sell her child to an old roue for a £1000 a year. Some of the domestics had hastily got horses from the stables, and with a great show of zeal, if not with much inclination in reality for the job, they professed their readiness to pursue the fugitives. It was not until Mrs. Dundas said, " I will give fifty pounds to whoever brings back my daughter," that ony of them really started upon the errand. That was a stimulant to exertion, that for a time led them on in the hazardous and uncertain chase.

CHAPTER III.

A LITTLE EXPLANATION.—CLAUDE'S COTTAGE.—THE WAYS AND MEANS.—A CARRIAGE LADY.

WE return to the fugitives. The whole scene that had taken place was, to Mary's apprehension, so like a dream, that she had ridden some miles from the " Oaks" before she could really venture to tell herself that it must be real. The road, after passing the immediate garden ground of the Oaks, skirted some meadows —or rather, we ought to say, that this was the road which the bold and adventurous Claude Duval chose to make for the occasion, for road it was not in reality. The fact was, that he had carefully considered the spot, and all its capabilities for advance and retreat, before he had conceived the enterprise, and he had taken care that no great impediment was in the way. A large ornamental gate at the end of the garden opened upon a little paddock that went by the name of The Shield, probably from the fact of its shielding the flower-garden from the impious gaze of any chance passengers from the meadows beyond, through which there were numerous footpaths. Across this shield, then, Claude led the way, every now and then looking back to see that all was well, and speaking a few words of encouragemene to his companions in the rear. There was another gate, but that was open ; Claud. Duval had propped it into that condition with a large stone some hours previously, and after they had passed through that, they were fairly in the open meadows, Claude paused for a moment.

"Let us listen," he said. "If there be no pursuit now, we need not harass Mary by a more hasty ride than is necessary. Do you hear anything, Gilbert ?"

The young sailor listened, but no sound came upon his ears. "No," he said, "all is still."

" I think so, likewise. Of course, pursuit there will be, but they have not yet sufficiently recovered from their panic to set about it ; and now tell me in which you would wish to go ?"

"; To London, where Mary and I can be united in those bonds that no one can tear asunder."

" Then to London be it."

"You consent, my Mary ?" whispered the young sailor to the still half insensible girl; all she understood was that he who was her heart's treasure asked her something, and she replied to him at once.

"Save me, Gilbert ! save me! anything, so that I am with you ; I will meet any danger, only save me from the horrors of calling that man by the name of husband."

" Enough," said Gilbert, " let us push on."

" This way," cried Claude, "this way."

The dashing highwayman, who so well became and justified his name, led them along two meadows, keeping close to the hedge, but upon emerging into a third, he rode completely across it, and pointing a little before him, he said—

" This is the high road to London."

In another moment, the horses having cleared a trifling obstruction in the shape of a newly planted privet-hedge, they all stood in the high road. It was planted upon each side by tall elms, through which the beams of the moon came straggling with great beauty, falling upon the roadway in speckled masses that looked alive as the shadows of the leaves of the tall trees moved in unison with the light and balmly air that agitated the umbrageous boughs.

"There, my friend—my true friend," said the young sailor, "I need trespass no longer on your kindness."

"Nay, I will see you safer than you are now. You know not the power, in these litttle country places, of such men as Sir Felix Moffat. Partly because they dread his vengeance, and partly for the fact that they expect his charity, most of the country people are willing and ready to commit any sort of iniquity that he or his agents may choose to dictate to them. Believe me, that the old principle of serfdom exists to a large extent yet in the country parts of free England."

By this time Mary had sufficiently recovered to be able to view her situation in a more calm and rational light than she had yet been enabled to do, and when the first joy of having escaped the obnoxious nuptials to which her tardy consent had been given was over, she burst into a flood of tears.

"My Mary," said Gilbert, "do not weep now that you have escaped."

"No—no!"

"Well, then, dear one—"

"Pardon me," said Claude, as he laid his hand upon the arm of the young sailor, "pardon me if I ask you to let those tears flow awhile without check or question; Mary will recover from this natural burst of feeling quickly, and be more herself."

"Thank you," said Gilbert, "you seem to understand the ways of women folks."

"I ought to do so," said Claude, with a smile.

In a few moments Mary's tears ceased, and turning to Gilbert, she said—

"Indeed—indeed, Gilbert, I thought that you were dead. The tale of the loss of your ship was proved to me, and all seemed so exact and circumstantial—"

"Pshaw, Mary! Never say another word about that. They made you believe I was at the bottom of the sea, and then, in your despair, you did not care what became of yourself, but yielded to your mother."

"I did—I did."

"Come, come, my darling, don't speak in that desponding sort of way; all will be well yet. You see, the old ship that I went out in did go down on the coast of Africa, dragging all hands into the deep with its old timbers, but I had had the luck to change out of her before that, you see."

"I ought not to have consented, Gilbert."

"To what?"

"To the unnatural marriage proposed by my mother."

"I don't know that, dear. When once you thought I was gone, it was rather a natural thing for you not to care much what became of you, and so you got tortured with saying yes to anything that you detested with all your heart."

"Yes, Gilbert, yes; oh, how good you are to forgive me!"

"Forgive you? May I sink the first craft I put foot into, if I don't love you more than ever."

"Hark!" said Claude.

"What is it?" said the young sailor; "pirates on our lee?"

"Gunners, I'm afraid. Do you hear nothing?"

"I am foolish at listening to land noises. But I think I hear the sound of horses' feet upon the hard road, for all that; and if it be any one who wishes to interfere with me, I think they will find it a harder road than is at all agreeable."

"This way," said Claude. "Come under the shadow of the old elms. This way. It may, after all, only be some traveller, and if so, he will pass us at once."

It was easy to hide in the deep shadow, close to the bank, of the old trees—that is to say, if no one bent more than a passing glance upon the road; and as our friends accordingly so bestowed themselves, in a few moments a horseman came on at a good round trot, and to the surprise of Claude and his friends, he, the horseman, appeared to be enjoying a conversation with himself.

"To London they will go," said a voice, "and if once we get ahead of them, and rouse the police, it will be all right."

"Yes," said another voice, "and then the fifty pounds will be ours."

It was evident now that the horse carried double, and just as it was passing, Claude called out in a loud voice—

"Help! help!"

The man who sat foremost on the horse pulled up as he heard the cry, and said, in a voice not destitute of apprehension in its tones—

"What is it?   Who calls for help?"

"I," said Claude.   "Only stop a moment, I want to get rid of two rogues, do you know; I'll make it worth your while, gentlemen, to stop a moment."

He dashed out from among the deep shadows, and laid his hand upon the bridle of their horse, and then he added—

"I have them!"

"Hands off!" said the foremost rider, "hands off.   Do not delay us.   We have nothing about us, if you be a highwayman."

Claude clapped the muzzle of a pistol to the forehead of the speaker, and said, in a calm, quiet tone—

"Dismount."

He rolled to the ground in a moment, crying, "Murder!" which so alarmed the other, that he followed his example.   A slash with a small riding whip he carried, given with all the force he was master of, sent the horse off at full gallop, to the astonishment of the two men.

"Now, my lads," said Claude, "I'm only hammering the flints of my pistol a little, so if you like, while I am about that little job, you can run—for whether you do or not, I intend to shoot you.   I'm bound to practise upon everybody I meet riding double after sunset, you see; so——"

With a roar of fright the two men scampered off.   Claude fired one shot after them, but he took care it should fly above their heads, and then, laughing, he returned to Gilbert and Mary, saying—

"The pursuit is stopped, I think.   Those two fellows would have roused the police against us, but it is all over now.   Let us come on at once, my friends.   It is but a sharp hour's ride to London, after all."

They all started forward at a rapid pace until they came to a rather steep hill, when Claude, who was in advance, set the example of walking his horse up hill.   Mary and Gilbert being a little in the rear, the former took the opportunity of saying to the latter—

"Who is this good and valiant friend who has done you such good service, Gilbert?"

"Humph!" said the young sailor, "if I were to be run up to the yard-arm for it, Mary, I could not tell you."

"Not tell me?   And why not, Gilbert?"

"For the best of all possible reasons, my darling, and that is—that I don't know!"

It will be recollected, that before Claude made the astounding declaration from the steps of the terrace of who he was, Gilbert and Mary had reached the garden, and although they had heard him say something in a loud voice, they were not sufficiently near to catch what it was.   No doubt, too, they were too intensely interested in each other to pay much attention to extraneous words.

"But you don't really mean to say, Gilbert, that this gentleman is a stranger to you?"

"Indeed I do, although I only hope I shall know such a noble fellow as long as I live.   I'll tell you how I came to know anything of him."

"Do, Gilbert, do."

"I only landed at Sheerness yesterday, and upon making inquiry about you, I, of course, found out you were living with your mother about this place.   It took me the whole day, though, to get the news, and then this morning off I started to you, for, you see, then I knew not a word of this marriage affair, or that you had been imposed upon with any notion of my death."

"Yes, Gilbert, yes—go on."

"Well, when I got about a couple of miles from here, I went into a sort of inn to rest myself, and there, for the first time, I learnt that Mary Dundas was to be the bride of Sir Felix Moffat."

"Oh, horror!—horror!"

"It was horror to me, Mary. For a time it almost took away my senses, and I sat in a little kind of arbour in the garden of the old inn, with my head upon my hands as nearly mad as any christian could very well be."

"My poor Gilbert!"

"I thought over all our old affections, Mary, and how I had loved you since you were a little wild chit of a girl, running about the lanes and culling wild flowers to put in your hair, and how it cost me an hour's chase to catch you, and get a kiss of those pretty lips.—By-the-by—a-hem!"

"What, Gilbert?"

"I should like one now!"

"Hush, Gilbert, hush. Go on with your story."

"Well, well. There I sat thinking of past times till the night came upon me. Ah, how well I recollected when I used to call at your mother's cottage before I went to sea!—Even then, Mary, there was a look of craft and subdued ambition upon the old woman's face, though she was pretending to be humble, and to live in a cottage, and all that sort of thing."

"My mother had fallen from wealth to poverty. Gilbert. She was once in the midst of all the gaieties of London, as she tells me."

"Ah, there it is—'What's bred in the bone you can't get out of the flesh.' The old lady thought that by this marriage she would get back again, no doubt, to the old haunts. Well, as I was saying, I sat till dark, and then the thought came over me of going to see you, and asking you yourself if this wedding were a thing of your own choice or not."

"But, Gilbert, you ought to have known—"

"Well, well, perhaps I ought; but only suppose, now, that you had heard all of a sudden that I was going to marry some girl with plenty of money, what would you have thought, Mary?"

"It would have been too dreadful for thought, as it is now too dreadful to be dwelt upon, even as a supposition."

"Very good. Then don't you wonder at my doing and thinking all sorts of odd things."

"I will not, Gilbert; and so you come here?"

"I started to come; they told me of a near cut across the fields, and I took it, and of course, as folks always do when they try near cuts that they know nothing about, I lost my way. I got into such a collection of fields, and lanes, and trees, and hay-stacks, that it would have puzzled a conjurer to find out his latitude. I completely lost mine."

"And what did you do?"

"Why I stood still in a little green lane that did not seem to have been trodden since the flood, and I shouted. That brought two men to me, and while I was civilly asking them the way to Hampton, one of the rascals struck me, unawares, a blow upon the head."

"The villain!"

"Yes, I felt partially stunned, and then they robbed me of all the money I had as well as the ring that you had given me, Mary, and which I held as more precious than my life."

"But you recovered it? I have it."

"Yes, I will tell you. Just as I was recovering a little, and as they were going, I fancy, to give me a finishing touch with the bludgeon they had first struck me with, a man on horseback leapt the hedge, and attacked them both."

"That man was our friend, yonder?"

"It was. He routed them and took one a prisoner. It was the one who had the ring, luckily. The other got away with my money. From the rascal we took we got all the news about your projected marriage, for it appears by some mean or another that he knew all about it.   Then it was that after I had told my new friend all the story, he said with a smile—'Come, this will be a little adventure ; I will help you in it.' It was he who way-laid both the parsons, and tied them to two trees, and such a bawling as they made, I never shall forget, and it is to him that I owe the joy of calling you once more my own Mary."

———

CHAPTER IV.

A LADIES MAN.—KISSING GOES BY FAVOUR.—THE SILK PURSE.—OFF WITH BOOTS.

The explanation of the young sailor, rapid as it was, was quite sufficient to make Mary fully acquainted with all that had passed, save and except the one important item, concerning which she may be well pardoned for feeling a deep curiosity—namely, the position in society, and the name of the stranger who had done her and Gilbert such good services.   There was all the air and manners of a knight-errant of old about him, and the way in which he had conquered the difficulties of the position in which she had been placed, combined with his strikingly handsome appearance, and his amusing manners, made an impression upon Mary, that if her heart had not been previously occupied by Gilbert Rushton, might easily have ripened into a more tender sentiment. As it was, she could admire, without loving. By this time the brow of the hill had been reached, and the varied scene, illumed as it was by the moon's refulgent rays, that was   presented to the gaze of the travellers, might well excuse the delay of a few moments in its examination. Gilbert and Mary found their unknown friend gazing around him with evident pleasure.

"Behold," he said, " what is to be seen here. It is an every-day sight, but yet falls not upon the senses."

" It is beautiful," said Mary.

" Yes.   This light of the moon, as it shines upon tree, and hill, and vale, seems to mistify, in a manner of speaking, every object.   It would be something strange, indeed, that would not look beautiful in such a light."

" You should see the ocean by it," said Gilbert.

"Ah !" said the stranger, " that is what I should like to see."

" Yes," said Mary , " and then Mr. — a—a——"

Claude smiled as he placed his hand lightly upon hers.

" You shall know who I am before I leave you," he said. "After giving that information to your enemies, I ought not to withhold it from you ; but not yet—not yet."

Mary looked all the vexation she felt at the innocent little *ruse* for the discovery of the name of her unknown champion, being so very easily seen through, and Gilbert only whistled slightly, as though he would have said—"That had better have been left alone ;" and so, indeed, it had, so far as regarded the effect it had produced. There was nothing, however, in the behaviour of their unknown friend that could in the smallest degree lead them to suppose that they had given him any offence, and this was no piece of acting upon the part of Claude, for he was not in the smallest degree hurt at the natural curiosity of Mary.   After gazing for a short time at the sweet landscape laid out before him, he said—

" We must not linger here.   Do you not see, Gilbert, the dark cloud that hangs over London, even from here ?"

' I do.'

' And you, too, Miss Dundas ?"

" Yes. It makes one shudder to look at it."

"It disappears when you get once fairly beneath it. Your path now is all before you, and—and——"

He paused.

"You have something to say," remarked Gilbert, "which you hesitate to give utterance to. Is that necessary with us, whom you have placed under such heavy obligations?"

"Perhaps not; but yet I do not feel that I ought to be prying into your affairs. The fact is, I was going to ask you frankly, what you intended to do."

"And," said Gilbert, with the permission of Mary, I will as frankly tell you. May I not?"

"Oh, yes, yes," said Mary.

"Then I intend to take Mary to my old aunt Rushton, who lives at Richmond, and there let her remain, until in calm and cool judgment she makes up her mind what to do."

"My mind," said Mary, "is made up."

Gilbert Rushton looked at her with fond affection, and then, after the silence of a few moments, he said—

"Mary, if I were not so sure of your faith, I should not probably propose the measure I have; but yet, with the consent of your mother, I may call you mine."

"And, in the meantime," said Mary, "what a joy it is to have broken off that dreadful marriage."

"One question more," said Claude.

"Speak it."

"Is your aunt at Richmond in such circumstances that she can well afford not only to keep Mary comfortable, but to protect her in the event of her retreat being discovered?"

"Circumstances!" said Gilbert, with rather a confused look. "We sailors have so little to do while at sea, with the affairs of life on shore, that we hardly ever think of how folks live. I honestly think that she is about as poor a gentlewoman as can be."

"That is bad," said Claude.

"It is. The fact is, it was no small trouble to her, poor soul, to fit me out for sea, after I had got my rolling as a midshipman, on board the Hawk line-of-battle ship. I hold the rank of lieutenant now, but I have no ship."

"Then the long and short of it is," said Claude, "that you ought not to place Mary with your aunt unless you can place some gold along with her. What is your own opinion?"

"Just that."

"Well, we shall see. Now, ride on. Hark, I hear the sound of wheels in the valley below."

"And I, likewise," said Gilbert, "but I don't see how the sound of wheels can much interest us, or make our position better than it is. It is doubly provoking, too, that the scoundrels who attacked me in the lane took away what money I had with me. By-the-by, my good friend, how did you in such a magical way procure these horses for our use?"

"In a magical way, if you like to think so," said Claude, coughing; "all you will have to do when you reach London, will be to oblige me by leaving them at a certain stable, that I will give you the direction to, and there will be no further trouble upon that score."

"It shall be done."

During the progress of the last portion of this little dialogue, the party had gone on, and were now descending the hill at an easy pace. When they reached the foot of the declivity, Claude paused, and turning to Gilbert, he said—

"Will you do me the favour to ride on, until you come to an inn on the right-hand side of the road, called the 'Red Rose?' There I will request of you to bait the horses, and await my coming."

"Certainly," said Gilbert. "You have but to direct us, and we will comply with your wishes in any way."

Claude waved his hand in adieu, and they both trotted briskly on the road; not knowing what might be the motive of their friend for this manœuvre, they made it a point of honour not to turn a glance in the direction where they had left him. Claude watched them till a turn of the road hid them from his sight, then in a deep-toned voice that had something of dejection in it, he said—

"And they are innocent as I once was."

This thought for the space of some few moments seemed to produce such a degree of dejection as completely to unman him who had given utterance to it, but it was only for a few moments, after all. Suddenly, as though he had been touched by the wand of the enchanter, he looked up. Fire flashed in his eyes, his mouth lost its downcast expression, and raising himself in his stirrups, he shouted rather than cried—

"Hurrah for the road!"

The sound of his voice seemed to have an equally inspiring effect upon his horse as well as upon himself, for the animal gave a bound that would have unseated any less-practised rider, and then darted forward at full speed. In about a minute and a half the highwayman suffered his gallant steed to dictate the pace at which they should go, and then he gradually drew the rein, and patted the arch neck of the noble creature.

"So ho, boy," he said, "so ho! You, too, if you had the power, would cry hurrah for the road, and in truth, in your own fashion, you do cry it. Well, we have now a little bit of work to do. Ha! ha! how the blood dances in my veins, when I hear the sounds that assure me a traveller comes. Listen—listen, my steed, listen! Do you not hear the grating of wheels? Ha! ha! 'Tis well, 'tis well. Now to work."

No doubt at that moment everything was forgotten by Claude Duval save the wild and adventurous calling in which he had made himself so celebrated. He rode to the top of a small hillock that was close at hand, and then holding his hand to the side of his face, so as to shut out surrounding and distracting objects, he took a long and steady look in the direction whence the sounds of the approaching carriage proceeded.

"'Tis well!" he said, at length. "'Tis well, and of the right sort."

Without another remark, he dashed down the hillock, and at an easy canter went along the road in the direction that the carriage was now rapidly approaching. The moon had by this time climbed to such a height in the heavens, that it had entirely lost its distinctive character, which had given it its name of the harvest moon, and it shed a clear silvery light upon the scene below, untinctured by any of that golden radiance which had been its peculiar characteristic only a short time before. The highwayman glanced up at it, as though he would have wished that some light cloud would cover the fair face of the queen of the night for a short time; but if he had any such feeling it very quickly passed away, and he trotted forward with the same joyous look as before, as though he were going upon some ordinary pleasurable errand, and not by any means upon one that perilled life and limb. As he was approaching towards the carriage, and that vehicle itself was going at a fair speed, they soon came tolerably close to each other, and then, to the astonishment of the postilion, Claude stopped, and in a loud, clear voice cried—

"Hold! The blood of those who resist be upon their own heads!"

"Murder!" cried the postilion, "it's—it's Duval!"

With the rapidity of magic, Claude cut the traces of the horses, and then as he passed the postilion, he said—

"Stir on your life. I have a long arm, and will reach you, if you afterwards hide yourself in the bowels of the earth."

"Murder, sir! No, sir! God bless you, sir! I won't stir for a month, sir, if so be, sir, as you says don't, sir. Oh, murder! spare my life and take my goods. I have got a large family, sir, and nothing a year."

" Peace !"

" Yes, sir ! Peace it is. Oh dear ! oh dear !"

All this was transacted in so much less time than it has taken us to relate, that Claude was at the window of the carriage before the inmates could recover from the first surprise of the affair, or comprehend why it was that the vehicle was stopped at all. The windows were up, but Claude let one down quickly, and as he did so he caught the flutter of female apparel.

" Ladies !" he said.

Bang went a pistol from within the carriage, and a voice said—

" Yes, and gentlemen likewise."

" Very good," said Claude, " but you are a bad shot, sir."

He saw the hand that had fired the pistol, and reaching his own arm into the carriage, he seized it by the wrist with a clutch of iron.

" Now, sir," he said. " Come out, and let me look at your quality, if you please. You have had your shot—what have you to say to me, that I should not have mine?"

By main strength, Claude pulled the person who had fired at him right through the window of the carriage, to the great detriment of his person and his apparel in the process. By the light of the moon, Claude saw that his prisoner was a young man of moody-looking aspect, and slim figure, which was quite a mercy, inasmuch as it not a little facilitated his passage through the window of the carriage. Some ladies in the vehicle screamed loudly while the operation was going on.

CHAPTER V.

THE CHASE.—THE HIGHWAYMAN VICTORIOUS.—NIGHT AT AN INN.

No doubt he who had fired the pistol so unsuccessfully at Claude, expected nothing but instant death for the attempt, and to the best of his ability he struggled with his captor.

" Fool," said Claude " will you force me to do a deed that I shrink from ? I forgive your foolish sport, but I require the submission of a prisoner."

" You will not take my life?"

" I take your life ? Pho—What is your life to me? Stand by yon tree, sir, and by the Heaven above us, if you stir hand or foot for flight, I will be after you like your fate."

The young man complied, and Claude dismounting, approached the carriage door. He seemed quite regardless of the chance of some one else being there who might fire at him.

" Ladies," he said, " a thousand pardons."

" Who are you ?" said a soft voice.

" A gentleman, madam; indeed, I may say that, take me for all in all, I am one

" More sinned against than sinning,"

for you can, in the tenderness and delicacy of your feelings, have no idea of how many evil deeds are placed at my door of which I am as innocent as you are guilty."

" Me guilty ?" cried the female voice.

" Yes, madam," added Claude, in a low voice of most musical accent. Yes, madam, guilty—deeply guilty."

" Oh, no—no."

" Yes, of enslaving the affections of all who know you."

The lady was silent, and Claude continued—

" As a remembrance of the pleasure of this meeting, I will trouble you for your purses, rings, and watches, ladies."

A faint scream came from another corner of the carriage, and then another lady said—

"Mr. Highwayman, go away—go away, and let the carriage proceed at once. We don't intend to be robbed."

"Robbed, madam? No, indeed, you nor any other lady shall ever be robbed while I am on the road, I flatter myself; I keep this road very clear of robbers, indeed. But by your voice I know that you are beautiful, so I feel that you will at once comply with my request to have some little remembrance of you."

"Well, I cannot say but that you are very polite."

"Very," said the lady who had first spoken to Claude. Before he could make any reply to these speeches the first lady cried suddenly—"Mr. Percival, am I to be pinched black and blue because a highway gentleman happens to be polite?"

"Mr. who?" said Claude. "Who dares pinch you, madam of any colour but the delightful and natural one you possess, while I am here? , He must be a ngularly bold man."

"It's my husband, Mr. Percival, up in the corner here."

"Is this possible?"

"No—no," cried a man's voice. "I—I—no—no."

"Pray, sir," said Claude, "step out."

"I have got no money, not a farthing, and no watch, and no jewellery but a mourning ring upon my finger, and you would hardly take that."

"Come out, sir."

"But—but——"

"Ladies," said Claude, in his softest accents, "allow me the pleasure of handing you out of this bear's den, and then I can ferret out the odious animal himself."

"It's all your own fault, Mr. Percival," said the lady. "It's all your own fault, and I hope it will teach you not to be so handy in pinching one, as you usually are, you mean-spirited ugly ——"

Claude had taken the hand of a young lady—he felt it tremble in his—and assisted her from the carriage,

"Be under no apprehension," he said. "Not the smallest hurt shall be done to you, or to any one whom you may wish to protect."

"Spare all," she said.

"I will."

Claude next handed out the other lady, who, although double the age of the young one, who could not be above seventeen at the most, was still a comely woman. They were both very elegantly dressed, and when they stood upon the road, Claude glanced around him until he saw a pretty green spot among some trees, where the short grass was a much more inviting place to stand upon than the road.

"Yon grass plot," he said, "will be more befitting the tenderness of your feet than this rough road."

Upon the instant, and before the slightest opposition could be made to him, he lifted up the young lady, and with all the tenderness in the world, he carried her to the grass plot.

"The devil, sir!" cried an angry voice now from the carriage, while a fist was flourished in the air. "The devil, sir! What do you mean by carrying my niece?"

"Your niece, is she?" said Claude. "She has the disadvantage of a very ugly and disagreeable uncle. Lie down, sir!"

Neither of the ladies could help laughing to hear the uncle of the one and the husband of the other addressed as though he were some vicious dog, merely, and when Claude now took up the elder of the ladies, and likewise carried her to the grass plot, the conquest of her affections appeared to be quite complete.

"Oblige me, ladies," he said, "by remaining where you are for the present, if you please."

"Have mercy, sir."

"Mercy! Oh, it is not needed. There will be no harm done. This is a mere farce."

He walked to the carriage, and holding open the door, which had a tendency to swing shut, he said to the gentleman within—

"Now, Mr. Percival, I will trouble you to alight, or if it be more convenient or pleasant to you from where you are, to surrender to me your money and valuables. I am quite ready to take them."

"There is my purse, and the deuce comfort you with it."

"Thank you."

"The idea of carrying my wife! I—I could—I don't know what I could not do."

"Therefore," added Claude, "it is much better to leave it undone, you see, sir; and now I warn you, if you attempt any act inimical to my safety, I will scatter your brains in this carriage with as little remorse as I would those of a mad dog."

Mr. Percival sank to the bottom of the carriage, as though he were half dead already, and Claude slammed shut the door. In another moment he was with the ladies, to whom he said—

"Who is the young man who fired at me?"

"My step-son," said the elder lady. "I hope you will forgive him for so foolishly firing at you."

"It is done. But now tell me, what is your husband?"

"A stock-broker."

"He has given me this purse. Is it all he has? I ask you, ladies, to tell me the truth in this matter, as you are ladies, and as I have, I trust, behaved to you with gentleness."

"I can say nothing," said the young lady.

"Nor I," said Mrs. Percival, "My husband is rich, and his boots may be worth something, but you cannot expect me to tell you where he has hidden his pocket-book, and his watch and seals."

"I owe you many thanks," said Claude, "and now my time presses, or what a pleasure it would be to me to enjoy a dance upon the green lane by the light of the moon. It cannot be, though, and now permit me to hand you back to the carriage. The postilion, when I am gone, will soon find a means of repairing the traces, and you can pursue your journey in absolute safety then."

"We have not forgotten," said the young lady, "that you asked us for our money and jewels. There are mine, with one exception."

"Make what exception you please," said Claude, "I do not desire to know of it. It may appear strange that, with my feelings towards you and all of your sex, that are admirable, I should lay this species of contribution upon you all, but if I were not upon the road, believe me, you would have some vulgar species of ruffian, who would add insult to injury, and perhaps violence. I pray you, therefore, to pardon me."

"We do—we do."

"I am much beholden to you."

"Let me tell you that the only thing I wish to retain is a small purse of beads, with a few valueless coins in it. You can inspect them."

"Certainly not."

The ladies handed to him their purses, which he found by the weight to be tolerably well filled, and then they would have given him their rings from off their fingers, but it was a sacrifice that he would not permit.

"No," he said, "I shall be quite content."

So saying, he handed them back to the carriage, within which the stock-broker was foaming and fretting, but quite in his mind at ease regarding the articles he had hidden in his boots. Claude was determined to possess himself of those articles, let their value be what it might, but he wished to do so without, in the smallest degree, compromising her who had given him the information concerning them. When he reached the carriage, he said to Mr. Percival—

" Sir, what you have handed to me is a sum not at all consistent with your station. Will you amend it ?"

" I have no more."

" Well, I never leave a gentleman the means of following me quickly, and so as I would not be so harbarous as to cripple you, I will content myself by taking your boots."

" My boots?"

" Yes, sir, only your boots."

" Then you must be the devil himself. Permit me time to take them quietly off. and you shall have them."

" I will assist you, sir. The least I can do when I am about to take your boots from you, is to help you off with them."

Claude duly handed out the stock-broker, who, with a groan, found his cunning artifice detected.

" It is all in vain," he said, " I can give you what you want, without at all disturbing my boots. My pocket-book is in one, and my watch and seals in the other."

Claude smiled as the articles were handed to him, and opening the pocket-book he took from it £1000 in bank notes, and then handed it back with all its papers untouched.

" This is generous of you," said the stock-broker, " for, to tell the truth, the papers in that pocket-book are worth more to me than £1000."

" Then," said Claude, " perhaps you will tell me if the numbers of these notes be known to you ?"

Before an answer could be returned to this most extraordinary question, the young man who had fired at Claude, and who had been spared by him on condition that he remained quiet, called out—

" Help—help ! thieves !"

Claude turned in a moment.

" Is this right ?" he said.

A pistol was in his hand, and presented at the young men, who cowered down expecting to be shot, but the young lady in the carriage leant from the window, and clasping her hands, cried—

" For my sake, spare him. I implore you to spare him, sir."

" 'Tis done," said Claude, " and when you tell this story, do not say you had to ask twice for me to spare one who shot at me once, and then broke his faith, by which I risked my life."

Claude felt that the call of " Help !" from the young man was not a mere impulsive thing, but that there was some special reason for it, and he glanced around him to note if he could observe any signs of approaching succour at hand. He gave a low and peculiar whistle, which had the effect of bringing his horse immediately to his side. On the instant he mounted, but still he was loath to leave the spot until he was sure from what direction the danger was coming, for that there was danger, he did not, for a moment, entertain a shadow of a doubt. It was soon made apparent to him. From the road whence the carriage had proceeded, he heard the sound of horse's feet, and he felt convinced that the number was considerable from the great accumulation of the sounds. He turned to the young man, who was still by the tree, and in a voice, the determination of which could not be mistaken, he said—

" Another word for help, and it is your last. No more intercessions shall save your life, and I will not allow my own existence to be trifled with."

The young man was still. Sweeping up the road, and talking and laughing as they came, now there appeared a party of about twelve horsemen ; Claude could plainly hear one of them say as they came within sight—

" Yes, it's an odd termination to a wedding. They say Sir Felix has broken a blood-vessel with vexation."

Claude bit his lips. He knew now that the approaching party consisted of some of the guests from the residence of Sir Felix Moffat, where he had made himself anything but popular by the part he had taken in putting an end to the festivities contingent upon the wedding that he had so signally and providentially, for the happiness of Mary, intercepted. His determination was taken in a moment. It was one of those strangely bold ones which most thoroughly had made his name so famous. He dismounted at once, and, in all appearance, strange as it may seem, he said something to the horse, who immediately trotted a short distance upon the road, and then vaulted over a hedge into a meadow close at hand.

In another moment Claude got into the carriage, and then, before he closed the door, he said to the young lady—

"What is his name?"

He pointed to the young man by the tree.

"George Percival."

"Very well. I thank you. George Percival, if you don't come here and quietly sit down in the carriage, I will shoot you."

Master George thought that it was good policy to come at once rather than throw away his life for the foolish bravado of not coming just because he was ordered so to do. He stepped into the carriage, which quite easily and conveniently held them all. Claude made him a place by his side.

"Now," he said, "if either of you two gentlemen contradict me by a word, I will not only blow his brains out who does so, but the other's likewise. As for the ladies, I only rely upon their gentleness. What they may choose to do, they must do unharmed by me."

Not one said a word. Claude then let down the front window and looked out to the postilion—

"Silence," he said, "on your life!"

"Oh, murder, yes, sir."

"That is well. The weather has been decidedly pleasant to-day, ladies."

Any one would have thought by the tone of Claude that he was quite at his ease, and that nothing of a very particular character was going on, so wonderful a command had he of his nerves and his voice. But now the horsemen, whose approach had been detected by the quick, listening ear of George Percival, before Claude was at all aware of their approach, made their appearance upon the spot. The affair began to get quite critical. By the light of the moon the ladies looked at Claude to see if his firmness in any way failed him, but they could not perceive such to be the case. His countenance was perfectly calm and unruffled.

———

CHAPTER VI.

THE HUNT FOR A LIFE.—LONDON.—THE OLD INN.—THE HAUNTED CHAMBER.

"HILLOA!" cried the foremost of the horsemen. "Did any one from here call for help?"

"Yes," said Claude. "We did. We have been robbed."

"Robbed?"

"Yes. By a highwayman; I only wish you may catch him, that's all. Oh, he has gone off at a canter."

"The deuce take me," said the young man, "if I can stand this."

"Perhaps you can this," said Claude, in a whisper.

George felt something cold touch his forehead. He put up his hand, and found it was the muzzle of a pistol that was indenting his skin. The effect was instantaneous. He shrank back with a shudder.

"Who has robbed you?" said several of the horsemen, crowding to the carriage window, "Who is it?"

"Why no other than the well-known audacious highwayman, Claude Duval."

" Claude Duval ?"

" Yes, that's his name. Do you know anything of him ?"

" Too much. He has left such a scene of confusion at the house of Sir Felix Moffat, that I don't know how it will end.",

" Can such things be ?"

" They not only can be, but they actually are, I can assure you, and if you will tell us which way he went we will take a ride after him, desperate fellow as he is."

" You must have passed him," said Claude, " for he went the very way you came, only just now."

" Did he ? Confound him ! I'd ride to the devil after him. Come back, my friends. Let us make a hue and cry after this fellow. It will be some sort of satisfaction to our friend, Sir Felix, as well as to ourselves, if we only can succeed in catching him to-night."

" And a great surprise to me, too," said Claude.

" A surprise, sir ?"

" Yes ; don't you know that the fellow has as many lives as a cat, and that it is fairly thought by some folks that he never will be taken at all, but will go out some day like an *ignis fatuus,* and no one know what has at all become of him !"

" There may be people superstitious enough to believe such nonsense, but we are not of the number. Come, my friends, come, let us ride back, and try our fortune against this Claude Duval."

The horsemen all turned, and with one accord, spreading themselves along the road, they went the way they came.

" Ladies and gentlemen," said Claude, " I thank you. I rather think, by your very kind and discreet silence, you have saved my life. Be assured that to those who preserved silence without threats, I am deeply grateful. To the others, I think I may cry quits, and be off."

Claude had opened the coach door, and then, before any one could be aware of what he was about, he had gallantly kissed both the ladies, and sprang from the vehicle into the road.

" This is unpardonable !" said Mr. Percival, furiously.

" No one asked your pardon," said Claude, " so it is easily withheld."

" Confound it !" muttered George Percival, " I have known my cousin Emily now for eight years since I came here, and never kissed her yet."

" And never will," said the young lady.

" Bravo !" cried Claude. " Ladies and gentlemen, I look forward to the pleasure of our meeting again, some day or night. Gentlemen, good night. Perhaps we shall meet again."

" Yes, at Tyburn !" said Mr. Percival.

" Well," said Claude, " it may be so—you know best : but if we do meet at Tyburn, I shall be in the crowd and you in a cart. Postilion, mount your horse, and push on."

" Yes, sir. Oh, dear, master! what a night this is."

" Remarkably fine, I think," said Claude. " A little dew falling, that's all."

He walked up the road, in the direction that his horse had gone, and in a very few moments disappeared from their sight, although they all looked after him from the carriage windows. Then they heard a whistle, similar to the one which had before summoned his horse to his side, and in a moment or two after that, the hard beating of a horse's hoofs upon the road. He was gone.

" Now for it," said George: " I'll do something."

" What—what ?" said his cousin.

" Why, I will take one of the coach horses and ride back after these gentlemen on horseback. and let them know the truth."

" Beware !"

" I don't care for your cautions, Emily. I shall call you the highwayman's bride after this, for you know he kissed you."

" And spared you," said Emily.

The young man sprang from the carriage, and ran up to the horses to get one out of the harness, and put his threat into instant execution. The postilion shook his head.

" No, no, Master George, don't you do it."

" Don't do what, fellow?"

" Don't you be putting your not overwise head into the net, Master George. I have known you and your family some time, and give you advice, gratis, sir, and that is, to let Claude Duval alone so long as he lets you alone."

" But, confound him, he don't."

" Yes, sir, he does now."

" I do not care one straw; if all the world stood between me and him, I'd have some try for revenge. Get out this off-horse for me, Peter."

" Very good, sir. Wilful people must have their way, but sooner or later they are sure to run their heads against something."

With this wise aphorism, Peter no longer hesitated to make the effort that was necessary to get out the off-horse, and in a few moments George was duly mounted, although the mission he was going upon was neither a very safe, nor, under all circumstances, a very proper one. As he passed the carriage windows he said to his father—

" Don't go from here, sir, till you see me again. If you do, and should happen to meet the highwayman, Emily, here, will tell him that I have gone to get help to apprehend him."

" Yes," said Emily, " and I could tell him that George Percival thought it required twelve men, besides himself, to take one highwayman."

With this taunt—which was tolerably well-deserved—ringing in his ear, off set Master George at a tolerably smart pace, for the coach-horse had had some rest during the proceedings of the last quarter of an hour. We may now leave the party in the carriage, in order to follow the more immediate fortunes of Claude Duval. It will be recollected that they had distinctly heard him whistle for his steed, and then, by the rapidly succeeding sound of footsteps, they could entertain no doubt of the fact that he had ridden off. They were right. The secret by which Claude had contrived to hold a strict oral communication with his horse is easily explained. There was a particular phrase which he, Claude, always used when he wished the creature to go and take what pasture it could in the open country, whilst he himself perchance passed some portion of his time in sleep beneath a tree, and the sagacious creature, of its own accord, knew what direction to go in. Hence was it that the horse had so instantly leaped the hedge into the meadows upon Claude speaking to it. Upon hearing his well-known whistle, as it was close at hand, it at once returned to him. The great object of Claude, now, was to reach the inn where he had told Gilbert and Mary to stop at, in order that he might hand to them sufficient of the money he had taken from the Percival family to make Mary's presence at the abode of Gilbert's aunt anything but a burthen to her. With this he determined upon handing to them all the gold and silver, let the amount be what it might, and keep back the notes for a time. For all he knew, the stockbroker might be well acquainted with the numbers of the notes, and if such were the case, his gift of any of them to the innocent young lovers might be the means of bringing them into the greatest possible danger. More than once he paused and listened intently to feel assured that pursuers were not upon his track. No sound of such a nature met his ears, and after proceeding thus about two miles with caution, he banished all such apprehensions, and setting off at a good gallop, the hedges and trees appeared to fly past him with great rapidity. Nothing of any moment occurred to Claude, now, until he saw the old sign of the inn of which he was in search, swinging by the road side, and strongly illumined by the moonbeams that happened to fall full upon it. The landlord of the house was at the door, straining his eyes down the road, and the moment he saw Claude, he came towards him.

" Anything amiss, my friend?" said Claude.

" I don't know, but here's a lady and gentleman waiting for some one, and by the description, it must be you."

" It's all right," said Claude, " I sent them. Many thanks to you for your caution, though. It might have been all wrong."

" Of course it might, and what seemed so odd to me was, that though they both described you exactly, they did not seem to know who you were."

" True. They do not know who I am. I hope you did not enlighten them on that score, landlord ?"

" Not I, Claude. I never give folks more news than they can give me, unless I know them well. But I'm glad all's right. Come in."

Claude Duval at at once entered the inn, and here we may say that Claude owed much of safety to his trusting disposition, He put so much confidence in people, that, as he was accustomed himself to say, he shamed many a man from betraying him, who, if he had thought himself in the least way suspected, would not have hesitated to do so. The landlord had had the precaution to place Gilbert and Mary in a room free from the usual interruptions incidental to a small country inn, and no doubt, during the short time they were together, the young lovers found time and opportunity for some of that delightful interchange of sentiment, which certainly constitutes the essence of a feeling that, once dying in the human breast, can be replaced by no other. Claude looked at them both gravely, and then said—

" You have no refreshments."

" We did not think of it," said Mary.

" Ah ! that's my fault," said Gilbert. " I will ring."

" Never mind. The landlord will in a moment bring us a bottle of his best wine, and then I have something to say to you both, which I hope you will take in good part as it is intended."

" How is it possible that we can take ill anything from you," said Mary, " to whom we owe so much ?"

Claude smiled as he said—

" Mary, you will really make me believe at last that I have done something deserving thanks ; but here is the wine, and now, Gilbert, pledge me in a bumper to Mary's health and happiness."

" Right willingly," said Gilbert ; "and now——"

" Hush," said Claude, sadly. " My heart tells me what you are going to say—you would now ask me who I am ?"

" You are right."

" I grieve, then, to say that there are circumstances that compel me to keep that a secret for the present."

Both Gilbert and Mary looked disappointed.

" I say only for the present," said Claude; "but I have a question to ask of you both, which is—have you seen enough of me to give me the privilege of a friend?"

" Oh, yes—yes," cried Mary.

" Quite enough," said Gilbert, as he grasped Claude's hand; "quite enough. Ah !—what it this?"

" Money," said Claude, as he left in the hand of the young sailor a purse ; " it is money. You want some, and I can and do lend you some for the exigency of the moment."

" Mary, we ought not to accept this?"

" Nay, I say you ought, or else shame upon the feeling of friendship which you have only just now said existed between us."

" Take it, Gilbert," said Mary. " It comes from a friend."

" Well," said Gilbert, " I will repay this as soon as I can draw a bill for my pay in advance upon a Navy Agent in London. How much is this, sir ?"

Claude looked a little puzzled.

" I really," he said, " don't—exactly know."

Gilbert elevated his eyebrows, and looked, as he might well look, rather surprised at a man offering another the loan of a purse of money, without knowing the amount it contained ; but the fact was, that Claude fully meant the money as a gift, and as it was all he had, with the exception of a few guineas, he did not very much care to count it.

" Well," said Gilbert, " if I, as a sailor, had done this, folks would have said it was just like me."

" Count it, Gilbert," said Mary.

" I will."

Gilbert counted out the gold, and found there was £103.

" This is too much," he said, " I don't want one half of it

A bell at that moment rang violently, and Claude started to his feet, and moved to the door.

" What is it ? what has happened ?" said Mary.

" Hush !" said Claude. " Hush ! a moment, be still. It may be of importance to me. Only a moment. Put up the money. Secure your horses at the Old King's Head, in Southwark. Good by."

The landlord made his appearance at the door of the room.

" Your horse," he said, " is ready—quite ready."

" I understand," said Claude.

CHAPTER VII.

MORE PERILS.—THE WOUNDED HORSE—THE LEAP—THE CHAMBER AT THE INN.

CLAUDE was gone before either Mary or Gilbert could say a word in reply to him, although they both rose to follow him. The landlord stopped them.

" Let him go," he said. " Let him go. He is the best judge of his own affairs, you may depend, and if you are real friends of his, you will let him go at once, and say nothing about him to a living soul."

They looked at the landlord in amazement, as well they might. They heard a loud shout below, and then a pistol-shot.

" By Heavens !" cried Gilbert, " it don't suit me to be cooped up here, while a friend perhaps is in danger. Get out of my way. Don't fear anything, Mary ; keep where you are, and I will soon be back to you."

" Gilbert, Gilbert !"

He was past the landlord, and down the staircase in a moment. When he reached the door of the inn, a most singular scene presented itself to him—a scene that for a moment almost deprived him of the power of action, so strange to his apprehension was it. Surrounded by several men on horseback, who were aiming blows at him, and preventing him from mounting, was Claude Duval, now making an effort to get on his horse, then stopping a moment to ward off some blow that was more maliciously aimed than another. Such a sight as this filled Helbert with indignation. He felt as if he were nerved by the strength of ten men, and glancing round him with flashing eyes for a weapon, the first thing he espied was a stable-fork hanging against the wall close to the horse-trough of the inn ; to seize this formidable and dangerous weapon was the work of a minute, and without thought, he dashed into the midst of the throng, knocking down all before him. This attack, so sudden and so furious, was most completely successful. The horsemen shrank back as they would from the attack of a maniac, and Claude in a moment was free to mount. He did not lose the opportunity. When once in the saddle, he waved his hand, and cried in a loud and ringing voice —

" Hurrah ! hurrah ! for the road."

" Now, gentlemen, try your mettle in a race. Gilbert, I owe you my life. God bless you and Mary, if those should be the last words that pass between you and me in this world."

By a slight movement of his knees, he made his horse fully understand what was wanted of him. There was a bound and then a rush, and Claude Duval was off like the wind.

"Forward!" cried one of the discomfited horsemen, "forward! follow him. Never mind his companion here; we will come back for him."

Gilbert Rushton stood the picture of amazement, with the pitchfork in his hands, while Mary, who had flung open one of the front windows of the inn, stood, with terror in her looks, regarding the scene below. Fortunately, although every one of the horsemen knew her, not one looked up, so intent were they upon the capture of Claude Duval. Being in her wedding dress, with only a loose cloak over her that Claude had lent her, she must, if she had uttered the least cry to attract any attention, have been at once recognised; but, fortunately, she did not. Surprise and terror kept her silent, not design. The whole of the mounted men dashed off in good style in the track of Claude Duval.

"Gracious Heaven!" said Gilbert, "what is the meaning of all this?"

The landlord tapped him on the shoulder.

"My friend," he said, "did you hear what they said?"

"Who?"

"The horsemen."

"Confound their sayings! what are they to me? How dared they attack my friend in that dastardly way, and why should he be pursued as though he were some notorious malefactor, that the hands of all men are raised against? I repeat, what is the meaning of all this?"

The landlord shook his head.

"My dear sir," he said, "you and the young lady have two good horses; for the love of Heaven, then, mount and be off."

The young sailor passed his hand over his eyes as he muttered to himself—"Is it all a dream?"

Then suddenly he looked up and saw at the window, Mary, and his eyes brightened.

"No—no!" he said. "At least, that joy is real."

He threw down the pitchfork, which, up to this moment, he had held in his hand, and dashed into the house again.

"Mary, are you ready?" he cried.

"Yes—yes."

"Come on, then. We will mount, and take the road to London, which is the same that our friend and his pursuers have taken, and we may find at last some clue to this mystery. The horses! the horses!"

"All ready," said the landlord.

"What's to pay?"

"Nothing."

"Nothing! How's that? It is something odd to stop at an inn and have nothing to pay, is it not?"

"No, not here; I never charge any friends of *his* anything."

"Ha! And who may he be?"

"Oh, that's neither here nor there. I wish you a good and prosperous journey, sir."

The landlord turned upon his heel and walked into the house.

"Well," said Gilbert, as he helped Mary to mount, "of all the inexplicable inns that ever I heard of, this is the most inexplicable; and of all the odd friends I ever met with, our late one is the oddest."

"I am bewildered, Gilbert."

"And so am I."

"But—but surely there must be some mode of arriving at the truth, and at an explanation regarding all these things?"

"That there may be, Mary, but as yet, at all events, it is far beyond my limited comprehension. Let us be off, for if ever there was an enchanted inn, where all the people are cracked, this is the one."

"Go—go—go, at once," cried the landlord, looking from one of the upper windows of the inn. "Go, while you can, young man, with a whole skin."

Gilbert shook his head at this, and then having ascertained that Mary was quite ready, they both set off from the inn door at a rapid canter on the London road, which was the same that Claude and his pursuers had taken. We may now safely leave Mary and her lover, the gallant young lieutenant, to pursue their journey, while we scamper upon the road with the reader some few miles in advance of them, and keep company with Claude Duval. The importance now, after what had happened both at Sir Felix Moffat's and upon the road, of making good his retreat, stared Claude Duval sufficiently in the face, and he gave his good steed the rein, a thing he seldom did, for he was always much more intent upon saving the good qualities of his horse, than upon using them. But the present was an emergency which banished all scruples, and, accordingly, he flew along the road like the wind.

"They must have indeed rare cattle," he said, "if they beat me at this sort of thing; and after a mile or two more, I think this speed may be with safety relaxed. Ah, that must be the toll-house light. Why, I am further on my road than I thought by a good mile."

"That's him!" cried a voice from behind a hedge, to the right-hand side of the road. "That's him! He has escaped them!"

"Stand!" said another voice.

Two men, well mounted, came out into the middle of the road.

"Ha! ha! George Percival," cried Claude, "is that you?"

He had recognised the voice behind the hedge, and without paying at the moment any attention to the two men in the road, he fired a pistol in the direction of George Percival's voice. Claude considered that, after all that had passed, this young man was pursuing him with too implacable an enmity.

"Help! he has hit me!" cried George.

"Serve you right," said Claude.

"Stand! or we fire!" said one of the two men. "You are our prisoner. We know you, Claude Duval."

"Then, gentlemen, you have the advantage of me," said Claude, "for I neither know you nor wish for such very doubtful acquaintance."

As he spoke, he dashed forward without giving them a moment's time for further consideration. The pistol was in his hand, which he had just discharged at George Percival, and although two shots were fired at him, one of which slightly touched his right cheek, he knocked down one of the men by a stunning blow with the barrel of the pistol. The other made a vain attempt to impede him, and on he darted. He then replaced the discharged pistol in his pocket, and took out one that was loaded, and presented it over his arm at his enemies, but he did not pull the trigger.

"Pho!" he said. "I will not waste powder and shot upon one man; and there is but one, for his companion is in the road."

Claude put up the pistol and rode on; but scarcely had he got a hundred yards off, when he heard the man behind him calling—

"Shut the gate!—shut the gate!"

"Ah!" said Claude, "he means the toll-gate, and there are two high garden walls on each side for a leap."

"Open!" shouted Claude, when he came nearly to the gate.

"Ha! ha! no," cried the toll-man. "You are cotched, Claude Duval; your time has come, and I've got the five pounds for shutting the gate on you."

"Surrender," said the man from behind.

Claude turned his horse's head so rapidly, that he threw down both horse and rider that were behind him by the rush he made against them both. Then turning back again, after a gallop down the road of about fifty yards, he came on clear at the gate, crying—

"Catch who may—catch who can! That's the game we play at on this road."

By a prodigious effort, his horse not only cleared the prostrate steed and its rider which lay in the way, but the gate likewise, coming clear upon the head of the toll-man, who, not at all expecting such a feat lay within human power, was exactly on the other side.

"Hip! hip! hurrah!" cried Claude. "A cheer for the girls whom we love!"

Like a flash of light he went down the road. The toll-keeper never spoke again, and when the hores and his rider gathered themselves up, the one was lame, and the other half stupified by his fall upon the hard road, where his head had come in contact with a stone that had made his eyes flash fire again, and fifty Claude Duvals, and as many turnpike-gates, appeared to be flashing before his vision. When in about ten minutes more the whole of the party that had been so signally defeated at the inn by Gilbert arrived at the toll-bar at full gallop, they found the gate fast and no one to open it. This was a serious delay, for after calling several times upon that man who would never again hear the voice of mortal, one of the party had to dismount and clamber over the gate to find the means of opening it. The first thing he did in the semi-darkness of the place was to stumble over the dead body of the gate-keeper.

"Help!" he said. "Here has been murder done here!"

"Murder?"

"Yes. Here is a dead man."

"Open the gate! open the gate!" was now the cry. "How can we come to you if you don't open the gate?"

After some fumbling, all of which delayed time, and so far was eminently in the favour of Claude, the man found the fastenings of the gate, and swung it open, when the whole party passed through. They looked for a few minutes in silence at the dead body, which they did not raise to see how it had come by its death, and then one in a loud voice, and with much energy of manner, said—

"Friends, all our duty now is to hunt this highwayman to the death. Do you not see that confusion and murder are upon his footsteps? Let us not waste another moment's time. Keep on after him."

"Ay! Ay! Hunt him down!" said another.

They now dragged the dead body into the toll-house, and without waiting for the man who had been thrown down to recover sufficiently to go with them, they pushed on after Claude Duval. He was three good miles ahead of them now, and the lights of London were gleaming upon his eyes, as he made his way towards that city in which he certainly knew there was much danger for him, but likewise much security. Claude had travelled far enough, and from the adventures that he had passed through during the last few hours, his clothing exhibited symptoms sufficient to draw upon him the attention of the passengers in the streets. But then the hour at which he arrived in London was one at which but few people were stirring. It was nearly one o'clock in the morning, and the good folks of that time were not so fond of turning night into day as they are now. Even the watchmen confessed to being mortal, and shut themselves comfortably in tair boxes and slept. Occasionally, from the corner of some small thoroughfare, the cry of drunkenness and riot would come, and then all would be still again, and for the space of a few minutes London would seem like a city of the dead. Claude pursued his way at a fast walk until he reached Finsbury-square, then by no means the aristocratic-looking place that it is now, but infinitely more rural, inasmuch as it was backed by the Finsbury-fields, in which buttercups and daisies flourished upon spots now sacred to the twin demons of dirt and drink. Alas! is it not sad that poverty should necessarily be squalid! Claude and his horse both sniffed the grateful perfume from a second crop of new-mown hay in the fields, but although they both would willingly have taken that direction, it did not suit his mind at that time, and turning off to his left, he at once plunged amid that labyrinth of streets, now sacred to the well-known region of the Knights of the White Cross. He had not to proceed far before he reached his destination. He drew up at an old-fashioned looking inn, that seemed te occupy, with its numerous suits of rooms, one half of a street. An emblazoned sign proclaimed it to be " The Porcupine."

CHAPTER VIII.

MR. PETERSON.—THE MYSTERIOUS DISAPPEARANCE.—THE DEAD BODY.—AN ALARM.

THE Porcupine had but a dubious reputation with the magistracy of the good city of London, and yet they found it hard to fix anything of a very particular character upon the old man. How could the landlord pretend to know, when a gentleman well mounted stopped at his door, if he were a lord or a highwayman?

It would be going rather too far upon the part of the keeper of an hostelry, who professed to find good entertainment for man and beast, to be very urgent in his inquiries respecting the private history of those who came upon the strength of such a general invitation to partake of his hospitality. But yet folks, inimical to the law—personages that Newgate might be said to pant for—had been known to walk in at the open door of the Porcupine, and when the authorities walked in after them, lo! they were not to be found. This was mysterious, to say the best of it. Then, the landlord, one Hugh Peterson, was also so ready to oblige the police. All the keys were so immediately at their service, and he never made the least secret of any part of his house—that what could they say ? Indeed, he would himself, not unfrequently, quite assist them in ekeing out a description of some gentleman, who was by them ' wanted,' and assert how he had seen —

"The very modal of such a man,"

in his coffee room, and be himself quite lost in wonder as to where he could have got to out of the way ! All this, then, we say, had given the Porcupine an equivocal reputation ; and, by the conduct of Claude, when he stopped at it, we should say it deserved such a repute. He paused for a moment or two, and looked up and down the street to see if any one of an obnoxious character were at hand, and then, with a silver whistle which he took from his pocket, he blew two peculiar blasts. The patience with which Claude waited after this, was in its way something quite exemplary. The delay lasted about five minutes, but he was not tempted to repeat his challenge to the inn : nevertheless, he kept his eyes with tolerable intensity fixed upon the exterior of the building, until a small window was suddenly thrown open upon the first floor, and a night-capped head appeared.

" Who ?" said the voice appertaining to the head.

"The moon is on the wane," said Claude, "and the Porcupine must take care of its young."

The manner in which he repeated these words, evidently showed that they constituted a kind of pass, and the landlord, for it was no other than Mr. Peterson himself who looked from the window, suddenly shut it, saying as he did so—

" It is he, himself. Who would have thought it ?"

Claude had not now to wait many moments before one of the very numerous doors of the old inn were opened for him, and the landlord appeared, partially dressed.

" Come in," he said. " Come in."

" All's right," said Claude.

" Stop !"

" Stop for what, Peterson ? What's amiss ?"

" Look there. Who's that ?"

Claude glanced in the direction to which the landlord pointed, and he saw a man scamper at headlong speed round the corner of the street, and in a moment disappear in the darkness beyond, for the mazy flitter of the oil lamps only confused the moonlight, and made the streets much more foggy and uncertain than as if they had not set themselves up at all in competition with the bright and beautiful luminary that was at that moment rolling through a sky of deep, transparent blue, spangled with millions of stars.

"Who was that?" said Claude.

"A spy. Do you know, captain, or count, I suppose I ought to call you, for that's the name most of the family like to give you, do you know I have had my own thoughts and ideas about some fellows that have been lurking about the old inn lately."

"Indeed!"

"Yes; they can't get the upper hand of old Hugh Peterson by fair means, so they want to do so by foul, which is a mean thing, to say the best of it; but I'll show them a trick or a double or two yet."

"Not a doubt of it."

"Come in."

"With the horse?"

"Yes; it will do all the same. You must get the creature to stoop—but if a highwayman's horse won't do all that a christian can, he ain't fit for the trade of his master."

"I believe," said Claude, as he fondly patted the animal and dismounted, "that I have as true a friend here as any man need wish to have."

"Now for it."

The landlord held the door open, and Claude led in his steed by the bridle. The creature trod as carefully as though it felt the necessity of secrecy in its movements, and when the door was closed again, and barred and locked, and a total darkness ensued—a darkness that really seemed as if it might be felt —you could hardly have heard the breathing of the creature, so still did it keep itself.

"I'll bring a light in a minute," said the landlord.

Claude heard him walking swiftly away, but in less time than he had said, he re-appeared with the lantern.

"Now follow me," he said, "and I'll show you a new way to the stables. This way, there is no stairs and nothing to run against. By all that's good, I hope that fellow saw you come in."

"You hope he saw me, Peterson?"

"Yes, I do, for so sure as he lives his occupation is gone."

"How can that be?"

"Just this way. He will be off the first thing in the morning to the Mansion House, and tell them all that he saw; Claude Duval come in here on horseback by the tittle door near the front entrance, and if that don't damnify him, I don't know what will. Who do you suppose would believe such a tale? If they come down to me about it, I shall say the fellow must have dreamt it, and tell them to look at the door and fancy how a man on horseback could come through its entrance. Then they may search the place and find neither horse nor man answering the description, and the fellow will get his discharge for romancing. Ten to one but they send him to a prison for a week for trying to impose upon the authorities. Ha! ha! ha! That would be good."

"I hope it may be as you say."

"It will be—it must be. Stop one moment."

They had passed along a narrow passage and completely through two rooms, when the landlord desired Claude to stop. It was only that he might unlock a door, and then, when it was thrown open, there appeared a sloping sort of wooden pathway with pieces railed across as a foothold for horses. A rush of cold air came from this place, and there was upon that rush of air unequivocal symptoms of the vicinity of stables.

"This is what I call rather an ingenious mode of going to rack and manger," said the landlord.

"It is, indeed," said Claude.

"Now, look sharp. Just hold the horse half a moment, and you shall see how the affair is managed."

"The landlord suddenly exerted all his strength upon a portion of the wall, and it gradually gave way before him, revolving upon a centre. A dim light shone through the opening, and Peterson said in a suppressed tone—

"Joe! Joe!"

"Here you is," replied some one.

"Lend a hand here to the horse. Give him a good feed, and mind, above all things, that you attend to the bell,"

"I sleeps under the manger," said Joe, "and it's close to my ear. Lord bless you, master, if so much as a mouse's tail was only to touch it, I could not be off hearing of it."

"Very well, Joe. There will be no inquiry without occasion, and when there is, there will be no hurry."

"All's right, master. Woa! so ho! You are a nice 'un. Ah, you are one o' the right sort, you are—sleek and slim as a young lady."

The revolving portion of the wall was just by a manger in the stable, and was so well contrived, that it might defy all ordinary examination. Of course, if any one came prepared to make such a discovery there, it was to be made; but the secret was in few hands, and those few all interested in its preservation.

"I must confess," said Claude, "that the more I think of the mode of entrance to the stable, the more I am of your opinion, Peterson, that no one will believe it. And now I may tell you that I have had a narrow escape."

"I thought as much, or you wouldn't be here at such a time, captain."

"No—I should hardly have disturbed you."

"The disturbance is nothing. I'm always glad to see you by night or by day, for the sake of those that you have been a good friend to. And now, if you like, I can show you where to stow yourself, that if they find you out, they must be greater conjurors than ever I took a police-officer to be."

"I shall be beholden to you, for, to tell you the truth, I am somewhat tired and have done a day and night's work without much rest, Peterson. But I don't think that any one is upon my track now."

"Don't make too sure of that, Claude Duval. However, we will take good care of you. Safe bind, you know, safe find, and——"

Peterson stopped abruptly, for a tremendous hammering at the front door of the inn came upon his ears.

"That's my friends," said Claude, "I'll be bound."

Peterson shook his head.

"That's the game, is it?" he said. "Why didn't you say you were close pursued, captain? I wouldn't have wasted so much time. But come along. All's right. I give 'em leave to do their worst. We'll have a good laugh at them yet at breakfast time."

"I hope so."

"And I am sure so. Now look you here. Upon the road, and well in your saddle, you are everything; but here in a house you are rather out of your element, you know."

"I confess it."

"Well, it's no odds; I know what I am about; so follow me, and all will be right. This way—keep close, and don't go much to the left. That will do—here we are."

They had ascended a small flight of twelve stairs, and the landlord entered a room, comfortably furnished, into which he showed Claude. He placed the lamp upon the table, and took a key from his pocket.

"You see that door," he said, "in the corner? It looks like a cupboard, and if is a cupboard too, and yet, not only a cupboard. The back of it slides up, minds like a window sash, and it takes you into a narrow space between the walls to many of the rooms of this house. But mark me, I don't wish you to stay there, for, after all, it is dangerous, and some of these days will he found out. But I do wish you to make use of that passage and this key, as a means of getting from one room to another, without the trouble of doing so by the common entrance. You understand me ?"

" I do."

" Well, you will find many a cupboard opening by a sliding back from that passage. I will place lights in some of the rooms, and in every one that is looked at; and as they send a few rays through the crevices of the cupboard, you will find that a sufficient guide to know what rooms to venture into."

Bang! bang! bang! went some one at the door, and a loud voice cried—

" House! house! house!"

" Be careful," said the landlord. " I now leave you to yourself, for it won't do to keep them at the door any longer. The moon will be all the light you want just now."

The landlord abruptly left the room, conveying the lantern with him. Claude found that the room was well-lighted by the moon's rays, but it was far from an agreeable thing to know that there were some twelve or fourteen men at the door of the inn, thirsting for his life.

" I have chosen my course in life," he said, in a low tone, " and I must abide its chances."

The key was in his grasp, but before he made any use of it, he was anxious to catch a glimpse, if that were possible, of his enemies in the street. The house, however, had so many windings and turnings about it, that he found, when he came to look from the window of the room in which he was, that it did not command a view of the front of the old building, but looked into a much narrower thoroughfare, full of mean, squalid habitations, that, though under the magic influence of the bright moonbeams, could hardly be made into beauty or to produce a picturesque effect. Under these circumstances, he at once made use of his key.

He unlocked the door of the cupboard, and found, as the landlord had told him, that the back of it easily slid up like a window-sash. This was likewise the back of another cupboard in another room, so that for a few moments Claude was puzzled to know where the passage was that Peterson had mentioned to him. A slight touch, however, to one side of the walls of the first closet showed him that it was of the same construction as the back panelling. He raised it, and at once saw a dark and dreary-looking passage about four feet wide. Before he plunged down it, he thought he would try and obtain a view of the street from the adjoining room, for he heard that Peterson had not yet let in his foes.

CHAPTER XI.

A LITTLE DISTURBANCE.—THE BRIDE AND THE BRIDEGROOM.—THE LOVER OF A NIGHTCAP.

CLAUDE was so far gratified, that the room into which he stepped did give him the prospect into the full street that he wanted. He felt that the danger of his being seen was too small to take it into account, and, accordingly, without hesitation, placed himself close to the window to watch the proceedings without. From the general appearance of the party, he saw that it was the same that had followed him up with so much pertinacity from the house of Sir Felix Moffat, but how they had contrived to discover that he had come to the Porcupine, was eyond his comprehension. It certainly was just possible that accident brought them there, but it was very improbable that such was the case, when to reach that part of London they would have to pass many more unexceptionable places of entertainment. They were parleying with the landlord at the door, and Claude ea d one say suddenly,—

"It's no use mincing the matter; I am an officer, and am fully well assured that a man we are in search of is here."

"A man, sir?" said Peterson.

"Yes. You may as well save yourself from the consequences of a rigorous prosecution by giving him up, for the house is surrounded at every outlet, and we are determined to have him."

THE SECRET TRAP IN THE PORCUPINE INN.

"Well, gentlemen, perhaps you will tell me who it is, for as I have several guests in the house, I only want to rouse up the right one."

"You know who it is. We want Claude Duval, the famous highwayman, and we know he is here."

Mr. Peterson put on one of the most incredulous looks in the world.

"Lord bless you, gentlemen," he said, "I should go right down crazy if I thought any such person was in the house as a highwayman."

"We shall see."

"Certainly. Come in, gentlemen, come and search where you like; I can only say that we have a lady and gentleman sleeping in the best bed-room. They are a newly married couple, gentlemen, and I hope you will not disturb them."

"We shall do our duty."

The party entered the house, with the exception of two, who were left to guard the door with pistols in their hands. Claude thought it then high time to leave the window and betake himself to the more secure retreat of the narrow passage. He felt that his head was continually encountering huge cobwebs, but the exigency of the moment enabled him to think nothing of the crawling of the spiders about his neck, which would otherwise have been anything but bearable.

Holding out both his hands to feel his way—for although he did not expect any obstacle, yet he could not help, in the intense darkness, fancying there might be one—he stepped on for the distance of about thirty feet, and then he found there was an abrupt turn. Suddenly a faint glimmer of light streamed into the passage, and then, by applying his ear to the wall, he heard the voice of Peterson say—

"Well, gentlemen, I hope you will soon be done, since you have begun at the top of the house and intend, you say, to go regularly down it."

"Jukes," said a man, "come here."

"What is it, now?" said some one, with a voice like a Polar-bear.

"Why, I don't like the look of this panelling at the back of the cupboard. When I was here last, I recollect it looked suspicious, but now I am quite resolved to satisfy myself about it."

"As you please, gentlemen," said the landlord. "The house is old, and may have odd places in it that I know nothing of. They say, that in old times, many a long year ago, it was part of an old convent."

Claude did not wait to hear more. He felt that the passage between the walls was discovered, and that, consequently, it was no longer a tenable place of refuge for him. He hastened on, blundering against many things in the dark, against many turnings and projections, until he saw again a faint light through some crevices. He cautiously slid up the panel that hid the room from whence the light proceeded, and at once—for the door of the cupboard was open—he saw into a chamber with a large four-post bedstead. From the appearance of the clothing that lay about upon chairs, Claude could at once see that a lady was in the room, and it at once struck him that he had pitched upon the bed-room of the married folks that he had heard the landlord speak of. He was considering what do, when he heard the sounds of feet in the passage behind him, and voices came upon his ears. To close the sliding-panel was the work of a moment, and then he stood in the cupboard, the door of which was open, gazing into the "Porcupine's" best bed-room. Truly the position of Claude Duval was now a fearful and complicated one, and nothing but some extraordinary movement, combined both of skill and courage, could save him. He did not hesitate, but dashing into the room of the married couple by means of one of the secret modes of entrance at the back of the cupboard, he stood before their bewildered eyes, covered with dirt that he had got in abundance from the secret passage between the walls of the old inn. A death-like silence was in the room. To tell the truth, Claude felt all the disinclination in the world to disturb the good people in the bed-chamber; but desperate emergencies require desperate remedies, and he had no other resource. The lady sat up in bed and uttered a cry of alarm, when she was sufficiently recovered from her first fright to do so; but the husband—yes, the husband, who certainly, if anybody ought to have done so, should have been the man to take the initiative upon the occasion, shrank under the bed-clothes, and shook like an aspen leaf.

"What do you want?" said the lady.

"My life," said Claude,

"Your life! and who is your life?"

Probably she took it as some sort of declaration of attachment uttered in the high-flown language of a melo-drama.

"You mistake me," said Claude. "I am pursued by those who would take my life. That is what I mean."

"But—but——"

"You would say, how can you assist me?"

"Yes—I ——"

"Your husband shall be my preserver, but I will repay to you the service. Sir—sir!"

"Mercy—help!" cried the smothered voice of the man under the bed-clothes, "murder! I am not here."

"Oh, Alfred," said the wife, "how can you be such a coward; and you an officer, too! I am surprised at you. I am indeed. Alfred! Alfred!"

———

CHAPTER XII.

CLAUDE'S ESCAPE—DEATH OF THE SPY.—A LITTLE ENCOUNTER.

CLAUDE's position was one of the greatest danger, but he did wait with as much patience as he could command for the lady's indignations to have their proper effect upon Alfred, and they certainly had some, for a head, enveloped in rather a remarkable looking blue silk nightcap, popped out from among the bed-clothes. The face beneath the nightcap presented quite a picture of serious alarm, and the eyes glared upon Claude with such agony, that at any other time he could not have restrained from laughing at such an apparition of fright.

"Can it be possible that you are an officer?"

"In the militia," said the lady.

"Oh," said Claude, "that is it. Now listen to me, sir. My life is in danger. It hangs upon the events of the next five minutes. I dare say there are plenty of unoccupied beds in this house. I will trouble you to go and find me one."

"Me, sir?"

"Yes, you; and that upon the instant too. I will not be trifled with. Rise, sir, at once, and leave the room. By the by, I will borrow your nightcap."

"Good God," said the lady, "what is the meaning of this?"

"Simply, madam, that to save the life of a fellow-creature, who, whatever may be his errors, has never failed in his devotion to your charming sex, I am sure you will permit me to lie down by your side for a few minutes only, and my honour may be——"

The lady gave a faint scream.

"Gracious providence, sir," she said; "you don't talk of getting into bed, do you?"

"Precisely so, madam."

At this, even Mr. Alfred plucked up something of a spirit, and shaking his head, he said—

"No—no, that won't do. You have come into my bedroom, sir. You have seen my wife in her night-cap and thingammy, and I warn you to mind what you are about, or you will rouse the British Lion, sir."

"If you consider yourself that individual," said Claude, "I may as well tell you what in the event of your refusal, I mean to do."

"What, sir? What?"

"Why, I shall be under the disagreeable necessity of throwing you out of the window. I will not blow out your brains first, because that would make a noise, but cutting your throat is an easy and quiet process, and that I may do; so as there is no time to lose, pray make up your mind, sir."

"Maria!" gasped Alfred, "Maria!"

"Well?"

"I think I'll go.   Life is—is——"

"Oh, you mean-spirited wretch!"

"Sweet, you know, and—and—I'm a-going.   Oh, have mercy upon me, sir. Who are you?"

"It cannot matter to you who I am," said Claude.   "But I warn you if you say one word about what has happened, and so be the means of my capture, although I may not be able to reach you myself from the prison to which I should be consigned, I have associates who will hunt you from one end of the world to the other."

Claude caught the nightcap from his head, as he stepped out of bed, and put it on himself.   Alfred made a bolt at the door of the room, and was gone in a moment.

"Madam," said Claude, as he at once got under the clothes into the place left vacant by Alfred.   "Madam, trust me."

"Oh, I shall never survive this night," said the lady.

"Yes, you will, madam.   I am only sorry you are yoked to a husband who would rather leave you in the way yours has done, than be thrown out of the window.   I would have had my throat cut twenty times, and been thrown out of one hundred windows, before I would have stirred from the side of so much loveliness."

"Don't speak to me."

"But, my dear madam—"

"Don't come any nearer, or I'll scream.   Indeed, I will, and then you will be taken, and serve you right."

"No—no.   Do not say so."

"Oh, I shall never forget this dreadful night.   Keep away, monster!"

"Madam, I am upon the extreme edge of the bed, and if I move only another half inch, I shall fall out upon the floor.   Mind, if anybody comes into the room, you are to call me my dear, and Alfred."

"Was there ever such assurance!"

"Scarcely ever.   My assurance is as scarce to be met with in a man, I should say, as your beauty in a woman."

A loud crash at this moment came from somewhere in the house, and Claude listened eagerly for the sound of approaching footsteps.   He had been most careful to fasten up the sliding panel at the back of the cupboard, so that there should be no suspicion excited by finding that open, that all was not right in the chamber.   The fact was, that the officers, although they had found out the secret passage, by dint of tapping upon the wainscot, and ascertaining by the sound that there was a circuitous hollow space behind it, had not found out any of the regular modes of entrance to that hollow space, but had reached it by knocking a hole in one of the panels in a room which they selected for the purpose of a careful examination.   Thus, then, was it that Claude heard a grand crash, which was occasioned by their breaking out the passage again into another room, not far from the bed-chamber in which he was.

"They come," he said.

"Mercy!   Oh, mercy, what will become of me, to be found in such a situation as this?" said the lady.   Oh, sir, be you whom you may, this is most ungracious and unmanly conduct of you."

"Nay, do not say that," replied Claude. "The secret of the whole occurrence rests with yourself and your husband.   He, surely, for his own sake, will keep the tale to himself, and you know that you have been compelled merely to endure my presence for a few minutes."

"Yet, sir, it is ungracious to compel me."

"Very well," said Claude. "It shall never be said that I owed my safety to such an act.   I will rise, madam, and defend myself against my foes as best I may; and when you see me weltering in my blood upon the floor of this room, you will then, at least. admit that I have not used arbitrary power over a lady, even to preserve my life."

He made a movement to rise.

"Stop a moment," she said. "How am I to know that this is not all a fiction? If you were, indeed, in such danger as you say, the whole affair would assume a widely different aspect. But how can I be assured of that?"

"By my telling you, madam, who I am, and so placing my life in your hands!"

"Tell me, then."

"I am Claude Duval."

The lady gave a start and a slight scream.

"What! Can I believe my eyes? Are you Claude Duval, the—the highwayman, and the man who is always so kind and so gallant to the ladies, that they never regret even being robbed by you, you do it with such an air, as one may say?"

"I am that individual, madam, whatever may be my merits or demerits. You have but to say, when the officers who are searching about this house for me, come into this room, which assuredly they will—'Here is Claude Duval,' they will at once attack me. I will not be taken, and they will kill me, so that you will have the satisfaction, if you please, of being my destruction."

"No—no, I cannot."

"You will not?"

"You have conquered. I cannot betray you, much as I condemn your life, and your presence here. No, I cannot say to any one—die!"

"Then I owe you my life; that is clear and distinct. I owe you my life, for it would, without your generous aid, have inevitably been sacrificed this night. I will not speak of my gratitude, but—"

"Hush! speak not at all. They come."

A confusion of voices outside the door of the room now came upon Claude's ears, and he heard the landlord say—

"Stuff! You know as well as I do, that the house is part of an old convent and, no doubt, there are all sorts of odd hiding places and corners in it. I am by far too much occupied in my bar to ferret them out. You may come as often as you please and do so; only if you break the walls, I shall fully expect that you will make them good again."

"That may or may not be," replied some one. "What do you say is in this room?"

"A gentleman and his wife, who came to town from Guilford only to-day. You will be the ruin of my inn if you go into folk's bedrooms disturbing them in this sort of way."

"We must do our duty, Mr. Peterson."

"Confound your duty, it will spoil my business; of course, I can't help it—but I have no doubt the lady and gentleman won't sleep another night in a house where they are liable to such visits."

"Oh, they won't mind us, when we tell them what we came about."

"Won't they?"

The principal officer tapped at the chamber-door; and then, after a short pause, Claude, in a capitally assumed voice, called out—

"Who's there?"

"Police officers, sir, in search of a highwayman," was the reply. "We are very sorry to disturb you, sir, but we are bound to search every room in the house."

Without waiting for any further parley, the officers opened the door, and with lights in their hands, walked into the room. Claude pulled the silk nightcap right down to his eyes, and muffled himself up to the chin in the clothes, as still in the assumed voice he said—

"God bless me, Maria, this is very unpleasant, indeed."

"Very," said the lady, faintly.

"Come—come," added Claude. "Landlord, do you call this a quiet house, where people are woke up in the middle of the night with a cock and a bull story about a highwayman? You may be all housebreakers yourselves, for all I know."

"It' all right, sir," said the principal officer, exhibiting a small staff with a little gilt crown at the top of it. "It's all right, sir. We shall not disturb you longer than just the time it will take us to be quite sure he has not slipped into this room and hidden, which he might do without your hearing, sir."

"I should say not," said Claude.

"Oh dear, yes, sir. He's as cunning as a fox, and has as many tricks as one, but he won't get the better of me very easily. No, no; I know a trick or two —and, though I say it myself, it's very difficult to deceive me."

"So I should think. Maria, my dear, we will leave here in the morning."

"Yes," said the lady; "yes, Alfred."

"Confound you all," said Claude, "have you done? I can tell by my wife's voice that she is as near fainting as possible."

"We are going, sir.—He ain't here, Grubbins."

"No, that's clear enough."

At this moment the door of the room, which had only swung shut, was flung violently open, and the husband—the veritable Alfred—made his appearance in the picturesque costume of a shirt only.

"I can't stand it," he cried, "I can't stand it any longer—I'm a desperate man. My brains are like a flue—I can't and won't put up with it—I'm really mad. Where's my wife?"

"Why, landlord," said Claude, "you told us you would shut up that poor lunatic; and you know when we saw him last night we would have left the house if you had not strictly promised he should be shut up."

"My wife—my wife!" roared Alfred. "Death and the devil—my wife!"

"I did promise to shut him up," said the landlord, "and forgot. Come along, Tommy, come along—no violence, Tommy."

"Who the devil do you call Tommy, sir?" cried Alfred. "Don't stand between me and the bed."

"Come, come, Tommy," said Claude, "go away."

"What is the meaning of all this?" said the principal officer.

"It's my poor brother Tom, sir," said Peterson; "the family cannot keep him among them. He ain't very dangerous; but he will have it that every woman he sees is his wife, and if we ever neglect locking him in his own room, he is sure to alarm the whole house.

"I ain't Tommy—I have no brother. That's my wife."

"You hear, gentlemen?"

"Poor devil," said the officer, "he ought to be in Bedlam."

"I think he is happier out," said the landlord.

"That may be all very well," said Claude; "but I don't see why I and my lady are to be disturbed, because your mad brother is happier out of Bedlam. Upon my word this is too bad. Don't faint, Maria, don't; I am here, you know, your Alfred."

"The lion is roused!" cried the husband. "He calls himself Alfred, and my Maria his Maria! Death and the devil! Murder! Curse all the world!"

"Take him away," said Claude.

"Do I smell a rat, or do I not?" said one of the officers.

"You had better call the cat," said Claude, "for fear."

"Come on," cried the principal officer. "Lay hold of your brother, landlord, and keep him under lock and key. We have wasted time enough with his folly. Push him along. We will lend you a helping hand if he be obstropulous at all. Be off, Tommy. Be off. What, you won't—won't you?"

"I ain't Tommy! I never was Tommy. I am Alfred, and that's my Maria. I ain't mad now; but I am going fast—fast. I shall be quite so in a little while if this goes on. Maria! Maria! I ask you if you don't know me, and acknowledge me as your husband. If you say no, I shall be satisfied that I am nothing but a madman."

" Answer him, my dear, to satisfy him," said Claude.

" Poor fellow. Take him away," said the lady.

Alfred, upon this, made a dash towards the bed, and Heaven only knows what might have resulted if the officers had not rushed upon him in a body, and laid hold of him tightly.

" Open the door," said one, "and we will take him out. Why he is as mad as a March hare. It's too bad to let such a dangerous lunatic be about, it is, indeed. You are to blame, landlord."

" I fear I am," said Peterson; "but if you knew all, gentlemen, you would alter your opinions; and so I will only take him up into his room till morning, poor fellow. Ah, gentlemen, once he had a fine mind, had Tommy. But now, you see what a wreck it is. He reminds me when he talks of the old harp in the drawing-room, with one half of the strings broken. Once it was all sweetness and melody, and now what a humdrum it is."

Alfred was forcibly removed from the room, and the door was closed again upon Claude Duval and the lady who had so delicately acted her part in the drama of his preservation. She had not said a word too much upon the occasion, and scarcely one too little.

———

CHAPTER XIII.

CLAUDE LEAVES THE PORCUPINE.—THE RECEIVER OF STOLEN GOODS
IN FINSBURY.

OF course, the search through the remainder of the inn for Claude was perfectly fruitless, and the officers were compelled to leave the house at length, with but a half conviction that they were mistaken, and yet with a complete one that, let the facts be how they might, they were baffled.

" Now," said the lady to Claude, after the room door had been closed for some few minutes. " Now, sir, you can with safety to yourself leave me."

" I will do so."

" I have but one request to make of you, and I think I am, after what I have done for you, entitled to have it granted."

" You have but to name it, and it is granted."

" It simply is, that the transactions of this night may be buried in oblivion, and that you name them to no one either in jest or earnest. Do you promise me that much ?"

" I do, upon my life and honour."

" I am satisfied. Now go."

Before Claude could get out of the bed, the room door was opened again, and the landlord made his appearance. Claude was taken completely by surprise at the manner in which Peterson spoke, but he soon found that there was good and substantial reason for it; and in a moment the conviction crossed him that the perils of that night were far from over.

" Sir," said Peterson, " I have come to apologise for the manner in which you have been disturbed."

" Don't mention it," said Claude; " I understand it all now. I don't think anything of it."

" Thank you, sir—you are very kind."

Peterson threw a small piece of paper on to the bed, and then at once left the room. There was light enough to read anything by, and Claude felt confident that upon that piece of paper he should find the reason of the mysterious conduct of the landlord. He looked at it earnestly. It contained the following words :—

"Be cautious! eight officers came into the house—seven only left. Is the eighth hiding in your room?"

Claude crushed up the little piece of paper in his hand, and lay down quite flat in the bed again. There were several considerations of moment connected with this alarming fact. Of course Claude was not, to say, afraid of the one officer; but he did not wish to commit Peterson in any way. The one man who had staid behind might, or might not, have an understanding with his companions who had gone. If he had, they might yet be lingering close at hand, in waiting for some intelligible signal. If he had not, cupidity alone could have prompted him to remain, for there was a reward offered for his, Claude's, apprehension. How was he to be baffled without killing him or compromising the house and its land-lord? That was the question.

"Are you going?" said the lady.

"In a moment."

"Is this your good faith, your lingering here after all I have done for you, when you may safely go? Is this generous—is it just?"

"I go," said Claude, as he sprang from the bed; "I go. God bless you, madam, I owe you much, and am overpoor in expressing my thanks."

Claude was not sure that he should be permitted even to leave the room without some interruption. He thought it most probable that the officer who had remained was the one who had said he smelt a rat, and who had been advised by him, Claude, to call the cat. If it were that man, Claude felt certain he should know him again, for he had regarded him particularly. Upon the landing he paused a moment. He heard a stir in the room he had just quitted, and then he knew that the officer was there. That was an important piece of intelligence, and he ran down the stairs as fast as he could. At the foot of the stairs he met Peterson with a light.

"Have you seen him, captain?"

"Yes, above."

"I thought as much. There is only one way now—only one way. Come on after me as quick as foot can fall. This way—this way. Don't mind what noise you make—come on quickly."

The landlord ran along a passage of some twenty feet in length, and then un-barred a door at its extremity. He still kept saying "Come on! come on!" and Claude followed him with a light and rapid step. The door, when opened, only showed a continuation of the passage; but soon the landlord stopped at a door to the left, which he flung wide open, and then when Claude was about to pass its threshold, he called out—

"No, no, no!"

"Not there?"

"No. Not unless you wish—But no matter. There is but one way. I don't like it—I shake at it—but there is but one way.

"What do you mean?" said Claude. "Explain yourself, Peterson. Why are you shaking in that way for, man? What do you purpose, that it has such an effect upon you"

"Only one way—only one way!"

"I insist upon knowing what you mean."

"Yes, captain, you shall know, of course you shall know, and you only. The secret must be kept locked up in your breast and in mine. This way—this way."

"What secret? What secret?"

"Patience, captain. Only a little patience. Follow me, and you will soon know. Trust to old Joe Peterson. There's only one way. If there were anothr you should take it. On—on through this room. You are sure he is up stairs?"

"Quite, but——"

"Hush! I know who it is. It's Wilkins. He shot poor Dick Harding—don't you recollect hearing of it, captain?—poor Dick Harding, who was as kind a soul as ever lived. He shot him last year, and did it wantonly, too. Oh, he's a regular brute is Wilkins."

"Confound him, is that the fellow?"

"Yes, captain.   He came in, but he did not go out."

The landlord had now opened another door about twelve paces from the one he had so ostentatiously flung aside, and that led into a room comfortably furnished, but he did not pause in it.   Passing on, he unlatched a door that conducted to an apartment so long that it passed at the back of the room, the door of which

THE ATTACK UPON CLAUDE DUVAL IN FINSBURY-SQUARE.

was thrown open. There Peterson paused, and opened another door that afforded a clear view into the first room, so that as he and Claude stood in it,   they could see across the first room,   right through its wide open door,   into the passage beyond.

"Wait here," said Peterson.

He drew a table as he spoke, so that it was visible through the two open doors; and then placing a chair by it, he added—

"You have nothing to do, captain, but to sit down here."

"This is mysterious, indeed," said Claude. "I know that whatever you do is for my benefit; but still, Peterson, I should like to know what it all means, and what in the end it is all to come to. I should have thought closed doors would have suited us better than all these open ones."

"Don't ask."

"But why not? Am I a child, Peterson, that I am to be told to do this, or to do the other, and know not a why or a wherefore?"

"You will thank me for not telling you. Sit down, Claude, and if you have any faith in me at all, ask nothing. Ah! I hear something."

Rapid footsteps approached.

"It is the officer," said Claude, as he took a pistol from his pocket. "He surely will not be so foolish as to encounter me?"

"What would you do?"

"If he will rush upon his own destruction, let him."

"Captain, put up your pistol. There's no occasion for it in the world. Put it up, I say, and sit still. When he comes to yon open door, and asks you, which he will, to surrender quietly, all you have to do is to pay no attention to him."

"But the doors are all open. He will come."

"Let him."

Peterson went into the room adjoining the passage, and Claude, with a perfect faith in the good feeling of Peterson towards him, and knowing that the existence of his house depended upon the police having nothing actually against him, he felt that he ought to submit to the plans dictated by him, Peterson. He accordingly sat down by the table, and looked through the outer room into the passage beyond, where he momentarily expected to see the officer; and he was not for many minutes kept in a state of suspense. Guided by the light which the landlord had placed upon the table at which Claude sat, and which sent some beams right through the outer room into the passage beyond, Wilkins the officer, for it was he, soon reached the spot. He had in his hand one of those short, stunted-looking pistols, so much patronised by the police in days gone by; and that he presented full at Claude through the open doors, as he said in a firm voice—

"Claude Duval, I know you. I suspected from the first the whole trick. You are my prisoner."

Claude only looked at him.

"Your time has come, Claude Duval; you are wanted. You know that sooner or later this hour would be sure to arrive; so it is quite useless to resist your fate. I tell you, you are wanted."

"By whom?"

"By me. I am not a man to be trifled with, and I will have you dead or alive; I have made up my mind to it, and set my life upon this task."

Claude still looked at him.

"Come out," added the officer. "None of your deep-laid tricks.—Come out, or I will shoot you dead as you there sit. I have shot as determined a man as you are before to-day.—Come out, I say."

"That is reasonable."

"What is reasonable? Come, come, this sort of thing won't do. Do you yield yourself up, Claude Duval? If so, you may depend upon the best treatment from me; and it may do you good at your trial that you did not resist."

"If you want me," said Claude, "take me; it is worth while coming across a room to do so.—I am am here and you are there; you talk a great deal, but you do little, Mr. Wilkins."

"Very well, I will come and take you; and, mark me, Claude Duval, I have taken a solemn oath; may I be smothered if I don't shoot you through the head if you make the least movement that I think looks like opposition."

As the officer said this, on he came.—On—on across the threshold of the room that opened to the passage, he made his way step by step. His eyes were fixed upon Claude, and the little plethoric-looking pistol was presented.

"Surrender! surrender!" he cried. "Now Claude, no resistance. If this were the last moment you had to live, you——"

"It's your last," said Peterson, suddenly emerging from the gloom of the room and standing close to the door of connection between the two apartments.—"It's your last, Wilkins, the murderer."

The floor opened, and down went the officer. One wild shriek came up from the deep abyss, and then all was still.

"Good God!" cried Claude.

"Hush!" said Peterson, "hush!"

He caught up the light from the table, and holding it over the aperture, looked keenly down.

"Hush! hush! It's all over."

Claude heard the rush of water. He sank back into the chair again, and said—

"This is horrible!"

"Humph! I don't see it," said Peterson. "You must have died by his hand, or he by yours. Now neither has happened. He as been, as it were, his own executioner; and if the spirit of poor Dick Harding was not there to receive him, it's an odd thing to me. He's gone for ever."

Claude shuddered.

"Peterson," he said, "I don't know that I can blame you. It was a case of life and death, and that man has perished; God be merciful to him. I had no idea you had any such contrivances as this in the house."

"It's no contrivance of mine," said Peterson;—"it's no contrivance of mine. I found it out by accident, only myself, captain, and an awkward accident it was. I only saved myself by holding on to the edge of this deep hole."

"Hark! what's that?"

"What?"

"I hear a cry," said Claude. "An awful cry. It comes from below. Do you not hear it? It is horrible! The wretch is not dead; he has found some resting place."

"No, no; impossible!"

A convulsive shriek came from below. It was the last cry of the man who had said he had set his life upon a cast, and who had so awfully—

"Stood the hazard of the die."

The trap-door, which was composed of two portions, slowly closed of itself. It looked like the grave yawning over its victim. Peterson shook so that the light got loosened in the stick. At the moment that the double-doored trap closed, it fell from the stick, and all was darkness.

"What's that for?" cried Claude.

"An accident, only an accident," said Peterson. "Don't stir, for your life's sake. The slightest step upon this trap, and down it goes."

"Be careful yourself."

"I will—I will. I must come your way, and by keeping close to the wall I am safe enough. Remember, captain, that this is one of the secrets of the old Porcupine that only you and I know."

"And Wilkins."

"Why do you mention him? He has gone to his account. All's right. This is your arm I am touching?"

"My arm? No!"

"God, what is it then? Something soft and warm."

The landlord made a leap into the room where Claude was, and upset the table, crying.—

"Off—off. Keep off, Wilkins; you—you brought your death upon yoursef. It was your own doings. You know it was your own doings. Off—off—off!"

Claude heard a heavy fall.

" Peterson! Peterson!" he called.

There was no answer. The landlord had fallen upon the floor of that inner room in a swoon.

CHAPTER XIV.

CLAUDE IN DANGER IN FINSBURY SQUARE.—A REMARKABLE CHANGE.

THE situation of Duval was anything but a pleasant one. He had seen quite enough of the Porcupine Inn to feel abundant faith in what the landlord had stated regarding the odd and secret places in it; and there he was in the very focus, as it were, of such mysteries, with the only person who could guide him clear of them in a state of insensibility. Call for assistance he could not think of, and he was fearful of moving much lest he should fall down some other trap-door that might be as conveniently placed for his reception, as the one that had already received its victim was for the reception of the unfortunate Wilkins. All he could do was to wait, with what amount of patience he could command, for the revival of Peterson. At length that happy event seemed to take place. The landlord uttered a deep groan that seemed to come from the bottom of his heart.

" Peterson!" said Claude. " Peterson!"

" Ah, yes," replied the landlord, in a vacant sort of way.

" Rouse yourself, man."

" Ay, yes."

" Come, Peterson. Bethink you of where you are, and don't be foolish, man. Get up and show me the way out of this abominable place."

" I begin to comprehend a little," said Peterson. " Ah, it's all coming back to me now, I recollect. What on earth made me faint, I wonder? I am not in the habit of that sort of thing."

" I should suppose not. But never mind the cause of it. Let it suffice now that you are recovered, and that, consequently, you can lead me out of this place, for which I assure you I have no sort of affection."

" I should wonder if you had."

" Get up then."

" All's right. Only tell me, did Wilkins call out again after the trap closed, or was it after all only my fancy that made me think so?"

" He did."

" It's a very dreadful thing then. But still he brought his fate upon himself."

" To some degree, that is true," said Claude. " But let us forget the past. It is irremediable. and we may only embarrass ourselves by recurring to it."

Claude was glad to find that Peterson had no recollection of the immediate cause of his swoon, namely, his supposition that he had encountered some one in the dark. Of course it could only be a matter of imagination, and it was quite as well that the landlord should not be unmanned by a recollection of it.

" Do you know the way," said Claude. " in the dark?"

" Yes, pretty well. But I would rather have a light for all that; it was stupid enough of me to drop the candle."

" Don't say any more about it, but lead on. There, I have got a hold of your coat, and will follow closely in your footsteps."

" Are you sure it is you that have hold of my coat?"

" Don't be a fool, man Of course I am sure. Why, you are quite wandering in your intellect to-night, Peterson. I can't think what has come over you, man."

" Nor I neither."

Claude Duval had really no great faith in the guidance of Peterson, considering the state of mind he was in; but there was no resource. He knew nothing of the route he had to take himself, with the exception of a steady determination not to pass through the open door leading to the room where the yielding trap was, and that he felt confident he knew the direction pretty well. Peterson avoided that door.

"Well, you are right enough now," said Claude.

"How do you mean, captain, by right enough?"

"You know your way I mean."

"Yes, yes, for the matter of that I know my way; but I would give something if I could tell what was that I touched in the dark. The idea of it comes over me with a cold shudder now; and when you said it was not you, my heart seemed to leap into my mouth, and then I seemed to step down a trap myself, and I knew no more till I was speaking to you about my recovery. Answer me one question, captain, if you please, and answer it candidly."

"What is it?"

"Do you believe in ghosts?"

"No."

"Are you only saying that to encourage me, or do you really think what you say?"

"I really think what I say. If there were any such things as ghosts, Peterson, the world would not have wagged so many hundreds of years without the fact being established, which you know is a long way off from being the case."

"There is something in that," said Peterson.

During the continuance of this little dialogue, the landlord had been leading Claude from those strange chambers, which had echoed with the death shriek of the officer; and suddenly upon opening a door there came quite a blaze of light upon their eyes, compared with the profound darkness of the place they had been in. This effect, though, was only comparative, for all the light only came from a little oil lamp, that was upon the first step of a small flight of stairs.

"Thank God!" said Peterson, as he put up a bar against the door they had passed through, "we are out of that part of the house."

"It was not wanting," said Claude.

"Far from it. I don't think, captain, I shall ever venture there again. It don't rightly belong to the inn, you know, but is part of the old original convent, they say."

"And the water?"

"What water?"

"The water I heard splashing down the trap."

"I know just as much about that as you do, captain, surmising that you know nothing at all. Where it comes from, or where it goes to, is a mystery. I only hope neither you nor I will ever have occasion to go near it again."

"Amen!" said Claude.

A very few moments now sufficed to carry them to the habitable part of the inn; and then Claude taking from his pocket-book the notes he had relieved the stock-broker from the care of, he showed them to Peterson, saying—

"I think the numbers are known of these, for they came from a man of business. What shall I do with them?"

"I know some one who will deal with you for them. They will go famously on the continent. But you must want rest now. It is nearly three o'clock in the morning, and the best thing you can do is to go to bed till the dawn."

"But my horse?"

"Trust me, that's all right; I rang the bell, and that's quite sufficient for my stable-man. Your horse was put in a secure place, you may depend."

"Then, Peterson, I will lie down for an hour or two."

"Good."

"But remember, I must be off before the daylight has fairly opened its eyes."

"I shall be up and stirring. There is the disposal of the notes to look to. But that can easily be done. It is only in Finsbury that we have to go. Come this way, captain, and I'll show you to your room."

Claude followed him to a bed-room, and soon cast himself upon a bed, having only taken off his coat and boots. Bidding the landlord, then, a brief good-night, although he might more properly have said good-morning, Duval was in a few moments fast asleep.

"Lucky fellow," said Peterson. "He can sleep, but I am afraid I can't.— What could it have been that I touched in that room? What could it have been? I shall not forget to-night soon."

*   *   *   *   *   *   *

To Claude the few hours' rest he got seemed merely like so many minutes. He was quite astonished when he felt some one shaking him, and heard the voice of Peterson crying to him—

"Up—up, captain. The sun is rising, and you must follow the example."

"Agreed," said Claude.

He sprang from his couch, and stretched himself.

"Cold water, Peterson, and in plenty, if you please. It is the only thing that will thoroughly wake me up. Ah, what's that?"

A confused noise, and then some moans came upon his ears.

"It's the couple in the next chamber," said the landlord. "When the officers were gone, I unlocked the door of the room in which I had confined the husband, and told him I was very sorry but couldn't help it. He is taking his revenge out upon his wife, I suppose."

"Which he shall not do," cried Claude, "while my name is——"

At this moment the cries became so loud, that the landlord ran out of the room to ascertain what was going on; and scarcely had he left it a moment, when there rushed into it the lady in her night-dress, crying as she did so—

"Help! help! He is really mad!"

Claude caught her in his arms.

"You are safe—quite safe," he cried, "with me."

"Ah, you here!" she said; and then shuddering, she closed her eyes, and fell into a swoon.

There came into the room, through the casement, sufficient of the rays of the young day to fall upon the face of the lady, and clearly render it observable by Claude. He was surprised at her youth and beauty; and as she lay helpless in his arms, he could not help feeling how blessed he should be if he could call such a creature his own. Certainly Claude should not have done so, but he pressed his lips to those of the young bride, and as one kiss is apt to provoke an appetite for more, he took a dozen. Then she recovered a little; and with a long drawn sigh, looked up in his face, amazed.

"Where am I?" she said.

"With one who loves you."

"My husband?"

"Does he love you? Can such a man love you as you should be loved? Ah, no! It is reserved for me, beautiful Maria (Claude recollected her name at the moment) to convince you of what love really is."

"I must not listen to this."

"I adore you!"

"Where is she?—where is she?" cried a voice in the passage. "Where is she?—I will have her life—I will be hung for Maria! Only let me find her, and kill her, and then they may hang me. I am really mad now! Where is she?"

"It is my husband!"

"Fear nothing," whispered Claude, as still holding her in his arms, he set his back against the door of the chamber. "Fear nothing, dearest, I will protect you. He shall not enter here."

"I will kill her!—I will kill her!" cried the husband again; "get out of my way! She came into this room. Death and the devil, I will kill her and be hanged for Maria."

"Don't be a fool," said Peterson, in the passage.

"I will—I will."

"Come, come, Mr. Finch, your good lady has gone down stairs, I think, and if you must go after her, that's the way."

"Ten thousand devils, I will have her life—I insist upon being hung for Maria—I will be hung for Maria!"

They heard him go down the stairs—at least, by the voice they felt certain that he had; and then Claude spoke—

"So your name is Finch?" he said.

"Yes—yes."

"I will never name you other than Maria; Finch is only the name of your odious husband. How came so much beauty and excellence to be thrown away upon such a man? Maria, I love you; do not turn from me; I love you with the love of a thousand Finches."

"No—no."

"I say, yes. No one but yourself in this world dare say no to such a truth. Am I not bound to you by the strongest ties of gratitude? Have you not this night save my life?"

"Let me go—let me go, sir."

"Nay, but one kiss."

Again he pressed his lips to hers; she struggled to free herself from his embrace, and in a tone that even made him sensible, at even such a moment as that, that his behaviour was not exactly the thing, she cried—

"Unhand me, sir, if you are a gentleman. Do not let me think that I have fallen into the grasp of a ruffian!"

Claude let her go in a moment.

"Pardon me," he said. "Do not go until you have pardoned me for a rashness—a presumption that ——"

"No more, sir—no more!"

"You will kill me if you are so wicked. If I have not your full forgiveness I may as well sacrifice my life to those who will be only too glad to take it. Maria—Maria, don't turn from me in anger."

"Do you deserve, sir, aught but anger from me?"

"Nay, Maria, do not treat me according to my deserving, but according to your own gentleness."

"Peace, on, peace. My name is Finch."

"Odious name! I cannot call you by it. As Maria, say that you forgive me; or bid me at once give myself up to the officers of justice, and I will do it. You will then be avenged."

"Avenged? I want no vengeance. Let us now part, sir, once and for ever."

"No—Ma——"

"Yes, it must be so. If you do love me, you will permit me now to leave this room and retire to my own."

"What? to await the ire of an infuriated husband?"

"By the time he returns his passion will be gone. He is only this way by fits and starts, and his threats mean nothing, although I admit at the time they alarm me much, and to-night they were worse than usual."

"If you must go, I will keep this in remembrance of you."

As he spoke, Claude snatched a ring from her finger; but she clasped her hands entreatingly, saying—

"Oh, restore me that! It was his gift, and he will miss it."

"Come for it," said Claude, "to-night at eight o'clock to No. 5, Spring Gardens, and ask for Count Stofet."

"I cannot, I dare not, I ——"

Claude stopped her mouth with kisses. He pressed her to his heart. The door was opened.

"Mrs. Finch, go to your room at once," said Peterson. "Your husband has hurt his foot over something, and his coming limping up stairs."

She darted from Claude's arms, and was gone in a moment.

"Confound you," said Claude, "I could knock your head off."

"My head off?"

"Yes! But no matter, she shall yet be mine!"

CHAPTER XV.

LIFE IN THE WEST.—CLAUDE AMONG THE FASHIONABLES.

PETERSON shook his head at Claude.

"Well," said the latter. "What now, stupid?"

"Ah, captain, captain! But it's no business of mine. Look out. Is it early enough for you still, or have you put off too much time with Mrs. Finch, to go to Finsbury about the notes?"

"Excuse me," said Claude, looking rather confused "" I have been rather, in a manner of speaking, forgetful, Peterson; but if I have said anything harsh, pray forget it,"

"Don't mention it. She is a nice-looking creature."

"Don't say another word about her to me just now, Peterson. I am sorry for her, poor thing, for she is united with one who cannot make her happy. Come, if you are ready to go out, I am. I suppose my horse is all right?"

"At the side door."

"Good. I thought once last night it was a doubtful chance whether I ever bestrode my good steed again."

"Things looked queer; but come on. You may make up your mind now that Wilkins was quite alone, and had stayed thinking to outwit his comrades; and a pretty piece of business he has made of it."

Claude found a boy holding his horse at the side door of the old Porcupine. He gave him a guinea—Claude always paid his way manfully; and then mounting, he said to Peterson—

"How will you get on?"

"I will walk upon the pavement, captain, and seem to take no sort of notice of you; but when you see me stop at a door, you can stop likewise, for it will be the one you want."

"Very well, I will go at a walk, so you will have no trouble in the matter."

"That will do. How clear the streets are. We seem to have London to ourselves."

"It looks likes it. Hark! what is that?"

"St. Paul's striking four."

They crossed Finsbury-square, and Peterson took his way down a street called Green-street, at the north-east corner of it. It led them somehow to the back of Bishopsgate. Suddenly he stopped at what, to all external appearance, looked like an empty house. Stooping close to the ground, he found an obscure bell-handle, which he gave a hearty pull at. The street door then opened as if by magic.

"Go in," said Peterson.

"Whose shop is it?" said Claude, as he dismounted. "I know some of the folks in this line. What's his name?"

"Lake."

"Lake—Lake! No. I don't know him by that name. Will you hold the horse a minute or two, Peterson?" Is the fellow trustworthy?"

"Of course."

"Humph!"

Peterson held the horse while Claude crossed the threshold of the house. He was hardly two paces in the passage when a harsh voice cried—

"Who is it?"

"What's that to you?" said Claude. "It's a customer: that's enough."

"Turn to the right."

He found a door a few paces to the right, which conducted him into a squalid parlour. It was full of miserable worn-out furniture, and in one corner was a wretched pallet bed, on which lay an old man, that there was no difficulty in at

SIR FELIX MOFFAT ATTEMPTS TO SHOOT CLAUDE DUVAL.

once seeing was of the chosen people. He glared at Claude from amid a mass of filthy bed-clothes, and then said—

"It is Duval!"

"You know me?"

"Yes. It is my business. What have you got, my pet? I am glad to see you here. You will come again. I often thought I ought to have you for a customer; but you used to go to Lyon's."

"I did."

"Well, you will come to me again. What have you got for the old man, my pet?"

Somewhat amused at the singular mode of address of the old receiver of stolen goods, Claude handed him the notes, saying—

"I'm afraid of getting anybody into trouble about the numbers. They may be known; but I am not at all certain."

"And you don't mind me getting into trouble?"

"Not a bit."

"Ha, ha! my pet, I like you. A thousand pounds in notes! Ha!—Humph! Dear, dear me! Worth nothing. I shall have to send them to Germany, and then have them all sent back, for they won't pass now even at the Roulette tables of the German princes, who support themselves by keeping gaming-houses. And yet, my pet, I will give you something for them. You shall have—you shall have two hundred pounds in good notes, that you shall."

"Be quick."

"You will take it—you are satisfied?"

"Oh, yes."

The old man fell back among the pestiferous bed-clothes with a deep groan. Claude thought he was taken suddenly ill, or was, perhaps, dying, and he said—

"What the deuce is the matter now? Is the devil going to have his own at last?"

"No—no! Oh, dear—oh, dear! Oh! he says he's satisfied, and I might have offered him less. He says he is satisfied!"

"Ha!—ha!" laughed Claude. "That's it, is it? Comfort yourself. I would not have taken less, you old rascal; so hand out the notes. Quick! Be quick about it, for I am in a hurry."

"Yes, my pet, yes; and so you would not have taken less?"

"Not a farthing."

"What a comfort."

The old man dived his hand among his bed-clothes and produced a pocket-book, from which he took two £100 notes, and handed them to Claude, saying—

"There, my pet. There, you are a rich man. I shall never see my money back again, I know; but then you are my pet, and that makes all the difference."

"For all I know to the contrary," said Claude, "these two notes may be in the same predicament as mine. If such should be the case, and I find you have played me a trick, you may depend upon me coming back and smothering you."

"My pet—my pet!"

Claude made no further remark, but rose and left the house.

"You have mode short work of it," said Peterson.

"Yes. I have got two hundred pounds in notes of him. I suppose I may depend that they are all right, Peterson, and not stolen ones?"

"Oh, yes; but it is too little by at least half. It is scandalous."

"Never mind, I can afford it. Here's one of them for you, and the other will provide us with a little pocket-money."

"I do not require so much as £100, captain. It's too much, indeed it is."

"Pho, not a whit. Put it in your pocket, man; I'm glad I have the opportunity of handing it to you. Don't have any scruples about it."

"Well, all I can say is, that as long as the old Porcupine has got one quill to rustle against another, there's a home for you, captain, and confusion to all your enemies. If you are hard pressed by the Philistines, and should be a hundred miles off, make for the old inn; and the moment you cross its threshold, I'll answer for your safety."

"Thank you, I know that, and it's no slight thing."

They had now reached Finsbury-square again, and Claude had just turned his horse's head westward, when from Chiswell-street there dashed out four men on horseback.

"That's him !" cried one, pointing with the handle of a riding-whip at Claude. "That's him. Down with him !"

"Indeed," said Claude.

The whole four horsemen made a rush at Claude, and the one who had the whip struck him a blow with the lead-loaded handle of it, which, if it had hit him on the head as it was intended, would have finished his career, to the great detriment of this faithful chronicle of his sayings and doings. But such was not to be. Claude swerved a little, and the blow fell almost harmless upon his shoulder. He then drew one of his holster pistols, and fired it clean in the face of the man with the whip, who fell across his horse's neck with a peep sigh. At this moment Claude was dismounted, and this was rather cleverly effected. One of the four assailants had sprung off his horse, letting the animal go where it liked, and it did gallop into the city, and then taking advantage of Claude being occupied with the others, he seized his right leg and fairly canted him over his horse's side. A couple of pistols were fired at him the same moment by the two mounted men, who kept their steeds and were unhurt; but the shots missed him, and in a moment he played one of them the same trick as regarded the unhorsing as had been played himself. The only man who was now mounted tried to cut Claude down with a police cutlass; but Duval drawing from his breast a small bright pistol, shot him in the arm, and he dropped the cutlass. One of the dismounted men made a rush to lay hold of Claude by the legs as he tried to mount again, but he was met by such a kick from the heavy boots that Claude wore, that he lay upon the road quite insensible. The affair was now merely a struggle between Duval and the only one of his assailants who was in a condition to follow him, to see which would be first mounted; and Claude won that battle. He could have shot this remaining man the moment he got into the saddle, for he had his other holster pistol ready at his hand. He half drew it out, but then, thrusting it back again with the words, "Blood enough already !" he started at a gallop towards the City-road. The man, who did not want for courage, was after him in a moment, shouting as he went—

"A highwayman ! stop him !—stop him !—a highwayman !"

The cry was of little use at that time in the morning in the streets, for they were nearly deserted; and at the busiest part of the day, that was no very great thoroughfare, bustling as it is now. The man fired at him once, and Claude heard the bullet whistle past his head. He took no notice of it, however, but rode on, for he was quite satisfied that the other's horse was no match for his steed. Claude's only danger was in the event of meeting with horsemen, who, in consequence of the hue-and-cry kept up by his opponent, might try to capture him. But this was not likely at such an hour. For a mile all he met was a market-cart, the driver of which drew up as near to the curb as he could to get out of the way. The man, whoever he was, fired again, and then Claude turned in his saddle rather angrily, and looked back. He saw sufficient to put him quite at his ease regarding his enemy. The horse was terrified at the discharge of the pistol, and was rearing in rather an uncomfortable manner; then it suddenly dashed into a gallop and fell, throwing its rider some yards over its head.

"That will do," said Claude.

A ten minutes' swift canter brought him to a turning to the left, which upon pursuing, conducted him to the back of the Strand. Then he let his horse subside into a walk.

"This won't do," he said. "I must not show in my true character for some time, or London, and perchance its environs too, will get too hot to hold me; and yet, I wonder if Mrs. Finch will come for her ring ?"

It was sparkling on his little finger.

"She is pretty, engaging, and captivating. I don't know when anyone has so touched me as she has. If she don't, if she cannot or will not, I can and will seek her out. I can almost fancy now I feel her soft lips close to mine. I will risk something to press em once more; ay, that I will."

He paused at a livery stables near Charing Cross, and rang a bell that, without dismounting, he could reach. It was answered by a man in stable costume, who respectfully touched his cap.

"Is William here?" asked Claude.

"No, my Lord Count," said the man.

"Very well. Take the horse, and when you see him, say that I am in town again."

"Yes, my lord."

Claude dismounted, and abandoning his horse—which showed not the least sign of having had a gallop—to the man, he walked very briskly in the direction of Spring Gardens.

"I will do the gentleman awhile," he said, to himself, "and mix in some of the gaieties and the frivolities of this great city, to which my title of Count gives me admittance; thanks to the folly of the young Lord Glosy. Ha! ha! f h e only knew who it really was now that he introduced as the Count Stofet!"

He laughed as he walked on, and soon reaching the quiet aristocratic thoroughfare called Spring Gardens, he knocked ond rang at a large house, a plate on the door of which announced that it was No. 5.

    *   *   *   *   *

It will have been observed that during the late affray in Finsbury Square, Peterson, the landlord of the Porcupine, had been remarkably quiet, taking no part in it at all. This was sound judgment, for, completely unarmed as he was, he could have done nothing effectual, and would only have brought suspicion upon himself, and hindered himself from being of the remotest benefit another time. Besides, he had great faith in Claude's power to cope in the fair open air with four adversaries. The result was favourable to Peterson's powers of judgment, and when he saw Claude, to all appearance uninjured, fairly ride away, he ran home alone, telling himself as he went, that he believed Claude Duval had both the devil's help, and his own luck. The fact was, that in the contest that had taken place in Finsbury Square, the great difference between Duval and his opponents consisted in that he was fighting for his life, and they only for a reward. He knew that if he were worsted in the contest his death upon the gallows-tree was certain, and he felt that it was best to die in the midst of a manly struggle to keep his life and liberty than be made the holiday show of a crowd that would have gaped at his dying agonies, and made food for after gossip of his last convulsions. Hence arose, then, that daring recklessness which actually made such a man an equal, and more than equal match for four others, who were not actuated by any such motives. The pistol shots were all that he had to dread, and anyone who knows anything of fire-arms, knows how very little, in a struggle, such a weapon is to be at all depended on.

CHAPTER XVI.

DOINGS AT THE PALACE.—A MAID OF HONOUR.

THE hour is six, and the scene we would present to the reader is a very different one to what we have had occasion to bring under his notice. Just rid the mind entirely of all that is poor, squalid, or ungraceful, amid the numerous images that the fancy will suggest, and step into an atmosphere of so different a complexion, that while inhaling it, and feasting the eye upon the many charms of art that meet it, one may well, for a time, forget that there is such a thing as misery in the world. In an apartment of most luxurious proportions and appointments sits one who, by the negligent attitude he assumes upon the silken couch, and his dress of in-door ease, is evidently the temporary or the permanent master of the place. Rich draperies hang from the windows, shutting out the noisy world, and the too glaring light of the day; for although it is long past mid-day, the sun has not yet got below the house tops. A chandelier, looking as though it were composed of millions of sparkling jewels, depends from the ceiling. The floor is covered with rare carpeting, and strewed here and there, in apparent confusion, but not taste, are many articles of furniture, contributing to ease and to splendour. And all this reflected by mirrors placed upon every wall, so that to the unpractised eye that apartment might seem of immense extent. He who sat, or rather lolled, upon one of the couches, however, did not cast one glance around him upon the beauty of his house. A small table, richly inlaid with pearl, was drawn close to him, and upon it was one of those tall-necked bottles that proclaim the vintage of southern Europe. Occasionally he raised a glass of the sparkling liquid to his lips, and then he would sink back among the luxurious cushions of the couch, and appear to be half asleep. This was only in appearance, though—the brain of that individual was sufficiently active. Our readers will not believe that we are introducing them to any one remarkable for indolence, either mentally or physically, when we announce that the personage surrounded with all this splendour is no other than Claude Duval! Yes, vulgar robbers retire into caverns and fastnesses deep in the earth when they require repose, or they make a home along with the owl in some dim old ruin, the haunt of—

"———— Spectres terrible, and wailing night-birds,
Soothing the fancy with a dream of horrors."

But Claude Duval did no such thing. When he for a short time—sometimes it was for days, and sometimes for weeks—retired from business, he at once plunged into an elegant line of life, that presented for him many opportunities. Fascinating in his manners—distinguished in his appearance—and with a delightful air of majesty about him, he was just the sort of person to make his way among a certain set; and although there doubtless were exclusive circles among the aristocracy that required to know something more of a man than they could know of him before they admit any one to their families, he did not regret that he was not welcomed to such frigidity. The acquaintance of a young nobleman of undoubted rank, a Lord Glosy, had stood him in good stead as an introduction, and few personages at the time were more popular than the mysterious, handsome, dashing Count Stofet. Where he derived his countship from—where were his domains, and what were his resources, were all profound mysteries; but that he had the means and the habits of a gentleman, and that he had resources in abundance, were facts totally evident to all who in any way came in contact with him. He gamed, intrigued, and rioted with the best of the set, among whom he found a ready-enough welcome; and, when in town, he was always to be found at No. 5, Spring Gardens. He kept but one personal attendant, and that was a young man named William, to whom he, Claude, had behaved with singular kindness. William knew who and what his master was, and kept the secret faithfully; attending upon him with all the zeal and devotion as though he had been a veritable count, and his good will was of the greatest importance to him. The room in which Claude sat was one of three that were on the same floor. One was a reception-room, one a bed-room, and one a kind of private apartment—half drawing-room, half boudoir, in which he commonly himself sat. That is the room in which we find him. Claude touched a small hand-bell of richly wrought silver that lay upon the table, and William in a few moments appeared.

"Well, William," said Claude, "how goes it with you?"

"Quite well, sir, thank you."

"I'm glad to hear it. Is your mother well?"

"Oh yes, sir. Thanks to you, the old dame looks younger and more hearty every day. She loves so the little cottage you bought for her; and her prayer each day is that you ———"

"There—there—Enough, William—enough.   If she be happy, and you are pleased, I am quite satisfied."

"But our gratitude ——"

"Say no more about it, William.   How much worse a use have I made of many a few hundred pounds than those that gave your mother, in her old age, a home!"

"Instead of the workhouse, sir," added William, as he wiped a tear from his eye.   "And I, too, was quite destitute and could do nothing for her."

"Anybody been, William?"

"A few cards left, sir.   Lord Glosy has called here, and offered me a guinea the last time, to tell him who you were."

"Ha, ha!"

"And the little marchioness, sir."

"Ah!"

"She came once and told me she had heard that you were a married man, and had a wife in Hungary—I think she said it was in Hungary."

"That is good.   Who could have imposed upon the marchioness with such a story, I wonder?   So, those are all the calls, William, that I have been honoured with?"

"All sir—here is a letter that came to-day."

Claude opened it, and read as follows—

"MY DEAR COUNT—One of those general entertainments at St. James's, at which it is possible to poke in a friend, takes place to-night.   If you should chance to be in town, I will call at twelve for you.—Yours truly, GLOSY."

"To-night?" said Claude.   "To-night?   Humph!   I may be busy.—By-the-by, William, how are you off for money?   You should always speak to me upon that score, as I am apt to forget you."

"You seldom forget me, sir.   The last supply was considerable, and I have some of it left, and I have paid up everything, sir.   Yet, if I am not to have the pleasure of seeing you again for another month, it may be necessary to meet some tradesman's bill; and I know it is your wish that everything should be paid the moment the demand is made."

"It is, William.   Get change for this £100 note, and take of it what you think you will want.   Give me back the remainder."

"Yes, sir."

"You feel quite sure, William, that there has been no suspicious inquiries, and that I am by no means in any way confounded with a certain desperate character called Claude Duval?"

Claude smiled as he said this.

"Oh, yes, sir, quite.   Who would fancy, for a moment, that the Count Stofet was anybody but just what he says he is?   You may trust to me, sir, to let you know as soon as the least shadow of suspicion arises.   We servants are in a position to hear much more than our masters."

"I believe it, I believe it.   Go for the change, William; and when you come back, it will be time to light up; I shall remain in to-night until Glosy comes, and then I don't know but I may go to this palace ball."

"I would not, sir."

"Why so, William?"

"Because, sir, it is generally understood that your title is a Hungarian one, and you may meet with some real noblemen of that country, who may, by the officious zeal of some of your friends, be brought to speak to you."

"Well, that would be a little awkward.   I will consider of it."

William left the room, and Claude threw himself back upon the cushions of the couch, and taking from his pocket a small morocco case, he opened it where there were some memoranda.

"Let me see," he said.   "What have I in the shape of amusement, now that I am in London for a few days."

He commenced reading from the memoranda—

" ' Laura B., age eighteen—has a lover, but can be easily got away from such a spooney. A blonde, rather plump and playful, not over-wise.'

" I have got nearly sick of blonds," he said, as he turned over the leaf. " Humph ! what have we here ?"

" ' Clara A. Dark, graceful, and agile. Age, about twenty. Her husband a clerk in the customs.'

" Ah," said Claude. " Clara is really worth looking after : I recollect her well. The jealousy of her husband first put it into her head that there were other men in the world worth looking at besides him. A common enough case. Let me see who comes next.

" ' The Marchioness of C. Little, plump as a partridge in full feather, lively, neither fair nor dark. Her husband at Constantinople as attached to the Embassy.'

" Ha, ha ! and did the stupid marquis really suppose that his wife was to lead the life of a nun, while he was flirting with the blue-eyed and the black-eyed beauties of the Bosphorus ? No, not exactly, if I can help it. She has called here, too, William tells me. She is mine ! Well, well, I must pay some attention to the little marchioness."

He read again from the pocket-book.

" ' Maria R. Husband a lawyer. She difficult, but a beautiful creature—hair dark as a raven's wing—age about twenty-three. Husband forty, at least, and as ugly as Satan. She married him for his money, and despises him for buying a wife.'

" Ah," said Claude, "that name, Maria, puts me in mind of Mrs. Finch. How dark it is getting ; I can scarcely see to read "

A French clock upon the chimney-piece began to strike ; Claude counted the silvery sounds—1—2—3—4—5—6—7.

" So late ! Where can William be, I wonder ? Oh, if Mrs. Finch should, after all take it into her head to come ? No—no. It is next to impossible. She is not the sort. Besides, the hurried manner in which I gave her the address was such, that, no doubt, she forgot it in her confusion the moment it was uttered. No, there is no chance, I fear, of her coming. Ah, William."

" Sir, as I turned the corner——"

" Yes—yes."

" The marchioness——"

" Oh, only her ?"

" If you don't want to see her, you need not. She tried to catch my eye to ask me if you had returned, but I would not see her, sir, so that it is quite at your option to say you are here or not here, you know, sir."

" Yes—yes. And yet——"

He rose, and paced the room in anxious thought.

" If I could only feel quite sure that Maria would not come, if I could only banish from my mind the idea that it is possible she may come—I would not have her arrive while the marchioness is here, for £1000, that I would not, and yet there is no probability of her coming. Not the least—not the least. William !"

" Yes, sir."

" I will see the marchioness."

" Very well, sir."

" And, mark me, William. If a lady should come in the course of the evening and ask for me, you will show her into the reception-room quite quietly, and then let me know by coming and saying—' I have delivered the note.' You understand ? Those words will let me know that she is here."

" Yes, sir, I will be careful."

" Do so. Ah, there is a summons at the door. It is, no doubt, the marchioness ; I wonder what her servants think of her coming here ?"

" They fancy she calls upon the celebrated court milliner, Madam Stockwellini who occupies a part of the ground floor."

" Grand—grand. If it be her, show her up at once."

" Yes, sir."

William left the room, and as he went down the stairs he muttered to him-self—

" I wonder how much of this £100 he wants back, or if he will forget it altogether ?   I have known him do such a thing as that before now.   How I am grappling money ! I shall be rich some day—quite rich, and what care I how it is got ?   He thinks me quite a pattern of gratitude.   Gratitude ? ha, ha ! I will stick to him as long as he has got plenty of money, but no longer."

Claude had no suspicion of William.   He fully believed him to be the simple-minded, honest fellow that he appeared.   This was a mistake, indeed ; Claude should have asked himself what right he had, as a general thing, to find common decency of feeling, common honesty or faith, in human nature more than any one else ?   He waited somewhat impatiently for the appearance of the marchioness, of whom he has himself, by the little memorandum he has read concerning her ladyship, given quite a sufficient description.   There are only two classes of society in England that completely throw off all virtue, and abandon themselves to their worst passions, and those are the low and the high.   If we wish to find real worth and real modesty of mind and manners, we must look to the educated middle class—not to folks with money, and who can keep up a grand appearance, for among them there is as much vice as among the squalid denizens of the courts of St. Giles's ; but to those who, whether they be poor or rich, are mentally cultivated and have tastes that render vice hideous.   The door of Claude's room was thrown open, and the well-instructed William merely bowed as he ushered in the lady, without announcing her at all by name.   Claude rose to receive her with a fascinating smile upon his really handsome features.

CHAPTER XVII.

A LITTLE DISTURBANCE.—THE MILLINER'S APPRENTICE.

" IT is impossible !" cried the marchioness.   " The Count Stofet in London ?'

" To his happiness—yes," replied Claude.   " What could keep him long away from the atmosphere of your presence, lovely Marchioness ?"

" Ha, ha !   Well, that is something new, count.   You have managed to survive a whole month in some totally different atmosphere."

" But I am overjoyed now that my hour of exile is over, to find I have, while absent, filled so important a place in your ladyship's recollection."

" In my recollection ?"

" Yes, else the period would not have been computed so exactly ; I have been from London one month to-day, and it has appeared to me an age.   You are more beautiful than ever, if that be possible.   More fascinating you cannot be !"

" Indeed ?"

" Yes.   Permit me upon those lips to——"

" Count—count !"

" Marchioness ?"

" Well, you certainly are the most impudent, ugly fellow, that I have known for a long time past.   If I had had the least idea of such rudeness I should certainly not have come myself with an invitation to a little supper at two this night."

" Two this night ?   To-night, or rather to-morrow morning, I'm afraid, I have got to go with Glosy to the palace."

" The palace ?"

" Yes.   He has dropped me a note to that effect."

" Why, surely you are aware, count, that nobody goes there who has the least regard for his or her character ?"

"Indeed?"

"Certainly.   The decidedly bad, indeed, I may say, indecent lot, that is to be found there, puts it out of my power to go. But if you must, and I suppose you must if you have promised poor stupid Glosy, you need only walk through the rooms, and then you can come to my house."

CLAUDE TAKING THE RING FROM MRS. FINCH.

"That I will do; and now that you have honoured me with this visit, permit me upon those vermillion twin-cherries you have by way of lips, to——"

"Count—count!   Are you quite sure——"

"Of what?"

"That the door may not suddenly open?"

"Quite certain. You are positively radiant with beauty this evening, my most charming marchioness. Ah, who is like you? Who, of all the fair beings who flit about the realms of fashion, are to be compared with you? You stand alone the queen of love——"

"Count—count!"

"Of beauty, of my affections. I seem to you——"

"I have delivered the letter," said William, just popping his head in at the door sufficient to make himself heard.

"D—n it," said Claude.

"I said so," screamed the marchioness. "The door was open, and I'm ruined."

"Stuff, my dear madam. You'll take a deal of ruining yet. I—I upon my word it is very awkward, but some one has come upon business of the very first importance, and I am under the painful and cruel—oh, how cruel!—necessity of seeing him directly."

"Her you mean."

"No, on my honour. What her in all the world is to be compared with you? No, marchioness, you, and you only, are my heart's idol. Do not fancy you share the throne of my affection with any one; I have not words to tell you how I love you."

"Very well. How long will your business occupy you with her?"

"I hardly know."

"Well, be it a long or a short time, I will wait here for you. This is your private room, and I know you will not bring any one in here who comes upon business; so I will take a glass of wine, and look at a book or a newspaper or anything, until you are quite at leisure again, dear count."

"Ah, how good of you, dear marchioness. But it is impossible."

"What is impossible?"

"For you to stay here."

"Not at all; I have only to will it, and here I am, you see. The impossibility vanishes."

"It seems to do so, and yet remains. I am going to bring my man of business into this room, and where we shall be all night settling our affairs, and you will be so good as to recollect your carriage waits."

The marchioness rose with sparkling eyes and flushed cheek.

"Very well, you ought to make your lawyer—I suppose it is your lawyer?"

"Yes—yes."

"You ought to make him come at more reasonable times, count. Since my presence here is such an affliction, I will leave you; and I don't think I shall be at home to-night at all, at any hour."

"Very good."

The marchioness bit her lips and walked to the door. Then making a rapid step or two, she opened the door of the reception room, and standing in the very centre of it, she saw a female closely veiled.

"Ha! ha! A female lawyer," she exclaimed. "Count, I have done with you."

"Pho!"

"Sir, dare you laugh?"

"Ay, dear marchioness, I can't help it. Have done with me? Impossible? You and I are made for each other, and what Providence has done you cannot undo. I will be with you at two, you may depend."

"The doors will be closed against you."

"I will break them open."

"The other guests in my house shall, by force, remove you, impertinent villain."

"I will fight them, and kiss you, my dear marchioness; so don't say another word about it. Good evening. William, see my sister, the marchioness, to her carriage."

"Sister?" screamed the marchioness.

"This way, madam," said William. "This way, if you please."

Claude shut the door of the room into which Mrs. Maria Finch had been shown, and the marchioness had no opportunity of denying the relationship that Claude, to blind the eyes of Mrs. Finch, had so suddenly and odiously foisted upon her. He bowed low to Maria.

"Your sister was that, sir?" she said.

"Yes, madam; and you are Maria——"

"My, name is Finch, sir. I come upon an errand, and for a purpose that— that—that——"

She was evidently too much flurried to continue speaking, and she placed her hand upon her bosom, as though by pressure she could brink back that calmness that was never again to be an inhabitant of it. As yet, Claude could not see her face, for she was closely veiled; but the tones of that voice had taken too strong a hold upon his imagination and his memory to be forgotten.

"Compose yourself, I pray you," he said. "Can you be safer than with one who loves you as I love you?"

"No—no. No more of that. I know my danger."

"Do you?"

"Yes, I—I—say I know and feel my danger."

"Nay, Maria, it is I who ought to feel any danger, knowing that you are aware of my secret. You only in this house, with the exception of my personal attendant, know who and what I really am. A word from you would call those around me who would eagerly seize Claude Duval, but who are all smiles and sweetness to Count Stofet. Do not talk of your danger. You are safe, but I am truly upon the brink of a precipice."

"No—no."

"Yes, say 'No.' You will not betray me? You will not consign me to a death of horror and indignation? No; beauty such as yours is ever merciful and good. Will you not let me see that face that is already engraven on my heart?"

"Sir, sir, I did not come to listen to such language. Indeed, I do not."

"Nay, dear one."

"Peace, sir, and hear me. I have come——"

"Do not speak in this room of anything that you wish not to be by chance overheard. Follow me into an apartment where you may say what you please in safety."

"Dare I?"

"Think what a power over me you have."

"Yes—yes. I will follow you."

Claude led the way into the room that had been so recently vacated by the angry marchioness, and handing Mrs. Finch a seat, he stood close at hand, as though he were only eager to listen to what she had to say, and to obey her commands, be they what they might. She drew aside her veil. She saw into his face, but she did not see into his heart!

"Sir," she said, "you may possibly put a wrong construction upon my presence here."

"Madam, I never put a bad construction upon the actions of a beautiful woman. Say what you please—do what you please; and I pray you, Maria, to consider this your home, to do as you please with it, as it is mine. I scarcely dared to hope that you would come; but now that you have, I pray you to banish all fears, and consider me your friend."

"The ring, then, sir. Restore to me that ring you took from me. I have, as yet, with some difficulty, been able to conceal its loss from my husband; but I cannot do so for long. If he should discover it he will be furious, and in his passion I know not what I may have to suffer."

"Can a ring be of such moment?"

"Yes, he gave it to me, and sets a superstitious store by it. It is for that I have, after much mental torture, gathered courage to come here."

"You shall not come in vain, Maria."

"You will, then, return it to me?"

"Yes; and if you could give me back my heart as easily as I can give you back the ring, I might be happy."

"You must forget me."

"Forget you? Oh, no—no—no!"

Claude affected to cover his face with his hands, and to be terribly cut up. It was really too bad. He actually fell upon a couch, and groaned. Mrs. Finch was affected.

"Cease these idle regrets," she said; "I am another's. Give me the ring, and let me go in peace. I have already done you a service, which I will not regret of. I have no other cause to do so than what has already passed. You shall have my best wishes and hopes that you will abandon the line of life that you are in, and take to some honest course of industry."

"What an angel of compassion and goodness you are to take so much interest in the fate of such a one as I am. You pity me?"

"I do, indeed."

"If you could but love me!"

"This is too much. Give me the ring, and let me go."

"Yes—yes, I will. Fate has separated us for ever. I can but look back upon this meeting with you as I could upon some dream; the spell of the magic beauty of which still haunts the mind. Oh, why, Maria, did I ever see you?—why did I ever hold you to my heart in these arms?—why imprint warm kisses on your lips?—why——"

"Peace—peace! I may not—must not, hear this, sir."

"And now I am desolate."

"The ring, sir—the ring!"

"In a moment. Yes, the ring. It is a ring—your wedding-ring, that separates us, and it is a ring that has brought us together this night. You shall have it back again, indeed you shall; and when I am no more—which will be before the dawn of the day that is soon to come——"

"No more!"

"Yes. Do you think I can live, and not see you?—do you think I can live, and not hear your voice?—never again hold your hand in mine—never strain you to my heart, and rain soft kisses on your lips——"

"Hold, in mercy!"

"Do you think I can live and not love you—not adore you? D——n! William, what now?"

William stood two paces within the door.

"Please, sir, a man is below, more like a madman than anything else. He has frightened Madame Stockwellini nearly into fits, and broken down the middle door in the passage. He is raving about his wife——"

"His what?"

"His wife; and says his name is *Pinch.*"

"No!" shrieked Maria. "Finch—Finch!"

"The devil!" cried Claude.

"Save me—save me!" she cried, as she clung to Claude's arm. "I ask you to save me. When he is in such a mood he is mad—quite mad, I tell you. Oh, yes—yes, and I am lost!"

"Not at all. We will delude Finch yet. Let me think but for a moment. William?"

"Yes, sir."

"You will sit here and be an efficient member of the Secret Police of London, and this lady, mind, has come to you about a ring that she has lost or had stolen from her. She has offered a reward of five guineas for its restoration, and you will do the best you can, and give her an answer to-morrow at this hour."

"Yes, sir."

"Mrs. Finch, do you understand the plot?"

"Yes—yes. I see it."

"Let your husband make his way in here. He will find you gravely talking to William about your lost ring. I will keep out of the way, of course, as he might recollect me again, although I am differently dressed. My opinion is, that this device will save you ; but mind you come to-morrow for the ring, and you shall save it.'

"Why not now ?"

"It would not look well in the plot."

"Where is she ?" cried the voice of Finch, at this moment, upon the stairs. "Fire and fury ! Brimstone and the devil ! I'll be hung for my wife. I insist upon being hung for my wife !"

"You hear ?" said Claude.

"Heaven help me !"

"I will help you, and you will have the ring to-morrow."

Claude left the room, and as he did so he muttered to himself—

"I wonder if Adele, Madame Stockwellini's pretty little apprentice, is in the house ? She is really a charming girl, and I don't know but, after all, I like her quite as well as I do Mrs. Finch, though her beauty is not quite so matured as Maria's."

———

CHAPTER XVIII.

KENSINGTON GARDENS.—THE ROBBERY.—THE VICTIM.

THE voice of Finch was still loud upon the stairs.

"Where is she ? I followed her here. I watched her, and I insist upon being hung for Mrs. Finch ! It's difficult to get the better of me. I know she is here. Fire and fury ! Fifty thousand devils ! Lumps of brimstone ! I'm a desperate man !"

"You hear him !" said Mrs. Finch to William.

"Yes, madam. But you have only to obey the directions of Claude Duval, and all will be well."

"If I have nerve enough."

"It is a matter of necessity. I pray you compose yourself."

I will if I can. Let me consider. What am I to say ? What am I to do ? Oh, I recollect now. I am to talk to you about a ring that I have lost, and you belong to the secret police of London."

"Exactly so, madam. Ah, he comes."

The door of the room was opened, and Finch appeared upon its threshold. The moment he saw his wife he uttered a kind of howl of the most unearthly character, while she and William affected to behold him with the utmost surprise. If they had not known him at all, certainly his appearance was sufficiently striking to warrant a good stare at him when he did make his appearance. By the violence of his exertions to get up the stairs quickly, he had torn his coat most ludicrously, and his hat seemed as though it had been kicked from one end of the street to the other. How it come to be in such a plight was a perfect mystery, but so it was, and as a shocking bad hat has more effect upon a man's general appearance than anything else, Mr. Finch had the full benefit arising from a very shocking one. His arms were elevated above his head, and his eyes flashed like those of a maniac,

"I see her !" he cried ; "I see her ! She is here ! I see her, and I live yet ! Fifty thousand fiends !"

"Sir," said William, gravely, "this is a most unwarrantable intrusion. Do you come upon any business ?"

"Business !" cried Finch. "Business ! why that is my wife !"

"Very likely, sir. The lady was just stating to me that she had a husband. But really, sir, your presence here, and your violent conduct, is most unsatisfactory."

Finch was thunderstricken! To follow his wife to a strange house, and find her with a strange man, and then to be told in a calm, soft voice, that his presence was most unsatisfactory! It transcended all that he could even have imagined in the way of cool assurance. It was something beyond belief; and he glared at William as though he began to suspect it was all a dream.

"Am I awake?" he said. "Am I awake?"

"You ought to know that best, sir," said William. "I can only speak for myself, and say that I am wide awake!"

"Will nobody convince me that I am awake?"

Mrs. Finch reached out her hand towards him, and plunged a tolerably long pin, right up to the head, in a soft part of his anatomy, as she said—

"Allow me to convince you!"

He gave a tremendous jump, and a roar that must have been heard all over the house.

"Oh, good gracious! What was that! I am awake—I am awake. I feel that I am. And you, madam; what have you to say for yourself? Remember the lion may be roused! How do you explain being here? Have a care what you say, madam: I am a desperate man!"

"And pray, sir," said Mrs. Finch, mustering up courage to play the part she had been told to play; "and pray, sir, what excuse can you make for following me here?"

"Excuse? excuse?"

"Yes sir, excuse. Surely you will not be so bold as to say that you suspected my conduct required watching?"

"Ha! ha!" laughed Finch, hysterically. "I—I—really, madam, when one comes to consider what happened last night at that odious Porcupine, one may be excused for a little suspicion."

"Well, sir," said William, "my time is precious, and I cannot waste it upon you. This lady came upon business; and all I can say is, that I will do my best to restore her ring to her."

"Her ring—her ring?"

"Yes," said Mrs. Finch. "I lost the small ring that you gave me, and I was very anxious to recover it again before you should miss it, as I knew its loss would vex you; so I came to this gentleman."

Finch shook his head.

"Maria—Maria," he said, with a look of what he thought was infinite wisdom and cunning. "Maria, Maria, that won't do. The loss of the ring is all very well. That is nothing. Even I lose things sometimes. But what has that to do with coming here?"

"Why, surely the police are the natural people to apply to?"

"The police?"

"Yes," said William, with much gravity. "The secret police, of which they do me the honour of saying that I am an efficient member. This lady offers five guineas for the recovery of her ring; and I will do my best, if it has been stolen by any of the adroit thieves of the metropolis, to get it back for her, although I feel that it will be a difficult job rather."

Finch looked at his wife and then at William, and then at his wife again, with wonder depicted upon his countenance; and when the explanation was over, he placed his finger by the side of his nose, and said—

"Oh! I see."

"Yes, it's plain enough," said Mrs. Finch.

"Really now, upon my word," added Finch. "This only shows how folks ought to be careful, and how easily they may be mistaken, upon my life it does. The secret police, eh? Well, for my part, I hardly thought there was such a thing in London."

"Oh, yes," said William, with a slight smile. "There are more secrets in London, sir than you suspect."

" Is it possible ? Then, if I were to be robbed of anything, and were to come here, there is a good chance, is there, of your knowing something of it ?"

"A capital chance. I should say that our information regarding some robberies is most accurate and quick. Indeed, we know as much about them as though we had ourselves committed them."

" This is very satisfactory. My dear Maria, pray excuse me for saying what I did. I am buite satisfied. I am not a man, as you will see, sir, to be imposed upon; and I flatter myself I can see through anything in the shape of an imposition in about half a moment, and with half an eye ; but this is quite a discovery. You may depend when I lose anything I will come to your office."

" I shall always be glad to see you, sir. And this lady may depend upon our utmost exertions being made for the recovery of her ring."

" Ah, Maria, you will excuse me ?"

"This time," said Mrs. Finch : "but it ought to be a lesson to you when you are inclined to let your hideously jealous temper get the better of you. Indeed, it ought."

" It shall—it shall. Come home, my Maria—come home. Sir, I beg your pardon, and am your very humble servant. The Secret Police ! And what a handsome place, too ! Upon my word, now, the more one lives the more one learns."

"Not a doubt of it, sir," said William ; " and it is astonishing what an amount of deception there is in London."

William bowed Mr. and Mrs. Finch very politely from the room, and then he sat down to laugh.

" What an idiot that man is," he said. " It's quite a disgrace to take in such a fellow. I hardly ever knew any one so positively soft before. Well—well, Claude must have his intrigues, I suppose, during those intervals he does not devote to the road. He says, they keep him alive ; but we shall see if some day one of them does not act the other way, and is the death of him. I foresee that if ever he is taken, it will be by being betrayed by some woman. I wonder where he is now ?"

William might have gone on wondering for some time, probably, before he could hit upon where Claude Duval was ; but if the reader will be so good as to remember what Claude said at the termination of the last chapter, he may be able to form some notion upon the subject. Duval had mentioned, by the name of Adele, a young girl who was an apprentice to Madame Stockwellini, the milliner, who occupied part of the house in Spring Gardens, in which he, Claude, had his magnificent apartments; and that he, with his perception of the beautiful, should be smitten by Adele, is not a fact to be wondered at. This young girl was truly beautiful ; and had she been in an exalted station of life, would have become one of those fair celebrities, the force of whose charms is handed down from generation to generation, coupled with a thousand regrets that so much beauty should be so frail and evanescent, as only to bloom for an age, and to leave the world nothing but the report of the wondrous charms and weak reflexes of them, achieved by the skill of the painter and statuary. But she was poor and friendless. Madame Stockwellini had, so she said, taken her from charity as an apprentice without a fee ; but then Madame Stockwellini could not exist without some one about her to whom she might play the tyrant, and the apprentice without a fee became the slave of her mistress's caprice and passions. Alas, poor Adele ! She was in this most miserable situation when Claude Duval chanced to see her. The reception-rooms of Madame Stockwellini were below Claude's apartments, but the whole of the upper part of the house above where Claude resided likewise belonged to the court milliner, and Adele had frequent occasion to go to and fro from the lower to the upper part of the house, upon messages and errands of one kind and another. It was upon one of these occasions that Claude met her upon the stairs, and was fascinated by her grace and loveliness. He had spoken to her, and she had shrunk from him ; but yet the words of kindness that came from his lips were grateful to the feelings of that young creature, who was surely made to love and to be loved ; and more than once she would begin with the hope that the handsome count—

for such, in her own mind, she called him—would meet her, and tell her again that she was fair. Yes; the temptation was strong, and the victim were weak. Claude, when he left the room for the purpose of allowing the affair between William and Mr. Finch to go on properly, had "wondered" if Adele was above in any of the rooms belonging to Madame Stockwellini; but he could not go up to see, lest, by so doing, he should encounter any others of the establishment, and a general scene take place. He lingered on the stairs, and fate was propitious to him, for he had not waited long ere he heard a light footstep coming down. A glance showed him it was she whom he sought.

"Adele!" he said, quickly.

She almost screamed at the sight of him, for she did not know he had returned. In her fancy he was somewhere in the country, enjoying the aristocratic amusements of his station. Of course, she only knew him as the Count Stofet.

"Adele, are you shocked to see me, that you almost scream?"

"No—no—but——"

"But what, my darling? Do you not believe that I love you?"

"I must not, sir—I ought not to hear you say this. I am a poor girl."

"Would all the riches of the world make you the more beautiful, Adele? Oh, no—no."

"Leave me, sir."

She disengaged her hand, which he had taken, from him, and then darted up the stairs again. Heedless of all the consequences, and thinking of nothing at the moment but of the marvellous beauty of that child of poverty, he ran after her. He just saw her flit into a room to the left, upon reaching the landing above, and then the door was made fast.

"Adele—Adele," he said; "is this kind to one who loves you?"

"Oh, leave me—leave me. If Madame Stockwellini were to know of this, I should be half-killed."

"Indeed you would not, for if Madame Stockwellini or any one else presumes to lay a hand upon you, I will put it out of their power to do so again. Adele, I love you."

"Oh, do not speak so loud: you will be heard, count."

"But I am forced to speak loud, or you would not hear me through the door. I swear to you, if you will grant me a few moments' interview, that I will leave you; but if you keep me from the sight of you, you will drive me mad, and I don't know what I may then do."

"No—no, do not ask me. I ought not."

"Nay, Adele—this is foolish prudery. You trust me, or you trust me not. If you do not, you doubt my honour: if you do, yours is safe."

She opened the door. Tears stood in her eyes.

"Speak," she said. "What would you say, sir?"

Claude at once walked into the room, but did not close the door. He thought it was much safer open, as he could then hear if any one were on the stairs. He saw that there was a cupboard in one corner of the room likewise, and that gave him more confidence in his situation.

"Now, Adele,' he said, with a smile. Alas! there was too much fascination in those smiles. "Now, Adele, can you feel that there is anything to dread from one who loves you as I love you?"

"I do not know, count. I pray you leave me."

"I will quickly; but hear me first. I tell you that from the moment I first saw you, I felt for you an attachment that will remain while life is mine."

"Nay, sir—consider the difference in our station."

"Does that make you less beautiful, or deprive me of my eyes, by which I see that you are fairer than any who yet blessed them by appearing before them?"

"I cannot answer you, sir. And yet——"

"Well—and yet? What would you say, fair logician? What is that?"

"Hush! Oh! fly—some one comes! I know the step! It is Madame Stockwellini!"

CHAPTER XIX.

TRUE LOVE.—A YOUNG HEART.

"CONFOUND her," said Claude, as he darted to the cupboard, and at once made his way into it, to the vast detriment of several bonnets, that all went flat with a crash, as he closed the door, and held it shut, for there was no fastening that he could feel upon the inside.

MRS. FINCH PAYS CLAUDE A VISIT.

"What's that?" said Madame Stockwellini, as she entered the room. "What's that?"

"What, madame?" said the trembling Adele.

"I thought I heard a noise, and I'm sure I heard a voice as I came up the stairs."

Adele replied to one-half of this interrogatory, by saying—

"Doubtless the voice was mine. I often speak to myself."

"Speak to yourself? And, pray, why do you speak to yourself?"

"Because I am alone in the world, madame, and have no friend to whom I can speak; so I unburthen my sorrows to myself, and to Heaven."

"You vile little wretch! Dare you say you have no friend, when you are perfectly aware that I took you out of charity as an apprentice, and without a farthing of premium?"

"I work very hard, madame."

"Hard! Hard! If you were to work your fingers off, it's no more than you are bound in common duty and decency to do, considering all that I have done for you, you most ungrateful hussy."

"I do not think, madame, that I am ungrateful."

"Indeed you do not? Oh, that I had left you to starve! Oh, that I had left you to the workhouse!"

"Do people starve in the workhouse, madame?"

"Oh, don't speak to me, you odious little brute. I have a great mind to spoil your baby-face, by giving you a good knock with this bonnet-stand, that I have."

Madame Stockwellini, whose real name, by-the-bye, was Stockwell, did not know what a capital thing it was for her that she did not carry her threat against Adele into execution, for if she had, Claude Duval would most certainly have come out of the cupboard and throw her headlong down the stairs.

"Madame," said Adele, "I would rather avoid these altercations. I strive to do my duty by you, and I can do no more."

"Indeed, you reptile; that's your opinion, is it? You talk of your duty to me, when you know you actually refused to wait upon Lord Spoonhey with his cravats."

"Yes, madame, and I will refuse again. I will wait upon any ladies cheerfully, but I will not wait upon gentlemen; and if you think I am wrong, I am informed you can take me before a magistrate and get me punished."

"And so I will!" cried Madame Stockwellini. "That's a good thought; and so I will! I'll bring down your proud poverty-stricken spirit, my lady, that I will, pretty quickly."

"I am ready, madame, whenever you like. In my own defence it will be my duty then to state to the magistrate, that I first of all refused upon principle to go to Lord Spoonhey's; and then that I had the particular reason for refusing, because I heard him say to you—'I don't mind a cheque for fifty pounds, madame, if your little apprentice is civil. Send her home with the cravats.' And then you said—'I will; but be cautious, my lord. Remember, that one's character is good till it is found out!'"

Madame Stockwellini staggered back, until she reached the wall of the room, the support of which came quite welcomely to her aid; and she glared at Adele, as though she were at her last gasp.

"Where?—where?—when," she cried, "did—did you hear that?"

"Yesterday, madame."

"And—and perhaps you would not swear to it?"

"I would swear to it, as it is the truth."

"But you—you have got no witness?"

"Yes, madame, I have. Another person in your establishment heard the words. I do not intend, unless it should strike me as necessary to produce the testimony, to say who that other persons is; and as you have no less that twenty-two at work in the room below for you, I do not think you will easily discover my witness!"

Madame Stockwellini was petrified. She made a vain attempt to rally her courage, and to threaten, and be violent, but she could not manage it. She felt like Macbeth that "the better part of her was cowed," and at last she rushed to Adele, and folding her in a crocodile-kind of embrace, she cried—

"My dear child, we will not quarrel, as you so charmingly say, and you will find me a mother to you. You are very much mistaken, indeed, in the construction you put upon the words you overheard me say to Lord Spoonhey ; but we will drop that subject. Come down stairs, my dear, and we will not quarrel any more."

"Thank you, madame, I will come directly."

"Do so, my chick!"

Madame Stockwellini, shaking in every nerve, went below, where she found it absolutely necessary to compose herself by a glass of something very hot, and sweet, and strong. When she was gone, Adele burst into tears. She was hurt to the soul that he whom she supposed to be the Count Stofet, and who said he loved her, should have overheard the cruel contention she had been compelled to have with her mistress ; and when Claude Duval stepped out of the cupboard, she could only say to him—

"Go, sir, go—oh, go."

"What! and leave you thus?"

"And if you do indeed love me, you will go, and from this time forget that there is such a person in the world as the poor friendless and wretched Adele."

"No. By Heaven, Adele, you give a false description of yourself."

"A false description, sir?"

"You are neither poor nor friendless. I am your friend ; and I will prove myself such if you will permit me, charming Adele ; and as for that Lord Spoonhey, who has insulted you, I will make him bitterly repent that he ever looked upon you with other eyes than those of respect."

"Oh, no—no!"

"Nay, but ——"

"Hear me, count. If you value my good opinion at all, you will get into no quarrel upon my account. It would only end in bestowing upon me an unfortunate notoriety that would kill me. I ask of you, as a favour, that you will take no notice of what accident has revealed to you."

"Adele, you have but to command me."

"It is well, sir. Now leave me."

"Not before telling you how much I love you, and admire your spirit and conduct to Madame Stockwellini. Oh, Adele, can you be insensible to the adoration with which I regard you ?"

He clasped her hands in his, and stealing his arm gently round her waist, he for one moment held her unresistingly to his heart, and imprinted a kiss upon her lips.

"By this kiss," he said, "I swear I love you."

She started from his embrace.

"No, no," she said, "it is ruin, degradation, disgrace! Unhand me, sir, if you be not a ruffian. Must I speak twice ?"

He let her go. Flushed and panting, she stood before him like some beautiful statue. He feared he had offended her, now, past all reconciliation, and he was mortified that he had been so precipitate.

"Adele," she said, in a mournful voice. "Adele, speak to me."

"Go," she said.

He dropped upon one knee at her feet.

"If you part from me in anger," he said, "I know not what may be the result, but I feel desperate thoughts rising up within my heart. Adele—Adele, you do not know how truly I love you."

"Let this be our last meeting, count," she said, in faltering accents; "you know and feel as well as I do that fate, destiny, or accident, call it what you will, has placed an insurmountable barrier between us. You cannot make me yours."

"And why not?"

"Your rank."

"Perish the rank that would say to my heart, 'Love not where you see beauty and intelligence, unless there be something else united with it of vain and empty value.' No, Adele, I am not one who values the title appended to his name a rush."

Claude Duval might very well, indeed, despise his assumed courtship. But the reader will see how he avoided saying anything about matrimony. Adele saw that likewise.

"Well, sir," she said, "if you have said all you have to say, and explained all you have to explain, you can now leave me."

"But not without your forgiveness."

"You have it. Now go."

It was rather difficult to stay after this, but still Claude Duval lingered. He was, indeed, fascinated with the beauty of Adele, and the difficulty he had in inducing her to deviate from her rigid principles of right, only the more inflamed his passion for the fair girl. More than once he really felt tempted to candidly tell her who and what he was, and make her his own; but he shrunk from doing so; and having risen from his humble posture at her feet, he said—

"Yes, Adele, I will leave you now, since you command me so to do; but you will permit me to see you again. I cannot live if I do not at times look upon your face, and hear your voice. Say that you do not banish me from your presence altogether?"

"Let chance decide," said Adele.

"Be it so. I will take measures to get my affairs in such a shape, that not being, as I am now, dependent upon a proud and haughty family of high lineage, I can offer you my hand as well as my heart."

Claude—Claude, this is too bad! A slight flush of colour came to the cheeks of Adele. It was the first time he had spoken of his hand as well as his heart, and it awakened a thousand hopes of the future. She did love him. Alas, poor Adele! He saw the effect he had produced, and he took the opportunity to approach her once more and hold her in his arms. It was but for a moment, and then she recovered herself.

"Leave me! leave me!" she said, "or I shall feel that you do not love me, and that you are unworthy."

"We shall meet again, here, at this hour to-morrow—or—or in my rooms, Adele."

"Oh, no—no—no."

"Well then, here."

She did not reply, but he read her assent in her looks, and he was quite satisfied. He felt that the interview had continued quite long enough to expose her to much animadversion; and once again half devouring her hand with kisses, he said—

"Farewell, until to-morrow."

Claude then slipped quietly down the stairs. He and his man William quite understood one another. When it was safe for him to enter his rooms, a red wafer was always stuck upon one of the panels of the door. The wafer was there now, for Mr. and Mrs. Finch had departed some time before Claude's interview with Adele had been brought to a close. He at once entered his room.

"Well, William?"

"All's right, sir. The Finches are gone."

"And the scheme answered, I suppose?"

"Oh, yes, capitally; Mr. Finch will always come here if he should happen to lose anything; and he has gone away with the most complete conviction that it was only to spare his feelings about the loss of her ring that his wife came here."

"Well, I almost doubt if she will come again now."

"Indeed, sir?"

"Yes. She may have really come for the ring only; and yet there is some hope. When a woman despises her husband, she is the easy prey of any one."

"That is a true maxim, sir," said William; "but Lord Glosy, if you recollect, will be here shortly."

"Ah, I was forgetting him, upon my word; there are so many calls upon one's time in London."

"And the—marchioness, sir?"

"Ah, to be sure, she will expect me at her house before the morning, notwithstanding all her affected indignation, and she shall not be disappointed. When I do spend a short time in London, I am generally pretty well used up with one thing and another. Look out a ball dress, William."

"Yes, sir."

Claude Duval was soon equipped in a rich and fashionable ball dress of the period; and true to his appointment, Lord Glosy came to take him to the palace, where one of those general entertainments was taking place, at which numbers of persons were admitted who by no means found place in the more select ceremonies of the monarch, which were confined solely to persons who had been duly presented at the court.

"You are quite ready, I see," said Glosy, "and as fresh as a rose."

"Why, yes, I wear pretty well," said Claude.

"My dear count, you have not began to wear yet. You talk of wearing half a dozen years too soon."

"You flatter me, Glosy. If I could make any pretensions to your look of high fashion and breeding, I might be vain, indeed."

This was attacking Lord Glosy upon the weak side of human nature in general, and his weak side in particular. Never was any young man of really good position so accessible to personal flattery. He adjusted his cravat, cast a glance at himself in the mirror, and then, with the most self-satisfied air in the world, he said—

"A-hem! Well, joking apart, I think I am rather the thing."

"Quite the thing," said Claude; "so now let us be off."

Lord Glosy's curicle was at the door, and he and Claude Duval stepped into it, and were off at the tearing pace fast young noblemen think is so very desirable so very striking, as an indication of style.

CHAPTER XX.

THE ROBBERY AT THE MARCHIONESS'S.

At that period there was a degree of laxity about the minds of the nobility of this country, which, although it may now be as much the case, is certainly more concealed. People of decent connexions, and moving in the first circles of society, do not now boast of their vices and make ornaments of them as they used to do. Outward decency is now the fashion of all courts, whatever amount of hidden vice the age may really have to account for. The state of the Continent, too, made the court less particular by far as regarded the standing and condition of the persons admitted to its precincts. It was thought to be so important that monarchy should rally round it as many friends as possible, that some very exceptionable, and in every respect doubtful, characters were at times to be met with in the Saloons of St. James's.

Hence, perhaps, it was that Lord Glosy found no difficulty in procuring a card for his friend, Count Stofet—a count whom no one knew, and who certainly ought to have been introduced by the ambassador in *charge d'affaires* of the court from which his countship was derived; but, as we have remarked, there were circumstances thus happening upon the Continent of Europe which had given a heavy blow, and a great discouragement to courtly etiquette. The Lord Glosy's carriage had some difficulty in wading its way through the crowd of vehicles in St. James's-street; but, at length, the old gate of the palace was opened. A string of yeomen of the guard filled up the entrance, and in the open street was a company of the foot-guards. The martial music of a military band could plainly be heard from the court-yard of the palace, now called the Color-court, just within a great gate to the left. The admission cards of Glosy and Claude

Duval were slightly inspected by a couple of officials from the Lord Chamberlain's office, and they were returned to them to facilitate their re-entrance, should they, in the course of the night, leave the entertainment and wish to return to it again. After this brief ceremony, they had nothing to do but to pass in through a double row of yeomen of the guard, until they reached the gateway that had been appropriated for the entertainment.

"Now, count," said Glosy, "I shall, of conrse, be at the marchioness's to-night. I suppose if chance should separate us in this throng, as it may very well do, we shall for certain meet there at some hour before day-light?"

"You may depend upon me," said Claude. "The marchioness has taken a tiff at me, and let me know that her doors will be closed against me; so, you see, I am bound in honour under such circumstances to go."

"Indeed? Why, what have you done to her vivacious ladyship?"

"Nothing particular; but I shall be at her *soiree*, and I am very much mistaken if she does not expect me."

"But if she really carries out her sentence of exclusion, and has her saloons denied to you?"

"Ha! ha! That will be rich; I don't intend to take a denial, Glosy; a pretty woman cannot offend me; so I feel as easy about it as possible I do not, for one moment, believe that she wants to leave me off; but if she did, she would find it about as easy and as complete as shaking off her skin."

"You are an odd fellow, count. Do you dance to-night?"

"Perhaps a little."

"Well, then, I fancy you would just as soon be left to your own resources in the saloons of royalty, as be clogged with a companion; so don't mind me.— Find what fun you can."

"All of which means," said Claude, with a smile, "that you have some intrigue or adventure on hand in which you think a companion would be rather troublesome."

"No, I really protest——"

"Nay, don't begin protesting, or you will quite convince me of my correctness, Glosy. What's the odd's, man. Such things will happen, of course; so commence yourself, but recollect that some time before the dawn makes the ladies' cheeks look queer. You and I meet at the gay marchioness's?"

"Be it so."

Duval's suspicions regarding the wish of Lord Glosy to get rid of him were strictly correct; but our business is not with the faults or frivolities of Glosy, and we will permit him to

"Go where his pleasure leads him,"

while we remain by the side of our hero, Claude Duval.

"I suppose," he said to himself, "as I am here, I may as well dance as not, if I can see any one that my fancy can hit upon. It is always a hard case, in such assemblies as these, to find a natural face. There is always so much frigid artificiality. Ah! I prefer my little Adele to all the painted and bedizened dowagers, and expectant scions of the nobility, that fill these royal halls."

In this humour, Duval was probably disposed to be over and above critical in his choice of a partner, and, indeed, he took the round of the principal saloon twice, without being able to see any one to whom he would take the trouble of offering his hand for the dance. He knew that some small recesses were set apart for refreshments close to the saloon, and he sought for one of them, feeling a desire for a glass of wine. He found more trouble—so well concealed were these little alcoves by the heavy and gorgeous hangings of the room—in finding one than he anticipated; but at length he was successful. He saw a slight movement of a piece of tapestry, to which a gold cord and a heavy bullion tassel was appended; and by pulling the tassel, he found that the tapestry could be drawn aside sufficiently to allow him to pass from the saloon into a small, but exquisitely-furnished room, in the centre of which was a table spread with every luxury that could be procured in the way of fruits, confectionary, and wines. This room was lighted by several wax lights. This was the very place Claude wanted; and pournig himself out a bumper of pure Rhenish wine, he raised it to his lips, and was uopn the point of tossing it off, when he was astounded by a long slip of the wainscot opposite to him suddenly opening like a door. Some one put one foot into the refreshment-room, and then, apparently seeing him, cried "Oh!" and suddenly disappeared. The panel, for it was a complete one that constituted the door, was closed again in a moment. Duval's curiosity was very much excited; but it did not prevent him from drinking the wine that he had at his lips. Perhaps he drained the goblet a little hastier than he otherwise would have done; but that was all; and then he sprang to the panel, and made an effort to open it. That offort was a vain one.

"Who on earth, now, could that have been?" he said to himself. "I saw a foot, and it was a man's by the costume. Confound the panel; there must be some means of opening it from this side."

The door, for door it undoubtedly was, was so well contrived in the wall, that no casual observation could possibly have detected it, it fitted so admirably into the rich mouldingsof the highly-wrought wainscotting. Duval was not one of the sort to be deterred by difficulties. He knew that a door was there, and he knew that some mystery was connected with it; so, quite heedless of the danger it might lead him into, or indeed, which he ought to have thought of, the unjustifiable nature of the intrusion, he used all his endeavours to find out the means of opening it. Perseverance will do wonders; and Claude Duval at last found that what fastened the door was a long thin spring-piece of steel, painted so exactly like the moulding, and lying so flat upon it, as to utterly defy ordinary detection. Upon pressing one end of this spring with his thumb, the long panel opened at once and remained open. Duval took one of the candles out of the silver sconce, and held it at the opening while he looked carefully through that doorway, the discovery of which had come so unexpectedly upon him, in the old palace of St. James's. What he saw beyond was a passage, that did not at the first glance look very inviting, it was so very black; but as the candle recovered its perpendicularity of flame after being moved, and gave a better light, he saw that this apparent blackness arose from the walls and the floor of the passage being lined with thick dark-coloured velvet. He only hesitated a moment, and then, after ascertaining that he could easily open the panel from the passage-side, he closed it, and he heard the spring hold it with a snap. He kept the light with him; and, let that secret passage in the palace lead to where it might, Claude Duval's love of adventure made him determine to explore it. It was well, as regarded the secrecy of the proceedings, that he did close the panel as quickly as he did, for some parties the moment after came into the refreshment-room, and he could hear them talking.

"Good," he said, "I have got the discovery, such as it is, all to myself, that is quite clear; and all I have to do is to follow my nose and make the most of it."

He held the wax light so as to diffuse the rays that came from it as much as possible, and at a slow pace he proceeded along the passage, which was not wide enough to allow of more than one person traversing it at a time, except they chose to go in Indian file, one treading in another's footsteps. He took the precaution to count his steps as he went, and he fancied he had gone the length of twenty-two, when something amazingly like the shutting or the opening of a door close at hand struck upon his ears. Duval immediately got apprehensive that the light he carried might, by being seen, materially interfere with his adventure, and without any ceremony, he gave it a dab against the velvet wall that immediately extinguished it; he then threw it on the floor. The moment he had deprived himself of his light, he saw a faint glimmer proceeding. from some few paces in front of him, and, guided by it, he cautiously advanced If that passage had been laid down and covered with velvet for the purpose of preventing the sound of any footsteps traversing it being heard, certainly the greatest success attended the plan; for Claude, although he did not take any exceeding pains to produce such an effect, was quite struck by the still and ghost-like character of his own progress in that singular place. When he reached the spot from which the light proceeded, he found that it came through the partial opening of a door, but it was so very faint that Claude could not imagine what species of lamp or candle could send forth so very poor and sickly a ray. He soon, however, found from what cause this effect proceeded. The light that he saw proceeded from an inner room beyond the one the door of which he found partially open, and from that inner room came the sound of voices. Impelled by the most irresistible curiosity, Claude glided into the first room ; it was not sufficiently illuminated for him to see accurately what it contained ; but from the sparkle of the light from the other apartment upon gildings and rich mirrors, he had no difficulty in persuading himself that it was royally and luxuriously appointed. Creeping close to the door of the inner room, he was able to hear with tolerable distinctness the conversation that was taking place there. A female voice broke upon his ear.

" No, no," she said " I must and will go. I do not know what spirit of infatuation it was that brought me here to-night."

" It was love," said a man's voice, and yet there was something very effeminate in t he tones.—" It was love."

" Call it what you will," cried the other. " Love is folly. It now matters little ; I am an outcast, and go I must from England. I, of course, can find many an asylum ; gold will purchase me a welcome. And now farewell for ever. You must find some other mode by which I may leave the palace than by the panel ; I tell you some one was in the refreshment-room ; I saw him."

" I really think," said the man, " that your imagination must have deceived you, for the gentlemen-ushers, I know, were not ordered to raise the tapestry of the refreshment alcoves until twelve had struck by the gate clock. Perhaps you saw yourself in a mirror ?"

" No—no—no."

" Well, of course, it is possible ; but allow me to combat with all the arguments I can your intention of leaving England. What am I to do without you, now that the ladies-in-waiting or maids-of-honour have not given me any encouragement ?"

" Good God !" cried the female voice, " and has it really come to this ?"

CHAPTER XXI.

THE FAIR UNKNOWN IN ST. JAMES'S.

THE tone of agony in which these last words were uttered was really so intense that Duval was painfully affected by them, and he crept close to the door with the hope of seeing through the narrow opening of it who the parties were that consulted in secret converse together. He found that by pushing the door a little, which he was able to do without the least noise, he could readily open a space wide enough to enable him to see into the room. It was in more ways than one worth looking into, for it was most splendidly appointed, so much so, that it seemed quite a show ; but Duval was much more interested by the persons in the room than by the room.

One of these persons was a female in man's attire. An elegant court suit, complete in every appointment, to smart ruffles, wig, &c., so metamorphosed her that but for the voice, Duval himself would have been puzzled to say that she was not what she appeared to be. This person was leaning upon a table, with her face buried in her hands, so that Claude could not see if she were beautiful. That this was the person who by his presence had been checked in escaping through the refreshment-room, was, after what he had heard, sufficiently evident to him. The figure, in its graceful proportions, looked promising, and like that of some young girl, rather taller than the ordinary ones of her sex. After uttering the last few words, which Duval had overheard, she seemed to have completely given herself up to a species of despair, and the very agony of remorse. The other person in the room was a fat, fair, thick-lipped, sensual-looking lad, for he could not be called a man ; and he was a little—but only a little—beyond a boy. He was dressed in full court costume.

CLAUDE'S NIGHT-ADVENTURE IN THE RESIDENCE OF THE MARCHIONESS.

"Come, come," he said. "What's the use of all this? I'm sure, Hariet, I am willing to make you comfortable, if you will make me comfortable ; and I don't see why you should not stay in London somewhere, where I can come to see you."

"Peace ! peace !"

"Only," continued the fat youth, "I am so watched that I can hardly move but some one is at my elbow, with a 'Can I assist your Royal Highness to anything?' Plague take them all, if they would only leave me alone. All I want is, to be quite comfortable; and I'm sure, if I had as much to eat as I wanted, and as much to drink, and you to call upon when I liked, I should be quite comfortable."

"And this," said the female, looking up suddenly with vehemence, so that Duval saw her face; "and this is the animal for which I have sacrificed fame and friends, and made myself the thing I am? This is the man—no—no not man—for whom I have been disgraced and discarded from the court, which I can only enter in such a disguise as I now wear? Oh, Death! now is the time to come to me; and to be sure that I shall smile upon you, and cry welcome."

The fat youth glared at her in dismay.

"How very uncomfortable," he said, "and how hungry I am getting."

This was George the Fourth commencing life early! The female sprung to her feet.

"Let this farce have an end, sir," she said. "Let this farce have an end. I have done with you and you with me. I know that at Hesse Damsteads I shall still be welcome; but you know as well as I that it is of no use going there without money. I demand the means from you of providing for myself."

The fat youth's eyes goggled, and his fingers nervously twitched the table-cover.

"I—I haven't got above a £100, in the world," he said.

"A £100?—What, sir, is the use of a paltry £100 to me? I want at least a hundred times that amount, and then you will never hear of me again."

"What? a hundred times that? Why, that comes to—a—hundred—a hundred times is—I don't know how much exactly, but it's a large sum, and where am I to get it, Hariet? I wish you would not make me so uncomfortable. If you will stay now somewhere quite close at hand, I could often get you money, and that would be much more comfortable. How hungry I am getting, to be sure. Really, I could almost eat anything."

"Hungry?"

"Yes. Surely one can't help feeling hungry, you know; I am almost always hungry. Dr. Knott says, that if they could only push half the learning into me that they can things to eat, I should be the finest scholar of the age, and the most polished gent in Europe."

"You will always be just what you are," said the lady, "a glutton!—a vile sensualist, stuffed up with unmanly pride and bloated stupidity. Of course you will find your flatterers—you will find your sycophants, who will fawn upon you, because you are what accident has made you; but if ever you come near me again, I will put this sword into your heart, if you have one, which I doubt."

She drew the delicate-looking court-sword that she wore from its sheath, and while her eyes flashed with the fury of a woman who feels all the bitterness of having cast herself away upon a worthless wretch, she advanced a step towards him. He plumped down upon his knees before her, and cried—

"Murder! oh, murder! Hariet, spare my life—oh, spare my life! It is so uncomfortable to die while there is plenty to eat and drink in the world—it is indeed. Oh, have mercy upon me."

"It would be a mercy to society to make a corpse of you, but—Speak! how am I to leave the palace?"

"I—I don't know, Hariet. Can't you try the refreshment-room again? Oh dear, the thought of a refreshment-room makes me feel worse and worse, and I know there is no end of cheese-cakes there, of course. Well, well—don't begin again, and I will get you an order to pass the gentlemen-at-arms, and you can go out by the queen's staircase, and so on through the main court. I'll go at once. Dear me, how uncomfortable I feel—I havn't felt so decidedly uncomfortable for a long time."

"Go," she said. "Get the order at once—I will wait for you here. You ought to be able to write one.'

"Ah, they won't let me do that. That would be more comfortable. And so you will go, Hariet? Come, now——"

"The order!"

"Well, well—don't get in a passion, and I'll get it. Dear me, what a strange creature you are. Why you used to be quite good-tempered, and now nobody could possibly be more uncomfortable."

"I was mad!"

"Mad? mad? Oh, if I had only known that—if I had only suspected such a thing. Why, I might have had my eyes scratched out, or my nose pulled out of my face, at any moment. What an escape—what an uncomfortable idea! but you don't mean it, Hariet—I am quite sure you can't mean it."

"Die then, if you will not go."

She again advanced with the sword, and the prince quickly made his escape from the room by a door that Duval had not observed. Bolting it upon the other side, he put his mouth to the keyhole, and said—

"You don't catch me back again, Hariet; and as for getting out of the palace, you may get out or stay in, for all I care, one way or the other. If you had chosen to stay in London and make me comfortable, it would have been all very well; but as you won't, I am going now to get something to eat, and you need not expect to see me again."

She flew to the door, and made an effort to open it, but it was fast locked and bolted; and being of mahogany, any effort which she could bring to bear upon it to break it open, would be perfectly futile. She burst into tears, and sunk upon a seat. Duval had listened with great curiosity to the dialogue we have recorded; but while he despised the prince, he could not be said to have his sympathies very much enlarged for the lady. It was quite clear from the contempt with which she regarded him personally, that the intrigue with the fat youth had only been a mere speculation. But yet she was beautiful, and from the glances Claude got of them, he thought her eyes exceedingly fine and lustrous. No doubt the dress she was in added a kind of piquancy to her charms. She might in ordinary costume have after all been but an ordinary personage, for the taste of George was no criterion to go by. Yet it was not in the nature of Claude Duval to leave her in the condition she was in; and accordingly, so soon as the hurried steps of George in full retreat proclaimed that he was gone, Duval stepped boldly into the room. The lady heard the footstep, looked up, and uttered a cry of alarm.

"Fear nothing, madam," said Claude. "You want a friend, and I offer myself."

"A friend?"

"Yes, madam. You wish to leave the palace. At least, I gather so much from your interview with one who merits your utmost contempt. If such be your real intention and your real wishes, I will aid you as effectually as I can."

"Who are you, sir?"

"The Count Slofet, madam, at your service."

He raised one of her hands to his lips, as he spoke, and as she did not seem to think there was much harm done by that, he thought he would go a little further, and accordingly, rapidly clasping her round the waist, he saluted her lips. This the lady thought was a little too strong upon so very short an acquaintance. She disengaged herself from him, and placing her hand upon the sword that hung by her side, she said in a voice of real or affected indignation, Claude could not take upon himself exactly to say which.

"Am I at the mercy of a villain?"

"Madam," he said, "that is a very harsh word. Do villains kiss those whom they meet? He who has so recently left you, might merit the title; and if not that, he has such superior claims to that of fool!"

"If you can aid me to leave the palace, sir," she said, "do so, and I shall then ask but one other favour from you, which is, that you will forget the occurrences of this night."

" If that were possible," said Claude, " I would obey you; but when you ask me to forget you, you do ask an impossibility."

The lady bowed slightly, and merely said,—" Lead on, sir, I will follow you."

Claude intimated that the outer room was the route which they would have to take; for the only way he knew of getting out was by the secret panel in the refreshment-room, and that, if the room should happen to be clear, was quite available. Indeed, it was the route by which she had reached the room in which she had had her singular interview with the Prince of Wales. They were upon the very threshold of the corridor, when the door at which the fat youth had departed, was opened, and he appeared again.

" What," he said, " are you not gone?" Then seeing a stranger, he had to effect an immediate retreat; but Claude put into requisition that wonderful agility of which he was master, and as the Royal George escaped through the door he got such a kick behind, that he was sent sprawling some four or five yards onwards, where he lay yelling for help.

" His cries will alarm the palace," said the lady; " yet I sincerly thank you."

" Come on; he deserves both the degradation and the fears of his punishment. If we reach the saloon there can be no danger to you, and as for me, I do not think I have need to fear from the resentment of such a party."

" You mistake," she said. " Young as he is, he has creatures about him who will do anything if he should chance to have seen enough of you to be recognisable. You will be marked out for vengeance."

" I care not if I do you a service."

" This is generous, indeed, of you. Are you a rich man?"

" Quite the contrary."

The lady sighed. Perhaps if Claude had answered in the affirmative she would have had no objection to strike up a kind of partnership with him, and dignify his leisure. Claude did not fancy her quite well enough for that sort of thing.

CHAPTER XXII.

ANOTHER ADVENTURE IN ST. JAMES'S.

" LET us hasten," she said, when they reached the outer room; " oh, let us hasten."

" Certainly," said Claude; " I have no particular wish to linger here, although I have the temptation to do so, by the presence of so truly engaging a companion."

" Compliments, sir," said the lady, " will be much more applicable at some other time; at present I should take it as a good favour now if you would spare me them."

" Perhaps," said Claude, " you and I, madam, will differ very much as to the definition of the word compliment. Now, to tell the plain truth, I never compliment anybody; least of all, should I think of complimenting you."

" And pray, sir, what would entitle me to such an exception?"

" The absolute impossibility of saying anything which would, in your ease, transcend the truth, and so be entitled to be called a compliment."

As Claude Duval said this, he very gallantly kissed the lady, but she got into a state of passion that astonished him; and drawing the sword she wore, she made two such resolute thrusts at him, that if he had not possessed more than the ordinary share of agility, that adventure, in all human probability, would have been his last. He felt himself compelled to disarm her, which he did after a brief struggle.

" This is not," he said, " what I ought to have expected from you. Let me beg that you will banish your anger, and forget the cause of it. There is one thing hat I dislike myself above all others, and that, consequently, I never force upon nybody. It is unwelcome caresses."

"I have had enough of them," she said. "Return me the sword, and you will have no further cause to wish it in your hands instead of in mine."

Claude handed it to her in a moment, and in such a way, too, that by the lightest movement as he held it by the blade, so that she might grasp the hilt, she might have run him through the body. She saw that, and she said—

"You have true courage, sir."

"Think you, there is any danger?" he said with a smile.

"I don't know. You have heard that an angry woman is capable of anything?"

"Yes; but you are not particularly angry with me?"

"You are certainly the most audacious——but no matter what you are. Befriend me so far as to get me clear of the palace, and I will not forget that you have done me a great favour. We may meet again, sir."

"I trust so," replied Claude. "Pray remain here in the secret passage while I ascertain if any one is in the refreshment-room. If it be vacant, you will have no difficulty in escaping at once through the grand saloon. Have you a carriage?"

"Do not trouble yourself, I can take sufficient care of my own safety when I am once clear of this hateful place; and there is one more favour I shall ask of you, sir."

"You have but to name it."

"It is that you will make no effort to follow me after I have left the palace."

"I give you my word of honour," said Claude, "that I will not, and I will likewise do my best to prevent any one else from doing so, should I see a disposition so to annoy you."

"I thank you."

While the lady waited some paces off in the narrow secret passage, Duval used all his endeavours to ascertain if any one chanced to be in the little room into which the secret panel opened. From the stillness that there prevailed, he came to the conclusion that it was empty; and turning to the disguised lady, he said—

"Now, madam, follow me quickly."

"Are you quite certain," she said, "that no one is there? I would not have this place known generally for the world."

"I am as certain as we may hope to be," said Claude. "We must run some trifling risk."

He opened the panel as he spoke, and to his satisfaction found that he was right. The room was quite vacant. The lady was out of the secret passage in a moment, and the panel was closed.

"Now," said Duval, "I will see you safely through the saloon, and then bid you adieu."

"There is not the remotest occasion for that," she replied; "let us part here, sir."

"If it must be so, I bow to your wishes, madam. You were pleased to say that we should meet again: may I still entertain that hope, madam?"

"Give me an address."

Claude gave her the number of his residence in Spring Gardens, which she repeated twice over, and then said—

"That is sufficient. Do not seek me, and upon that condition I make a promise that I will call upon you some day. But if you, from the indulgence of an indiscreet curiosity, make any exertions to discover who I am, I will take measures to be revenged sufficiently upon you."

They reached the door of the refreshment-room together, or rather, the hangings which served in lieu of a door, and the full blaze of the saloon burst upon them. It was much more crowded than it had been when Claude was in it last, and he thought that there seemed an unusual excitement about the people, who, in some places, were gatered together in little knots, as though some more than usually interesting subject of discussion had suddenly arisen among them. The disguised lady slipped from his side in a moment, and he was alone, although in the midst of such a glittering throng. In the course of a moment or two, however, he was joined by Lord Glosy, who said—

"Why, count, where have you hidden yourself for the last hour? I have been looking for you everywhere. There's quite a commotion in the saloons."

"I am not aware that I am to plead guilty to hiding anywhere." said Duval; "but what is the commotion about?"

"Oh, the most absurd thing in life. A rumour, how or by whom originated nobody seems to know, has got about that the notorious highwayman, Claude Duval, is in the palace."

"You don't say so!" said Claude.

"Yes, that is the absurd report; but how is it possible? How could he get admittance even with all his impudence? and they do say that there never was a fellow of his trade with a larger stock of that commodity on hand."

"If he really has got admittance here," said Claude, "it must have been by the assistance of some fool who did not know him."

"Precisely," said Glosy, as he arranged his cravat. "Have you met with any amusement, count?"

"Not the remotest. The mantle of dulness appears to me to be over the whole party, and I don't care how soon I leave to go to the marchioness; but don't let me drag you away, Glosy, for what may be dull enough to me, may have some charms for you."

"Oh, not at all—not at all. Ah! my Lord Staytope, how are you? Allow me to introduce my friend Count Stofet to you."

Claude and Lord Staytope bowed, and then the latter said—

"Have you heard the comical report?"

"What report?" said Claude.

"Oh, about Claude Duval, the highwayman, being here. It seems that in one of the ante-rooms an officer from Bow-street was placed so that he could see every one who passed without being seen himself, as that would naturally enough have looked offensive, and he declares that Claude Duval, disguised in a magnificent court suit, passed into the saloon."

"Why did he not arrest the fellow?" said Claude, as he took from his pocket a diamond snuff-box, and regaled his nose with a pinch, and then handed it to Lord Staytope.

"Upon my life, now, do you know, Glosy," said his lordship, "that did not occur to me, and I'll be off and ask about it directly. That is a magnificent box of your's, count."

"A trifle," said Claude. "I picked it up one day."

Lord Staytope made his bow, and shuffled off to retail, as his own, the question of "why did not the officer apprehend Claude Duval at once when he saw him?" to which the simple answer was—"that not being quite sure, as there are remarkable likenesses in the world, he hesitated until the opportunity had passed."

"Well," said Claude, "I think I shall go, Glosy, do you know. This is really a very slow affair, indeed. What an absurdity about that impudent fellow, Duval, to be sure. Ah! here comes Lord Staytope again, and full of news.— Ah! my lord, I guess by your countenance that that most impudent of highwaymen is really caught at last—is he not?"

"No—no. Really, no. My countenance is very deceiving. Ha! ha! At least the ladies say so. Ha! ha!"

His lordship's countenance had about as much expression as might be found in an underdone muffin. He laughed so much at his own highly facetious remark, that it was some few moments before he could add that half-a-dozen of the yeomen of the guard, together with the Bow-street officer, were keeping watch behind a seam in one of the ante-rooms, to pounce upon whoever might be pointed out as the remarkable likeness to Claude Duval, always provided that the person who enjoyed so unenviable a physiognomy, should not be some known nobleman or gentleman. This was news, indeed, to Claude Duval. It was important in more ways than one. It, in the first instance, assured him that he was safe in the saloon, inasmuch as the lynx-eyed officer was behind a seam in an ante-room ; and in the second instance, it convinced him of the impropriety of taking his departure by the regular route. The natural enough idea, under the circumstances, of making use of the secret passage, came across him. Let it lead where it might eventually, it could not lead him into greater danger than awaited him between the saloon and the palace gate.

"Well," said Glosy, "shall we be off?"

"Ah !" said Claude, suddenly, "who is she?"

"Who?—who?"

"There—there! With the ringlets—there! Ah, she has gone—disappeared in the throng; what a charming creature, to be sure."

Claude had wisely indicated a part of the saloon where there was the greatest number of persons ; but as for any charming creature in ringlets, poor Glosy might well look puzzled, inasmuch as there was no such person.

"I should have liked to see her," said Glosy, " as I dare say I could have told you who she was. But come on."

"Nay, my heart is enslaved. Will you bear with me for half an hour longer now ? I begin to think, since catching a slight glance of that fair face, that the saloons of royalty are not really so dull, after all."

"Ha ! ha ! upon my word," said Glosy, "that is good, very good, indeed. Come, then, and let us find out your beauty in ringlets. I shall know her, I daresay, directly I see her, and may get you an introduction. Come ; which way did she go, count?"

Glosy slid his arm quite affectionately within Claude's, and they walked together in the direction where the latter had seen the imaginary pretty face and the ringlets. Of course it was the intention of Duval to shake off his too obliging companion as quickly as he could; for the danger, although not just then in the saloon, might invade it at any moment.

"Do you see her?" said Glosy.

"Really, no," replied Duval, with the most perfect sincerity. "I think she went this way."

He dexterously continued to get as close as possible to the opening into the refreshment room, where there was the secret panel, and then suddenly pausing, he cried—

"She is upon the other side of yon throng of persons, Glosy. Will you do me the favour of going to look at her, while I wait for you here? I should like your candid opinion upon her."

Highly flattered at the idea of his opinion being asked, Glosy replied—

"Certainly," and was off at as quick a pace as the usages of the very polite gentry in which he lived permitted.

The moment he disappeared behind the throng of persons that Claude had pointed out, Duval entered the refreshment room. To his horror, Lord Staytope was there, eating confectionary in a manner that looked as though he was not likely to leave off for some time.

"My lord, my lord," cried Claude, "they have caught him, and are calling for you in the ante-room."

"For me? Good gracious. For me? You don't say so?"

Away flew Staytope, with a raspberry tart in each hand, and Claude, touching the spring in the wall, in a moment passed into the secret passage.

CHAPTER XXIII.

THE ESCAPE FROM ST. JAMES'S

THE panel closed with a snap. Claude drew a long breath.

"Safe at last," he cried, "Safe from the worst danger, being beleagured in a crowd. Confound the fellow, what officer can it be who is sufficiently familiar with my features to recognise them in even such an unlikely place as St. James's Palace? Well, well, it don't much matter. It will only make him a little more particular in identity another time; for when he finds I don't pass his post again, he will get nothing but derision and incredulity for his pains."

There was nothing to interest Claude Duval connected with the refreshment-room, and he accordingly did not pause for one moment upon the other side of the panel; but on he boldly traversed the secret passage until he reached the room through which he had so recently conducted the disguised lady. The light which had at first attracted him to that apartment, was still burning in the inner room; and after listening for a moment or two, Claude felt convinced it remained quite vacant as he had left it. He hoped to get through the door-way by which the Prince of Wales had made his escape; and upon touching it, he was agreeably surprised to find it open; for although there might be other modes of emerging from the other room, yet he, Duval, could not see any regular door. He made no doubt but that he was rapidly approaching the private and domestic portions of the old palace. What might be the difficulties or facilities in the way of his leaving the building by the route he had chosen, was entirely a matter of conjecture. He was supremely ignorant of the topography of the place, and had nothing but chance for his guide. He only felt he had escaped one danger, even if he fell into another. But then he was armed, and the stake at issue, with him, was his life. If taken, he knew that an ignominious death awaited him; and he felt that he would by far rather die with a good sword in his grasp, than by the rather revolting formalities of the law; not one of which would, in his case, be abated. He loosened the court sword he wore in its sheath, and keeping his pistols ready to his hand, he passed on. The room in which he found himself, after passing through the door that the Prince of Wales at one time halted, was handsome and spacious—if we may except the roof, which was much too low to give anything like dignity to the apartment. Claude's head only just cleared a large chandelier that hung from the ceiling, the glitter of the cut glass of which made it look like a collection of brilliants. He took the light from the other room with him.

He found he had quite a choice of modes of leaving this room, for there were no less than four doors opening from it. To hesitate would have answered no purpose at all, so he opened the first that come to hand, and found that it led him to a picture gallery of considerable length, but still low in the roof. He shrouded his lamp with his hand, and glanced around him. Not a soul was there to impede him or ask him questions, and he strode on holding the light above his head in such a way as to shed the most diffused rays around it. He soon came to a staircase, the balustrades of which were richly carved and gilt. After descending about twelve steps down this staircase, he came upon a landing place where there was a brilliant light and some exquisite statues. This landing was about twelve feet square; and as there was so much light there, Duval placed his lamp upon the stairs, to relieve himself of it. From this landing, which, by-the-bye, was richly carpetted, several rooms seemed to open, and one of them had the door about an inch open. From that room there came the subdued murmer of conversation; and Claude, with great daring, stepped up to the crevice and peeped in. A glance showed him the King sitting upon a very low chair or stool, while opposite to him stood a man advanced in years, and in a clerical costume.

"Very well," said the king rising, "let it be so."

This was all that Duval heard George the Third say, and then fully expecting, by the backward movement of the clerical-looking personage, that his interview was over, and that in another moment he would come out, Claude took two strides backward. At the moment, however, he felt that total escape was out of the question, for whether he went up stairs or down, he could not get sufficiently far off in a moment to escape being seen, so he stood quite still, and in an easy

CLAUDE'S RECONTRE WITH THE WATCHMAN IN WESTMINSTER.

attitude. The elderly clerical personage in another moment backed himself out of the royal presence, and then, upon turning, was face to face with Claude, who made him a profound bow. The bow was returned, and then, in a soft silky sort of voice which is only acquired amid the hypocricies of a court, the clerical personage said—

"Your lordship is in waiting, I presume?"

"Precisely," said Claude.

They both bowed again; and then as the clerical-looking personage edged off towards the staircase; Duval thonght the best thing he could do was to keep close to him and they descended the staircase together. A gentleman usher suddenly made his appearance, and gave a slight start upon seeing Claude.

"I—I was not aware that—your grace," he said.

Now, Claude kenw that he could not be called a "Grace," and he at once concluded that the person he was with was no other than what he had suspected from the first moment, the Archbishop of Canterbury; so he said at once—

"His grace will leave now. The carriage is close at hand, I presume?"

"In the court," said the bewildered gentleman-usher; and then casting sidelong glances at Claude, in whose appearance there was to him one of the profoundest of mysteries, he preceded them both along a couple of rooms, in the furthest of which Claude felt, by the coolness of the air, that he was not far from the open court-yard.

"His majesty seems remarkably well," said Claude to the Archbishop.

"Very," was the reply. "Thank God, very."

"Oh, it's all right enough," thought the usher; "but how he came in, and who he is, may I be shot if I have the smallest idea in this world. It's a perfect mystery to me."

"Yes, do not," said the archbishop to Claude, "trouble the saloon with your presence, my lord, to-night. Perhaps you are in too close personal attendance upon his majesty."

"Yes," said Duval. "Like your grace, I fix my thoughts on higher, and, I hope, better subjects than dancing, and such like frivolities."

"Allow me to say," replied the archbishop, "that for a young man, that is rather an extraordinary state of feeling."

"I believe that I am singular in my views upon more than one subject."

"Your grace's carriage waits," said the gentleman-usher, making a very low bow. Duval kept quite close to the archbishop, and kept on talking as they crossed the threshold of a large door-way, and at once emerged into the open air, which was inexpressibly cool and grateful to Duval after the heat of the saloon.

"Yes," continued Claude. "It is something rare at a time like the present, when the most pernicious doctrines, respecting church and stare, are freely broached, to find any one who has entirely passed through the fiery ordeal of scepticism unscathed—at a period when a neighbouring kingdom—after your grace, certainly—when a neighbouring kingdom is in the most lamentable state of irreligion."—Claude fairly pushed the archbishop into the carriage, and followed him with all the coolness in the world. As he allowed himself to sink back upon the luxurious cushion, he continued—"I repeat that it is truly a rare thing to find true piety in Europe; and the enviable and most desirable position that England occupies, I feel confident, is owing to the personal piety of the king."

The two footmen of the archbishop were touching their hats, and waiting for orders.

"Home," said the primate.

In another moment the carriage took the round of the court-yard, and rolled under the gateway into Pall Mall, along which it sped rapidly.

"You are for Lambeth, probably?" said Claude.

"I am; and if I can set your lordship down anywhere, it will give me great pleasure."

"Thank you. Did you hear the report that the highwayman, Claude Duval, was in the palace?"

"I did; and his majesty was much annoyed at the supposition, which he did not, and could not, believe for a moment."

"Indeed, and why not?"

"It is so very improbable, my lord; so very impossible, I had almost said."

"Not at all, not at all, your grace; and if I had had the slightest idea His

Majesty was so incredulous, I should not have scrupled to have introduced myself to him."

"Introduce yourself?"

"Yes. I am Claude Duval. Did you not know that?"

The archbishop slipped off his seat to the floor of the carriage as he gasped—

"You Claude Duval? You the—the notorious—I mean the—the—Are you Claude Duval?"

"I am, indeed, your grace; and if you give the least alarm, I shall be compelled, I own most reluctantly, to make a vacancy in the See of Canterbury. You perceive I have the means, your grace."

Claude just slightly showed the bright barrel of one of his pistols, and the archbishop took such a fit of shaking, that Claude was really afraid the unwonted motion of the carraige upon its well-made springs, would alarm the two footmen behind; so he said—

"I must really trouble your grace to take things with a little more christian fortitude. Look at me. Do I look like one from whom you have anything to fear, beyond such a demand as professionally I feel that I cannot part from you without making? Come, sir, sit down in your proper place."

The archbishop gathered himself from the bottom of the carraige, and resumed his seat.

"I really took you," he gasped, "for some lord in waiting; and yet I wondered I did not know you."

"I was in waiting," said Claude, "and rather anxiously, too, before you so opportunely made your appearance to release me from a very serious embarassment; for, to tell you the truth, I had not at that moment any very clear idea of how to leave the palace; but as it it has turned out it is all well; and I will now trouble your grace for your watch, money, and jewels."

"Young man, young man, did you ever ask yourself when this mode of life was to end? Let me exhort you to repent, and to give yourself up to that offended justice which cries out for you. I will send you a book of prayer for your last moments, and even you may hope, by repentance and faith, to escape the dreadful doom that otherwise in the world to come awaits you."

"Have you quite finished?" said Claude. "Because, if you have, I beg to remind you of my little professional request, for your watch, money, and jewels; and to hint that I am of an impatient tenor of mind, and rather apt of a moment to lose my usually mild and quiet way, and get a little violent."

With a groan, the archbishop took a small purse from his pocket, and handed it to Claude.

"The watch?"

"Really, young man, you see that we are in quite a street of a populous character, and anybody but me would give you up to the strong arm of the law."

"You will immortalise yourself if you do," said Claude, "for I shall blow your brains out in the carraige here; and you will be talked of in the same breath with me while London is a city. It strikes me, however, very forcibly, that you prefer an archbishopric, with all its nice little annuities, to even the fame of capturing the famous Claude Duval."

With this Claude caught the right reverend personage by the cravat with one hand, just to hold him steady, while with the other he emptied his pockets in a trice. A remarkably handsome gold watch, superbly jewelled, and a much larger purse full of notes and gold, were Duval's prizes.

"Now," he said; "I will trouble your grace to put me down. I see we are close to Downing Street, and I am going from home at every step of your horses."

The archbishop pulled the check string, and Claude alighted.

"I have the honour of wishing your grace a remarkably pleasant drive," he said; but before he had got twenty paces off, he heard a shout behind him of "stop thief! stop thief! A highwayman!"

Upon turning, he saw the two footmen of the archbishop in pursuit of him. No doubt their master had told them who he was.

CHAPTER XXIV.

THE HUNT THROUGH WESTMINISTER.

"THAT's all you get," said Claude, "for trusting to the generosity or gratitude of a parson. If I had only now put a couple of slugs into his brains, all would be well enough.

"Stop him!" shouted the foremost of the footmen. "Stop thief—stop thief!"

This footman had in his hand one of those long sticks which the fraternity hold in so martial a manner over the roof of a carriage, and Duval, turning suddenly upon him, caught it from his hands, and with one blow smashed it over his head. He continued belabouring him with it until the other footman came up, who had the fool-hardiness to lay hold of Duval by the collar, a step which he soon found abundance of reason to repent, for dropping the remainder of the stick with which he had been belabouring the first footman, Duval only paused to be quite certain he had got a good hold of the second one, on each side of him about the loins, and then he canted him over his shoulder on to his head, and he lay upon the pavement without sense or motion. The sudden stoppage of the carriage, however, and the vociferations of the footmen had some effect, and the few watchmen who were in the street had taken the alarm, and were hurrying after Duval as fast as their infirmities would let them ; for watchmen in those days used to be chosen upon the rule of contrary, and he who was least capable of doing the duties of his post was sure to get the situation. The archbishop too, was, leaning from his carriage, and calling out in as loud a voice as so distinguished a character could command.

"A hundred pounds reward for that fellow ! It's the notorious Claude Duval. A hundred pounds reward for the man in the court suit ! A hundred pounds !"

Claude's danger was more increased by these words of the archbishop than by anything else. There are all times in the streets of London ; whether by day or by night, idlers and disreputable characters, who, for a tenth part of such a sum as a hundred pounds, would hunt to the death their own fathers ; and some of these hearing the shouts of the footmen, and the words of the archbishop, at once started in pursuit of Claude Duval. In the course of five minutes he had about twelve desperadoes upon his track. Now, the most unfortunate thing for him was the dress he had on. It was quite sufficient to describe him by in a moment, and the cry of stop the man in the court suit was so significant that it would at once enable anybody to see that he was the party who was to use the officer's phraseology upon such occasions, "wanted." The difficulty of getting rid of such apparel, and substituting anything in its place, was immense ; but yet Claude did not absolutely despair. Few persons were better acquainted with Westminster than himself, and he dashed down a bye-street with an expectation of baffling his foes yet, and a feeling that the chances were all in his favour. His principal difficulty, he considered, was in the fact that they were so close upon his heels, that he had not time to attempt to get into any of the houses ; he was compelled to pass on so rapidly, for that was the plan he would have adopted, desperate as it looked, if he could only have had two or three minutes to himself to find some door that was not sufficiently well secured to resist the vigour with which he would attack it. Besides, Duval was no dispicable hand at a pick-lock, and fortunately he had one with him.

"Confound the rascals," he muttered to himself, " if I can but get round some corner, and baffle them for the space of half a minute, all will be right enough."

A corner of a street was close at hand ; but just as Duval got up to it, a watchman bounced round it, and made an attempt to hit him on the head with his bludgeon ; Claude caught the stick in its descent in the hollow of his hand, and wrenched it from the guardian of the night in an instant ; and then, before a word could be spoken, it came down upon the watchman's skull with a most ominous crack.

"The very thing," said Claude, as he stooped, and with marvellous celerity got the huge top-coat of the watchman off, and put it on himself. He then ran round the corner, and there stood the watch-box of the man whom he had left certainly not in a state to give any information. He stepped into the box in an instant, and wrapping the cloak closely round him with the collar up to his neck, he was quite sufficiently disguised at that hour of the night. Scarcely were these arrangements completed, when three of the foremost of his pursuers came up, and paused, evidently at fault. A lantern hung outside the box in which Claude had ensconced himself so snugly, and by its light the three men were directed to him.

" Has any one passed here, watchman," said one.

" Arrough. then, by the holy father if you don't move on," said Claude, speaking in a rich Irish accent, "I'll be after taking you to the Round-house, my darlints."

" We are looking for a highwayman."

" Faith, then, by my soul, it's me that's thinkin' you wont have far to look for to see one, if you'll just take a mighty nate glance at each other."

By this time four or five others had come up; and if any suspicion had been excited by Duval, his situation would have been rather critical; but he sustained his character too well to have any fears of the result, as long as he kept within the box. If he had come out of it, the shoes, with diamond buckles in them, and the silk stockings that would have shown below the watchman's coat, would have quickly enough betrayed him.

"He must have passed this watchman," cried one. " He came all the way along here."

"By all the saints," said Claude, " the only man, woman, or child that has been past here, was a gentleman with a mighty fine suit of clothes on him, and a sword by his leg, and he went on as fast as he might, and down Peter-street."

"That's him! That's him!" they all cried, and they set off in the direction Duval had mentioned, as if their lives depended upon the speed they made.

The moment they were gone, Claude emerged from the watchbox, and approached the watchman, who by this time had risen to a sitting posture, and was rubbing his head; Duval saw that he had on a pair of grey worsted stockings in the form of overalls, that came above his knees, and it struck him that with that addition to his disguise, and the watchman's hat, he should be quite perfect.

"My friend," he cried, " I will trouble you for your worsted overalls."

' Murder!" said the watchman. "He has come again!"

"Another such cry and it is your last," cried Duval, as he drew his sword and flashed it before the eyes of the watchman. The argument was irresistible, and lying flat upon his back, the guardian of the night made no sort of resistance. In half a minute, Duval was completely equipped in the watchman's stockings and hat; and then taking the lantern from the nail upon which it had been hanging in front of the watchbox, he cried, in stentorian accents—

"Past two and a cloudy morn!"

"Won't I be after you soon," muttered the watchman, as he lay on his back on the pavement.

' I will trouble you," said Claude, " to get into the box, Charley."

The man did not dream of making the slightest resistance now; and rising, he made his way into the watchbox, only in a whining tone hoping his honour would not think of taking away a poor fellows coat, without giving him a trifle towards another."

" Oh, certainly," said Duval. " You shall have nothing to complain of."

When he was fairly in the box, Claude pulled it from the wall by an effort of main strength, and at the same moment sent it over upon its face, with a bang that was enough, not only to break it to pieces, but to dislocate every bone in the body of the watchman. Feeling then tolerably well assured that it would be some time before he could possibly emerge from such a prison, Claude walked off very composedly, crying every now and then in a voice that was morally certain to awaken the whole neighbourhood—

"Past two and a cloudy morn!"

His object was to get to his own home as quickly as possible now, and change his costume preparatory to going to the marchioness's assembly; for notwithstanding all the adventures of the night, he was still determined upon so doing. With this intent, then, he retraced his steps until he reached Whitehall, where he found a crowd of people assembled round the carriage of the archbishop, and he had the hardihood to push his way into the throng, and ask what was the matter.

"Oh," cried one, "Claude Duval, the famous highwayman, has robbed the Archbishop of Canterbury, and murdered his two footmen, that's all. They have sent to Bow-street for some officers, and they will soon have him, they say."

"Yes," added another. "He is in a court suit, and he cannot escape for long."

Under these circumstances, Claude thought it might not be quite so advisable to go to his own home, for as being likely enough seen to enter that house as he was then dressed, when the story of the watchman of whom he had borrowed the coat, &c., began to be told, it might be the means of breaking up his little household in Spring Gardens, which for more reasons than one, he was particularly averse to.

"What is to hinder me going as I am to the marchioness's?" he said. "It will only be looked upon as a good joke. I'll do it."

As soon as he made this resolve, he started off along Pall Mall to the residence of the marchioness, which was close at hand; and as he went, he called the hour in the same vociferous manner in which he had already respectfully announced it. As he proceeded, he was challenged by more than one watchman for coming on to their beat; but he took no notice of such little interruptions, only replying to them by such a flourish of the stick he had taken from the other watchman as rendered it a matter quite of policy, to let him to go on with a curse or two. In this way, then, he traversed one-half the length of Pall Mall, until he saw by the chaises and coaches close to the marchioness's, that her rout was by no means over. When he reached the door he found two of her ladyship's footmen standing on the lower steps; and as he passed them to reconnoitre a little, one said—

"Hilloa! stop! watchman! Will you come inside and earn half-a-crown and a pot of ale?"

"By my soul, yes," said Claude.

"Very well then. Our mistress expects a gentleman will call here to-night that she has made up her mind not to admit to the saloons. She thinks he will try and force his way in, and she threatens to discharge us all if he does. Now we don't like to be rough to him, but you can, you know, stop him; so if you will just come inside the hall we will put you behind a screen, and when we call for you do you come out and take him to the watch-house, if he won't go away quietly."

"Won't I thin," said Duval, "every mother's son of him shall be locked any way. An what's the name of him, young man?"

"He is the Count Stofet.

After this, Claude could have no doubt but that he was the person the marchioness was so urgent to exclude; and as he well knew it was only a piece of temper upon the part of her ladyship, and for the purpose of enjoying a kind of triumph over him, since he had declared that in spite of her he would come, he was not a little pleased at the singular combination of circumstances that had bought him fairly into the house without any violence.

"This way—this way," said the footman. "What's your name?"

"Dennis Bulgruddery," said Claude.

"What a deuce of a name, but that don't matter. You shall soon have the ale, just sit down quietly here behind the screen, and you will earn your money easy enough. Perhaps the count may not come, and of the two we would all rather he did not, for we don't want to show him any incivility, as he is liberal enough to us.

"Blur an' ounds!" cried Duval, "then you'll object to me giving him an ilegant top on the head of him wid my persuader here?"

"Yes, we should. All you have got to do is to stop him from coming into the house; and if he is violent and tries to force his way in, we will give him in charge."

"It will do natily and nicely, darlints; only don't forget the same ale and the half-crown, any way."

"You will have both. Now be quiet."

"Asy—asy it is."

They showed Claude a seat behind a screen in the hall, from which he could command a good view of the staircase leading to the marchioness's saloons, although he could not see the door. He was afraid at first to make anything in the shape of a movement, for fear he should be interrupted; but after the ale had been brought, he felt that he was quite at liberty to take his own course, and he determine upon surprising the marchioness.

———

CHAPTER XXV.

THE MARCHIONESS'S ROUT.

His first act was carefully to divest himself of his disguise, and to trim up his court suit as well as he could from the rather rough treatment it had received from the watchman's coat; and then, after arranging his hair, and putting himself into presentable trim, he glanced around him for some hiding place for the watchman's apparel, but no one presented itself; and seeing close to him a staute of Venus, as large as life, he put the coat and hat upon it, and regretted very much that in consequence of the legs being fixed to the pedestal, that he could not slip on to them the worsted overhalls; but he contrived to wrap them in such a manner round the limbs of the statue, that at first sight it would seem to have them on. He then waited an opportunity of slipping up stairs, and one soon presented itself.

A party of eight persons arrived, all laughing and talking very loudly, for they had come from some other entertainment, where they had not been very scrupulous as to the manner in which they had sacrificed to Bacchus; so Claude found the opportunity a capital one, and slipping up along with them, he reached the door of the saloon without being noticed by any of the marchioness's attendants, who were all perfectly possessed of the fact that upon no pretence whatever was the Count Stofet to be admitted.

While the others were being announced, he quietly slipped into the rooms and lounged about at his ease. He well knew that although the marchioness might give stringent orders regarding him to her servants, she would say nothing to her guests of such an affair; so he was not at all surprised at the calm manner in which he was welcomed by those whom he encountered in the gaudy saloo .

But it was the marchioness herself that he looked for, and her ladyship was in an inner saloon, with what she called a select circle about her. No doubt she fully believed that she had taken such steps for the exclusion of the offending count upon that evening, that it was impossible he could triumph over her by making his appearance in spite of her interdiction.

"Ladies," she said, "of course you have all had lovers of all kinds and descriptions, some impertinent and some modest; but a young friend of mine lately spoke to me about a lover of hers in a way that quite surprised me."

"Indeed," cried everybody.

"Yes, my dear friends," said the marchioness. "It appeared that this lady had done her lover the honour to invite him to an entertainment, but preceeding the night upon which the entertainment was to take place she discovered something that induced her to alter her mind with regard to him, and to forbid him from coming to the party."

"And very proper too," said three ladies in a breath.

"No doubt of that," said three more.

"But that," continued the marchioness to the admiring throng which pressed closer around her, in the hope of hearing some bit of scandal of the most delightful character. "That was not the difficulty, ladies; and what perplexed this young lady was that the wretch said, that having had an invitation to the entertainment, he would not take a denial, but attend it in spite of her."

"In spite of her?" said eight ladies.

"Yes. He said, come he would, whether she forbade him or not; and that she had no power to keep him out. Now ladies, as this young friend of mine is in great distress upon this account, I would fain seek your advice, by asking you what she had better do under such extraordinary circumstances?"

"Keep him out, by all means," said the whole lot.

"Yes, ladies, that is quite agreed; but the means of doing so? That is the question? What would you do, and how far would you go in strong resources, provided he should have come to the door, and made an effort to force his way past the servants?"

"Really, my dear marchioness," said the ugliest of the party, "I should call upon some gentleman to draw in my defence, for there's no saying how far such a man might go."

"I should give him to the watch," said another."

"And I," said a third, "should stand myself in my hall, with a drawn sword and run him through, if he persisted in entering the house without my permission."

"But the lady," resumed the marchioness, "has plenty of servants to keep the fellow out, and surely they ought to do it."

"But, what," said Claude Duval, suddenly making his way into the circle of ladies, "but what, my dear marchioness, if he come down the chimney?"

The marchioness gave a shriek, and then cried—"There he is!" while the throng of ladies immediately called him their dear count, and hoped he was quite well?"

"Perfectly, ladies," he replied. "Ah, I need not ask of you such a question; your blooming cheeks and love charming eyes sufficiently assure me of the fact."

"You monster!" cried the marchioness.

"Monster?" cried all the ladies. "Call the handsome Count Stofet a monster. Why we have been looking for him all the evening. Surely, marchioness, the case was not your own, and you really could not wish to exclude the count?"

Her ladyship bit her lips with rage, and her eyes flashed as though fire were in them.

"Audacious man!" she said; "how dare you intrude here? You have suborned my servants; but not one of them shall remain another day with me."

"My dear marchioness," said Claude, "do not blame your servants, for they have not the remotest notion of my presence here. On the contrary, they have got even now a watchman in the hall to take me into custody, if I should attempt to cross, so do not blame them, my dear marchioness; and above all things, too, I beg of you not to make a scene. If you must say something angry to me, let it be elsewhere than here."

"Where, sir?"

"Oh, anywhere; up stairs will do."

The ladies tittered, and the marchioness seemed, upon the point of doing something, violent beyond all precedent, but Claude spoke again, saying,—

"Madam, I said, that in spite of all the impediments you could possibly throw in my way, I would be here to-night, and I have kept my word. Having done so, I am satisfied; and, if you wish it, I will now leave this house at once, and in that case with an equal obstinate adherence to my word, I promise you that it's threshhold shall never again be crossed by me."

At these words the marchioness turned rather pale. She had wanted to triumph over Claude, not to lose him.

"Say the word, madam, and I am gone."

"How very affecting," said all the ladies.

"You deserve that I should say go," the marchioness said, in a low voice.—"Your audacity deserves as much."

"I acknowledge it, madam."

ANNETTE PROTECTS AND GUARDS CLAUDE.

"Then, for that acknowledgement, I will pardon you."

"How very affecting," said all the ladies again, and Claude, with a slight smile upon his face, made a low bow. He then, said, "Perhaps the watchman, who is waiting in the hall may now be dismissed, madam; and your servants informed that I am no longer one of the prescribed."

"Will you oblige me, count, by yourself giving these orders?"

" With great pleasure, madam," said Claude ; and he went down into the hall anticipating much amusement from the consternation of the domestics, as well as on account of his inexplicable appearance, as the equally inexplicable disappearance of the Irish watchman.

At his appearance in the hall, the servants, all of whom knew him perfectly well by sight, looked as amazed as though they had seen a ghost, and his name passed from mouth to mouth in accents of fearful consternation.

" You can let the watchman, who is behind the screen," he said, " go, and the half crown you promised him, I will pay."

" Yes, yes—sir," exclaimed one of the servants. " How did your honour get in ?"

" That is of not the slightest consequence," said Claude, " I am here, let that suffice now. Tell the watchman he may go to his ordinary duties, for he is not wanted here. Remove the screen."

They did so, and then, to their intense surprise, was the Venus decorated, if we may be allowed the term, with the watchman's coat and hat, and with the grey worsted overalls upon her legs. Claude, while the servants were gazing in with wonder, not altogether unmingled with fear, at this spectacle, went up stairs again.

It was now getting time for the route to be over, and, indeed, a number of the guests of the marchioness had already left ; Claude was rather surprised at not finding his friend, Glosy, there, and as he thought it would be anything but prudent for him to go home to Spring Gardens, he had no wish to leave the marchioness's house, just then.

The guests, however, were going so quickly, that it was really a very difficult thing to stay. After some consideration with himself, he hit upon a mode of proceeding which no one but himself would, for one moment, have had the audacity to dream of.

What it was will be speedily seen in its action.

He approached the marchioness, and with much grace of manner, announced that he had come to bid her adieu.

" Allow me to hope," he said, " that I have a full pardon for the past, and that all that I have done may be attributed to its right motive, namely, intense admiration of yourself, without the countenance and acquaintance of whom, believe me, I could not, and would not, exist in the world of fashion in London. May I hope for the happiness of seeing you soon ?"

" You may hope."

" But will that delightful hope to-morrow be converted into a certainty ?"

" At what hour will you be at home, count, and disengaged ?"

" All the evening."

" It is well. Perhaps I may come that way."

Claude said all the evening, because he fully expected to be quiteengaged. during that time with others, and he knew that the marchioness would be sure to call upon him at some other time than that which he specified. Her jealous disposition always taught her that little piece of deceit, and he was quite prepared for it.

He then bade adieu to some others of the guests with whom he was personally acquainted, and who were all upon the point of leaving, and then with all the coolness in the world, when he reached the landing, instead of walking down stairs he walked up.

No one noticed this remarkable divarication from the ordinary route upon the part of the Count Stofet, or if they did they were much too well bred to take the smallest apparent heed of it. It was no business of theirs, and in the course of another quarter of an hour, the last carriage rolled away from the door of the witty, elegant, beautiful, but not very particular marchioness.

Duval did not stop till he got to the top of the staircase he was ascending, that is to say, upon the landing from which opened the principal bed chambers of the house, and then he paused to hear that last guest depart, and to listen to the fastening up of the outer door by the servants of the marchioness's establishment.

"All's right," he said, "I shall be much safer here to night than I should be at home."

Probably if he could have gone home he would, for to tell the truth, Claude was by no means very much infatuated with the marchioness. The pretty girl at the milliner's, Madame Stockwellini's, was much deeper in his heart than any marchioness was ever likely to be, but yet she was attractive, and besides there was a kind of catch attached to the matter, which made it to him rather delightful.

All was profoundly dark in the suite of rooms in which Claude now found himself, and he held his hands out before him, lest he should run against something, a contact with which might possibly be more energetic than pleasant.

He knew perfectly well that the bed-room of the marchioness was upon this floor, and it was there that he meant to conceal himself until all the guests had left the house. How far he was warranted in such a step as this is best known to himself, and to the lady. There can, however, be but one opinion regarding the singular audacity of the proceeding.

After peeping into a room or two, Claude came to one which from its style of appointment he guessed perfectly well was that of which he was in search. A light was upon the dressing table, and he had only just time to hide himself behind one of the curtains of the bed, when he heard a footstep rapidly approaching the room.

He considered that this must be the marchioness, but he was mistaken in that conjecture, as it appeared.

CHAPTER XXVI.

HOUNSLOW HEATH IN OLD TIMES.

CLAUDE DUVAL had hardly been two minutes in the room; when carrying a small silver hand lamp, the waiting maid of the marchioness made her appearance, Claude knew this girl by sight, and he was in hope that she would merely place the light upon the dressing table, and then leave the room, but in that hope he was doomed to be signally, and completely disappointed.

The very first thing she did was to begin altering the arrangement of the curtains of the bed, so that Duval felt that his discovery was certainty. With such a coincidence he thought the best thing he could do was what he did do, namely, step out of his place of concealment at once.

"How are you, Annette," he said, as he suddenly confronted the girl.

She gave a loud scream, and dropped the hand-lamp which she had in her hand; the scream was just loud enough to be heard all over the house, and Duval felt that any further concealment in that room would be impossible now. Although, before he emerged from behind the curtain he had fully intended to request Annette to say nothing to her mistress of his being in the chamber, which considering all things, was rather a cool idea of his.

"Why did you call out in that way?" he said.

"Why did you pop out in that way?" said Annette. "What business have you here?"

"It is not business at all," said Claude; "but you, with your foolish squabbling have spoilt the whole affair, so off I must go. Now, mind, Annette, you have seen no one."

"But—but——"

"Duval did not wait to hear what objection the waiting-maid had to keeping his secret but he at once dashed from the room, and placed himself in an obscure corner of the landing-place. He was not at all disappointed as to the result of the outcry that Annette had made, for in a moment the marchoiness came up the stairs. She passed him, and went into the bed-room, saying—

"Annette, was that you?—what is the matter?"

"Oh, madam, 1 thought I saw——"

" What ?—what ?"

"A ghost, madam !"

" You silly girl. I did think that you were above such folly as that. Really, Annette, 1 shall have to part with you if anything of this sort happen again."

"I am sorry, madam, but I did think at the moment, that I saw something in the room, and I screamed ; but if I have frightened your ladyship, I am very sorry."

"You have not frightened me, girl ; but folly of any kind or description always annoys me. You can go, now, I shall not want you any more to-night."

Annette left the room, and as she passed Duval upon the staircase, she placed her finger upon her lips to intimate, in all probability, that she had said nothing of his presence in the house. He comprehended in a moment what she meant, and nodded and smiled his thanks. When she had got down the staircase some distance, she beckoned to him, and when he crept softly to where she was, she said—

" For Heaven's sake, come now, count! I will let you out."

" Nay, Annette, I am decidedly too late to go anywhere else to-night, and must needs stay here."

" But you cannot ; it is impossible, I tell you. There is a reason."

" What is it ?"

" That I dare not tell you, but there is a reason ; and I beg of you to go. Besides, you will compromise me now by staying, for I told my mistress that I had seen a ghost, and if she should see you now, she will guess that it was you whom i saw, and that I only mentioned a ghost to screen you."

" There may be something in what you say," replied Claude, " and if anything could induce me to leave at once, it would be that, by staying I did any mischief to you. But cannot you conveniently hide me somewhere ? I tell you in confidence that I have a particular reason for not going home to-night."

" No—no, I cannot."

" Nay, think again, Annette. Think again. What the duce is that ?"

The sound of some one ascending the staircase to where they were, came upon the ears of Claude. It was the footstep of a man, treading vere cautiously, but yet firmly enough to be heard by both Claude and Annette, as they were upon the staircase. The waiting-maid caught Claude by the arms, and dragged him into a room, that opened from one of the steps, whispering as she did so—

" Do not speak or move."

" But I may look ?"

" No—no."

The person who was coming up the stairs, had no light, so that although Duval did keep in such a position that he could command a good view of the stairs, he would not have seen who it was, if the marchioness had not emerged from her bed-room, and leant over the balustrades of the staircase with a light in her hand, aying—

" Is that you, Charles ?"

" Yes," replied a man, and at that moment, as he passed, Duval saw that it was a celebrated political character of the time. He smiled as the earl (for such he was) passed up the staircase, and when he had disappeared in the bed-room of the marchioness, he said to Annette—

" So that was the special reason, was it, why you was urgent upon me to go ?"

" It was."

" Well, I won't deny but it is a good one, and now that I know as much, I will go, and if you can let me out of this infernal house without any of the servents being aware that I am here, I shall be much obliged."

" I can do that," said Annette. " Come this way, at once."

Duval said no more, but holding by the balustrade of the staircase, he crept after the waiting-maid into the hall, where a lamp upon a marble slab was still burning, by the light of which he saw that the street-door was formidably barred and bolted."

"If you leave here," she said, gently, "you must permit me to let you out my own way."

"Pray, what way is that?"

"I must not betray to you the secrets of other people; and, in order that I may not do so, you must permit me to blindfold you; and you must give me your word of honour that you will not peep or make any effort to find out the secret?"

"Humph. Cannot you unbar and unbolt a door, Miss Annette, without making all this fuss about it?"

"The door is securely locked, and the key with my mistress, and no one can get in or out of the house by it, without her express permission, but there is a mode of letting you out, if you will agree to the terms."

"Very good; be it so, only I do think you might trust me."

"I dare not."

Claude was quite curious to know what this mysterious mode of exit from the marchioness's house could be, and he the more willingly consented to be blindfolded; inasmuch as, whatever it was, he had very little doubt that it would not escape his perception. Annette placed a handkerchief securely over his eyes and then turned him round several times, so as to confuse him a little. He then suddenly found cold air blowing upon his face.

"Lift your feet," she said. "There is a step."

He did so.

"Go on, now, go on."

He half stumbled over some obstruction, and then felt quite confident he was in the open air, but Annette spoke to him again, saying—

"Go on—go on."

He did go on, and the result was, he rolled down the four stone steps leading up to the door of the marchioness'. Fortunately for him he did not hurt himself to a greater extent than a few bruises amounted to, and then tearing the handkerchief from before his eyes, he found himself in the street. The door of the house was fast shut, and he did not hear the least noise, so he began really to wonder how it was that he had been let out so readily.

He was determined to find out the secret, but he thought it highly probable that Annette might for a few moments, until she should hear him go away, be upon the watch on the inside of the mysterious door. So he played her a trick, by walking off with as much sound upon the pavement as possible; after which he tripped back again upon his toes, as gently as he could.

All was profoundly still in the hall, for he placed his ear quite closs to one of the panels of the door, and if anything had been stirring within, he must have heard it. He then set about, as well as he could, by the dim rays that came from the nearest street-lamp, examining the door.

"Ah, I have it!" he said, suddenly. "Of course one of these long panels is moveable, and if I could only find out how, I could at any time enter this house."

As he spoke he tried and pressed the panel in all directions, and suddenly it slipped aside, passing into a recess made for it, in the thicker portion of the door.

"That will do," he said, as he closed it carefully up again. "Who knows of what use, upon some such emergency, the knowledge of such a mode of getting speedily into this house may be to me?"

"Hilloa!" said a watchman, suddenly coming up. "What are you doing there? Cracking a crib, I'll be bound. You must come along o' me, young fellow."

"Hush!" said Claude. "Hush!"

"Eh?"

"Hush! Don't speak so loud. There's something very odd going on in the passage now."

"Is there? In the passage?"

"Very curious, indeed. It's in the passage. I really would not lose it, for I don't know how much."

"You don't say so?"

"Hush! Come softly, or else it may leave off. Come very softly, and listen. Hush—hush!"

The watchman crept up the steps as though he were treading upon eggs, and when he got to the door, he inclined his head towards it, and Claude, at the moment that it was about six inches from the panel, gave it such a rap, that the skull of the watchman nearly cracked the door.

"There, do you hear it?" said Duval.

In another moment he was off like a shot, leaving the half-stunned watchman sitting upon the top step, with such a singing in his ears as he had never heard in his whole life before.

Whether he should go home or not, was still with Duval a most doubtful question. If he could, by any possible means, have got rid of the court suit he wore, he would not have minded; but then it was at once as a proof that he was the person who had robbed the archbishop; and as his grace had offered a very liberal reward, he (Duval) could not doubt but that there were persons lingering about Charing Cross ready to pounce upon him the moment he should make his appearance.

Still it was an awkward thing to be kept out all night, and with that daring which was a portion, and a very large one, too, of his character, he at length stepped out quickly towards Spring Gardens.

The distance was by no means great, and he was soon at that entrance to the street of his abode which is nearest to Pall-Mall. He was rather surprised to see no one peeping or prying about, and he almost began to think that the affair had been given up as a bad job. With this idea, each moment gathering strength as he went on, step by step, to his own door; he was, perhaps, not so much upon his guard as he ought to have been, for he was rather taken by surprise when a man rushed out from a dark and deep doorway, crying, "I have you," and clutched him by the collar.

"What's the matter?" said Claude.

"Not much; only you are my prisoner."

Claude gathered all his strength into one effort, and fairly lifting his opponent from the ground, he held him for a moment in the air.

CHAPTER XXVII.

THE SUDDEN CONFIDENCE.

"Murder! Let me go," said the man. "Help!—murder!"

"Once, twice, thrice," said Claude, and then away went the man over the rails of a neighbouring house, and down the area, with a crash.

Duval did not wait one moment then to see what was the result of this affair, but dashing on to his own house, he took a key from his pocket and opened the street door. He had it still in his hand when he saw four men coming from some hiding place over the way, at full speed, crying, as they ran—

"That's our man! that's our man! We have him now. That's the fellow."

"You don't say so," said Claude, as he just slammed the door shut in time to exclude them. Is was a massive door that, and, although they all four made a rush at it, with the hope that it would give way, it remained firm as a rock, and they only got some bruises for their pains.

In another moment Duval had put up a chain and a bar, which materially added to the security of the place; and then, as the officers began to knock furiously for admission, he quietly made his way up stairs.

"Is that you, sir?" said William, meeting him on the top stair, with a light in his hand.

"Yes, William."

"What a dreadful knocking, sir."

"Yes, there are some unfortunate friends of mine at the door, that's all. Your best plan is to let them in at once; but mind, the Count Stofet has not come home yet. Give me the blue bag that is hanging behind the door in my bed-room."

The bag was handed to Claude in a moment, and with it in his hand, up the stairs beyond his own room he went, but without any appearance of hearing, although the knocking at the door below was perfectly frightful.

In a few moments it would be quite obvious that every one in the house must be roused up; but Duval, with the blue bag in his hand, groped his way up to the top of the house, and then he tapped at a small door of one of the attics. He knew that that attic was the only one occupied that night, and that then [it was only so occupied because Madame Stockwellini would have nobody belonging to her establishment sleep upon the premises. The occupant was Adele, the young apprentice of the fashionable milliner.

Claude tapped twice at the door, and then a low faint voice asked "who was there?"

"It is I," he replied. "Do you not know me?"

"The count, Stofet?"

"Yes."

"Shame upon you, sir. Away to your own apartments. You have affected to love me, but you do not. No—no. You cannot; I command you to retire, sir."

"Adele, I will obey you, if you persist in that demand, and in ten minutes I shall be a dead man. There are those now below, clamorous for admission, who must take my life, since in no other way can they conquer me; I am glad I have come to say, farewell to you, Adele—God bless you!"

The door was opened in a moment.

"Hold," she said, as she slipped out upon the landing, and laid her little hand upon his arm, swear to me that all you say is true, and use the name of God in the oath."

"I swear to you, Adele, in the name of God, and that it is true."

"Come in."

She dragged him into the little chamber, and closed the door, over which she spread her arms, as though that frail defence would avail against Claude's enemies.

The awful knocking at the street-door continued; still, William was determined to give his master as much time as possible to perfect his arrangements for escape, whatever they were.

"Speak to me," cried Adele. "What have you done that men should seek your life? Tell me all. Speak, freely."

"Adele, I am not what I seem. I am not Count Stofet, but I am one with whom the law is at variance."

She shook, as though some sudden spasm had seized her.

"No! no!" she said. "Tell me that you are poor—wretched. Tell me any-thing—but that you are a criminal."

"I am criminal, as the world will have it, Adele. My acts are those that will take me to the scaffold. You can save me, or you can give me to my foes.—Alive I will not be taken, but before I can kill four men I shall fall.

"Speak again," she cried, with frantic earnestness. "Are you guiltless of bloodshed?"

"No. In self-defence I have killed men, but it was only after feeling and knowing that it was a question of my life or their's. For the value of what could be got by my destruction, I have been attacked, and I have defended myself."

"And that is all?"

"It is all, Adele. I have many a time spared those who would not have spared me, and when I saw a road to safety open without a deed of violence, I always took it."

"Who—who are you?"

She seemed hardly able to put that question, so great was her agitation.

"They call me Claude Duval."

She clasped her hands and uttered a low, wailing cry. Then bending upon him a look of inexpressible tenderness, mingled with woe, she said—

"I have heard of you, and the worst I have heard of you is that you have a hollow heart—that you glory in lighting up the flame of affection in some pure and gentle bosom, which you afterwards leave to all the horrors of despair and bitterness. Is it so?"

"No—no—no."

"You—you love me, then. Oh, no—no. You are what you are, and there is a gulph between us which I will not, and you dare not, cross. Go, sir—go, sir."

"To my death? Yes."

"No—no. I had forgotten, but what can I do—a poor, weak, and helpless girl? Tell me what I can do to save you. Alas! alas! I am utterly helpless!"

"Hark! The knocking ceases. The outer door is opened, Adele, and those who have come in will not be content unless they search the whole house. It is here, and here only that I must hide, and you can hide me. How comes it that Madame Stockwellini allows you so well got up a bed-room, although it is an attic."

"She sleeps here herself at times."

"Ah, that accounts for it in a moment, then. All you have to say, Adele, is that I am not here."

'But there is no hiding place."

"Yes; I am more fertile in expedients than you, of course.'

As he spoke he approached the bed, which was a very large and well-filled one, and to the amazement of Adele, he got fairly under it, between the feather bed and the mattress, and by dint of pushing the feathers about, he left the surface very little off the level, notwithstanding he was beneath it. Right up at the top portion, by the bolster, he kept a breathing-space, and then he called to Adele, saying—

"Leave yon little light still burning, and get into bed at once; never mind me. Let them come into the room, and all you have to say is that you are alarmed, but you know nothing."

The young girl could not but see at once that this was a very likely plan to succeed, and she got again into bed and covered herself with the clothing. Her light weight upon the feather bed was but little inconvenience to Claude, although it came partially upon him, and he quietly waited the result of the search that the house was soon to be subjected to.

He heard Adele weeping.

"Be of good cheer," he said. "All will be well."

He heard her praying, and then he did not speak. He—even he, with all his boldness, and all his recklessness—dared not attempt to stop the current of that innocent young creature's communion with her maker. He felt that for such as she was, prayers had been fashioned, while he was beyond their gentle influence; never, probably, in all his wild and wayward career had Duval felt so much as upon that occasion. While that young girl prayed it seemed as though a voice kept whispering to him "She feels the need of prayer, and rebel art thou!"

More worldly considerations, however, soon put to flight such feelings, new and strange as they were to Claude Duval. The sound of voices, and the banging of doors warned him that the officers were prosecuting the search with vigilence.

"Adele," he said, "remember upon your calmness all will depend."

"I will be calm," she replied. "I will be calm.   They come."

"Hush.   I hear them."

From the noise and general confusion upon the staircase leading to the attics, it was evident that some more persons were joining in the hunt for the despoiler of

ADELE.

the archbishop than the four officers who had made such efforts to get into the house.

"As he is nowhere else," cried one, "he must be up here, for how could he get out of the house?"

"No how," cried another. "We shall find him, and he will lodge in New-gate, in spite of all his fine clothes.   We shall find out that he is some old hand, when we once get a good look at him."

"Oh, the villain," said a female voice. "The idea that I should arrive in town at such an hour, and find the house in confusion and all sorts of thieves in it."

"That is Madame Stockwellini," whispered Adele.

"Hush," said Claude.

By this time the whole of the party had reached the stair-head, and then one of the officers after asking for silence, said in a loud voice, for the special benefit of the culprit, let him be where he might—

"You had better give yourself up at once, and make no resistance. We are well armed, and it is our duty to take you dead or alive; and you will find that it is a duty we will not flinch from. You had better take your chances of a trial than have a pistol-bullet in your head to-night."

All this spoke pretty plainly the language of fear; and, after waiting for a few moments, in the intense hope that some reply would be made, and finding that nothing came of it, the officers proceeded to make their search.

"All these attics belong to me," said Madame Stockwellini, "and I keep stock in every one but my own bed-room, where one of my girls sleep to keep it aired when I am out of town; so you can shoot who you like in any of these rooms, gentlemen—but mind you don't make a mess, that's all, my good men. If you can shoot him on the stairs it will be better, of course. It's a mercy I just came in in time with the keys."

"We should have had to force the doors, ma'am," said one of the officers; "that would have been our duty, ma'am."

"But, talking of keys and locks," added Madame Stockwellini, "how can the wretch be in any of my rooms that I had the keys of?"

"Lord bless your innocence, ma'am, such fellows as this here one we is arter mind no more a lock being in the way than nothing at all. I'll be bound, ma'am, if he's one of the regular old hands, that he'd pick a lock faster than you'd open one with the regular key."

"Gracious goodness! then there is no knowing what mischief has been done to the stock. Shoot him, by all means, my good man."

The officers now proceeded to search all the attics first, but that in which Claude really was; and while they were so occupied, Madame Stockwellini knocked at the door of Adele's room.

"Adele!" she cried—"Adele! get up immediately, and let me in. Do you hear my voice, you contemptible little wretch?"

"The door is open, madam," said Adele; "the door is only upon the latch, madam."

In another moment in walked Madame Stockwellini, little imagining who was now the principal tenant of that bed-room, to which she had returned so unexpectedly.

"You vile little hussy!" cried the lady. "How dare you go to the frightful extravagance of burning a light while I am away?"

"I bought it, madame."

"Then it only shows that you have a great deal too much money. I always did think that eighteen-pence a week was too much for an idle vagrant, that only did eighteen hours work a day."

Duval really felt the greatest difficulty in preventing himself from jumping up, and taking Madame Stockwellini by the throat, and then and there holding her tight until she apologised to Adele, for addressing her in such a tone, and in such a language; but he comforted himself that he might have yet an opportunity of saying something to her, before he left that little attic apartment.

CHAPTER XXVIII.

THE ESCAPE WITH THE HORSE.

" AND so we buy candles, do we ? " added Madame Stockwellini, in a sneering tone, as she disencumbered herself of some of her outer apparel. " We cannot be in the dark, and so we must buy candles. Dear me, we are mightily afraid of the dark, to be sure. Perhaps now, we will be so kind as to move our fine lady-limbs out of the bed, and go and finish our night upon the sofa in the show room below."

"Madame," said Adele, who, probably, at any other time would have obeyed the order, without a murmur. " Madame you cannot ask me to go down stairs, while the house is full of men ?"

" Oh, dear, of course, we are mightily afraid of the men—we are. Bless and save us ; of course all the men must be attracted by our baby face ; but we will soon see, my fine lady, whether you will obey my commands or not."

Madame Stockwellini approached the bed, on violent thoughts intent, but at that moment the door of the room was thrown wide open—she had only left it partially closed—and the officers appeared at the entrance.

"We can't find him," said the principal one. " He must be in this room, for we have been in every other one in the house, and can't find any trace of him."

" In this room ?" screamed Madame Stockwellini. " Oh, no—no—no, I shall faint, right off, if anything is said again. The idea, of a man being in the same room with me, and that room—a bed-room, too—is too much."

The officers grinned at each other, and proceeded to look round the room, despite the scruples of Madame Stockwellini. One of them spoke to Adele, saying—

" My dear, how long have you been in this bed ?"

" Since ten o'clock last night," replied Adele.

" And how long have you been awake ?"

" Since a violent knocking at the street-door."

"Then he can't be here. Besides, we have peeped everywhere that a cat could hide in. Its no go. The fellow has done us, unless, on going over the rooms again, we find him in some out of the way corner we have missed. I'm very sorry to have disturbed you, my dear, and a pretty little creature you are too. The old woman, I take it, your mother here, was never like you, even when she was your age. Good-night, my little lass. Lord love you, I have got one of my own at home your age, but no more to be compared to you, than a warming-pan is to a Stilton cheese."

" And pray, sir," said Madame Stockwellini, " who did you call an old woman ?"

" No offence, ma'am. I always call my wife the old woman. We can't always be young, you know ; and as for beauty, why neither you nor I need say much about that ; but we are as God Almighty made us, for all that."

" You impertinent thick-headed blockhead. You scum—you dirt. You horrid deaths-head-on-a-mopstick.looking poor low-brought-up wretch."

" Come on," cried the officer. " The old lady has got her jawing tackle on, and there's no knowing when she'll leave off. Did you look at the window, Jem ?"

" Yes. No one has been that way. It's a lost game."

Before Madame Stockwellini could gather breath for another load of abuse against the officers, they hastily left the apartment to her, to Adele, and to Claude Duval. Little did Madame Stockwellini imagine that there was a third person in that chamber. She flew to the door, and closed it with such a bang after the retreating officers, that she nearly knocked the last one down ; and then turning to Adele, she gratified herself by levelling against her all the abuse which she was debarred from uttering to those who had really offended her ; but Adele bore it all patiently, with the hope that Madame Stockwellini would, when she was tired, go herself and lie down, for the short time that it now wanted to daylight, upon the sofa in the show-room ; but in that expectation the young girl was doomed to the most complete disappointment.

"Get up, you idle hussy," screamed the lady. "Get up this moment, and be off with you. Do you dare to hesitate ? I'll pull you out of the bed pretty quickly if you do."

Adele knew that this was no idle threat, and she rose, saying as she did so—

"I leave my reputation in the hands of one who ought to suffer anything rather than endanger it."

Of course these words were intended for the ear of Duval, but to the fashionable milliner they were perfectly inexplicable.

"You do what with your reputation ?" cried she. "What do you mean, you mean-looking thin wretch ?"

Adele made no reply to this; but slipping on a large robe de chambre, she quitted the room, leaving Claude to the tender mercies of the lady, and the lady to the tender mercies of Claude.

Now the idea of allowing any one of the weight of Madame Stockwellini to come plump upon the bed while he was between it and the mattress was what certainly never occurred to Claude Duval, for one moment. That he must do something in self-defence, he felt to be quite evident, and his only difficulty was to think upon what it could be, so as not in any way to compromise Adele, for he recollected her words to him, and of course he felt that what for him might be only an adventure to be laughed at, was destruction to her. While he was vainly endeavouring to think of some plan of operations, the lady locked the door, but she left the key in the lock.

"Dear me," she groaned. "Well, after all, travelling is tiresome ; but I do hope I have got rid of Stockwell. The idea of the wretch sending to me for money, and threatening that if I did not give it, he would find out that my first husband, Captain Gogerty of the Mary Ann, laden from Hamburgh, was alive. Dear me, now if he should be alive after all, instead of drowned, as I hoped he was, what on earth shall I do ? What a fool I was to marry that Stockwell just because he was so big; I do hope the beast will drink himself to death soon, that I do, and then if Gogerty is really dead, I shall be free to marry somebody else, and he shall be the biggest man I can find, of course."

By this time the lady, if we do not profane the title by calling her one, had got off several articles of apparel, and then Claude thought it was high time to do something. He had only been waiting until a favourable opportunity offered of saying something. Suddenly, in a deep sepulchral voice, he said—

"Stir an inch and you are a dead woman, in the fangs of the hideous monsters of the North Sea.—Scream, and you will be torn piecemeal by the howling fires of the ice-frowning mountains of the pole !"

She did not speak. Absolute terror, without any sort of denunciation such as Duval had levelled at her, would have kept her silent. All she did was to open and shut her mouth something after the manner of some large fish who finds himself or herself most unexpectedly on *terra firma*.

"I am the spirit," added Claude, "of Gogerty.

> Full fathom five my corpus lies,
> Of my bones are coral made,
> A scaly fish scooped out my eyes,
> So list to what I've sung and said.

Sit down, wife, in the chair by the bed's foot, or it will be worse for you."

Madame Stockwellini sunk into the chair indicated with a deep groan, and then Claude began slowly to rise up, holding the feather bed between him and the lady.

"I come, I come," he said, "from my watery home. I come to tell you that I must have vengeance on Stockwell,"

" Yes—yes—yes, good Mr. Ghost," faltered madame.   He lives at No. 2 Para-dise-row, Windsor Old Town."

" Peace, I know.   O woman of many sins, make thy peace with thy conscience for a dismal fate awaits thee !   O woman of foul and most abusive tongue, take that !"

Suddenly Claude flung the feather-bed right upon the terrified lady, and over she went chair and all with it upon her.   He did not wait to see if she was smo-therd or not—indeed he did not care—but at once turning the key of the door, he left the room with the blue bag in his hand that he had been so solicitious to take with him.   It contained a complete change of apparel, but as yet he had had no opportunity of putting it on.

He listened at the head of the stairs for some few seconds ; and as the house seemed pretty quiet, he thought he might venture to descend.   He fully intended to leave, but ten minutes time in his own rooms would be very valuable to him before doing so.

When he got within view of his own landing, he leant over the balustrades, and saw his man William standing at the open door of his rooms.   He coughed, and William looked up.   By the light that came through the open door, he could see that it was his master, and he ascended a few steps, saying—

" They are gone."

Upon this Duval at once made his way to his own rooms, and the moment he got there, he began rapidly changing his dress, speaking to William as he did so—

" I am tired of London, William," he said, " and shall be off for a week or two to the country.   You will keep everything in order while I am away ?"

" Yes, sir."

" And you will write to me to the post-office at Hounslow, as usual ; letting me know what is taking place here, and particularly the news of the house, and what this Madame Stockwellini, confound her, is about ; and—and what Adile, the little apprentice is doing."

" Certainly, sir."

Claude by this time had put on a pair of white pantaloons, horseman's boots, a waistcoat of plumb-coloured satin, and a scarlet coat.

" Now, William," he said, as he went to the door, " I shall, as usual, leave you in full charge and authority here ; depending entirely upon your vigilance and sagacity."

" You shall not be disappointed sir.   At what time may I hope to have the pleasure of seeing you return here ?"

" When I am least expected," said Duval ; and in another moment he was gone.

" So" said William, when he was alone.   " So, he will come back when he is least expected ?   I could have told him that.   He always does.   Well, I am of course faithful to him.   Why, I gain more by being faithful to him in one month, than I could sell him for, out and out.   No ! No ! I don't kill my goose that lays me the golden eggs ; but when I take it in my head to retire, I may as well do so with a few extra hundreds as not ; and then Claude Duval look out, for I can place you securely in Newgate, and then I will do it.   Yes, then I will do it, for I shall not feel at all comfortable if I retire, and he is alive.   He would think it the finest joke in the world to come and rob me of all I had, that he would, just for the girl's sake.

The look of diabolical hatred that was upon the face of William, would have been amply sufficient to warn Claude of his danger in that quarter, if he had chanced to see it.   But he did not.   He was on his route to the stable, where he had left his trusty steed, which had now had a good rest, and was ripe and ready for the road.

Upon reaching the street from his lodgings, of course, Duval had kept his eyes open, to see if any of his old acquaintances, the officers, were on the look-out ; but only one man, skulking about the corner of Spring Gardens, met his gaze ; and that one permitted him to pass on with nothing more than a temporary glance.

The fact was that, although Claude Duval's costume, as we have cursorily described it, would have soon got a mob about him; now it was, then, nothing more than an ordinary kind of flash costume, affected by young bloods, as they called themselves, and rather military in its character, for there then was not by any means that uniformity and precision in the costume of the soldier that there is now.

Duval, therefore, neither expected, nor met with any interruption on the score of his costume.

He walked rapidly on until he reached the stables, where he had put up his horse, and, although the hour was a very early one, indeed, his ring at the ostler's bell was quickly enough replied to.

A boy with a profusion of red hair upon his head, opened a small wicket in the great gate.

"All's right, Mike," said Duval. "I see you are determined to earn a guinea, sharp and well this morning, by bringing me out my horse."

The boy's eyes brightened at these words, for to tell the truth, he had but in a half-awake kind of way opened the door. Without wasting time by a word, off he was again, and then in an incredibly short space of time, the one half of the great gate slowly revolved upon its hinges, and Claude's gallant steed made its appearance. At the sound of his voice, as he addressed some kind words to it, the creature rubbed its head upon his breast, and shewed the most marked signs of attachment to him.

"He knows his master," said the boy, "as well as I shall know a guinea, when I see one."

Claude smiled as he tossed the boy the coin.

"I should not have forgotten my promise," he said. "Good-bye, Mike."

The boy touched the front portion of his hair, and in another moment, Claude was off.

CHAPTER XXIX.

HOUNSLOW HEATH BY DAY-BREAK.

"To Hounslow Heath," said Duval, as he turned his horse's head westward. "A sharp canter in the cool morning air, will not do me or you any harm."

He patted the horse's neck, as he spoke, and then putting the creature to the pace he wished, away they went at a good eleven miles an hour, from the dense city of smoke and disorder. It was not long ere the fresh fine air of the open country saluted agreeably the senses of both horse and rider.

"Ah," said Duval, "how I love the country, after a brief stay in London. How freshly, and beautifully upon my senses comes all the sights and sounds of country life. How I love the tall trees—the murmuring brooks, and the meadows. Who with a heart at all susceptible of real beauty, would shut himself up in the brick and mortar haunts of men, when he could breathe the pure air of the open country; and look upon its thousand beauties and glories? It is truly a great privilege, after mixing in the follies and the frivolities of the city, for awhile to be able to fly from it to such a scene as this."

As he spoke he drew rein. He had ridden six miles, and he stood upon an eminence, which commanded an extensive view around him. To his right lay Hounslow Heath, with its dark patches of verdure ; and to his left was a village, the faint blue smoke from which was tinting the fresh morning air. It was the dawn of a new day, and the eastern sky was glowing with the early beams of the sun.

Each moment every object was brightening beneath the influence of the coming day. The distant bark of a watch-dog; and now and then a faint tinkling of a sheep-bell, were the only sounds that came upon the ear to disturb the holy calm of that sunrise in the open country.

"Yes," said Claude, "this is beautiful, and peaceful, and happy-looking; and yet there are people who will prefer the dim of crowded streets—the vile congregation of odours—and the strife and the contamination of a great city, to all this. Will Heaven help their tastes? Perhaps they pity the dwellers amid trees, meads, and flowers, and think them but a species of barbarians for their taste."

He allowed the horse to have his will for awhile, in cropping the sweet soft herbage at his feet, and in good truth, Claude Duval himself could have lingered there for hours, watching the advance of the daylight, and listening to all the sounds, that gently announced the life of country activity that was coming, had he not felt that it was not in his vocation to be such an idler, and that safety for him could only lie now in deeds of daring, and activity of spirit. He felt that his path in life was chosen, and having been so chosen as it was, he felt that pursue it he must, let it lead to where it might.

With a start he awoke from a kind of reverie into which he had fallen, and that start aroused his horse too.

"Hurrah for the road!" he cried. "Hurrah for the road, and no skulking. What am I thinking of?—Of turning hermit, and foreswearing the world? Ha! ha! No—no, Claude Duval, your time has not yet come for any such fancies. With youth and warm blood in your veins, you must fulfil your destiny."

He cantered down the further side of the little hill, upon the brow of which he had paused, and made direct for the village of Hounslow, which was close at hand. As he rode on he thought for a few moments of how he was breaking a kind of implicit engagement with Mrs. Finch, but that did not disturb him much. He felt that at any time upon his sojourning in London for a short time, he should be able to find that lady, and as regarded the scent of his identity, he did not give himself any concern about that.

"It is indisputably true," he said to himself, with a laugh, "that most gentlemen of my fraternity have been betrayed by women, but then that was always by some woman whom they had used too well, and I, as I use them all badly alike, run no such risk; and yet—and yet, I do almost love Adile. She is really beautiful, and really good, and even I almost at times dream that I could be happy with her in some little domestic cottage, covered with roses and honeysuckles in summer, and full of earwigs and cockroaches in the winter."

By the time Duval had drawn this picture of rural felicity, he had reached the village of Hounslow—he only paused as he rode through, to say something to the keeper of the little post house; and from the manner of the woman whom he addressed as she looked out of the window upon his call, it was tolerably clear that she knew who he was.

She called him Captain, and promised to attend to his letters.

"Good-by," he said, as he waved his hand. "I shall not forget you when good things are going."

The post-mistress nodded, and shut the window.

"She must have the first pretty-looking gewgaw," said Claude to himself, "that falls in my way; for I am really much indebted to her for her care of my letters, and I suppose for not, when I come for them, screaming out, 'This is Claude Duval.'"

Another mile of road brought him to a very old delapidated-looking road-side inn, called the Royal Oak. The roof of this ancient hostel contained a world of red tiles. The door was a study for an antiquary, and a huge chesnut-tree that grew against one corner of the house seemed to be, as in all likelihood it really was, its principal support. Duval dismounted at the door of this place with all the ease as though it were his own house.

"Turn the horse into the paddock, Bradshaw," he said to a man, who made his appearance in a lounging manner from the stables; "I shall stay three or four hours."

"Yes, captain," was the reply. "Nothing amiss I hope, captain?"

"No, Bradshaw, thank you. All's right; but I am sleepy, that's all. Is Ben up? I want a bit of breakfast."

"All ready, sir; you'll find master in the bar-parlour. Ah, here he is."

At this moment a jolly-looking personage made his appearance at the door of the hostel, munching a new roll; and at the sight of Claude, he cried—

"Ah, captain, who'd a' thought of seeing you this morning?"

"Is there anything extraordinary, Ben, in a man coming at breakfast-time to a place where he knows he will get a good one? Have you got room for one?"

"To be sure, captain—in course we have. Come in. But I thought you were down west a long way."

"Not I. I have been in London a few days, and got heartily tired of it, as usual. No news stirring, I suppose, in this neighbourhood?"

"Not a word, captain, except that Claude Duval has found Hounslow Heath too dangerous a spot now, and has gone far abroad."

"You don't say so?"

Both Duval and the landlord indulged in a hearty laugh as they together crossed the threshold of the Royal Oak.

In the bar-parlour of the house there was about as ample and substantial a country breakfast laid as any man — or dozen of men — could well have desired. A huge round of beef made the table groan at one corner. At another there was a ham of Herculean dimensions; and the basket of fresh-boiled eggs looked something prodigious. There was tea, and there was coffee likewise; but the host of the Royal Oak had a large silver tankard of ale by his side. The milder infusions and decoctions were for his wife and three buxom daughters. Some perfectly astounding loaves of brown bread, and a large platter of cream-cheese, completed the table arrangements.

"Are they all well?" said Claude.

"Oh, yes, all but Betsy. She's rather off her feet, I think."

"That's your eldest?"

"Yes, and here she comes. Well, my lass. Here's the captain. How are you this morning?"

"Better, father," said Betsy, who was only six feet high. "How are you, captain? Have you brought me the ear-rings you promised me some time ago? You can't think how delicate I have got lately; father, cut us a round off the beef, mind, and give us a dollop of fat with it, and draw us a quart of ale. I don't think I can take much more than that, this morning."

"You will be able, perhaps," said Duval, "to subsist until your appetite comes back to you."

"Yes," said Betsy, quite gravely, and not seeing in the least that Claude was having a laugh to himself at her expense.

Sue, another of the gigantic daughters of the landlord, now made her appearance, with a bunch of radishes; and after the compliments of the morning, she said—"Here, Bet, a radish or two will do you good," upon which recommendation, Betsy consumed about two dozen.

The third daughter was named Kate, and was no way inferior in size to her sisters. The mother was not by any means an out of the way big woman, and it was quite amusing to see how she and the father regarded their gigantic progeny, and evidently thought everything they did and said, to be little short of miraculous; and when they spoke to them or of them, they called them their children, which was truly ludicrous, when applied to such gigantic monsters of size.

"Come, my loves," said the mother, "attend to the captain—you know what a little eater he is, and what a deal of encouragement he wants to get him to take anything."

"I am really so afflicted," said Claude, "to see Betsy not taking anything; I am certain she has not had yet above two pounds of the beef and one whole loaf."

"I have had a trifle of cream cheese," said Betsy, in rather a languid tone.

"But I am certain it was not above three-quarters of a pound," said Claude, gravely. "You are in a very poor way, Betsy, and really, if you don't eat, you will fall off."

"Well, I must try," said Betsy.   "Father, give us hold o' the ham, and draw us another quart of the old ale."

"Yes, my love," said the father ; "now do try an egg."

"No, father, I seems to turn agin eggs this morning—I have tried eighteen of 'em, and could hardly fancy 'em."

CLAUDE'S ADVENTURE WITH SIR C. FARROUGH'S DAUGHTER.

With this amiable family, Claude Duval breakfasted ; and at the conclusion of the repast, he presented the delicate Betsy with a pair of ear-rings, with which she was specially delighted. He then told the landlord that he should be glad of a couple of hours' sleep, as he had been up all night, and was shown to a room, the windows of which he darkened by closing the shutters ; and then, merely pulling off his coat and boots, he lay down, and, with a remarkable facility that he had of almost commanding sleep at will, he dropped off into a sound repose.

It was one o'clock in the day when Claude felt some one shaking him by the shoulder, and upon looking up found it was Ben.

"Anything amiss?" he said.

"No. Not that I know of. There are two men below that seem rather inclined to stay. They came well-mounted, and their horses are in the stable. I thought they rather looked at your horse, for he was having a rub down after being tired of the paddock. Will you get up and have a look at them?"

"I will at once."

Duval's toilette was soon made. A slouch of cold water over his face and head, and his boots and coat put on, was all that he required, and then he followed the landlord down stairs. Ben told him as they went that the two men were in the coffee-room, as a large irregular apartment upon the ground-floor was called, but in which not a drop of coffee had ever intruded ; and Claude, without any ceremony, walked in.

The two strangers started at his appearance, and exchanged with each other significant looks.

"A nice day, gentlemen," said Claude.

"Very, sir," said one.

Duval then slightly bowed, and saying—

"I shall perhaps have the pleasure of seeing you again," he left the room.

The moment he reached the bar-parlour again, Ben eagerly asked him if he knew them.

"Not personally," replied Claude ; "but that they are after me, I don't entertain a doubt for a moment. I will go now, not upon their account, but because I intended to go at any rate. Let me have my horse."

At this moment the coffee-room bell rang smartly ; and when Ben returned from answering it, he said—

"They have ordered their horses directly."

"Good," said Claude. "You can let me have mine first, and then you can serve them as soon as you like."

"Won't I," said the landlord, "and if they find their girths all right in a gallop across the heath, my name is not Ben, and I have not got one of the loveliest young families in the country. Ah, captain, what a wife Betsey would make."

"Yes," said Claude, "especially if you happened to run short of provisions. I should expect her to eat me by dinner-time, if the breakfast was not a tolerably ample meal. But the horse, Ben, the horse, if you please."

"All's right," said Ben.

***

CHAPTER XXX.

THE FIGHT ON THE HEATH.

THE landlord left the bar-parlour to expedite the getting ready of Claude's horse, and he had hardly been gone a moment, when both the strange men came out of the coffee-room.

They glanced around them, and upon seeing Claude, a look of a significant character passed from one to the other of them. The tallest of the two came up to Claude, and said—

"Are the roads safe, my friend ?"

"No," said Claude.

"No? Indeed, you don't say so. Why, are there any highwaymen about these parts, do you know ?"

"Oh," said Claude, "you need not be particular as to any highwaymen being about here.   There are plenty of thieves of all sorts to be met with as well as they on the road.''

As he spoke he made a dart out of the house, for he heard the tramp of his horse upon the stones in front of the old Inn.

"Stop, stop," said the man who had spoken to him, " I only want to speak to you a moment."

" I am busy, and can't wait," said Claude.

" Then, by Heaven, you shall : for, if you don't stop, I'll send a bullet through your skull."

The man, followed closely by his companion, rushed to the door after Claude as he uttered this threat ; but Duval had reached his horse, and placing his left hand upon the pummel of the saddle, he was in the seat in a moment, and the bridle firmly in his hand.

" Blaze away," he said.

Bang went the pistol ; but, at the moment it was fired, the landlord had—quite accidentally, of course ?—ran up violently against the man who fired it, and away went a pair of slugs about twelve feet above Claude's head.

"Hark ye," said Claude, " I don't want to make a disturbance opposite an honest man's door, so as to bring disrepute upon him ; but if you have the pluck to do it, follow me.   I will wait for you a couple of miles or so down the road."

With these words he gave one slight touch to the flank of his horse with his right heel, upon which was the smallest spur that ever was made, and away he went like the wind.

" Our horses," cried the two men.   " Our horses.   Get us out our horses, directly.   Confound you, landlord, for a fool or a rogue; don't you know that that is Claude Duval, the great highwayman, and he will escape us yet if we are not upon his track in a moment ?"

"Lor !" exclaimed Ben, " you don't say so, gentlemen ?   Oh, it's enough to give one the stomach-ache to think that the notorious Claude Duval has been in one's house, and one has not nabbed him.   Cut away after him as quick as you can.   Didn't you hear him say he'd wait for you ?"

" He wait for us !" said the latter of the two men.   " I think I see it.   A highwayman wait for a couple of officers—I think I see him doing such a thing. No—no.   We may catch him yet by raising the country after him ; but with all his bounce he knows a trick worth two of waiting for us.   Why the deuce don't you get us our horses ?"

" They are here, gentlemen—they are here.   It's all right ; I only wish you may catch him—that's all."

" I strongly suspect you," said the officer, who had not yet spoken, " of being his accomplice."

" Me ? Me ?"

" You—you.   He has been here for some time, and was evidently on capital terms with you and your family."

" I course, but how was I to know he was Claude Duval the highwayman ?   I always thought he was a traveller in the hard-ware line.   I can't tell who's who when they come to my house.   You may be the greatest rogue in all the world, for all I know ; and though you are both so bold-looking, you may be all of a shiver of fear in case Claude Duval should be waiting for you a couple of miles on, as he said he should.   I know I should.   Why, I wouldn't be in your shoes for— dear me, how much ?"

The two officers cut Ben's speech short by mounting their horses and at once taking to the road after Claude, who by this time, at the rate he travelled at, must have been considerably in advance of them, and in a condition completely to give them the slip if he felt so inclined.

After he, Claude, had got about a mile off, he stopped to have a laugh at his adventure at the inn, and to give his horse a rest after the sharp gallop.

"It was absurd enough," he said, " Ben running against that fellow just as he was on the point of firing at me. Well, it may have saved me, though those fellows are generally slovenly shots ; and the safest thing in the world, when they do pull a trigger, is to be aimed at by them."

The manner in which Claude examined his pistols showed, however, that if the two officers did venture after him, he did not wish to be trifled with, and that it would be at the risk of their lives.

He never for one moment thought of being worse than his word, and not waiting for the officers, although he had from his experience of similar adventures upon the road, the greatest doubts as to whether they would come so far as one mile after him, to say nothing of two.

He knew that the next mile would bring him to a barren bit of country, where there were very few houses ; but he knew that in more than one of those houses he could find not only a shelter but a welcome. With a wise forethought, he had made earnest friends with the poor occupiers of many a lone cottage around the suburbs of London. They had felt what it was to have a generous friend in the hour of distress ; and Claude had, as regarded his money, often verified the old proverb of " Lightly come, lightly go."

People who take a peculiar view of Claude Duval's transactions, will probably say it was easy enough to be generous with what don't belong to you. But then there are some who would be generous under no circumstances at all, whether the means legitimately belonged to them or not ; so we can still lay claim for Claude to some sort of virtue upon that score.

As he had mentioned a couple of miles or so, he did not wish to meet the officers earlier ; so he rattled on until he came to the extensive barren spot which we have mentioned, and where, amid the heath, only now and then the gable-end of some white-washed cottage was to be seen.

There, then, he waited for whatever adventure it might please fate to send him. He kept a wary eye upon the road to London, for there was just a possibility of the officers coming, and that was all.

He had waited many minutes in this place, so full of beauty, barren as it was, before he heard the sound of a horse's feet upon the heath ; but it came from the opposite direction to that in which he expected the officers. As he looked anxiously to see who was approaching, he was rather surprised to observe a young girl of about fifteen or sixteen years of age, attired in a handsome riding-habit, and mounted upon a small chesnut palfrey, emerge from a lane on to the common. The flush of youth and beauty was upon her face ; but a glance at the horse was sufficient to show Claude that it had had a hard gallop.

The creature was panting, and the foam was hanging to the bit, while its reeking sides testified likewise to the violent character of the exercise it had taken. When he looked again, Claude could not but see that there was an appearance of alarm upon the countenance of the young lady ; and he at once came to a correct conclusion upon the subject ; namely, that the little steed had run away with her.

With all that easy grace of manner that he found rarely failed to be for him a sufficient introduction to any one, Claude approached her ; and slightly bowing in the saddle, he said—

" Can I be of any service to you ?"

" I know not, sir," she replied ; " but I have certainly lost my party. Something came over my usually quiet little pony, and at a headlong speed, for the distance I fancy of more than three miles, I have been brought here."

" I guessed as much," said Claude, " from the state of the animal. Permit me to protect you back. The roads are not particularly safe just now. If you will tell me in which direction lies your home, I will do myself the pleasure of acting the part of an escort to you."

" I am truly obliged, sir," she said. " I am the daughter of Sir Clement Farrough, and my home is at Farrough Lodge, which should not be very far from here."

"I know it well," replied Claude. "It is only a sharp trot of some few minutes."

"Indeed? I am truly much beholden to you, sir; but my father will be able to thank you better than I can."

While this little conversation was going on, Claude had quite forgotten the fact that the two officers might be coming after him, and that a rather disagreeable encounter might possibly take place in the presence of the young lady; doubly disagreeable, too, as in all probability it would have the effect of disclosing to her who he was, before he had taken her in safety to her own home.

That all this was really to be expected was soon rendered sufficiently manifest by the appearance very shortly, at some distance off, of the two officers and a farmer-looking man on horseback, whom they had met upon the road, and tempted to accompany them, by the promise of a handsome reward for so doing, provided the whole three should succeed in capturing the renowned Claude Duval.

They all three evidently hung back, and as Claude saw that such was the case, he resolved to make an attempt to free himself from the encumberance of their presence by one of those bold actions which he so frequently owed life and liberty to.

"I am truly glad," he said to the young lady, "that I am with you; for to the best of my belief those fellows are no better than highwaymen."

"Highwaymen!" exclaimed the young lady. "I was told that the well-known Claude Duval, kept this road all to himself."

"And I too have heard the same; but there will be interlopers and trespassers upon everybody's manor house. Have you anything of importance that you would be loath to lose?"

"I have a watch that was my mother's, and I would not willingly part with it. It is of considerable value, too."

"Then you shall not part with it," said Claude. "I will soon disperse those fellows for you. Do not stir from where you are, and you will see what real cowards these kind of men are."

As he spoke he turned his horse's head in the direction of his foes, and approached them at a gallop. Of course such a proceeding, of all others, was calculated in the greatest degree to astonish the officers, who fully expected that if he galloped at all, it would naturally be in the opposite direction to that in which they were to be found. The farmer-looking personage was seized with a panic, and at once rode off as hard as he could make his nag set foot to the ground, so that the two officers were alone.

CHAPTER XXXI.

CLAUDE IS TAKEN PRISONER.

CLAUDE did not pause in his career until he got close up to the officers, and then drawing a pistol from one of the holsters of his saddle, he cried—

"I will soon rid the world of you two. You shall drink my blood, or I will drink yours."

Bang went the pistol; but he purposely missed the man he fired at.

The words he spoke, and the daring of the whole affair, combined with the discharge of the pistol, had such an effect upon the spirits of the officers, that they both turned, and setting spurs to their horses, they galloped off by the road that they had come as fast as they could persuade their horses to go.

Claude pursued them for some short distance, and fired another pistol at them, which had the effect of adding wings to their flight; and then he quietly trotted back to the young lady, who had been a spectatress of the whole of the strange proceeding.

After this, if she had not a tolerable respect for the prowess of her champion, it was not his fault; and if she had not seen the whole affair with her own eyes, she might well have doubted that one man, be he ever so bold and resolute, could strike terror into three.   But such things are of much more frequent occurrence than is generally supposed. The courage of a man depends almost solely upon what he is fighting for.   He who engages in a contest merely for money, does so with a widely different feeling to him who feels that his life is dependant upon the issue.

Such a man as Claude Duval had everything to fight for ; while those who, in most cases, attempt his capture, have only the prospet of the acqustion of a few pounds to urge them on.

"This is an exploit, indeed," said the young lady, when Claude got back to her. "You are as redoubtable as any knight of old romance."

The paleness of her face, and the slight quiver of her lip, showed that, notwithstanding she spoke of the affair in a tone and with a manner that was more in jest than in earnest, she had been very much frightened at the encounter.

"It would have been the delight as well as the duty of any knight to have protected you," he replied.

"You did not kill either of them ?"

"No, nor wound them either. I have the greatest repugnance to shedding even bad blood. I fired twice at them, but I purposely missed them."

"You are in the army, I presume, sir ?"

"Yes, in the 'Rifle' Brigade ; but this is not my uniform exactly. This is my fancy merely to dress in such a way when I am on the road ; and now if you will trust yourself to my guidance, I will take you in safety to Farrough Hall, the chimney tops of which we shall soon see."

"With pleasure," replied the young lady. "I shall at least feel that I am safe from highwaymen."

"That you shall be truly ; and yet it is a strange thing, but I was actually robbed yesterday upon this very heath."

"You robbed ?"

"Yes, strange as you may think it ; I was taken unawares, and actually robbed by a man in a gig—a fat man——"

"Why, sir, look there. There is a fat man in a gig."

Claude Duval affected for the first time to glance in the direction of one of the roads that traversed the common, and there, sure enough, was a gig coming slowly along ; within it was a man, who was not only fat, but of such a size that it was quite a wonder how he got into the vehicle, or how, having once got in, he ever got out again.

"That man," said Claude, "who is, to look at, a highly respectable man, took me at unawares, when I was off my horse, and half asleep beneath a tree, and robbed me, and then drove off."

"You astonish me!"

"Look at him, if you please ; and as you are a resident of the neighbourhood, perhaps you may know him by sight."

The young lady shook her head. No, she knew nothing of the fat man. She had never seen him before ; and what was more, she considered it quite incredible that he could be a highwayman at all.

"The rascal!" said Claude ; "I fully believe that his fat is all a sham ; but if you will do me the favour to pause for a few moments only, I will make him restore what he took from me."

"Certainly—I will wait by this tree."

"I thank you. I will make short work with him."

"Would it not be proper, sir, to apprehend him ?"

"Yes, highly proper ; but then I should be kept in England to prosecute, and a beloved mother and sister expect me by a certain time on the continent, so I cannot encumber myself with a prisoner, or the trouble of a prosecution. Ah, how often such fellows escape from such reasons."

"They do, indeed," said the young lady, "and it is a sad pity that they should. I will wait for you, sir. I shall never forget the singular adventures of this day."

Duval, with an amount of assurance that certainly could have been but rarely equalled in this world, rode up to the gig; and addressing the driver, he said,—

"Come, I am glad I have met with you ; I now insist upon restitution,"

"You insist upon what ?" said the corpulent gentleman, suddenly drawing up and fixing his staring eyes upon Claude ; "you insist upon what ?"

"Restitution. Your money, watch, and valuables are mine, or as good as mine. You may give them up without having a bullet in your brains previously or not, as you like ; but give them up you shall, some way or another."

"Murder !" cried the old gentleman. "It's a highwayman, and in broad daylight, too !"

"Quick," said Claude. "That young lady is waiting for me, and nothing can be more unpolite than to keep her long. Be quick, I say, or I shall be under the necessity of shooting you, and she and I will bury your body on the heath."

From the appearance of the old gentleman and the blue color that appeared about his nose, Claude really thought he was going off in a fit of apoplexy from fright, so he hastened to say—

"You will have no harm done you if you comply with my request, and then you can pursue your journey with perfect safety, and you will be a little lighter than you were before, which will be a great consolation to the horse. Do you hear ?"

The old gentleman only goggled his eyes at Claude, but he said nothing ; and as his watch-seals, together with nearly a foot of gold chain, were hanging out of his fob, Claude laid hold of them, and by one vigorous pull possessed himself of a valuable gold repeater.

"Have you much money about you ?" he said.

The old gentleman only stared a little more wildly than before, and Claude was so amused at his manner, and the effect which the robbery had upon him, that he forbore to trouble him further, contenting himself with the really valuable watch-chain and seals that he had taken from him. He gave the horse, which was a strong but sluggish beast, a smart cut with his own riding whip, and the lazy animal, astonished at being so wakened up, started off at a hard canter, and soon carried the old gentleman far away over the common.

"I have got my watch back again," said Claude, as he rejoined the young lady.

"I am glad of that. Did he resist ?"

"He threatened a little, that was all ; but upon finding I was resolute he told me to take it, and I did. I am afraid he will soon make it up by some other robbery ; but the career of such a man must be cut short some day. It is quite melancholy to think how people can give their minds to such a life."

"It is indeed, sir. Honest industry surely ought to have charms that would more than compensate for all the robber's gains, even if the end of his career was not certain to be disgrace and death."

"Exceedingly true," cried Claude. "But, my dear miss, did you ever hear of honest industry getting its reward in this world? Did you ever hear of it getting ordinary comforts ?"

"Often."

"Indeed !"

"You seem to doubt it, sir ; but I feel assured that a honestly-earned crust and a draught of spring-water caught in the palm of the hand from some stream, is a banquet far more delicious than an Apician feast which is corrupted by injustice and stolen from the resources of others."

"Humph !" cried Claude. "This is our way. By a trot of half a mile down this shady lane we shall come to the hall, or close to it. Ah, who have we here ?"

From the lane to which Claude alluded, there came four persons on horseback. One was an old gentleman with white air and without his hat, another was a young man about nineteen or twenty years of age, and the two others were ladies. The moment the young lady who was with Claude saw them, she exclaimed in eager delight—

" That is my dear father!—that is my father !" and springing forward, she in a moment was by the side of the old gentleman without a hat. The others crowded around her, each expressing the greatest joy at beholding her again, and so completely unhurt ; but upon her saying something, suddenly they all turned towards Claude, and the old gentleman, with all the others following him, rode up to him.

" Sir, I am extremely obliged to you," said the father.

" Sir," said Claude, " you are extremely welcome."

" My daughter, Bena, tells me that she had the good fortune to meet you on the common ; and that you have, since that time, protected her from some dangers."

" From three highwaymen, father," said the young lady, who rejoiced in the rather singular name of Bena.

" Yes," added the father, " as I hear, from three highwaymen ; but I really was not before aware that our neighbourhood was so infested."

' Ah, sir," said Claude, " you don't know what troublesome and bad characters you may have near you, when you least expect them to be near at hand."

" That is very true, sir," said the old gentleman. " Allow me to introduce you to my son, and to my other two daughters, Nock and Krutz."

" Sir !—"

" Oh, you are surprised at the names of my family ? but that is the fancy of an old maiden aunt of the children, from whom they had great expectations, and who would name them, Nock, Krutz, and Bena. My son was permitted to have an ordinary appellation, so he is named Walter."

Claude did indeed feel a little surprised to find such an odd-named family, but he was by far too polite to make any remark about it, merely contending himself by replying with a bow to the communications of the father.

When they reached Farough Hall and were fairly seated in one of its handsome reception-rooms, Claude at once cast off any shyness of manner that might at first have beset him ; though not having made up his mind as to what course of conduct to pursue in the present adventure. He turned with a smile to the baronet, and said—

" I greatly regret that I am compelled to appear in riding costume ; but if you will permit me to seek it, I can find in my vallaise a more suitable coat, at all events."

CHAPTER XXXII.

CLAUDE'S PECULIAR POSITION AT THE HALL.

" Now I am glad to hear you say that," cried the baronet, " because that shows, my young friend, that you have gracefully yielded to the request that we have all made you to stay a few hours with us. I will give the necessary orders to have your vallaise, which I presume is strapped to your saddle, taken to a room at once. Now pray do not disturb yourself, I beg."

" I am much beholden to you," said Duval, " but the fact is, sir, that my horse, from long association with me, and much petting upon my part, would not rest or eat unless I paid him a short visit in his stable to assure him by my presence that all was right. It's a singular whim of the animal's, but a fact that I cannot get over, so I just indulge him in it."

" Well sir, in that case, then, of course you must. Simpkins, show this gentleman the way to the stables, directly."

" Yes, sir," said Simpkins, who was a very prim-looking servant out of livery, and who evidently at the word stables turned up his nose as though he thought it far beneath his dignity to know even of such a portion of the premises.

Of course Claude's great object, wherever he was, was always to know where his horse could be found at a few moments notice, for in his mode of life it was quite impossible that he could say with certainty one moment from another that he might not require to be off and away, and he would as soon think of going without his horse as without his head. He followed Simpkins with all the gravity in the world, and that individual upon reaching a lawn at the back of the house, called upon Robert to do the rest of the honours of that portion of the premises.

SIR C. FURROUGH TREATS CLAUDE WITH GREAT DEFERENCE.

Robert was rather a rough-looking specimen of the groom gems, and when Simpkins was gone, Claude took from his waistcoat-pocket a guinea, and handing it to Robert, said—

"It's a fancy of mine always to take a look at my horse in his stall, and it's a fancy of his to expect me."

"Certainly, sir," said Robert, as he gave the guinea a twirl with his finger and thumb. "And a very good fancy it is too. This way, sir, if you please. This way."

Duval soon had all the information he wanted of the whereabouts of his steed, and then he returned to the drawing-room in which the baronet and his family were seated. A servant had charge of the little vallaise which Claude usually had at the back of his saddle, and only waited the baronet's orders where to take it.

"Ah, my friend," said Sir Clement to Duval, "you will be put upon your mettle shortly if you leave us to-night."

"Indeed, sir ?"

"Yes; I have just had information that Claude Duval the famous highwayman is in this neighbourhood, and as a magistrate, I am asked, by a couple of officers who will be here directly, to back a warrant for his apprehension."

"Really," said Claude. "May I proceed now at once to change my coat."

"Oh yes, certainly ; Simkins, take that genleman into my room."

Claude vanished after Simpkins in a moment, and was conducted, vallaise included, into a sumptuous dressing-room adjoining a bed chamber of commensurate appearance. There he rapidly made the alteration that was so desirable in his costume, and then, without waiting one moment longer than was absolutely necessary, he repaired again to the drawing-room:

"Oh, my dear sir," said Sir Clement, "you dress with military expedition. The too officers who are seeking for that notorious rascal, Duval, are anxious to see you, to ask you, as you have been riding in the neighbourhood, if you have observed anything of such a person as the highwayman."

"Indeed, no. The only highwaymen that I have seen consisted of two fellows, that I had the honour of preventing from interfering with your daughter on the Common. Perhaps one of those was the man these officers seek."

"Oh, no, sir. Oh, no. Claude Duval does all his robbing alone. As a magistrate, I have heard of some of his tricks, and I am quite sure that he would never admit a companion to share with him either in his dangers or his plunder. He is, I assure you, sir, a very desperate character."

"And a most impertinent fellow too, I should think," said Claude.

"As you say, a most impertinent fellow. Well, Simpkins, you can tell the officers that this gentleman is here, and will cheerfully answer any inquiries they may have to make."

"Yes, Sir Clement. They are both here on the door mat, and will come in directly."

"Let them come by all means," said Claude. "I am sure that any information I can give concerning that notorious character, they will be most welcome to."

Upon this the two officers, one of them looking very rueful from a hurt he had got in a fall from his horse, made their appearance in the room. All the precaution that Claude took was to place himself with his back to the window, so that his face was rather obscured than otherwise. To that and to the slight alteration he made in the costume he wore, he entirely trusted.

"We are sorry, sir, to trouble you," said one of the officers, "but understanding you had been upon the road, we make bold, sir, to ask if you had seen Claude Duval."

"No," said Claude, "I saw nobody at all answering the description of the fellow ; and as I am well acquainted with his person, I can satisfactorily assure you that he did not pass me."

"Thank you, sir. His lordship has been kind enough to back our warrant against him, and to say that he will lend us what help he can to nab him to-night on the heath, if so be he should be bold enough to show himself there.

"I wish you success," said Claude.

The officers then bowed themselves out of the room, and Duval fully believed that he had succeeded in deceiving them. Whether such was or was not the fact, we shall speedily see.

The baronet began to speak very freely to Claude about his family, and he particularly praised the sweet disposition of her who was named Bena, and whom Duval had first met with previous to his introduction to the rest of the family. Probably the baronet thought that if the new acquaintance should turn out to be a young man of good family, it would be no great harm to make a favourable impression upon him. Of course, Claude, who was quite sufficiently wide awake to perceive this little scheme of his host, made suitable replies, and in the midst of the conversation, Simpkins made his appearance, saying in a respectful voice—

"Dinner is laid, Sir Clement."

"Dinner?" said Claude; "I am afraid I am inducing you to sit down to that meal at a very early hour, Sir Clement."

"Oh, no, no—not at all, my dear sir—not at all. We are really quite countrified and primitive in our habits here. I live, as you see, a quiet life of a country gentleman among my really amiable girls, who will make the most excellent wives, though I say it. But it will be a sad blow to me, my young friend —a very sad blow to lose any one of them, particularly Bena."

As he spoke, the baronet affected to dash a tear from his eye, and then he added—

"She is like her mother—but never mind—never mind. I am content to suffer any privation so that I only see my children comfortably settled in life."

"A most praiseworthy object," said Claude. "My uncle the duke often says— a—a—hem! I mean my uncle merely—often says that it is only in the sweet calm of domestic life that true happiness is to be found in this world, whatever state of things we must look for in the next. That is his opinion, Sir Clement."

"How very true, my dear young friend. How very true. After you. Nay, I could not think of taking precedence. His uncle the duke," added Sir Clement to himself, as he followed Claude into the dining-room. "His uncle the duke? That stepped out now completely unawares. His uncle the duke? I saw from the first he was a most distinguished young man. His uncle the duke? What a chance for Bena."

The dinner was duly laid with quite a profusion of old plate, though Claude could not help noticing that the crest upon it was not always the same; indeed, if he had known more of his host he would have been aware, that he was one of those city baronets, who having made money by trickery in trade, have had the luck, if there be anything lucky in obtaining such a handle to one's name as Sir in these degenerate days, to be made a baronet on account of some Royal gorge in the City during his sherivalty, and that he was positively going to get his daughter wedded to the aristocracy.

"You do, indeed, keep primitive hours," said Claude. "Why, it cannot be very much past mid-day."

"Only two, about two," said Sir Clement, taking out a very handsome gold watch from his fob.

"That's a repeater, I presume?" said Claude.

"Yes, and considered a capital one," replied Sir Clement, as he handed it to Duval. "Those brilliants round it are considered of the very first water, and match the ring on my finger."

"Do they match it?" said Claude, dubiously. "At this short distance, and by this light, I really don't see that they are exactly of the same lustre. Nay, my dear Sir Clement, don't trouble yourself—don't indeed; it's only imagination, I daresay."

"It's not a bit of trouble, my dear sir," said the baronet, as he worked the ring from off his finger, and handed it to Duval; "it's not the smallest trouble, I assure you. Pray compare the ring-joint with those round the watch."

"Ah!" said Duval, "I now see that I was wrong. They are precisely similar; and they both put me in mind, do you know, sir, and you, my charming young ladies, of a singular adventure I met with one day in Oxfordshire."

"In Oxfordshire?" said the delighted Sir Clement, who was the happiest person in the world at that time, to find the nephew of a duke so very communicative and affable in his house, and to hear him call his daughters dear young ladies ; "in Oxfordshire—an adventure in Oxfordshire, girls—do you hear that ? How very singular and how very delightful."

"Oh, very," said all the young ladies together.

"But I am afraid," said Duval, "that I shall bore you by telling it to you, and I would not for the world, after the kind—the very kind reception I have had here from you, sir, and from the bright eyes about me, that make these brilliants look by comparison but poor gems, after all."

"Oh, no, no," cried everybody; and then the young ladies whispered to each other what a charming compliment that was about their eyes and the brilliants on papa's watch and ring.

"Well, then," said Claude, "since you are kind enough to say that it will not bore you to hear the anecdote, I will briefly relate it to you."

"Fill the gentleman's glasses, Simpkin," said Sir Clement.

Claude sipped his wine ; and then, with an engaging smile, he thus spoke, while every eye was upon him, and every ear drunk in the soft melody of his tones—

"I was taking a quiet canter through Oxfordshire some few years ago, when, it being autumnal season, I found, as the day darkened, that a raw and gusty air got up, accompanied by dashing rain, so that it became highly desirable to find shelter somewhere. I rode on at a rapid pace, the gloom still gathering around me, until in the distance I saw lights, and urging my tired steed still more quickly forward, I, to my great satisfaction, soon reached a large old-fashioned looking inn, by the road-side.

"The sign of this inn I cannot just at this moment call to mind, but whatever it was, the indication of it made a terrible creaking, as it hung by some iron-work to an old tree, that was before the door of the ancient hostel. I drew up in a moment, and the ostler taking my horse, I strode into the house, and asked for a private room, and specified that there was to be a good fire in it. Well, sir, and ladies, they did show me into a private room, but I found that the fire had only just been lit, and that the chimney did not draw well, for the room was full of smoke. In answer to my remonstrances, the landlord said—

"'I would have accommodated you, sir, with a better room, but the fact is, a gentleman is now in occupation of our best room, and he has got such a beautiful fire, that it would do your heart good to look at it.'

"'Is he,' said I, 'really a gentleman?'

"'Oh, dear yes, sir,' replied the landlord; 'he is a real gentlemen ; spends his money like a prince, sir ; and won't drink any but the very best of wine."

"'Give him the compliments, then, of a stranger,' I said, 'and ask him if it will be agreeable to him for me to sit by his fire, and share his society for the evening, as I shall put up here to-night.'

"Well, the landlord took my message, I presume, to the gentleman; for in a few moments he came back, to say that the gentleman sent his compliments, and begged to say that nothing would give him more pleasure than my joining him in his room. And upon this polite invitation I went to the stranger's apartment, and found him by the side of a roaring fire, and a very tempting-looking bottle of claret at his elbow. We were mutually polite, and soon got to be quite at home with each other.'"

CHAPTER XXXIII.

DUVAL RATHER ASTONISHES THE BARONET AND HIS FAMILY ; AND HAS A FIGHT
ON THE HEATH.

"Simpkins," said Sir Clement, "attend to the gentleman's glass."

"Thank you," said Claude, " thank you."

"Pray go on," said Bena, "with the very entertaining story, sir."

"With great pleasure," said Duval; "but after all, you see, Sir Clement and ladies that it is not one of those stories which are entertaining as they go on ; but the conclusion, I promise you, will surprise you a little.   Well then, as I was saying, I and the stranger got quite intimate and delighted with each other ; and at last, as the discourse turned on the beauties of the country, he suddenly said— ' I received rather a check one day in my admiration of the picturesque, for not far from this house I was robbed by Claude Duval, the celebrated highwayman.' 'Indeed !' I replied, ' I was not aware that he practised in this part of the country at all.' ' Yes,' replied my new friend, ' he robbed me in a most ingenious way : he took advantage of my having dismounted to tighten my horse's girths, and gave the creature such a slash with a riding-whip that sent it off at a gallop ; and, as I was on foot and defenceless, he took from me my watch and money.' We then had another bottle of claret, and were getting on capitally with each other, although neither party had mentioned who or what he was, by a sort of tacit consent that was evaded, when he sudddenly said to me—' That seems a remarkably pure brilliant in the ring you have upon you litttle finger, sir.' I thought this, at the time, only one of those common-place remarks that, o vera glass of wine, anybody may make to another, and I drew the ring from my finger and handed it to him, saying, ' Yes, it is considered pure, and matches with the jewels round my watch,' for it was a most singular coincidence, Sir Clement that, like you, I had then a watch surrounded with brilliants of the same lustre as my ring."

"Very remarkable," said Sir Clement.   "You hear that, girls !   How very curious to be sure things do come about."

"Very, oh, very," said all the young ladies.   "Pray go on, sir."

"I took out my watch," added Claude, " to show him that the brilliants resembled that one in the ring; and he took about five minutes comparing them, and then, with all the coolness in the world, he took up my ring—as I might this of yours, Sir Clement—"

" Yes, yes,"

" And put it on his little finger—as I put this on mine."

" Exactly.   How very droll."

" Well, Sir Clement, he then took up my watch—as I do your's now—and with all the assurance in the world, he put it in his pocket in this way—just as I put yours in my pocket now."

" Precisely," said Sir Clement.   " Upon my word and honour, it was a very cool proceeding on the part of a stranger."

" Very.   A most impudent thing, I call it."

" Uncommonly so."

" Well, then, up he got in this way, while I stared at him, in utter amazement, as you might stare at me ; and leaving the table as I do now, just in this way, he made towards the door, and said, " Sir, I have made perhaps more free than welcome with your watch, and your ring but when I tell you that I am no other than Claude Duval, you will scarcely feel any amount of surprise at my doing so ; and I have the honour of bidding you good day, and more wit.' That was just what he said ; and then, Sir Clement and ladies, out he went from the room as I do now, and shut and locked the door behind him."

As Duval uttered these words, he walked out of the dining-room with Sir Clement's watch in his pocket, and his ring on his finger, and finding the key in the lock of the door on the outside, he rapidly turned it so that the worthy baronet, and his family, together with Simkins, who was officiating at the side-board were made prisoners in a moment. Before he left the door, Claude heard Sir Clement roaring out—

"Capital! Capital! Excellent! Upon my word this is capital. Ha!—ha! ha! Really this is good. Ha! ha! ha!"

It was now that Duval felt all the importance of knowing his way direct to the stable, and he flew rather than walked in that direction. He felt confident that not for many minutes could the delusion in which he had temporally wrapped up the senses of Sir Clement last, and that there was no time to lose. The moment he got within sight of the stable, he saw the man to whom he had given the guinea, and he said to him—

"Robert, earn another guinea by showing me how quickly you can saddle my horse, and bring him out to me here."

"Yes, sir," said Robert, and he vanished into the stable like a shot. Claude felt certain he should be in the saddle in the course of a few moments. He felt how very precious every one of those moments were, and he had the greatest difficulty to keep himself from entering into the stable and helping Robert to bring out the horse. Suddenly he heard the violent ringing of a bell in the house, and he said to himself, "They are now beginning to suspect that all is not right. Oh, for my horse."

Robert, at that moment, made his appearance with the steed already caparisoned for the road. "That's right," said Claude, "there's nothing so delightful to me as a scamper by night. Where does that little door in the w l lead to Robert?"

"Into the meadows, sir."

"Open it then. That will be my way. Here is your guinea, my man."

Tingle, tingle, tingle, went the bell again.

"There's two gentlemen in front of the house, sir," said Robert, "who offered me five shillings for letting of 'em know when you went to bed, if so be as you slept here, and the same money for letting of 'em know if you ordered your horse."

"Five shillings, Robert? I have outbid them, then. Open the door, and then be busy in the stable ; and say nothing, and hear nothing until you are forced, and I'll turn their silver bribe into a golden one. Here are five guineas, Robert, and remember that I trust you."

"You may, sir. If you were the devil himself I'd lend you a helping-hand ; for this money will make my old mother comfortable for the winter that's coming, and it's her last, I dare say, poor old girl."

Robert flung open the gate, and Claude, waving his hand to him, darted on horseback into the meadows. The bells in the house were now ringing with a fury that threatened the absolute dislocation of every wire in it. But Claude Duval was off.

Close to the small gate-like-door, at which Robert had let him out, was a remarkably beautiful row of poplars, and Duval crept close under them, walking his horse, until he should come to some gap in the hedge that would enable him to get into a lane which he saw was close at hand, and which, no doubt, communicated with the high-road. He did not by any means court a collision with the officers, any more than he took pains to avoid one, although of the two he would certainly have preferred avoiding them, because he did not wish to take a life or lives, which, in the event of their attacking him, he might be obliged to do.

It would appear, however, that in their measures for the apprehension of Duval—whom, notwithstanding the change in his costume, they must have recognised when they came into Sir Clement's drawing room—they did not wholly trust to Robert and the five shillings they had with such remarkable generosity promised him ; for suddenly, as Claude emerged from the trees and was thinking of dismounting for the purpose of clearing a sufficient gap in the hedge for his horse to pass through, he heard a whistle sounded.

"Halloa!" he said, "the enemy is nearer at hand, probably, than I thought.—Well, the lane will be as good a place, and perhaps better, than the meadow in which to meet them."

With this he cantered back about a hundred yards, then putting the horse to speed, he gave him his head and over he went, clearing the hedge in beautiful style, and alighting in the lane.

Bang went a pistol, and a bullet whizzed past Duval's head.

"Oh!" he said, "that was a coward's shot, let it come from whom it may;' and then glancing in the direction from whence it proceeded, he saw a man crawling down, and creeping along, close to the hedge, with the recently discharged pistol in his hand. Now, Claude always kept one of his large holster pistols loaded with good-sized shot, and drawing that weapon from his saddle, he took good aim at the man, and fired it."

"That wont kill you," said Claude, as the man uttered a loud shriek, and rolled over and over at the foot of the hedge. "That won't kill you, but it will make you rather uncomfortable, my friend, for some time, I think."

"Surrender, Claude Duval!" cried a man springing out of the hedge, and then another followed him, and then a third appeared, armed with a pitchfork. The two first who appeared presented each a pistol at Claude, and from their general aspect he could see that they were officers.

"The game is up, Duval," said one of them. "You are wanted. Your time has come, and we must have you; sooner or later, you know, it was sure to come to this, so it is of no use shirking it. You are wanted. Resistance is useless. We have lots of help, and you can't escape this time. I warn you not to shed blood uselessly, but to give in at once, for you have not the ghost of a chance of getting away from us now."

"You are very kind," said Duval; "and I daresay that advice is quite disinterested. That my time to die with the moon or the sun above me, as the case may be, will come some day, I don't doubt; but I have a sort of faith that it has not come yet, so blaze away."

"Don't be a fool, Duval," said the officer. "Don't be a fool. I have made up my mind to have you dead or alive. I have a dozen men armed, at all parts of the lane, and you may throw away your life if you like, but that is all you can do."

"Hark ye," said Duval, "I have never any faith in those who talk much of what they are going to do. If you were serious you would do it, but I have an opinion of my own to the effect that you dare not. I'll trouble you to get out of my way."

Claude, while he was speaking had prepared himself for the bold dash he now made. Touching his horse on the flank with that peculiar movement that the creature had been taught to understand was a signal that all its best energies were required—in a moment he bounded forward with a tremendous leap that cleared one half the distance between him and the officers. They both fired their pistols, but in that moment of surprise and hurry, it is not to be wondered at that they missed him, Claude. The man with the pitchfork made a savage thrust at the horse which would have killed the noble creature had not the flap of the saddle partly saved it. As it was, it inflicted a long graze on the skin, ripping it up completely for the space of about a foot or more.

If anything more than another was calculated to thoroughly infuriate Duval, an injury wantonly inflicted upon his horse would be that thing. His eyes flashed fire, and swerving in the saddle he caught the pitchfork by the prongs and tore it from the hands of the man who had made so cowardly a use of it. He tried to escape, but Duval was too quick for him, and with a crashing blow that had quite a horrible sound upon his head, he struck him to the earth with the handle of the fork.

One of the officers sprang forward and caught the bridle close to the bit calling out "I have him—I have him!"

"Hold him tight then!" cried Claude, as he again urged the horse on. The officer was galloped over in a moment, and away went Duval down the lane with his blood throughly heated now by the little battle that had taken place.

The officer's assertion that there were others, in the lane to oppose him, was pretty well borne out, for a man suddenly started up and pointed a gun at him He pulled the trigger, but the gun missed fire, and Duval cried as he passed on —"Thank your stars for that. It has saved your life."

Taking then the bridle in his mouth, Duval with a loaded pistol in each hand galloped down the lane. Another shot was fired at him and struck his hat. He immediately discharged one of his pistols in the direction whence it come, but with what effect, at the speed he was going at he could not tell.

In one minute more he was out of the lane, and in the high road to Hounslow. "Hurrah!" he cried. "Hurrah, for the road! hurrah!"

Then like the wind, he and his horse went off, leaving behind them but a barren triumph for the officers and the people they had got to assist them in attempting his capture. The man who had wielded the pitch-fork was dead; and the officer who had spoken so grandly about Duval's time having come, and his determination to have him, sat in the middle of the lane examining the contusions he had received from the horse galloping over him. At a short distance off, a great lubberly looking fellow was blubbering at the pain he suffered from the charge of shot that Claude had favoured him with; and upon the whole a more lugubrious looking party than that which made its way back to the house of Sir Clement Farrough after the battle, could not very well have been conceived.

"I ought to know the time of day," said Duval, as he drew rein, at about three miles from the lane where the fight had taken place; "I ought to know the time of day, for I have watches enough."

There was by the road-side a pleasant-looking little copse, only protected by a swinging gate, so Duval opened it, and led in his horse, in order that it might crop the sweet herbage. He carefully examined the wound the faithful creature had received; and although it was only a superficial one, he felt the necessity of having it attended to; and observing a finger-post at some short distance off, he went to it, and saw that it pointed "To Guildford."

"I will go there," he said. "It can't be many miles; I will go there and get a farrier to sew up this skin-wound in my horse, or it will grow serious if neglected."

Could he have had any hope of getting in sufficient time to Guildford to do his horse any service, Claude Duval would willingly have gone on foot, and led the faithful creature; but that was out of the question; so he at once mounted and rode sharply, convinced that the delay was of far more importance to his wounded steed, than anything else.

He met with no adventure upon the road, and with but very few passengers indeed. The few that he did meet with, he paid no attention to, nor did they trouble him with any attentions, so that he reached Guildford in the quietest manner possible.

His first inquiry was for the best farrier in the town, to whom he could apply to for the hurt his horse had received?

CHAPTER XXXIV.

DUVAL STOPS THE OXFORD COACH, AND THEN MEETS WITH A SINGULAR ADVENTURE.

THERE was no difficulty in such a place as Guildford in finding not merely a farrier, but a skilful one; but along with his skill the farrier was possessed by the very demons of loqacity and curiosity, and he nearly drove Claude distracted by the questions he asked, and the questions he implied.

"Perhaps, sir," he said, "your horse was where he ought not to have been, when he met with this accident? Was it an accident, or was it wilful, sir? Do you come from London, sir; or out away further into the country? Did you meet with a highwayman, or didn't you, sir? Beg pardon, sir, for asking so many questions. A fine horse, sir; indeed, I may say a very fine horse, sir. Got him a bargain I hope?"

"I forget," said Claude.

"Forget, sir? Dear me, how very extraordinary. It won't be a bit the worse for this little scratch. It's, after all, only a skin-wound. Going to London

CLAUDE AND THE SUPPOSED MANIAC.

I suppose, at once, sir? Don't happen to know anybody I suppose, sir, who wants a good horse? Much rain on the roads, sir, the way you come? Didn't happen to hear if anything in shape of a highwayman was about the commons?"

"I heard nothing, and know nothing," cried Duval. "I am not at all inquisitive, and never pester strangers with impertinent questions."

"And very right, sir, on your part. I only wish all the world was of your opinion. Folks come here and go on talk, talk, talk, and asking so many questions, that one can't get in a word even edgeways. Did you say it was accident this cut on the horse, sir, or done on purpose? In a hurry, sir, or travelling only for pleasure? Going to see a friend in this part of the country perhaps, or on business of importance? Got a beautiful bay horse to sell, sir. Tim! Tim! Tim!"

" Yes, master."

" Tie this bandage carefully while I show this gentleman Scud Away. That's what we call the bay, sir, and a finer creature you never clapped eyes on. This way, sir—won't take you half a minute. Don't want a new set of harness perhaps, and don't know anybody that does? Name ain't Smith, is it, sir?"

Duval saw that the loquacity of the farrier was a kind of insanity, which it would be no use to try to combat with, and which it was quite unnecessary to answer; so while Tim, the man, was putting a bandage over the skin-wound on the horse, which, to do the talkative farrier justice, he had sewn up with great skill, Claude accompanied him to the stable to look at the fine horse, Scud Away.

The farrier opened the stable door, and Duval followed him; but the moment he got about half a dozen paces in, the farrier turned round, and placing his back against the door, said—

" Claude Duval, I know you."

Duval started at the moment—as well he might—but he did not lose his presence of mind for anything like an appearable lapse of time, and with admirable coolness, he replied—

" Well?"

" I tell you what it is," added the farrier, " I'm the best boxer, or the best wrestler, in the county. How far have you come? Did you meet anybody worth robbing on the road? What did you really give for the horse now? I intend to arrest you. The money I shall get for your apprehension will be very useful. It's of no use your looking big, for I mean to do it."

" I have not the slightest desire," said Claude, " to look bigger than I am. But since you are the best boxer and the best wrestler in the county, perhaps you have no objection to a fall."

As he spoke, Duval flew upon him with a vehemence that the farrier did not expect, but he nevertheless maintained his ground.

" Easy—easy," he said. " Now for it. You talked of a fall, and you shall have one. To prison you go, and it's odds, but you carry with you a broken bone or two. Now, my man, I'll show you a trick."

" Is it anything like that?" said Claude, as he suddenly let go his hold of the farrier's waist, and dropped to his feet, when seizing his legs about a couple of inches above the ancles, he tossed him over his head in a moment.

The farrier lay stunned, for the stable was paved with rather large round stones, and his head, thick though it might be, was not exactly calculated to resist a hard knock against one of them.

" Fool!" said Claude, " I hope I have not killed him; but he forced it on me. The fellow surely must be a little insane to go on in such a way; and yet, how in the name of evil fortune, came he to know me? If he can so surely recognise me, others may. It is time that I left Guildford behind me as far as possible."

Duval left the stable and the farrier, and when he got into the yard again, he found that his horse was all ready, and Tim was putting the head-gear to rights.

" I wouldn't ride him no further than I could help, to-day, sir," said Tim.

" I will not. He shall have rest enough. This crown-piece is for yourself. I have already settled with your master."

Duval mounted, and at a quiet canter left the stable. He would have been well enough pleased to have galloped from Guildford; but his consideration for his horse prevented him; and, notwithstanding all the danger that might beset him—for the farrier, in all probability would give an alarm, and raise a hue-and-cry when he recovered—Duval went at an easy pace. He took care, however, to look to his pistols, and to see that they were all ready for active service, in case any extraordinary occasion for their use should arise.

More than once, when he found himself upon anything like an eminence, he looked around him, long and carefully, in the direction of the road he was leaving, to note if any persons were upon his track; and those who had not known how very anxious he was to spare his horse, would have been not a little surprised to observe the look of keen anxiety that was upon his face.

There did not seem to be any danger though; and he had got a good three miles from Guildford, when, upon reaching the top of a considerable hill, he glanced back again, and he saw, coming along at a hard gallop, no less than six well-mounted men.

They were more than half a mile from him, however, and the hill was before them.

"Ah," said Claude, "this is what I fully expected, so I am not at all taken by surprise, which is one comfort, at all events. Now, if things were just as they ought to be, I should no more have any objection to a sharp gallop of half-a-dozen miles, than to eating my breakfast; but I cannot venture upon it now. We must house ourselves, my brave steed, somehow or another."

After a little consideration he waited upon the brow of the hill, until, by the gestures of the approaching horsemen, he felt quite satisfied that they saw him clearly, and then waving his hat, he made as though he had started off at a tearing gallop; but he pulled up before he had got twenty yards, and being then quite satisfied that the brow of the hill was between him and his foes, he looked anxiously about him for some place of shelter.

"They will assuredly pass on if we can but get under," he said, as he patted the neck of his horse.

After trotting a little way, he saw among the trees, to the right-hand of the road, the top part of a mansion; and feeling that it was only for a short time that he required a place of concealment, he made up his mind to ride up to it and get within its gates, if possible, by adopting a plan which he had found successful in more than one similar instance, which was, to boldly ask to see the owner of the house, and when favoured with an interview, to regret, in the most gentlemanly manner, to find that he was not the gentleman whom he (Duval) had thought resided there, and so comfortably put off the time until the outside danger had passed away.

In some cases when he had done so, the people had been so favourably impressed by his gentlemanly and engaging manners, that they had pressed him to remain, and take rest and refreshment, both for himself and his horse.

There was a slight hedge by the road-side, and then a small meadow, and beyond that appeared the wall of the gardens of the house; but Duval could not find any entrance. It was probably on the other side, so as time with him was by far too important an object just then for him to tamper with it by skirting the estate, which would no doubt have enabled his foes to see him, he pushed his way through the hedge, and dismounting, he led his horse close along under the wall, which was of unusual height, with the hope of discovering some door.

He fancied he could hear the thundering sound of the horses' feet of his pursuers, as they, with very little diminished speed, came up the hill. His situation was now in truth a most critical one.

Had there been sufficient wood about the spot for him to trust to as a concealment, he would have done so; but there was not, and he felt quite certain that upon reaching the brow of the hill, and then missing sight of him, they would pause and look carefully about them, when, if he were still without that high garden wall, he must inevitably be seen, and a contest for life and death must ensue.

Just as he had almost made up his mind that such must be the case, and that there was really no help for it, he came to a small door in the wall. To try it, and find it fast, was the work of a moment. It was of no strength, however, and that was no time to stand upon any ceremony, so Claude, placing his elbow against it, with one push sent it in, nearly falling after it himself. He had destroyed one hinge, and the whole of the lock.

There was not a moment to lose, and accordingly, propping the door open, he led his horse through it ; the creature, after a glance at the height of the opening, stooping with great precision just sufficiently low to go comfortably through it. Then Duval replaced the door in its proper situation as well as he could, so that it could show no signs of having been broken through to the casual observer, although a touch would have sent it down again.

He found himself in a spacious garden, well laid out in gravelled walks, and abounding in fine shrubbery. It was evidently a well kept place ; and as he was looking about him for the most eligible path to pursue, he heard a light footstep upon the gravel path close to him, and in a moment there appeared round some bushes, a young lady of the most fascinating beauty, attired with great elegance, and carrying in her hand a small boquet of flowers.

At sight of Claude she smiled, and advancing more rapidly, she said to him in the most winning accents—

"Ah, what joy is this. So, my own one, you have come at last ? How long I have expec'ed you ! Have you no smiles for your own Clara ?"

Duval was, to tell the simple truth, so utterly astonished at this address, from one who was a perfect stranger to him, that for once in the way, even he, with all his admirable tact and self-command, found himself perfectly at fault.

"You do not know," added the young lady, as she came quite close to Claude, and looked confidingly and affectionately in his face. "You do not know how long and weary the hours have been to me without you. How I have wept and sighed for you to come ! but now that you are here, all is joy again. Yes, all is joy again."

She fell upon his breast, and burst into tears ; and while she sobbed bitterly, he was compelled to place his arm around her waist to hold her up, or she would have fallen.

He was compelled to let go his horse, for he could not very well attend to his horse and a young lady as well, so that the animal sought out a comfortable grass plot, and began to cropt the sweet herbage at its leisure, leaving its master in what may be called a very interesting situation.

"I beg you will compose yourself," said Claude. "These tears will be injurious to you. Pray be calm."

She only wept the more.

"What in the name of fate," thought Duval, "is the meaning of all this ? If it be some crafty mode of insuring my apprehension, I am done, and shall I be taken, for I cannot be such a brute as to shake off this young creature."

As he spoke, he felt rather inclined to press her closer to his heart, and he was pleased to find that her sobs were not so very frequent, and that she was evidently each moment becoming more composed and rational. Suddenly, with an alarmed look, she gazed in his face, and then a blush overspread her face and extricating hemself from his arm, she said.

"Where am I ? Oh, where am I ?"

"That," said Claude, "is a question which I am sorry to say, I have the greatest difficulty in answering. I can only offer you all the service in my power."

"But !—but !—Oh, God ! what has happened ?—what can have happened ?—Where am I ? What place is this ? Uncle, uncle, where are you now ? Oh, save me, save me !"

A pretty garden-seat was close at hand, upon which she threw herself ; and then, wringing her hands, she gave herself up again to the most hopeless sorrow, sobbing as though her heart would break. Claude every moment got more and more puzzled to know what to say or to do. He gazed upon her as h ough he almost doubted if she were a being of this world or not ; and then he said to himself—

"Is this all a dream, or am I really wide awake ? Let me see. There is my steed, and here am I. Everything is too clear for a dream. It is ; it must be a reality. But what it all means, passes conjecture. I am fairly bewildered."

He thought he would wait until this fresh burst of feeling, upon the part of the mysterious young lady, had passed away, before he said anything more.

CHAPTER XXXV.

CLAUDE DOES A LITTLE HARM TO DO A GREAT GOOD.

AFTER a time, as in the former instance, these tears of the young lady gradually subsided; and then Duval, burning with curiosity to know who and what she was, and what was the occasion of her very strange conduct, approached her, and spoke kindly to her.

"If there be anything," he said, "that I can do for the purpose of alleviating the great distress under which your feelings evidently labour, I beg that you will command me fairly; for in some sense I look upon myself as a sort of knight-errant of old, and feel bound to redress what grievances I can in my progress through life."

"Thank God," said the young lady. "Thank God that I am able to speak rationally to you now."

"Rationally?" thought Claude; but he said nothing, and the young lady continued.

"Yes, I am now able to implore your protection, if you be a gentleman, and not leagued with those who would be my destruction, and who will be it, if I be not rescued from their dreadful hands."

"I assure you," said Duval, "that I am leagued with no such persons; I am here alone, knowing no one in this place, and I have seen no one but yourself.—Pray tell me what it is you would have me do."

"But, you are true? Oh, pardon me, sir, for suspecting all whom I see in this place. You are true?"

"Yes. But when I tell you how I came here, I think you will acquit me of being in any way connected with your enemies. I broke into the garden, I assure you, and know not whose house it is that I see yonder among the trees; so, if you have any grievance, pray speak it freely to me."

"I will—I will. Your words speak to me a language of sincerity, and I will not doubt you. My uncle, Mr. Briarley, has placed me here that he may keep all that my poor father left to me. He lives at Oxford, and will be in this house to-night to threaten me further. Oh, if you can take me from hence, I pray you do so. If you would have the blessing of an orphan, aid me in escaping, for I shall die if I remain here.

"But what house is it? Who keeps it?"

"It is a madhouse."

"A madhouse?"

"Yes. This is an asylum for those upon whom the Almighty has cast that heavy infliction. It is a lunatic asylum; but, alas! how it belies that word asylum. I am not mad, I assure you, sir. Indeed I am not.

"Mad!" exclaimed Duval. "Certainly not. That is to say I—I don't think you are, and hope you are not."

The singular first reception that the young lady had given him, at that moment flashed across his mind, and made him doubt very much how far he was really called upon and justified in interfering in her case. She could not but observe his indecision, and with a look of the most poignant grief, she said—

"Ah, sir, you think because you find me here, that I am indeed one of those who are deprived of reason. You think so because you find me here, sir. Oh, do not fancy because you find me in such a place as this, that I am mad. You are here, and you are not mad."

This was a very plausible sort of argument, but it was nothing else but plausible and, Claude might have truly said, "Yes, I am here, but I have not committed myself by any extraordinary speeches as you have." He did not like, however, to make the affair a matter of argument, and he merely said—

"I repeat that I shall be delighted to render you any assistance. Do you know me?"

"No—no."

" Are you quite sure that you have no sort of knowledge of me ?"

" Ah," she cried, " now I understand you. When first I saw you I was suffering under the effects of some drug that they give me here, and which, for the time, is potent enough to unsettle my mind completely. The effect of it, however, does not last long, and it always goes off with a feeling of great distress and floods of tears. I know not what I may have said to you while under the influence of that drug, but believe me, whatever it was, I am not truly accountable for it."

" If that be so," replied Claude, " it is one of the most atrocious affairs that ever I heard of."

" Hush! hush! Oh, save me :"

" What is it ?—What do you dread ?"

" The man who keeps this place is approaching ; I know is footstep. It is too late to save me now, but promise that you will come here to-night at half-past twelve, and take me away ; I will be upon this spot, for they do not always lock me up, and I think I can get away at that time. It is my uncle who pays the people here to keep me and to own that I am mad, and this is his day of visiting me. He will come from Oxford, and his name is Briarley. Say, oh say, then, you will come."

" At half-past twelve ?"

" Yes, yes. You will promise me ? Oh God, he will not promise !"

" I will," said Claude.

Joy beamed in the face of the young creature, and she bounded away from the spot, and was in a moment lost to sight amid the intricacies of the path that wound among the thickets, and the flowering shrubs of the garden. Almost at the same moment, a man of vulgar and course aspect, attired in a sort of demi-clerical costume, made his appearance, and stopped short, when he saw Duval gazing upon him, with the utmost surprise.

Duval was determined to let him speak first, so he pretended not to see him. In the course of a few moments the individual strutted up to him, and said—

" Hilloa! Who are you ?"

" A gentleman," said Claude.

" And pray, sir, how the devil did you get here I should like to know ? Will you oblige me by answering me that question, sir ?"

" Oh yes, of course. You see that part of the wall over there, where the fig tree is trained ?"

" Yes. Well, sir, well ?"

" My horse is passionately fond of green figs, and although he was coming along the road outside in the quietest manner imaginable, no sooner did he see a branch of your fig tree projecting over the wall, than he made one leap and over he brought me. I fancy he thought it would not be safe to try such a leap again, for he obstinately refused to take me back again ; so if you will show me the way to the regular entrance, I shall be very much obliged to you, indeed, sir."

" And, sir," said the asylum-keeper. " do you think to gammon me into a belief, that there is any horse in the world who can jump a wall eighteen feet in height? No, sir, I am not an idiot."

" Very good," said Duval ; " I did not ask you to believe it. Here we are, that's all I have got to say. There is the horse, and here am I."

" But—but—the devil, sir !"

" Ah, I don't know where he is. You ought to know better about your own acquaintance, than I can by any possibility expect to do."

" But I don't believe it, sir : I don't understand it."

" Sir, I am not bound to furnish you with belief or understanding. It is quite sufficient if I supply you with an extraordinary fact. Whether you believe it or understand it, is to me a matter of the most supreme indifference."

" Very good, sir—very good. We shall soon see, sir, who will have the laugh. I flatter myself that I am not quite alone in this place, and that those who are in my employment here, will not be very scrupulous in executing my orders. I will have you taken up, sir, for being found upon my premises—no doubt with a highly felonious intent.   My name is Riggles, and I put up with nothing.”

With this, the madhouse-keeper started off as hard as he could to the house, no doubt to give the alarm to his myrmidons that some one had got into the garden ; and in all likelihood, he thought that Claude was safe enough until he returned ; for the little door in the wall, as a means by which the stranger had entered the place, had never once occurred to him.

Duval considered now that all danger from his Guildford pursuers must have passed away, and accordingly his impulse was to leave the lunatic asylum garden as soon as possible.   One note of a whistle brought his horse to his side ; and then again displacing the little door in the wall, Duval and his steed passed out as easily as they had come in.

He took some pains to replace the door, so as, if possible, not to point it out immediately as the mode by which he had made an entry into the premises ; and then mounting his steed, he rode off at the same easy pace at which he had came from Guildford.   He could see nothing whatever of his pursuers from that town.

“ This will not do,” said Duval, to himself ; “ I am really doing no business of any importance ; I must take to the road in earnest now, or I shall find my supplies run rather short when I reach London again, where I have several affairs on hand that may cost me something.   Adele, Adele, I feel that I love you better than any one now, and that I cannot keep for very long absent from you.”

Finding that his horse was rather inclined for a sharp canter than otherwise, Claude would not baulk the creature, but let it take it’s own pace down one of the beautiful green lanes that lie between Guildford and Hounslow Heath. They had not proceeded far, when Duval heard quite distinctly the sound of horses’ feet, and the grinding noise of carriage wheels.   He got to the side of the road, and waited until he saw a very strong vehicle make its appearance.   A coachman, with an immense powdered wig, was upon the box, and two footmen were behind.

“ Come,” said Duval ; “ here ought to be some sport.   It will keep my hand in, at all events.”

Darting suddenly out into the centre of the road, with such a bound of his horse, that he made as sudden an appearance as though he had sprung out of the ground, he called out—

“ Stop, stop !   A toll here !”

The coachman pulled up so rapidly, that the pair of greys drawing the carriage were thrown upon their haunches, and the vehicle gave a tremendous lurch.

“ Hark you, my fine fellow,” said Duval, as he presented a pistol at the coachman.   “ Move another inch, and I’ll knock that powdered wig about your ears with a couple of bullets in a manner that you won’t like.”

“ Who are you ?” gasped the coachman.

“ The lord of the manor,” said Claude ; and then feeling satisfied that the coachman was by far too terrified to stir, he cantered to the door of the carriage, just as a fiery-faced individual looked out with rage in every distorted feature, crying—

“ Coachman, drive on !   What is it ?   The devil seize you, what do you mean by stopping.   Drive on !   drive on, I say !   Am I, the under-sheriff of the county to be kept one moment ?   Drive on, I say !   Drive on !”

“ He dare not,” said Claude.   “ It is of no use, sir, your bullying the poor man.   I have ordered him to stop, and stop he will.”

“ You—you ?”

“ Yes, even I.”

“ And who, in the name of all that’s abominable, are you ?”

“ It is of little consequence who I am.   Let is suffice that I have taken it into my head to establish a toll in this lane, and here I am to enforce it.   Ah, you are not alone —a lady, I perceive.   Madam, I beg you will not be alarmed in the least.   The under-sheriff, madam, seems rather a hot-headed kind of man, but you should be firm with him.”

“ A highwayman,” said the gentleman, “ by all that’s abominable !”

"Now, sir, your money, watch, and jewellery."

"Gracious heavens!" cried the lady; "are we to be robbed?"

"No, madam," replied Claude; "you may give me what you like, but I will take nothing from you without your consent. As for the under-sheriff, he will see the force of this little argument, as my time is rather precious."

Duval rested a pistol-barrel upon the edge of the coach window as he spoke, and the sheriff changed colour. That is to say, his face turned from a glowing red to an odd-looking purple.

It was at this moment that Claude fancied some shadow crossed his face, and looking up, he saw the two footmen with their staves uplifed ready to bring them down upon his head.

"That's right, my fine fellows," he said. "Defend your master, and hang the consequences. I'll find you work enough."

He raised the pistol, and fired it at the two footmen; but he took care that the bullets should go over their heads, for he guessed that that would have as good an effect for all his present purposes as shooting them both outright; and so it did, for they both fell off the back-board of the carriage, and lay in the road as bereft of all movement as though the pistol had, with the utmost impartiality, divided its contents between them.

"Are you a murderer?" said the lady.

"No madam. They are both unhurt."

"For God's sake, Mr. Up-horne, give him what he asks for, and let him go at once. Do, I implore you."

"You rascal," said the sheriff, "you will swing for this. I will have the whole county raised about you. It will be the very worst day's work you ever did I should like to know who you are?"

"I'm not an under-sheriff," said Claude, as he pocketed a magnificent gold watch and seals that were handed to him, and then a purse tolerably well filled. The lady, too, handed a small purse.

"Is it your own own money madam," said Claude, "or this man's?"

"My own."

"Then keep it."

"You are Claude Duval," said the lady. "You have convinced me by that one act. I never heard of any other—other——"

"Highwayman put in Claude, as he saw that the lady hesitated about the word no doubt for fear of offending him. "I am not at all nice, madam, about a word or so. You would say that I am the only highwayman who knows how to behave himself to a lady; and I really believe it is a melancholy fact in these degenerate days."

Claude deliberately took a pinch of snuff.

"So you are Duval, are you?" said the sheriff. "By the lord, I'll have you hung, you rascal. Just let me get a good look at you, that I may know you again, you thieving vagabond."

"Perhaps that will clear your eyes," said Duval, as he flung the whole contents of his snuff-box right into the sheriff's face. Then turning his horse's head from the carriage, off he went at a hand-gallop.

CHAPTER XXXVI.

THE OXFORD COACH DOES NOT REACH ITS DESTINATION.

"Well," said Duval, as he rode off, "this is doing business, at all events. I wonder now if I shall have the luck to come across that Oxford coach? If I do, folks will say it is rather an audacious thing; but they have been so much in the habit of saying that much of me, that I have got used to it, like the eels to being skinned, I suppose. But no matter; a light heart, a pair of bright eyes, and a

pocket full of money, give me ; and I am happier than a king.   But the bright
eyes must belong to some bewitching little creature who is willing she should
be kissed—some such a one as my Adele.   Ah, but I must not forget my appointment at the madhouse.   No, I will not let that slip my memory.   But
now for the Oxford coach.   I wonder if that young creature's uncle will be upon
or within it ?"

CLAUDE SHOOTS THE BULL-DOG IN THE FIELD.

Duval knew right well the route that the Oxford coach would take ; so he
hovered about a gloomy spot of the road, that in its aspect was enough to fill
any one with gloom and fearful presages.

This spot of road consisted of a hollow of about a quarter of a mile inex-
tent.   The road at this spot was only just wide enough for two vehicles to pass

one another, and in the centre of the hollow, during the rainy seasons, the vehicles had to pass right through a little sheet of water, that swept over the road.

Now the road was free from that incumbrance, but what with the gigantic fir trees that rose to an immense height upon each side of it, and the swampy character of the roadway, and its distance from any habitation, except some very miserable cottages indeed, whose wretched inhabitants bred ague and fever by living in such a damp hollow, the place, take it for all in all, was the gloomiest between London and Oxford.

It was there, then, that Duval purposed waiting for the coach, with the benevolent view of lightening it of some of the weight it carried in the shape of metal.

The twilight was coming on, and by the time the coach might fairly be expected at that spot, no doubt it would then be sufficiently dark for any daring deed to be perpetrated. Duval backed his horse between two of the lofty fir trees, and there he waited with all the patience of a sentinel for the approach of the vehicle. Occasionally he whiled away the time by humming the air of some ditty then popular in London, and at times his thoughts wandered to the fashionable lodging in Spring Gardens, and to the fair Adele, to whom his imagination clung with a tenacity rather unusual with him.

"Yes," he said, after rather a long pause, "I do begin to think really that I am in love at last, and that Don Cupid has sent into my heart one of his most fiery darts, with the name of Adele upon its point. She is, without doubt, a beautiful young creature; and there is such an exquisite charm about her youth and innocence, that it is quite out of the question to look upon her and to hear her speak, and not to love her. I feel—"

Duval stopped short, for amid the solitude with which he was surrounded, he felt certain he heard the sound of coach-wheels traversing the road from the direction whence he fully expected the Oxford coach to come.

"Ah!" he said, as he patted the neck of his steed. "The time for action is coming, and you and I, my gallant friend, must have an eye to the preservation of our reputation. It comes—it comes, and tolerably rapid, too; but they will decrease speed upon reaching the hollow, and then will be my time. Ah, this is life! This is what I enjoy, now. This is what I feel to be something great and worth living for. I will stop that coach; and all its passengers, with all their hopes and all their fears, shall have a story to tell of how one man said 'Hold!' and how, then, they all obeyed him. Ha, ha! It has been so, and it will be so again and again!"

The coach appeared in sight—a misty, bulky-looking object in the gathering twilight. The lamps would not be lighted until at the place where they next changed horses, so that the vehicle looked dark and lumbering, as it came carefully guided down into the deep hollow, where Claude Duval was waiting for it with all the impatience of some ardent sportsman for his game.

One touch to his horse's flank, and, like a flash of light, out he bounded into the centre of the road.

"Stand and deliver!" he cried.

The coachman impulsively pulled up with a suddenness that brought the leaders upon their haunches, and then he cried—

"Good Lord! who is that?"

"Drive on!" shouted a voice. "Drive on! Over him—over him, coachman! I will stand all the consequences!"

The coachman, in another moment, might have recovered from his first state of stupefaction, and obeyed this order, but Duval, making for the horses' heads, at once cut the reins close to the bit, with a small but exquisitely sharp knife he snatched from his pocket.

"We shall be smashed," said the coachman. "The leaders will start off."

"Let them go then," said Claude, as he severed the traces, and unhooking the guidechain, the leaders were free, a circumstance they did not omit to avail themselves of in a moment, for they started off as if a thousand fiends were pursuing them.

"Stoop, coachman!" cried the same voice that had urged the desperate measure of riding over Duval. "Stoop, while I have a pop at him!"

"Why don't you stoop, coachman?" cried Claude. "The gentleman behind you wants a pop at me, and I am quite willing to let him have first fire, because I feel that my turn will come."

The coachman did stoop, and so low, too, that he rolled off the box on to the wheel horses, and then to the ground, where he lay upon his back, roaring, "Murder!"

"If you don't cease that noise," cried Claude, "I'll request my horse to stop it, by putting his near fore-foot in your mouth. Now, sir, where's this pop you were so anxious to have at me?"

The passenger who had been so violent, stood up upon his seat behind the coachman, and peerseted a large horse-pistol at Claude's head.

"Blaze away!" cried Claude, as he carelessly handled one of his own long, thin, bright-barrelled holster pistols. "Blaze away, sir; but remember I have second fire, and in that case it's a pity if you have any one dependant upon you."

The passenger slowly let his arm drop, and the pistol hung by his side. He muttered something that was unintelligible to Duval, and then sunk backinto his seat.

"You are wise," said Duval, "What's the use of a man throwing his life away in the defence of a few guineas at the utmost? Pho! pho! sir, you know better."

The coachman was now profoundly still. The extaaordinary threat of Claude that he would speak to his horse to silence him with his foot, had had its due effect. The wheel-horses of the coach were, however, evidently getting uneasy at finding there was no controlling hand over them, and Duval thought the best plan was to save accidents, and give them their liberty at once; so when he cut their traces, off they went after the leaders, although not at quite such a break-neck kind of pace.

It has taken some time to tell all this, but the real space occupied in its transaction was short indeed. You could not deliberately have counted thirty ere it was all done; and the inside passengers had hardly become thoroughly alive to what was going on, before Duval made his appearance at the coach door, and just projecting the barrel of one of his pistols in through the window about six inches, he said—

"If there be any ladies here, or a nervous gentleman, he need not be at all alarmed. Only I warn people not to hide their watches in their boots, or to stuff their purses under the seats of the coach, for I know as well what any one has, as he or she does themselves. I want your watches, rings, and purses, ladies and gentlemen, if you please. One lady only, I think?"

"A poor w—w—widow, sir," stammered a voice in the last extremity of fear.

"Fat, and old?"

"Fat and old!" screamed the lady: "certainly not. How dare you, you ugly, impudent fellow, say such words of me? I declare, if I were a man, I would never cease following you up till I got you hanged."

"Ah! my dear madam, what a release flrom his earthly troubles it must have been to your poor husband when he died Now, gentlemen, I will trouble you, if you please, to be quick."

"I am very poor," said one.

"And I never travel with anything of value about me," said another. "I am not such a fool."

"A guinea, and some silver, is all I have," said a third. "You will find this anything but a good night's work, Mr. Highwayman."

"I always take my chance," said Claude. "Of course, I cannot expect more than you have; but, if I don't get two watches out of four people inside a coach, and some well-filled purses, I have a very troublesome habit."

"And what may that be, pray?" asked one of the insides, in a very soft tone of voice.

"I generally blow out somebody's brains. But upon this occasion, gentlemen, for fear I should be mistaken, I will be content with one watch."

Claude paused, and then he heard one of the passengers say—

"Give him yours."

"Not I," said another, "give him yours."

"Nay, why should I be the victim?"

"Now," said Duval, "I increase my demand to three watches; and if I don't have them in the time I count three, I will fire into the coach, and you may take your chances of what may ensue. One—two—thank you, gentlemen."

Three watches were duly handed out to Duval; and then he said—

"Now, madam, I can, even, by this light, see that you have a watch by your side."

"But you would not rob a lady?"

"Pho! pho! I am quite convinced you are a man in petticoats, or you never would have talked of taking any pleasure in seeing any one hanged."

The widow, with a groan, handed Claude a watch of considerable value, saying—

"I wonder at three sticks, calling themselves men, allowing themselves to be robbed by only one highwayman."

"Oh," said one of the passengers, "the pleasure of seeing you disgorge something out of your unhallowed gains, quite reconciles me to my loss, I assure you, madam."

"Who is the animal?" said Duval.

"Fat mother Bonus, they call her at Oxford. She keeps a pawn-shop, and lends money at the trifling rate of two hundred per centum to the improvident gownsmen. I am a poor man."

Claude laughed as he said—

"Is your watch a silver one?"

"Yes, and I value it, for it was my father's."

"Take it back then, sir, by all means. Come, gentlemen, your money—your money, if you please. Be quick, Mr. Briarley."

"Good gracious!" cried one of the insides, "he knows my name. Who are you, and where do you come from, you infamous rascal?"

Duval had been most anxious, all along, to find out which was Briarley, the uncle of Clara, the young lady at the madhouse; and now that he had made that discovery, he at once dismounted, and opening the door of the coach, out he handed him on to the road. He did not ask him to give up his papers, but by giving his pockets a flap or two, Duval found out a large leathern pocket-book, which he at once appropriated and placed in the breast of his own apparel. Briarley dropped down upon his knees in the road, crying—

"Take everything but my papers. Spare my papers, and take all my money. I will send you £100 where you like; but give up my pocket-book. You had better kill me than take that; and there's not a thing in it that will fetch you a penny piece. Oh, good sir, do give me back my pocket-book."

Claude mounted again, and his principal object being now accomplished, which was to get hold of Briarley's papers, which he felt convinced, by the outcry the fellow made about them, were in the black pocket-book, he prepared to leave the spot.

"Gentlemen on the outside," he cried, "I shall not trouble you, with the exception of my friend who wanted the pop at me, and he I will take his pistol from as a present."

"There's one of them, then," said the outside passenger, who now thought he had Duval at a disadvantage, and fired right at his face.

It was not a bad shot, for the bullet tore a slight furrow in Duval's cheek, which, however, at the moment, he did not feel at all. He pointed his own pistol at the man, who roared for mercy, and rolled himself about the coach top in the most horrible and extraordinary manner.

"Take the reward of treachery," said Claude Duval, as he pulled the trigger of one of his long, bright-looking holster pistols.

CHAPTER XXXVII.

DUVAL RESCUES CLARA, AND BORROWS A HORSE FOR HER.

THE pistol which Duval fired at the crouching, roaring man upon the coach top, was only loaded with small shot, and he watched an opportunity of discharging it when none of the little leaden pellets would hit his face.

Mingled with the report of the pistol, came such a yell from the outside passenger, that the place rang with it again.

"Now we are even again," said Duval. "You can try your luck a second time, if you like."

"Oh, good gracious, no. I'm all in pieces! I'm a dead man. I'm done—done—done!"

"Farewell to you all," said Claude. "I'm afraid the Oxford coach will be very much behind its time to-night; but these things will happen sometimes, you know, and you must take the world as you find it, and don't give way to grumbling."

With these words, he put his horse to a gallop, and did not pull up until he was four miles from the spot where he had stopped the Oxford coach.

A gleaming light was at a little distance before him, and after shading his eyes with his hand for a few moments, and regarding it attentively, he said—

"It's all right. That's the Roebuck, and I'll stay there for the night. In the morning will be time to get in the saddle again, and to make my way to the mad-house. I feel more tired than usual after to-day's work."

At a gentle trot he made his way to the little road-side inn, and calling out loudly—

"Frank! Frank!" a poor miserable-looking man made his appearance with grin of fatuity, and in a little squeaking voice, cried—

"Is that the good captain? Has he come to do good to our eyes at last? Ha! ha! Is that the captain, let me ask? He! he! he! I hope it is the captain?"

"Well, old Screw-'em-all," cried Duval, as he dismounted, "how does the world use you now, eh?"

"He! he! it is the captain. I said it was the captain. But don't call me Screw-'em-all, captain. My name is Bowles, you know. Why, good heart alive, any one to hear you talk would take me for a miser."

"And how far wrong would they be?" said Duval, with a smile. "I never met with or heard of such a miser as you are. Confess, now,—do you ever cook anything for yourself, or your wife? or do you really still depend for your own eating solely upon what any chance guest at this dog-hole of an inn may happen to leave upon his plate?"

"We—we must be economical," said the old man. "In these times we must be economical, good captain. We don't know what we may come to. He! he! Don't fancy that I am a miser, good captain, for misers have chests of gold, but what have I?—Not a penny—not a penny. I am miserably poor, as all the world knows. Most miserably poor. He! he!"

"Poor?" exclaimed Duval, as he followed the old man into the inn, after a half-starved-looking boy had taken his horse; "poor do you call yourself? Why, if I wanted a thousand pounds upon any sudden emergency, I should be down upon your strong box in a moment, with a certainty of getting it, too. Poor, indeed! No, that won't do by any means—no, no."

"My strong box!—my strong box!" cried the old man. "Oh dear—oh dear!—Wife—wife—Lucy! The captain fancies we have got a strong-box with a thousand pounds in it! Oh dear—oh dear! I shouldn't believe my eyes if I saw a thousand pounds!"

"Oh dear, how can the captain say that?" cried a little shrewish-looking woman with a red nose, as she made her appearance in the room where old Bowles had conducted Duval. "But the captain is always at his jokes, he is."

"Well," said Duval, "it is no joke that I am desperately hungry, so let me have something to eat as soon as possible; and as I am tolerably sure you have neither of you had anything to eat for the last fortnight but cheese-parings and crumbs of bread, left by some chance visitor, you had better sup with me."

The old man's eyes glistened, and he rubbed his hands together, as he cried—

"Sup with the captain!—sup with the captain! Do you hear that, Lucy, my dear?—Sup with the captain! It's the honour of the thing that I look at, not the eating and drinking. Oh dear, no—it's the honour of the thing, Lucy, that we look at."

"To be sure," creaked the old woman; "to be sure it is, Peter. But the captain is like me—he is a free heart, and gives away with an open hand; just like me is the captain. Ain't he, Peter?"

"Yes, Lucy, and like me, too. There's nobody in all this world, or the other either, who knows what I give away. He! he! he!"

"Nor ever will, I'll be bound," said Claude. "What you both give away any one might paste on to his spectacle glasses without dimming them in the least. But be quick about the supper—I know you can put a supper upon the table if you like, and you know that I shall not look twice at the bill."

The old couple, upon this, half-starved as they were, bustled about, and it was astonishing how in the course of half an hour they had managed to kill, pluck, and dress a couple of fine fowls, which, with some fine crisp rashers of ham, made truly a very delectable kind of supper, and saluted the appetite of Duval in a most pleasant and becoming fashion.

"Fowls are very dear," said the old man, "just now; but we thought you'd like them, so we killed them. He! he! he! It's not an economical supper at all, and I'm afraid we shall have to charge you a good price."

"Bother you!" said Duval, "don't talk to me about your prices. Charge a guinea a couple for your fowls, if you like, and another for cooking them."

"Lucy, do you hear that?" said the old man. "What a man the captain is, to be sure. Do you mean it, captain?"

"Yes, I do."

Old Bowles rubbed his hands together, and looked as delighted as possible; so that when he and Lucy sat down to the festive board, they really for once in their ves looked pleased and happy.

Duval cut one of the fowls into three portions, and handed the old couple one ach; and then he said, as if a sudden thought had struck him—

"The deuce take it! my horse has a bandage on him; I ought to have spoken your boy about it. Can you ring for him?"

"Bells," said the old man, "are not economical. The wires will wear out; but I can tell him in a minute. Don't you stir, captain, the young rascal shall come in here to you, he shall."

After screaming out "Bubble!" for about five minutes, which was the boy's somewhat singular name, he came suffthing into the room with a lank, half-starved look.

"Bubble!" said Duval, "don't touch the bandage on the horse's side, and mind you give him a first-rate feed."

"Yes, sir," said the boy, "this here's the place for first-rate feeds, above a bit. Oh, my eye, how my inside is a rumbling!"

"You wretch!" exclaimed Lucy. "You ungrateful, guttling, guzzling wretch. You think of nothing, from morning till night, but of eating and drinking, and drinking and eating."

"I'm forced to think on it, Missus," said Bubble. "When a chap is always hungry it makes him think on it, whether he will or not, and there ain't much chance of being anything else in this here blessed crib."

"It's a disease," said old Bowles, lifting up his hands. "It's a disease that the poor boy has got that makes him feel always hungry. Don't scold him, Lucy. He can't help it. Go to the cupboard, Bubbles, and help yourself."

"Yes, with the deal shelves," said Bubbles, "for there's nothing else there that a half-starved mouse wouldn't turn up his tail at, and give up the blessed ghost at once."

Duval was much amused at this scene, but he had sent for Bubbles for a purpose, and beckoning to him, he put into his hands a whole loaf that was upon the table, and the third of the fowl that he had divided, saying—

"There, Bubble, don't say you have not had a supper to-night."

"Oh, murder!" cried old Bowles, springing up and throwing Lucy over, chair and all. "Oh, murder! I can't sit and see this. Oh dear, oh dear! Put it in the cupboard, Bubble, and we will warm it up to morrow by—sitting on it."

"Doesn't you wish you may get it?" said Bubble. "Lor' Missus, how can you lay on the floor a showing of your rum-looking old legs in that way? Thank you, captain; and if ever you wants a boy to go through fire and water for you, only come to me, and I'll do it pretty quick."

With this, Bubble vanished from the room, but not before Duval had given him a pantomimic hint to draw himself a pot of beer from the bar.

Both Lucy and the miserly old Bowles groaned over the loss of the third of the fowl, but they found by Duval's manner that to say anything would be utterly useless, and as for making any attempt to get the eatables away from Bubble again, that would be about as absurd a project as the fabled one of extracting a lump of butter from a dog's throat.

Duval carved the other fowl for himself, and he was much amused at the manner in which the old miserly couple pretended to eat, but in reality took very little, and pocketed at sly moments when they thought he was not looking, many pieces of both ham and fowl, with the hope that they would be able to dish them up to some one and get paid for them again the next day. They could not bring their minds to enjoy the supper, although they were actually treated with it by their liberal guest, whose pursuit in life they both knew very well, but never betrayed on account of the liberality with which, at times, he spent his money with them at their old inn.

Duval always knew that when he choose, he might stop in perfect safety there; provided he was sufficiently cautious himself not to permit of his being dogged to the old place.

In the present instance he felt quite confident that such was not the case, and he was well enough pleased to find some six or eight hours of calm and quiet rest, both for himself and for his horse. Some old wine was produced by the old man, for well he knew that Duval would not drink any of an inferior quality; and so, after about an hour, Duval was shown to his chamber by Lucy.

"What's the reward for him, Lucy?" said old Bowles to his wife, as they were clearing away the remnants of the supper. "What's the amount of the reward that's out for the captain, now?"

"Two hundred poonds, I think," said Lucy.

Old Bowles shook his head.

"Two hundred. No—no, it would not pay—it would not pay. You can't, Lucy, invest two hundred pounds to bring you in anything like one-fourth of what Duval spends with us in a year. He! he! So you see, Lucy, the best way is to take the greatest care of him. He's worth much more than two hundred down to us—oh, yes, much more. But what a shocking thing it was to see him give Bubble the third of a fowl, and a whole loaf. I shall not forget that for weeks—weeks. Couldn't we deduct it from what Bubble gets in some way?"

"It would be very difficult," said Lucy, "as he gets nothing at all from us, but liberty to sleep in the stable. I don't see very well, Peter, how it is to be done."

" Well—well, I must think of it—I must think of it. I shall never forget it, I'm sure, while I live. A whole third of a fowl to Bubble! Dear—dear, it's enough to break one's heart, to say nothing of the whole loaf. Yes, to say nothing of the whole loaf. It is a dreadful circumstance. But shut up for the night, Lucy. It's quite clear we must take every care of Claude Duval."

Perhaps Claude would not have been quite so comfortable at the old inn, had he known upon what calculation he owed his safety : and yet probably in the calculating cupidity of old Bowles, he had as safe a reliance as upon the feeling of any one else, although they might be of a more pleasant and generous sounding a character than those of the miser.

*   *   *   *   *   *   *

The morning dawned in beauty, and Duval, after paying his host and hostess even beyond their expectations, mounted his horse, and was on the road again before eight o'clock. He trotted gently to the neighbourhood of the madhouse, and then riding into a road-side meadow, he turned his horse loose to graze upon the rich young grass, while he himself sat down under a tree, fully intending to occupy the next half hour in a careful view of the pocket-book he had taken from Mr. Briarley.

The book was one of those that are usually carried by professional men, and are of great size, having no encumbrance in the way of fastenings.

" There should be something here," said Duval, as he opened it, " to account for the state of anxiety that Briarley was in to get it back ; and we shall soon see upon what particular documents he fixes his affections."

The contents of the leathern case, for indeed it might rather be called that than a mere pocket-book, were in truth most voluminous and multiferiour. There were notes of all kinds and descriptions, relating to legal and parochial business in Oxford ; but what surprised Duval more than anything, especially when he thought of the anxiety of Briarley to get the case back, was the absence of all money within it. Neither note, cheque, nor order for money was to be found, although Duval looked with tolerable care on the papers as they lay at his feet for any such documents.

Finally, however, in a compartment of the case that he had at first rather neglected, he found what, no doubt, constituted the value of the affair in the eyes of Briarley, and which likewise he was very glad to find, for the sake of Clara, the young girl at the madhouse.

CHAPTER XXXVIII.

CLAUDE COMES TO LONDON AGAIN, AND VISITS ADELE, AND AN ARTIST'S STUDIO.

THE document that Duval thought, and justly so, was of importance, was tied up with red tape and endorsed—

" Deed of assignment from Clara Briarley, to William Briarley of the Down Common Estate, Oxon."

"This must be the matter of importance," he said, "that Briarley was very anxious to get back. Humph ! Let me see. ' In consideration of £4000 had and received.' Ah, I understand it all now ; the price of the liberty of Clara would have been her signature to this document, and then in all probability they would not have kept faith with her, but she would have died in that miscalled asylum. I am glad to be able to counteract this villany." There was nothing else of any importance in the pocket-book, and Duval, after carefully placing the prepared deed of assignment in a side pocket. carelessly enough bestowed the pocket-book with the remainder of its contents into one of the ample pockets in the skirt of his over-coat.

He had scarcely completed these arrangements when a loud voice aroused his attention, by calling out—

"Hilloa! hilloa! you fellow! What do you do there? Don't you know you are trespassing? How dare you come into my meadow, and turn your horse loose in it, eh?"

Claude's steed gently cantered towards its master, and a rough farmer-like-looking personage followed it. He had a thick stick, with a large knob at the end of it, in his hand.

CLAUDE CONDUCTS CLARA TO THE ARTIST'S HOUSE.

"My friend," said Claude, "you must forgive us our trespasses, as we forgive them that trespass against us."

"What do you mean by that? Don't you think you are going to gammon me, young fellow. I'll have you in the cage and your horse in the pound, or else my name ain't Giles Gobblings any way."

"What for, Giles Gobblings?"

"Why, for tramping down my grass here, besides letting the horse eat some of it up. Do you think I rent meadows to turn your horse into?"

"Certainly not," said Claude; "I will pay over and above for what my horse has eaten or destroyed. Will that satisfy you?"

'No it won't. I'll have the horse in the pound, dang my buttons if I don't. I have said it, and my name is Giles Gobblings."

"Come and take him, then," said Claude. "Will you? And now I warn you, if you so much as lay a finger on him, I'll give you such a thrashing at you never had in all your life."

"I don't care for such a whipper-snapper as you," said Giles Gobblings. "If I fell upon you I should crush you. Your horse goes to the pound, and you to the cage, or else my name ain't Giles Gobblings."

With this, Giles made an attempt to seize the horse by the bridle, but Claude Duval gave him such a cut across the knuckles with his riding whip, that he uttered a yell of pain, and began calling out—

"Pinem! Pinem! Pinem!"

Duval could not, for the life of him, make out what he meant by Pinem: but he soon found that it was the pet-name of a ferocious looking blear-eyed bull-dog, who made his appearance in answer to the summons, with his tongue lolling out of his mouth, and seemingly as intent upon acquiring a pound of somebody's flesh as ever Shylock was. Duval drew out a pistol from his pocket and shot Mr. Pinem in a moment.

"You and I," he said, "can settle this matter without any dogs as witnesses."

The farmer was infuriated at the death of his dog, and grasping the stout stick he advanced upon Duval. At the moment that he was about to commence an attack with it, Duval ran in upon him, and grappled him so closely that their faces were not six inches apart. Under such circumstances the stick was completely useless. A brief struggle ensued, and the farmer began to call out lustily for help, for he found that with all his brute strength he was no match for his young and agile antagonist. Down he went to the ground, and Duval above him, with a concussion that seemed enough to shake the earth, and which did for a few moments deprive him of breath.

"Now," said Duval, "you will be a little more civil another time."

"Murder!"

"Say that again and I'll make it one. Do you see this?"

Duval pushed the barrel of a pistol into his mouth.

"Oh, yes—yes; spare my life. I'm a miserable man. Spare my me, only, good sir, do. Master Briarley, Master Briarley, where are you now?"

"Of whom do you speak?" said Duval. "Did you mention the name of Briarley?"

"Yes, sir, I did. I've got to go with him to the 'sylum, to witness a deed as his niece, Miss Clara, is to sign, if you please, sir, to let me go."

"And when are you to meet him there?"

"Soon, sir, if you please. Your horse may take what he likes, only let me go, for I'm to have twenty pounds for the job."

"Now, mark you, Master Giles Gobblings, if you set any value upon your life, you will be pleased to tell me, at once, why it is you are to get this twenty pounds you speak of, for it can't be for witnessing a signature, you know?"

Giles Gobblings wriggled about a little on the ground, and then he said—

"Why, no, sir; but if the young lady were to say anything arterwards about the matter, as if she had been forced to sign, or anything of that sort, I'm to swear she did it with free will, you see, and owned she had had the money, and all that sort of thing, and kissed her uncle, and—and—dear me, I've got it all set down on a bit of paper somewhere."

"And did it never strike you, Master Giles, that you were to play the part of a great rogue in this transaction? I say, did that not strike you?"

"Folks must live, and crops is bad."

"Very good. Now I will trouble you to get up. Is that your farmhouse yonder, that I see the chimneys of among the trees?"

"Yes, it is, and if you'll only come there I'll give you the best jug of ale you ever had in all you life; dang my buttons if I don't."

Duval began rummaging in his pockets, and having found some pieces of strong cord, he tied Giles Gobblings' ankles together, and his wrists behind his back, despite his protestations and prayers for mercy. He was afraid to cry out loudly for help, since the pistol barrel had rattled in so very ominous a manner among his teeth ; and he began to shed tears in great abundance, for he had an awful misgiving about the fate that was intended for him, by one whom he found to be completely his master.

"You will come to no harm, if you will only be quiet," said Duval. "That paper you mention, upon which Mr. Briarley wrote your instructions, I should certainly like to have, although, perhaps, after all, an easy death now is preferable to being laid upon a bed of sickness, as one day you might be."

"Oh dear, no—no. It's in my waistcoat pocket. It's in my waistcoat pocket."

"Oh," cried Duval, "is it.—Ah, sure enough, here it is. And this is the hand-writing of Mr. Briarley, is it, Master Giles Gobblings?"

"Yes, it is. Won't you let me go now?"

"I cannot let you go just yet, but you shall come to no harm, I will promise you that much, although you may be for an hour or two rather uncomfortable."

Mr. Gobblings glared at Duval, with both wonder and fear depicted upon his countenance, but he was not for a long time kept in a state of ignorance as to what was to be done with him. Duval cut rather a stout branch of an alder tree, that was close at hand, and providing himself with a piece about six inches long, he made Gobblings take it in his mouth like a bit, and then he twisted some cord round each end of it, and tied it firmly at the back of his head.

"How do you feel now?" said Duval.

Gobblings made an ineffectual attempt to answer him, and from that, Duval was satisfied that the gag was as effectual as he had fully intended it should be. He then laid Gobblings close under the hedge-row, saying—

"Some one will see you, I daresay, in the course of the day, but until they do, I am induced to think that you are tolerably harmless. You can, to yourself, you know, swear as much as you like. Perhaps it will do you good to do so; and if you feel an inclination, pray don't baulk it at all upon my account. I now bid you good morning, and have no doubt but you will hold deep and cunning ruminations with yourself upon the state of the crops in this field, of which you have a capital view ; and as regards an attentive study upon the weeds in the hedge, the opportunity you now have of taking a good look at them cannot be sur-passd.'"

Mr. Gobblings made a vain attempt to return what, no doubt, would have been some very furious answer, but the gag effectually prevented him, and the cords that held his wrists and ankles as effectually stopped him from rising. He could only roll about a little, and as Duval had placed him in a kind of rut or drain close to the hedge, he could not get fairly out of it.

"Now then," said Duval, as he sprang upon the back of his steed; "now then for Clara and the asylum."

The hour had arrived when he had promised the imprisoned girl that he would make an attempt to rescue her; and at a sharp trot he made towards the same part of the wall of the lunatic asylum, where there was the little door that he had broken through upon the former occasion. All was quiet ; and, dismounting close to the door, he led his horse right up to the wall. He felt certain that the creature would wait for him, and he hoped that the time would not be many minutes that he would have to be in the garden. The grand thing was to ascer-tain if the door had been re-secured or not.

A touch convinced him that it was in the same state as he had left it the preceding day. He did not enter the garden with any degree of precipitation, but after listening for a few moments to be quite certain that no one was at hand, he cautiously pushed the door open sufficiently wide to enable him to enter the garden, and then he stepped lightly in. A glance was sufficient to show him that he was alone; and then, gently closing the door, he began to hope that Clara would not be long in coming to him, as the time was past. In the course of a few moments, he heard the sound of voices, and feeling confident, from their momentarily greater distinctness, that the speakers were approaching where he was, he concealed himself tolerably well behind a sycamore-tree, and awaited their arrival.

Presently, round the same angle of the shady walk which Clara had turned when he first saw her, two females appeared. One of them he saw was Clara —the other was a female of large proportions, and most inconceivably ugly. She was dressed in a style of flaming vulgarity, and from the manner in which she walked and talked to Clara, it was quite evident that she considered herself as exercising some sort of authority over her.

"May I rest here, madam?" said Clara, when they reached the garded-seat that was close to the spot.

"Very well, you may," said her companion, or keeper, whichever she was. "I only hope that you see your own interest in what I have said to you?"

"Oh, yes, I hope so."

"Of course, your uncle's affection for you wlll always procure you a comfortable home, and it's much better for a man to have an estate than a mere you ng girl. You would, if you kept the property, only have a parcel of fellows running after you for the sake of it; whereas, if you have nothing in the world but what depends upon the will of your uncle, Mr. Briarley, you will, when you do marry, be able to say that you were chosen for yourself alone."

"Certainly, madam. 1 am very glad that in some way the usual dose that confused my faculties has been omitted from my food last night. I do not feel this morning confused at all, as since my residence here I have been in the habit of feeling."

"Oh, nonsense, child, that is all your fancy; you have had no doses; you have made up your mind to do what's the right thing by making over your property to your uncle, and that's why the Almighty makes you feel better this morning."

"Do you really think so, madam?"

"I do, of course. 1 hope you will never forget your reliance upon providence, and I can assure you, that when you have signed the deed that your uncle ought to have been here with before now, that you will thank us all for our kindness to you, and of course you will never be mad enough to say you were ever in a lunatic asylum, for if you do, you will never get a husband as long as you live, I can tell you; so I hope you will not be so foolish. I expect your uncle here every minute, and he is going to bring a very respectable man with him, a Mr. Gobblings, to witness the little transaction."

"Oh, God," cried Clara, "is there no hope for me? What if I don't sign, after all?"

"Your life, wretch, shall be sacrificed if you falter in the least. We are above all law here. You are within these walls; and if you do not do as you are advised, there are cells here that will be good coffins, and that keep secrets quiet as well as graves."

"I am lost, I am lost!"

"What do you mean, hussy?"

"He does not come! Oh, God, he does not come! He forsakes me——"

"Do you mean your uncle?"

"No, no, no. I tell you, madam, I will not sign the document that will make me a beggar; I will not do it. Kill me if you will, but 1 say again I will not do it."

"That's right," cried Claude, as he sprang forward; "I am a witness to that."

With a cry of joy, Clara dropped upon her knees.

"Oh, God be thanked! He is come, and J am saved!"

The large female's huge face became of a purple colour with rage. She rose and made an attempt to fly from the spot, no doubt to seek assistance; but Duval caught her by the head-dress, crying—

"Stop a moment, madam," and then all the head-dress, including an immense wig with a forest of black ringlets, came off in his hand.

The large female, who was no other than the wife of the keeper of the lunatic asylum, tried to take advantage of this accident to escape, but Duval was too quick for her, and held her tight by the back of the neck.

"No, my dear madam," he said, " we cannot spare you just yet, I assure you. You are too good company by a vast deal to be easily parted with; and without your wig, you really do look particularly fascinating, I assure you."

CHAPTER XXIX.

LONDON AGAIN.—DUVAL VISITS HIS LODGINGS, AND DOES AN ACT OF JUSTICE.

THE large female uttered a shriek.

Duval faced her about in a moment, and looking at her sternly, he said—

" Hark you, madam, I don't wish to say anything uncivil to a lady, especially one so very delicate and lady-like looking as yourself; but if you don't be quiet I shall be under the disagreeable necessity of digging a hole in the ground and of stuffing your head into it."

" Monster, who are you?"

" Clara," said Claude, " open that door at once, and we will be off. It will be necessary to take this sweet creature along with us a little way."

"Then I won't go," said the lady resolutely; " I will raise an alarm. Help—help—mur——"

Duval still had the interesting creature's wig in his hand, and he at once put a stop to any further vociferations by cramming it into her mouth as far as it would go. She kicked, and plunged, and turned very red in the face. Clara was alarmed, and said—

"Oh, do not smother her. You have stopped her mouth completely. She cannot breathe."

" Oh, yes," said Duval; "rather than choke, she will make her nose do duty. Open the door. That's right. Ah! what bell is that ?"

"It is the great gate-bell. We are at the back of the house," said Clara. "Oh, we shall be stopped! Let us hasten—let us hasten! It is my uncle arrived !"

"Don't be alarmed. All will be well. We have plenty of time. My horse is without; and if they have got anything on four legs that can beat him, I will give in to them as soon as they like."

Duval caught up the wigless lady, and handed her through the door in the garden-wall in a moment. The horse stood in precisely the same spot in which he had been left by his master; but he testified, by his movements, how well pleased he was to see him again. Clara, in obedience to Duval's directions, carefully closed the door again.

"Now, Clara," said Duval, "have you the courage to wait here for me two minutes quite alone? I give you my word that I shall not be longer gone, and I give you my opinion that you will be perfectly safe."

"Yes, yes ; anything you wish."

" Very good."

To the astonishment of the lady of the asylum, Duval lifted her on the horse, and then, with great quickness, springing up before her, he cried—

"Madam, you and I will take a little ride. If you don't hold me tolerably fast, I'm rather afraid you will fall off. So ho! boy—off and away!"

One touch to the flank of the gallant steed, and away they flew in a direction towards the open country like the wind.

The large female shrieked with dismay, but she held Duval with the clutch of a tigress. A gallop of a few minutes' duration took them out of sight of the lunatic asylum, and then Duval drew rein close to a not very savoury heap of manure by the road side.

"Now, madam," he said. "Now, madam!"

"You wretch, what do you mean ?—what do you want, you odious monster ?"

"I want you to dismount, madam, if you please."

"Then I certainly will not, you murdering vagabond, I'll cling to you till I see some one who will take you into custody. Oh, you will find that I am not a female to be so easily frightened as you seem to fancy, you highwayman."

"Then you decline dismounting?"

"I do. and you can take that in the meantime. You find I have got rid of what you stuffed into my mouth, and I can speak now."

With this the lady, who had managed immediately upon being ridden away with in such a way to take the wig out of her mouth, dealt Duval such a cuff upon the side of the head, that she made his ear sing again.

By a peculiar movement of the rein, Duval made the horse give a sudden demi-vault of a tremendous character, and being quite unprepared for such an undulation, the lady found herself, with a grand squash, fairly landed in the midst of the manure heap.

"Good day, madam," said Claude. "Sweets to the sweet !"

He turned at once, and at the same speed he had used in riding away from the asylum with its mistress, he rode back to where he had left Clara. As he got near to her, he saw her beckoning him to be quick; and by her manners she was evidently in a perfect agony of tears. When he got up to the spot, she said,

"Oh, let us fly at once. They seek me now in the garden."

"Do they so?"

"Yes. I have heard their voices, and I nearly fainted with dread, lest you should be too late to aid me."

"All's right. I did but go a little way to dispose of your friend. Place your foot upon mine, and give me your hand. That is right. You will find a comfortable enough seat behind me, here. Are you all right?"

"Yes—yes."

"Hold me tight, then, by the belt I have on, and you need fear nothing. We shall go a few miles, perhaps, rather fast ; but do not fancy there is any danger in so doing. Only fix your mind upon the pleasant idea that you are leaving the odious house behind you."

"Yes—yes, I will. Oh, how shall I thank you ?"

"Don't think of that."

The garden door opened at this moment, and three or four men made their appearance. With one voice they all cried—

"There she is !"

"Ha !" cried Claude; "yes. Here is your victim, that was. Here is she who is rescued from you, and who will yet live to call you all to account.'

"Villain, who are you ?" cried the asylum keeper.

"The Lord Chancellor, of course," said Duval. "Who else should I be, I should like to know ? If you've a mind for a race, and have very good nags, come out. The roads are good, and you will find me some few miles a head !"

"Fetch the blunderbuss ! Fetch the pistols ! Call the dogs !"

"Ha ! ha ! ha !" shouted Claude. "Off and away. "Hurrah for the road Hurrah !"

He gave the rein to his horse. The creature lowered its head, and for a moment was still. Then shaking its mane, and giving a loud snort, off it flew at a pace that made Clara close her eyes, to shut out the terrifying effect of the flying objects that seemed to dash past her in their headlong progress.

"So —so. Gently—gently !" said Duval. "Gently."

The pace became steadier. but not a jot slower, notwithstanding the double urthen that the creature had upon its back : but Duval was not what could be called by any means a heavy weight, and Clara was decidedly a light one; besides, she sat back, so that the total weight was not near so distressing to a horse as though it had been concentrated in one individual.

A small, low, heavy market cart appeared suddenly from a cross lane, and dawdled out into the very middle of the road, in order to cross it, and continue its progress still in the lane.

Duval waved his arm, but the driver of the market cart did not, or would not, understand—perhaps his conduct was the result of a little of both—but he stopped his vehicle exactly in the centre of the road, and with a half-stupid, half malicious kind of grin, waited the issue.

Duval did not relax his speed for one moment, and over went the horse, making the most magnificent leap of the cart and its contents. There was a bunch of turnips on the top of all the other things, and that the horse struck with his hind feet. It did not look more than a touch, but away flew the bunch of turnips, as though it had been discharged from a cannon, and taking the driver of the cart on the side of the head, it sent him sprawling and howling into the ditch, that ran in not very savoury streams by the side of the road.

"Bravely done !" cried Duval, as he patted the neck of the gallant and high-spirited creature. "Truly, when I love thee not, chaos has come again. Away—away! Look up, Miss Clara. Is not this delightful ?"

Clara opened her eyes for a moment, but she closed them again, saying—

"I am terrified. We fly—we fly!"

Another minute, and Duval thought that they had placed a sufficient lapse of country between them and the lunatic asylum to justify him in relaxing the speed at which they had been travelling. He was the more inclined to do this as a hill was in front of them. By a gradual tightening of the bridal, he soon reduced the gallop to an easy canter, and then he spoke to Clara, saying—

"Open your eyes now. They are too bright and beautiful to keep closed. We are not now going at a speed that will alarm you, and the asylum is five miles behind us."

"Five miles !" said Clara, as she gazed round her. "Is it possible, my friend, that we have come that distance in so short a space of time ?"

"It seems incredible, but it is so, for all that ; and you see the horse is not at all distressed, notwithstanding. But now you must tell me what notions you have of your course. Where do you wish to go? Have you any friend upon whom you could rely for protection ?"

"Alas ! no—Yes."

"No and yes ? I don't quite comprehend that."

"I meant that I had no relation to whom I could apply; but there is a friend with whom I should be quite safe, if—if——"

"If what, Clara? If you have any doubt of him you had better not trust him."

"Oh, no—no. I have no doubts—I only asked myself if it would be proper for me to go to him at all."

"Oh, then, he is your lover ?"

The bright flush that instantly spread itself over the face of the fair girl, and which Duval caught a glimpse of, was quite a sufficiently conclusive answer without any words passing upon the subject, and he said at once to her—

"No one but yourself can be a competent judge upon that point. If there be an honest, honourable man who loves you, and you find yourself deserted, and more than deserted, by your relatives, go to him at once, and laugh at what the world will say."

"Do you think so ?"

"On my soul I do. The opinion of censorious people never has any effect upon me. No doubt, whoever this lover is, he will be quite delighted to see you, and the very best thing you and he can do is to get married as fast as possible."

"You are a true friend," said Clara, "and I will follow your advice."

"Very good. Only tell me where he lives, and I will take you to him. Who and what is he ?"

"He is a young artist, and his name is Theodore Atherton; I can take you to his abode. It is in the north of London, and he is, I am afraid, very—very poor."

"But you are not?"

"I hardly know. I am, I suppose, possessed of something, or else my bad uncle would not have taken such measures to get it from me; but he always said it was some mere trifle that had been left me by my father's will, and that he really had in a great measure to pay for my education out of his own pocket."

"Indeed?"

"Yes, that was the language he always held to me; but his conduct of late, of course, gave me reason to think I was differently situated."

"You may well think so. And now, tell me, did you never hear of a place called the 'Down Common Estate?'"

"Oh, yes, that is where my uncle lives."

"Do you know what it is worth?"

"I once, by accident, overheard that it was worth £1200 per annum; but I always understood that it was my uncle's property, although I may have some slight claim upon its revenue, which he wished me to give up to him."

"Well, listen to me. I stopped the Oxford coach last night, and took from it your uncle's pocket-book."

"You?"

"Yes, and in that pocket-book was the deed that you were to be compelled, under threats of the most diabolical description, to sign this morning, if you had not escaped from the asylum. In that deed the whole of the Down Common Estate is mentioned, together with the furniture, plate, knives, carriages, and everything belonging to the house called Down Common Manor House. That is what you were to have been desired to surrender, and the deed is a proof that it is all yours."

"You do astonish me."

"Very likely, but it is an agreeable surprise, I hope?"

"Yes—yes. Oh, how happy I can now make poor Theodore."

"I hope he deserves it. Does he so?"

"He does, indeed. You don't know him as I know him, sir, or you would not find it necessary to ask that question of me."

"I only asked it for one simple reason."

"May I know what that is, sir?"

"Certainly you may. I only thought at the moment that if he loved you a you ought to be loved, it ought not to have been left to the chance arrival of a stranger to rescue you from the perilous and extraordinary position you were in at the lunatic asylum; but he may have some good and sufficient reason for not having achieved that adventure very likely."

"Yes, he has—I feel assured that he has. Oh, sir, you do not know him, or you would not doubt him for a moment. He is all goodness—all nobleness—all courage and generosity."

CHAPTER XL.

ADELE GETS A NEW SITUATION.—A FRACAS.

"THERE is London," said Duval, as they reached the summit of the little hill they had been ascending.

"Indeed! Have we made such rapid progress in so very short a space of time? I really thought that we must be far off yet."

"No. We have travelled, Miss Briarley, quicker than you could imagine; but we will not go through the streets of the metropolis in this fashion, as it might subject both of us to remarks. I will put up my horse, and we will get a coach at the end of Oxford Street."

" I am a great trouble to you."

" Oh, no. I am so rejoiced at rescuing you from that dreadful house, where you must have seen and heard enough to drive you mad in reality, that I think

CLAUDE WAITS FOR THE OXFORD COACH.

nothing a trouble connected with the whole affair. Only tell me that you do really wish to place yourself under the protection of the young artist you have named, and I will take you to him forthwith."

" Indeed I do. Such is my wish, I assure you. It is the true wish of my heart. You do not know him, sir, but I do. I can forgive your doubts, but I know his truth and the loyalty of his love for me."

"That is quite sufficient. Five minutes more will take us to the top of Oxford Street. We will then get a coach and drive to the address of this Mr. Theodore, who is one of the happiest of men, to have inspired a tender sentiment in such a bosom as yours."

To this Clara made no reply. It sounded so like a common-place compliment, that she did not like to here it come from the lips of one to whom she owed so much as she did to Duval. He could not but feel that she shrank a little from him, and their conversation was rather restrained than otherwise for the next few miles.

The end of Oxford Street was gained at last, and Claude Duval seeing a lumbering hackney-coach disengaged, handed Clara into it, telling her to wait for him a moment, while he went to put up his horse, which he did at a first-class livery stables in the immediate neighbourhood. Duval often put up his horse at strange places without exciting the least suspicion of who he was.

"Now, Clara, he said, "have you given the coachman his instructions where to take you to?"

"I have," she said. "He knows the way well."

"That will do," said Duval, as he threw himself back in the coach; "that will do. And now, my dear girl, tell me how long you have loved this young man whom you speak of?"

"He has loved me," said Clara, "for more than two years now."

"Indeed," said Duval, as he took hold of her hand in a careless manner, and held it in his own. She tried gently to withdraw it.

"Why, Clara," he said, "is this not rather prudish to me?"

As he spoke he placed his arm round her waist, and drawing her towards him, kissed her cheek. Clara burst into tears.

"Tears!" cried Duval. "Have I produced them, my fair one?"

"You have—you have. Oh, sir, how ungracious it is of any man, under any circumstances, to force his attentions upon a young girl; but how doubly ungracious—how base it is of him to do so, when her natural feelings of gratitude have allowed her to give him the opportunity."

The colour rose up to Claude's face in a bright flush. No man living was more likely than he to feel keenly such a rebuke as this. It sunk deeply into his heart, and for some few moments he was profoundly silent. But he withdrew his arm from around Clara, and suffered her to escape, sobbing, to the other corner of the coach. She wept really bitterly.

"Well," said Duval at last, with a feeling of desperation. "Well, I am a most unlucky fellow. Of course, now, the sooner you get rid of me the better, Miss Briarley. Some devil took possession of me at the moment; but the fact is, I am never alone with a pretty girl, but I am sure to say or do something foolish. I know you can't and won't forgive me, so I will not ask you."

"No—no. Do not say that, my friend. Let this little affair pass over. It is enough that you regret; and now I feel that we know each other, and understand each other, far better than we did before. Is it not so, my kind friend?'

"You certainly know me better," said Claude, as he took the fair hand that was presented to him in reconciliation. "I don't think I shall commit myself again in such a way with you; so if you can forgive it and forget it, do so."

"With all my heart; and you will not pay me any more compliments upon what you are pleased to call my—my——"

"Beauty, which transcends the——"

"Ah. Stop—stop."

"There I go again," said Claude. "It is a bad habit, I am afraid, I have got, and sometimes it will at unawares show itself; so if it does so, I pray you pardon it as a little vice of custom that means nothing bad. Why, what is the coachman stopping for, I wonder?"

"Because," said Clara, clasping her hands, "we are at Theodore's door. Oh, sir, will you go in and see him first, and prepare him for my presence? I wish you to do so that you may satisfy any doubts of his honour that my still cling to you, despite all I have said."

"I will go to him, if you please, Miss Briarley, but not from any doubt that I now have. I only go, if it be your wish that I should do so. Shall it be so?"

"Oh, yes—yes."

Duval then left Clara in the coach, and having ascertained from a woman who opened the door of the house in answer to his knock, that the young artist was in his own rooms upon the first floor, Duval ascended, and tapped at the door of the front room. A voice from within cried to him to enter, and opening the door, he found himself in an artist's painting room.

The walls were adorned by some excellent copies of the great masters; and some unfinished portaits in the room proclaimed that the young artist had resorted to that profitable branch of his art, most probably, more from necessity than from choice.

Theodore himself was a young man of engaging address; and, as he advanced towards his visitor, Duval thought he had scarcely ever seen any one with so engaging and gentlemanly an exterior.

"Sir," said Duval, "I hope my visit will not be considered as an intrusion; but I have come to say a few words to you concerning a Miss Clara Briarley."

The face of Theodore turned as pale as death, and he was compelled to lean upon the back of a chair for support, as he said faintly—

"Good God!—you do not bring me ill news of her?"

"Before I answer you any question, sir, will you allow me to ask you one?"

"Certainly. What is it?"

"When did you last see the young lady?"

"Before her uncle took her to Bath, sir."

"Bath! Bath! Fiddlestick, sir. She has no more been at Bath than you or I have. What put Bath into your head?"

"This letter, sir, from Mr. Briarley, her uncle. I own that its contents rather surprised me, but they held out a hope that I dared not trifle with. You are at liberty to read it, sir. I have no secrets that concern Mr. Briarley, or my love for Clara, his niece."

Duval took the letter, and read the following lines—

"Sir,—My niece, Clara, has candidly made a confession to me of her esteem for you. She is going with me to Bath for a short time; but the moment we return I will do myself the pleasure of calling upon you. In the meantime, believe me to be—Yours, very truly,—W. Briarley."

"What a piece of villany," said Duval.

"Villany sir!—how?—in what way? How is this letter a piece of villany? Pray, sir, explain yourself. You put me upon the rack."

"Upon this letter, sir," said Duval, "of course, you waited patiently for the return of Clara with her uncle, from Bath?"

"Not very patiently; but I did wait, of course. Under such circumstances it was no use my going to look after her; and yet, the time has seemed to me very, very long indeed. I endure much suspense."

"No doubt of it. I can now tell you that that letter was written to keep you quiet—to prevent you from making any troublesome enquiries about Clara, and it has succeeded. Her uncle placed her in a private lunatic asylum for the purpose of terrifying her into signing a deed, that shall convey to him all she possessed."

"Oh, Heaven!"

"Yes, sir; and there she languished until chance brought one to her aid, who rescued her."

"Heaven bless him!"

"You knew that she had property?"

"Yes, I did. I knew that her father left her something, and that her uncle was her guardian; but I could not believe in such villany as you have detailed to me. Oh, Clara, Clara! Tell me where she is, sir. Let me fly to her.—She re-sisted her uncle?"

"She is free from him, but she is pennyless. She now, at this present moment, is literally possessed of nothing but the clothes she actually wears."

"Then she is mine!" cried Theodore, with animation in his tones, and throw-ing off his dressing gown preparatory to putting on his coat. "She is mine, and no one can say to me that I loved her but for herself alone. She is mine, and mine only. I will toil for her; if needs were, I would beg for her. Heaven bless her! she is mine. The most welcome words I have heard for many a long day, are these which tell me she is pennyless, for now I can offer her a heart and a home. Take me to her, sir. Where is she? Oh, where is she?"

"You deserve her," said Duval, as he strode to the door. "You deserve her, sir, and I have only to ask your pardon."

"My pardon? For what?"

"For submitting you to a little trial of affection, sir. Pray forgive me for being a little suspicious. There are so many rogues in the world: highwaymen and all sorts of iniquitous characters: that I feel quite refreshed in meeting with an honest man. Will you do me one favour?"

"Name it, sir. If within my power, I——"

"Oh it is very simple. All I ask of you is to stand where you are for three minutes and then I will bring you the address of Miss Briarley; I promise you that, sir, upon my honour."

"I do not know you sir, I——"

"Then know that it was I who rescued her from her uncle and his good friends and rascally accomplices, at the lunatic asylum."

"I will refuse you nothing. How can I thank you, sir?"

"Just by waiting three minutes where you are. I do not ask of you anything else. You may watch the time if you please."

"I will not be impatient."

Duval immediately left the room and walked quickly down the stairs, and out of the street door, to the coach that was still waiting close to the curb-stone, and which the young artist could not see on account of the lower half of the shutters in his room being closed in order to give him a top-light for his studies.

"Will you permit me," said Duval to Clara, "to take your place in the coach, while you go up-stairs? You will find your lover in the first floor; and if it will give you any satisfaction to hear me say so, I assure you that he is in every way worthy of you. Now don't say that that is a compliment to you. It is one to him only, and a very high one indeed."

Clara Briarley looked her thanks, but she did not say anything. Duval helped her to descend from the coach, and then he saw her ascend the staircase. He flung himself into the vehicle and closed the door.

"Well," he said, as he threw himself back on one of the seats; "this for me is rather an extraordinary adventure, I confess; it is a little out of my line, too, I rather think. Nobody would believe that I had allowed myself to be re-pulsed by an amazingly pretty girl, and then made no end of highly moral speeches, and after that, to sit down in an infernal old hackney-coach, while she went up-stairs to throw herself comfortably into the arms of another. That is, I confess it, not at all like me."

He shifted his position uneasily, for in good truth the charms of Miss Briarley had made a great impression upon him, and the one kiss he had stolen from her had set his soul in a ferment; and yet there was an innate gentlemanly feeling in Duval, which in the presence of virtue always made him respectful.

"Well, well," he said, "let her be happy with him, who is a thousand times more deserving of her than I. What could I bring her to?—A happy home?—No. A contented fireside, and an honest position in life?—No. Sorrow and shame are all that I have to offer to any one."

Claude Duval let his head drop upon his breast, and felt rather affected. He was aroused by some one looking into the coach with a full stare at him.

CHAPTER XLI.

DUVAL'S GREAT DANGER IN THE STREETS OF LONDON.

"Well," said Duval; "who are you?"

The face of the person who glared into the carriage, was about as ugly a one as Dame Nature, in some eccentric freak, had ever thought of producing to astonish the world with; and the small-pox afterwards had made no small havoc with the skin. There was a fearful obliquity of vision likewise.

"Well, who are you?" cried Duval, again.

"Humph!" said the man.

"What do you mean by humph?"

"Only that you are my prisoner, Claude Duval, that's all."

With one blow of his clenched fist, Duval hit the ugly man right upon the nose, and he flew backward right up the steps of the house, and into the passage.

"Coachman!" cried Duval; "drive on."

"But, but—" said the coachman.

To tear down the front window, and project his arm through the opening with a pistol that he clapped against the back of the head of the coachman, was the work of a moment, while in a voice that to the affrighted ears of the man sounded like his death knell, Duval cried—

"Drive off, or by the Heaven that made me, I'll blow your brains out this moment!"

The slash that the affrighted coachman gave his horses was prodigious. They started off with the old crazy vehicle at quite a pace, and just as they turned the corner, Duval heard several voices crying—

"Stop him! stop him! A highwayman! stop him! Stop the highwayman!"

What a pang such cries shot even to the bold heart of Duval! For a moment —but only for a moment, he quailed before them, and fell back in the old coach. And then, ashamed of his own temporary weakness, he sprung forward again, and cried to the coachman, in a voice that was not one to disobey—

"Quick! quick! qicker still, or your life will answer for it."

There was a little square window at the back of the coach, and by kneeling on the seat, Duval could just look through it; and then he saw his danger.

By the rapidity with which the coach had started from the young artist's door, a party of about six men, who had been in the company of he whom Duval had knocked down so unceremoniously, had just been eluded.

That party had been foolish enough to hide in a doorway a little behind the coach. Had they hidden in advance of it, nothing could have been easier to them than to have rushed out and stopped it; but nobody can be wise at all times, and even police officers are mere mortals.

Immediately following these men was a rabble rout of people, who had joined the chase on the cry of "Stop him!—stop the highwayman!" being raised by the officers. It was quite evident that the present state of things could not last many minutes in the streets of London.

The coach rattled on; but Duval undid one of the doors, and only held it closed, so that he could fling it open in a moment, when he should think it desirable to leave the company of the crazy old vehicle.

"Round the next corner," he called to the coachman; "round the next corner with you. You will find ample payment upon the seat of the carriage."

As he spoke, Duval threw a couple of guineas upon the carriage-seat, and in another moment the vehicle, at the great risk of turning over, twisted round a corner. For a few moments Duval knew he was out of sight of his foes. He sprang from the coach, and calling out—"Drive on—drive on!" he rushed up the steps of a house, and knocked sharply at the door, without caring to whom it belonged, or thinking for a moment upon what excuse he had to make. Before the door was opened, however, a brass plate upon it caught his eye, upon which was the announcement of Doctor Smithson.

"Ah! that will do capitally," said Duval.

The door opened, and he entered the hall. It was closed again, just as the rabble rout of his pursuers turned the corner of the street, and went on full tear after the hackney-coach, in which they believed him they sought still to be.

"Is Doctor Smithson at home?" asked Duval of the powdered footman who opened the door.

"Yes, sir. Walk this way if you please."

Duval was shown into a handsome room, and as he thought it would be highly imprudent to go forth until the chase, and the excitement contingent upon it in the neighbourhood, had died away, he thought that he might as well give the learned doctor a fee, and keep him in talk as long as he possibly could.

In the course of a few minutes a little primly-dressed elderly man, with his white hair violently drawn back from his forehead and the sides of his head, and tied behind, entered the room.

Duval bowed, as Duval could bow; and the doctor was at once convinced that he had a gentleman in his consulting-room—that is to say, a gentleman if it be true that manners make the man—a proposition which we think our readers will with us pause over a little ere they receive it as a dictum of wisdom.

"Doctor Smithson, I presume?" said Duval.

"Yes, sir—yes, sir—certainly," said the little doctor. "Pray be seated, sir, if you please—a-hem! Pray be seated."

"I have come to consult you professionally," said Duval, as he took a guinea from his waistcoat pocket, and placed it upon the table, at which the doctor made a kind of salam. "I expect," added Duval, "that mine is a most singular case. Have you had much experience, sir, in affections of the brain?"

"Oh yes, yes. I am now attending a lady, who fancies she is a local post-office, and will swallow any letter she can get hold of, seal and all."

"Really! Well, doctor, my case is, if anything, more singular than that. I will detail it to you."

"Do so, sir—I shall be most happy to pay any attention to it, I assure you, sir."

"Well, sir, I have one of the most strange and curious propensities in the world. I am at times seized with a desire to order my horse, and to gallop to one of the roads, a little way out of town—the western road usually; and then, with a pair of pistols, all ready primed and loaded, I stop folks, and cry—'Stand and deliver!' and take possession of their purses, watches, and rings, whether they like it or not. At times, too, I stop a coach, and actually, in my frenzy, rob all the passengers, and then I gallop up to town again, and for a little while the fit goes off. Now, sir, is not this a most distressing case?"

"God bless me! yes, it is," said Doctor Smithson. "A most distressing case, indeed. Dear me, yes. Well, I really do not think that in the whole course of my practice I have met with anything so truly singular as your symptoms."

"They are positively distressing, sir, I assure you."

"So I should say—so I should say. But what do the people whom you, in your partial aberation, stop on the road, say to it?"

"Oh, they take me for a highwayman."

"I don't wonder at it, my dear sir. Let me feel your pulse. Ah—oh—hem! Rather fibril. It is a most remarkable case. Pray, sir, what do you do with the things that, in your mania, you take from the people?"

"I sell them, and eat and drink up the proceeds."

"You don't say so?"

"Indeed I do. Of course, it's a very distressing thing, but I am afraid if I go on in this sort of way, that people will give me the character of a professed highwayman, and instead of according to me their pity for my slight hallucination, will be hunting me up some day, and actually put me in Newgate."

"I should not wonder, my dear sir. What do you eat and drink usually? Dt is a great thing in these cases. Are you abstemious?"

"Remarkably so. A roast duck and a pound of ham will, with the assistance of a couple of bottles of wine, always make me a snack before dinner."

The doctor opened his eyes to an unusual width, and then he said—

"My dear sir, I'm very much afraid that you eat a little too much, just a little, you understand; and that that circumstance has much to do with your truly distressing case. Of course, I shall be happy to prescribe for you. When did you last feel the paroxysm come on?"

Duval suddenly put his hand to his head, and in a startling voice, cried—

"'Tis coming now!—'tis coming now!"

The little doctor sprang to his feet.

"No—no," he cried. "Stop it, stop it; don't go mad here, my dear sir, whatever you do, I beg that you wont."

"But I can't help it," said Claude; "I'm off now. Hurrah for the road! Your money, watches, and rings, gentlemen. Hurrah! hurrah! for a dark night and a lonely road. Fire away! What ho! my gallant steed.—Hilloa!"

"Murder—murder!"

Duval rushed past the doctor, and in a moment left the house, and took his way down Charlotte Street, Fitzroy Square, at a rapid pace. There was not the least appearance of any of his pursuers about the spot, and as soon as he turned the corner, he lounged along at his ease. He kept, however, a sharp eye upon any passengers whom he might chance to see eyeing him rather curiously.

His first idea was to go to the stables at the top of Oxford Street, where he had left his horse, and gallop into the country again. But when he came to consider that he must have been recognised by some one who might yet be about the streets, he thought it would be more prudent to go to his lodgings, in Spring Gardens, for a short time. At all events, he could stay there until night, and then, if he choose, be off to the road again. Besides, he could send his man, William, for his horse, which would be better than running the risk of fetching it himself.

Upon the whole, then, there seemed to Duval so many more reasons for going to Spring Gardens than for taking to the road again at once, that he bent his steps in the direction to his fashionable lodgings at once. He was as well acquainted with the by-ways as with the highways of London, and he went by rather a circuitous route to Charing Cross, as he was attired in rather a suspicious-looking costume. He could not help thinking as he went along how anxious Clara Briarley and her lover, the young artist, would be about him when they heard—which they must have done—that hue and cry raised after him; but he knew that they would soon be able to conclude he had escaped, for if he were captured, the news of such an event would soon enough be patent to the whole town.

It took Duval somewhere about half an hour, taking the very circuitous route that he did, to reach Charing Cross; and then he rapidly went over the road, and was upon the point of going down Spring Gardens, when he saw a small throng of persons coming up towards him upon the pavement.

"Why don't you let the girl go?" cried a voice. "She tells you she never touched your ribbons and laces."

"I let her go?" screamed a woman, whom Duval at once recognised as Madame Stockwellini; "I let her go? Not I, indeed; I will have her up to the justice's, that I will. I charge her with stealing ends of ribbon and bits of lace. I'm a respectable woman; and I'll see if a month at Bridewell won't bring down her pride a little."

To the amazement of Duval, he saw that Adele was in the hands of a constable, and that several people were trying to persuade Madame Stockwellini to allow her to be let go.

Adele herself spoke—

"I am innocent—indeed I am—I am innocent! Do not suppose me guilty; I would scorn guilt, and welcome death far rather. Oh, save me—save me! I am indeed innocent!"

"None o' that bawling," said the constable. "You is gived in charge, and I

^must take you off. I don't see nothing to make a rout about—lots o' people is ^took off as well as you. Come on."

"Drag her along!" cried Madame Stockwellini; "I'll bring down her nasty pride, I'll be bound. I pay rent and taxes, and I'll give her a month at Bridewell, I will. Drag her along!"

CHAPTER XLII.

DUVAL RESCUES ADELE FROM MADAME STOCKWELLINI.

"MERCY! mercy!" cried Adele. "Is there no one who will help me now Have I no friend?"

"Stop!" cried Duval, as he strode up to the group. "What is all this about? Hold, I say!"

Adele knew his voice; and, with a cry of joy, she broke away from the officer, saying—

"Ah, Heaven has at length sent me a friend. He will protect me now!"

"I will," said Claude. "Fear nothing, Adele, fear nothing."

"And pray who are you, you rapscallion?" shouted Madame Stockwellini. "Who are you, that dare say you will protect anybody that I say I shall prosecute?—you ill-looking vagabond!"

"Come, come." said the officer, as he took from his pocket a little staff with a gilt crown at the end of it; "come, come, this sort of thing won't do. Don't interfere with me, young man, or I shall have to take you into custody."

"Really?" said Duval. "How many like you do you think now, at a moderate computation, it would take to do so? I am quite sure that the ladies and gentlemen present can hardly keep themselves from laughing at the idea."

Being called ladies and gentlemen, quite pleased the few persons who had been attracted to the spot by the arrest of Adele, and they all laughed outright together, upon which the constable, who was rather a short tempered man, as constables are rather apt to be, made a dart at Adele, and catching hold of her by her long hair which hung upon her neck, he cried—

"You may all laugh and be hanged, for I care; but I will have my prisoner for all that."

"Then take the consequences, idiot!" said Duval, and with one blow of his fist he sent the constable flying like a shot, and in his course he chanced to come right against the stomach of Madame Stockwellini, who fell down in a moment, with the constable rolling over her.

"Off with you!" cried a man in the crowd that was now rapidly collecting; "off with you before the officer gets up. Do you want a coach?"

"Yes," said Duval.

"Follow me, then."

The crowd cheered Duval, as with the half-fainting Adele upon his arm, he made his way towards Charing Cross. No one made the least attempt to stop him, and a coach being procured from a stand that was close at hand, Duval handed Adele into it, and they drove off, saluted by a loud cheer from the assembled people. Duval had merely told the coachman to drive on up the Strand, without giving him any more precise direction, but it was necessary to tell him where to go to directly.

"Adele," said Duval, "dear Adele, you are safe now—you are quite safe now."

"Ah! yes, I know that you, count, would save me."

"Do not call me count. Recollect that you know really who and what I am. Have you any friends in London?"

"Alas! I have no friends at all."

"But me?"

"Yes, I ought to have said but you. You are a friend to me, and you will tell me what I ought to do. You will be my guide, and my protector. I rely wholly upon you."

Alas! it was something like the lamb relying upon the wolf, this.

"Then, my dear Adele," said Claude Duval, "I must find a home for you. Hilloa! coachman, drive out of London by Kentish Town."

CLAUDE AND ADELE IN THEIR QUIET RETREAT IN KENTISH-TOWN.

"All's right, your hon

"And now, my own charming Adele," added Duval, "you may dismiss all your fears. I will find you a lodging in a quiet suburb of London. You may depend upon me for supplying you with ample resources, and you may be much happier, if you will, than you have ever been yet."

"You are very good to me. But I can work, indeed I can."

"But you shall not, Adele. I do not protect you by halves. Do you think I would let you work while I can with ease provide most amply for your wants? No—no. You must not think of working, Adele."

"But—but indeed I would rather, and you can come and see me sometimes, ou know, for me to thank you for your great kindness to me."

"Oh, yes, you may depend upon my coming to see you, for you know I love you, Adele. You know how truly and fondly I love you. Ah! my dear girl, can you be insensible to how very happy we may be in each others society? Beautiful Adele!"

He clasped her to his heart, and for a few moments she permitted him to hold her in his arms; but when he got a little too warm and ardent with his kisses, she gently yet firmly disengaged herself from him, saying—

"Do not—oh, do not make me think ill of one to whom I am so deeply indebted. Do not make me suspect the motives of one whom I would fain always think a true and a sincere friend."

"Think nothing," said Claude, "suspect nothing, charming Adele, but that you are beautiful, and that I love you dearly and fondly, and that I will always stand between you and all harm."

"But—but——"

"Nay, you are full of reservations, dear one. Calm yourself, I pray you, and get rid of all these strange doubts and fears. See, we are gitting quite into the open country. How charming everything appears. The birds are singing their madrigals on every hedge. Behold how delightfully in the clear fresh breeze of Heaven, the branches of the old trees sway to and fro. Look at the sunlight upon many a flower, and ask yourself, if after all it is not a happy accident that has released you from the thraldom of Madame Stockwellini, and the dreary workroom in Spring Gardens. Why, you will be as happy out here in the open country, as the day is long. Will you not, my fair Adele?"

"I think I shall be happier."

"You will indeed. Your taste cannot but be pure, for you are young and beautiful. Why, such a being a you are, Adele, was born to life amid the birds and flowers, and not to waste your sweetness in the service of such a woman as that from whom it has given me so much gratification to rescue you. You will here, with all the sights and sounds of country life about you, feel really what it is to live, and in a week you will fancy yourself a new creature."

"You make me feel happy by what you say."

"I am glad to hear it. You will not fail to find that what I say is true, and in a short time you will smile with pure joy to find what a happy change has taken place in your condition."

"Shall I indeed?"

"Yes, dearest and best—my own charming Adele."

Again he clasped her to his heart, for Duval really loved this young and innocent girl as much as he could love any one. He loved her before a thousand Mrs. Finches or a thousand marchionesses. But by this time the coach had reached what was then the really quiet and noval little village of Kentish Town. It was not what it is now, a mere suburb of London, and almost as town-like as any of the streets in the actual city. It is rather a sad thing that London has gone out of town, and destroyed the beauty of the seclusion of many such spots. But it will go yet much further, and the lover of nature will have to travel far before he can look upon a true and real green field, or a real growing flower.

By this kind of discourse, Duval certainly fully succeeded in restoring the spirits of Adele, so that when they alighted from, and dismissed the coach, there was quite a smile upon her lips. Duval gave her money to go into a linen-drapers shop, and purchase a hood and mantle, as she was not clad for the streets, and then they dined together at a pretty little country-looking inn, with a world of ivy growing all over the front of it, and the dinner was so nice, and everything was so quiet and so serene, that certainly Adele had not been so truly happy for a long long time.

But it became necessary that they should seek for some lodging, and having settled everything at the Inn, they strolled through the village, until, at a pretty vine-covered cottage, they found a lodging to let.

"Would you like this place?" said Duval. "It is humble but very pretty."

"Is it not far better and prettier than I thought I should ever be able to call home?" said Adele. "It is charming."

They entered the cottage, and found that they might be well accommodated. An old woman kept the place, and she said—"Is the young lady your sister, sir?"

"No," said Duval. "My wife."

Adele turned pale, and trembled. She was not prepared for this; but the words had been spoken, and she had not at the moment the courage to contradict them; and when the moment was passed, she felt how very awkward it would be to do so. When, however, the lodging was taken, and she was alone with Duval, she clasped her hands and fell upon her knees, saying,

"Oh, spare me! Spare me!"

"Spare you, Adele? What do you mean?"

"You will not—you cannot wish to bring me to disgrace—to shame—o infamy. You have said that I am your wife, when you know that I am not. Why did you say so? Was it honest? Was it right for you to say as much? Let us go from here, and at some other place make no such statement. Say that I am your sister if you will, and I will love you as a brother may be loved, but I am not your wife."

"Adele, you have no confidence in me."

"Yes—yes. Abundance, if you will not yourself destroy it."

"But you shall be my wife if you will not despise an alliance with me; I make you a solemn promise to that effect. Have you ever found me deceive you in any promise that I made you? No, Adele. Do you think that I could have said to this woman here that you were my wife, unless I intended to make you such? If you refuse me, it is another matter."

"Refuse you?—oh no—no."

"Rise, then, dearest Adele, and feel assured that in saying you were my wife already, I could have but one object in view, and that was to spare you the fuss, and the observation, and the inquiries, that in a little place like this you would have been directly subjected to, if I had announced you as only going to be married. Do you not see that?"

"I think I do."

"Of course you do. You could not fail to see it. The idea of my deceiving you should not for one moment find a home in your heart. No, my Adele, I love you too well—by far too well for that. Let me only see your smile again, and then all will be well."

"You will not deceive me, then?"

"No, I swear I will not—I swear it by your own beauty. Could I be happy if you were wretched? Ah, how can you think so lightly of my love?"

"I will not again, Duval; you have convinced me now. How foolish I was not to see that you were right, and had a kind object in calling me already your wife."

"It was foolish, but yet natural enough, my darling, for all that; and we will not speak of it again."

"And so you really love me, then?"

"As Heaven is my witness, I love you."

"We shall then, I think and hope, be happy—very happy."

She flung herself upon his breast, and wept aloud in the fulness of her heart.

CHAPTER XLIII.

DUVAL PICKS UP A TRIFLE ON HAMPSTEAD HEATH.

AT twelve o'clock that night Duval was upon Hampstead Heath. It was in his neighbourhood now, and he thought he might pick up a few trinkets to give to Adele.

The night was rather cold, and a heavy wind was sweeping over the heath, and yet at times the clouds would break up a little, and show the bright stars, peeping down from the blue crevices upon the world. It was, take it as a whole, just the sort of night that a gentleman of Duval's profession would have chosen for the purpose of carrying on business. It was not too dark for him to see what he was about, and yet it was quite dark enough for him to make a rapid escape, if it should become at all necessary for him to do so, in consequence of being assailed by overpowering odds, or from any other inciting circumstance.

At that time, however, Hampstead Heath was not a very favourite place for Knights of the Road, for there were too many first-class villas and other residences in the neighbourhood, to make it very safe ; and it was not a high-road to anywhere of importance.

To be sure, a good portion of the traffic of the northern road in the winter time, when the ascent of Highgate Hill was worse than that at Hampstead, would partially cross the heath, and make way up Swain's Lane : but at the season when we find Duval upon the heath but little plunder was to be expected.

If there were a chance of doing any good at all, it consisted in waylaying some of the resident gentry, who might be coming home late, or from some other cause might be out upon the road.

But then, as we have stated, Duval was near home, and so he had thought it just worth his while to go out upon the heath for an airing to himself and to his steed, which he had managed to get from the stables where he had fortunately left him.

For some time he met no one but a poor-looking man, who said "Good night, sir," as he passed him, and to whom he, Duval, made a civil rejoinder. His horse was pretty well used to all sorts of country, so that Duval did not at all scruple to ride off the high-road a little on to the open heath.

There were gardens at the back of some villas, close to where he happened to be, and, all at once, he heard distinctly a scream ; but whether it come from any one in one of the villas, or one of the gardens, or upon the heath itself, so sudden was the sound, that he could not take upon himself to say.

He listened attentively for a repetition of the sound, and he was not disappointed ; for, in the course of a few minutes, it come again, and then he was able to fix its locality better. He felt quite clear that the sound was in the open air, and that it proceeded from the garden of a mansion close at hand to where he was, and which was enclosed by a rather high brick wall. He rode quite close to the wall to listen, and then he heard a man's voice say,

" I tell you I watched you all the evening. I saw everything. You looked, but I did not hear anything you said. I could guess all though, and I am a desperate man. You and the major quite understood each other."

" You are madly jealous," said a female voice, of much younger tone than the man's. " You are madly jealous. And so you would kill me like a crack-brained Othello ?"

" Don't speak to me ; I believe Othello was right after all. Don't speak to me. I waited until I could take you at unawares, and now, my lady, that I have got this rope well round you, I can dispose of you without any kicking or scratching."

" But you surely do not mean to kill me ?"

" I surely do though—but not upon my own premises. I will take you out by the door in the garden-wall to the heath, and there kill you, and in the morning I will make quite a wonder as to what has become of you, and so escape any suspicion. It will be thought you committed suicide, and I will depose to such persons expressions as shall strengthen the idea. Come on. Come on."

"Mercy!"

"No—no. I am a desperate man, and will have no mercy. Horns are on my head, and no wonder they drive me half mad. I saw you wink at Sir Barnaby Grubbs too, and I am quite sure that you trod upon the toe of Lord Lovehemhall. Oh, I have eyes in my head, and something else on the top of it. I'm a desperate man! I'm a desperate man!"

"In mercy spare me!"

"I will not. It is quite music to me to hear you say that. I only wish all your lovers heard you, madam. If the devil himself were to come and ask me to save you I would not."

There was now a scuffling noise, and the jealous husband was evidently dragging his wife towards the door he had mentioned in the garden-wall. Duval had made up his mind to interfere with the affair from the very first. It was not exactly the thing for him to stand by, and let a jealous husband have his own way ; and now, feeling quite sure that his horse would stand profoundly still and wait for him, he dismounted, and guided by the scuffling noise in the garden, he found the door in the wall, which in a few brief moments would doubtless be opened to let out the disputing couple.

"I will see the end of this adventure," said Duval to himself. "By the sound of the lady's voice she should be young and fair, and if she be, why I will take her part from pure love of the young and the fair ; but if she be not, why I will yet see justice done to her, for then I should say she is decidedly innocent.'

Suddenly a door in the garden-wall was opened, and two person came out. The one was a female, and she was evidently being pushed forward by the other, who was the husband.

Duval had been now for so long upon the heath, that he was able to see pretty clearly about him, notwithstanding the darkness, and although he could not take upon himself absolutely to say that the lady was young, he saw by her figure that she could not be old.

Her beauty by that light was not to be thought of ; but he was soon recalled from his reflections by the rather violent conduct of the pair.

"You dare not—you cannot kill me," said the lady. "All this is merely done to terrify me. You could not for your life and soul's sake commit so unmanly an action as to kill me, sir."

"Dare I not? We shall soon see that. In such cases as mine there can be but one course to pursue, and that must consist of the death of the object ; I will kill you, and then I will leave England."

"Help! help!"

"Nay, madam, it is of no use your calling help here. You know as well as I do, that this is a very unfrequented part of the heath, and that your cries cannot be heard."

"But I am innocent—indeed I am!"

"The major!—the major!"

"Well, I repulsed him."

"Wretch! Then you own that he solicited you?"

"I do. But surely that is no fault of mine ? If I repulsed him, what more could the most virtuous woman the world ever saw do, I would ask?"

"It is quite sufficient. I am a desperate and dishonoured husband, and as I said before, the devil himself should not save you."

Upon this, Duval thought that there was a capital opportunity of saying something ; and assuming suddenly a deep, low, and sepulchral voice, he stepped forward, saying—

'Who calls on me?"

'Gracious Heaven," cried the lady, "what is that ?"

"I was called and I have come!" said Claude, advancing so that in the dim light he was faintly seen.

The husband staggered back until he reached the wall close to the door, and then in a voice of great trepidation he said—

"Who—who are you!"

"When such deeds as that which you contemplated are doing," said Duval, still speaking in a strange and monstrous voice, "I am always there; but I do not appear—I dare not appear—unless I am called upon. You mentioned my name and I am here. What would you with me?"

"You—you don't mean to say that you are the—the devil himself?"

"Exactly."

The husband turned round and fled with the greatest precipitation towards the house. Fear had taken the most complete possession of him; and from the sound of his footsteps it was quite clear that he was taking the nearest route that he could, quite heedless of flower-beds or other vegetation that might be in his way, to his home.

The lady likewise turned and fled, for whatever might be the slight nature of her objections to a murderer-lover, she certainly did not seem to think one from the infernal regions at all desirable.

"Stop," cried Duval.

She only fled the quicker; but owing to the intense darkness in the garden, for it was, in consequence of the numerous trees within it, darker than the heath itself, she caught her foot in some flowering shrub, and fell to the ground. In a moment Duval was up to her.

"Do not be at all alarmed," he said, in his natural voice. "I am a gentleman, and thought it would be a good thing to punish your jealous husband by giving him a good fright."

"Are you, indeed, a gentleman?'"

"I assure you I am."

"But the—the certain party is called the Old Gentleman I have heard?"

"Yes. But if there were light sufficient, you would soon see that I was certainly not the Old Gentleman."

"Should I?"

"You would, indeed. What do you think of me now?"

Duval raised her up, and kissed her cheek.

"Well, I don't know what to think; but be you whom you may, or what you may, you have certainly done me a service; but do you know that I am bound round by a cord, that my husband put on me at unawares?"

"That I will soon release you from, if you will stand still for a few moments. I have a sharp knife in my pocket, and I can feel the cords, I dare say, and so cut them without doing you any harm. Will you trust me?"

"Yes. Oh, yes."

Duval found no great difficulty in cutting the cords that held the lady in bondage, and then he said,—

"It is a monstrous thing that your husband should let his jealousy of you go to such a length."

"Alas! sir, it is; but what can I do?"

"Be revenged upon him in the only way that is in your power, and in the way that all wrongfully jealous husbands should be served. Give him real cause."

"Ah, now I am afraid that you are really the devil, or you would not so advise me. No—no! No more kissing, if you please. One Satanic salute is quite enough."

"Well, I ought to have a kiss as payment for cutting the rope that bound you."

"You paid yourself before-hand. But as my husband really seems to think that you are the evil one himself, you will do me a signal service if you frighten him out of his jealousy."

"I will do so with pleasure; but how would you have me proceed? Shall I follow him now into the house—or in what way shall I accomplish the object?"

The lady seemed to reflect for a moment or two, and then she said—

"It is worth the trying. I only wish I knew that you were a man of honour, sir, whom I might trust."

"I have no means of convincing you. Of course, name-assertion is no proof. If you will trust me, well and good; if you will not—good night."

It is very questionable, indeed, if Duval would have gone had the lady echoed his 'god night;' but she did not put him to that trial, for she said—

"I will trust you—follow me. I will lead you into the house by a way that will enable you to reach our bed-room. Once there, I must leave it to your own ingenuity to frighten my husband; who, I think, will now abandon his attempt upon my life for to-night; but who, if he be not well terrified, may renew it on another occasion.'"

"Take me where you will," said Duval; "I will obey your orders; and you will find your confidence not at all misplaced."

CHAPTER XLIV.

DUVAL FINDS THAT SPRING GARDENS IS TOO HOT TO HOLD HIM.

THE lady took Duval by the hand—he took good care to give to hers some gentle sqeezes as he went along—and she led him into the house and through several rooms, until she came to one in which she left him for a moment or two, saying—

"Be not impatient; I will soon return to you."

The room was profoundly dark; but in the course of a few moments he saw a dim light coming through the crevice of a door leading into some other apartment; but before he could make up his mind whether to go towards it or to stay where he was, it opened, and the lady made her appearance.

"This way," she said, "this way."

Duval sprang after her, and in a moment more found himself in a very handsome room, fitted up as a sleeping chamber. The general appointments of the place were really superb; and it was quite evident that some more refined taste than that of the jealous husband—or probably than that of the lady, who may, or who may not, have given him cause for such jealousy—had at one time presided over the appointments of that room.

"A handsome chamber," said Duval.

"Hush!" cried the lady. "Hide yourself in that wardrobe. He will be here shortly. Hide yourself at once; and remember that I leave all to your discretion."

"You may, indeed, safely do so."

"I hope I may."

She pushed him into the wardrobe, and scarcely had the door been closed upon him before the husband entered the room. The tone of his voice was very much subdued, as he said—

"Madam, you must know as well as I, that that appearance on the heath was all a delusion. It was only some man who had chanced to overhear what was going on between us."

"I should be very sorry," said the lady, affecting to shudder, 'to think that he was really what he said he was; but you ought to know best."

"I! How should I know?"

"Why, you must be probably aware that jealous people are generally waited upon by something from that place which it is as well not to mention; but as you stooped to the contemplation of actual murder, it is not very hard for one to think that the evil spirit himself may have thought proper to appear to you.'"

"Stuff—stuff!"

" Very well."

" I have no sort of fear of the—the—"

" The what ? Why do you hesitate at pronouncing his name, if you have no fear of him ?"

" Because I think it is just as well not to be too familiar with such names, madam, in ordinary discourse. That is the reason, however you may be inclined to attach some other to it. Therefore, I particularly desire that you drop the conversation, and come to bed at once. I am willing, if your conduct for the future is what it ought to be, madam, to forget the past."

" You will ?"

" Yes ; I say I am willing to do so, only you must never again speak to Lord A., or the Mayor, or, or—in fact, I will give you a list of people you must not speak to on any account, and then you are sure to be right."

" But will not that look very awkward in society ?"

" Society be hanged, madam. Do you want to drive me mad again ? Society be hanged !"

The husband by this time had got into bed, and the lady having only partially disrobed herself, put on a very elegant night-gown trimmed with rich lace, and in the quietest manner in the world slipped into the bed likewise, saying—

" Shall I leave the light ?"

" Yes, leave it, confound you. What a life you lead me with your dancing and your flirting, and your——Hilloa ! what's that ? Why the light has gone out."

Duval had found a pair of silk stockings in the wardrobe, nicely knotted together, and he had thrown them with so good an aim at the candle, that he at once extinguished it.

" It's very extraordinary," said the lady, " for it was a whole candle, as you yourself saw."

" Yes—yes," stammered the husband. " I--I can't at all make it out, my love."

" Don't my love me, sir. By your violence and your threats you have brought the devil on the premises, and now heaven only knows when we shall get rid of him again."

" But, my dear—Good God, you don't really think, or really mean to say that —that—that——"

" Yes, I do ; and I shouldn't at all wonder if, not only me, but all the servants in the place were to be smothered with sulphur before the morning. Oh, you have much to answer for, and if the devil——"

" Hush ! Good gracious. Hush, don't mention him, I beg of you. If anything more than another will be likely to——the Lord have mercy upon us, did you hear that ?"

Duval had given utterance to a hideous groan from the wardrobe, and so ghostly and horrible had he made the sound, that even the lady herself could not help giving a slight start of alarm.

" Mercy !" said the husband. " I begin to think he is here, I begin to feel sure. Oh, wife—wife, by your conduct you see you have raised the thingamy."

" I ? You mean by your conduct. Did you not upon the heath actually say such things and contemplated such things, that the enemy of mankind thought proper to make his appearance to us ? There it is again !"

Duval gave another groan more hideous than the first, and the husband was so alarmed, that forgetting all his caution about not mentioning that name which is not usually mentioned to ears polite, he cried—

" The devil ! devil ! Oh, the devil is here, and we are lost—lost—lost !— Help ! Help ! Murder ! What's to be done now ? The devil is here ! He is here, I know. Speak to him, wife, and ask him what he wants."

" What do you want ?" said the wife, in an affected, trembling voice ; " oh, what do you want here ?"

" My due," said Claude Duval.

" And good Mr. D. what may that be ?"

" A groundlessly jealous husband.   A man who, because his wife is fair and pleasant, must, forsooth, fancy her criminal.   Such is the man I want."

" Merciful Providence," said the husband, " that is me."

" It is," said Duval; " are you prepared?"

" No, I am not.   I am quite the reverse of prepared; I don't wan to be

CLAUDE'S ADVENTURE WITH "JEALOUS HUSBAND'S" WIFE.

ealous a ry more.   I am [e]fectually cured—most effectually cured.   Say no more to me, I beg.   I am not the man that I was.   I will no more threaten my wife."

" But yet, as a token, it is necessary that I should hold your hand in mine for a moment.   One moment will suffice.   Your hand will turn perfectly black, so that, whenever you look at it, the memory of my visit should be with you."

" Oh, no—no—no."

" It must be so. I come—I come—I come."

As Duval took good care to make his advance quite manifest, as regarded the side of the bed he was upon, the husband, whose fears had almost worked him up to madness, sprang out at the other side, and with a yell of horror darted from the room.

" A thousand thanks," said the lady. " I do think you have made an impression upon him, that he will never in this world forget. I owe you very much."

" But he will be back again ?"

" Certainly not ; I make no doubt but that he will lock himself up in his study for the remainder of the night ; and the discomfort he will there experience will be a proper punishment for his conduct towards me."

" I quite agree with you, my dear madam. He will be cold and uncomfortable in the study as a punishment, while I shall be warm and snug in his bed as a reward."

" Sir ?"

It was very dark, but Duval succeeded in stopping her mouth with a kiss, and then he whispered—

" Do you think I could be insensible to your beauty ? Ah, no ; what I have done, has been done for the love I bear towards you."

" Help !" said the lady in a whisper. " Help !"

*   *   *   *   *

The faint dawn of the morning was upon tree and flower, and upon the wide expanse of the majestic heath, as Duval emerged from the garden-gate of the mansion in which he had made himself so very useful. He paused to glance around him upon the beauty of the young day. A slight smile was upon his face.

" What a remarkably unreasonable thing," he said, " it is of that husband to be jealous, to be sure. Really he must be one of the most suspicious of men, to be at all suspicious of such a wife. Well—well, I came upon the heath to get a trinket or two for Adele, and I must confess that the toilette-table of that happy couple has furnished me with a few as pretty pieces of gold and jewels, as I have seen for some time."

As he spoke, he held up to the faint light a pair of sparkling bracelets. At that moment through the dim mist that was upon the heath, he saw something coming towards him that looked of a stupendous size. He drew back in alarm, but that feeling did not last above a moment, for from amid the white mist his faithful steed emerged, and with a great show of tenderness, rubbed its head against him. The trappings and saddle were wet with dew.

" Ah, my friend," said Claude Duval, " I should wrong thee much, if I were to say that I did not expect thee here this morning. I fear that the hours have seemed long to thee."

He patted the neck of the faithful animal, and then with his handkerchief carefully wiped the dew from its face and mane, the horse all the while, by every means in its power, testifying its satisfaction at again meeting with its kind master, for Duval was truly kind to the noble creature.

" We must not linger here," said Duval, " or the master of yon mansion may take a fancy to a morning walk, and then may set us down as something not quite so respectable even as his infernal friend of last night."

With this, Duval mounted his steed, and leaving the heath to brighten and grow beautiful, as the long slanting rays of fair sunlight shot across it from the rapidly awakening east, he took his way to Kentish Town again.

At that early hour in the morning the whole village was wrapped in repose, and Duval, as he cantered through the little high street, did not see one person. He paused opposite to the cottage where Adele lodged, and the moment he did so the casement was opened, and she looked out to him with a smile upon her sweet face.

"Ah, you are returned," she said.

"Yes, for a moment, my Adele—only for a moment. I must to London now; but be assured I will be with you again as soon as may be. In the meantime here is a little remembrance of me."

"Ah, I need no remembrance of you."

"Nay, but take them and call them what you will—a remembrance or a present, Adele."

He threw the pair of bracelets into the room through the open window, and then waiving his hand, he urged his horse on, and at a sharp pace he made for London.

"That girl loves me now," he said to himself; "and she thinks there is no one in all the world like me. She believes in all my promises. What will she think of me when she finds them all broken? No—no, they will not be all broken. The principal one, and that is that I will love her always, shall be kept. How can I cease to love you, my dear Adele? but as for matrimony, why that is quite another thing, and I am afraid that just yet I cannot very well bring my mind to it."

As Duval came to this conclusion, he reached the stables where he usually put up his horse; and after doing so he walked to Spring Gardens. Duval was at that time particularly anxious to get to his lodgings, for he wished very much to know if, by any accident, he had been by any one recognised upon his rescueing Adele from the fangs of Madame Stockwellini.

He did not, even if madame found out where Adele was, anticipate that she could do much against her, for he could easily see that the charge professed to be brought against the young girl was one of the vilest trumped-up ones that could be thought of; and that fact he did not doubt would be at once apparent to any justice before whom the malice of the fashionable milliner might take her.

From William, however, he felt quite confident he should be able to hear all that he wished to know, and so it was that he made his way so quickly to his lodgings.

By the aid of his latch-key he easily let himself in, and he crept very slowly up stairs, for he did not want to disturb any one, as he knew he could get into his rooms by the master-key he had to the doors of every one of them; and he would have had no objection to take a nap of an hour's duration upon one of his couches before he saw William.

By the time he got to within sight of his own rooms he was rather surprised to see straggling with the daylight a faint gleam from a candle or a lamp, coming from under one of the doors. This was the more astonishing to him, as he knew that William had no reason to expect his return, and why he should sit up, he (Duval) could not conceive.

Of course, after making this discovery, Duval, with the utmost caution proceeded the rest of the distance up the stairs, and when he got to the door from under which the light came faintly streaming, he laid his ear quite close to its panels and listened attentively. All he could hear was a confused murmur of voices; but that was amply sufficient to let him know that some one besides William was there; and now it required no small amount of boldness to do what Duval did, which was to open the outer door gently and stand close to a very light inner one that had been set up to keep out the cold air, and there to listen to what was going on in his apartments.

CHAPTER XLV.

DUVAL AVOIDS THE SNARE LAID TO CATCH HIM BY WILLIAM.

THIS inner door was so thin and light, and ornamental, that it afforded very little obstruction to sound; so that Duval, when he placed his ear close to it, had no difficulty at all in distinctly comprehending anything that was taking place in the room.   William was speaking in a steady, business-like tone to some one.

" I have thought the affair over," he said, " in every shape and way ; and for a very long time I felt that it was to my interest to be faithful to him ; but as I think that his career is nearly over, for I know that the greatest exertions will soon be made to take him, I fancy I may as well get what I can by the transaction."

" Assuredly," said another voice.   " Most assuredly.   You take an exceedingly sensible view of the affair ; and as you have sent for me to advise with you, quite confidentially of course, I have no hesitation in saying that I can get you a £100 at least.

" Are you sure of that ?"

" I am.   The fact is, that the old king and the bishop are so dreadfully wroth at the visit of Duval to the palace, that they will pay almost anything to be certain of his destruction."

" Do you think his capture alive is a great object ?"

" It may be."

" Well, then, I tell you it can't be done ; and if you and I are to do the job between us, we must kill him."

" Kill him ?   Won't that be attended with no small amount of risk ? I, some-how, from all you have told me of Duval, don't like the idea of having anything to do with him in a scuffle, although we may be two to one."

" A scuffle ?   Do you think, that knowing him as I do, that I would go into a scuffle with him if we were six to one ?   No—not I.   But I have a plan—I have a plan—ay, such a plan !"

" Indeed ?"

" Yes ; it's one that can't fail."

" Well, that is the strongest recommendation to any plan that I ever heard of in all my life.   What is it ?"

" I will tell you.   When he comes here again, you, from your lodging opposite —for you must take one forthwith, and be in it to-morrow morning—will be able to communicate with me.   I will, when he is here, place a wafer on the middle pane of glass in the left-hand window of this room.   By that you will know that he is here.   Then, the first bottle of wine he has I will so drug that he shall soon, after drinking any of it, fall fast asleep in his chair.   You un-derstand ?"

" Yes, perfectly."

" When that is accomplished I will remove the wafer, and then you will know he is asleep and helpless, and you can come over, and from the open doorway shoot him dead, and we can easily say he resisted, and we were forced to take his life to save our own.   After having once tried to effect his arrest—"

" Oh, yes, it's easy enough, but why don't you shoot him ?   What is to hinder you from shooting him ?"

" Because I don't see why I should do all the work, and you have half the money.   If I hocus him and get him all ready for death, and open the door, and betray him to you, you may as well, I think, pull the trigger that will finish the whole affair.   If you will not, our bargain is off."

" Well, well.   I will do it."

" Agreed then.   Our bargain is made, and whatever we get we divide fairly, guinea for guinea."

" Certainly, that is well understood ; and, I take it, it will be the best day's work you or I ever did, William."

" Will it ?" muttered Duval to himself, as he carefully closed the outer door again and slipped down the staircase.   " Will it really ?   We shall see that. This is one of my luckiest escapes, after all.   We shall see, master William, if diamond cannot cut diamond."

Duval did not pause, but without making the least noise he left the house, and repairing to an hotel in Covent Garden he easily got admittance, notwithstanding the early hour, and was soon seated at a luxurious breakfast, at which, if any one had seen him, they would scarcely have suspected he was cognisant of a well-laid plan against his life.

But Claude Duval was celebrated for his remarkable *sang froid*.

While at his breakfast, Duval matured the plan he intended to adopt in this emergency, the only part of which that touched him at all, being the treachery of William, whom he had loaded with benefits and favours of all kinds and descriptions.

Pray, who was the worst member of society after all, William or his master?

At about ten o'clock in the day, Duval started to Spring Gardens as if nothing at all were the matter, and letting himself in as usual, he walked up stairs, treading as he went sufficiently heavy to give to William the most ample notice of his coming.

The obsequious traitor met him on the stairs, within a few paces of the top.

" Well, William, any news?" said Duval.

" No, count, none." William always called his master count if he spoke to him on the staircase or on any of the landings of the house, for fear any one might be lis.ening, which in a house so full of people was by no means an unlikely circumstance.

" Well, I did not particularly expect any. Help me off with my coat, William. I will dine here to day."

" Am glad to hear you say so," said William, as he closed the door of the splendid room. " I am very glad to hear it indeed."

" Why so ?"

" It's so much more cheerful to have you here."

" Ah, I dare say it is ; and now, William, my man, you must get me a nice little dinner to day, for I have no appetite for anything that is not more than tempting."

" I will do my best, sir."

" That will do. We ought all to be abundantly satisfied with any one who does his best. I am."

Duval strolled into the adjoining bed-room, and made some slight alteration in his dress. When he came out again a glance showed him that a small red wafer was fastened on the centre of one of the panes of glass of the window specified by William in his conversation with his friend.

If the smallest doubt had remained in the mind of Duval as regarded the reality of the treachery of William, and his perseverance in the diabolical plan that he had heard hatched, this observation of the wafer would have removed it effectually ; and the scheme he had concocted became at once a fixed resolve in his mind.

Duval sat down with quite a bland smile upon his face.

" William," he said, " has there been any disturbance in the house ?"

" A little *fracas* between Madame Stockwellini and her pretty apprentice they call Adele, that is all. I understand the milliner gave her to a constable, but some one rescued her, and she disappeared."

" Indeed ! Why, William, that must touch you home, for, if I mistake not, your heart was a little smitten in that quarter, was it not, William ?"

" A very little."

" Well, I would set you up in a snug inn, as I have often told you, any time you like to marry—although, of course, I should be loath to lose you, William. Good and faithful servants like you are so scarce."

" And good masters, too, sir. God bless you ! you have been a kind friend to me, sir, always."

William wiped his eyes with the corner of a table napkin he had in his hand, and Duval was so disgusted at the rank hypocrisy of the rascal that he was compelled to rise and pretend to look out at the window in order to conquer the propensity he had to catch William by the throat, and there hold him until he breathed his last.

As he stood at the window, he saw that one of the casements on the second-floor of the house immediately opposite was opened just far enough to permit the end of a telescope to be projected out of it, and he did not doubt but that there was the accomplice of William gloating over the presence of the wafer on the window-pane.

Suddenly there was a slight tap on the outer door, and upon William opening it, Duval was not a little surprised to see Mrs. Finch.

"He is at home," she said.

"Oh, sir," said William, "I forgot to say that this lady has called several times when you have been from home, sir."

"Once more I see you," said Mrs. Finch.

William prudently left the room.

"My dear madam," said Duval, "I have only just come home from the country. I have not had the pleasure of seeing you for a long time. How fair and blooming you look."

Duval kissed her cheek, and in a faint voice Mrs. Finch cried, "Don't!" and then burst into tears.

"My dear madam," said Duval, "I sincerely hope that nothing particular is the matter. Why those tears? Has that brute of a Finch dared to say anything or to do anything to cause them to flow?"

"Oh, count, he is a raging lion!"

"Is it possible?"

"Yes, my—my dear sir, and an iron chain, too—he is a raging lion, is Finch, and a large iron chain."

"May I beg you, madam, not to be so alarmingly metaphorical, but to tell me at once what he has done. The rascal shall bitterly repent causing pearly tears to flow over the cheek of beauty. Ah, my dear madam, he is not the man to appreciate you."

"He is not! he is not! But you are not single, count—you are not single."

"And you, alas! are double."

"I am—I am! Oh, cruel fate! Don't!—don't!—That makes eight times you have kissed me, and I have not been here much above as many minutes. Don't!"

"But is it possible for any one to avoid kissing you? that is the question; and I put it to your good sense if it be possible to avoid it, my charming Maria."

"Well, perhaps it would be difficult."

"The difficult would become the impossible."

"Ah, now, that makes —9, 10, 11 times. Oh, don't! I came here only to ask your advice, for Finch declares he will not come home again, and has been away two days and three nights. What am I to do?"

"Make yourself as comfortable as possible, and give me your address, so that I may pay you a visit; for it is very likely that Finch, being a little jealous of me, may watch this house, and in that case he might rush upon you and do you some injury when I was not by to protect you from the brute."

"That is true. When shall I see you?—12, 13.—No more kisses, I beg. I am staying at No. 2, Queen Square, and I do think I shall be at home from dark all the evening. Don't come.—14, 15,—oh."

"Perhaps I won't; and now my dear Maria, I wish you good morning, for I expect some visitors of importance, and really have some business to transact that will entirely occupy me. I will come at seven."

Mrs. Finch nodded, and having reckoned 16, 17, 18, as the number of kisses with which Duval had indulged himself, she left the room, no doubt considerably comforted in her domestic afflictions, considering all things.

Duval paced the room in silence, and ever and anon he glanced at the wafer that still stuck to the window-pane, and sad thoughts came over him—

"Oh, that this man had been honest to me," he thought. "Had he asked me any favour, I would have done it for him. If I could only find one who was not a traitor in this world, I would pay any price for the luxury of such a friend!"

Duval had such a friend in the fair, and gentle, and loving Adele, if he would but have believed as much, and not continued merely to think of her as the toy of an hour, that might he cast aside when the glitter of its fascinations and the gloss of its beauty were gone.

But the day was creeping on apace, and as he had ordered his dinner unusually early, the time would soon come when the diabolical scheme of William would be attempted to be carried into execution ; and if he, Duval, for a few moments thought of other things to the exclusion of that most monstrous piece of treachery, the wafer on the window-pane was sure to bring him back to the sad contemplation of what might have been his doom.

William was more than usually attentive to his master, and particularly fawning and obsequious in his address and manner towards him. He was just the man to be so under the circumstances. He was each moment afraid that his villany would peep out of his eyes or blazon itself upon his face, so as to become patent to all the world, and therefore was it that he took no end of pains to try to glaze it over to the only man who, beside his associate, who was on the watch in the house opposite, knew anything of it.

Surely, there was something more than chance in all this ! Surely, Duval had some mission to fulfil yet in the world, and he was not to die by the hands of those men.

But yet, as the time came close, and as William began to lay the table for the dinner of that master whom, Judas-like, he was about to betray, Duval had to look continually at the wafer to assure himself [that there could be no sort of mistake upon the subject. And as often as he did look at that wafer, so often did he feel a kind of rage rise up in his heart against the man who had so grossly abused his bounty.

Perhaps even William could not help noticing that his master was ill at ease, for he said, with a tone of voice that had guilt in every accent of it,

" Are you quite well, sir ?"

" Oh, yes, quite ; I never was better, William."

" How glad I am to hear that, sir. It is so—so very pleasant and satisfactory to me. It is, indeed."

CHAPTER XLVI.

DUVAL ROBS THE BANKER IN CLEMENT'S-LANE, AND CALLS ON MRS. FINCH.

Duval felt as though he could have really forgiven his man, William, anything but this rank hypocrisy ; but still he did not betray himself ; but sitting down to his dinner as if nothing were the matter, he said to William,

" Are we well stocked with wine ?"

" Pretty well, sir."

" That's right. Always keep up our stock, William, for we don't know what may happen."

" No, sir. We don't know what may happen, as you very truly say, sir."

Duval just caught sight of William's face in the glass, and he saw come across it a most diabolical smile. That was sufficient ; and Duval from that moment got rid of all compunctions regarding the fate of William.

" Well, William, I think we will have some of the old madeira to-day."

" Very good, sir ; I happen to have a couple of bottles in the wine-cooler, all ready ; for I thought you would probably drink it to-day, sir."

" Very good, William ; and now that we are quite alone, we will take a glass together."

" Thank you, sir."

Of course, as William knew perfectly well who Duval was, there was not upon all occasions such ceremony between them, and at odd times, when the humour took him, it was not at all unusual for Duval to say,—" Here, William, take a glass of wine with me," so that his doing so upon the present occasion did not seem to the traitor to be anything extraordinary or out of the way. Nay, if it had upon his mind at all any special effect, it was only to convince him more and more of Duval's total want of any suspicion of what was going on.

The wine was duly produced, and, by the slightest glance at the bottle, Duval felt convinced that it had not been at all tampered with, and, consequently, he felt rather curious as regarded the mode in which William purposed giving to him the dose that was to put his resistance out of all question.

He was not long kept in a state of suspense.

In the glass that William placed before him, Duval's watchful eye at once detected about a couple of drops of some perfectly limpid-looking liquid. So slight was the effect produced upon the richly cut chrystal by this small quantity of fluid, that had not he (Duval) been looking for some such thing it must have quite escaped him.

"Fill, William," he said.

William filled both the glasses. In Duval's there was a slightly tinged look about the wine for a moment, and then it passed off, leaving the pure-looking madeira as clear as a chrysolite.

Duval took hold of the glass, and was in the act of raising it to his lips, when he suddenly paused, and put himself into a listening attitude.

"What is it, sir?" said William.

"Well, William, that is what I should like to know. I thought I heard something on the stairs."

William cast a hasty look at his wafer on the pane of glass. He thought that perhaps it had come off accidentally, and that his accomplice, conceiving that the signal was given to him, had, perchance, come over to do the deed of blood; but no, the wafer was all right as before.

"I don't hear anything, sir," said William.

"Nor I, now. Perhaps it was all imagination after all. Fill your glass, William; I know this is prime wine, and I will for once in a way give you a toast."

"Thank you, sir, I shall drink it with peculiar pleasure, I'm sure; and I am truly obliged for all favours, past and present, sir."

"Oh, don't mention them. Fill—fill, William."

William filled his glass, and then Duval, raising his voice, said, "I give you, William, the——. Ah, what is that I hear again—an odd noise on the staircase?"

"Confound it," said William, springing up half wild at the delay. "Confound it; I will soon see what it is, sir. if it be anything at all. Perhaps it is only some infernal cat or dog. I will be back in one moment, sir, if you please."

"Do so."

William passed through the outer room, and opened the door leading to the staircase. He was not gone for half a minute; but during that half minute Duval *changed the glasses*, giving to William the one that had had the two limpid drops of something mysterious at the bottom of it, and taking the other, which he had no doubt was perfectly pure, to himself.

The moment he had made this exchange he went rapidly after William; so that the perfidious valet thought he had been followed instanter. Of course nothing was seen upon the stairs, and William said—"What was the sound like, sir?"

"It sounded to me more like some person trying to come very softly up the stairs with creaking boots on, than anything else. William."

"It's very odd, sir; for not only did I hear nothing of it, but I am quite certain that there is no one on the staircase."

"Well—well, it is no matter; I don't see why I should all of a sudden be so nervous and so fidgetty. Let us come and take our wine, William, and dismiss it from our minds."

"Yes, sir, that is, indeed, the best way. I am quite anxious, sir, to hear that toast you were kind enough to propose giving. Will you be so kind, sir, as to let me know it?"

"Certainly," said Duval; "but let me remark that it is a toast that must be drank with a full bumper, and without any reservation. You must drain your glass."

"Trust me, sir."

"DIAMOND CUT DIAMOND."—THE BANKER AND CLAUDE.

They both sat down to the table, and Duval raised his glass—the one that he felt quite sure now it was safe to drink out of—to his lips, while William took the drugged portion to himself, and looked, or effected to look, as pleased as possible.

"May we all meet with our deserts!" cried Duval, and then he tossed off his glass of madeira. William did the same.

"It's rather an odd toast, sir," said William, his eyes sparkling with triumph; for now, in his own mind, he felt certain that his master had taken the drugged wine. "It's rather an odd toast, sir, don't you think?"

"Why?"

"Why, because really if we all had our deserts, we should some of us be poorly enough off."

"Do you think so, William?"

"I am sure of it, sir. Now you, sir, might be hung some of these odd fine mornings, you know."

William was getting bold and impertinent, for well he knew that in the course of five minutes or so the powerful narcotic must begin its drowsy work.

"You really think so?"

"In faith I do, sir."

"And yet how much worse than I there are in this world, William. Just fancy now, some cringing hound, who has been feasted, and petted, and made much of by a generous master, suddenly turning upon him and betraying him, merely for filthy lucre. Oh, William, are you such a hound?"

"I, sir?"

"Yes; if you are, down upon your knees and confess at once. Confess that you had some abominable plan against my very life. Nay, move your hands towards your breast an inch, and I will blow your brains out as you there sit. I make no doubt but that you have a weapon concealed about you. Stir an inch, I say, and you are a dead man."

William sat and trembled.

"I say confess!" cried Duval. "Confess!"

"I have—nothing—to confess. You are mad or dreaming, sir. What have I done? Nothing—absolutely nothing."

"Granted, William; but by this time you would have done something, if I had not taking the opportunity of changing the glasses, while you went to see what it was made the imaginary noise upon the stairs."

It was quite a sight to see the expression of William's face as Duval made this, to him, terrible revelation. Horror was depicted upon every line of his features. He made an attempt to rise from his chair, but the time had arrived for the powerful narcotic to begin its work, and his enfeebled limbs refused him support. He fell back again with a deep groan.

Feebly—very feebly only, he gasped—

"Mercy—mercy."

"Yes," said Duval, "such mercy as you intended for me, William, will I show to you. No man can complain of having anything meted out to him is his own measure."

William's head sunk upon his throat. He was fast emerging into a state of absolute insensibility, and if Duval had not risen and clutched him by the throat he would have fallen to the ground.

"Vile traitor," said Duval, "I will not take your life, but into the snare you and your associate have laid for my destruction, shall you and he both fall."

Duval hastily stripped off the embroidered dressing-gown that he himself wore, and wrapped it sufficiently about the now insensible form of William, whom he then placed upon the couch where he had himself been sitting. He propped the arch traitor up, so that he might he fairly seen from the door of the room, and then he crept to the window, and taking care that nothing but his hand was visible during the operation, he at once removed the wafer, which had been for so long a signal upon one of the panes of glass.

That done, he left the rooms, and letting all the doors be open behind him, he ascended a few of the stairs leading to the second floor, until he got to a dark corner, and then he waited the result of his arrangements.

Duval was not kept long in suspense, for in a very few minutes he heard the street door open and shut, and then the footstep of a man upon the stairs came plainly upon his ears. He had the advantage of looking down from the dark corner in which he was on the much lighter staircase below, and he saw William's associate coming stealthily on.

The fellow seemed as though at every step he expected to meet with William, and by the time he got to the top of the stairs, he said—

"Hist! Hist! Where are you."

"Here," said Duval in an assumed voice. "It's all right. Shoot him—shoot him. He sleeps, and all the doors are open."

"I'll do it."

"Quick—quick."

The man drew from his pocket a pistol with a long bright barrel, and then boldy entered Claude Duval's apartments, with the full belief that he had it in his power to take the life of the man for whom so handsome a reward was offered.

Owing to Duval having spoken in a whisper, the fellow had been completely taken in, and had thought that to be sure it could be no other than his vile associate William who had addressed him.

CHAPTER XLVII.

THE ADVENTURES OF A LONG NIGHT IN LONDON.

Duval quickly waited the result.

Bang went a pistol, and in another moment, with a face as pale as death itself, William's associate came out of Duval's apartments.

"I have done it—I have done it."

"What have you done?" said Duval suddenly, at one leap clearing the half-dozen stairs between him and the villain, and alighting close to his feet. "What have you done?"

The fellow's hair stiffened on his head, for he knew Duval by sight, and there was no room for the intrusion of a doubt but that Claude actually stood before him, while only a brief minute since, he thought, he had seen him, half-sitting, half-reclining helplessly upon a couch, and had shot him there and then dead !

"What have you done?" added Duval, as he took a firm clutch of the assassin by the collar.

The man could not speak. He only glared at Duval, and went back until the balustrades of the staircase prevented him going any further; and then Duval by one effort cast him over, and he fell a height of twenty feet to the marble-paved hall beneath.

Duval looked over, and saw him lying without sense or motion. So he at once went into his own room again, closing the door after him as he proceeded. Upon the couch was the dead body of William. The bullet from the pistol of his accomplice in crime had struck him in the face, and had gone right through his head. His death must have been instantaneous.

"An easier exit than you deserved," said Duval, as he looked at the body; "but no matter, you have met the fate you deserved, poor fool; and now these rooms are no more for me."

In the course of the next quarter of an hour, Duval had got about him all his papers and little things, chiefly arms and trinkets, which he had any regard for; and then throwing a large cloak over his shoulders, he cast one more glance around him upon the room he was not likely ever to see again.

"Farewell," he said; "I have passed some pleasant hours here, and in good truth, I did not think that my leaving would be such a one as this. Fare-well."

He closed all the doors after him, and locked them up; and then he composedly walked down the stairs. In the hall there was a crowd of people round the dead body of William's friend, whose skull had been shockingly fractured against the marble flooring. Duval, as he was passing out, was stopped by a man, who said—

"There's been a murder here, sir."

"Well, my friend, what then ?"

"Oh, I beg your pardon, sir, I only thought you might like to know about it, sir, as you come from up-stairs, that's all, sir."

"Not at all," said Duval. "It's no affair of mine."

He left the house quite composedly, and was soon in the busy bustle of the Strand ; but as he walked along, very serious thoughts came over him indeed, and it was not very often that serious thoughts and Claude Duval ever associated much together ; but upon this occasion they did.

"What," he said, to himself, "what would have become now of poor Adele, if by the rarest accident in the world, I had not found out the murderous and diabolical intentions of William ? She, poor girl, would have been left entirely destitute among strangers, and I tremble to reflect upon what her fate might have been."

There was abundance of truth in this mental speech of Duval's. If he had been murdered, the situation of Adele would indeed have been most pitiable, and the more Duval thought of it, the more horrified he got.

Now it so happened, that about a year before this time, Duval, having been very successful on the road, had had a sum of £500 to spare, which, with the idea that some day it might be most peculiarly useful for him either to bribe his way out of prison or for some other highly pratical purpose, he had deposited in the hands of a banker in Clement's Lane in the City, giving the name of Smith as he did so. And now as he neared Temple Bar, he thought that if he were to give that sum into the hands of Adele, it would be a something for her to fall back upon, in case any untoward accident should suddenly deprive her of his protection, and, in his profession, such a thing might happen at any time, and if it happened at all, would most likely be when the least expected.

Duval was, as the reader has found, very much a creature of impulse, and all this had scarcely flitted through his mind when it was decided upon, and at a rapid pace he was making his way towards the banking-house in Clement's Lane, where his money was.

The streets of London were not then near so much crowded as they are now, so Duval got on up Ludgate-hill, through St. Paul's Church-yard, and so on by Cheapside and the Poultry, to the place of his destination without much hinderance or difficulty, and at length dived into the dingy banking-house, where, summer and winter, candles had always to be kept burning.

The clerks looked dim and faded by the spectral light, and the few people who stood by the counter, looked like anything but beings of flesh and blood.

"Oblige me with a blank cheque," said Duval to a bald-headed old man, who had glared at him for some seconds without speaking.

"Have you an account with our house, sir ?" said the old man.

"Yes, my name is Julius Smith, and I have an account with your house."

"Oh very good, very good, Sir Julius—Smith—hum—ah. Oh yes—I see. We have not had the pleasure of seeing you for some time, Mr. Julius Smith, I think, if I may presume to say as much.—Hum—ah !"

"You had better take a good look at me now then," said Duval, "for it may be as long again before you have the pleasure of seeing me here."

"Hum! Ah! I will bring you the blank cheque in a moment, sir, if you please. Mr. Julius—Smith. Hum—ah ! In a moment."

Duval thought that this reception at a banking-house was rather a strange one ; but he waited patiently for the return of the old clerk, who, in a few moments, came hobbling back, and said in a soft oily tone—

"Will you be so good, Mr. Smith, as to step this way ?"

"Certainly," said Claude Duval. "Any way you like, so that you transact my business for me as quickly as possible, for I have no time, sir, to lose."

" Oh, sir, there will be no delay, only Mr. Stubbs, our principal partner, wishes to speak to you for a few moments, that is all, Mr. Smith."

Duval followed the old bald-headed clerk through the intricacies of a number of desks, and then through a half-glass door, and then through one covered with green baize, and so into a dingy-looking room, where, with a multitude of books before him, sat Mr. Stubbs, the senior partner of the banking-house.

" Mr. Julius Smith," announced the old clerk, and then he left Duval alone with Mr. Stubbs, who was a florid, insolent-looking man, of about fifty years of age, with a very odd crop of wiry-looking hair standing up quite on end, like the bristles on the back-bone of a pig, and something of that colour too.

" Well, Mr. Smith ?" said the banker, putting his pen behind his ear.

" Well, Mr. Stubbs ?" said Duval, reaching imself a chair, and sitting on it.

" I believe, Mr. Smith, you left with our firm a considerable time since the sum of five hundred pounds sterling ? That is correct I presume, Mr. Smith ?"

" It is correct ; and no one ought to know that better than you, sir. I have now come to take it away again, and will give you a cheque for the amount."

" Not so fast, sir—not so fast. I am a man of business, Mr. Smith, and I strongly suspect that five hundred pounds was not honestly come by ; and until you give us a reference or two as regards your respectability, we shall not pay it again."

" Indeed ?"

" Yes, sir, indeed. So you can do your worst or your best, Mr. Smith. I am not a man to be trifled with, or bullied. Oh, no—no! How do I know but there may be some very peculiar circumstances connected with— Hilloa ! what are you about, sir ?—what are you about ? I will call a constable, sir."

Duval had risen, and very calmly locked the door of the room ; and then, advancing to Mr. Stubbs, he took a pistol from his pocket and said—

" Sir, if you make the slightest disturbance, I will blow out your brains with more satisfaction than I would those of some mad dog !"

The bristly hair of the banker actually moved upon his head, and his face turned of a blue colour, as he shrank back in his chair in a perfect paroxysm of fright—so much so, that he could not speak a word.

" Now, sir," said Duval, " understand me. I am this day going to commit suicide. Do you hear me, sir ?—Su-i-cide !"

" Ye—s."

" Very, well, sir ; since you refuse me my money, I will go into the other world arm-in-arm with you."

" With me? Oh, don't !"

" Yes, sir, with you. I will here, in your own private room, blow your brains out with one barrel of this pistol, and my own with the other. It can, you see, make no difference to me, although it may possibly make just a little to you."

" A little ?" gasped the banker. " Oh, it makes a great deal—it does, indeed, my dear sir."

" Well, you may save yourself."

" May I—oh, may I, indeed, sir ?"

" Yes, easily. Before I take leave of this world, I want to hand some money to a friend, and that was why I came for my five hundred pounds. Now as you have given me some trouble, I will have interest for my money. Give me a blank cheque, and I will draw for a thousand pounds ; come with me to the counter and tell them to pay it ; and then you shall only walk with me a little way, after which I will let you go."

" A thousand pounds? Oh, dear—oh, dear ! Cent per cent !"

" Exactly. Do you refuse ? Because———"

" Oh, no—no ! There is the blank cheque—there it is !"

" Very good," said Duval, as the terrified banker gave him a blank cheque from his drawer ; " very good, sir."

He then filled it up for the sum of one thousand pounds, after which he rose and said—

"Now, Mr. Stubbs, you and I will go out together; and if you attempt to leave my side, or by word, or look, or gesture to give any alarm or indication that you are in a coerced condition, that moment shall be your last. I am a man to keep my word. My name is not Smith. Take your hat, sir; we shall have to go out of doors together."

"Will you tell me who you really are?" said the terrified banker.

"Oh, yes, I have no objection. They call me Claude Duval!"

"Then my money is gone," said Stubbs, wringing his hands; "then I feel now that my money is gone. I shall never see it again."

"You are right; you never will; and take this to your heart, if you have got one, that you pay this day five hundred pounds for your own insolence and folly. Of course you thought me some one who upon the least hint of anything wrong, would be glad to get away, and leave you the money; but you have mistaken your man."

If the banker had such an idea, and there can be very little doubt but that he had, he certainly mistook his man, for certainly Duval was just the very last person in all the world to be so intimidated.

The banker's face assumed the most lugubrious expression that was possible conceive.

"You—you—will take," he said, "your own five hundred pounds, and let this be an end of the transaction."

"Certainly not. Not one penny-piece less than a one thousand pounds now. You will pay the extra five hundred pounds for the little pleasantry of the last quarter of an hour; so now you had better come out with me, and put as good a face on the matter as possible. I know if I am taken that death is my lot, and before I go to the other world, I am quite resolved to send you there."

The banker groaned and followed, or rather went ahead of Duval into the open part of the premises.

CHAPTER XLVIII.

MR. FINCH IS AT HOME.—THE ESCAPE BY THE ROOF.—AN ODD ADVENTURE.

THE clerks bowed and smiled as their principal passed them.

"Tell them to pay the cheque," said Duval, in a whisper.

"Thompson," said the banker, "pay this gentleman's cheque at once, if you please."

"Yes, sir," said Thompson, with a smirking alacrity that made the banker mentally resolve upon his discharge. "Yes, sir. How would you like it, Mr. Smith—notes or gold, sir?"

"Notes will do."

"Thank you, sir. One thousand. That is right, Mr. Smith, I believe. A very nice day, sir."

"Mr. Smith and I will soon be back, if any one asks for me," said the banker, in much about the tone of voice that any one would be supposed to use if he were bidding good bye to the Revd. Ordinary in front of Newgate, previous to being turned off. Claude Duval easily put the notes in his pocket, and taking the arm of the banker, out they sallied into the open street. Claude stuck to him like a leech.

"Beware," he said. "The least attempt to escape, or to give the least alarm, and you are a dead man."

The banker groaned.

"I will not take you far from your business," added Claude. "Indeed, I will not take you one step farther then is consistent with my own safety. Why do you shake in that way?"

"My money. My five hundred pounds! All at one swoop. In a morning. Oh, my money! It will kill me."

"Oh, nonsense. Don't you believe it, sir. It will do no such thing. You can very well afford it, and it will be a useful lesson to you not to attempt to cheat anybody again unless you thoroughly know your man. There's no saying how much the experience of to-day may really and truly be the means of saving you."

"You are only joking. You will give me back my own?"

"You may as well ask me for my eye-balls. This way, sir, if you please. This way. How mild the weather is to be sure. Is it not mild, sir? Come, sir, is it not mild?"

"Oh, very, damn it!"

"Sir, I am surprised at you. I really wonder that a man of business cannot keep his temper."

"But who in the name of all that's abomiable could keep his temper when he was being robbed of five hundred pounds?"

"Robbed, my good sir? Robbed? Really I never in all my life heard a term so misapplied. You embarked in a speculation, in the speculation of frightening me, by which you thought to get a sum of five hundred pounds; but luck was against you, and you lost that amount."

The banker groaned, and while he was so groaning, Duval looked about him for some mode of disposing of himself. He had no wish to be encumberd by his company for a longer time than was necessary under the circumstances. A rather large gloomy-looking private house was close at hand, and Duval, with his characteristic decision, at once pitched upon it as the assistant he wanted to get rid of the banker, and he approached the house, still taking care that the banker did not give him the slip, for a race through the city after him would have been anything but an agreeable thing; and then he knocked smartly at the door.

"Are you going in here?" said the wretched man of money.

"No, I am only going to make a call and leave something."

"Then you will let me go now?"

"In a moment or two I will."

The door of the house was opened by an extremely corpulent red-faced girl, upon whose head was some prodigious head-dress, that, like Joseph's coat, was "of many colours." There was a look upon her face of wild indignation at the sort of startling knock that Duval had given at the door, and the moment she got it open, she likewise opened her mouth to commence a volley of expletives, but Duval was too prompt for her.

"Here he is, my dear madam," cried Duval. "Make much of him, I beg of you."

With these words in his mouth, Duval gave the banker such a tremendous push into the passage, that encountering the rather corpulent female, over she went, and the unhappy man above her, and they both rolled, and kicked, and scratched, and fought in the passage, while Duval deliberately slammed the street-door, and at a rapid pace sped from the spot.

He was far enough away before anything in the shape of explanation could be entered into between the banker and the lady.

"This is not a very bad day's work," said Duval; "and now for Mrs. Finch. Her address is in my memory; and that it is somewhere hereabouts, I am quite certain."

He had no difficulty in finding the address that Mrs. Finch had given him, when she said that she resided now alone, as her husband had left her, and upon inquiring for her, Duval was shown into rather a handsome room, which showed that however Mr. Finch might have deprived her of his sweet company, she was by no means without some sort of resources with which to carry on the war with society. Of course, Claude Duval announced himself as Count Stofet, and by the servant, who showed him the way up stairs, he was treated with a wonderful amount of respect in consequence. After he had waited for a few minutes, Mrs.

Finch made her appearance, rather elegantly attired in a morning dress of the current fashion.

"Oh, sir," she said, "is it really you?"

"Look again, my dear madam, and convince yourself," said Duval; "but I too plainly see that you are unhappy; your eyes look red with weeping. Has Finch been here?"

"Ah, no. But yet, how, under my distressful circumstances, can I be otherwise than unhappy?"

"Nay, my dear Mrs. Finch——"

"Oh, do not call me by that odious name."

"My dear Maria, then, I should say, how can you be otherwise than happy while you have the three blessings?"

"Three blessings?"

"Yes, youth, and health, and beauty."

"Ah, sir, you are a flatterer, you are indeed. But oh! tell me, as you are a true friend, what I ought to do. I shall never be happy with Finch. My heart tells me that you love me. To live with one who really loves is a great satisfaction. What ought I to do?"

"Why, as Finch has thought proper to abandon you, my dear Maria, what can you do but turn to him whom Providence has sent to comfort you? and that I am that person your own heart truly tells you. Forget that such a person as the odious Finch ever existed; and you and I, in our affection for each other, will defy the world. You are very comfortable to all appearance here, and I will call upon you as often as I possibly can."

"You will, indeed?"

"Indeed will I."

Mrs. Finch, with a deep sigh, sunk into the arms of Duval, and then the door opened, and the servant flew in, crying——

"Oh! Mum! Mum! Here's Mr. Finch at the door, mum!"

With a scream, Mrs. Finch started from the embrace of Duval, and he, with an emphasis that he seldom troubled himself to use, said—

"D—n Mr. Finch!"

"Oh, hide yourself. Hide yourself," cried Maria.

"But where? Confound it, where am I to hide? I'd much rather, if you will allow me, kick him down stairs, or throw him out at the window. Pray do not disturb yourself, I will do either in a moment."

"Oh, no—no. If you really have the shadow of a regard for me, I pray you not to let him see you. Oh, sir, let me, if possible, while I may, keep up the semblance of virtue, if I have it not. I implore you, sir, to hide yourself."

"As you please. I will do your bidding. So adjured, I cannot refuse to do so. Where shall I hide? Only tell me where and I will do so. I pray you dispose of me as you like."

"Here—here. This way. Come, I pray you."

Duval followed her into an inner room, and frantically opening a large cupboard, Mrs. Finch pushed him in, and closed and locked the door upon him, leaving him so cramped up that it was with the greatest difficulty he could breathe, for the space between a shelf and the door was about an inch or two too narrow to hold him. He, however, by a violent twist of his arms, succeeded in turning round, and then he knocked the shelf down pretty easily, and had plenty of room in the cupboard, so that without any sensations of bodily pain, he could listen to what was going forward in the room adjoining.

For a time all was quiet enough, for the servant took good care not to let Mr. Finch in until she was sure her mistress had disposed of Duval, and then Mr. Finch was permitted to ascend the stairs. He walked into the room adjoining that in which Claude was in the cupboard, and in a high constrained tone of voice, he said—

"Maria, I have come to say that I have no more suspicions of you, and that while we both live, I hope that we shall live quietly and comfortably together.

Human life is so very uncertain, that I do think, Maria, we ought to pass the remainder of our days together."

Mrs. Finch was thunderstricken, as well she might be, by this speech from her husband. It was so essentially different from anything he was in the ordinary habit of saying, that she could only glare at him with astonishment and dismay.

CLAUDE AND MRS. FINCH SURPRISED BY THE SERVANT.

" Yes," added Finch, " I am satisfied."

" What—do—you—mean ?"

" I mean, Maria, what I say. That I am satisfied, and I am now going to live here contentedly, while I can. You cannot be sorry at the idea, that, from this time, you will hear no more of my suspicions or of my jealousies. I am quite an altered man now,—oh quite,—quite. Time was, when I should have been ferocious, but that time has passed away."

"I am—very glad."

"You look very glad—very glad indeed."

"Yes—Oh yes. Well, you have found that you have nothing at all to be jealous about?"

"Nothing whatever, and as the day is advanced, I shall not go out any more, now, but stay here and enjoy myself in your society."

"You—you will?"

"I will, Maria. Unless you have any particular objection, in which case, I don't know what I might think. Have you any objection? Speak; have you, I say?"

"Oh no—no—no."

"That is well. I began to fear that you had. That is well, quite well.—The day is near its close. Let us have some wine—some wine that makes people's hearts glad. Ha! ha! some bright generous wine."

Mrs. Finch glared at her husband with feelings that, as the novelists' say, may be better imagined than described, for she had not now the remotest doubt in the world but that he was mad. The difference in his style and manner, was too great to be accounted for upon any other principle; so she did not for one moment attempt to get him to go away, as she considered that such an attempt would in all probability produce such a paroxysm of his disorder, as might terminate in something very fatal to her, and probably to himself likewise.

Mrs. Finch was a weak woman, not a bad one, and she did not wish any further harm to come to her husband than might result from her own unfaithfulness to him.

"Be calm," she said. "You shall have wine."

"Calm?" he said. "Did you say calm? I never was so calm in all my life! Don't you see how very calm I am?"

"Oh, yes—yes."

She found that contradiction only made him furious, so she wisely now abstained, from anything of the sort. Once she made a sort of pretence to leave the room, by saying—

"I will order the glasses, and take care that you have them nicely polished, which I know you are rather particular in," but he started up with fury in his looks, and cried—

"Do you want to leave me?"

"Oh, no—no," she said, "I only——"

"Then only sit down. I am quite calm—amazingly calm; and I have got rid of all my suspicions!"

He placed such a marked emphasis upon the word suspicions, that Mrs. Finch could not but think he meant more than he said. By getting rid of his suspicions a man might mean that he had converted them into certainties; so that upon the whole, Mrs. Finch did not feel quite so happy as she expected to be, as that day declined. If by any means she could have liberated Duval she would have felt much easier in her own mind, but as the only exit from the room in which he was happened to be through that in which Finch sat, she could not attempt it on any account.

The house in which they were was a very old one indeed, and had been built in a curious and capricious fashion, most likely from generation to generation, as new rooms were required in it. Mrs. Finch occupied three apartments, that is to say, the front room in which she and her husband now sat—the back one in which was Duval, and a bedroom above it, which was reached by a little spiral flight of steps in one corner of it. There was no other outlet from the bedroom, unless any one chose to get out at a trap-door which was in its roof, and so on to the roofs of the neighbouring houses, which might be gained by a jump over a fearful chasm about eight feet in width.

But it must be borne in mind that of all this architectural blundering, Claude Duval was quite ignorant. He only fancied himself in a back room on the first floor, and that, of course, he should find a door opening from it on to the landing.

By a very slight exertion of strength, although certainly it might have been attended with much more noise than under the circumstances it would have been at all prudent to make, and then he fancied he could have made his escape ; but he had a hope that Mr. Finch would leave, notwithstanding he heard his conversation tolerably distinctly.

CHAPTER XLIX.

THE FEARFUL NIGHT AT MRS. FINCH'S LODGINGS.

THE sound of Mr. Finch's voice latterly had been rather passionate, and Duval, with his ear placed against the panel of the cupboard door, did not miss one word of it.

" Confound the fellow," he thought, " I wish I could think of any mode of frightening him away without compromising Mrs. Finch at all, I would put it into practice."

This was easier to be wished than to be carried out, and after racking his imagination, Duval found that there was nothing for it but patience, and that he must, like other people, await his opportunity instead of trying to create it.

The wine was brought to Finch, and his wife had a hope that he would soon drink enough of it to confuse his faculties, and probably fall asleep, but although he took, with great rapidity, about six glasses, they seemed to have no more effect upon him than as if he had taken so much water. Had Mrs Finch been more versed than she was in the eccentricities of human nature, she would have suspected from that very circumstance of the wine not having its usual effect upon him, that something of an all-engrossing character was weighing heavily upon his spirits ; but she had not information sufficient to enable her to reason in such a way, and she could only wonder at a phenomenon that she in her limited experience could not account for in any way.

" More wine," said Finch, " more wine, Maria. Why don't you drink ?"

" I have taken one glass."

" One glass ? What is one glass ?—Nothing at all.—Take another. Who knows how long we may live ? The term of life is short at the longest, and while we do live, we ought to enjoy ourselves the best way in our power. Drink, I say, drink."

She tremblingly took another glass, and then laying her hand on his arm, she said, rather to hear what he would say, than with any hope of gathering safety from his words—

" And you have banished all your suspicions, then ?"

" All, all. Every one of them. Every one of them, I say. What have I to do with suspicions now ?"

" What do you mean by *now* ?"

" I mean the present time, Maria. I repeat that suspicions are odious, and that I have done with them. They are all gone. I have passed them. But drink. Why don't you drink ? Don't you recollect that I used to say I should be hanged for you ?"

" You did."

" Ha ! ha ! It was a droll thought, was it not ? What strange things we say in our rage at times, do we not ? Very strange things. The idea of my being hanged for you ! Why that could only happen in the case of one circumstance, namely, my murdering you. That is the only way it could happen."

" What the deuce," thought Duval, " has this stupid fellow got in his muddle brains now ?"

" But you have now no such thoughts ?" said Mrs. Finch.

" Certainly not. How truly absurd it would be of me to say I had any such thoughts. I am weary. We will retire early to-night, Maria. I have not had a long night's sleep for many a night. I say, we will retire early, Maria."

"As you please. I will just see if the bed-room is right, and then, when I return, I will have another glass of wine——"

"No—no.—I say no."

"What, must I have no more wine? Do you think I have had enough then, or too much perhaps? Well—well."

Mrs. Finch tried to speak in a jocular tone, but she very much belied her heart in doing so, and Finch sternly replied to her—

"You may have what wine you please, Maria, and as much as you please, but you do not leave this room until you and I go together to our chamber. Do you understand that?"

"I hear, sir, but I will not be dictated to in such a manner; I will not be made to drink or not to drink, to stay or to go, like a child."

"You will not?"

"I will not. It is time that this farce should end. If you are out of your mind, which I thoroughly believe you are, I will for your own sake, as well as for mine, summon the people of the house. I will go and come at my pleasure, Mr. Finch."

"Bravo!" thought Claude.

Finch was staggered, and for a few moments he did not speak. Then, suddenly, with a strange wild hilarity of manner, he cried—

"Go—go. Ha! ha!—Go at once, Mrs. Finch, go at once. I will sit here. There is no other outlet from the rooms, I know. Go, Mrs. Finch, go. But do not deprive me long of your admirable company. Ha! ha! I have no suspicions now—no suspicions; I am quite a happy thriving sort of husband with no suspicions. Ha! ha! ha! All is right. Go, Mrs. Finch, go."

This conduct upon the part of Finch was still more perplexing than before; but Mrs. Finch availed herself of the opportunity to go into the next room where Claude Duval was in the cupboard, and she took good care to close the door of communication between the two apartments.

She approached the cupboard.

"Hist! hist! It is I—it is I. Do you not hear me!"

"Yes; but I can't get out."

"Oh, I had forgotten. Here is the key. Oh, what will become of me? Have you heard anything?"

She unlocked the cupboard-door, and Duval stepped out into the room.

"I have heard all," he said.

"All—all?"

"Yes, every word that Finch has said; and do you know, Maria, I think him in the most dangerous mood he has ever been in yet. I will not leave you while he is in the house. When such a man alters so completely, you may depend upon it that he means mischief."

"You make me tremble."

"Be under no alarm. I will remain here. Give me the key of the cupboard. I will lock it on the inside, and so if he should take it into his head to come to it, I shall be safe, at the safe time that I can get out at any time I please. Give me the key. Quick!"

"Oh, Heaven—what will happen?"

"Maria, are you coming?" roared Finch, from the next room. "Where are you, Maria?—Are you coming?"

"Yes—yes. Instantly."

"Go to him," said Duval. "You owe the poor devil as much countenance as you can give him. Go to him, Maria, and depend upon my continued presence here to protect you; and I am but an indifferent judge of human nature, and a bad prophet, if you will not need my protection. How dark it gets."

"It is late."

"Maria, I say! Where the deuce are you, Maria?"

"I come—I come. Farewell."

"Fear nothing," whispered Duval, "I will be near to you. Fear nothing, now, Maria. Go to him at once. Go—go."

Duval kissed her cheek, and then she went into the front room. Claude kept the cupboard ready open so that he could pop into it in a moment and lock it on the inside; but he was by far too anxious to listen to what might pass in the front room, to get into the cupboard before there was any obvious necessity for it.

"What were you about?" cried Finch. "But no matter—no matter; life is so very short. Drink—drink, I say."

"Only one glass more."

"As you please—as you please, Maria. What do you think there is beyond the grave? Have you any serious belief that way?"

"Surely, yes, there is another world, and there is a God."

The head of Finch sunk upon his breast for a few moments, and he was silent; then in a low strange voice he said—

"Murder!"

"What say you?" cried his wife. What do you mean?"

"Say—mean?—I said nothing."

"You did, indeed. You said, murder!"

"I say murder? No, no. That is all imagination. Only a day-dream. Why should I say murder? Oh, no—no.—We will go to bed early, and have a long night's sleep. Oh, how I want a long night's sleep. My eyes have not closed for a long time. My heart and soul are weary. More wine. Let us have some more wine. Ring for more, Maria. Ring."

More wine was brought by the servant, and still Finch drank of it, and still it had no effect upon him. He was dead to all such ordinary impulses. Possibly it might have added a something to the insane feeling that had thoroughly taken possession of him, for if ever any man was mad, Finch was at that time; but as regarded the production of intoxication it was lost, if loss it was for any man, under any circumstances at all, to avoid such a degradation.

Lights were brought along with the second bottle of wine, and then Finch got rather gloomy, and at times he would sit with his head resting upon his hands, and then he would start up and pace the room with disordered strides, muttering to himself; and once he caught up his hat, and Mrs. Finch with quite a gush of satisfaction thought that he was going.

"Oh, if I could only leave you," he said.

"And why not?"

"I have no reason. Let it only suffice, that I cannot, that is all. I cannot, no—no, I must stay. It is my fate, and it is your fate. I must stay."

"I do not understand you. If you will stay, you will stay; but if you choose to go there is nothing to prevent you that I can see, and I am sure any explanation that you think we ought to have, will be much better had in the morning than now."

"Explanations in the morning!" gasped Finch. "Oh yes, there will surely be some explanations in the morning."

"You are full of riddles. You seem to have a something on your mind to say, and yet you never say it. Why is that?"

"I know not. Drink more wine—oh, if I could only induce you to drink more wine. Come, another glass—only another."

As his face began to assume a threatening aspect again, Mrs. Finch did not think it quite prudent to refuse the proffered glass, and she sipped its contents.

All that we have related had taken a much longer time in the passing, than it has taken us to tell. There are some actions of the human mind occupying hours, that can be told in a few words, so that the reader will not be surprised that a clock in the hall of the house suddenly struck the hour of eleven. Finch sprang to his feet.

"To bed! to bed!" he cried. "It is more than time. Come, Maria, we will to bed, and, as you say, there will be explanations required in the morning. We will now to bed."

"So soon ?"

"Soon ? It is not soon. No—no, it is late—very late. What is there in all the world worth keeping awake for, that any one should care to keep from sleep ? Let us drink some more wine, and then to bed—to bed. You look as though you had a dread of something horrible upon your mind, Maria."

"What should I dread ?"

"Ay, what ; and so we will go to bed dreading nothing. Come—come. I wonder what the matter will be to-morrow ?"

"Why do you say that ?"

"But it won't matter, one jot to—but, come, come ; I am in good truth very weary. What a fool I was to say I should be ever hanged for you, Maria. But that was when I only suspected."

He suddenly sprang to the only door of egress from the small suit of rooms, and locked it. In another moment he caught up both the candles, and still kept crying—

"To bed—to bed !"

Mrs. Finch humoured him, so she followed him through the back room, up the little corkscrew of a staircase that led into the bed-room above. Duval heard them go, and as the light disappeared, he opened the cupboard-door, and stepped out on the soft carpetting of the room.

"What on earth," he said to himself, "does that idiot of a Finch mean ? I never faced a man so altered in all my life. He must be thoroughly and completely mad. I have a sort of dread of something, I know not what, tugging at my heart. What can be the meaning of it ? Well—well, I will stay here and be within call in case anything should really happen, and in the meantime, if a glass or two of wine should happen to be left in the next room, I don't see or know anything in the world to prevent me making free with it."

Duval trod very lightly, but he went into the next room and helped himself to the wine that was upon the table. On a sideboard, too, in the room he found some fruit and some biscuits, so that after all, he found a very tolerable supper, if it were not exactly the one he would have chosen.

All this took him up some time, and by the time he had finished off the wine, the clock on the staircase struck twelve. Duval counted the strokes, and as the last two or three sounded in the silence of the house, he thought he heard a strange noise. He listened very attentively, and then fancied it must be rain upon the window panes, for the night had set in a very wet one ; but after a few moments more listening, he felt satisfied that that did not sufficiently account for the noise, which was like some one moaning from afar off.

The door between the room that he was in and the back one had swung shut, but now he hastened to open it.

CHAPTER L.

THE MURDER AND THE DEATH OF THE MURDERER.

ONE of those strange presentiments of evil, which have at times, when probably least expected, attacked the best and the strongest of us, now came over Claude Duval, and if one man more than another had been picked out from the whole population of London as less likely than his fellows to be the slave of such fancies, that would surely have been our hero ; but now he gave way more than he had ever done to a superstitious feeling.

We have mentioned that the door of connexion between the two rooms had of its own accord swung shut, but now Duval had his hand upon the lock, and he flung it open, and entered the back room.

The moment Duval got there, the odd noise which came upon his ears in the other room so very faintly and indistinctly that he was at liberty to mistake it for any other sound he liked, could no longer be mistaken for anything but what it really was, namely, the moaning of some one in great mental and bodily pain.

The sound, too, localised itself more than it had done before, and he was able to tell himself that, without a doubt, it came from the room above.

The reader has seen and heard enough of Duval to feel assured that he was not a man to shrink back, when anything in the shape of energetic action was required, and now with a bound he reached the little corkscrew-like staircase that led up to the sleeping-chamber of Mr. and Mrs. Finch, and ascended it at a pace that soon brought him to the door of the room. It was fast.

Duval knocked sharply.

"Oh—mercy!" he heard a voice say, from within, and then something sounded like a heavy fall.

He knocked again.

"Who is there?" said a voice.

"Open the door, or I will knock it in," said Duval.

"Wait—wait," said the voice again.

Duval did wait while it would just have been possible for anyone to approach the door from the other end of the room, and open it, but no longer. When that brief period had elapsed, he felt pretty sure that there was no intention to let him in, so placing his knee against the door, and his shoulder to the upper part of it, he, by one vigorous and muscular exertion, smashed it in. It took yet another push before he could make a sufficient opening for himself to pass through, and then he did so with an expedition that brought him at once into the middle of the room.

The sight that there presented itself to Duval, was one that he had little calculated upon, and one that almost for the moment unnerved even him, albeit he was unused to the melting mood. Upon the floor, just at the foot of the bed, as though she had in her last agony fallen off it, and no doubt that was the noise he had heard a moment or two before, lay the dead body of Mrs. Finch, weltering in blood! A knife, with which the fatal and unmanly deed had been committed, lay by the side of the poor victim.

For the space of time that half a minute might comprehend, Duval gazed upon the poor remains of her for whom, in his way, he had felt some amount of affection, and then with a start he glanced round him, crying—

"Where is the murderer?"

That Mrs. Finch had perished by the hand of her husband, and that jealousy had been the cause of the commission of the dreadful act, there could not be a doubt. But where was he? That was the mystery.

A candle was burning upon the dressing-table, and shedding its shadowy ray upon the scene of blood, but no Mr. Finch was to be seen. Duval hastily looked into every possible hiding-place in the room, and satisfied himself thoroughly that he was not there. It was then only by the merest accident in the world that Duval happened to look up to the ceiling, and there he saw the little trap-door which was called a fire-escape, and which communicated with the roof of the house, open wide.

Of course this was the route by which the murderer had escaped, and this equally, of course, was the route by which Duval was determined to follow him. A chair was in such a position upon the floor, that by standing upon it any one might reach the trap-door's edges with both hands, and so in a shorter space of time than we could possibly take to tell how it was done, Duval had raised himself bodily through the trap.

There was a dull, dreary, vacancy between the trap-door and the outer roof, so that Duval paused a moment to try to pierce with his eyes the obscurity of that place, lest the murderer should there have hidden himself. The outer trap, though in the actual roof, being open, was sufficiently convincing that that was not the case, and that the wretched man had sought to get right away, by that means, from the scene of his crime.

In a moment Duval was on the roof of the house. It was quite a relief to be there in the cool night air, although it did rain, after being for the short space of time even that he had been in the heated atmosphere of that bed-room, where the odour of blood was upon every mouthful of its air, and he paused a moment to draw a long breath or two of the cool, damp, atmosphere. He did not lose any time by so pausing, for while he did so, his eyes were getting accustomed to the night air and the dim light that it carried with it.

Then at each moment he found he could see clearer, many objects appeared to come out of the darkness, and to make themselves visible to him. Chimney-stacks—gable ends of old houses—quaint old water-spouts, all came out of the darkness and presented themselves to him; and then at some distance off, close to a parapet, beyond which was the deep chasm we have noticed between two houses, separated from each other by a space which upon level ground any one could jump easily, but which at that giddy eminence, from relative circumstances, something fearful, Duval thought he saw something crouching.

A dark object. Yes! He was certain something was lying in the gutter close to the parapet. He kept his eyes upon the object, and in the course of a moment or two it slowly moved. Suspicion was now converted into certainty.

"Nothing would be easier," said Duval, "than to shoot him from where I am, but I must have the rascal alive if possible, and give him up to justice for the foul and dreadful deed that he has done."

Duval did not at the moment reflect how very ticklish a thing it would be for him, circumstanced as he was, to appear as evidence against Mr. Finch. No, at the moment he forgot everything, but that a very foul murder had been committed, and that he was cognisant of the facts.

Slowly and very circumspectly, indeed, he crept along the roof towards the spot where the murderer lay crouched. Duval wanted to seize him before he could make an attempt to spring across the chasm from one house to the other, for in that neighbourhood he felt that if once he did so, he might find some means of escape, as there were houses about it where any criminal would find secrecy and comfort if he had money in his pocket, and that, probably enough, Finch had, if he had contemplated for some time his crime, and the circumstances of it seemed to point to the fact that it was a premeditated thing.

Duval did not make the slightest noise, but the murderer was glaring about him in order to debate upon the best means of escape, and just as Duval was within half-a-dozen yards of him, he saw the crawling figure coming over the house-top towards him.

On the instant, with a cry of terror, the murderer sprung to his feet in the drain close to the parapet of the house.

"Hold!" cried Duval. "Resistance is useless."

Another moment and he would have had him in his grasp, but Finch made a spring to clear the chasm between the two houses, and leaping short, he fell right down into the street beneath, disappearing from before the eyes of Claude Duval as though he had sprung down some deep well.

"Gone!" said Duval.

He heard a loud crash far below, and then all was still; crawling close to the parapet, he looked over, and strained his eyes to see into the profound depth, but all was as dark as any dungeon for a few moments. Then, however, a light flashed upon the scene from a doorway, and he saw a man appear shading a light with his hand.

"What was that?" said the man.

"I'm sure I heard something," said a female voice, "I'm quite certain I heard something," and then a woman made her appearance in the street.

At that moment the rain put out the light, and all was pitch darkness again. Nay, the gloom appeared to be much more profound than before, in consequence of its temporary dissipation by the light that for a few short moments had glanced upon surrounding objects.

"He must be dead," thought Duval.

The man then who had had the light, began to call—"Watch! Watch!" so Duval lingered to see what would ensue, and in the course of a few minutes, as the man kept up his cry for the watch, the dubious gleam of a watchman's lantern came upon the scene.

"Watch! watch!" continued the man.

Duval could hear with perfect distinctness from where he was, every word that was uttered by any one, as the sounds ascended freely.

CLAUDE ENACTS THE GHOST TO GREAT PERFECTION.

"Coming," cried the watchman.   " What is it now?"

"I don't know," said the man, "but something has happened."

"Ah," said the woman, "that it has, Mr. Watchman. Bring your lantern this way. We don't mind a glass of something nice and warm, Mr. Watchman, if you will find out what it is."

"Thank you, ma'am, it's a dirty, cold sort of a night, ma'am. Nobody knows what we goes through."

"My light went out," said the man, "but something seemed to come down from the top of that house, and I never, in all my life, heard such a crash, upon the pavement."

"We'll soon see what it is," said the watchman.

The guardian of the night then moved slowly along with his lantern close to the ground, moving it along in circles, so as to illuminate every portion of the pavement by turns, and the man and woman followed him, notwithstanding the rain, and at last they came upon the dead body of the wretched husband.

"Hilloa!" cried the watchman, "it's murder!"

"Murder!" echoed the man and the woman.

"Yes, it's blue murder, and I shall have to take everybody up. He's a dead man, as sure as a gun."

Feeling then that the matter was one of sufficient importance to warrant him in so doing, he dropped his lantern and began springing his rattle.

Duval thought that he had seen enough, and that it was time for him to provide for his own safety. Nothing would now have been easier, than for him to have gone back through the trap-door in the roof of the house into the chamber of death again, and so have made his way out of the house, but he had an insurmountable repugnance to passing through the room in which was the dead body of Mrs. Finch. He prefered running into any risks, and falling into any danger, rather than do so, and therefore he made up his mind to jump across the chasm, which Mr. Finch had lost his life in attempting.

To Duval it was one of the most ordinary feats in the world to do such a thing, and he was over in a moment, alighting fairly upon the parapet of the house opposite, which was the one from which had come the man and the woman who were still busy with the watchman.

The rattle was going still vigorously, and from far off it was being answered, and presently, like so many Will o' the wisps, watchmen, with their lanterns swinging to and fro, might have been seen hurrying to the scene.

"Enough!" said Duval. "I have seen enough of all this, and I am sickened at the night's adventures."

With this, he began to turn his whole attention to providing for his own safety, and creeping along the parapet of the house, he began to look for some window, by which he might get into one of the rooms.

He was not long in finding an attic window, but do what he would, he could not see sufficiently through it into the room, to be at all able to say if this apartment was inhabited or not, so he was forced to chance it. The rain beat in that direction, so the slight noise he made in opening the window, which to such a room was not the most elaborately fastened one, was completely smothered, and presently he got one of the little doors of the miserably latticed frame-work open. It was no easy thing to get into the room through such a small opening, but Duval made a spring through the casement, and fell upon a bed, from which somebody immediately set up a shout of dismay, and began calling out—"Murder! murder!" with all their might.

The voice was that of a woman, and Duval felt how utterly in vain it would be to say anything deprecatory of the uproar she had made, so he tried all he could to disentangle himself from among the bed clothing, and to get away.

CHAPTER LI.

DUVAL GETS INTO THE COUNTRY AGAIN AFTER SOME SERIOUS PERILS.

SUDDENLY the voice of the female, whom he (Duval) had so very unceremoniously disturbed in her bed, ceased, and he considered that no doubt she had fainted from excess of terror. He snatched from the bed what by the feel of it he felt confident was a sheet, and hastily throwing it over his head and wrapping it completely round him, leaving only the smallest possible space for him to breath through, he made his way to the door of the room, which he conjectured, and rightly too, was opposite to the window. The door was not fast in any way except by the mere latch, so that it yielded to his touch in a moment, and he stepped out on to the landing.

Duval was above the middle height, and now that he was from head to foot enveloped in a white sheet, he looked quite gigantic and awful. An attic door was opened next to that from whtch he had emerged, and an old woman appeared with a light in her hand.

"Dear me," she said, "what is the matter? Is it fire? Eh? Is it fire? Oh, gracious! A ghost!"

She had caught sight of Duval, and she immediately fell backwards into her attic, candle and all, and rolled out of sight.

"That will do," said Claude Duval. He had by the aid of the old woman's light seen the situation of the staircase, and now he began to descend, hoping that his ghastly appearance would have the same terrifying effect upon everybody else whom he might chance to meet, as it had had upon her. When he reached the second floor landing a door opened, and a man rushed out on to it with a lamp in his hand, crying—

"What in the name of all that's abominable is this disturbance? Are we never to have a quiet night's rest in this house? Am I and Mrs. Jenkins to be night after night continually—The devil!"

"Repent!" said Duval, in a deep sepulchral voice.

Down went the lamp, and with a shout of terror the man flew into his own room again.

"This will do capitally," thought Duval. "I do believe I shall work my way to the street by the assistance of this sheet."

He descended the next flight of stairs without any opposition, and gained the landing of the first floor; but he had not had time to cross it, when the flash of a light came up from below, and a voice cried—

"Hilloa!—Hilloa! Who calls murder?"

Duval made no answer, and then a female voice, cried—

"I insist, Mr. Watchman, that you go up and see what's going on. I heard murder called by somebody up stairs."

"Well—well, I'm going," said the watchman, and then Duval heard him stamping up the stairs, and in a moment or two the faint reflection from the light of his lantern was plainly visible. Duval took his station exactly at the top of the stairs, and if he looked tall to any one who was on the same level with him, he must have indeed looked immense to anybody coming up the stairs, and looking up to him. He did not utter a word as the watchman was approaching; but he trusted entirely to his appearance.

"Come, Mr. Watchman," said the woman's voice, "get on, will you. How do we know but there may be murder doing in the attic's while you are creeping up the stairs like a snail?"

"I creeping, mum?"

"Yes, you know you are, and if I don't complain to the parish, I am not a Christian woman, that's all. It's my honest belief that you are afraid to go up."

"Me afraid?"

"Yes, you. And for all your thick stick, and your great white coat, I believe you are as great a coward as ever lived—that I do; so you had better go on, for my husband knows the turncock, and he knows the lady that washes for the overseer's wife, so you will run a good chance of losing your situation if we make any complaints against you."

"Good gracious," said the watchman, "protect me from female women, when once they do begin to talk."

"What's that you say, sir?"

"Nothing, mum, nothing ; I was only a saying that I like to protect women, mum, that's all."

"Oh, very well."

Up came the watchman, and when he got within three stairs of the top of that flight, he saw the lower part of the sheet in which Duval was enveloped, and he came to a dead stand still.   Then slowly raising his eyes he looked up—up—up to the tall figure in white, until it appeared to him as if in height it were endless. Human nature—at least, watchmen's nature—could not stand this, and backwards he went lantern and all on the woman, who was following him so closely behind with so many threats and expostulations if he did not do his duty. The consequence was that they both rolled into the passage together, and Duval thought that he could not do better than embrace that opportunity of leaving the house.

Gathering up the sheet, then, so that it should not impede his progress, he darted down the stairs ; and scrambling over the watchman and the lady who lay roaring in the passage, he made for the street-door, which was open ; but there the first obstacle he met was a man who was running in, and as Duval had by this time nearly got rid of the sheet, so that he did not by any means present so ghost-like an appearance, the man was not a bit confused, and made an attempt to seize him, crying—

"Who are you ?"

"Don't ask ridiculous questions !" said Duval, and with one blow he sent the man sprawling upon top of the watchman and the female. Divesting himself then rapidly of the sheet, he flung it above the whole party, and, finding a table and two chairs in the passage, he likewise accommodated them with those upon their backs, so that they, no doubt, thought that the ghost was amusing himself by lying upon the whole of them.

In another instant Duval was in the street, He did not run, but his walking pace was something uncommon, and he very soon, indeed, left that neighbourhood behind him. His first care was then to procure his horse, and then, when he was fairly mounted and upon the road to Kentish Town, he began to breathe a little freely, and to think over the events of that most extraordinary night.

Such thoughts could not be pleasing to him, for he could not by any amount of sophistry conceal from himself the fact that in all probability the lives of both of those unfortunate persons, Mr. and Mrs. Finch, had been sacrificed upon his account. That he was the person of whom Finch was jealous, and that that jealousy had driven him out of his senses—as it is a passion well able to do— and that under an accession of that species of insanity he had murdered his wife, there could be but little doubt ; and then the horrid end of the unhappy man himself, as a fit sequel to that drama of blood, made Duval shudder to think of it.

He let his horse lapse into a walk, and the most serious thoughts that had ever touched him crept over him.

"To-day," he said, "within the space only of a few short hours, four people have come by their deaths through me ; and, although, William and his associate amply deserved their fate, I cannot say so much of Mr. and Mrs. Finch. Am I to become a destroyer ? Are my footsteps henceforward to be tracked by blood ?"

He shuddered from top to toe.

The rain was still coming down rather thickly, and the night was intensely dark, so that, although he held his hands close to his face to see if there were any blood upon them, he could not tell. The mere idea, however, that such might be the case, at once turned the current of his thoughts from any idea of proceeding to the cottage where he had left Adele.

"No—no," he said, "I dare not go to her with probably the evidence of murder clinging to me, although I did not do the deed. I must wait until the morning's light shows me if I have such marks upon my hands or clothing."

With this idea, instead of going to the right to get to Kentish Town, he galloped up the Hampstead Road, and drew bridle at the Load of Hay, nearly opposite to a cottage which had been built by Sir Richard Steele. A dim light came from a room over the stables of the Inn.

"Hilloa!" cried Duval. "House! House!"

"Hilloa, yourself," answered a voice, "what's the row?"

"I want shelter till morning for myself and my horse. Can I get it here to-night?"

"Oh, yes," replied the voice, now much more respectfully. "I burn a light in my room over the stables on purpose to let everybody in. I'll be down to you directly, sir."

Duval had not to wait many moments before the ostler and a boy made their appearance. The boy was rubbing his eyes with his knuckles very hard.

"Come, bustle—bustle, Dick," cried the ostler; "take the gentleman's horse into the stable. This way, sir, if you please. You won't mind sleeping in a double-bedded room, I suppose, sir?"

"Not at all, if the other bed is vacant."

"Why, sir, it ain't quite vacant in a manner of speaking, I rather think."

"Which means that some one is there. Who is it?"

"Oh, a very respectable man, sir. It's Mr. Racefoot, the Bow Street runner, sir. We ought to be safe enough while he's in the house—oughtn't we, sir?"

"Oh, very."

"Then you don't mind, sir?"

"Not a bit, now that I know what a very unexceptionable man is in the other bed. It is quite a pleasure to feel so sure a protection against thieves and highwaymen, as one must do in his company."

"Oh dear yes, sir, in course—in course. This way, sir, if you please. Mind the step, sir."

"Thank you, I see it."

Duval followed the man up a crazy flight of steps, and then through a door that opened into the first floor of the old Inn, (the ancient structure has long since been swept away); and then cautiously opening a door, upon which in quaint letters was painted "32," he said—

"This is the room, sir. At what hour would you like your horse in the morning?"

"As soon as you are up and about."

"That's as soon as we can see, sir."

"Then that will do for me very well. Good-night, my friend."

"Good night, sir, and a good night's rest; you will find it a very nice bed, sir, and well aired."

The ostler put into Duval's hands a little miserable light, and then left him by himself just on the threshold of the double-bedded room. Duval closed the door very gently, for as the officer had said nothing he considered that he was asleep, and as yet he (Duval) had no wish to disturb him; for well he knew that that officer had been several times specially upon the hunt for him, and for all he (Duval) knew to the contrary, he might be then only resting a little before proceeding in the morning upon the same errand.

Duval, as he advanced into the room, shaded the little light with his hand, so as to keep its rays out of the eyes of the officer as much as possible; and after noticing that the curtains of the bed were all drawn close, he tripped up very lightly to the dressing-table, upon which it appeared that the officer had laid a variety of articles, that upon going to bed he had taken from his pockets.

There were a pair of hand-cuffs—a pair of pistols—a stout cord—a knife—and a pocket-book, which was lying open at a part that had evidently been recently looked at, for the book had a marked inclination to remain open at that point, and some writing was upon the page thus exposed, and Duval read as follows—

"Memorandum—To devote my whole time to the apprehension of Duval, by which I shall get enough to take a farm in the country, and retire from the profession.

" Memorandum—Duval is not quite six feet high, and his real hair is a very dark brown—He has a slight scar upon one hand, they say.

" Memorandum—To take him alive if possible, but at all events, to take him any way, and by no means to let any one else have a share in the transaction, as what is quite enough for one is by no means enough for two."

" Well," whispered Duval to himself, " this is pleasant, I must confess."

He tried the pistols and found them both loaded, and very carefully primed; so the first thing he did was carefully to shake out the priming of both of them, and to wipe the pans quite clean, so that there should be no chance of an explosion. He then considered what it would be best for him to do. No doubt the most prudent thing would have been to have retreated at once, and got clear away; but then Claude Duval was by no means the sort of man to do the most prudent thing, so that although that course occurred to him naturally enough, he quickly dismissed it from his consideration.

" No," he said. " I will not let this man disturb me from a few hours repose. I will lie down; and as I generally awaken at whatever time I determine to do before closing my eyes in sleep, I will take my chances. He seems sound asleep enough at all events to be harmless for some hours to come."

CHAPTER LII.

DUVAL'S ADVENTURE WITH THE OFFICER, AND THE ROBBERY OF THE BARNET COACH.

FEW indeed could have been found to lie down to sleep in the manner that Claude Duval did with that officer, who was so intent upon his capture, in the other bed; but it happened to be just one of the things in which he (Duval) took a kind of reckless delight.

Indeed, of the two it is doubtful if he would not rather that the officer should awaken and have some talk with him, than continue to give him the security of his sleeping. But probably the officer had fatigued himself very much during the day, for certainly he slept as calmly and as soundly as any man well could.

" Never mind," said Duval. " Never mind. He will perhaps awaken in the morning, and then I shall be able to say something to him; and as it is, until then I shall indulge myself with a quiet nap."

With this Duval drew the curtains of his bed, so as only to leave him a little crevice through which he could take a peep at what the officer might do; and besides, Duval knew very well that at the slightest noise he would be sure to awake, for it was a peculiarity of his to do so.

" Good night," he said.

It might be that Duval pronounced these words rather loudly, but certain it is that the officer moved very uneasily in his bed, and murmured something, but as Duval made no further remark, and as all was still, he soon subsided into the deep sleep that he had been in during the whole of the proceedings that we have detailed.

In five minutes Duval was asleep.

How long a time he had slumbered, Duval had at the moment of awakening no means of knowing, but he was aroused while it was still quite dark, by hearing some sounds from the road-way, and the clatter of the hoofs of horses.

He rose in his bed and listened, and then he heard a voice say in clear tones—

" Hilloa, ostler. Have you had anybody pass here lately, well mounted ?"

" No," said the ostler. " I haven't."

" Well there's been a murder in London, and people are going all over the country roads to pick up a man who is suspected. A servant at the house has described him well, and if he be the man he will swing for it yet for murder will out.'

"To be sure it will," said the other. "What sort of man is he?"

"Tall and well looking. It's a woman he has cut the throat of. He is well dressed, and has taken the road by one of the avenues from London."

"Murdered a woman, has he," said the other. "Well, that's a good bit worse than murdering a man, to my mind, at any rate. Surely a man may keep his hands off a woman. But no such a one has passed here. If he should, and you or any of your people can come by him, I will soon mention it."

"Thank you. Are we right for the heath?"

The clatter of the horses' feet now sounded upon the hard road, and then all was profoundly still, and Duval was in his own mind not a little puzzled to account for why the ostler did not mention him when the men described him, even so slightly as they had done. There was not light enough for him to see his watch, so he could not find out what the time was, but as he lay awake he thought the dawn was coming, as the chamber grew lighter, or he got more accustomed to its darkness, and could faintly distinguish the dim outline of objects better.

"I won't sleep any more," he said to himself, "for I feel sufficiently rested by the repose I have had."

In the course of another quarter of an hour he could have no sort of doubt but that it was the daylight that was close at hand, and he was thinking of getting up, when he heard the ostler whistling and hissing under the window as if cleaning a horse.

"He is mindful of my orders," said Duval, "and no doubt is now getting my horse ready for me. I will get up, and perhaps it will be as well if I get out of the room, after all, before my friend in the other bed wakes up."

With this idea Duval rose, and as he had not taken the trouble to disencumber himself of anything but his boots, one may reasonably suppose that his toilette was tolerably quickly performed. But he was disappointed in his idea of getting so quietly away, for in putting on his second boot he quite forgot the officer in the bed at the other end of the room for a moment, and stamped the heel of it upon the floor, to get his foot right into it, with a force that was enough to have awakened the soundest sleeper the world ever saw.

"Hilloa!" cried the officer. "What's that?"

"The devil!" cried Claude.

The officer sprang up to a sitting posture in his bed and glared at Claude as though he thought him a spectre. Then he repeated his question in a highly exclamatory tone of voice—

"Who are you?"

"Don't trouble yourself," said Duval. "Don't put yourself out of the way. I have got it on, now."

"What on?"

"Why my boot, to be sure. Didn't I wake you up by knocking it down at the heel?"

"But how the deuce came you here?"

"That's self-evident enough, I think. It's a double-bedded room, and you didn't want both the beds did you? Be a reasonable man. Good morning."

"But I must know who you are."

"Oh, nonsense. Why, I should like to ask? I don't see the smallest necessity in life for your knowing who I am, my good sir. You don't find me asking all sorts of impertinent and ridiculous questions about who you are. Come, come, you had better take another nap."

"Now by all that's impertinent, I never was treated in such a cavilling-like way in all my life, by any one. I'll pretty soon convince you that I am one who will be answered; I don't find a man in my bed-room, and part with him again in this free and easy sort of style, I can tell you."

"Dont you?" said Duval as he put on his hat and adjusted it in the glass; "I don't see myself how you are to hinder it. Everybody has his peculiar way with him, and I must say you have described me very nicely indeed by the words free and easy; so, I leave you to the benefit of your definition, my friend.

I am all ready. Good morning. Don't put yourself in a rage; now, I can see you are doing so."

"Not put myself in a rage?" roared the officer.

"No, it's the very worst thing you can do. I see by your complexion that you are a bilious man, and if you put yourself in a passion you will be ill."

"Ill? The devil."

"I speak to you as a friend. Good morning."

Duval opened the door of the room and walked out, but the officer was not to be so coolly baffled. He sprang from his bed undressed as he was, and running to the table where he had laid his pistols, he caught one up, crying in a loud voice—

"Stir another step, and I fire!"

"Fire away," said Duval, "only remember that it will be my turn after you have had yours."

"I do not wish to take your life. Why will you force me to use a weapon against you?"

"Upon my word you are considerate," said Duval; "you do not want to take my life? How very kind, to be sure you are, my dear sir. And, pray, upon what pretext do you interfere with me at all? I came to an inn—a public place of entertainment, and am shown to a bed, and then because I don't happen with all the submissiveness in the world to answer your questions, not put in the most civil manner, you take credit for not upon the instant blowing my brains out."

" I am an officer in search of a criminal."

" Very well."

" And therefore I have a peculiar duty in speaking to any one whom I may mee ."

"t Very good."

" Under these circumstances I feel justified in asking you who you are, sir?"

" Well, I am Smith, cousin, four times removed, to Jones, who is distantly related to Thompson; so, now again I have the honour, of course feeling deeply grateful for your kindness in sparing my life, to bid you good morning, sir."

The officer was evidently puzzled and staggered by the cool manner of Duval, but he did not make any further opposition to his leaving the room, only laying his pistol upon the bed, he began dressing himself with as much speed as he could put into the operation.

Duval accordingly went down stairs, and upon issuing into the open air, he found that his horse was at the door nearly ready for the road.

"That will do," he said. "What do I owe you?"

" Whatever you please, Claude Duval," said the ostler.

" Ah, you know me?"

" Yes, I do, but I should'nt if you had not left in the pocket of your saddle a letter addressed to you by some one. It's never wise for gentlemen of your profession to do that sort of thing."

" No. You are right. But my friend, I heard you questioned by some mounted man about a murderer.—How came you not to suspect that I was the person they were in search of——"

" I did suspect it, but I knew you didn't do it."

" You know I didn't do it?"

" To be sure I did. The man who after receiving a pistol shot almost in his face, and only missed being killed by it by next thing to a miracle, and then didn't reply to it though he had a pistol in his hand, because the man who had fired at him begged for his life on account of his children, is not the man to cut the throat of a woman."

" And who did that?"

" Why, you did, Duval, and my brother was the man. He was guard of the Oxford Mail at the time and an outside passenger lent him the pistol.—He has often told me the story."

Duval nodded.

"I recollect it, now," he said. "It was more than two years ago."

"It was."

"Well, I thank you. You are quite right. I had no more to do actually with the killing of the poor creature they spoke of, than you have. The real murderer is dead, and I think it was in trying to get out of my way that he came by

CLAUDE'S ADVENTURE WITH THE POLICE OFFICER, ON THE NORTH ROAD.

his death. I will be off now, as your friend up-stairs is dressing himself not a bit faster than he can't possibly help, to come after me."

"He does not know you?"

"No, but he has his suspicions that I may be some one whom he would like, in the meantime, to get hold of, and I don't want to be troubled with him. Impede him with his horse as much as you can."

"Leave that to me, Duval."

"There is a guinea for you."

"No, Duval, not a farthing. Not a farthing from you. My poor brother owes his life to your forbearance, and his poor children would have been orphans if it hadn't been that you had a kind, a noble heart, in your bosom. Any service that I can do for you I would run a hundred miles to do, but I won't take any payment for it. Oh, no, I am paid enough."

"Ostler! ostler!" cried the officer, from the window.

"Yes, sir."

"My horse, directly, ostler. I shall be down in a minute. Get my horse out, for I want to be off."

CHAPTER LIII.

THE OFFICER IS CAUGHT IN HIS OWN SNARE.

AFTER giving this order, the officer pulled his head in again, and Duval, with a nod to the ostler, gave his horse the start up the little hill that is just beyond the "Load of Hay."

The animal had been well fed, and well groomed, so that it was in every respect well fitted for the road, and Duval felt the greatest confidence in his being able to beat the officer at a race on the Heath, if such a thing should be at all a matter of necessity.

"I might have asked the old ostler," he said to himself, "how the fellow was mounted, as that would have been some sort of guide to me how to act. But it is better to suppose that he is well-mounted than ill, so here goes for a sharp trot to the old Heath."

Duval avoided the village of Hampstead by leaving it upon his right, and cutting through the fields to the lower Heath. To be sure, he had to leap a hedge or two; but that, to him and his horse, was nothing but sport; so that in an incredibly short space of time they were both upon the Heath close to the high road that cuts it into two portions, and from the left hand of which, looking westward, you have so fine a view of that picturesque space of ground, while to the right you can see the dark cloud that hangs over London, and when the sun shines brightly you may distinguish its church steeples, and some of its most prominent buildings.

Duval was always pleased with the view from Hampstead Heath, and he paused to look at it as he always did, and not unfrequently when other people would have thought, and with some reason too, that he had little enough time to spare for such matters.

"Yes," he said, as if pursuing a train of reflection that he had not given utterance to until then; "I have had many a good gallop on these roads and meadows, and on this wild Heath, and I hope to have many more yet. But I must not altogether forget my friend of the double-bedded room, nor must I forget that I have one waiting for me at Kentish Town, who will think my absence strange. Yes, Adele, I must not forget you."

Raising himself in his stirrups, he cast an anxious eye on every part of the Heath, and after a few moments he was convinced he saw some one on the lower Heath trying to make a horse leap a hedge, while the animal evidently did not like the effort.

By shading his eyes with his hands, and by looking very carefully at the person, he felt quite convinced that it was no other than the officer with whom he had had the little wordy contention in the double-bedded room.

"So, so; he is following on my track as nearly as he can. Well, we shall see what will be the result; no doubt, by this time, he is beginning to have a suspicion that I am the man whom he seeks, and if so he will risk something to catch me. Well, it is his business, and if he will run into danger, he must."

After a few moments reflection, Duval now determined upon riding along the public road right on into the country, for of all things he did not wish to bring any danger into the immediate neighbourhood of where Adele was residing. He only paused until he saw that the officer had succeeded in making his horse leap the hedge, and by the style in which the animal eventually did the leap, he, Duval, saw that it was a good one.

Patting his steed affectionately on the neck, he said—

"Well, my friend, perhaps you will be put to your mettle to-day, after all, so let us keep the start that we have got."

With this, off went Duval at a slashing canter that soon left the Heath far behind him.

He had not got on above two miles though, when he saw a stage coach approaching him rapidly from the other direction, and as they neared each other the coachman slackened his speed, and cried—

"Shall I give you a lift, sir, horse and all?"

Upon this, several of the outside passengers laughed, for that coachman was considered to be rather a wag, and any of his jokes were sure to be greeted by uproarious laughter, whether they happened to be good ones or not. It so happened, however, that in picking up Duval for a butt, he certainly made a very serious mistake, for in an instant Claude drew a pistol from his pocket, and presenting it at the facetious coachman's head, he said—

"If you don't pull up sharp, I'll blow your brains out."

The coachman turned as pale as death, as he said in a faltering voice—

"Who—who are you?"

"A highwayman, to be sure. Who else should I be ? Now, Mr. Coachman, as I know you take your money at your last stage, I will trouble you to refund it to me, for I look upon myself as general proprietor upon this road."

"Gemmen," said the coachman, with a rueful look to those who had laughed so loudly at his joke, "are you going to see a poor fellow robbed in this way ? It's my own coach too, and my own money."

No one laughed now, but everybody looked the picture of dismay, and the one who had laughed the most, cried,

"You brought it on yourself; give up your money, and don't lead us all into danger by your obstinacy."

"Don't trouble yourself, sir," said Duval, "I shall come to you presently. If you don't produce your money, Master Coachman, you have not another moment to live, and I will then have your skin along with it."

The coachman, with a groan, handed to Duval a small leathern bag of money.

"Very good," said Duval, "now be off with you."

As he spoke he clapped spurs to his horse, and went on his road at a full gallop, for he had already in this little affair which had come upon him at unawares, put off much more time than he wished, considering that he had such an enemy in the immediate vicinity, as the officer who had made it the object of his life to take him, alive or dead.

Duval always went upon the good principle that it was foolish to despise any enemy ; but if he had not gone upon such a principle, the officer would not have been one who could be thought lightly of as a foe, for not only was he naturally a very determined man, but Duval, by the accidental inspection of his pocket-book, had been made aware of how important a point, in his speculations, his capture was. It was, therefore, with a kind of conviction that he or that officer would not live much longer, that he now spurred along the road again after robbing the coachman.

He did not trouble himself even to look at the amount of booty he had secured by his encounter with the coach, but making his way right on through Hendon, he soon got into the beautiful green lanes near Mill Hill, some of the houses in the neighbourhood of which he could already see.

More than once he paused as he got upon high parts of the road, and looked in the direction from which he came, but he could see nothing of the officer, and he began to fancy that he must be some three or four miles the start of him, when through a hedge about half a mile only in his rear, he saw him suddenly emerge into the high road.

Duval was so astonished at this sudden appearance of the officer, who must have crossed the meadows with a rare knowledge of the locality, that for a moment or two he stood stock-still, not attempting even to preserve the little dis. tance that there was between them.

The officer raised a shout of satisfaction when he saw Duval, in the midst of which our hero thought he heard his own name mentioned.

" He is resolved upon his own death or mine," said Duval, " but I will baulk him while I can. Nay, this looks so like fairly running away that I cannot do it. I will meet the fool, and if he will throw away his life, why he will, and there's an end of it."

With this feeling uppermost in his mind, Duval checked the impulse to speed that he had given to his horse, and being in the centre of the roadway, he firmly awaited the arrival of the officer.

When Duval's pursuer saw that this was the case, he gradually slackened his speed, and only came on at a gentle trot, and when he got sufficiently near to Duval, he called out—

" Surrender yourself. I know you now. You are Claude Duval! Surrender yourself. I have made an oath to take you, and I will keep it or kill you, so help me Heaven !"

" And does it not strike you," said Duval, in a clear loud voice, " that there is another alternative, namely, that I may kill you, and then ride off in safety ?"

" I know that I run many risks."

" Come on then. I am waiting for you."

They both put their hands to their holsters, and produced pistols, but Duval was willing enough, for more reasons than one, to let the officer have the first fire, and he cried—

" Blaze away, my friend. It will not be the first time I have given one of your fraternity a chance shot at me."

" You are a bold rascal, at all events," said the officer, " and it is a pity you did not take to something else than this trade which you now see brings you to so lamentable an end."

As he uttered these words, he fired at Claude, and when the smoke cleared away and he saw his opponent still sitting as before upon his horse, he cried with rage—

" That is the first shot I have missed for one while, but I don't miss a couple."

Then before Duval could say a word, he discharged the other holster pistol at him, but as they chanced to be the weapons from which Duval had drawn the bullets, of course no damage was done.

" Confusion !" cried the officer. " Some more than human influence mars my aim."

" You are a dead man !" cried Duval, galloping up to him and placing the muzzle of a pistol against his cheek. " You are a dead man !"

" I know it."

" Will you yet save yourself by making me a promise, that you will cease this pursuit of me ?"

" No—no ! Take my life if you will, but the pursuit of you I must continue if I live."

" Why this must be sheer insanity," said Duval. " Are you really in your senses or not ?"

" I am as sane as you are, Duval, to the full, and I still say that I must and will have your life or your person to hand over to the law."

" Take that then," said Duval. " You are a greater fool than I thought you. But I should not feel myself justified in shooting you in cool blood in this way. I believe you are a madman."

With one blow of the pistol-barrel, Duval knocked him off his horse, and then, without pausing to see how he fell, or what became of him, he turned his own horse's head towards Hampstead again. He had not proceeded far before he saw approaching him a complete cavalcade of horsemen; but instead of making the least attempt to get out of the way, Duval rode into the very midst of them, calling out, in a loud voice—

"Help, gentlemen—help! I am an officer, and was in pursuit of the notorious Claude Duval. We have had a tussle together, and he lies on the road a little hurt, I think, about a quarter of a mile, and I ask you all to help me to take him."

"Won't we!" cried the horsemen, with one voice; and off they went in the direction Duval intimated, leaving him to pursue what route he liked at his leisure.

He galloped through Hampstead, when the few shops of that then very rural village were only just opening, and never drew rein until he reached the cottage where Adele was most anxiously waiting for him.

CHAPTER LIV.

THE OFFICER GIVES DUVAL YET A LONG CHASE TO THE NORTH.

Perhaps, of all the adventures that Duval had been engaged in, this one, which had terminated in the tragical end of Mrs. Finch, was, to him, the most unsatisfactory, and the most full of painful recollections. He was, to be sure, a man of reckless impulses and ungoverned passions, but when ever indirectly he produced such a catastrophe as that which he had witnessed at the house where Mrs. Finch had breathed her last, it made even him think a little.

"Would to Heaven," he said to himself, as he reined in his steed opposite to the little cottage where Adele resided. "Would to Heaven I had never seen Mrs. Finch, or that she had so for resisted me in the first instance as to make me feel that a pursuit of her would be but folly. Who would have dreamt that ever the utmost jealousy or such a man as Finch would have carried him to such a length !"

Duval was right enough so far. No one would have thought that Finch was the sort of person to do the deed which we have seen he did do; but then, no one can properly estimate how far human nature may be completely transformed by passion.

Duval dismounted, and tying his horse to the little gate of the garden of the cottage, he strode along the gravel path towards the humble but pretty abode.

The hour was still so early, that the shutters of the lower room were not unbarred; but the ear of affection is watchful, and Adele heard the footstep of Duval upon the path. She opened the little casement from which she had last bidden him adieu, and with a fresh morning face full of beauty, she welcomed him.

"Are you quite well, Adele?" he cried.

"Oh, yes; quite well now."

That one word "now" spoke volumes; and as she disappeared from the window to come down and let him into the cottage, he sighed as he said—

"Yes, I will be true to this young girl. Constant, in what the world understands by constancy, I may not be, but I will never desert her, and leave her to shame and ruin."

The door opened, and Adele, taking him by the hand, led him in, saying as she did so—

"How long and weary the hours are without you."

"Are they, really, Adele?"

"Can you doubt it?"

"No, no. I will doubt nothing that you say, Adele—nothing; and you shall be my only joy, dear girl. Time was when I have thought I loved, but until I saw you, I never, in truth, knew what real love was."

"You flatter."

"Indeed I do not. Come, Adele, we must make a bargain with each other that we are to have implicit faith in what each may say; and so, as we will always be complimentary, never will there be a happier couple than we shall become."

Adele smiled, and she would fain have induced Duval to remain, and to pass the whole day with her; but he was in too feverish a state of mind concerning what had taken place in the City, to do that. He felt nervously anxious to know what complexion the dreadful murder of Mrs. Finch had to the public; so in about two hours after, taking some things from the vallise that he always had strapped to the back of his saddle, and with these disguising himself, he put up his horse at an Inn in Kentish Town, and taking advantage of a stage-coach that passed the door of the cottage, he went right into the City.

Duval was not kept long in suspense regarding the light in which the murder of Mrs. Finch was viewed, for upon a lamp-post he saw a placard which stated that, "Whereas, a dreadful murder had been committed, by a man unknown, upon Mrs. Maria Finch; and that it was supposed that the murderer, upon being pursued by Mr. Finch along the tops of some houses, had thrown down that gentleman to the pavement below, by which he was killed at once." The placard then went on to state that, "A Reward of One Hundred Pounds would be paid to any one who would give information as to who the party was who called upon Mrs. Finch upon the evening of the murder, and a reward of another hundred pounds upon his being lodged in any of His Majesty's jails."

"Pleasant," said Duval, as he finished reading the placard; and then a rough voice behind him, said—

"By your leave, sir!"

Duval stepped aside, and found that he had been impeding a bill-sticker in his work. This man in a few moments appended a smaller bill to the foot of the other one, which contained a full description of Duval, given by the servant of the house where the Finches had lodged.

"A bad job, sir, that ere murder," said the bill-sticker.

"Very."

"They'll nab him, sir, don't you think?"

"It is very likely."

Duval walked slowly away. He had certainly all the information he wanted, and made more than was at all agreeable upon the subject of the murder; and, galling as it was to be supposed to be the guilty party, he did not see the smallest chance of being able to prove the contrary; for Finch was dead who might have owned to his share in the dreadful deed.

"Well," said Claude, "all I have to do is to take care of number one. I am willing to admit that my conduct in the transaction was bad enough; but it was not so bad as they would fain make it out. I did not kill either of them, although I may have been the indirect cause of the death of both. I will to the road again, and try to banish these uncomfortable thoughts, or I shall know no peace of my life. This affair will blow over in a little time, and the secret must remain in my own bosom."

There was no conveyance from the City to Kentish Town, where Duval had left his horse, so he resolved to walk the distance; and, by getting across the fields by Finsbury, and then making his way by Islington, he knew that an hour's sharp walking would take him as nearly as possible to his place of destination.

With this intention, Duval struck off as nearly as he could for Finsbury fields, which, at that time, were quite clear and open as the Kentish Town fields are in our own time, and he thought certainly of nothing less than of meeting with anything in the shape of an interruption by the way. Fate, however, had decreed it to be otherwise.

He had got clear of the houses pretty well, and was in the neighbourhood of some citizens' villas, not far from Finsbury, when he heard a loud voice cry—

"Stop! Stop! Stop!"

This was not a species of invocation which Duval was likely to let go quite unheeded, especially as he was upon foot. Had he been well mounted, probably he would have treated it in a much more supercilious manner. He turned on the instant, and saw a mounted man coming at a smart trot towards him, up a lane in the immediate vicinity.

"Hilloa!" cried the horseman, again. "Stop, my friend."

"What for?" said Duval.

"Only to answer me a question. Have you seen a man on a very dark bay horse in this neighbourhood?"

"No."

The mounted man came close up to Duval, and they both looked in each other's faces for a few moments in silence. To the intense astonishment of Duval, this mounted man was no other than the officer with whom he had had the encounter near Golden Green, and whom he had succeeded in playing the trick of giving him into custody; and no sooner had Duval made this discovery, by an attentive perusal of the officer's face, than the officer found out, by the same process, who he was speaking to.

"By Heaven!" he cried, "it is Duval."

"Right," said Duval. "You never spoke a truer word in all your life, my friend."

"You are my prisoner now. Scoundrel, your career is now, at last, at an end."

"My dear sir, you flatter yourself," said Duval.

Quick as thought, then, and before the officer could possibly divine his intention, Duval stooped, and seizing him by the foot, fairly canted him off his horse into the roadway. The officer made two or three plunging attempts to rise, but the large riding boots he wore impeded him, and Duval had time to spring into the vacant saddle.

"Now, my friend," he shouted. "My career is not quite over yet. If you want your horse again, you must look for him some miles from London, and for fear you should be disappointed taking the wrong direction, I am going north. Good day!"

The officer, without troubling himself by any further efforts to get up in a hurry, pulled a pistol from his breast-pocket, and fired it at Duval. The bullet just slightly touched his left arm.

"All right," cried Duval.

No one knew better how, at a moment's notice, to start a horse to a full gallop than Duval, and before the officer could get at another pistol, he was off like the wind.

"Stop him! It's Claude Duval," roared the officer. "Stop him! Help—help! It's Duval, the highwayman! A hundred pounds to anybody who will stop him. Help—murder—help—watch!"

As Duval galloped on the sounds died away, and by the time the old houses of Upper Islington appeared, he was in complete solitude and silence, and the officer's voice had faded away in the dim distance.

"A narrow touch, that," said Duval, as he slackened his speed a little and looked around him.

Not a soul was visible, and from the high ground upon which he was now, if any one had been in his proximity, he must have seen them easily. The horse upon which he rode was a good one, and far from being in the least distressed, seemed very much to have enjoyed the gallop it had had over the fields; and then, Duval was rather a lighter weight than the officer, so that it was something like a relief to the steed to change its rider in such a way.

What was to be done now, might have puzzled some folks, but Duval was a personage of rapid resolves; and after a very few minutes consideration, he made up his mind to ride to Kentish Town, and then, when he got very near to where his own horse was put up, and which by that time would of course be quite fresh and rested, he would be able to get rid of the one he rode, by dismounting and letting it go loose. He did not think it at all prudent to ride it to the door of the Inn where he had left his own steed, for in Kentish Town he was as yet unknown, and that would have been, in all probability, a means of identifying him, more complete than pleasant to him.

He was not, however, forgetful of the probability that he should be followed by some person whom the discomforted officer might stir up to such an enterprise quickly, and he knew that where he had left that very unlucky individual, a fresh horse could easily be procured; so he paused about every five minutes to take a long look around him.

Upon one of these occasions it was, that he saw three men on horseback coming on as rapid as the nature of the ground over which they proceeded would permit them, in his direction.

"Humph!" said Duval, "people don't cross a ploughed field, if they can help it. They think it a near cut, or they would have found out some better path. No doubt they congratulate themselves now upon the likelihood of coming up with me, and taking me very comfortably, so far as they are concerned, to town. We shall see."

Duval had gone so much to the right, that in the course, even of a very few moments, he arrived at Newington Green; but still, if he could strike across the country, he was not so far from Kentish Town as any one would have supposed, and it must be recollected, that at that time there was by no means the amount of obstruction in the shape of buildings and enclosures that all that part of the suburbs of London now present.

Crossing the Green then, he dived down a narrow lane and soon came to a low hedge, beyond which stretched the open fields; and at some distance off, he could plainly see the cottages in Kentish Town, and mark the whole of the straggling road right up to Highgate.

It was now that he put the capabilities of the officer's horse to the proof. He did not think it wise to give the creature a heavy leap to do in the first instance, for well he knew that such a course of proceeding will sometimes shake a horse at the outset of his career, and make him lose speed for a mile or two; so Duval sought for a gap in the hedge, through which he charged him, and then walking him for a few moments on the turf to get him accustomed to the feel of it after the roads, he gradually urged him on, and in the course of three minutes was flying over the meadows at a tremendous rate.

Two magnificent leaps of enclosures were now taken with ease by the horse, and without relaxing in his speed in the least degree; and Duval seemed to be approaching the houses in Kentish Town with magical rapidity.

Our hero now did not pull up to look about him; but when nothing but a level meadow was before him, he at times swayed himself half round in his saddle, and took a keen glance along the fields.

He saw his pursuers about half a mile behind him. They seemed, however, to feel that their cattle were unequal to the leaps that were necessary in the cross-country ride, and they were making for the high road.

"That will do," said Duval.

He now felt quite certain that he should be able to reach the Inn at Kentish Town, and to get his horse out and be off before they could reach him by the road. His great object was that they should have no knowledge of where he had put up his horse, for of all places in the world he did not wish any inquiry to be made concerning him in Kentish Town, and that was on account of Adele.

On he went at the same slashing rate; and now, before you could well have counted twelve, he was at the back of Kentish Town; but an unlucky obstacle presented itself to him in the shape of the long straggling grounds belonging to a market gardener and florist.

To coast this place would have put off more time than Duval felt at all inclined to waste, so in the first instance he jumped the hedge, and let his horse alight in the middle of a bed of asparagus, and then on he went right through a whole rotation of crops, until he reached the gravel path that led out into the village; but there he met the gardener himself, who, being a very irascible man, at once flung a long rake at his head.

Duval had no wish to ride into the village, and as it was quite immaterial to

CLAUDE ASTONISHES THE LANDLORD OF THE ROAD-SIDE INN.

him whether he dismounted where he was or elsewhere, he flung himself hastily from his horse, and catching up the rake, he felled the gardener with one blow of its handle, breaking it in two by the process.

"I can't stand upon trifles," said Duval, and in another moment he ran out into Kentish Town, and found himself exactly opposite to the Inn where he had left his horse. The officer's steed which had done him such good service, he left in the nursery-garden to amuse himself with such dainties as he might there find suited to his palate.

Without the least appearance than of hot haste, Duval went into the Inn yard, and asked for his horse. He held up half-a-guinea between his finger and thumb to the ostler, as he merely uttered the two words—

"Be quick!"

The sight of the glittering coin was quite a magical stimulus, and the horse was out and saddled in an incredibly short space of time. The half-guinea was transfixed from Duval's finger to the hand of the well-pleased ostler, and in another moment Duval was in the high road, and firmly on his saddle.

"Now," he said, as he patted his steed. "Now, those gentlemen behind us if they are inclined for a little excursion of some twenty miles or so into the country, can have it."

He trotted on until he got to the rise of the hill, and then he took a long look behind him. The three horsemen had got quite clear of the village, and were pointing him out to each other.

"Very good," said Duval. "Half a mile is a long pull up; and if you catch me you will have me, my friends, but not before."

The whole of that neighbourhood was well known to Duval, and he fancied that Swain's Lane was not quite so bad an ascent as the high road to Highgate, so when he got to that turning he at once took it; and at a long gallop, which his horse in ascending hills had not his equal at, away they went up the lane, and in a very few minutes were in Highgate.

Upon the level through the town then, Duval went leisurely, for he was determined that his horse should have every chance, and although he did not believe that the ascent of Swain's Lane had winded him in the least, he was resolved to give him all the advantage in his power.

Highgate, then, so far as regarded the level upon which the village is actually situated, was cleared at a rapid walk only; but after getting to the descent on the other side, just past the Wrestler's Inn, Duval gave his horse the rein, and away they went towards Finchley at a tremendous pace.

"Bravely done," cried Duval. "Bravely done, my gallant steed! Why we must already have made the half mile that was between us and our foes a whole one."

He kept his ear on the stretch to catch the sound of the horses' feet of his pursuers, but no such indication of their approach reached him, and he concluded rightly enough, that they were toiling up the steep bit of the hill, and so going leisurely enough.

In a few moments Duval was right down in the valley by Finchley, but he did not pause. He left East Finchley well to his left, and keeping still the high road, he ascended to a rising bit of country again, from which he could at intervals command extensive views for many miles round him on all sides.

CHAPTER LV.

THE RACE CONTINUED, AND THE CATASTROPHE AT THE ROAD-SIDE INN.

THE only thing that Duval felt at all solicitous about was, that he should to a certain extent keep his enemies in view. He did not like the idea of their leaving the high road perhaps, and lulling him into a feeling of false security, and then pouncing upon him at some moment when he did not expect them. Therefore was it that he paused now upon the high ground in the immediate neighbourhood of Finchley, to reconnoitre the surrounding country.

He took care to get so far to the roadside that the identity of himself and his horse would be very much lost against the trees and the bushes, if his enemies should happen to be looking for him.

Not for the space of about half a minute had Duval been waiting, when he saw coming from Finchley, a poor-looking boy, rather sadly mounted upon a miserable-looking nag, and as he neared the spot where Duval was, he saw that he was one of the postboys belonging to the post-office, who for a few shillings a-week and a red jacket, risk their necks twenty times a week at the very least.

Duval waved his hand to stop him, and the boy pulled up with an uncomfortable jerk.

"Any of my friends down the road?" cried Duval. "We are after a highwayman, my lad."

"Oh, is you," said the boy; "I'm glad to hear you say that, for I was half afraid you was him, and you'd rob my letter bag."

" Oh, dear no."

"Well, they are all a-comming; they have got a couple of young chaps from the village to come with them. They say they will be sure to have him. I suppose you do not like to try it alone?"

"Certainly not."

"Well, I must push on whether I meets him or not. A post-office boy mustn't wait for nothing, no how."

"I suppose not."

"Oh dear me, no. Good day. Kim up, will you."

After a short wrangle with his horse, off went the boy, again, at the same rattling kind of half-trot, half-gallop, which only such horses ever think of perpetrating.

"So," said Duval, "they are getting reinforcements, are they? Well, be it so. The more the merrier. Now, I dare say I might manage to play them the old fox's trick of doubling upon them; but I am inclined for a gallop, so I will lead them by the nose some twenty miles or so further yet; and if they are not pretty well knocked up by that time, for the pace it is that will do it, they are better mounted, and better horsemen than I like them to be."

Duval, however, was resolved not to start until he actually saw his enemies, for it was only by keeping them constantly in sight from the high portion of the road that he might encounter, that he could gather any amusement in the chase.

But in a moment or two, his attention was directed to the sound of wheels in the direction of which he was galloping, and a man in a cart appeared round a turn of the road.

"Hilloa," said Duval. "If you meet some men on horseback, just say that Duval is only a little way ahead, and they may get pretty close to him at dinner time, as he means to put up at a respectable house on the road."

The man in the cart stared, but Duval did not want to give him the opportunity of making any remark, but dashed on at his old pace. He knew that his message would be delivered, for his pursuers would stop every body they met now for a certainty, to ask news of him, since they must have lost sight of him since he turned into Swain's Lane, and he did not wish that they should go straggling about the country in search of him, and so raise a great alarm on his account.

For the next three miles, Duval did not in the least slacken his pace, and it was a tremendous thing to take a horse for that distance at such a speed. Gradually, however, then, he drew up, and stopped at the door of a road-side Inn.

The landlord came out in a moment, and with a profusion of bows, wanted to know if his honour would bait there.

"No," said Duval, "I only want a pot and a pint of your best old ale, landlord, if you please."

"A pot and a pint, sir?"

"Yes, the pint is for me, and the pot is for my friend."

The landlord stood in the middle of the road, and shading his eyes with his hand, he gazed all round him to see for the friend, but finding no one but Duval, he shook his head, saying—

"I don't see him, sir, if you please."

"Never mind," said Duval, "only be quick with the ale, or else I shall have to ride on to the next house."

This was a threat to the landlord of a road-side inn which was not at all to be despised, and accordingly the pot of ale and the pint were produced in two foaming tankards. Duval drank the pint in a moment himself, and then taking the pot in his right hand, he leant over his horse's neck, and held it to the creature's mouth.

It was gone in two or three seconds, and the horse gave a snort of satisfaction.

"Well, I never!" said the landlord; "that's the finest and maltiest old ale as is, and almost too good for christians, and the idea of a horse whipping up a whole pot of it is—is——"

"What is it?" said Duval.

"Oh, nothing at all, sir, if you thinks proper, nothing in all the world, sir, in course."

"Very good—there's your money."

Duval threw half-a-crown on the ground, and then with a slight touch to the horse, as a hint that the creature well understood, off they were again like the wind.

"Stop that man! Stop that man!" roared a person without his hat, rushing out of the puble-house.

"What him, sir?" said the landlord.

"Yes; stop him! stop him!"

"Lord bless you, sir, he's a mile off by this time. He's had a pint of the old ale himself, and his horse has had a pot. Do you know him, sir?"

"Do I know him? To be sure I do. He took a hundred pounds from me all in gold, one day, on Finchley Common. It's Claude Duval the highwayman."

"Claude Duval?"

"Yes, I should know him again, if it were a hundred years hence. All I got for my money was a good look at him; that I have dreamt of him ever since, and now I shall dream of him still more, for here I have missed him by a hair's breadth only."

"Missed him, sir? Why you don't mean all for to go to say as you'd a inter-fered with him."

"Wouldn't I? I was taken by surprise when he robbed me, and was not very well, but if I only had a chance of meeting him again face to face, I'd soon rid society at large of such a vagabond—that I would. I shall always regret that I did not notice him till he was going away—that I shall."

The landlord put his hand up to his eyes, and took a long look down the road.

"What are you looking at, landlord?" said the bold guest.

"Well I—no—yes. To be sure."

"What is it, landlord?"

"Why, if he isn't a-coming back for his change, as I'm a sinner. Yes, he is."

"Murder!—Help!—Hide me somewhere, landlord. Put me in the cellar—in a cask—under a bed—anywhere, and don't say I mentioned him. Murder! Murder!"

The bold guest rushed into the Inn in a frantic state, and the landlord laughed so, for Duval was not coming back at all, that he was forced to hold by the horse-trough to keep himself up.

While this farce was going on at the Inn door, Duval had made great progress on his road, and began to get into a very beautiful and finely wooded bit of country. The ale that the horse had taken seemed to stimulate him to every exertion, and if it had been at all necessary, which under the circumstances it was not, Duval could have made an amazing ride of it.

As it was, he pulled up, and finding that he was quite alone, and that not even a house was near him, he dismounted, and seizing the branch of a tree that grew in a hedge-row close at hand, he clambered up to a considerable height, so that he had quite a bird's-eye view of the surrounding country for many miles in all directions : and such a view anywhere in England is very charming, the country lying before the eye, as it does, like some immense garden in the highest state of successful cultivation.

Upon more than one occasion, Duval has shown that he was rather an enthusiastic lover of nature ; and now as he took such a long view from the old tree, of all the rich landscapes spread out like a moss before him, he would have been delighted to have been permitted to linger for an hour to gaze at it, had not the urgency of his situation warned him, although he was probably in no immediate jeopardy, he had no time to lose.

Far off, looking like bestud by insects, he saw a cluster of horsemen coming on at what, at that distance even, his practised eye told him was a good pace.

"So," he said, "they think to run me down at last. But they will be mistaken. If I am ever nabbed it will be by treachery, and not by a race across the country. Let them come, I am right glad to see that they place such value upon my word, as to believe that I am to be sought in the north, only because I said as much."

He came down from the tree, and again mounted his faithful horse, which had as docilely as a dog waited for him at the foot of it, and then he took the road again.

"Let me think," he said. "If I were to pause, it would take them now half an hour to come up to me. That is not time enough for me to dine in ; I must have three quarters of an hour at the least ; so I must find some means of detaining them upon the road."

What those means were to be, Duval did not know at the moment. All he had made up his mind to was, that he would stop and dine somewhere, notwithstanding the pursuit that was so steadily kept up after him. But he was turning the matter over in his mind, and there was but little doubt that his futile genius in such matters would hit upon some scheme to accomplish what he desired.

He was not galloping now, so that he had an opportunity of looking about him a little, and in the course of a few moments he was rather startled to see the head of a man, as it appeared, just peering over a hedge at him.

"Hilloa !" cried Duval. "Who are you ?"

No answer was returned, and upon riding up to the hedge he found that it was a scare-crow in the field beyond it. A coat, trowsers, and an old hat stuffed out with straw, and supported upon a stout stake, made up the illusion.

Duval could not but laugh at the idea of his saying—"Who are you ?" to the scarecrow ; but he had not ridden half a dozen paces from it, when the idea struck him that it might be the means of procuring him the delay necessary to stop and refresh both himself and his horse.

Duval was quick in action, and with him the conception of every plan was quickly enough followed by its execution. He glanced round him, until he saw a tall chesnut-tree which would just suit his purpose, and then dismounting, he proceeded to carry it out.

He made his way through the hedge, and got possession of the scarecrow, which he threw over into the road. Following it there, he lifted it up, and by a happy jerk he cast it right into the middle of the chesnut-tree, where it lodged securely enough, presenting as nearly as possible the appearence of some one hiding in the tree.

"I think that will do," he said ; "and if it does not, it is not a bad joke, and I will keep a good look-out notwithstanding."

He immediately mounted again, and rode on, when to his good satisfaction he met a groom upon horseback. Duval on the instant rode up to him, and said—

"I have been robbed on this road."

"Robbed, sir ?"

"Yes, and by the notorious Claude Duval ; I have had my watch, a diamond-ring, and sixty pounds taken from me, only half an hour ago, and I hid in a hedge after he had left me, and saw him turn his horse adrift and climb up a large chesnut-tree and hide in it."

" The deuce he did, sir ! Then we will have him—I will go back with you, sir."

" No, I cannot, I am on a very particular business, indeed, which must be transacted quickly—my dinner," added Duval, to himself, " or I would go back with you at once. If you can get any assistance on the road, take him, and as I come back I will join you. I am Sir Marmaduke Tompkins."

The groom touched his hat.

" Which tree is he in, sir ?"

" It's a large chesnut on the right-hand side of the road as you go to it from here, and it's near a gate with a lot of brambles stuck in it to shut up the field."

" I know it, sir—I know it. It's just a little way on, sir, a big tree with a large branch coming right over the road?"

" The same."

" Thank you, sir; I know it it, sir."

" Very good. I believe there is a large reward offered for the apprehension of this Claude Duval. . Of course, in my position of life, the money is of no sort of consequence to me, so you can share it with any persons who may assist you in apprehending him ; and when you have him safe, I will take care that justice is done you, and that you are not cheated out of it."

" Oh, sir, you are very good."

" Not at all, my friend, not at all. I am sorry that my pressing engagement, indeed, prevents me from having the pleasure of going back with you."

The groom, who was only out to give a horse an airing, was not at all sorry that the sham Sir Marmaduke could not go back, for he hoped to have most of the reward to himself, by the knowledge that he thought he now possessed of the whereabouts of the notorious Claude Duval."

He rode on until he came to the tree, and one glance was sufficient, by showing him a portion of the scarecrow hidden among the branches, to convince him that the information that had been given him was quite correct.

" Oh, it's all right," he said. " There he is. Of course he has got fire-arms, and will have a pop at anybody who pretends to look at him. Dear me, what shall I do? I have heard a good deal about this Claude Duval, and they say he's a most desperate fellow, and no more minds blowing a fellows brains out than he would of lighting his pipe. I must be very careful, for what's the use of the reward to me if I am a dead man before I get any of it?"

Having arrived at this highly philosophical conclusion, the groom was half afraid to look up into the tree, for fear of encountering the much dreaded glance of the highwayman's eye, and he began to think that after all it would be better to share the danger and the reward with some one else.

In this state of mind he waited quietly enough, keeping only now and then an eye on the tree, for fear the highwayman should suddenly slide down its trunk and escape, and waiting with great impatience for some assistance to arrive.

Of course, in due time, up came the mounted party in pursuit of Duval, and with a groan the groom noticed their numbers. He made up his mind, however, to make the best of a bad job, and to pocket, with perfect security, what he could ; so, riding forward, so as to meet the party at some distance before they reached the tree, he said—

" Gentlemen, I can tell you of a good thing, if you will let me have some of the advantage coming from it."

" What is it?" cried one. " Be quick, for we are busy."

" But you can't be after anything that will pay you as this will," said the groom.

" You don't know that, young fellow. We are after Claude Duval the notorious highwayman, and there are sufficient rewards offered for him to make us all, and you too, if you could find him ; so if you have anything to say, say it quickly and at once, for you find we are not upon any trifling business."

" Claude Duval did you say ?"

" Yes, to be sure. Are you deaf ?"

" No—no. But—speak low or I don't know what may happen. I beg, gentlemen, that you will speak low."

" What for ?"

" Listen to me. There are five of you and one of me. Now if you will promise me upon your words, all of you, a sixth part of what you get by taking Claude Duval, I will put you in the way of getting him without much trouble."

" You will ?"

" If I don't you have nothing at all to pay me, so you are quite safe enough."

" True—true, we are," said the officer, who was the chief person of the party. " Upon my word you shall have the sixth of whatever we get if you do what you say. I make you that promise with all these four persons as witnesses to it."

" You all hear him ?" said the groom.

" Yes—yes. Of course we do."

" Then, after robbing Sir Marmaduke Tompkins of sixty pounds, and his watch, and a diamond ring, only half an hour ago, he turned his horse adrift and got up into that chesnut-tree, where he is now hiding."

The five pursuers of Duval gave five starts at this most unexpected and extraordinary information.

" In that tree ?" cried the officer, who had pursued Duval with such pertinacity ; " in that tree ?"

" In—that—tree," said the groom, solemnly.

" Come on, then. We will soon see that. Come on."

They all trotted up to the tree followed by the groom, and then the first thing the officer said was—

" There he is, sure enough."

" And I can see his eye," said one of the others.

" Look out," cried a third. " I can see the barrel of a pistol. He has got up there to shoot us as we pass."

There was a general scattering of the party now all over the road, each one being anxious that if any one were shot it should not be him ; and the groom held his that to the side of his head, and cried—

" Oh, don't—don't. Murder !"

This panic, however, when it was found that no pistol was fired from the tree, gradually subsided, and the officer, gathering courage, cried out in a loud voice—

" Claude Duval—the game is up now. You are wanted, and you cannot escape. We see you, and that is sufficient. You had better come down from that tree a live man, for if you don't you may be quite sure that you will have to come down a dead one, or so badly wounded that you will wish yourself dead."

" Lord bless us !" said the groom, " what does he say ?"

" Nothing at all."

" Ah !" said one of the men, " he is all the more dangerous on that account, I know."

" He's only plotting and planning something," said one of the young men from Highgate, " and I'll go home."

" And so will I," said the other hero from the same place.

" What ?" cried the officer. " Go home now, will you, my lads, while we are on the point of catching our man ? You must be mad. My idea is that he has hurt himself in some way, and has crawled up the tree to hide."

" But why don't he speak ?"

" Oh, he is too much chagrined to do that."

Upon this the two young men who would have taken flight home, again plucked up a little courage, and remained ; and the officer again spoke in a loud tone of voice to the scarecrow—

" Claude Duval, do not be foolish. You had much better give yourself up to us gently. Who knows but there may be some flaw in the indictment against you even at the Old Bailey, and then you may get off this time; but if I am compelled to shoot you, you have no chance."

"What does he say?" cried the other.

"Oh, he's as obstinate as the very deuce. He won't speak."

CHAPTER LVI.

DUVAL OUTWITS HIS PURSUERS, AND DINES WITH THE LORD MAYOR OF LONDON.

WHEN they found that they could not get a word from the figure in the tree, they grew more and more cautious, for to their imaginations there was something extremely exciting in the fact of the great highwayman being in a tree, and keeping that contemptuous silence.

"I really," said one, "would not fire into the tree. Who knows but it may explode some mine and blow us all up."

"Eh?" cried the officer as he started back. "What do you say?"

The man repeated his view of the case.

"Oh, stuff!" said the officer, "I can't think that at all possible. How can he blow us up?"

"I don't know. He's an outrageous kind of chap, and has as many doubles and twists as an old fox that has lost his tail."

The others laughed at this illustration, and that set the officer's mettle up a little.

"Nonsense," he said; "no doubt he thinks by preserving this silence and mystery, that he will frighten me, as he has already frightened you; but I am not exactly that sort of man; so if he don't come down and give himself up, I shall fire at him. I feel that it is my duty so to do."

Upon this the officer came under the tree again, and in a solemn voice he said—

"Claude Duval, you may fancy this is a very fine joke, but I can assure you that it is not; I am determined that I will take you; I have made up my mind to it, I tell you, and set my life upot it. Eh? Did you speak?"

"He didn't say nothing," said one of the others.

"But he moved," said one.

"Did he move?" cried the officer, turning round sharply to the man who had spoken last. "Are you quite sure you saw him move, my man?"

"Oh, yes, sir."

At this moment a very large chesnut, that had remained an unwonted time upon the tree, suddenly fell right on the crown of the officer's hat, and as it come from rather a considerable height it dwelt his hat a smart rap, and splitting open rattled four chesnuts about his ears.

For the moment this event took him so much by surprise, that he sat upon his horse perfectly motionless, but looking as white as a ghost. Then he cried—

"Murder, what was that? Stop him! Murder!"

A roar of laughter from the men, who had seen exactly what it was, at once awakened him to the fact, that at all events there could be no danger where there was so much hilarity.

"It was only a chesnut, sir, as fell on your head," said one.

"A chesnut?"

"Yes, that was all. He is pelting you with chesnuts, that's all, sir. It's just his way to be always up to some joke or another."

"Joke, does he call it—eh? Joke! By the holy—I'll joke him."

Full of anger, the officer at once now presented his pisto at the scarecrow in the tree, and pulled the trigger.

Bang! went the well-loaded weapon, and a shower of leaves and two more chesnuts came down upon the officer. But to the great surprise of the whole party there was the figure in the tree, sitting on a branch to all appearance as calm and as composed as though nothing at all out of the common way was taking place.

"Confound him," said the officer. "I must have hit him."

"He don't move, sir."

"But I could not miss him. Claude Duval, you are wounded. Are you intent upon

CLAUDE FINDS AN EASY DUPE IN MR. SCHOFFER.

self-destruction that you remain in that tree so perversely ? Come down, and no further harm will be done to you ; but if you remain there you will be destroyed, and your dead body will hang as a scarecrow amid those branches."

The figure maintained its position.

"Did he move ?" said the officer.

"I think I saw him move a little," said one.

"I saw him wink his left eye," said another.

"His eye? Can you see his eye?"

"Yes. If you come here, sir, and look right along where I'm pointing to, you'll see his eye just above a little branch of the tree that bends round in this way, just as I'm a-bending my finger. Do you see it, sir?"

"I—think—I——"

"Don't you see it a glistening?"

"Well, I wouldn't like to swear to it, but I do think that I really, now you mention it, see a something like a human eye. Yes, surely—upon my word, though it is difficult to say. One is rather apt to imagine the eye, but I feel quite sure I can see his nose and a part of his chin."

"That's very near it, sir."

"Yes, we may safely conclude, under such circumstances, I think, that the eye is there likewise."

"Quite safe, sir."

"Well, my friends, you know that this affair has already cost me a good deal of money, and that when I have paid each of you what I have promised you, and that groom what I have promised him, I shall not be very much the gainer by apprehending Claude Duval; but if any one of you will climb up the tree and fairly make him come down, I'll stand a five pound note down on the spot."

The men looked at each other rather dubiously.

"Recollect," added the officer as he took out his pocket-book, and produced a five pound note from its capacious enclosure, "recollect that five pounds are not easily earned every day in the week as by climbing a tree."

"It's an awkward job, sir," said one.

"Oh, very," said another.

"Five pounds," added the officer, holding the note at arms length. "Five pounds."

"Hang it all," said one. "I'll do it."

"Will you, my friend? Then the five pounds are yours, and what is more, I will remain with a loaded pistol pointed at the tree, so that if needs be I can render you effectual assistance. My opinion is that when he sees we will have him down, he will give in with a good grace at last."

"I'll try it, sir. I should think he'd have shot some of us already if he had had any pistols, don't you think?"

"Of course he would. It is as clear as possible. There is no danger whatever in going into the tree! I would do so myself, only I think I can be of more use here where I am. Take the note, my friend, and I hope it may do you a deal of good."

"Thank you, sir," said the man, cramming the note into his pocket. "Thank you, sir, I hopes as it may. Bill, will you give me a leg-up to that first branch?"

"All right," said Bill. "I'll do it."

"Very good."

The man slipped off his coat, and Bill gave him the leg-up to a low branch of the tree, which, when he once got a fair hold of, rendered the rest of his progress easy enough. The others all watched his proceedings with intense eagerness, and the officer, with one eye shut, and a pistol pointed towards the seeming figure in the tree, kept on the watch.

The adventurous man went cautiously from branch to branch until he came near the scarecrow, and then the interest of those below became painfully intense. They saw him kick it with his foot, and then they heard him shout out—

"Oh, my eye!"

"Is he dead?" said the officer.

"As mutton!" said the man.

"Then, my friends, that first pistol shot of mine must have done the business. Is he shot right through the head? I aimed at his head!"

"Everywhere," said the man from the tree. "Catch him, some of you, I'm going to throw him down."

At this intimation, far from coming forward to catch the supposed dead body, they all retreated, officer included, some paces further off than they were, and then they saw their comrade lay hands on the dead body. They saw it fall from branch to branch, and at length down it came to the ground, and lay huddled up at the foot of the tree.

" How light the poor fellow fell," said one.

" Very," said another.

" I take you all to witness now," cried the officer, " that before I shot Claude Duval I said all I could to him to get him to come down from the tree and give himself up quietly, but he was so obstinate that he would not. You will all, I am quite sure, be able to depose to that much, my friends."

" Oh, yes—yes."

" Very good. Then now we will get a hurdle, and placing the body upon it, we will take it to the watch-house at Hampstead. Come on, my friends. He is quite dead."

Curiosity, joined to a thorough conviction that Duval was quite dead, induced them all now to come forward, and at the same moment he who had ascended the tree came to the lowest branch and dropped to the ground, after hanging by his hands a moment.

" We are all done," he said, " except me."

" What do you mean?"

" Why you may have Claude Duval among you."

So saying, he picked up the scarecrow which was as light as possible, and flung it right among the advancing group.

The scene that ensued beggars all description.

Some fell flat down upon the road, and bellowed as though they were at the last gasp, others fought madly with their comrades to get away, fancying that they were obstructing them in some way, and one and all raised such a chorus of shouts and yells that the one who had produced all the confusion, by, in a moment of thoughtlessness, throwing the scarecrow among them, thought his safest plan would be to take to flight with what he had got, so off he went with his five pound note in his pocket, and catching his horse and his coat he quickly disappeared from the scene.

The unfortunate officer was knocked down and trodden over by the whole party, and as the scarecrow likewise had come right against him, he was more bruised and bewildered than any of them. It was not until one suddenly cried out—" Why, it's Farmer Stubbins' scarecrow !" that anything like order was restored, and then as they regarded the cause of their terror with careful looks, and glared at each other like men in a dream, the conviction certainly crept over them that done they were to all intents and purposes.

The officer sat on the ground looking half stunned, and there we shall leave him and his companions while we follow the fortune of Duval, who had been so successful in playing off such a *ruse* upon the enemy.

A quarter of an hour more saw him quietly trotting down the hill of Hampstead.

" I wonder," he said, " how long they will continue staring at the scarecrow in the tree ? But it don't matter. The north road, for about a week, now will be too hot to hold me, so perforce I must go west for a little time, whether I like it or not. I can easily ride into town of an evening, and visit Adele."

With this intention, when Duval got quite to the foot of the hill, where Chalk Farm Tavern stood, he turned up a shady lane to his left, of which there are now no traces, and soon got across a few meadows to where Regent's Park now rears its aristocratic abodes. Then it was only a large tract of not very inviting fields, rather damp in bad weather.

Striking across these fields, he so easily made his way to the west end of the town, and came out into the western road about half a mile below Tyburn Gate.

" Good," he said, " I have made a tolerably short cut of that, at any rate.

Something seems to tell me that I shall have some luck on this road. I am glad I relinquished my original intention of going on northward to dine, for I should soon have had the whole country about my ears. I will make a stop at the Old Hats, at Ealing."

Having made this determination, Duval went down the road at an easy canter. He passed the old wall of Kensington Gardens, and rapidly leaving Bayswater behind him, he was quickly at Shepherd's Bush, then a little straggling collection of about twenty houses only. He took the right-hand road and soon reached Acton, which was something, even then, of a village of importance, with its church standing more prominently forward than it does now.

A very short ride then brought him to the Old Hats, which then stood quite alone by the road-side, and was an old-fashioned, long straggling one storied house.

This hostel was well-known at that time to the knights of the road, as being kept by a man who never asked any questions of any one who made no demur at the bill.

Duval drew up at the door, and the ostler at once made his appearance and took charge of his horse, while he strolled deliberately into the house, as though no price were on his head.

———

CHAPTER LVII.

THE OLD HATS, AND WHAT HAPPENED THERE TO CLAUDE DUVAL.

"That's Duval the highwayman," said the landlord of the Old Hats, as Claude descended from his horse at his door.

"You don't say so ?" cried the landlady.

"Yes, I do, my dear."

"What, the famous Duval the dashing highwayman, who is so fond of all the ladies, and such a very nice man ?"

"Humph!"

"The good, handsome Duval—the——"

"My dear, he won't thank you to be bawling out his name in that sort of way, I am sure. It is enough that you and I know him, without letting everybody in the house into the secret of who he is ; and you know likewise perfectly well that young Mr. Schoffer is here now on his way to dine with the Lord Mayor ; and his father, you know, as well as I can tell you, is Alderman Schoffer, so of course he would feel bound to try to apprehend Duval, and then only think what a pretty disturbance there would be in the house."

"He apprehend Claude Duval ?" cried the landlady. "Why Duval would eat him up,"

"Very likely, my dear, but would it do any good to our house to have the son of Alderman Schoffer eaten up in it by Claude Duval ?"

"Well, who said it would ?"

"Nobody, my love, only don't be bawling Duval's name out so loud, for we don't know what may come of it. You know our mode of carrying on business, is to charge well and ask no questions, and you know that no class of customers pay us better than the——"

"Knights of the Road," said the landlady.

"Precisely, my dear."

"I know all that quite as well as you do, and I am quite as little likely to do any mischief to any guest. As for young Mr. Schoffer, as I say, Duval, from what I have seen of him, would eat him up with half a grain of salt."

"Very likely, but——"

Tingle, tingle, tingle !

"Ah! there's the bell, I declare—it's the coffe-room bell, and young Mr. Schoffer is there. I only wish, wife, you had not kept me talking here, I could have met Duval, and got him to go into the bar-parlour, or some other room, but now——"

Tingle, tingle, tingle !

" Are you going to answer the bell, Peter, or is Mr. D. to pull it down, I ask you?"

" Coming, coming, coming !" cried the landlord, as he made a rush now to a long low-ceilinged dingy room, that was called the coffee-room, because not a drop of that beverage was ever within its doors, and there he found Duval taking off his riding gloves, and young Mr. Schoffer the alderman's son looking at him with amazement, for that young gentleman had been to school in Holland, and had very little experience of life. He probably thought no one would venture into the coffee-room at the Old Hats, while so very important a personage as himself was there.

" Well, landlord," said Claude, " have you anything very tempting in the house that one can have to eat ?"

" Oh yes, sir."

" What is it?"

" Why, sir, we have something of all sorts. There is a roast haunch of as fine mutton as you would wish to see."

" Uncut?"

" Oh yes, sir. Nobody but the cook has so much as looked at it ; and then there is a——"

" Stop ; don't let me hear any more. Bring me the haunch at once—one of your home-made loaves, and a bottle of your best claret. I only want a slight snack, and that will do very well for me—only pray be quick."

" Certainly, sir."

Young Mr. Schoffer by this time began to think that the new comer must be somebody, from the deference with which he was treated by the landlord, and his own off-handed manners. The young man was sufficiently new in the world to be completely taken in by dashing manners, whether in man or woman, so he thought he would do the civil thing by the new comer, with the hope of finding out who he was.

" A remarkably nice day, sir," he said.

" Very," replied Claude.

" Perhaps, sir, you would like to sit here, as it is more in the light ? I will give you this seat, sir, if you prefer it."

" You are very kind," said Duval ; " but where I am will do very well indeed. I would not incommode you on any account. What a time this tiresome land-lord is to be sure. Here have I been waiting for dinner no less than three minutes and a-half."

As he spoke, Duval took from his pocket a superb watch, set in a circle of bril-liants, and glanced at it.

" He must be some nobleman," thought young Schoffer. " I'll get into talk with him, and show him that I, too, have a watch."

With this he took out his watch, which, by comparison with Duval's, was but a very shabby affair ; and by way of letting the supposed nobleman know that he was somebody, he said—

" How slow the time goes to be sure. My father, the alderman, told me to be at the Mansion House by five, and it is now only half past three. I am going to dine with the Lord Mayor, sir, you must know."

" Oh, indeed."

" Yes, sir. The old gentleman has got the gout, and can't go, so he gave me his invite, and I am to go, you see, sir ; and he has written to the Lord Mayor to say as much, and his lordship sent back a very flattering reply indeed, saying he should be happy to see me."

" You don't say so, sir ?"

" Oh yes, sir ; it's true, upon my life. My father is Alderman Schoffer : a well-known man in the City, sir."

" Very likely, sir, indeed."

" Humph !" thought Schoffer.   " I did think he'd be forced to tell me who he was, after I had said that. How close he is to be sure. I'll try him again, though." Then turning to Duval, he added, " My curicle, sir, is in the Inn-yard, and I am going to drive myself to town, you see, sir."

" Very probable."

" I have managed very nicely, I think, for I have put the card of invite in the box under the seat of the curricle, besides my white gloves and a charming bouquet. I rather think I am a bit of a manager—don't you think so, sir ?"

" Your forethought." said Duval, " is only equalled by your subsequent discretion, my good sir."

" No—you really don't say so, sir."

" Indeed I do ; and your experience of the world will let you see at a glance that I am not the sort of man, my dear sir, to say what I do not think."

This compliment to young Mr. Schoffer's experience of the world quite won his heart ; and if it be true, as some cynics have asserted, that mankind are always better pleased to be praised for those virtues and those qualities that they do not possess than for those that they do, the satisfaction that beamed from the young man's countenance is easily accounted for.

" Sir," he said, " you don't know how happy I should be to take a glass of wine with you."

" With great pleasure, sir," said Claude. " I will but just finish the little snack that I am taking, and then we will manage a couple of bottles of our host's claret here."

" Certainly, sir, certainly."

" I presume you have been in the army ?"

" Not exactly, sir."

What not exactly being in the army could mean, Claude Duval did not stop to inquire. It was quite sufficient for him that the young gentleman was highly flattered at the supposition ; and when Duval had finished his repast by making a rather considerable inroad into the haunch of mutton, they both sat down by each other as comfortably as possible.

After a few glasses of the really excellent claret had been despatched, Claude Duval said—

" I have been riding so much to-day, that I feel really fatigued with that kind of exercise, and yet I must get to London."

" My dear sir," cried the young Mr. Schoffer, upsetting his glass of claret on his pantaloons in his eagerness : " my dear sir, if you will condescend to accept of a seat in my curricle, I shall be proud of the honour of driving you to town."

" Really, sir, I fear that it would be too much of an intrusion upon your kindness."

" Not at all—not at all, sir. Only say that you will do it, that's all, my dear sir."

" Well, since you are so very kind as to make me such an offer, and in so gentlemanly a way, too, I feel that I ought not to think of refusing it."

" Of course not, sir, of course not ; and I hope you will not think of such a thing for a moment. You cannot think, sir, how very comfortable two can ride in my curricle. I have no servant with me, because I always can put up the horse and vehicle at father's old shop—I—I mean in the city—dear me."

" Exactly, sir. Shall we have another bottle? Claret is not a very insidious wine."

" Why really, sir, I'm almost afraid to venture, as I shall have to drink a good deal of wine at the Mansion-house, for the Lord Mayor is sure to keep his eye on me, and to cry out—' Come, come, Mr. Schoffer, don't shirk your glass.' "

" Very likely."

" Yes, sir. Our present Lord Mayor actually began life by dealing in rags and bottles."

"You don't say so."

"Yes, and so he got on by degrees, until he is the great man he is now ; and they do say that in a box under his bed, he still preserves the original black-dolly that used to swing outside his door [in the Minories, where he first set up in business."

"It shows a proper and profound humility. How did he get on in his business then?"

"Oh, very well indeed. They say he swindled—no—I mean he got the better in business, and you know, sir, in business that nothing that keeps to the windward of the law is swindling.

"Certainly not."

"Well, sir, he got the better of everybody, and from one thing to another, he deserted the bottle business, and took contracts for the army."

"That I should think was profitable."

"Oh, yes, sir, there was not a pair of breeches went to our army in Flanders but were made by the present Lord Mayor of London."

"Really I quite congratulate you upon the useful and ornamental position in which your house stood with the military character of the nation."

"Thank you, sir, you are very good."

"Not at all ; modest minds like yours should always be properly appreciated, in my opinion. Permit me to hand you the decanter."

"Thank you."

The young scion of the city house had not a head-piece that was either proof against Duval's flattery or the claret which was so liberally administered to him, and he soon showed signs of having had quite enough. It was no part of Duval's scheme to render him quite helpless.

"Bless me," said Duval, suddenly looking at his watch. "It is time to start for London."

"Is it!" cried young Schoffer, starting to his feet. "Let's be off then. My curricle ! Hilloa, there, my curricle !"

"All right," said the landlord. "It is at the door."

———

CHAPTER LVIII.

DUVAL MAKES A GOOD THING OF A MANSION-HOUSE DINNER.

IN the course of another five minutes Duval and his new friend were seated in the curricle together. The young man took the reins—nobody is so tenacious of driving as your half drunken man—and away they went at a good pace from the Old Hats.

The open air, however, soon began to have a very insidious effect upon the head-piece of Schoffer, and from the manner in which he swayed from side to side, it was quite evident to Duval that in the event of their meeting any other vehicle upon the road, the chances of a collision were hardly doubtful.

"Well," he said, suddenly. "I have had a lesson. That is beautiful."

"A lesson ?" said Schoffer, speaking thickly. "A lesson, my dear friend, did you say ? What's—what's beautiful ?"

"Your driving ; and as I have had the advantage of seeing it, of course I have had a lesson in the art."

"Oh, ah, yes, to be sure. Come up, will you ! I rather think there are not many, sir, who can come near me in this sort of thing."

"Not one."

"No, really though, you ain't joking ?"

"Joking? Perish the thought."

"Then you do think I drive rather uncommon well ?"

"I am certain of it; and I have, contingent upon that conviction, a very great favour to ask of you, my friend."

"Name it—what—is—is—it?"

"It is that you would let me try to put in practise the admirable lesson in driving that you have given me, by allowing me to take the reins for a minute or two only, now that we are still in the country. I own that with you by my side I should feel very diffident about driving in London, but here nobody sees us."

The young dupe smiled blandly.

"Well—well," he hiccuped, "nobody sees us here; I don't mind for once in a way. There, my fr—friend. Take the whip and reins, and I will tell you when you go—go wrong, I will."

"A thousand thanks for that kindness," said Duval, as he took the whip and reins from the hands of the young man. "There now, how stupid I am."

"What's the row?"

"I have dropped the whip, and owing to sitting in an awkward position I have got the cramp in the calf of my right leg, and can't move. Oh, oh!"

"I have had the cramp in my calf sometimes," said Schoffer.

"Then it must have been all over you," said Duval. "My dear friend, will you get the whip?"

"To be sure I will. Don't you move. All's right. I'll get it. Don't you trouble yourself, my dear friend, I'll get it in a moment. All's right. Some people couldn't have taken as much claret as I have and been so decidedly so—sober—very sober."

He rolled, rather than stepped out of the curricle, and the moment he gained the road, Duval made a slight noise with his lips, and at the same instant gently jerked the reins, and off went the horses in the curricle at a sharp trot, leaving the unfortunate owner of the vehicle in the middle of the road with the whip in his hand, glaring after it, as it rapidly retreated from his sight, in such a state of bewilderment that he was unable even to cry out about it.

Duval never even troubled himself to look back. He was quite satisfied that pursuit was out of the question, and he knew that Schoffer was not so tipsy as not to be able to take care of himself so far as regarded any danger to life or limb, so that he looked upon the whole affair as quite a professional thing.

Tyburn Gate was very soon gained, and then Duval thought it was time to think upon what he was to do to carry out the plan he had determined upon in his own mind of going to dine with the Lord Mayor in the character of young Schoffer. He recollected that in the plenitude of his foolish confidence the young owner of the curricle had mentioned that under one of the seats were his gloves and his card of admission to the banquet at the Mansion House; and now Duval drew up at an Inn some few paces up the Edgeware Road, and pausing at the door, he made the examination of the seat and found the articles named.

Fortunately Duval, by merely getting rid of his riding-boots, was in a fit dress to go to the City feast. To be sure, he wanted a pair of shoes and another cravat, and then he would do very well, but both of these appendages to his costume were easily enough to be got in London.

Leaving the curricle in charge of the ostler at the door of the Inn, he entered it, and gave his order for a bottle of wine and for a hair-dresser to be sent for. The style of the 'turn out' at once insured him every attention, and the best hair-dresser in the whole neighbourhood was speedily in attendance.

"My good fellow," said Claude Duval, "I want you to dress and powder my hair for an evening assembly, and I want you to take a couple of guineas and get me a pair of dress shoes and a lace cravat."

"Oh, yes, sir; certainly, sir."

"The change, if any, I desire that you will be good enough to keep for your trouble."

This was quite sufficient to induce the barber to obey the orders of so munificent a customer with the greatest possible alacrity, and in the course of twenty minutes Duval was fully accommodated with all that he required.   The curricle was at the door, the horses having been refreshed with a little hay and water, and off went our hero again at a slashing pace to the City.

At that time the Mansion was easier to get at than it is now, when you have to thrust your way through an army of omnibuses and cabs.   The streets of the

CLAUDE HAS A CONFIDENTIAL INTERVIEW WITH THE LORD MAYOR.

city were bustling and animated, but that was all.   There was none of the **wild** rushing of vehicles which characterize the present day.   Without, then, being forced naturally to relax his speed, Duval got to the Poultry.   There he certainly found a collection of carriages conveying persons to the banquet.

A constable stepped up to him, and exhibiting a little gilt staff, he said to him, respectfully—

"Sir, you cannot pass this way ; you must go down King Street, unless you are going to the Mansion House."

"But I am," said Duval.

"Beg pardon, sir : will you be so good as show me your card ?"

"Oh, yes ; certainly."

The constable looked at the card, and then in a loud voice, he cried—

"Make way for Mr. Schoffer—way for Mr. Schoffer to the porch. Make way ; move on."

This was a common form observed there to all the guests, and was for the purpose of keeping the route as clear as possible, as well as informing the servants who were drawn up at the door of the Mansion House, who it was that had arrived.

"I want some one to take charge of my carriage," said Duval ; "and to take it to some livery stable."

"I'll see to that, sir," said a man in the Lord Mayor's livery.

"Very good."

"Mr. Schoffer !" cried a tall footman, as Duval entered the Mansion House. "Mr. Schoffer !" shouted another, as he went up stairs. "Mr. Schoffer !" bawled a third, and he entered a brilliantly-lighted room, where there was an assemblage of at least a hundred persons waiting for the welcome and momentarily expected announcement of dinner being on the table.

"Ah, Mr. Schoffer !" said a little fat man advancing, "glad to see you in the City again. Hilloa !"

Duval bowed.

"Why, you—you are not my old friend Schoffer !—You—you——"

"I am his son, sir," said Duval.

"Bless my heart and life, my dear boy, I am very glad to see you, indeed —very glad. And how is your worthy father ?"

"As well as the gout, sir, will let him be. He has sent me as his unworthy representative here."

"Unworthy ? dear me, no—no—not at all. Come this way, and I will introduce you to the Lord Mayor."

"I shall esteem it a great honour, sir. May I be so rude as to inquire the name of my father's old friend ? He will be sure to ask me who it was that treated me so kindly."

"Oh, yes, to be sure. Tell him it was Sheriff Buggins."

"I will sir ; and permit me to say that this is the proudest moment of my life, when I find myself treated with such distinguished courtesy by no other than the great Sheriff Buggins."

"My dear young Mr. Schoffer, really such penetration at your age is truly wonderful ; my young friend, I will likewise introduce you to the City Remembrancer, so called on account of forgetting everything. Come along."

With this, the exemplary sheriff led Duval to the Lord Mayor, to whom he formally introduced him. His lordship held out one finger for Duval to shake ; but as Duval saw the pompous and insulting trick, he only met it by one of his own fingers ; so that the most comical effect in the world was produced. The Lord Mayor was one of those large pompous men who acquire a reputation for amazing sagacity by scarcely ever opening their lips. He only glared at Duval.

"A long-headed man, the Lord Mayor," whispered Sheriff Buggins confidently to Duval.

"Yes, and thick, too," replied Duval.

"Oh, very, very."

"So I thought. I am much obliged to you for this kind introduction, and I am quite sure, my father will be very much pleased, indeed."

"Don't name it, my dear young sir. You must come and see me and the girls at Twickenham—Mrs. Sheriff Buggins will be quite delighted, and so will the girls."

" And so shall I, sir."

" Look—look—look !"

" At what, sir ?—where ?"

" The Lord Mayor is consulting his watch. We shall soon now have dinner announced. That watch, sir, cost three hundred pounds. It is studded with diamonds ; and inside the outer-case is the Lord Mayor's arms, two donkeys on a field azure, and an owl for a crest, with the motto of ' Business is business.' "

" Hem !" said the Lord Mayor.

A buzz of approbation at this remark ran through the assembly, under cover of which Duval said to himself—

" I will have that watch, and, if possible, the gold chain that that piece of hog's flesh they call a Lord Mayor has round his neck."

Duval was not without hopes of getting something from the worthy sheriff likewise, and some of the other guests looked promising in the way of watches and pocket-books ; so that, upon the whole, Duval was not without a hope of paying himself very well for his trouble in coming to the Mansion House.

" Dinner waits !" cried a loud voice at the door of the drawing-room, in which the guests were assembled.

If etiquette and the customary form of English gentry would have permitted such a thing, what a grand rush there would have been ; but they were a little too civilised for that. England is not America, and so the guests, according to rank, proceeded in a long, gay, sparkling, procession to the feast. Duval took care to keep very close to his friend the sheriff, by which means he secured a capital place at the principal table close to the Lord Mayor.

" I beg pardon, sir," said a lacquey to Duval, " but that seat was reserved for the Recorder."

" Eh ?" said Duval.

" That seat, sir, was reserved for the Recorder."

" Oh thank you," said Duval. " I am very comfortable ; I don't at all prefer the corner."

" Deaf as a badger," said the flunkey, and he moved away to state the difficulties of the case to the learned personage whom it concerned, and who it appeared laughed it off, and left Duval in his seat, for he was not interrupted again.

The feast now began, and Duval was truly astonished to see the great execution which the guests did upon the rich viands that were placed at their disposal. He ate but very little himself, for his mind was intent upon some plan of operation by which he could contrive to possess himself of the Lord Mayor's watch ; the chain and seals of which hung temptingly out of his fob. He did not sit absolutely next to his lordship, so it was by no means easy. A cabinet minister occupied the post of honour, but luckily for Duval that personage all the time he was there was in a perfect agony to get away, and left as soon as with any decency he could.

Duval popped into the vacant chair in a moment, and the sheriff joined up close.

" Hem !" remarked the Lord Mayor again.

CHAPTER LIX.

A LITTLE DISTURBANCE IN THE CITY.—DUVAL'S ESCAPE.

It was quite evident to Duval that his worship the Lord Mayor considered that a great breach of etiquette had been committed by Duval taking possession of the vacant chair of the minister of state, and that the " Hem !" was the mode in which he so expressed himself.

Under any other circumstances, Duval would not have troubled himself upon the occasion; but now he had an object in view, and leaning towards the Lord Mayor, he said—

"My lord, I was stopped on Ealing Common as I came here, by the celebrated Claude Duval."

"Ah!" said the Lord Mayor.

"I should not trouble your lordship with so very trivial a circumstance were it not that after robbing me, Duval said—'I know, Mr. Schoffer, where you are going, and you can tell the Lord Mayor that I fully intend to dine with him to-day.'"

The Lord Mayor upon this gathered in all the breath his lungs would hold, and puffed out his cheeks like a grampus, looking unutterable things the while. He stared at Duval as though he would eat him up, and then in a low mumbling voice like distant thunder, he said—

"Claude Duval, the highwayman, dine with me?"

"He said so, my lord."

"Bah!"

"Exactly, my lord. I consider that last remark of yours as highly intelligent and satisfactory; but for all that, Claude Duval, who they do say would keep his word in such a particular if he died for it, declared his intention of dining with you to-day."

The colour slightly faded from the face of the Civic King, and he ran his eye along the line of familiar faces on each side of the table, almost expecting to find some strange physiognomy among them that should seem like what he could picture to himself Duval's would be; but no, all were known. He never thought for a moment of suspecting his informant; besides, had not Sheriff Buggins introduced him as young Mr. Schoffer? and that was conclusive.

"He not only, my lord, swore he would be here, but that he would rob you of your diamond ring."

"My ring—my ring!"

"Yes, my lord, that one on your finger which becomes you so well, and which upon no other finger would look as it does; and if Duval——"

"Hush, don't speak so loud young man. I don't want all the world to know that it is possible any highwayman could have the impudence to come here."

"Impudence indeed, your worship. It shall go no farther."

"I would not lose this ring for a thousand pounds—No."

As he spoke, he drew it from his finger and handed it to Duval to look at. The guests at the table, in the midst of the clatter of knives and forks, and the constant changing of plates, paid no attention to the whispered conference between the Lord Mayor and his neighbour, young Schoffer. It was not then that the attention of his worship was required to the general company. After dinner it would have been quite another thing.

"It is a handsome ring," said Duval, "a very handsome ring, indeed."

As he said this he dropped it on to the floor, at the feet of the Lord Mayor.

"My ring—my ring," said his lordship, as he stooped to pick it up.

Claude stooped at the same time and adroitly drew the gorgeous watch from the fob of the Lord Mayor, who was so intent upon picking up his ring that he never missed it, or felt the slightest movement of it escaping.

"I am so sorry your lordship troubled yourself to stoop," said Duval; "I would have got it in a moment for you."

"Don't mention it," said his lordship, looking almost purple with the exertion of stooping. "I would not lose it for a thousand pounds, that I would not—eugh!"

"It was very awkward of me to be seen to drop it."

"Don't mention that, sir—don't mention that, sir. Do you think you should know this Claude Duval if you were to see him again?"

"Oh, yes."

"Ha, that is a very good thing indeed. Just look around you and tell me if you observe him."

Duval affected to look very carefully all along the tables, and then he shook his head dubiously.

"I should hardly think, my lord, that he has ventured to come. I don't see anything of him."

"Hem! I'm very glad of it indeed."

"The probability, my lord, is that he will hide somewhere, and pounce upon you when you least expect it."

"Gracious! in my private room perhaps."

"Nothing more likely. I hope you will permit me to accompany you there to look for him. If you could take him into custody it would be very much talked of. There could be no danger here, I should say."

"Let me think," said the Lord Mayor. "Ah—hem! Mr. Sheriff, will you have the goodness to take my chair for a few moments?"

"Certainly, my lord. I am much honoured."

"Come," added the Lord Mayor, to Duval, "follow me. We will, at all events, give such directions as shall prevent the possibility of his escape if he is now in the Mansion House, or of his entrance into it if he is not—hem!"

Duval followed the Lord Mayor through a little door in the end of the dining hall, and after traversing a short passage, they reached a small room, which was lighted by an elegant lamp upon the table.

"Now, my young friend," said the Lord Mayor, closing the door, "what do you advise?"

"Are we quite alone, my lord?"

"Oh, quite—quite."

"And can no one overhear us?"

"This, sir, is my private room, and no one presumes to overhear anything that takes place within it—hem!"

"Then, sir, I would advise you not to make the smallest resistance, but to take things perfectly easy."

"Eh? What do you mean, sir?"

"That I am Claude Duval!"

"Ah!" cried the Lord Mayor, and staggering back, he fell into the recesses of a great arm chair.

For a moment Duval thought he would have fainted away, but he did not. His face only assumed a purple hue, and his eyes opened particularly wide, and he glared upon Duval as though he would devour him.

"Yes, my lord," added Duval, in a low cautious tone, "I am Claude Duval. I said I would dine with you, and I have dined with you; I said I would have your diamond ring, and—I have it."

As he spoke, he slipped the magnificent ring from the finger of the bewildered Lord Mayor.

"I said I would have your gold chain, and lo! I have that likewise; and now, my Lord Mayor, upon your making the least outcry for the next half hour or so, I shall be under the disagreeable necessity of throttling you."

His lordship only groaned slightly.

"I have the honour to bid you good evening, my lord. Your dinner was excellent—your wines first-rate, and I must say that I have enjoyed myself very much indeed."

"He—has—enjoyed himself," gasped the Lord Mayor. "Hem! Oh—oh—ah!"

Duval suddenly started, for a confused clamour of many voices came upon his ears. The more he listened the louder the sounds grew, and then stepping to the door of the private room he opened it a little way and listened. He could hear that it was from the dining hall that the confusion of voices proceeded, and feeling confident that, with amazement and terror combined, the Lord Mayor was incapable of making any resistance, or giving any alarm, he walked hastily down the narrow passage connecting the private room with the banquet hall, and listened at the door that led into it.

" Yes, gentlemen," he heard a voice say—" He left me in the road and drove off with my curricle, and I do believe he is a highwayman. I am young Mr. Schoffer, I can prove it. He is a highwayman. I have walked all the way, till I got a hackney-coach at the top of Oxford Street. Oh, gentlemen, I am an injured individual."

Duval easily recognised the voice of young Schoffer, and for the moment he felt rather undecided what to do.

" Justice," shouted Schoffer. " My curricle—my horse—my card of admission—my gloves—my everything. I had to bawl out thieves at the top of my voice, before I could get into this place at all, and now I bawl out murder !"

About thirty voices said something all at once, and Duval felt all over the door for some mode of fastening it.

" Where is the Lord Mayor ?" shouted some half-dozen people at once. " Where is the Lord Mayor ?"

" I only hope," thought Duval, as he shot a small bolt into the socket, " that you won't find the Lord Mayor yet awhile."

With a conviction, then, that there must be some other mode of outlet from the Mayor's private room than through the banquetting hall, Duval returned thither, and found his lordship still seated on the large chair, and looking about him as before.

A glance showed Duval a small door opposite to the one at which he had entered, but he had hardly time to reach it, before he heard a crash, and felt certain that the little door leading from the banquetting hall to the narrow passage was broken open. There was now no time to lose.

" All's not lost that are in danger," said Duval, as he pulled open the little door and darted through it. He closed it after him, and finding a key in the lock upon the outer side he rapidly turned it, and then hurried along totally in the dark. He knew that the Mansion House was a tolerably modern building, and that he was not likely to fall down any trap-doors or secret places, so he darted on heedless of the total darkness until he came bump against a wall.

" Where there is a wall," he said, " there is a door somewhere, so I have but to go on feeling for it. I must take care, though, that I do not make a precipitate tumble down some staircase."

As Duval was on the first floor of the building, this was by far the greatest risk that he ran ; but he came to the handle of a door, which he tried to turn but found it fast. As he stood for a few moments quite still, he heard a rattle sprung fiercely.

" What the deuce are they at ?" he said. " Do they want to summon all the watchmen of the City ?"

He made another attempt at the door and shook it. From the manner in which it shock, he felt confident it was only slightly fastened, so placing his shoulder against it, he forced it at once open with a crash. The room beyond it was quite dark, and the first thing Duval did was to tumble over a chair.

" Confound the chair," he cried.

Almost as he spoke, a door nearly opposite to him suddenly flashed open, and he saw right into the banquetting hall. How he had got round to it again he could not conceive, but there was really no time for reflection. The danger was imminent, for a number of persons armed in different ways were about to come through that doorway.

As Duval was in the dark they could not see him, and he had time and presence of mind enough to shrink back before any flash of light could fall upon him. He had now no resource but to go on pursuing the wall, and as he did so, he reached the head of a flight of stairs, and slipped down several of them.

He heard the trampling of feet behind him, and once he heard quite distinctly, a loud voice say—

" No doubt it is Claude Duval, as the Mayor says."

" Ah," thought Duval, " they know me then do they ? Well, they will not get me quite so easily for all that now, I take it."

He flew rather than walked down the flight of stairs now, and was in a moment or two at the foot of them. A faint light, as if reflected from some apartment, flashed upon him, and a man came towards him with a branch candlestick carrying three lights in his hand.

"Who's that?" said the man.

"I!" cried Claude, and rushing forward he knocked him down, candlestick and all, before he could say another word.

"Stop him!" shouted another voice.

Claude drew the dress sword he wore, and dashed on. He came to another little flight of steps, but they ascended instead of descending, and then he bounced into a room in which were some dozen of lackeys. One of the windows was open, and a glance told Duval that it looked out on to the landing of the stone steps in front of the Mansion House. Turning to the lackeys for a moment, he cried—

"If any one is in love with death let him follow me!" and then he sprang out into the open air.

"There he is! there he is!" cried a hundred voices.

CHAPTER LX.

DUVAL'S GREAT PERIL IN THE CITY, AND STRANGE PLACE OF REFUGE.

Duval felt at the moment just a little staggered at the exigence of his position, but he felt that if anything was to be done for his safety it must be done at once. Each moment brought with it many dangers.

Without more hesitation, then, than was sufficient to let him see his way down, he rushed from the elevated portion of the Mansion House and reached the street. One man made a plunge at him, crying—"I have him."

"Not yet," said Duval, as he run him through the breast with the sword he still had possession of.

The man fell back with a groan, and his fate seemed rather to stagger those who were pressing on with speed, and a lane was kept for Duval, through which he made his way, brandishing the sword. In this way he darted down Mansion-house Street, and gained Bucklersbury before any one could muster courage enough to lay hold of him. There was one thing, however, that had a prejudiced effect upon his safety, and that was that he kept the drawn sword still in his hand.

A watchman in Bucklersbury threw himself in his way, crying—

"Just stop a bit."

"Out of the path, idiot!" cried Duval.

"Not quite so foolish," said the watchman, and he made a blow at Duval with his bludgeon.

Duval did not want to kill him, but he caught the bludgeon in its descent, and twisting it out of the hands of the watchman he dealt him a blow on the head with it that sent him reeling into the road-way.

A loud shout behind him now warned him that the mob and the officers were close upon his heels. He paused for a moment at the corner of a court to take breath.

"Whither shall I fly?" he said. "Of a truth I did not exactly calculate upon being thus hunted through the streets of London. This is something more than a perilous adventure, and how it will end yet has to be seen."

"Stop him! stop him! Stop thief!" cried many voices.

"Indeed! Well, be it so; I will run, and let the peril be his who is fool enough to overtake me."

Duval dashed down the court.

He had not the remotest idea where the court led to, but he took it at a venture.

It was only when some distance down it that he thought of the rather disagreeable chance of its having no outlet.   Suddenly he came to what appeared the end of it, and he paused irresolutely.

A boy was standing upon a doorstep, and to him Duval said—

"Can't I get out of this court but by going back ?"

"Oh, yes, sir," said the boy, pointing to what looked like a doorway. "There is the way out.   It leads into Cannon Street."

"Stop him ! stop him !   A highwayman !" chorussed a crowd of voices, and Duval had just time to dart off in the direction the boy had pointed out to him, when his foes rushed down the court in a dense throng.

The little alley into which he had plunged was so dark that for a moment he thought the boy had deceived him, but as he ran on he found such was not the case, for the passage widened and he got into another court somewhat similar in size to the first one he had at such a venture darted down.

Then in a moment or two, he get out into Cannon Street, along which he went at a great rate ; but the mob kept close upon his heels, and the worst of the affair was, that it was a time of night so very few passengers were in the streets, that he, as he ran, became quite a marked object, and his dress sufficed to attract the observation of the few people he did chance to meet.

If he had seen any open door he would not for a moment have hesitated to enter the house to which it belonged ; but none such presented itself, and he was compelled to rush on a fugitive hunted through the streets of the City.   And now he heard behind him a hard and rapid tread upon the pavement, and upon looking round, he saw one man, who had outran all the others, and was gaining fast upon him.   This man did not speak, for well he knew that by doing so he should only lose his wind, and so incapacitate himself for continuing the chase.

"He runs well," thought Claude Duval.   "Perhaps he would like to be a little in advance."

With these muttered words, Duval slacked his pace a little as though he were quite exhausted, upon which the man, with a short cry of satisfaction, made superhuman efforts to come up with him.

Gradually Duval let him get nearer and nearer, and he heard him say—

"The reward will be mine."

Suddenly then, with the rapidity of lightning, Duval dropped upon his hands and knees on the pavement, and in an instant the fast runner, who was unable to check his headlong speed, flew over him, and went rolling and scudding along the pavement heavily for about twenty feet, when he was caught by a post, which knocked the little remaining breath he had completely out of his body.

"How do you feel now, my friend ?" said Duval, as he walked leisurely past him.

The man was incapable of answering a word, for he was effectually stunned by the fall he had had, and there Duval left him lying without seeking to inflict any further injury upon him.

Duval now hoped that he had distanced his foes, and thrown them off the scent. He looked about him to see where he was, but he was not sufficiently conversant with the City to feel quite certain upon that point, so, at a venture, he took the first turning that he came to.   He found that that brought him out close to St. Paul's Church-yard, and he had hardly had time to assure himself that it was the cathedral he was close to, when from Cheapside about twenty people suddenly turned, and exclaimed—

"There he is !   There he is ! Seize him ! Hold him, somebody.   Stop thief ! —stop him !"

Duval had sufficiently recovered now to be in good breath, so off he started round St. Paul's, hoping to get into Newgate Market, and admist its intricacies, find some mode of baffling his pursuers.

He did, by great swiftness, reach Paternoster-row, but some of his enemies kept close upon his heels, and as he fled down Ave Maria Lane he was compelled to turn and face two men who pressed him closely.

Here it was that Duval gave evidence of that great personal strength which, to look at him, no one would believe he possessed, and which he only put forth when very much pressed or very much angered.

He seized the foremost of the two men, and fairly lifting him off his feet, he flung him with such force against the other that they both fell, greviously hurt, and

THE DEPUTY-GOVERNOR OF NEWGATE SHOWING CLAUDE HIS CLOAK.

bellowing for assistance.   Duval by that action got a start of nearly the whole length of Ave Maria Lane, and he came out into Newgate Street.   He then ran round the corner of the Old Bailey, and when there he paused to listen which route his pursuers had taken.   He soon found that some were coming after him down Newgate Street, while from Ludgate Hill another party of some thirty or forty persons advanced with furious cries.

Duval now showed that remarkable presence of mind and daring which had preserved him in many dangers. He hit upon a scheme, the daring insolence of which was almost certain to make it succeed. He knew that day and night warders were up in the lobby of Newgate, and that a light was there, so he boldly ascended the rugged stone steps, and knocked authoritatively at the little wicket.

"Who's there?" growled a voice from within.

"A gentleman from the sheriff," said Duval, in a clear voice; and then in a moment the door was opened, and the turnkey, with a very much softened voice, said—

"Pray, sir, walk in. Anything amiss, sir?"

"Not much," said Duval. "I suppose the governor is asleep by this time—is he not?"

"Why no, sir. He is at my Lord Mayor's entertainment at the Mansion; but Mr. Smithers, who acts for him, is only lying down, sir, in his room."

"Take me to him at once, then," said Duval. "I have a message to him from the sheriff."

"Yes, sir. Hilloa, Watkins!"

"Here you is!" said a half-drowsy man, getting up from a bench upon which he had been indulging himself with a nap. "Here you is. What's the row now, old fellow—eh?"

"Show this gentleman to Mr. Smithers' room, Watkins. He comes from the sheriff with a message."

Upon this intimation, Mr. Watkins was all alive; and, indeed, the appearance of Duval in his handsome apparel was quite sufficient to give a colour to what he said, so Mr. Watkins went before him with a light, and after conducting him through some windings and turnings, paused at the door of a room, and tapped at it.

"Come in," said a voice.

Watkins opened the door, and said in a humble voice—

"A gentleman from the sheriff, sir, if you pleases."

"Oh! ask him to walk in. Pray be seated, sir. I hope nothing is amiss in the City?"

"Nothing of material consequence, I believe, sir," said Duval; "but it has been proved that, by some means, the notorious and impertinent Claude Duval has found his way to-night into the Mansion House; and some say he has left, and some say he remains, and that it is a companion of his who has left; so my Lord Mayor and the sheriff have requested me to ask you if you have any one here who knows him by sight, and if so that you will be good enough to send such a person at once to the Mansion House."

"Certainly, certainly, sir. I do think we have several officers in the prison who can recognise him. Will you excuse me a moment, sir, and I will give the necessary orders?"

"Oh, of course. Pray do not hurry yourself upon my account, for I have made such speed from the Mansion here on foot, not being able to find my carriage in the Poultry, that I am really glad of a little rest."

"Pray draw near to the fire, sir, and make yourself quite at home. I shall be back in a few moments."

"Humph!" said Duval, when he found himself alone; "I am to make myself at home, am I? Well, I should not wonder, but that is just what I shall have to do in reality some of these days in this not very comfortable building. However, I think that by this rather hazardous adventure I have distanced and outwitted my pursuers. A capital fire, this—Egad, I will make myself at home, too."

With this he drew a chair near the fire, but he took good care to keep an eye upon the door, and an ear open to any sound that might apprise him of danger.

Such precautions were, however, quite unnecessary, for Mr. Smithers had not the remotest suspicion regarding the genuiness of the mission upon which Duval said he had come. In about five minutes, back he came.

"I have sent three of our officers, sir," he said, "who know Duval by sight very well, indeed; and if he be still in the Mansion House among the guests, you may depend they will find him out."

"His lordship will be very much obliged to you, indeed," said Duval, "for this promptitude, and I only hope that they may be as successful as their zeal deserves."

"It seems," said Mr. Smithers, "to be the general idea that he has escaped, and is somewhere in the street; for a mob of thirty or forty people has just passed Newgate, shouting for him, and no doubt eager to catch him, on account of the large reward that has been offered for his apprehension."

"That is their motive no doubt, sir. But the Lord Mayor is decidedly of opinion that he is still in the Mansion House."

"If so, sir, you may depend my officers will have him."

"I am rejoiced to hear it."

Duval now intimated that he must leave; but he kept protracting the time by thanking Mr. Smithers in the most engaging manner for the kind alacrity with which he had acted upon the occasion; and Smithers fancying by the style and appearance of Duval, that he must be some person of consequence, was a very mirror of urbanity and suavity.

At length Duval thought that all danger from the mob must have ceased, and he gave a slight shiver, as he said—

"I shall feel cold, I daresay, in the night air, going back."

"My dear, sir," said Smithers, "will you do me the favour to accept a loan of a cloak? I have one quite at your service."

CHAPTER LXI.

DUVAL GETS TO THE OLD HATS, AND RESCUES HIS HORSE.

Duval could scarcely refrain from a smile at the great alacrity of the Deputy Governor of Newgate to assist him in his escape, by lending him a cloak to cover up his evening dress.

"My good, sir," he said, "you are veay kind, and if I thought it would not be putting you to any inconvenience——"

"Oh, none in the least."

"Then, sir, I accept your kind offer with pleasure, and perhaps you will add to your kindness by letting somebody fetch a hackney-coach for me?"

"Of course, sir. I was just going to propose it. I will fetch the cloak in a moment if you please."

"Mighty complacent," thought Duval, when he was once more alone. "Now this fellow will be ready to eat his own head off when he finds what a mistake he has made. In good truth it was a lucky thought this of coming to Newgate. But here he is; I must be careful not to abate in my assumption of a good character to the last. By-the-by it will look bad not to give him some name."

Mr. Smithers made his appearance with a large and handsome cloak upon his arm. It was made of blue cloth, and lined with rich crimson plush.

"This, sir," he said, "will at all events keep the cold out, and a coach will be ready in a few moments."

"I do not know how to thank you for this kindness," said Duval, as he put on the cloak. "You shall have this back in the course of to-morrow. My name is Franks—Sir Willoughby Franks."

Mr. Smithers bowed.

"It don't look exactly the thing for a baronet to be running about the streets of the City at night; but you must know, this Duval actually stopped Lady Franks one night upon Ealing Common, and the Lord Mayor knowing that I felt rather sore upon that matter, said to me, 'Sir Willoughby, I am quite sure you will do anything to capture Claude Duval.' 'Indeed my lord,' I said, 'I will.' 'Then,' he added, 'if you don't mind taking your carriage and going as far as Newgate, I think you will do us good service.' So you see I come."

"Yes, Sir Willoughby. It was very good of you to come, indeed."

"The coach is ready, sir," said a man at the door.

"And so am I," said Duval, "Mr. Smithers, good night. Lady Franks and myself will be very glad to see you at our little park close by Watford at any time that may suit your convenience. Nay, my dear, I beg that you will not leave your room to see me off. Now, really!"

"But allow me, sir—the honour."

"My good, sir."

Mr. Smithers would insist upon it, and accordingly with all due ceremony Duval was seen to the door of Newgate, where a hackney-coach, the driver of which had been awakened from a comfortable snooze on his stand by Fleet Market, was in waiting. In got Claude, and then waving his hand to Smithers, he said in a loud voice to the coachman—

"Drive to the Mansion House as quickly as you can, my friend. Good night, Mr. Smithers. Good night."

"Good night, Sir Willoughby."

Off went the coach, and the wicket-gate of Newgate was shut, to keep out the cold night air that rather set in that direction. The moment the coach got half way up Newgate Street, Duval pulled the check-string, and the driver pulled up.

"Did you go for to want anythink, sir?"

"Yes, my friend, I have altered my mind; I wont go to the Mansion, but if you will drive me to the corner of Oxford Street, I will give you a guinea for the job."

"Won't I, your honour? All's right. Lor, if this isn't the governor o' Newgate, I'm smothered. He's arter some cove now, I'll be bound, as has been and gone and done somethink in the robbery line, or the murdering for all I knows on."

The horses' heads were turned in the direction of Holborn, and Duval was fast carried away from the scene of his dangers in the City. He wrapped the cloak well around him, for the night was very chilly, and as the vehicle rumbled up Holborn Hill, he could hardly keep from laughing aloud, to think how easily he had duped the Deputy-Governor of Newgate.

The coach made good progress, and they reached the corner of Oxford Street in perfect safety; but as they turned into that then tolerable thoroughfare, Duval heard the sound of horses' feet in the direction of Holborn.

He had kept both the glasses of the coach down, in order that nothing might impede him in hearing if any pursuit were attempted, and he now placed his ear outside one of them, and listened intently. He became convinced that some three or four horsemen were on the road, but whether they were after him or not, of course he had no possible means of judging.

Suspicion haunts the guilty mind, and Duval could not help fancying that he was pursued.

"It is possible," he thought, "that some suspicion may have arisen; and if so, I will die game at all events." The thought then struck him that he might make a friend of the coachman, and accordingly he carefully let down one of the front windows, and leaning out, he without stopping the coachman, just touched him on the arm, as he said—

"My friend, a word with you."

"Oh, lor! How you did frighten me to be sure, sir. I was a thinking, you see, and in what you calls a brown study, and didn't expect nobody to say nothink."

"Listen to me. If any one should stop you, and ask you if you took up a fare at Newgate, it will be a five pound note in your way to say 'No!'"

"Will it, sir?"

"Yes, and here it is. You can keep it whether you are asked the question or not; but mind, no shuffling."

"Lor bless you, sir, shuffling? No, indeed! Haven't I got a matter o' nine babbies at home, and did I ever so much as see a five *pun* note in all my life? Oh, no, sir; only you say what I am to do and I'll do it."

"Then in plain language, I suspect that you may be stopped and questioned, and I don't want anybody to know that I am here, or where I came from. I will leave the management of the affair to you."

"All's right, sir! I supposes as you is the Governor of the stone jug, and arter some desperate rum un?"

"Exactly."

Duval resumed his seat, but he carefully felt the priming of his pistols, for he felt a sort of presentiment that some danger of not a very common-place character was at hand; and with all his usual strength of mind, his very mode of life had tended to make him rather superstitious.

"I hold the lives of two men in my hands at all events," he said, "and woe be to those who may tempt me too far. I will have, and I have had, great forbearance, but I will not be hunted like a wild beast to the death, without turning upon my pursuers."

The horsemen had turned into Oxford Street, and in a few moments Duval was quite convinced that his suspicions that they were after him were correct, for one of them cried out with a loud voice—

"Coach! Coach! Stop! Coach there!"

The coachman paid not the remotest attention to the cry to him to stop, nor did he urge his horses a bit the faster. He treated the matter just with cool indifference, and heard it as though he heard it not.

But the horsemen were tolerably well mounted, and were not to be baulked in that sort of way, and as of course any attempt to escape with a couple of hackney coach horses would have been truly ridiculous, the mounted men soon reached the vehicle, and one riding to the head of the horses, stopped them. Another spoke angrily to the coachman.

"Why did you not stop when I called Coach?"

"'Cos I was hired. I couldn't take you."

"Did you take up a fare at Newgate?"

"Newgate?"

"Yes. Answer me directly. Where you fetched from the stand at Holborn Bridge to take up a person at Newgate?"

"N—o! Why you are out o' your mind. My fare comed out o' Gray's Inn, and my stand was opposite the old pump. Ask the gemman hisself as is my fare. I knows what you is—you is highwaymen, and wants to rob a poor fellow. Watch, watch, watch!"

"Hold your row, will you, and drive up to the next lamp? We want to speak to your fare."

"Werry good."

"Danger," said Duval to himself; "three men well mounted and well armed. I must be off. Oh, if I only had my horse now with me, I would desire nothing better than to give them a run; but on foot they are just one too many for me."

As he spoke, and as the coachman drove very leisurely to the nearest lamp which was on the near side, Duval opened the door of the coach on the off side, and merely held it from flapping wide open by one hand, while with the other he had one of his pistols ready for immediate action.

"Here ye is," said the coachman as he drew up, so that although he was pretty close to a lamp, not much of the light of it could come into the coach. At the same moment, too, a watchman crossed the road from the other side of the way, calling out—

"What's the row? I'll take you all into custody. Who was it called out watch? Here I am."

The mounted man who had given his orders in so very peremptory a manner, now leant from his saddle to look into the coach, and when he saw Duval he said—

"All resistance is useless. You are a prisoner. If you stir hand or foot, I will put a pistol through your brain. I am not a man to be trifled with."

"Very likely," said Claude. "For whom do you take me?"

"For Claude Duval!"

"Then you ought to be more careful."

Bang went Duval's pistol, and the man fell over his horse's neck, instantly exclaiming—

"He has killed me! Help, help! He has killed me!"

Duval had kept his hand still upon the handle of the opposite door of the coach, and the moment he had pulled the trigger of his pistol, he opened it and dashed out, upsetting the watchman in the mud and rolling over him. With an execration Duval rose, and only waiting to deal the prostrate watchman one hearty kick, he darted over the road, and dashed down what is now Wells Street.

All this was done with such rapidity, that the horseman who was close to the horses' heads of the hackney-coach, and another who was just behind it, hardly knew what had happened, except that a pistol shot had been fired by some one, before Duval had vanished from before their eyes like a phantom. Perhaps, too, there was some little fear mingling with their other feelings, when they saw their comrade fall.

"After him," cried one of them recovering from the momentary confusion into which he had been thrown. "Come on. He went this way. Shoot him down if you see him."

They both started off in the direction Duval had taken, and when the hackney coachman found himself alone, he placed his finger by the side of his nose, and in a low voice he said—

"Five *pun* for that ere job. Good! Off I goes, and not never a one on 'em knows my number, I'm sure."

With these words he turned round his horses, and in a few moments was going at an easy pace down Wardour Street, quite satisfied with his night's work.

Duval did not go far up Wells Street, but turning off to the left, he at a slashing pace made his way to the upper part of Oxford Street. Fortunately for him, the officers did not turn in that direction, but rode on stopping to ask every passenger they met if such a person as he, Duval, had been seen; but no one could give them any information, and they rode right out into the fields where the Regent's Park now stands, before they began to think that they might as well give up so fruitless a chase.

They then made the best of their way back to Oxford Street, where they found about half-a-score of watchmen round the dead body of their comrade, who had received Duval's pistol-shot in his head, and had only lived long enough to utter the few words that we have recorded, before he fell from his horse to the ground.

In the meantime, Duval pursued his route on foot at a good round pace towards the Old Hats Inn, which he reached as the Acton church clock struck the hour of five in the morning.

———

CHAPTER LXII.

DUVAL MEETS WITH A STRANGE ADVENTURE AT EAST ACTON.

IF the young City gent, instead of making the best of his way to the Mansion, when Duval so unceremoniously ousted him from his curricle, had gone back to the Old Hats, he might have done him, Duval, a much greater amount of injury than he did, for he might have laid hands upon his horse.

As it was, however, we have seen that he did not adopt that course, but rather chose to make the attempt at the Mansion House, which, although it had certainly placed Duval in no small peril, we have seen, signally failed in making him a prisoner, or in killing him, either of which objects would have been not at all displeasing to those who called themselves the authorities.

But still Duval knew that there had been time enough ever since his escape, to send an express to the Old Hats to detain his horse, for he had, it will be recollected, lost considerable time in Newgate. It was, therefore, with some slight amount of anxiety that he now approached the ancient Inn. All was profoundly quiet, and from that Duval drew a favourable omen, and he boldly rung the ostler's bell.

In a few minutes a voice from within called out to know who was there.

"My horse," said Duval. "I want my horse, and here's half-a-guinea waiting for you, if you bring him out quick."

"Oh, you are the gentleman who went away in the curricle?"

"Yes—I am he."

"Very good, sir. I will be with you directly."

"All's right," thought Duval. "Only let me get into the saddle, and I care for nothing. Ah, what clattering sound is that I hear upon the road? Surely I am not at this critical moment pursued? That would, indeed, be too provoking. By all that's unlucky, yes, I feel assured of it; some half-dozen horsemen are on the road, and I don't exactly know anything more likely to get folks into a gallop, such as they are coming at, than a chance of catching me."

With this conviction on his mind, Duval hammered at the stable-gate, and called out in a loud voice—

"Quick, ostler, quick."

"Coming, sir."

The stable-gate was opened, and the ostler appeared with Duval's horse, all ready for the road.

"Hilloa," he said, "are they friends of yourn, sir, as is coming from town at such a slashing pace? My eye, ain't they doing it!"

Duval did not waste his time by replying one word, but vaulting at once into his saddle he faced round on the road, with his front to his pursuers.

"That half-guinea, sir," said the ostler.

"There is a whole one.—Halt!"

That word "halt" was pronounced by Duval, with such a sudden and startling distinctness, that the horsemen, one and all, on the instant drew up. Then one who seemed to be the leader of the party, cried out—

"Who says halt? Are you anybody in authority?"

"Of course," said Duval.

"Who are you, sir? We are officers, and after the notorious highwayman, Claude Duval. Perhaps you are a magistrate, sir?"

"Oh, my eye!" said the ostler.

The officer who had last spoken, trotted up to the spot where Duval was standing mounted, and the moment he turned his eyes upon him, he turned pale with passion, as he said in a hoarse, excited tone—

"Confound your impudence! you are Claude Duval! But your race is run at last. Surrender, or I will have your life—you vagabond!"

"Keep off," said Duval, "if you are a wise man. I am not used to be called names, my friend."

"You ain't, ain't you? We will soon see what you are used to. Come on, my men, here's our customer; come on, here's Duval, and we must have him dead or alive. Here he is on his horse; we are just in time. He is afraid to run away; we are sure of him now."

"Well," said Duval, "you are the greatest fool in your business I ever met with yet. Come on, my men."

Duval uttered these last words so ironically that the officer's rage very much increased; and but that he felt very sure indeed that any movement of that sort would be the signal probably for a pistol bullet in his brains, he would have made a dash at Duval, and tried to capture him alone.

The others here rode up, but they trotted back again about twenty paces from Duval. That was quite a sufficient indication that they considered the service they were on to be one of no small danger, and Duval took advantage of their momentary hesitation to increase their too evident fears.

"Hark you," said Duval, "there are six of you altogether, and I think that you are in force enough to get the better of me; but in so doing, it strikes me very forcibly that you will run some risks, and some of you I should not be at all surprised to find stretched in death upon the road. I feel that I am to take the lives of three of you, and if you think that my capture is worth the risk of which three it shall be, why you may set about it at your earliest convenience."

The officers looked very shy.

"What!" cried the chief of them, "do you mean to say that you shrink from seizing this fellow now that you are face to face with him?"

"Of course they do," said Claude. "They are wise enough to prefer enjoying life a little longer to even dying with the glory of having contributed their lives to the death of Claude Duval; and you will do well to imitate them, for I warn you that the first among you who makes a hostile demonstration against me, will not live another minute. Now take your own course: I am not going to wait here while you consider whether you can screw up your courage or not."

Duval very slightly half turned, and the officer, who may be said from courtesy to have command of the party, immediately took a pistol from his pocket, and fired it at him.

"All's right," said Duval. "You will find it much more difficult to hit with a pistol bullet than it looks, my friend. It was not a bad shot, but what do you think of this?"

As he spoke he produced one of his pistols; but the officer, with a cry of alarm, got behind his men. They, however, were by no means anxious to act as a shield to him, and they dispersed right and left immediately, leaving him fully exposed to Duval's fire; but the slight tinge of anger which at the moment might have induced Duval to shoot him, had passed away, and he no longer thought it worth his while to take such a life. However, to his great alarm, Duval kept him covered with the pistol, until unable any longer to stand such a state of mortal apprehension, the officer fairly turned and galloped away.

This served quite as a sufficient impulse to his men to follow his example, so that for the time being, Duval got rid of them without firing a shot.

"This is a panic," he said to himself, "and wont last long. I must take advantage of it while it does remain."

With these words he gave the word to his horse, and off for the Old Hats he went at a speed which defied all pursuit. He thought it would be much better to get out of the high road as soon as possible; so observing to his right-hand a green lane, that in the early morning looked very rural and inviting, he at once turned down it, and went half a mile at a good pace without a pause.

The lane, even during that brief space, had taken several turns, principally to he right, so that Duval did not know very well where it led to, as he had never to his knowledge been in its intricacies before. Of course, it could not take him out of his way, as his way just then was any way that promised him temporary safety, until the ardour of the pursuit contingent upon his escape at the Mansion House had quite subsided; so he trotted up the lane.

It was quite a beautiful and charming thing to hear the wild birds twittering and singing in the luxuriant hedgerow; and as the sun rose higher and higher in the heavens, Duval felt all that charming influence which the cool pleasant vital morning air is sure to impart, and more particularly so to one who like him was a lover of nature.

"Well," he said, as he paused and listened to the song of the thrush, "I yet hope that the day will come when I may be able to retire from the din and bustle of this kind of life in which I am engaged, and far off in the quiet country, lead a life of ease and serenity. If they would only let me do it, I think that I would make an effort to get together a couple of thousand pounds or so, and go off at once to some midland county, and turn squire."

CLAUDE SAVES MAY FROM THE DAGGER OF HER FATHER-IN-LAW.

Duval himself, as he went on, could not help smiling at the conceit of his finding capital on the road in the character of a highwayman, and then becoming with it the great man of some village far away from the scene of all his exploits.

"I wonder," he said, "if I could really so settle down? I doubt it."

A dog suddenly bounded to his side, and then a lad came lounging along the lane.

"Hilloa, my boy," said Duval, "where does this lane lead to ?"

"To East Acton, sir. It's only round them alder trees to the right there, sir."

"Thank you. Humph ! East Acton," said Duval. "I must have come a tolerable round to get here ; but it is a quiet enough village among the tress, and perhaps after all it will be no bad plan upon my part to pass the day there. I will look about me first though when I get fairly into the village."

He only walked his horse now that the boy had told him it was so very near at hand, and then he found that he had been correctly enough informed, for upon turning the alders, he found himself in the village ; but a sight met Claude's eyes which induced him to come to an abrupt standstill.

In the centre of the main, and indeed only thoroughfare of the village, was a man holding a couple of horses, and from the accoutrements of the steeds it was quite evident to the practised eye of Duval that they belonged to the New Mounted Police, which had during the last six months been organised as a body of men ready to take the road against any highwayman who might become too notorious in any district. It was from this small body of mounted police that the horse patrol eventually sprang, and which gave the first very severe blow to highway robberies.

Now, Duval was anything but afraid of two men, but then it was his policy invariably to avoid an encounter with any one if he could, and accordingly he drew back under cover of the alder trees again. Upon glancing round him, then, he saw that he was close to a park paling, immediately above which was a bord announcing 'This Mansion and Offices to Let.' By rising in his saddle a little, Duval could get a tolerable view of the mansion, and seeing all the shutters closed, he concluded that it was empty.

"This may be as good a chance as any," he said, "for all I know. I may find this, if it be really deserted, a capital place to retire to for a day or night either ; and if any one be in it, it is most likely only some old couple to take care of the house, and I can coax or frighten them into silence for a few hours at all events."

He gave his horse as good a run as he could, and leaped him over the park paling with ease.

"That will do," he said, as he immediately dismounted, finding that by so doing both his own and the horse's head were beneath the paling, and free from observation from the village or the lane.

A little in advance of him he found a shrubbery, and having made his way into it, he tied his horse to the low bough of a young sycamore, about the roots of which was some fresh, inviting grass, which he knew would engage the attention of his four-footed friend for some time. With a light step then, and keeping all his senses on the alert, Duval went up a long shaded avenue towards the mansion.

Once he paused, for something amazingly like a faint scream came upon his ears.

"What can that be ?" he said. "Surely it was a scream, and yet it is possible it might have been the sharp sudden cry of some startled bird ; and yet it did sound strangely. However, I will walk slower and listen."

As he went on, no other sound met his ears until he came to the termination of the shady walk in which he was, and which he found ended in a pretty flower garden, that had been for some time suffered to go rather to decay. Then, the moment he stepped into it, he heard the cry again precisely as before, and it seemed to him evidently to come from the house.

"This is more than strange," he said, and he hastily crossed the little garden, and keeping some shrubs between him and the mansion, he reached an angle of it where there was a window rather close to the ground.

Putting his ear close to this window, Duval heard a loud voice saying something : but what were the precise words he could not distinguish. It was sufficiently evident, however, by their tone that they were words of violence and menace. This was enough for Duval, and he immediately sought the means of gaining admittance to the house.

This was by no means a very easy matter, for the window by which he had listened was defended by some ornamental iron-work, and, although it could not have offered any protracted resistance, yet Duval's object was to get into the mansion quietly, if possible.

CHAPTER LXIII.

DUVAL SAVES A LIFE, AND BECOMES SMITTEN WITH A BEAUTY.

ANOTHER cry, similar in tone to the two that he had before heard, acted as a powerful impulse upon Duval, and he ran round the house in order to seek for some mode of entrance into it. He tried three doors, but they were all fast. A fourth, however, yielded to his touch, as it was but upon the latch. He found himself at once in the house.

The moment he got in, he listened attentively; but for a few moments he could hear nothing. Then there came the sound of that man's voice again—for a man's it undoubtedly was—and it sounded to him harsher than it had done before. Yet Duval could not hear what he said.

"That sound, however, will guide me," he said. "I will find out what is going on in this house now, surely."

There were sufficient windows open in the place for him to be able to see well about him; and as he came along corridors and through rooms, he still at intervals could hear that loud angry voice. Duval was most anxious to ascertain from what room it came, and he, after traversing at least a dozen, and ascending one staircase and descending another, at last paused quite irresolutely, for he knew not which way to go. He had not long to wait, however, for a renewal of the sounds, and then he quite started to find that he was so near at hand to them.

They evidently proceeded from a room a little way from him on his right hand. He dashed towards it at once; and, opening the first door that presented itself, he found himself impeded by a curtain of some thick substance that hung in front of it facing the room. Behind that curtain, he felt convinced, were the persons whom he sought.

He now paused and listened, for he was anxious to ascertain the state of affairs in the room before he hazarded anything by a hasty, and perhaps ill-timed, interference. The stern, harsh, high voice of a man came upon his ears, and it was quite evident that the man spoke without the smallest thought that in that house he could be heard by any one but the party for whom his speech was intended.

"I tell you, girl," said the voice, "that you are here beyond all human aid—and you cannot expect any convulsion of nature in your favour. If you prefer death to signing this paper, you will get it; and then, knowing your handwriting so well as I do, I will sign it for you, and all will be as I wish it."

"Oh, no—no—spare me! A dreadful thought comes across my brain! Tell me, did you kill my mother?"

Perhaps Duval had heard as sweet voices; but he never had heard one that was more full of soft natural music than that which sounded in his ears. The man replied instantly—

"The knowledge of such a fact may perhaps influence your determination. Listen to me, Annette. When I married your mother, who had been then a widow two years, and who I found was most warmly attached to you—her only child—it was by pretending affection for you that I succeeded in winning her. Now, I tell you that I always hated you!"

"Hated me?"

" Yes, I detested you, and your mother likewise ; but I know that she had considerable property, which was to descend to you at her death, and I married her solely with the view of getting that property."

" But yet, you do not tell me if you took her life."

" I did."

" Oh, horror! horror !"

" Ha! ha! And so you had so slight an appreciation of my character as to fancy that I would let a human life or two stand between me and my objects !—No! Not twenty lives should warp me from a purpose once fully entertained and resolved upon."

" Monster !"

" Rail on. It matters not. This old mansion is deserted. No human ears but mine will give heed to what you say! You are here shut up from all the world. You have no chance—no hope of succour, so I will freely tell you all. I prepared a deed, the effect of which, provided both you and your mother signed it, would be to vest the entire property in me. If you had both signed it freely, you might have lived : she refused, and she died."

" You got not her signature, then?"

" I wrote it myself after her death. I am an adept at such matters. It is now your time, Sign, and live ; or refuse, and die, and I will sign for you. Choose !"

" You cannot be so base ?"

" Can I not? You will see."

" You asked me to call you father. Can you look upon me, and talk of killing?"

" Yes, I can talk of killing ; but upon your own head be the death you prefer to the mere parting with certain gold or gold's worth. You are more fond of possessions than I am, for you hesitate about even saving your life at the expense of this, which I would not do ; for, much as I love the riches of the earth, I yet hold my life as my chief possession. With you, however, the case seems to be different."

" No—no."

" But I say yes, girl ; and every moment that you delay signing this document, convinces me of that fact."

" No—no, it does not. You have made with me a fearful confidence. You have told me secrets which the grave alone can hide and if I sign that deed, who shall assure me then that you will not kill me ? You are too candid with me to permit me to live ! I am lost !—lost !"

" Not quite," said Duval, as he dashed aside the curtain, and made his way at once into the room—" Not quite. We will have something of a fight for you yet, unless this man is such an abject coward that he dare not raise a hand in his own defence."

With a shriek of joy the young girl flung herself at Duval's feet, and the father-in-law was so absolutely staggered and confounded at the sudden appearance of Duval, that he stood like a statue for several moments, and all his faculties appeared to be in obeyance.

" Villain !" said Duval. " Did you think that Heaven had nothing but a miracle by which it could stay such an arm as yours?"

The man recovered his senses, and drawing a knife from the breast of his apparel, he made a rush at Duval ; but the latter had fully expected that some effort of violence would be made, and he was prepared for it. He met the would-be assassin by so tremendous a blow in the face, that it stretched him on the floor at the farther end of the room in a state of insensibility.

" Saved ! Saved ! I am saved !" shrieked the young girl.

" Yes, you are safe now. But calm yourself, and tell me who you are, and how you came here ?"

She could not reply to him ; but, bursting into tears, she wept like a child.

" Do not try to check those tears," said Duval, tenderly. " Your feelings must have vent.   Your heart has been surcharged with grief and horror.   Weep freely ; you will be better."

She did weep freely.   When the feelings once break bounds, as well might we try to stem some torrent that is leaping its maddening course from crag to crag of a mountain, as stay them.   But, at length, they subsided into sobs, and then the first articulate sounds she uttered were—

"Take me from here!   Oh, take me from here, I pray you!   I feel as if I should die, if I remained longer in this dreadful place !"

"But your worthy father-in-law must be handed over to the police.   I rather think you will feel, no doubt, desirous that such should be the case, do you not ?"

"Oh, no—no.   I only wish to leave here.   Let him be.   Heaven, in its own way, and in its own good time, will punish him."

"Well," said Claude Duval, "if such be your wish, I, of course, can have no other.   Where would you like me to take you to ?"

"Anywhere but home."

"You forget that I don't know where your home is, nor have I the smallest knowledge of who you are, except that you are that man's daughter-in-law.   I am a complete stranger here, and my coming was one of the most accidental things that could possibly take place."

"Ah, no !   Heaven sent you.   But I will tell you all as we leave this house. I have a friend in London—an old friend of my own father's.   He is an attorney, and lives in the Temple.   Oh, sir, if you can but take me to him, all will be well. He disapproved so much of my mother's second marriage, that ever since that event we have seen nothing of him ; but I know he will protect me."

"In the Temple ?"

"Yes.   It is not so very far.   We can get to the village of Acton, and get a coach easily, or we will walk.   Anything, so that I soon leave this dreadful place."

Now, as regarded Duval, it was not one of the most safe or practicable things for him just then to go to the Temple, inasmuch as to do so would be to march into the very locality from which he had only recently escaped with no small difficulty.

These considertions crowded rather upon the mind of Duval, but he did not say anything at the moment as he saw that the young girl was in a state of great anxiety to get out of the mansion.   He just gave one glance at the prostrate form of the wicked father-in-law, and then he supported her from the place.

Duval took her by the same way that he had come, and pausing by the young sycamore tree, he said—

"This is my horse, and whatever mode of conveyance we may hit upon to the Temple, I must first place him in safety."

"Oh, my friend, there will be no difficulty in that.   I know persons in the village who will be kind to your steed, if I ask them ; and then we can easily find some means of getting to the City.   There is no sort of difficulty, my dear friend ; but it would vex me much if you were to leave me until I am in safety.   I seem to feel when I am by your side a sensation of security, which I should be loth indeed to lose.   You will stay with me ?"

"I will ; and having made you that promise, you may rely upon my carrying it out.   Allow me, however, to take my own course in so doing "

"Oh, yes—yes."

"Then, I decline going into East Acton ; and if you will allow me to place you on the saddle of my horse, I will likewise mount, and he will carry us both well to Hammersmith, where, if you have no particular objection to that course, I would like to go to the Temple by water."

"Your way, my friend, shall be my way.   Have you not saved me from death? I will go with you anywhere."

"Then let us lose no time."

With this, Duval assisted the young girl to the saddle, and springing upon it behind her, he held the reins in his right hand, while with his left he held her securely on her seat, and off they went down the lane at an easy but very fast canter, indeed.

Duval knew the way across the country to Hammersmith very well indeed, so he did not find it at all necessary to relax in his speed in the least; and as the total distance was something under two miles, it was soon performed. More than once during the ride the young girl had turned her face to his with such a look of sweet confiding affection, that Duval, who was by no means to be classed among the least susceptible of human beings, began first to admire and then to feel for her something akin to love. Poor Adele, at Kentish Town, to whom he had sworn so much affection, was, for the time being, completely forgotten; and he thought he had never seen a face and eyes so beautiful as those that now beamed upon him.

She was not above nineteen years of age, and of a very different style of beauty from Adele; so that she came before the senses of Duval with all the charms of contrast.

"How could any one," he said, "be so barborously wicked, as to think of injuring you?"

"Ah, my friend, all the world is not so good as you are."

This was rather a home-thrust to Duval. It was taking his goodness by far too much upon credit, in consequence of this one good act he had done in rescuing her from her evil father-in-law. For some few moments he made no reply to the speech, but then he said in a low tone—

"Do you love any one?"

She looked at him with a calm indifference, that at once convinced him no one had possession of her heart.

"None as I ought to love you," she said, "for have you not saved my life, and, but for you, what might I not be now? I am yet too young to bid the world good-by, do you not think so?"

CHAPTER LXIV.

DUVAL MAKES A GOOD BOOTY IN THE TEMPLE.

Duval was silent for a few moments now. The words of the young girl had made him reflect a little; and even he had a dread of breaking down that good opinion of hers, which from his gallant conduct in rescuing her from her father-in-law, she evidently entertained. At length he broke the silence by saying—

"And so your hand is really disengaged?"

"Ah, I understand you now," she said. "You wanted to know if I had any lover?"

"Just so."

"Then, I have none. I fancy I must be very ugly for no one ever yet took the trouble to whisper love to me."

"Then you are wrong."

"Oh, no, no, I assure you they never did."

"You mistake me. I meant that you were wrong as regarded fancying that you were ugly, for you are quite the reverse."

"Am I so?"

"Indeed you are, for you are very beautiful. I have seen many faces, and some among the many that I have at the time thought to be quite matchless in their beauty; but when I look upon you, I alter my opinion, because I find you without compare."

"You flatter me."

"No, I am not given to flattery. On the contrary, those who know me best accuse me of being rather too free-spoken. You may believe me, when I praise I feel much more than I express in the words that I am able to use."

Upon this the young girl was silent for a few minutes; she was evidently revolving in her mind what Duval had said, and at length very timidly she said—

" You will not tell me I am beautiful again ?"

" Why not ?"

" I don't know, but yet I feel that I would much rather not hear that from your lips."

" If you do not hear it from my lips, you will be sure to see it in my eyes. But if it pains you I will certainly not say as much again, nor will I tell you that I love you."

" Oh, do not—do not !"

Duval was silent, and by this time they had reached Hammersmith, where he dismounted, and determined to put up his horse, while he went by water to the Temple. He did the most prudent thing he now could, which was, to put up his steed at the largest inn he could see, where it was much less likely to attract any attention there as if it had been placed in charge of some little public-house ; and then with the fair young girl upon his arm, he went down to the river-side, and engaged a boat with two good rowers to carry him and his young and beautiful companion to the Temple.

That at that time Duval did not for one moment contemplate any evil to the young creature who had been so saddly thrown upon his protection, is quite evident from the fact of his going to the Temple at all, for there she had informed him that she would meet with a powerful protector in the shape of a member of the legal profession ; so that if he had had in his mind any dishonourable thoughts concerning her, he would not certainly have taken her in the first instance to the only one who in all probability would and could oppose him, and make any step inimical to her peace and reputation attended with disasterous consequences to him.

As the boatman, aided by the tide which happened to be running down, and so was perfectly favourable to their progress, made rapid way, Duval and the young girl sat in the stern of the boat, conversing in a low tone.

" And so you are quite sure," he said, " that the person you are going to will prove a kind friend to you ?"

" Oh, quite—quite. He is very old, but he will and can protect me, and he will get others to do so likewise. He will too, being in the law, know exactly what to do as regards my mother's husband."

" You do not like to call that man father ?"

" Oh, no—no. That is too sacred a name. I would have all children call their mother's second husband by merely that name, and never by that of father."

" Indeed ?"

" Yes, I think that that ought to be the childrens prerogative, and the only sort of reproach that the mother ought to hear for marrying again with the children of a former union about her."

" You have thought, then, upon this subject ?"

" Not much, but I have heard such a sentiment, and I so fully agreed with it that I at once adopted it. Oh, how very beautiful this progress through the water is. Will you always call me May ?"

" Why May ? It is not your name ?"

" I was born in May. All those with whom I am very intimate, call me May. My poor father would never call me by any other name.'

" Well, May, I will call you by that name since you wish it. But now, are you not curious to know who I am ?"

" Oh, you are kind and good."

" Humph. But do you not feel that you would like to know my name and condition ?"

" I might, but I ought not to ask you. You will tell me at your own time, and until you do so, I can only love you and admire you for the service that you have done to me."

There was something most engagingly beautiful in the confiding innocence of this young girl. Duval loved her more and more each moment, and the image of Adele faded more and more from his imagination ; and yet he trembled to think upon what might be the double result of the ruin of the fair young creature now by his side, and the desertion of Adele, who for him had sacrificed so much, and who truly loved him.

"No—no," he said to himself. " I will not, and need not desert Adele, even if I do love this young creature, who is so rapturously beautiful ; and how to help loving her I know not. Truly, in all my adventures I never met with such a world of fascinations as she in her one person comprehends."

By this time the Temple-stairs were in sight, and one of the rovers paused a moment, as he said—

" The tide is high enough to land your honour on the terrace of the garden."

" Will that do ?" said Duval to May.

" Oh, yes—yes. Anywhere so that we get into the Temple at all ; and from one of the gardens, now I bethink me, there was an entrance to the chamber of my mother's old friend."

" That will do well, then," said Duval. " Let it be the garden."

Upon this the two watermen pulled lustily, and in the course of seven or eight minutes more they had the boat just on the level of the stone coping to the long gravel-walk of the garden of the Temple.

Duval sprang on shore, and then assisted May to do so, after which he gave the two rowers a half-guinea, saying—

" Keep where you are until I return, and you shall have as much again for taking me back."

The payment was so much more than they could have thought of demanding, that they were quite profuse in their thanks to Duval, and one of them said—

" We shall be here, your honour. There's no danger of our forgetting a customer that pays so well."

" Very good," said Duval. " I will be back as soon as possible, and if I detain you an unreasonable time, that shall be likewise remembered, and well paid for."

With this he placed May's arm beneath his, and as they paced along the garden path, he said—

" Now, how will you find out your friend ? Had you not better make an inquiry of the gardener, who is rolling yon path ? He doubtless knows every resident in the Temple."

" Oh, yes—yes. That is a happy thought. I will ask him at once for the precise house.

May did this, and was at once directed to one of the houses which could be got to from the garden. She pointed out the house to Duval, saying—

" Come, my friend, we will go and see my mother's old friend."

" You would prefer, perhaps, going alone ?" said Duval.

" Oh, no—no. You will come with me—you would not deprive me of the pleasure of showing to him my preserver ? Do come—do come !"

Duval did not much relish the idea of going into a lawyer's chambers in the Temple ; but as he was then pressed by May to do so, he yielded, thinking that, after all, if by any accident he was to be recognised, surely, after what he had done in saving May from death, even her legal friend would hardly think of denouncing him.

They ascended a small flight of stone steps, and went into a sort of vestibule, where they met a woman who had been cleaning the chambers.

" Is Mr. Arrowsmith within ?" said May.

" Oh, yes—you will be sure to find him," said the woman. " He is sure to be in while the sun shines."

Neither May nor Duval could understand this very enigmatical answer of the woman. Why he should be always in while the sun shone was rather extraordinary.

" What do you mean ?" said Duval.

"Mean? Why I mean what I say, that such as he don't go often out in day-light.   It don't suit their goings on."

"What goings on ?"

" Oh, don't ask me. The least said is soonest mended, of course, and it ain't no business of mine."

MAY DEFENDS HERSELF FROM THE YOUNG LAWYER IN THE TEMPLE.

With this, the woman made a hasty retreat, and left May and Claude on the threshold of the chambers, both of them wondering at the oddness of her words and manner, as connected with an old and respectable practitioner of the legal profession.

" The woman must be out of her wits," said Duval.

" Indeed it does seem like it," said May.

" What will you do ?"

"Oh, I will go in at once, and speak to my mother's old friend ; and then, when I introduce you to him, you will find how kind and good he really is."

" I hope so."

They both went into the chambers ; and then Duval, finding that they were in a kind of outer room, said—

" I will wait here, May, while you explain to your friend the circumstances that bring you here ; and when you have done that, you can call to me, and I will come in at once and speak to him ; but I will not intrude at the first part of your interview."

" As you will, my friend ; but why not come in now at once ? Mr. Arrow-smith will be well pleased to see you."

" Why, I feel a little diffident," said Duval.

This excuse went down very well with May, who did not happen to know that diffidence was not exactly one of Duval's failings, and she accordingly opened a door that led into another apartment, and went in. The door swung shut after her ; but Duval had noticed that there was in the wall a window, with a curtain to be seen on the other side of it ; but he did not fancy exactly that that curtain was so good a fit as to prevent him from peeping into the adjoining apartment ; and he meant to form his own conclusion regarding May's legal friend, before he made his appearance before him, if he made it at all.

" Now that she is in safety," he said to himself, " I can leave her so, and my disappearance will do her no harm, if I happen but to like the looks of this Mr. Arrowsmith ; and it is not very many lawyers that I do like the look of."

With this, Duval tripped across the outer-room very cautiously, and placed himself at the window in the wall, which commanded a view into the inner one ; and he found that the curtain by no means fitted so well as to exclude any obser-vation, while from the window being the only obstruction, everything that passed, to the minutest word, could be heard perfectly well by Duval.

He now saw and heard enough to invite all his attention, and to alter the whole circuit of his thoughts regarding any ideas of going away alone.

CHAPTER LXV.

DUVAL DOES GOOD SERVICE TO SOCIETY AT LARGE IN THE TEMPLE.

THE room into which Duval looked was a large and handsome one. In the centre of it was a table laid out with all the materials for a very luxurious break-fast, and the whole place was very well furnished indeed.

At the table sat quite a young man, whose bloated and dissipated countenance bore sufficient testimony to his habits. He was attired in a splendid morning-gown of brocade ; and the untasted breakfast before him, had given place to a liquor-stand, that had greater attractions.

The room was strewn with whips, sticks, swords, boxing-gloves, and apparel of all kinds and descriptions, such as what was then considered a fashionable. London blood of the first-water might be supposed to indulge in, and find his enjoyments.

When May entered, it was with a quick step and a sparkle of the eye, for she expected to find the gray-headed friend of her mother in that room, instead of the dissolute young spark who sat in it.

" What the deuce now, Mother Simpkins ?" he said, as the door was opened " I thought you had done with all your mopping and brooming for to-day, surely Ah ! who are you, my dear ?"

The sight of a young and charming girl like May filled the libertine with as-tonishment, and he rose with his eyes wider open than they had been for many a long day.

May paused and looked embarrassed. Then in her low, sweet tones, she said—

"I am afraid, sir, that I have made some mistake."

"I hope not," said the young rake.

"I come, sir, to see Mr. Arrowsmith."

"By Jove, then, it is no mistake, for that is my name."

"But Mr. Arrowsmith is an elderly gentleman."

"You mean the governor?"

"The who, sir?"

"The old man, my governor. I am young Mr. Arrowsmith, as you see, my dear. The old brick is ill at his house at Islington, but I am here quite at your service, my dear.

"Oh, sir, is he very ill?"

"Why, they do say that he won't get up again. If I thought he would, I should not have made quite so free with the crib here. But come, my duck, you are only gammoning. I suppose Mother Phillips sent you here? Come, own it now, and sit down and make yourself comfortable. Upon my life you are the nicest little girl I have seen for many a long day."

"Sir," said May, who only felt disgusted at the coarse manner of the young man, without understanding his allusions. "Sir, as the friend I expected to find here is not here, I will leave you now, and trouble you no further."

"No, by Jove, you won't, though."

As he spoke he darted past May, and turning the key in the lock of the door, he put it in his pocket, and then with a loud laugh, he added—

"No, you don't go quite so easily as all that comes to. You have come here, and here you shall stay for some time, at all events. Come, come, let us have no nonsense. You are a very pretty girl, and I can pay well."

"Help!" cried May.

"Oh, it is of no use your crying out. No one will pay the least attention here."

"But I have a friend without!"

"Then he has gone, or he would hear you and knock at the door, in which case I should have to go out and start him, which would not take me much trouble to do."

"Let me go, sir!"

"Not a bit of it. Come, a kiss, my charmer. A kiss at once, and no nonsense about it."

"Sir, hear me for a moment, I beseech you. It seems to be my unhappy fate to-day to fall into the company of ruffians. My mother was your father's friend; my father, too, knew him well. I came to seek him, sir, and not to be insulted by his son."

"Oh, stuff. Don't I tell you that the old boy is on his last legs? You won't see him any more, and I am master here now; so the best thing you can do is to make a friend of me, and you will not find me a very bad one."

"I despise you and your friendship, sir. Unlock that door, and let me go at once. I command you, sir."

"What! are you an actress? By Jove! you must be. I never saw anything so prettily done. Bravo! But all this nonsense won't do, so a kiss I will have."

May, as he approached her, darted round the breakfast-table, and snatching up a knife that was upon it, she cried—

"I will die first, sir, before you shall approach me. I am but a poor, weak girl, but at such a time as this Heaven will lend me strenght to cope with you. Look to your own safety, coward that you are!"

The countenance of the libertine became immediately flushed with anger, as he cried—"What! will you defy me?"

"I do defy you!"

"Then you shall suffer for it, you little idiot. What the deuce did you come here for to play these heroics? Will fifty pounds pay you? I have five-hundred pounds in that desk there. Take what you like of it, only leave me enough to carry on the game till the old man is gone, and then you may have as much more, for he has plenty of money."

"Let me leave this place, sir!"

"Oh, you won't? Well, we shall soon see how you will like to carry on the war. I will let you into the secrets of a little fencing. I am the best swordsman in London; and mind, now, I don't intend to get a scratch from you; but I will disarm you pretty quickly, and if you get hurt, mind, it is your own fault, and you can't blame me."

With this he took a sword from a corner close to the door, where there were several, and drawing it, he cast the scabbard to the ground, saying—

"Do you surrender?"

"Help!" cried May.

"Do you surrender, I say?"

"Coward, you would not dare to brag thus to a man, if one were only within my call!"

"Would I not? I am always ready and willing to fight the best man in all England. I am a first-rate fencer, as I tell you, and my courage is true as steel."

"I am delighted to hear it," said Duval, in a voice that rung through the rooms again; and then, with one rush against the locked door, he dashed it open, and appeared, with a face glaring with passion, in the room.

Arrowsmith rushed to the farther end of the apartment, and stood upon his guard, and May, passing him, at once threw herself upon Duval's breast, crying—

"Save me—oh, save me from him! Save me, my friend—my preserver a second time!"

"Fear nothing," said Duval. "Fear nothing."

"And who are you?" cried Arrowsmith, "that dares to break my doors open, and intrude upon my privacy?"

"Your superior," said Duval.

"My superior? Insolence!"

"Beware, sir. You have already quite a sufficiently long account to settle with me as it is. You had better not add another item to it. May, will you wait for me in the outer room?"

"Oh, come away—come away at once," cried May. "You need not pursue this any further. You have come in time to save me from this man, and that is enough. I beg of you to come away now at once. He is far beneath your further notice."

"So far, May, you are right; but I cannot go without punishing him for his dastardly conduct. Hark you, sir; you call yourself the best swordsman in England. I have no such extravagant pretensions; but with one of your own weapons I will try your skill."

As he spoke, Duval snatched from the corner one of the swords, and rapidly drawing it, he flung the scabbard at his foe, and stood upon the defensive.

"Be off with you," said Arrowsmith, "and take your girl with you. I don't want to have anything more to say to either of you."

"Not so easily," said Duval. "You must apologise to this young lady, and humbly too, for your conduct towards her; or else I will force you, in self-defence, to exert some of your much-boasted skill in swordmanship, unless it all deserts you when you face a man."

Young Arrowsmith was close to the door of a cupboard that was in the room, and now, suddenly, before any one could be at all aware of his intention, he darted his hand into it, and drawing it out again armed with a pistol, he levelled it at the head of Duval and pulled the trigger.

The aim was good, but the weapon only flashed in the pan, or that might have been the end of the career of Duval, who, with all the coolness in the world, said,

"Well, sir, you must confess you have had all the chances; now defend yourself. May, you will only be my destruction if you call for help, or in any way interfere,"

Thus spoken to, the young girl dropped upon her knees close to the shattered door, and covered her face with her hands to shut out the sight of the conflict which immediately began upon both sides with fury.

When the young libertine saw that fight he must, he made up his mind to defend himself with desperation, and in every way to do his adversary all the mischief he could, whether in fair fight or not; but for all that Duval was prepared, and a more consummate master of the sword than he, Duval, was, could not be found.

From the moment that the two weapons crossed each other and wrung together, the young rake had no chance, and he seemed to feel that himself, by the desperate mad way in which he fought with his powerful antagonist.

Duval let him exhaust himself, merely acting for his own part on the defensive, and parrying all the furious assaults which the other made against him. This he did with an ease and coolness that drove Arrowsmith quite frantic.

"Coward!—coward!" hr cried, through his clenched teeth; "you know you are a coward. You are fighting the safe game;—you dare not attack me."

"Do you wish it?" said Duval.

"You dare not; you dare not ! Coward!—coward!"

"Very good. Now, look to your guard."

Duval immediately commenced a rapid assault. His sword flew from point to point like a flash of light; and then, before three minutes had passed, he suddenly took his opportunity, and ran the libertine right through the body.

With such tremendous force was the thrust given, that the sword, with a crash, went right through the cupboard-door against which Arrowsmith stood, and the hilt struck against his chest before it stopped.

The wretched man uttered one cry, and then there he remained pinned to the cupboard-door. Duval let go the sword, and turning round, he caught May up in his arms and dashed out of the chambers in which such a horrid scene had been enacted. He knew that the wound he had given to his antagonist was mortal, or he would not have left even such a man as that without some sort of help.

May had fainted, but her light weight was nothing at all to Duval. He rushed across the Temple Gardens with her as easily as he would have carried some ltttle child, and in a very few seconds he reached the water side.

The tide had sunk a little, but the boat was there with its two rowers.

"Take her !" cried Duval, and then one of the men stood up and received the insensible form of the young girl, and laid her carefully in the boat. Duval sprung in after her, crying—

"Push off ! push off !"

———

CHAPTER LXVI.

THE RACE ON THE THAMES AFTER DUVAL AND MAY.

The boatmen at the moment looked rather astounded at these hasty and violent-looking proceedings, as well they might ; but they did not every day get a customer who paid so magnificently as Duval ; and as their politic virtue took its hint most decidedly from this priorite advantage, they did not feel called upon to take any steps in the matter, but such as might seem pleasing to their customer.

"Pull away again !" cried Claude Duval. "Pull away. You will find it pay you well."

"All's right, master," said one. "We have no doubt of that, when we have you for a fare."

"The young ooman ain't hurt ?" said the other.

"Not a bit," said Duval. " The only mischief that has been done has ensued in protecting her from a rascal."

"All's right, then. Pull away, Bill."

They bent to their oars with right good will, and the boat not being by any means heavily laden, shot through the water swiftly, propelled by the powerful strokes of the two strong and, what was more than strength, and always is, skilful watermen who conducted it.

Duval had been rather glad at the moment to find that May had fainted, and so had escaped the sight of that final and really dreadful and sickening catastrophe in the chambers; but now he wished that she should look up again.

"May," he said. "May, you are quite safe now."

"Safe as a coffin," said one of the watermen.

"Will you be quiet?" said the other. "Haven't I been for a year and a half telling of you not to mention such things in wherries, and yet you always will? Do you want this to be the unluckiest boat on the river?"

"I didn't give it a thought at the moment, mate," said the other, "and I won't say it not never no more, no how."

"Mind you don't, or else you and I will have to go out o' partnership together I can tell you. I don't like it."

May made no answer to Duval, so finding that she was still in a state of syncope he dashed some water on her face from the river, as it rushed and gurgled past the boat. She gave a slight shudder and opened her eyes.

"All is well?" said Duval; "you are saved from that bad man."

"Saved?" she said, and it was evident by the tone in which she said it, that she was as yet not sufficiently recovered to be quite conscious of the meaning of the word even when she uttered it.

"Yes," said Duval; "look at me. Do you not know me?"

Both the watermen seemed to lend rather attentive ears to what might be the reply of May. Probably, in their minds, there might be yet some lingering doubt regarding the work they were doing; but if they had any idea that Duval was an enemy of the young girl's, it would have been quickly enough dispelled by the trustful manner in which, now that reason and recollection had both come back to her, she looked up into his face and spoke to him.

"Oh, yes, yes," she said. "You are my preserver. I owe you my life, and more than my life. You will not desert me now? Oh, tell me that you will not, for I feel that I have no friend else in all the world but you."

"Depend upon me," said Duval; "I will not fail to protect you against all enemies, whether secret or open. Do not weep; you have no cause now for tears. All is well."

"Where is he?"

"Whom mean you?"

"That man in the Old Temple who is so unlike his father, and yet bears his name. Oh, sir, was it not most villanous to speak to me as he spoke, and to threaten me as he threatened, when my sole object of visiting that place was to ask protection? I did not—I could not think that in the world there could be any one so base as he."

Duval was rather glad that by speaking on, May had lost sight of her first question regarding the fate of the young man in the Temple, so he avoided a repetition of the question by saying—

"Do not agitate yourself upon account of the past. Believe me that you are quite safe now, and that all will be well. I am with you, and you already know that I have both the will and the power to protect you."

"Oh yes, yes—both will and power; and I am so poor in thanks."

"I desire none."

"Sir," said one of the watermen, "just look in our wake half a minute, will you, and tell us what you think of that?"

"Of what?" said Duval, turning his head hastily.

He soon saw of what, for there were two boats evidently chasing them as hard as four rowers in each could do so. Had Duval changed colour, or shown anything like trepidation, the watermen would likely enough have lost confidence in him;

but he did not. He always rose superior to the occasion, let it be what it might ; and now feeling pretty well assured that the two boats were actually in pursuit, he said—

"Do you know what stairs they come from ?"

"The Temple," said one of the watermen. "I saw them push off in no end of hurry and bustle."

"And you think they are after us ?"

"Sure of it."

"Then, my friends, I tell you that they are after me from no good cause why they should be so after me. This young girl has enemies. Only this morning she would have been murdered by one of those enemies but for my active interference. I say this much to you to convince you that if you exert yourselves, it is not in a bad cause ; and in addition, here are twenty guineas in this purse. Follow my directions, and I will give them to you. You will run no risk, for come what may of it, all you have to say is, that I told you I was escaping from the bailiffs. Such things, you know, are quite common and of every-day occurrence, both on the river and on land."

The watermen looked at each other for a few moments in silence, and then one said—

"It's all as true as if fate had spoke it ?"

"It is true," said Duval.

"All's right," said the other. "All I have got to say is, ' Pull away, Bill.' "

"Here you are, then."

They bent to their oars, and scarcely had they done so, when a loud, clear voice came across the surface of the water, crying—

"Boat a-hoi! Boat a-hoi! Police!"

"Don't heed them," said Duval, as he flung the purse with the gold in it to the bottom of the boat, as a proof that he meant to be as good as his word. "Don't heed them, but pull away."

"They near us !" cried May.

"Yes, they will near us," said one of the men; "and in the long run they would overhaul us ; but a stern chase is a long chase, and we may put you ashore somehow yet before they make way enough to get within boat's length of us."

"Yes," said Duval, "that will be it. Oh, that another pair of oars were in the boat ! Put us on shore anywhere you like as near Hammersmith as you can, and we will then shift for ourselves. Pull away. Look how they are striving at their oars !"

"Ay, ay, sir. It's quite a kind of race between the two of 'em and us, and then between one of 'em again the other; but easy will do it yet. They go three feet for our two ; but it takes a deuce of a while at that rate to get over a quarter of a mile."

"You are right. May, there is no cause for apprehension ; I pray you to be tranquil. It will be better for you not to look at these pursuing boats. You but vex yourself to see them."

May could not keep her eyes off them, however; and now for the space of about ten minutes, not a word was spoken in the boat ; but the two men rowed as though it were for life and death. The boat shot through the water with amazing speed, and although the wherries that were in pursuit had four watermen in each, yet by that very fact they were heavier laden than the one in which Duval and May were ; so that their increased number of rowers was by no means all gain with them.

"Hooiah !" cried one of the watermen, suddenly. "They have run one into the other. There's beauties !"

It was a fact that, in the anxiety of the watermen in the two pursuing boats to get a-head of each other, they had run so close alongside that they each had for a moment to stop their oars. Perhaps you could not have counted eight before they were in full pursuit again; but still, that was a great gain to the boat in which were our fugitives.

"If they come that sort of game again," said one of the watermen, "we can take you easy up to tne bridge and land you comfortably where we took you from."

"I hope they may," said Duval. "But don't trust to that. It is not very likely. Only see in what a mad sort of manner they make the boats spring out of the water, to make up for the lost time. Ah, we shall beat them yet!"

May held one of Duval's hands in both of hers, and wept freely. She knew that he had fought with the young man in the Temple, who had treated her in so villanous a manner; and although if she had been put upon her oath, she could not positively have taken upon herself to say what had been the issue of the combat, yet the fact that her preserver was then with her, and unhurt, was to her mind a pretty good proof that something serious had happened to the other party.

"They will drag you to a prison," she whispered; "and it will be all upon my account."

"No! We shall beat them! Be under no apprehension."

At this moment a sharp crack, that could not be mistaken for anything else but the report of a pistol, sounded across the water; and the watermen involuntarily paused a moment upon their oars as a bullet plunged into the water about twenty feet to the stern of the boat.

"On—on!" cried Duval; "it's no matter. We are out of pistol-shot. Pull away, now!"

"All's right, sir. But they do seem rather bent upon it, don't they now? Pull away, Bill."

Bang went another pistol-shot, and that was echoed by a shriek from May; for in all this she could read nothing but the total destruction of the man who had done so much for her, and who she felt was incurring all this danger for her sake and service alone.

As before, the shot fell short, and Duval said in a cheering tone to the watermen—

"They will soon get tired of that sort of thing. We are completely out of range of their pistols, and at every shot they retard their own boat by confusing their rowers. We gain upon them now—and there is Hammersmith. Pull on— the twenty guineas are nearly earned already, my friends."

"They shall be quite, sir," said one of the men. "Don't you cry, my dear girl. It will be all right soon now. Let them blaze away as much as they like."

As Claude Duval sat, he now became aware of a new danger, which neither the watermen nor May had an opportunity of noticing. They merely looked to the wake of their boat, and her whole attention was fixed upon the pursuers. It was Duval only who looked out narrowly ahead, and as he did so he saw a long narrow wager boat, with six rowers in it, coming right towards his wherry. It was evident from the manner of the rowers in the long boat, that they intended to make an effort to stop him, for two of them stopped their oars, and got out a couple of boat hooks as they neared.

"Do you know those people?" said Duval, pointing to them.

The watermen both looked, and then one said—

"They belong to the club. What business have such tailors with us?"

"They are going to try to stop us."

"Are they?"

"Don't you see? They are sidling up so as to get alongside us. Let them take the consequences."

"You be still, sir. Leave Bill and me to manage them. We know how to do that sort of thing best. You keep quite quiet, sir, and depend upon us that they shall not stop you."

"That will do," said Duval.

He shrunk back in the stern of the boat along with May; but he kept himself for all that ready for action at a moment's notice, if there should arise any occasion for his interference in the matter.

The affair now assumed a very exciting aspect indeed. The two watermen in what might be called Duval's boat, felt that they dare not relax in their speed, lest they should bring themselves within pistol shot of the men who seemed well enough disposed to use such weapons against them, from the pursuing wherries.

On the other hand they were called upon to navigate their boat with very great skill, so as to avoid getting into such a position with the six-oared wherry

THE FLIGHT ON THE THAMES.

that was coming down upon them in the opposite direction, as would give that craft any advantage over them. But they were experienced men.

It was easy to perceive that their blood was up; and that now, quite irrespective of the money that Duval offered to them, they were far from being disposed to give in to their pursuers, as to the boat that in a few moments would be sure to meet them.

CHAPTER LXVII.

AN ESCAPE, AND THE STRANGE MARRIAGE IN WILSDEN CHURCH.

THE fear of poor May would have been excessive, had it not been that courage and confidence are really as contagious as fear. One glance in the calm assured face of Duval gave her wonderful nerve; and as he saw that she was glancing at him for strength to bear what was about to take place, he smiled gently.

"You are confident?" she said.

"Very," he replied.

"Then I will trust all, and look at nothing."

She lay down by his feet and covered her face with a portion of a cloak that she wore.

"That is a wise determination," said Duval. "Do not stir until I call upon you by name to do so. Hear what you may, and fancy what you may, remain as you are, and you will be quite safe."

"I will," she said.

Duval hardly thought that it was possible she could have constancy of purpose enough to remain so hidden. He only hoped that she would; but his attention was soon drawn from both hopes and fears as regarded that minor subject, by the rapidity of the occurring events around him.

It was quite clear that the two pursuing wherries had in some way managed to let the parties in the wager-boat know that they wished the wherry with Duval and the young girl to be stopped; but it was equally clear that owing to the lightness of the craft, the party of six rowers resolved to do the work as carefully as possible. They no doubt considered themselves to be more than a match for three men and a young girl, and so they wished to get alongside and grapple with the stouter boat.

The watermen were not slow to perceive all that could be done, and all that could not. He who was on the river side of the boat said to his companion who was nearer shoreward—

"It will be your job, Bill."

"Yes, I know it," said the other. "You ship your oar in time, and I'll do it."

"Very good. Now pull away, and here we have 'em."

"Hilloa!" cried the steersman of the six-oared boat. "Ship your oars, will you? There's something wrong about your cargo."

"Where did you buy them whiskers?" said one of the watermen. "We know a fish would give any money short of a groat for 'em."

"Come—come, no insolence. Pull alongside. Out with the boat-hooks."

"Can you swim?" cried the waterman who was named Bill. "'Cos if you can't, you'd better give us a berth longer than a boat-hook, that's all."

This language from the watermen, served to enrage the six men in the wager-boat, and with some amount of skill they pulled, so as to come broadside down upon Duval's wherry. But the two old hands that had the conduction of the latter, were more than a match for the amateurs in handling the oars.

In a moment, whisk went the boats head round crossways to the river, and then with two vigorous sweeps of their oars, the watermen shot the head of their boat right over the shallow side of the other.

It begun to fill with water directly, and there was such a scrambling among the six rowers with their fancy jackets, and the steersman with his uncommonly knowing cap, as never was seen. The state of consternation they got into was excessive, and all idea of interfering with Duval's boat, was lost in the fear of a grand upset of their own.

"Back—back!" they all shouted. "You will sink us. Murder! Help!"

"Back it is," said Bill.

Another sweep of the oars in the contrary direction disengaged the two boats, but the six-oared wherry was nearly full of water, and upon the point of sinking.

"Now, gentlemen, I tell you what it is," said Bill. "If you sit uncommon steady, and bale it out, you won't go down; but if you don't, you will, and let me give you an old waterman's advice : Don't poke your nose into another man's affairs. We have a proverb on the river that says—'Nobody sees anything but his own wherry,' and it would be a good thing for you to mind it."

Not the ghost of an answer was attempted to be returned to this speech, for the six rowers felt that indeed their only chance of safety lay in slowly and cautiously baling out the water from the boat, as otherwise the slightest thing would have upset it, and at once precipitated them all into the water.

"Give way now," cried Claude Duval. "Pull hard, and we shall soon be to land. The others have gained upon us now."

"Ay, ay, sir. But not enough for mischief, and they won't fire at us now for fear of killing those pretty fellows with the white jackets, who we can manage to keep in our wake now pretty well. I do consider that that job was done in a business-like-way now."

"Just enough and no more," said the other.

"It could not have been better!" cried Duval. "I owe you a world of thanks for it. May, look up. The danger is now over."

May uncovered her face. It was very pale.

"Don't you take on, Miss," said Bill. "All's right now."

"Are we indeed saved ?"

"Yes," said Duval. "We shall land directly now."

"They are giving it up," said Bill. "Look, the other two are putting-in at the nearest stairs. They think now that as they don't know exactly what sort of a dance we may lead them up the river, it will be best for them to land and get up a riot along shore."

"Not a doubt of it," said Claude Duval. "But if we do get to Hammersmith and have but five minutes the start of them, I will give them leave to do what they like and can. Can you ride, May ?"

"Oh, yes. They say I ride well."

"That is everything."

In the course of about six minutes now the keel of the boat grated on the pebbly beech at Hammersmith ; and Duval taking May in his arms, sprang on shore with her.

"The money is in the boat !" he cried. "Take it, and my best thanks with it. If ever we meet again, which I hope we may, I will thank you again ; and if we don't, I shall not forget the good and gallant service you have done me to-day."

"Nor I," said May, as she waived her hand to the two men.

"It wasn't done for the money," said Bill ; "but my heart, after a little while, was in the work ; so God bless you my pretty little lass, and good luck to both of you."

Duval waived his hand, and then placing May above the water-mark on the beech, he put his arm in hers, and as they walked up to the Inn, where he had left his horse, he said—

"There is not nor can there be any occasion for your joining your better and more innocent fortunes to mine ; I must perforce escape the best way I am able ; but you need not be under any fear. You are far more sinned against than sinning. Can you bethink you of any home to which you could go ?"

"Alas! alas! Not one."

"Is that possible ?"

"It is too true. We had never many connexions, and no relations in this quarter of the world; I believe there are some people in Canada with whom I may claim kindred, but—but none in England. He to whom I thought that I was going in the Temple, was the only one I know would afford me an hour's shelter, and now that that hope has fled, I am desolate, indeed."

"Not so ; but—but——"

"You mean to cast me off—I am a trouble to you ?"

"Ah, May, how much you misconstrue my motives! I did not think, and I do not think you a trouble. Far—very far from it, indeed. But what I was so anxious about, was not to compromise you in any way by taking you about with me."

"Compromise me?"

The tone in which these words were uttered made it quite clear to Duval that in her own innocence of heart, May did not know what he really meant.

"Listen to me," he said. "If I continue to protect you, the world will think and speak ill of you. I was in hopes that you knew some family where you could go; for, as you tell me, your wicked uncle wished you to sign a deed transferring property that belonged to you to him, that is a sufficient proof that you need not be a burthen to any one. I would have bought you a horse, as you say you can ride, and I would have seen you to any one's door who would have received you."

"Alas! there is no one—not one!"

"That is very awkward."

"I can feel, though, how much I may be a burthen, and perhaps a disgrace, to you, and I will leave you."

"No, May, no; that you must not do. It is I who may be to you a burthen and a disgrace; but I have no time now to explain all this to you—I am on the brink of a precipice. If I am taken by those who are my pursuers, all is lost with me. Let us place some miles of cross-country between us and this place, and then I can talk more freely to you; but for the present we must remain together. Be of good cheer."

"With you, I am sure to be happy."

By this time, for Duval had not for a moment paused in a rather rapid walk, they had reached the door of the inn where he had left his horse. They entered the house, and Duval gave May into the charge of the landlady, while he sallied out to a livery-stables in the vicinity. There he quickly enough found a horse for forty guineas that would suit May, and he rode it back to the inn door himself; where by that time, as he had previously ordered that it should be, his own steel was waiting ready saddled.

May had no riding-dress, but Duval bought a large and handsome shawl, and completely wrapped up her feet in it, tying it round her waist so that she was completely protected from the cold. He then lifted her on the horse he had purchased, and he saw in a moment, by her management of the rein, that she was an accomplished horsewoman.

"Are you comfortable?" said Duval.

"Quite."

He paid trebly for the slight accommodation they had had at the inn, and then off they went.

The horse that May rode turned out to be a capital one; and as Duval's steed had had a good two hours' rest, it was in good condition, so they both made good speed, and in the course of an hour they had placed no less than eight miles of cross-country between them and Hammersmith.

About half an hour after they had quitted the inn, a party of twelve mounted officers of the police rode up to its door, and the principal of the party called out in a loud voice—

"Ostler! ostler!"

"Yes, sir. Here you are!"

"Did a man put up a dark bay horse here about an hour or two ago?"

"Without any spots?"

"Yes."

"Uncommonly full and bright in the eye, and thoroughbred?"

"The same."

"Then he did, in course; and a better bit of blood I never came near. As quiet as a lamb, too, in the stable, so long as you were kind to it and patted it a bit. Why, it was as playful and gentle as a cat, it was."

"Had he a young girl with him?"

"To be sure he had, and as pretty a little creature she was as ever you laid eyes on. They both went off a goodish time ago. She had a clever little na. he gave a matter of forty pounds for to Mr. Snaggs, as keeps the stables up above here."

"Confound it, then, we are too late! I'd give another forty pounds to see them both. Which way did they go?"

"Well, it's lucky I can tell you. A man came here to have half a pint of something, and said he saw them both go over Fulham Bridge; so that's the way you will find them."

"Thank you—thank you. Come on; they are on the other side of the water, it appears, comrades. This is the way over Fulham Bridge."

"Is it?" said the ostler, when they were gone. "If they went over Fulham Bridge, I'll eat it, all the old wooden piles and all. No—no, I ain't going to peach upon a man as gives me a guinea to myself!"

CHAPTER LXVIII.

MAY'S DISGUISE.—ADELE WAITS IN VAIN FOR DUVAL.

"I THINK," said Duval, as he and May paused upon some high ground in the neighbourhood of where Kensal Green Cemetery now stands; "I think we may give ourselves joy that we are past all pursuit now."

"Do you think so?"

"Yes, May. Take a long look around you—your eyes are rather younger than mine—and tell me if upon the roads you see any one in haste."

May did look anxiously in the direction from whence they had come; but she could see no one. All was calm and still, and the only objects that met their gaze were a few labouring men in the fields, and in the lanes now and then a farmer's cart rumbling along lazily.

"We have distanced them, then, truly," added Duval; "and I should feel happy and comfortable enough, but for one thing."

"What is that, my friend?"

"It is that, frankly speaking, I don't know what to do with you. Nay, do not weep, my dear girl, I pray you. It is because I have known you now long enough to love you, and seen enough of your courage and gentle disposition to feel that you ought to adorn some happy home, that I feel sad, and wonder what to do with you."

"Alas!" said May, "you do not know what a grief it is to me to hear you speak in such a strain as that. Only let me be ever near you, and you will find me a dear friend, and one who for you will share any dangers that the world can present!"

"Ah, May, you know not what you say—indeed, you do not! The time might come when you would call me a villain for taking you at your word."

"Oh, no—no—never!"

"Do not be too sure. But yet——"

"Why do you pause? Ah, I am all confidence with you, and have no secrets; but you pause in speaking to me. Why is it that you fear to trust me as I trust you? Speak to me freely, my friend; I will not misconstrue what you may please to say to me, for well I know that you will say it in kindness only."

"Then, May, I was going to say, that what suppose I were to ask you to become my wife?"

May looked down, and a flush of colour came over her cheeks, as she said—

"I did not think that I was asking you to say that."

"I know you did not; but I am unmarried, and what would you say to me if I were to ask you?"

" Alas! I have no one in all the world now to cling to but you! What should I say to you, my friend and my preserver, but yes?"

"And not knowing, then, who I am, you would venture, May, to accept me?"

" I would; I know what you are, if I do not know who you are. You are brave and generous—and those are surely two qualities that bespeak others. And you will tell me who you are?"

"Yes, May, I will give you back your 'yes' again into your own keeping; and then I will tell you who I am. Remember, that the consent you have given to be mine, I make now no account of, inasmuch as you gave it in the most positive ignorance of whom it was you were about to unite your fate to. You have not the least idea to whom you speak, and you have a perfect right to retract your words."

"You terrify me," said May.

"Nay," added Duval, with a smile, "I do not mean to do that. Calm your fears, my dear girl, and tell me what in your imagination you suppose me to be. Speak quite freely, I shall not feel hurt by anything you may say of me. What condition of life, now, do you suppose I fill?"

" By your dress then," said May, " you are in the army."

" No."

" Then—then I know not what to say, or what to think. You will tell me at once. It cannot be anything very bad, or you would not smile."

"Indeed; but it is something very bad. Did you ever hear of Duval the highwayman?"

May turned very pale and started. She looked fixedly at Duval, and then in a low tone she said—

"Is that your name?"

"It is," he replied. "And now, perhaps, you know worse of me than I deserve, for I have heard enough of myself to know that my character is coloured one way or the other by the feelings and the prejudices of those who converse of me. Some will have it that I can be nothing more or less than a common ruffian, robbing and killing upon the highway. Others again would make me out as something almost more than mortal, and with circumstantial tales of chivalric conduct, and of hair-breadth escapes and rare generosity, fill up my character; but you, May, must, when you think of me, take a middle course; and not thinking me anything so good as some make me out, believe me to be not so bad as others would fain paint me."

" Duval!" said May, as if talking to herself. " He is Duval of whom I have heard so much. He is Duval. Oh, I might have made a guess at this surely. Surely I might have thought that no one but such a man could do as he hasd one."

"Indeed!" said Duval. "Then you have heard of me. Well, May, now that I have made this revelation to you, listen to me: I do not by any means press upon you my offer lately made to you, but if you even still say yes, say it, and I will make you as happy as I can; but if you prudently say no, I will at once set about placing you somewhere, where you can live in repute and peace, and I will find some lawyer to interest himself concerning your property, and you will only have to remember me as one who was happy enough to have the opportunity of doing you a service in the hour of danger and of difficulty."

Tears were in May's eyes as she looked up to him.

"Take me, Duval," she said, "I am yours and yours only."

"Is this possible?" he said, as he placed his arm round her waist, and drew her close to him. "Is this possible, that knowing who and what I am, you will really join your pure fate to mine? Oh, think again, May, think again."

"No, I will not think again. I have made my resolve and I will abide by it. You have said that you will make me your wife, Duval, and if you abide by that promise, I abide by my consent."

He kissed her cheek as she leant from her saddle towards him, and then with a smile, he said—

" Let that kiss ratify our mutual pledge. Come on, dear one. We will ride to yon village, and then while partaking of some refreshment, we will converse further of the past and the future."

" What village is it ?" said May.

" It is Wilsden. We have come right across the country. That square tower you see yonder belongs to the ancient church. Come on—a quarter of an hour's trot will take us to it. You must, after all the fatigues of the day, have much need of rest."

" I do not feel as yet tired. The excitement of the many events that have taken place has been sufficient to obliterate all those of fatigue."

They now rode on : the little time they had passed to have so very important a conversation, had sufficed to give the horses a rest, and in less time than Duval had mentioned, they were in the winding lane that leads to the village of Wilsden. They soon emerged opposite to the ' Old Cage,' with its picturesque window, and its projecting direction post. Duval pointed to it with a smile, as he said—

" The good folks of this place once thought that they would place me in there, but they reckoned entirely without my consent."

" Is it not then dangerous for you to come to this place ?"

" Oh, no ; it was some time ago, and it is very unlikely that they will again recognise me. Besides, there is a hostel here, where we shall be perfectly safe for a time, and where we can take some refreshment."

Turning to the left from the ' Old Cage,' instead of going right an towards it, Claude Duval paused at the door of an old, straggling, long, low-roofed public-house, and taking a whistle from his pocket, he blew a long shrill note upon it. In a moment, an elderly man came to the door and looking up scrutinously at Duval for a moment or two, his face then lit up with a smile, as he said—

" Oh, it's he—it's he ! What, art in this part of the world now ? No good to be done here. The high road is the place."

" I know it," said Duval, as he dismounted and assisted May to do the same. "We only halt here for a short time to rest, and to take a look at the old church."

" Ay—ay—Well, come in, come in, I hardly knew you. Why, it is a matter of I don't know how many long months since you have been this way.—Come in, come in."

" All's right, I presume ?" said Duval, as he stooped to cross the threshold of the old place. " You have no suspicious character here, I hope ?"

" Not one," said the old man ; and then sidling up to Duval he whispered— " Who is the young miss ?"

" My wife, man. Did you not hear of my marriage ?"

" No, surely."

" Why you must indeed then be out of the world. Pho ! Pho ! I got tired of a single life, so I married. Don't you approve of my choice ?"

" To be sure, Duval. As far as beauty goes, you could not have done better, and I noticed how she sat her horse—it was first-rate ; only it does seem an odd thing for a gentleman in your profession to marry. A very odd thing, I may say."

" Don't it ? But if you knew more of me, you would find that that's nothing at all to the many odd things that I think of doing at times ; so now get ready the best you have in your house, and as quickly as you can too, for our stay is never very long in one place."

" I know it—I know it ! All's right. A couple of chickens and a knuckle of ham. We have got, too, some of the old Madeira left. All's right ?"

" Yes," said Duval, " that will be all right."

Giving his arm then to May, Duval led her into a room above stairs, which for a little old country place was rather prettily furnished : and when he had found a large arm-chair for her to sit down, he said—

" Do you know, May, I have been thinking, that the old church in this village would be a nice quiet place to get married in."

"As you pleas ," said May. "If it suit you it will me."

"Well I will think about it, and at all events when we have had our refresh-ment here, we will walk to the ancient structure and have a look at it, and you shall then make up your mind about it."

The chickens and the ham, together with the old bottle of Madeira, were no fiction, but in a very short space of time, indeed, were laid before Duval and May, and it was something at once delightful and yet sad to see with what a childish confidence that young girl regarded the man, from whom many would have shrunk aghast, and from whom, indeed, much was to be feared by youth and innocence. But yet in the character of Duval the reader has not failed to detect one strong pervading principle, and that was a horror of anything positively wrong towards one who in entire innocence trusted him. Even in the case of Adele, it will be remembered that he was very explicit, before he really took her from the paths of virtue and innocence and made her his. And now as regarded the young creature who was with him, her innocence of heart and purpose were so very clear and manifest, that he shrunk from by word or look outraging her confidence in him.

To marry her, though, he had made up his mind ; and we may safely say, that not one thought of Adele now crossed his mind.

When the repast was over, Duval, after paying liberally for what he had had, ordered the two horses to be brought after him by a lad, while he and May went to look at the church. When they got there, they found the door of the sacred edifice open, and the clerk within it engaged on some official duty. Duval immediately addressed him—

"Is the clergyman's name—a—a—dear me," he said, "I know it as well as my own——"

"Millikin, sir," said the clerk. "The Reverend Joseph John Millikin, if you please, sir."

"To be sure—yes. Dear me, I do believe my memory will take wing altogether some of these days, and I shall forget that I am an earl—a—a—I mean a gentleman."

The clerk had caught the word earl, and he bowed until his nose nearly touched a flat tomb-stone.

"Be so good," added Duval, "as to say that a lady and gentleman would be much obliged to the Reverend Joseph John Millikin, if he would just step down to the church for a few moments. I knew him long ago, and he will be doing me a great favour by so doing."

"Oh, dear—yes, sir," said the clerk. "My lord, I mean. He will be sure to come. There is nothing in the world that the Reverend Joseph John Millikin, B. A., thinks so much of, as the dear and excellent nobility of this admirable country. I feel highly honoured, my lord, by the favour of being permitted to carry the message. My name, my lord, and your ladyship, is Peter. Peter Smith, my lord and my lady."

"Go !" said Duval.

The clerk bowed himself out of the church, and when he was gone, May looked at Duval and said—

"Do you want the clergyman here ?"

"Yes, dear, to be sure I do. I mean to make him marry us. Why do you start ? Is it not better that he should marry us at once, dear one, than that we should trouble ourselves with banns and licences ? Here is a church, and all we want is a parson to perform the ceremony."

CHAPTER LXIX.

DUVAL AND MAY ARE MARRIED IN WILSDEN CHURCH.—AN ADVENTURE.

WHILE Duval and May walked to and fro in the old church, the clerk must have made good speed to the parson's house, for in a much less space of time than Duval thought it possible the Reverend gentleman cou'd arrive in, a very fat

CLAUDE FORSAKES ADELE.

man appeared at the church door. His cheeks were of a brilliant hue, and his little eyes were quite sunk in the fat that puffed up around them. His costume at once proclaimed him to be the clergyman.

As he advanced up the aisle he paused to make two very formal bows, for he had been duly impressed by the clerk with the idea that it was an earl that wanted him. Duval without any ceremony walked past him to the door of the church, and taking the key of it from the outside, he brought it in and locked the door.

The fat parson stared until his little eyes seemed to be almost ready to jump out of his head upon observing this, and then before he could gather breath to speak, Claude said—

"Sir, I have sent for you to do a little job for us here, in the due and proper exercise of your calling.

"Ah—yes—a—my lord, certainly. Why—why this lady—this young lady is Miss——"

"He knows my uncle," said May, as she clung to Duval. "He knows my uncle—oh, Duval, save me—save me!"

"Duval!" shouted the little fat parson. "Why, gracious goodness, amen! it isn't the horrid highwayman? Murder—help—thieves—murder—sacrilege! I'll ring the bells—I'll ring——"

"Hold, sir," said Duval, as he took a pistol from his pocket, and held it to the level of the face of the astonished parson. "Hold, sir. If you are in love with death you will make an alarm ; but if life has any charms for you, you will be prudent enough to take the only step you can that will preserve it, and that is to be quiet."

The terrified parson stood trembling before Duval. It was some few moments before he could find breath to speak, and then he said—

"You have decoyed me here to kill me. I am as good as dead already. I have heard quite enough of you to know my fate."

"If you have heard any truth of me," said Duval, "you ought to know that you are in no danger, unless it should chance to be of your own seeking, and arise from your own folly. You are a clergyman, and I require you to marry us forthwith. There may be some little singularity in the proceedings, but we will waive all that. It is the actual ceremony that we wish to be performed in a church."

"But, oh good gracious! There ought to be banns or a licence, and the parties ought to reside in the parish, and I have not any book."

"We will trust, sir, to your memory, as regards the last objection, and the others I have already said are of little amount. Come, sir. Quick, if you please. Among other things that you may have heard of me, may be that I am rather impatient."

The pistol was still in the hand of Duval as he spoke, and the sight of it had evidently a very trembling effect upon the clergyman, whose face looked absolutely shining with perspiration.

"Oh, dear—oh, dear," he said, "I am a miserable sinner. We are all miserable sinners ; but I am the worst of all. The bishop will take my gown from me for this, I feel assured, and if I don't marry you, you will shoot me."

"Decidedly. But you need be under no fear of the bishop for this ceremony ; we only wish it to be performed for our own private satisfaction, and shall make no mention of it. Come, sir, be quick."

The tone of voice in which Duval spoke, was too peremptory to be resisted, and the terrified parson began the service. He did manage to get through it in a sort of way, and Duval very gallantly placed a rich diamond-ring, which he took from his own finger, upon that of the bride, and the ceremony was over.

We believe seven minutes is the orthodox time for the performance of that awful ceremony, which makes or mars a man for ever, but upon this occasion it was got through in three, at the very outside, and the Amen was duly pronounced.

"Sir," said Duval, "we are very much obliged to you, indeed, and will now wish you a good day. But let me tell you that it will be very unsafe indeed, if you should think of peaching upon this subject, to do so until to-morrow. Then, if you like, you can say what you please, and exaggerate or diminish the facts in any manner to suit your own fancy, and your own interests."

"Oh, dear me, I won't mention it all," said the parson. "Not at all. I wouldn't have it mentioned for the whole world. You be so good as to hold your tongue about it, and I will hold mine."

"Very good. You may rely upon me and upon this lady."

As he spoke Duval gave his arm to May to conduct her from the church, and in in a whisper as he reached the door of the picturesque little edifice, he said to her—

"We had better be off at once. I do not think that our fat friend here will say anything, but still he is not implicitly to be trusted with the secret of my presence in this neighbourhood."

"Oh, yes, let us leave at once," said May. "Your safety requires it, and that is reason sufficient at once."

Duval opened the church door, and handed May out. The boy with the two horses ran up the pathway just outside, and the moment he saw Duval he said—

"Father says, sir, that off and away is the word."

"Does he so?" cried Duval. "Then he is right. I know. Here's a guinea for yourself, my lad."

"Thank you, sir," said the boy. "Thank you, sir. There's been a man peeping in at one of the windows of the church, and only a little while ago he set off at full speed into the village, and that was what made me get so close to the church door with the cattle, sir."

"All's right," said Duval, as he instantly assisted May to the saddle. "All's right. That clerk of the church, I think, May, has played us a trick. I quite forgot him. Tell your father, my lad, that I will see him soon, and thank him."

"Is there danger?" said May.

"No—no—not danger. But I have no doubt—Ah! there they come. Well done, Master Parish Clerk, I shall owe you one for this."

As Duval spoke, there appeared coming towards the church four or five men on horseback, and about a dozen on foot, variously armed. In the centre of the throng was Peter the clerk, whose curiosity having been excited by the church-door being locked, had peeped through one of the windows, and seen quite enough to convince him of the peril in which the Rev. Joseph John Millikin was in, and the name of Duval striking his ear, he had at once become alive to the whole proceeding, and had gone to alarm the village, and brought a force that he thought would be amply sufficient to capture the highwayman.

If Peter and his friends had only been five minutes earlier, certainly the peril to Duval would have been very great, for he would have found it no easy matter to leave the church, but as it was, being mounted, he thought but little of the danger to which he was exposed. His knowledge, too, of the locality was quite perfect, and that was a decided point in his favour.

"Don't be alarmed," he whispered to May. "There is a lane close at hand which leads into the high-road, and if we can once reach it, which I think we may, we will lead them a pretty dance yet. You see the end of those trees where the rookery is?"

"Oh, yes—yes."

"Make for there, then."

May did so, and Duval, with the most admirable skill, made his horse go partially sideways through the churchyard, keeping his face pretty well to his foes, while May trotted to the point he had indicated to her at the end of the rookery. Duval had forgotten that there was a little paling, and a gate to prevent cattle straying into the churchyard, but it was not so high as to stand in the way of such steeds as he and May had.

"Seize him! seize him!" cried the voices of all the people who were coming after him. "Lay hold of the highwayman! seize him! To gaol with him! Shoot him!" cried one.

"Try it," said Duval. "Are you sure you know me? I am Duval, with a thousand pound reward on my head. Why, it would make any of you for life. Why don't you come on? It is but the chance of a bullet through your head, you know."

At this intimation the mob of people, which was each moment increasing, hung back a little, and only one voice cried—

"As the constable of this village, I take you into custody, you most horrid and notorious malefactor."

"Very good," said Claude Duval. "I am quite at your service. Pray come on—come on. Surely there are enough of you?"

Some one fired a gun at him, and then the bullet that had been hastily crammed into it whistled past his head. In a moment he clapped spurs to his horse, and dashed forward towards the throng, crying—

"Who did that? Show me the man!"

Horsemen and those on foot alike turned upon this sudden and unexpected movement of Duval's, and one over the other they tumbled in an ineffectual attempt to get out of the churchyard. The man with the gun was thrown down and trampled on by his neighbours, and Duval then, seeing the state of confusion into which they were all thrown, thought that he could not have a better opportunity of joining May and being off, which, after all, was his only policy; so he turned his horse's head abruptly, and made for the rookery, and the little gate that led into the lane close to it.

May was close to the gate. "Over!" cried Duval; and in an instant she made the horse leap the little obstacle. Duval followed her. There was a loud shout from the rustics in the churchyard, who, when they found that Duval did not absolutely ride over them, had recovered from their first fright; and then both Duval and May darted up the lane at a great pace; but before they reached the top of it which joined the high-road, they were encountered by two horsemen, who blocked up the narrow road-way, and one of them said—

"Claude Duval, I arrest you in the king's name!"

"Indeed! How do you mean to do it?" cried Duval.

"I say I arrest you in the king's name. I am the sheriff of the county—the high sheriff."

"Are you?" said Duval, as he dashed against him, and overthrew him, horse and all, by the suddenness of the shock. "Are you? There, now: I have converted you into the *low* sheriff, and down you go, in my name or your own, just which you like."

"Help!" cried May. "Oh, help!"

Duval turned with rapidity, and found that the other horseman had seized her by the arm. If anything were more calculated than another to make Duval thoroughly angry, it was to see anybody attempt any violence to a young girl. We are afraid his sympathies did not extend beyond the young and the pretty. He spurred forward, and seizing the man by the collar, he dashed him from his horse; and the man, as he half scrambled to his feet, drew a pistol, and snapped it at Duval. Luckily for the latter, it only flashed without discharging. The man immediately rose, and ran back as fast as he could towards the churchyard.

"It's my turn," cried Duval; and taking from his breast one of the pistols he always kept loaded with a good charge of shot instead of a bullet, he took good aim, and pulled the trigger. A yell from the man, and his rolling over and over in the lane, were sufficient evidences that he had been hit, and then Duval called out to May—

"On—on! We shall have the others upon us if we don't make speed. Come on, May!"

It was well, not only that May was so capitally mounted, but that she was so well able to manage her steed, as was the case, or she would have hardly been able to keep up with Duval, notwithstanding he did not by any means put his horse to its utmost stretch of speed. As it was, however, they both at a very rapid pace went down the road that led towards Harlesdon Green, but Claude did not pursue that for long. He turned to the right, and made towards Neasdon as quickly as he could, for he thought that by going that way, he would easier get across the country to some other district. There were no signs or sounds of pursuit, and still taking advantage of every turning to the right that they came to, they at length emerged in the Edgware Road, very nearly as high up as Crincklewood.

"Safe enough now," said Duval, " I think, May."

" Oh, yes—yes. But what a fearful risk for you to run."

"Nay, I confess that you have chanced to be in the midst of my adventures on the road; but I have been in many a worse strait than I was a little while ago. I hope you will never—never again be in the midst of such a scene."

" Did you kill that man in the lane, Duval ?"

" Certainly not," he replied, laughing. " I only left with him a few grains of shot as a remembrance of me, and as a verification of his story when he tells it."

CHAPTER LXX.

THE HOUSE AT HORNSEY.—DUVAL SETS UP HOUSEKEEPING.

DUVAL did not think it at all prudent to continue so near to Wilsden, or the Edgware Road, after all that had happened, and the hue-and-cry that would certainly be made after him, but taking advantage of a lane to the right near the Brent River, he led the way down it, and contemplated crossing Hampstead Heath, and getting right away by Highgate.

" My poor May," said Duval, " you have but little rest indeed now that you have joined your fortunes to mine."

" Your dangers," she said, " shall be my dangers."

"Nay, indeed—I hope not. My first endeavour will be now to place you somewhere in safety. You are most unfit to battle with the world as I am forced to battle with it ; and my duty is to save you from its rude shocks. We need not ride so fast now. There is an inn not far from Highgate where we may rest in safety."

" Anywhere with you, if you are safe," said May. "But you must not be so cruel as to deny me the privilege of sharing your dangers."

" In what way could you ?"

" By accompanying you on your expeditions. You will find me able and willing to assist you.'

" Alas, my poor May! You speak with the simplicity and the innocence of a child of these affairs. No, May, I have not had much time for thought, but still I have had sufficient to come to some sort of resolution ; and it is, now that I have you whom I may truly call my own, to amass a certain sum, and then for ever leave this most hazardous line of life."

" Oh, what joy it is to me to hear you say so."

" I sincerely hope that we shall both have the joy of being able to carry out such a resolve. I think if we can get together the sum of ten thousand pounds we can go to the South of France, and purchase some chateau there, and live in peace."

" It is too much ; limit you desire to less, Duval. With half the amount let us fly from England for ever."

" Well, be it so. We shall perhaps be as happy with five thousand pounds as with ten ; so we will make the smaller sum the limit ; and as I shall now have a real object in view beyond the mere wants and extravagances of the passing hour. I shall feel much happier than I have felt."

By this time they had got right across Hampstead Heath, and up the long lane or road that leads to Highgate ; but just as they reached the high road, they heard the sound of horses' feet in a considerable number rapidly approaching as from London. Duval did not then wish for any useless contest, and as it was just possible they who were approaching might be enemies, he rode through the old churchyard, which, although it took him some little way out of his route, yet got him clear of the approaching horsemen. A man was in the churchyard working upon a monument.   At the approach of Duval and May, he looked up and said, respectfully enough—

"This, sir, is not a thoroughfare for horsemen."

"Then, I am sorry I intruded, my friend," said Duval; "but as we are more than half way through, we will go out at the opposite gate."

The man shifted his position, and Duval took a passing glance at the monument upon which he was chiselling some letters.   He had only completed one word, and that was the name *Adele*.   It was but a mere coincidence that the name of the dead who there reposed should be the same as that of the young girl at Kentish Town, to whom he owed so much faith, but whom he had so completely forgotten; but at the moment it quite unmanned him, and placing his hands over his eyes, he uttered a deep groan.

"You are not well," said May, looking at him anxiously.

"Oh, yes—yes."

"Nay, your are ill—very ill, Duval.   Speak to me.   Tell me what it is.   Your looks are wild, and you are pale and flushed by turns."

"A mere passing feeling of indisposition, May.   Heed it not.   Believe me, it is nothing.   Nothing at all.   There, I am better again, as you see.   It has passed away."

"And how sad and ill you looked."

"Which I certainly ought not to have done with you by my side.   But say no more about it.   We are clear of the churchyard now, and only look what a magnificent view you have now of the country lying betwixt us and London from this height upon which we stand."

"It is indeed very beautiful; but the daylight is fading fast away.   Look how dim and hazy the distance gets."

"It does, indeed.   But where we are to shelter ourselves for the night, is not far from here."

Duval was glad of any theme of conversation that would suffice to distract his mind from a recollection of Adele, whose name had been so strangely brought back at such a moment to his memory; and he continued to talk of the sunshine, and the view, and the evening star that was twinkling faintly in the twilight, until they reached an inn, half-way between Highgate and Hornsey, and they found rest and shelter for the night, under the name of Captain and Mrs. Smithson.

Duval rose early.   He had formed a determination of leaving May at the inn for a few hours, while he rode off to Kentish Town to see what had become of Adele, for much as his feelings had calmed down and chilled towards her, he could not but feel how much she had sacrificed for him, and that she was entitled to all the protection he could afford her.   He hoped that he should be able to keep secret from her his marriage with May; and if so, he flattered himself that all would be well.

It was easy for him to plead some urgent business as an excuse to May; and leaving her in bed, he took a hurried snack for breakfast, and mounting his horse, he rode off to Kentish Town.   The distance was by no means great, so that Duval reached the cottage at a very early hour indeed, and before any one was stirring. He turned his horse into the little garden, and coming under Adele's window, he cast up some gravel from the garden path at it.

In a moment or two it was opened,

"It is you!" cried Adele.   "Ah, yes, my dream is prophetic.   I thought you would come soon."

Duval could not speak.   His heart smote him at that moment for his ungenerous conduct to that fond confiding girl; and he felt that for the future whenever he was in her company, his feelings would be under fear and restrait.   Adele opened the cottage door, and with all the warmth and tenderness of manner that belonged to her, she led him into the little dwelling.

"Ah," she said, "what a truant and a wanderer you have been; and bu that I know well no other can hold my place in your heart, I should be so jealous, oh, so jealous! my Claude."

She smiled as she spoke, as though jealousy and she could never be companions, and it was quite a joke to think of her own Claude Duval, who had with so many oaths and protestations sworn to love her so well, giving her any cause of such uneasiness.

"Of course, Adele," he said, "I cannot be always master of my time."

"No—no, and it is selfish of me to ask you to come oftener. But you know how very dull I am without you."

"Yes, and I will come often."

"That is enough, more than enough. You know that this is your home; so now you will stay and tell me all your adventures since last I saw you. You must omit nothing, for you know how deeply interested I feel in the most trivial incident that concerns you."

"You are too good to me, Adele."

"No—no. You must not say that, for have you not been very good to me? Was it not you who took pity upon me when I was poor and homeless, and had no friend in all the world to stand by my side, and to say a kind word for me or to me? Ah, it is you who are too good."

Duval felt almost suffocated. He sprung to his feet.

"I must go—I must go!"

"Go? Oh—no—no."

"Yes, Adele, I must go. You see, I have a friend who is in some danger, and it distracts me to think of it. Indeed I must go, and at once too. Do not attempt to stay me. I will come to you as often as I can; but if I am away at times longer than you expect, think but that something very important indeed keeps me from you."

He paced to and fro in the little chamber in evident perturbation of spirit, and as Adele looked at him, her eyes filled with tears, and she was ready to sink to the floor, to see him for the first time in so strange a mood.

"Oh, Claude—Claude! I am sure that something has happened."

"What?"

"That I know not, I would I did—but you are not accustomed to be thus moved. It is some more than commonly serious a thing. Oh, tell me all. I implore you to tell me all. Anything in the world is better than this frightful suspense."

"Peace! Peace!"

"Nay, I will kneel to you. Why should I not? I only kneel to Heaven and to you. You are my hope here—heaven is my hope hereafter. I implore you to tell me what it is that has so strongly wrought upon you?"

"I cannot, I cannot."

He pushed her from him, and rushed to the door of the chamber. He paused only a moment upon the threshold, and taking a well-filled purse from his pocket, he flung it towards her, and then rushed at full speed down the little staircase.

"No—no!" cried Adele. "One moment. Only a moment."

"I cannot! I dare not!"

He reached the little passage and dashed open the door. His sagacious and familiar steed came up to him, and Duval sprung upon its back. Adele rushed into the garden.

"You cannot leave me thus? Oh, tell me—tell me what has happened. What has filled your mind with this dreadful confusion of thoughts? Speak to me, Duval."

"Farewell!"

"Not for ever? Oh, not for ever?"

"Farewell, Adele!"

He gave the horse an impulse forward, and dashed from the garden. He was afraid to look behind him, but he heard a shriek upon the morning air, and he knew it came from the young creature who now felt that she was deserted. If he could but have closed his ears against that sound, he felt as though he should have been happy enough perhaps in time to come ; but from the moment that he heard it, he knew that it would haunt him sleeping and waking.

"Oh, that I could have played the hypocrite," he muttered, "and seen her at times and lulled all suspicion ; but it is not in my nature : I could not do it. We must meet no more, since we cannot meet as once we met. I must banish thought!"

He drew up abruptly at the door of a public house, which was just being opened, and in a loud voice cried—

"Brandy!"

"Brandy, sir?" said a man who had just pulled down a shutter. "Yes, sir, in a moment, sir. How much?"

"A pint!"

The man stared, but he brought out a pint measure full of brandy. Duval raised it to his lips, and crying—

"To Adele!" he drank about half of it, and then throwing the measure and the remainder to the ground, off he galloped.

"Stop, stop! Oh, murder!" cried the publican, "he hasn't paid. Help! Police! Watch! Call the military! He hasn't paid!"

"Lor!" said the ostler, as he sat down on a truss of hay to laugh. "Lor master, do you know who that was?"

"No! Oh, dear no."

"Well, it's Duval the highwayman! Lor bless you, he only forgot it, and next time he comes this way it will be all right enough. I wouldn't mind waging an old horse-shoe now agin a sack o' oats, that something has put him out of his way."

Duval had, as the ostler said, quite forgotten in the excitement of his feelings that any payment was required for the brandy, nor did it once cross his mind even after he had galloped on. That scream of Adele's was still wringing in his ears.

He reached to within a quarter of a mile of the inn at which he had left May awaiting his return, before he pulled up and permitted his horse to go at a walk, and then he put to himself the question of—

"What will she do?"

This was a question of fearful significance, and one that was much more easily asked than answered. Perhaps the brandy helped Duval just then to get over it for he added to himself—

"Oh, she will be well, quite well. In a few days, or weeks at the utmost the disappointment will wear off. There was a hundred pounds in the purse, and that will help her on a little, and I will make inquiry about her, and she shall never want—no, no! and some of these days, when all this burst of feeling has passed away, all may be well, and we may meet again and be quite good friends. Oh, quite."

And so Duval tried to console himself as he stopped at the inn door.

CHAPTER LXXI.

DUVAL GETS SOME GOOD BOOTY ON THE NORTH ROAD.

MAY was up and waiting for him, not with impatience, for he had hardly led her to expect that he would return quite so soon. She had thought that very probably the business he spoke of might carry him to London, in which case he could not have got back in anything like the time that he did.

She flung herself into his arms.

"How good of you to come to me so soon, Duval. You thought that I should be lonely, did you not?"

"In truth, I did, May. Let me hope that you have breakfasted well and been happy and comfortable?"

"As happy as I could be with the thought that you might be running some risk."

"No! I was in no danger. The service that I went upon was not what I may call professional, although I certainly did not expect to be back so soon."

MAY.

"Ah, then, I dare be sworn you have been on some errand of kindness and charity to some one. It would be so like your kind and generous nature, which I know would shrink most sensitively from giving pain to any one. Is it not so? Ah, you turn aside your head. You would not tell your May even what good you do."

If the bitterest reproaches had been heaped upon the head of Duval by any one for his conduct to Adele, they could not have effected him half so much as did these innocent words of May, giving him credit for a consideration and a kindness that he certainly that morning had been very far from exercising. He hastily turned the conversation, by saying, as he walked to the window—

"It is time that we left here, May. Of course we will not live at an Inn, and I still feel much inclined to carry out my half formed determination of yesterday, and find a house for you."

"But will not the expense be great, and so at variance with our project of getting money enough to leave England?"

"I think not. It will, in my opinion, be the cheapest and the best thing we can do; besides, it will provide me with a refuge that otherwise I should not have. With the feeling that I had a home to come to, I should not spend anything like the money that I now do out of doors; and besides, I should know that you were safe."

"I daresay you are right, Duval. I will in all things submit to your judgment, for you must know the best."

"Nay, your opinion and your wishes will always guide me. But we will go at once, if you are ready."

"Quite—quite. Always ready to accompany you. Are you not my husband? My only hope now in this world?"

The thought of how he had deserted Adele, to whom he had been an only hope, prevented Duval from making any reply to May, and he left the room affecting to be anxious about the horses. When he reached the open air, he muttered to himself—

"When—oh when, shall I ever lose the recollection of the despairing cry of Adele, when she found that I was leaving her for ever! It is a weakness thus to torment myself; but I find that it will take much time yet before I recover from the shock I have this morning experienced."

The two horses were soon ready, and Duval and May left the Inn, and proceeded on the road to Hornsey, which little picturesque village was close at hand. May might have noticed, and probably did, that there was an amount of dejection about Duval's manner, such as was rather foreign to it, but she did not think proper to question him as to its origin.

When they reached Hornsey, almost one of the first objects that presented itself to them, was a very large old rambling house which was to let, as a board nailed to the front of it intimated.

"Behold!" said Duval. "The very thing. Do you think that will suit us for our first attempt at housekeeping, May?"

"If you like it, yes," replied May. "Shall we look at it?"

"By all means."

The gate-bell was rung, and an old woman showed them the house, which was partially furnished, the sum of fifty pounds being required for the goods that were in it. The rent was very inconsiderble, and as the reader is well aware that Duval's money was got easily enough, it may be supposed that he was not disposed to be very particular with regard to terms. The house was in the hands of a person about half a mile off, and without tiring the reader with details, we may say that in the course of two hours the fifty pounds was paid, and under the name of Mr. and Mrs. Smith, Duval and May took possession of the house. The old woman petitioned for, and got the place of servant to them.

"Now," said Duval, "this for a gentleman of my profession is rather an audacious proceeding; but it seems to me, that all I have to do, is to take care that this immediate neighbourhood is free from my exploits. I will come here only when I feel assured that I can come with safety to this establishment, and my professional pursuits will take effect upon other roads."

"But you will not forget," said May, as she looked tearfully into his face. "You will not forget that the object is to get sufficient to leave England, and at once to put an end to all the risks and anxieties of this frightful line of life?"

"Be assured that I will not forget that, May.   You have now given me by your love a stake, as it were, in life; and for your sake, as well as for my own, I will now try to save myself upon many an occasion when otherwise I should have been something more than careless, perhaps, of my safety.   Now, farewell. I will leave you to get your house a little in order.   But beware of making any confidence in your servant.   She might seem all that you would wish her, and yet be most dangerous."

"Trust me," said May, "I will be careful.   But I shall see you again to-day, Duval?   You promise me that?"

"If possible; yes."

Duval rode off, but the fact is, he would certainly not have left home so soon, had it not been that he was so full of anxious thoughts regarding Adele, that he felt the quiet of the house he had taken with its pretty garden, would not suit him, and that some Life on the Road was now necessary to bring his mind back to its usual state.   He was convinced that nothing but the excitement of danger would have the least effect upon his spirits.   He rode up a lane that led towards Highgate, and thus got out on the Great North Road.

"Once again," he said, "once again, after all this turmoil with girls—this, deserting, and this marrying—I am on the road.   I already feel lighter in spirit and more like myself, and if I do not have some adventure before midnight, it shall go strangely with me.   Let me see—I will pick up some money and then dine at an inn, and wait until sunset, which will give my horse a capital rest, and thus until midnight my life will begin.   Who shall say that I do not stand a good chance of taking home, by the light of to-morrow's dawn, some of the five thousand pounds that May thinks will be enough for happiness? Hilloa! What have we here?   The St. Albans waggon, I declare."

Slowly creeping along the road with its team of eight horses, came the waggon from St. Albans.   It only took eight hours to do the distance in, and as it had started at a very early hour indeed in the morning, it had actually neared High-gate by the time that Duval was upon the road.

Duval would hardly have thought it worth his while to interfere with a waggon and the sort of company that was usually to be found in such vehicles, had it not been that he saw the driver leading by the bridle a very handsome saddle-horse, and the idea struck him that the rider might be inside the waggon, for he knew that it was not unusual for persons who were carrying sums of money, or valuables, to ride in the waggon for safety's sake, as so many daring robberies had been committed upon the roads lately.

Duval rode up to the man who was driving, and said, with all the calmness in the world—

"My friend, whose horse is that?"

"Not yourn," replied the waggoner.   "You go your ways and I'll go mine."

"Have you made your will?" said Duval.

"My will? what do you mean by my will?"

"Just what I say.   If you have got anything to lose it will be a good thing if you have made your will, for I am going to blow your brains out for being insolent on the highway."

"Oh, murder!" cried the waggoner, dropping on his knees, as Duval levelled a pistol at him.   "It's a highwayman, as sure as a gun.   Oh, dear sir, spare me. I'm a poor man with a large family."

"Are you?   Why the greatest favour I could do you would be to put you out of the world under such circumstances.   But stop your team, and keep quiet, or you will never see your large family again."

"Oh dear, yes, sir—oh, yes.   The Lord have mercy upon us!   Woa! woa! Oh, yes, I'll stop 'em, sir, if you please."

Duval left the waggoner holding fast the leading horses of his team, and then, the waggon having stopped, he went to the back of it, and drawing aside the canvas, he cried—

"Your money or your lives!"

A chorus of screams came from some half-dozen females who were in the waggon; and then one voice cried—

"Oh, good sir, spare us all—we are helpless women, and the only gentleman here is the tax-gatherer."

"Murder! I'm a dead man!" cried another voice.

"The tax-gatherer?" said Duval. "Where is he?"

"Scrambling under all our feet, sir, to hide himself."

"Oh, is he? I'll soon have him out. Come out, you rascal—come out, will you? How dare you insult all these respectable, handsome, and accomplished ladies, by crawling about among their feet? It's really most disgraceful!"

"So it is," cried all the women at once. "Pull him out, sir, the ugly wretch! You are quite a gentleman, sir."

"And such a nice-spoken man," said another.

"And such eyes," said a third.

"Come out and be killed, Mr. Tax-gatherer," said a fourth, "and don't make the gentleman angry."

Duval leant as far off his horse as he could, and after routing about a little among the straw near the back of the waggon with his left hand, he got hold of the tax-gatherer's foot, and out he pulled him.

"Oh, murder!—murder!—spare my life, and take the assessed taxes."

"Come," said Duval, "your money—quick!"

"Oh dear—oh dear, I shall lose my situation."

Duval placed the muzzle of a pistol against his head, and added—

"If you detain me much longer, I shall have to shoot you first, and take your money afterwards; I call all the pretty girls in this waggon to notice what a deal of trouble you give me."

"Oh, yes, yes," said all the females at once, "it is abominable;" and then one added—"It's a wretched thing that a tax-gatherer should be so troublesome. Anybody but so very polite and handsome a gentleman would have shot him at once."

The poor tax-gatherer, who was by no means well-looking, saw that everybody was against him, so with a great many groans he produced a little yellow bag half full of money, which he handed to Duval, saying—

"I take you all to witness that I am robbed of the assessed taxes—I call upon you all to witness that. I'm a ruined man!"

"Pho! pho!" said Duval, "you know you will make a good thing of this, for you will pocket as much again, and say that I took it."

"So he will," said all the ladies.

"Oh, murder!" cried the tax-gatherer; "I only wish the waggon would break down with you all. Indeed, I wonder it don't with such an ugly lot."

"Ugly!" shrieked all the females at once; "ugly!"

They sprang upon the unfortunate tax-gatherer, and Duval putting his horse to speed, left them in the midst of a desperate fight with that unhappy individual. He galloped on until he had placed two or three miles between him and the waggon, and was not very far off from Barnet. He then looked at the tax-gatherer's bag, and found there were in it one hundred and seventy pounds in gold.

"Not a bad morning's work," said Duval. "I will try yet another adventure this morning, and then I will turn in somewhere to dinner, for I won't go home until midnight."

Duval when he made up his mind to an adventure had seldom to look far before finding one; and almost as he spoke he heard the sound of horses' feet upon the road before him, and in the course of a few moments a lady and gentleman on horseback appeared.

"Shall I stop them, or shall I not?" said Duval. "I won't alarm the lady if she be young and pretty, especially if I like the looks of her companion, too; but we shall see—we shall we!"

As the parties rode up, the young lady appeared to be in great dejection, and the gentleman turned out in appearance to be anything but a pleasant-looking personage. There was a disagreeable foxy look of low cunning and malice about his face, and Duval heard him distinctly say to the young lady—

"If you were to cry for a month, Jane, you should not get it from me. I don't care what are the consequences to you, I will show it to father, and have my revenge on the fellow, He threatened me once, and I have not forgotten it."

"But, George," said the lady, "how mean and dastardly it is of you to take such a revenge as to steal, and then show my letter."

CHAPTER LXXII.

DUVAL IS HUNTED, AND FINDS REFUGE IN A CAVERN NEAR MILL HILL.

THE words had come so plainly upon the ears of Claude Duval, that he could not help being struck by them. No doubt the beauty of the young lady, too, had a great deal to do with the sympathy which he felt upon the occasion.

"Who is that?" he heard the gentleman say, if we may call one a gentleman, who would speak to such a companion as he had with him, in such a strain. "Who is that, I wonder? I don't like the look of that man, Jane."

The young lady was weeping, and did not look up; and the sight of her tears at once determined Duval to interfere in the matter. He considered himself as a sort of knight-errant, called upon to succour, in particular, distressed damsels; and riding up to the gentleman, he said, in a very solemn tone—

"George, my boy, how are you this morning?"

Upon this, the gentleman started, and drew back his horse's head, while surprise seemed to choke his utterance.

"As usual, I suppose," added Duval. "Answer me, sir, for I have many souls to see to-day."

"Souls!" gasped George.

"Souls!" said the young lady, looking rather alarmed. But Duval, still preserving the utmost gravity of countenance, and speaking in the same mysterious deep tone, pointed to the young lady as he said—

"With you I dare not converse. Purer spirits than I am only have power to do so. Your presence nearly blinds me, and causes me the most excruciating pain; but such is my inheritance. It is George, your brother, he only that I dare speak freely to, for he is mine."

"What—what do you mean?" cried George, his face turning very pale, and the hair almost bristling upon his head with fright.

"I mean that which I say. I dare not speak that which is not. I ask you again, if you feel well?

"Yes—yes—pretty well. Oh, dear Jane, speak to him. It's the—the—I'm sure it is the——"

"Devil!" said Duval. "That is what you were going to say; but it's better not said, young man. I have travelled some distance to meet you this morning. We have not met for some time."

"Oh, dear—oh, dear—Help!—Murder!"

"Your outcries are of no avail. I want a letter that you have about you, and which is addressed to Jane."

"Yes, good Mr. D—no, I don't mean that—anything you like, only let me off, do, this time. Only say you have not come for me, and you may have everything else."

Duval pointed upwards, as he said—

"It is the higher and nobler intelligence—the first cause of all, and the Lord of all, only that can issue his fiat to part the body from the spirit; and your time has not yet come. Give me the letter."

" Yes. oh, dear, yes. I didn't, indeed, think of meeting with you, sir, this morning. Indeed, I didn't. Here's the letter, sir. It's from young Lieutenant Hill, sir, to my sister Jane, and ——"

" Hush! Do you think that anything has been hidden from me? I yet retain sufficient of my celestial gift to dive into the secret thoughts of men. You would tell me nothing. You were about, from mere revengeful motives, to show this letter to your father."

" Oh dear, yes. Have mercy upon me, good Mr.—oh dear!"

Duval took the letter, and handing it to the young lady, he said—

"It is yours. If ever again this brother of yours—this fool, whom I know well—crosses your fair purposes, take a small roll of brimstone, and wrapping it up in a piece of paper, upon which the name 'Satan' is written in blood, cast it into any flame, and I will come and take note of what is doing. Farewell! —Farewell!—Farewell!"

With these words, Duval uttered a mournful groan, and struck his chest as though he were in great agony ; and then giving his horse the rein, off he galloped, leaving the young lady and her brother, as thoroughly terrified and bewildered by what had passed, as any two persons could possibly be.

Duval was so mightily amused at this adventure, that when he got about half a mile off from where he had left the young lady and her brother, he fairly stopped to laugh aloud.

" I would wager anything now," he said, " that that fellow passes some sleep-less nights, and will be afraid to venture out in the dark for the next six months to come. I never did in all my life see such a picture of absolute fright as he presented. I only hope Miss Jane, who I think shrewdly suspected the trick, will take care to profit by it, so as to keep her cub of a brother in order. He will be terrified to death if she now and then threaten him with the little bit of brim-stone that I mentioned. Ha! ha! ha! Who says now that I don't do some good ?"

" Not I," said a loud voice.

Duval started, and turning in the direction from whence the sound proceeded, he saw right on the hedge by the road-side, a man on horseback, on a rising ground in a meadow.

" Well," said Duval, " who are you ?"

" I think, my man," said the stranger, " you will soon find that out. Your rigs are over at last. Duval, your race is run, and you may as well as all those have done who have gone before you, and had their career upon the road, give in with a good grace."

" Upon my faith," said Duval, " you speak in riddles. You seem to know me, so if you have anything about you worth the taking, you may consider that, in the exercise of my vocation, it is mine."

" Certainly," said the man. " The only thing I have about me that will fit you, are a pair of as well made handcuffs as ever held the wrists of a highwayman together, and they will be yours shortly."

" Indeed ! Are you quite sure of that ?"

" Quite ; you are a prisoner now."

" Well," said Duval, " that is news, and pray what name do you go by when you are at home ?"

" Brand."

" Ho! ho! In good truth I have heard of you, Mr. Brand. You are an officer of the police, and as report says you are bold one. And so you have laid your plans so that you have encompassed me at last ?"

" I rather think so, Claude Duval. It is my business to take you if I can. I dont believe that you have quite made up your mind to die by a bullet upon the road, so your best plan is to take the thing easy, and give up, in which case I promise you good treatment."

" You are very kind. I suppose you will take care, you mean, that I am hanged with all due ceremony ?"

"With the hanging part of the business I have nothing to do. My work is to lodge you in Newgate, and then they may do what they like with you; so give up at once, and save the unpleasant consequences of a resistance, that will be of no sort of avail."

"Upon my word," said Duval, "you are the most jocular person, Mr. Brand, that I have come across for a very long time, indeed. What if I decline to give-in in the nice easy way that seems to be so satisfactory to you?"

"In that case, instead of your living carcass, I shall carry your dead one to London."

"Indeed! Well now, Mr. Brand, allow me to give you a word or two of advice, since you have favoured me with so many. I am fond of a joke; and can give and take one as well as most people. But there is such a thing as carrying a funniment a little too far, and my temper, folks say, is just a little hasty. Now, Mr. Brand, you are safe just now, but I won't take upon myself to say how long you will be so; and my sincere advice to you is, that the healthiest thing you can do is to go while you can."

"I would under any other circumstances."

"And why not now?"

"Because, Duval, I am quite aware you are speaking under the most serious misapprehension. You are now in rather a narrow country road."

"Granted."

"Well, you have behind you six men hidden in ambush, whom you have passed. Before you there are six more likewise, and well armed. The hedge is too high for you to jump or to scramble over; and here I am with a pistol in my hand, and there you are in a trap."

"Thank you for your information."

"You need not attempt, by riding on and by violence, to get off. The trunk of a tree is down across the road, about a hundred yards in front of you, so that you cannot get on; and by this time, those behind you have barricaded the road in your rear, to allow them time to do which, I have thought proper to engage in this entertaining conversation."

"Upon my word, Mr. Brand," said Duval, " you are a clever fellow; and it's only a pity you were not brought up to some business in which your abilities would have met with a better reward than they will in the ticklish one you have chosen."

"I am quite content," said the officer, " with the emoluments of my business; and the reward for the apprehension of Claude Duval, you will grant, may not be a ba windfall."

"Take it then," said Duval. "There it is in full; and much good may it do you, Mr. Brand."

As he spoke, Duval drew a small but rather long barrelled pistol from a secret pocket in his saddle, and levelling it at the officer, he pulled the trigger. There was a sharp report, a shriek, and the officer fell from his saddle to the grass, where he lay dead; for the bullet with which the pistol was loaded had passed right through the centre of his forehead and lodged in his brain.

"Now," cried Duval, as he replaced the pistol in its secret receptacle, and armed himself with another loaded one, "let those stop me who dare. Their deaths be upon their own heads."

He touched his horse with the spur, and the creature at once bounded forward as though mad. The short distance of a hundred feet or so were passed in a few moments; and then, sure enough, as Mr. Brand had predicted, there was the immense stump of a tree, with many branches sticking from it in all directions, thrown across the roadway, and behind it, half a dozen well armed men. Duval felt now that to hesitate would be to be lost, for they could make a target of him easily from behind the tree. He trusted, therefore, to that good fortune which had so many times, in the most desperate state of his fortunes, befriended him, and giving his horse another impulse, on he dashed. The horse had courage enough for anything, and at once was among the branches of the tree. It was next to impossible that the creature could keep its feet under such circumstances, and it stumbled to its knees over one of the long loose branches. This stumbling, however, had the effect of saving Duval's life, for the whole six men at the moment fired at him, and the shots all went over his head. Infuriated at the attack upon him by so many, Duval, without waiting for his horse to move, shot one of them with the pistol he had in his hand. Then a strong man grappled with him; but one ringing blow upon his forehead with the barrel of the discharged pistol sent him reeling to the ground.

Duval had rapidly flung himself off his saddle at the moment that the horse fell, and now he held it by the bridle close to the head, and assisted it to rise. He thought the best thing he could do was to lead it now through the branches of the fallen tree.

" You are dead men if you resist me!" he cried. " I fight for my life! Cowards, make way!"

It so happened that at this moment the men in the lane who had been mentioned by Mr. Brand as lying in ambush, so as to let Duval pass, and then close up the rear against him, hearing the contest going on in front, rose up from amid the brushwood, where they had been concealed, and ran on to lend what aid they could, for they were not aware of the death of Brand; and thus in the hurry and excitement of the moment, they, with the heedlessness of people not accustomed to having fire-arms in their hands, discharged a volley at Claude Duval and his horse, as they intended, without reflecting that whatever bullets missed him were likely to find their way among the party on the other side of the fallen tree, who were their own companions.

One bullet knocked off Duval's hat. Another caught him just on the top of the shoulder, making an ugly kind of furrow in the flesh and skin; but in the excitement of the moment, he felt nothing but a sudden stunning sensation; and then, two of the four men who remained to dispute his passage across the trees, fell wounded, and uttering the most dismal cries.

The two who remained did not seem to think themselves at all a match for Duval, although encumbered as he was with the care of his horse; if they had flung themselves upon him, they might have brought him down, in which case victory would be declared for them; but, on the contrary, they began scrambling up the hedge, heedless of thorns and blackberry twigs, and only intent upon getting quickly out of the way of further danger, which appeared to them to be most immediate and imminent.

CHAPTER LXXIII.

THE DEATH OF DUVAL'S HORSE, AND THE CHASE.

It was not likely that Duval would trouble himself much with those of his foes who chose to leave him the field of battle; so he turned all his attention to the extrication of his horse, from among the branches of the tree, which being in the course of the next few moments effected, he sprung to the saddle, and giving the creature a powerful impulse forward, both with spur and rein, off he went at a tearingmad sort of gallop.

" Hurrah!" he cried. " Hurrah! Safe at last. Mr. Brand, you are not the first clever person who has laid a trap for another, and been caught in it himself. Hurrah!"

The exultation of Duval at finding he had escaped from such a really serious danger, was so great, that he did not, for some few minutes, notice that the horse went on very unsteadily; but just as he plunged into a narrow lane, that was much darkened by the tall trees in the hedgerows, almost at places meeting overhead, he did fancy that the gallant creature staggered.

" What ho!" he cried. " Steady!

The words had scarcely escaped his lips, when the horse fell, and Duval was precipitated over its head. It was well for him that his pace was not then great, or from such an accident, the knight of the road might have brought his course to a close. As it was he was rather shaken; but feeling satisfied that no bones were broken, he was quickly enough on his feet.

CLAUDE SEEKS REFUGE FROM HIS PURSUERS IN A CHESNUT TREE.

The horse lay panting upon its side.

Duval rushed up to the creature, and knelt by its head. It was then that for the first time he saw it had received one of the pistol shots in its neck, and that all its progress from the scene of the conflict was marked by a track of blood. It had no doubt fallen at length from pure exhaustion.

Duval would rather have encountered any amount of danger to himself, ay, and he would have suffered great personal injury, rather than he would have looked upon the sight that he now saw in the lane, of his horse dying before his face. That such was the fact, there could be very little doubt from the aspect of the creature. Its eyes were but dimly turned upon Duval, and it drew its breath by short fitful inspirations. The shot in the neck had wounded some blood-vessel of importance, and the hot blood was now weltering forth in a stream.

"Alas," said Duval, as he rose, "my poor steed, my gallant and courageous companion, with whom I have gone through so many adventures, and who has carried me through so many dangers in safety, must we indeed part at last? This is indeed grievous to my spirit. Most grievous."

He stood with his hands clasped before him, gazing upon the horse, which each moment was faintly dying. At length a sharp convulsive shudder pervaded the limbs of the creature, and the mouth opened twice as though gasping for breath. Then all was still. The gallant steed of Claude Duval had breathed its last.

For a moment Duval covered his face with both hands, and he shook as though some convulsion in imitation of that which had announced the demise of the horse had come over him. Then he took his hands away, and said calmly—

"That is over."

Even as he spoke he bent forward, and inclined his ear to listen, and in the distance he heard loud shouts, and the tramp of the feet of men and horses. It seemed as though a multitude of people were not far from him. He clambered up the hedgerow, and grasping the branch of a dwarf oak tree for support, he shaded his eyes with his hands. He looked in the direction whence the noise came. To his surprise he saw forty or fifty country people, some armed with pitch-forks, some with flails, and with them about eight or ten men on horse-back, who seemed to be directing the others how to proceed ; and by their pointing out different parts of the ground to each other as they proceeded, Duval could not entertain a doubt but that they were his enemies.

"They trace me by the horse's blood," he said, "and, perhaps, by some of my own; but I am not yet conquered."

Springing down from the top of the hedgerow, he commenced the work of reloading all his pistols ; and taking those from the saddle of the dead horse that were always kept there, he bestowed them handily about his person, and there he stood considering for a few moments what he should do.

While he so stood he heard the riot of the pursuit approaching him closer and closer ; he could almost at times distinguish what the people said ; and more than once, he was certain that he heard the word " Murder !" repeated.

"Ay," he said. "Murder is the word. They have murdered you, my poor horse; but it will yet go hard with me if I do not avenge you upon some of them. Oh, that I knew the precise hand that fired the shot that has laid you low, I would manage, despite even the seeming desperate crisis of my fortune, to lay him low."

"This way ! This way !" he now heard a loud voice say. " He is in the lane! Come on !"

"Is he in the lane ?" said Duval, as he glanced round him, and then, with amazing speed, he took to his heels, and ran until he came to a stile that seemed to lead into some sort of plantation or preserve. He thought that it would be safer to get into that woody retreat than to remain in the open lane ; so, vaulting over the stile, he dived at once among the trees, and the thick underwood that was outstretched in every direction, no doubt, as a shelter for the game that was there preserved.

It was quite a relief to Duval to get into this thick, woody retreat, after the sharp run he had had, and he plunged on, now and then, torn by the briars; but feeling a sense of security, as each moment took him further and further into the intricacies of the preserve. Twice he started a pheasant, which flew up above his head with a sudden whirr, and once a hare rushed almost past his very feet.

" I shall baffle them for a time," he muttered. "If they even find that I have taken such a place of retreat as this, they will find it difficult to attack me here ; and if they are disposed for a species of warfare in which I can use

my pistols with advantage upon them, they may have it, and take the consequences."

There can be no doubt but that in the then imbittered state of Duval's feelings,
he would not have scrupled at the taking of more life than he ordinary would
have liked to level his pistols at; but the death of his horse had certainly for
a time soured all the milk of human kindness in his disposition.

Every few minutes he would now pause, and inclining his ear close to the
earth, he would listen for the distinct shouts of his pursuers. Upon one of these
occasions he heard a loud and continuous Hurrah! and biting his lips with vexation, he said—

"That shout of poor triumph is over the remains of the horse. Well! Well!
let them shout. It certainly is a great thing for some fifty people to be so elated
that they have found a dead horse in a lane; but if I don't change the character of
their shouts for some of them shortly, I am not Claude Duval."

With these words, he hurried on; but, at length, thinking that he had placed
a sufficient distance between himself and his pursuers, he paused to rest himself,
and he sat down upon the gnarled roots of an old elm tree, which afforded him
a convenient seat.

"So," he said. "Here I am on foot at last, and when shall I get such
another horse as that I have this morning lost? I may look long, indeed, for
one; but still, one I must and will have. Well, it is something that he has
only fallen dead into the hands of the enemy. After the many escapes that he
and I have had together, I would not have had them take the gallant creature
alive. Let them now make the most of him. Ah! what is that?"

A loud shout now sounded in fearful proximity to him, and he sprang to his
feet.

As he did so, he felt a sudden tinge of pain from the slight shot-wound in his
shoulder; and, upon putting his hand up and glancing at it, he found that the
blood had trickled right down his arm to his elbow; from whence it was falling
drop by drop upon the ground.

"It is so, by Heaven!" he said, after a moment's thought. "They traced the
horse by the spots of its blood, and now they are tracing me by mine; I should
have thought of that. They, doubtless, have found quite sufficient evidence that
I have crossed the stile into the plantation, and like blood-hounds they are upon
my track again."

He took his cravat, now, and made it into a bandage for his wounded arm,
tying it sufficiently tight to prevent the bleeding from being at all excessive; and
then feeling satisfied that he should no longer leave such an audible trail behind
him, he clambered on through the trees and underwood.

He did not intend, unless absolutely forced to it, to leave the shelter of the
preserve, for in the open country he would have no chance; but he hoped where
he was to succeed in keeping his enemies at bay until night; and then, under
cover of its friendly shadows, he might escape.

He paused again to listen.

His enemies were certainly nearer than they had been.

"Let them come," he said. "Some at least of them come to death. If I
have not the lives of half a dozen men in my hands, it will cease to be a matter
of regret to me; for I shall myself have gone from this world. Alas, my poor
May, what will become of you? and you too, Adele, that I did not mean should
ever want, you will miss me!"

He saw close to him a large tree, and the thought occurred to him that if he
climbed it and hid among its branches, those who were pursuing him might
possibly pass.

"Amid all these trees," he said, "although they may fancy I may be hidden
in one, they cannot pitch upon which, and it will take them until sunset to climb
into one half of them to see; and as for firing at me in the tree, even if they
take that mode of trying if I am here, the merest twig or folded leaf thicker
than common will alter the direction of a bullet. Yes, the tree will be the

thing ; and if it does come to a fight, I think they will be more happy to get out of the range of my fire, than I out of that of theirs."

Active as Duval was, it did not take him many minutes to climb up into the tree ; but when there, he was rather surprised to find a smell of smoke pervading its branches, as if from recently burnt wood.   He was just asking himself what this could be, when he heard voices close at hand, and peeping down from his leafy covert, he saw a man and a boy come cautiously near to the spot.   The man was a large coarse-looking fellow, with a hideous squint, and the boy was one of those little wiry vagabonds only to be found in rural districts, and who are quite created by the game-laws: Both were dressed in a costume something between gamekeepers and poachers.   Duval set them down at once for the latter.

"What's all the row in the croft?" said the man, " eh, Peter?   What's it all about ?"

"Don't know," said the boy.

"You ought to know, then," cried the man, dealing him a box on the ears. "Take that, and find out.   You never know nought."

"Do that again," said the boy, "and I'll put my knife in thee."

"Ha! ha!" laughed the man.   "Try it, Peter, try it, my boy.   Only try it, that's all."

"Then don't hit me."

" Only now and then, Peter my boy, just to bring you up in a quiet way loike. Now, what's the row in the croft?"

"They're hunting a highwayman."

"Oh, is that it.   Humph, well I only wish they may not get him, the wretches. I hope he'll give 'em as many turns and doubles as an old fox.   The idea now of a-going and a-hunting a fellor cretur, just for saying stand and deliver, on the highway ; but there's nothing, Peter, but parsecution in this here world.   You daren't do nothing as is pleasant.   If you knock over a brace of partridges, or throttles a hare, they has you up, so we oughtn't to wonder at society, Peter."

"Shouldn't I like to cut old Squire Adams's throat," said Peter.   " I'd like to do it with a blunt knife, with a lot o' notches in it, and keep him a squalling for half an hour, I would."

This, to the perception of the big man, was such a happy conceit, that he was compelled to hold his sides while he laughed ; and then shaking his hand at Peter, he said—

"Ah, my boy, you will be hanged, of course, but you'll do some funny things afore that comes to pass, I do think.   We are best under ground though, while this hunt is going on.   Let's get into the Old Cave, my boy."

CHAPTER LXXIV.

DUVAL GETS OUT OF THE FRYING-PAN INTO THE FIRE.

THOSE words, Old Cave, rather struck upon the ear of Duval as being a little remarkable ; but after a moment's consideration, he made up his mind that they referred to some public-house in the vicinity, for he well knew what odd, fantastic names were given at times to these establishments.

"Ah!" said Peter.   "I does like the Old Cave."

"And so does I," said the man, " and if it wasn't for that, I don't think at times there would be a place for a poor fellow to hide his head in ; and yet they call this a Christian country."

"They does—they does," said the boy.

Duval began to think that there was something more in the Old Cave story than he had at first supposed, for if it had merely referred to some public-house, it was natural enough that Peter and his not very respectable-looking friend would have gone off to it at once, instead of lingering upon that spot.

All Duval's doubts and cogitations upon the subject were, however, soon at an end, for he saw enough in a very few minutes more to convince him that the words, Old Cave, for once, must be taken in their literal sense, and by no means figuratively applied to any public-house.

The man, after listening for a few moments, and apparently satisfying himself that no one was within hearing, said—

"Very good! It's all right, Peter. Now for it, old fellow, and if we don't light a good fire and enjoy ourselves a little before the others come home, it won't be our faults."

"Not a bit of it," said Peter.

With this, the man went to an old broken down trunk of a tree that was near at hand, and having stooped over it, he pulled out a kind of plug of wood, made from the roots of some other tree, and which evidently sufficiently stopped up the hollow trunk to give it only the appearance of incipient decay, if any one looked into it, while in reality it was no more than a mere shell.

"Now, Peter," he said, "you go down."

"Here you goes," said Peter.

The boy, with great dexterity, swung himself up to the top of the old decayed trunk of the tree, and let himself right down, disappearing entirely from before the eyes of Duval.

"All right?" asked the man.

"Yes," said Peter. "All's right. Nobody at home, though."

Duval was a little curious to see how the man would get down, and replace the wooden plug in the tree, seeing that it was of rather a bulky appearance, and must have been weighty. But that was done with considerable tact. He just balanced it at the side of the hollow trunk against a projecting branch that was sufficiently strong to hold it, and then having gone down the hollow, he put up one hand and pulled it slightly, when it fell into its place.

"Well," thought Duval, "that plan is worth the knowing, at any rate, if one should be hard pressed by the Philistines at any time, and certainly I should not feel any scruples in the world in making use of it, under such circumstances."

The cogitations of Duval concerning the old cavern, however, were soon put an end to by the appearance of his enemies in the immediate vicinity of the tree in which he was hiding. Half-a-dozen well-armed men came just under the tree, and one said—

"I feel quite sure that he is in the preserves somewhere."

"Well," said another, "if so, he is as good as taken, for it is not very large, and somebody is placed at every possible outlet, and within sight of each other, too, to give the alarm."

"Then we shall starve him out?"

"Not a doubt of it; and in the meantime I shall amuse myself by going through the wood, and sending a good charge of shot into a few of the trees, upon the chance of his hiding in some of them, for that's not the most unlikely thing in all the world."

"Far from it."

Duval set his teeth with anger, at the idea of being thus baited by a parcel of men whom he had not injured, and whose circumstances were such that it was not at all likely he would ever come in contact with them. The man who so kindly proposed to fire into the tree, was a kind of under-gamekeeper.

More men kept straggling in as the others spoke, and Duval had the satisfaction, if it were any, of hearing the most complete arrangements made for watching the preserve night and day, in order to entrap him, while there was a talk of getting more officers from London for the purpose of hunting him out of his place of concealment.

"This little wood," he thought, "will be too hot for me, probably, in a little while; but it will be bad for the healths of some of you, if you stop my progress from it."

Duval had not quite made up his mind what he should do, but as he did not feel any pangs of either hunger or thirst, he felt that he could afford to wait in the tree a considerable time, and perhaps wear out the vigilance of his foes.

The man who had so coolly announced his intention of firing into the tree, was very deliberately now loading a double-barrelled fowling-piece, and when he had done so, he pointed it at a chesnut tree, some dozen yards or so from the one which Duval was hiding in, and fired.

"Have you caught him?" said one, as a few leaves and short branches came whirling to the ground.

"Never mind," said the man. "It was a scattering shot, and if he should chance to get one of them in his eye, he won't see his way quite so plain on the highway, if he should ever come to it again."

Duval had vehemently sought the hilt of one of his pistols, but he immediately relinguished the hold again, for he felt how imprudent it would be to shoot that man, although the temptation was very great and the provocation for doing so immense.

"Well," said the fellow, "I will take it for granted that he isn't in the chesnut."

"No," said another, "and for all I have heard of Duval, if you were to riddle him with shot, and he had made up his mind to stay in the tree, stay he would in spite of you."

"Yes, that he might, but I don't think he'd feel comfortable; so here goes into the other tree."

The fellow now levelled his gun at the tree in which Duval was, and the only precaution that he, Duval, took, was to cover up his face with the lappet of his coat.

Bang! went the second barrel of the gun, but as good fortune would have it, so far as Duval was concerned, not one of the shots touched him, although some half dozen of them lodged in a limb of the tree not twelve inches from his head.

"Hit him now, Sam?" said one of the men.

"No, I don't suppose I have, and I didn't say I should; but I could hit such a goose as you at three times the distance."

"Could you indeed, Sam. Why you are quite a wonderful character. Do you think Squire Adders will like to supply you with powder and shot to spoil the trees with, stupid?"

"You mind your own business."

The man who was named Sam, then walked sulkily off, reloading his gun as he went.

"Well, my fine fellow," thought Duval, "it certainly is possible that I may have to leave this preserve without paying you the little debt that I feel I owe you; but I won't do so if I can help it, you may depend upon it. Sam, they call you. I won't forget that."

"Now my men," said a person suddenly arriving. "Any news of the person we are in search of?"

"No sir; Sam has gone blazing away into the trees, but we can't see any traces of him."

"Sam's an idiot."

"Well, sir, we did tell him not do it, but he said he would, and now he's gone off to spoil all the fine old wood in the plantation, besides frightening the game out of their nests, and making them clear out of the preserve, sir, for a month to come."

"Dear, dear, that any body should be so pested with an idiot! Which way did he go?"

"Right on, sir, by those sycamores."

Upon this the person who appeared to be in great authority, from the respect he was treated with by the others, went off at a quick pace after Sam, and Duval was not a little pleased at the idea that something like retributive justice might overtake the man, who, because he had a gun in his hand, could not refrain from doing or attempting to do injury.

After this, the men left the vicinity of the tree in which Duval was hidden, and he had the satisfaction of knowing, that sentinels were placed all round the wood, at such intervals, that they could see each other, and so spread a general alarm should he make any attempt to leave it.

Once again, and only once, Duval heard one of Sam's barrels go off, but after that all was still enough, as no doubt he had been stopped from carrying his project of firing into the trees any further. It, therefore, was become a very serious thing with Duval to consider what he should do in this emergency of his fortune.

If he should leave the tree, or attempt by a rush to get away, he felt that he would be only making his situation a great deal worse than it was, inasmuch as he was now under cover, whereas he would be at the mercy of his enemies, to be chased through the open country ; and without his horse, what could he do ?

"No," he said, "if I do anything it must be by finesse, under cover of the night; but it is by no means a pleasant idea to sit in a tree till then."

It was rather a grave question, though, when he came to consider how he could by any means better his condition ; and then, after a time, his thoughts reverted to the old cave, and scarcely had he turned his eyes in the direction of that singular place, when he heard a noise, and the plug of wood that filled up the strip of the aged tree, was raised from within, and the man made his appearance.

"Humph," he said. "It's all right. Peter, come on, my boy, come on."

It was evident that he was well accustomed to lodging the loose piece of aged root upon the projecting branch of the hollow trunk, for it was done in a moment ; and then he scrambled out, being followed by Peter, who was on the ground with the agility of a monkey in a moment.

"Come on, Peter, my boy," he said. "Let's go to Mill Hill, and see what's doing. Who knows but there may be something for honest folks to pick up ?—such as a stray duck, or a hen, or even a shirt, or a pair of stockings, hung on a hedge Always keep your eyes open, Peter, and be industrious. Doesn't the copy books say that Satan always finds some work for idle hands to do ?"

"Hold your gammon," said Peter.

"Gammon ! Do you call that gammon ? Oh, Peter, I'm very much afraid as you don't mind your chatechiz, you bad boy. Come on, you wiper, will you, and mind you keep your eyes open, and is down upon everything like a shot, if you thinks it worth the taking."

"I hear you."

"Well, Peter, it is a good thing that you does. Take that."

"Oh, murder ! what do you kick me for ?"

"Why, Peter, you said you heard me, and I thought you might as well feel me too, you is such a forward, nice, boy ; so now come on, and whatever you do, Peter, always be civil to everybody as is bigger than yourself."

CHAPTER LXXV.

DUVAL FINDS A TEMPORARY REFUGE IN THE CAVE.

DUVAL, if his circumstances could have permitted him, would no doubt have enjoyed quite a hearty laugh at the peculiarities of Peter, and the man with whom he appeared to be very closely associated; but the fact was, that Duval's whole attention was too much engrossed in his own affairs just then, to smile at the peculiarities of others.

When the man and Peter had got fairly away, and Duval could no longer hear their footsteps upon the decayed leaves of the preserve, he began to ask himself whether or not it would be prudent to go himself into the cave that they had just left.

"What can they be," he thought, "but poachers? and from the advice of the man to Peter, it appears that they are not very particular about what they do, so long as they are doing something. I might surely be safe enough with such people, and, besides, I can pay them well, which is rather an important element in the transaction."

There was now only one consideration that made Duval pause a little before venturing to the cave, and that arose from an expression of the man's to the effect, that there was nobody at home, which would lead to the supposition that others besides himself and the boy Peter were in the habit of visiting the cave, in which case there might be rather too many to trust himself and his liberty to. If they had been members of what was called the "London family," that is to say, cracksmen and highwaymen by profession, Duval knew that he would have been safe enough, if a thousand pounds had been the immediate price of his death or capture; but with such personage as those who might use that cave— half-poachers, half-poultry stealers, and in fact, wholly anything that would soften the rigour of poverty in the country—he felt that he should hardly feel at ease.

After about ten minutes spent in arguing the matter pro. and con. with himself, he at length said, suddenly—

"I will chance it."

When Duval made a resolution he was not long in carrying it out, and form the moment he said "I will chance it," he began to make his preparations for the risk. Cautiously he descended from the tree, for although no one was at hand, he felt that it would be highly desirable to make as little noise as possible.

He trod lightly upon the ground, and reached the tree, or rather the old decayed stump of tree, which served as the portal of the cave, concerning which the man and Peter had spoken. To him it was not a matter of any difficulty to remove the plug of wood that stopped it up; and as he had tolerable tact, he quickly balanced it as he had seen the man do.

All below seemed to be as dark as night, and yet if they, Peter and his friend, had gone down in safety, there is no reason upon earth why he, Duval, should not. While he paused for half a moment, he heard, or fancied he heard, a footstep coming towards the place. That at once determined him, and drawing up his feet as he had seen the man do by the aid of a couple of branches of the old stump over head, he at once let them down into the cavity, and felt that he stood upon something. Then he pulled the plug of wood into its place, and narrowly escaped a severe blow upon the head with it as it came down.

The sensation that Duval felt now, was anything but an agreeable one. He was in a place that he could not move in, in any direction but downwards or upwards, and he was in total darkness. There was no hold for his hands either anywhere, so he was forced to trust to fate or providence.

Cautiously he put down one foot off the little kind of ledge that he stood upon, and then he felt another such a one below, at a distance of about six inches, and from that moment he felt quite easy as to the mode of descent, for that he was on the top stairs of a little flight of steps was sufficiently apparent.

He descended very carefully, for he was rather afraid of hitting his head, but after getting down no less a number than eighteen of the little steps, he found that they ceased, and that he stood upon ground and not upon wood, of which they were composed. Yet he was in the most profound darkness, and he felt all round him without being able to find any mode of outlet. Under these circumstances he proceeded right on for about six steps, and then has he kept his hands stretched out before him, he felt something move to the touch.

At first he started back, for he thought that in the darkness he had touched some person, but it was only for a moment that such an idea took possession of him, and he immediately advanced, and found that what he had touched was a blanket, apparently hanging in the way of his further progress.

After a moment or two's consideration, Duval did not make any effort to tear the blanket down; but he moved his hand across it until he reached the edge of it, and then he drew it aside, and in a moment he saw where he was.

The blanket covered the entrance to the cave, which was about thirty feet in length, and as many nearly in breadth. The roof was rather low, but by the light of a turf fire which was faintly burning in one corner, Duval was able to look pretty well about him, at the rather singular place in which he found himself.

CLAUDE IN THE POACHERS' CAVE.

The walls were evidently of nothing but hammered earth, and projecting from them in some places were the gnarled roots of old tress, which flourished in the little wood overhead. The floor was earth likewise, but hammered quite hard; and from the state of the atmosphere, it was quite evident that there was some mode of ventilation, and some sort of chimney by which the smoke from the turf fire made its escape.

Of furniture, there was nothing in the place but a very rough wood table, evidently put together with no skill, and some stools apparently got up by the same hand. An old chair was in one corner, and upon some shelves fastened by some screws to the walls, there were many little odd articles, and a quantity of cooked and some uncooked meat as well as some bread.

A large pitcher was in one corner with a piece of thick board over it, and upon peeping in, Duval found that it contained ale of some kind by the odour.

"Well," said Duval, "one might live here a little while in preferance to a jail above ground. It is rather dark, though."

Upon one of these shelves he found a candle in a little square lamp of clay by way of a candlestick, and he speedily ignited it at the turf fire, which spread an agreeable enough kind of warmth in the atmosphere of the place; but what most surprised him was that he could perceive no dampness in the cave.

From this latter circumstance he came to the conclusion that it was very old indeed; and that from the constant presence of the turf fire, which no doubt was never permitted to go out, it had got in time so warmed, and the walls and floors so baked, that the damp vapours of the earth could no penetrate into the place.

"Very good," said Duval, "I am here certainly an uninvited guest, but I will make myself as welcome as I can for all that. If anybody comes, they will perhaps be pleased to recollect that if they have the secret of my being here, that I have the secret of this place, so that we shall be even."

With this, Duval placed upon the rough table some of the cooked meat, and pouring himself out a portion of the ale in a brown jug that he found, he sat down, and was quite determined to enjoy himself as well as he could.

In the midst of all this though, Duval was not unmindful of his safety, for he looked carefully to his pistols, and ascertained that they were in excellent order, and he kept his ears open to the lightest sound that might warn him of the approach of any one.

Half an hour thus passed away, and Duval had, by an ample meal from the flesh of some venison and a ham, fortified himself against the pangs of hunger, at all events for the rest of the day; and as he had considerably rested himself, he rose, and taking the candle in his hand, he determined to make what discoveries he could in the cavern.

At first sight it would seem that there was in that place nothing to see but what you might take in at a glance; but Duval soon found that such was not the case. He found in one corner another odd dingy blanket hanging up, which by the action of time, and the smoke and heat, had got so much the colour of the wall, that until you got quite close to it, it would be impossible to distinguish the one from the other,

"Oh," said Duval, "my obscure friends of the cave have got an inner apartment, which I will take the liberty of examining."

With the candle in his left hand, he, with his right, moved the old blanket aside, and found that upon the other side of it there was a cave about half the size of the outer one, and in this inner cavern it was quite evident that people were in the habit of sleeping, for the floor was covered in many places with old clothing and rushes, and such other substitutes for beds or mattresses as the neighbourhood might afford to those who were not very particular.

It was while Duval was looking round him at this inner cave, that he thought he heard a slight noise over head, and after listening attentively, he was convinced that a footstep passed over the roof of that part of the cave.

"Some one comes," he said. "I will take my seat by the fire and take the affair easy. The more confidence I show that I feel myself, the more I shall make those feel who may call this place their home."

With this view, Duval sat down by the turf fire again, and kept his eyes fixed upon the blanket that stopped up the entrance to the cavern. Each moment he felt more and more convinced that some one was coming, and he could see that the blanket was slightly agitated by a current of cold air that came from the preserve above.

Another moment and Duval could hear the lump of wood pulled back into the hollow of the tree, and then a footstep came down the little narrow stairs. The blanket was pulled aside and a man came into the cavern.

" Good day, my friend," cried Duval.

At the moment, the man was so terrified that he stood as though he had been turned to stone. Then, with a shout of dismay, during which the words—" I didn't do it!" came from his lips, he turned and tried to escape from the place, but that was just the thing that Duval did not mean that he should do.

Springing from the old chair by the corner near to the fire, Duval caught him by the back of the neck and dragged him into the cave again, for he had got to the foot of the little flight of stairs.

" Oh, no—no," he cried. " it wasn't me. Murder ! murder ! They did it among 'em, they did. and buried the body under Smythe's bed. Oh, I didn't do it, and they wouldn't give me my share. Oh, good sir, let me go, do—oh dear, oh dear !"

" Don't be a fool," said Duval.

" No sir. Oh dear sir, no. Would you like a nice young hare, sir ?"

With this, from under his smock-frock the man produced a leveret that was quite warm, it having been only recently secured in the preserve above the cavern.

" Anything, sir, you like, only don't have me up about it. I'm as innocent as a lamb, sir, indeed I am, and you see I'm quite a boy."

CHAPTER LXXVI.

DUVAL REACHES HIS NEW HOUSE AT HORNSEY.

DUVAL found it quite in vain to attempt to say anything while the fears of this man overcame him in such a way, but he took care to keep between him and the opening of the cavern, so that he should not have the opportunity of making another bolt to escape him. Duval could see that notwithstanding he was a long hulking sort of fellow, he was very young, and he calmly waited until he had said all that his fears dictated.

" Have you done ?" said Duval, when from sheer want of breath the other paused.

" Oh dear, yes sir. Anything you like."

" Very well. Listen to me then, and in the first place you must know that I am not only well armed, but that I am accustomed to defend myself, so any atttempt at mischief on your part will in all likelihood fall on yourself. Do you understand me ?"

" Oh, dear yes, sir."

" Very good. Now who are you ?"

" Why, sir, you'd hardly believe it; but they will try to make out that I am a poacher."

" Indeed. Well how many of you belong to this cavern, or know of it, and make a practice of coming to it ?"

" There's six of us, sir, besides Peter ; but Peter is only a boy you see, sir, and I don't count him."

" Very well. Now I will calm your fears by telling you that I am a highwayman, and that I came into this place only to save myself from those who chased me into the wood."

" Why—then you are Claude Duval !"

" I am."

" Oh, lor! What a treat. Oh, dear. I heard 'em all on the road looking for you. Oh, how comfortable I feel, to be sure. I thought you were some officer from London, and that you had no end of others, all ready to pounce upon a fellow.

I feel quite another thing now. My name, do you know, is Luke. They call me lanky Luke, but Luke without the lanky is my name."

"Am I welcome here?'

"To be sure. Yes—Oh, of course you are. They won't find you in this out-of-the-way place. You are as welcome as flowers in May. And yet—yet—now I think—

"What do you think?"

"Ned is a thorough bad one, and so is Bill, and they lead the others. No, you had not better stay here, Duval. There are some of the fellows, and Peter the boy too, that you mustn't trust to. Be off with you before they come. I know 'em. I know 'em."

There was such an air of pitiful sincerity about the manner in which Luke uttered these words, that Duval felt it as far beyond the reach of art, and he believed him implicitly.

"I am much obliged to you, Luke," he said, "for your friendly caution, but my danger in the wood while daylight lasts is so great that I feel myself compelled to risk something here, and to try to make some terms with your companions. I can pay them well."

"There's something in that," said Luke.

"When do you expect them?"

"They may come at any time, or not at all to day for all I know. But now I am here I'll stay if you make up your mind to do so, and I'll say all I can to make things pleasant. How came you to know of our old cavern, though? We thought we had the secret all to ourselves."

"It was a mere accident made me acquainted with it, Luke, which it would be no use imparting to you. I will pay liberally for shelter until dark, and then I will leave, and the secret shall remain with me as safely as if you had it only in your own bosoms."

"Hush!" said the poacher, and he put his hand up to his ear in an attitude of listening.

"What do you hear?"

"Some of the lot coming. They may take your being here amiss, or they may not. It's just as it happens. But mind you, I will be your friend; and if anything really goes amiss, I'll let you know."

"Thank you," said Duval, as he held out his hand to Luke, who gave it a friendly pressure. "Thank you : it is a strange thing that, in the worst extremity of my fortunes, I never failed to pick up a friend ; and it is equally true as strange, that that friend never repented of holding out the hand of kindness to me."

"All's right," said Luke.

Duval could now plainly enough hear the sound of footsteps approaching down the little nearly perpendicular stairs, and in the course of half a minute more the blanket was drawn aside, and two men, of about as repulsive aspects as could very well be imagined, made their appearance in the cavern.

It happened that the first person they cast their eyes upon was their companion, Luke, and they did not see Duval, who was close to the turf fire, and rather in the shade. If they did observe the figure of a man, they, of course, concluded it was one of their own comrades. One of them said—

"There's no end of row in the preserve. They say that Duval, the highwayman, is there, and that they are determined to have him out somehow."

"He was there," said Duval, stepping forward, "but he is here now."

The two men started back, and one of them pulled from under his smock-frock the barrel and the but of a gun, so made, that they could be secured together at any time, and commenced fitting the pieces, while the others got far off in the cavern, and after a moment or two, owing to the surprise of the sudden sight of a stranger, he cried,—

"What's all this? Are we sold at last? Keep off, will you!"

" We ain't quite done yet, Ned," said the other, " while I have got my little single barrel here."

" I don't know," said Duval, " what you are both putting yourselves out of the way for. My name is Claude Duval; and I found out your cave by mere accident; and being hard pressed by my enemies, in the preserve above, I came to it as a temporary refuge. What you can have to say against that, or how it will serve you to make a riot with me, I don't know?"

" But how are we to know who you are?"

" Stand out of the way!" said the man with the gun. " Stand out of the way! Ned and I'll put an end to the matter, by shooting him at once. That will be the best plan of all. Stand out of the way!"

Ha k ye," said Duval; "if you don't this minute put down that gun, I will make you."

" You make me?"

The last three words were scarcely out of the fellows mouth, when Duval made such a dash at him, that not having his fingers actually upon the trigger, he could not discharge the piece as he had fully intended to do. Duval wrested it from his hands, and turning it round, dealt him such a blow upon the head with the but-end of it, that down he went insensible; and the gun broke in two where the screws were that fastened the but-end on to the barrel.

" Take that," said Duval. " If you think that I am going to stand here and let an idiot like you present a gun at me, you are very much mistaken indeed. Now, Mr. Ned—if that's your name—I have had no quarrel with you. You are poachers, and perhaps something else and worse. I am a highwayman. What in the name of all that is ridiculous should set us by the ears together?"

" I don't know," said the fellow, " I don't want to quarrel with anybody, not I; only Luke had no business to bring a stranger into the old cave."

" No," said Luke, " nor did I."

" That is true," said Duval. " I can tell you, Mr. Ned, that Luke, far from bringing me here, found me here, and was as much surprised as you can be. I found out your cave by an accident; and to save your comrade Luke, here, from any suspicion of having brought me here, I will tell you how I found it out. I was hiding in a tree not far from here, and saw a man and a boy open the trap. The boy was called Peter."

" It must be so," muttered Ned.

" It is so."

" Well, well, Claude Duval, we don't wish to do the thing that's unhandsome. We are poachers, and if the secret of our cave is known, we may as well go and give ourselves up, and get transported at once, for our living has gone likewise. If you keep our secret, and be off soon, there's no harm done, except to George's head, which you needn't have gave such a crack to."

" There I differ from you, friend. It was quite evident from George's conduct, that his head was very hard; and I felt, therefore, that it required a very good crack to produce any effect upon it; so in that way he has got no more than he deserves, you see. I will keep the secret of your cave to my dying day, and beyond that if you wish it; so don't be putting yourself and your comrades out of the way on that score. Deal fairly with me, and I go at dark; but I tell you that I am not afraid of you nor all who may come here, and that I will make such a racket about your heads if you play any pranks with me, as shall make you remember to-day as long as you live. I don't say that as a threat, but as a warning."

" Oh, well, well, there's no occasion," said Ned, who was evidently cowed, as all bullies are, by the manner of Duval. " There's no occasion to make any disturbance. It's all r ght now. The others will drop in soon, and then you can make yourself quite comfortable, you know."

" I intend," said Duval; " and if I mistake not, some of them are coming now."

Duval was right, for in the course of a moment or two, Peter and the

man with whom he seemed to have so close an alliance, offensive and defensive,
made their appearance; accompanied by a coarse, brutal-looking man, with
violently red hair. At the sight of Duval, there was a general consternation;
but Ned took upon himself to explain, and to smooth over every fear and indignation which the others felt; although to Duval's apprehension his manner of doing
so was anything but pleasant, as to him it just translated itself into—'Don't say
anything just now, as it may be dangerous, but wait a little until i give you a hint
to speak, and then we will do something.'

In the course of five minutes more another man made his appearance, and to
Duval he was the most repulsive looking of the whole lot. He was short and
thick set, having a kind of roll in his walk, as thought very unsteady on his feet.
His features were thick and coarse, and his head was of that shape and make,
commonly denominated a bullet-head. His hair was nearly black, and he had
the peculiarity of never looking any one in the face. From the physiognomist
expression of this man, it was evident that obstinacy was his prevailing characteristic, and that he was decidedly one of the most wrong-headed brutes that ever
the Almighty permitted to exist.

By some means this man evidently was looked upon by the others as a sort of
leader, and his opinion was eagerly listened to.

CHAPTER LXXVII.

THE FATE OF THE ROBBERS IN THE CAVERN.

In a clamouring sort of way it was explained to this new comer who and what
Duval was, and he regarded him in silence for some few moments beneath his
knitted brows.

"How now!" he at length cried. "Are we to be turned out of house and
home by highwaymen? Eh? Eh?"

Duval made him no answer.

"What do you mean by this?" he cried. "Are you dumb?"

"He's rather a dangerous fellow," said one of the men. "Don't go near him,
captain. There's no knowing what he may do all of a minute."

"Oh, ain't there, indeed?"

With this the fellow waddled up to Duval, for all he could accomplish in the
way of walking was something in the shape of a waddle; and setting his arms
akimbo, he cried—

"Look, Mister Knight of the Road. We don't let lodgings here, and I
should advice you in a friendly way to take yourself off about as quickly as you
conveniently can. Do you here?"

"I hear," said Duval.

"Well, and hearing, do you understand?"

"Perfectly; but I don't intend to go."

"You don't intend to go? Come, that's a good one. I'll soon see whether you
intend to go or not. Oh, I am used to such customers as you are, as my friends
here know well enough. Are you a bruiser or a wrestler? Speak the truth."

"A little of both."

"Oh, you are—are you? Then here goes for a tumble. Don't you interfere,
my lads. These long slabs of fellows are easily upset, and you'll soon see how
he will lower his tone after taking the measure of our floor on his back. Now
old chap, just look to yourself, for I am not at all particular, when I get a chap
in a hug, where I pitch him to."

"Then I must not be particular, I suppose?" said Duval.

"Not a bit."

The man upon this made a rush at Duval, and caught him round the loins,
but notwithstanding the heave he made, and which brought up almost all the

blood in his body to his face, he could not move him, and then he was forced to let his pent-up breath go. This was just the moment that Duval was waiting for, and taking instant advantage of it, he fairly lifted the ruffian off his feet, and gave him a tremendous fall into a far corner of the cavern.

"Will that do?" he said.

The fellow lay without breath or motion.

"You have killed him," said one of the others.

"Not at all," said Duval, "such a fall as that may break a bone perhaps, but it don't kill. Throw a pailfull of water over him if you have got one, but you will soon find him get up again."

"Murder!" said the discomfited fellow, in a low voice.

"There, you see," said Duval, "I told you so."

Two of the others now helped the captain, as they called him, to his feet. His face was of a ashy paleness, and he shook so that he could scarcely manage to stand at all. After a great effort, however, he managed to put on a sickly kind of grin, and holding out his hand to Duval, he said—

"Well, old fellow, you wrestle well, very well. I don't mind a few falls. Come. we will make merry now."

"As you please," said Duval. "All I can say is, that I came here for shelter, and I have met with nothing but attempted violence, since I have been in the place, from one and another of you. I promised to keep your secret, as indeed, why should I not? for what earthly good could it do me to do otherwise? and ye yet have made repeated attemts against my life."

"Oh, well, we understand each other now, old friend. Let beggars be beggars. The past need not trouble us now; come, we will be merry. Get out some of the old wine, comrades."

"What, have you wine here?" said Duval.

"Oh yes. The fact is, a great lord's mansion in this neighbourhood is shut up, while he is somewhere abroad, and there's a good cellar of wine that we have found the way into, and on drizzling, dark nights, when it's difficult to see your hand before your face, we bring away a few dozen. By the time he comes back, he will have an empty cellar."

Duval looked at his watch, and then he said—

"It wants yet some time to the period when I shall make an attempt to leave this place, so I will take a glass with you, at all events. At dusk I will try to get away."

"That you will easily manage. There is no moon to-night, and the trees in the old preserve cast such shadows, that as long as you make no noise, you may get along famously. Come, master, let us enjoy ourselves while we can; life's short, you know."

As the fellow said these last words. he winked at the man who had been first seen by Duval with the boy, and that worthy burst into a great laugh. This wink and the laugh that followed it, set Duval thinking what it could possibly mean, and from that moment he became all but certain that there was some plot on the alert as regarded him.

"I will watch these rascals narrowly," he said, "and woe be to them if they try to play me any trick. They may succeed, since there are so many to one, in killing me, but they shall find I am not to be very easily overcome."

There was now a general kind of a bustle in getting more lights, during which the man named Luke contrived to pass Duval and slightly pinch his arm to attract his attention; and then he said in a whisper the one word, "Poison."

Duval did not by any imprudent start or exclamation betray that a communication of such a character had been made to him. He heard it as though he heard it not; only by a slight touch of Luke's foot with his own he managed to let him know that he was fully cognisant of the friendly warning.

It certainly had not entered into the imagination of Duval to conceive that even these men could be such desperate villains as to try to take his life by poison; but yet he could not for a moment doubt the truth of the communication that was made to him by Luke, and of course he determined to be upon his guard.

And now they cleared the table in the middle of the cave, and began to place glasses upon it, and the captain cried out in a loud, boisterous kind of voice—

"My shoulder ain't quite so supple as it was, but we will make merry for all that, and live till we die. It ain't always the strongest that live the longest, is it, Mr. Duval?"

"Certainly not."

"Ha! ha! You never uttered a truer word than that in all your life. Now comrades, quick, and get all ready. Who knows how many of us may be alive and kicking by cock-crow?"

"Life is proverbially an uncertain possession, I admit," said Duval, "and therefore I am a great advocate for enjoying it while we can."

"And so am I, so am I. I will just pop into a cellar and get the wine, and then we shall be all right."

With these words the fellow went into the inner cavern, and after being absent for about five minutes, he returned with two wine bottles in his hand, and placing them down at the top of the table, but carefully putting his hand upon one of them, he said—

"We don't want more than one light; surely we can see the way to our mouths. One light will be plenty; there is no knowing what little odd crevice the light might get through, and give the alarm against us if we had too much of it in the old cave. There, that will do."

Two lights had been lit, but now one of them was extinguished, so that quite a semi-darkness reigned in the old cave, and even the ferocious countenance of the man who called himself the captain of the gang, was but dimly visible; but yet his eyes evidently had about them a fiendish, malicious twinkle, which more and more had the effect of convincing Duval that Luke was right in the warning that he had given to him.

"Come now, sit down, old fellow; all's right," cried the captain. "The brave and honourable guest that we have here, will take his own bottle all to himself, you see, while we drink together. It looks more like as if we thought something of him, you see; and so we do, and I hope we shall have him with us a long time, that I do."

"Thank you," said Duval. "I am, then, to drink by myself?"

"If you please, and then you can fill as often as you like, you know, without at all waiting for us."

"Oh, thank you; that will do."

The candle was just about half arms-length from Duval, as he sat by the captain, and that latter personage, since he had taken his seat, no longer kept his hand upon the bottle that he intended for himself and his comrades.

"Come, come," he said "we waste time."

"Yes," said Duval, placing his right hand on the bottle intended for him. "We do. But I hope to be better acquainted with all of you, my friends!"

As he said these words, he waved his left arm, so as to give emphasis to the words, "all of you;" and at once upset the candle, and rolled it on to the floor when it went out. A nearly complete state of darkness ensued, for the turf fire was at its lowest ebb now, and taking advantage of the moment, Duval *changed the bottles*, taking the captain's one for himself, and placing his by the captain's hand.

"Holloa," said that personage, "all's right; light up again. Light up. That will do.—We have no stint of matches. There's no harm done."

"I really," said Duval, "must apologise."

"Not at all, not at all. There's no occasion. Accidents will of course happen at times to the best of us."

The candle was speedily enough lighted, and when it was placed upon the table again, they found Duval's right hand still clasped round the neck of the bottle, as it had been before the upset, and they little suspected that it was not *the* bottle that he had had his hand on before.

The captain glanced at him, and was satisfied. He laughed, as he said—

"Upon my life, you are a great orator, Mister Duval, for you suit the action to the word, you do, and away goes the candle. But it's of no consequence; all I say is, drink."

"With pleasure," said Duval, as he poured out a glass of the wine.

CLAUDE STOPS THE MUSICIAN.

"Now, my lads," said the captain, " now, my lads, push me your glasses, and I'll fill them. All's right, you know! All's right! We shall yet live many a long day, I hope, ay, and a night, too, in our old cave, that has sheltered us so long."

"Not a doubt of it," said Duval.

The glasses were all filled, and while the captain was busy doing so, Duval caught the eye of Luke, and shook his head. Luke slightly nodded, and Duval then felt certain that he fully understood him, and would not drink the wine.

"Bumper! bumper! all," said the captain, as he raised his glass. "Now, Mister Duval, when we take a glass in this sort of enjoying way, the first thing we drink to is the old cave."

"Very good."

"So, my boys! I give you the toast of 'The Old Cave!' and Mister Duval will drink it, I know, in a bumper at once, and leave nothing in the glass. 'The old cave! The old cave!' Are you all ready?"

"Yes, yes! All ready, captain!"

"Then here goes, and much good may it do us."

"Amen!" said Duval, as he drank his glass of wine clean out, while the captain and his beautiful companions did the same, with the exception of Luke, who clearly enough tossed his glass of wine over his shoulder, and then put down the empty glass as though he had drunk it.

When this was done, and the captain saw that Duval's glass was quite empty —indeed he had watched him drink it that there should be no mistake about it— he leant back almost to the verge of falling, and laughed cunningly.

"I wish you would let me know the joke," said Duval.

"Oh, it's nothing—it's nothing. Take another glass, that's all. I like to see you enjoying yourself. Don't we, comrades?"

"Oh dear yes," they all said.

"I, of course, will take another glass," said Duval. "But you must all fill, and this time I will give you a toast."

"Hurrah! All's right! Put your glasses this way, comrades. We will all fill, of course. Glass for glass. And now let us have the toast of Mister Duval. How do you feel, Mister?"

"Quite charming," said Duval. "Quite charming."

CHAPTER LXXVIII.

DUVAL REACHES HIS HOUSE AT HORNSEY AGAIN.

At this reply of Duval's regarding his feelings, the captain roared again with laughing; indeed, his conduct was so indiscreet, that more than one of the rascals winked at him to be cautious. He was a little more quiet accordingly.

"All's right," he said. "All's right as possible. Silence for Mister Duval's toast. Here we are with our glasses quite full. By-the-by, Mister Duval, how do you like this wine?"

"Very well indeed."

"You like its flavour?"

"I do. I flatter myself I am a pretty good judge of Port wine, and this appears to me to be particularly pure and good. I feel tolerably convinced that there is nothing in it."

"Oh!—oh! That's good. Oh! oh!"

The captain got into such a convulsion of laughter that he nearly fell off his stool, but Duval did not make any remark about his conduct, and as the others called loudly now for the toast, Duval rose to propose it,

"Gentlemen," he said, "the toast I have to propose is one that is common as an expression in society at large. I don't pretend that it has any over-particular application to the present company, except so far as we are all a little adverse to the laws, and therefore may be able to fully appreciate the sentiment: Are you all ready, gentlemen?"

"All—all."

"Then I give you 'The cunning fox that outwitted himself!'"

The glasses were all emptied, including Duval's, with the exception of Luke's, and he got rid of his wine as before.

The fellows looked at each other a little uneasily, for they did not at all like the complexion of the toast, and the captain for a moment or two turned serious, but he soon rallied, and then he said—

"Pray, Mister Duval, what is the explanation of that?"

"There is no explanation at all. Only it is as well I think to drink to the cunning fox who outwitted himself, because there is really no knowing what may happen to him in consequence."

"Well, you are a strange fellow."

"Allow me to return the compliment."

"Come—come, we won't quarrel about nothing."

"I never was further from any desire to quarrel than now," said Duval. "I must confess that I am perfectly satisfied, and your wine is excellent, let it have come from whose cellar it may. I don't think a whole bottle of this would do a fellow any harm."

"You don't?"

"Certainly not. Why should it?"

"Oh, there is no reason at all why it should. How do you feel now? Pretty well—eh? You don't feel at all queer, do you?"

"Not in the least."

"But I do, captain," said a mournful voice from the lower end of the table. "I do, I can tell you. Oh, what have you been about, you stupid fool? I don't feel all right at all."

"Why, what's the matter with you?"

"That's just what I should like to know. I—I shall go down in a minute or two. I know I shall. Oh dear—oh dear!"

"Good gracious," said the captain, "what is the meaning of it? Mister Duval, ain't you ill? Don't you feel queer? Tell me only that you feel queer rather, and it will be such a satisfaction. You must, you do feel queer!"

"Not at all."

"Then—I—do."

"Well," said Duval, quite calmly. "I thought you did not look the thing exactly, my worthy friend, several times during the last few minutes; but you ought to know best, of course. I hope there was nothing wrong in your wine?"

"Wrong—wrong! what do you mean? Oh—oh. The old cavern is beginning to go round and round with me."

At this moment, two of the gang fell from their stools to the floor of the cavern, where they lay perfectly insensible, and Duval, seizing the captain by the arms, bawled in his ear—

"Here's to the fox that outwitted himself. Ha! ha! my friend. Life is short. I changed the bottles!"

The captain upon hearing this fell backwards, stool and all, and Duval rose to his feet saying—

"I cannot say what abominable drug was put in the wine that it was intended I should drink. You know best yourselves, and you must take the consequences of it; and whatever they may be, you will recollect that I have nothing to do with them. I hate poison, and poisoners. There cannot be, in all the catalogue of crimes for which the worst of the human race have been famous, any one that can for enormity come near to poisoning. I now leave you to take the consequences of your own acts."

Not one of the villains was in a condition to answer him; and then, by a slight glance at his watch, Duval saw that the night-time must have arrived, and he prepared to quit the cave. It was then that Luke stepped up to him, saying, in a voice that was struggling with emotion—

"Duval, after what has happened here to-night, this is no place for me. Will you let me go with you?"

"Certainly I will, with pleasure."

"And you will trust me?"

"Most assuredly. You have already done me too great a service for me to dream for a moment that you would play me false now. Come with me, for I can very well imagine that these rascals were never fit companions for you, and probably after this night they might guess that you had some hand in the business, if they live over this affair, which they know best about."

"Oh yes," said Luke, "they will live, but they did not at all intend that you should. The poison is only, after all, a very powerful sleeping draught and while you were under the influence of it they would no doubt have given you up to the officers or murdered you. They will not awake for a couple of days, I dare say, and then they will feel, as the captain himself was so anxious you should feel, rather queer."

"Come then, Luke. Let us leave this place at once. It is no fit one for either you or I. I do not desire any further revenge upon these rascals than I have had. Let them lie like drunken swine where they are, until they recover in the ordinary course. We will leave them."

"Oh dear, won't you take me?" said a voice.

Duval turned and saw the boy. He shook his head at him as he said—

"No, you are by far too amiable a youth for me to have anything to do with. It's a good thing for you that they were not liberal enough to give you a glass of wine, so you can stay and nurse all your friends here, who may be in need of your assistance."

"Go to the deuce," said the boy.

Duval took no further notice of him, but proceeded at once with the assistance of Luke to leave the old cave, and in the course of a very few minutes they were in the open air. It was indeed, to Duval, a most exquisite relief to be able to breathe once again the cool, pure, fresh air, and for some minutes he could do nothing but stand still and inhale it with rapture as it came sighing and faintly whistling amid the old trees.

"This is pleasant," said Luke, " after being so long in the cave."

"It is delightful. I only wonder how those late friends of yours could bring their minds to pass much of their time in such a place. I would rather, ten times, lay my head in the open wood upon a few decayed leaves than I would sleep upon a bed of down in such a place as that we have just left."

"It is not very inviting, but I hope never to see it again; and I daresay you don't want particularly to do so?"

"Far from it, Luke; I am to the full as sick of it as you can be. It is a pity that there should be such a place and in such hands; but as it really has afforded me a shelter for a few hours, I will not betray the secret of its existence. How shall we get clear of the wood? Probably, Luke, you know more of it than I do?"

"Oh yes, I know every nook and corner of it, and every tree. There will be no difficulty in our leaving it."

"Think you not? Are you aware that it is well guarded at every outlet upon my account, and that there are sentinels placed all round it within hail of each other on purpose to intercept me, if I should make an attempt to leave it? for they are pretty sure that I am in it somewhere."

"Oh yes, I know all that; but if you will follow me, Duval, and trust to me, I will take you quite clear of it easily."

"Lead on, then."

Upon this, the first thing that Luke did, was to lie flat upon the ground for a few moments and listen intently. Then as he rose, he said—

"Do you mind wet feet?"

"Not particularly, if there's any good to be got by wetting them."

"The good will be the escape from the wood."

"All's right then, I don't mind wet feet at all, so lead on. If that is the only harm I shall come to in getting out of this place, which they think will prove such a trap for me, I shall think little of it."

"Don't speak then, except in a whisper, and come as close after me as you possibly can. In a little while we will leave this place behind us."

Duval could not at all conceive how it was that he was to escape from the wood, but he placed the most implicit confidence in his new friend and followed him closely. And now, even in the darkness, which was tolerably intense, it was quite a wonderful thing to see with what tact Luke made his way through the wood. He never for one moment appeared to be at a loss, or deviated to the right or to the left of his even course with any appearance of hesitation. On he went, until suddenly pausing, he laid his hand upon Duval's arm, and whispered—

"There is one of the sentinels."

Duval was for a moment a little startled at this intelligence; but looking forward in the darkness, he saw the dim outline and the figure of a man with his arms across his breast leaning against a tree.

"That's the fellow," said Luke, "that went about the wood with a double-barrelled gun, firing into the trees."

"Is it?"

"Yes. He is well known as a brutal felow."

"Then, my friend Luke, do you know it will be a very severe trial to me to be forced to leave this place without punishing him in some sort of way for his brutality."

"It will be hazardous."

"Never mind that. Will it seriously jeopardise our escape? for if so, I will give up the idea; but if it will not, I must confess it will give me great pleasure to be even with him, and pay him the debt I owe him, which else will accumulate with interest in my imagination."

"It may be done. You do not want to kill him?"

"Oh, no—no."

"Well, immediately in front of him there is a deep stagnant ditch, full of duck-weed, and anything but in a savoury condition. Now I may as well tell you that the course by which we were and are to escape, is under a little bridge of some length, that will take us clear of the wood, and beneath which there is a running stream. No one will think that you have a sufficient knowledge of the place to venture under there in the dark, as it looks bad, and you will not be able to stand upright there.

"Is it close at hand?"

"Quite; half-a-dozen steps to the right here would take us to it now; so what you are going to do, do quickly."

"I will only send him into the ditch."

Duval with this crept gently forward until he got quite behind the tree against which the man was leaning, and then he doubled his fist, and suddenly dashing out he knocked him down; but scarcely had he touched the ground, when Duval stooped over him, and lifting him up bodily, threw him right into the centre of the ditch, with a loud splash.

Of course this was quite enough to spread an alarm among those who were placed to watch the outskirts of the wood, and the consequence was, that they began calling to each other. Luke seized the arm of Duval, and said to him—

"Come, come, quick."

"It's done," said Duval, "I am ready."

They heard the man splashing about in the ditch as they rapidly left the spot, and then Luke led the way into the little stream. The passage under the bridge looked rather frightful. Indeed it was quite a matter of courtesy to call it a bridge at all, for it looked much more like a drain than anything else; but Duval followed his guide, and in about two minutes they both freely emerged from it, never at any time having been above their knees in the water.

"We are safe now," said Luke. "Here is the high-road.

CHAPTER LXXIX.

THE FORGED BILL, AND THE LAWYER'S CHAMBERS.

BY a scramble up a rather steep bank, they both reached the high-road in safety.

"I owe you much," said Duval.

"No—no, not at all. But let us push on, and get out of this neighbourhood as quickly as we can. Don't you hear the fellows calling to one another to keep a good look out?"

"I do."

"Well, they will soon be running about everywhere. What direction would you like to go in? for I know all the roads well enough, and can easily take you by any one you like.'"

"I want to go to the village of Hornsey; but it is a good distance from here of course."

"Yes; but the London road will take us, and then we shall have to turn off to the left and get round Highgate, which will be rather a long stretch; but that won't matter. I only wish we had a couple of good horses; we would soon do it."

"Ah, my friend," said Duval, "this morning I had as good a steed as ever man bestrode; but the rascals killed her."

"So I heard. Let me think"—

"Of what?"

"Why, of how to get steeds. There's a good horse or two in the stables of the rector of this parish."

"You are not very particular, my friend, then, about how you get a horse, or how you meddle with the parson's property?"

"Not at all. Of course, knowing that all that the parsons have is robbery, I don't mind taking a little of it when I can."

"Very good."

"Well, as I was saying, if we could only get hold of a couple of good horses out of the rector's stables, it would be a capital thing, I think. What do you say to it, Duval?"

"I say yes, if it can be done; it is quite clear to me that before I am twenty-four hours older, a horse I must have, and it is very immaterial about whose stable it comes out of, provided it is a good one, and I can make it attached to me; which there is no great difficulty in doing if you try it."

"That I believe, Duval, that I believe fully; and if you give your free consent to the plan, I will take you to the rector's stables at once."

Duval was rather amused at the extreme coolness and simplicity of Luke, for he talked of stealing a couple of horses from the rector of the parish as calmly as though he projected something that was not at all of an out of the way character; indeed, if he had proposed going to lunch with the rector, it would have been done in much the same easy tone of voice.

They had both walked, or rather run on, for they had got into a half run, rather rapidly; and by the time this little conversation regarding the rector's horses was over, they had got quite out of ear-shot of the men who were keeping guard at the little wood. Luke led the way now from the main road into a lane, and then crossing a stile, he said to Duval:—

"We have only to get across a couple of meadows, and we shall come to the rector's stables; which, I have reason to know, are not very well taken care of."

"One would think, though," said Duval, "that if the horses are valuable, they would be taken care of well."

"Yes, but the rector is not quite aware that the man who is supposed to sleep at the stables has gone off to drink at the 'Crown' every night, and that the horses are left to look after themselves in the best way they are able."

"That will do," said Duval; "it would be quite a pity not to take some advantage of such a providential dispensation."

They now crossed the two meadows in perfect silence, and crouching down close to an iron hurdle fence, Luke listened for a short time; and then he whispered :—

"All is right; there's not a mouse stirring. Come on, this way; creep through the fence, and there's less chance of being seen."

They crossed the fence in this way, and then Luke led Duval right into a stable yard; and pointing to a door, he said :—

"There's a couple of capital nags I'll be bound may be got out of there; but the door is locked, I dare say, though I have known it to be left open as careless as possible; and so it is now—look."

The stable door was only on the latch, and both Luke and Duval entered it. The place was much too dark to make any choice of cattle in, so Duval made up his mind to be satisfied for the present time with the first horse he could lay his hands upon; and accordingly he led one out into the yard.

Luke in a moment appeared with another.

"Don't mount," he said; "let's lead them to the high road first."

This was good advice, but Duval said in a whisper—

"Can you find a saddle?"

"Oh dear yes, to be sure; it would be a poor look out to go away without one. The harness-room is close at hand here. Only wait a few moments and I'll soon bring the requisites."

Luke was quite as good as his word, for he was back in a very short time, well loaded with all the requisites for a couple of horses.

"You seem," said Duval, "to understand this sort of thing, and to be particularly conversant with these premises likewise."

"Why yes, I am a little—just a little. You see I was once a groom to the rector, and that's how I come to know the place."

"Oh, indeed. Then you probably know the horses likewise?"

"I know that there isn't a bad one in the stable, though I can't exactly say what ones we have hold of, for the old man has been buying some fresh bits of blood since I was with him."

While this little bit of conversation was going on, both Claude and Luke were busy in putting the saddles upon the horses, and as they were both pretty good adepts at that sort of work, they got done—notwithstanding it was in the dark—pretty well at about the same time, and they gently led the horses away. It was necessary to pull up one of the iron hurdles to get the horses past that fence, but there was no difficulty in doing so, and then they quickly enough crossed the meadows. They had to skirt the one next to the lane until they reached a gate, which Luke unfastend, and then they got safely into the lane.

"Now for it," said Luke; "get on, Duval, as quick as you like, on the London road; and when you come to the turning to the left, that will lead round by Finchley to Hornsey, I will call to you, sir."

"That will do," said Duval.

He urged the horse on, and he was not a little gratified to find, by the pace of the creature, that it must be one of no ordinay value. The canter that he put it to was remarkably easy too, so that he was well satisfied with his bargain. The darkness effectually prevented him from seeing the colour or any of the points of his steed; but upon the principle that a good horse cannot be of a bad colour, he made up his mind that his was a beauty.

Several times he glanced behind him to see how Luke was getting on, and by seeing that he kept the relative distance between them without breaking at all into a gallop, he was satisfied that his new friend's steed had likewise turned out to be of the r ght sort, and that they were both superbly mounted.

"To the left," cried Luke, suddenly, and Duval at once obeyed the direction, and found that they were among those beautiful green lanes that lie so thickly over that part of the country.

"The first to the left," again cried Luke; "and then the second to the right, if you please."

"Come," said Duval; "you had much better take the lead in these lanes, for I confess I don't know them sufficiently well to be quite certain about my route; I might succeed in floundering through them somehow, and in getting to my destination, but not with expedition; so I will follow."

"Very well, sir; I will lead now, if you like; but recollect, that although I have made very free with you, Mr. Duval, during the time that we were making our escape from the cave and finding a horse a piece, I am not unmindful that I am not a companion for you."

"How do you mean, Luke?"

"Why, sir, as I have told you, I was the rector's groom, that's all; and before that I was a poor country fellow—and since that I have been a poacher, sir."

"And what follows from all that, Luke?"

"Why just that as I have left the poaching, I must take to some sort of service again, that's all, sir. I understand a little bit of gardening—and I understand a horse, and, in fact, there's few things in and about a country house that I could not turn my hand to."

"Why, Luke, I can find you a master, then."

"Can you, sir? Really! and without a character, too?"

"No: with a good character. I will take you myself. At Hornsey I have a house—and a garden—and a wife."

"You don't say so, sir?"

"Indeed but I do; and when I am away on the road it would give me a good deal of satisfaction to know that there was some one there upon whom I could depend as completely as I can upon you. So, if you like to enter my service and stay at home, you may do so, and I can promise you liberal wages, at all events, and a good home."

"Can you doubt, sir, for a moment, that I would grasp at the opportunity? It's the very thing I would like above all others."

"Then let it be considered as settled, Luke; and now we will push on for Hornsey at once, and when you get there you may consider yourself quite at home."

"Well," said Luke, "this is indeed a change in my fortunes that I little expected or calculated upon. It has been a lucky thing for me that you came to the old cave, though those rascals were very near taking your life."

"Which they would have done but for you."

"Well, I am glad, indeed, that I had it in my power to warn you of your danger in time. I can just fancy how furious the captain will be, when he finds it all out. Turn to the right, now, sir, and then we can push on for a mile without turning."

They rode on, and in due time drew up at the garden gate of Duval's house at Hornsey.

It may be well supposed that the long absence of Duval had very much terrified May. At the sound of his footsteps now, she at once rushed out to meet him, and not observing that any one was with him, she cried—

"Oh, Claude, Claude, where have you been?"

"In all sorts of places, my dear May," he said. "But I am safe you see, and although I really intended to have been here many hours ago, this will be a good lesson to you after all—Never expect me until you see me."

"I will think of nothing but the joy of seeing you here."

"That will be sufficient, May, and the pleasure of seeing you obliterates all the past from my recollection. Luke, take the horses. I will get a light and come to you, and show you the stables in a few minutes."

"Yes, sir," said Luke.

"Who is that?" whispered May. "Who is that?"

"A friend who chooses to serve me in the capacity of a servant. He has saved my life, and I have taken him into my services. He will be here always when I am absent, and he will nurse sweet flowers for you; and in fact he will be serviceable in many different ways, and I believe truly may be thoroughly trusted."

"If you trust him," said May, "I will."

"That is right; and now let us find something for supper, for to tell the truth,

LUKE IMPLORES CLAUDE TO TAKE HIM WITH HIM.

I am rather hungry, and I promise you, May, that I will not leave home again until——"

"Until when?"

"To-morrow night, dear one; and then I hope to be back to you before the dawn of another day, for it is not often I meet with such adventures as have fallen to my lot during the last four-and-twenty hours."

CHAPTER LXXX.

DUVAL ROBS THE ST. ALBAN'S COACH, AND RESCUES A PRISONER.

DUVAL passed the whole of the day ensuing at his house at Hornsey. He did not anticipate anything in the shape of danger there, for he felt quite confident that he was unknown in that neighbourhood, and that he and Luke had not been traced from the wood in which there had been so much peril.

May would fain have persuaded him to remain yet longer, but as the twilight approached, the temptation to take to the road again was too strong for him to resist; and in reply to her entreaties, he said—

"I will promise you one thing, May, and that is to be more than commonly cautious, and you shall be treasurer, too. There is all the money I have; and if I am successful, I hope to add soon a good round sum to it."

"And then you will leave this mode of life?"

"I will."

"You solemnly promise me that, Duval?"

"I do, indeed. As soon as we can call three or four thousand pounds our own, I promise you that I will forsake these perils of the road; but until then, May, it is my destiny to go out and take my chances upon the king's highway."

May felt that it would be quite useless to attempt to dissuade him from going, so she was fain to content herself by the promises she had succeeded in getting from him to the effect that he would be more than commonly cautious in his proceedings, and careful of his safety. She told him that such a promise gave her much satisfaction, but Claude Duval replied with a smile—

"I make the promise to you as you ask for it, but my own opinion, May, is, that safety is not procured by taking care. My experience has taught me that the impunity with which I have hitherto proceeded in my adventurous career, has arisen from no care-taking, and that I have far oftener owed my safety to some piece of recklessness upon my part than to any foresight."

"Oh, no, no, I cannot think that, Duval."

"It is natural enough, May, that you should not think it. I could hardly expect that you would. But I know it as a truth beyond dispute."

"Then I will bind you by no promises, Duval, for it is your safety only that I care for; so that that be accomplished, I care not how. But before you engage in any unusually hazardous adventure, I would ask you to bestow one thought upon me."

"A thousand," said Duval, with a smile.

"Then I will be content."

The night was now creeping on; and agreeably to the order he had received to that effect, Luke brought Duval the parson's horse, which had turned out to be such a capital one; but the moment Duval looked at it, he cried—

"Hilloa, Luke, this is not the horse. It had one white foot and a small light brown star upon the forehead; I noticed as much this morning."

"Not a doubt of it, sir. The horse had one white foot, and a light-coloured star on the forehead, just as you say."

"Where are they now, then?"

"Why, you see, sir, as the horse happens to suit you, it is just as well that nobody should know him but ourselves, so I made bold to alter those little peculiarities. I have dyed the foot, sir, and dyed the star."

"Oh, that is it."

"Yes, sir; I will warrant now that not all the cunning and all the learning in all the world, could make that foot white again, or re-produce that star. It is rather a secret, the dye, sir, but it is quite effectual."

"I am very much obliged to you, Luke, for your forethought, and I suppose I might meet the parson himself that owned the horse, without the slightest danger?"

"That you might, sir; you might meet him and ask him the time of day, and what he thought of your horse, and yet he could not fancy it had ever been in his stable. It's a glorious creature, and worth as good a hundred pounds as ever were counted out."

Duval mounted, and patted the neck of the animal, as he said, "I don't quite think I shall ever make such a pet again of a horse as I did of the last one I had. But time may do wonders, and I naturally take to an animal after a little, and get up quite an affection for it."

"You will like this one, sir. May we expect you at any time, sir?"

"Hardly; and yet it's time to get home before the first cock crows; so if you are up and stirring about that time, it may be as well to look out for me."

"I will, sir."

Duval waved his hand to May, who was stationed at one of the windows of the house to see the most of him as he should trot away, and then he went off at a good pace from the gate that led to his stable.

It was very customary with Duval to wear a large horseman's cloak over his clothing when he sallied out in this manner to look for plunder on the road; and when he got some mile or two from his starting place, let that be where it might, would divest himself of the cloak, and rolling it up after the fashion in practice among cavalry soldiers, he would strap it to the back of his saddle.

He wore the cloak upon this occasion, and moreover, the hat he wore was very capable of acting as a further disguise, for one of the flaps had a loop and a button, which he could either let it down by, or fasten it up with, so that in a moment or two his appearance could be very strangely altered indeed.

These were the only precautions in the way of disguise that Duval ever took.

He trotted through the little district of Crouchend, and taking his way right on to the North-west, he got to the neighbourhood of Muswell Hill, and so on, to the High Northern Road, running directly through Highgate, at the large Inns in which village it was customary for the coaches starting from Inns in the City to change horses, so that at that time the North Road was at all times rather an animated one, and not as it is now, one of the quietest, although very far from being one of the least picturesque of the roads out of London. The railway has destroyed the coaches with their cheerful horns and merry look. But the beauties of hill and dale cannot be changed, and let the march of improvement proceed, but it cannot improve upon nature.

"Well," said Duval, as he trotted through Highgate; "there ought to be some business to be done between this and Barnet. We shall see.—We shall see."

Just before he reached the "Wrestlers' Inn," a four-horse-coach, that had been changing, then started at a rattling pace down the slope towards Finchley Common, but Duval had no idea of interfering with the coach. Its four horses were about two too many for him to manage, so he let it go on, and gently trotted on until he passed the valley close to East-end Finchley, and commenced the ascent upon the opposite side, which would take him right on to Barnet.

"Now," he said, "there ought to be a chance, and I won't be extremely particular as to the shape in which it presents itself."

He took off his cloak, and carefully rolled it up, and strapped it to the back of his saddle; and then he looped up his hat, so that he had a clear view around him; and then loosening his pistols in the holster of his saddle, and setting himself firmly in his seat, he felt that he was ready for any adventure.

Scarcely had Duval made these brief arrangements against the peace and order of society at large, than he heard the tramp of a horse, and from the shortness of the step, he could tell that it was a very small horse that was approaching. Drawing off a little to the side of the road, he waited its approach, and in a few moments he saw a man mounted on a poney, that ambled along pretty well, though evidenly hardly equal to the weight of his rider.

"Stand!" cried Claude.

"Oh, lord! who's that?" cried the rider.

"The devil! if you like," said Duval, as he rode up to his side. "Now, sir, who are you?"

"Oh, don't. I am nobody, sir, if you please. Who are you, pray?"

"I am somebody. But I will trouble you for your cash, sir. Nobody and you can't complain, as I rob nobody."

"No, sir; that is, yes, sir. But I'm a poor singer, sir, at one of the playhouses, and I have only got a matter of fifteen shillings in all the world."

"Whose horse do you ride, then?"

"It's my own, sir, if you please. I ride into town and out every night, and I find it good for my health, you see, sir; and as I have not much time to spare, perhaps you will be so good as to let me go at once."

"Well, if you are a singer, let me have a touch of your quality in that line; I am something of a singer myself, and am very fond of music. Come, sir, strike up. Let me hear the quality of your voice."

"Very good, sir. What do you think of this?

> 'Since laws they were made for every degree,
> To curb vice in others as well as in thee,
> Some day we will have your company
> At Tyburn Tree.'"

This *slight parody* upon Macheath's song in the Beggar's Opera, was so well sung, that Duval no longer doubted the fact that it was a professional musician whom he had thus stopped on the highway.

"Hark you, my friend," he said. "You have a very good voice, and a very good wit. It is a good thing for you that I can appreciate both, and particularly the latter, even when it is directed against myself. If I do ever get to Tyburn Tree, you are quite welcome to come and see me there; but now as you ride for your health, give me leave to tell you that you make one great and almost fatal mistake."

"Mistake, sir! Pray what is it?"

"You ride too small a horse, and to convince you of it, I will trouble you to dismount and walk the rest of the way, while your little pony, who is not at all fit to carry so very good a singer, enjoys a run upon Finchley Common until the morning, and don't let me catch you on its back again, that's all, my worthy friend."

"But really——"

"Come, come, no buts for me. What do you take that to be, eh, my accomplished acquaintance?"

"Oh, dear! I can't exactly pretend to say, but it feels very like the muzzle of a pistol trying to get into my ear."

"Very good indeed. If, then, you have no desire that such an ear-wig should make any further progress into your brains, you will be wise enough to dismount at once."

The singer took the hint, for there was a something in the tone of Duval's voice that, when he chose, was very convincing indeed. The moment he was on the road, Duval turned the head of the pony in the other direction, and started it off at a gallop, leaving its discomfitted owner some six miles from London on foot and no time to spare.

"Good night," said Duval. "You can beguile the tedium of the way, you know, by practising a little more of the song you have been so very obliging as to sing to me just one verse of."

Humming the tune which the musician had sung with so much effect, Duval went off at a trot, and he had not got a quarter of a mile from that spot where he had liberated the little pony, when he heard the sound of wheels; and as a man on foot passed him, he called out—

"What coach is that coming on the road?"

"The St. Alban's coach," said the man.

"Thank you! thank you!"

The man passed on, and Duval, after listening for a few moments, and finding by the sound of the feet upon the road that it was but a two-horse coach, and that it was coming along very deliberately, nodded his head as he said:—

"Be it so. I will stop the St. Alban's coach, and see if there be anything to be got inside or out. It will be a hard case if I cannot make something like a decent night's work out of a whole coach-load of people.

——

CHAPTER XXXI.

A SCENE ON THE ROAD.—THE MADMAN AND HIS KEEPER.

Duval stopped short on the road side, so as not to be actually in the way of the coach ; and then he watched it carefully as it came on with its lights casting a bright glow like an immense fire of flame on each side of the road, lending a passing lustre to the trees and bushes, and awakening the birds who were slum· bering amid the still leaves.

"Coach ! coach !" shouted Duval.

The coachman pulled up on the moment, thinking that some passenger was on the road side waiting for him.

"Here you are, sir," he said, "outside or in ?"

"A little of both, my friend," said Duval, "and I have to advise you, if you do not mind a bullet in your brains, to sit quiet and hold your reins very steady. Stir onward another foot and you are a dead man ! Phillip, keep a good aim at the coachman's head while I speak to the passengers."

Duval had upon more than one occasion found it to be a very good ruse at night, to affect to speak to some associates, who, from not being seen, inspired all the more terror, as folks did not know then on which side to look for the danger.

"Oh, they are highwaymen," cried the coachman, "and there's no end of 'em. I can see their eyes glaring through the hedge like glow-worms. We are all dead men !"

"Peace !" cried Duval. "Not a hair of anybody's head shall be hurt, if no resistance be offered. Comrades, reserve your fire, and by no means use your pistols unless I give the word."

With this, having fully convinced everybody that the coach was stopped by a whole gang of desperadoes, of whom he was the captain, he rode up to the side of the coach and said—

"Are there any ladies here ?"

"Oh, yes, yes," said a female voice. "Pray spare our lives, good Mr. High-way-gentleman. Me and my niece Jemima, are the only ladies here. Oh spare us, do, good sir."

"Be under no apprehension, madam, No violence is intended on any account if none be offered."

Dexterously taking from its socket one of the coach lamps, Duval now held it close to the upper part of the door so that it shed a clear light within the vehicle, while the shaded side of it was towards his own face, so that he was not at all confused by the glare.

The coach contained two ladies and two gentlemen. One of the gentlemen was a mere youth and looked very pale—the other was rather a ferocious-looking man, with a countenance expressive of great intemperance ; and as the light fell upon him, he cried—

"What, are we to be robbed by vagabonds? I only wish I was armed, I would soon put an end to this affair. Ah, that I would ; bother me if I wouldn't.—Ah !"

"Sir !" said Duval. "I will attend to you in a few moments. Where is Jemima ?"

"Oh, gracious !" exclaimed an old lady who was wrapped up in a wilderness of shawls, "he wants my niece. Oh, sir, she is in the corner, sir. Pray have mercy upon us all."

"My dear madam, you have no cause for apprehension; but I must see Jemima, if she pleases."

Upon this, rather a pretty looking young girl of about fifteen years of age emerged from the corner, and Duval said to her—

"I am afraid you are frightened, but you need not be, I will trouble your aunt for her money. I don't intend to ask you if you have any. Now, madam, be quick."

"Oh, dear, yes. There's my purse, and much good may it do you, you vill— no, I mean you nice man."

"I have no money, sir," said Jemima.

"But my father-in-law has," said the pale-faced youth, suddenly. "He has not only got a hundred pounds in gold with him, that he was going to bribe a madhouse-keeper to keep me, when I am not mad at all, but he has just put his gold watch in one of his boots, for fear you should see it."

"Oh, I'll serve you out for this, Master Harry, or the sun shan't rise to-morrow," growled the man with the rather forbidding face. "You young rascal!"

"What's all this about a madhouse?" said Duval.

"Nothing—nothing, at all," cried the man. "You mind your own business. All you have got to do is to rob us, my fine fellow, and be hanged for it at some other opportunity."

"You are a bold man," said Duval. "Now, my lad, I ask you again what is all this about that you say concerning a madhouse? Never mind this man. I will protect you effectually from him. You tell me the truth."

"The truth," said the lad, "is, that by his ill usage, this man killed my poor mother; but as I am still in his way, he is going to put me in a madhouse, and my hands are tied, and there is a man on the roof to help him. Nobody but this young lady here will believe that I am not mad. Oh, sir, if you can but find out a Captain Russel, who lives somewhere near to Whitehall, and tell him that the son of his old friend, Mr. Ambrose Hill, is in such a difficulty, he will save me."

The tone of voice in which this speech was spoken, rapid and affecting as it was, savoured nothing of insanity, and Duval could not help saying to himself,—

"If this be madness, there is the strangest
    Method in it that e'er I saw."

Twice or thrice the man of whom the lad so spoke made efforts to interrupt him, but a warning glance from Duval had the effect of letting him see that a per-severance in such a course might be dangerous.

"Well, sir," said Duval to the father-in-law, "what have you to say to all this?"

"Oh, the boy is mad!—mad!"

"You and I differ in opinion. Allow me, my lad, to assist you from the coach. What do you think of him, Miss Jemima? Has he shown any symptoms of madness since you have been in the coach with him?"

"Oh, no, no."

"He is as mad as a March hare, sir," said the man. "A likely thing that if he were not he would find time in the midst of what he call his afflictions to praise this young lady's eyes in such an extravagant manner, that the aunt was quite shocked."

"But the young lady was not, and by saying that of him, you have given me the most convincing proof of his perfect sanity that you possibly could, for even by this light I can take upon myself to say, that I have rarely seen such eyes, and rarely expect to see such."

"They are very, very beautiful," said the youth.

Duval smiled as he helped him out of the coach, and released him from a rope that tied his hands behind his back.

"Stay close to me," he whispered to him, "I will protect you from any one who means ill to you."

"Oh, how can I thank you!"

"Hush, we shall have plenty of time to talk. Now, sir, I will trouble you for the hundred pounds you have with you, and the gold watch you have so cleverly hidden in your boot."

"There's the money, and I only hope—well, well, my turn may come some day."

"Help!" cried young Harry, "help! oh, help!"

Duval turned hastily, and he saw a rough-looking fellow holding the lad by the collar, and trying to drag him away.

"I belongs to the 'sylum," said the fellow. "He shall come along o' me. We is paid for his being mad, and that's all we cares about. Come on, will you."

The pistol that Duval held in his hand was a heavy one, and without reversing it he gave the fellow such a crack on the head with the barrel of it, that he danced again, and then Harry having the use of his hands, ran in upon him, and with more power than one would have expected from him, stripling as he was, knocked him down, and left him rolling in the road, from which he very comfortably slipped over a little stone parapet into a drain, that was conveniently close at hand.

Duval was sufficiently put out of temper at all this not to be very particular in his treatment of the father-in-law; and as he was not very quick or inclined to get the watch out of his boot, Duval dismounted, and asked Harry to hold his horse for a moment.

"Now, sir," he said, "the watch!"

"You have got quite enough already. Be off with you, while you are in a whole skin," was the reply.

Scarcely were these words past the lips of the father-in-law, when he found out the truth of the often disputed proposition, that there is a retribution in this world; for Duval caught him by the leg, and in a moment he found himself on his back in the road, with a tolerable collection of contusions acquired in the process.

Duval then did not trouble himself further to search for the watch; but having a horsewhip tucked into a place in the saddle of his steed that was made to receive it, he now possessed himself of it, and began belabouring the father-in-law at such a rate, that he did not know how soon to produce the watch.

"Oh, murder," he cried, "murder! here's the watch! Stop it—stop it! Oh, oh, help. Stop the whip!"

"Oh, you have had enough of that, have you?"

"Yes. Gracious goodness, yes."

"Then, sir, take this lesson from me, and never show your brutal temper when you find that you have met your master. What is your name, sir?"

"Oh, oh, my name is Watts."

"Very well, Mr. Watts, now you may get up and resume your seat in the coach at soon as you please, for I and my comrades will soon be off now. Hilloa, my gallant Phillip, you can draw off your eight men, and you, Stephen, can get out of the way with yours. Don't shoot the coachman, he has behaved very well."

"That's a mercy," groaned the coachman, "for I have been giving of myself up for a dead man anytime this last ten minutes, that I have."

Mr. Watts gathered himself up from the middle of the road, and with many groans got into the coach again. Duval shut the door, and then in a loud voice, he cried—

'Coachman, drive on."

"Oh, dear, won't I," said the coachman, "with all the pleasure in life, I'll drive on. Good night, gentlemen; you might have behaved much worse than you have; and if ever you stops me again, I only hope you'll be just as civil and considerate as you have been to night. Come up. Cluck—cluck!"

The horses started into a good trot, and the St. Alban's coach quickly disappeared from the scene of Duval's encounter with it on the North Road. The young lad, who had been by Duval rescued from his father-in-law, remained close to the horse, and then Duval spoke to him—

"Well, Master Harry," he said. "Who do you suppose I am?"

"A kind friend to me."

"That is a good answer; but you have heard of such a person as a highwayman, I suppose?"

"Yes, and I have heard them spoke badly of, while I have heard such a person as a father-in-law spoken well of; but now I feel that in both cases people are wrong: for the highwayman has been a kind friend to me, and the father-in-law has been the worst of foes. Oh, sir, believe me, I am very grateful to you indeed."

Duval could not but be very highly pleased, indeed, with this speech from Harry Hill, and he replied to him, by saying—

"What would you like to do? Have you a home that you could return to, if I were to take you there?"

"Oh, no—no. This man Watts is master of what was my home. It is Captain Russel, close to Whitehall, that I would like to go to. He was an old friend of my fathers, and I can at once throw myself upon his protection."

"Are you sure of him?"

"As sure as I am of you."

"Very well then. I will charge myself with your safe conduct to Captain Russel. He will no doubt be easily enough found; and as I do not intend to remain on the road longer to-night, you shall ride behind me, and I will take you to my home, where you can rest till morning."

CHAPTER LXXXII.

DUNAL FINDS HIMSELF IN HIS OLD FASHIONABLE QUARTERS.

THE young lad seemed hardly able to speak for thankfulness to Duval for this offer, and the latter was so much pleased with the liberality and the frankness of Harry Hill's ideas, that he felt as if he could have gone through any danger for him.

"If this Captain Russel be really the friend you believe him, your misfortunes will be at an end, and you will have the sasisfaction of defeating your uncle. But how was it that you accuse him of killing your mother? I think you made such an accusation."

"I did—I did."

"Well—well, Harry, if it distresses you to say any more upon that subject, do not do so."

"Oh, no—no. It is not talking about it, that now can add to my distress. I have gone through so much sorrow, that it lies too deeply to be lightly ruffled by mere words."

Duval was quite charmed by the elegant, yet simple phraseology of the lad—for after all, he was no more; and as they cantered on towards Hornsey, he felt quite a pleasure in listening to him.

"When I spoke of Mr. Watts' murdering my poor mother," added Harry, "I did not mean that he actually lifted his hand against her, and killed her; but she died through remorse and sorrow at having married such a man. My poor father had not been dead long, before she began to think that this Mr. Watts would be a good husband for her; and despite all my prayers and entreaties, and cold looks and open remonstrances of her friends, she married him."

"Ah," said Duval, "when a widow is bent upon marrying again, all the world may rise up in arms to prevent her, and produce little effect."

"She soon found, sir, that it was only for what she had in goods and money that he married her; and to get entire possession of both, he wearied her with solicitations; and when she was, for my sake, firm against them, he commenced a career of ill-usage which soon brought her to the grave."

'Well, I won't say, serve her right, Harry, because she was your mother, and I respect you; but I will say, that if a woman, with a child or children,

CLAUDE RUSHES OUT OF HIS HOUSE TO THE ASSISTANCE OF LUKE.

marries again, she don't fall exactly within the sphere of my sympathies, let what will happen to her."

"She died," added Harry, "leaving me the old house, and all its contents. This Watts' tried to persuade me to let him have everything, on condition of giving me one hundred pounds per annum; and when I would not, he commenced a series rather of annoyances than absolutely ill-usage, and finally spread about, without my having the least idea of it, a report that I was mad, and yesterday brought a madhouse-keeper to the house, and treated me as you saw."

"Well, Harry, never mind. I will take you to Captain Russel, you may depend, and all will be well. I only hope that you will not be deceived in him."

"My father saved his life once."

"That ought, indeed, to constitute a bond of union between you and him; but we shall see. You can make yourself quite comfortable for the night, and all will be well. In the morning I will lend you a horse, and we will ride to the neighbourhood of Captain Russel's house together."

"But, my dear friend, can you do that with safety?"

"Yes, certainly. I can put on a very different aspect to that in which you now see me, and you will find that I can make my appearance in Whitehall without a tremor."

"I am glad to hear that, for not even to save myself from my mother's bad husband, would I have you go into any danger."

"Do not fear for me. And now here we are close to my hourse, Harry, where I can promise you safety and quiet rest, at all events; and in the young fresh hours of the morning, we will mount and go to London."

They had ridden at a good pace, so that now Duval drew rein opposite the garden gate of his own house at Hornsey, and in a moment or two, Luke spoke—

"Is that you, sir?"

"Yes, Luke—all's right. I have got a gentleman with me."

"Very well, sir. I will open the gate if you will ride in, sir. It's all clear, right on to the stable, sir. I will get a light directly, if you please."

Luke thought that it was much better, considering who and what Duval was, not to get a light until the horse was right into the yard, and the gate shut after him, as then no one could see who it was that had ridden in. But in a few moments the lantern was brought, and then Luke was not a little surprised to see a youth with Duval.

"You need not think anything of the young gentleman's presence," said Duval. "He knows who and what I am, and I am quite sure he may be thoroughly trusted with the secret of my residence here."

"I should," said Harry, "be almost induced to kill myself, if I imagined you thought me capable of any baseness towards you."

"Make yourself quite easy upon that head," said Duval. "I have no such thought, believe me; so now come in. We shall want both the horses to-morrow morning, Luke."

"Very good, sir."

Duval and his young companion went into the house, where he soon introduced him to May; but notwithstanding they rung repeatedly for Luke, he was not to be found; and as May had let the person who usually did the domestic work of the place go to bed, they were obliged to wait upon themselves.

We can account satisfactorily for the absence of Luke.

When he let Duval and Harry Hill into the premises by the garden gate, he had seen, or thought he saw, the figure of a man skulking along the road-way just opposite. Not feeling quite certain that such was the case, although his, Luke's, eyes were pretty well schooled to out-of-door sights, he had said nothing to Duval upon the subject; but the moment he had put the horse in the stable, he left the premises by another gate, and crept cautiously up the road close to the hedge, for the purpose of discovering if he were right or wrong in his conjectures.

Luke had not got on far in this way, before he ran against a man crouched down close to an old chesnut tree that was nearly opposite Duval's gate.

"Hilloa," said Luke. "Who are you?"

"Who are you?" said the man.

"Only a poor fellow looking for a job, sir."

"Ah, indeed, you are looking for a job—are you? What kind of a fellow are you?"

"Well, sir, I hardly know. The fact is, I am not very particular what I do, so that it is honest, and I can earn a shilling or two, for times are very hard, perhaps as you know, sir."

"Are you belonging to this place?"

"Lor' bless you, no, sir, I am on the tramp, and don't know what place it is. But I suppose it is Hampstead."

"Humph! I suppose you are a desperate coward?"

"Coward? No, sir, that I am not. I am afraid of nothing in the world, and my friends won't give me any help, because they will have it that I am as strong as a horse, and they keep on saying, ' Why don't you go for as soldier?' till I'm sick of hearing of them, sir, that I am."

"Well, my good fellow, I do think it is quite providential your coming across me, for the fact is I can give you a job that will not put shillings, but guineas into your pocket. What do you say to that, my friend?"

"Say to it, sir? Lor' bless you, you have only to tell me what it is, and it is as good as done out of hand, sir."

"Then I can do you a good turn. In that house opposite to us, there is a man that I have a warrant to apprehend. Now, he is rather a troublesome fellow, and as I am only single-handed here, of course, I am very glad to get some assistance."

"Yes, sir; who is he?" said Luke.

"Why, his name is Noakes, but that is of no sort of consequence. All you have to do, is to help me to secure him, and I will put a pair of handcuffs upon him, and take him away, and for the job, I will give you a couple of guineas."

"But are you sure, sir, he is the man?"

"Quite. By mere accident, I was here some days ago, and I saw him come out. I know his face so well, that I cannot be mistaken. He is the man."

"But surely, sir, you can get some of your friends that you have told about him being here to help you?"

"Why, you idiot, do you think I would be fool enough to tell anybody, when I want him all to myself? No, hardly. If you don't like the job, say so, and be off at once. It is quite clear to me that your courage is oozing away, and that you will be of no use to me."

"Then, sir, you are much mistaken," said Luke. "I only like to know as much as possible about what I am going to do always; and if you will assure me I shall have the two guineas, you may depend upon me flying at him the moment you say, ' There he is!' and laying hold of him with a grip, that he will find it no easy matter to get out of."

"You are a fine fellow, and I will make your reward no less than five guineas. There, what do you say to that?"

"Nothing at all, sir, but that I would lay hold of the devil himself by the tail, and hold him till you came up, for that money."

"Come on, then!"

"What, are you going to ring at the gate, sir, or to knock at the door?"

"Hardly. What I am going to do, is to make my way into the garden of the house, through that hedge, which I see is the only fence to one part of it, and then we can be guided by circumstances."

"So we can, sir—so we can."

Now, if this officer, for such he was, who had chanced to see Duval as he came out of his house, and who had been prowling about ever since, had not been so full of cupidity that he wanted all the reward for the capture of Duval himself, and so could not bring his mind to inform any of his brother officers, there is very little doubt but that the career of our adventurer would have ended on that night, for in a couple of hours, with the certainty that Duval was in that house, the officer could have brought to it a sufficient force to have rendered the success of an attack quite certain, so far as regarded the death of Duval, if he had chosen that rather than captivity; but he could not do that. The idea of achieving the affair single-handed, or with such adventitious assistance as the sum of five guineas could afford to him, was really too seducing.

And when we come to consider that the reward for Duval was near to one thousand five hundred pounds, we can hardly wonder that the imagination of the officer was led astray by the glitter of such a sum.

Little did he imagine the snare he had fallen into in speaking to Luke, and making to him his proposals.

They now (that is, Luke and the unsuspecting officer) crossed the road-way, and after some little trouble, forced a passage through the hedge that had been spoken of into the garden of the house, and when they were there the officer said—

"Now, my friend, the grand thing will be to get him out of the house, you know, for in the open air we can do much more than any where else ; and he cannot dodge, as he might, up and down staircases, and through rooms that he knows all about, but of which we know nothing at all."

"But is he alone in this house?" asked Luke.

"No, there is a young girl, and a sort of stable fellow, or gardener, who, I dare say, is as great a rogue as his master ; but that is all, and if we are not a match for them, I think it will be a very odd thing indeed."

"Oh, very—very."

The officer now, by the dim night light, began carefully looking at his pistols, and Luke said to him—

"Lor, sir, you don't mean for to go to say as you will shoot him ?"

"I don't know what I may do, my good friend. At all events, it makes no sort of difference to you, you know, whether I shoot him or not."

"Oh, dear no. As long as I get my money, what can it matter to me whom you shoot ?"

"Exactly. Now I would give something to know where that gardener sort of fellow may happen to be. But there is one good thing in this affair, and that is, that as we are on the side of the law, all the alarm that is given is all the better, you know, for us. What now, if you were to get up to the house and call out in a loud voice 'Hilloa! Hilloa!' I rather think that the fellow I want would come out to see what was the matter, and then I could pop him down in a minute. I don't want to kill him, but I shouldn't mind wounding him in a way that he was quite helpless; for if I can a get him to Newgate with a breath or two of life in him, it would be a great thing to me.'

"Then you'd shoot him as he came out of his own house to see what was the matter ?"

"Of course I should."

"Very good. I somehow don't fancy, do you know, calling him out without having a pistol in my hand. Will you lend me one of yours, and then I will do it in a moment ?" ·

"Oh, stuff! you will just make a blunder if you have any fire-arms. I have only one pair of loaded pistols with me. You be off, and call him out while I hide behind this apple-tree, and I'll manage him."

"I don't like."

"You don't like ? What do you mean by you don't like ? Are you going to tell me that after coming thus far, you are going to draw back ? Are you afraid, or do you want more money ?"

"Why, perhaps I am a little afraid, as I have got no pistol. I should feel like a lion, if I had a pistol."

"Well—well, take this, then. It is loaded carefully, so do mind what you are about with it, and don't fire unless you see me in a difficulty.'

"A difficulty ?"

"Yes, if you see me in a decided difficulty, blaze away, but not before, mind you ; and now let us get on."

"Well," said Luke, "do yo know it strikes me that you were never in such a difficulty in your life as you are in now, and you never will be in such another in this world, whatever your troubles may happen to be in the next."

"What do you mean? Are you mad?"

"Not at all; but the Noakes that you want out of this house, is Claude Duval the highwayman, and I am his man, the gardener sort of fellow.   W do you think of your difficulties now? I think you will indeed be inclined to admit that you are too clever by half."

At these words the officer was so completely staggered that he stepped back and tumbled right on a currant bush.

"Get up," said Luke, "and don't bury yourself. Now I have a proposal to make to you, my friend, which it will be the wisest thing in the world for you to adopt, because it gives you just a chance of getting away."

"Murder!" said the officer; "I'm a dead man!"

"No you ain't, but you may be, you know. There's no saying what may happen in a little time.   I am quite resolved that you and I shall fight a duel."

CHAPTER LXXXIII.

THE DUEL BETWEEN LUKE AND THE OFFICER, AND ITS RESULTS.

THE officer did succeed in scrambling to his feet, and as the moon just then peeped out from behind a dense mass of clouds, and shone with great brilliance, he and Luke could see each other remarkably well.

"A duel?" said the officer. "What do you mean by a duel?"

"I mean a fair fight, at about twelve paces; you may fire at me, and I will fire at you. If you hit me, you may go off; but if I hit you, I will bury you in the garden."

The officer shook again.

"Let me go," he said. "You may take my word now, after what has happened, that I won't say one word about this place, or who lives here; only let me go in peace."

"Yes, I will trust you just as much as I would trust a famished fox in a poultry-yard. No, you must fight. Come, you can stand where you are, and I will go back twelve paces, or thereabouts. We will fire together, and when I say one, two, three, it will be the signal, you know."

As he spoke, Luke backed along the gravel-path of the garden, but before he had got to the distance he thought of going, the officer rapidly raised his pistol and fired saying—

"Take that, then, if you will have it; and I hope it may do you some good, you scoundrel."

"I'm hit," said Luke.

"A good job, too."

The officer ran towards the gap in the hedge; but although Luke had fallen, he still kept his hold of the pistol he had in his hand, and levelling it after the officer, he pulled the trigger, just as he was scrambling through the gap in the hedge.

With a loud cry the officer fell backwards, and rolling twice over, there lay without motion upon the pathway.   In another moment, out rushed Duval with a light in his hand; but the wind blew it out instantly. He then flung it down upon finding that the moon was shining brightly, and he called in a loud voice—

"Luke, Luke, what is all this? Who fired a pistol just now? Where are you, Luke?"

"Here, sir," said Luke, faintly. "This way, sir. Here I am on the grass-plot."

"Duval went forward in the direction of the sound immediately, and to his astonishment, he saw Luke lying on a small grass-plot that was close to the gap in the hedge that had been made by the officer.

"Why, Luke, what's the matter? Speak to me, I beg of you, and tell me what has happened!"

"He has done for me, I think, sir."

"Who? who?"

"An officer, sir, who has been dogging about the place for I don't know how long. He and I have had a shot at each other; but the treacherous rascal took me at unawares, and hit me."

"Where, Luke, where?"

"Right in my ribs here, sir, I feel the blow of the bullet; and I'm as sick as a dog. I must be bleeding inwardly, sir, as there's none on my clothes; but a man can't get a pistol bullet in his stomach and live, I know. Good-by, sir; I have done all I could for you, and now I am going."

"No, no! I will carry you into the house and see what can be done for you. There's many a bad wound, Luke, got over when it's least expected. Be still and I will carry you gently into the house, my friend."

With these words Duval lifed Luke from the ground and carried him into the house, right into the room where he and May had been sitting, and where another candle was upon the table. May was excessively alarmed; but when she saw what she thought the dead body of Luke, she almost fainted.

"Get some warm water, May," said Duval, "and some linen; tear up anything so that you are quick. Our friend Luke is badly wounded, I am afraid, by some one who came to take my life; but I hope he may recover yet. I will but dress the hurt the best way I can, and then go for the nearest surgeon."

Upon this, May summoned all her presence of mind, and left the room to get what Duval required.

"How do you feel now, Luke?" said Duval.

"Not any worse. I don't know how it is, but the bullet went in here, and I don't feel much of it."

He pointed to his breast as he spoke, and Duval at once tore open his waistcoat, in which there certainly was a little jagged sort of hole; but, singular to state, there the bullet had stopped, as if after perforating the waistcoat, Luke had been shot-proof—for certainly, wound there was none.

"Why you are not hurt a bit," said Duval; "it's all fancy, my good friend. I rejoice to say that you are not hurt in the least. Here, swallow this glass of brandy, and you will be all right again in a minute."

Luke could hardly believe his senses, but he tossed off the glass of brandy that Duval offered him, and then he said:—

"But I felt it hit me, sir."

"Well, then, Luke, you are a necromancer, for the bullet, if it did hit you, has flown off you again as it would off a plate of steel, for touched you are not."

"But it knocked me right over, sir. Oh—oh—oh! Here it is! oh!

"What is the matter, Luke?"

"Only look here, sir. Now I understand it. Here's a five shilling-piece, sir, that you gave me to get a new pair of bridle-ends with; I put it into my waistcoat pocket, and only see, sir, if the bullet has not dented it right into a cup shape. No wonder it knocked me down. It is this, sir, that has saved me, or I should have been a dead man."

As he spoke, Luke took from his waistcoat pocket the crown-piece that had saved his life, and sure enough the ball from the pistol had indented it so that it would have held a tea-spoonful of any liquid. At this moment, May, still pale with anxiety and fright, returned with warm water and some linen for bandages; but Duval turned to her with a smile, saying,

"Our friend is all right again."

"Right!" cried May; "is he not shot?"

"No, this coin in his waistcoat pocket saved him. He will, I fancy, keep it as long as he lives as a curiosity, for he will never have the opportunity of getting such another. These things don't happen twice in the course of ones life."

"Indeed they do not," said May.

"I will keep this crown-piece as a remembrance of to-night's adventure," said Luke, "if you permit me, sir?"

"Permit you? Certainly I will."

"But there were two pistol shots,' said Clara. "Don't you remember, Claude, that you started up at the first, and that the second sounded in our ears before we could leave this room?"

"There were, indeed,' said Duval. "Who fired the other, Luke?"

"I did."

"You did? and pray with what effect? for now it appears if the officer is off and away, this will be no home for me another hour. We will pack up and be off, May, for he will soon bring force enough to make it a matter of impossibility for us to cope with them. This is no home for me."

"Nor for me," sobbed May.

"Stop a bit," said Luke. "I strongly suspect that unless he had a five-shilling-piece in the middle of his back, you will find him lying in the garden. He had his shot at me first, and it was, as you see, sir, a tolerably good one; and then as I lay upon the ground, fancying my life not worth the next two minutes' purchase, I had my shot at him."

"He fell?"

"He did; and if I am any judge of such matters, we shall find him there still."

"Oh, this is terrible!" said May.

"It is to your gentle spirit," said Duval; "but what would you have me do, May? This man, for the mere love of money, comes out armed with deadly weapons, for the purpose of taking my life. What would you have me do? Am I to sit calmly, and allow these men to come at their good pleasure, and drag me to a felon's cell, or, for fear he should not be able to do so with perfect safety to himself, maim me first, and convey me bleeding to the prison?"

"Oh, Claude! do not speak so."

"And yet it is so, May. I rob upon the highway for my subsistence, but I do not take life. On the contrary, I have allowed many a rich booty to slip through my fingers rather than I would obtain possession of it at the price of blood."

"That I am sure of, Claude."

May clung to him and wept, for she had not yet seen Claude look so severe, or heard him speak about his position, and the perils that surrounded it, so seriously before.

"Say no more," she said; "oh, say no more! I will now return to my chamber. Settle this unhappy affair yourselves, and I will ask no further questions concerning it. It is better that I should know no more, for then my imagination will be free from anything to brood over, in the solitary hours when you are far from me."

"You are right, May! you are right! Go to your room, and leave Luke and me to settle the affair entirely."

Upon this, May retired at once from the room, and then Duval, turning to Luke, said, "Come, we must go and see what amount of mischief has been done to the officer. The moon is yet shining brightly, and we need no other light. Come at once!"

"I will follow you, sir."

Duval and Luke now made their way to that spot in the garden where the officer lay, and by the bright beams of the moon they now observed him lying upon his back, and Duval, who was walking first, took but one glare at his face, and then, turning to Luke, he said,—

"Quite dead!"

"I thought as much by the way in which he fell. He went over and over, as like a rabbit when you have hit it by a good shot as possible. Well, I do not feel many compunctions, for his attack upon me was so dastardly; it was like a murder."

"It was, Luke; but what are we to do with him?"

"Bury him, sir!"

"But where, Luke?"

"Here, in the garden, sir. We can easily find some odd corner in which to place him. It is the only safe and easy thing that can be done. He's dead, and no one will hear any more of him in this world, sir; and it's a comfort to know that in all ways he brought his death upon himself, and that neither you nor I can really be blamed for it at all."

"Yes, Luke, that is something; and as you say, I do not see any other mode of disposing of him than by burying him; so it is better that we should do so at once. Get a couple of spades, and we will both set to work."

"Ay, sir," said Luke; "we will soon get a trench big enough to put him in comfortably. He was a very bad fellow, sir; worse, I should say, for the most part, than officers in general; for everything he wanted to do had something treacherous about it."

Luke went to a little tool-house that was in the garden, and soon returned with a couple of spades, and then he selected a very retired spot where the ground would not have to be disturbed again, in which to dig the officer's grave.

"Here, sir," he said, "nothing will grow, and it ain't at all likely that any one who may have this house after you will dig up this bit of the ground; you see, sir, not a bit of sunshine can get to it at any part of the day, and then it is always dark, dreary, and damp; so it will just do for a grave, for it seems to be just cut out for one."

"Come on, then. Let's be as expeditious as possible in getting this rather ugly job over, Luke."

They began now working away, and as they did it with a right good will, it was truly astonishing to see what progress they made. In something less than half-an-hour they had a grave dug for the officer; and then, as Luke wiped his brow, he said, in a low voice,—

"I hope that young gentleman you brought here with you will know nothing of this job?"

"It is not likely, Luke. You had hardly left us with the horses when I showed him to bed, for he was thoroughly tired out and could hardly keep his eyes open. Before, however, I retire myself to get an hour's sleep, I will take care to ascertain what he has heard, and what he thinks of it."

"Do so, sir; for this is a secret that it will be much more satisfactory to think remains in your and my keeping than in any one else's. I will fetch the body, sir."

"You have no repugnance, Luke?"

"Not a great deal, sir. Of the two I would rather this affair had not happened; but the fellow firing at me in such a cowardly way first, has put out of my head all feeling for him, and I am quite sure that such a man is a good riddance to society."

With this, Luke went away, and presently came back, dragging the dead body along by the heels.

"I could not make up my mind to lift him," he said; "so there he goes into the grave. Fill up, sir, as quick as you can."

They both worked away in silence, and trod down the earth over the body until the grave of the officer was filled up.

CHAPTER LXXXIV.

DUVAL PLAYS AGAIN THE MAN OF FASHION IN LONDON.

DUVAL was anything but well pleased with the whole of this adventure. It involved the taking of a life, and the smuggling up of a dead body, in a way that was anything but gratifying to his feelings; and yet, although he considered the thing in every possible light, he could not see how it could have been otherwise managed.

"Luke," he said.   "There is now another bond of union between you and I, in the recollection of this affair."

"Ah, sir, there needed no other than what there was.   You have given me a home, and you are very kind and good to me."

"But I owe you much, Luke."

CLAUDE SELLS HIS HORSE TO COLONEL LANE.

"No, sir, indeed, you do not ; and I only hope the death of this man will not give you any uneasiness."

"That I cannot help."

"Ah, sir, I feared as much, notwithstanding what you said upon the subject, and the manner in which you tried to carry it off ; but the more you think of it, I fancy, sir, the more you will see and feel that nothing else could have been done but what was done."

"That, I freely admit, Luke; and it is a positive fact, unless I had chosen to give myself up to the first officer of the police who chose to come, and demand me to lead me forth to execution. It is not exactly the deed itself that has brought regretful feelings to my mind, but it is the necessity for it."

"Well, sir, it is a pity, if you look at it in that way."

"It is; but now go to your rest, Luke, and I will go to mine, and above all things, keep this affair from the knowledge of your mistress. Her gentle nature would be horrified at it, and the idea that the garden held such a secret would haunt her day and night, to her great detriment and unhappiness."

"I would not, sir, wish that she should know it for worlds."

"That is right, Luke. Let the horses be got ready to-morrow morning at an early hour; for the young gentleman and I are going to town upon his business."

"It shall be done, sir."

Duval went into the house again, and it required all the gentle converse of May to sooth him into even a partial forgetfulness of the scene in the garden; but when the bright morning came, many of the gloomy feelings that the night's adventure had engendered in his mind were dissipated, and he could almost smile at his own fears. He took a more rational view of the whole affair; and if he regretted it none the less, he did not so closely as he had done associate it with his feelings.

The young lad whom he had rescued from the unjust father-in-law, looked as happy again as he had looked over-night; and after partaking of a capital breakfast, he and Duval mounted, and set off for London.

Duval, upon this occasion, rather astonished the young lad; for as he was going into a portion of the City where he would probably meet with people of fashion, he had attired himself in conformity with their usages.

Duval, however, did not wish to be at all known as the Count, with the highly fashionable reputation that clung around him during his sojourn in the handsome apartments in Spring Gardens; and, accordingly, he had with great art disguised himself so that those who had known him most intimately would not have recognised him.

As one part of his disguise he wore a handsome pair of jet-black moustaches, which were so well put on that it would really be next thing to impossible for any one to detect them being false. His hair was naturally of that colour, but by wearing it in so many different fashions he could give quite different aspects to his face; and upon this occasion he wore it in long curls right on to his shoulders. His dress was a very handsome suit of velvet, so that he looked remarkably well.

"Now, my young friend," he said, "you know what I am, and who I am; but my secret I know well is safe with you, and if you meet me anywhere after to-day, all you have got to do is to cut away and affect not to know me."

"Oh, that I could not do."

"Oh yes, it is by far the best plan."

"But my grateful feelings towards you would not let me do it. If I meet you I must long to shake hands with you."

Duval was sensibly affected at this kind and artless gratitude from the young lad; but he spoke to him very severely upon the subject, saying in a low voice :—

"Nay, it would give me the greatest pleasure perhaps to shake hands with you, but if you chance to see me it is quite impossible for you to tell how I may be situated. Recollect that my life is one of the strangest vicissitudes and most hair-breadth escapes; and by your recognising me at some inopportune moment, it is just possible you might be involving me in the greatest danger."

"If I were to do that I should never forgive myself."

"I know it would give you great pain, and therefore it is that I ask you to make me a promise."

"I cannot refuse to make you any promise that you may choose to require of me."

"It is just this, that let you see me where you may, you will not recognise me, ner in the least way affect to know me unless I make the first advance towards you. If I do so, you will then feel assured that you will do me no harm by speaking to me. Will you give me your word to that effect?"

"I will—I do."

"Then I am quite satisfied, my young friend; and believe me it will be no small gratification to me to see you well and happy in the time to come."

"And I, you, Duval; perhaps I shall be able to assist you in getting clear of this terrible line of life, which will kill you if you do not leave it."

"Perhaps so. But let us talk of your own prospects. I will make such inquiry at Whitehall as shall quickly find out this Captain whom you wish to see, and then I will wait to discover if he be the friend you expect or not."

"Of that I have no doubt."

Thus discoursing they made their way to London, and notwithstanding they made anything but speed, the distance was so short that they were soon at Whitehall. That spot filled Duval with painful recollections. The thought of Adele, which he had in a great measure managed to shake off, would obtrude itself upon him; for it was close to there in Spring Gardens that he had first seen and loved her.

The gloom of his heart spread itself over his face, and his young companion said to him :—

"You are not well, Claude."

"Oh yes,—yes I was only thinking of some one this place put me in mind of, that is all."

"Ah, that was some one doubtless to whom you had been kind and good as you have been to me. It is strange, indeed, that you, whom most men would consider to be without the pale of the law, are more generous than those that live within its closest precincts, Duval."

"Say no more upon that head. I will inquire for your father's friend at once."

With a sudden impatience that the young lad could not account for, Duval now set about the inquiry concerning the Captain, that his young companion wished to see, and he was quickly successful; for he found that he was the chief of one of the public offices which abound in that quarter of the City.

"Now," said Duval, "my young friend, you will go to this gentleman; but do not say anything of me; I will wait for you here; and if your reception by him be all that you wish, I should like you to come out to me, and tell me so."

"I will—I will."

The lad, who owed so much to the gallantry and the kindness of Duval, was not absent above ten minutes when he came back; and standing by the side of Duval's horse, he said—

"It is all right. I have been received in the kindest manner. Of course, in obedience to your commands, I have said nothing of you; but will you now permit me to ask him to see you?"

"If you like."

"I will this moment."

With these words in his mouth, he at once went back to the Captain; and then Duval, as he held the rein of the horse that he had lent to his young protege in his hand, urged both the animals forward.

"It is well that we should part here," he said. "He can but do himself harm now by any further connexion with me; and an interview with this personage of whom he speaks, can do me no good. So, farewell."

A sharp trot took Duval past Westminster Abbey, and then stopping at the first livery stable he came to, he rode down the gateway, and put up both the horses at once. On foot then, he, by a circuitous route through the Park, got again to the immediate neighbourhood of St. James's. That Duval had a design in all this, who shall doubt?

In St. James's Street, at that period, there was one of the finest establishments, resembling the modern club, that ever was set going in London. It was kept tolerably select, and the utmost surveillance was kept up at the door, that none but the elite of society should enter.   Trusting to his appearance, which was highly favourable, Duval strolled up to the door of this establishment, and walked in.

Far from any opposition being offered to him in so doing, the doors were most officiously held open for him by the servants. He entered what was called a news-room, and there found some gentlemen killing time in the best way they were able.   He heard one say to the other——

" Is it time yet ?"

" Hardly, my lord," said the other.   " It will be a bore to be too soon at the affair, and I cannot help thinking it will be a bore when we get there."

" Why, the fact is, the Prince is rather too young for this sort of thing, just yet."

" That's what I think, my lord ; and the mystery of the thing is, that we don't know who is invited, and who not.   It appears that the Prince has given half a dozen tickets to some, to bring with them whom they please, while others have had no end of difficulty in getting one."

" Why, how many will be there ?"

" It is limited to thirty, I understand ; and all that is on the tickets are the two letters, P. F."

" And what do they mean ? for although I have a ticket, to tell the truth, I did not look at all at it."

" Why the letters mean Prince's Fete, I believe ; but let us be off. It is a sharp-enough ride to Kew now, and we cannot be much too soon I should say."

" Very good.   Come along."

" Gentlemen," said Duval with all the cool impertinence in the world, " if you are going to the prince's fête at Kew, I can assure you that you are in good time, for His Royal Highness told me only two hours ago, that he hoped no one would come very early, as he had taken a small quantity of claret last night, and was as even princes may be at times."

The two gentlemen bowed, and one of them said——

" We have not the pleasure of knowing you, sir."

" I am Baron Hoge, a noble of the Roman Empire, a general in the Sicilian service, and a relative of the queen."

The two gentlemen bowed again.

" But," added Duval, " I don't trouble the queen much, for my age and my taste, I must confess, incline me more to the amusements of the prince, who, if he were a little older, and not quite so selfish, and a glutton, would be very good company, and make plenty of amusement for men of the world."

" You speak freely, sir."

" I do. The fact is, none of the family much mind what I say ; but you will do me one favour, gentlemen, if me meet, as no doubt we shall at this fête, and that will be to say nothing to the prince of me, as he and I are going upon a little expedition soon, and he don't want any one to know that I am in the country, as it might get round to the ears of the Queen ; and there is a certain little blue-eyed cousin of hers, whom she is rather irate at, for admiring your humble servant."

All this was said with such an air of engaging frankness, that, men of the world as these two persons were, they were completely taken in by it, and one said——

" Allow me, then, Baron Hoge, to introduce myself ; I am Lord Austincourt, and this is Colonel Lane.   We are both upon tolerably good terms with the prince, and hope to lead a pleasant life with him for the next dozen years to or so, as he certainly seems to be in the vein to emulate his illustrious and much-talked-of antecedent, Prince Henry, afterwards King Henry the Fifth."

" He may wish to imitate him," said Duval, " but the copy will be more unlike the original than I am unlike Hercules, I fancy.   Have we time and in-clination for a bottle of Bordeaux before starting ?"

" Both, I hope," said Lord Austincourt.

The bottle of wine was brought to them, and after duly discussing it, Duval sent a message to the livery-stable for his horse, describing the one of the two he wanted ; and as he had quite arranged that he was to accompany his two new acquaintances to Kew, he mounted at the door of the club, and their horses having been brough round from a neighbouring stable, they did the same.

He saw that they very much admired his steed, and he said in reference to it—

" This is a kind and good creature, and will do almost anything. I thought it cheap at two hundred pounds."

" And so it is," said Austincourt. " I will give the money for it now at once, if you want to part with it."

" No," said Duval. " It is my favourite horse for common use, although I have some in my stable that cost me more than double the amount."

" Can he leap ?" cried the colonel.

" A little. Do you see that cart ?"

A cart was creeping lazily along, drawn by a donkey, and carrying vegetables ; and as he uttered the last words, Duval put his horse at it, and the leap right over the cart was done in a capital and clean style.

" By George !" said the colonel, " I should like to have him. Will three hundred tempt you, baron ?"

Duval hesitated a moment, and then he said—

" Well, i don't know but that, upon two conditions, it might."

" Name them—name them."

" First, you must let me ride him to-day."

" Oh yes, certainly. By all means."

" Then you must come for him yourself to my place, that I will give you the address to before we part to-day."

" That I will with pleasure."

" Well then, colonel, he is yours at three hundred pounds."

The colonel took out his pocket-book, and at once, in the presence of Austincourt, handed out three notes of one hundred pounds each to Duval, who put them very coolly into his pocket, and then Lord Austincourt said—

" I envy you your bargain, colonel, and if I had been flush of cash just now, I would have bid another fifty ; but I am devilish short, so it is no use talking about it. Let us push on now, for it is near eleven o'clock, and after all we ought to be in tolerably good time, if we are not early."

CHAPTER LXXXV.

DUVAL MAKES A BRILLIANT DAY AT THE PRINCE'S FETE.

Upon this they all increased their speed, and Duval enjoyed a most delightful ride to Kew.

It is perhaps necessary that we should now say a few words regarding this fête or private entertainment, which the Prince of Wales was then giving. George, Prince of Wales, afterwards George the Fourth, was then but a very young man, and could hardly be said to be out of tutelage. Already, however, he had begun to give ample evidence of those luxurious habits which stuck to him through life, and which have clung to his memory with no enviable reputation.

He had become the petty tyrant of all around him ; and having just awakened to the fact that there was no ordinary limit to his powers of self-indulgence, he had commenced that course of selfishness, gluttony, and animal gratification, which he became so famous for, and which royal and illustrious personages are but too apt, by the grace of God of course, to fall into.

The old palace at Kew had been for a short space assigned to him as a residence, where it was supposed that he was completing some portion of his education ; but he soon contrived to convert it into the scene of his illicit pleasures, and there were those around him, who took good care to encourage the growing foibles and vices of the young prince.

A man in such a position will never want sycophants, and already the Prince of Wales had his party in the nation, and was accustomed to pass the night with some of the most worthless characters among the aristocracy that could be got together.

This meeting at Kew was intended to celebrate one of those early orgies for which he afterwards became rather too well known, and which he only abandoned when failing health forced him so to do, and he found himself deserted by all save that bloated female member of the nobility, who, after his death, and while the clay of the debauchee was still warm with recent life, robbed the chamber in which he breathed his last, and decamped with the spoil.

But then she was a marchioness !

The only person that the young prince was most particularly solicitous to keep his orgies a secret from, was the queen, and this anxiety did not arise out of any filial respect, but simply because Her Majesty had it in her power to materially interfere with his enjoyments, by turning him out of the palace at Kew at a moment's notice, as it was in her keeping specially ; and when she indulged herself with a walk in its garden, and tittulated her royal nose with a pinch of the snuff she was so vulgarly fond of, she little imagined that those groves, and walks, and fountains, and sweet retired places, had recently rung with the vacant laugh of the courtezan.

"Have you been to one of these little meetings before, baron ?" said Lord Austincourt to Duval.

"Not here," replied Duval, with a laugh that conveyed the idea that he knew all about them somewhere else ; and as the colonel and his lordship had not been to any such parties elsewhere, they set it down in their own minds that Duval knew a little more than they even did of the freaks of the young prince.

The aspect of appearances at the gate of the gardens and palace at Kew, was not such as would have led any one to suppose that the heir-apparent to the crown of England was there. Only one servant was on duty, but then the grand object was that the whole affair should be kept strictly quiet.

There was one little difficulty that Duval had to contend with, and that arose from the fact that he had no ticket, and for the last mile he was full of thought as to how he should get over this trouble. Accident furnished him with a good opportunity for accomplishing it.

During the ride, Lord Austincourt had produced his ticket and replaced it in the pocket of his over-coat, and it so happend that the horse which his lordship rode limped a little just as they got within sight of the royal abode.

"Hilloa !" said the colonel, "your horse has fallen lame, Austincourt. That's a pleasant job."

"Is he, though ? Do you see it, baron ?"

"Yes," said Duval, "but it's probably of no sort of consequence. He has picked up a stone, most likely ; you see this bit of road is full of them. I will dismount and look at his foot for you."

"Oh no—no, I will dismount myself. I could not think of troubling you."

"Don't mention that. It is no trouble, I assure you, and I am rather a good hand, they say, at anything of this sort; my horse will stand still, or rather, I should say, your horse, colonel.—Excuse my saying mine."

As Duval spoke, he dismounted, and so did Lord Austincourt, and as they both stooped to examine the horse's foot, in which was a small stone, it was the easiest thing in the world for Duval to take his ticket of admission to the prince's fete from his pocket.

"There, it's gone, now," said Duval.

"Upon my word, I am very much obliged to you, baron. I would not have this horse go lame on any account, for I value it very much, and, as all the world knows, I am in no cue just now to buy another."

They both mounted again, and in a very short time they reached the gate of the gardens, at which it was customary for the private friends of the prince to enter. Then, as they dismounted, the servant blew a whistle, and in a few minutes three grooms came to take charge of the horses,

"Hilloa!' said Austincourt, "there is De Lohm, the prince's valet. I'll be sworn he has come to take the tickets, and if so, it is a very private affair indeed."

"It is so," said Duval, with a nod of the head. "Even I am provided with a pass, which, upon any ordinary occasion, would not have been requisite, as you may very well suppose."

"Certainly not. He is coming," said the colonel.

"Gentlemen," said the valet, bowing, "I will have the honour of taking your tickets."

"Certainly, good Lohm," said Austincourt, "certainly. I hope both you and the prince are blooming to-day?"

"Quite well, my lord!—at your lordship's service."

Duval handed his ticket to the valet, who looked at him scrutinizingly; but the ticket was a pass that he dared not dispute, for on one side of it were the letters P. F. and on the other a G.; and that G. was written by the royal fingers of the prince himself, with a peculiar flourish at the tail of it that the valet knew perfectly well, so he bowed and said,—

"Pass on, sir, if you please. This is perfectly right and regular."

"Anybody here?" said Duval.

"Almost all invited, sir. Thank you, colonel,—all right. Pass on, if you please."

"Confound it," said Lord Austincourt; "where is my card? I had it only half-an-hour ago. Where the deuce did I put it? I have not so many pockets, either. Hang the thing!—Did you not see me with it, colonel?"

"Certainly; and the barons, likewise."

"Yes," said Duval; "you took it out of your pocket to look at to be sure. You had it."

"Certainly I had, and I put it in this— no, it must have been this pocket— No. I have not got it, that's quite clear, De Lohm."

"It is a pity, my lord,"

"It is. But here is the colonel, who know; I had it and here is the baron."

"Yes," said the colonel; "we are both witnesses to that effect; you know it, baron, as well as I?"

"It is a pity!" said De Lohm; "but there is another witness to the fact that my Lord Austincourt had a ticket, and that is myself, for I sent it to his lordship at the express command of the prince. Pass on, my lord; it is all right. No doubt it has come out of your pocket upon the road, and that shows what a good thing it is to have nothing on the ticket that the uninitiated can understand."

"You are very right, De Lohm," said Austincourt, "and very obliging. I am not the man to forget a little courtesy of this kind; and, as you say, the ticket will be an enigma beyond their guessing to any one who may chance to find it."

The valet bowed, and the three visitors passed the gate of the royal demense.

"Provoking!" said Lord Austincourt, "the loss of the card; "but it was very obliging of De Lohm. Don't mention it, either of you, to the prince. It is just one of the little things that he will pretend to make a great fuss about."

"Not a word of it," said the colonel.

"And my lips are sealed!" said the mock baron. "I know George quite well enough to be perfectly aware that if you tell him anything, he generally gets hold of the wrong version of it."

Both the colonel and Lord Austincourt laughed at this remark from Duval, and it tended more and more to confirm them in their belief of his position, for if he had not felt quite upon easy terms with the prince, he would surely, they thought, never have ventured upon talking of him so freely.

Duval cautiously allowed his new friends to take the lead, and they went along the paths in the shrubbery that led to the palace with practised familiarty, and at length emerged upon an exceedingly pretty lawn, in the centre of which was one of the most gorgeous flower-beds that the imagination could conceive.

"'That is a beautiful sight!" said the colonel, as he looked at it. "They are all rare green-house plants, and are taken in at night, but in the daytime they are so well arranged, that they really have all the appearance of growing and flourishing in the open ground."

"They have, indeed," said Duval.

A loud roar of laughter at this moment came upon their ears from the palace, and then all was still again, as if by magic.

"Ah!" said the colonel, "they are at it, I hear, already."

"Not a doubt of it," said Austincourt. "But I would always rather be a little later, for if one comes early on these occasions, one is obliged to out with all one's good jokes at once, and then for the rest of the affair look as dull as ditch water. Come on; I wonder where they are?"

"Oh, in the painted room, of course."

"Do you think so? I thought the sounds came from the queen's parlour."

Duval said nothing, but he put on a quiet kind of smile, as if he could have said a great deal if he had so chosen; and no doubt his two companions so translated it. There is nothing like saying nothing to give a man a reputation for knowing a great deal.

"Let us go in," said Austincourt.

"Agreed," said the colonel.

They all three reached a little low-arched door, which any one would have thought opened upon some of the domestic offices of the palace, and Lord Austincourt tapped at it with a ring that was upon his finger. It was immediately opened by a man elegantly dressed in a court suit, who said not one word, but merely bowing, waved his hand for them to enter.

"Which room, Collins?" said the colonel.

"The Painted Saloon, sir."

"Oh, so I thought. Come on, my lord. Ah! there they go again; I wonder what that is at. Nothing very humorous, I'll be bound. A small joke goes a long way at times in certain places, and with certain people."

"It does indeed," replied Duval, to whom this remark appeared to be more particularly applied; "but by the laughter now, one would really suppose it was anything but a small joke."

"Ah! but a great noise is no—"

"Hush! Hush!" said Lord Austincourt. "Pray recollect where you are, and bear in mind the old saying, that walls have ears sometimes."

"Thank you for the caution."

At this moment another person habited like the man at the little door stepped up to them, and said:—

"Allow me, gentlemen, to show you into the prince's presence. This way, gentlemen, if you please."

A door was thrown open, and a blaze of light from a room that was closed against the daylight, and then brilliantly lighted up with wax candles, shone upon them.

CHAPTER LXXXVI.

DETAILS SOME SINGULAR PROCEEDINGS IN KEW GARDENS AND PALACE.

Duval was certainly not at all prepared for the extraordinary scene that presented itself in the room where the Prince of Wales was enjoying himself with his b on companions; he had thought all along that it was rather an odd thing to hold such a class of entertainments in broad daylight, but it had not struck him that that was a state of things that could be easily remedied.

The fact was, that every shutter or loop-hole through which a ray of sunlight could make its way into the room, was scrupulously closed; and it was all lit up in the same way as it would have been had the hour been midnight.

The apartment was rather spacious, and the ceiling was a higher one than is generally to be found in those plain Dutch-looking palaces, that we owe partly

CLAUDE AND MAY.

to the no-taste of King William and Queen Mary, and partly to the almost lower taste of Queen Anne. It was painted, in some allegorical subject, the details of which had nearly disappeared in the course of time, and all you could see was a a leg or an arm, or some flaunting piece of drapery that happened to stand out in bright relief from the rest of the subject.

A large oval table was in the centre of the room. The floor was covered with crimson cloth, and a large chandelier, carrying about thirty or forty wax lights, hung from the ceiling.   Upon the table was a perfect chaos of decanters, glasses, bottles, and fruits of all kinds and descriptions ; and sitting round the table was a party of about twenty persons, each one of whom appeared to be perfectly at his ease.

At one end of the table, upon a large chair which he occupied in a sprawling manner, was the then young Prince of Wales.

No notice whatever was taken of the new comers, and Duval was glad that it was so, as he wished to avoid anything like an inquiry as to who he was.

The colonel and Lord Austincourt managed to find places for themselves, and Duval sat next to them.   The door of the room had been noiselessly closed again by the man who had opened it for them, and the fun and jollity went on, without the least interruption, fast and furious.   It seemed as though there was enough wine upon the table to effect the complete intoxication of the whole lot; but Duval wondered that no attendant was present.

" Help yourself, colonel," said Austincourt.   " I suppose, baron, you feel yourself quite at home here ?"

" Rather.   If he catches my eye it will bring him down a degree or two."

" Who ?   The prince ?"

" Yes.   He is perfectly safe with me ; and, yet, nothing will get it out of his head that if he and I were to have a word or two about anything, I must forthwith go and tell all about these little entertainments, when nothing could be further from my thoughts than such baseness."

" It would be very unfair."

" Oh, most grossly so after actually assisting at them,"

" You are a man of honour, baron, and I am very happy to make your acquaintance.   Allow me the pleasure of drinking a glass of wine with you ?"

" Certainly.   With pleasure."

The wine was drank, and then the prince called out in his thick, husky voice—

" Come !   Come !—Who was that had a toast to propose ?   Let us have the toast by all means.   Here we are all waiting.   Come—the toast.   I think it was you, marquis, that had it.   Get on with it."

" The toast—The toast !" cried everybody.   " The marquis's toast !   Bumpers ! Ha !   Ha !   Fill to the brim !   Bumpers !   The toast of the marquis—Silence —Order—Now, marquis !"

A lazy, dissipated-looking young man rose to his feet ; and tossing off a glass of Burgundy that he had just filled, he flung the glass on to the floor, as he said,—

" It is nothing particularly new that I have to propose.   It is the health and well being, as regards looks and condition—confound all the rest !—of an animal."

" An animal !" cried one.

" Order—order !   Silence."

" If you say another word now," said the prince to him who had interrupted the marquis, " I shall have to pour a decanter of Rhenish down your throat."

" Order !   Order !"

" Yes," added the marquis, " it's the health, I say, of an animal, and rather a remarkable one too."

" Hear !   Hear !   Order !   Order !"

" Sometimes this animal is fair, and sometimes it is dark, and sometimes it is neither the one nor the other.   At times, too, you will find the specimen tall, and at times short ; and sometimes this animal is all that is pleasant, while at other times it is as loud and as disagreeable as a gale of wind, and as chilly as winter.   In fact, gentlemen, I give you, as a toast, Woman !"

" Hurrah !" cried the prince.   " Now, that's what I call very clever.   Who could have supposed now what the marquis meant ?   Let us drink the toast, gentlemen."

" When people are hanged for wit," said a voice, " the marquis will be brought in not guilty."

A loud laugh followed this speech, and then Duval saw that several of the guests dropped under the table and brought up cool, fresh bottles of wine ; and upon glancing there, he saw that several ice-pails, crammed with bottles, were placed quite handy to the reach.

" The prince's toast !" cried a voice; and then the cry was echoed by every one at the table ; and the prince, as well as he could, considering that he was so far gone in wine, tried to look amiable and modest.

" Well, gentlemen," he said, "I will give you a toast. I believe it is very usual to drink the health of King George ; but I will give you King Wine and all his family !"

The sycophants of the prince, of whom there was a goodly number present, were quite uproarious and frantic in their applause of this toast. These parties affected to be in the most rapturous state of delight upon the occasion, and the prince, as he winked his fat, sleepy-looking eyes round the table, looked satisfied.

This toast was drunk with all the possible noise and rioting that could be appended to the operation, and from what was taking place, Duval began to entertain far from an elevated idea of the wit of the party.

But what was wanting in wit was made up by noise ; and in our readers experiences of parties, no doubt, that is found to be very generally the case, as well in other places as where Royalty may be the presiding genius.

"Drink away," said the prince; " whatever you do now, mind you don't spare the bottle."

" That we won't," said Lord Austincourt, " for we know it costs no one anything that is here."

"Oh, are you there, Austincourt ?"

" Yes, your highness."

"Oh, don't highness me. When one of these affairs are going on, all the world knows that I am plain George, and no highness at all ; so I request every one of you to call me so."

" Hear—hear—hear !"

"Damn it we are not deaf !" cried Colonel Lane, shrinking from his next neighbour, who, with stentorian lungs, cried—" Hear ! Hear ! Hear !" in his ears.

This little incident produced another roar of laughing, and then the prince called out—

" Now, Austincourt, let us have your toast. We generally have a tolerably good one from you upon these little entertaining occasions."

" Oh, yes," cried a man opposite to Austincourt. " He lies in bed for a week to think of his one solitary joke, and it would be quite a cruelty not to give him an opportunity of coming out with it as early as possible."

" Well," said Austincourt, " I would rather lie in bed than I would do as some folks do nothing else but *lie* out of it."

This was a pretty good retort, but it looked too severely personal to be much laughed at ; and the man who had provoked it bent forward, and said, in bland tones—

" Did you mean that for me, Lord Austincourt? Because if you did, I will throw this decanter at your head."

" I'll be hanged if you do," said one who sat next him. " It is my decanter. Throw your own, if you please."

This produced a roar of laughing, during which Lord Austincourt and the personage at the other side of the table said, no doubt, very cutting things to each other, which were completely lost in the shout of uproarious mirth. When he could speak from laughing, the prince said—

" Enough of this. Don't you all know that there must be no offences taken at this table ?"

" Nor given either," said the man who had quarrelled with Austincourt.— " Nor given either."

"Certainly not, major, I agree with you there. I am quite sure Austincourt meant nothing; so now let us have the toast. Come, Austincourt. If you do lie in bed a week to think of it, it ought to be a good one."

Lord Austincourt rose, and in a solemn tone, he spoke—

"The toast which I am about to propose, is one that I feel quite assured will be received upon its merits, by this assembly, in the most cordial—pleasant—delightful—joyous—agreeable—heartfelt manner. It is a toast which we all have in our hearts, if at odd times it does not show itself exactly upon our faces or in our actions. It is a toast that I feel assured one illustrious personage will feel delighted to drink, and, in fine, it is one that, while it ought to bring tears of sensibility from the feeling bosom, at the same time is calculated to strengthen those delightful ties which bind us all to that which is right and delightful. Gentlemen, I give you a toast which may be summed up in one word, and that is—Morality!"

The exquisite gravity with which Austincourt communicated this toast was admirable; and before he had got to the end of his prologue, every one was almost bursting with laughter; but when he really uttered the word Morality, the smothered mirth burst into a shout.

"Good—good! Capital!" cried several; and the full glasses were drained to honour that word which found not the faintest echo in any one heart that was there present. We have no sort of hesitation in saying that the most really feeling person there present was Claude Duval the highwayman.

An hour or more had now elapsed, and the quantity of wine that had been drunk was rather formidable; and yet, beyond a few red faces and a considerable amount of noise no one seemed very much the worse for what was going on.

The prince's face was probably the reddest of the lot. He was decidedly the youngest man present, and although his head and his stomach might stand excesses with less apparent actual mischief than those of his companions, he was likely enough to show the encroaches of the wine cup superficially much more than they would.

"What's the time?" cried somebody.

"Helloa!" cried the prince, "a fine, a fine!"

"Oh, I forgot it was against the rules to mention such a thing as the lapse of time here. I beg to be excused, gentlemen; I really sinned in the most inadvertant manner possible."

"Never mind that, you must drink a pint of claret off at a draught, and if you had used the word clock, or actually announced the hour, you would have had to take a quart."

"But I could not."

"That's nothing to do with it; you must have done it. Is he to have the pint, George?"

"To be sure; give it to him."

The unfortunate who had made himself answerable to the fine of drinking a pint of claret, was about the most intoxicated of the whole party; or probably he would not have been so forgetful of where he was as to subject himself to such a penalty; and now a pint goblet was procured, which was filled with claret and placed before him.

"Drink! drink!"

"Well, if I must, I must. Here goes."

"He is spilling it!" cried one, "he is spilling it!"

"Then give him a quart," said the prince, "and that will make up for the deficiency."

It was in vain that the culprit protested that he had been drinking the pint in the most *bona fide* manner. A quart goblet was filled and placed before him, and amid the uproarious shouts of the assemblage he began to drink it. There was then something like silence for a moment as he completed the draught, and took the goblet from his mouth. Then he let it fall, and it struck into a thousand fragments. He tried to speak, but he could not, and falling backwards, he lay upon the floor in a state of insensibility that looked almost like death.

One would have thought that this catastrophe would have excited some degree of interest, if not of alarm; but it did not do so. All that took place was a great shout for some one of the name of Stevens, and in answer to the call there came into the room a well dressed man. A glance showed him what had happened, and with a bow he retired again; but he had hardly been gone a moment when he came back with another, and between them they carried off the insensible form of the first who was prostrated by the spirit of the wine of that bacchanalian meeting.

Duval began to think of what it would be best to do, and he made up his mind now as soon as possible to secure what booty he could and then get away. He noticed that the prince had a superb watch set with diamonds and hanging by a rich chain of exquisitely-worked gold round his neck. Upon his fingers, too, shone several diamond rings; and Duval did not doubt but that the jewellery he had about him was worth some thousands.

There was certainly one difficulty attending those costly gems and works of art, and that was that if he, Duval, fully succeeded in getting possession of them, it would be no easy matter to find a purchaser for them; ; but that was a matter which he reserved for future consideration entirely. At present, he bent all his energies to the acquisition of the costly jewellery of the Prince of Wales.

When Duval made up his mind to a think of that kind, one may very well imagine that no ordinary difficulties would be allowed to stand in his way in the shape of prevention for long; but there was one thing that a little distracted him, and that he felt must be well arranged beforehand, and that was the getting away quickly with his horse, which he would not have left behind for all the jewels that glittered upon the fingers of the Prince of Wales, and his watch into the bargain.

CHAPTER LXXXVII.

DUVAL ASTONISHES THE PRINCE, AND LEAVES KEW PALACE.

AFTER some thought, Duval was convinced that the best thing he could possibly do was to get out of the room quietly without observation, and make some inquiries about his steed.

It so happened that this could be done easier no v than before, for the prince had began to amuse his royal mind by throwing glasses of wine at the wax candles in the chandelier; so that not only were his guests sprinkled with the wine and little bits of half melted wax, but the lights were, many of them, put out, and the room looked nothing like so bright and so brilliant as it had.

Duval rose while the prince was blundering through some foolish anecdote; and stooping, so that his head did not reach much above the level of the heads of those who sat along the side of the table, he reached the door unnoticed; and opening it suddenly, he ran violently against the person named Stephens who had been called to carry away the gentleman who had been forced to take the undue quantity of claret.

"I beg your pardon, sir," said Stephens. "I really beg your pardon most humbly, sir."

"It's of no consequence," said Duval. "I shall want my horse at a minute's notice, that's all, as I have to ride to town for the prince. How can I get it?"

"I will take care of that, sir, if you will do me the honour of telling me your name, sir."

"They will know me at the gate, as the gentleman who arrived with Lord Austincourt and Colonel Lane."

"That is quite sufficient, sir. Any time that you think proper to leave, if you will go to the gate, the horse will be there waiting for you, sir, in charge of one of the grooms."

"Thank you—that will do."

Duval at once rushed to the banqueting-room ; but he found that some change had taken place in the feature of affairs, even in the few minutes he had been absent.

One or two of the guests had left their seats ; and although not bad enough to be taken out of the place by Stephens and his comrade, yet had thrown themselves upon a couch or two at the farther end of the room, in the hope of recovering their faculties a little, which had begun to be bewildered by the wine, and perhaps more still by the noise and riot.

There was a vacant place next to the prince.

Duval glanced round him and saw that the place he had occupied before was filled up by some one in the course of the changes that had taken place. He at once sat down on the chair by the prince.

This was a cool thing enough of Duval to do, considering that the prince knew nothing of him ; but he relied upon the quantity of wine that the heir-apparent had drank to make him not over particular, provided he had a good companion next to him, as to who it was. Master George was speaking at the moment, so he did not notice who sat down by him.

"Hilloa !" said the prince, when he happened to look in the direction of Duval. "Hilloa !"

"Exactly," said Duval. "That's just my opinion."

"The devil it is !"

"Yes, George. Do you see that light now at the corner of the chandelier ? I will hit it with this glass of claret, or else you may call me what you like—a highwayman, if you please. I will bet you what you like, too."

"Done !" said the prince. "I have been trying at that candle for the last half hour myself, and I do believe it has a charmed life, for I can't hit it. Let us try for a cool hundred who puts it out first."

"Done," said Duval. "You try first."

"Well, that's generous. Here goes."

The prince poised a glass of claret in his hand, and then let it fly at the light ; but the fact was, that, as he said, he was very much deceived as to the position of the wax candle, and the only effect of the shower of wine he sent at it was to sprinkle his guests well who happened to be near; but that was highly amusing to royalty, and he laughed outrageously.

Duval now raised his glass, and a voice—it was that of Lord Austincourt—cried out—

"Bravo, baron !"

"Oh, he's a baron, is he ?" muttered the prince. "D—n the fellow, I don't know him."

Slash ! went Duval's glass of wine, and the candle was at once extintinguished.

"Bravo ! bravo !" cried everybody ; and there was a great banging upon the table. "That was well done. By Jove, it is getting rather dark, though. Go it. Have them all out. Ha ! ha ! Bravo, baron !"

These and such like cries resounded through the room ; and the prince, turning to his neighbour on the other side, said, in a tipsy tone—

"Lend us a hundred pound note."

"Haven't one farthing to bless myself with," was the cool reply, with a shrug.

"By Jove, you must trust me, baron."

"Don't mention it," said Duval. "The pleasure of seeing you happy, and free from troublesome thraldoms, if it be only for one hour, is so great a pleasure to me, that I can think of nothing else."

"A devilish gentlemanly, sensible fellow, that," muttered the prince to himself.

Duval had the diamond-mounted watch of the Prince of Wales now safely in his own pocket. At the moment that the prince had thrown his glass of wine at the candle, and when all eyes were fixed upon the flame, Duval had quietly and dexterously possessed himself of the watch, and at once transferred it to his own pocket.

"Well, you lost that cool hundred, George," cried one, from the lower end of the table.

"Yes, stupid," said the prince.

By mere accident the tone of the prince was such an exact imitation of that of the person who had made the rather foolish remark, that the roar of laughter that followed was perfectly prodigious; and the prince was highly delighted, for he fancied he had, at all events, for once in his life, said a very good thing, indeed. He smiled with gratification; and when the person who had refused to lend him the hundred pounds to pay Duval said suddenly—"I'll stake you another hundred, George, you don't hit that other corner chandelier," he took up a glass of wine, and jerking it slap into the speaker's face, he cried—

"I have won, by Jove!"

It was really amusing now to see the cool gravity with which the person whose face was streaming with wine, took this insult. He did not wince at it in the least, or make the slightest spluttering, but filling his glass, he said, calmly—

"That was a royal joke. We will pass it round;" and then, on the moment he discharged his glass into the face of his next neighbour.

The prince almost shrieked with laughing, as every one now threw a glass of wine into his next neighbour's face; and it was done so rapidly, that Duval felt himself drenched by the glassful thrown at him by the person on his right-hand before he could rise to save himself from the infliction.

"Oh! Oh! you will kill me among you!" said the prince. "Oh, but this is good—I shall crack my sides! Oh, dear—Oh, dear, I never laughed so much."

Duval poured himself a full glass; and as he dashed it in the great round fat face of the prince, he said—

"Yes, it is a royal joke, and now it has passed round and gone home to roost at last."

It would be impossible to describe the effect produced by this bold act upon the part of Duval. The prince sat, looking the picture of discomfiture, and several of the guests rose. Others were so tickled at the comic appearance of the prince's face, with the red wine trickling down it, that if their lives had depended upon their preserving their gravity, they must have roared outright with laughter.

Duval thought it was time to go, and he rose; but he would not hurry away for fear it should be thought that he was flying from dread of the consequences of the act he had done, and done so boldly, too. He threw another glass of wine at another candle, and that left only five alight, so that the place was in a very dubious twilight, indeed.

"By the Lord, we shall be in the dark," said Austincourt, "if this sort of fun goes on!"

Duval left the room as Austincourt spoke, and he met Stevens in the ante-room.

"My horse," he said.

"Is at the gate, sir, as you ordered it to be."

"That will do; I shall be back in two hours if the prince should ask for me. He won't keep a very exact account of how the time goes now, I rather think?"

"Not very, sir."

Duval at once walked out into the garden. The sudden transition from the light of that room to the daylight on the outside was quite painful to the eyes, and made Duval wink again for a few moments. But that was but a very evanescent effect, and was gone almost as soon as it was noticed to appear.

Duval had taken the most special care as he made his way to the palace long with the Colonel and Lord Austincourt, to note the route through the grounds;

so that upon the spur of any moment, he might be able to make his way to the gate at which he had come in. That route led round some shrubberies, that in places were very thick and shady.

Duval heard a footstep.

"Some new guest," he said, "I presume. Ah, whom have we here?"

A well-dressed youth made his appearance coming on towards the palace.— Upon sight of Duval he paused; but in a moment seemed to recover his courage, and he advanced, and said—

"Is the prince in the room?"

The moment this youth spoke, Duval was convinced of what at first sight of him he had suspected—namely, that it was a young girl in male attire.

"Yes, my dear," replied Duval, "he is in the room."

"Ah, you know me?"

"Of course I do. You are one of the prettiest creatures it has been my lot to look for many a long day."

"Ah, then," laughed the girl, "you don't know me. I was afraid you re-cognised me; but your last words convince me that, although you have found that I have no right exactly to wear this apparel, you don't know who I am."

"You are right; but I can add something to that, which is, that I care not who you are, while I can see what you are."

A slight flush came over the beautiful face, for indeed it was beautiful, and in all the first freshness of girlish charms, and she said—

"How, sir—would you insult me? What mean you?"

"Simply that you are the fairest of the fair."

"Oh, that, indeed; and who are you, sir?"

"The Baron Hoge."

"Well, that's not much information; but you will now, sir, do me a singular favour."

"Anything that is in my power."

"Very good. Get out of my way, and you go your path, while I go mine."

"How can you be so cruel?" said Claude, as he caught her suddenly in his arms, and before she had power to resist, kissed her lips some half dozen times. "Good-day," he then said, "we shall meet again, I feel assured. How long will you remain here, beautiful being?"

"You are most insolent, sir, and I am truly surprised at you. How dare you kiss me in this way? I dare you, sir, let you be whom you may, to call at No. 10, Clarges Street, and ask for Marianna de Courcy."

"Thank you; of course I shall not think of calling, and so once more, adieu!"

The rather questionable young lady smiled and passed on, while Duval made his way towards the garden gate of the royal domain.

As he proceeded on he reasoned with himself.

"This carouse in the old palace will last the remaider of the day and all the night likewise, or I am very much mistaken. I should like to come back to it when the shadows of the evening are on the wane into night. Ah, and I will, too!"

He reached the gate, and there, sure enough, his horse was waiting for him. He mounted, and then beckoning to the man at the gate, he said to him :—

"Look at me well, my friend, so that you may know me when I return, for I can't find De Lohm to get my ticket back from him again, and the prince will be furious if I don't come back soon."

"Oh, sir, we shall know you; it will be all right, be assured of that, sir."

CHAPTER LXXXVIII.

DUVAL RETURNS AT NIGHT TO THE ROYAL CAROUSE.

The object of Duval was to ride home to Hornsey for the purpose of calming any fears that May might have at his long protracted absence, which neither he nor she had at all expected.

CLAUDE DINES WITH PRINCE GEORGE AT KEW PALACE.

Knowing, however, as she had known, that he had gone upon an expedition that might possibly be attended with some risk, he felt particularly anxious to assure her of his safety as well as to prepare her for a more continued absence in case he should persevere in his intention of returning to the fete of the Prince of Wales at Kew.

That he did intend to return was pretty evident.   The royal carouse at the old palace in Kew gardens had too many temptations for one like Duval to resist it. He felt that while even he could not help despising the royal entertainer, that there was yet much in the entertainment to enchain the imagination, and to take the fancy prisoner.

"Yes," he said, as he pursued his way at a rapid pace.   "Oh yes, I will return there, and see what may yet be done ; I have a shrewd suspicion that as the night comes, what is now wild riot will very materially alter its character, and we shall have some rich and rare scenes, which it will be well worth my time and attention to study.   Yes, I am decided : I will go back."

It was still daylight when Duval reached Hornsey ; but Luke was on the watch for him, and at once opened the garden gate for him to ride in, so that he should not be exposed to the curious gaze of their neighbours. It was so rare a chance for Duval to reach his home at such an hour as that, that there was more positive danger of observation in the few moments that it took him to pass from the road into it than in half a dozen of his usual exits or entrances from his pretty rural abode.

"All right, Luke ?"

"Yes sir, everything is as quiet as possible, sir."

As he spoke, Luke glanced about him rather nervously.

"Why, what's the matter with you, man ?"

"I don't know, sir, but the fact is, I have been a little nervous all day ; and I can't get that man out of my head that lies over there, sir, in the shade of the old trees."

Luke indicated the grave of the officer in the corner of the grounds, and Duval could not but see that his imagination was quite real, and that he was in a state of fear that he found it difficult to repress.

"Why, Luke," he said, in an encouraging tone, "I should hardly have expected this of you, do you know."

"No, sir, nor I ; and if you were always at home I dare say the case would be very different ; but as you are not, you see, sir, it alters it very much ; and I get brooding on things that it would be quite as well not to think of if one could possibly help."

"Oh, well, Luke, you must not mind all that ; you will shake it off in a little time, man ; and if you feel dull in the old house, why you might come out for a ride with me now and then."

"Ah, sir, I should like that very much."

"You shall, then ; I am going out to-night, but it is not on the road, Luke, or you should go with me ; it is on a special invitation to supper, where I cannot introduce any one, I fear ; but I will think of it within the next hour or so. How is your mistress, Luke ?"

"She is quite well, sir, I believe."

At this instant May made her appearance to answer for herself ; and the radiant look of joy that spread itself over her face at the appearance of Duval, was a sufficient answer in the affirmative as to her being quite well.

"How good of you," she said, as she accompanied him into the house, with her arm linked in his. "How good of you to come home so soon this evening. I feared you had been attracted by the spell of some wild adventure, and had gone off to carry it out, and that I might not see you for many a long hour."

"I have, May, been attracted by the spell of an adventure, and it is but to tell you that I may not return for the whole of the night, that I have ridden some miles even now."

"And you are going again ?"

"I must."

"Ah, Duval, you do not love your home."

"In good truth, if I do not love the home, I love the fair and gentle spirit that gives to it all its beauty, May ; so we will just take a little refreshment, and then I must be off ; and as I eat, I will tell you where I am going'"

It was not commonly the case that Duval told May of any of his adventures ;

but upon this occasion he could not help thinking that a slight description of the prince's doings at the Royal Palace at Kew would be amusing to her; besides, it would have the effect of setting her mind at ease as to where he was going, and, at all events, of convincing her that it was not upon some expedition of great danger.

"How strange," she said, "that one who might be so great, prefers to be so little! How can he find enjoyment in such vulgar luxuries?"

"May, we all act up to our perceptions and capacities. The notions of George, Prince of Wales, are no higher than those of vulgar sensual enjoyment; and so, having large means of seeking such enjoyment, he follows the bent of his inclination."

"It must be so. But you will be very careful, Duval, not to excite a suspicion of who you really are?"

"Believe me, May, that I will be so careful. I do not think that there is the slightest chance of detection, as long as I keep my head clear; and that, I think, I can do, notwithstanding all the rich temptations to the contrary. So now, as the shadows are each moment deepening, I feel inclined to be off again."

"Must you, really?"

"I much wish it, May."

"Ah; then, I will not oppose you. Go, Duval, and may Heaven protect you, for my sake. I know that you have not a bad heart, Claude Duval, and so, although—although——"

"Although what, May? Nay, speak freely to me."

"I was only going to say that, although all the world would condemn your course of life, that I still thought you deserving of some of Heaven's care. You deceive no one. I do not believe that you ever left any poor heart to break through trusting you."

Duval shook a little. A recollection of Adele came vividly to his mind at the moment, and he could not make any reply to May for a few moments. When he did speak, all he said was—

"Come—come, you are getting quite tearful and sentimental, May. You must not send me away in such a mood as this. Let me see you smile before I go."

"I will smile when you come back, Duval. That will be the better compliment of the two, will it not?"

"Well, perhaps it will, May; and now, for another thing, I am thinking that it will be very much conducive to my safety in this little affair, if I took Luke with me to put up my horse somewhere, so that I should not be dependant upon the palace servants to get him for me at any sudden moment."

"Oh, yes—yes."

"You will not mind, then, for a few hours, being left in the house by yourself, May? I will get back as soon as possible."

"Oh, no—no! When the question concerns your safety, Duval, all others give place to it at once."

"You are too good to me."

"That is impossible. Take Luke with you, and I will shut myself up in our chamber, and not stir from it until I hear your voice. Go now—go at once, Duval, for perhaps then you will be the sooner back to me. The hours will seem very long, indeed, until I see you again. You will think of that?"

"In good truth I will, May; and, perhaps, I shall get home again much sooner than I at present think."

"Ah, now, you shall go at once, Duval, that you are in such a kind, good mind. I pray you to go."

Upon this, Duval went to Luke, and told him that he would take him with him; but Luke, after the first feeling of pleasure at getting out a little from the house, looked rather serious, as he said—

"Ah, sir, you are going to take me out from kindness to me; but your good, kind lady will then be all alone, and she will feel very solitary, indeed, in the house, and every slight noise will fill her full of fears when she knows that there if no one on the premises that will protect her at all."

"Don't think of that, Luke. I have arranged it all with her; so get the horses ready, and let us be off at once."

In another ten minutes they were both on the road; but Luke was mounted upon a nice hackney that Duval had empowered him to buy in Hornsey, hoping that it would come in usefully for May, when the days were fine and serene enough for her to take a canter in the neighbourhood.

As they rode along, Duval told Luke all about the adventure at Kew Gardens; for in case of anything going wrong, Luke would be much more likely to be of efficient a sistance to him by knowing the whole of the circumstances, than as if he were in ignorance of the most important of them; besides, Duval felt certain that he might safely depend upon his discretion, as well as upon his courage.

"What I want you to do, Luke," he said, "is to put up with the horses some-where as near the gate of the palace garden as you can find a place of entertain-ment; and thus, if I am forced to leave in a hurry, which may be just possible, I can come to you direct, and mount and be off. After about four or five o'clock in the morning, I should like you to keep the horses saddled for any emergency."

"I will, sir. It will be much the safest plan."

"Very good, then, we will push on, Luke, for now we perfectly understand each other upon this point."

With this, they put their steeds to a steady canter, by which they got over the ground in capital style; and in a much less space of time than we would have thought it possible to go such a distance across the country as from Hornsey to Kew, the deep shadows of the old trees in the Royal Gardens came upon their sight.

"Here we are, Luke," said Duval.

"So soon, sir?"

"Why, yes, I confess that we have done it rather well, considering the real distance that it is; but here we are, to all intents and purposes, Luke; and now the only thing is to find out where to put up the cattle. A little place will be the best, as they are not so likely to be importunate about your saddling the horses early in the morning."

"Very good, sir. I think I see a swinging sign a little further on. Look, sir, is there not something of the sort?",

"I think so, too; but it seems to be a waif, or a stray upon the road-side, for there is certainly no house near it."

"Let us go and see, sir."

They rode up to the swinging sign, which was creaking to and fro, making a melancholy monotonous tune of its own, as a light wind, that had got up since the sun had set, took hold of it, and made a little sport with it.

"There is a direction on it," said Luke. "Are your eyes very sharp, sir? Mine won't read it."

"I will try, Luke."

Duval raised himself in his saddle so as to get very near to the sign, and im-mediately beneath he found a wooden hand, with a preternaturally long finger pointing down a lane, and on it was written "The way to the White Lion."

"All's right," said Duval. "That is the way to the White Lion, so at the White Lion we will leave our steeds. It is not two minutes' walk, or one minute's run, from the gate of the Palace Garden."

Duval did not intend to go to the White Lion; but he rode sufficiently down the lane to look at the situation of the house, so as to be sure to know it again; and then he dismounted, and gave his horse to the care of Luke, saying—

"Don't expect me till you see me; but I think I shall not wait until sunrise. However, I must be guided by circumstances, so that, perhaps, I ought not even to say that much; so now good evening, Luke. Have you money?"

"Oh yes, sir."

"Very good. Never omit to ask me for whatever you want in that way, as my exchequer is easily filled again if it does sometimes get a little empty."

"Oh, sir, you are very good, but I want for nothing with you."

Duval turned out of the lane again, and on foot made his way to the gate of the royal gardens. He had in his mind some slight misgivings about whether he should be let in again or not, but he advanced boldly, and seeing a sentinel, he cried—

"Open the gate!—open the gate!"

"Sir, I—I—

"It's all right, Jack," said another, coming up at that moment. "I recollect this gentleman."

The gate was opened, and Duval taking a coup'e of guineas from his waistcoat pocket, gave one to each of the sentinels, who bowed to the very ground upon receiving so unexpected a gratuity.

"I'd give more than this by a good deal," said Duval to himself, "as the price of my admission to this place."

"Now, Jack," said one of the sentinels to the other, "that's what I call a real out-and-out gentleman."

"I believe you," said the other. "Mind you, I don't mean to say what we shall get as the company goes away, but I always think a good deal of the first guinea."

"So do I."

"Do you know who he is?"

"Not I; but he's somebody, I can tell you, for I heard say as the prince was a little within bounds when he was a looking at him. We shall find out before the night's over I dare say, no doubt. The fun hasn't half begun yet.

"No, but it will soon."

"I believe you my boy! Mother Lee is come, and brought some of the young ones with her, I take it."

"Not a doubt of that. All those young gentlemen as come in with a special order was *gals*."

"I knowed it, I knowed it! Ah me! there is goings-on here that would make some folks open their eyes a bit, I rather think. But we makes a good thing of it; so the least we say is the best, I take it; and all's right is the *mottor*."

While this delectable little bit of discourse was going on at the gate of the palace garden, Duval, with as good a resolution as he could suddenly bring to bear upon the matter, was making his way through the rather intricate garden-paths to the palace.

The night had quite dropped upon all things by this time, and the garden bore such a very different and mysterious aspect in the deep shadows, that he might well, as he did, pause more than once to ask himself if he could possibly be right in the course that he was taking.

After he had thus stopped for the third time, he found no difficulty in pursuing his way, for a loud ringing peal of laughter from one particular direction warned him that there was the palace, or, if not, that he should quickly enough fall in with some of the madly-joyous guests of the Prince of Wales.

"Ah!" he said, "that is the direction; I shall have no longer any difficulty in finding my way now."

He took, as nearly as he could now guess, the route that would bring him to the spot where the sounds were made, but he found that some plants in a large flower-bed obstructed him. Duval was not very particular, so he strode through the flower-bed at once, heedless of the mischief that he was doing; and then he heard some one say in a low voice—

"Who are you, pray? Answer at once!"

The voice was decidedly a feminine one.

"Oh," said Duval, "I am your very humble servant."

"Go away directly."

"How very cruel it is to say, go away directly," said Duval, as darting forward he caught by the arm a figure that he could only just contrive to catch a faint glimpse of in the dim light among the old trees.

There was some sort of summer-house upon the spot, and the figure by a sudden wrench got out of his grasp and rushed into it.

"That was well done," said Claude; "but I am after you, for all that, my fair one, for a fair one you are, or you would not be here, I feel quite assured. Why need you be so very particular?"

He tried the summer-house door, but it was fast shut. He tapped gently enough at it, but that produced no effect.

"My dear," said Duval, "I have made up my mind to speak to you, and to have a look at your face as well as I can see it by the light; and I shall be under the disagreeable necessity of breaking down the door, if you don't open it."

"Begone!" said the voice from within the summer-house.

Duval laughed, as placing his shoulder against the little frail door, he at once forced it off its hinges. The moment that he did so, there was a sharp crack, and a small pistol-bullet came with a dash through one of the panels of the door, escaping Duval only by a hair's breadth.

"Take the reward of your folly!" said the voice. "You have brought this upon yourself, and it but serves you right."

CHAPTER LXXXIX.

THE ADVENTURES AT KEW HAVE ALL THE CHARM OF ROMANCE.

DUVAL was on the point of saying something, but he checked himself; and willing to have some sport with the young lady who could be bold enough to carry fire-arms about with her, and use them upon so small an amount of provocation, he thought that if he affected to be hit by the bullet, he should probably have a chance of seeing her more readily.

Full of this idea, he uttered a low groan, and then was profoundly still.

"I have killed him," said the voice again, and immediately from the little summer-house came the figure. "I have killed him. I am sorry—more than sorry that it is so; but I have killed him. Where are you? Why don't you speak, unhappy man? If you have breath to do so, tell me where you are."

"I am here," said Duval, faintly.

"Where?—where? Oh, I can see you faintly now. Why did you persevere so madly, and bring such a fate upon yourself? Are you very badly hurt?"

"Not that I know of," said Duval, in a sprightly manner, and suddenly seizing the figure in his arms. "Now, tell me who you are, or you won't get away from me again so cleverly as you did before. I forgive you the pistol shot, with all my heart; but I am sure that you are beautiful. I can stand any fire but that from your displeasure."

"You are a singularly bold man."

"I always was."

"Are you a friend of the prince?"

"My being here ought to answer that question."

"Tell me who you are."

"The Baron Hoge."

"Very well. Now I ask of you a favour, and I make to you a promise at the same time that, if you grant it to me, I will truly keep."

"Name the favour, and without the promise, I will at once grant it. If you really wish to get rid of me at once, I will go; and I much regret that, in the impulse of the moment, I have intruded upon you so much as I have."

"Go, then. That is the favour. The promise is that you shall hear of me again. Does that satisfy you?"

"It does. Good-night."

In a moment Duval left the spot.

That this young lady—for that she was young, her voice was a sufficient testimony—was one of those damsels who had been brought to that place upon the occasion of the *fete*, he could not doubt; and yet there was a style and manner about her that created a feeling in the mind of Duval that there was some mystery connected with her. He did not expect to hear anything further of her, notwithstanding her promise; but he now made the best of his way towards the palace.

A loud ringing peal of laughter now broke upon the night air again, and so Duval was, as before, guided in the direction in which he had to go, and he suddenly came from out of a small trim path of the garden in front of the palace.

The blinds and shutters of the windows were so well arranged, that scarcely a ray of light got out into the night air to show what rooms were occupied and what were not; but yet there was a kind of halo of brightness about the building which led him to the belief that in many parts of it lights were burning.

Duval looked about anxiously for the little door at which he had before entered the banquet-hall, where the prince and his mad companions had held their carouse; but he was puzzled for a time between several doors, and hardly knew which to choose. At length, in impatience rather than in any certainty of being right, he pushed at one and found it yield to the pressure of his hand.

"This will do, and shall do," he said.

He hardly stepped within the door-way, when he heard the wild laughter of some of the half intoxicated guests; and guided by the sound, he went until he came to a large velvet curtain that impeded his progress. He drew it slightly aside, and found that it opened upon the same room that he had before sat in; but the company was rather altered.

Some strange faces were there that he had not seen upon the former occasion; and about a dozen ladies were present attired in the most extravagant style of fashion. The whole party were hand-in-hand in performing a wild kind of dance round the table in the middle of the room, to the dim light of only three or four of the wax candles that still remained in the chandelier that had suffered so much from the wine that had been from time to time cast at it.

Duval looked for the prince, and presently he saw him come round along with the tipsy dancers. He passed quite close to Duval, so that by merely stretching out his hand he could have touched him; but he let him pass.

The mad dance, which resembled some tipsy revelry, such as one sees in the old mythological pictures of the Italian Masters, continued; and the love of frolic came strongly on Claude Duval. When the prince got round to where he was again, Duval put out his foot, and the Prince at once tumbled over it, dragging with him the two ladies whom he had by the hands: The others who were following could not stop themselves, and the consequence was, that like a pack of cards that had been set up on end, the whole of the party were sprawling upon the floor.

The prince being the first to fall, had a tolerable weight to bear, and he roared out for help in such a comical voice of distress, that it was with difficulty that Duval kept himself from shouting with laughter. If he had done so, however, it would have exposed him to the suspicion of being the author of the trick, so he wisely kept silent as far as laughter was concerned, and stepping into the room, he sat down upon a sofa in a distant corner of it.

A table was close to him, upon which was some very elegantly got up confectionary, and while the disordered company was still floundering about upon the floor, Duval amused himself by throwing mince and raspberry tarts at the few lights that remained in the chandelier, by which process he succeeded in extinguishing them, and producing intense darkness in the saloon.

"Murder!" cried the prince, "Murder!"

"Lights!—lights!" shouted some twenty voices.

No one paid the slightest attention to their cries. Whether the attendants were not within hearing, or really thought it was only part of the fun, it is hard to say ; but certainly no one put in an appearance with a light, and Duval, in whom the spirit of mischief was now fairly awakened, crept to the side of the table, and by giving it a powerful lurch, at once scattered the whole of its contents on to the floor.

Suddenly a bell rung.

It would appear as if the servants had been waiting for this signal, for the door at once opened, and a stream of light came into the saloon at once.

" Lights—lights!" cried the prince, " I am half killed. Lights here, I say !"

Several branches, containing six or eight wax candles, were now brought into the saloon, and the scene of disorder that they made apparent astonished even those domestics, who were not astonished at mere trifles during their time of service with the heir-apparent.

Amid the wreck of the contents of the table lay one-half at least of the guests still upon the floor of the room. The wine was running about in perfect streams hither and thither ; and some of the ladies, who had looked so very elegant only a short quarter of an hour before, were in the most woeful plight indeed, with their dresses torn and soaked in different coloured wines, that had rolled over them from the table.

The prince sat in the midst of the wreck, looking the very picture of distress and dismay. His eyes were goggling out of their orbits, and his cheeks seemed swelled out to more than their usual dimensions, and Heaven knows that was needless.

" Murder ! murder !" was the only word he kept at intervals, as he could collect just sufficient breath to do so, gasping out.

Duval thought it would be prudent to keep as much as he could out of the way, so he assumed a horizontal position upon the couch, and drawing one of the pillows, with which it was richly and plentifully furnished, partially over his face, he watched the uproar.

As the lights enabled them to see what they were about, some of the guests began slowly to gather themselves to their feet and look about them with dismayed aspects. They then lifted the prince to his legs.

" Oh, dear," he said. " Oh, oh, what's it all about ? Murder! I didn't tell anybody to do all this. How dared anybody ? Oh, let me sit down. I am half dead, I declare. I am—I am a dying man."

They helped him to a seat, upon which he sat with many groans, and the ridiculous appearance he cut with his face and head all streaming with wine, was enough to have provoked laughter in any one but a court parasite.

The ladies wept plentifully over their disordered finery, and such a scene of ludicrous woe was never before exhibited in that place. It was with difficulty Duval kept from roaring again with laughter, but by dint of cramming a corner of the pillow of the couch into his mouth, he did manage to keep quiet.

" You fell down, my dear George," said a young lady.

" Go to the deuce," said the prince.

The young lady wiped her eyes, and retired rather a little discomfited at the failure of her attempt to pour consolation into the royal ear ; and then, after looking rather wildly about him for a few moments, the prince said—

" Where's Lane ?"

" Here," said Colonel Lane. " I hope your highness is not hurt ?"

" Well, Lane, I hardly know ; but how did it all happen ? that was what puzzle l me."

" It is easily enough explained, your highness. Somebody fell, and then we all fell upon him."

" Good gracious, that somebody was me, for I felt as if the whole palace lay upon me, and that my inside was crushed quite flat, and that I never should breathe again. Oh, my poor stomach. It's dreadful to think of what a crush I have had to be sure."

" Never mind, your highness ! A good glass of Claret will set you all to rights again.   The only mysterious thing is, to me, how the table got upset in the midst of it all."

"But it ain't upset," said another.

"And yet every bottle and every glass that was upon it is now upon the floor. How is that to be accounted for?"

THE PRINCE IN THE YELLOW ROOM AT THE PALACE.

"Let's go into the Yellow-room," said the prince.   "Oh, dear, I feel a little better.   Let's go into the Yellow-room.   We shall do very well there, and we intended to go there, you know, soon."

"Oh, yes—yes," said all the ladies.

The prince was getting better, although when he rose from the chair upon which he had been seated, he staggered a little.   The wine that Colonel Lane had persuaded him to drink had warmed his blood a little, and as he had in reality received no very serious injury, he was rapidly getting the better of his fall and his fright.

"Oh, George," said one of the ladies, "only look at me ; I am ruined, I assure you."

"My dear, I don't doubt it."

A very little joke goes a long way when it comes from the lips of a prince, so everybody shouted at this, and Duval having adroitly risen from the couch and joined the throng, said to the colonel—

"I am afraid there is some one amongst us bent upon mischief to-night, colonel."

"Oh, baron, are you here? I missed you. I thought you had left us somehow rather early."

"No, I wish I had, for I am afraid I am cut in the arm with a bit of broken glass. I distinctly saw some one upset the table sufficiently to throw everything off it on to the floor. It was quite a cruel thing, I think, to do."

"Can you identify who did it?" said the colonel eagerly.

"Not I. And between you and me, colonel, I think it would not be the province of a gentleman to do so, even if I could."

"You are right, baron : I like your nice sense of honour in this affair. You are quite right. It would not be the thing, as we are all here amusing ourselves, although that was, in my opinion, decidedly carrying the joke too far."

"So I think."

"You know it might have been attended with serious consequences to many of us."

"Exactly so, and, as I tell you, I am hurt."

"Now—now !" said the prince. "Let us make our way to the Yellow-room, my friends. We have had, I do think, quite enough of this one, surely. Come along—Come along. This way. I begin to feel very much better again, really ; but it was past a joke for all that—par past a joke."

"It was, your highness," said Lord Austincourt ; "and I don't at all envy the feelings of the person who could perpetrate it."

"Nor I," said several.

"I only wish," said one of the ladies, "that I knew who had upset the table, I would pretty soon sicken him of any such proceedings for the future. Look at my beautiful cherry satin ! It is quite destroyed. Only look, George."

"Well—well, I'll give you another."

"Oh ! how very kind ! Now you are a duck."

"Oh, be off with you ! Do you want to smother me? Protect me, Lane, from these women ! Recollect who I am. It's high treason to smother the Prince of Wales ! But come along to the Yellow-room ; it is all ready lighted, I have no doubt ; and there we will have some rare fun ; and after that we will have a run through the palace, and make quite a jolly night of it. Oh, we will manage to enjoy ourselves in some way or other; for if you don't enjoy yourself, what's the use of your life, I should like to know, eh ? Come on—come on ; this is the way. Don't you look so serious, Celia. Take my arm, if you must—only do look a little pleasant."

These last words were addressed to the young lady who had been requested only a short time before, by the prince, to go to the deuce, and she gladly accepted the peace-offering in the shape of the prince's arm, to the Yellow-room.

That Yellow-room deserves a few words of description, at our hands, in this place.

This Yellow-room, then, was, in the first place, the largest in the whole palace. It was called the Yellow-room, because it was covered over all the walls with yellow drapery of the richest and most exquiste character.

The roof was very richly painted in some mythological subject, and the floor was covered with a Persian carpet with most brilliant yellow flowers upon it. Take that room for all in all, and it certainly was one of the most beautiful in the palace.

CHAPTER XC.

CLAUDE DUVAL HAS BUT A NARROW ESCAPE AFTER ALL.

DUVAL was rather too intent upon what the human occupants of the Yellow-room were about to pay a great deal of attention to its decorations, although, at first entering it, he was much struck, as no one could fail of being, with its light and beautiful character.

Around the walls of this room, there were elegant couches, covered in yellow satin; and in the centre of the apartment there was a rather long, narrow table, upon which was a collection of the rarest fruit that could be procured for money.

Wine was laid upon a buffet in a deep recess, over which hung a small chande- lier. The general lighting of the room was a whole galaxy of wax candles—there must have been forty at the very least in one chandelier that depended from the centre of the ceiling.

Duval noticed that that chandelier hung very high up, and that it seemed to be much, too much condensed for beauty; but he found out in the course of the evening that there was a meaning in that, although he had no means just then of finding it out, or even suspecting it.

"Now," said the prince, "all we have got to do is to make as merry as possible, and quite forget the mishaps of the other room. I don't feel any the worse, I assure you all, now; therefore, it is all right."

This was just the sort of selfish exposition of the prince's character that those who knew him well might expect from him in a moment of incaution. He did not feel any the worse—therefore it was all right. It mattered nothing at all what anybody else might chance to feel upon the occasion.

Several of the ladies began waltzing, with a freedom of gesture such as is not exactly found in private society; and the prince cried out—

"Bravo! Bravo! That is capital. Suppose we all have a dance now? It will be good fun."

"Take your partners, gentlemen," cried Colonel Lane, in rather a significant tone of voice.

It was evident that two or three of the ladies were contending with each other for the honour of the prince's attentions, and one said to him in a coaxing tone of voice—

"How well you look. Ah, if you were not a prince, I should love you very much, indeed. You have got the most charming colour, too, to-night that can be conceived."

"Have I, Louisa?"

"Perhaps," said another lady, as she dealt Louisa a box on the ears, that nearly felled her to the floor. "Perhaps you would like a little more colour, and if I mistake not that will go some way towards giving it to you."

For a moment or two Louisa was staggered and stunned by the blow; but quickly recovering, she snatched up a large pine-apple that was upon the table, and attacked her assailant with it with such vigour, that in a few moments she left nothing in her hand but the little bit of stalk, while the face of her foe was com- pletely covered with the smashed fragments of the pine-apple, and presented truly a most ludicrous spectacle to the whole room.

The prince was so highly amused and delighted at this little affair, that he was compelled to lie down upon one of the couches to have his laugh out. The enraged ladies were separated by some of the guests, and made to promise good behaviour upon pain of expulsion; and the prince chose some one else for his partner, so that they were both disappointed.

Claude Duval offered his arm to rather a pretty young girl, saying—

"Are you better engaged?"

"Oh, no," she said; and then looking at him, she added—"You are not one of the regular guests here."

" No; but I shall be."

" Very good."

She placed her arm within his without any further ceremony. Some one then clapped his hands together, and a wild kind of galop began right round the room, which was very exhilarating, and very easily kept up by all who were at all sober enough to keep the step. Duval was wondering what it would all lead to, when suddenly the prince called out—

" Now !"

In an instant, by some means from above, every light in the chandelier in the middle of the ceiling was extinguished ; and the small chandelier that was likewise over the buffet, shared the same fate.

An intense stillness reigned in the room, only broken by some very low, half-smothered laughs now and then.

" What is the meaning of all this ?" said Duval to his fair companion. " Is it any trick ?"

" Don't you know ?"

" No—on my faith I don't."

" You are cold-hearted."

" I am not generally accused of being so ; and you are, I do think, the first female lips from which I have ever heard such a remark. What do you mean by it ?"

At this moment, he felt the cheek of his fair companion touch his ; but before he could speculate upon the proceeding, she was violently torn away from him and in the darkness, although he struck out, he could not tell which way the person who had laid so insolent a hand upon her, had taken her.

" I only wish I had you by the throat, my friend," said the irritated Duval, " whoever you are."

A low, smothered laugh was the only response to this ; and he began to be afraid that whatever trick was going on, it was in some way specially levelled at him. A feeling of anger took possession of him, contingent upon such a supposition.

" I warn you all," he said, " I am not the safest person in the world to play practical jokes upon."

There was another laugh, and then a voice that sounded very like that of the prince, said—

" Who the deuce is that talking nonsense in the middle of the room, I wonder? Is it a methodist parson ?"

More subdued laughter followed this, and Duval got just a little more aggravated.

" If I am in the middle of the room," he thought, " I have some power of mischief close at hand."

He then carefully groped his way to the table, where the fruit was lying in such abundance, and soon placed his hands upon some rather large specimens of the rich and rare productions of Pomona. In all his movements, though, to find the fruit and the table, he took care not to lose his perception of the part of the room from which had come the voice, that sounded like that of the prince.

Taking up, then, a large pear in one hand, and an apple of rather gigantic proportions in another, he flung them in the direction of the voice. The apple did not seem to do any execution ; but the pear did, for a loud voice called out on he moment—

" Oh, the deuce—the deuce ! What the devil is that ? I'm smashed with something or another in my eye !"

There was something extremely ludicrous in the voice in which this was uttered, and no one could mistake that voice for any other than the Prince of Wales'.

Duval felt quite encouraged by the success of the pear, and hastened to follow up the attack in all directions. There was certainly no want of amunition on the long table in the centre of the room, and he flung with all the force he could, pineapples, pears, bunches of grapes, apples, oranges, and many other matters that came readily to hand.

The confusion that reigned in the room began really to be something terrific, and shouts and cries for lights resounded from all quarters, and then Duval, finding that the fruit was all gone, began to throw the dishes and plates, and the clatter they produced was something quite prodigious.

"I have him!" cried a voice, and at the same moment, Duval felt a hand laid upon him with a firm clutch. He did not wait for that clutch to tighten itself, but, by a violent jerk, he at once freed himself, and darted from that part of the room. A door was suddenly opened, through which there came a gleam of light. Duval sprung through the opening in an instant, upsetting a servant who was bringing in two wax lights. They were both extinguished, and the passage in which he found himself was in the most impenetrable darkness directly.

The servant, who had been thrown down, said not a word upon that account. The fact was that the servants were too much accustomed now and then to a little rough usage in the way of practical jokes, for which they always got well paid, in the long run, to say much about them.

Duval had no immediate intention of going back to the yellow-room, but he held out his arm before him as he went along the passage in which he now was, and moved slowly, for fear of a fall down any staircase that, for all he knew to the contrary, might be close at hand. Suddenly a low voice, in sickly sycophantic accents, said—

"Is it your royal highness?"

Duval was an excellent mimic, and he replied in so capital an imitation of the somewhat plethoric voice of the Prince of Wales, that his closest intimates might have been deceived by the tone in which he spoke.

"Yes—yes. It is I. There's a row in the yellow-room."

"Will your highness put on a cloak? It is not very cold out, but it would be a sad thing for your highness to take cold."

"Thank you. Give it me."

"I will get a light if your highness pleases?"

"No—no. Better without. I am feeling for the cloak. You can easily hand it to me. This way."

Duval kept his hands out before him, and in a moment or two he grasped a cloak, which he put on, and then the same voice said—

"If your highness will come straight on, I will lead your highness to the summer pavilion, where the young lady is waiting for you. She is very beautiful, indeed."

"Do you know her?" said Duval.

"Oh, dear, no, your highness. I have been very careful, indeed. She is about sixteen years of age at the outside, your highness, and you may take my word for it, that it is a real affair. Of course, there are too many who would be glad, by any trick, to try to get an interview with your highness; but I trust I have been always found equal to the task of keeping them at arm's length?"

"Yes—yes, you have. Go on—go on.'

Duval kept up the imitation of the voice of the Prince of Wales so capitally, that this man, who was a kind of valet or confidential messenger to the prince, did not suspect, for a moment, but that it was his royal master whom he was conversing with.

Having no longer any fear of a fall down any steps, Duval went quickly on, and his guide opening a door, in the course of a few moments, slipped out into the garden. Duval followed him, but he took good care to keep the cloak so much shrouded round him, that it would be very difficult to detect that he was not the prince. Besides, the man who led the way was so prepossessed with the idea that it was his master that followed him, that he did not look for any little discrepancies in height or in person, that might have caused a doubt in his mind. When we are convinced of anything, or fancy that we are so, the very senses themselves will aid in the perpetuation of the common delusion.

It was quite a relief to Duval to get out into the open air. The night was so calm and still now, that not a leaf stirred upon a tree, and a holy and beautiful repose seemed to be upon the whole face of nature. Duval could just see the dim figure of his guide, as he went rather rapidly on before him down one of the garden paths, and he followed him at what speed he could command.

Once or twice the man turned, and upon those occasions he would make a low bow, saying—

"It is not far, your royal highness ; the little pavilion is close at hand."

"That will do," said Duval.

Suddenly the man paused, and allowed Duval to get quite up to him, and then he said, in a low tone—

"It is here, your highness, and I can assure you that she is a lovely girl, indeed. She has the most beautiful blue eyes that your highness can conceive, and the most lovely raven hair floating down her shoulders in the very greatest luxuriance. Her mouth, too, is the most perfectly beautiful that ever I saw. Believe me, your highness, I would not have troubled you about her, had she not been what I may call perfection itself."

"Humph !" said Duval.

"If I might say only one word against her, your royal highness, I might possibly say that—that——"

"That what ?"

"That knowing your royal highness' exquisite and admirable taste, she is—is not just——"

"Why do you pause ? Go on. What the devil do you mean by all that stammering and stuttering ?"

"I humbly beg your royal highness' pardon. I was merely going to take the liberty of observing that the young lady, perhaps, was not quite fat enough."

"Oh !"

"I sincerely beg your royal highness' pardon, for taking the great liberty to mention such a thing. The young lady has been rather particular, and would not come unless I gave her a key of the little door in the garden wall, and she likewise has the key of the pavilion ; so that she can go where she likes, and keep out all intruders until your royal highness came."

"Very good. Tell her I am here."

"I will, your highness. No doubt she will consider herself to be very highly honoured, indeed, your royal highness. I will take the liberty of announcing your royal presence."

CHAPTER XCI.

DUVAL SUCCESSFULLY PERSONATES THE PRINCE IN THE PAVILION.

DUVAL was so thoroughly disgusted with the tone and manner of this man that it would have given him the greatest possible pleasure to kick him from out of his path ; but he felt that he should very much like to speak to the young girl, who could be so weak and so infatuated as to come to that place, in such a manner for an interview with really the most contemptible of all the debauchees who made rude riot in the palace.

With this feeling, then, Duval controlled his great inclinations to take summary vengeance upon the valet, and allowed him to have his own way in the affair.

"You will wait within call," said Duval.

"I will, your highness. Here is the pavilion. A-hem !" The valet tapped at the door of a little fanciful building that they had now reached, and which was quite surounded by rare plants and flowering shrubs—"A-hem ! The prince is here."

"Are you sure ?" said a female voice.

"Yes, my dear. Quite sure. It is the prince."

"Let him come in, then. The door of the pavilion is open. Can you get a light? It is very dark."

"Oh, yes. I have some phosphorus matches."

"Give them to me."

Duval stepped into the little pavilion, and the door was immediately closed. He heard the sound as of some one sobbing, and then a voice of great sweetness, said—

"Oh, sister, why did you not let me go?"

"Be quiet, Alice," said another voice.

"What!" said Duval; "are there two of you?"

"Wretch!" said the voice that had spoken second. "Wretch—Monster in human shape! Do you not know me now?"

"I certainly have not that honour."

"Not that honour? True, it is an honour; but you have no honour, wretch. Do you not know that you married me?—that you pretended, although your rank would prevent you from acknowledging me in public as your wife, that you would always do so in private, and that you would be faithful to me, and to me only?"

"But, my dear," said Duval, "when and where did I wrong you? You must be under some mistake."

"No, wretch!—no—no—no!"

"But I say, yes—yes—yes."

"The only mistake I ever made, or dreamt of making, was in trusting to your honour. Then, I own, I did mistake; but you know as well as I do, that we were duly married by the profligate parson, that you think so clever a reprobate, named Evans. You know that that was now nearly two years ago."

"Two years!"

"Yes, two years. Oh, it is a very convenient thing to affect to recollect nothing, you base man—you worse than base—you utter shameless profligate."

"But how can it be two years ago? Why my man says that you are not above sixteen, and he doubts if you are that."

"Do not—oh, do not add insult to injury by pretending not to know who it is that speaks to you. True it is, that in order to get admittance to this place and to secure an interview with you, I got my younger sister, Alice, to pretend to wish to see you, and so your man-of-all-work, your Mr. Jenkins, was deceived, and I came with her."

"Oh that's it, is it?"

"Yes, that is it; and I ask you now, prince though you are, what reparation you can make to me for the injuries that you have done me? You cannot pretend not to know me."

"It was very kind of you to bring Alice here; I am told that she is young and pretty, and I am master here. Perhaps Alice may find some little difficulty in getting away again."

"Oh, no—no," cried the other voice. "Oh, have mercy upon me, and let me go at once—Eliza, I told you how I shrank from coming here, but you would make me. Let me go at once or I will kill myself."

Here the younger girl burst into such a passion of hysterical weeping, that Duval could not think of keeping up the delusion regarding his identity any longer, but spoke in grave accents, saying—

"Listen to me:—I am not the prince, but I am one who, having by accident become acquainted with your position here, will befriend you; and you may well believe me when I tell you that upon such a night as this, in such a place as this, you will need a protector."

"Not the prince?"

"No; does not my voice, now that I no longer take the trouble to mimic his tones, assure you that I am not the prince?"

"Oh, yes—yes. I am lost—lost!"

"And I am saved," said Alice.

"You are," said Duval. "Dry your tears, Alice. I pledge you my word of honour that pure as you came to this place, where dissipation and infamy stalks abroad without disguise, pure you shall depart. I will stand between you and all harm, and woe be to him who will be so bold as to make the attempt to pass me."

"Oh, sir. How can I thank you?"

"Don't thank me at all. Get a light, if there is the means of doing so in this place."

"Sister, sister," said Alice, "you can get a light."

The sister obeyed without a word, and a light was soon procured, with which she made her way close to Duval, and holding it up, she looked keenly in his face.

"Well," he said, "are you satisfied?"

"I am, I am. You are not the prince."

With these words, the sister placed the light upon a table in the little pavilion and sitting down upon the chair that was nearest to her, she began swaying to and fro and wringing her hands, and sobbing so as to present a picture of the greatest grief. This poor victim of the prince was a very handsome girl; but it was the sister, Alice, that attracted the attention of Duval; and as he looked at her, he felt, indeed, that the encomiums of the valet were very far from being, overrated.

He felt that he had never seen such blue eyes as Alice's, and such an exquisitely-shaped face, so full of gentle, girlish beauty, before; and he was right enough, for she was fascination itself.

"Listen to me, both of you," said Duval. "Will you attend to me?"

"Yes, sir—Oh, yes," said Alice.

"Will you?" he added, turning to the sister.

She made an impatient gesture, saying then, with a sudden feeling of anger—

"I will see him—I am determined to see him. I have come here with an object and I will carry it out."

"Be it so. If such is your determination, I will help you to see him; but it will only be upon one condition."

"What condition?"

"That you will let Alice at once leave this place. It is not a fit one for her, and no one ought to know that better than you. If you will wait here while I see that she is off these premises and in perfect safety, I will return to you, and I give you my word of honour that I will bring the prince to you."

"I consent. Go, Alice—go."

"She should never have come," said Duval. "Any way to get the chance of an interview with the prince, would have been better than bringing her to this den of infamy. Come, Alice, I will take you out of the gardens at once. Come— trust to me."

"I will, sir," said Alice, as she timidly placed her arm within that of Duval's. "I will trust to you."

The sister, who, no doubt, had been the victim of a mock marriage with the Prince of Wales, leant her head upon her hands, and took no further notice of Duval nor Alice. It was quite evident that her own injuries so completely filled up her mind, that she was rather dead to those of others, or to the danger that her fair young sister might incur by coming upon such an expedition to the Royal Palace and Gardens of Kew. This kind of half indiffence to her sister's welfare, did not speak well for her in the estimation of Duval, and he rather thought but little of her in comparison to what he might have done, had she exhibited a different feeling.

Duval, though, ought to have made more allowance for the great change that injuries of a serious character make in the feelings.

Alice clung to him with an evident feeling of safety in his presence; and looking up in his face, she said—

"Indeed, sir, I did not wish to come here, and I came with fear and trembling; but my sister would have it."

"Never mind it now," said Claude, " you will be perfectly safe. Do not say a word, let what may happen, but leave all to be settled by me. Alice, I promise to keep you safe, and to see you out of the garden."

With the young girl hanging upon his arm, Duval now left the pavilion, and he took care to take the very opposite direction to that in which he believed the valet

THE QUARREL BETWEEN THE TWO YOUNG LADIES IN THE YELLOW-ROOM.

to be waiting his orders, under the impression that he was the Prince of Wales. The great object of Duval was to get to the gates, and take Alice fairly out. After proceeding a little way, he said to her—

"Have you far to go to get to your home?"

"Oh, no—no. We live very close at hand, and we have no father. Alas! alas! what will become of my poor sister?"

" Her fate is a sad one, Alice, but it behoves you to look to yourself, and to take her situation as a warning. It was a very ill-advised step, the bringing you to the palace."

" Yes—yes, I felt that it was, but my sister would fancy that if she saw the prince, she would be able to work upon his feelings, and induce him to do something for her, as our mother is very poor."

" The prince will do nothing but what his own most selfish nature dictates; but as I have promised your sister that I will get her an interview with the prince, I will do so. Here we are at the gate of the gardens. Shall you know your way when you are on the outside of this place ?"

" Oh, yes—yes. Quite well."

" You are then saved from the consequences of coming here; but you must consider that it is only owing to a fortunate incident that you are so. Good-night, Alice."

She placed her hand within that of Duval's, and thanked him with so much eloquent sincerity, that he was much affected by it, and could reply nothing to her. Indeed, Duval was glad when she was gone, for he felt that if he had remained much longer in her fascinating company, he must have surrendered his heart to her.

The thought of the one fair being who loved him, and whom he had at the old house at Hornsey, made him glad to keep out of the way of temptation—for of all the temptations that this great world could offer to Claude Duval, that which was comprised in a pair of bright eyes, was the most hard to resist of all.

" Yes," he said, as he watched her pass through the gate, " yes, she is gone. Peace go with her—She is wondrously beautiful."

The servants at the gate had made no hesitation in allowing Alice to leave the gardens, and no doubt the quiet and respectful manner in which they behaved was greatly owing to the liberality with which Duval had treated them when he came back to the gardens after he had been home.

When Alice was fairly out of sight, Duval returned towards the pavilion.

" Well," he said, " poets and painters may talk in what rapture they please about the beautiful in nature; but there is not, and there never was, and there never will be, anything in the world one half so beautiful as the face of a young girl, rich in all the charms and graces of early youth, and stamped with loveliness by the hand of Heaven."

So enraptured was he by a recollection of the fair face of Alice, that he quite lost his way in getting back to the pavilion, and was a good ten minutes in finding it again. Indeed, he began to dispair of doing so at all, when he suddenly emerged from a path and found himself close upon it.

The little light that had been lit within it, was too faint to do more than shed a very dreamy-looking halo through the stained glass windows; and Duval at once entered the little building. The sister of Alice was still there, and she had something in her hand which she hastily hid at the entrance of Duval.

" You have returned ?" she said. " Can you fulfil your promise of procuring me an audience of the prince ?"

" Yes, I have returned; but I should have expected that your first question would have been concerning the safety of Alice."

" Well, is she safe ?"

" I hope so; and now if you like to follow me, I will get you the interview with the prince that you require."

The young person immediately rose.

" Oh, yes—yes, take me to him! I will not ask to see him again; but do take me to him now! At once let me confront the base deceiver! He did marry me, and I will have justice! Take me, sir, at once !"

" Come on, then. I will do my best to comply with your wishes; but I tell you beforehand, that justice you will not get."

" I will—I must."

" Very good, I will not argue the matter with you any further. You can try, but one would have thought you had had sufficient experience of your royal admirer to know that there was nothing in the shape of justice to expect from him."

"Heaven will avenge me."

"That is quite another thing."

"I will follow you, sir; but do not attempt to drive me mad by speaking to me in such a strain. He must and he shall listen to me, or I will find a means to make him."

Duval somehow had taken rather a dislike to sister Eliza, so he did not offer her his arm, but she took a good hold of the cloak that he wore, and was evidently determined that he should not escape her, if it were at all possible to keep him from doing so by what strength she possessed.

CHAPTER XCII.

DUVAL MAKES A GOOD NIGHT'S WORK AND ESCAPES.

DUVAL felt rather annoyed at the pertinacious manner in which the young lady clung to him.

"You need not be afraid," he said, "I do not wish to leave you. I will be as good as my word, you may depend, and introduce you to the prince; but when I have done so, you will be so good as to conclude that our acquaintance ceases."

"I have met with so much treachery," she said, "that I may be well excused for being suspicious of anything in the shape of a man. But I will trust you, sir."

"You may with perfect safety, and I beg you to believe that I pity you."

After all, Duval began to think that he was taking too harsh a view of the behaviour of this poor mentally benighted creature, and he felt that great allowance ought to be made for the state of suffering she must be in He determined that she should be introduced to the prince, whether he might like it or not, and whatever might be the result; but a little difficulty suddenly presented itself; for Jenkins, the valet, seeing Duval emerge from the summer-house, with a cloak on, and take his way towards the palace, must needs come officiously forward with a half bow.

Duval walked fast; but Jenkins got sufficiently close to him to say—"Has your highness any commands?"

"How is this?" said the lady. "Are you one of the royal family, too?"

"Be off, Jenkins," said Duval, once more assuming the tone of the Prince of Wales; and the wily valet, finding that he was not wanted just then, effected a very precipitate retreat.

"Tell me who you are," said the betrayed girl. "Why did that man call you, 'your highness?'"

"Do you think," said Duval, "that the only highness in all the world is the Prince of Wales?"

"No—no; and yet——"

"And yet you would say, that it sounds strange to your ears to have any one else so distinguished. Rest content, madam. You are in very good hands, and you may rest satisfied, that what I have promised I will perform. I will keep my word with you, and show you to the Prince of Wales. I fancy, that is all you require at my hands?"

"It is all," said the lady; and by the tone in which she spoke, it was quite evident that she entertained a much higher sense of the importance of Duval than she had done before. Those two words, 'your highness,' had had all their effect.

"Ah," thought Duval, "now I am quite convinced, that vanity is the rock upon which this girl has been wrecked. If the Prince of Wales had appeared to her only as plain Mr. Somebody, he would not have conquered."

This was a view of the case, that again had the effect of turning Duval's warm heart from the girl. "All for Love," was a motto that he never despised; but he had a hearty contempt for any one who was taken by the mere empty glitter of a name.

"Do you admire the prince very much?" he said.

"Oh, no—Not at all."

"And yet you married him, or fancied that you had married him. Oh, Eliza, if that is your name, you took the wrong road to happiness, most decidedly; but I do not want to play the part of a monitor to you on any account. I will give you the opportunity of saying what you please to the prince, and then you will not be troubled with me any more."

She followed Duval in silence.

The numerous doors that opened from the palace into the garden, Duval had found, by experience, were for the most part open; and, indeed, it would seem as though everything as regards safety and privacy, was left to depend upon the persons at the gates of the garden; and free ingress and egress to the palace was quite an understood thing among the guests who were in it, living a time of such wild riot with the prince.

Duval made his way to one of those doors, and giving it a slight push, it yielded at once. Just within, he encountered one of the royal servants, who bowed very lowly to Duval, and moved aside to allow him and the lady to pass.

"Where are they all now?" said Duval.

"In the Cedar-room, sir."

"Oh, very good."

Now, Duval knew just as well where the Cedar-room in the palace at Kew was as if he had been informed that the prince and his associates were in some particular spot of the moon; but he neithter liked the servant nor the lady to suppose that he required any information upon that point, so he walked on, thinking, no doubt rightly enough, that the noise and racket would be sufficient to direct him to where the mad revelry was removed to.

The poor deceived creature whom he had under his care, now clung to him again with fear; for much as she had hoped, and planned, and prayed for that interview with the prince, which she had been at such pains to get, she now shrank from it with real terror.

"Do you hesitate?" said Duval. "If you do, there is yet ample time to retreat, and I will see you safely out of the gardens, as I saw your sister only a short time ago."

"Oh, no—no—I will see him."

"Very good. You shall."

At this moment, a wild roaring laugh and shout of revelry came upon their ears, and so near at hand did it seem to be, that even Duval started at its contiguity. He did not see any door, but he felt certain that nothing but the thickness of a wainscot-wall divided them from the room in which the riot was going on upon so noisy a scale.

"Come on," said Duval, "you have nothing to apprehend if you are only true to yourself, and steadfast in your purpose. The prince will be surrounded by too many eyes to behave otherwise than courteously to you, let you say what you may to him. It is your privilege to speak if you like, and his penance to listen."

Duval felt certain that by going on he should come to some door leading into the room from whence the boisterous sounds had proceeded, nor was he disappointed in such an idea, for a door quickly presented itself, over which, in a niche, burnt a small silver lamp. Duval turned the handle of the lock, and opening the door sufficient only to enable him to do so, looked into the room.

There, sure enough, was all the wild crew, with the prince, and Colonel Lane, as a sort of president, was mounted upon a chair placed upon the top of the table, with a field-marshal's cocked hat and feathers on his head.

A few lights were scattered about here and there, and the prince sat with his back to the door, lolling in a large easy-chair, above the back of which his head only slightly projected. The whole party was much too far gone in wine, and too intent upon their own noisy enjoyments to pay the least attention to the opening of the door or the appearance of Duval at it, so that he was permitted in perfect peace to note all the particulars that we have recorded.

He drew back his head again just as the prince said—

"Now, I will give you a toast such as none of you ever heard of before or ever will hear of again."

"'Tis he !—'tis he !" said Eliza.

"You hear his voice then ?" said Duval.

"I do. Yes, it is his voice ; but I am very much afraid, from the sound of it, that he is—is—is——"

"Drunk, you would say. Well, I must say that I am rather afraid, likewise, that he has had about enough to drink, and it is entirely for your own consideration whether, seeing, or rather hearing his condition, you think proper to enter the room and have anything to say to him. As for getting him out of it to speak to you, you need not think of it, for he would not move."

"I know it—I know it."

"Then you will risk all the consequences of going into that room and speaking to him in the mood that he is in ?"

"I have made up my mind to higher consequences than merely speaking to him, let his mood be what it may."

Duval stepped aside and held the door a little way open, and the deceived one made her way into the room at once and up to the chair upon which sat the prince. Duval likewise entered the room and closed the door behind him, for he was not a little anxious to see how the scene that was going to occur would go off, considering the state of the prince and the violent cause of wrong under which the lady suffered.

The first thing she did was to proceed right in front of the prince's chair, and there she stood looking him in the face in profound silence. No doubt, as her wrongs were uppermost in the mind of that poor creature, she thought they must be so in the mind of him who had wrought her so much woe. She did not seem capable of comprehending that in all likelihood she was all but completely forgotten.

The ladies who had, in the Yellow Drawing-room, adorned the elegant leisure of the company, were not there, and the appearance of this young female confronting the prince with such strange and stern silence, and looking almost like an apparition, had the effect in a few moments of attracting great attention.

All the boisterous noises ceased, and even Colonel Lane pushed his field-marshal's cocked-hat on one side to listen to what was going on.

The prince drew back as far as he could in the easy chair, and with fear struggling between anger and alarm, he said—

"Who the deuce are you ?"

"Oh, George—George," she said, "you wretch !"

"Bravo !" cried everybody, and a positive shriek of wild laughter shook the very room. They all thought it was some joke got up on purpose to have some fun with the prince.

"What do you mean by calling me a wretch ?" said the prince. "Get out, madam. Damn it, what do you mean ?"

"Do you pretend not to know me, you monster in human shape ?—Do you pretend, you lump of atrocity, not now to know your victim ? Oh, George—George, did I—ought I to expect this reception from you ?"

This was considered as such a capital piece of acting by the prince's guests, that some of them nearly went into hysterics with laughter at it. "Go it !" cried some. "Give it him again !" cried others. "Capital ! Oh, excellent ! Ha ! ha ! ha !"

"But really," said the prince, "I—I—This is some mad woman. Murder ! What does she mean ? I can't stand this, you know. Lay hold of her, some of you, and turn her out."

"No—no—no!" cried a dozen voices.

"Do you not remember Eliza?" said the accuser, coming still closer to the prince. "Wretch, do you not know me now? Did you not wrong me? Did you not promise to be mine, you vile lump of vanity and deceit?"

The prince's countenance was at this moment a fine expression of surprise, and age, and fear. He did now recollect her, and how she got there was to him the greatest of mysteries. He felt that he would give anything to be out of her way; and yet, from the look of her, he dreaded to make a movement to leave the easy chair, lest she should pounce at once upon him.

"Come, come," he said. "Be calm—be calm, now. Come, come. Hilloa, now—be calm——"

What further he said was completely drowned amid the incessant roar of laughter from the guests, and then arose a general cry of—"Silence! Order! Order!" The fact was, that they did not like to lose one word of what was going on, considering it as the highest amusement of the evening; but they had not the remotest idea that it was real upon the part of the girl, although the terror and confusion of the prince was too good by a long way to be simulated by him.

Comparative silence was restored, and then she said—

"Tell me now—do you know me, or do you not?"

"Oh, dear me, yes, I suppose so. Just be so good as to call again to-morrow, Eliza. I—I—you see I can't speak to you now—that's a good girl."

"Am I your wife, sir, or am I not?"

"Just whichever you please, my dear, only do go."

"No, sir, I will not go. I have come here on a great errand—a pious errand, and I will not go."

"Capitally you do it, too," cried Colonel Lane.

"I never saw anything half so good on the stage," cried Lord Austincourt; "and I don't believe I ever shall."

"Take her away!" cried the prince. "Take her away. Where are the servants? Take her away!"

"And do you think," she said, "that I will allow myself to be taken away? Did you not say that you would live with me in a cottage, you monster? and that although you could not exactly introduce me at court, yet that you would always consider me as your wife? Answer me that."

"Oh, yes, of course; now go away."

"Will you come with me at once, then? Our little boy is very like you, indeed."

At this the laughter burst out afresh, and the prince, who was getting desperate at his situation, made a slight movement to get up from the chair; but Eliza darted in an instant behind it, and throwing her arm round it, she fixed him by placing her left arm just under his chin, and so pinned his head to the back of the chair, at the imminent risk of choking him, and the figure he cut was so ludicrous, that Colonel Lane rolled off the table, chair and all, with laughing.

CHAPTER XCIII.

THE COMEDY ENDS IN A TRAGEDY.—THE DRESSING-ROOM.

DUVAL saw this scene with conflicting emotions, and had it not been that he felt certain that the prince was being really desperately frightened, he would have stepped forward to try to get Eliza away from that scene which so ill accorded with even what she was; but the prince was undergoing a kind of mortal retribution for his sins, so Duval would not interfere with him, at least for yet awhile.

It was in vain that he struggled to free himself from the arm of Eliza, and the guests feeling fully convinced that it was all a piece of acting upon the part of the female, would not interfere to spoil the fun, on any account.

"Murder!" he gurgled out, for the pressure upon his throat was rather severe. "Murder! help!" but not one hand was stretched forth to save the heir-apparent from what looked remarkably like strangulation.

"Gentlemen," said Eliza, "you laugh at my misery; but you see before you one who is the poor victim of this man's baseness and duplicity. You see me in my youth lost—lost for ever."

"Bravo!—bravo!"

The prince got very red in the face.

"But," continued Eliza, "I will not live to be the scorn of others who are happy in their virtue, and in their innocence. I will not continue to exist in a world that can have no further charms for me, but which must be but a place of pain so long as I draw the breath of life in it. I will die."

"Capital!—capital! What a piece of acting, to be sure."

"In this little phial," continued Eliza, "I have the means of death, and I fully intend, if George will not be mine in this world, that he shall in the next. Drink, George, you will be quite as happy in another world, as you would be upon the throne which you fancy awaits you in this."

The prince kicked dreadfully, and made a violent effort to escape; but with her right hand, which she had kept at liberty, Eliza produced a small bottle from the bosom of her dress, and extracting the cork with her teeth, she jammed the mouth of it against the lips of the prince, crying—

"Drink—drink, and die!"

This the guests thought was the crowning portion of the joke, and they roared again, while the prince fought and spluttered until he got fairly out of the clutches of Eliza, and rolled on to the floor. Then she lifted the bottle to her own lips, and drained it to the dregs, saying, as she cast the empty bottle from her—

"It is done—it is done! God forgive me, now."

She staggered back and would have fallen, but that Duval darted from the corner in which he had ensconced himself to be a spectator of what was going on, and caught her in his arms. The guest began now to look a little serious at each other, and some of them rose in confusion.

"What does it all mean?" cried Colonel Lane. "Is it not all a joke? What is it to end in?"

"It's a mere piece of acting—a jest, is it not, baron?" said Lord Austincourt, advancing to Duval.

"I know no more of it than you do, gentlemen," said Duval. "All I can say is, that if it be a piece of acting, it is the best done thing that I ever saw; but, to me, it has such a very serious look, that I will not answer for its not being real."

"Real!" cried a dozen voices at once, in all the different accents of consternation.

"Good God! Look to the prince," said Colonel Lane. "This may be a serious night's work, indeed. Raise up the prince."

Some two or three of the most sober of the guests got the prince to his feet, and then he began to be dreadfully sick; and to look about him, like a man in a dream. It was quite clear that he was very ill. In point of fact, it was only the sudden accession of sickness of the prince that upon that occasion saved his life, although those around him did not exactly suspect that he was in such imminent peril.

Duval carried Eliza to a sofa, upon which he laid her, and then he approached the throng that was round the prince, just as Lord Austincourt was saying to him—

"How does your highness feel? Would you like a physician sent for at once? Only say yes, and I will mount and fetch one."

"No—no," said the prince, faintly. "I will lie down in my own bedroom a little. I shall be better. Oh, dear!"

"Allow me to help him," said Duval.

Lord Austincourt allowed Duval to take a sort of precedence in assisting the prince, and, in fact, Duval half carried him out of the room. Colonel Lane went first with a light to show the way, and all the guests who were equal to the task of ascending a flight of stairs, followed the prince, with Duval on one side of him and Lord Austincourt on the other.

"How do you feel ?" said Duval, as they reached a flight of some twenty stairs that led to the upper floor of the palace.

"Oh dear, I don't know—I don't know. But I do believe—Oh—oh !—I do really believe———"

"What, your highness ?" said Lord Austincourt.

"That you were all in a plot to murder me. What else could you mean by setting that mad woman on me ?"

"We really thought it was a joke."

"A joke ?—a joke ? Oh—oh !"

"If we had not, we should in a moment have interfered, but I declare that the impression was that it was an excellently acted and well-got up dramatic performance."

"What! was it a joke when you saw, first of all, that I was half-choked ; and then that she poured a bottle of poison down my throat? Oh, don't tell me. Give me some brandy or I shall faint away. A joke, indeed! The deuce take such jokes. A capital idea to joke away my life in such a manner,"

"We are all very sorry," said the colonel.

"Ah, so am I—so am I. I will lie down for a little, and see if I get any better. Sorry, indeed! That's a poor sort of consolation to me when I am half dead."

They had now reached the prince's bed-room, adjoining which was a little dressing-room, fitted up in the most gorgeous manner possible. Duval placed him upon the bed, and then he whispered to Lord Austincourt and the colonel—

"The best thing will be to take all the men down to the saloon again, and I will talk his highness into good humour again. You know I have some little influence upon him, and will soon put everything to rights."

"Ah, yes," said Lord Austincourt, "that will do."

"Very good," said the colonel. Then raising his voice, he added—"We will leave your royal highness with the baron, who will pay you the most affectionate attention."

"D—n the baron," said the prince

"Ha ! ha !" laughed Claude Duval. "Very good! Go off, all of you at once now, and leave me to bring him round."

"We will—we will !"

"That's right. Be off."

Lord Austincourt and the colonel, by their joint influence, got the whole of the guests to leave the bed-room, and Duval was left alone with the prince and one solitary wax-candle that was placed upon a marble-table attached to the wall by a splendid mass of gilding in the shape of a lion's foot, with no end of claws.

"How do you feel now ?" said Duval.

"Who are you, sir ? I don't know you," said the prince, shading his eyes with his hands, "I don't know you at all, sir. Confound you, I do believe you were the impudent fellow who sat next me in the painted-room, below."

"The very same," said Duval.

"And who won some money of me about throwing wine at the wax-lights in the chandelier ?"

"The very same."

"Humph !"

"There is only one little thing that your royal highness has forgotten."

"And what's that, eh ?"

"Why, that you did not pay the money !"

"Oh, indeed!   Well, I can dispense with your company, sir, at once, if you please.   Go and order some of the servants to come to me!   If you can find my valet you may be of some service."

"Hark you, George, Prince of Wales," said Duval.   "I am not exactly the sort of man to trifle with ; and now I tell you clearly and distinctly, that if you don't lie still and keep quite quiet, I intend to blow out your brains."

"My brains ?"

"I beg your pardon.   Of course, I mean only to allude to the few that you possess, that's all.   Do you understand this ?"

As he spoke, Duval produced a pistol which he held against the bloated cheek of the royal libertine.   The prince turned pale, and fell back on the bed with a groan.

"I'm a murdered man !" he said, "I'm a murdered man !"

"No, you are not any such thing. If you only remain quiet and keep your own counsel, all will be well. I intend to appropriate to my own use some of the little valuables that are on the tables in your dressing-room, that is all. You will experience not the slightest difficulty in replacing them."

With this, Duval took up the light, and advancing to the bed-room door, he carefully locked it and put the key in his pocket, for he was rather apprehensive that the prince might give him the slip while he was in the dressing-room, if he did not take some such precaution. He then went into the dressing-room, and in a very few minutes succeeded in putting into his pockets a number of little articles, composed of solid gold, and appertaining to some of the more intricate operations of the toilette.

A stand, with about half a dozen diamond rings and brooches, was upon the table, and that, too, Duval took possession of, so that he returned to the bed-room very well contented with what he had.

The prince still lay upon the bed.

"Now, Master George," said Duval, "if I might offer a piece of very sincere advice to so very great a man as you, it would be to hold your stupid tongue about this transaction, for if you will speak of it, and, in consequence, any trouble comes upon me, I shall be under the disagreeable necessity of at once declaring to persons who may interrupt your festivities here all I happen to know of the goings on at the old palace at Kew, and that may have the effect of rather altering the state of affairs in this pleasant suburban retreat; and as the summer is coming on, you know that would be rather a loss to you, and your enjoyments for the next few months; for if Kew is shut up against you by order of the queen, it is not likely that any other similar place will be opened to you."

"Oh, dear—oh, dear! How very true."

"You feel the force of my remarks ?"

"I do, to be sure, of course I do. There's only one thing that I should be very much obliged to you to leave alone."

"Name it."

"It is a brooch, set with the queen's hair. I don't care a straw about it, but if she don't see me wear it when I go to take a stupid family dinner at Windsor there will be an explosion, that's all."

"I shall certainly, then, leave it to you," said Duval. "Here it is ; you will find it, when I am gone, upon this marble table."

"You will really leave it ?"

"I have left it."

"Then, I won't say a word about the robbery; and you had better be off as soon as you possibly can out of the palace, for others may get suspicious. But I should like to know who is implicated in bringing you into the palace at all."

"No one. Do not suspect any one, for all are innocent of such a thing. Each of your guests, no doubt, thought me a friend of some other one, and you thought the same thing ; so I passed muster very well indeed."

"You did ; and now, if it is not asking too much, pray tell me who you are, my friend ?"

"First of all, what bell is that that keeps tingling at some distance off in the palace ?"

"Bell? Did you say bell ?"

"Yes, I did. Ah, who is that ?"

A sudden violent knocking came at the door of the room, and Duval had a strong suspicion that as he lay, the prince had some means of ringing a bell, and this knocking at the door of the room was the reply to it.

Just showing the prince the pistol that he still held in his hand, Duval said, mildly—

"I think you have played me false, as all your race are accustomed to do. Folly and selfishness are your characteristics; and it is only that I have a good command of my temper that saves your utterly worthless life."

Duval proceeded then to the door of the bed-room, and opened it so suddenly, that a servant fell upon his hands and knees into the room. Another one Duval seized by the collar and flung right on to the bed to the detriment of the prince; and then knocking the one further into the room who had fallen upon the threshold, Duval closed the door, and locked it on the outside. He put the key in his pocket, and then hurried down the stairs.

———

CHAPTER XCIV.

DUVAL IS BETRAYED BY A JEW, BUT GOOD FORTUNE ATTENDS HIM.

THE great object of Duval was now to leave the palace. He had been quite long enough in it to see all that his curiosity prompted him to see; and as regarded the profit of the adventure, he had certainly been long enough in Kew to make that tolerably complete.

Upon reaching the foot of the stairs, he was at the moment rather confused to find his way out of the palace; and really whether to turn to the right or to the left, he could not take upon himself to decide.

While he was in this state of uncertainty, a bell rung very violently, indeed; and Duval asked himself if it boded danger to himself or not. He mechanically laid his hand upon the double-barrelled pistol, upon which he knew he could depend, and listened.

The bell rung again, and that it was a peal of alarm there could not be a shadow of a doubt.

"Ah," said Duval, "that comes, I'll be bound, now, from the prince's chamber. He thinks, after all, that he will capture me; but they will find it a more difficult matter than they perhaps imagine, to lay hands upon me with any safety."

Feeling then the necessity of coming to some decision as regarded the way he was to take to get out of the palace, he turned to the right; not with any very particular idea that that was the route that would lead him to the garden, but with the notion that it would consume less time to try it and come back again if it were the wrong route, than to hesitate about it.

"Confound that bell," he said, as a third time he heard it pealing through the palace.

In a few moments Duval came to a door, which he pushed open, and found that it led into a bed-room. A slight suppressed shriek convinced him that some female was there.

"Bother you," said Duval, "I don't want to intrude upon you."

"Who the devil is it?" said a gruff voice, in unmistakable male accents.

"Nobody," said Duval, as he closed the door again, and finding a bolt upon the outside, he at once shot it into its socket.

Duval now ran down the passage he was in for a considerable distance, until he came to another flight of stairs, which ascended again to the upper floor; but it was no part of his wish to get up again, so he glanced round here for some door by which to leave the passage. As he did so, he heard a scuffling noise, and a man came rushing down the stairs, crying as he came—

"Help—help! The prince has been robbed. Thieves and highwaymen are in the house! Help! help! Murder!"

"You don't say so?" cried Duval, stepping up to him.

"Oh, yes. Help!—help!"

Duval seized him by the throat.

"Another word, my friend, in such a tone as that, and it is the last that you will be troubled to utter in this world. Do you understand me? I am rather serious."

The man's knees knocked together with fright.

" Where does yonder door lead to ?"

" To—to—that door?   That one ?"

" Do not trifle with me.   Most folks find that a rather dangerous pastime. Where does yonder door lead to ?"

" To—to the library."

" And the library ?"

" Op—opens on to the south lawn."

" That's enough.   Recollect now that there are six of us, and while I go the other five have their eyes upon you.   Sit down upon the bottom stair of this flight, and as long as you sit still you are safe, but the moment you move you will have your brains blown out."

Down flopped the man on to the stair indicated in a moment, and there he sat trembling in every limb.

" Oh, yes.   I'll sit still.   For how long would you like me to sit, sir?   Only mention the time, sir."

" Half-an-hour."

The door to which Duval had pointed was fast, but one rush at it burst it open, and Duval passed through it into the library.   That library was a magnificent room, with five long French windows opening on to one of the lawns of the garden.   Duval had one of the windows open in a moment, and out he dashed.

" Thank the fates," he said, " I am in the open air once more, and all is well. What did that frightened fool say this was?   Oh, the south lawn.   South—ah, yes.   Then my way is to the left if I would reach the lodge gate, and I shall not be exceedingly particular about how I reach there.   The beds and the flowers must suffer for my being rather in a hurry.   I hope Luke will be at hand with the horse."

Duval dashed on in the direction that he knew must lead him towards the gates, but he had not gone far before he came to one of those little kiosk-like buildings which were sufficiently numerous in the grounds, and a female voice cried out—

" Is it you ?"

" Of course it is," said Duval; " but I am rather busy."

" Ah, that is so like you," said the voice.   " I will speak to your grace, if it be only for a moment."

" Good night," said Duval.

He dashed on, but he found his course suddenly impeded by a complete maze of flowering shrubs, some one or other of which met him at every turn, and somebody caught him round the waist from behind, saying—

" Come.   Stilla is in the shell-room waiting for you.   Come, she is more than beautiful to-night."

" I cannot."

" Oh, it is not the duke !"

" No," said Duval, " but it's the devil, if that will do as well."   As he uttered these words, he, with one spring, cleared the bush that was in front of him, and alighted upon a path, which he pursued rapidly with a well-founded idea that it would lead him to the lodge-gate.

He heard the female whom he had quitted so very abruptly, and who had mistaken him for the Duke of something, utter a loud scream, and wishing her in a place that it is not polite to mention, he increased his speed, and to his great satisfaction, upon a sudden turn of the path, found himself in sight of the lodge.

There were several paths that led to this lodge, and the one that Duval was pursuing was in truth the least important of the whole of them; but he was well enough pleased to find that it brought him out so close to the gate, which was plainly discernible by the light of a lantern, shaded with blue glass, that hung so that none of its rays went outside the royal premises.

As he reached the gate, and a servant stepped up to open it with the most respectful movement, Duval heard the clatter of feet, and a voice cried from one of the other paths—

"Keep the gates shut, Wood! Keep them shut. Let no one leave this place. The prince's life has been attempted!"

"Yes," said Duval, "keep the gates close shut, Wood, whatever you do, until you see me again. I am going for a guard. Be very vigilant, Wood. Mind that."

Wood, which was the name of the man who was on duty at the gate, was rather confused, and Duval was not the person to fail to profit by that confusion. He swung the gate open and left the garden. The excuse he had made, too, warranted him in going fast, so that he disappeared in the darkness of the night before the man at the gate or the persons who were rapidly approaching it by another path from the garden, could make up their minds whether he was to be stopped or not.

Duval's great object now was to meet with Luke and the cattle, so he ran to the top of the lane, and taking from his waistcoat-pocket the little silver whistle that he had there, he blew it with a long, faint sound.

It was immediately answered, and the sound of horses' feet came sharply upon his ears. Duval ran forward to meet the sound, and he then called out—

"Luke—Luke!"

"Here, sir," said Luke. "All's right."

"That will do. Ah, I see you now. How dark the night has got all of a sudden."

"It has, sir. A regular bank of clouds has come up and covered all the sky. Is there any particular hurry, sir?"

"Why, I think there is rather, Luke. But you see I am here, for all that, and all safe, too."

"I'm glad to here it, sir. We will show them a light pair of heels, if need be; and if they will come too close upon us, and get into danger, well and good: they must take the rough with the smooth. This way, sir, for home."

"But I am for London, Luke."

"Oh, then that's quite another thing. We must go to the right." --

"Yes, Luke, to the right it is. The fact is, that I have about me some little articles of value, that I would rather at once dispose of before I go home. I know a Jew in Gray's Inn Lane who will deal with me, and who can easily dispose of them through his connexions abroad. We will take a trot to his house and turn the trifles into cash, and then we will go home; where, I think, after what has happened, I shall feel inclined to remain for a few days, for it strikes me that this little exploit of mine will make a fuss."

"Would it not be better, sir, to defer going to the Jew until the hue-and-cry is over?"

"Why no, Luke. The fact is, I daresay some very heavy reward will be offered for me, and the little things I have taken belonging to the prince, to-morrow, and I want to dispose of them and be out of the way before that fact is known to my old acquaintance, Moses Monti, or he might be tempted too much, as, after all, you know, Luke, he is but human."

"And a Jew, sir."

"Well—well. As regards that, Luke, I have found in my career quite as much double-dealing, and perhaps a little more, from those who called themselves Christians. It is very seldom that a Jew will betray you; but still I never like to rely too strongly upon any man's virtue, so I will go to him at once, before he has the opportunity of reflecting how much he might make by concocting some plan for my arrest."

"There is good reason, sir, in what you say. Do you hear anybody after us, sir?"

Duval listened. - "By all that's uncomfortable, yes! I hear the dash of horses' feet. You have your arms ready, Luke? We shall have to give them a taste of our quality."

"We will, sir."

They drew up in the middle of the road and awaited the approach of the horsemen. When they were tolerably near, Duval cried out, in a loud voice—

"Hold! What do you want on the road at such a pace?"

"That's the man!" cried a voice. "Fire at him! He is far better dead than alive. Fire away!"

Bang—bang, went a couple of pistols, and then a couple more, and still the voice cried out—

"Fire away! Kill him, my men: I will hold you harmless."

"Now, Luke," said Duval. "Fire!"

Luke and Duval fired together.

"Keep at it," said Duval, and he discharged two more pistols.

"Down with the villain," cried the voice again. "Fire away, my lads, fire away!"

Only two more dropping shots were fired, and Duval then discharged the only pistol he had loaded.

"Now, gentlemen," he said, "if you are disposed for a race, I am ready; and if you can load again as you gallop, I can do the same; and we will stop again at the most convenient open spot we come to, and have another little blaze away. Come on. Hurrah for the road!—Ha!—ha!"

Away he went, and Luke by his side. In the space of a few minutes, they placed a mile between them and their foes, not one of whom felt disposed to follow them. Duval, however, with the bridle of his horse freely clutched in his teeth, kept both his hands at liberty, with which he succeeded in loading his pistols again; but when he found that his opponents had evidently had enough of the affair, he relaxed in his speed, and allowed his horse to go at an easy trot.

"That's over, Luke, I think," he said.

"Oh, yes, sir. It was something like a little battle while it lasted. One bullet went right through my hat, sir, and another has had the kindness just to touch one of my knuckles, but it did it very gently."

"They were all chance shots, Luke. Nine folks out of ten fire half a mile over your head with a pistol. They level at you, and then give the trigger a pull that elevates the muzzle an inch or so, and that, in twenty or thirty paces, comes to something rather prodigious. I have really got to care little for a pistol shot, for what with badly made weapons and bad marksmen, it is a hundred to one that you escape; and in the dark, to tell the truth, I do think there is quite as much danger as in the light. But here we are in London. They have done some good, at all events, for they have brought us to town quicker than we should otherwise have reached it."

"That they have, sir. But I don't care how soon we leave it again, and get to our quiet home in the country."

"Nor I, Luke; for, to tell you the truth, I am much more in the humour now to lie down and have a long sleep, than to go to the Jew's in Gray's Inn Lane; and, but that I feel how much better it is to get rid of the swag, and have the affair all over as far as I am concerned, I would go home; but I shall soon rouse myself up again. We will get on a little faster."

They increased their speed a little, and in a short time reached Gray's Inn Lane, which was then a long straggling thoroughfare, with fields upon the east side of it, and a great many lonely places between Holborn and Battle Bridge, which latter place was really then quite out of town, the Fleet river flowing along its lowest part, and irrigating a number of chesnut trees, for which the spot was rather famous; and upon the hill of Islington—or Isledon, as it was then called—there were but two or three detached houses.

————

CHAPTER XCV.

THE BETRAYER IS CAUGHT IN HIS OWN SNARE, AND DUVAL ESCAPES.

"This is not the liveliest spot in the world," said Duval, as they reached Gray's Inn Lane; "but if we find our friend, the Jew, stirring, it will do very well for us."

"It is an early hour, sir," said Luke.

"Yes, but only look, Luke, how everything is gradually brightening beneath the influence of the new day. The morning is stealing upon us now rapidly, and it will be rather lighter than I should wish, I fear, before we see the old house at Hornsey again."

"It will, indeed, sir. Is this the place?"

Duval had stopped opposite to what seemed to be nothing in the world but a dead wall. Nevertheless, there was a little, low, dingy-looking door in it; but there did not seem to be any means of opening it, or of conversing with the inmates of the place, if there were any.

"Look about you, Luke," said Duval, as he dismounted; "and let me know if any one is watching us."

"Not a soul, sir," said Luke, after he had cast a cautious and searching glance around him. "Not a soul, sir."

"Very good. Then it may be useful for you to know, Luke, that under the step here, which you see is of wood, and not above six inches from the ground, having a hollow space under it, there is the handle of a bell."

"It is ingeniously placed, sir."

"It is, indeed. If you listen sharply you will hear it ring. I have not been here often, but each time that I have come I have heard its tingle."

Luke did listen; and the moment Duval gave the bell a jirk, a clear but distant sound of a bell came upon his ears.

"I heard it, sir."

"And so did I. We shall soon be answered."

In the course of about a minute, the upper part of the little dirty door was opened upon a separate pair of hinges to those which belonged to the whole structure, and a form appeared.

"Who is it?" said the Jew, shading his eyes with his hand, and peering out into the darkness.

"Look again, Moses. Don't you know——"

'So help me, Abraham! it's Claude Duval.'

"It is; and I have some little trinkets, and other matters, for you to look at which I don't choose to carry home with me."

"Oh, you nice young man! You shall come in directly. I will go and fetch the key. I only now do the best of business, you beauty."

The Jew shut the little wicket, and hurried off for the key. During his absence, Claude said to Luke—

"You can wait in the lane, Luke. I will be as short a time arranging matters with the Jew as possible. You know the little bell move; if anything should occur which makes it necessary for you to communicate with me, you can ring it, and I will come at once to the wicket."

"I will keep a sharp look-out, sir."

"Do so. It will not be for long. A quarter of an hour at most."

The Jew at this moment made his appearance again, and opened the door for Duval to enter. He poked his old face right out into the lane, and seeing Luke, he said—

"Ha! my dear Duval, you have got a friend? Do you think he has any silver spoons about him? There's a good market for silver spoons."

"I'm sure he has not, Moses."

"Oh, what a pity."

The Jew closed the door; and as he hobbled before Duval through a little dim looking court-yard about twenty feet square, which led to one of the dirtiest houses, as far as outside show went, that could be conceived, he said, in what Duval thought rather a particular manner—

"Does your friend wait for you, my dear Duval?"

"No, he goes home at once."

"Oh, dear! Bless you."

"Why, Moses, how polite you are this morning."

" It's because it's so early, my dear Duval. I like to get up early. I always like a long day, as the gentlemen say at the Old Bailey, when they are sentenced to be hanged! Ha!—ha! That's a good joke! A long day—Ha!"

" Very good, indeed," said Duval, " considering who it came from. But I hope you have plenty of money in this old den, for I have those things to show you that must not go for a trifle."

" Money? Did you say money, my dear? Oh, it never was so scarce. Money is hard to get."

" I never heard of its being otherwise, Moses."

The Jew coughed, and led Duval into a small room upon the ground floor of his house. Upon a table in the middle of the room was a pair of scales for weighing articles of gold and silver, and various other articles useful for testing the quantity. In the centre of the table was a hole that seemed to be partially closed by a conical bag of green cloth, the narrowest part of which hung downwards. It was into this orifice that Moses slipped the articles that he purchased of the cracksmen and highwaymen, who come to his fence, and below there was a confederate to receive them, and lay them away at once in a place of safety.

" Ah, well, my dear," said Moses. " What was you have to get? I half made up my mind to buy no more, it is so difficult to get rid of anything now-a-days. I seldom get above fifteen shillings back again, as I'm a sinner, for what I give a pound."

" Gammon, Moses."

" Gammon do you call it, my dear Duval?"

" Yes, and you know it, you old rascal. What you mean to say is, that you get about five pounds for every one pound. That is nearer the mark. But what do I care if you got twenty? It is all the same to me, so that you give me what satisfies me. What do you think of that?"

As he spoke, Duval laid before the Jew the watch and seals of the Prince of Wales.

" Ah! dear me," said the Jew, as he looked at the superb articles, and his eyes sparkled again. " What a capital imitation, and what really good gilding."

" Indeed? Do you think that the Prince of Wales is likely to wear imitation diamonds, and a gilt watch?"

" The Prince of Wales, my dear?"

" Precisely so; and here are a few odds and ends from his dressing-table. Now Moses, I don't wish to be kept here an hour or two, trafficking and bargaining with you. I am tired, and want to get home. I have set the price of two hundred upon these things, and if you like to have them, there they are. If you will not say so at once, and I am off, for I will not haggle about them."

" Two hundred! Two—two! Oh, Abraham, look down! Two hundred! Oh—oh—oh! Two——"

" Very good. I am off, then. I regret having given you and myself so much trouble. They don't suit you, and that's enough."

Duval began pocketing the trinkets with great speed; and the terrified Jew caught hold of the watch-chain, crying—

" Hold, my dear—hold! One hundred I will give!"

" No—no."

" A hundred and fifty? Well—well! Oh, gracious, I shall be ruined, I know! but I will give it. Two hundred! Mother of Moses, what will become of me? I feel that I am ruined; and yet I will give the money rather than you should be vexed, my dear Duval. Lewin—Lewin, my dear, come here."

" Who the deuce is Lewin?" said Duval.

" It is my little boy, and here he comes."

A Jew lad, with the strongly marked features of his race, crept silently into the room.

" My dear Lewin," said Moses, " you will run to our friend, Shadrach, in Field Lane, and tell him to give you two hundred pounds on my writing till to-morrow; and you will be quick, Lewin."

"Yes," said the boy.

The Jew wrote about two lines of Hebrew character upon a slip of paper, and then gave it to Lewin, who just glanced at it, and a flush came over his face for a moment, that Duval thought rather singular considering the little moment of the affair.

"Re, ort much belies you, Moses," said Duval, "if you have any real occasion to send out to a friend for two hundred pounds."

"I am poor—I am poor!"

"Poh!—poh! How long will this boy of yours be gone? I am not disposed for any delays."

"You know Field Lane, my dear Duval? It is only just down the hill, you know. He will be back in a few minutes. Will you have anything to drink?"

"No—no; I have had quite enough already during the night, and might have swam in choice wines, if I had cared to do so. You have got a bargain, Moses, for I believe the diamonds round the watch are worth double the money you are about to give for the whole lot."

"Oh, no—no—Oh, dear, no," said Moses. "You are very much mistaken, my dear Duval. Diamonds are down now, very much down, indeed, my dear; and, you know, I shall have to send the things all abroad. And then our expense! and the ship, perhaps, may go to the bottom before they get to Holland. My dear Duval, you should think of all that."

"Well—well, I am satisfied, if you—Hilloa! That's rather a sharp ring at your bell, Moses."

The bell tingled furiously.

"Oh, dear, dear!" said the Jew, "that's the way with them. If they have such a thing as a two-ounce old snuff-box to part with, they come and ring the bell as if they had all the diamonds in the world in their pockets, and are willing to take half-price for the lot."

The Jew hobbled off to the door, and Duval followed him across the court-yard. The little wicket was opened, and in a sharp voice, for Moses had not wished to be interrupted until he had quite concluded the little business that he was upon, he cried—

"Who is it? Who is it?"

"Duval!" cried Luke. "Are you there?"

"Yes, Luke."

"Open the door! Open the door!"

"No! No! By Abraham, no," said the Jew, placing his back against it. "No, you shall not—Help! Murder!"

"Open the door!" cried Luke, again. "You are betrayed, Duval. The Jew has betrayed you, I say."

"Ah!" cried Duval, as he clutched the Jew by the throat, and sent him spinning across the court-yard. "What say you?"

"A Jew boy is bringing at least a dozen officers up Holborn Hill, and they are well armed."

The door was secured by a bolt on the inside, and Duval in a moment undid it, and admitted Luke.

"The horses, Luke!" he said. "The horses!"

"All safe! I have put them out of sight, that's all."

"Is there time to mount and be off?"

"No—no. Oh, no!"

"Very good. Then, this shall be our fortress for a little time, at all events."

As he spoke, Claude Duval bolted the door again firmly, and turning round he caught the Jew by the arm as he was approaching it, and cried—

"You old rascal, so you would give me up, would you?"

"Mercy—mercy!"

"You don't deserve as much as one would give to a mad dog, you old villain; for I trusted you, as well you know. Come along; I will not let you out of my clutch again."

The Jew seemed to be half dead with terror, as Duval dragged him back into the little parlour again. They had hardly reached it, when a heavy shower of blows sounded upon the little door; and then, there came a sharp ring at the bell. No doubt some of the officers had reached this spot a few moments before the boy, and had not known how to ring for admission.

"What is to be done?" said Luke.

"I'll be hanged if I know," said Duval. "It's rather awkward. Suppose we knock Moses on the head, and then see if there is a back way out of the house?"

The Jew fell upon his knees when he heard this, and in the most abject manner, begged for his life. The ringing continued with rapidity; and the banging on the panels of the door was sufficient to convince both Duval and Luke that they would not stand such an assault for long.

"Oh, spare me ! Spare me!" cried the Jew. " Rachael—Rachael, where are you ?—my little grandchild, where are you ?"

The door of the room opened, and one of the most beautiful children that Duval had ever seen, appeared. She was dressed in the richest costume ; and when she saw her grandfather, for she was the Jew's grandchild, upon his knees, and Duval in a threatening attitude standing over him, she raised a shriek of alarm, and springing forward, clung to Claude's arm in an agony of terror.

"Oh, kill me ! kill me!" she said ; " but spare him ! He is old—very old. You will not kill him?"

"For your sake I will not," said Duval. " Do not cry so, my dear. Your grandfather has done us a grievous injury ; but for your sake I will spare him. Be of good cheer."

"Blessings on you," said the young girl, and she clung round Duval's neck with an affectionate caress.

The old Jew shook like an aspen leaf, as he kept on mumbling—

"It's false ! It's false, I say ! I have done nothing. Nothing at all, I say. It is not true."

Bang—bang ! went the blows upon the door, and the bell rung furiously. Much less time had elapsed in all these circumstances taking place than we have taken to tell of them ; but yet the danger was, in truth, most imminent.

CHAPTER XCVI.

THE ESCAPE FROM THE JEW'S HOUSE; AND HOME AGAIN.

"I HAVE it," said Luke. " I have it, sir."

"What !" cried Duval. " What do you mean?"

"The little girl will not refuse to assist us, so far as she will feel certain that no harm will come to her grandfather."

"Oh, no—I will not refuse," she cried, " Bid me do anything, and I will do it. You have spared his life. I begin now to understand what he has done to excite your anger. Oh, it was not well done, grandfather : it was not, indeed. He would have betrayed you to your enemies ?"

"He would."

"Then, if you will yet spare him, I will do for you all that it is possible for me to do."

"Your plan, Luke !" said Duval. Your plan !"

"It is just this. I think that, by putting on your coat and hat over the Jew, and wrapping his face up with a handkerchief, on the plea that he resisted, and you were forced to do so, you may pass him off for yourself. He is rather tall, you see ; and if we can only get the officers to be off with him, it will do. The little lady can have no objection to a proposal that will only for a little time inconvenience her grandfather, and do him no real hurt, as the officers will be glad to release him the moment they find out their mistake. Shall it be tried?"

"Yes," said the girl. " I feel bound to do or to try anything that will be for your good. It shall be done at once, and I will get this gentleman—(indicating Duval)—a long dressing-gown of grandfather's to put on, so that he shall not be known."

"And me, too," said Luke. " Let me have something."

"You shall."

"It will do very well, I do think," said Duval.

"Oh, no—no," said the Jew, as he cast a reproachful glance at the young grl. " Are you, too, against me? Does my own flesh and blood turn against me, and side with the Gentile? My curse will fall upon your head!"

"No, grandfather," said the girl. " When you are more calm, and feel that your life has been spared, you will be thankful."

She left the room as she spoke; and Duval, as he seized upon the Jew, said—

Come, Moses; for once in a way, we will do you the honour of making you ook like a highwayman."

In the hands of Duval everything in the shape of resistance, upon the part of old Moses, would have been worse than madness; so he gave in with as good a grace as he could, and only uttered deep sepulchral groans. From the silence at the door leading into the court-yard of the Jew's abode, any one who did not know them so well as he (Duval) did, might have supposed that the officers had left the place; but he felt well convinced that they were only adopting some mode of forcing the door open, and that with suddenness they would be upon them.

Stripping off his coat, Duval enveloped the Jew in it, and then he tied a handkerchief so round his mouth, that while it did not stop his breath, it did most effectually gag him. Cutting down a thick bell rope, then, that hung by the side of the chimney-piece, Duval bound the Jew round and round with it, so that his arms were confined to his sides, and he was made completely captive.

The young girl returned with two long Jewish coats, that buttoned all the way down from the neck to the toes, and both Duval and Luke were in a moment or two enveloped in them. The change in their appearance was most remarkable.

"Hark! there goes the door," said Luke.

A sudden crash had proclaimed that the outer door was burst open by the officers. Duval immediately threw the Jew on the floor, and affecting to hold him there, he cried out—

"Help! help! This way—this way! We have him all right. Officers, this way."

Luke flung the house-door open, and the officers at once rushed into the little room. The young girl clasped her hands with a look of terror, and Duval called out—

"It's all right. We have him here a prisoner. Take him with you—you had better get a coach and take him off in it, for he is a desperate fellow. I will hold him to the floor."

The principal danger was that the Jew boy would blow the plot up by declaring that Duval was Duval, and his grandfather was the person in the predicament of being tied up with the bell-pull; but Luke got over that by the moment he saw the boy rushing to him, and catching him in his arms, and crying, as he fairly carried him out into the yard—

"Oh, my dear nephew, I am so glad you have come back in safety with these gentlemen."

"But—but," cried the boy.

"Ah, yes—it's all right."

They reached the yard, and then Luke said to him—

"Hark you—you are a very clever fellow, I daresay, but I have a knife here with which I'll cut away at your throat till your back bone stops me if you so much as say another word, good, bad, or indifferent, unless I bid you. Now look to it."

As he spoke, he, Luke produced a knife, and the Jew boy fell upon his knees in a moment. There was a door in the yard that seemed to lead to some out-house, and holding the hopeful young gentleman by the hair of his head, Luke peeped into the place that the door concealed. It was a coal-cellar.

"Now, my lad," said Luke, " I will give you a chance for your life."

"Oh dear, sir, how good of you."

"Well, perhaps it is. But you will oblige me by going into that cellar and waiting there until I come to fetch you out; and if you attempt to stir or make the least disturbance while you are there, as sure as you are now a living boy, I will rid the world of you, and put an end to your career in this life."

"Oh, mercy—mercy!"

"Go into the cellar."

" I will, sir—I will. Indeed, I will."

The boy crawled on his hands and knees to the cellar-door, and when he got quite close to it, Luke expedited his progress into it by a kick that sent him sprawling to the farther end of it with such a howl that he, Luke, was afraid might reach the ears of the officers ; so he closed the doors rather abruptly.

" He is safe, at all events," said Luke. " Confound him ! he would have spoilt all our plans. Hilloa ! here they come."

What attracted the observation of Luke now was the curious manner in which the officers were bringing out the person whom they supposed to be Claude Duval. They had wrapped round the unfortunate Jew, in order to secure him still more effectually, a large rough, great coat belonging to one of themselves, and as that held his feet together, they had no resource but to bring him out something after the fashion of an Egyptian mummy, one of them holding his feet, and the other of them holding his head.

" A coach—a coach !" cried one. " Has Jones got a coach ?"

" Yes, yes," cried Jones, running into the yard from Gray's Inn Lane. " Here's one at the door. It's all right. The man would not come without double fare, as it was a Newgate job, and I agreed to give it to him."

" Oh, that's all right. It ain't a shilling or two, or a pound or two, that will matter in the affair. Hilloa, Mr. Jew. How much do you expect, now, for giving us the affair ?"

" That, my dears," said Claude Duval, imitating capitally the Jewish accent. " That, my dears, I shall leave to you altogether."

" You will ?"

" Yes, my dears, just what you think proper I will take."

" Will fifty pounds do ?"

" Yes, my dears, very well, indeed. I don't want to make a large profit by it, my dears, for you see this Claude Duval did't behave well to me, at all ; so, I will take the fifty pounds ; and the satisfaction of knowing he will be hung up to dry, my dears, will be worth as much again."

" Well, I take you all to witness," said the principal officer, " that he says he is satisfied with fifty pounds, and that after that, Claude Duval is to be considered our capture."

" Yes, yes. Oh, yes."

" Oh, yes, my dear," added Claude. " It's all right ; I don't want to go back from my word, I swear it by Abraham."

" Then," said the officer, taking out a black pocket-book, " there, Moses, is your fifty pounds, and that settles the business. Take it ; it's a good note. You needn't look at it, and your liberality in the affair won't be the worse for you, if ever your little establishment here should be routed out, which you know may be some day."

" I know it," said Claude. " Have you got him safe in the coach, my dears ?"

" Oh, yes, yes. All's right."

" Then be off with you. Rachael, my little love, you will shut the door after the gentlemans."

" Yes, grandfather, I will."

There was no doubt upon the minds of the officers that all was right ; but the confident manner in which the beautiful young girl spoke, would have dispelled any if it had existed. They had put the old Jew in the coach, and perfectly well tisfied with their bargain, as they now expected all the reward for taking Duval. They ordered the coachman to drive as fast as he could to Newgate.

Two of them went inside, two got on the coach-box with the coachman, and the rest held on behind or scrambled on to the roof ; for they were resolved that Claude Duval, whom they fancied they now had at last in their clutches, should not escape from any want of care upon their parts.

" They will not hurt him ?" said the little girl to Claude.

" Not at all ; they dare not. They will find out their mistake when they ge. to Newgate, and then they have no sort of authority to detain him a momentt

It was a thousand pities that your grandfather conceived the idea of betraying me. cannot think what could have induced him to do so."

"Ah, sir, he is getting old now, and the love of gold is now day by day, and hour by hour, growing upon him. He wishes to amass a large sum, that he may leave England, and go and lay his bones in Jerusalem."

"Oh, that is it! He is going out of business!! That accounts for the whole affair in a moment. I must now, my dear, bid you a good day, for every moment that I linger here is full of danger."

Duval had again carefully secured about him the rich property that he had brought with him to dispose of to the Jew, and then shaking hands cordially with the young girl, he hurried from the house. In the yard, waiting rather impatiently for him, he met Luke.

"Come, sir, oh, come," said Luke. "Recollect how short the distance from here to Newgate is, and how at any moment, even before getting there, for all we know to the contrary, the deceit may be discovered."

"You are right, Luke ; I am off directly. Where are the horses ?"

"This way, this way."

Luke led the way into the lane, and under cover of an archway, both the horses were quietly standing. To mount was the work of a moment, and off they set at a hard gallop down the Gray's Inn Lane northward, for that was then the nearest route to Hornsey, as they could get across the fields by Islington.

They had hardly got to Battle Bridge, when they heard a great shouting noise behind them. Upon turning to look in that direction, they saw two mounted men, with arms in their hands, in hot pursuit of them.

"Ah," said Duval. "They have found out their error at last."

"But there are only two of them, sir."

"So I see, and we will give them a little race into the country. There is a lane just by here, called Maiden Lane, which is our best way, as it escapes the hill. We will take that, Luke, and if these fellows choose to come after us, which I don't think very likely, they will find it to be the worse for them."

Maiden Lane, at its commencement, then had a few little rather poor cottages sprinkled here and there, but it was not the squalid den of infamy that it is now. Those who know nothing of that part of London, as it is at present, and who fancy that they must go eastward of the Royal Exchange, or to the river's banks to look for squalor and filth, had better visit Maiden Lane, and walk the first half mile along it, from King's Cross, where they will have an experience of what frightful odours—low language—drunkenness—and filth, really are, such as they may almost in vain seek for elsewhere; and yet in that immediate neighbourhood insane attempts are made to construct long rows of handsome houses, and to found almost a new city.

We warn all persons seeking a home in that locality, that Maiden Lane and King's Cross are under their noses. If, after such information, they can relish the neighbourhood, Heaven help their tastes.

It was up Maiden Lane then, as it was, and not as it is, that Duval and Luke, at a swinging gallop, took their way, with the two boldest and most talented officers of Newgate after them. It was quite clear, from the manner in which those two officers rode, that there was no shrinking upon their parts, and that they had quite made up their minds to do the job upon which they had come, or to see some much more substantial reason than danger, for leaving it alone.

"Ah," said Duval, as he listened to the loud tread of their horses' feet in the lane, "those are men who will not be deterred by a trifle. I deeply regret that they have come upon such an errand."

"But you do not think for a moment, sir," said Luke, "that they can get the better of us, surely?"

"No, Luke, **that is not** the ground upon which I regret their coming ; but I do not like to take life, **and I am** much afraid that these men are of that order, that unless I do, they will not be easily disposed of. But it must be so, I suppose."

"You should not forget, sir, that it is to death they would drag you, and that all their seeming courage is merely because a large reward is offered for you. Self defence is a better motive than that."

CHAPTER XCVII.

DUVAL IS CAUGHT IN A TRAP, BUT TRICKS HIS CAPTORS.

DUVAL was rather surprised to hear Luke argue the matter so well as he did, for what he said was really very much to the question.

"Luke," he said, "you remove many of my scruples, I know, and feel the truth of what you say, that it is, after all, nothing but the love of gold that brings these men after us, and that makes them seem so bold and so full of daring, and I will defend myself to the last against them."

"Do so, sir. They come well armed against us, and they deserve all that they get."

"They do—they do."

"Shall we stop, then, sir, and meet them ? There is a nice little hillock close a-head of us, where we can conveniently come to a pause, I think, sir."

"I see the hillock, Luke ; but let me advise you never, if you are going to exchange pistol shots with any one, to take the high ground. You chances of being hit, if you do, will be ten to one in comparison to what they would be if you occupy a low position. When you are upon an elevation, the bullets that otherwise would go over your head, will hit you almost to a certainty."

"I see, sir—I see—I understand. Then we will wait in the hollow, sir. It strikes me that the moment we come to a stand they will do so likewise."

"It is more than probable, Luke, especially if they see us with arms in our hands."

"Our best plan, sir, will be to take one of them a-piece. There's the fellow, with the red coat, I will pay all the attention I can to him, sir, if you please, if you will tackle the other ; and by that means I don't think we need waste a shot."

"Upon my word, Luke, you take the thing coolly and quite philosophically. But let it be as you say. You attend to the one in the red coat, and I will keep my eye on the one with the blue."

"Do so, sir, and between you and me, I would not give a dump for their lives. But that's their look out, not ours, you see, sir. They will have it, so we can't possibly help it."

The manner in which Luke reconciled himself to the necessity of killing the two officers, or, at the least, of very seriously wounding them, would at any other time have been quite amusing to Duval, but at that period their circumstances were of rather too serious a nature to permit him to have the laugh that Luke's calm philosophy really provoked.

"Halt," he said. "This, I think, is the lowest part of the road, my friend ?"

"It is, sir ; and there they come, thundering on. Ah, no, they are already pulling up. They don't like the look of us, after all, and are rather afraid to come to close quarters. It is as I all along suspected, sir. They don't want to come to a fair fight, but they relied upon running us down in course of time, and getting all sorts of help to be upon us."

"Likely enough !"

"I am sure of it, sir; and it's a nasty, sneaking spy-like mode of doing business, such as I don't like at all ; so for that, if for nothing else, I'm glad enough that we have put a stop to it by a halt. Why, what are they about now, sir ?—what the deuce is the meaning of that, I wonder ?"

One of the officers had taken out a white handkerchief, and fastened it at the end of his riding-whip, and with that fluttering in the morning air, as a " Flag of

Truce," for such he intended it; he gently walked his horse forward to where Duval and Luke were staying.

"He wants to talk us over, Luke!"

"Talk us over?"

"Yes. That white handkerchief shows that he has got a something or another to say, and that while it flies, he will not attempt any violence, and hopes that he will receive none. I will go forward and hear the fellow."

"Don't, sir—oh, don't."

"Nay—but, Luke, you see it is a regular flag of truce, and it would look bad, indeed, not to go."

"I would not trust him, sir."

"You would not?"

"No, I would not trust one of those fellows upon their oaths, much less upon the strength of a white pocket-handkerchief. Don't you go, sir! Take my word for it, it is only a take-in. They can't fight you by fair means, and they want to try to do so by foul. That's the long and short of it, sir."

"If I could but think so for a moment——"

"Do think so, sir! I don't like the talking part of the affair at all; but if it must be, you stay where you are, and let me go. You will then see if they mean fair or not."

"No—no! If there be danger, let me face it."

"I implore you not, sir!"

"Nay, Luke, I find that you don't know me yet. I have always found the greatest safety by meeting danger half-way; and, besides, if yonder fellow means any treachery, it by no manner of means follows that he is to succeed in it. I will keep such a wary eye upon him that he shall find it a difficult matter to wink without my cognizance of the act. Be under no apprehension; all will be right, Luke. Wait for me where you are."

When Luke saw that Duval would not be persuaded not to meet the officer with the handkerchief at the end of his riding-whip, he made no further opposition, but only took care to place himself in such a position, with a pistol in his hand ready for immediate use, as would give him a chance of shooting the officer if he should see occasion, upon a sudden emergency, so to do.

Duval rode forward about a couple of dozen paces, and then he called out—

"My friend, I think you and I are quite near enough to each to hear anything you have to say!"

"That is as you please, Duval," said the officer. "I have no sort of desire to intrude further upon you than you think proper, and I hope you will listen to me calmly."

"Oh, I am quite calm; only I think the sooner you manage to come to the point the better it will be."

"I will come to it at once—a-hem!"

"Very well, go on."

"I was going to say, that that was a capital trick you played those idiots who brought the jew to Newgate, instead of you, in the hackney-coach; but with that I personally have nothing to do, although my friend yonder has."

"Oh, he is one of the idiots, is he?"

"Why, a—in a manner of speaking, yes; but I beg to state, Duval, that it will be quite impossible for you to escape, and you had much better take your chances of a comfortable trial at the Old Bailey, than be shot down like a dog on the highway."

"Is that all you have got to say?"

"Why, to a reasonable man, as I fully believe you are, that ought to be enough, and I trust you will see the propriety of coming quietly back to London with me!"

"Upon my word," said Duval, "you are the most impudent fellow I have met with for some time."

"Impudent?"

"Yes, to be sure.   Is it not the very height of impudence to make such a proposal to me while a breath of life is in me?   I am amazed at your infernal assurance."

"You really are?"

"I really am."

CLAUDE RETALIATES UPON MOSES, THE JEW.

"Then you refuse the excellent advice I offer you?"

"Rather!"

"Then perhaps you will have the kindness to take that."

As he spoke, the officer fired a thick, short, holster-pistol right at Duval's head. The contents blew off his hat and singed his hair, but owing to the fact of his horse causing him to stoop at the moment, the villanous attempt did not do him any further injury ; but really, in the confusion of the moment, Duval could not take upon himself to say whether he was hit or not ; but of the two, he rather thought he was.

The moment the officer had fired this dastardly shot, he turned round and tried to get away to his companion, but Luke came on at a pace that seemed as though he were flying, and then suddenly bringing his horse to so dead a stop that he threw the creature upon its haunches, he called out—

"A fair shot for a foul one !"

With the pistol that he had kept ready for service in his grasp during the whole of the interview, he levelled at the officer, and hit him exactly between the shoulders.   With a loud cry of agony he fell forward on his horse's neck.

" If that has not done for you," said Luke, " there is no virtue in a couple of ounce bullets."

The officer's horse made a mad plunge forwards and then half fell, flinging his rider to the earth ; and the other officer seeing that he was now left alone, at once turned, and went off as fast as his horse could take him.

" Oh, sir—sir," cried Luke, " he has killed you ! I expected it would end in this way, and it is but a poor satisfaction to me, that I have been able to avenge your murderer—for it was a murder."

" Wait a bit," said Duval.

" What, sir. are you not mortally wounded ?"

" Not that I know of, Luke," replied Duval, shaking his head ; " I don't feel quite so clear-headed as I did, but I don't think there's much more harm done. I fancy if there were a bullet or two in my brains, I should feel rather more confused than I do now, and that's going away fast."

" Oh, sir, how pleased I am, to be sure ! I made up my mind that you were done for."

" Did you ?"

" Yes.   When I saw the rascal fire slap at your head, sir, what else could I possibly think of it ?   I really thought he had blown your head almost off, and I felt as if I were going mad."

" It was my hat, Luke.   I am pretty right again now.   By Heaven, it was as foul and dastardly a shot as I ever heard of one man firing at another.   What has become of the rascal ?"

" What, sir, did you not see me settle him ?"

" Settle him, Luke ?   Is that a delicate way of saying that you have killed him ?"

" If a couple of bullets through his back will do it, I have ; and did he not deserve it, sir ?"

" He did—he did.   He was an assassin, and all such deserve death from any hand that has the power to inflict it upon them.   This is the closest touch that I think I have had yet for my life.   When I heard the report of the pistol, I gave it up as a done job ; and if he had but fired another at me, he must have hit me, for I was too confused to resist him."

" Thank Heaven, sir, the rascal did not fire again ; but the fact was, he thought the first discharge had done the job, and was willing to get away then as quickly as he could."

" Where is he, Luke ?"

" There !   Lying on his back in the road."

Duval shook his head again, for he still felt to a degree confused at the nearness of the pistol-shot.   Luke thought it was with disapprobation of the death of the officer, and he said—

" Surely, sir, you think he deserved it ?"

" You mistake me, Luke.   I am not shaking my head at that, but to settle my own brains a little.   They seem to have given quite a jump ; but that feeling will soon pass away.   I think our best plan is to get home as quickly as we may."

" It is, sir."

" Come on, then.   We will leave the field of battle to the enemy, if they think proper to come and claim it. It is quite sufficiently satisfactory to us to have obtained the victory."

With this they went off at a canter, leaving the dead officer lying just where he had fallen. His treachery had been really of so glaring a nature that Duval did not feel at all inclined to prefer any ordinary scene towards the dead body, nor did he feel an atom of pity for a man who could behave in so glaringly treacherous a manner towards him.

"I feel, Luke," he said, "that I am deeply indebted to you for the manner in which you have seconded me in this affair. I was really at the time unable to defend myself, and the probability is that if you had not advanced in the manner that you did, the other officer would have come up and finished me."

"It's very well sir, as it is; and here we are in the high-road of Holloway. We shall soon be at home. The best way now, sir, will be down the Seven Sisters' Road, and then up Hornsey-lane."

"Precisely; and I don't know how you feel, Luke, but I will say for myself that I never felt more inclined for a rest than I do now. I am thoroughly weary."

"Ah, sir, if you had not been so, you would not have been so easily taken in by that rascal of an officer. I thought you had not quite your usual judgment and sharpness about you."

Duval smiled at this opinion of Luke's, and in the course of twenty minutes were at the garden-gate of Duval's house at Hornsey.

CHAPTER XCVIII.

THE COURT JEWELLER IN ST. JAMES'S, AND THE ARREST.

"HOME again," said Duval, "and I am not sorry for that, Luke, for to tell the truth, I am for once in a way fairly fagged."

"And no wonder, sir. I think that eight or ten hours' sleep will do one no harm, and I am quite sure that you want it."

"I really think I do. But neither you nor I must give way to such a long repose as that."

"Not both of us at a time, sir. You go to rest, and I will still manage to keep my eyes open for a few hours."

"No, Luke. Bolt and bar the place up—make the doors and windows secure, and then I think we may both repose without any harm coming to us."

"Then I will sleep in the stable," said Luke. "There's nothing to me so capital and luxurious as a bundle of straw just opened, and then to get right inside of it, with a couple of horse-cloths. The straw makes a pleasant rustling that sends you to sleep, and you are soon as cosey and as comfortable as possible. If anything should happen, too, I shall be sure to hear of it in the stable. So you may rest, sir, quite at your ease."

Duval could not but laugh at the idea of comfort that Luke had, and then surrendering to him the horses, he went into the house where, as a matter of course, he was warmly welcomed by her who was his wife both by an union of affection and of ceremony. Duval took care, however, before he indulged himself with any repose, to hide, in a secure place, the booty he had brought with him from the palace at Kew, and which he had made so unsuccessful an attempt already to dispose of. That the articles he had got possession of were of great value, there could be no sort of doubt, and the greatest difficulty was to realise their value.

Duval made up his mind, if he could find no other mode of doing so, to take a trip to Holland, and try to dispose of the plunder in Amsterdam, which was then a great mart for every description of valuable property, as France was in a very disorganised condition, politically.

Nothing occurred for the whole of the day to give the remotest alarm to Duval; and as he had made up his mind to remain at home for some time, until the affair at the palace had quite blown over, he amused himself about his house and garden.

"Ah, now," said she whom we feel has a right to be called Mrs. Duval, "if you could only always lead this life, Claude, how happy we might be."

"Do you think so?"

"I am sure of it. Here this day is passing away quite delightfully, and I am sure that nothing can be more pleasing to you than walking in your garden and tending the animals that are my only amusement when you are out of the place."

"Well, I admit that I am fond of a country life, but how long that fondness would last I cannot at all pretend to say. It is possible enough that after a time I should weary of it."

"Oh, no. The country has a thousand charms that you could never weary of. Were the season always the same as it is now, or were there perpetual winter, or even perpetual summer, I grant that the sameness of the country would become in time very tiresome, indeed; but, on the contrary, there is in the country perpetual change."

"Well, perhaps I might be happy enough in it."

At this moment Luke came up to where Duval and his wife were, to ask something concerning the horses, and Duval turning to him, said:—

"I wish, Luke, that you would mount one of them, and go and try to purchase for us a newspaper; it is just possible that we might find something about our recent adventures that it may be as well for us to know."

"Yes, sir; I shall be able to get one at Islington."

Luke made good speed to Islington and back, and brought Duval a newspaper then published, called the "St. James's Chronicle." There was a look about the face of Luke that convinced Duval at once that there was a something in the paper interesting to him.

"There is a paragraph for us, Luke?"

"Yes, sir; and an advertisement."

"Indeed! That is a rarity. Let me see it."

Luke pointed out a particular part of the paper, and Duval read as follows—

"To the Baron Hoge:—If the individual calling himself the Baron Hoge, will return to Mr. James Sanderson, 24 St. James's Street, the various little articles taken from K., he will receive a five hundred pound note, and no questions will be asked or inquiries made concerning him."

"This does, indeed, concern me; and yet I don't know what to do exactly. If I thought I could rely upon this promise in the advertisement, I would not hesitate a moment to part with the things. I know that their intrinsic value is much more than five hundred pounds; and yet it is a much larger sum than I ever expected to realize for them."

"Why, sir," said Luke, "the fact is, that I daresay there are certain parties who are quite as anxious as we can be to keep the secret of the affair at Kew Palace; so that perhaps it really is true that they would gladly enough give the five hundred pounds to hush it all up."

"That is likely enough, Luke. You would then counsel me to venture to St. James's Street with the booty?"

"No, no, sir. Let me go. Then if there is any treachery, it won't be so bad as if they got hold of you."

"No, Luke, that would not be fair."

"Oh yes, sir, it would. And I feel quite assured that my mistress will consider that it is the best plan."

"No; I would have neither of you go," said Mrs. Duval. "I would forego the money, and wait until some favourable opportunity should arise of making one-half the amount by the jewels."

"Ah," said Duval, "do not forget that you are the banker, and that my object is to make enough to prevent me from being under the necessity of pursuing this line of life.—Did we not agree fully upon that? Recollect what a lift the sum of five hundred pounds is towards that object. I think I will go."

"But the frightful risk!"

"The more I think of it, the more I am inclined to think that the advertisement is quite genuine."

"Oh sir, do let me go," said Luke.

"No," said Duval, with a sudden resolution. "Saddle me a horse, and I will go at once, Luke. The whole affair will be over in a couple of hours. I will ride in sharply and ride out as quickly. I do not think there is any real danger. I will dress myself as quaintly as I can, and take the plunder with me. Do not be under any apprehension; I suspect that I know too much of the proceedings at Kew, to make it safe to apprehend me."

Poor May burst into tears, for she had a kind of presentiment, as she said, that this affair would turn out to be most disastrous to Duval; but she well knew that when he had made a determination, to try to turn him from it by speaking of its dangers was utterly futile, so she only said—

"For my sake you will be as careful as is possible for you to be, Claude; you will promise me that?"

"I will, indeed. I will neglect nothing that shall in any way contribute to my safety; and there is one thing that I beg of you to remember, and that is, that let what will happen to me, you can do me no good; let you hear what you may, I beg and implore that you will remain here at home, and take no step, in the mistaken idea that you can do me a service."

"But—but——"

"Nay, I must get you to promise me that much."

"I will, then. I do. I rely upon your judgment wholly; and if you are of that opinion, I will promise to follow the course you point out."

"Here's the horse, sir," said Luke.

Claude went into the house, and made some slight change in his apparel. He likewise carefully secreted about him all the articles that he had brought away from the Prince of Wales's bed-room and dressing-room at Kew, so that there should be no cavil about his keeping his part of the agreement; and then, with a cheerful air, he started from his home on the very perilous expedition.

There were several circumstances that induced Claude Duval to think that upon this occasion he was going upon a safe errand. In the first place the value of the articles was much over the sum offered, so it was evident that sum was considered to be a sort of compromise of the affair; and in the second place, he knew that the Prince of Wales had everything to dread from a public exposure of what took place at the palace at Kew. The reader will easily imagine, that although we have, from the most authentic sources, the whole of the particulars of that night at Kew, we have been compelled to suppress a good portion of it.

Heaven forbid that our pages should be like those of many who pander to the worst passions of beauty at the present day. We flatter ourselves that we can present life, in its most stirring scenes, to the reader, without outraging modesty and virtue.

It will be understood, then, that there was much more to tell about what passed at Kew upon that night, than the reader of this work is aware of; and so it was that Duval thought that the Prince of Wales would hardly provoke such a disclosure by any act of treachery to him.

"No," he said, as he rode along. "The sum of five hundred pounds is but a small one in such a quarter; and I quite understand that it is given to hush up the transaction."

So far Duval was right; but it will be seen that there were other circumstances in the affair which he had not, and which, indeed, no one would have taken into account. But we will not anticipate.

At the pace at which Duval rode, he soon reached London; and then suffering his horse to subside into a quiet trot, so that no appearance of undue hurry should be about him when he should reach St. James's Street, he quietly entered that aristocratic thoroughfare.

No. 24 was a jeweller's shop, and the words on the window of "Jeweller to

His Royal Highness the Prince of Wales" by no means tended to diminish
Duval's faith in the *bona fide* character of the whole transaction. Nothing was
more natural than that the prince should have entrusted to his jeweller the conduct of such an affair.

Full of these ideas, and really not anticipating any danger, Duval halted at No.
24, St. James's Street.

To be sure, there was nothing in the appearance of Duval to lead in the least
to the idea that he was a highwayman ; and when he entered the shop, he was
received with the greatest possibile civility.

"Is Mr. Sanderson within ?" he said.

"Yes, sir. Certainly, sir. Pray, step this way."

Duval followed the shopman to a private counting-house, that was built in the
yard, and there he was introduced to a very staid-looking personage with a bald
head, who was Mr. Sanderson. When the door was closed, and the shopman
out of hearing, Claude Duval said, in soft and bland accents—

"Sir, I came here in consequence of an advertisement addressed to the Baron
Hoge."

Mr. Sanderson gave a jump.

"You—you have some little articles for the prince then, I presume, sir ?" said
the jeweller, all of a shake, and looking as nervous as possible.

"I have, sir," said Duval. "I have placed the most implicit confidence in
the advertisement, and have come here relying upon the prince's honour to accept
the terms offered. I hope that I have not misplaced the confidence that I have so
promptly shown ?"

"You have not, Mr. a—a Baron Hoge. The prince is extremely desirous that
the whole affair should be forgotten, and he is quite willing to pass it off as a
joke merely. Some of the little relics that you took with you, were presents from
different members of the royal family, and, therefore, he will freely give five hundred pounds for their restoration."

"Very good," said Duval, as he laid the articles before the jeweller. "There
they are, and you have nothing to do, but to give me the money, and I will be
off at once, Mr. Sanderson."

The jeweller rapidly glanced over the articles, and then compared them with a
written paper that he had close at hand.

"Quite right, sir," he said; "quite right. I will hand you the money
directly."

With these words he proceeded to an iron chest that was let into the wall,
and speedily abstracted from it a note for five hundred pounds, which he handed
to Duval, adding—

"Now, sir, I only hope that you will make good use of this money. You are
a young man, quite a young man, and I am an old one, so you will excuse me
for offering you friendly advice. With that sum of money you can surely find
some honest and reputable means of getting a living."

"Sir," said Duval, "far from feeling any offence at what you say, I thank you
for having so much kindly interest in me as to say it. I will bid you good morning,
well pleased that I trusted to your word and that of the prince, and came here."

"Yes—but really now consider, Mr. What's-your-name—you will not bring
yourself to a bad end ?"

"It is very kind of you, sir, to speak to me in such a way. I will consider."

"That's right. That's right. You have something in your face, and tones,
and manner, that convinces me that you are not a bad—not a very bad young
man. I was not prepared to see a person like you, indeed, I was not; and I feel
a degree of kindly pity for you. Remember, now, that if you really feel an inclination to change your mode of life, you will find a friend in me."

"I will not forget it, sir. Friends are too scarce now-a-days for me to hold
lightly so kind and generous a one as yourself."

Duval shook hands with the old gentleman, and walked out of the counting-
house, with his five hundred pounds in his pocket. He thought that the shop-

man cast a very odd look at him, and then through the window into the street, and a faint suspicion crossed the mind of Duval at that moment for the first time that all was not right.

At the door there was his horse, and no one offered to in any way interrupt him. The suspicion that had crossed his mind that there was some lurking treachery somewhere, vanished again ; and he gave the boy a shilling, and placed his foot in the stirrup to mount.

At that moment he felt himself clasped round the body by a powerful pair of arms, and a voice cried in his ear—

" You are my prisoner, Claude Duval !"

CHAPTER XCIX.

DUVAL FINDS HIMSELF IN NEWGATE RATHER UNEXPECTEDLY.

So unexpected an arrest as this was, must have confounded Duval, unless he had really been something more than human. No other mode than that which had been adopted, could have so effectually secured him ; and from the moment that the arms were cast around him, Duval might be said to feel that he was in experienced hands.

All he could do was to kick vigorously.

" You are my prisoner," said the voice again, " and you may remain so without injury or with it, as you think proper."

" Not yet," said Duval.

By such an effort as few men could have made, he succeeded in turning round to face his assailant ; but he had scarcely done so, when four men rushed round them, and he found that they had arranged how to set to work with him, for one took possession of an arm, another of a leg, and so on, until, if he had had the strength of a lion, he would have been overpowered most completely.

" Very good," said Duval. " I'm taken, that's all."

From that moment he abandoned resistance, for he felt that it would be quite futile against his foes; while in its result it might inflict some injury upon himself, that might incapacitate him for any future efforts for his escape.

" Do you give in, Claude Duval?" said the officer, who had first laid hold of him ; " do you give in ?"

" Yes, rather. It's long odds, one to five, don't you think, old fellow ? Of course, I'm like the bit of iron that bends when it can't help it, if you call that giving in."

" All's right. Now for the darbies."

" Oh, anything you like in a quiet way."

Duval had a knack of sticking out the bones of his wrists, to enlarge their apparent circumference ; and the first pair of handcuffs the officers tried to put upon him were, consequently, found to be too small. Another pair was fitted on which he knew perfectly well he could, with some little difficulty, get his hands out of when he choose.

They then let him get up, or rather they lifted him up, for in the first brief struggle, he and the four officers had gone to the ground together ; and then he stood fairly clutched between two of them, and a prisoner.

" Where's the coach ?" said the principal officer.

" Coming," said one of the others; " there it is."

A hackney-coach lumbered up to the goldsmith's door, and then one of the officers tied Duval's ankles together with a silk handkerchief, saying as he did so—

" He is a slippery customer, and you cannot make too sure of him."

" Wait a bit," said Duval, " you are not quite sure of me yet."

" Ain't we, though ? It strikes me you will dangle for this affair though, Master Duval."

" What affair ?"

" Oh, you are as innocent as a babby, of course.   Now help him in, Joe ; you get up behind, Bill.   We will get inside along with him."

At this moment Duval cast his eyes towards the jeweller's window, and he saw the shopman standing close to the door rubbing his hands together, as though he thought what was going on quite a capital piece of work.

"Ah, my friend," said Duval, "I shall recollect you!"

The shopman immediately disappeared.   By this time a crowd of persons began to collect, and the questions of " What is it ?" "Who is it ?" were asked eagerly.   It was the officer who got up behind the coach, that, in the pride of his heart at assisting at such a capture, cried out—

" It's Claude Duval !"

The news spread like wildfire among the crowd, and a wild kind of shout rent the air.   People ran up to the spot from all directions, and "Duval! Duval! Duval the Highwayman, is taken!" was shouted by many lips.

Duval looked quite calm and unconcerned as he heard all this, and he was observed to smile slightly as the coachman began to swear dreadfully upon finding that his progress was impeded by the people, who would crowd around the vehicle with the hope of catching a glimpse of the celebrated personage.

"You should have kept your own secret," said Duval, "and then the people would not have know that it took five of you to overcome me, and then that you had to do it by surprise."

" Never you mind about that," said the officer.   "Surprise or not surprise, we have got you, that's enough for us."

" Mind you keep me."

" That we don't care about.   We will lode you in Newgate ; that will be enough for us.   If they let you go, it don't matter to us a brass farthing.   It's not my business."

" Perhaps it may be, though."

" Drive on, will you, coachman ?   Drive on !"

The coachman proceeded with difficulty, amid a yelling and shouting crowd, that each moment was on the increase.   The officer who had taken his station behind, in resisting the intrusion of some of the more clamorous and curious of the mob, kicked at several of them, and the consequence was, that he was pulled down and severely maltreated by the people.   The officer who was upon the box with the driver, presented a pistol at some that would stop the horses, and threatened to fire ; and by the time the coach got to the neighbourhood of Charing Cross in its route to Newgate, it was compelled to come to a dead stop, being hemmed in by a mob of about a thousand of the roughest of the London population.   The officers who were with Duval looked pale and anxious.

" Pull them out !" cried a loud voice, and then there was a yell of execration at the officers.   The one that was upon the box was afraid to use his pistols, and gave them up to the crowd.   If he had used them, there can be no doubt but that his own life would have been instantly sacrificed.

"A rescue ! a rescue !" cried a loud voice.   " Let's set him free, for Duval always gave to the poor, what he took from the rich !"

" Hurrah ! hurrah !" shouted a thousand voices.

" We shall all be murdered," said one of the officers.

Duval began to think that there was a chance of escape, and so there would have been, but a tradesman upon the spot, who was a constable in his own right, suddenly rushed out with a staff from his shop, and in a little squeaking voice, he cried—

"Disperse, you wretches, disperse !   Look at me and tremble !   Disperse ! Here I am !"

This produced such a roar of laughter, that for the moment all the vigorous intentions of the mob, regarding the rescue of Duval, was forgotten.   The valorous constable was seized upon in a moment, and a voice cried—

" Hang him ! hang him !"

"No—no," shouted another; "here's the parish pump; give him a good du king."

"Hurrah!" shouted the multitude, and in the course of half a minute the constable in his own right was held under a large pump, while the handle of it was worked with a vigour that threatened to work it off.

MAY REMONSTRATES AGAINST CLAUDE'S VISIT TO THE JEWELLER.

The coach moved on a little.

"Stop the coach," said somebody.   "We will let Duval off; and as our hands are in, we will pump upon the officers."

This suggestion was received with uproarious delight; but at that moment that both Duval and the officers thought it would be acted upon, there arose a scream—

ing yell from the mob, and its members began to fly in all directions. The principal officer thrust his head out of the window of the coach, and cried—

"A troop of cavalry, by all that's good! We are saved!"

In the course of a minute the mob had evaporated, and Duval could see the red coats and flashing weapons of the soldiers through the coach windows, as they surrounded it.

Twelve dragoons had been sufficient to disperse the mob, and leave a perfectly clear space for the coach.

"So much for popular support," thought Duval. "Well, I am not disappointed, at any rate."

The two officers on the seat opposite to him were whispering together, and he heard one say—

"Yes, it's the colonel who has managed that for us."

The moment Duval heard the colonel mentioned, he began to think; and the idea that Colonel Lane was somehow connected with his arrest, pressed itself slightly upon his imagination. He would have been glad to think that Sanderson the jeweller really had no hand in the treachery, but under the circumstances, it was very difficult to acquit him by any course of reasoning.

A sergeant who was in command of the little party of dragoons, now came close to the coach window, and said—

"Have you got your prisoner all safe, officers?"

"Oh, yes—yes."

"Very well; our orders are to see you safe to Newgate."

"Thank you. I do believe you have saved our lives, sergeant."

"Who sent you?" said Duval, and the sergeant thinking at the moment from the tone that it was one of the officers, promptly replied—

"Oh, Colonel Lane ordered me off."

"And how is he?"

"Pretty well, thank you."

"Remember the Baron Hoge to him when you see him."

"The who?" The sergeant looked closely into the coach, and was mortifi d enough to find that he had been conversing with the prisoner instead of one of the officers.

With an oath, he turned his horse's head from the coach, and trotted on in advance of his men.

"You are a cool fellow, Duval," said the officer.

"Why not?"

"Well, of course, there's no reason why you should not," he said; "but it's a fact, for all that. I don't wish you any harm; but you know, in the way of business, when we had information of where you were likely to be, it was not a very probable thing that we should neglect it and keep out of the way."

"Certainly not. I don't blame you. If you can tell me one thing, I should be much obliged to you."

"What is it?"

"It's just this. Did Sanderson, the jeweller, give you information that I was to visit his place, or that I was likely at all to be there? I should like to know that.—Yes or no."

"Well, it's no harm telling you that he did not."

"But his shopman did?"

The officer nodded, and added, "He is well paid for it, too, I rather think. Colonel Lane, I fancy, has some particular charge against you, Claude Duval, or else he would not be quite so angry."

"Oh," said Duval, "I think I understand it all now."

"How do you mean?"

"It's of no consequence. I am obliged to you for the information you have given me. It can do no one any harm, and it prevents me from being angry at an innocent person. I had reason to suspect Mr. Sanderson of acting treacherously by me, and it is a great relief to me to find that he has not done so."

"You may make up your mind to that, Duval," added the officer. "It is very doubtful even if the old gentleman knows of the matter yet. But here we are at Newgate."

It was not in human nature for Duval to feel nothing of a gloomy tendency as he was helped out of the coach into the lobby of Newgate; and there came a bright flush to his cheek as he heard the principal one of the officers who was with him, cry out—

"Claude Duval!"

At the sound of that well-known name, there at once ensued quite a commotion in the vestibule of Newgate. It was repeated from mouth to mouth, until every officer of the prison, who was not upon actual duty in some of its gloomy passages, came to the hall to have a look at him; and in the course of a few moments, the governor himself reached the spot.

"What is all this?" he said.

"Claude Duval, sir."

"Is it, indeed, so? Are you Duval?"

"I am."

"Then you are as welcome here as you possibly can be. Get No. 27 ready for Duval, directly. So, your career is at an end, is it?"

"Who says so?" said Duval.

"I do; and all the country will say so."

"Indeed! Then you and all the country are very much mistaken, I can tell you. There's something at my heart and brain that tells me I shall yet weather through this storm."

"If you do," said the governor, "I'll make you a present of this, my fine fellow."

As he spoke, he pointed to his head; but Duval, with a laugh, said, "It is not worth the having, or I should certainly claim it."

"Load him with the heaviest irons," said the governor, "and visit him every hour. I will see the Lord Chief Justice about you, Mister Duval, and he shall direct what course is to be taken concerning you. Come into my office, Mr. Edwards, and I will give you a receipt for the body of this most notorious reprobate."

The governor was lashing himself into a passion, for he was quite provoked at the calm smile that was upon the face of Duval, who, since he had heard that it was not the old jeweller who had betrayed him, while speaking so kindly to him, had felt quite comfortably at his ease.

When the governor left the vestibule of the prison, the officers and turnkeys smiled at each other, and one put his tongue in his cheek as he said—

"The old one is quite vinegary to-day; but come on, Duval, we must obey orders, you know; we will make you as comfortable as we can, for all that."

"Your wish to do so is quite enough," said Duval. "Don't get yourselves into any trouble on my account; I am used to roughing it, rather. All I want just now is leave to write a letter."

"To whom?"

"To Mr. Sanderson the jeweller, of 24 St. James's Street. You won't, I suppose, suspect him of being a pal of mine, will you?"

"Hardly, Duval. You shall have the means of writing your letter; but you know that in Newgate there is such a thing as garnish."

"I know it, and a good thing it is too, when you have got it to give. There is twenty pounds among you, and if I can get the letter delivered by some of you, I will make it as much again."

CHAPTER C.

DUVAL IS MYSTERIOUSLY TAKEN FROM NEWGATE.

THE liberality of Duval to the jailors and janitors of the old prison of Newgate was by no means thrown away. The higher authorities, such as the sheriff, and the governor, and the chaplain, no doubt, felt a degree of exultation at having at length in custody so noted a criminal; but at that time it is a certain fact that there was no character so popular, and so much thought of, with all the lower officials connected with the criminal law, as a highwayman.

To be sure, when we say highwayman, there were at the period some upon the road, who, like the highwayman in *Roderick Random*, were bullies when they thought they could do so with safety, and as pusillanimous as possible under different circumstances; but such men as Duval, Turpin, and a few others, were not obnoxious to such a reproach.

Then, again, whenever they did come into contact with the officials of the law, they treated them with boundless liberality; and it was quite a little fortune for the lower personages attached to Newgate to have such a man as Duval in the building. Can we wonder, then, at the frequent escapes of highwaymen in those days from the great metropolitan prison?

The cell into which Duval was conducted, those who had a kindly feeling towards him could not change, inasmuch as it was specified by the order of the governor; but in every other respect he had it all his own way. When writing materials were brought to him, he wrote the following letter to Mr. Sanderson, the jeweller in St. James's Street.

The original of this letter is now in existence, and was found among a heap of documents appertaining to the early part of the reign of George the Third, in St. James's Palace.

" Newgate.

" SIR—You were kind enough to say that if I wanted a friend, you would like to hear from me. I have now something to complain of which I think would be put to rights if represented in the proper quarter.

" I trusted to your word, Mr. Sanderson, and came to your house in perfect confidence. I was arrested almost upon your doorstep, and certainly in consequence of some one giving information to the officers that I was likely to be there.

" The one who gave that information, Mr. Sanderson, *was not you.* If it were, I should lose all faith in human nature, and never again take upon myself to decide upon an honest heart or a kind face in a human being. If you can do anything for me, I ask it of you. If you cannot, I thank you for the kind things you said to me, and still remain your debtor for them, and am—Yours ever,

"CLAUDE DUVAL."

It was a rule of the prison that all letters written by any of the prisoners to any of their friends in the world outside, were to be submitted to the chaplain first, and if he did not find them stuffed with cant religious phrases, he very commonly intercepted them; but Duval's liberality to the turnkeys got over that difficulty, and his letter, which, no doubt, would have been suppressed, never found its way to the chaplain, but was taken direct to St. James's Street.

" Now," said Duval, as he flung himself upon the little straw mattress in his cell. "Now for a rest. There's no very great likelihood of any calls, so I shall try to get a sleep; after that I will just turn over in my mind what had best be done if Mr. Sanderson fails me."

With that happy constitutional indifference to surrounding circumstances, which carried him through so many difficulties and dangers, that would have appaled ordinary men, Duval threw himself on the mattress and closed his eyes. The cell was very dark and he was very soon fast asleep.

How long he slept he had no means of knowing, but he was suddenly awaked by some one crying out—

" Hilloa there !"

"What now?" said Daval, looking up.

"Get up; you must come before the beak."

"Indeed! Is there any letter for me?"

"Why, yes; Bill Lee, who is on the outer lock, has got one that he will slip into your pocket, as you go out. It appears they want to get you committed to-day, as the sessions are on, so that they may hang you comfortably out of hand in the course of the next half dozen days."

"Very much obliged," said Duval, as he gave himself a shake. "I'm all ready."

The governor and the chaplain now appeared at the cell door with a couple of sturdy officers.

"Duval," said the governor, "you must come to Bow Street now, and then you will hear the charge that is to be made against you."

"I am quite willing," said Duval. "Indeed, I'm not a little anxious to hear it, for feeling that I am as innocent as any lamb, it surprises me what charge human impudence can bring against me."

The two officers laughed at this, and the governor called out in an angry voice—

"Silence! Don't let us have any laughing here;" and the chaplain, addressing Duval, said—

"Unhappy young man, your criminality is so great that nothing can save you in this world; and, therefore, I recommend you to plead guilty, and to devote all your time to prayer, and in attempting to prepare yourself for the world to come."

"Thank you," said Duval. "It is quite time enough for the world to come and I to make acquaintance when I get there; and as I am in this world for the present, I shall attend to it. As for pleading guilty, I dare say it would save some trouble; but as I am by no means of a lazy disposition, I shall fight it out to the last."

"Hardened wretch!" said the chaplain.

"Canting rogue!" said Duval.

"How dare you, you reprobate, speak to me in such a way?"

"And how dare you commence abusing me, I should like to know? Is it because the agents of the law have placed me in prison, and are about to try me for my life, that you are to come here, and by virtue of a black coat, begin calling me names?"

"Bring him along," said the governor. "Bring him along."

It was quite evident, from the manner in which Duval was hurried from the cell to a hackney-coach at the door of Newgate, that there was a hope of getting him to Bow Street and committing him for trial before its transpiring that a criminal of such celebrity was there at all. Just as he passed the man who was at the outer gate, Duval felt something like a twitch at one of his skirts, and he said—

"Thank you."

"For what?" said the governor.

"Why, for amazing kindness, of course," said Duval; "what in the name of all that's wonderful, could I otherwise thank you for, eh?"

"I suspect—Well—well! It don't matter."

The governor looked inquiringly about him; but the face of the man who was at the outer door was so stolid, and, indeed, so stupid-looking, that it was quite impossible to fix him as having done anything to call forth the thanks of Duval. But the prisoner now was very anxious to read the note that he felt quite sure was in his pocket, only he feared that if he took it out while he was in the coach, that he should implicate some of the turnkeys in the vestibule; and he thought he had better wait until he had come into contact with other persons, one of whom might be as well suspected of giving it to him as the man who really had.

With this idea, then, Duval controlled his impatience until he got to Bow Street.

The coach rattled along with unusual speed to the police-office; and it was quite clear from the two or three ordinary loungers that were about the door, that there was no idea so notable a character as Claude Duval was to be brought before the magistrate at such a time.

Duval was taken into the court by a private door, and there he was kept in a little room while some communication was made to the magistrate; after which he was at once hurried into the public court, in which there were not above twenty people, but there was a strong muster of officers about its doors.

"What is this?" said the magistrate, affecting an ignorance which certainly was not the case, as it had been all pre-arranged that Duval should be brought up, and committed for trial.

"This man, your worship," said the Governor of Newgate, "is charged with highway robbery."

"Oh, indeed. Who is he?"

"Claude Duval."

"Really? Well, we have heard of you, Mr. Duval, before to-day. What evidence have you, Mr. Governor, against him?"

"Here is a witness, your worship."

Duval was rather amused as well as surprised at the manner in which the business was being conducted; and when a man stepped forward, whom he did not recollect to have ever seen in his life before, and was swore, he could not make out what it was all about.

"Well, sir," said the magistrate to 'the witness. "What have you got to say in this matter?"

"My name is Phillip Jarvis," said the man. "I am a commercial traveller, and was crossing Ealing Common on the evening of the 24th of October last, when I was stopped by a highwayman, and robbed of eighty seven pounds, ten shillings, and eight-pence, all done up in a canvas bag."

"Should you know the robber?"

"Yes."

"Well, look round the court, and point him out if he be here."

"That is the man!" said Mr. Jarvis, pointing to Claude Duval. "I will swear to him."

"Very good. Is there any other witnesses?"

"Yes," said the clerk. "Call Thomas Singleton."

Upon this, another man stepped forward, and upon being sworn, he said—

"I am an agent; and was crossing Ealing Common upon the night in question, when I heard a kind of altercation going on, and having been warned that Claude Duval the highwayman was in the neighbourhood, I hid in a hedge, and I saw the prisoner at the bar rob Mr. Jarvis of a canvas bag, that seemed to be very heavy."

"Can you swear to the prisoner at the bar?"

"Yes, clearly and distinctly."

"Well," said the magistrate with a shrug; "that looks about one of the clearest cases that ever come before me. What have you to say to this, prisoner? You can say anything you like, you know, or nothing, just as it may suit you."

Duval put his hand into his pocket, and felt that there was a letter there. He took it very calmly out of his pocket, and while the magistrate looked at him in some amazement, and the governor and the officers wondered how he got it, he opened it, and read the following words, clearly written—

"Ask if your counsel, Mr. Charles Braithwaite, is in the court, and trust all to him. This is from the friend to whom you have very judiciously written, and who has not betrayed you."

Duval crumpled up the little note in his hand, and said in a calm cool voice—

"I will leave this most unfounded and infamously got up charge against me, in the hands of my counsel, Mr. Charles Braithwaite, who I believe is in court."

"Counsel?" said the magistrate. "Do you mean to tell me that the eminent Mr. Braithwaite is your counsel, prisoner?"

"I do."

"And I am here," said a gentlemanly-looking man, advancing towards the bench. "I am here to look after my client's interests in this matter. Your worship, I presume, will do nothing hastily. We deny that there is the slightest foundation for the charge, and shall be prepared to prove an alibi of the most satisfactory nature by this day week, to which time I have to request that the prisoner may be remanded, according to all established usage in such cases."

The magistrate, and his clerk, and the governor, and the chaplain, all looked at each other in evident perplexity. They were perfectly startled at the idea of Duval having counsel ready, when they thought that he could not be aware, until he was actually brought to Bow Street, of what was going on against him. The object was, to commit him upon the charge brought against him, and then leave his character to hang him upon it. That Colonel Lane was at the bottom of the proceedings, there could be no sort of doubt whatever.

The magistrate, after two or three preparatory "Hems," said—

"Really, Mr. Braithwaite, you see the sessions are on, and it is an object to society to—to try this man during their duration."

"But, sir," said the counsel, "it is a far greater object to society that an innocent man should not suffer. I believe I have a right to demand this week's remand; and if you will not grant it, the judges will traverse the trial until next sessions, upon my application to that effect."

The magistrate looked up at the ceiling as if he were intent upon the evolutions of some flies, who were there disporting themselves, and then as he bit the end of his pen, he said—

"Well I—a—I—that is, I suppose I may as well remand the prisoner until this day week?"

"I think so," said the counsel.

"Very well, then let it be so. Prisoner, you are remanded until this day week at twelve of the clock, when I think it will be my duty to commit you for trial."

CHAPTER CI.

DUVAL HAS A DISTINGUISHED VISITOR IN PRISON.

DUVAL did not think it incumbent upon him now to say another word to the magistrate. He felt that some one was interesting himself strongly in his fate, and he did not for a moment doubt in his own mind but that that some one was Mr. Sanderson, the jeweller, of St. James's Street.

The governor of Newgate, however, did not feel inclined to let the affair blow over quite so easily, and after a little whispered consultation with the chaplain, he said—

"If your worship pleases, we can bring another case against the prisoner at the bar, upon which your worship will be able to commit him at once."

"This is monstrous," exclaimed Mr. Braithwaite, with warmth, before the magistrate could reply. "This is truly a most monstrous proceeding. One would be half inclined to think that the great object of those who had brought the prisoner to this court, was to get him hastily committed for trial, so that before he could scarcely be said to know what he was accused of, he might be convicted and hung! If the jury at the sessions were only one half as eager to convict as certain parties are to commit, there would be an end to justice."

"Well—well," said the magistrate. "Let the affair stand over until this day week."

"But—" interposed the chaplain.

"Sir," cried the counsel, "do you not hear that one of the most upright, and vigorous, and intellectual magistrates of the city has said that the affair shall stand over until this day week? Do you want, sir, to insult the bench by endeavouring to make it eat its own words, and stultify its own decisions?"

This adroit appeal to the vanity of the magistrate settled the affair. Shaking his head with great pomposity, he said,—

"I have decided upon this case, and I particularly desire that no one will interrupt further. Officer, you will immediately remove the prisoner, and call the next case."

"Very good," said Mr. Braithwaite, with a scarcely perceptible smile, "I shall call upon my client, to whom, of course, I have free access, in the course of the day."

"I shall be happy to see you, sir," said Duval.

In the course of the next five minutes, Duval was removed from the court, and placed in the hackney-coach again, and rapidly drove towards Newgate. The chagrin of the governor and of the chaplain was quite manifest, and Duval was at no loss to clearly understand that there had been a vigorous effort to commit him upon a charge which was in no way connected with the one for which he was really to suffer. That the malevolence of Colonel Lane, concerning the horse-selling affair, was at the bottom of the whole transaction, he did not doubt for an instant, and he felt that if he had been committed at that time while the trials at the Old Bailey were proceeding, there would not be the slightest chance of his living another week.

"Well, Duval," said the governor, "you manage your affairs pretty well, I rather think."

"Ah !" said Duval.

"Here you are, apprehended in the morning, and you are taken before a magistrate in the afternoon, and yet you contrive to have engaged counsel who knows all about your case."

"Ah !" said Duval.

"And," added the governor, getting warm as he went on, "and who defies the ends of justice by getting a whole week's postponement, by which time the sessions will be over, as he and you both know perfectly well."

"Ah !"

"What the deuce do you mean by only saying 'Ah' to me, eh ? What do you mean by it, I say ? It's infamous—it's most infamous and unjustifiable conduct from first to last."

"Ah !"

The governor looked at Duval as though he would very gladly have taken his life ; but in the presence of others he dreaded to give utterance to his passion. The two officers who were likewise in the coach were half-suffocated in the attempts they made to keep themselves from laughing outright ; and the discomfitted governor was fain to crush himself up into a corner of the coach in silence, where he tried to comfort himself by reflecting upon how uncomfortable he could possibly make Duval in Newgate.

As for the chaplain, he was too much confounded at what had taken place before the magistrate to be able to say a word. His wits, at the best of times, were none of the clearest ; and the extraordinary way in which Duval had managed to get counsel to meet the charge that was professed against him, puzzled him completely.

Upon the arrival of the coach at Newgate, the governor appeared to recover a little of his equanimity. Perhaps finding himself in his own territory, as it might be called, had the effect of restoring him to something like a reasonable condition. He did not, however, forget that he had such a grudge against Duval, that he would do his very best to pay it off.

"Where's Foxton ?" he cried, as soon as they were fairly in the vestibule.

"Here, sir," said an individual, whose cunning leering expression of countenance showed that he was well adapted to be the tool of any one's bad passions ; "I am here, sir, if you please. Happy to wait upon you, sir."

"Oh, I think, Foxton, you said you had the keys of those cells, where the— the——"

"Water comes in, sir ?" said Foxton.

"Well, well, I daresay it has gone out again; you will see that this prisoner is put into one of them. He is a sly fox, and rather a slippery customer; and I am resolved, that as he is to be kept for a week, I will keep him safely. Mind, all of you—if Claude Duval escapes, I will discharge every official in Newgate that has had anything to do with his safe keeping; so now you are all warned, and you may make the best of it."

CLAUDE SURPRISES AN ATTENDANT OF THE PALACE AT KEW.

Bang! came a single knock at the door of Newgate, and the governor hearing it, angrily said—

"Who is that? Who is knocking now? This is not the time for visitors. What do you want?"

A man's head appeared above the railings at the top of the little half door, and a hand presented a paper; while the voice belonging to the hand, said—

"Where is the governor of Newgate?"

"Well, and what the devil——"

The governor took the slip of paper with a jerk, and holding it to the light, he read it in silence. Then looking round him with astonishment, he cried—

"Why this is an order from the Lord Chief Justice of England, to permit the bearer to have a private interview with Claude Duval."

Upon these words, the turnkey who had charge of the wicket, conceived it to be his duty to open it, and a plainly dressed, but gentlemanly man, stepped into the vestibule of Newgate in a moment.

"I am the bearer of that order," he said, "and I presume there will be no difficulty in complying with it?"

"Why, no, no—of course not," gasped the governor. "Who said that there would be any difficulty? Of course the order of the Lord Chief Justice is patent here; but how the devil he came to give it, or to know anything about Claude Duval being now in Newgate, is beyond my comprehension entirely."

"Probably," said the stranger, as he regaled his nose with a pinch from a diamond-mounted box. "Probably that is not the only little affair that is beyond the comprehension of the governor of Newgate."

"Sir, do you come here to insult me?"

"Oh, dear no. I came to speak with Claude Duval; but it does not seem to me that the order of the Lord Chief Justice has any very great respect shown to it in this place. I should be sorry to be compelled to state as much to his lordship."

Upon this the governor began to see that he was going just a little too far, and that the well-dressed stranger with the superb snuff-box, was not to be trifled with.

"Sir," he said, "every possible respect will be shown to his lordship's order. Pray excuse me, I am very much vexed at several little affairs. I assure you, sir, that the governor of a prison has a vast deal to try his temper."

The stranger bowed.

"Here, Foxton, show this gentleman into the private consulting room, and let Claude Duval be with him. Pray, sir, be so good as to follow that person, and you will met with every accommodation that Newgate can afford to you."

The stranger followed Foxton, and Claude Duval, to whom the whole scene was very amusing, was conducted after him, but not until the governor had cast upon him a most malignant look, which had in it the promise of as much annoyance as the most concentrated hatred could possibly suggest.

Duval only smiled in reply to the look from the governor, and followed the mysterious stranger.

The room to which he was conducted was one that in the building was usually devoted to the purpose of prisoners' interviews with their counsel, and although tolerably dingy, was yet comfortable, compared with the portion of Newgate devoted to the criminals. There were seats in it, and writing materials; and whatever it was in reality, it was supposed to be strictly private.

The stranger flung himself into a seat, and a silence of some few moments' duration ensued, and then Duval took a seat himself, upon which the stranger gave a slight kind of start, as though he thought it rather a liberty. That start did not escape the keen penetration of Duval.

"Well, sir," he said, "I am Claude Duval, that you have honoured Newgate with your presence to see. Pray, what have you to say to me?"

"That," said the stranger, "I will soon explain to you. Certain circumstances have enabled me to come to the knowledge that you were one of the company at a little entertainment or supper, or something of that sort, call it what you will, which was given by the Prince of Wales at Kew."

"Indeed?"

"Yes, I know that for a fact, and my present visit is one connected with that circumstance."

"Very well, sir—go on."

"Of course you are in a very unpleasant predicament here, and the authorities will find no difficulty in getting charges enough against you by which to insure your conviction, and then the execution of so notorious a criminal as you are will follow promptly, as a thing of course. Of that your own judgment, however, must inform you as well, if not better, than any one else can tell you."

Duval merely inclined his head.

"But," added the stranger, "if certain persons in a very high position in life, indeed, chose to interest themselves in your favour, you would upon this occasion, at all events, be allowed to go free, and it would depend entirely upon yourself whether or not in time to come you make yourself criminal to the laws of your country."

"Very good, sir."

"But you may very well be aware that there is no effect without a cause, and that if those certain persons high in authority stretch out a hand to save you, it must be on account of some act of yours pleasant to them, for which they do you that service as a kind of return."

"Perfectly clear," said Duval; "and pray, sir, what is the act that you require me to do to entitle me to the kind and greatful recollections of certain persons in high authority?"

"It is simply that you will give to me a full and particular detailed account of all you heard and saw at the palace at Kew, and inform me who where the associates of the Prince of Wales, and in what manner he passed the time upon the occasion of your presence at the little entertainment."

"Is that all?"

"Yes—that is all. It is a piece of information that certain high persons are very anxious to get at, and it is hoped that a consideration for your own safety will induce you freely to give it."

"Very good, sir. You may tell certain high personages, that if I had been the invited guest of the Prince of Wales upon the occasion you allude to, it would be a base and unmanly act for me to partake of his hospitality, and then turn informer regarding the manner in which he spent his own good leisure among his friends; but being there without being an invited guest at all——"

"Exactly. There is the difference."

"Why, it would be to play the part of the basest and meanest spy that ever lived, were I to turn round and tell that which I was never asked to see."

"Do you refuse?"

"I do, sir. You can tell the high personages from me, that they are mistaken in their man. I will not be their informer of all the little tittle tattle that may have reached my ears. I will not intrude into any man's privacy, and then blazon forth what I chance to see and hear. I have been treacherously taken, and if I am to suffer death, I will suffer it without the feeling upon my soul that I am a paltroon and a spy."

"Then you intend to keep to yourself all you saw and heard at Kew?"

"I do, sir, and I will."

The stranger took rather an elaborate pinch of snuff from his richly-mounted box.

CHAPTER CII.

DUVAL FINDS THAT HONOUR IS SOMETIMES REWARDED.

Duval felt more indignation than he expressed at the proposal that was made to him by his singular visitor; but if the room in which the conference took place had not been quite so dark, that personage would not have failed to see by the expression of Duval's face that he was fully in earnest in his refusal to give the information that was required of him.

"Sir," said Duval, after a pause, "if you have anything else to say to me, say it at once, and go."

"You are too hasty, Duval, very much too hasty," said the stranger, as he calmly replaced his snuff-box in his pocket.

"In what respect, sir?"

"Why, in your refusal to embrace a chance of escape, which no other man in your position would hesitate about for a moment. Think again. Do not be angry. I offer you the terms that I think you ought to expect. In clear and plain language, I tell you that if you choose to inform me in detail of all that passed at the palace at Kew, you shall be free within twenty-four hours from the charge that has been brought against you."

"And I, sir, as clearly and distinctly reject your terms."

"Well, if you will fall, you may; but it is new certainly to me to find a man at your age so in love with death."

"I am not in love with death, but I am with honour. Perhaps you will think it strange to hear a man who lives by plunder talk of his honour; but I think that it is more disreputable to act the part of a spy upon any one's private actions, than it is to cry 'Stand!' to a man with a full purse upon the highway."

"Indeed!"

"Yes, and it is always my greatest pleasure to rob some one who is in place or power in the country, or in the church, for example."

"Why so?"

"Because I am then quite aware that I am only robbing the thief, as such folks it is well known only live and fatten upon the plunder of the people."

"Well, Duval, I will leave you then to your fate. You have had a fair chance given to you of escape from this rather awkward dilemma in which you now are, and you reject it; therefore, with that rejection my mission here is at an end."

"Very well," said Duval. "That being the case, then, you can go at once; I have no wish in the world to detain you."

"What if I were to tell you that I am from the queen?"

"It makes no difference to me who you are."

"What if I were to tell you that it is of the greatest possible importance that the Prince of Wales should keep secret his orgies at the palace of Kew, and that the queen most specially desired to know all about them?"

"I don't care what you say or what you tell me. I have given you an answer, and I will abide by it."

"Very good. I have the pleasure, then, of bidding you good-by, and of considering you one of the most obstinate of men that ever I encountered in all my life."

"As you please, sir."

The stranger moved to the door, and called to the turnkey, who was within hearing, in a loud voice—

"You can take Duval to his cell again," he said. "He and I have had our conference. Show me the way out of the prison."

Duval was reconducted to his cell, and the stranger, with the same calm impassable manner that had throughout characterised him, left Newgate.

"There," said Duval, as he threw himself upon the little hard mattress in his cell. "That bother is over; and now, I suppose, they will let me have some sleep."

With that strange facility in taking repose that Duval had, he was sound asleep in a few minutes. How long he so slept he knew not, but when he awakened he found a light flashing in his eyes, and a couple of men in his cell. The governor, too, stood near to its entrance.

"He's awake now, sir," said one of the men.

"Do your duty then," said the governor.

"What the deuce are you after now?" cried Duval. "You don't hang a man here before trial, I suppose?"

"Oh, dear no, Claude Duval," said one of the men. "We have only come to accommodate you with a few steel ornaments, that's all. We have been some time getting them ready, as they are extra strong, out of compliment to you, and now we have come to put them on."

"Please yourselves," said Duval. "It's some satisfaction to think that you are afraid of me, as you evidently are."

"No, Duval," said the governor, "we are not afraid of you; but, as I told you, now that we have got you, we mean to take care of you. If you get out of my clutches, I will consent to eat those irons that are now about to be rivetted upon your limbs."

"Rail away," said Duval. "You can't place your irons upon my spirits, and I intend to laugh and be as merry as possible in spite of you and all your chains. Ha! ha! Why, now to look at us, any one would think that I was the governor and you the prisoner. You look as gloomy as if you had just come out of the pillory."

"Have your joke, Duval," said the governor. "Have your joke. The laugh is, I take it, rather on the wrong side of your mouth. We are quite used to the bravado of criminals when first they come here; but the air of Newgate has quite a wonderful effect in bringing that down."

"It will fail for once," said Duval.

The two men now set to work to fix a remarkably heavy set of fetters upon his limbs. One of them had brought into the cell a little portable anvil, and a basket of blacksmith's tools, by the aid of which the rivets were to be perfected, and he said in a coaxing tone of voice—

"Now, Duval, be so good as to stand still, and I shall not hit your shins with the hammer."

"If you do," said Duval, "it will be the worse for you, my man. I like a joke as well as most people, but I give as well as take; so you will bear that in mind."

The man did not seem at all inclined to despise this warning, and he set about his work, accordingly, with the very greatest possible circumspection; but the hammer had not descended twice to rivet one of the fetters round Duval's ancle, when there came a tap at the door of the cell. The governor opened it sharply, and said in an angry voice—

"Well, what now?"

"Oh, if you please, sir," said a turnkey, "there is somebody else in the hall with a order from the Lord Chief Justice to see Claude Duval, if you please."

"The devil there is!"

"Come—come," said Duval, "don't swear, Mr. Governor. Why may not my friends get orders from the Lord Chief Justice, if they can induce his lordship to give them?"

"But—but it's enough to drive anybody mad. It's one of the most extraordinary things. The Lord Chief Justice must be going out of his mind!"

"You had better not say that again, or perhaps he might recommend to the city authorities a new Governor of Newgate."

"Confound you, and the Lord Chief Justice, and the city authorities, all in a heap! What, in the name of all that's abominable, can it mean? Where is the order, you fellow?"

"Here, sir, if you please."

The governor snatched a piece of paper from the astonished turnkey, and read it in silence.

"Ha!—ha!" he laughed angrily. "Another private interview with Claude Duval. I won't permit it—I won't. If the Lord Chief Justice was to come himself, I wouldn't permit it. It's too bad. It destroys all authority, and so I'll just tell the person who has had the impudence to bring this order."

"You had better mind what you are about," said Duval, "or else when I see his lordship I will complain of you."

"When you do see him," said the governor, "it is to be hoped he will have a black cap on his head, before he bids you good-by again, my facetious friend. Ha!—ha!"

Pale with anger, the governor dashed from the cell to repair to the hall of the prison, and get rid of the second visitor to Duval.

"Your governor," said Duval to the two men, "is a nice, pleasant, lively sort of person to live with, I should think."

"Don't blame us," said one of the men. "It ain't our fault that you are to have the heaviest irons on you that were e er seen in Newgate yet; but you know we must obey orders, or go."

"Of course you must. I don't blame you in the least. You only do your duty; and for the matter of that, the governor only does his in trying to hold me tight; but he might do it after a little pleasanter fashion than he does."

"So he might, Duval; but you will excuse us, as we are forced to do our work properly, you know."

"Oh, don't mention it. You may rivet the fetters as tight as you like. I don't intend to try at the rivets to get rid of them, when I set about it, you may depend."

"I say, Bill," said one of the men, "I think I hear some one in the passage. I should not wonder if it's that old Bennet; he is always peeping and prying after us. Just run out, and pretend to tumble over him, and give him a good kick."

"Won't I?"

Bill run out of the cell, and the moment he was gone, the other man handed Duval a file, merely giving him a nod as he did so. Duval concealed it in the breast of his apparel in a moment, as he said in a low voice—

"This won't be the lowest priced file you ever parted with, my friend. I will find you out."

"Hush!"

"Why, there's nobody there," said the other on returning. "Why did you send me out on such a fool's errand for? Thinking, to be sure, there was some one to run against outside, I nearly fell down myself when I found nobody. What a fellow you are with your jokes."

"Upon my word, Bill, I did not intend it for a joke. I thought there was somebody there, and you know old Bennet is always dodging about, and watching everybody in the prison, so that he may go and whisper all sorts of things to the governor."

"Why, yes, that's true enough; but somebody is coming in earnest now, I take it."

The sound of footsteps were now quite plainly discernible in the passage leading to the cell, and Duval was full of wonder to know who his next visitor was likely to be who had got an order in so high a quarter as the Lord Chief Justice to visit him. In his own mind, he thought that it would be another attempt to get from him some particulars of what took place at Kew; and he made up his mind that, let the consequences of his obstinacy be what they might, he would not play the part of a spy, and report those things that might do the greatest injury to the Prince of Wales if known. It must not be supposed, however, that Claude Duval was actuated by any very tender feelings towards the Prince of Wales in the matter; but he acted purely and entirely upon principle—the principle of not purchasing his safety, or even his life, by betraying the secrets of any one whatever.

The door of the cell was opened, and the governor appeared at it, to the surprise of both of the men who were fitting on Duval's fetters, and of Duval himself, with quite a hideous smile upon his face. No doubt, he intended it to be a very remarkably pleasant one, but it sat very ill upon his coarse sensual features.

"Duval," he said, "here is a visitor."

Behind the governor stood a gentleman, enveloped in a very large Spanish cloak, with rather a broad brimmed hat pulled far down over his brow.

"Very good," said Duval. "What does he want with me? Let him speak his mind at once; for when these little pieces of rough jewellery are fitted upon me, I hope I shall be allowed a little peace and quietness."

"Come this way, Duval," said the governor.

"What! and drag after me, by one leg, all these fetters that you have been so good as to accommodate me with?"

"Take them off—take them off!" said the visitor hastily.

"Do you hear?" said the governor to the two men. "You are to take them off. The gentleman says you are to take them off. Off with them directly."

The two men looked at each other in amazement, but they were not slow in obeying the last order. The one rivet that had been made fast round Duval's ancle was speedily struck out, and he was free from the heavy irons that had begun to weigh upon his limbs.

"Come on, this way, Duval," said the governor. "This gentleman will speak with you, and you will find him a friend."

"That is more than I have found you," said Duval.

The governor made no reply to this, but he preceded the gentleman, and Duval followed. They reached a little arched room, in which the gentleman paused, and turning abruptly to Duval, he said—

"You will be free directly, and have a couple of hundred pounds, if you will put in writing all that you know of a certain entertainment given by a certain person, at Kew. Is it a bargain?"

"No," said Duval. "It is quite the reverse. Mr. Governor, there is no occasion to give you or this gentleman any further trouble. You may as well take me back to the cell, and allow your myrmidons there to finish that nice little job of the fetters; for I am sure that this person and I shall not agree."

"Yes, we shall," said the stranger, as he took hold of Duval by the arm. "Come—come. We shall agree well enough."

"No—no."

"But I say we shall. Are you not aware,' and here the visitor lowered his voice so that only Duval could hear him. "Are you not aware, that if the secret of what went on at Kew that night were to be known to the court and the parliament, it would almost be the ruin of the Prince of Wales?"

"I don't know any such thing of my own knowledge," said Duval; "but it don't matter, for I am not going to tell."

"But, you see, it is who were there that is wanted to be known."

"It matters not; my lips are sealed upon the subject, and you will, as a gentleman, oblige me by not pressing me upon it."

CHAPTER CIII.

DUVAL QUITE UNEXPECTEDLY FINDS HIMSELF AT HOME.

By this time, they had all three—that is, the governor, the strange visitor, and Claude Duval—reached the hall or vestibule of the prison, and what astonished Duval was, that the governor hardly dared to walk erect, but kept himself at a bowing angle the whole of the way, and tried to look as amiable as he possibly could.

Duval was perfectly puzzled to know what it could all mean, and he was upon the point of shaking off the hold that the stranger had of his arm, when, to his surprise, he heard him say—

"I cannot talk with Duval in the prison here, Mr. Governor; you will be so good as to allow us to go outside."

The governor groaned.

"Outside? Out—out in the street?" he gasped.

"Just so," said the visitor. "Place your arm in mine, Duval, and we will see if any one will stop us; I rather think they will not, as far as I can judge of the matter."

"Oh, won't they, though," cried the man, who was on the lock, as it is technically called. "Won't they, though? Just try it, though, that's all, and you'll soon find out if anybody will stop you!"

"You rascal!" cried the governor, "what do you mean by talking in that way? Open the wicket, this moment, and let the gentleman go out if he chooses to do so. Open it directly."

"But lor, sir," said the man, "he wants to take Claude Duval with hi!"

"I don't see that," said the governor, "and what I don't see, I don't see any occasion for any one else in Newgate to see."

The man looked so amazed, that he was quite incapable of turning the key in the lock of the door, and the governor sprang forward and did it for him. The mysterious stranger who had Duval under his convoy and protection, merely gave a kind of short nod to the governor, and then conducted Duval out of Newgate, and fairly down the steps into the Old Bailey. Duval was himself so perfectly astonished at this unexpected turn that events had taken, that he began to doubt if he were awake; and as, still arm-in-arm with that most mysterious stranger, he walked towards Ludgate Hill, he said, in a tolerably audible whisper,—"Oh, this is a very absurd dseam!"

"No," said the stranger, "this is no dream."

"But I tell you it must be."

"But I tell you it is not. Allow me to explain to you, that it was by the express order of the Prince of Wales that Mr. Sanderson, the jeweller, inserted the advertisement in the newspapers to the effect, that the articles and jewels taken from Kew would be paid for, and no hinderance given to your departure in safety from St. James's Street."

"I thought as much, and yet I was betrayed."

"Not by the prince, nor by Mr. Sanderson. The fact is, that Colonel Lane, seeing the advertisement, and being perfectly savage at a little horse transaction in which you were engaged with him, went to Mr. Sanderson's shop, and gave his attendant or clerk, whichever he is, a twenty-pound-note to let him know by a particular signal when you were there, and he had officers stationed in the immediate neighbourhood, who arrested you, as you found out."

"They did, indeed."

"And you very fortunately, instead of flying into a passion, and proclaiming all you knew, wrote to Mr. Sanderson, who immediately communicated with the Prince of Wales. He attacked Colonel Lane upon the subject, and the excuse of the colonel was, that if you were not put out of the way, you would sell your information regarding what you saw and heard at Kew to the prince's enemies."

"It is untrue."

"Yes, but the prince could not know that, and he sent a person to you to ascertain that fact. The report of that person was so satisfactory, that the prince thought he was bound to save you."

Duval withdrew his arm from that of his companion, and bowing, he said, "I now know to whom I am indebted for my liberation. Your royal highness will not find me ungrateful."

"Ah, you know me, then? I am, indeed, the Prince of Wales. Did you know me in the prison?"

"I did not, your highness."

"Well, I thought you would have recognised me; especially when the governor let you see by his conduct that he was no longer master in Newgate."

"No, your highness, I had no means of coming to such a conclusion, for I naturally enough looked upon the affair of the person who called upon me about what took place at Kew as genuine."

"Well, Duval, you are now free. There is a five hundred pound note for you in addition to what you have, and I hope that for the future you will do me the favour of leaving me alone."

"That your highness may depend upon; and in all this transaction, now, there is only one thing that I have deeply to regret."

"What is that?"

"The loss of my horse."

"Oh, you need not regret that for long. The fact is, that it was the horse that Lane wanted; but I made him give it up; and if it is not now awaiting for you at the corner of Fleet Market, in charge of a man, I shall be very much surprised."

"Ah, your highness," said Duval, " now, indeed, permit me to say, that you have acted like a prince."

"For once, I suppose, you would add ?" said the prince, laughing.

"No," said Duval, "I had no such thought of your highness.   A man, be he a

CLAUDE IS TAKEN BEFORE A MAGISTRATE.

prince or a peasant, who can do a noble act, will do many ; for it will be in his nature."

"Upon my word, Duval, you should be a courtier, and you would make your fortune.   You have quite mistaken your vocation by going upon the road.   But if I am not mistaken, there is your horse."

"Ah, yes—it is, indeed," cried Duval; " and now, like the world in general, I have no sooner got rid of one piece of regret, than I get up another."

" What is amiss now ?"

" I am much afraid that your highness will suffer some inconvenience from the mode in which you have taken me out of Newgate. If I thought that, I would rather go back again."

" Don't you be afraid upon my account, Duval. It is ill fighting against me, I am more powerful, to tell the truth, for evil than for good, which, I presume, is, after all, the case with most persons in my station of life. No one will think it to his interest to carp much at my acts, and, therefore, the affair will subside. There is your horse, and now be off with you."

" I am eternally your highness's debtor," said Duval, as he sprang upon his horse.

" Oh, don't mention it," laughed the prince. " The best thing you can do is now to forget all about it. I wish you would turn to some better mode of life than highway robbery."

I will, your highness, if I can ; and you may depend that if once I get into Newgate again, by force or by fraud, I will let you know as quickly as possible."

With these words, Duval gave the rein to his horse, and clattered through Fleet Street at a good pace.

" Confound the fellow's impudence !" said the Prince of Wales, as he walked slowly in the direction of St. James's.

" Hurrah !" cried Duval, as he passed through Temple Bar, to the great terror of a watchman, whose box was against one of the pillars of the old gate, and who was half asleep. " Hurrah ! this is not such a bad job, after all."

" Oh, you wagabone !" cried the watchman. " I do believe you are a high-wayman."

" You are right," cried Duval, " I am."

The watchman sprung his rattle, but Duval with a laugh set off at a hard gallop, and taking a turn to the right, soon left the Strand, and began making his way westward so as to get as soon a posssible into the more direct route to Hornsey.

" I shall be home," he said, " now, before the news of my arrest can have reached those who are interested in my fate ; and upon the whole, I take it, that this is not the least extraordinary of my many adventures. I will keep my word though, and the Prince of Wales, for the future, shall be saved from any attack on my part, be the opportunity ever so tempting."

The slight pursuit of Duval by the Temple Bar watch had not lasted three minutes, and he laughed it to scorn. In the course of a quarter of an hour more he had shot across the fields towards Battle Bridge, and went up Pentonville Hill at a brisk pace. Islington church-clock struck the hour of eleven.

" In good time," thought Duval. " So that I get home before midnight, it is not so bad. This has truly been for me a busy day's work. I wonder what any-body would have given for my chance of sleeping in my own bed to-night, at four o'clock to-day !'

The Angel, at Islington, then quite a suburban public-house, and not—as it is now—the centre of attraction for a legion of omnibusses, and another legion of idlers and pickpockets, was soon passed, and Duval made his way along what is now the High Street, Islington.

That thoroughfare was at that time completely shaded by rows of magnificent trees, which are now all gone, with one or two exceptions, so that the pretty out-of-town appearance of the place is nearly destroyed. Surely it would have been well to have preserved the stately trees of Islington.

Taking a turning to the right, Duval got into the high road to Hornsey, and as there was no great danger of encountering any one in such a retired road, Duval put his horse to a canter, that got him over the space between him and home in an extraordinary short space of time. He drew up when he got to his own garden fence, but not before.

A voice called out to him—

" Claude ! Claude ! can it be really you ?"

"Yes—yes. What is the matter? Is it you, May?"

"Oh, yes. There is nothing the matter now that you have come back. I will open the gate. Oh, this is joy, indeed! And you are indeed well, Claude?—tell me that you are?"

"To be sure I am. But what put it into your head that anything was amiss with me?"

May cou'd not reply to him, for she had run round to the gate to let him into the garden; but when he got in, she would not let him dismount from his horse until she had taken him by the hand, and looked as well as she cou'd in his face to assure herself that he was as usual.

"Why, May," he said. "What has terrified you?"

"Oh, Claude, there has been a man going through the village crying an account of your arrest."

"Confound the fellow, I only wish he had waited until I came home, I would have given him something to cry about. But where is Luke?"

"He has gone to town, Claude, to get the truth concerning you."

"That is a pity, May. Make it a rule, I beg of you, never to take any steps concerning me until you hear positively from me, with full directions what to do. Here I am, you perceive, quite safe and sound. I wonder how that rascal could so soon have found the means of crying the news of my arrest."

"Was it true, Claude?"

"Why, in a manner of speaking, it was; but it could not have been a very serious affair, you know, when I am here. They don't let such folks as I am away again very easily."

"But you have been in danger?"

"A little."

"Oh, Claude, Claude, you will break my heart if you do not leave this frightful mode of life, you will, indeed. Incessant terror while you are away from home is already beginning to tell upon my health. You wil: kill me, Claude, indeed you will."

"Nay now, May, you are out of your mind to talk in such a way. That fellow who came to cry the account of my arrest has frightened you, I fear."

"He has. But not so much, Claude, as you terrify me. I am sure we have got money enough now. A very little, with peace, and calmness, and serenity, will be better than wealth with such a heart-beating as I endure from day to day. You do not know what I suffer, Claude."

"Come—come, May, you must get the better of all this. Since Luke is out, I must put up the horse myself, and you will help me. Have you had any other alarm?"

"Oh, no, no. None in the least. But was not that enough?"

"Why, yes; but I rather think now that I have got a friend at court, who will prove to me a very powerful protector. Come, dry your eyes; and now that the horse is all right, come in-doors, and I will tell you all that has happened to me to-day."

May was somewhat comforted by the confident and easy manner in which Duval spoke of the day's occurrence; and when he told her from first to last all that had happened, she was most deeply interested, and at different parts of the narration did not know whether to weep or to smile.

"And so, you see," added Claude, at the conclusion, "I have something like a claim now upon the Prince of Wales, for I have kept his secret, and will keep it; and I hope and expect that if anything should go amiss with me, in time to come, that he will recollect that I have placed him under some obligation."

"Yes, Claude; but you never told me what you really did see and hear at the palace at Kew?"

"Of course not."

"Of—course—not, Claude, do you say?"

"Certainly; would that be keeping the prince's secret, were I to tell you?"

"Why, no—not exactly; and yet——"

"And yet you think I might as well, and so I will, May, at some other time; but for the present let me feel that I am really and truly earning my liberty at his hands, by not even informing you of those particulars which he evidenly dreads should be made public. Ha, I hear Luke's whistle. He will be truly rejoiced to see me safe at home again."

CHAPTER CIV.

DUVAL RECEIVES RATHER A MYSTERIOUS LETTER FROM A LADY.

TRULY, Duval, with all his love of stirring adventure, was not at all sorry to find himself snugly under his own roof, after those events which, in their bodily fatigue and mental excitement, were sufficient to break down the strongest frame.

The sleep that he dropped off into scemed as though it would last for an age, so preternaturally deep was it. The day after the escape from Newgate had yet some hours past its meridian before Claude Duval opened his eyes and looked about him.

May was seated by the bedside.

"Ah, Claude," she said, "you are awake now. I thought that so long a sleep would surely injure you."

"Long? Have I slept long?"

"Indeed you have, Duval. You have slept thirteen hours."

"The deuce I have. Then it is the first time in all my life that ever the world caught me napping for half the time: but I recollect I did feel such a sense of absolute fatigue, that let me have been in what unluckly position I might, I think I should have closed my eyes in repose. But I feel wonderfully refreshed now, and I may truly say, Duval is himself again."

"Ah! those are cheering words; and as you promised that you would remain at home with me for some time, Claude, I am not afraid to hear them, nor that such a feeling will induce you to break your word."

"Did I promise?"

"Indeed you did. You have slept off the recollection of your promise along with the recollection of your fatigue."

"It looks like it."

At this moment there came a tap at the door of the chamber, and upon May going to see what it meant, she found Luke, who was looking very pale, and terrified. He had a letter in his hand, and he said—

"Oh, we are found out at last! This was thrown over the wall."

"What is it?" cried Duval.

"A letter, Sir. It was thrown over the garden wall exactly where I was at work, and it is addressed to you, so that it is now quite clear that some one knows where you live. Oh, sir, your best plan will be to be off at once."

"We will see about that, Luke. Give me the letter. It will really try the evidence of my own eyes to convince me that the letter is addressed to me. Hand it to me, Luke."

Luke brought it to him, and he stood pale and agitated by the side of the bed, while May, with her hands clasped on his breast, was evidently in a state of the greatest terror.

"What can it mean?—Oh, what can it mean?" she said.

"Hush—be still!" said Duval. "It is certainly addressed to me, and that it should be so, I admit, is a most mysterious circumstance. We will see what it contains. The inside may possibly enlighten us as much as the outside has astonished us."

With these words, Duval hastily tore open the letter, and found the following lines, in a handwriting that he was by no means familiar with:—

"To Claude Duval, Hornsey.

"These few words come from a friend, if you will let her be such. You are required to be at the statue of King Charles the First by Charing Cross at the hour of six to-night. You will there find one whom you once knew, and who, by accident only, has discovered your abode. To neglect this will be death."

Duval read the letter in a sufficiently loud voice for both Luke and May to hear it, and at its conclusion they all three looked at each other in no little surprise.

"'To neglect this.' said Duval, quoting the letter, 'will be death.' What do you say to that, May? Come now, Luk, we will take you into the council. What do you say of this affair—ought I to attend to it, or ought I to neglect it?"

"Not neglect it, certainly, sir. It is no idle threat. It is quite clear that whoever wrote it knows your place of abode here."

"Just so; then if it cannot be neglected with safety, it must be attended. Now let me urge upon your belief, May, that the only way to defeat danger is to meet it."

"I am full of terrors," said May.

"I own that you are; but if you reflect a little, I think you will be convinced that they are vain ones. Whoever wrote that letter it is quite clear that she, if it be a she, knows my place of abode. With that knowledge, nothing could be easier than to compass my destruction, for a sufficient force could be got to surround the house to cause my destruction. The writer of the letter has not done so, and therefore, will not do so."

"Do you think that a direct consequence, Duval?"

"Not a direct one, but sufficiently so. I will and must go, May; and I beg that you will be under no sort of apprehension of the consequences. I am a tolerable judge of these matters, and I am convinced that there is not any danger in this affair but such I can overcome."

May looked still terrified, but yet her reason was convinced by what Duva said; and she could not but admit that to remain in the state of doubt and anxiety that would ensue if no notice were taken of the letter, and if there was an expectancy each moment of some frightful catastrophe occurring, would be intolerable.

Duval, upon this, rose, and ascertaining that it was but three o'clock in the day, he set about amusing himself in his garden as best he could. It was with an uncomfortable feeling, though, that he at times could not help regarding the spot where the constable lay buried; and he saw that Luke could not pass that part of the garden without a very perceptible shudder of dread.

Duval took occasion to speak to him of it.

"Luke," he said, "you will never be happy here."

Luke was silent for a few moments, and then he said, sadly—

"I am afraid I shall not, sir; and if there were any other reason for leaving this place, I must confess that I should be glad to see you in some other."

"I will remove, Luke, I think. But tell me now—do you not think that the body of the officer is more likely to be found if we move, than if we stay? Some one else might put a spade into the spot, you know, Luke."

"They might, indeed, sir."

"Then, Luke, that has to be considered in the question of removing, you know; but we will talk it over another time. I think I had better take you with me to this appointment by the statue of King Charles."

"I shall be well pleased to go sir," said Luke. "If you let me keep tolerably close to you, and yet not seem to be with you, the probability is tha I may be able to warn you in time, if any treachery is intended."

"Not a doubt of it. So you will understand, Luke that we both go. We will leave here at seven o'clock, and quietly walk our horses the distance; so that they will be quite fresh for a good gallop, if such should become desirable. I will leave it to you to get everything ready, Luke."

"You may depend upon all being right, sir."

The time soon elapsed, and by seven o'clock Duval took leave of May, again and again begging her not to consider the affair he was going upon as anything serious ; and he jestingly warned her that if she took so much to heart his going upon such little adventures, he should be obliged, contrary to his inclination, to keep things secret from her, that otherwise he should be glad to tell her.

This was a remark that had some effect upon May, and induced her to show much less fear than she really felt. She managed, with an appearance of cheer. fulness, to bid Duval adieu ; and just as the twilight was deepening into darkness, he and Luke rode from Hornsey, by the quiet lane close to the garden wall that led to Crouch End.

Luke spoke to his master as they trotted at a gentle pace along that lane, which even now goes by the name of Duval's Lane.

"Do you really, sir," he said, "not guess in any shape or way from whom the letter comes?"

"I am quite abroad upon the subject, Luke. I have turned and twisted the matter about in my brain in every way, and exhausted conjecture, and can come to no conclusion regarding it. It remains as it was at the first, a mystery."

"It is very strange, sir."

"It is, indeed ; but, doubtless, it will soon be clear enough, for we are near the place of appointment, and it is near the hour of eight."

Luke, no doubt, had been cherishing in his own mind an idea that Duval had something like a good guess, if not an actual knowledge, of whom the letter came from, and what the mysterious rendezvous meant ; but now that, from the manner in which he was answered, he felt quite certain that such was not the case, he felt much more anxiety upon the subject of the issue of the adventure than he had done before.

They rode on in silence, and as the night happened to be a very cloudy and dark one indeed, there was nothing to relieve the imagination from the most gloomy thoughts. Duval was more than usually silent, for the real truth was that he was painfully anxious regarding the letter, as he could not for the life of him fix it upon anybody in his own mind.

"Confound it," he suddenly exclaimed. "I cannot make out how any one could get at my address."

"Nor I, sir," said Luke ; "but there are horsemen ahead of us, and I would recommend you to speak low, sir."

"Thank you for the caution, Luke. The best way will be for us to preserve silence until we are no longer in their immediate vicinity."

With the intention to pass the horsemen, who were in the lane, just within about a couple of hundred yards of its termination in Holloway, Duval put his horse to more speed ; but as he was about to pass, one of them called out—

"Have you come up the lane, sir?"

"Yes," said Duval, "for some distance."

"Have you met any one, sir? We are on the look out for Claude Duval the highwayman, who we have some reason to think is in the neighbourhood, and if you have leisure to join us, sir, you may be in at the death or the capture of him."

"Thank you. I am sorry I can't stay. How do you know he is to be met with hereabouts?"

"Why the fact is, there's a man living in Islington who is ready to swear to him, and he has seen him pass his house, and go down the lane four or five times lately at a speed as if he were going home."

"Well, gentlemen, I can only wish you may get him ; and express my sorrow, that neither myself nor my servant can remain to aid you in your public duty of catching a highwayman. I have heard that he is rather a desperate fellow, though, and I would advise you to be as careful as possible in your proceedings."

"We shall, sir. Good night."

Duval, in the most courteous manner, bade them good night, and rode on, followed by Luke, who, after a time, said to Duval—

"Ah, sir! the reasons for leaving Hornsey seem to multiply rather, don't you think?"

"They do, Luke. Of course, I always did look forward to the time when the place would no longer suit me. Nothing was more probable than that I should be seen at last about the neighbourhood; and now I will make up my mind to a removal, despite all consequences; and those who may chance to find the dead body of the officer in the garden, may make the best of it. They cannot take upon themselves to say who put it there, and we may manage to leave Hornsey yet without any one being aware that we have resided in that house except ourselves."

"And our unknown correspondent, sir."

"True; but that correspondent will, I think, be no longer unknown after to-night. Hark! it is eight o'clock. Let us make some speed, for the interruption of these fellows in the lane has made us just a few minutes behind our time."

They increased their speed now, and when they got near to Charing Cross, they separated; for they did not wish to seem to be in company in any way. Duval rode right on down St. Martin's Lane, and Luke made his way down a street or two that led him to the Strand, so that he would come out by Northumberland House, at the corner of which he purposed waiting to notice how his master got on.

It will be remembered that in those days the streets of London were not blazing with light as they are now. Most of the shops were closed after nightfall, as the most daring robberies were committed, if they were not, and the miserable oil-lamps in the streets shed but a very dubious twinkling ray around them.

For the sake, too, of getting the best of the beams of light from the wretched lamps on to the pavements, they were so low, that any one could with a stick demolish one of them in a moment; and the consequence was that, frequently before half the night was over, one-half of the lamps had fallen victims to the drunken frolics of troops of inebriated persons from the taverns, or to the more systematic efforts of the thieves to leave the streets in darkness, so that they might, with greater security, carry on their depredations.

There was a lamp at the corner of the Strand close to Northumberland House; but as it was not desirable for Luke to be seen, he very coolly put it out, and halted in profound darkness. He then fixed his eyes upon the statue of Charles the First, which sat quietly upon its pedestal, only partly relieved against the dark night sky in its upper half, and against the dim and dusky houses for its remainder.

Duval had purposely gone very slow down St. Martin's Lane, so that he might give Luke ample time to get round by the Strand, and to take up his station so that he could watch what was going on. It was, therefore, some few minutes after Luke had put out the lamp before Duval appeared. Then, however, he, after some time, came trotting up to the statue.

It was not more than six minutes after eight at that moment.

"All's right," said Luke to himself. "We are here; but I don't see any one else upon the spot to meet us."

These words had hardly, in a sort of suppressed manner, escaped the lips of Luke when, from the direction of Whitehall, a carriage rapidly approached, and made its way towards the statue, where Claude Duval was waiting.

As far as Luke could judge of the carriage, it was a handsome one, drawn by two very stately dark brown horses; and there was a footman hanging on to it behind, attired in rich livery; for a watchman, who had recently made an appearance upon the spot, turned his lantern now in the direction of the carriage, so that Luke caught for a moment or two a very good view of it, indeed.

"What on earth can all this mean?" he said to himself. "This is, indeed, a rather strange adventure."

CHAPTER CV.

DUVAL IS TAKEN TO A HOUSE WHERE HE MEETS AN OLD FRIEND.

As the more remarkable events of that night occurred, of course, to Duval, who was the person appointed to meet the unknown, we will now leave Luke to his own cogitations, and to take what steps may seem to be most expedient, contingent upon what he sees, while we accompany Duval throughout the proceedings of the night.

Like Luke, he, upon reaching the place of appointment, and finding no one, was rather disappointed as well as surprised; but he had not had many minutes to reflect upon the matter, before he heard the rattle of the wheels of the carriage upon the rough paving.

Duval did not at the moment pay much attention to the sound; for in such a neighbourhood, it was not at all an unusual one, and he could not think it possible that his unknown correspondent was likely to come to meet him in a carriage and pair, with a coachman and a footman in attendance to see all that passed, and possibly listen to what was said. He was soon, however, undeceived, for the carriage was driven close up to the iron railing surrounding the base of the statue.

Duval drew his horse back a little, for he yet could not think that it was for him the carriage came; but suddenly, one of the windows was let down, and a voice said—

"Is it C. D. ?"

"Yes," said Duval, "I am here. What is it you require of me ?"

Anxious to discover, if possible, who it was that had written to him, he made his way up to the carriage window, but to his surprise, he found a young gentleman there, whose countenance he could only dimly see, and who, from the little that he could observe of his dress, seemed to be attired in the first style of fashion; the wig was powdered, according to the prevailing mode, and there was a very deep lace ruffle upon the wrist of the hand that was placed upon the sill of the carriage window.

"I am here," said Duval; " what would you with me ?"

In the space of about half a minute, the young gentleman did not make any reply, and when he did speak, it was in a very strange, muffled voice, that Duval thought was either struggling with deep emotion, or was very much disguised.

"Will you have confidence ?" he said.

"Confidence in whom ?" said Duval; " you will possibly see reason sufficient why I should not have the greatest confidence in a total stranger."

"A total stranger ?" said the young man, mournfully.

"Perhaps I wrong you by saying so much," added Duval, "and by having any doubts upon the subject; but you may easily put an end to them by telling me who you are."

"No—no !"

"Is there very great occasion for so much mystery ?"

"There is. If you will put up your horse somewhere in this neighbourhood, and then trust yourself with me, you will soon know all. You will be in perfect safety. No treachery is intended. That I will swear. The expressions in the note that was sent to you, and which you may consider to be of a threatening character, were put in, in the dread that you would not come."

"But that note purported to come from a female ?"

"Yes, it did come from my sister, and it is to her that I will take you, if you will trust yourself; she will explain to you the meaning of it. If you will not come, I have only to go back to her as I came, to tell her."

The young man paused, and Duval said,—

"What would you tell her ?"

"That C. D. was afraid, after all."

Duval felt the hot blood tingle in his cheek.

"You would, then, stain your lips with an untruth," he said. "I never was afraid, and am not now likely to be the slave of such a feeling, because I have met with a beardless boy whom I do not happen to know, or to recognise. You know, or you ought to know, that caution is compatible with courage. It is the coward, not the brave man, who is reckless."

"As you please. Will you come, or will you not?"

Duval hesitated for a moment or two. All his reason told him that it was the most desperately incautious and foolishly hazardous thing that he could do to go; but then there rose up in his mind all that love of adventure, which took him into so many difficulties, and that daring nerve and courage which took him out of them.

"I will go," he said; "I will go with you."

"Rightly decided," said the youth; "I will wait upon this spot, while you dispose of your horse in some way, for it might be an encumbrance where we are going, and it had better be where you yourself know you can find it at any moment you please, than in my keeping."

"I shall not be many minutes," said Duval; "I have made up my mind to trust you, and having done so, I will trust you implicitly."

"It is well," said the youth.

Upon this, Duval hastily rode away from the carriage, and as he had agreed with Luke that he was to be at the corner of Northumberland House, he at once made his way to him.

"Luke—Luke," he said.

"I am here, sir."

"Take my horse. Lead it, and follow yonder carriage as closely as you can consistently, without being seen. I am going I don't know where in it; but if there should be any danger, and you should hear a pistol shot, you will be so good as to take it as a pretty good hint that you may interfere."

"I shall, indeed, sir. But who is it?"

"That I am still in the dark about."

"And yet you will go?"

"I have promised, and must. But as far as I can judge, there is not the least cause for any alarm, Luke. I do not think by going in that carriage I shall be taken among the class of people that would be likely to do me any harm. Take the horse."

Duval dismounted, and Luke took hold of the bridle of his horse. The faithful dependant would fain have said something more to Duval to dissuade him from running too great a risk, but he was off before Luke could think of some way to shape the remonstrance, so that it would not sound offensive, or as if he doubted the carriage or the discretion of his master.

"Heaven help him!" said Luke.

Duval did not hurry back to the carriage. He was resolved to keep himself perfectly calm, and cool, and collected, so that he should be able to notice any little circumstance that might in any way help him to a knowledge of his position, and aid him in case there should chance to be, contrary to his expectations, danger.

The footman was standing now at the carriage door, and the steps were let down. Duval would not betray the slightest hesitation nor the slightest hurry. He got into the vehicle as calmly and coolly as though it had been his own, and he was only going to pay some ordinary visit. A rapid glance assured him that the young gentleman was alone in the carriage. That was not what he, Duval, had expected.

The steps were replaced, and the door was closed. It was quite clear that the servants had their orders beforehand, for there was no command now given; and in the course of a few moments the carriage was driven off in the direction of St. James's Street.

"You have trusted me," said the young gentleman.

"Yes, you see I have."

"Then it is very imprudent, indeed, and I grieve to say that this reckless spirit will one day be your destruction. How can you know but that this is only a plan to take you to a prison?"

"It is not so."

"You speak confidently, Claude Duval; but you cannot know as much. Your heart tells you that it may be so, notwithstanding your words admit it not."

"No," said Duval, "my heart tells me no such thing. It is quite clear that you are well to do in the world, be you whom you may; and I do not think you are quite insane."

"Quite insane? What do you mean?"

"Ah, I have heard that voice before, somewhere," cried Duval; "but for the life of me I cannot, at this moment, recollect where. You were off your guard for a moment, young gentleman, and spoke more naturally; and so you have unwittingly convinced me that I do know you, or rather that, under some circumstances, I have known you."

"You are mistaken."

"Not so; I have a good ear and a good memory. I am not mistaken, I feel assured. But it does not matter; keep your secret as long as it pleases you to do so: you will, no doubt, reveal it at your own good time."

"I will. But you were talking of my being insane to betray you. What brought you to that conclusion?"

"Simply this, that here you are evidently in possession of the comforts of life and its luxuries, and it would be insane to barter them all and step out of the world at your age, merely for the stupid gratification of playing a dishonourable trick to Claude Duval."

"But how do you mean that I should barter my advantages, and step out of the world by playing you a trick? I do not comprehend that."

"Then I will enlighten you upon that head by informing you, that if I saw any reason to believe that such treachery was intended me, I would blow out your brains without any compunction at all upon the matter."

The young man laughed slightly.

"Very good, Duval," he said; "and do you suppose that I am not armed? Do you fancy that I have come upon such an expedition as this without weighing all its perils and chances? Oh, no; you have your equal in me so far as that goes, Duval, and your threats I laugh at."

"Laugh as much as you like. My threat was only one, and that was contingent upon your own conduct. But if you have only got me here to have a wrangle about the consequences of betraying me, the sooner it is brought to an end the better; and if you will order your coachman to stop, I will get out of the carriage and leave you."

"Oh, no; it is not for that object. It is to ensure your happiness that you are brought here to-night. It is to give you a chance of acting the part of—of—"

"Go on. Why do you hesitate?"

"I was going to say, Claude Duval, that this is a crisis in your fate to-night. You may or you may not see it in its proper light; but if you do, you may be happier than you have been, and you may emerge from a line of life, that if you persevere in, will destroy you."

"If your intentions are really kind towards me," said Duval, "however ill-directed and inefficient they may be, I will thank you and not regret this meeting. There is a something in your tone that assures me you are not an enemy; and I can see, or rather hear, that you are struggling with deep feelings."

"I am—I am!"

"Ah!" said Duval, "that tone again! How will I know it, and yet how strangely it baffles me to say where I have heard it. Speak again, and speak in your natural voice, and then, I feel confident, that I shall soon be able to tell you who you really are."

"No, Duval, you will not."

"But I am certain I shall. You are now again disguising your tone, and I grant that you baffle me, and I can do nothing. I never before felt such a difficulty in a recognition."

"You will yet be foiled until the time comes for me to tell you of my own free will."

The carriage suddenly stopped.

"Are we at our destination now?" asked Duval.

"We are. Will you still be trustful, or, even now, would you like to leave me? You are free to do so if you have such an inclination. But I pray that you will not, for as yet you know nothing of me and my motives; and if you come not further, you will be tortured by a thousand doubts and conjectures about what might have been."

" I know it, and so I will escape that most miserable condition by still accompanying you. Lead on—I will follow.

The carriage door was opened, and the steps let down in silence by the footman. Duval sprang out of the vehicle, and found that he was at the door of a very great house, indeed, in a wide handsome street. An oil lamp was burning over the door, and as the noise of the arrival of the carriage had, no doubt, warned the servants within that there was an arrival, the entrance to the house was then open, displaying within a very handsome hall, paved with marble, and well lighted.

Duval just eyed all this askance, for he was much more intent upon noticing his companion of the carriage, who sprang out after him.

Duval was rather surprised at the slight and diminutive appearance of the young stranger; but he saw, by the light of the oil lamp above the door, that he was most superbly dressed.

"This way," he said, and ascending the steps, he rapidly crossed the hall, followed by Duval. A pair of doors, covered with crimson cloth, were opened by a domestic, and discovered a flight of stairs, conducting to the upper chamber. The young gentleman ascended, still followed by Duval; and then opening the first room they came to upon the landing, Duval found that it conducted him into a very magnificent drawing-room.

It had seldom been the lot of Claude Duval to look upon such an apartment as that into which he was ushered by the young gentleman who had been his mysterious fellow-companion in the carriage. It was fitted up entirely in crimson and gold, the walls being covered with the most costly brocade, upon which, upon a light ground, were raised flowers in a deep crimson, interspersed with golden threads, that had an eminently rich effect.

The ceiling of the room was elaborately painted, and the carpet was as soft as driven snow. A crowd of costly pictures, of a corresponding colour to the walls, with a few varieties, which were a great relief to the eye, in white satin, of which material the curtains of the windows were composed, completed the character of the room, and made an ensemble of the most delightful description.

One chandelier of cut glass, in which there were some three dozen wax candles, lit the apartment. A bright sea-coal fire burnt in the grate, which might have been dispensed with, for there was a warm south wind blowing over London, and the temperature was high; but the pleasant sparkle of the fire, and the bright jets of flame that it produced, had a very comfortable look.

This apartment might well claim, as it did, from Duval more than a passing glance, and it really for a few moments distracted his attention from the young gentleman who had in so mysterious a way conducted him to it.

"So," said the young gentleman, "this room has charms for you, Duval? Look at it well; could you be happy in such a house as this? Speak, and speak freely: I wait your answer."

CHAPTER CVI.

DUVAL MAKES A DISCOVERY, AND SAVES A LIFE.

" I do admire the room," said Duval.

"And would be content with such a home?' cried the young gentleman eagerly. "Is it—it would be if you saw your way—your ambition to call yourself the master of such a place?"

" I cannot go so far as to say that."

"And why not? Is it not to your taste? Is there anything wanting in the rich and rare appointments of this place that you cannot say you envy it and would gladly call it yours?"

" I am not disposed to be so critical as to say that anything is wanting to the place; and as I am not   want of a home at present, and, to tell the truth, can do very well without all this glitter, I may say at once, that envy it I do not. Will you permit me to ask, young sir," said Duval, with some asperity of manner, "if you have brought me, at considerable trouble, to admire your upholstery? Carving and gilding, and rich stuffs, are things very well in their way, and which I am far from despising; but I certainly should not have come from my home for the purpose of seeing them, unless I had thought some higher purpose was to be achieved."

"You are right, Duval," said the young man; "a higher purpose is to be achieved. I did not bring you to this place merely that you might look upon such baubles with an eye of admiration."

" State your purpose, then."

The young gentleman paced the room several times in silence, and some powerful emotion appeared to come over him. At length he spoke—

"Duval," he said. "Look at this place once more. The whole house is in the same rich taste, and it is all mine. It was all my sister's—My poor sister! Alas! alas!"

" Is she dead?"

"Dead! dead! Oh, what a happy thing it would be if she were dead! But she may be soon. Who know—who knows? I have almost a thought that she will be soon; but that is not the question now. I tell you, Duval, that this house, with all it contains, is for a brave heart to win."

" You indeed surprise me."

"Listen:—I had a sister; she was young and innocent, and there was one whom she had seen, and whom she loved. She trusted him. I will not say he took her from a happy home to be his minion, for home she had not; but he did say that if she would be his, he would love her well, and truly, and constantly. All her joy was to be with him;—to watch his every look—to hang upon his words; and day and night her study was to please him: But he was a villain."

" A villain?"

" Yes; was it not the act of a villain to win the young heart of a confiding girl, and then desert her—leave her to shame and to desolation? I ask you, Duval, if that was not the act of a villain?"

Duval was silent. The still, small voice of conscience told him that he, too, was obnoxious to such a charge.

"If aught of this concerns me," he said, "go on and let me hear it. If not, I only occupy your time and my own, too, for no available purpose, and I will go at once from here. I cannot feel a great interest in the woes or the joys of people of whom I literally know nothing."

" Nay, but stay a little. Let me finish my sister's most sad history. She loved her betrayer still."

" Well?"

"And, notwithstanding all the deep and greivous wrong that he had done to her, she yet cherished in her heart of hearts a love for him, which was as boundless as eternal space. It is woman's poor nature so to do and so to cling to their destroyers. A period of great desolation came over her when he left her. Poverty, in all its guant, hideous aspect stared her in the face. For some time sickness and want assailed her; but she at length found one by the side of her couch who made her many promises. He was a man of wealth and rank, and was enamoured of the still girlish beauty she possessed."

"And she was comforted," said Duval. " It is an old story: such things happen every day. In your youth you may think it rare, but my large experience can inform you that it is not so. Say, now, what it is that you would have me do contingent upon all this?"

" Much—much."

" Please, then, to enlighten me concerning it. for as yet I must confess that I am much in the dark. Your sister, of course, yielded to the promises of her new friend, and was happy enough ?"

"She yielded."

"To be sure, and yet you think this such a very strange affair?"

"But she was not happy enough. A kind of madness took possession of her brain. Her new friend, as you call him, lavished wealth upon her. He gave her gold and jewels—he gave her a house, with all its costly contents; but he could not give her peace and joy.

"Was she discontented?"

"She was, for yet in her heart she clung to the memory of her first love—to him who had been her destroyer; and she longed to look upon his face again. She watched for him—she placed others upon his steps—and at last, accident enabled her to trace him to his home. She thought that then, as there might be yet for her some lingering sparks of affection in his bosom, she would fan them if that were possible, into a flame again; and with such love as she had for him once before, she might——"

Here the young gentleman paused, and it was quite evident that he was deeply affected by what he was saying.

"I pray you to proceed," said Duval. "Let me know all your story, since you thought it proper that I should do so."

"You shall know it all. Duval, you cannot—you cannot be so cold-hearted —so cruel—so obstinate."

A clock upon the chimney-piece at this moment struck the hour, and the young gentleman, with a start of alarm, counted the strokes.

"He will be here—he will be here," he cried. "This time in another hour he will be here."

"Ah!' cried Duval, " now again you speak in your natural voice, and I ought to know you, yet does the recognition baffle me. I know the voice, but I do not know to whom it belongs. Speak to me clearly and candidly. Who, and what are you?"

"You do not know me yet?"

"In truth I do not."

"Oh, Duval, can it be possible? The lights are dim—very dim, or you would see in me your once loved but long lost——"

"Ah, I know you know! You are Adele!"

"I am—I am!"

She sprang forward and fell into the arms of Duval, who, forgetting at the moment how deeply his faith and truth were pledged to another, and how much he had injured the young Adele, clasped her to his breast and covered her face with kisses. For a moment or two she yielded to the fascination of that caress which she had not for so long felt wound about her; but then a sudden thought seemed to come across her, and bounding from his arms, she cried—

"Duval, you are a villain! You love me not—you never loved me!"

"Say not so, Adele; you wrong me by the doubt."

"I do not wrong you, but I tell you, Duval, that your soul is a selfish one, and knows not what real love is. I did think that you loved me; but it turned out to be only a dream—a mere delusion of the passions. You loved yourself only."

Duval was silent. He could not but feel that to a great extent he merited the reproaches of Adele. His conduct to her had been anything but what it ought to have been; and even in the utmost extent of his ingenuity, he found it difficult to think of anything in extenuation of the past. He looked conscious of guilt.

Adele saw he shrunk before her, and she spoke in a more kindly tone.

"Oh, Duval, well you know that I am your victim. Well you know that you see before you one who fell not for the love of guilt, but for the love of you; and well you know that for the first fresh face that dawned upon your passions, you left me to ruin, to misery, and perchance to death. Was that manly?—Was it honest?"

"It was not, Adele."

"Then there is some grace in you yet, and I will not heap reproaches upon your head. Once more I ask you to look around you, Duval, and tell me how you think that I am housed. Speak, I say, or you will drive me mad—quite mad!"

She pressed her hands upon her head, and a strange expression came across her face. Duval had never before seen such an expression upon the face of Adele, and he dreaded to look upon it. The effect upon him was to convince him that positive or incipient insanity was there; and if anything could have touched his consience, it was the thought that to him and to his conduct regarding her, was to be attributed that wreck and the overthrow of her reason. With an air of profound affliction he spoke—

"Adele, can you not forgive me the past?"

"I can and will, but it must be from the pleasant feeling of the present and the future. Duval, tell me in a word—Will you be mine? Speak to me or this moment is my last. It had better be so.—Ha! ha!—I often ask myself why I live at all."

She hastily approached a cabinet that was in the room, and flinging open one of its richly panelled drawers, she took from it a pistol, and having rapidly cocked it, she held it to her head, adding—

"It is but one pang, and then all is past—one momentary pang! Why do I not do so?"

Duval was alarmed at the idea that she might really pull the trigger of the pistol, and before his very eyes, doom herself to death. He was afraid to make a rush forward to try to disarm her, as her finger was upon the trigger, and the least pressure would discharge the weapon. Commanding his feelings at the moment, he spoke in a calm tone—

"Adele," he said, "I have in good truth a brighter opinion of you than to suppose for a moment you would stoop to such an act."

"What act?"

"Suicide. It is, after all, the cowards refuge from pain. Tell me what you would have of me, and you will still find that I cherish an affection for you. You have not sent for me here to be a spectator of your death—I am quite sure you had some other purpose."

A confused look passed over the face of Adele, and she repeated the words "other purpose" in a low tone, as though she were trying to make them a key to the remembrance of something that had escaped her memory. The pistol trembled in her grasp.

"Oh, yes," she at length said, "I had another purpose. Do you still love me, Duval?"

"I do—indeed I do."

"On your soul, do you love me?"

"On my soul, I love you, Adele. I love and pity you, my poor girl.' Come to me and tell me all that you were going to tell me. Put aside that murderous weapon. It ill befits you to have it in your hand. Come to me, Adele, and let us talk of the happy past."

"No—no, not of the past—of the future we will talk."

With a slow staggering step she came towards Duval, and sinking upon her knees at his feet, she suffered him to take the pistol from her hand. She looked up in his face with a strange glance, and then Duval saw that the expression of her eyes was totally different to what it had ever been before, and he trembled at the thought that already madness had made its home in her brain.

"Listen to me," she said. "He who came to me in my distress is Lord Clifdean. He is rich, and he gave me this house and all that it contains; but I do not love him. Love him!—Oh, how I hate that man! It is my own fancy to dress in this way, for then I know that I am not likely to be recognised by any one who knew me in the time gone past. Do you think they would know me, Duval?"

"I am certain that they would not. If I did not know you, Adele, it is most unlikely that any one else would."

"Hush! Let us speak low. You will not shriek at a little danger Duval for before we can be as tender and as loving as once we were, something in the shape of danger must be met. Oh, yes; I had a plan, Duval. What was it? What was it?"

"Nay, I know not, Adele."

"Ah! I remember it now, Duval. You see, I am waiting for a visit from Lord Clifdean; he will be here presently."

"Don't you think, then, Adele, that in such a case my presence will be just a little awkward?"

"No; I want you here. It is part of the plan, Duval, that you should be here. He will come shortly to pass the evening with me. Through yonder door is a small room, where you can remain, Duval.

"I would rather not."

"But you must. I tell you that this house, and all it contains, belongs to me; but he must be got rid of. From that small room, Duval, you can easily shoot him."

"Shoot him!"

"Yes, and why not? Shall I not be free, then, again? Do I not hate him? Shall I not then be able to come to you again?"

Her eyes flashed in so strange a fashion, and she began to get into such a state of ungovernable excitement, that Duval was obliged, for the sake of calming her down, and preventing her from probably at once laying violent hands upon her-self, to say, in soothing accents: —

"Oh, yes, yes; certainly. I did not at the moment quite understand. It is just as you say, Adele."

"Why, then, that is well. I say, that from that room you can shoot him, and then we can find some mode of disposing of the body, for when he comes here, he always comes on foot, and he goes out gently, opening the street door for him-self, so that no one but I know when he has left the house; and then when he is no more, we can be happy again."

That poor Adele's intellect had quite given way before the shock of his deser-tion of her, Duval could not now doubt; and probably nothing that could possibly have happened with regard to her could have had a greater, or anything near so great an effect upon him. He sat looking into her face pale and agitated, and it was some few minutes before he could command himself sufficiently to speak.

"Adele," he then said, "come sit beside me, and let me talk to you. What kind of man is this Lord Clifdean?"

"I hate him!"

"Yes, but why is it that you hate him? Has he been unkind to you? Come, tell me all about it. Is he young or old, married or single?"

Before Adele could make any reply to Duval, there came a sharp, rapid knock at the door of the house.

―――

CHAPTER CVII.

DETAILS WHAT HAPPENED AT ADELE'S HOUSE.

DUVAL, when he heard that knocking, sprang to his feet, for he did not doubt for a moment but that it was Lord Clifdean, in whose house, above all others, considering his (Duval's) former acquaintance with Adele, he did not wish to be.

"He comes! he comes!" said Adele.

"Who? Tell me at once if it be the man you have named to me. Is it Lord Clifdean?"

"It is; hide yourself, and remember, Duval, you are to kill him—nothing short of his death will do—you must kill him. If you will not, there will be more deaths than one, for I will kill him, and then myself."

"Adele! Adele!"

"What mean you? do you shrink, or tremble, or recoil from the act? Only say so in truth, and then I shall know what to do."

"No, no," said Duval, terrified by her wild look. "I do not shrink. Hide me —I will do it."

The fact was, that Duval wanted time for reflection as to the best course he could pursue; and in order that he should have such, he allowed Adele to take him by the arm, and lead him into the small room adjoining that magnificent one in which this strange dialogue had taken place. He was only just in time in reaching his place of concealment, for a rough voice from the outer room called out, while she was still with him :—

"Adele! Adele! where are you?"

"'Tis he," whispered Adele. "Remember!"

Without another word, or waiting for any reply from Duval, she entered the outer room again, leaving him in no small perplexity as to how he ought to act under the most singular circumstances in which he there and then found himself.

There was a small lamp in the room, placed upon a bracket, so that he could see pretty well any object in it; and although Adele pulled the door after her, it did not close at all properly, but left a crevice of about two inches in width, through which Duval could see the whole of the outer room, and which enabled him to distinctly hear every word that was uttered therein.

Duval thought his then present situation one of the most disagreeable he had ever been in.

"Here I am," he said, "an interloper in a man's house of whom I know nothing, and playing the part of a spy under circumstances that make it specially disagreeable; and yet what on earth can I do? I cannot drive that girl to suicide, and as for shooting this Lord Clifdean who is with her, that is quite out of the question. Well, I must just wait, and be guided by circumstances as to what I can do."

There was nothing in it, however, but to be patient, and to trust to circumstances dictating a course of conduct to him; and in the meantime he was certainly a listener, in spite of himself, to the proceedings in the other room.

"I am here," he heard Adele say. "Are you not late to-night?"

"Not that I know of, my dear," said the man's voice. "So, you are dressed *en cavalier* to-night, eh?"

"Yes,' said Adele; "I have been out, and you know I always prefer this costume upon such occasions, as it, at all events, saves me the trouble of hiding myself from the gaze of the men, although not from the observations of the women."

"And they all fall in love with you?'

"Probably enough."

"Well, I don't wonder at that, for without any flattery to you, Adele, you do look the most charming of all charming youths. I have no doubt you could make a capital match if you liked; but it would be a dreadful deception."

"I don't intend to try it."

"Ah, you little rogue, you are too well satisfied as you are. I am sure you have already made a good match."

"Indifferently good."

"Say you so? By all that's magnificent, if you go on as you do, you will make up a good round sum in the year, my little expensive beauty."

"Oh, that's nothing."

"Humph! It's all very well for you to say, 'Oh, that's nothing!' but, to my humble apprehension, it is something, and something worth consideration too. But let us stop this talk—I hate any conversation about money—I pray I shall be always able to get enough of it somehow or another; so let us talk about something else, you beauty, if you will."

"Oh, that's nothing."

"Well, then, let us have a glass of wine, and talk of the weather, or of what you will."

"Very good, my lord. You are very good indeed; but I cannot drink wine, and you know I cannot. I don't know how it is, but there is in my brain a strange feeling."

"By Jove, Adele," said his lordship, "and if you encourage such nonsense, you will go out of your wits, I assure you, love. Shake off such odd fancies, and be a good girl, as you are a charming one."

"No, I cannot shake them off; but I will order your wine, and I can talk to you while you drink it."

With this, Adele rang for a servant, and ordered some wine, and in a few minutes the noble acquaintance was provided with the description of rich drink that he best loved. He was about to say something to Adele, when she rose saying :—

"I will be with you directly—I think I left my handkerchief in the next room —indeed, I am pretty sure I did."

She went from the gorgeous apartment where his lordship sat, and made her way to the little room where was Claude Duval. The propinquity of these two rooms was such, that it would have been hazardous in the extreme to speak above the faintest whisper. She placed her mouth close to his ear, and whispered the two words " Do it !"

Claude made no reply, and then she changed the words to the certainly more expressive ones of " Kill him!"

Duval shook his head.

She stamped in rage, and the protector called out from the next room,—

" Hilloa, Adele, what is the matter now? Are you getting into one of your little tiffs ?"

" No, it is nothing," she said.

" Oh, very well. Don't hurry yourself. You certainly do manage to keep a good bottle of wine in the house.'"

Adele again approached Duval, and holding him by the collar of his coat, she whispered the words " Kill, kill, kill !"

There was so odd a look about her, that he almost dreaded to tell her that he would not. Nevertheless, it was absolutely necessary that he should say something, and he (Duval) could not relish the idea that she should go back into the er room with the idea of expecting each moment he (Duval) was going to commit a deliberate and cold-blooded murder. He spoke to her in the very lowest tone he could possibly assume which could have the least chance of making her understand what he said.

" Adele, for the love of Heaven—for your own peace of mind—for the love of me, I beg and implore that you will banish from your mind all idea of this dreadful deed !"

" No—no !" she said.

" Eh ?" said his lordship: " Did you speak?"

" No. I am coming directly."

" You will give it up ?" whispered Claude. " It would be base and cowardly, it would, indeed, Adele."

" Kill—kill !" was her reply.

" Nay, consider. The time will come, when even you would most bitterly repent such an act—when you would fain recall it at the price of your existence ; for the memory of it will live after you. There will be a retribution in this world as well as in the next !"

" Coward !" she said, " you shrink from it ; but I will let you see that I do not. I have the means of putting in his wine a poison that will quickly do its work ! I would have liked that, for the love of me, you had done the deed, as then—But no matter ; I see you will not, so I will. Remain where you are, and for your life's sake, interrupt me not !"

Before Duval could say one word in reply to this, she went into the outer room again, leaving him in the most painful state of mind that can be imagined.

That she was to a certain extent insane, he could not doubt, for her conduct sufficiently proved that fact ; but that there was a certain dangerous method in that insanity was likewise pretty evident.

From what she had hinted, it was clear to him that she had an idea that if she could only get him to commit the murder she proposed, there would be such an union of guilt between them that he would never be able to leave her. So far she showed the most cunning calculation ; but in the idea of the crime at all, and in fancying for one moment that it could be concealed, their was madness. Now, however, after the threat that she would poison Lord Clifdean, Claude found himself in the miserable position of being, by his silence, an accomplice in the deed, or under the necessity of proclaiming her guilty intentions to his lordship.

Neither alternative was likely to be very pleasing to Duval.

Over and over again he bitterly regretted that he had met her at all, or that he had not left the house at once, upon discovering who she really was; but it was too late to think of such things now, and it would have been but a cowardly thing to go away now that he was aware of her murderous intentions towards one who, whatever might be his faults, had, at all events, lavished wealth and comfort upon her with a profuse hand.

What to do, he knew not; and at length he felt that he could only assume such a position in the little room as should enable him to watch all that went on in the larger one; and if then he saw enough to convince him that Adele was really intent upon carrying out her threat of poisoning Lord Clifdean, he felt that, let the consequences be what they might, he must interfere.

The idea of poison was to Duval, who really had a brave spirit, truly detestable; and he looked upon it, as every one with a particle of courage or honesty in their disposition must look upon it, as the most truly despicable crime which human nature had it in its power to commit.

"It must not be," he said to himself. "I must stop here, and then I must try and save her from the possible consequences of this attempt. Alas! poor Adele! how are you changed!"

Well might Duval say—"Alas! poor Adele! how are you changed!" for she was changed, indeed, from the gentle, kind, and loving creature she had been when first he knew her, and when he had warped her poor spirit from the path of virtue. That change though, he should have told himself, was one which he of all men had the most to answer for. It was a change wrought in what had been a pure soul, by the consciousness of having for ever lost that purity!

But yet she was not to commit murder in consequence; and so, in stopping her from a perpetration of that dire offence, Duval was right.

"How is it, Adele," said Lord Clifdean, "that within these last few weeks you are so changed?"

"Changed, my lord?"

"Yes, to be sure; you don't seem like the same girl, and you go about whispering to yourself as though you had something very bad indeed upon your mind, and were making a continual effort to reason yourself out of the misery it occasioned you."

She covered her face with her hands for a moment or two, and then suddenly withdrawing them, she said—

"It is nothing."

"I am glad of that, my poor Adele. If it be illness that affects you, I will get the highest medical aid that the country can possess for you. You know that I love you, you little gipsy."

"Oh, no—no! Do not say that."

"It's true enough, though, whether I say it or not, so it may very well be said. Come now, cheer up, you little troublesome monkey; the summer is coming, and I will take you a trip somewhere, where new scenes, and new faces, and new habits, manners, and customs, will amuse you."

"No—no!"

"No? Why do you say no? I should have thought now that a few months in Paris or Naples would have been just what you would have liked above all things."

"Oh, peace—peace! do not speak to me in that way. If I am in truth a little mad, you only make me worse by any kindness. Why are you not harsh, and cruel, and unfeeling to me? That is what I want you to be."

"You do?"

"Yes, in good and solemn truth I do, my lord."

"There's no accounting for tastes ; I should have thought, now, that kindness upon my part to you would have been everything."

"It is everything that is calculated to drive me mad."

"You are a very strange girl, indeed."

"Hush! what is that? A disturbance in the street!"

"Is there?"

Lord Clifdean rose from his chair and approached the window. He pulled aside the blind, and placed his face so close to the glass that he could see into the street. While he was so occupied, Adele deliberately emptied a small vial of some clear liquid into the decanter from which he was taking his wine.

CHAPTER CVIII.

THE MURDER PREVENTED.—THE DEATH OF ADELE.

CLAUDE DUVAL saw her do it. A cold shudder came over him as he so saw her, for he felt that he could not remain where he was and allow the murder to be done, and he likewise felt that to prevent it, he must denounce Adele.

Bitterly he regretted that he had met her; but there was no time for reflection now. If Lord Clifdean did but attempt to raise the wine to his lips again, Duval felt that he must be prevented drinking. There was only a faint chance that he might not feel disposed to drink any more.

It was a very faint chance that, indeed.

"Why, Adele," said his lordship, "I don't see any disturbance in the street. It must only be a carriage passing."

"Perhaps it was nothing more, after all. Come away from the window. I thought I heard a noise; but, if there is nothing, why there is an end of it."

"Exactly so, as you say, Adele, there is an end of it; but what on earth is the matter with you, you strange girl, to-night? You don't seem to be yourself at all."

"Am I not?"

"Indeed you are not. I never knew you so cold in your conduct, although, I must confess, you have some fancies that would make any one stare, who did not know you."

"Perhaps I am more myself," said Adele.

"How do you mean?"

"I mean, that perhaps my present conduct is, after all, much more natural to me, than my previous behaviour, my lord."

"Oh, nonsense! Come, now, only tell me, you little provoking creature—is there anything that I can get you that will contribute in any way to your happiness? Have you a wish ungratified? If you have, let me know it, and if it be within my means, you shall be pleased."

"No—no—no! Peace, oh, peace! Do not speak to me in that way. How dare you speak kindly to me? It is what I do not want from you! Oh, if this night you would but say something harsh, and cruel, and selfish, how much I should be obliged to you!"

"Well, that is a strange fancy, if ever there was one; so, you would prefer that I should say harsh, and cruel, and selfish things to you, than kind ones?"

"Oh yes, much—much!"

"Then I cannot do so, Adele, for I do love you, you little mad-headed wayward girl. You are not like many in this great city, who are hardened in vice, and who will smile when their hearts are not at all in unison with the feeling. No, Adele, you, at least, are one upon whose sincerity a man may count. You never would tell me the name of him who deserted you, but I have never ceased to wonder how he could do so, for he might go far, indeed, before he found your equal in beauty and in sensibility. Shake off, then, I pray you, the wayward childlike fancies that beset you, and which at times quite mar your better nature. Be what I am convinced you really are, and you cannot then help being charming."

"Charming, indeed!"

"Yes, I repeat the word, charming! Come, let me see you smile."

"And so you love me?"

"Indeed I do. Have I not done and said all I could to prove that I love you?"

"Well, my lord, drink your wine, and I will tell you who it was that so strangely deserted me at the time that you first saw me in accidentally riding through Camden Town."

"I don't want any more wine."

"Thank God!" said Duval. He was so delighted to hear Lord Clifdean say so that he almost uttered the exclamation aloud.

"No more wine!" said Adele; "well, that is a strange idea! I shall fancy that you don't like it, and then I shall fancy that if you don't like the wine, you don't like me, and so I shall not tell you who it was that deserted me."

"I don't know that it will at all contribute to my happiness to know, Adele," said Lord Clifdean; "but as you seem to be a little tiffed about the wine, I will take another glass just to please you."

Duval's spirits sank again.

"Come now," added Lord Clifdean, "let me see you smile like a good kind girl, as I know you are at heart, and then I shall believe that you are not ungrateful."

"Ungrateful!" cried Adele; "how dare you talk to me of gratitude?" she said, delighted to have at last found something that she could find fault with in what his lordship was saying; "what gratitude do I owe to the man, who, for the gratification of his own passions, places me in this gilded cage? Ungrateful, indeed! No, sir, I may seem to smile, but gratitude is not due from me to you, and well you know it."

"Upon my word," said his lordship, "this is a most extraordinary humour you are in, Adele."

"It is not, sir; it is a natural one. Now you know me better than ever you did."

"In good truth I do; but I am inclined to think that something you do not think proper to tell me has disturbed your spirits and produced in you this strange tone of feeling; so, Adele, I will leave you, and I feel quite sure that upon reflection, you will find that I have shown more temper and patience, and you have shown more wilfulness and caprice, than ought o have been expected from either of us. I will now go; and when I think you have had time to recover from this odd state of mind, I will come back to you."

"Thank heaven," thought Duval; "he is too much offended to drink any more wine. She has overdone it now."

Adele covered her face with her hands for a moment, and his lordship rose.

"Oh, forgive me," she said. "Indeed, I am not myself to-night. Before you go, dear, oh do drink to my health and better feelings."

"That I will do with pleasure, my poor Adele; and I beg you to believe that I love you sufficiently well to look over this little ebullition of passion of to-night, although I hope it is the first and the last time that I shall be a witness to it."

As he spoke, Lord Clifdean filled himself a glass of wine from the drugged decanter. Duval felt that to let him drink it would be the most dastardly thing that could be imagined. Had he been quite other than he evidently was in his conduct to Adele, it would have been a base thing to have him poisoned. Had he been as cruel and as vindictive and heedless of her feelings as he was all the reverse, Duval was not the kind of man who, upon such an emergency, could possibly remain a quiet spectator of such an act. The glass of wine was just about half-way to the lips of Lord Clifdean, when Duval darted from his place f concealment into the room, and in a clear, firm voice, cried,—

"Hold, my lord! Do not drink that wine!"

In the surprise of the moment, Lord Clifdean dropped the glass, and it was shivered to atoms. Duval seized upon the decanter, in which was the remainder of the drugged liquor, and flung it to the ground, dashing it to pieces, so that every drop was spilt.

The shriek that Adele uttered was perfectly ear-piercing, and Lord Clifdean looked from one to the other with surprise, not unmingled with dismay.

"Good Heavens!" he cried, "what is the meaning of all this?"

"Death!" cried Adele. "It means death. That is the meaning of it. Ha! ha! Think you I am foiled? No. When I resolve upon a deed, I will do it. You will say that there is madness in my brain, but I say that there is not. Oh, no—no! Duval, you are my destruction. For you I would have done this. For the love of you I would have sinned, so that angels might have shunned companionship with me. For you I would have loaded my soul with guilt that would have weighed it down to perdition. But all is not over yet. I am foiled with poison, but there are other means yet."

"Poison, said you?" cried Lord Clifdean.

Before Duval could make any remark, Adele sprang to a couch that was at the further end of the apartment, and hastily turning up its mattress, she took out a pistol, and levelled it at Lord Clifdean. This was just one of those emergencies in which the cool, dashing courage of Duval was sure to show itself to advantage. Without the hesitation of a moment, he sprang forward to Adele—she pulled the trigger, and the pistol exploded. The bullet hit a looking-glass, which was shivered to pieces, with a crash, and then Duval closed with her, and took it from her hand in a moment.

"Mad! mad!" he cried. "My lord, she is quite mad, and will require restraint. Oh, Adele!—Adele! how is it that your mind has thus gone from you?"

"How?" she cried; "why, because I was deceived, and then deserted, by one who swore to love, but who heeded not the oath, and played the part of a villain. You—you deserted me, Duval, and from that moment I was mad!"

Duval shrank back with the discharged pistol in his hand, and upon the moment, Adele, seizing the favourable opportunity, darted past him, and made towards the door of the room. Lord Clifdean, had he possessed the presence of mind in emergencies that Duval had, might have stopped her with ease, but after what had passed, it was perhaps more natural for him to do what he did, namely, get out of the way as quickly as he could, so that from him she met no opposition, and before Duval could get round the table to stop her, she had succeeded in opening the door and was bounding down the staircase of the house.

"On, my lord," cried Duval, "come with me after her. She is quite mad, poor girl, and will yet do some desperate deed. Her own life will in all likelihood be the next sacrifice, if we do not stop her."

"For Heaven's sake, tell me who you are," said Lord Clifdean.

"Never mind, my lord, who I am. Let it suffice that I have been a good enough friend to you to save your life, by preventing you from drinking the poisoned wine, and, likewise, by opposing myself between you and the pistol, which else might have proved your destruction. Will you follow me, and see what we can do for the poor girl?"

"I will. What you say is true. I will follow you."

Duval was down the staircase in a moment, and he saw Adele at the street-door, which she apparently found some difficulty in opening. He made sure that he had her then.

"Adele!" he cried, "no one will harm you. Turn to me. Oh! do not fancy that any one will harm my poor Adele. All will be forgiven!"

"Yes, all—all!" cried Lord Clifdean.

With a frantic shriek, Adele redoubled her efforts to open the door. Another moment and Duval would have had her in his grasp; but she succeeded, and the street-door being flung open, she darted out into the night air.

Duval ran after her at full speed, and Lord Clifdean, at a much better pace than could have been expected from him, likewise joined in the race, keeping pretty close to Duval.

It is probable enough that if Adele had been encumbered with the usual apparel of her sex, she would soon have been caught, as it is not by any means favourable to a race; but it will be remembered that she was dressed in male attire, so that there was no encumbrance to her movements, and she fled with a speed that set even Duval, who was an accomplished runner, at complete defiance. The dark clothes, too, that she wore, made it much more difficult to keep her in sight than it otherwise would have been; and the slight figure that bounded along Whitehall, after traversing the streets that led to it, looked more like a spectre than a living thing.

"Stop her!" cried Duval; "stop her!"

He was in the hope that some watchman might dart out suddenly upon the fugitive, and resist her flying steps; and then it all of a sudden struck him that to cry "Stop *her*," was no guide to the watchman or any one else who might be inclined to assist in the race, and he changed his shout to "Stop him!" being much more descriptive of the sham apparent youth who was darting along with such speed.

Just at the corner of Parliament-street a watchman made a vigorous effort to stop the flying figure; but it only resulted in the guardian of the night rolling into the kennel, while the speed of Adele had scarcely been perceptibly diminished for a moment. The corner of the street leading up to Westminster Bridge was now gained by Adele, and at the moment that it was so, the idea that she intended to drown herself came across the mind of Duval with such a fearful gush of conviction, that he could hardly persuade himself that some one had not actually whispered it in his ear.

"Lost! lost!" he cried. "Oh, Heaven! she is lost!"

Lord Clifdean arrived panting at the corner of the street.

"After her, my lord," said Duval. "After her to the bridge; she will throw herself over; I will take a boat."

Lord Clifdean was too much out of breath with the run he had had to be able to reply to Duval; but he fully understood what he meant, and at once acted up to that understanding, for he continued his course on to the bridge without a moment's more pause than had been just necessary to hear what Duval said to him.

Duval then darted down the stone steps at the side that led to the river. It was quite a miracle that he did not fall down the whole flight and injure himself severely, for he missed his foot-hold, and had to jump about a dozen of them, and only alighted safely at the bottom, by one of those accidents which at times save men from the direst consequences of a too hasty action. The tide was very low just then.

"A boat!" cried Duval, "a boat!"

"Ay, ay, sir," said a lazy voice, "I'm coming. Where do you want to go to?"

"To the devil!" said Duval, as he dashed right into the water, and scrambled into a wherry. It was fastened to some other by a cord, but Duval had his knife out in a moment and released it. Seizing, then, the oars, he shot out into the stream in a moment, to the intense surprise of the waterman, who had only got as far in his preparations as to have his arms in the sleeves of an overcoat he was going to wear, as the night was rather chilly.

The dark shadow of the old bridge was upon the water as Duval urged his boat in that direction. He looked up at it as well as he could, and then he heard a loud shriek and he saw a small figure on the parapet.

"Adele! Adele!" he cried. "No, no! Do not! Oh, God spare her! Adele! Adele!

There was another shriek, and Duval was too terrified for the space of a moment or two to say another word.

"Help! Oh, help!" cried a voice from the bridge.   That voice was the voice of Lord Clifdean.   "Help! help!"

Another moment and the light figure came dashing through the air with a wailing shriek.   It turned over then, and as Duval *felt* sickened at the sight, it fell into the dark water of the river

CLAUDE HAS A VISITOR FROM THE PRINCE IN NEWGATE.

CHAPTER CVIII.

POOR ADELE COMES TO A SAD END.

IN the course of his eventful career, Duval had passed through many a scene that, for a time, had filled his soul with horror.   Often had even his bold spirit shrunk almost aghast from what human nature was capable of doing under circumstances of undue excitement; but never had he felt such a pang of terror and of regret as when he saw that young girl, who had been to him a gentle and a loving companion, come dashing from the parapet of Westminster Bridge, head-foremost, into the river; and never could he forget the frightful splash with which the dark waters opened to receive their victim.

It was scarcely to be wondered that for a moment or two, notwithstanding all the strong purpose that had brought him to that spot, he was completely unnerved, and incapable of moving.

But that purpose had been to save Adele, and it was not for many moments that terror allowed it to sleep in his bosom. With a sudden shout, he aroused himself, and in a voice that sufficiently betrayed the extent of his feelings and the bitterness of his regret at the fate of the young girl, he cried out,

"Adele—Adele! I am here—I am here yet to save you! I am here!"

Alas, she heard him not!

With a vigour that at any other time he might have been quite incapable of, he rowed towards the spot of the river where she had fallen; and with an intense anxiety that was nearly maddening, he waited to see if the body would rise again to the surface of the stream. While he so waited, a voice from the bridge cried loudly,

"Save her! Oh, save her! and receive your own reward!"

That word, reward, was loathsome to Duval at such a moment. The idea of being rewarded for saving the life of Adele was an insult to the feelings that prompted him to make the attempt; but he let it pass. His eyes were fixed upon the water, and he made no answer to the voice from the bridge.

Yes, she rose again to the surface. Cleaving the dark heavy mass of water, the body rose again, and with a cry of joy, Duval caught at it. He grasped a portion of the clothing, and the skirt of the lightly made coat, the fashion and the fit of which were more looked to than the durability, came away in his hand, and the body sunk again to the bottom of the Thames.

"Lost! Lost!" cried Duval. "She is lost!"

With a full conviction, now, that she had really achieved the death that she had sought, Duval gave himself up to despair.

"My poor Adele!" he said; "my poor beautiful Adele! I did love you, and I was mad to leave you to the scorn and the pity of the world, and to your own sad thoughts, which have driven you mad! I am your murderer! I who swore to protect you and to love you! Yes, I am your murderer!"

Virtually, Duval was, indeed, the murderer of that poor lost one. The sin of weaning her from the path of virtue to a life of shame, was bad enough; but the sin of deserting her afterwards was ten times greater. At least, he should have abided by her, and strove to stand between the world and the young creature, when he had parted her from it by his seductions.

For a moment or two, he had covered his face with his hands, but he let them drop from before his eyes, and then, the moment that he did so, as though fate would have it, the body of Adele rose again to the surface of the water, and this time it was so near to the boat, that with a little effort he could easily reach it, and he instantly did so.

"Save her! oh, save her!" cried the voice from the bridge again. "Save the poor girl!"

The voice so startled Duval at the moment, that he lost his place in the little frail wherry, and with the insensible form of Adele in his arms, he fell into the river, the boat upsetting as he did so, and the oars floating away under the arches of the old bridge.

Duval could swim tolerably well, and that was not a moment in which to neglect the practice of such an accomplishment. Supporting the inanimate form of Adele upon his left arm, he struck out with his right towards the shore, which, in the course of a few minutes, he gained. A throng of people with lights had there assembled, for the men whose boat he had taken so very unceremoniously, had raised an alarm about it; but when they saw, which they had soon enough seen, that his object was to save the life of some one who came over the bridge, they understood that it was not a daring robbery, but a kind action, that had to be done, too, promptly if it were done at all effectually, to wait for any explanation.

So the whole of the affair was well enough seen by the waterman and others upon the river's bank, and Duval was welcomed by friendly cries and voices, instead of in a hostile manner.

"This way!—this way!" cried a dozen voices, and two or three men sprang into the water to help him.

"Thank you," cried Duval; "thank you. You will easily recover the boat. I could not help it."

"Oh, hang the boat!" cried one. "Lay hold of me. That's right! Hurrah! All's safe now. Is the poor young gentleman dead, sir?"

"Poor young gentleman? Oh, I understand you. This is a girl whom I hold in my arms, poor thing!"

"A girl! Oh, dear—oh, dear!" A general feeling of intense pity and grief ran through the whole assemblage at this announcement, and many a one would gladly have stretched out an arm to save Duval the trouble of carrying Adele; but, dead or alive, he would not part with her, but held her more closely to his heart, whilst a shower of water from his and her clothing marked their progress.

"No—no," he said. "Alas! poor thing, I much fear that she is past all human aid. Show me to the nearest public-house, my friends, and get a medical man. But she is dead—quite dead!—I am sure of that. And yet nothing shall be wanting to set that at rest beyond a doubt. Poor, poor Adele!"

A public-house near the bridge was open, and into that Duval took the body of Adele. A neighbouring surgeon from Parliament Street was soon knocked up and upon the spot in the course of a very few minutes.

"Tell me, sir," said Duval, "is her spirit really fled, or is this but a case of suspended animation?"

The surgeon shook his head.

"We will try what can be done," he said, "but there is scarcely a hope."

The landlady of the house and the female servants did all that could be done, assisted by the medical man, for the restoration of Adele, and Duval paced to and fro in front of the house more like a madman than anything else. The gray light of early dawn was just beginning to creep over all things, when the surgeon came out of the house. Duval sprang towards him.

"Well, sir," he said, "well, sir! she—she—"

"Is quite dead!"

Duval started as though he had been shot, and then entering the house, he ascended the stairs, and guided by the voices of women, he reached the room where the corpse lay. Without any ceremony, he opened the door and entered the apartment. The landlady was just about to throw a sheet over the body of poor Adele, and the clothing in which she looked such a pattern of youthful fashion and beauty, lay upon a chair by the bed-side. A couple of servants belonging to the house were crying in the room. They were quite young girls, and were too much shocked at the scene to control their tears.

At the sight of Duval, there was a feeling of alarm, but he checked it by saying,—

"Pardon me for this intrusion. I have only come to take a last look at this poor girl. I knew her, and I loved her; but she has gone now where she will be happier far than she was ever in this world; much—much happier!"

With a gasping sob, he bent over the corpse and kissed the cold lips. The landlady and the servants were deeply affected. He then turned to them, and in a voice of great emotion, he said,—

"For what you have done to bring back to this world the spirit of this poor lost one, God bless you all!"

Without another word, then, he left the room, and before any one could question him, he was out of the house.

Duval was indeed deeply affected at the death of Adele, and he walked for some distance from the public-house towards Charing Cross quite in a state of abstraction from surrounding objects. Indeed, he hardly knew why he walked in that direction, and it was not until some 'one said to him suddenly, "Oh, sir, is it indeed you?" that with a start he turned round. It was Luke who spoke to him, and who was close to the curb-stone, mounted upon his own horse, and holding his (Duval's) by the bridle.

"Oh, Luke, she is dead!" said Duval.

"She, sir?"

"I forgot, I forgot: you know nothing of it. I have had a fearful adventure this night. But it is over now, and I will mount and be off."

"Why, sir, your clothes are all wringing wet."

"Yes, I have been in the river. But at some other time I will tell you all about it, Luke. I cannot command my feelings sufficiently to do so now. Recollect, nothing must be known of all this at Hornsey. How came you to find me out?"

"Oh, sir, I saw you scampering along the streets, and I was so bewildered that I lost you, and have been walking the horses up and down here for an hour, thinking it was more likely you would look for me about here than anywhere else. But you don't look at all well, sir; you are as pale as death, and your eyes—"

"Peace, Luke! oh, peace—do not now remark upon my looks. I have gone through enough to-night to make any one look strange and full of excitement. But all that will pass away, and in a little time I shall be myself again."

Luke was silent. He could see that his master was under the influence of much more powerful feelings than ever he had seen him moved by, and he found that it was better not to speak to him, but to allow the excitement of his mind gradually to subside, which it would be sure to do in course of time.

Duval mounted, and at a trot led the way to his house at Hornsey. It was a great relief to Duval to feel he was once again upon his gallant steed and rapidly leaving London behind him. When he got quite clear of the houses, he put the horse to a gallop, and the exercise tended more than anything else could have done to calm down his feelings. In Hornsey Lane he paused, and turning to Luke, he said:—

"My friend, I would not pass such another night as this for the wealth of England."

"I hope, then," replied Luke, "that you may never be again called upon to pass it. But I am glad you are getting better."

"Yes, Luke, and I think I can command my feelings sufficiently to allow me to explain to you the night's proceedings. I am quite sure that my confidence will not be misplaced, and it will be a great relief to me to find some friendly bosom into which I can pour my grief; for, indeed, and in truth, I never felt such grief as I now feel in all my life."

"It is a grief to me to hear you say so," said Luke.

"I know it is. But we have now about a mile to go, and while we walk our horses over that distance, Luke, I shall be able briefly to tell you all that has happened to-night, and why it is that it has had for me an overwhelming and a powerful interest."

Luke was all attention, and then Duval detailed to him how he had first got acquainted with Adele, and how he had taken her to lodge at the little cottage by Kentish Town—how he had left her eventually, and then how she had procured so oddly an interview with him that very night, when she wished to be the destruction of Lord Clifdean, which he, Duval, felt himself bound, as a man, to prevent.

When Duval, however, came to that part of his sad story which comprehended the death of Adele, his voice failed him a little, and he was scarcely able to proceed. It was with great difficulty that he did at length succeed in informing Luke of the catastrophe that had taken place; and then he concluded his narration.

"You know all now, Luke," he said, "and you can judge how deeply I must feel these events."

"I can, indeed, sir," said Luke. "But still there is one thing you ought to consider, and that is, that the poor girl was not in her right senses to-night, and that, after all, poor thing, it was insanity, rather than any other feeling, that has produced all the mischief."

"I wish I could persuade myself, Luke, that I was less to blame in the affair than I feel that I am; but I cannot. That she loved me dearly and fondly is beyond the shadow of a doubt; and it is that love that has brought her to death."

"Why, yes, sir," said Luke. "Perhaps, in a manner of speaking, you may say that such is the fact; but you know that after all it is not what exactly happens that we ought to look to in this world, but what we want should happen. Now, you never intended that Adele should go mad and drown herself."

"Oh, no—no!"

"Very well then, sir. That she did so is not so much your fault as you seem to think; and if Adele had not gone out of her mind, there is very little doubt but she might have been happy and comfortable enough with Lord Clifdean."

"It is very kind of you, Luke, to try to comfort me, but I am afraid your reasoning is more specious than true. The past, however, cannot now be recalled."

"Certainly not, sir; and, therefore, we ought to make the best of it by thinking of it in a very quiet way, and not making it too much a source of discomfort for the present. But here we are at home, sir. I suppose you will give up the idea of moving?"

"I don't know that, Luke. I am beginning to get rather tired of this place, and I know it is distasteful to you."

"I should not be telling the truth to you, sir, if I were to say it were not, for after what has happened in this garden respecting the death of the officer, who lies buried there, I do not like it; but in time, perhaps, I might get over such a feeling."

"There is no occasion," said Duval. "I will look about, and try to find another house. A man in my profession, Luke, ought not to stay too long in one place.

"Certainly not, sir. I am quite of that opinion. Let me take your horse. I have him, sir."

CHAPTER CX.

DUVAL DETERMINES TO SEE ADELE BURIED IN PEACE.

It was with a very heavy heart that Duval rode within the gates of his house at Hornsey. The events of that night had made an impression upon him that would not easily be mastered, and that would never be wholly effaced. He began to think that there was not quite so much glory and high-mindedness in breaking the heart of a young girl as he had flattered himself there was.

This affair with Adele was a rough lesson to him, but it was a lesson that in every way was calculated to do him some good. Alas! it is a thousand pities that one human being is compelled to look for the experiences that will be beneficial to him, in the sufferings of another! But it is so.

There was one thing, now, that suddenly struck upon Duval's mind, and that was, that it would be necessary to say something to May about this night's adventure. Duval was by no means an habitual perverter of the truth. He rather, on the contrary, loved it, and purchased it, from a conviction that it was the very easiest and the best policy; but it was quite out of the question to think of disgusting May with the details of such a story as that connected with the fate of poor Adele.

Yet it was necessary to say something.

"Luke," said Duval, "I will not hatch up any story to tell your mistress about this night's adventure. I will only ask her not to press me for an account of it."

"Oh, sir, do you think that will do?"

" Why not, Luke ?"

" Why, sir, I don't mean to say that my mistress is quite so curious as some ladies, sir ; but still, human nature, you know, sir, will be human nature, under all circumstances."

" I understand you, Luke: But I will will try it, and if I find that she has any great and overbearing curiosity upon the subject, she must then be told something; and upon the same principal that listeners seldom hear any good of themselves, she will find that the too curious are apt to be put off with what is not exactly true."

Luke smiled, and Duval having given him his horse, proceeded into the house. He was met by May, who was enraptured to find that he had returned ; but as she held him in her arms, she cried out—

" Oh, Claude, what is this ? Why, you have been in the water somewhere."

" May, my love," said Duval, " will you do me a favour ?"

" Oh, yes, surely."

" Then let me beg of you to be so good as not to ask me where I have been to-night, or rather, the past night, or anything concerning my adventures."

" If you wish it—" said May, with some degree of hesitation.

" I do, indeed."

" Oh, then, believe me, I will not ask you ; and yet I shall now be thrown upon my own surmises, and it would be better always to trust me, Claude, than to leave me to think and to create what most likely I shall in my own mind about the matter. But that is for your consideration entirely."

" Ah !" thought Duval, " I begin to see that I must get up some story or another ; and that Luke is right."

Duval, notwithstanding he had now the conviction that it would be necessary to tell May something that should appear probable as an account of what had happened to him during that eventful night, was too fatigued to call upon his imagination for the concoction of any tale at that time ; and he was but too glad to lie down and rest, for even highwaymen, like ordinary mortals, want sleep. When he did sleep, his brain was full of vexing images. At one moment he would fancy himself in the Thames swimming for his life, and poor Adele clinging to him, and shrieking in his ear for him to save her ; and then again, he would see her pouring the drugged wine into a glass for Lord Clifdean, while he, with all the wish to interfere and prevent him from drinking the fatal liquor, would feel as though paralysis had laid hold of all his energies, and he could not move or speak.

Such a feverish sleep did not tend greatly to relieve Duval from the sense of fatigue that had been upon him. He was glad when May roused him, and told him he was moaning so sadly in his sleep, that she could not bear to hear it.

" Oh, yes," he said, " I was dreaming of I know not what. I think a canter on my horse will do me good. Will you spare me for a few hours, May ? I will return before sunset."

" Ah, now you are intent upon some dangerous expedition, Claude."

" No, in good truth, I am not. I assure you I have nothing whatever on hand now; and it is purely for the purpose of trying to chase away the fancies of my brain, that I wish now to take a scampering ride for a few miles. You will see me return to you quite a different being, and then, May, as I can well perceive that your curiosity to know what it is that has so much disturbed my brain is very great, when I come home again I will tell you all."

" Ah, do Claude."

" Humph !" thought Duval. " I must invent something or another, that shall sound as like the truth as possible, and yet be as far from it as darkness is from light."

Luke was ordered to saddle the horse that Duval had recently ridden ; but before it could be got out of the yard, there came through the village a news-boy with his horse, shouting some extraordinary intelligence.

A that time, if anything happened of an out-of-the-way character, either in politi? or domestic life, the Grub-street printer would get hold of it, and in quite an incredibly short space of time, it would be printed upon a flying sheet, and boys, with tin horns, would go all over the town and its suburbs, making the most tremendous noise, and selling the intelligence to all the lovers of the marvellous.

"Just printed and published," shouted the boy at Duval's house, "at the small charge of one half-penny," the horn here made a dreadful blast, "the full, and true, and particular account of the murder in the Thames of a young lady of quality in boy's clothes—here you have it." Again the horn split the ears almost of all within hearing, with something between a groan and a shriek.

Luke turned a little pale as he said, "Oh, sir, that surely don't refer to—to——"

"To what, Luke?"

"To your adventure with the young creature that drowned herself?"

"Hush!" Duval listened to what the boy was crying, and he soon satisfied himself that, at all events, there was sufficient connection between his story and that which had really happened to make it very suspicious that the one was engrafted upon the other. He called to Luke directly.

"Luke, go and buy them all of him, and tell him to be off directly, and not even have any more or he will repent of it. If May hears the affair, she will couple it with my wet clothes, and immediately jump to the conclusion that I am the hero of it. Run, Luke, run. Pay him for the whole lot, and send him off."

"I will," said Luke, and then going very quickly out by the garden-gate, he caught the boy by the throat, just as he was putting the diabolical horn to his lips again, and stopped him, for he only succeeded in producing a melancholy howl, instead of the full-toned blast he had calculated upon, and drawn in his breath for.

"Stop, you young rascal," said Luke. "What do you mean by making that horrid noise, eh?"

"Here you have the full, true, and particular——"

"Silence!"

"Account of the murder on the Thames——"

"Will you be quiet?"

"Of the young lady in a pair of——Oh dear, what do you mean by shaking a cove in this way? for I didn't go for to do nothink. Let a cove alone, will you? Murder! Maydn't a cove pick up a living in a quiet way? Oh, dear. Murder!"

"Hold your noise, will you? How many of those papers have you got?"

"Only three dozen at a halfpenny each. Here you have the full, true, and particular account of the——"

"Silence! There is half-a-crown, and there is a shilling to put to it, and if they don't pay you handsomely, I don't know what will; and now you be off out of Hornsey as quick as you can, for if I catch you again within half a mile of this house, I'll break every bone in your skin."

"What, you'll buy 'em all?"

"Every one."

"What will you give for the horn?"

"Why," said Luke, as he took it in his hand and slily pinched it quite flat about the middle, with his finger and thumb, "I don't want the horn at all; but I warn you to be off, young fellow, for I am a man of my word, and if I catch you here again you shall smart for it."

"Oh, won't I be off?" said the boy; "rather!" And then away he went, at a scamper, adding to himself, "and won't I bring another three dozen to Hornsey as soon as I can get 'em neither?"

"Have you got rid of him, Luke?" said Duval.

"I have, sir; and you may depend the papers are all about poor Adele, sir. Just read one and you will soon see that there is just enough truth in the account to make you feel sure about it."

"You are right, Luke," said Duval, after slightly casting his eye over the paper. "This is an account, as far as it goes, of that unhappy girl. Poor—poor Adele! Little did you ever suspect that you would come to such a fate as this and little did I ever dream that I should hold in my hand a paper that in such a way concerned you. Well—well, the bitterness of death is past with you, Adele. It is those who stay behind you who suffer. Luke, I should like to know what takes place with regard to her. No doubt, there will be a coroner's inquest held upon her poor remains. You are unknown at the house where the body lies; will you go and be present, and watch what transpires, and let me know the whole particulars?"

"I will, sir. I will go at once."

"Do so; you cannot miss the public-house. It is quite close to the bridge; you can go, you know, as a perfect stranger, and put up there for a little time; but I need not tell you how to manage, you will do it quite right, I know. Be off at once, Luke. Take my horse, as it is saddled, and I will wait your return here; I will not ride out, as in that case, we should have both to leave the house, which I avoid letting occur if possible."

"I will go, sir," said Luke, "of course; but yet I cannot help thinking that if you could dismiss the matter altogether from your mind, it would be the better now for your peace."

"Perhaps it would, but I cannot do it. No, Luke, that poor, young creature, who was, when first I knew her, a thing of innocence and love, seems ever haunting me; and at odd times I think that she walks even by my side, and I turn rapidly in the expectation of seeing her. Go, Luke, I cannot chase from my mind the sad thoughts of her, and, therefore, it is as well to feed them."

Luke felt that it was now useless to reason with Duval upon the subject, so he mounted at once and started for London. May was very well pleased that Duval remained behind, and as they sat in the garden together, she put him in mind of his promise to tell her his last night's adventure.

"To-morrow, May, to-morrow," he said, "oh, let it be to-morrow. I pray you not to ask me now: I cannot tell you. Believe me it is nothing that at all concerns my safety; but—but it implicates the life of a dear friend, who, in times past, did me some kind service, and so I feel sad."

"And you will be attempting some desperate act for him!" sighed May.

"Oh, no—no, he is dead!"

"Dead?"

"Yes, May, so there is nothing to fear from my attempting any dangerous act, you see. And now let us talk of something else, and when my feelings are a little more rational, dear, I will tell you the melancholy story of my poor friend who is now with the dead. You shall then know it all, May."

"I am content, Duval, and I regret now that I urged you upon the subject, since it evidently gives you so much pain. Can you forgive me?"

"Freely, May, freely; you could not know that it would give me so much pain: and now we will talk upon a subject that is, I know, most grateful to you, and that is, the possibility of my being enabled to leave the road."

"Oh, yes, talk of that, Claude."

Duval was very glad to find some theme for conversation in which May was sufficiently interested that she would not wish to question him upon anything else; and so the time passed well enough for about two hours, and then the shades of evening were beginning to creep over the landscape, when the sound of horses feet in the lane leading from Crouch End to Duval's house, struck upon his ears.

"It is Luke," he said.

"Has he been to London for you?" said May.

"He has, on an errand of no great importance, but still one that I wished performed, and if I had not sent him, I must have gone myself. I will go and meet him."

Duval sallied forth, and met Luke in the lane.

"Well," he said, "you have heard all?"

"I have, sir. There has been an inquest on the body, at which I was present. Twelve stupid tradesmen from the neighbourhood have been muddling their brains with beer, and trying to think on what they know nothing of, and what, if they knew all about, they would not understand."

"You are right, Luke.   Well, and what happened?"

ADELE TEMPTS CLAUDE TO SHOOT LORD CLIFDEAN.

"Ah, sir, I saw her!"

"You saw her?"

"I did, sir. I went into the room where she was lying, when the jury went to view the body; she looked calm and beautiful, with just a faint smile upon her half-parted lips.   She is happy now, sir."

Duval covered his face with his hands, and the tears trickled through his fingers.

"Luke," he said, "I thank you—I thank you—Go on. Tell me all that passed. What did they say of her?"

"Why, sir, some of the people wept, they could not help it."

"No—no, they could not help it."

"It was such a piteous thing to see one so young and so fair lying there in death. Others again did not weep, but they said " Poor thing !" and one wondered how her mother would like to see such a sight. Another hoped there was no one in all the world who loved her."

"No more—no more ! Oh, no more !"

"And another said he was quite sure there could not be, or she would never have come to such a fate as that."

"Then he lied !" cried Duval. "He lied in his throat, for I loved her ! Oh, yes, I loved her, and I deserted her ; why I know not, but I did—I did, and now I am punished for it. Oh, Adele ! what would I not now give to look upon you once again in life !"

"Alas, sir, that is all past."

"It is, Luke—it is ; and these are all vain and idle regrets now. But the feeling that has been awakened in my breast, by the fate of Adele, will never pass away. My heart has received a blow which it never can recover. The time may come, and no doubt it will come, when I shall smile, and seem to be gay and reckless ; but still there will be one spot in my heart that no revelry can reach, and that will be sacred to my sorrow for Adele."

"You think too deeply, sir, of the matter."

"That is impossible. But come, Luke, and put up your horse. You will find me in the lane here. I feel as though in the house I should be stifled. Come out to me when you have attended to the horse, and tell at full length all that took place."

"I will, sir."

Luke went into the stable with the horse, while Duval paced the lane to and fro in such an agony of remorse as he had never thought to have felt : but the few simple words in which Luke had described the appearance of the dead Adele, cut him to the soul.

CHAPTER CXI.

DUVAL MAKES A RESOLVE, AND PROCEEDS TO CARRY IT OUT.

In the course of ten minutes, Luke came out to Duval, and they paced to and fro in the lane together.

"Now," said Duval, "tell me all. Conceal nothing from me. You cannot say anything that can touch me closer than what you have. Let me know all that passed at the inquest."

"Yes, I will do that. I took care to spend my money freely, so that the landlady was very well pleased to have such a guest, and I was not denied access to the room in which the inquest was held. The coroner was a very old man, and evidently so deaf, that it was with the greatest difficulty he could be made to comprehend what was going on at all. The only evidence that was taken down was that of the watermen who were by the stairs close to the bridge when you brought her on shore, and the people at the public-house who received her lifeless remains."

"Was there no conjecture concerning me ?"

"None, sir, of a positive character. It was thought that you had tried to save her from motives of humanity, and that then finding that she was past human aid, you had abruptly left the public-house rather than be troubled any further in the affair."

" Well, Luke, well ?"

" That is all, sir."

" All? No, surely, they must have come to some sort of a decision regarding the case. What was the result of the investigation?"

" Why, sir, they considered she did it herself."

" Yes, yes, poor Adele! they are right there, and I did all I could to save her, you know, Luke; but mortal means could not do more than I did."

" Certainly, sir, and so there's an end of it."

" But the verdict, Luke—I want to know particularly the exact terms of the verdict of the jury."

Luke was silent.

" Why is this, Luke? Why will you not tell me all? What is there to keep a secret from me? I charge you, as you have any friendly feelings to me, to tell me everything. You keep me on the rack by this strange silence. What on earth is the meaning of it? Speak, Luke, I implore you!"

" Then, sir, I must tell you."

" You shall, Luke—you shall. Tell me, I beg of you."

" Then, sir, they found a verdict of suicide, and—they——"

" Well—well ?"

" They ordered the body to be buried to-night in a cross road, with a—take——"

" What? The fiends! They dare not—God! they shall not! I will tear their selfish, cold hearts from their bosoms, rather than they shall do so. No—no! It is not in human nature. You cannot mean that, Luke?"

" Such was the verdict, sir."

" Oh, monstrous!—most monstrous! But I say it shall not be! No! If my blood should flow like water in stopping such a deed, it shall not be. Horror!—horror! Oh, Luke! did not your blood freeze within you at the thought?"

" I felt hot and cold, sir, by turns."

" Yes, of course you did. Why, they must be fiends and devils in human shape, to think of such a thing. No, Luke, it must not be. Oh, Adele, Adele! My poor Adele!"

Duval threw himself upon the ground in an agony of remorse, and it was with great difficulty that Luke could persuade him to rise again. Such a paroxysm of passion, though, could not last very long, and after about ten minutes he was much more calm. Clutching Luke by the arm, he said :—

" Luke, by all your hopes here or hereafter, sware to assist me in preventing this most vile and abominable desecration of the dead!"

" I will assist you, sir."

" To the death you will do it ?"

" I will."

" You will spare no pains—you will shrink from no danger—you will risk all to aid me in this great act ?"

" Before God, sir, I will."

" Why, then, 'tis done, and before to-morrow dawns, poor Adele shall sleep by the side of many not half so kind and good as she was before madness turned aside her better nature, in consecrated ground. She shall be buried in the old church-yard, Luke, here at Hornsey. Will that do?"

" Truly, sir, and it shall be done, too. But you and I will not be enough to do that. We shall want help."

" We shall, we shall. Let me think. Oh, let me think who will help me in this emergency. I have it. Saddle both the horses, Luke; we must go to town. What is the time, now?"

" Only eight, sir."

"Four hours. That will do. Only four hours; but yet, time enough for all that. The horses!—quick, Luke. We must now be off to London."

Luke did not wait to be bidden again, but hastily proceeding to the stable, he prepared both the horses for the road, and brought them out to the door. May heard the sound of their feet, and came out hastily to know what was going on.

"Oh, Claude," she said, "I thought you were going to remain at home for this one night at the least."

"And so I was," he replied; "but you must forgive me for breaking my promise for this once. Luke has brought me news that enforces my presence in London. I will return by daybreak, or, perhaps, much earlier still. Be content, for in good truth I must go."

May was rather alarmed at the violence of his manner, in which there was a sort of wild vehemence that she had never witnessed before, and she shrank back in dismay. In another moment he had mounted.

"Farewell!" he cried.

'Oh, no—no—do not say farewell! It seems as though there was a doubt if we should meet again."

Duval was off. He had tried to say something; but what it was he knew not and, in the then excited state of his feelings, he could not pause. It was only the galloping pace at which he went to London, that gave him anything like ease of mind.

Luke kept close to him.

At the pace they went, the green fields of Islington were soon left behind them, and before nine o'clock they found themselves in Holborn. The great agony of Duval was that the body might be possibly removed from the public-house without his knowledge, and that there would be a difficulty in finding where it was conveyed to.

"Luke," he said, "we will ride to Westminster at once, and you can go to the public-house and glean what intelligence you can concerning the desecration of the dead. If the body be still there, perhaps the people may know exactly of where it is proposed to take it."

"Very good, sir," said Luke. "You come very slowly after me, and wait at the corner of Parliament Street. I will bring you all the news that I can collect."

Luke rode on, Duval at a slower pace after him, till they got to Westminster, and then Duval paused, while Luke went on to the public-house. He was not gone long before he returned to bring important tidings.

"The body, sir," he said, "is to be taken right awaw to Camden Town, to be buried in some cross-roads there that you and I have often passed."

"And she, too! Poor Adele!"

"But it appears, sir, so the landlady tells me, that the surgeon who came and tried to restore her, has offered ten guineas for the body, and the police hearing of it; have taken possession of the house, for fear any attempt should be made to remove it. There are now half-a-dozen constables in the place waiting till the time shall come when the body can be taken to be buried, between the hours of twelve and one."

Duval shook his clenched fist in the air, as he said—

"Let them multiply the six by sixty, and then they should not do it."

"It will be desirable, sir," said Luke, "to keep a sharp watch upon the public-house, for they will start at the latest, I suppose, by eleven o'clock; and there's no knowing what whim of going earlier still, or perhaps to some other spot altogether to that mentioned, the officers may not take."

"True, Luke—true. You will go and keep watch while I—What o'clock is that?"

"It is the Horse-guards clock striking ten."

"Very well, Luke. There is yet time——"

Before Duval could say another word, a band of disorderly young men, with loud shouts, and yelling, and every description of indescribable noise that the human lungs could produce, rushed from George Street, and came over the road in the direction where Duval and Luke were.

"Who are these, sir?" said Luke. "Are they mad or drunk?"

"Perhaps a little of both," said Duval. "They are a set of riotous young bloods, who have of late infested the town, committing all sorts of outrages. They call themselves the 'Mohocks.'"

"Keep close, sir; they are upon us."

Before the words had well escaped the lips of Luke, he and Duval were surrounded by the mad roaring party, who, with shouts and yells, danced round them.

"Who wants a ride?" cried one. "We can borrow a horse here for an hour or two, and then turn him loose to find his way home."

"Did anybody ever see a man tossed in a blanket?" cried another, "because we can break into some house and get one, and toss these two fellows."

"Indeed, gentlemen!" said Duval; "so you are as blind as beetles, and as deaf as bats, are you? If I mistake not, I hear the voice of Lord Leighton among you. Hurrah for the Mohocks!"

The noise ceased in a moment, and a single voice cried out—

"Who the devil are you?"

"Guess again," said Duval.

A street lamp was hastily taken from its place, and held up to his face, and then one cried—

"Why, it's the count, to be sure: and we have all been wondering what has become of him for some months now."

"Yes, gentlemen," said Duval, "I am the count; but pressing personal business has taken me from London. What a pleasure it is to meet old companions on the first day of my return!"

"Hurrah!—hurrah! All's right. Come with us, count. We are going to upset the Strand to-night."

"My old and attached friends," said Duval, "will you, as you are gentlemen, and as what you do is for the pure love of fun and frolic, listen to me for a few moments before we go upon our errand of riot and racket? I have something to say to you all that concerns you all."

"Say on. What is it?—what is it?"

"I came here upon an errand of such a nature, that I know there is not one of you but will cry—'Bravo!' to it. I know you all will. You have good, kind, hearts, and above all, you shrink from any act which gentlemen might blush for."

They were all silent upon this, and stood waiting in mute wonder for what Duval was going to say next.

"There's a watchman listening!" cried one.

"Down with him," shouted all the others, and then with one shout like a parcel of fiends, they pounced upon the unfortunate watchman, and closing him up in his box, they threw it with a frightful crash upon its face, and there left it.

"Go on, count—go on."

"I will, my old and kind friends. You must know that a young girl, alas! she yet is in her teens—one of the sweetest, gentlest creatures that Heaven ever gave the breath of life to—graceful as a young fawn, and soft-spoken as an Eolian harp when only touched by a zephyr—her long glossy hair, and her sparkling eyes were—But I tire you all by this description. God help her, she is dead!"

"Dead!" cried everybody.

"Yes, you shall hear. Despair took possession of her young and tender heart. Poor thing, she thought that in all the world there was no one to love her, and last night she plunged into the river."

The Mohocks gathered closer round Duval.

"Yes," he added, "she plunged into the river, off Westminster Bridge, and was drowned."

"Poor thing—poor thing!"

"Alas! yes, I knew you would say poor thing; but only listen. To-day, some twelve greasy, mechanical, thick-headed lumps of stupidity—your chandlers and your bakers—fellows whose honour lies in keeping short weights, and drinking heavy wet—decided that the poor and sad remains of this young creature, be-cause she had, in a moment of frenzy, compassed her own death, should be as-signed to a grave in a cross-road, and—and——Oh, my friends, I cannot tell you!"

"Why, they would dash a stake through her!" cried one.

"Oh, God—God," said Duval, "they would! You are gentlemen—you have hearts and souls, and you have strength and daring to do deeds of violence for frolic's sake. Oh, aid me to do one in the sacred name of justice, and of kind-ness to the dead!"

A shrieking shout of approbation followed this appeal.

"Will you let them do it?" said Duval.

"We won't!" cried every voice. "We won't. Hurrah for the Mohocks! It shan't be done. Down with them! Whoop! Hilloa!"

Duval held up his hand.

"Gentlemen," he said, "let us be discreet in this affair. I am informed that it is intended to place the poor girl in a grave by some cross-roads close to Camden Town; shall we go there and wait for them?"

"We will—we will!"

"Yes!" cried one, "and if they say much about it, we will give them the stake, instead of the poor girl. Come on—come on. Hurrah for the bold Mohocks! Hurrah!"

"Luke," said Duval, in a whisper to him. "I will go with these gentlemen, you keep in sight of the public-house, and if you discover any change in the destina-tion of the corpse, spare neither whip nor spur to come to me and let me know; but if they start with it, and you see that it takes the direction to Camden Town, all will be well."

"I will be on the alert, sir,"

"Do so, Luke; and, oh, remember that this is a matter that lies very near to my heart, indeed."

Luke nodded, and rode off to the public-house, and then Duval, who had made such a favourable impression upon the Mohocks, walked his horse, while they surrounded him in a disorderly throng.

They numbered about twenty, and such was the terror with which they had inspired the watch, that it was very rare that they were at all interfered with, and for some years they kept London, after night-fall, in a state of alarm and terror.

The fact was, however, that they were principally young members of the nobility—officers of the guard, and idlers connected with the public offices, so that money flew about in abundance, and the impunity with which they carried on their games, might be said to be in a great degree purchased.

Duval, at the time he had occupied his splendid apartments in Spring Gardens, in that very home where he had first made the acquaintance of poor Adele, was well known, in his assumed character of a foreign count, to most of the dissolute young men upon the town. His bold daring character was just what they admired, and it was no wonder, therefore, that now they eagerly followed him upon the expedition he had planned for them.

CHAPTER CXII.

A NIGHT SCENE IN HORNSEY CHURCH-YARD.

HAVING thus enlisted the Mohocks in his enterprise, Duval did not feel the slightest doubt about being able to carry it out with perfect safety. His intention had been, after discovering exactly where the body of poor Adele was to be taken, to go to some of the kens of London, and there enlist a sufficient force of the "family," as the thieves were called, to enable him to accomplish his design.

We need hardly say that it was much more agreeable to Duval to have his present associates, than the rabble route he might have been compelled to avail himself of for want of better. As for the Mohocks, it was, of all others, the very adventure that they liked, for it was defying the authorities, and taking the part, as it were, of a girl—not that they were always, when they had wine enough, very particular in their conduct regarding the fair sex whom they might meet in the course of their parade through the streets of the metropolis. But they assumed a certain amount of chivalrous feeling towards the fair sex, whether they carried it out or not.

"Well, count," cried one, "where, in the name of all that is diabolical and wonderful, have you been all this time?"

"Out of England," said Duval.

"Out of England? Why, how did you live? You don't mean to say you have been existing upon frogs in France?"

"No, but a man must go now and then and look after his property, you know, or the day might come when he would lack the means of enjoying himself in London."

"By George, that's true," said one, who was just a little more drunk than the others, and, therefore, less scrupulous about what he said. "That is strictly true. But we have often raised the question among ourselves, count, of where the devil is your property, and what the deuce do you live on."

"Why the fact is," said Claude Duval, with a laugh, "I take solids and fluids, and perhaps rather a larger portion of the latter, at times, than I ought."

"Oh, but that ain't it at all."

"What is it, then?"

"Why, we are puzzled to know where the money comes from; that's the question, my dear count."

"Oh, I understand you now. I have a number of tolls in the country. You see, there are certain roads that belong to me up and down, and I make the folks who use them, pay handsomely for passing."

"That is in your own country, count, of course?"

"Oh, yes, in my own country, as you say, most truly and decidedly. Of that there can be no mistake."

"And a very comfortable way of making money too," said the drunken Mohock. "I should like to do it myself."

"You?" cried another. "Why, how, can you desire a better business than you have?"

"Business? I scorn the word."

"It is a business, though," said a third, in a low tone, "and a deuced good one, too, that with a little management with a pack of cards, brings in a couple of thousands a year, quite comfortably."

He who uttered these last words fully intended to utter them in so low a tone, that they should not be heard by the person to whom they applied, for he had no wish to make himself the champion of fair play at the card table; but, unfortunately, the words, "cards," and "two thousand a year," struck upon the ears of the gambler, and in a blustering tone, he cried—

"Did you speak to me, sir?"

"No, but he spoke of you," said another, "and that is much the same. The most prudent thing you can do, captain, is not to hear."

"Not hear, sir! I say I will hear, and chastise likewise. By the powers of all mischief, sir, I will cut off the man's ears, who insinuates aught against my honour."

"Gentlemen, gentlemen," said Duval, "let me beg of you to recollect that we have a project on hand, which ought not to be trifled with, or for a moment delayed or interfered with by private disputes. After we have done that which we have made up our minds to, regarding the young girl who is to be buried, it will be quite time enough to settle any little personal affairs. Let me beg of you for the present to let this altercation drop."

"I am willing," said he who had spoken of the other's luck at cards, "I am quite willing."

"But, zounds, sir," said the captain, "I am not, unless, indeed, you apologise. Then, indeed, it is quite a different affair, and, by my beard, I will look over it. Ah!"

"Apologise!" cried the other. "I apologise to a thing like you? The only apology I owe is to society for having the bad taste to associate with a swindler and a card shuffler, a man who picks up a living by the aid of loaded dice, and by nicking the edge of the ace of spades. Apologise, indeed! No, worthy captain, you must put up with what little affronts you get, and put them against other matters of a more satisfactory character, if you please."

That a speech of this kind could pass without a riot of some kind or another, was quite out of the question, and for the moment, despite all that Duval could say, poor Adele and all the wrongs that the authorities contemplated inflicting upon her poor remains, were forgotten in the present affair that had so unfortunately risen.

"A ring, a ring!" cried half-a-dozen voices. "Two to nothing on the captain! Bravo, my lord! Give it him! Give it him! Captain, have you made your will? A ring—a ring!"

These, and such-like expressions, were shouted by those who were quite delighted at the idea of a fight; and the captain, who was one of those bullies which London is at all times so full of, at once drew his sword, crying out as he did so—

"Even yet, if his lordship will admit that it was all a joke, I will forego my otherwise just resentment."

"No," said the young man who had spoken disparagingly of the captain's card morals. "I am sorry that I cannot say that. What I said I stick to. It is true that I did not intend the words to reach the captain's ears; but as they did reach them, it only convinces me that they are even larger than I thought them; so I am quite willing to take the consequences."

This sally produced a roar of laughter; and opposite a lamp in the street, the whole party stopped, and made a ring for the combatants. The young lord— for such he was—drew his sword and stood upon the defensive. He was a very slim, small young man, and looked anything but a match for his bulky antagonist, who was a well known skilful master of his weapon. The face of the captain was very pale, but whether that was with passion or the consequence of some lurking fear of the issue of the combat, it is hard to say, except upon the general principle, that a gambler is in general a coward at heart.

"Now, captain," said the young lord, "since we must have a tilt for this, pray come on, and don't let us waste time."

"Once for all: do you apologise, my lord?" said the captain. "I should be very sorry to deprive the peerage of such a promising subject as yourself. Do you apologise?"

"Certainly not, and I shall not be at all sorry to deprive the commons of such an unpromising subject, as you are captain; so come on, if you are not afraid."

"Afraid! Zounds, that word sticks in my throat! Boy, you have your own death to answer for. I call upon you all, gentlemen, to witness that this is a fair fight."

"Quite fair! Quite fair! At it, Mohocks! Whoop—at it! This is brave fun. Go it! Three to fifty on the captain, in spade guineas!"

LORD CLIFDEAN AND ADELE.

Enraged at the ridicule that was cast upon him, the captain made a furious attack upon the young nobleman, who contented himself with standing coolly and calmly upon the defensive; but he did not give his foe an inch of ground. That was a little fact that was by no means lost upon the observation of the Mohocks, and in the excitement with which the combat was regarded, a deathlike stillness prevailed for a few minutes, interrupted only by the sharp ringing of the swords, as the blades rapidly passed over each other.

A window was thrown open in the house close to which the fracas was going on, and a man appeared in his night-dress, and began crying—" Watch ! watch !" He was glad to disappear though, for some half-dozen of the Mohocks pelted him with stones so effectually, that they broke every pane of glass in the window, in the course of two or three seconds.

The combat still raged furiously.

From his higher situation on horseback, it was easier for Duval to see the combat than any one else, and after a few minutes, he decided in his own mind as to how it would terminate. The attack of the captain was one of those furious onslaughts that not unfrequently at once decide a conflict by the surprise into which they throw an adversary, but if unsuccessful, such a course was sure to be disastrous to him who should attempt it, as exhaustion must follow it in a very short time, and then the other party would have all the advantage.

The captain soon found out the state of affairs, and it was evident that both his strength and spirits were flagging fearfully. With a shout, the Mohocks gave way behind him, so as to allow him to retreat if he thought proper, and then the young nobleman, with the agility of an antelope, darted in upon him.

There was a loud shout from the Mohocks, and in another moment the captain was run through the body. The hilt of the sword of his adversary struck against his chest.

Duval felt sickened at the sight.

With a screech, for that is the only word that can adequately describe it, the captain held up his hands above his head, and then, as the sword was dragged from him, the blood spouted after it, and he fell upon his face.

" Twenty to nothing on the captain !" said a voice.

" Oh, gentlemen," said the young nobleman, " you all saw that this unfortunate affair was forced upon me."

" It was ! It was !"

" From my soul I do regret the necessity I was under of killing this man but after our swords had crossed, it was either my life or his, and I naturally hesitated to allow him to murder me. I could not help it—indeed, I could not."

" It's all right !" shouted half-a-dozen voices, and then Duval spoke in a serious tone, saying—

" I saw the whole of the affair, perhaps better than any of you, and I can say that it was a combat forced upon our young friend here by the captain, and which he could not avoid, and yet preserve his standing and character as a gentleman."

" I thank you count, for that testimony ; and yet I do regret the deed. Is—is he quite dead ?"

" Quite," said one. " Quite. His blustering is all over now. What is to be done with the body ?"

" Prop it up against a doorway. The police will find it," said another. " There you are, captain, and, after all, you have come to a more honourable end then ever I expected you would come to or perhaps than you expected yourself. I was going to propose shortly, that this man who is now no more be prevented from joining us in our frolics, and I know I should have had to fight him."

The dead body, all ghastly and bloody as it was, was dragged to a door-step, and there propped up in a corner, being partly wedged in behind a column that supported one side of a balcony. His hat and sword were laid upon his lap, and then the Mohocks turned carelessly from the spot.

" Old friends, you do not forget," said Duval, " the expedition we were upon? Let me beg that it may not be further interrupted. Remember, that the time is rapidly drawing near when she of whom I spoke to you will be in the hands of those who persecute beyond the grave."

" Forward !" shouted the Mohocks. " Whoop ! Forward. All is right. Come on. Hurrah ! hurrah !"

With wild and frantic shouts, quite forgetful, in the course of a few minutes, of the fearful tragedy to which they had been witnesses, they now darted forward, keeping good speed with Duval's horse, although he put it to a trot, and following him in a disorderly and madly riotous kind of procession towards the spot upon which he had been informed that poor Adele's remains would be taken to, to undergo the degrading ordeal that the obtuse barbarity of a now obsolete law suggested.

The amount of estimation in which the defunct captain had been held by the Mohocks was quite sufficiently testified by the ease with which he and his fate were alike forgotten. The only one of the lot upon whose face and conduct there was a kind of shadow, was the young nobleman who had been the unwilling means of ridding the world of a blackleg.

As Duval rode on, this young man placed his hand upon the mane of the horse, and kept equal pace with it.

"Ah," said Duval, "you feel the death of the captain more than there is really any occasion for you to do, I think."

"I am glad to hear you say that," replied the other, "for I do feel it. It is a selfish thought, but I wish if he were to fall, that it had been by some other hand than mine."

"The fight was as fair a one," said Duval, "as ever mortal man witnessed; except that he had all the advantages in strength and weight, and that you let him try his skill in a first assault, and, moreover, he forced the quarrel upon you; so, my friend, it strikes me that beyond the natural regret that a brave heart must feel upon such an occasion, you ought to be satisfied with yourself."

"I am pleased to hear you say so much, count, about it, and I daresay that a very short space of time will suffice to rid me of the feeling that I now have."

"Not a doubt of it; and the good work that you are about to help me to do to-night, will go far to chase it from your mind. Am I riding too fast for you?"

"Not at all. I suppose, count, you knew this young girl who has come by so melancholy an end?"

"I did."

"I guessed as much, and I give you my word for it, that she shall be placed in the grave without the frightful ceremony that those who probably are far less acceptable in the sight of Heaven than herself, poor thing, would fain, in the brutality of their imagination, carry out."

"A thousand thanks for that assurance," said Duval. "I own that I had set my life upon saving the body of the girl from such a sacrilege, and I would have died by her side, rather than it should have been accomplished, and they might have, if they had chosen, placed me in the same grave with her, poor young thing; but now I feel assured that we shall conquer those who will bring her body to the cross-roads, and that all will be well."

"It shall be well. Be quite easy upon that score, count."

Duval now felt a thorough assurance that all would be well as regarded the obsequies of poor Adele. He felt that the only atonement he could now make to her for the past, was to prevent her remains from being outraged; and in his inmost heart he blessed the chance that had brought him into communication with the Mohocks, who were sure to be ripe and ready for such an adventure as that which he had proposed to them.

"This is the spot," said Duval, as they reached the then dreary-looking suburb where the cross-roads intersected each other.

CHAPTER CXIII.

ADELE IS BURIED, AND A REAL PASTOR IS FOUND.

For half-an-hour the wind had been rising, and each moment increasing in gusty power. In the streets of London its effect had scarcely been visible; but now that Duval and his friends were in the more open country, it swept and careered past them with a vehemence that rendered it impossible they could disregard its presence.

Accompanying this wind, for it was a blustrous one from the south-west, there came, at times, a dashing splash of rain, as some cloud surcharged with moisture would be hurried over the night sky; and each moment the air got darker and darker, until, at last, the Mohocks could hardly see each other's faces.

"A blustering, riotous night, this, count," said one. "Is this the place that the performance was to take place at?"

"It is, I take it," said Duval. "Let us halt here. I shall have due notice when they are coming."

"Hilloa! there's a dash of rain. Who caught it?"

"I had some of it," said Duval; "but such weather is all in our favour."

"It is," said another, "only it would have been much more in our favour if any one had had the prudence to bring a bottle of something strong and good with him; for here we are in the outer regions of civilization, and with nothing in the world to drink but rain water. That, I guess, you may have, if you open your mouth, and place yourself against the wind."

"Never mind the drink just now," said the young man who had slain the captain. "We know where to go and get plenty of that when we have settled this affair we are upon; and, recollect, friends and comrades, that this is not a piece of mischief."

"Oh, don't tell us that," said one, "or we shall all be off at once."

"No, that I am quite sure you will not," added the young nobleman. "If we do make a little more noise than the fat citizens of London exactly like, I still think we may set up to be the reformers of the age. Don't we admonish the watch to leave well alone?—don't we point out to the authorities how very bad the lighting of London is, by showing them how easily the lamps may be put out from Temple Bar to Charing Cross?"

"Hurrah! so we do!"

"Don't we improve the public thoroughfares, by, at times, moving some stupid tradesman's unsightly sign, and placing it in some other position, where its truely ridiculous character is fully seen?"

"We do—we do!"

"And don't we give an elegant finish to the education of the citizens' daughters whenever we chance to catch any of them going home from the Ranelegh Gardens, or from somebody's dinner?"

"Whoop!—hurrah! We do!"

"Then, gentlemen, we are the reformers of the age; and well does it now become us to step between the corpse of a young girl, and those who would do more than death has done—those who would desecrate God's image, and in the sight of Heaven, commit a deed too revolting to think upon!"

A shout from every one of the Mohocks, proclaimed the success of the appeal to them from the young nobleman; and Duval felt that there would be no flinching from the act that would save him the grief of thinking that Adele, whom he had loved so well, had came to so dreadful an end.

It was just as the shout from the Mohocks was dying away on the night air, that a horseman rode rapidly up to the spot and drew rein close to the group of dark figures that stood on the cross-road.

"Luke? Luke? Is it Luke?" cried Duval.

"Yes, sir," said Luke. "They come."

There was a commotion among the Mohocks at this news, and even in the very faint light of the night sky, the flashing of their drawn swords was visible, as they prepared themselves for action. Duval had, however, arranged in his own mind what was the best mode of procedure, and he now spoke in a voice of entreaty—

"Gentlemen," he said, "it is not a fracas with a few constables that we want but it is to rescue the dead girl from them. I propose that we all retire to the shadow of this hedge here, close to Pancras Lane, and there wait until they have reached their destination and laid down the body. We can then pounce upon them."

"That's it, that's it," cried one. "They will take to their heels and run with it else, if they see us here in any force."

The advice of Duval was fully taken, and in the course of a few moments the whole of the Mohocks were stooping down under the hedge, so that their heads should not be seen against the night sky. Duval dismounted and gave his horse in the care of Luke, and alone he stood upon the spot of the cross-roads which was intended, but not destined, to be the grave of the poor, lost Adele.

The flicker of the torches now rapidly approaching the spot, soon announced that Luke's information was perfectly correct, and that no sort of alteration had taken place in their intention regarding the place in which the remains of the suicide were to be placed. Duval, too, could hear the grating sound of wheels, but there was no tread of a horse, and he concluded, which was right, that the body was being conveyed to its last resting-place in a truck drawn by hand.

Oh, how his heart and conscience smote him at that moment, as he remembered what that poor and delicate young creature had been once, and what she was now! He almost staggered as a gasping sob came from his lips; but feeling all the necessity for controlling such feelings, he quickly recovered, and stood to all appearance firm as a rock.

"They come," called out Luke, "sir, they come."

"Hush," said Duval, "oh, hush: I see them plainly."

Straggling on came the gloomy procession, with the lanterns that lighted it upon its way, nearer and nearer still to the spot at which those who brought the dead little thought to encounter any one who cared sufficiently about one who had been so unhappy as to seek the repose of death, would be there to say them nay.

The wind that still moaned and howled across the fields, dashed the lantern to and fro in the hands of the bearers of them, and Duval could hear the jest and the loud laugh of the men who came to play a part in a scene which one would hardly have supposed anything human could have been got to participate.

The party conveying the corpse consisted of some twelve or fourteen persons actually on duty upon the occasion; but there were about as many others mere stragglers, whom curiosity had attracted to accompany them.

In the course of a few minutes, one cried out in a loud voice—

"Come on you fellows, with the truck and the corpus; here we is. This here is the place; and when you get there, just begin on the grave no quicker than you can, do you hear!"

"Oh yes, sir. We will make quick work of it," replied a voice.

"Mind you do, for this is a deadly-lively sort of a night to be out in, and if I had not had the thought to bring with me a drop of something to keep the cold air off my stomach, there's no knowing what might have happened."

"Lord, sir! what could happen?"

"Could happen, you booby? I'm delicate."

"Perhaps you wouldn't mind, sir, just giving us a taste out of that bottle? We have had a long pull, sir, with the truck."

"Wretches! how dare you ask it? Ain't I a constable in my own right, and a free vintner of the City of London? You ain't delica e. Come on— come on. This is the place. Ha! ha! this is the place. Now, my good fellers, make short work of it."

In another moment the cavalcade had halted, and by the flaring light of the lantern, the constables saw Duval standing upon the very interesting spot of the cross-roads where they had intended to dig the grave, with his arms folded across his chest, and looking more like a statue than a living man.

"Hold!" said one of the men. "Here's somebody here."

As this man spoke, he held up his lantern, so that its light fell full upon Claude Duval.

"Somebody there?" said the constable who had the direction of the barbarous ceremony. "Who the deuce is it?"

" We don't know, sir."

" Hilloa !" cried the constable in his own right, walking close up to Duval, and taking a look at him. " Who are you, my friend ?"

" Not your friend, certainly," said Duval.

" Come—come, no insolence, or else I shall have to take you up. I'm a constable, sir, in my own right, and a free vintner of the City of London, sir, so mind I don't take you up."

" What for, sir ?"

" What fo ?   Did you ever, sir, hear of an authority like me saying what for he did anything, sir—eh, sir ?"

" No—nor knowing what for, neither."

" Then get out of the way and move on."

" Nay, this is a public highway, and I insist upon my right to remain here as long as I like. There is plenty of room for you to pass upon either side of me, if you please to do so. Go on, and do not trouble me with your nonsense."

" Nonsense ? Did you say my nonsense ?"

" I did."

" Oh, very good. Then, sir, do you see that staff—that constable's staff? It has a little gilt crown at the top of it, sir. What do you say to that ?"

" I do not see that it in any way concerns me ; but if you have any disposition to resort to violence, do you see that sword—that long sword ? It has a sharp point, Mr. Constable."

The constable in his own right, made a start back on to the toes of one of his party, for Duval drew his sword suddenly from its scabbard, and the bright steel flashed in the light of the lantern.

" Oh, Lord, sir !" said one of the men, " don't interfere with him. He's a gentleman you may depend, sir."

" A gentleman !" cried the constable, catching at the word with great satisfaction. " A gentleman? Then I am satisfied. When I meet a gentleman I am always satisfied, sir. I am your humble servant—I may say I am your very humble servant, indeed—a-hem ! The constable knows always what is due to a gentleman who won't get out of the way or move on."

" What brings you here ?" said Duval, giving his sword a slight sweep round him so as to keep them from thronging too close upon him. " Why is it that you are all here at such a time as this, and what is it that you came to do in such a spot ?"

" Allow me, sir, to explain," said the constable. " You see, sir—you will see it's all right when you hear the particulars—there's been a young gal, sir—she has been and drownded herself in the Thameses, sir, and a crowner's 'quest has brought it in self-murder. She hasn't got no friends, and nobody cares about her, so she is to be buried here in this cross-road with a stake through the body."

" What !" cried Duval, in a high voice, as he stepped up to the truck in which the body was, and placed his back close to it. " Are you men that you can find it in you hearts to do such wrong to the poor lifeless body of a young girl ? Have you human hearts in your bosoms ? Have any of you children ? How can you tell what amount of wrong or sadness unsettled the reason of the young creature whom you would pursue beyond death with your barbarous usuages ?"

" Oh, we haven't got nothing to do with that, sir—oh, dear, no ; and besides, we beg to assure you, sir, that she has no friends at all."

" Why, then, the more need that all of you should befriend her, and feel for her, poor thing."

An incredulous laugh came from the constables, and they looked at each other, as much as to say—" Well, that is a good joke."

" My dear, sir," said the chief constable, in a soothing tone to Duval, as he rubbed his staff up and down his nose. " My dear, sir, you really should consider ! Suicide you know—Oh dear ! *Felo-de-se*—Ah ! shocking !—You wouldn't, sir, all for to go for to have such a one placed in a respectable churchyard, by the side of some person of propriety ?"

"Why it was only last week," cried Duval, "that a countess swallowed poison. What cross-road was her ladyship buried in, and who drove the stake through her aristocratic clay ?"

"Oh, but a countess, my good sir,—a countess ! Now do consider. Oh, oh ! that is really too bad. A countess is quite another thing ; so if you will be so good, sir, as just to step aside, we will dig the grave and pop in the girl in a very short time. Now, my good fellows, set to work, will you. It's a coming on to rain, and I am quite sure this gentleman don't wish to be any hinderance to us in this little affair. Rather a rummy sort of night, sir, aint it ?"

The men made a movement towards the truck that contained the body, but Duval, as he laid his left hand upon it, and elevated his sword in his right, cried—

"Touch but a hair of her head ! lay but one sacrilegious finger upon her, and, by the God of Heaven, I will lay you dead at my feet ! What ho, Mohocks ! To the rescue ! Ho !"

With a wild shout that made the air ring again, the Mohocks dashed out from their place of concealment upon the bewildered constables, and began with the scabbards of their swords, and with various hedge stakes that they had got hold of during the time they had been hiding, to lay about them with such effect, that in the course of a few moments half-a-dozen of the escort of the body of poor Adele were prostrate on the ground. One of the constables made an attempt to draw the truck away ; but Duval, with one blow of his clenched fist, sent him sprawling into a ditch by the road-side, and in the course of three minutes the Mohocks were masters of the field—for those of the constables who were able to do so, ran off to town again as fast as they could, shouting, " Murder !" as they went.

"Hip ! hip ! hip ! hurrah !" shouted the Mohocks, and then with one wild ringing " Hilloa !" they proclaimed the victory. Duval spoke in a tone of excitement.

"Come on, my friends," he said. " I will draw this truck containing the remains of what was once so full of life and beauty. It is a duty that I owe to her memory. Come on. Let us be off and away before the constables can get any assistance."

Duval had not to draw the truck alone, for half-a-dozen of the Mohocks helped him with it, and so poor Adele was led to the grave.

CHAPTER CXIV.

THE ATTEMPT TO ARREST DUVAL.—ITS FAILURE.—THE FLIGHT.

YES, poor Adele had some honour done to her remains now that she was no more. Who would have thought that the bearers of her corpse to the grave would include several noblemen and some officers of the army, all of whom became afterwards distinguished men? There was one among the lot, too, who became a judge; but it would be hardly fair to name him in connection with so very riotous and illegal a transaction.

We will let his lordship have the advantage, if it be any, of the doubts as to his identity. In modern times, people would be sure to say it was Lord Brougham ; but as the song of Guy Faukes classically observes—

"He didn't live till arter that;"

so it could not possibly be him.

"Where are we to go, count ?" said one of those who were most forward in dragging away at the truck.

"I hardly know," said Claude. " I did think of the little grave-yard at

Hornsey ; but I am afraid you will think it too far off, so I will yield to any suggestion you like to make upon that subject. I feel myself already somewhat your debtor for the gallant manner in which you have aided me, that I do not like to dictate to you where you shall take the body."

" Oh, that's nothing. Hark, ye friends—the count feels very strongly upon this affair, and is very anxious that the poor girl should be buried in Hornsey churchyard. It can't be very far, so let us go there."

" Hurrah !—Yes—That will do."

" It's a good thing, too," said one, " to get to a distance ; for, you may depend upon it, those rascals that we have routed will not put up with the defeat quite so easily, and if we were to make a pause near at hand, they would be down upon us with all the rabble they could collect."

"It is more than probable," said Claude.

" But that would be good fun," said another.

" Nay," said Duval ; " let us bury the young girl first, and then, no one will be more ready than I to have a bout with the watch, and with all that they can possibly attempt to bring to their aid. Come on, my friends, and let us place the girl in her grave."

" Yes—yes," cried everybody. " That will do. The count is quite right. Business first, and fun afterwards."

Duval was well pleased that the affair, so far as regarded the taking Adele to the churchyard of Hornsey, was so satisfactorily settled. He thought that by proceeding rapidly that distance, the watch would be thrown off the scent completely for a time ; and he did hope to get Adele placed quietly in her grave before the authorities could interrupt the ceremony.

After that, as he truly said, Duval had no particular objection to a disturbance with the constabulary.

There was no doubt, too, that the Mohocks looked forward to another riot as part of the night's entertainment ; but they had been a little touched by what Duval had said of the young girl, and they were quite willing to carry out the enterprise they had so excellently begun, before thinking of anything else.

Duval abandoned his horse to the care of Luke, and he would not leave the truck in which were the remains of Adele. He considered it to be a duty that he owed to her to keep by it ; and, besides, his familiarity with the road enabled him to go by much nearer a route than probably the Mohocks would have taken.

Once only he went on in advance a little ; but it was only to open a gate by which means they could all cross a meadow that cut off a good quarter of a mile of the road, and he was back again in a few minutes.

The distance, what with talking and laughing—for, to tell the truth, the Mohocks did not proceed very reverently with their burthen—did not seem long ; but when Duval knew that they were close at hand, he stopped the cavalcade and spoke seriously.

" My dear friends," he said, "the great object will be not to let the authorities know at what part of the churchyard we place these poor remains of what was once so beautiful. If they know, they will, to-morrow, when we are none of us here to resist it, have them up again, and make a point of carrying out their barbarous idea, which we have to-night defeated. Therefore, I make it a particular request that what we now have to do, as five minutes' walking will take us to the churchyard, be done in solemn silence."

" Agreed—agreed."

" That will insure success." said Duval.

From that moment not a soul spoke except the very lowest possible whisper to his neighbour, and the cavalcade assumed, therefore, a much more strange appearance.

One or two persons whom they met, got as quickly as they could out of the way ; and as the rain, which was now falling fast, pattered upon the ground, it was the principal sound that was heard in the stillness of the country, into which they had now fairly got.

"You seem to be wonderfully well acquainted with the neighbourhood, count?" said one of the party.

"I am," replied Duval; "yonder is the old tower of the church, with its clustering ivy, and you may just see, in the dim night light, the tops of a few of the grave-stones."

LUKE ALARMS THE CRIER OF ADELE'S DEATH.

"I do."

In less time than the five minutes that Duval had mentioned, the party came down the little slope that lies to the south of the church-yard, and Duval, opening one of the gates of the region of departed humanity, admitted the truck. It was quite evident that the Mohocks had all the place to themselves, and a more favourable night than the one upon which the adventure was taking place could not have occurred, as it happened, for the soft, thick rain that was falling kept everybody within doors, and the little village of Hornsey was as quiet as some isolated region.

A feeling of awe crept over the hearts even of those riotous young men, the Mohocks, and they no longer needed the injunction to silence; for after they had entered the precincts of the church-yard, they were so far awed with veneration, that they felt something akin to a religious reverence of the spot in which they found themselves.

"Halt!" said Duval; and those who were dragging the truck, brought it to a stand-still upon a grassy slope of the church-yard. Duval, in a voice that showed he was making an effort to subdue some powerful emotions, spoke.

"It is not enough, my friends," he said, "that we place this poor dead girl in her grave, but we must adopt some means of preventing that grave from dese-cration after we have left it, and if no one of you has any plan for that purpose to propose, I think I know of one that will do."

"Name it," said the Mohocks.

"It is just this," said Duval. "Let us dig two graves. Into one of them we will place the corpse, and we will raise over that no mound of earth to mark the spot, but over the other we will raise a mound, and that shall be simply so that when they come to it, they will find nothing; and as for any regular search through the burial-ground for the body, that would not be permitted by those who have the remains of their friends and relatives here lying. Shall we adopt that plan?"

"Yes—yes."

"But," said Luke, suddenly, "it may be done easier than by digging a grave. We need to dig but one, and we can easily carry the displaced earth to some distance off, and make a mound with it as though there were a grave beneath, when there will in reality be none."

"Yes, that will do," said Duval. "I thank you, Luke."

"Let us set to work here," said one of the Mohocks, "for there is no turf to displace."

In the truck that carried the body were all the tools in the shape of spades and pickaxes that the men had brought with them to help to bury the body in the cross-roads, so that there was no lack of tools to set the work a-going.

None work so well or so quickly as those who work with a will, and it was truly astonishing in what an incredibly short space of time a grave was dug. Every spadeful of earth was carried about thirty yards' distance, and then patted into a mound exactly resembling the top of a grave. To be sure, they did not dig a very deep grave for poor Adele, but it was deep enough; and when they had got about five feet below the surface, they looked at Duval as well as they could, and one said—

"Will that do, count?"

"Yes—oh, yes," said Duval. "It will be upon the secrecy regarding the spot more than the depth, that the safety of the body will depend. Five feet is as good as fifteen feet for that matter. Have you enough earth to cover it in flat?"

"Just about."

"Then—then I will fetch the body from the truck."

"No, count," said one, "your feelings are too much interested in this affair. We will fetch the body. You loved the girl."

"I did," he said. "I did."

"Then you be quiet. We will fetch it out of the truck in a moment. You stay where you are."

"No—no," said Duval, "I feel that I ought. I shall not be many moments in doing this last mournful duty to one whom I did, as you say, love."

The truck was not far from where the grave had been dug, and Duval, sum-moning all his firmness to his aid, went towards it. The body lay in the truck, covered over only by a couple of old sacks; Duval very tenderly removed them.

He was very glad to find that poor Adele had been dressed again in the clothes that he had last seen her in, for he had rather dreaded that such was not the case.

It was the decent compassion of the females at the public-house by Westminster Bridge that had done that.

"Poor Adele!" sighed Duval, as he raised the body in his arms. "Poor—poor Adele!"

'Let me help you, sir," said Luke, close at hand.

"No, no! But where are the horses, Luke?"

"Just here, sir ; tied to the railings of a tomb."

"Get me my large riding cloak from the back of my saddle, Luke, if you please."

"Yes, sir, in a moment."

Luke guessed what the cloak was wanted for. He shook it open, and while Duval held up the body, Luke carefully wrapped the cloak round and round it.

"That will do," said Duval. "I thank you, Luke."

With the still form in his arms, then, Duval walked to the grave, and knelt by the side of it.

"She is here," he said.

There was a death-like stillness, and every eye was fixed upon the mysterious looking form in the cloak. Duval did not speak for some few moments ; but he laid the body very gently in the grave, and tucked in the cloak upon all sides of it. One of the Mohocks, with all the tenderness of some one providing for the repose of a much loved child, assisted him.

"I thank you," said Duval at last. "I thank you for that. Is there any one here, who—who would like to see her face, before the earth covers her, I hope for ever and ever?"

No one spoke.

"I think," added Duval, "that even I should like a last look at those features that I knew so well. Luke, are you here, Luke?"

"Yes, sir."

"Can you get a light that will live only for a moment or two? I think you usually have the means of doing so with you, Luke."

"I have now, sir," said Luke.

The Mohocks now gathered closely round the grave, while Duval knelt at the head of it. Luke took from his pocket some phosphorus matches, but the rain would soon have put them out. He, however, contrived to ignite one inside his hat, and then to light a wax taper, which he sheltered in a similar way. By holding his hat in a particular direction, he let the few flickering beams fall upon the head of the grave.

Duval then, with slow and trembling fingers, took off, from the face, the fold of the cloak that he had placed over it. The light fell upon the pale, worn features.

"Behold her," said Duval.

Not a word was spoke for the space of about a minute and a half, as the Mohocks gazed upon the face of the dead. Then one of them only, in a very low tone, said—

"Poor thing!"

Duval could not speak. He tried to say something, but he found that he could not, and he covered over the face of the corpse again with the piece of the cloak.

"Rest in peace!" said Luke.

"Amen," said some one of the Mohocks ; and then, as if they had all been relieved from some spell that had fallen upon their faculties, they drew long breaths, and one said—

"Shall we fill in the grave?"

Before Duval, to whom this question was addressed, could reply to it, there glided from behind a tomb-stone, to his side, a figure, and a mild voice said—

" What is the meaning of all this ? Is your errand impious or gentle in the home of the dead at such an hour ?"

Duval sprang to his feet, and grasped the intruder by the arm.

" Who are you?" he cried. "Speak ! On your life, tell me who you are, and what is your business here ?"

" Young man," said the stranger, "there is no occasion for any violence to induce me to tell you who I am. I only beg that you will be equally candid and explicit with me. I am the clergyman of this parish, and there stands the church that I preach in. From my window I saw a crowd of dark figures in this place, and it was my duty to come among you, to know what you were about."

" The parson !' cried one of the Mohocks. "Then she is lost."

" Who is lost ?" said the clergyman, mildly.

" Away with him !" cried another.

" Hold," said Duval. "In, perhaps, a kindly spirit, this reverend man has come among us. Who shall say that when he hears what brought us here, even he will condemn us ?"

" I condemn none," said the clergyman. "Thank God, I condemn none. Tell me the reason of this assemblage, and why at such an hour you open a grave in this sacred place ?"

" Do not mistake," said Duval ; " we came to place the poor remains of one who has gone from the world in this spot, not to desecrate what ha already been placed here."

" That is well," said the clergyman. "But where there is secrecy there is ofttimes guilt. Will you tell me all ?"

CHAPTER CXV.

DUVAL GOES THROUGH ONE OF HIS GREATEST DANGERS.

THE manner of the clergyman was so mild, and yet, at the same time, so dignified (a very rare thing among clergymen), that the Mohocks regarded him with an involuntary respect, that they would have withheld from one of his cloth who had not been what he was, a real, kind-hearted, generous christian divine. There was a pause of silence when he asked if they would tell him all. That pause was broken by Duval, who said—

" Yes, I will, sir, tell you all, and I bespeak your pity, for one who was, after all, more sinned against than sinning. You see before you in this shallow grave, the body of a young girl—she was very beautiful, and very innocent, sir ; but she fell a victim to the flatteries of one who thought he loved her. It is needless to say by what designs and violations her heart was broken ; but, at length, her reason yielded, and with an impulse clearly and purely maniacal, she plunged into the Thames, and in death sought that peace she could not know in life. She was very young and very fair."

" Go on," said the clergyman.

" I will—I will. A coroner's inquisition was held upon her remains. The verdict was one of self-murder ; and in accordance with a barbarous custom—or a barbarous law, I know not which—she was to be interred where four roads met, and a stake—Oh, God !—it is too horrible—You know, sir, what I mean. We rescued her, and brought her here to place her in peace in this consecrated spot, and to commend her to that Almighty being who sees all hearts, and who in her's may find more to pity than in those of her judges. Poor—poor Adele !"

The clergyman placed his hand upon Duval's shoulder.

" And all this is true ?" he said.

Duval stooped and again uncovered the face of the corpse. At that moment, the little wax taper that Luke had had alight, went out, but the clergyman had just caught a glimpse of the cold, pale face of the dead. His voice faltered as he spoke.

" Young man," he said, " you have judged this young girl not as those who are perhaps, much older than yourself have judged her. You have resisted the authorities, and I dare say committed an assault in so doing. You have trespassed upon the ground where you certainly had no right, and all I can say is, that—that you are quite right, and from the bottom of my heart, I commend you all for what you have done!"

" You do?" cried Duval.

" You do?" shouted the Mohocks.

The clergyman held up his hand.

" Silence!" he said. " Silence! Remember where you are, and in what presence," he pointed to the copose—" I repeat, that to my thinking, and as I will answer for it before heaven, you have done a meritorious thing—a noble thing; and I will repeat, if you please, over this poor corpse, the service of the dead."

Duval could not speak, but he seized the hand of the clergyman in both of his own, and shook it heartily, There was more in that mute action than in all the words he could have uttered.

The Mohocks stood around the grave, and in a moment every head was uncovered. The clergyman, too, took off his hat, and Duval held it for him. The rain came slowly down, and upon the grave-stones it pattered with a melancholy monotonous sound; beyond that, all was so still that those who in the silence and darkness of the night surrounded that grave, might have been a band of spectres instead of living, breathing men, who passed the greater part of their lives in riot and debauchery.

In a low, rich voice, the clergyman began the service for the dead, Oh! what a soothing balm it was to the heart of Duval, to hear those words,—" Forasmuch as it hath pleased Almighty God to take unto himself our dearly beloved sister, Adele." They appeared to take away, at once and for ever, much of the agony that had clung to him since her death; and he shed tears in silence as the service continued.

It was Luke who, at the appropriate words, cast a handful of earth upon the body, and then in a few moments more the service was over, and poor, lost Adele had, after all, a decent and a holy burial.

The service was over—the clergyman had repeated every word of it from memory. He was too well versed in the services of the church of which he was a member to need a book, which always mars the effect of the simplest and most eloquent prayer in the whole church service in our estimation.

" Now," he said, " I have done my duty by this poor soul who has gone from us, but who is not lost. Oh! believe me all of you, it is not what poor, erring, weak human nature does or what it does not do that will be judged in heaven, but it is the heart that will be looked at and judged of, not the actions; and I say to you all, that verily there are many who are condemned of men that will not be condemned of God, and, perchance, this erring sister of ours will be one of that great number."

" Oh, how can I thank you?" said Duval.

" Hush! not a word in that strain; I have but done my simple duty. How could I have entered again that building devoted to the worship of heaven, if I had shrunk from doing what I have done, feeling it to be right?"

" Shall we fill in the grave?" said one of the Mohocks.

" Yes," said the clergyman, " I will stay to see all finished."

" We have a dread," said Duval, " that those of whom we took the corpse will come in the light of day and drag it from its grave again to perform the unholy and frightful rite that we prevented."

" Not while I live," said the clergyman, " shall they touch a hair of her head. They shall not remove from this ground one stray weed that grows upon its surface. Banish your fears—it shall not be."

" We proposed levelling this spot," said Duval, " and some distance off we made a mound, so that the enemies of the dead might be deceived, and not know where to search."

The clergyman was thoughtful for a moment, and then he said,—

"I am old, it is true, and cannot night and day be here. There is no knowing what the bad passions of some men may induce them to do. Superstition and brutality are sad prompters, and it will be as well to carry out your plan. Raise the mound where you intended, and leave this spot unmarked by any sign that she whom you have done this much for to-night sleeps beneath it; and yet I cannot think but that some signal judgment of heaven would alight upon any one who would dare to lay a sacrilegious hand upon her whom we have committed to the earth in the name of God."

Duval had great faith in the protection that the clergyman would extend to the remains of Adele; but he was yet well-pleased that the little artifice by which the constables would be put upon a false scent was not decidedly objected to by him. It was to be supposed that if it were to be discovered that they had deposited the body in Hornsey churchyard, and it was wanted to be exhumed again, that the first person applied to would be the clergyman of the parish, so that there was great safety so far; but still, the secrecy concerning the spot at which the interment had taken place was a great point.

In the course of ten minutes more the grave of Adele was filled up, and patted down so flat with the shovels, that it was impossible for any one to say that the spot had been recently disturbed; and the loose earth that had been carried away, was made into so shapely a grave-mound, that it would, by any one not actually knowing what it was, be taken for one.

"It is finished," said Duval.

"And let us hope happily so," said the clergyman. "Now, I beg of you all to retire quietly from this place. Take with you every vestige of what has been doing here, and rest in peace that the good work you set about is perfectly accomplished."

"We will!" said the Mohocks. "We will!"

"Hush! hush! Not a word more."

"Farewell!" said Duval to the old clergyman, as he took him by the hand again; "farewell! I shall never forget this night, nor you. It is you, and such as you, that make me religious. I shall think more sincerely upon subjects that I have much slighted, after this night, than I ever thought of them before."

"Now see," said the clergyman, "how I am repaid already. A good work is never without good friends, and you may always know a good work by its friends too; and if the result of this affair has been to awaken one human soul to the sublimity of religion, it is a glorious and much to be praised consummation."

"I say," whispered one of the Mohocks to another, "it is all very well to bury the girl decently, but I shan't stay if we are to be favoured with a sermon."

"Nor I!"

"Let's move on, then. We must get the count away, too, for he is so pleased with what the parson has done in the way of reading the service for the dead over the girl, that, out of complaisance, he will stay all night."

"Not a doubt of it. You call him."

"Count!" cried the Mohock. "Are you thinking of moving off, now?"

"I am," said Duval.

"Is that your title, or only your name, young man?" said the clergyman to Duval.

"They will tell you it is my title," answered Duval uneasily, for he did not feel as if he could tell a direct untruth to that old man, after what had occurred in the churchyard.

"Then I hope that was has passed to-night will really have its effect upon you, and that you will carry with you serious resolves to do all the good you can in your station."

"I will."

"I much suspect that you are yourself the hero of the story you told of the young girl who now sleeps in peace?'

"I am so, sir," said Duval frankly; "but I truly repent for the past; and the events of the night are some evidence of the sincerity of that repentance."

"A fault truly repented of, is half extenuated," said the clergyman. "Good-night. If you should at any time wish to see me, you will find no difficulty in so doing, for I shall live and die in this neighbourhood, to which now I am greatly attached."

"Good-night!" said Duval. "I will pay you a visit, sir, and that, perhaps, at an earlier period than you imagine, for, to tell the truth, I shall be glad to converse with you."

"The count is turning spooney," said one of the Mohocks.

"He is, decidedly," said another.

"We must get him away, then, at once. Count, all your friends are ready, and think of going."

"I come—I come," said Duval. "Luke, where are you?"

"Here, sir," said Luke, "I am here, if you please. The cattle are all right. I have them both in hand."

"Hilloa! who are you?" said a voice. It was one of the party of Mohocks who spoke.

"What is that?" said Duval, who was ever upon the alert, on account of the ticklish tenure upon which he held his liberty.

Before any of the Mohocks could reply to him, a man made a dash towards him, and laid hold of his collar, saying as he did so, in a loud voice—

"Claude Duval, you are my prisoner!"

"Claude Duval!" cried the clergyman, in amazement at finding who it was that he had been conversing with. "Claude Duval the highwayman?'

"Yes," said Claude, "but nobody's prisoner yet."

"Yes," said the man who held him, "you are mine. Your tricks are over, now, Claude Duval."

"Certainly not. That's one of them."

As he spoke, Claude seized the man with a gripe of iron, and closing with him, he gave him such a fall that he lay upon the ground as motionless as though he had come down from the clouds, and every bone in his body was broken by the concussion with which he had met the earth.

"Fire upon him!" cried a voice.

"Yes, kill him!" cried another.

Duval stooped, and a couple of pistols went bang! bang! as rapidly after one another as you might repeat those two words. The bullets flew a couple of feet over Duval's head.

The flash of the pistols, however, had had one effect, and that was to show Duval exactly where Luke was with the horses, and he at once made a dash over the tomb-stones in the direction of them, for were he once mounted, his chances of escape would be greatly increased.

The Mohocks had been so astonished at the whole affair, that they had not known what to do; but now they recovered, and one called out, in a sharp, clear voice—

"This won't do. Mohocks, to the rescue!"

"Hurrah!" cried the others, and a rush was made at a small party of officers that were in the churchyard, that at once carried them off their feet. They were seized, and in a moment canted over the railing of the graveyard into the meadow beyond, and one of them falling when he got there, rolled with a loud splash into the New River, that was close at hand.

"Luke! Luke!" cried Duval. "The horses!"

"Here!" said Luke, in a clear voice; and at the moment he ignited one of the phosphorus matches that he had.

The match was as instantly extinguished by the wind and the rain as it was lit, but still it had had the effect of again guiding Duval to the exact spot where Luke was, and in another instant he had his hand on the neck of his horse.

"All's right, Luke!" he said. "Mount, and be off!"

"With you, sir, I will."

"I mean it.'

Duval was in the saddle in a moment, and then, in a loud voice, he cried,—

"Mohocks, good night, and good luck to you all. May you never know what it is to have an unhappy half hour. I owe you more than I can express for your kind aid to-night. So, once more, good-by."

"Stop—stop!" cried several.

"Are you, really——" said one.

"Claude Duval!" shouted Claude; "quite at your service, gentlemen. The highwayman, who never deserted or deceived a friend, or flinched from an enemy. Off and away, Luke! Good-night."

CHAPTER CXVI.

DUVAL DETERMINES UPON A HASTY REMOVAL.

THERE are some birds, who, when they find themselves in any danger, fly in any direction but that which leads to their own nest; and upon the present occasion, Claude Duval imitated those sagacious feathered beings, for he took a route, then, directly opposite to the one that would have led him to his own house and garden at Hornsey.

Luke followed him closely.

Never, positively, had Duval felt so fully alive to the fact that he was in a very critical situation as upon that occasion. He knew perfectly well that if he were taken then there were no extenuating circumstances that could save him, and that all the sins that could by any possibility be laid to his charge, would be raked up for the purpose of destroying him, if possible. The very fact that ought to have said something for him, namely, that he had succeeded in acting in opposition to a cruel and barbarous law, he felt conscious would tell against him in the greatest degree.

Alas! if Claude Duval once got into the hands of the authorities now, the Mohocks, although they might, in truth, have all the will to do so, would have little power to aid him.

The many hair-breadth escapes that Duval had had, and the many dashing exploits he had been the hero of, had had the effect of incensing the authorities against him to a most serious degree, and, with a kind of *esprit de corps*, that surely might have been better directed, the constabularly of London felt that to catch Duval would be one of the greatest and most gratifying exploits they could possibly perform.

They had sworn to see him hung, but then, as the cookery-book very sagely remarks, "First catch your hare!" and, although Duval was in danger, he was not yet caught, and if caught, the hanging was not a sequel to the adventure that any one could calculate upon to a certainty.

He fled like the wind.

It was a happy thing, and Luke felt in the fullest degree that it was so, that Duval had quite completed the burial of poor Adele before the officers pounced upon him. Had that affair not been quite complete, the odds were that he would have been taken in consequence of clinging to the spot upon which he had determined to carry out the sad ceremony of the burial of the dead; but all that was done, and in a much more wonderfully satisfactory manner than even he had dared to hope he should accomplish the purpose, and the poor lost one was consigned to the grave.

It was the feeling that all that was done, and done so well, too, that gave Duval coolness and courage now for anything that might happen, and render him equal, or more than equal, to any emergency.

The idea that the officers would pursue him, was, of course, uppermost in Duval's mind, and a very natural idea it was, for he could not consider it to be

CLAUDE IN HIS ILLNESS ATTENDED BY MAY.

very probable that they would make an attack upon him without having the means of carrying it out.

In this, however, a little time served to show—as it shows all the world in many things—that Claude Duval was rather mistaken, for after a hard gallop of a couple of miles through the green lanes at the back of Highgate, our hero began to feel convinced that only one horse's footsteps echoed behind him, and that that sound proceeded from the hoofs of the gallant steed that carried Luke.

" Hilloa, Luke," cried Duval, reducing the speed of his horse, and then turning to face Luke.

"I am here, sir," said Luke.

" All's right?"

" Yes, sir, all is right, I think you may fairly enough say now, if you like, sir. They would need to be well mounted and bold riders that would follow us."

" And bold fighters likewise, Luke."

" They would, sir."

" Listen—can you hear anything on the road?"

Luke dismounted while Duval held the bridle of his horse, and bending low down to the earth, he listened intently for a few minutes, and then he said—

" The road is clear, sir."

" Then we are fairly off."

" We are. It strikes me, do you know, sir, that if the officers had any horses at all at hand, that they had completely knocked them up in getting to Hornsey, and that they had no legs with which to begin a chase of us."

" Like enough, Luke, like enough. But how could it happen that they came upon us at all?"

" Upon that point," said Luke, " I cannot hazard a conjecture, unless it happened that some one of those who were put to flight when you and the Mohocks got possession of the corpse, happened to know you, and went at once to town and gave the information that you were somewhere about here."

" I do not, myself," said Duval " see any other probable mode of accounting for the sudden character of the attack. But it is over now ; and one thing is a pleasant thought to me."

" I know what that is, sir."

" Yes, Luke, you can guess it. You know that the burial of poor Adele, in a consecrated spot, and there being read over her sad remains the service for the dead, has been balm to my very soul. And now, Adele, farewell ! I will not think with so much of sorrow upon your fate as I did, for I have done what I can ; and, after all, this is not so delightful a world that you, or any one else, need care much about quitting it."

" Talking of quitting," said Luke, " I think that, after what has happened, our house—if I may make so bold as to call it such—at Hornsey, will be rather too hot to hold us."

" No doubt of that."

" You will really move, then, sir?"

" I really will ; and I can very well understand that that is a determination that gives you considerable satisfaction, Luke."

" In good truth it does. sir ; and no man will turn his back upon a garden with more satisfaction than I shall upon that, which I have certainly taken some pains to cultivate."

" Your wish will soon be gratified, Luke. But where are we now? I don't this lane."

" I do, well. It is no thoroughfare."

" No thoroughfare, Luke ? then it certainly is not the place for us. Let us get out of it as quickly as we can."

" Nay, sir, if you go on you will come to a gate that can easily be opened, and that leads through a couple of meadows to East Finchley, and when once there, I think you know the road, sir, and the neighbourhood, quite as well as I do."

" I think I do," said Duval. " Come on."

A canter of about three minutes led them to the end of the lane, where, as Luke had said, there was a gate, the white rails of which they could only just very dimly see. Luke dismounted to open it, as he was very well acquainted with it ; and as he swung it wide, he said, in a low voice—

" There's a board up, warning off all trespassers, under all the pains and penalties of the law; but I don't think it very likely that we shall be troubled by any one, sir."

"Nor I, either, Luke. They will find us rather a trouble, I think, if they interfere with us."

Both Duval and Luke were soon in the first of the two meadows; and Luke being mounted again, they reached the second field without the shadow of an interruption; but just as they got half way across it, they heard a voice say—

"Hilloa! who's that riding across the meadow? This is no thoroughfare: Who's that, I say?"

"What! don't you know?" cried Duval in a bantering tone.

"Hush!" whispered Luke, " it's the parson that owns these fields, and one half of the neighbourhood. I know his voice."

"The deuce it is!"

"Yes. He is coming this way. What on earth can keep him out of his bed at this time of night I can't think; but speak low, sir, till we get into the road, and then, I think, we can bid him good-night pretty quickly."

Claude Duval had rather a deeply-rooted antipathy to parsons in general. Perhaps we ought to call it a strong prejudice, for such to some degree it was, and always is to have an antipathy to any particular class of men who cannot all be bad and selfish. Recent events, however, had gone far to remove such a feeling from the mind of Duval; and the kind and truly Christian-like manner in which the clergyman at Hornsey had behaved, had had the effect of modifying the feelings of our friend towards the Church.

"I am disposed to be civil to him if I can," said Duval to Luke, in the same kind of tone in which Luke had spoken, "and I only hope he will allow me to be so.'"

"Come—come," cried the parson, as he reached where Duval was gently walking his horse now. "I must know who and what you are, before I let you go any further across this meadow."

"Are you mad," said Duval, "that you talk of stopping a couple of well-mounted men?"

"No, I am not at all mad, but if I raise my voice, I rather think I can bring plenty of help about me; so now, who are you?"

"Mr. Smith."

"Oh, and who are you?"

"Mr. Jones," said Luke.

"Indeed, Messrs. Smith and Jones, I shall take the liberty, then, of having you apprehended. Hilloa! hilloa! help here! Thieves! thieves!"

"Stop, Mr. Ginfall," said Luke, who knew the parson both by name and sight very well. "Stop, sir. We are doing no harm to you, and none to your meadow at this season of the year. We wish you good night, and don't wish to have anything further to say to you.'

"Oh, don't you?"

"Certainly not, sir."

"Indeed! How came you to know my name, fellow? But that don't much matter. I'll have you both apprehended, and I shall be able to see to the exact hour, for there is light enough for me to see my watch, and it is now a quarter to three precisely."

"Is that a good watch?" said Duval.

"A better than you will ever handle," replied the parson.

"Don't say that," cried Duval, whose patience had been upon the wane for the last five minutes. Turning then suddenly, he caught the parson by the collar, and with one lucky, or with perhaps, we ought to say, unlucky catch at the watch, he got it out of his hands in a moment, and placed it in his own pocket.

"I will keep it for your sake," said Duval. "Come on, Luke.'

"Murder—murder!" shouted the parson. "Bring the blunderbuss! Peter! Murder! Help! Two highwaymen!"

"Confound him!" said Luke, "he will raise the village upon us. Make speed, sir. This way. The fence is so low that you may jump it easily. This way—this way, sir; all's right."

Duval dashed on after Luke, and the little fence that was by the side of the meadow offered no obstruction to their progress, for the horses' just saw it and were over it in a moment, without minding it as a jump, or considering it as one.

"Over," said Duval. "Now, shall we show the parson a light pair of heels, Luke, or shall we play with him a little?"

"Oh, let us be off at once," said Luke.

"Very well—as you please. Here goes, then. Good-by, Mr. What's-your-name, and if it had not happened that I feel a little tender towards parsons just now, I rather think I should have felt it incumbent upon me to let you know that I am not to be roughly spoken to with impunity."

"Oh, come on, sir," said Luke.

"Why, Luke, what on earth are you afraid of? The parson is very quiet now, and has even given up the hue and cry after us, that he seemed so delighted to set going a little while ago. Surely we may take things easy."

"I don't know, sir. I would rather he had gone on with the hue and cry. This silence is suspicious."

"Is it?"

"I feel assured, sir, that it is."

"Well, Luke, I do not feel at all prepared to say that you are wrong in such a matter. It may, as you say, be suspicious, so we will go on, and I think this turning to the right——"

"Oh, no—no!"

"Why not? It leads towards Highgate, I think."

"Yes; but you have to go right past the parson's house, and he has had time to get in doors by now, and to take measures against us. Let us go to the left, I beg of you, sir. It won't matter much, you know."

"Upon my word, Luke, I am surprised at you. What on earth is the matter with you to-night, or rather this morning?"

"I hardly know; but I feel nervous."

"About passing the parson's house? Now, take my word for it, Luke—whenever you feel nervous about anything, face it at once, and you will soon get rid of this feeling. If you avoid all the nervous feelings that come across you, you will run the risk, at last, of being frightened at mere shadows of the imagination; and not knowing whether there was real danger or not, you will always fancy that you have escaped something, when, in reality, there was nothing to escape; so, come on at once, and when you have passed the parson's house you will laugh at this little presentiment. Come on."

"I hope you are right, sir; but whether or no, I will follow you, let it lead me to where it will."

Duval dashed forward, and Luke came after him about half-a-dozen paces only. As it turned out though, that was rather an important difference.

The moment Claude Duval got opposite to the parson's house, a voice cried out—

"That's the man! Fire!"

A tremendous report immediately took place, and Duval reeled upon his saddle, as he called out—

"Luke, I'm hit!"

"Oh, no—no!"

"Yes, I—I—home, home!—The horse!—Oh, I die!"

Duval fell from the horse to the ground. Poor Luke was for a moment bewildered; and then, acting upon the last commands of his master, he seized the horse by the bridle, and went off at a fearful pace.

CHAPTER CXVII.

DUVAL FINDS THAT LUKE WAS RIGHT IN HIS FOREBODINGS.

DUVAL'S usual good fortune had forsaken him. He lay upon the ground quite dead to all the events of this world, although the vital principle had far from fled. Insensibility had supervened, though, and to all appearances the career of that daring spirit was over.

That Luke believed he was no more may be taken to be an ascertained fact, for if he had not fully thought so, he would have remained where he was, and clung to him at any risk; but seeing, or believing that he saw, Claude Duval was no more, he felt that his duty was to obey his last orders, and proceed home to break the sad news to his mistress.

We will leave Luke to take this course, while we remain by Claude himself to see what becomes of him.

When he fell, the persons who had fired upon him were for a few moments too much terrified at their own success to be able to come forward and take all the advantage of it that they might.

The tremendous report of the blunderbuss had astonished them quite as much as it had Duval and Luke; but when they saw, which they could only just do, that one of the two had fallen, and that the other had ridden off from the spot with the horses, they gathered courage.

"Lights, lights!—this way!" cried the parson; "this way, my men. We have done for one of the fellows."

Perhaps, for a parson, it was rather an extreme measure to order a blunderbuss, loaded with heaven only knows what, to be fired at Duval or at any one; but we must take human nature as we find it, and we decline to make fancy parsons to please the prejudices of any class of people.

In the course of a few minutes more there was a rather dense crowd of some dozen or so people around Duval, and as they all believed he was dead, there was that strange feeling of awe over the assemblage which usually attacks all persons when in the presence of such a spectacle.

The dominant feeling was one of pity for the young and handsome form that lay there so still.

"He might have been taken up," said a man, who had come out of a house at some little distance off. "Surely there was no occasion to take his life?—who did the brutal deed?"

"Come, come, sir," said the parson, "mind what you are saying."

"I always do mind what I am saying," replied the man; "but I am not going to shrink from saying what I think for fear of you, you may depend."

"Silence, sir; I know you quite well. Your name is Smith."

"Very good; it is Smith—but I presume that my name being Smith does not incapacitate me from having an opinion about a murder, sir?"

"A murder"

"Yes, I repeat it—this is a murder, and whoever did it will be answerable for it to the law."

"Oh, dear," cried a voice, "I had the blunderbuss, and master told me to fire it, and I did, and down went the man off his horse; that was all I had to do with it, sir.'

"And quite enough, too."

"Hark you, Mr. Smith," said the parson, in a voice of suppressed rage. "I know you well, sir. You are a very troublesome man in this parish. You are continually babbling about the churchwardens' accounts, and it was you, sir, who prevented them from having their nice little annual dinner, sir. You never come to the church, sir. because you pretend it is more pleasant to pray at home; and you don't pay me my Easter Offerings, sir; but I can tell you that some of these days we will get a law passed to fine and imprison people who don't go to church."

"That I should not be at all surprised at," said Mr. Smith. "There have been such laws, and there will be again in England such laws; but for all that, I say this is a murder."

Before the wretched parson could make any reply to this reiterated charge, the sound of rapidly approaching horses' feet upon the road came upon the ears of every one present.

One of the parson's servants called out in a voice of alarm,—

"We shall be killed! It's the other man coming back again with his friends! We shall all be killed!"

At this intimation, although it only arose from the fears of him who uttered it, it was quite ridiculous to see with what wonderful alacrity every one drew away from the dead body, as they supposed it to be. The parson and his servants tumbled over each other in their anxiety to get into their house; and in the course of half a minute, the only person who remained by Claude, was Mr. Smith, the troublesome parishioner.

"Poor fellow," he said, as he glanced at Claude Duval; "his race is run, let him be whom he may."

The horsemen rapidly approached, and it was quite evident from the pace they were coming at, and the darkness of the road, that if not prevented, they would scamper over Duval as he there lay. That, however, was an act which Mr. Smith did not like to see perpetrated, dead as he thought the person to be in whom he felt interested; and, accordingly, he stood in the middle of the road, and called out in a loud voice,—

"Stop! stop!"

The horsemen heard him, and pulled-up on the moment. They were five in number, and one, who was a little ahead of the others, called out in a voice of authority,—

"What is it? Is there anything amiss?"

"Yes; a man has been shot, I believe, and his body lies on the road, here, just by me."

"A man shot? That is rather serious."

As he spoke, this person hastily alighted from his horse and approached the spot where Mr. Smith might be said to be, in a manner of speaking, keeping watch over the body. As the man came forward, it was easy to see by his costume that he was a police officer, for although the police at that time wore no set uniform, yet they, by general consent, attired themselves in a style that was perfectly well known, the red waistcoat being always, too, a distinguishing mark of the profession.

"You are an officer?" said Mr. Smith.

"I am."

"Then you are the very person to take cognisance of this affair. Who or what this man may have been who lies dead in the road, I don't know, but I have every reason to believe he has been shot by the servants of the clergyman living at that white house opposite, and I believe that the servants in so doing, acted under his orders."

"It's rather a serious thing," said the officer, "to shoot down a man on the public highway. What was the pretence, sir?"

"Of that I know nothing; something has been said about a highwayman, but of my own knowledge I know nothing about him."

"Can you light your hand-lantern, Josephs?" said the officer to one of those who were with him.

"Yes, sir."

"Do so, then, and hand it to me; I will take a look at this dead man. We may possibly know him."

By the assistance of a phosphorus match, the officer who was named Josephs by the other soon lighted a lantern that he had in the huge pocket of his over-coat. It was a little lantern that, but the magnifying glass attached to it was a good one, and that, by the aid of a powerful reflector likewise, enabled it to send forth one clear and bright ray of light upon any object to which it might be directed.   The principal officer directed that ray right upon the face of the seeming corpse.

"Do you know him?" said Mr. Smith, as he saw the officer give a slight start upon seeing the features.

"Know him? In truth I do."

"Who is he, then?"

"Why, it's no other than Claude Duval, the highwayman. We were as near as possible to nabbing him to-night in Hornsey churchyard, but he got away from us, and we were inclined to give the thing up as a bad job."

"Claude Duval is it?" said Mr. Smith.   "Well, his adventurous career is over now, I fancy. He is a fine-looking fellow."

"I believe you," said the officer; and then with a deep sigh, he said, "I don't know how it will be settled now."

"How do you mean?"

"About the reward, sir; oh, dear—oh, dear! it's an unlucky piece of business. I don't think we shall get anything, and I don't see how those who finished him off in this way are entitled to anything, for they did not, I suppose, know who he was?"

"That I cannot tell."

"Well, well; we must do the best we can. Hilloa, comrades!—this is no other than Claude Duval."

At this intimation, the other officers hastily dismounted, and holding their horses by the bridles they congregated round the body with looks of great interest.

"What are you going to do, Mr. Bland?" said one.

"Oh, we will take him to town of course,' said Bland, who had, as it were, the command of the party. "It's no use leaving him here; and all I can say is, that I will do my best to get the reward among us."

"Thank you, sir," said the others.

"But how are we to take him?" said one.

"Why," said Bland, "the very best way will be for you, Josephs, to place him over your horse, and then you can lead the animal."

"But it's a deuce of a way," said Josephs, "and I am one of the worst of walkers that can be."

"But somebody must take him."

"Let me," cried another of the officers. "Place him astride on the back of my horse, and tie him to my back so that he don't slip off, and then we shall get on capitally. My horse is quite strong enough to carry double, I assure you."

"Oh, yes, yes," cried all the others. "Put him on Phillips's horse. That will do. That's the best way."

The fact was, that they did not very well like the job of carrying the dead body, and he who was named Phillips, as he had expressed his indifference upon the subject, was anxiously accommodated by his comrades with the situation at once.

"Two of the officers picked up from the ground the miserable form of poor Duval; and having placed him on the horse, they tied him fairly to the back of Mr. Phillips, and these proceedings were just completed as the parson gathered courage enough to come out of his house with the blunderbuss again, which he had reloaded.

"Hilloa!" he cried. "What's all this? I shall fire, if you don't mind."

Perhaps the parson would have had no objection to making a chance shot, in the hope that it might possibly rid the parish of the troublesome Mr. Smith; but the officers were not exactly the sort of men to put up with any nonsense, and Bland called out at once in reply—

"We are officers, and if you do fire upon us, I can promise you that we will not be backward in returning the compliment. Where are your pistols, my men?"

Now, the parson had no objection to firing blunderbusses upon other people, but he had no idea of being subjected to any danger himself; so upon the intimation that pistols were forthcoming, he at once bolted into his house with very undignified precipitation.

"Let's be off," said Bland.

"It's your best plan," said Mr. Smith, "and if you want my evidence of what I know of this transaction, you will easily find me here. My name is Smith, and everybody about this spot knows me perfectly well."

"Thank you, sir. We will trouble you if there should be any occasion," said the officer. "Good-night, sir."

"Good night," said Mr. Smith, and away went the officers with poor Duval in rather an awkward position behind one of them on the horse.

"To London, I suppose, sir?" said Phillips to Bland.

"Oh, yes. The best thing we can do is to go to Newgate direct, and I shall make a claim on our behalf for the rewards as it says in the offer made from the Secretary of State's Office, that whoever brings in Claude Duval dead or alive to Newgate shall be entitled to it."

"To be sure it does, sir."

"Then we must have it," said another.

"I think so," cried a third.

"Push on, then," said Bland, "and let me get a receipt from the governor of Newgate for the body, and I rather think that upon that we shall get the money. But you know that it is only five hundred pounds now for him."

"I thought it was double that?" said Phillips.

"Yes, if committed, but it is only five hundred pounds to lodge him in jail, and as you cannot very well commit a dead man, there will be no more for any one, you see."

"Oh, oh—that's it! Well, we must put up with what we can et. It's of no use grumbling."

"Not a bit," said Josephs, "and in my idea, a hundred pounds a-piece is no bad thing among us for our night's work."

This was a sentiment in which the rest of the officers were tolerably sure to concur, and so the party trotted on towards London in tolerable comfort. To be sure, they would rather have had Claude Duval a prisoner in life than in death; but then they looked upon it as now quite past praying for, and like wise men, they behaved accordingly.

At the rate they travelled, for they were not very particular about the comfort of the supposed corpse, they very soon left the open country behind them, and made their way through the streets of London towards the gloomy prison of Newgate.

As they ascend Snow Hill the clock of St. Sepulchre—that clock, the sound of which has so often echoed in the ears of unhappy wretches, as they took their last look at the world before the hangman launched them into eternity, to use the newspaper phrase—struck five, and each moment the sky was getting lighter.

The morning was very close at hand, and but for a bank of dark dense clouds that lowered upon the horizon, no doubt the first faint beams of the early sun would have shone upon London.

"Here we are," said Bland, as he stopped at Newgate, and hastily dismounted from his horse. "Here we are, at last, and I am, for one, tired of the saddle."

"And I," said Phillips, "am tired of my friend behind me, here."

The others all laughed at this, for they had been very far from envying Phillips the companionship of the dead, and all along they had been rather fearful that he would insist upon some of them taking their turn in carrying the supposed dead body of Claude Duval.

"Come," he added, "take him down among you, at all events. I wonder, now, if we shall get the reward? Ah, he little thinks he is at the gate of——"

"Newgate!" shouted Duval, in the ear of Phillips, at this moment, with a power of lungs that made the Old Bailey echo again.

CHAPTER CXVIII.

IT IS FOUND THAT DUVAL IS NOT DEAD YET.

It would be quite impossible for any language to sufficiently point out the effect produced upon the officers by this sudden exclamation from Claude Duval. We can but very faintly state some of the more immediate results.

THE COMBAT BETWEEN THE TWO MOHOCKS.

The man to whom he, Duval, was tied upon the horse, was so terrified at what he foolishly conceived to be some frightfully supernatural sound from the lips of the dead body, that he began bellowing for help, as though a thousand devils had got hold of him.

The other officers, one and all, made a grand rush into the vestibule of Newgate, for they seemed to have an idea that the cry from the lips of the supposed corpse could only be the prelude to something yet more dreadful.

The man at the wicket-gate, thinking that his head was high enough from mischief, at once sat down upon the stone-floor with his keys in one hand, and a little stone-bottle in the other, from the contents of which he had been solacing himself upon the occasion of the arrival of the officers with the supposed dead prisoner.

"Murder—murder!" still shouted the officer on the horse. "Take him away some of you. Murder—murder, I can't stand it! Help—help!"

These vociferations made the matter rather worse, for they impressed the others with a belief that the dead body in some extraordinary way was serving out their companion for his share in the transaction.

But Duval thought that he had terrified the officers enough now. He had fully intended to give them a fright, and he had done it; but when that was once accomplished, he did not care to continue the affair.

"Hilloa!" he said, in a loud voice, "are you all so much afraid of one man that you run off as though you were shot?"

Duval had already made rather an energetic effort to free himself from the bonds that held him to Phillips, before he spoke. If, in the surprise of the moment that had come over the officer, he could only have freed himself from the man he was tied to, he would, no doubt, have fairly got away, even then.

The officers, however, had been too careful in securing what they considered to be the important dead body, and Duval, in a very few moments, had found that, dead or alive, he was a prisoner.

"Why, he ain't dead!" cried one.

"Not dead?" shouted all the others.

"Not yet," said Duval.

A great revulsion of feeling took place on the instant, and they rushed out from the lobby of Newgate and surrounded the horse with its double burthen.

"Why, good gracious, how is this?" cried the chief of the party. "Do you mean to tell me, Duval, that you are not dead?"

"Certainly I do."

"Then I am as glad as if any one had given me a thousand pounds, that I am."

"Ah," said Duval, "that is the difference, I suppose, between taking me in dead, and getting me committed and hanged; but all are not lost that are in danger, I can tell you."

"I don't say they are; but yet I shouldn't quite like to be in your danger, after all, old fellow. Lay hold of him, comrades. He's a slippery customer, as we all well know. Hold him tight!"

The officers had now fairly recovered from their first fright and surprise, and the idea of losing Duval by any desperate effort upon his part, was so harrowing to them, that the precautions they took against such a catastrophe looked truly ludicrous.

It was absurd, for instance, to see so many men all holding fast by one, while Mr. Phillips, whose mind seemed to be a little unsettled by the fright he had had, kept calling out—

"Take him away, will you! Take him away! Why don't you untie him from me, and take him away?"

"Stop a bit," said Bland; "there's a time for all things. When I see Duval inside Newgate and the lock turned upon him, I shall think he is safe, but not before."

"Then," said Duval, "you had better let me ride in, horse and all. I will do it, if this fellow before me will give me the rein."

"Yes," said one, "and if you had the rein, Duval, you would be on Hounslow Heath, perhaps, before another hour was over."

"To be sure he would," said Bland. "Hold him tight, whatever you do."

"All's right, sir. Wouldn't it be best to lift Phillips and him off the horse together, and so take them into Newgate?"

"To be sure it would. That's a good idea. Now for it. Lift them both off. That is the thing."

The officers, by their united strength, fairly lifted Duval and their comrade—still tied together—off the horse, and carried them up the steps and so into the lobby of Newgate. Duval felt that under the circumstances he was in, any attempt to escape could only result in his incurring personal ill-usage that might have the effect of incapacitating him for some future exertion which might be required for the purpose of giving him a chance of escape; so he very wisely, as he was taken, made the best of a bad business, and did not exhaust his strength, or court a hurt or two by showing any restiveness upon the occasion.

When they got him into the lobby and the door locked, they felt satisfied that he was secure, and they speedily released him from Mr. Phillips.

That officer looked more dead than alive when he was released from such close acquaintanceship with Duval. The sound of that unexpected voice was still ringing through his head, and he was glad to stagger to a seat, where he sat looking pale and distressed.

"Why," said Duval, "I had no idea of giving you such a fright as that, my friend."

"A fright, indeed!" he gasped.

"You should take things as they come in an easier fashion. You all of you understood that I was dead?"

"And you were alive all the time," said Bland.

"Not exactly. The fact is, there was something in the blunderbuss that was fired at me that must have hit me in some odd way on the head, and for the time knocked me into insensibility; but the ride restored me, and I don't feel much hurt."

"There is blood running down your face," said one of the turnkeys.

Duval put up his hand and withdrew it dabbled with blood.

"Ah!" he said quite calmly, "that's were it hit me, then, and the bleeding will put me all to rights. It can't be much of a hurt, for I feel as much as usual, except a little confusion in my brain."

"You know where you are, though?"

"Rather," said Duval.

"And you know what will be your fate now?" said another.

"No," said Duval, "nor you either. I do not profess to be a conjurer, and I feel quite sure that with that muffin-face you are not one."

This sally produced a general laugh among the officers at the expense of the man who had spoken, so that he was fain to get out of the way and not attempt again to set his wit or his malice up against one who could so successfully turn him into ridicule.

The governor of Newgate had been sent for, as so very important, and we may add, so very unexpected a prize as Claude Duval was not an every day or an every night occurrence, and the officers knew very well that the governor would not grudge being roused up upon such an occasion, as the authorities were so, exceedingly anxious to get Duval hanged out of the way.

In the course of about five or six minutes, the governor made his appearance enveloped in a dressing-gown and carrying a light.

"You don't mean to tell me that you have Duval?" he cried, as he reached the lobby.

"Yes, sir; here he is."

"Let me have a good look at him; I know him by sight well enough. Ah! in good truth it is Duval.—You are quite welcome to Newgate once more, and I don't think this time any very illustrious personage will trouble himself to release you: you understand me?"

"I do," said Duval.

"Very good. Now, Mr. Martin, where are you?"

"Here I is," said a gruff spoken individual, cruelly marked with the small-pox, advancing from a dark corner.

"Oh, very good ; you will accommodate Duval with a good set of irons, and place him in—let me see : No. 10—no, 11 ;—No. 11, Mr. Martin, if you please ; that will do best—No. 11."

"I hear you," growled Martin.

"And to-morrow morning, Duval," said the governor, as he turned to retire to his own apartments again ; "to-morrow morning the judges will decide upon what is to be done with you."

"No they won't," said Duval. "The jury will have to decide, and if I happen to like the verdict, I will submit to it. If I don't, I won't."

"You won't?"

"Certainly not."

"Very good ; we shall soon see that. Take him away. Oh, dear me, how very sleepy I am to be sure!"

The governor, yawning at a dreadful rate, retired from the lobby, and then there commenced the process of searching Duval, which the officers went through in the tried and practised manner that they were able to do from long usage. They took from him his pistols and his money, together with two watches and a rather formidable-looking clasp-knife, that when open was so fixed by a spring in order that it might be serviceable as a dagger, and a very fearful looking weapon it was.

To all this, Duval made not the least opposition, for he knew the folly of doing so. On the contrary, he joked and laughed with the officers all the time, so that he was on very good terms with them by the time the search was over.

"Come now," he said, "you know very well you have found everything now ; and as I know you are anxious to do so, I would tell you if there was any little affair you had overlooked."

"Oh, no, it's all right, Duval. You take things easy."

"Of course I do."

"And you don't bear any malice?" said the officer who had been named Josephs by his comrades.

"Malice!" cried Duval ; "certainly not; why should I? All you do is your duty. It is your business to catch me if you can, and it is my business to keep out of your clutches. I don't think there is one man here who would do me any harm merely for the sake of doing it."

"Not one, Duval," they all cried.

"And I," he continued, "can answer for myself, that I wouldn't, except in the way of self-defence, if I was jammed in a corner and couldn't help it, hurt a hair of the head of any of you. Don't fancy that I have any ill-will against you for this affair. It was, as I say, your duty to take me, and here I am."

"That's the right way to view it, Duval," said Bland ; "and now all we have to do is to see you to No. 11. Are you ready, Martin?"

"Here you is," said Martin, appearing with a very heavy set of fetters slung over his shoulder, and a blacksmith's hammer and a small portable anvil in his hands. "Here you is—all's right."

"Are these little fancy ornaments for me?" said Duval.

"Yes, they are."

"Very good. I wonder, though, that you don't have something just a little better in temper than such bits of iron as this."

As he spoke, Claude Duval took the fetters from the shoulder of Mr. Martin, and placing one of the long pieces under his foot, he, with a sudden jerk, bent it quite double.

"There's a pretty bit of stuff for you," he said.

"Ha! ha!" laughed Martin ; "steel will break, but iron will bend, so you see the iron does the better for us; you won't break these with a jerk, but you might a piece of finer stuff. Come on ; we know pretty well what we are about."

"Ah, but," said Duval, "what would resist the sharp tooth of a file the best, eh, Mr. Martin?"

"We don't allow files here."

"No; but, at times, they make their way here without asking leave ; and then they slips through the iron in a minute or two, that's all."

"Ha!—ha! Come on, will you ? You are a droll chap, I will say ; but if you get out of this,"—Mr. Martin jingled the fetters boisterously—" if you get out of these, I'll forgive you."

"I am particularly obliged," said Duval ; "that will be very consolatory to me in my last moments."

The officers laughed ; and then, by the light of a couple of flambeaux, they led Duval to the cell that had been named by the governor as his place of confinement for that night, at all events, in Newgate.

It was one of the strongest cells in the prison, that No. 11, and the passage to it was so tortuous, that no prisoner could take upon himself to say in what part of Newgate it was situated, so that every plan of escape from it would be wanting in the rather essential particular of knowing which way to go, even if, by extraordinary good luck, the imprisoned one should get out of the cell itself.

It was in vain that even Duval, with all his tact, strove to recollect how many turnings to the left, and how many turnings to the right there were as he proceeded ; but, perhaps, his head was still a little confused, and, indeed, the blood kept trickling down his face in rather an alarming manner.

"You had better have that ugly knock on the head seen to,' said Bland. "I will send for the surgeon."

"Oh, no!" said Duval, "give me some cold water, and it will be all right enough by-and-by."

"Nay, but it is our duty to let the surgeon of the prison know if anything is amiss, or if we bring in a wounded prisoner, so you go and rouse him up, Josephs. We don't wish you to be more uncomfortable than you need be, Duval."

"Thank you. I shall do very well. But if it be your duty to have this surgeon, have him here at once. I don't care about it one way or the other."

Mr. Josephs fetched the surgeon, who, yawning with sleep, came half dressed to the cell, and looked at Duval's head.

"I can't make out," he said, "how you could have come by such a hurt. If it had only gone a quarter of an inch to one side, it would have laid open an artery that would have bled you to death in a quarter of an hour."

"You don't say so ?" said Duval.

"Yes I do. Something must have hit your head in a very sharp oblique fashion. You won't feel it to-morrow, I daresay. It won't bleed any more now, but keep it tied up."

"Thank you ; I will. Perhaps the next time they fire a blunderbuss at me, I shall not be so lucky. I do believe it was loaded with a pewter quart pot, for something nearly as big appeared to me to go past my head when I fell."

The surgeon looked at Duval for a moment or two, as if he would fain discover whether he were joking or not ; but the impassible look of Duval's face baffled him, and repeating the words "quart pot," he left the cell, and repaired to his own apartment in the prison.

Martin, then, with great tact and skill, rivetted the irons upon Duval ; and when that operation was concluded, they all bade him good-night, and left him alone—certainly not in his glory.

"This is pleasant," said Duval. " I wonder if this is in truth my last adventure, or if I shall live to once more snuff the morning air upon a lonely road with a good horse under me ? We shall see."

CHAPTER CXIX.

DUVAL IS BROUGHT TO TRIAL IN A VERY SUMMARY MANNER.

In Duval's cell, the only sleeping accommodation consisted of a sloping board, fastened at one end to the wall, and a sort of rough quilt with which he could either cover himself up, or manufacture a kind of pillow, according as he might think proper so to do.

Duval preferred the latter mode of disposing of the quilt, and in the dark, as well as he could, he doubled it up, and placed it upon the board, so that he could lay his head upon it. Then stretching himself at full length, he said—"Good night," and fell asleep.

What an amiable thing is that light-hearted carelessness, that enables some men to sleep almost at will! Perhaps the great majority of cases in which we are informed that such a power exists or existed are doubtful; but there can be no question but that some men do possess the faculty, and Claude Duval was among the number. Probably he slept more soundly in that gloomy cell of Newgate than many a profound worshipper of pleasure did that night upon a bed of down.

How long he remained in repose he had no possible means of knowing, but he was awakened by some one calling out—

"Hilloa! hilloa! Duval, rouse yourself."

"Well," he said, "here I am. What now?"

"You must get up."

"Very good. Anything else in a small way that you would like? You have only to mention it."

"Come this way."

Duval gave himself a shake or two that made him falter rather again, and then he was tolerably awake. A dim kind of twilight only entered the cell, but in the corridor outside it the daylight was sufficiently apparent.

"What's the time?" said Duval.

"Eight," said the turnkey.

"Oh. Then I suppose I may make so bold as to ask at what time you breakfast here, my friend?"

"You will have yours directly. The sheriff is waiting to see you in the lobby, and you will be taken before a magistrate at once, committed for trial—tried as soon as possible, and hanged off-hand like a brick."

"You are too good," said Duval. "The breakfast, however, as the first of the promises, I have no sort of objection to. The others will all keep."

"Perhaps so."

By the time this little dialogue was at an end, Duval and the turnkey had reached the lobby of Newgate. There was some dozen or so of persons, and the governor was talking to one of the sheriff's who had his gold chain round his neck, and looked very fierce indeed, and full of authority.

Upon the entrance of Duval there was some little bustle, and the governor came towards him, and spoke, saying—

"Duval you will be allowed half-an-hour for your breakfast now, and after that time you will be taken before a magistrate, and a formal charge made against you, upon which I daresay, you will be committed for trial, so that we shall soon have you back to us again."

"You have no right," said Duval, "to prejudge even the examination before the magistrate, in that way I can assure you that I am not by any means so fond of your society as to wish to come back again to this place. I speak in all candour, although the remark I feel myself compelled to make is not very flattering to your powers of entertainment."

A slight smile came over the face of the sheriff, as he advanced to Duval with something in his hand—

"Claude Duval," he said, "it appears that a considerable sum of money was found in your possession, and although there is every possible reason to suspect that that money is the produce of highway robberies, yet I am satisfied to take the responsibility of lending you sufficient for your support, and for the expenses that will be necessarily contingent upon your defence."

"I am much oblige to you, Mr. Sheriff," said Duval.

"Here are fifty pounds," added the sheriff, "and I should say that such a sum ought to be amply sufficient."

"I have no doubt but it will, sir, and I again thank you for the liberality which has induced you to place such a sum in my possession."

"I am very sorry for you, Duval," said the sheriff, "for I have every reason to believe that you have abilities and education both, that fitted you to be among different members of society than you are."

"It may be so, sir, but the time is past now, and as I am what I am, society, you may depend, won't let me be anything else. I did hope that I should be able to leave England, and that Claude Duval would have been soon forgotten; but that, perhaps, is only a dream."

The sheriff shook his head as he walked away, saying in a low tone—

"Claude Duval will not be forgotten while the English language is spoken, I think."

"What will you have for breakfast?" said Bland the officer.

"Oh, are you here, my last night's acquaintance?"

"Yes; and I will send one of my men to get whatever you like."

"Very good. In the first place here are five guineas for my footing in the prison, and I hope you will all get something good to drink with them."

"You are a generous fellow," said Bland.

"He is—oh, crikey, he is!" said Morgan. "Five shiners to drink! Let me see—this is Thursday. Why, I shall be drunk till Friday night."

"But what shall we get you, Duval?"

"A pint of the best sherry that the city can furnish," said Duval, "and two dozen of native oysters, and as much fine bread and fresh butter as you think a hungry man is likely to consume at a sitting. Take that guinea and never mind the change."

"Ah," said Josephs, in a whisper to an officer who stood next, "ain't he, after all, a fine fellow? Lor bless you, he knows how to do it as well as ever a lord in the whole kingdom, he does!"

"I believe you," said the other.

The administration of the criminal laws was at that time very loose indeed, in its minor details. The most notorious criminals, if they only came into Newgate with plenty of money, could just live as they pleased; and, indeed, if they particularly desired it, they could have a convivial party now and then, at which they would be surrounded by their friends, and all sorts of jollity would go on to the accompaniment of the clank of fetters.

It was Jerry Abershaw, they say, who actually did dance a hornpipe in his fetters in the lobby of Newgate, and so brought that barbarous and stupid exhibition into vogue at the Minor Theatres of London.

The eatables and drinkables that Duval had ordered were speedily procured, and he had no cause to find fault with the quality of what was procured for him. After a breakfast of that description, which was at once light, nutritious, and substantial, but which none but a strong, healthy man could have ventured upon, he felt that he was capable of going through any fatigue that the day might present to him.

The half-hour soon expired, and just as St. Sepulchre's church clock chimed that period of time past eight, Duval was handed into a hackney-coach at the door of Newgate, and two officers accompanied him. Upon the box by the side of the coachman another rode, and a fourth went behind in the fashion of a footman, so that Duval was pretty well taken care of.

Bland and Josephs were the officers in their side of the coach along with Duval, and they had not gone far before Bland said to him—

"Do you know, Phillips is very bad this morning. You frightened him to such an extent last night, that the doctor says his brain is touched by it, and that it is doubtful if ever he gets the better of it."

"I am really sorry for that," said Duval. "It was the impulse of the moment that made me bawl in his ear in the manner I did; but, really, I only meant it for a joke."

"We all feel that; but it's no joke to him, poor fellow, though."

"Certainly not; but I can only regard it deeply, after all. If I get through this affair, and he still continues so bad, I will do something for him."

Bland and Josephs exchanged glances, and then the former said—

"It is kind enough of you to say so, Duval, but I can't help thinking they have made up their minds about you."

"What do you mean?"

"They will commit you to-day and they will try you to-morrow, and to-morrow is Friday, you know."

"From which you would infer that they have quite made up their minds to hang me on Monday?"

"It looks like it, don't it?"

"It does; but they may find themselves mistaken for all that. I cannot pretend to say that they can't get the better of me, but I don't think, and I won't think it. The last thing a man should do is to give himself up, and that I never mean to do. No, not if the rope were round my neck."

"That's pluck, at all events."

"You may call it what you please, but it is my determination. You know that I have been in Newgate before to-day?"

"Yes, and I'll be hanged if I could ever make out how you got out. There was a mystery about the whole affair that to me is quite inexplicable. I only wish you would tell me how it was."

"It's another person's secret."

"Oh, well, if that's the case, I can't expect to know it, and perhaps, after all, the other person will come and open the door for you again."

Duval was silent. He did not like to say yes or no to that question. If he said yes, it might lead to too much talking, and, besides, he had no such expectation. If he said no, it would make the officers think that he had no friends, and that he should be abandoned to his fate, and that was a feeling regarding him that he by no means wished to get up.

After this, they proceeded in silence for some time, and the coach finally drew up at the door of the police-office at Bow Street. There was no knowledge, as yet, in London that Duval was taken, so that the crowd that would have been at the office, had it only been popularly know that he was to be brought up, was not to be seen. Some half dozen people, lounging about the doors, as disreputable people will lounge about such doors, for no earthly purpose, one would think, but that the police should get familiar with their physiognomies, were only to be seen, and Duval entered the office with the officers without exciting any sensation beyond a passing stare.

The night charges from the various watch-houses had not come in, but everything had been very well managed, and the magistrate, precisely as nine o'clock struck, was on his seat, and Claude Duval was placed before him.

"What is the case?" said the magistrate.

"Highway robbery, your honour," said the officer.

"Prisoner, what is your name?"

"Claude Duval."

"Oh, very well. Now, where is the evidence?"

"Here, your worship," said a man stepping forward. "I prefer the charge against the prisoner at the bar."

"Very good. Swear the witness. Now, sir, make your charge."

"My name is Ambrose Wilkins, I am a lawyer's clerk, and was sent by my master to collect some rents at Guildford. I was on horseback, when about two miles and a half on the London side of the town, I was accosted by the prisoner at the bar, who said—'My friend, do you carry weight with you.' I said I did not know what he meant, and he then added—'Are you a man of metal?' as I understood him, and then I tried to get away and called out murder, and he took hold of me by the collar and asked me who I was, and I told him I was a lawyer's clerk, and had the money of my master with me; upon which he said—'Very well; you can tell your master that a verdict that he is a great rogue has gone

againt him on the Guildford road, and that the damages have been assessed at
what money you had with you,' and so he took the money from me."

"How much was it ?" said the magistrate.

"Sixty-two pounds."

"And can you swear to the prisoner at the bar ?"

THE BURIAL SERVICE IS PERFORMED OVER ADELE.

"I can."

"Very good.   Have you any observations to make, prisoner, upon the subject,
or any questions to ask the witness."

"Yes," said Duval.   "When did the transaction take place ?"

"On the twenty-sixth of last October."

"Was I on my white horse ?"

" Yes."

" Will you swear that?"

" Certainly I will."

" Very good.   What time in the evening was it?"

" Half-past ten as near as possible."

" That is all I have to say to you. You are an excellent witness.   You may go down now."

" Call Mr. Skinner," said the magistrate.

" Oh, you knew all this beforehand, then?" said Duval.   " Pray, Mr. Magistrate, what made you suddenly aware of the name of the next witness?'

A flush came over the face of the magistrate, and then with a pompous air, he said—

" Prisoner, I would strongly advise you to attend to the case that is being brought forward against you, and not to indulge in extraneous remarks to the bench."

" Thank you," said Duval.   " I'll attend to it; but it don't require a necromancer to see that this affair is all cut and dry. Is there any clever sharp attorney here, who will for a good fee see to the affair for me?"

" Yes," said a voice, and a young man stepped forward at once.

" Who are you, sir?" said the magistrate.   " How dare you interrupt the case. Go out of the court, sir."

" I will not," said the young man.   " I am an attorney, and it is the practice of all courts to allow a prisoner at any moment to stay the proceedings until he has made an arrangement with his legal adviser. I demand that right for Claude Duval, and you cannot refuse it to him. If you do, I will make an application within this hour to the Lord Chief Justice."

The magistrate turned rather pale.

" Well—well," he said.   " I am more inclined to be indulgent than otherwise. I will adjourn the case for a quarter of an hour, so that the prisoner may consult you, and then it will be resumed."

The officer of the court summoned Duval into one of the small cells at the back of it, and they locked him up along with the solicitor, who said to him at once—

" Duval, did you do the robbery?"

" No."

" You did not?   Pray do not deceive me."

" I will not.   Have you heard the evidence already given?"

" I have."

" Then I will tell you that I never was upon the back of a white horse in all my life, and that last October I was not near the part of the country spoken of."

" Can you prove where you really where?"

" No.   That I cannot, upon that particular night."

" Well, Duval, it is a got-up case against you for the mere purpose of expediting proceedings, that is all.   They want to hang you on Monday to get rid of you, and as they know that you have really committed many highway robberies, they think it is just as well to get up a clear case which is a fiction, instead of taking the trouble to procure complicated and possibly defective evidence on a real one."

" I suspected as much.   What had better be done?"

" I shall insist upon a remand for a week.   If the magistrate will not grant it, but insists upon committing you, the judge will traverse the trial until next sessions; so, after all, take it in any way or shape, they shall not hang you next Monday."

CHAPTER CXX.

CLAUDE IS TRIED, AND THE RESULT IS RATHER EXTRAORDINARY.

It was quite clear to both Duval and his attorney, that the magistracy, and perhaps others higher in authority than they, were determined to hang him if they possibly could, and that in the most summary manner possible. Whether they will succeed in doing so, we shall soon see.

The short time that the magistrate, in order to keep up a semblance of equitable proceeding, had allowed to Duval and his legal adviser, quickly expired, and again Duval was put to the bar.

"Well, prisoner," said the magistrate, "you have heard the evidence against you. Do you wish to add anything to your former statement?"

"The prisoner made no statement," said the attorney, "except a clear and positive denial of the protested facts deposed to against him."

"We hardly expect him to admit them, sir."

"Very good; he does not admit them, but as he is taken by surprise upon the charge, and it will take him some time to get his witnesses to refute it, I have to request a remand for a fortnight."

"A man who gets his living by highway robbery," said the magistrate, with a sneer, "should hardly complain of being taken by surprise, when he is charged with such an offence before a police court."

"And yet it is so," said the attorney; "and I must say that such a remark from you, sir, filling the situation you do, is entirely unwarrantable and uncalled for, and aside from the purpose. You have no evidence before you that my client is such a person."

"Common report is tolerably conclusive upon the point."

"Common report is bad evidence. How would you like for the Secretary of State to turn you out of your situation, because common report said that you were very unfit for it indeed? You would naturally demand that some charge should be brought forward against you, and that you should be called upon to answer to it."

"That is not a case in point," said the magistrate.

"Very well. It is not my province to argue such matters with you; but according to all usage, I demand a remand for my client, in order that he may be able to meet the charge against him."

"I have considered the case," said the magistrate, half shutting his eyes, and putting on a look of candour he was far from feeling, "and I must say that a clearer case never came before me. Here is a man who is a notorious highway robber, brought before the court upon a clear and simple charge of that description, substantiated upon oath by respectable witnesses. My duty is plainly before me, and I followed it without direction."

"The witnesses may be mistaken," said the attorney.

"Oh, no, sir—no."

"Or perjured."

"Really," said the magistrate, "I cannot sit here to listen to such aspersions thrown out upon the character of respectable individuals; my only course is to commit the prisoner for trial at once."

"You must not do so, sir."

"Must not?"

"No, you dare not, if you have the sense to see how dangerous it may be to your own position to do so. Recollect, sir, that the judges of this land are not men who in matters of this sort will be trifled with, and that it does not tell well for a magistrate that a judge does that which he ought to have done."

"I very much doubt if any judge will interfere in the case. I shall commit the prisoner for trial at the Old Bailey. The Grand Jury is now sitting, and there is very little doubt but that a true bill will be found, and the whole affair settled very shortly."

"There is no doubt at all, sir," said the attorney, "if every one is of your mind in the matter."

"If you are insolent, sir, I will have you turned out of court."

"Beware," said the attorney, "or I will have you, before you are a month older, turned off that bench."

The magistrate shook a little at this, for there was a look about the face of the attorney, which showed that he was a man well qualified to carry out any threat of that kind. But yet, the magistrate did not alter his determination; and Duval was duly committed for trial at the Old Bailey upon the charge of highway robbery, and the witnesses bound over in their own cognizances to appear and prosecute.

Duval was about to say something; but a look from his attorney, and a slight shake of the head, stopped him. After all, what would have been the use of anything he had said to the magistrate who, by pre-arrangement, was evidently resolved upon committing him for trial?

How far this kind of conspiracy among the authorities, for the purpose of hanging Duval on the next Monday morning, might speed it, was quite impossible just then to say. The solicitor was rather afraid it was more extensive than would be pleasant to grapple with; but that was a state of things which, if it were the case, would easily develope itself upon a little inquiry.

Duval was taken back to Newgate.

While the examination and the short interruption to it had taken place at Newgate, the news had spread like wild-fire in the neighbourhood of the police-office, that Duval, the celebrated highwayman, was in custody, and by the time he reached the outer door of the office again to be conveyed back to prison, the officers who had him in their custody rather shrunk to find that the whole of Bow Street was a mass of human heads.

A loud shout from those who were the nearest to the officers proclaimed to those who were most distant that the prisoner was brought out, and such an effect had that shout upon the nerves of the officers, that they hastily drew back in alarm, fearing that some rescue of their prisoner was about to be attempted.

"So, Duval," said one of them, "you have got your friends about you?"

"Pho!" said Duval. "They are no friends of mine."

"They seem to welcome you?"

"Yes, they would be quite as much amused to see me hanged. You need not be afraid. I have no faith in mobs, except so far as a noise goes, and the breaking of a few windows."

"Then you will not try to get away?"

"Come, come," said Duval, with a slight laugh. "Don't try to commit me mo e than the magistrate has done. Just ask yourselves what you would do if you were Claude Duval, and in such a delicate situation as I am. Don't be too hard upon human nature."

"Come on!" said the boldest of the four officers. "I think with Duval, that mobs only make a noise and break windows. We shall soon be at Newgate, and it won't do to seem to be afraid now."

Thus urged, the other three laid hold of Duval, and brought him to the door of the coach. The official persons belonging to the police-office assisted them so far, so that there was no great difficulty of procedure in the matter, and they tumbled him into the vehicle and shut the door upon him, amid the houting and shouting of the mob.

It is strange how fond mobs are of that class of criminals, whose offence is against property only, while those who commit offences against the person, are held in high detestation. It can only arise from the fact, that the vast majority of persons making up a mob, have nothing in the way of property to lose, but everything in the way of life; but, certainly, Duval, who was well known to confine his highway depredations to the rich, was in high favour with the multitude. But being in high favour with a couple of thousand people or so in London, and being rescued by them from four constables, are very different things, indeed.

Duval seemed to have a pretty good appreciation of the kind of valour that actuates a London mob.

The officers proceeded in the same order that they did before, that is to say, two of them got into the coach with Duval—one on the box with the driver, and one behind, and then off went the coach.

Now, the officer who was behind the coach was in rather a ticklish position, for there was a certain number of blackguards who were particularly anxious to ride behind it themselves; and after proceeding for some distance, they summoned up courage to attack the officer, by laying old of his leg to drag him down.

The officer kicked at them, but that only added fuel to the fire of their exasperation, and in another moment they had him down among them, and a struggle began which would have ended, no doubt, in his death, had he not called loudly for help.

"What's it all about?" said Duval.

The officers looked rather pale, for they thought that now had commenced the rescue they had dreaded, and that in all likelihood they would all be murdered. Duval saw the situation they were in, and hearing the frantic cries of the man who was among the mob, he said—

"Take these handcuffs off me, and I will save your comrade."

"You will escape, Duval."

"No, I promise you that I won't. Be quick, or he is a dead man."

One of the officers thought that the very best thing he could do was to release Duval from the handcuffs, and while the other looked on with a pale face, he unlocked the shackle, and Duval had his hands free.

To dart out of the coach was now to Duval the work of a moment, and plunging among the crowd, he got hold of the officer who was being maltreated, and by an exertion of strength such as few men would have been capable of, he carried him in one hand, while with the other he fought his way to the coach again, and when he reached the door of it he threw him in and jumped in himself after him.

"Now drive on," he cried. "All's right. What the deuce did one of you venture behind the coach for? You might have been sure the mob would be at you."

The officer seemed to be more dead than alive when he was cast into the coach by Duval, and he lay by the feet of his comrades without moving until the coach had proceeded some distance; but fright, and the prospect of the dreadful death that had seemed to await him, had more to do with the prostrated condition in which he was than anything in the shape of real injuries, for, with the exception of a number of contusions, he was not hurt.

Now the coach had reached nearly the outskirts of the mob, and by passing through Lincoln's Inn it was thought that the worst of the populace would be got rid of, as that was so very unusual a route for any vehicle to take, and, in fact, would not be allowed upon any occasion but one of emergency to the authorities. The officers raised their injured comrade from the straw at the bottom of the vehicle, and seated him by them.

For a few moments he looked about him as if bewildered, and then one of them said to him—

"Come, it's all right now, Jones, ain't it?"

"Am I saved?"

"To be sure you are. Don't you see you are in the coach with us, and we are almost clear of the mob?"

"Yes—yes. I am saved?"

"Come—come, cheer up; you ain't much hurt, now, I dare say. No bones are broken, are they?"

"Oh, no—no! I begin to feel that I am safe now. They would have killed me—indeed they would, and you were a long time, all of you, coming to my rescue, though I did call out for you loudly enough."

The officers made no reply to this, but they looked rather askance at Duval, who said nothing.

"I gave myself up to death," continued the officer. "There was one fellow who tried to throttle me, and I think in another moment or two he would have done it. That was what made me feel so queer when I got into the coach."

"Oh, well, it's all right now. Don't say any more about it, old fellow."

"Oh, yes, but I will though; and I promise you that I will stand a very handsome treat for the way in which you got me out of the clutches of the mob. It w s a brave and well-done thing."

"Come, Duval," said the officer who had released him from the handcuffs, "I must put the darbies on you again, or when we get to the stone jug, we shall be blamed about it."

"As you please," said Duval.

"What!" cried the officer, who had so narrowly escaped with his life from the mob. "What, do you mean to say you have let Duval have his hands free, and a howling mob about you?"

"Yes," said the officer, as he fastened on the handcuffs again to Duval's wrists, "and I feel that it's an unfair thing not to tell you all about it; but it was Duval, and Duval alone, who went out of the coach among the mob, and rescued you. It was he who did it while we waited here, and you owe him your life."

The officer looked aghast.

"Can—can," he gasped, "this be true?"

"I believe it is," said Duval; "but I don't see anything very extraordinary in it, after all. I certainly could not have done it if your friend here had not released me from the darbies."

"Then to you, Duval, whom I am assisting to take to prison, and perhaps to death, I owe my life?"

"Perhaps so."

The officer held out his hand.

"Will you shake hands with me, Duval? Will you, indeed?"

"Oh, yes."

They shook hands.

"Now hear me," said the officer. "If I forget this day, and what I owe you, may I fall into the same, or a worse danger, and may there be no one to stretch out a helping hand to me. It's no use me saying any more, but I mean what I do say, and I will keep my word."

"Ah," said one of the others, "it don't much matter, but Duval will be hanged on Monday."

"No," said the officer, whose name was Jones. "No, Duval will not be hanged on Monday."

"How do you know that?"

"No how," he replied, "but I hope he won't, that's all."

Upon this reply, the other two laughed aloud.

"Come, that's good," said one; "but, however, Duval, you have done a good thing in saving Jones, for it might have been any of us, and we all owe you a good turn for it. We will tell enough of the story at Newgate to do you some good, and that is all we can do for you; but your affairs look bad."

"I know they do," said Duval; "but yet I don't despair."

"No," said Jones, "never despair."

There was a peculiar meaning in the tone of the officer as he now spoke that convinced Duval that he had some design in his mind concerning which he did not wish his brother officers to have any suspicion, and Duval began really to gather hope that the officer would and could do him a good turn.

CHAPTER CXXI.

DUVAL IS PLACED UPON HIS TRIAL AT THE OLD BAILEY.

AFTER passing through Lincoln's Inn, it was quite evident that the mob was got rid of, and that there was no more danger to apprehend. The officers looked all the better for the change.

"This has been a close touch," said one of them, "for notwithstanding all your opinion of crowds, Duval, they would have knocked us on the head and carried you off, as soon as look at us."

Duval smiled, but it was quite clear that he had a very different opinion, and then one of the officers said to him—

"Where did you put the body of the young girl, Duval, who was to have been buried in the cross-roads?"

The countenance of Duval flushed with passion.

"Attend to what concerns you," he said. "that is my business."

"Oh, well, I didn't mean to offend you at all about it; I only asked, tha was all."

"Then you will not know."

"Very good; it don't matter to me a straw whether she is buried in a church-yard or a cross-road; but it was that affair that brought us upon you."

"I know it."

"And that may bring you to the tree, you know; so it only shows what nonsense it was, after all."

"You can think what you like," said Duval; "but if I had all this to do over again, I should only look to see that it was done as effectually as it is done; and one great consolation to me is, that she is safe."

"Well, and so are we, for here we are at Newgate."

It was quite evident, from the manner of the governor of Newgate, that he expected Duval would be committed for trial, for the first words he said to the officers were—

"Committed, of course?"

"Yes, sir."

"All's right. The grand jury is sitting."

"So, governor, you are in the plot?" said Duval.

"Plot? What do you mean by plot?"

"Why the plot to hang me, to be sure. No one knows better than you what I mean. You want to get rid of me by Monday, don't you now? But you won't. I have made up my mind that you won't."

"Very good, Duval; if you are satisfied, I am quite sure we are. Take him to his cell again. Where's Jones?".

"Jones! Jones!"

"He was here, sir, just now," said one of the other officers, "and he was so hurt by the mob, that it ain't at all likely he has left the prison."

"Yes, but he has so," said the man who was "upon the lock" at the outer gate. "He went out and ran as hard as his legs would carry him towards Snow Hill a few minutes ago."

Duval had no very special reason for supposing that Jones had gone upon business connected with his welfare, but the idea that such was the case took possession of him, and he waited with no small share of curiosity to know what the next twenty-four hours would bring forth. He knew that if the authorities chose, nothing would be easier than to bring him to trial on the morrow, in which case, if he were convicted, they might hang him on the succeeding Monday morning; but yet he had a sort of faith that such would not be his fate, and he went to his cell full of thought upon the subject.

Duval had not been above two hours left to the solitude of his cell in Newgate, when the door was opened, and the governor's clerk appeared.

"I have to inform you, Duval," he said, "that the grand jury has found a true bill against you for felony, and that you will probably be placed upon your trial to-morrow."

"Don't say probably, my friend," said Duval. "Say certainly, for you know as well as I, that all this was arranged beforehand."

"Oh, no; I don't know anything, but that Jones is a relation of my wife's, that's all."

As he spoke, the clerk dropped upon the floor of the cell a little piece of paper, and then hurried away, and the door was closed again by the turnkey who had come with him.

Duval was rather surprised, as he might well be, to see the clerk drop, in so mysterious a manner, a piece of paper in the cell, and he only waited until the bolts of the massive door were shot into their sockets before picking it up and examining it.

Upon the paper were these words—

"Do not prejudice yourself by any attempt to escape. All will be well. Those are working for you, who will not desert you."

"Now what am I to think of this," said Duval, "I wonder? I should like to know who wrote it, and how much reliance I ought to place upon it. Let me see. He said his wife was a relation to Jones. There's something in that, for Jones has promised to do something if his gratitude don't go off before a few hours are over his head, as the gratitude of human nature is but too apt to evaporate. Well, we shall see; but it is rather needless to tell me not to escape, for I don't think with the few means I have that I could do it. I don't like to lose all to-night though, nor will I, unless I have better reasons than I have at present for doing so."

In the course of another hour, Duval's rations for the day were brought to him, and then in a growling manner the man who attended upon him, said—

"Your lawyer is coming to see you."

"Very well," said Duval; "why don't you bring him here?"

"Oh, he is having a kind of palaver with the governor first, you see.— Ha! ha!"

Duval did not like to hear that exactly, but he did not think it was prudent to say anything to the turnkey about it, so he heard the information in silence, and it was full a quarter of an hour after the man had left the cell, that the door was opened again and the attorney was ushered in.

"Well, Duval," he said. "How are you now?"

"Much as usual," said Duval.

The attorney listened to the steps of the retreating turnkey, and then he said—

"In all my practice, and in all that I have heard of the practice of others who have had great experience, I never knew of such a determined attempt to get any one hung as the authorities are making in your case."

"Indeed!"

"Yes. There is something more in it than we are at all aware of. Do you know of anything which could bring down upon you the enmity of people in very high quarters indeed?"

"No—but I know of something that ought to make some people in high quarters be a little grateful to me."

"Ah then, that's the secret."

"How do you mean?"

"Why, that it's one of the most difficult and rare matters of the world to make a friend of one great person without making a foe of another."

"There may be truth in that; and now you mention it, I am rather inclined to think that there is a lady——"

"Who is anxious that you should be hanged?"

"Possibly."

"I will conceal nothing from you, Duval. When I reached the prison this morning, about half-an-hour ago, and, as your legal adviser, demanded an interview with you privately, which I am empowered in that capacity to do. I was shown into the private house of the governor, where he and the chaplain were waiting to receive me. With much politeness they informed me that I should be doing myself a professional injury by putting off your trial, or by any means rescuing you from your impending fate, while at the same time they intimated

CLAUDE ROBS THE PARSON OF HIS WATCH.

to me that the queen was engaged in some law suits in which I should be employed if I would assist in your condemnation."

"The queen?"

"Yes; they boldly mentioned Queen Charlotte, and the chaplain muttered something about the Bishop of London being anxious upon the point. Now, how is it on earth that you have succeeded in making such enemies as those, Claude Duval?   You have surely not robbed them?''

"No, I have not had the chance."

"Then, how is it?"

"By holding my tongue when they wanted me to speak, that was all.   I know something that they want to know, and they could not get it from me, so they would hang me in spite."

"And you would rather die than tell?"

"I would."

"Well, Duval, you are a brave man, I must say.   Is it a something that you feel yourself bound to keep it from me likewise?"

"It is.   A secret, if it travel out of the hand that holds it, is a secret no longer. But what reply did you make to the governor concerning his proposal to you?"

"Scouted it."

"I am glad to hear you say that.   Have you any news for me?"

"Yes; a man of the name of Jones has been to me, but I was very cautious with him, as I doubted him much."

"I think you may trust him; I saved his life this morning."

"So he told me; but of course, knowing that the authorities were not very particular about what they were doing in your case, I felt bound to be doubly cautious.   His errand to me was to concoct a plan for your escape at the trial, by preventing the witnesses from appearing."

"Can it be done?"

"It would be difficult and very liable to failure.   Of course, if it could be done, it must answer the purpose; but there is the doubt, and we are to have another meeting about it, for to tell you the truth, until I had seen you I did not like to enter into his plans, although he did seem anxious enough about your safety."

"In my opinion," said Duval, "you may trust him with the most perfect confidence; but by what you have said about the queen and the bishop of London, you have awakened in me a mountain of thought."

"What is it?"

Duval was silent for a few moments, and then he said—

"I do not think that I am betraying any confidence in what I am about to say to you, so I will say it at once.   The anger of the queen and the bishop has been vowed against me, because I have been able to do a kind thing to the Prince of Wales—and, in fact, I know what they want to know."

"Ah, I see."

"You begin to see?'

"I do.   The Whigs are in power, and they have taken the Prince of Wales by the hand, and promise him a greater sum of money in opposition to the Tory parties, which is supported by the queen and the bishop of London.   They are anxious to find such matters against the prince as shall have the effect, if laid before parliament, of making it impossible to pass the bill for the grant to him, and which they think, if passed, will bind him to the Whig party for ever.'

"Just so."

"And you know these things?"

"Some of them."

"I am glad to hear it.   The prince is the person to apply to.   Why, the the papers report that it was only last week he went at an early hour to the door of the queen's bed-room, and giving it a kick enough to break the panel, shouted out—'Bravo, Wilkes!'"

Duval laughed.

"I have heard as much," he said; "but are they not about to send Alderman Wilkes to the Tower?"

"So I hear; but they are rather afraid of a popular commotion, in consequence of such an act.   However, if at any juncture the prince feels disposed to assist his friends, this is it."

"What course would you advise me to adopt?"

"You should write to him, and I will undertake the delivery of the letter."

Duval paused for a moment or two, and then he said—

"There is one very serious difficulty in the case."

"What is that?"

"The Prince of Wales will be left to think that it is a threat that if he does not assist me, I will divulge to his enemies what I know to his detriment."

"Oh, you mustn't be so particular."

"Yes, I must. I would not have him think that on any account—no, not for my life's sake. But I will write to him, for a man in my extremity should do what he can to save himself. Yes, I will write to him, but you must be careful to let the letter get into no hands but his."

"That I will take care of. The prince is counting the popularity of the people now, as he is in full opposition to the court, and he rides every day in the park, and is ready and willing to answer any one who will speak with him. They say that he has been advised to such a course, and he is gaining friends every hour by it."

"Very well; then I will write, if you can provide me with the means of so doing in this place."

"I have them about me."

The attorney produced a little bottle of ink, with a screw stopper to it, and a piece of paper.

"Now, Duval," he said, "write your letter, and I think I can promise that in two or three hours at the outside, it will be in the hands of the Prince of Wales."

"Very good," said Duval. "I only hope it will be effectual." He then wrote as follows:—

"To His Royal Highness, the Prince of Wales.

"Your Royal Highness,—That which I happen to know, and which your Royal Highness thinks, in honour, I ought to keep locked up in my own bosom, shall there remain, and go with me out of the world, if I am doomed to die. Such is my fixed determination, and, therefore, I do not write to say that anything will unclose my lips, but I write as a man who is to undergo an unjust trial may write to a prince who may think proper to save him. I am accused of commiting a robbery, on the evening of the 24th of last October. I do not recollect where I was upon that evening, but I do recollect that I never saw my accusers.

"They are going to try me to-morrow, and hang me on Monday. It is not fair, for I have no time to inquire of others where I was and what I was about upon the date in question; I ask, therefore, for delay, and that I should not be caught and murdered like a mad dog, upon a charge that I am innocent of.

"Long life to your royal highness. This is from your obedient servant, and one who hopes yet to live a little longer to be so,—CLAUDE DUVAL."

"What do you think of it?" said Duval, when the attorney read it.

"It will do very well."

"Then take it with you. It is but a clumsy affair, I admit, but a man can't be supposed to write his best in a cell in Newgate, with his life hanging upon a thread."

"Certainly not. I will take care the prince has it, and will bring you back his answer as soon as I get it. Be of good cheer, for there's great hopes now for you."

CHAPTER CXXII.

DUVAL GETS A ROYAL AUTOGRAPH.

DUVAL felt his mind a little at ease now that he had made some sort of effort towards his deliverance from the straits he was then in; but there was one thing that he had nearly forgotten, and that was, that there was a house of his at Hornsey to which it behoved him, at all events, to pay some little attention.

He was only just in time to call the attorney as he was going away, and speak to him upon that subject.

"Perhaps," said Duval, "you are not aware that I have a wife?"

"Indeed, no."

"Well, it's a fact, and it's possible enough, you see, that she would like to know how I am. The public papers will soon enough tell her where I am; so I should be obliged if you will send to the address I will give you, and say that things are going on as well as may be with me."

"You had better write, and I will post it."

"Ah, well, perhaps that will be the best; and yet I don't know either. Might not that have the effect of opening the eyes of other people to the fact that I have a home?"

"It is possible; but I presume you don't keep house in the name of Claude Duval, do you?"

"Not exactly."

"Then there can be but little difficulty in the matter after all; but if you prefer it, I will send to your home, or if it be not a very great distance off, I will go myself."

"It is not a great distance, and if you can go, you will be able to say more in a few words than I could write in a hundred."

"I will, then. Give me the address, and I promise you that I will go before I see you again."

Duval gave him the exact name and address of his house at Hornsey, and then he said,—

"Now, sir, I am going to say something that you ought to have said, and that is, that I look upon all that you are doing for me as done in the way of business, and I shall, if I am so lucky as to get free, be quite prepared to pay you handsomely; and if I do not escape from this affair, then she to whom I have given you a message will discharge your claims against me."

"Oh, don't mention that."

"But it is right that in a business matter your remuneration should be placed upon a right basis."

"Very well, Duval; I see you know how to manage lawyers now. Good-by, and expect good tidings from me."

"I will."

The lawyer left the prison, and Duval was alone.

"Now," said Duval, "I will leave a memorial in this cell that I have been here, and when any one else is in this dismal place, he will call it Duval's Cell, and it shall be known as that for many a day to come; so here goes. I wonder if it will be well seen in a good light?"

Duval had an old nail in his pocket that he had picked up unobserved by the officers in the hackney coach that had conveyed him to Bow-street and back again to Newgate, and with the sharp end of it he succeeded in cutting on the flat stone wall of his cell the following verses, which are still to be seen in Newgate, although the cell that was occupied by the celebrated highwayman is no longer in use, but the officials know it, and some who have been many years in office in Newgate call it Duval's Cell.

"Claude Duval was in Newgate thrown,
　　For a crime that wasn't a bit of his own;
　　And the beaks declared, that decreed it should be,
　　Duval should swing on the gallows tree.
　　　　　　　　　　Higho, chivey, higho!

"But Claude Duval knew a thing or two,
　　And of tricks of his trade he knew just a few;
　　He laughed as he sat in the old stone cell,
　　And he thought a fresh canter were just as well.
　　　　　　　　　　Higho, chivey, higho!

" ' The time hangs heavy,' said Claude Duval;
' 'Tis better to list to the wild birds' call,
Than wait for the beaks with the darbies ringing,
Which isn't the very best sort of singing.'
Higho, chivey, higho!

" He took a thought of his galloping mare,
Of swag on the roads, so rich and so rare;
And when the beaks thought they would give him a fall,
' Good-day, to your honours,' says Claude Duval.
Higho, chivey, higho."

"Plague take it! I am not in the verse-making mood to-day," said Duval, as he put the old nail in his waistcoat pocket, "so I shan't do any more; and what I have done I don't much like. One can't be always up to the mark; and when the mind is weary and the spirits flag, and you feel half worn out, and just for all the world as if you could lie down and go to sleep for an age, and bid the world good-night, without caring if the morning between you and it came again, how the deuce can you compose either prose or poetry? So there's an end of it. And now for a slumber."

Duval threw himself upon the floor of the cell; but he had not been there above a moment or two when, as if the fates had determined to keep him from any repose, the door was opened, and in walked the governor, with his clerk a few paces behind him.

"What the deuce now?" cried Duval. "I tell you what it is, I shall leave these lodgings without any notice, if you don't leave me alone, and let me have a little quiet."

"Duval," said the governor, "I come to you as a friend to you. Of course you can easily conceive that I pity very much the melancholy situation you are in at this juncture."

"No, I can't," said Duval.

"But I assure you——"

"Oh, then I agree with you. I have not the smallest doubt of your assurance."

The governor looked angry.

"Give me leave to say, Duval, that this is not only a foolish, but it is an ungrateful reception to one who comes to do you a kindness."

"It would be," said Duval.

"And it is."

"I shall be better able to say yes or no to that proposition, Mr. Governor, when I know what it is that you call a kindness."

"Very well. Be it so. In the first place, then, I may remark that I am very much afraid that I am outstepping the lines of duty in coming to you at all, just now, and that I ought not to do it."

"Well, it's quite optional, you know," said Duval. "There's the door, and you can but go again. There's one thing, too, you may make sure of, and that, is that I shall not come to you "

"Well, well! we will let that pass."

"Go on, then."

"I have had a conversation with a gentleman upon your case, who feels that it would be a sad thing if a young man of your talents and general acquirements were to go out of the world in such a dreadful way, as by the hands of the hangman!"

"Give my compliments to the gentleman, and tell him that I quite agree with him."

"I will; but he and I have arranged that such an appeal is to be made in your favour to high quarters, that we are fully sure that at the last moment you will be saved."

"Thank you!"

" You don't seem to be much elated at it."

" Oh, yes, I am ; but I never make much account of things before they happen, so you see I am never greatly depressed at misfortunes, nor over-elated at the idea that anything extraordinary is likely to occur in the way of good fortune to me. It is much the best to take everything in an easy way."

" Perhaps it is ; but, of course, if we are able to do anything for you in the way we wish, it must be upon the plea that you are very contrite for the past. In fact, we can urge nothing else."

" Oh !"

" And so you quite comprehend that—that, in fact——"

" I'll be hanged if I do," said Duval ; " and I suppose you will tell me I shall be hanged if I don't ?"

" Ha ! ha !" laughed the governor, in a forced manner. " Ha ! ha ! A very good joke ; but not, just now, very seasonable, I think. Were I you, I should be rather too seriously inclined to joke as you do."

" Were you me, governor, you would do as I do ; but, as you say, truly, all that is not to the purpose. What more have you to say as a consequence of this new-born sympathy with me ?"

" Why, I have now to point out to you the course which the gentleman and I have decided upon as the best for you to pursue, in order that you may aid our exertions as much as possible."

" Oh ! very good. What is the course ?"

" It is, to-morrow, when you are put upon your trial, to plead at once guilty to the indictment."

The clerk, who was about three paces behind the governor, immediately held up a piece of paper above his head, so that Duval should see it, upon which, in large characters, was the one word—

" No !"

Duval nodded, and the clerk immediately put the paper into his pocket again. The governor had an odd sort of suspicion that Duval was looking at something over his head, and he faced about suddenly to the clerk, who, however, put on such a meek and stupid look that he disarmed all suspicion.

" You can wait for me, Mr. Brown," said the governor.

" Thank you, sir."

The clerk left the cell, and then the governor putting on a look of as familiar pleasantry as possible, added—

" Of course, this is a private interview, and on the whole, I rather approve of your being reserved before the clerk. Now we can talk freely.—You will, then, plead, as I say, guilty to-morrow ?"

" Oh, no."

" No?"

" Certainly not. I couldn't think of such a thing."

" But really consider now, while I convince you that ——"

" It's of no use your talking. Unless you can convince me that I did the special robbery they charge me with, which I am convinced I had nothing to do with, I will not plead guilty ; and as I know you cannot convince me of that, inasmuch as the robbery never was committed at all, and it is a mere made up case, you may spare your arguments on the subject, and me the trouble of listening to them."

" Do you really mean to tell me," said the governor, " that for a little peccadillo of this sort, you will refuse to save your life ?"

" Yes."

" Oh, nonsense, nonsense ! Now, Duval, you are joking with me ; but I find I must be more explicit with you. I am empowered by certain parties whom I must not name, to make you a certain promise, which is, that if you plead guilty, you will be reprieved on the scaffold."

" Ah, that will be too late."

" Too late ?"

"Yes, to be sure. If once you get me on to the scaffold, I'd just as soon be hanged as not."

"Impossible."

"Yes, I would; and besides, do you know, if it got as far as that through me pleading guilty, I'm afraid something might happen to the messenger with the reprieve, and he would arrive too late by a few minutes, so that I don't mean to run the risk, if it's all the same to you, Mr. Governor."

"Then do you mean to tell me that you are so pig-headed as to refuse an actual offer of your life from an illustrious person when it is made to you, just because it is done in the illustrious person's way, and not in yours?"

"That's just it."

"Very good—ve-ry good, Mister Duval. Oh, you will repent of this, that you will. Very good, sir; I have done my duty, and made the offer, and there's an end of it. Oh, it don't matter to me one straw one way or the other, so I bid you good-day, and leave you to your own folly and obstinacy."

"Thank you."

The governor strode to the door, and then turning round, he said in a softened tone—

"Oh, Claude Duval, do not send me away with a refusal to the illustrious person. Think again. It is for your own good I speak, Duval, and to save you from an ignominious death."

"How affecting!" said Duval; "if the gammon did not so much predominate over everything else, I do believe that you would draw tears from the fetters that I have on me."

The governor did not say another word, but bounced from the cell, mightily chagrined at his discomfiture.

"That's over," said Duval, and once more he laid himself down to rest; but this visit of the governor had had the effect of disturbing his mind, if it had failed in the object it was intended to promote, merely to betray him into going quietly to death, for there cannot be a doubt but that the object was to get Duval lulled into fancied security up to the very moment when the fatal cord would be about his neck, and then nothing would be easier that to destroy him.

A writer of the period, speaking about the abuses of Newgate, says—

"Claude Duval was once induced, or attempted to be induced, by every possible means, to plead guilty to the mock charge that was brought against him; but he would not, and to that constancy he owed his life, for there were two great personages in the realm, a male and a female, who wished him dead for vengeance's sake, and would have done anything that they could, without publicly exhibiting their malice, to destroy him."

These two personages were, no doubt, the queen and the then Bishop of London. The latter Duval had deceived at the Palace of St. James's, and the former he had annoyed by not disclosing what he knew of the Prince of Wales's proceedings at Kew, which knowledge was, no doubt, believed to be much more extensive than it really was.

"It is a hard thing," said Duval, "that my life should be so hunted. It is true enough that I have done many an act that makes me amenable to the law, but, strange to say, it is not for one of those acts that I am to be persecuted, but for something that I never did at all."

Duval thought over the matter, until, full of weariness, and amid the silence of his cell, he fell fast asleep, and was only roused by the door suddenly opening, and a voice uttering his name.

CHAPTER CXXIII.

DUVAL FINDS TWO UNEXPECTED WITNESSES IN HIS FAVOUR.

"Hilloa! who calls?" said Duval, as he sprang to his feet and rubbed his eyes to thoroughly awaken himself.

The gleam of a light that some one carried made him wink again, and then he saw the turnkey and his attorney at the cell door.

"Oh, it is you, sir?" said Duval.

"It is. Leave us, Mr. Turnkey."

"You must be busy, sir. It only wants twenty minutes of our time to shut all up for the night."

"I shall be ready to go in that time; and as you are a civil fellow, there is a guinea for you."

"Thank, your honour; you needn't hurry for a minute or two."

The cell door was closed upon Duval and the attorney.

"I quite forgot," said Duval, "when you were here last, that I had money, and there is no occasion for you to be any out of pocket. Take what you like out of that lot, and leave me a trifle. I shall not want any, I suppose, as, let what will come of it, my stay will be short in Newgate."

"No, Duval; keep your ready money. You don't know in what sudden emergency it may be useful to you, and I can put all down in the bill of costs."

"Very well. Mind you don't forget any of it."

"A lawyer is not likely to do that, Duval. But I bring you news—I have seen the Prince of Wales."

"Ah!"

"Yes—I handed him your letter, and he read it, while I walked, with my hat in my hand, by the side of his horse. He then took a pencil from his pocket, and wrote upon the back of your note what you will there see."

Duval, tremblingly, held the letter to the light which the turnkey had left with the attorney, and he saw, written in a straggling hand in pencil, the following words—

"You say that they will hang you like a dog; but I think I can bring a couple of cats to save you.   "GEORGE."

"Is that all?" said Duval.

"Yes; after he had written that, he just touched his hat to me, and off he rode. I must confess I didn't know what to make of it."

"Nor I."

Duval read the few words again, and then, with a shake of the head, he said—

"It's a royal autograph, at all even's, let there come what will of it; and I don't think he would have written these words without a meaning, though how two cats are to save me, I don't know."

"If the prince knows, that will suffice."

"Assuredly it will, and the more I think of it, the more I feel a kind of confidence that he will be as good as his word. Did you give him your address, so that he might send any one to you."

"I did—I give it to him along with the letter, and he put it into his waistcoat pocket, so it is just possible that I may hear something from him; and, in that case, I will let you know in the morning. And now, I may tell you that I have been to Hornsey, likewise."

"Ah! how is she when you saw there?"

"I found her distracted with grief, for the idea was that you were dead, as no news of your incarceration in Newgate had reached there. The mere fact that you were alive and well was so satisfactory, that it almost obliterated the grief at your rather equivocal position, and I left your wife much more calm than when I found her. I gave her what hopes I could of your safety."

"Did you see my man, Luke?"

"I did; the fellow was ready to eat me up with joy, and came part of the way back with me. He begged me to tell you that he had your horse quite safe in the stable, and that he hoped soon to see you on the back of it again."

"Amen!" said Duval. "No one can hope that more sincerely than I do, although I believe that Luke hopes it from the bottom of his heart. But now I have news for you."

THE EXAMINATION BEFORE THE MAGISTRATE.

Duval then briefly told the attorney how the governor had come to him to try to persuade him to plead guilty in the morning, and how steadily he had refused to do so.

"It is a mere plea to entrap you," said the lawyer; "but the best thing you could have done would have been to have deceived him."

" How mean you ?"

" Why, the fact is, Duval, you must fight such men with their own weapons. I should, if I had had any idea that such an attempt would have been made, advised you to seem to acquiesce, to throw them off their guard against you, and then in the morning I would have boldly pleaded not guilty in spite of them ; for it is just possible now that they will, as the grand jury is sitting, prefer another indictment against you."

" I did not think of that."

" No, it is not very likely that you would ; but it would be a very awkward thing if you were acquitted of the first charge, and then find that there was another quite ready against you."

" It would ; is it too late to retract the error, for I agree with you, that the only way you can meet such frightful duplicity, is by a course of conduct that will throw it off its guard. I will see the governor again, if you think it is worth while."

" I would advise you."

" Hush ! I hear footsteps ; some one comes."

The door of the cell was opened, and the chaplain of Newgate presented himself with such a pleasant sort of smile upon his face, that one would have thought his errand was quite one of mercy and love instead of the most rank hypocrisy.

" Duval," he said, " I have come here, as your legal adviser is present, not for the purpose of disturbing you in any consultation, for the time has come when he must leave the prison, but for the purpose of urging you once more in his presence to embrace the certainty of a reprieve that is held out to you, if you will only plead guilty to-morrow, so as to make your conduct look like contrition."

" Exactly so, sir." said the attorney. " Duval has been telling me that some such advice was tended to him, and I was just regretting, as you came in, that he had thought proper to reject so fair an offer."

" Were you, sir, indeed ?"

" Yes, he was," said Duval, " and I must own that the arguments he used rather staggered me ; but I suppose it is now too late."

" Oh, no, not at all. It gives me the greatest satisfaction and pleasure to think that you have so very judicious a legal adviser about you. The fact is, you see, sir,"—here the chaplain looked very mysteriously at the attorney—"the fact is, that there is a high personage who wishes to save Duval."

The attorney nodded.

" But," continued the chaplain, " of course a high personage must have something to go upon, and Duval pleading guilty with a contrite look, would be that something—you understand ?"

" Oh, it is quite clear."

" You are," said the chaplain, placing his finger by the side of his nose, " a very remarkable acute practitioner, indeed."

" Sir, you—really—a—a—upon my word—such flattery !"

" Oh, no—no ; not flattery. It is my candid opinion, and I will just confidentially tell you both what the high personage said,—' Let Duval,' said the high personage, ' plead guilty, and own the justice of his sentence—let him attend to the chaplain's exhortations, and show, by his speech and manner, that he is deeply impressed with the enormity of his offences—let him be conducted quietly to the place of public execution, so that there may be an impression made upon the multitude, and then he will be reprieved at the last moment for a certainty.' Those were the words of the great personage."

" And very satisfactory ones, too," said the attorney, giving Duval a slight kick as he spoke.

" Oh, very," said Duval. " Who is the great personage, sir ?"

" There," said the chaplain, " you must both excuse me. I am pledged to secrecy. I do not think, indeed, you will ever know exactly who the great personage is ; but provided you are saved, what does it matter ?"

" Oh, nothing at all."

"Then you consent?"

"Most assuredly I do. How can I do better than consent to what will save my life? By the advice of my solicitor, I assent in every way to the kind proposition."

"Ve—ry good. Then, Duval, let me congratulate you that next Monday morning your troubles will be over, and I am quite sure that I shall never hear you complain of the neat little arrangement."

"Of that I have no doubt," said Duval, "and I feel quite sure that you, sir, will perform your part in the affair. It would be quite as impossible for this roof to fall in upon your head suddenly, as for a minister of the gospel to deceive any one in such a matter as life and death."

The chaplain gave a start, and looked up at the arched stone roof of the cell.

"Oh, sir, it is not coming," said the attorney.

"Coming? oh, no—no! of course it is not. How very absurd of me! But, as you say, Duval, it is impossible that I can deceive you. So, now, good night. I hear the turnkey coming to tell us all that the time is up, and the cells must be closed for the night."

The solicitor shook hands with Duval, but the chaplain did not offer to do so. Perhaps he felt himself too Judas-like to do it. He rather hurriedly left the cell accompanied by the solicitor, who having previously come to a perfect understanding with Duval, only gave him a nod as much as to say,—"It's all right, now: you understand what the enemy would be at."

Duval listened to their retreating footsteps, and then as he flung himself down upon his rather hard bed, and covered himself up with the rug that was allowed him as a counterpane, he said—

"Oh, that human nature, and parsons in particular, should be so given to lying."

Duval was rather prejudiced against the church. For our own parts, we do not think that parsons nor even bishops are much more given to lying than other people.

Very probably that night in Newgate was not half so weary a one to Duval as it was to many out of it; but he had some very comical dreams.

His thoughts evidently were upon the curious note that the Prince of Wales had sent to him, and he fancied that after he had been condemned, and the judge had solemnly pronounced his sentence, two large cats came into the court, and one of them twitched off the black cap from the judge's head, while the other got on the front of the dock, and said—

"Claude Duval, lay hold of my tail, and fear nothing."

He then thought that he did lay hold of the cat's tail, and that she immediately after, spitting and foaming at everybody, swelled up to the size of an elephant, and then flew out at one of the top windows of the court, with him hold of her tail. The other cat then, he thought, cried out—

"This is the way we prevent a *catastrophe*."

Duval laughed so in his sleep at this, that it fairly awoke him, and he found himself cold and shivering in his gloomy cell.

"How ridiculous," he said, as he turned on his other side, and in a few minutes went to sleep again. That second sleep was a profound and dreamless one, and it was not disturbed until a rough voice cried—

"Six o'clock, Claude Duval, and here's an artist wants to take you off."

"Take me off?" cried Duval.

"Yes, he says it will sell capitally, so he begs that you will sit still for half an hour, while he does it. Here he is. The sheriff has given him a pass into Newgate."

"Yes, Duval," said a grinning ape of a fellow, sidling into the cell. "I will make a sketch of you in your fetters, and after your sentence it will sell well, and I will get you, if you please, likewise, to write your name at the corner, of which I will have a facsimile taken; so you see it will be all in proper business-like order, won't it, eh? Ha! ha!"

Duval made but two strides towards the unhappy artist, and seizing him by the nose, he held that organ as though it had been in a vice.

"Oh—oh! Murder! murder!"

"What's the row now?" said the turnkey, as he lazily returned to the cell.

"Nothing particular," said Duval. "I am only quietly advising this gentleman to take himself off, instead of me, that's all."

"Murder!—my nose! Help!—oh, death! Murder!"

Duval let him go, and then as he turned to leave the cell, he aided his retreat by giving him an impetus behind that sent him right into the arms of the turnkey.

"Ulloo! Where are you a-coming to?"

"Oh, let me go—let me leave the ruffian, who has no taste for the fine arts! Where's the door? Oh, he has ruined my nose."

"Be off with you, will you?"

The discomfited artist rushed along the narrow passages of Newgate, and was lost to both sight and hearing of Duval.

"Rather cool that," said Duval. "What next, I wonder. I suppose I shall ave some one coming to ask for my last dying speech and confession, and telling ne very composedly that it will be worth something as a business fetch after my execution."

"No, Duval," said the turnkey, as he came back, "they will get up that without troubling you, and I would lay a wager of a hundred guineas to one, that vey are getting all that up in the Dials now."

"I shouldn't wonder."

"Lord bless you, they set to work upon such matters in good time."

"They must, or they would not get them out in the way they do; but I suppose it is one of the things one must put up with as the price of celebrity. And now I don't care how soon I have some breakfast."

Duval's liberality had not been thrown away in Newgate. The turnkeys provided him with a luxurious breakfast, which he took good care to do justice to; and by the time he had finished it, he was told that the court was near the time f opening, and that his solicitor would be glad to see him.

Duval was full of impatience to see him, and at once requested that he might be rought to his cell. The moment the solicitor appeared, Duval said eagerly—

"Any news from the——"

"Hush!"

"Yes, yes. I understand; but you know who I mean?"

"I do. He has sent some one to me, who says, there will be distinctly proved n alibi."

CHAPTER CXXIV.

DUVAL IS TRIUMPHANTLY ACQUITTED AT THE OLD BAILEY.

THE tone and manner of the solicitor as he gave this information to Duval, as quite sufficient to show that he felt rather confident as to the result of the ial.

Perhaps he, the solicitor, had information that Duval had not, and so from at deduced a confidence that the prisoner could not feel. To the apprehensions of ur highwayman acquaintance, it did not seem that there was much in the nformation.

"You don't seem," said the lawyer, "to be rejoiced."

"No," replied Duval. "I must confess I expected something better than he production of people who would indulge in a little hard swearing at the rial."

"Never mind what they indulge in," said the solicitor, "so long as they save ou."

"Granted; but do you think really that so stale a device, as the attempt to prove an alibi will have any effect upon the court and the jury?"

"I do."

"Well, I defer to your better judgment, then."

"Understand me, Duval," said the lawyer. "You or I could easily have produced parties who would have deliberately sworn you were anywhere at the time that the alleged robbery was committed; but would the court believe them?"

"Hardly."

"Upon that, then, I ground my hopes. If the Prince of Wales should produce any one to make such a statement, the probability is, that it will be some one that the court must believe."

"There is something in that."

"There is everything in it; and now let me advise you to say nothing, with the exception of a general denial of the charge, for a certainty that you did not commit it, although you are unable to say where you were on the night in question."

"I see."

"You understand that if you were to make any statement, you might be severely committing those who will come forward, and——"

"Hush," said Duval, "I hear footsteps."

The attorney was prudently silent in a moment, and then the cell door was opened, and a couple of officers made their appearance, accompanied by the governor of Newgate.

"Your time has come, Duval," said the governor.

"What do you mean?" said Duval. "Do you want to hang me out off-hand without judge or jury?"

"No; but you must come into court to plead. You are wanted, and I hope if things should go wrong with you, you will at least admit that you met with civil treatment here from me."

"I think my best plan," said Duval, "is to admit nothing, but leave all that to my legal adviser."

"As you please," said the governor; "you will please to follow me, though, in the meantime, for the judge wont be kept waiting, if he can help it."

"Who is sitting to-day?" said Duval.

The governor turned to him with a smile, and mentioned the name of a judge who had acquired a very amiable notoriety for his severity and his liking to condemn poor wretches to the gallows when he could possibly find a pretext to do so.

"Oh!" said Duval, "it's he, is it?"

"Yes; a very humane man is he."

"Very likely. He is called the hanging judge, I have heard; but not he, nor all the judges, and all the princes in the land, can hang a man, unless he is proved to be guilty, in this country, that's a comfort."

"Oh, a great comfort!" said the governor. "A very great comfort, indeed, Claude Duval; and we all suspect very much that you are as innocent as one of the Babes in the Wood."

The chaplain was hovering round the door of the cell. There could be no means of doubt, but that all the officials of Newgate looked upon Claude Duval as a condemned man. It was so generally understood, that when a man of his notoriety got fairly into the clutches of the law, that there was an end to his career, that they could not for a moment bring themselves to think that he had a chance of escape.

"I will wait for you when the trial is over," said the chaplain.

"Thank you," said Duval; "but I shall go home when I am acquitted!"

"Acquitted?" said the governor. "Oh—oh!"

"Alas!" said the chaplain, "he is very obdurate."

"Yes," said Duval; "and, with all due deference to you, he will continue to be so. Lead on—I'll follow, Mr. Governor."

The governor seemed, as in truth he was, anything but pleased at the easy and confident air and manner of his prisoner ; but he could not believe it possible that he would escape the sentence of death that was virtually passed upon him by the judge and jury already.

The route from the cell to the court of the Old Bailey was then a much more intricate one than it is now, and it took about seven or eight minutes' walking to reach the dock. The moment Duval appeared, there was a buzz and a conversation in the court, which was crowded to excess.

The prisoner was surprised to see before him, and on both sides of him, nothing but a sea of faces ; but the fact was, that the news of Claude Duval's arrest, and committed for trial so rapidly, had soon spread over London, and everybody believing, as indeed they might well do, that the career of that famous criminal was just upon its end, the greatest exertions had been made by thousands to be present at his trial.

Of course, only those succeeded in getting into the court who, in the most liberal manner, feed the door-keepers ; and it was calculated that there was a crowd without, that, at a moderate computation, could not comprise less than three thousand persons, all eager for admission.

Upon the bench sat almost the whole of the high civic authorities who had a right to be there, including the Lord Mayor ; and there was among the barristers at the table, several Members of Parliament, and others who had been attracted by curiosity to see Duval, concerning whom the most strange and extravagant stories had been circulated.

In his anxiety concerning his own affairs, Duval had quite forgotten that he was such a public character as he now found himself, and he rather shrank from the amount of observation that he found he now caused.

The appearance of Claude, as the reader by this time is well aware, was strikingly in his favour ; and so far does appearance go with the mob of mankind, that there were many who thought, when they saw him, it would surely be a great pity to hang so very handsome a man.

Perhaps those who thought so were principally the ladies, for a very unusual number of the fair sex had pushed their way into the court to hear the trial.

It was asserted by the door-keeper, that since the court had been built there had not been so many ladies in it at one time.

The judge was evidently in no very good humour. The evident interest that the prisoner excited, from his youthful and handsome appearance, appeared to gall him wonderfully. Surely it could not be that his own ugliness looked so much the more ugly, in consequence of the contrast with the manly beauty of the man who came before him to be tried upon a charge affecting his life ?

Certainly, there was not a person present in the court who did not observe, when they turned their eyes again upon the judge, that there was a scowl upon his face that had not been there before.

It is not often that the Old Bailey practitioners of the law take a great interest in a prisoner ; but, upon this occasion, there had never been known such an attendance of gentlemen of the long robe.

When in court, all their eyes were bent upon Claude Duval.

The attorney-general, who was in court, bent a long and earnest gaze upon the prisoner, and then turned to his notes, which he diligently examined, for he was to conduct the case against Duval on behalf of the crown, which was prosecuting in that instance as was usual in such cases.

" Officers," said the judge, when he found that the buzz of conversation, and the hiss of many whispers, anything but subsided. " Officers, will you take into custody any one who you may observe disturbing the quiet of the court ?"

This was a threat that had its effect, although no one was taken in custody, but the officers made a show of great activity, and pushed some of the most quiet and noffensive of the spectators out of the place, so that the judge was satisfied that something had been done.

With his eyes half shut, then, he leant back in his chair, and calmly waited the course of events.

"Prisoner at the bar," said the clerk of the arraigns, "do you answer to the name of Claude Duval?"

All eyes were turned upon Claude, who in a clear musical voice, that was strangely in contrast with the rapid nasal twang of the clerk, said—

"I do."

The clerk then read the indictment in the way that indictments are usually read at the Old Bailey, that is to say, in such a style that if they were written in Sanscrit there would be about as much chance of learning what it was all about, as there is in a vain attempt to listen to the confused gabble of the clerk.

Everybody here knew that this was, after all, but a mere form, and they just heard towards the end of it that Claude Duval had done something against the peace of our Sovereign Lord, the King.

"Prisoner at the bar," then said the clerk, "do you plead guilty or not guilty to the charge that is entered in the indictment now read?"

The governor fully expected that he would plead guilty, and he had almost got ready to take him from the court again, when, to his indignation, Claude Duval said in a firm voice—

"Not guilty."

"Hurrah!" cried a voice in the crowd.

The judge sprang from his seat, but immediately resumed it again, and while his lips turned white with passion, he said in a low tone—

"Officers, bring that person before me, if you please."

This was easier said than done. The officers had all the will in the world to bring "that person" before the court, but either no one could find out who it was, or really no one would do so; and after the most anxious inquiries, no one, with any semblance of justice, could be laid hold of as the guilty party.

While the search for the indecorous interrupter of the court was going on, the eyes of the judge, with a flashing expression, were here, there, and everywhere, and at length they settled upon the face of Duval, which wore a very quiet kind of smile.

"Officers," said the judge again. "Where is the man who interrupted the court?"

"We can't find him, my lord,' said one of the officers.

"You must find him."

Again the officers pushed everybody about, and the Lord Mayor offered a reward of five pounds; but it was of no avail. The man could not be found.

"You cannot discover the author of the outrage upon the decency and the solemnity of the court?" said the judge.

"No, my lord," replied the principal officer.

The judge turned to one of the sheriffs.

"It is quite clear, Mr. Sheriff," he said, "that the officers of the court are entirely unfit for their duty."

The sheriff bowed.

"Therefore I hope they will at the end of the sessions be all discharged, Mr. Sheriff."

The sheriff bowed again, and the judge, although he strongly suspected that the sheriff would see him——further, before he discharged the officers of the court, was compelled to be satisfied with the bow of acquiescence.

"Let the trial proceed," he said. "Who conducts the prosecution in this case?"

The attorney-general rose, and said—

"I have the honour to appear, my lord, in behalf of the crown, in this case."

"Very well, Mr. Attorney general; pray let us get at the facts as soon as possible."

Again the judge leaned back in his seat, and half closed his eyes, which was with him a regular habit, and the attorney-general began his speech for the prosecution.

"My Lord, and Gentlemen of the Jury,—

"The facts which I have to lay before you regarding the criminality of the prisoner at the bar, and concerning which it will be your duty, in conformity with the oaths you have this day taken in this court, to come to a judgment, lies in an exceedingly small compass.

"Gentlemen, it is a fortunate thing for society that miscreants like the one who is now at the bar of this court, are at length most certainly stopped in their career of crime by some clear case like the present, concerning which, there can be no sort of cavil or doubt whatever.

"It appears then, gentlemen of the jury, that upon the evening of the 14th of October last past, the prosecutor in the case, who will appear before you, was passing along a rather unfrequented road near to Hounslow, and that he was then and there robbed by the prisoner at the bar of certain monies. Not only will this be deposed to by the person who was so robbed, but another witness, worthy of implicit credit, will give corroborative testimony.

"Under these circumstances, it is quite needless for me to take up the time of the court by any ony declaration of facts that will best come from the lips of the witnesses ; and, therefore, I will call the person who was robbed into the witness-box, who will clearly depose to that circumstance, and identify the prisoner at the bar as the robber."

The judge mildly nodded his head, as much as to say,—"That's quite enough —it's all settled."

The same shabby-genteel looking person who accused Duval in the police office was placed in the witness-box, and he told his story in as nearly as possible the same words that he had used when at Bow-street. The other shabby person then was called, and in the same cool manner corroborated the statement. Duval was asked at the end of each of their examinations if he had any questions to ask, and he replied,—

"No. What is the use of asking men questions, who do not come here to speak the truth, but to get up a case ?"

"Have you any more witnesses, Mr. Attorney," said the jude, "to call in this case ?"

"No, my lord: I think that the case is clear."

"Oh, quite. Well, prisoner, what have you to say in answer to this clear and conclusive charge against you ?"

"I must protest," said a counsel, rising and settling his wig upon his head, "I must protest against such language from a judge to a prisoner accused of an offence, and standing at the bar of this court."

"Protest, sir !" said the judge ; "what do you mean ?"

"I mean, my lord, with all due respect for the office you fill, purely what I say, and I again say it, that it is disgraceful for a judge to prejudge a case to the jury in the way that this case is attempted to be prejudged."

"Sit down, sir !" roared the judge ; "your speaking at all is a gross impropriety, and an intrusion, and an insult to the court."

"Indeed !" said the counsel, "that is a new doctrine in an English court of justice, that for a prisoner's counsel to speak at all is an insult to the court, and an intrusion ! I appear here for the prisoner at the bar, to answer the charge now brought against him, and I will answer it in spite of any judge."

CHAPTER CXXV.

DUVAL FINDS THAT THE PRINCE IS AS GOOD AS HIS WORD.

THE judge had just discretion enough left to see that he could not with any profit to himself contend with the counsel, who was only asserting a right, concerning which there could be no dispute. The fact was, though, that neither the judge nor any one else had had the smallest idea from the mode in which the case had been conducted, that Duval had any counsel to speak for him.

The crowd in the court was evidently quite delighted at the firm stand that the counsel made against the judge; and it was only the full and complete knowledge of the fact that the officers were keeping a wary watch, and were quite anxious to

pounce upon, and apprehend somebody, that kept a demonstration of satisfaction from taking place in the court.

"My learned friend," said the attorney-general, "appears for the prisoner. It would have been but usual upon the part of my learned friend and courteous to the Court, and to the prosecution, to have let us know that."

"The fact is," said Duval's counsel, "the case has been brought forward in so vindictive and unusual a spirit, that I thought I might as well be in the fashion, although contending for the right against all that was wrong, and all the power that authority could bring to bear against my client."

"Pray attend to the case, sir," said the judge; "we don't want any extraneous remarks."

"Oh, they are galling, are they?"

"Silence, sir!"

"I will not silence. I stand here as much upon my right as you sit there. I do not like—I do not invite collisions between the bench and the bar; but I have a duty to perform here to-day, my lord, which is a higher duty than your duty, and I will do it."

The judge half closed his eyes, and bent back in his seat as though everything were going on quite pleasant; and Duval, who had no idea that counsel was engaged for him, was wondering who the daring and evidently talented individual in the wig was, who was fighting his battle with such spirit and success.

"Go on—go on," whispered the attorney-general, who was very solicitous to put an end to the contention with the judge. "Do go on. This will do no good, you know."

"Not a bit; but if we find upon——"

"Well, well.—Go on."

The counsel smiled, for he was upon private terms of great intimacy with the attorney-general, and then addressing himself to the jury, he spoke to the case:—

"Gentlemen of the Jury,—Probably appearing here as I do for the prisoner at the bar, it may appear to you surprising, that up to this moment I have said nothing, nor in any way or manner interfered with the progress of the case. It might have been supposed that I would have cross-examined the two very glib and capitally spoken persons who came into court to give their evidence against the prisoner at the bar; but I felt, gentlemen of the jury, that by saying one word to either of those witnesses I should only be throwing away the valuable time of the court, and not at all advancing the interests of my client, who I shall be able to prove to you is as innocent as you or I of the charge this day brought against him, and distinctly sworn to by the two witnesses."

The confident tone in which the counsel pronounced this last sentence evidently had its effect both upon jury and spectators. The judge did not betray by the movement of a single muscle that he even heard what the counsel said, but the attorney-general looked inquiringly curious.

"If, gentlemen of the jury," continued the counsel "I had questioned those witnesses, I should have got nothing from them but an obstinate reiteration of what they had already sworn to. That swearing consists, gentlemen of the jury, of two points. The first is, that a robbery was committed in a particular place; and the second is, that the prisoner at the bar was the person who committed the robbery. Now, gentleman, with regard to the first half of the swearing, I have nothing to say. I do not know, and as far as regards my case and my duty to my client, I do not care, whether or not a robbery such as has been by the witnesses described was committed."

The judge made a note upon the paper that lay before him.

"But," continued the counsel, "as regards the other oiety of the swearing, I can say much; and it does materially matter to my client whether that he lives or not. Gentlemen of the jury, it is, to say the very mildest of it, a very great mistake, indeed."

The two witnesses upon this, looked very indignant, and whispered to each other.

"Gentlemen," continued the counsel, "I am in a position to prove to you that when the robbery was said to be committed, the prisoner at the bar was some ten or eleven miles from the place mentioned; and if such were the case, he must have had a very long arm, indeed, in order to rob the person who this day has deliberately sworn to his identity."

"You intend to attempt to prove an alibi?" said the attorney-general.

"No—it is no attempt.—It is positive and undoubted."

"Oh, very well. It is nothing to me."

"Yes, it is much to you. Gentlemen of the jury, my learned friend says it is nothing to him, but I say it is much to him, for I know my learned friend well, and I am perfectly aware that nothing will give him such genuine satisfaction as to see the prisoner at the bar walk from this court a free man this day after being acquitted by you of the crime so unjustly laid to his charge."

The attorney-general smiled slightly, and the brows of the judge came down so low over his eyes, that they were completely hidden, with the exception of a small twinkling spot at the corner of each.

"This robbery," continued the counsel, "was committed on the night of the 14th of October last past, between the hours of ten and twelve."

"Or thereabouts," said the attorney-general.

"Oh, we are not particular to an hour or two," said the counsel for Duval. "Only let us know your time, and we are satisfied."

"A witness may certainly mistake as to an hour or two. Perhaps the prosecutor had no watch with him."

"Let us have him up again, then."

"With all my heart."

The prosecutor was re-called, and it was evident to all the court that he was in a state of great agitation.

"Calm yourself," said the counsel. "Unless I am obliged to do so, I will not set about proving where *you* were on the night in question. It will be sufficient for me to prove to the jury that the prisoner at the bar was not upon the spot you mention, at the time you mention. Now, sir, at what hour did this robbery happen?"

"I may be mistaken as to the hour."

"Nothing more probable, and as to the identity of the prisoner, likewise."

"Oh, no!"

"Oh, no! You are quite sure of that?"

"I am."

"And will you deliberately swear that you are not mistaken as to the robbery altogether?— or that is the most likely mistake of all."

"No, I'm not mistaken as to that I was robbed."

"Very well—you were robbed. We will admit that fact, as we are in law forced to admit a great many fictions. When were you robbed, sir?"

"Well, I cannot swear to the hour."

"Will you swear to the place?"

"Yes, of course, I will."

"Yes, of course, you will. Why, the only wonder to me is, that you don't mend your evidence, and swear that it was in the county of Middlesex, or some adjoining county, at some time unknown!"

Even the jury smiled at this, and the spectators would have indulged in a roar, if they had only dared to do so ; but the judge looked too dangerous.

"I don't know what you mean," said the witness. "It is a hard thing to be robbed and then bullied."

"Oh, very hard, indeed ; but for all that, let us come to the point again. Where were you robbed?"

"Close to Hounslow Heath. In a road leading from the heath."

"Was it dark?"

"Oh yes, very dark, indeed. That I will swear."

"And it was not midnight?"

"No—no."

"Very well, then, it is quite clear that you depose to the robbery taking place somewhere close to Hounslow Heath, and at sometime between sunset, and the hour of twelve at night, and that the prisoner at the bar was the man. Are we to take that as your evidence?"

" Why, yes."

" Very good, you may go down, and I can only say you are a very capital witness in my opinion, whatever my learned friend who is for the prosecution may think of you."

The man looked confused and anxious as he descended from the witness-box, and the counsel turning to the jury, said in a solemn tone of voice—

" Gentlemen of the jury, it is not for me to say lightly that the witness who has just left the box has committed perjury. It is far more pleasing to my feelings, and I am sure it will be far more pleasing to yours, to believe that he is mistaken, and that in deposing to what he has in the court this day, he has deposed to what he believes to be the truth, however far from it it may be in reality. It is not at all necessary that I should go out of my way to fix upon that witness the stigma of perjury. It will be sufficient if I show you, as I have done, that he is a witness who is very likely to be very much mistaken, and then prove to you, upon other evidence, that the prisoner at the bar was not from the hour of sunset until midnight anywhere near the spot where the robbery was alleged to have been committed. That, gentlemen of the jury, it will be my task to prove to you by such witnesses as I think you will feel induced to place every credit in, and whose statement will be so clear and precise, that it will not admit of the shadow of a doubt."

" Then you really intend to call witnesses in support of the alibi plea?" said the attorney-general.

" I do."

" Well, I give you fair warning, that I shall cross-examine them. We all know how easily witnesses to prove an alibi can be procured in London."

The judge smiled slightly.

" Yes," said Duval's counsel, " and, unhappily, our experience in this court is sufficient to let us all know how easily witnesses may be brought forward to swear away a life upon the most broad and intangible assumptions."

" Call your witnesses," said the judge.

" I will, my lord. I now call the Countess of Downbourne."

" The who?" said the attorney-general.

" The Countess of Downbourne."

" Oh!"

The judge almost shut his eyes completely, as through the throng an elegantly dressed lady was conducted to the witness-box. She was duly sworn, and then the counsel said to her—

" Are you the Countess of Downbourne, madam?"

" I am."

" Do you recollect anything remarkable occurring on the fourteenth of October last?"

" I do. I went in my own carriage accompanied by Lady Hariet Scrope, as far Hadley to visit the earl of Bute. It was a very dark night, indeed, and after getting some distance up the northern side of Finchley, the postilion let the two right-hand wheels of the carriage slip into a ditch, and it was all but upset. We were in the greatest alarm, and as there was but one postilion, he was afraid to leave his horses. Our footman was thrown from behind the vehicle and severely hurt. Our cries for some time for assistance were quite unavailing; but at length, a horseman dashed up to the spot, and with great strength and gallantry rescued us from our perilous situation."

" Unhurt?"

" Quite so, for the carriage had not really upset, although if he had not arrived at the moment he did, it is highly probable that it would have done so."

" What happened next, madam?"

" We were profuse in our thanks, and as the footman was much hurt, he was left at the next inn, and we both requested the gentleman who had done us such good service, to accompany us the remainder of the way to Hadley, which he consented to do."

"In the carriage?"

"No; he rode his own horse by the side of it, now and then only exchanging a few words with us as we proceeded, and we both thought him a very great protection, indeed, upon the road."

"Did you part with him at Hadley?"

"No. He wished to bid us there good-night; but we prevailed upon him to enter the earl's house, and he supped with us, and slept that night there; for a heavy rain came on, and the earl positively would not let him go. In the morning we saw him again, and thanked him for the service he had rendered us, and then he left the earl's mansion."

"Did you know who he was?"

"No; but we all concluded that he was some cavalry officer."

"Did he say that was his calling or station?"

"Oh, no. We never, of course, asked him who he was, and he did not volunteer the information. It was a sufficient introduction to us that he had done us a very great service; and the Earl of Bute considered that, likewise, to be a sufficient introduction to him; so no questions were asked of him."

"Now, your ladyship will, I am sure, excuse me for what I am about to say; but as this is rather a grave and solemn judicial inquiry, we are compelled to be, consequently, very precise in what we do."

"Oh, I am quite willing to answer any necessary questions, and shall not feel in any way offended at them."

"That is the answer I fully expected from your ladyship; and, therefore, I ask you if, upon your solemn oath, you can aver that the circumstance you have narrated to the court, took place on the evening of the 14th of October last past?"

"I can aver it, upon my solemn oath. I have with me, now, a memorandum that I made upon the subject, in a pocket-book, and I know likewise, from other circumstances, that I am right in the date."

"Very well—that is all I have to say to your ladyship upon that point; and, now, I have to ask one important question."

There was a death-like stillness in the court, for any one could very well guess that that important question related to the identity between the gallant stranger, who, on that night of the 14th of October, had rescued the ladies, and supped with Lord Bute, with Claude Duval, the prisoner at the bar.

The judge looked stern and cold, and the attorney-general was evidently very much interested; for he knew the countess perfectly well, and was perfectly taken by surprise at her appearance and her testimony in court.

"Have you, madam," said the counsel, "seen the chivalrous stranger, who did you such a service, since that night?"

"Yes."

"Upon what occasion?"

"To-day in this court, arraigned for his life. That is the man!"

She turned, and pointed to Claude Duval, who bowed low in the dock; and, in defiance of the judge and the officers, a cheer burst from the crowd that was so simultaneous and so sudden, and included so many people in it, that the officers stared at each other in a state of bewilderment to know how to interfere with such an universal expression of opinion.

CHAPTER CXXVI.

DUVAL HAS A RACE THROUGH LONDON FOR HIS LIFE.

It is quite surprising how some trifle will, after all, turn the tide of popular feeling, and have its effect even upon the imagination of those who, in character and education, are above the crowd. Even the attorney-general began to look staggered, as he saw that the countess, without any hesitation, pointed out Claude

Duval as the gentleman who had behaved so gallantly upon the occasion referred to.

The counsel of Duval saw that he had procured, in evidence from the lady, all that he required, and he felt that to induce her to say another word would only have the effect of unmaking what she had already said.

"Madam," he said to her, with great courtesy, "I have only now very much to regret that public justice required your presence here upon this occasion, and now to state, that I will not further trouble you."

The countess was about to leave the witness-box; but the attorney-general rose, and in a bland tone, said—

"One moment, if your ladyship pleases."

"Certainly, sir."

"Did you miss anything after the departure of the prisoner at the bar from the Earl of Bute's?"

"Miss anything, sir?"

"Yes; I ask if you missed any property."

"Certainly not."

"Then your may depend upon it, madam, that you are mistaken in the identity of the prisoner at the bar, with the person who was so gallant to you upon the road. Allow me to beg that you will look at him again, madam, and in all seriousness again ask yourself if he is the man."

"I have sworn that he is the man."

"And to that, you still adhere?"

"I do, sir."

"Very well, madam. I hope without offence I may entertain an opinion, in which I have no doubt the jury will coincide with me, that you are most grievously mistaken. I will not trouble you further."

The countess withdrew from the witness-box at once, and then the counsel for Duval said in a pleasant kind of voice—

"The next witness I shall call for the substantiation of this alibi, is the Lady Hariet Scrope, who was with the Countess of Downbourne upon the occasion in question."

The appearance of the young lady who now stepped into the witness-box was very much in her favour. She was not above nineteen years of age, and of the most charming aspect that can be imagined; there was not one person in court, the ladies of course excepted, who did not feel that it was quite a treat to get a sight of so much beauty.

"Allow me, Lady Hariet Scrope," said Duval's counsel, "to ask you if you have heard the evidence of the Countess of Downbourne?"

"I have, sir."

"Upon your oath do you corroborate that evidence?"

"I do, in every particular."

"Then pray look at the prisoner at the bar, and to the best of your knowledge and belief, say if he is or is not the person who rescued you and the countess from your unpleasant position upon the night in question."

"He is that person. I have no doubt whatever upon the subject."

"You swear to his identity quite distinctly, then?"

"I do."

"Very well, Lady Hariet; I shall not trouble you further. My learned friend who is for the prosecution, may or may not have something to say to you."

"Nothing whatever," said the attorney-general, as he gave his brief a kind of push across the table, which his professional brother quite understood to mean that he had had enough of it.

"Then, gentlemen of the jury," said Duval's counsel, "I have no more to say or to do, but to submit to you the evidence now brought forward in favour of the prisoner, as one of the clearest and most conclusive alibis that was ever proved in a court of justice; and I feel quite sure that you will coincide with me in that view. As I have called witnesses for the defence, my learned friend who is for the prosecution, has a right of reply, and can, if he so please, comment upon this evidence. Whether in this judgment he will think fit to do so or not, it is impossible for me to predict. but——"

"I have no reply to make," said the attorney-general.

"Oh, very well," said Duval's counsel, and with a smile of conscious triumph he sat down at once.

There was a breathless stillness in the court, and the judge looked scowlingly over his notes, and beneath his shaggy brows at the jury. Then in a low but clear voice he commenced his summing up.

"Gentlemen of the Jury,—The prisoner at the bar stands charged with a highway robbery. It appears uncontradicted that he is the notorious Claude Duval, whose criminal course has been but too well known to the public at large. It appears that on the 14th of last October, the prosecutor, a highly respectable individual, was robbed on the highway, and without any doubt or hesitation he charges the prisoner with that offence, and swears to his identity. Another highly respectable individual corroborates that testimony against the prisoner. Well, gentlemen, the whole case lies in a nutshell, and a more clear and conclusive case of guilt, apparently, could not come before a court. The only way in which such a case could be met with a chance of success, was the old way of attempting to prove an alibi. Gentlemen, it was more than probable that such would be the line of defence, and it so has turned out; but if that alibi had been attempted to be proved by persons of such character and low standing in society as would have hinted to them a reasonable doubt upon their evidence, I should have felt it to be my duty to tell you to discard it altogether from your minds, and to regard it as an impious attempt of the accomplices of the prisoner at the bar, to get him free from the punishment justly due to his many offences; but, gentlemen, such has not been the case, for the parties who have appeared in the witness-box this day, in support of the alibi, are unimpeachable."

The jury tried to look very wise.

"I say, gentlemen," continued the judge, "those parties are quite unimpeachable in their character and in their evidence. As I sit here believing that I live, I fully believe that those ladies believe the evidence that they have given to the court. But, gentlemen of the jury, evidence is a thing that it is hard to give, and human nature is prone to err.

"Here, gentlemen of the jury, you have a man before you whose whole life is stained by cruelty, accused of an offence, which, with him, is a matter of ordinary occurrence in the history of his career, and defended by a story that is directly opposed to the history of his career.

"The learned attorney-general particularly asked one of the witnesses for the alibi, if she were sure that the prisoner at the bar, admitting for a moment that she was not mistaken, and that he was the person who had supped with the Earl of Bute on the night in question, had not stolen something from that nobleman's residence. Now, gentlemen, by profession, the prisoner is a highwayman, and, therefore, it is natural to suppose that he would steal anything when he could. But the witness swears that he did not, and that is a very strong argument in favour of the supposition that she was mistaken in his identity.

"Gentlemen, I can only recommend you to bring as calm a judgment as you can to bear upon this question, and to endeavour to decide whether the prosecutor and his witness were mistaken or not mistaken in their identity of a man who is in the pursuit of his regular calling, or whether the two ladies who have come forward to prove the alibi, are mistaken or not mistaken in their identity of a man who was decidedly not acting in conformity with his usual character. I have been accused of prejudging this case, but it is for you further to judge of it, not me; and I feel quite convinced, when I see the very intelligent countenances before me, that you will hesitate to let loose upon society a man who is a pest to it, and whose life is one career of rapine and robbery, and, for all we know, of murder, likewise.

"Gentlemen, the case is in your own hands."

This most intolerably one-sided summing up was concluded, and the counsel at the table below the bench looked at each other significantly. The attorney-general, if such a feeling can ever find its way into the heart of a government law officer, was rather ashamed of the affair than otherwise, and the jury looked so confused, that it was quite evident they did not know what to do.

After a brief consultation in the box, one of them turned to the judge, and said, in a very dispirited tone of vioce,—

"My lord, we wish to ask a question of the court?"

"Certainly," said the judge.

"If we find the prisoner guilty, will the ladies be accused of perjury: and if we find him not guilty, will the prosecutor be accused of perjury or not; and if we find him not guilty, will he be let go; and are we to consider if he did anything else beside the present robbery?"

The judge looked vexed.

"Gentlemen," he said, "you have nothing to do but with the specific charge laid in the indictment; and as regards a charge of perjury, surely people may be mistaken without false swearing."

"Oh!" said the juryman.

The jury then whispered together for some few minutes, and no doubt, by so doing, increased the state of confusion they were in, until at last they hit upon the plan, as juries usually do, of leaving it to the biggest man of the lot to decide the verdict.

"Come, Mr. Bailey," said one, "I believe you weigh thirteen stone, and you ought, if anybody ought, to decide upon the case."

"Well, really, gentlemen—ha! ha!"

"Nay, but you must, Mr. Bailey."

Upon this, Mr. Bailey placed his finger against the side of his nose, and said,—

"I tell you what it is; it won't do to offend the ladies by saying they were wrong, for we all keep shops, and who knows but they might find out who we were, and never come into our shops again?"

This was so alarming a suggestion, that the jury looked quite flurried and excited.

"And," continued Mr. Bailey, "not only might they prevent the people coming to our shops, but they might serve us out in other ways, you know."

"So they might," gasped the jury.

"Then my opinion," said Mr. Bailey, "is to bring him in not guilty, on account of the ladies, and I daresay the judge and the lawyers will find out some other case against him, so that he will be hung in the long run, you know, and the ladies not offended."

The rest of the jury felt quite enchanted at this view of the case, and at the admirable mode of getting out of the difficulty, and they fully concurred in the advice of thirteen-stone Mr. Bailey, who having originally been chosen to be foreman on account of his size, now turned round to deliver the verdict to the court.

The clerk of the assizes, then, seeing that the jury had agreed upon their verdict, rose up and said—

"How say you, gentlemen of the jury, do you find the prisoner at the bar guilty or not guilty."

"Not guilty," said Mr. Bailey, "on account of the ladies."

"What?" said the judge, sharply.

"Not guilty, on account of the ladies."

There was quite a commotion in the court, and although no actual cheering took place, there was that hum of gratification and general merriment, that sufficiently showed that the spectators were highly gratified at the result.

"I don't understand the verdict," cried the judge.

"It is quite clear, my lord," said Duval's counsel. "The jury means, that the prisoner is declared not guilty on the evidence of the ladies."

"Just so," said Mr. Bailey. "Not guilty."

"Not guilty!" said the clerk of the arraigns, and down he sat.

"Very well, gentlemen," said the judge, looking pale with rage, "that is *your* verdict. I only hope, with a Christian spirit, that none of you will personally have to repent of it on the highway."

CLAUDE PULLS THE ARTIST'S NOSE.

"My lord," said Duval's counsel, "I have to apply for the immediate discharge of my client from custody."

"Discharge?" cried the judge. "Discharge a man from custody who is loaded with crime, because, in their abundant stupidity, a jury has thought proper to pronounce a verdict of not guilty?"

Upon this a juryman, who was rather short-tempered, and who did not like his "abundant stupidity" alluded to, rose, and in a very fiery, sharp voice riel out—

"My lord, you are a *hass*."

The commotion in court upon this, was really tremendous. At first there was a movement to and fro of the people with wonder and surprise, and then they burst into one roar of laughter.

The judge looked petrified, and the counsel rose to their feet. The Lord Mayor, grasping the gold chain that was round his neck, as though he thought to be sure the next tremendous thing that would happen would be an attempt to take that from him, left the court to have a glass of something, and it was several minutes before anything like order could be restored. Then the judge, looking as pale as the paper before him, spoke.

"After this gross insult to the court," he said, "it does not become me personally to decide upon what ought to be done."

"My Lord," said Duval's counsel, rising, "I am quite prepared to say, that a juryman who could apply such an epithet to a judge upon the bench, is not fit to sit any longer in that box; but I do think at the same time, that when a judge, to the face of a jury, speaks of their ' abundant stupidity,' that it ought to be considered jurymen are human beings, and that it is more to be expected that some one or other of them should follow a bad precedent set by a judge, than have temper sufficient to give him a lesson in moderation."

"I am quite prepared," said the judge, "to——"

"Pardon me, my lord," said the attorney-general interrupting him. "I beg that your lordship will not consider that this interruption upon my part savours in the least of disrespect to your lordship; on the contrary, it is dictated by only one idea, and that is that this unhappy affair may be allowed to subside."

"Subside!" cried the judge.

"Yes, my lord, let me hope so. The juryman will no doubt leave the court, and another can be procured; and your lordship will allow me to say, that you are too well known for every stray word from an excited man to have any consequence in the world."

"Oh, I'll go," said the juryman. "I'll go."

"Go, sir, and be quiet, then," said the attorney-general.

The juryman bustled out of the box, and then Duval's counsel spoke again, saying—

"I cordially agree in the sentiments of my learned friend the attorney-general to the effect, that what has been said ought not to affect your lordship in the least, and I likewise sincerely hope that the matter may now be allowed to rest."

The judge, as one of the most important consequences of all this, was allowed time to think; and if he did think at all, it was quite impossible but that he would come to the opinion that the affair was one that was only the worse for him the more he strived in it; so with an affectation of coolness and temper he said—

"In all matters in which every individual is personally concerned, I am inclined to think that others are in a better position to come to a judgment than that individual himself. Therefore, I will take the advice of the learned counsel who has spoken, and pass over this circumstance with the contempt it deserves. I hope that juryman, who is so unfit for his office, has left the court."

"He has, my lord," said an officer.

"Very well, then. We would rather, I am sure, all of us, forget that such a thing has occurred, than again in any way revert to it."

This was a statement in which everybody fully coincided; but still there was the question with regard to Claude Duval's release still undecided. He was yet n the dock, and the officers that were about him did not know very well what to be at.

CHAPTER CXXVII.

RESOLVES RATHER A KNOTTY POINT OF LAW.

It was evidently the great object of Duval's counsel to get him, upon the strength of the acquittal, out of the court; and rising now again, he said—

"May I request of your lordship to order the discharge from custody of an innocent man, who has been declared not guilty by a jury of his countrymen?"

"Is it possible," said the judge, "that there is no other indictment against the prisoner than the one that has just been tried?"

"No other, my lord," said the clerk.

"This is too absurd," added the judge. "Is this notorious highwayman to be let loose upon society?"

"My lord," said the counsel, "with all due deference to your lordship, it is nothing to this court whether the prisoner at the bar be the most criminal or the most law-respecting individual in this kingdom. He is in due course, after being acquitted, entitled to his discharge."

"I knew that very well; but surely some other charge may be ready against him among the numerous crimes he has committed."

"That is an assumption, my lord; and I here ask boldly in this court, who but the judge accuses the man, I will not call him prisoner, at the bar, of any crime?"

"I do not accuse him of any special crime," said the judge. "Has Mr. Attorney-general nothing to say to this application for the release of Claude Duval, the notorious highwayman?"

"Nothing, my lord," said the Attorney-general, "except a devout wish that I may be able when he is released to keep out of his way."

There was a slight laugh at this, and then an officer stepped forward, and said—

"If the court will allow me, I should like to take Duval into custody, now, upon my own responsibility, and re-carry him to prison."

"Upon what charge?" said Duval, breaking the silence that he had imposed upon himself.

"Oh, there will come a charge," said the officer, "before the day is over, no doubt."

"This is monstrous," said Duval's counsel. "It is quite impossible that any English judge can sanction such a proceeding."

"Have you a distinct charge to make against the prisoner upon which you can take him before a magistrate?" said the judge.

"Why no, my lord. I—I merely would apprehend him."

"Upon speculation?" said Duval.

"Just so," said his counsel.

"No—no," said the Attorney-general, shaking his head, "this must not be it is too bad. It can't be sanctioned for a moment. I am no party to this proceeding."

"Let the prisoner be discharged," said the judge. "If any police officer or officers choose to apprehend, him it is at their own risk. Let him be discharged."

"Yes," said the counsel for Duval, "and allowed safe conduct to his home."

"I don't know that," said the judge.

"It is the case, my lord. A man is brought to cou compulsively, and he is not after acquittal thus to be taken advantage of."

"That rule applies very well to criminal c as jurisprudence there is processes, and so on; but I am not sure that in criminal ischare the prisoner at any precedent for such a course. All I shall do will be to d once, and I will repress any disturbance in court."

"He will come back to Newgate, I suppose, my lord, first?" said the governor of the prison.

"If he thinks proper," said the judge. " He is free now."

The officers hung back, looking as savage as possible, and Duval, placing his hand upon the side of the dock, at once vaulted out of it into the court with an ease and dexterity, considering the confined space he was in, that was little short of marvellous.

"No," he said, " I have had quite enough of Newgate, and very much prefer leaving the court by its proper door."

There was a sudden rushing movement in the crowd, and Duval found himself surrounded by about twelve strong men, who constituted themselves into a sort of body-guard to him, and began, with him in the middle of the throng, slowly making their way towards the door of the court.

Three or four officers made a rush to try to collar him ; but they were struck forcibly by those surrounding Duval, and in the course of a few minutes the arena of the court was filled with a mass of combatants.

The judge rose and abruptly left the bench.

The moment the door through which the judge had passed closed upon him, the restraint which had kept the people tolerably quiet was wholly removed, and the scene that ensued was one of the most fearful character, and such as never before or since had taken place in that or any other court of justice in England.

In addition to the dozen or so persons that seemed to be there specially for such a purpose, the whole of the mob now took part with Duval, and although the officers were reinforced by the whole body of them within the court, they could not make head against the people, and the most fearful disorder was the result.

The door-keepers and the police who were about the doors of the court closed them, but it happened that the doors were so constituted as to bear almost any possible pressure from without that could be brought to bear against them ; but from within they were by no means so secure, and in a very few moments they yielded to the people.

Duval and his friends clinging round him, rushed out of the court in a dense throng.

"Stop him !" cried the officers. " Stop Claude Duval ! Seize him ! Stop him—stop him !"

One drew a pistol, and was in the act of presenting it towards where Duval was, when a man wrenched it from his hand, and with the butt-end of it gave him a blow upon the head that knocked him insensible in a moment, and then the battle still continued right out into the roadway of the Old Bailey.

The dense crowd that was there waiting to hear the result of the trial, had procured authentic information from the juryman who had been so summarily ejected from the court only a short time before, and they were quite prepared to do battle with the authorities, and to facilitate the escape of Duval.

The shout that was raised by the mob was something appalling, and the officers shrunk back, rather aghast, at these demonstrations against them ; but still the strong wish not to lose the reward for the conviction of Duval was sufficient to induce them to run some risks ; and collecting together in a very compact body of about thirty, they made a rush to try to capture him, and they got to within half a dozen paces of him.

This charge was a well executed one ; but yet it failed, for only five out of the whole thirty of the officers succeeded in getting back again without serious hurts.

It was just after the defeat of this charge of the police, that Duval found some one grasping his arm, and a voice said—

"Don't let me be forced rom you, sir"

It was Luke.

" Ah, Luke," he said, " are you here?"

" I am, sir. Your horse is on Holborn Hill."

" That's right. If I live, then, for the next ten minutes, I will be upon his back. Come on, Luke. All's right. But you are hurt?"

Blood was flowing from Luke's mouth.

"Oh, no, sir. Only a cut-lip from somebody's knuckles, that's all; and I don't think the fellow who did it has much to crow about, for I pretty well smashed him."

The mob was so elated at the defeat of the officers, that at the corner of Newgate Street it would stop to indulge in three cheers, that must have been heard all over the city. Duval felt that at such a moment it was of no use to attempt to proceed; but when the cheering had subsided, he cried out in a loud clear voice—

"Let me proceed, good friends. My route is down to Holborn Hill.

Upon this, the dense multitude raised another shout, and slowly began to move down Snow Hill with Duval in the centre of them; and there can be no doubt now but that the mob was very much impeding his escape, although they did not mean to do so; for owing to being so jammed up among the multitude, he only got down Snow Hill at a slow pace, when he would have been glad to scamper at speed the whole distance from Newgate to Holborn Bridge.

Luke still kept close by him.

"Where is the horse, Luke?" said Duval.

"At the old Angel Inn, at the corner of the market."

"That will do. Let us get on as quickly as we can, for they will try it on again to capture me."

"They will, indeed."

Just as Luke made the reply to Duval, there arose a shout among the mob, that for a few moments neither he, Luke, nor Duval could catch the purport of, and then a voice, louder than the rest, cried—

"There he goes to fetch the soldiers!"

"Surely not?" said Duval to Luke.

"It ain't impossible, sir."

"Then there is really no time to lose, for, under the pretence of dispersing a dangerous mob, they will apprehend me, and if they do so, for the riot of which they will accuse me, they will soon find a grave charge against me."

Both Luke and Claude Duval now made the most strenuous efforts to get on, and Duval called out—

"Good friends, let me get to Holborn Bridge quickly, if you would really assist me to escape. Let me get on, I beg of you."

This appeal had some effect upon the people, at all events, and they did get on somewhat faster than before; but still, every now and then, the cry was raised that the soldiers were coming.

"Duval reached the corner of the old Fleet Market, next to the City, and he was upon the point of saying something to Luke, when two men made a rush upon him, while a third opened the door of a house, close to which he was, and the evident idea was that they would, in the surprise of the moment, from the suddenness of the attack, succeed in forcing him into the house, and getting the door shut upon him.

If they had done so, probably they might have been successful in disabling him in the passage, and capturing him; but Duval was not the sort of person easily to be taken by surprise; and although one of the officers got his arms around his waist, and held him tight, he caught the other by the throat, and in a few seconds his face began to turn blue, when Duval dropped him, and suddenly flinging himself backward to the ground, he gave the one who was holding by him such a damaging fall, and a crush beneath his weight, that he lay insensible.

With a yell and a shout the mob trampled over them both, and in another minute Duval was at the gateway of the Angel Inn by Fleet Market.

The inn is still there, and the old spacious yard may still be seen, in which Claude Duval's horse was standing on that eventful morning. All day both Claude and Luke had carefully avoided saying anything to the mob, concerning the fact that his horse was there standing, for it might have reached the ears of a thief, as well as those of a friend; and some persons upon the outskirts of the mob, might have managed to get there before him, and take possession of the animal, in which case Duval's escape would have been a very doubtful proposition, indeed, instead of looking very feasible.

"This way—this way!" cried Luke, and he dragged Duval through the throng into the inn yard, where a man was waiting with both his (Luke's) steed, and that of Duval; but the man had not the least idea that they belonged to two such personages, and when he saw the mob coming, he looked aghast; but when two persons sprang from out of the mob, and began to mount the horses, he thought it was time for him to interfere.

"Be off with you, will you?" he cried. "These ain't none of yours."

"Yes, they are," said Luke, as he dashed the disfiguring blood from his face. "Don't you recollect me?"

"Oh, lor! yes, sir, it was you as left 'em both."

"To be sure it was, and didn't I give you half-a-guinea?"

"And promised me another half if I didn't move from here, nor let any one but you have the 'osses."

"Yes, and there it is."

"All's right, sir."

Duval and Luke were mounted in a moment, and then, with a bound of the horse, reached the street, and spoke in a loud voice, so that he was heard by every one in the remotest part of the crowd—

"My friends, if you would give me a chance of escape, you will make way for me and my friend here. I thank you all for the kindness you have done me, in defending me from the Old Bailey to this spot; but now I am fairly mounted upon my gallant steed, I feel that I can distance every pursuit, if you will only clear the way for me, and let me be off."

"Which way, Duval?" shouted one.

"Up Holborn," replied Claude.

Upon this the mob swerved on one side, and left a lane, up which Duval and Luke could just pass one after the other upon their horses. The animals were rather terrified at the appearance of the host of faces upon each side of them, and they were inclined to be a little restive: but Duval, far from being at all put out of the way by such a circumstance, only looked upon it as an additional proof that they were quite fresh, and equal to any work that was likely to be required of them.

From all he (Duval) and Luke knew to the contrary, they might yet be compelled to have a race for their lives. Such, however, did not seem to be the case, for they both reached Holborn Hill without any appearance of a foe to contend with them.

Before them there was now no crowd at all to signify, for it was only the chance passengers who had stopped upon the pavement, to see what the disturbance was, who were there.

Duval turned and waved his hand, as, with a cheering voice, he shouted—

"Farewell!"

"Hurrah!" cried the mob.

"Now for it, Luke," said Duval. "The sooner we bid good-by to these streets the better; but still we must not do the thing at a very break-neck pace. Let us try a sharp trot."

"That will do, sir. It is a very good sort of pace over the stones."

"On, then."

They both set off at a trot: but the trot of those horses, when they were well put to it, was a pace that got over nearly ten miles in the hour; so the reader may suppose that Duval and Luke soon left Holborn Hill behind them. They rapidly passed St. Giles's Church, which was then not at all so surrounded by houses as it is now, and proceeding up Tottenham-Court-Road, one side only of which was slightly built upon, they were soon in the open country in the Hampstead Road.

"This will do," said Duval, as he drew rein.

"Yes, sir," cried Luke; "and allow me now to congratulate you upon your escape from what seemed to be the very worst predicament you were ever in; for, to tell the honest truth, I never again expected that you and I should be riding together on the high road in this fashion."

"My time has not come, Luke."

"It seems not, sir."

Duval inclined his ear for a moment towards the route they had traversed, and then he said—

"I hear horses' feet. Let us get out of the high road, Luke. But you have not told me how *she* is at home."

"Quite well, sir, and expecting you. When I started from the old place this morning, I thought that I was telling the most abominable of untruths, when I said that she might expect you to dinner."

"You ran a great risk, Luke. But here is a turning to the right, which will get us on our right path in a little time, I hope. I still hear the beat of horses' feet upon the road, Luke."

———

CHAPTER CXXVIII.

DUVAL MAKES RATHER A SUDDEN REMOVE FROM HORNSEY.

It was no false alarm that came on Duval's ears when he said that he thought he heard the tramp of horses' feet, for he really had done so; but the abrupt turn that he and Luke made to the right into a very nice and picturesque lane, seemed to have the effect of throwing the persons completely off the scent.

More than once, during the next half mile's progress, Luke got off his horse, and placed his ear flat to the ground to listen, and each time that he did so, he heard less and less of any tread of horses' feet.

"We have distanced them, sir," he said.

"Yes, Luke, I think so. And now, in your knowledge of this part of the suburbs of London, can you show me any very near way to Hornsey?"

"I can, sir."

"Then go first, and I will follow you."

"The nearest way is by trespassing on some lands belonging to a farmer, who is as savage, if a hoof be placed upon any of his fields, as if it were placed upon his own stomach; but I think we can be on and off his meadows before he can get anything like sufficiently near us to complain about it."

"And if he should," said Duval, "he can only move us off, and off we intend to go; so lead on, Luke, and we will trespass, so that we get on quickly."

"It will save, sir, half a mile."

"That is everything. I will follow you."

Luke, in his wandering expeditions in search of game in the neighbourhood of the metropolis, before he knew anything of Claude Duval, had had occasion to make himself so well acquainted with every lane, field, road, and, indeed, almost with every tree, that he could have sat down and drawn a pretty accurate map of the country to the north of the metropolis for many miles, had it been requisite, and such knowledge was of the very greatest possible importance.

It was quite singular to see the cunning secrecy with which Luke now proceeded. After traversing the lane for a little way further, the came upon a cluster of little cottages, and, to the surprise of Claude Duval, Luke turned his horses's head right into the yard of one of them, to the great danger of a brood of chickens there assembled.

"Hilloa!" said Duval. "This is not the way."

"Oh, yes, sir, it is."

"Come—come," cried a woman appearing at the cottage door. "What do you want here, you vagabond?"

"Only through your yard and garden into the meadows," said Luke, "there's a broken fence that we can easily go through.   It was in that state a year ago, and it would take your husband half an hour's trouble to mend, or you yourself could do it in that time; but I know you are too idle and fond of gossiping with your neighbours to do it, and he is too fond of the ale-house, so the gap remains —and here it is."

The woman stared at Luke as though he had been a conjurer, and there the gap was in the fence, that a little industry, such as few of this class of agricultural poor really possess, would have mended.

"We have been thinking," said the woman, "of stopping it up."

"Oh, no doubt," said Luke.   "Come on, sir."

Claude could not help smiling at the confident manner in which Luke had calculated upon finding the same the gap in fence that he had known a year ago; and after having passed through it right into the meadows, he said—

"Why, Luke, you know these sort of people pretty well, to be so confident that they would not mend the hedge."

"Oh, yes, sir, I do know them well.   They will now talk about mending it for another week to come, since we have ridden through it."

"But you think they won't mend it?"

"Not they.   The fact is, that one half of the misery, in appearance, of the class of people such as that woman belongs to who has just spoken to us, is a consequence of insatiate idleness, and love of drink."

"Ah, there is the evil, Luke."

"Yes, sir.   Now, that woman's husband is a day labourer, that is to say, he gets employment at hedging, ditching, trenching, hay-making, reaping, or anything connected with farming operations, all of which he understands pretty well, and his average earnings all the year round will not be more than eleven shillings a week."

"Not much, Luke."

"No, sir; but he makes it not half that."

"How does he manage that, Luke?"

"I will tell you, sir.   First of all, he spends out of that about three shillings at the ale-house.   Then the wife has a sum to pay weekly to a man who lets them have things upon credit, such as tea, gown-pieces, flannel, trumpery ribbons, fancy tea-boards, with staring patterns on them, and so on; for which, to cover his risk, as he would tell you, he only charges the moderate profit of two-hundred per cent., and in that way another three shillings of the money goes.   They pay two-and-sixpence per week for the rent of the cottage and the little patch of ground, and then, I would ask you, sir, what can be left to provide food and the proper necessaries of life?"

"Little enough, Luke."

"Too little, sir; for the moment such a man gets ill, or is out of work for a week, he comes upon the parish."

"Exactly.   I can clearly understand the evils of the system you point out, Luke; and until the poorer classes of England are temperate, and turn the tallyman from the door, they will remain the poorer classes, and only, year after year, be dull and stupid in misery and affliction."

"That is about it, sir; but here we are on the farmer's ground.   They are fine meadows.   You see yonder group of chestnuts, sir?"

"I do."

"That, then, is the point at which we must leave the meadows.   Close to them runs a lane that leads from Mussell Hill to Crouch End, and then, you know, sir, we shall be close at home."

"We shall, Luke.   But who is that yonder upon a pony?"

"The farmer himself, by all that's disagreeable!"

"Hoi! hoi!" cried a voice, and the farmer, mounted upon a sturdy pony that looked like a little dray-horse, came up at a clumsy galop towards Claude and Luke.

"Shall we distance him, sir?" said Luke:

"Not yet.   Let us hear what he has to say."

The farmer was coming obliquely towards them, and as Claude did not quicken his speed, they soon met.

"Hoi!" said the farmer, "just go back agin."

"What, that way?" said Claude.

CLAUDE AND LUKE TAKE A LEAP THROUGH THE OLD GAP

"Yes, to be sure."

"Why we have only just come that way, my friend, and it would look foolish to go back again.   There lies our way."

"But you are trespassing on my land.   Didn't you see the board as said all trespassers wur to be prosecuted?"

"No; but if I had I should not have minded it.   Good-day."

"Dang it, you shall go back, though."

"Shall, my friend," said Claude, "is a word that I don't understand, unless use it myself. You had better be civil, or I shall give you a thrashing, such as your own corn hardly gets."

"Oh, that's your game, is it ?" cried the farmer. "We will soon see how we can manage such a fellow as you are. I can't be quite alone, and if so be as I only just put this here whistle to my lips, and keeps on a blowing at it, some o' my men will soon be here."

"If you do put it to your lips," said Claude, "I will make you swallow it as sure as you are a living man."

"You will?"

"Upon my word I will."

"You had better not chance it," said Luke to the farmer. "My friend is a man who usually keeps his word."

"And in this instance," said Duval, "I will keep it to the letter, and you will find that you will be paying just a little too dear for your whistle."

The farmer looked doubtful for a moment or two, as to whether he should risk the realization of Duval's threat or not, and then with rather a sheepish look, he said—

"Well, I don't mind whether I gets my fellows here by a whistle or by going and calling on 'em; so I'll just trot off."

"A very prudent resolution," said Duval. "Come on, Luke. We have delayed more time with this man than would have taken us round by the high-road."

"I fear we have, sir."

The farmer, who began to be rather afraid that the trespassers were not exactly the sort of persons to be trifled with, made off in one direction, and Duval and Luke made off in the other. They made now such good speed that they soon reached a hedge that skirted the last meadow they had to cross, and just divided it from the high-road.

"This will do, sir," said Luke. "Both of our horses will take this leap without any trouble, you may depend."

"I feel pretty sure of that, Luke."

"You may, sir. Here goes."

Luke gave his horse a touch, and over he went to the other side of the hedge as clean as any one could wish. Duval followed him on the moment, and they were then both in a high road that to the right led towards Mussell Hill and so on to Hornsey.

"You know the way ?" said Duval.

"Every inch of it. To the right is—Hush! some one comes. Don't you hear a horse in full gallop, sir ?"

"I do. Let us get aside, Luke, beneath the shade of these trees, and see who it is."

They both got as close to the hedge as possible, where some very luxuriant plane trees spread their branches right out into the road-way, and at the pace that the horse they heard was coming at, they knew that it would not be a question of many minutes who was the rider.

There was here a slight bend of the road about a hundred yards off from the spot where Luke and Claude paused; and until the horse and rider had got past that point, they could not see anything of either. Suddenly the approaching person came into sight, and turned out to be, to all appearance, a mere youth, with a cap on the side of his head, although young as he was, he showed that he well understood the management of a steed.

"Why, he is quite a boy," said Luke.

"Yes—yes. That is, yes," said Duval abstractedly.

"What is the matter, sir ? Are you ill?"

"No, Luke; but—but if it did not seem to be too improbable, I should take upon myself to say that that travelling cap was mine."

" Yours, sir ?"

" Yes, it is. or the exact fellow of it ; it certainl aung up in my bedroom at the house at Hornsey, and how it came to be u...n the head of that youth, is to me most puzz ling. I will question him."

" Don't sir."

" Oh, nonsense, I must."

Duval now went out into the middle of the road, and the moment the youth in the travelling cap saw him, he uttered a cry of joy, and dashing the cap from his head, disclosed the features of May !

CHAPTER CXXIX.

DUVAL HAS TO TAKE REFUGE IN THE OLD CAVERN.

Poor May, if Duval had not at that moment supported her, must have fallen from the horse she rode. The sudden joy, so unexpected, too, as it was, of seeing him again, was almost too much for her, and if she had not—after an inarticulate attempt to speak—burst into a copious flood of tears, there is no knowing what dangerous swoon she might not have fallen into upon the occasion.

Duval was scarcely less surprised to see her than she had been to see him, and while he held one arm round her, he cried—

" Can I believe my eyes ? Is it really you, May, that I see before me ?"

" It is my mistress," said Luke, " certainly, sir ; and I'd lay any wager she was looking for us."

" I was—I was, indeed !" gasped May.

" Calm yourself," said Duval. " Believe me, I was, with Luke, hurrying home with as much expedition as I could possibly command ; but this happy meeting spares both of us, perhaps, another half hour's anxiety."

" Oh, yes—yes !" sobbed May.

It was quite evident that some littlet time must yet elapse before she could sufficiently calm her feelings to allow her to speak rationally in answer to Duval ; but, inasmuch as the tears and the excitement caused by our over-joys have less lasting effect upon us than those caused by our sorrows, she, in a comparatively short space of time, was able to smile in Duval's face, and to make an effort to dash aside the tears from her eyes, and to speak to him.

" Oh, Duval," she said, " only tell me that you are safe and well ! Tell me that much, and then all is well."

" I am quite well, dear one," he replied, " and I am safe as I ever am ; I am quite sure Luke will tell you the same."

" Ah, yes, we are much—very much indebted to Luke."

" No one can feel that more truly than I do," said Duval ; " and Luke knows that if I do not say much to him of the services he has rendered to me, I am not without thought concerning them."

" And if you will both be so good as to say no more upon that head," said Luke, " I shall be obliged."

Duval smiled, as he replied—

" Very good, Luke, we will spare your blushes, my friend. Services such as those you have rendered to me are far above being repaid by mere words ; so you are quite right in stopping me saying much about them."

" Oh, but," cried Luke, " I did not mean the stopping you to be taken in that sense."

" Never mind," said May. " You are our friend, Luke, and as such you must allow us to praise you now and then a little."

Luke shook his head, and then Duval, looking inquiringly at May, said to her—

" But how is it that, after I heard from Luke that he left you quite well and full of a hope of seeing me speedily, I now find you on the high-road, and in such a costume too? Have you, too, turned highwayman?"

"Alas, no!"

"Oh, you mean to be one, though?"

"No—no, Duval, and Heaven knows how happy I should be to take you from this most fearful and dangerous course of life."

"Ah, that is a hope that we will talk of another time; but now tell me how it is that you are from home, May."

"I will; but we must not remain here."

"Not remain here?" cried Luke and Duval, both in a breath, as they glanced around them with the expectation of some immediately approaching danger.

"No. Let us proceed, and place as large a space as possible between us and the old house at Hornsey."

"Ah! there is danger, then, there?"

"There is, Claude. It is true that Luke left me full of hope and expectation of speedily seeing you again; but scarcely had he been gone ten minutes from the house, when it was broken into by six men, who roughly demanded of me who I was, and required me to admit that it was your house. I steadily refused, but they only laughed at my refusal, saying that their information was too good to be effected by any obstinacy of mine in not confirming it, and that they had come there to wait for you in case you should have the luck to get free of your pursuers in the City, and to get so far with your life."

"The rascals!"

"I was terrified, and yet I preserved my presence of mind wonderfully, considering all things, and I would have left the house, but they divining my intention to do so, locked me up in my own bed-room, and being quite satisfied that they had me securely, they left me to myself."

"And you escaped?"

"I did, Claude. You know that this sort of clothing was in one of the wardrobes, and this cap hung upon a nail close to it. I hastily attired myself as you see me, and opening the window carefully, I made a safe and easy descent into the garden by the aid of the old vine."

"Yet it was perilous, May."

"Not at all. I had but to clutch firmly to the vigorous shoots of the vine, and to find a foothold, of which there were hundreds, and so I got in perfect safety to the ground."

"But you are mounted. There was no horse in the stable?"

"True; but I did not leave the bed-chamber without taking care to secure about me all the money that from time to time you have given into my keeping; so the moment I got free of the garden, which I happily did without observation, I ran to the livery stables that are not far from the church, and boldly walked into the yard and asked if they had a horse to sell."

"It was bold, indeed."

"Perhaps imprudently so, but they were all civility, and did not seem to have the least suspicion, but that I was some extravagant young gentleman who had more money than wit. I gave them fifty pounds for this nag."

"And not dear," said Luke.

"Do you think not?"

"I am sure of it. It is only fit for a light weight, but it is as neat a little animal, to all appearance, as I have seen."

"Then I have not thrown away your money, Claude."

"A plague take the money!" said Duval. "That is of the very least possible consequence. It is your safety that is everything."

May looked at him with a smile, as she added,—

"You see, then, that I am safe. They gave me a saddle and a bridle into the bargain, and here I am."

"But where were you going?"

"Ah, that is the most difficult question of all for me to answer. The fact is, I was so terrified and saddened at the idea that you would fall into the hands of the officers, that I knew not which way I rode, and it was pure chance that brought me in this direction."

"A lucky chance, dear May, indeed. They may stay as long as they like at the old house, waiting for me; and they may do what they like with it, when they find that I don't come. You have brought from it the most valuable of its contents, May."

"Yes; all the money, Claude."

"Nay, do not fancy for one moment that it was the money I alluded to. Indeed, and in truth, I had forgotten that again. It was, yourself, dear May, that I called the most valuable of the contents of the house; and, since you are here with me again, and we are all unhurt, if you were as poor as Job himself it would not concern me much."

"Nor me," said May.

"Nor me," said Luke.

While this little explanatory conversation had been going on between Claude Duval and May, they had all three pursued the contrary route to that that led to the village of Hornsey, and had made some progress in placing a large space of country between them and that place. After what May had detailed, it was quite clear that his old home was now no place for Duval; and as far as Luke was concerned, the reader is aware that he had his own reasons for wishing to inhabit any other place but that house, in the garden of which was a recollection that always distressed him.

The question, however, of where they should go, was one that very shortly soon arose in the course of their talk, and Claude Duval was just upon the point of turning to Luke to say something upon that point, when a faint 'Hilloa!' from a distance came upon his ears.

"What is that?" said May.

"I hardly know yet, replied Claude; "but it is worth our attending to. Such outcasts of society as I suppose we may consider ourselves to be, are interested in every unusual sound that may arise."

Luke was listening attentively.

"Suppose, sir," he said, "I ride back a little, and try and find out what it is about? I won't go far."

"I don't like you to rush into danger, Luke," said Claude. "You may be known personally, for all I can say to the contrary; and they may pounce upon you for having been seen in my bad company."

"I am not afraid of that," said Luke, "if you will only let me go."

"Hush!" cried May. "There may be no occasion; for, if my ears don't deceive me, I hear some one coming on horseback."

Both Claude and Luke listened now attentively for a few moments, and then they were enabled to confirm what May had said; and, as it was only by the sound a single horse that was approaching, they resolved to go on at a quick walk, and let whoever it may be overtake them.

It did not require many minutes for that to ensue, and a young man, mounted upon a very good-looking hack, was about to ride past, when Duval called out to him,—

"Hilloa, my friend! is anything amiss?"

The young man paused, and turned to the friends. He had the look of a stable-lad; and the moment he saw May, he cried out,—

"Why, that's the young gent as bought a oss of us. I hopes as how you likes him, sir, on the road?"

"Very much, indeed, thank you," said May. "I have seen no need to repent of my purchase yet."

"Nor, sir, nor you won't," said the groom. "The fact is, he ain't everybody's money, for he ain't up to much weight; but he'll carry you famous, and there isn't what you may call a vice about him as isn't all his little fun."

"You are riding fast," said Duval; "I hope there is nothing amiss?"

"No, gentlemen, nothing much amiss ; but it appears that Claude Duval, the famous highwayman, that you have heard of, no doubt, was to have been in guilty at the Old Bailey, this morning, and hung on Monday, but he away, after killing I don't know how many officers, and very nearly mu the judge on the bench ; and the officers say they have made up their minds to have him before night, and they are raising up all the constables, and the magistrates, and justices of the peace in the county ; and I'm sent to Highgate to give a letter there to the justices, about getting a lot of mounted men, you see, sir, on the different roads."

"Oh, I understand."

"They say they must have him, dead or alive, to-night."

"Well," said Claude, "if they must, of course they must ; but still it is possible enough that Claude Duval himself may object to it. We thank you for your news. You had better ride on now."

"Thank you, sir ; I will. They told me to make haste."

———

CHAPTER CXXX.

THE SITUATION OF DUVAL AND HIS FRIENDS BECOMES DOUBLY PERILOUS.

THE man rode on quickly to make up for the few moments' time he had lost in replying to the questions that had been put to him ; and until the sound of his horse's feet had quite died away in the distance, neither Duval nor his friends uttered a word.

It was May at last who broke the silence.

"Oh, Duval," she said, "this is really serious. The danger around thickens. It will not do now to hesitate. You must fly from this place at once."

"Over the tree tops, May ?" said Duval with a smile.

"Oh, do not jest at such a time as this !"

"Forgive me, May. I know that it is injurious to you to do so, for you are full of fears ; but yet I do not myself know that my danger is much greater than we formerly supposed it to be. It is true that the hands of all men are raised against me, and I may say, likewise, that my hand is raised against all men."

"This general rising, though, sir, of the country," said Luke, "is rather more serious than usual. It is seldom that the authorities make such a determined effort, without—without——'

Luke paused ; but Duval turned to him with a smile, saying—

"Do not pause in what you would say, Luke. I know the word that was upon your lips, but which you did not like to utter. It was ' succeeding.' "

"It was, sir."

"I am better pleased that you should say what you think ; and now that you are both full of the idea that there is really imminent danger, I will take whatever course you point out to me."

Duval looked at May ; but she shook her head.

"No," she said, "Luke is far better able to advise than I can be. Let him speak."

"Well, Luke, it remains with you," said Duval.

"I don't like it, sir."

"Like what, Luke ? What is it you don't like ?"

"That it should remain with me to decide. If you will think a little, you are much more able than I can be to come to some conclusion. Whatever you do, sir, I shall be apt to consider the right thing ; so only say what it is to be."

"I am inclined to think that this knowledge that we have got from the mounted man who has just passed us," said Duval, musingly, "alters the complexion of affairs, and is sufficient to induce an alteration in our plans."

"Decidedly so," said May.

"Well, Luke, I wait for you.'

"Time is precious, sir, and if you really do require my opinion, I will give it freely, and it is, now, that we should take to some of the roads leading right away out of the neighbourhood of London, and ride a good fifty or sixty miles into the country."

"And you, May—what do you say to such a plan?"

"I say yes to it, with all my heart."

"Then let us go."

The scheme was one of the very best that could be possibly thought of, for it was a fact that such strenuous exertions were to be made for the capture of Duval in and about that neighbourhood that it would have been hardly possible for him to have secured his safety, whereas, by riding quite away for some time, he at once altered the whole circumstances by which he was surrounded.

"The only question is, which road to go," said Luke.

"South," said Duval. "That is the road I shall like best, I feel assured; and so come on. We will soon leave danger, I hope, far behind us; and if we do not, and it should arduously meet or follow us, why we must show it a bold front, and defy it."

It was no very easy matter to get southward from where they were, as all the principal roads were to the right in one direction, and right into London in the other. Of course, Duval had no idea of going through the metropolis; but he thought that if he could get by cross-roads and lanes to the banks of the Thames, about Richmond, he would cross that stream, and then shape his course up one of the great roads that ran down to the south coast of England.

Whether or not Duval intended to transact a little professional business as he went along or not, we shall soon see. If he had any scruples about doing so, we must take them as entirely arising from the fact of his having May with him, and of the dread he felt at the idea of getting her into any danger.

For the next hour they rode on without exchanging much conversation with each other. The fact is, that they were each anxious in a different way, and such anxiety—we can truly say—was of the most unselfish description, for it was about May that Duval was full of thought, while she forgot all her own perils in consideration for his safety.

As for Luke, there can be no doubt at all but that he would have thrown himself in the way of meeting death, rather than any injury should have come to Duval, towards whom he had the strongest attachment.

There can be but little doubt regarding the wisdom of the course which Duval now adopted, and he was glad that May fully coincided with him in it. By taking a considerable round they managed to get into the neighbourhood of Fulham, and finally crossed the river by the aid of the old wooden bridge that connects that district with Putney.

"Now, Luke," said Duval, "our course is tolerably easy, I suppose?"

"Yes, sir, it is. Let us get towards the south-east, and we shall soon, I think, place a sufficient space of ground between ourselves and our foes, as to make it not very likely that they will interfere with us."

"But if we go right on in such a direction, my friend," said May "we shall reach the sea coast."

"We shall," said Duval, "and I think I shall not at all be disinclined to do so. What say you to a trip to Hastings? I have been told that there we may find some amusement, and possibly some profit."

"Amusement there is plenty," said May; "but when you talk of profit, Duval, I have a fear that you contemplate engaging in your dreadful pursuit."

"Oh, May, call it not dreadful, for who knows what it may not enable us to do? The object I now have in view is to leave as soon as I can this precarious mode of life, and retire with you to the country, and then, in a few years, I should hope and expect that Claude Duval would be forgotten."

"Never!" said Luke.

"Never what, Luke?" said May.   "Do you mean to say that such a happy state of things can never be accomplished?"

"Oh, no, you misunderstand me. I mean that Claude Duval will never be forgotten while the world stands."

"It may be so," said Duval.

"Alas!" sighed May, "I would have wished it were otherwise."

They had made good speed while they spoke, and where rapidly traversing a road in the direction they wished to go, when from a side thoroughfare there suddenly dashed out a lady upon horseback. It was quite evident that the horse was running away with her, and that she was fast loosing control over the movements of the animal.   Without a moment's hesitation, Duval rushed forward and caught the horse by the rein, and in a few moments, by firmness rather than by violence, succeeded in calming it.

"You are only alarmed, I trust?" said Duval to the lady.

"Oh, that is all," she replied; "but you must tell me to whom I am indebted for my safety. The horse would have started off, no doubt, in another moment or two."

"It is sufficent, madam," replied Duval, "that I have had the happiness of rescuing you. I have the honour to bid you good-day."

"Not so.   Here comes one who will be as grateful to you as you can wish, for he has the power to be so."

As the lady spoke, Duval heard the clatter of a horse's feet in the lane, and to his great surprise, no other than the Prince of Wales emerged from it into the high road.

"Hilloa! Emma," he cried "I thought you were gone. How did you stop that mad-headed horse, that you will ride in spite of all I can say to you to the contrary?"

"I did not stop it, George, but here is a gentleman who has left his party, and who has kindly done so.   If he had not, I don't know what might have been the result; but I will not ride the horse again, George."

"I'm sure," said the prince, "I am very much obliged to the gentleman, and beg him to accept my thanks."

"Your Royal Highness is too good," said Duval, as he took off his hat, and bowed as well as he could on horseback.

"The deuce take it—he knows me," said the prince.

"Ha, ha!" laughed the lady; "you are not so easily forgotten, George, if any one has once seen you. Your beauty makes an impression."

The prince looked rather annoyed at having been so easily recognised by any one; but after regarding Duval for a few seconds in silence, he said—

"It is the very man."

"What very man?" said the lady.

"I trust your Royal Highness," interposed Duval, "will be so good as to keep my secret."

"I will; and you be as good as to forget that you met the Prince of Wales along with——"

"A lady whom I do not know," said Duval, "and concerning whom I shall make no sort of inquiry."

The lady looked from one to the other of them, during this little mysterious dialogue, rather impatiently, and then she broke out with—

"But I must, and will, know who he is. Come, sir, who and what are you? I see by your appearance that you are a gentleman; but I want to know your name."

Duval was silent, and the prince said, with suddenness—

"No, this must not be, Emma. It really must not be. The gentleman has a good reason, of which I am well aware, to conceal his name, and I cannot have him pressed upon the subject. Who are these people watching us?"

"Friends of mine, your Royal Highness," said Duval; "but they neither of them know the Prince of Wales personally."

The lady had been looking keenly at May for the last few moments, and now she said, abruptly—

"Why is that girl dressed in men's clothes for?"

"Girl in men's clothes?" cried the prince, with sudden emotion.   "Is she pretty?—Where is she?   Oh, there—By Jove! she is an angel!"

CLAUDE CARVING HIS NAME ON THE WALL OF HIS CELL.

"I should not like to make that remark concerning a lady who was under your royal highness's protection," said Duval.

The pointed way in which Duval uttered those words, was quite sufficient to let the prince see that the admiration he evinced for May was not very pleasing to him (Duval), and the prince quite understood him.   The lady did so likewise, and gave a slight toss of the head as much as to say—" Pho! I don't care a straw about it."

The Prince of Wales was about to say something, when suddenly both May and Luke rode up to the party, and the latter said—

"We are lost, sir. There is a party approaching that we cannot contend with. We are hemmed in upon both sides."

"Oh, fly!" cried May. "Fly, Claude. We will remain her and detain your foes until you are far away."

Duval was annoyed that they should both come up to him and the prince, and so freely proclaim their fears.

"What is the meaning of all this?" he said. "I see no one but friends, and hear no one but friends."

Duval was not in a position to see or hear anything that was upon the high road, for he was some ten or twelve paces down the lane, whither the prince had slowly backed his horse, to carry on the little conversation he had had with his old acquaintance; but now that Duval rode out into the open road, he saw that to his right there was a troop of cavalry keeping watch, and to his left there advanced about a dozen mounted men, who were in civil costumes, and who, no doubt, were belonging to the police.

"Hemmed in, indeed," he said.

At once he trotted back to the prince, and in a tone of voice that shook just a little, he said to him—

"Your Royal Highness has already shown me such great favour, that I feel I am asking too much to request one more boon at your hands."

"What is it? Say on."

"It is, that you will let this lady, who is my wife, and this young man who is my attached and faithful friend, remain for a few minutes under your protection, for there is great danger to me and to them."

"But yourself, man," said the prince; "what are you to do?"

"I will take my chance, and fight my way through them if possible, and if I cannot, why I can but fall; and my last words will be thanks to you for protecting the only living beings that I feel anxious about, on account of their attachment to me."

"No," said the prince, "that must not be."

"You will not?"

"Don't misunderstand me. I will do more than you ask of me, but you must remain here likewise. If I have the power to protect them, I have the power to protect you."

Both Luke and May were quite amazed to hear Duval use the words Royal Highness, and they could not look enough at the person who bore that title. As for the lady who was with the prince, she seemed each moment to be getting more confused, and more angry at the mystery in which the whole affair was wrapped to her.

"George," she said, "this is folly. There is no time for you now to engage in foolish adventures on the road. Come away."

"Not yet, Emma," said the prince, and approaching May, he said in as engaging a tone as he could assume. "Be assured that I will not only protect you, but I will protect him, in whose fortune you are interested."

"My heart thanks you," said May.

"Oh, nonsense," cried Emma. "I wonder you are not ashamed of yourself to appear in the public thoroughfares in men's apparel. It is disgraceful!"

"Oh, madam," said Duval, "there are more disgraceful things than that, as no doubt you are well aware."

"What do you dare to mean to insinuate, sir? I am the Marchioness of Morton."

"I thank you for the information, madam. It may be interesting in case I should meet with the marquis."

"There, now, Emma," said the prince, "a pretty affair you have made of it by your anger: but that is always the way with you. The moment you lose temper you lose all sort of discretion. Now, if it were not that I know I can depend upon the honour of this gentleman, your imprudent declaration of who you are might be productive to you of many disastrous consequences."

The lady bit her lips with chagrin.

"Rely upon me," said Duval. "The words uttered in an incautious moment shall never pass my lips again; and if you even suspect that I could play you so treacherous a game, you shall have it in your power to do me a still worse turn should you see reason, by declaring that I am ——"

"Oh, no—no!" cried May—"do not."

"Nay, surely I may trust this lady with my name. May I not, madam?"

"You may," said the marchioness, with a mortified look. "I confess I am dying with anxiety to know who and what you are. If it be a secret, I will keep it."

"Then, madam, the world names me Claude Duval!"

"What! Duval the highwayman?"

"The same. But, although I may at times cry 'Stand!' to a true man on the king's highway, or give a temporary fright to a lady, I yet never broke my word or played a traitorous part to one who trusted me."

"That is true," said the prince; "so now, Emma, let there be no ill blood in the matter. I for one feel that I am under great obligations to Duval, and I will protect him as best I may. Get all of you behind me, now, and I will alone face these people who are close at hand, and prevent them from making their way down the lane."

"Do so, George," said the lady. "I am quite satisfied. I have been longing to have a good look at Claude Duval, the celebrated highwayman; but nothing was further from my thoughts than meeting him to-day."

CHAPTER CXXXI.

THE PRINCE SAVES DUVAL, AND THE LATTER ALTERS HIS PLANS A LITTLE.

It was quite evident, from the conduct of the party of armed men that was advancing along the road, that there was a strong impression concerning the whereabouts of Claude Duval. As it turned out afterwards, though, the troop of cavalry had nothing to do with the matter.

The fact was, that the soldiery were on their route to London, and had come to a halt, while one of the officer's horse was taken to a farriers, to have something removed from its foot.

Probably the officers who were really in pursuit of Duval, heard the clatter of the horses' feet belonging to the soldiers, and then their sudden halt, and thought that such sounds were indicative of the presence of Duval and his friends, for they came on at the most active pace.

By the time, however, that the officers had reached to within about twenty-feet of the lane, a little way down which Duval and his friends were, they saw that it was a party of military that had made the alarm, and not a little gratified were they, at the idea of such unexpected aid. It turned out that a magistrate was with the civil power, and when he saw the soldiers, he at once rode forward and demanded to see the commanding officer, who came forward rather sulkily, for nothing can be more annoying to the military than to be forced into coalition with the civil powers.

"Sir, I am a magistrate," said that personage.

"Very good, sir," said the officer.

"Perhaps, sir, you will be so good as to cast your eye over that prescript from the Secretary of State."

The magistrate handed a folded paper to the officer, who, to his chagrin, found that it was a general order to all civil and military powers to aid the bearer to the extent of their ability in the capture of Claude Duval, a convicted felon as he was called in the prescript, no doubt alluding to some former imprisonment of Duval's orm which he had made an escape.

" Very well, sir," said the officer. " Pray what do you wish us to do ?"

" Why, sir," replied the magistrate, " by making the most diligent inquiry, we have ascertained that the highwayman we seek, along with two other persons, no doubt as bad as himself, have come this way. A young fellow on a fleet horse has kept them pretty well in sight for some miles, and assures us that they are hereabouts. Now, sir, if you will let your men just block up a few of the lanes and roads, while we ferret out the culprits, it will be a capital thing."

" Very well, sir ; point out the spots where you wish me to place sentinels, and it shall be done ; but recollect that we have as little time to spare as possible, and are on the march."

" The secretary's order, I presume, sir, will put an end to any difficulty.'

The magistrate was getting a little out of temper at the superscilious manner in which he was treated by the officer ; and they both regarded each other with anything but amiable countenances.

At this moment, when something like a snarling disagreement was very likely between the civil and military authorities, one of the magistrate's party rode up in quite an excited state, and said—

" Please, your worship, there are people hiding in a lane quite close at hand here. There is the lane, by yonder tall alder-tree."

" Then," said the magistrate, " I have no doubt but that those are our men. Pray, sir, allow me some of your troop to assist."

" You had better have us all," said the officer. " Forward !"

The soldiers immediately moved on, and the magistrate would have been ridden over if he had not hastily turned his horse's head and kept in motion upon the road.

" You can make your arrest," said the officer, " easily enough ; I daresay, the sight of us will put all ideas of resistance out of their heads."

" I hope so," said the magistrate, looking rather pale ; " but Duval is a desperate fellow, and no doubt well-armed."

" You expect him to fire upon us, do you ?"

" Indeed I do."

" Halt !"

The troop halted on the moment.

" The first file of men will load with ball cartridge."

The soldiers with great activity loaded the carbines that hung by their sides, and when the operation was completed, the word to advance was again given, and the officer coolly said—

" If they fire at us, I shall treat them to a volley at once, which I presume will settle the business, so you can pick up your prisoner afterwards satisfactorily enough, Mr. Magistrate, I daresay."

" Alive or dead, certainly, I must take them to London."

" Very well. Of course, it's quite immaterial to me. They may shoot you through, and it's probable enough they will."

" Do you—you think so ?"

" Of course I do. They will know that you have much more to do with the affair than we have. It would be a foolish and shabby thing of them to fire upon us."

" I think I'll get behind your men, do you know, until it is ascertained what sort of a humour the rascals are in."

" Oh, no, you won't, sir. If you desert the officers we go on, and have nothing further to do with it. You don't suppose that we are going to catch your thieves and hand them over to you, do you ?"

" Oh, very well—very well."

The magistrate was evidently anything but well pleased at the post of danger hat he was made to occupy ; and the soldiers, who had overheard the little diatogue between him and their officer, were all on the broad grin at the idea that there really might be the fun of seeing the magistrate shot down by the highwaymen, which they would have considered rather a joke than otherwise.

In this way, then, the whole party proceeded towards the head of the little lane, some short distance down which the fugitives had taken refuge, while their royal protector kept at the head of it, as though with his single arm he could defend the pass against all the force that was being brought against it.

The marchioness, during the time that the colloquy was taking place between the magistrate and the officer in command of the troop of cavalry, had managed to get quite close to May, and to plague her with questions.

"Well, child," she said, "and what is your name?"

"May."

"And so, you go about with Claude Duval, in this kind of guise, eh?"

"No."

"How can you say 'no,' when I see you thus? It is quite shameful, that it is; but as I rather like your face, I will protect you; and if you will call upon me to-morrow, I will find some means of providing for you. What would you say now to going to America, if I gave you a good sum of money?"

"I shall decline, madam."

"Decline! What do you mean by that? Do you mean to tell me that you would refuse my bounty?"

"Yes, madam; and for the single reason, that I do not require it."

"Oh, very well. We shall see. Do you know it strikes me that you are an artful little piece of goods, and I can only tell you that if I see you, by look or gesture, attempt to attract the prince, I will have your life."

May smiled.

"Oh, you will find it no laughing matter. I saw the kind of look he gave to you, I can tell you. But I warn you, that is all."

May made no answer to this ebullition of jealous fright upon the part of the marchioness, who was not so blinded by personal vanity but that she could see that the charms of May were infinitely superior to her own, and she knew enough of the prince to be well aware of the power that a new face had over his fickle affections, especially when that new face was decidedly prettier than the old one; and that he was a little smitten by the features and the beautiful form of May, as it was shown rather to advantage in her male apparel, her ladyship was quite convinced.

Duval himself, when he saw that the marchioness began to speak to May, had not thought it a gentlemanly thing to move sufficiently near to them to seem to be overhearing what they said, so that he was not aware of the subject even of their conversation; but seeing the quiet smile that was upon the face of May, he thought that the marchioness could not be saying anything very unpleasing or provoking to her upon the occasion.

By the time her ladyship had thus given vent to the jealous feelings that were tugging at her heart, the magistrate had reached, with the soldiers, the top of the lane. The Prince of Wales was mounted upon a chestnut-horse of the most superb description. He never paid for it, to be sure, but that was no matter just then. When he saw the horsemen stop, he rode right to the corner of the lane, and blocked it up by moving his horse a little sideways, and there he remained looking full in the face of the magistrate, who, in faltering accents, addressed him.

"You are not the person we seek, sir," he said; "you don't answer the description at all. Pray remove from our path."

"Halt!" cried the prince.

The soldiers at once mechanically pulled up, and the officer, as his face flushed with passion, cried out—

"This is the coolest piece of insolence on the part of a highwayman that ever I heard of. Pray, sir, who are you?"

"A superior officer to you, sir, and I desire that you consider yourself as under my order. I am a general in the service."

"A what?"

"A general."

"A general rogue, I suppose. Come, Mr. Magistrate, if you don't lay hands upon one of your highwaymen, you are very amiss in your duty. Oh, you are waiting for your men? Very good. Here they are."

The party of constables that was with the magistrate reached the spot at this moment, and the magistrate, as he himself retreated a pace or two, pointed to the prince, saying—

"Lay hold of that one. He is an associate of Claude Duval's. Clap a pair of handcuffs upon him. He is a very dangerous character."

"You had better beware, sir, what you do," said the prince. "It is a pity, captain, that you do not know me. I shall have to place you under arrest, I fear, for this breach of discipline. I announce myself to you as a general in the army, and order you to place yourself and men under my orders. Do you still refuse?"

"There is but one general in the army of your age," said the captain, "and he has a higher title than that."

"Well?"

"Why, you don't mean to have the impudence to say that you are the Prince of Wales, do you?"

"Precisely."

"Oh, indeed! Well, of all the pieces of impudence that ever I came near, this is the worst; but there happens to be a brother officer of mine at the rear-guard who is personally well known to the Prince of Wales. Give my compliments to Lieutenant Fane, and ask him to ride up this way."

A sergeant at once trotted off upon the errand.

"A fine day, captain," said the prince.

"I don't care whether it is a fine day or not. Don't speak to me, sir. You are our prisoner."

"Very well. I merely remarked that it was a fine day; I thought that even a prisoner might take that great liberty."

"No, he may not."

"The insolence," said the magistrate, as he arranged his neckcloth, "the insolence of this man, whose features I do believe I recollect, is beyond everything. Officers, I think this man is a suspicious character. Do you know anything of him?"

Upon being thus appealed to, the officers shook their heads, and one of them said, in a tone of voice that was the very essence of lying impertinence—

"Oh, yes, your worship. He was brought before you for horse-stealing last May twelve months."

"I thought as much; and I have no doubt that the horse he is now riding is not his own."

"It is not paid for," said the prince.

"Nor will it ever. Ha! ha! Paid for, indeed! No, no!"

"Well," said the prince, with the most admirable temper, "I don't think it ever will be, if I may hazard a candid opinion; but the people will trust me, so it is their own fault."

"Well, of all the confounded impertinence," said the officer, "that ever I heard of, this is the worst. Oh, here comes Lieutenant Fane. It is a good thing always to proceed regularly in these cases."

"Did you send for me, captain?" said a young officer, riding up from the rear guard.

"Yes, Fane. Just look at that person on the chestnut horse, and tell me if you know him."

"Oh, I can't know him," said Fane, as he turned a supercilious glance upon the "person." In a moment, then, his whole manner changed, and instantly saluting with his sword, he exclaimed—

"It is the prince. I hope your royal highness is quite well?"

"Pretty well, Fane," said the prince.

The magistrate almost fell off his horse, and the captain drew back a pace or two, thoroughly bewildered.

"I want you, Fane," added the prince, "to be so good as to assure your captain that I am a superior in the service; and as a field-marshal, I am, I think, authorised to give him orders."

"Good God! your highness, who doubts it? There is surely no one who would not be anxious to obey your orders."

"I don't know that, Fane."

The captain advanced, looking as pale as death. He held his sword by the blade, as he said—

"To whom am I to surrender my sword, your royal highness, as I presume I am under arrest?"

CHAPTER CXXXII.

DUVAL FINDS THE PRINCE AN USEFUL PATRON.

THE manner of the officer was so extremely crest-fallen, that no one could help pitying him. The prince held out his hand for the sword as he said—

"Deliver it to no one but to me, sir, and I shall then have the satisfaction of returning it to you. You could not know that I was the Prince of Wales; but I did hope that I should not have been mistaken for anything but a gentleman."

"Pardon me, your highness. I—I——"

"No more, sir. Let the past be forgotten."

The officer bowed, and took his sword again, and stepped back a pace or two with a look of intense chagrin. The magistrate had taken his hat off, and he now spoke in a fawning tone of voice, saying—

"Of course, if I had had the least idea, your royal highness, that it was your royal highness, I——"

"Enough, sir!" cried the prince. "To business, now. What do you want with me? Speak at once, sir."

"Oh, nothing—nothing, your royal highness. I am searching for the notorious highwayman, Claude Duval, that is all."

"Very well, sir, you do not suspect that I am that individual, do you, nor that any of my friends, who are some little distance behind me in the lane, answer such a description?"

"Oh dear, no. I—that is——"

"Then proceed, sir, about your business. Good-evening, sir."

"I have the honour to wish your royal highness good-evening; and if your royal highness will allow me, I will proceed down the lane, and——"

"No, sir. I have some friends with me, whom I do not wish you to interrupt. They are ladies. You may or you may not understand me, but in plain language, you shall not go down this lane."

"But if your royal highness will consider."

"No, sir; I do not intend to consider your convenience half so much as my own. Captain, you will be so good as to assist me in holding my post here."

In a moment or two, with a clash and clatter of arms, a couple of dragoons were at the head of the lane.

"Well, really," said the magistrate, "this looks as like a collision between the military and the civil power as possible."

"The uncivil power you mean, I suppose?" said the prince.

"Oh, dear no, your royal highness," added the magistrate, who had never made a joke in his life, and did not understand one when anybody else made one. "Oh, dear no. I am a magistrate, and I have a strong suspicion that the parties I seek are in the lane."

"What, sir, do you mean to tell me to my face that I am screening from the law a highwayman?"

"Oh, dear no. I was going to add, unknown to your royal highness."

"Well, captain," laughed the prince, "it is quite clear that I and my friends will all be apprehended, if you and your men do not aid us against this very civil power here, for you see he will not understand that no means nay."

"May I clear the way, your highness?"

"Why, yes, perhaps it will be as well."

"Right face! Take open order!"

There was a great clattering of horses feet, and the dragoons filled up the entire road-way. The magistrate was beginning a speech, and was waving his finger in the air in a very oratorical manner, when the captain shouted—

"Charge!"

With a rush like a tornado, on spurred the dragoons, and the magistrate, with his posse of officers, had only barely time to turn and put their horses to speed, or they would have been ridden over by the superior weight of the dragoons. A panic evidently now took possession of the police, and they did not attempt to halt, although the soldiers were recalled by a few notes from the trumpet, and quickly came back again.

"Would your royal highness desire us to escort you?" said the captain.

"Oh, no—no; you go on as you were, and let this little affair rest quietly. They won't interfere with us again, I daresay. Good-day, Fane."

The lieutenant bowed, and the prince then, with a salute to the captain and the troop, turned his horse's head down the lane.

As may be well supposed, Duval and his friends had been rather anxious spectators and listeners to what had passed between the prince and the police, and while they could not but feel gratified for the firm stand which the prince had made for them, they felt that their safety could be but of a temporary character; and they were terribly anxious to quit the spot before the police should rally again, and think of returning, as it was probable enough they would.

"You are safe at present, Claude," whispered May, "but it will not last."

"I fear not."

"It cannot. We must take immediate advantage of the lull in the tempest of danger that has surrounded us, and fly."

"Hush—hush! the prince approaches."

"Duval," said the prince, "a word with you."

Duval rode to about a dozen paces off with the prince, who then said in a hurried tone of voice, as if he were ashamed of what he was about to say.

"I think you can be useful to me, Duval, in a little affair that I have on hand, that requires courage and address."

"I shall be happy to be of any service to your highness."

"Do you really mean that?"

"I do, indeed. I owe you my life, and I owe to you the safety of one who is dearer to me than my life."

"Oh, well, never mind that. It was not at all likely I was going to let them take you, Duval; but I can't explain further to you just now what I want of you. You must meet me in London."

"As your highness pleases."

"Of course, you know St. James's Park well?"

"Perfectly."

"Very good; then you know the wall of Carlton House—the wall enclosing the garden?"

"I do, your highness."

"That will do. You must be at that wall this evening, if possible, at ten o'clock. A man will come up to you and say, 'One, two, three,' to which you will be so good as to reply, 'Four, five, six,' and then you will submit yourself to his guidance. Are you willing to do this for me?"

"Quite so."

"And I may depend upon you as regards punctuality, and all that sort of thing?"

"Your highness may."

"Very well, then—that is all I need say to you just now.   Take care of yourself, Duval; you know that you are in rather a ticklish position.   Good-day."

DUVAL SEES THE SPECTRE IN THE OLD LODGING.

Without then taking another glance at Duval or his companions, the prince turned towards the lady he called Emma, and said, gaily—

"Now shall we be off?"

"It is almost time," said the marchioness, with an air of vexation.

The prince trotted off, and after hesitating for a few moments, and no doubt, during that short period, having something of a conflict with her temper, she went after him at speed, and they both disappeared round a turn in the lane, apparently rather on the wrangle.

"Well," said Duval, "this is rather a nice state of things."

"What do you mean, Duval?" said May.

Luke, too, looked inquiringly, upon which Duval, who had made no promise of secrecy, so far as they were concerned, told them exactly what the prince had said to him, to which they listened with alarm and surprise.

"What can it mean?" said May; "you do not suspect treachery?"

"Oh, no—no!"

"It is an odd thing," said Luke; "and yet it will be quite out of the question to attempt to dispute the commands of the prince. It would be as foolish to do so as it would be unfair."

"But the danger—the great danger," said May.

"That must," said Duval, "be encountered; and recollect that whatever danger I may now fall into, I have a powerful protector in the Prince of Wales."

"Yes, his will may be good to protect you, but his power may fail to do so. There cannot be a doubt but that if he could, he would; but even he dare not interfere too openly with the law."

"There is no human enterprise," said Duval, "without some risk; and so this one that I have agreed to go upon for the prince has its dangers; but as I have promised him to do so, I will keep my word and my appointment with him at any risk. You are of that opinion, Luke?"

"I am, sir."

"And you, too, May, upon reflection, will likewise be of it."

"Alas! I am already," said May; "and while I tremble at the risks you must run in going to London just now, I yet could not conscientiously advise that you should break faith with the prince after the generous manner in which he has befriended you."

"That is spoken like yourself, May."

"Ah, Duval, how could I feel otherwise? But I will rely upon you, for my sake, to be as careful as you possibly can of your safety."

"That I will."

"Then I am perforce content that you should go."

Duval now was evidently in deep thought for a moment or two, and then he said—

"May, and you too, Luke, I cannot come to a conclusion in my own mind whether or not it would be better for us all three to go to town or not."

"That I must leave to you, sir," said Luke.

"But you have an opinion?"

"I have, sir; and it is that we should all go. I think that there is greater safety by us all going. A lodging can easily be got for us while you attend to the affair that the prince wishes to employ you upon; and if anything should go amiss, we shall be at hand to aid you."

"And what is more," added May, "I shall be at ease in my mind, comparatively speaking, instead of being a prey to the frightful feelings of suspense that would come over me if I were some miles from you and could not see you frequently."

"It is decided, then," said Duval. "Let us all go to London. It often happens, and to none has it oftener happened than to me, that by going, to all appearance, into the very jaws of danger, I have escaped, while by taking a course that looked like almost the assurance of safety, I have dropped into great peril; so let us, with as light hearts as we can, proceed at once to London."

"That will do," said Luke.

They at once put their horses to the trot, and went down the lane at a good pace. To Duval himself it seemed, indeed, most singular, how a short half hour had so completely altered his whole train of thoughts. But a little while since and he had been intent upon getting as far from London as it was at all possible to get, even to going as far as the south coast, and now he was actually thinking, on what would be his most direct route to the Metropolis.

They went right on over the Surrey side of the river till they came to Battersea Bridge, which they crossed, and then made their way onwards right into the West-end of London.

The district now so fashionable, and which comprises Belgrave and Eaton Squares, was then but a sorry suburb of London, and it was there that Duval tthought it would be better to get a lodging for May and Luke and himself, so hat he might be close at hand to the prince.

Notwithstanding Pimlico was then anything but a choice or fashionable locality, there were some old, large rambling houses in it; and without meeting with any adventure worth the record.ng, Duval and his two friends found themselves near the back of old Buckingham House, upon the site of which some portion of Buckingham Palace now stands.

"Sir," said Luke, "if I might advise, I should say, let us put up our horses somewhere first, and then seek a lodging on foot. It will be necessary, too, that you think of some name to call yourself."

"You are right, Luke. What shall I name myself, May?"

"Call yourself Colonel Park," said May, "and we shall none of us forget the name, as we are so near the park."

"Be it so, then; I will be Colonel Park, and you had better be my brother John, and you Luke, what will you be?"

"Oh," said Luke, "I will be a confidential servant, supposed to be sent with you both by old General Park to look after your morals."

Neither Duval nor May could help laughing at the tone of serious mock gravity with which Luke made this speech, but they agreed that such should be his character, and dismounting, they got him to take their horses to a stable hard by, where he left orders that either Colonel Park, or his brother John, or himself, should have access to them at any time; for he did not know, of course, what sort of emergency might arise, in which Duval or May might require their steeds when he might not be at hand to get them.

"It's all right!" said Luke, when he returned. "The horses are very well housed now, indeed."

"That will do," said Duval, "and it was much better that you should take them, and that we should not be seen, as the ostler now cannot give any description of us to anybody who may be curious enough to inquire to whom the cattle belong."

"That is a great point," said May; "and now for a house."

After walking a little distance, they saw a large old-fashioned-looking house with an immense chestnut tree before the door, and in the window of which there was a bill announcing that there were lodgings to let.

Duval knocked at the door, and it was answered by a woman, whose rather fiery-looking visage seemed to proclaim that she was rather intimate with the brandy-bottle; but, after all, a red face is not an infallible sign of a hard drinker.

"We have come to look at the lodgings, madam," said Duval.

"Oh, any ladies?"

"No—only myself, and my brother here, and my servant."

"Very good, sir. Pray walk in. I only take in and do for gentlemen. I don't want lady lodgers. They are no end of trouble, and so mighty particular, and such a plague with their hooks-and-eyes and all that sort of thing, that I have made up my mind only to let to single gentlemen."

"A very wise resolution," said May; "you will find us very single, indeed, and giving no trouble. My brother the Colonel is very much out, and as for me, I am one of the quietest people in the world."

At the title of Colonel, which May took care to bestow upon Duval, the woman was evidently mightily pleased, and taking them up a rather crazy flight of stairs, she showed them a suite of ancient dingy-looking rooms. There were no less than five apartments all opening one into the other, and some of them having doors on to the staircase.

"This is the very place for us," whispered Duval to May. "It is cut out for us—we must have it."

"What's the rent?" said May.

"Did you ever see such nice rooms in all your lives, gentlemen?" said the landlady, who was determined to expatiate upon the accommodations of her apartments before she named the rent. "Large and airy they are, and as quiet as if you were at the bottom of a well, and as cheerful, too, as sunshine in May. The last gentleman that had them d ed, poor man."

"Of the cheerfulness," said Duval, "or that well-like feeling you describe?"

"No, sir, of the gout."

"Oh, that is quite another thing; and now will you have the goodness to name to us the rent of the suite of rooms."

"And only look out," said the landlady, throwing open a window. "There's a prospect of the park just over Buckingham House—that is to say, if Buckingham House wasn't there, you would see it as nice as nice could be."

CHAPTER CXXXIII.

DUVAL AND MAY GET SETTLED IN THEIR NEW LODGING.

It was quite clear that the landlady was determined Duval and May should not know the rate of her rooms until she had explained all their perfections.

"In this small room," she said, "the last of the lot, there's a turn-up bedstead, that you see, in the day time, stands up against the wall quite easily, and when you want it down——"

Bang came the bedstead down with a good sweep through the air, for the landlady had unconsciously touched a little button that alone held it up, and in an instant she was hidden from sight beneath it, being knocked flat by it in its downward progress.

"Ah!" said Duval, "when you want it down, down it comes."

"Murder!" shrieked the landlady.

May was forced to go and put her head out at the window to laugh, while Luke released the landlady. who rose in a very great fluster indeed, declaring that the bedstead had never done such a thing before, and she had had it seven years.

As it was only the sacking that had struck her, she had not sustained any serious injury, and Duval said to her, with a smile,—

"I think it would be a capital thing, if one had any troublesome visitor, to place him just under this bedstead, and then release it, when it would quite extinguish him."

"Oh dear, yes, sir, it would; I wonder if the tax-gatherer would like it, when he comes bothering?"

"He would not like it, madam; but I do not think he would venture up-stairs again. And now, perhaps, you will be so good as to tell us what the rent really is?"

"The rent, sir, for yourself, and your little brother, and your servant, sir, of the whole five rooms, with all convenience and attendance?"

"Yes—yes."

"Well, it will be two guineas a week."

"Very good, that will do. We will take them."

"Without extras?"

"What do you mean by extras?"

The landlady, by the readiness with which Duval had agreed to give the two guineas a week, was in an agony at the idea that she might have got more for the asking, so she immediately replied that she would make a little bill of the extras at the end of every week, and let him have it.

"All's right," said Duval.

"Yes, sir," said Luke, "and I dare say if the general comes to town, that he will be quite pleased to see you so comfortably situated."

"The general, I presume," said the landlady, "is your worthy father?"

"Yes," said Duval, "that is the old pump."

"The old who, sir?"

"The governor," said May. "The old pump we generally call him, out of affection, you know."

"Oh, dear me, really. Well, I suppose you can oblige me with a reference, gentlemen, of course."

"Yes," said Duval, as he laid two guineas upon the table. "There are two references, and if his majesty's head stamped in gold will not do, I am quite sure that nothing will."

"It's quite right" said the landlady, as she pocketed the guineas; "I am quite delighted to let my rooms to such highly respectable gentlemen, I assure you, only you will easily imagine that it's right of me as a lone widow, though I have left off my caps, to be particular."

"Quite; and now, madam, you will consider that we hold possession of this suite of rooms. When we want anything, we will ring the bell, and you can get it for us, and put it down in the bill."

This was precisely the arrangement that suited the landlady, and which suits landladys in general, for they can then make out a bill, the only limits to which depends upon the degree of elasticity of their consciences. With quite a profound curtsey she left the rooms; and then Duval, turning to May with a smile, said—

"Shall we be comfortable here for a little while?"

"Oh, yes, Claude."

"Hush! do not call me by that name. Landladys, in addition to having keys that will open all your locks, have frequently places from which they can overhear what you say."

"I will call you brother."

"Do so, and I will call you John. Of course, our stay here will depend entirely upon what the prince requires of me; and that I shall, no doubt, know all about to-night."

"I only hope," said May, "that he does not want you to take the dangerous part of some enterprise that he himself shrinks from."

"Oh, no, I do not anticipate that, May."

"Oh, now, brother," said May, with a smile, "you are forgetting, and doing the very thing you blamed me for. Can you not call me John?"

"Oh, dear, yes. John you shall be, and dear John, too. But now we will put our landlady's powers of entertainment to the test, by ordering something to eat of her."

Duval rang the bell, and the landlady herself answered it so promptly, that one could hardly, with all the charity in the world towards her, imagine that she could have been very far off. To be sure, the kitchen might be near at hand; but the promptitude of the landlady was such, that in order to account for it consistently, it ought to have been at the top of the stairs.

"Did you ring, sir?"

"Yes," said Duval "You will be as good so to get us something to eat as quickly as convenient, and go to the nearest wine merchant's and procure a bottle of Madeira."

"Certainly, sir. Oh, dear, yes. Perhaps chops, as being the sort of thing that can be got amazingly quick, will suit for to-day, gentlemen?"

"Very good: chops be it."

The landlady bustled off to execute the order, and then May said—

"Ah, I am afraid she was listening to our conversation."

" And so am I," replied Duval ; " but she cannot have overheard much of it, I think, after all, and we really said so little, and that little must have been so completely incomprehensible to any one who did not understand what we were talking about, that I have no apprehension."

"They are very curious old rooms," said Luke, suddenly coming into the apartment where May and Duval were sitting, after having taken a survey of the apartments.

"I think they are, Luke."

"I like them on that account," said May.

"Theie's no end of odd old hiding-places and cupboards, and all sorts of secret-looking nooks. I should not at all wonder if there were secret panels in the walls, and winding staircases, and all that sort of thing, in the old place."

" You don't mean that, Luke ?"

"Yes, sir, I do ; and I think it would be quite a capital thing if we could find out some of the odd hiding-places in the house."

"So it might, and to-morrow, Luke, we will have a good look about us. It is too late to day to do so, and I confess to being somewhat wearied ; and, indeed, I feel as if I wanted sleep."

"There is quite time enough, Duval," said May, "for you to take an hour or two's repose, before your time of appointment with the prince. Your eyes look languid ; and, indeed, I am full of astonishment at the little sleep that suffices for you."

"The fact is," said Duval, "I do get desperately sleepy ; and then, after a time, that feeling goes off, and I feel as if I could keep awake for a week ; but when it does come again, it is almost irresistible, so I will just partake of the land-lady's chops, and a glass or two of the wine that we have ordered, and then I will have a sleep until nearly ten o'clock ; but I must rely upon you, brother, John, to awaken me."

"Oh, yes," said May, "that brother John will do, you may depend upon it. How capitally we are getting into the habit of calling each other as we have agreed."

"Yes," remarked Luke, " and for my part, I almost feel as if there really were an old General Park, who has deputed me to look after you both, and take care of your morals, for I have repeated the name so often to myself for fear I should forget, that I can hardly believe it really means nothing at all."

Both Duval and May laughed at this speech of Luke's, and then the door opening in the midst of their mirth, showed them the landlady with a large tray in her arms, containing the repast that had been ordered.

" I hope, gentlemen," she said, "that I have not kept you at all waiting, if you please. I made all the haste I could."

"Not at all," said Duval " I think you have been wonderfully quick about it indeed, and very nice the chops look, too. If the wine only is as good, we shall be very well off."

"I hope it is, sir. I asked for the very best, and told them that it was for a real gentleman, that I did."

"Thank you, madam."

The table was laid with considerable activity by the landlady, and then she said with rather a confused air—

" Perhaps your luggage will soon come."

" There will be no more luggage than the two little vallises that you see," replied Duval.

"Oh, certainly, sir ; that is all right."

With this she left the room, and May looking at Duval, said—

"What did she mean ?"

"Only that she looked forward to having the rummaging of a lot of trunks and boxes, that is all. These kind of people like you to bring in a quantity of mis-cellaneous property, and then they think there is a chance of laying hold of some of it."

"I do not like that woman's manners," said May, with a slight shudder.

"Never mind her manners," laughed Duval, "as long as her chops and wine are good; so let us set-to at once with the eatables. Sit down, Luke. Come—come, do not hesitate; sit down and let us begin."

The chops and the wine both turned out to be excellent, and even May, although she had taken a dislike to the landlady, could not help owning that it might be by possibility a mere prejudice.

"We must not judge of people by their looks," she said, "for if we did, I am quite certain we should never have come to live in this place at all."

"Certainly," said Duval, "our hostess is not dangerous on account of her beauty, I must say. You will have no cause for jealousy, May, upon her account."

"Not the least."

"She will very likely be communicative enough to me," said Luke. "I will take an opportunity of getting into conversation with her domestics; and no doubt, in her great anxiety to ascertain from me all the particulars about General Park and the family, she will be very confidential herself."

"There is no servant here, that is quite clear," said May.

"No, Nor, to all appearance, any one in the house but herself," added Duval, "although I do not see that such a state of things, as long as we are properly attended to, ought to make any difference to us."

In such like discourse the dinner was dispatched, and then Duval, who felt that it would be quite impossible for him much longer to resist the feeling for sleep that had crept over him, went into one of the bed-rooms, and flung himself upon a bed.

In three minutes he was in profound repose.

When May ascertained that Duval was in sound repose, she returned to the room in which Luke was waiting, and in an anxious tone of voice, she said—

"Luke, I do not like this house that we have got into. Tell me truly what you think of it, and of the woman who seems to be the sole inhabitant of it."

"I don't know what to think," said Luke. "I know so little of the habits and of the people of London, that I am hardly able to come to a judgment."

"But you do not like the woman?"

"Certainly I do not, and yet I cannot say why; but if you will permit me, I will go down stairs now, and try to get into conversation with her, when I shall be better able to come to some opinion concerning her."

"Do so, good Luke—do so at once. There need be no hurry, for I will find some amusement, while Duval sleeps, from looking over the books that are here in tolerable profusion."

"I shall not be long gone," said Luke. "People either will not talk at all on their own affairs, or they will be so communicative, that they will tell you a great deal in a short space of time."

With these words, which were uncommonly true, Luke left the room, and May began to look over a quantity of books that were in one corner of the large and gloomy apartment.

Some of these books were upon a table, and some were upon the floor; but what attracted the attention of May was, that names seemed to have been erased from nearly every one of them. They were a strange collection, for there was something of every kind of literature extant, and among them some works in Latin that evidently were belonging to the Roman Catholic Church. Among the whole lot, there was only one that she cared to read, and that was a very fearful account of a discovery of an island in the southern ocean by some persons who had been wrecked, and who reached it after a weary sojourn amid the waste of waters on a raft.

There was a profound stillness in the house now; and the evening was visibly creeping on, so that May felt that she would have to procure lights soon; but while she could possibly see, she read.

The door of communication to the adjoining chamber where Duval slept, was open, so that she could hear his regular breathing as he slept; and as the night crept on, she became more and more absorbed in the interest of the book.

CHAPTER CXXXIV.

MAY SEES AN APPARITION IN THE OLD LODGING.

IF May had been asked to define why it was that she felt very odd and uncomfortable, she would have been puzzled to do so ; but if she had been required to say with perfect truth how she did feel, she must have replied, decidedly frightened !

Yes, as May sat in that large, solitary room, a strange feeling of fright came over her.

What was there to be frightened at ?   There she was, in apparently a secure enough temporary home close to many persons and many other houses.   There was nothing particularly solitary in the aspect of the house, and, more than all, she was so close to Duval that, as we have said, she could hear him breathing in the adjoining chamber ; and she knew that if she only raised her voice a little higher than ordinary, that she should awaken him.

And yet, with all these aids to calmness, and inducements to feel quite secure, May felt he heart beat rapidly, and her breath come and go in such strange spasmodic gaspings, that she began to be very much alarmed, indeed, at her condition.

" What is the meaning of all this ?" she said in a whisper.   " Is this illness, or what is it ?—What does it mean ?—What does it portend ?"

Such questions were easily asked, but by no means so easily answered ; and far from the strange feelings that crept over her subsiding, they seemed to be upon the increase, and to oppress her each moment more powerfully by their distracting pressure.

" This will not do," she said.   " It is a foolish, weak superstition.   I must shake it off.   Why, I never felt this in the old house at Hornsey, where I have spent nights alone, and when the hollow wind has been whistling through the chamber, and roaring in the chimneys !"

She shook, for she plainly heard something like a deep-drawn sigh from the apartment occupied by Duval.

At this moment, May had not happened to be looking in that direction ; but upon hearing that sigh, she turned her head towards the door of communication, and she distinctly saw a sight that served to freeze her blood, and in an instant to wrap up all her faculties in dread.

With a slow and stately movement, there came from the inner room a female figure, clothed in white drapery.   It did not seem to walk, and, indeed, May felt that walk it did not ; but it glided along, just touching the floor.   The face of the figure had a strange, misty look about it, and the eyes appeared to be fixed upon May.

Oh, what a horror it was to look upon those eyes !

The figure did not attempt to approach May.   If it had done so, she felt that there would have been some danger of it driving her distracted ; but it moved along the room diagonally towards the door that led out on to the stair-landing.

Almost petrified with terror, May continued gazing at it as it went along, and when it reached as near as might be the centre of the room, it paused, and seemed to be regarding her with a look of intense grief.

The pause lasted only a moment or two, and then it glided on again with the same strange and noiseless movement as before.

The door leading from the apartment on to the staircase had been carefully closed by Luke, when he had left the room, and even in the midst of her fright poor May wondered if the figure would open it, or finding it closed, go back again to the chamber from whence it had come.

The figure did neither.

Assoon as the apparition—for what else could May call it, or could any one have called it ?—reached the door, there seemed to be a very slight pause in its progress, and then it fairly appeared to pass through the solid door and to melt away before the eyes of the wonder and terror-stricken May.

It was gone.

May sprang to her feet and uttered a cry of terror. It seemed as if the departure of the apparition had had the effect of at once releasing her faculties from

THE APPARITION APPEARING TO MAY IN THE OLD LODGING.

the bondage in which they had been bound up, and of enabling her to utter a sound.

That sound was a loud shriek.

As she uttered the shriek, May rushed into the adjoining chamber, and was caught in the arms of Duval, who had sprung from the bed upon which he had been lying upon being aroused by that sound of fear from her lips.

No. 67.

"What is the matter?" cried Duval. "What is it?"

"Help!—Help!"

"Yes, yes, May; I am here. Do you not see me? What is the matter with you? What has happened?"

"Oh Claude, Claude!"

"Yes, May. That is right. Speak to me. What has produced this condition in you? Are you terrified?"

"I am—I am."

She would have fallen to the floor, had not Duval supported her; and as there was a large old-fashioned arm-chair by the side of the bed, he placed her in it, and entreated her to tell him what had caused her to cry out in such a way, and produced such a feeling of alarm within her; but for some time she could not speak, and only clung to his arm and looked wildly about her.

"May, May," he said, "I implore you to take me off the rack of dread that I am on, and tell me what has happened to terrify you in this way. Is it anything connected with Luke?"

"Oh, no—no——"

"Then what is it? You are not hurt?"

"Oh, no—no! Not hurt, Claude, but I am horror-stricken."

"Horror-stricken?"

"Yes, yes.—Oh, pray for me, Claude. Claude, it is a warning of something, I feel assured. There is danger somewhere. Oh, pray for me, Claude, do. I shall never recover this day—this hour——"

She burst into a flood of tears.

"Good," said Duval, "now she will be much better. After the rain, the storm vanishes. Weep on, May. These tears will save you, poor girl, from further suffering. Do not attempt to check them: they are blessed drops."

Poor May could not have stopped her tears if she had been ever so much inclined to do so, for they came in spite of her. It was nature relieving herself of the superabundance of excitement that had ensued upon the appearance of the spectre.

For more than ten minutes May sobbed, but then she was quieter, and she felt wonderfully better, and was able to look up in the face of Claude and speak.

"Oh, Claude," she said, "how weak you will think me, and how wicked, too."

"Weak and wicked?" he said, with a smile. "Why, May, you are quite resolved to bring accusations enough against yourself, I think."

"Yes, but I am indeed."

"Pray explain; and if you convince me that you are weak, you shall not convince me that you are wicked, May."

"I will tell you, Claude. You naturally wonder to have seen me in such a state of suffering, but I can tell you, Claude, that I have seen an apparition."

"A what?"

"An apparition! Nay, Claude, do not laugh at me, for if this were the last moment I had to live, or if my life depended entirely upon my stating the truth to you, I could say nothing but what I have said."

"May, I do not laugh at you. Do not fancy for a moment that I do. From my heart I believe that you believe you have seen an apparition."

"But you do not believe it, Claude?"

He shook his head.

"It would be very difficult, indeed," he said, "to induce me to believe it. should be sorry to feel that I was compelled even to doubt upon such a subject."

"I shall doubt no more."

May spoke with such a shudder, and in such a tone of voice, that showed her thorough and deep-seated conviction of the fact that she had seen an apparition, that Duval became not a little curious to hear what account she had to give of an appearance that had evidently terrified her so much.

"Well, May," he said, "since you will have it that you have seen this apparition, let me know all about it."

"You shall, Claude; but we will go into the other room, and then I shall be able to show you how it was that I saw it, and where it came from, and whither it went. Come, come."

Duval, to humour her, accompanied her, and she led him to the chair upon which she had sat when she saw the figure, and then drawing a little footstool close to him, she sat down at his feet, and held by one of his hands, to give herself a greater sense of security.

"Why, you tremble yet," he said.

"Oh, yes, I cannot but tremble. I do not wonder at that, Claude; the marvel would be if I did not."

"Well, now for the story."

"Yes, yes, you shall hear it. Oh, Duval, are you certain that we are alone in this room, even now? Do you feel assured that there are no beings of another world hovering around us, and watching us with eyes that we cannot see, and listening to us with ears that are not mortal? Are you certain of that, Duval?"

"How can I be certain of any such thing, May? Come, come, shake off these dreamy terrors, and let your better judgment speak for you. I'll warrant, now, by this time to-morrow, you will be the first to laugh at this story of an apparition, which now seems to take your fancy prisoner."

"No—no! Oh, no!"

"Well, then, go on and tell me all."

May began in a faltering tone of voice her narrative, and Duval listened in all seriousness to what she had to say, nor did he even interrupt her till she got to the end of the story. He could not for one moment doubt but that May was firmly convinced of the truth of what she had asserted. Her manner was quite sufficient to force him to that conclusion.

"Well, May," he said, "now that I have heard your ghost story——"

"You do not believe it, Claude?"

"Nay, there you are too quick. I do believe it. But——"

"Ah, I knew an exception was coming."

Duval smiled as he added—

"But, May, I likewise fully believe, that, overcome by fatigue, which you well might be, you went to sleep in that chair, and that then this vision appeared to you, or seemed to appear to you."

"Oh, no—no!"

"Yes, May, it must indeed have been so. Nothing else could by any possibility have produced such an effect. Half a minute's sleep would have been quite sufficient. as you well know, to set the imagination at rest from the control of the reason, and then who shall say what strange visions it may not produce?'

"Claude, it is impossible for me to take upon myself to say to a moral certainty that it is not so ; but this much I can say, that if I was sleeping then, I am now."

'Duval was silent for a few moments, and then he said—

'May, you will freely admit, I presume, that if there be any truth in the appearance of supernatural beings, that it is not a common phenomena?"

"Certainly not."

"Then when it does come, we ought to expect that it is for some object."

"Yes, Claude, we ought, indeed."

"Then, pray, May, what object can be obtained by a figure in white crossing a room, apparently merely for the purpose of giving you a fright? If this apparition had had anything to communicate, why did it not do so? If it came to give you a warning of any description, it failed to give it."

"I know," said May, mildly, and in a low voice, "I know well, that all the argument is upon the side of those who deny the existence of the supernatural, but nothing will shake my belief in what I have seen in this room."

"Then we will say no more about it, May, and you should, as forcibly as you can possibly do so, adopt another line of argument to the effect, that if everything you ever heard or read of——"

" Or saw, Claude."

" Well, or saw—be strictly true as regards apparitions, there is no reason why you should be frightened at them."

" There is more in that argument, Claude, than in a thousand against a belief in such things, and that is the feeling that I should like to cling to in the matter. But here is Luke."

Luke at this moment made his appearance in the room, and Claude turning to him, said—

" Well, Luke, have you made any discoveries regarding our singular hostess?" Luke shook his head.

" No," he said, " and I don't think that there is any great deal of chance of doing so. She seemed very well pleased to get me to talk to, and made all sorts of inquiry about General Park, which I answered in the best way I was able, without saying too much : but when I strove to induce her to be communicative in return, I found that she was not at all inclined to be so. But I don't like the place."

" Nor I," said May.

" But why don't you like it, Luke?"

" I will tell you, sir. The landlady had occasion to go to the door while I was talking with her, and I seeing a large cupboard in the room, I thought I would open it to see what she had in it, when I saw a large sack."

" A sack? What of a sack, Luke?"

" Nothing of a sack merely, but this sack had something in it that looked, by the odd shape that it made the sack assume, so like a human body——"

" A human body !" cried May.

" Oh, no, no !" said Claude. " Impossible. You found that it was no such thing, Luke?"

" I had no opportunity of coming to a conclusion upon the subject, for while I was making some efforts to untie the knot into which a piece of stout cord was drawn that fastened up the neck of the sack, I heard the woman coming back, and I had no resource but to hastily close the cupboard again."

" It is strange," said Duval, as he paced the room in thought.

CHAPTER CXXXV.

DUVAL GOES TO KEEP HIS APPOINTMENT WITH THE PRINCE OF WALES.

THE state of alarm into which May had been thrown, combined to this event of mysteries below-stairs by Luke, contributed largely to her fears. The apparition that she had seen had prepared her mind for any horror that might succeed it ; and, indeed, she felt as though it would be quite impossible that something of a fearful character should not come after such a circumstance.

" It was some few minutes before Duval spoke again, and then advancing towards May, he said, with a smile—

" Why, you are allowing yourself to be more frightened each moment. Surely you ought to arouse from your terror rather than improve upon it in this way."

" Yes, Duval, I should, but——"

" But what ? Come now—let me see you smile away those fears. What are you going to say ?"

" Just that every circumstance seems to add to those fears that you think so idle, or that you would fain, Duval, for my peace of mind, effect that you think idle. I cannot smile."

" Well, then, I must smile for both of us. In the first place, you sit half asleep in a chair, waiting for me, while I am wholly asleep, and some shadow from without, no doubt, passes across the wall of the room, and you take it at once for an apparition. Is it not so?"

"I wish I thought it so."

"Oh, you must. And then up comes Luke with a cock and a bull story about something in a sack."

Luke shook his head.

"Oh no, sir, it is no cock and a bull story—that is to say, not to my thinking—(Luke caught the expression of Duval's countenance, which was one that let him see he, Duval, wished him to alarm May as little as possible)—Of course, sir, it might not have been a dead body in the sack."

"Well, that is candid," laughed Duval.

"But then it might," said May.

"Or perhaps it was a sack of potatoes—or of lumber of any kind, or perchance a pig."

"It might have been a pig," said Luke.

"This is trifling with me," said May, "although I know and feel that it is done with the best motives of silencing my fears, if possible; but I tell you, Duval, that if I were to live for a hundred years from now, I should never get rid of the impression, and of the firm opinion, that it was a real apparition that I saw cross the room."

"Well, then," cried Duval, "if it were, I only wish it would be so good as to come again; and when it does come, be a little explicit about what it comes for, as I cannot, for the life of me, see the use of a ghost stalking through a room just to frighten somebody about nothing."

Both May and Luke looked in rather a scared way about them, and Duval seeing that, added—

"Now, Mr. Ghost, if you please, be so good as to glide this way, for you are particularly wanted, rather. Now is your time—we are all waiting for you, and are quite prepared to listen with the most respectful attention to any conversation with which you may be pleased to favour us upon the present occasion. Now's your time. Walk up, Mr. Apparition, if you please."

"Oh, Claude—Claude!" said May, "do not go on in that way—do not, I beg of you."

"It is just as well not," said Luke.

"Really now," said Duval, "this is too absurd; you see that your ghost will not come here; he is civilly asked to do so, and I warrant I should sit here for an age, and he would not have the common good manners to say, 'How are you?'"

"They can't speak," said Luke, in a low voice, "till they are spoken to—at least, I have heard say that such is the case."

"I did not speak to it," said May, with a shudder; "I could not do so. If my life had depended upon doing so, I could not."

"Then the ghost ought to have a placard pinned to his back to the effect that all questions would be answered if asked in a clear tone of voice, and I promise it that I will speak to it, and no mistake, if it will be so good as to come."

"Duval, you terrify me," said May, "by going on in such a reckless way, talking of things that are beyond our knowledge. It is not right—it does not sound right to hear you say such things."

Luke nodded very gravely in token that he fully coincided with May in her opinion of the impropriety of speaking of the inhabitants of a possibly other world in such a strain.

"I only wished," said Claude Duval, smiling, "to convince you of the absurdity of such a thing by what I have been saying. Do you fancy for a moment that if I had had any belief in such appearances that I would have turned them to such ridicule? No, I should consider them as part of the phenomena of nature, and as such I should have respected them as I would any other of the works of the creator."

There was a slight pause after this speech of Claude Duval's, and May was upon the point of saying something, when three distinct taps came upon the wainscot of the room in which they sat.

Luke turned as pale as death, and May looked as though she were ready to faint. Even Claude Duval could not help feeling at the moment some degree of surprise.

" Who heard that ?" he said. " Did you both hear it ?"

" Yes—yes,"

" What was it like ?"

" A tap upon the wainscot," said Luke.

" Yes," gasped May, " that was it."

" Then it is no ghost," cried Duval, " for how can that which in itself is immaterial make a material noise? This is some trickery, and I can only warn those who are practising it, that they will find it anything but a joke to encounter me."

" Oh, no—no !" cried May, " it is no trick."

" It must be, and it is," said Duval.

" Ghosts only come to one person at a time," said Luke, timidly.

" Oh, is that it," laughed Duval. " Are they afraid of their appearance being substantiated by witnesses ?"

" They say so," said Luke.

" Very good, then. You, May and Luke, go into the next room, and shut yourselves in, and leave me and the ghost to settle our affairs as best we may together. If he will be so good, then, as to appear to me, being alone, I am willing."

" No, Claude," said May, " could you suppose that we would leave you to the chances of such an encounter?"

" Don't think of it," said Luke.

" But I will think of it, and if you won't both of you go into the next room and leave me here for the apparition to come to me if it likes, I will go in there, and leave you both here."

He made a movement to leave the apartment, but May ran up to him, and clasped her arms round him, crying—

" No—no, Claude Duval, I implore you not to do as you project. Let me beg of you not. For my sake do not."

" It is for your sake, May, that I would do so. Let me ask of you, as a favour, that you will let me go."

Duval uttered these words so seriously, that May felt that it was not possible to prevent him. She released him from the hold she had taken of him.

" Go," she said, " but call to me if you see anything or hear anything, and if there is nothing, do not be gone long. Oh, do not keep me above a moment or two in suspense."

" I will not."

Duval, with a firm step, left the sitting-room, and went into the old bed-room in which he had enjoyed the short repose that he had been so much in want of. He closed the door with great care, and finding the key on the inside, he turned it in the lock, so that neither May nor Luke could come suddenly into the room and take him by surprise, for they might startle him by doing so without intending it.

The feeling that came over Claude Duval, when he found himself now alone after what had happened, could not be defined to be fear, although he felt a little nervousness, but it was rather the excitement of expectation that was at his heart.

The only thing that he seemed to be very sensitive about, even to the verge of what perhaps looked like fear, was that anything should be behind him ; so, with great alacrity, he placed his back against the door, and then, in a low but by no sort of means a tremulous voice, he said—

" Come."

This word had hardly escaped his lips, when a sort of current of air seemed to come through the room, and directly opposite to him between the two windows, he certainly saw a something, but what it was, he could not at the moment define.

Duval drew his breath shortly and thickly as he gazed. To him it looked like a figure, and for the moment he forgot the idea of Luke's, that such appearances must be spoken to before they can give any utterance to a sound. With amazing difficulty then, he uttered the one word—

" Speak !"

Duval had expected that some sound would meet his ears, but he was not prepared for the one that did do so. It was one of the most unearthly laughs that he had ever heard in all his life. It seemed to stop the very current of his blood to hear it, and to freeze his heart.

In a moment, the figure, if it were a figure, was gone. Duval turned and unlocked the door, and stood upon the threshold, looking into the next room more like a spectre himself than a living breathing man.

" Oh, Duval," said May, " thank heaven you are here again."

" All's right, sir, of course ?" said Luke ; " there was nothing ?"

" Nothing !" gasped Duval. He could not understand how after that horrid laugh they could both be sitting there so calmly, and could speak to him in such ordinary and common-place accents. That they could avoid hearing such a sound, did not lie within the compass of rational belief; and that, hearing it, they should think nothing or so little of it, was staggering.

Yet such seemed to be the fact. He walked right into the middle of the room, and then he said—

" What did you hear ?"

" Nothing !" said May.

" Nothing !" said Luke, and then they both looked at him as though they would add, " What was there to hear ?"

Duval sat down upon the nearest chair and drew a long breath. During the respiring it, he made up his mind that he would suppress the knowledge of what he had seen and heard, and he said—

" To be sure, what was there to hear ? Nothing—nothing !"

CHAPTER CXXXVI.

DUVAL LEAVES THE MYSTERIES OF THE OLD HOUSE TO EXPLAIN THEMSELVES.

THE manner in which Duval uttered these last words, was of itself in every way calculated to arouse the suspicion of May that there had been something to see or to hear; but she was so much affected at the supposition, that for some few moments she could only look at Duval imploringly, as though she wished him to tell her, but had not the power to ask him so to do.

Luke, after a glance at his master's face, felt quite convinced, that let him, for the sake of the serenity of May's mind, say what he would, he had seen or heard something in the inner room.

Duval could not help seeing what they both felt, and he spoke as calmly and firmly as he could to them.

" Let me beg of you both," he said, " to shake off these fears that possess you. Pray remember that I have an appointment that I must not break. It would be the height of ingratitude for me to break it. You know to whom I allude ?"

" The prince ?" said May.

" Yes, the prince expects me, and I must attend to the appointment I have made with him, or for ever forfeit his friendship by breaking it. Now, while I am gone, do not allow yourself to be overcome by vain fears, May. I put my trust in your natural courage to resist superstitious impressions ; and as for you,

Luke, in leaving to your care May, I leave you all that I hold most dear upon earth."

"You shall not put your trust in me in vain," said Luke. "I will protect her with my life."

"Of that I feel assured. You are well armed, and, if you like, I will leave you one of my double-barrelled pistols besides. Upon it, you know, you can depend thoroughly in any emergency that may present itself. And now, as you both see, the shadows of night are coming, and it is time for me to go."

"Yes, Duval," said May, as the tears gushed to her eyes, " go—go, at once, and banish me from your thoughts."

"May, is that a kind speech?"

She burst into tears.

"Nay, do not weep. You will soon get the better of this accession of fear. Believe me, I do not think there is anything to dread. My advice is for you to go and lie down and rest, for you must be in need of it, and Luke will remain in this room and keep a good guard, I am certain."

"That I will," said Luke, "and when you are gone, sir, I shall feel myself, no doubt, more free from any superstitious fears, for I shall know that I have a duty to perform, and I will fight out against them."

Duval was very well pleased to hear Luke say this much, for he knew that he was speaking his real sentiments upon the occasion, and that he might thoroughly depend upon him.

"Now, May," he said, "you hear what Luke says, and let me hope that you will feel more serene, and quite understand that in Luke you will have an efficient friend and protector. Are you content that I should go?"

"I am, Duval—I am, indeed."

"Then, farewell, for a brief space. Of course, I cannot take upon myself to say how long the prince may require my services; but if that time should extend beyond the night, I will adopt some mode of letting you know."

"I will go and lie down, Duval, for I am not fit to remain up. I am fatigued as well as terrified."

"Well, it is the best thing you can do. Let me escort you to the further room, and you will, perhaps, sleep the greater part of the time away that I am absent from you."

"I hope so. Indeed, I hope I shall, Duval."

"Be assured you will, if you keep yourself quiet."

Leaning upon Duval's arm, she went into the room where he had so firm an impression that he had seen the apparition between the windows. He could not help casting a glance in that direction as he entered the apartment, but there was nothing unusual. The evening, however, had dropped over the earth now so completely, that every object was confused in the room.

"You would prefer a light here," said Duval, "would you not?"

"Oh no, no; I am better without it—much better without it, Duval, for I shall close my eyes and hope to sleep in the darkness, when I could not do so if there were a light. Farewell! you will be very careful of your safety for my sake?"

"I will, indeed, dear May. Farewell!"

She followed Duval with her eyes as he stepped towards the door, and then when he was gone, she closed her eyes, and made up her mind to try to sleep.

Claude Duval did not shut the door, but he left it just about a couple of inches open, so that if there should be any alarm, Luke could have no sort of difficulty in hearing her call to him for assistance. Duval then spoke to Luke seriously in the outer room.

"Luke," he said, "I confess to you that I do not like this house—I confess to you that I have my suspicions that it is not one in which we would like to remain for long; but I think that I can manage so that you will be free from any attack to-night."

"How can you manage that, sir?"

"By speaking to the landlady of some unexpected luggage. Of course, if this be a house in which there is anything in the shape of plunder going on, it will be then put off until there is more to be got; but if anything should occur to induce you to think that it is decidedly unsafe to remain here any longer, or to get up so much fear in the mind of May that she cannot remain with anything like

LUKE IS CAUGHT IN A STORM WHILE SEEKING NEWS OF CLAUDE.

ordinary serenity, take her by one hand, and with a loaded pistol in the other, march out of the house at once."

"I will, sir—I will."

"Pass right through the park, then, and go out of it by the narrow gateway at Spring Gardens. Then go into the first hotel that you come to, keeping upon the right-hand side of the way, and wait for me."

“ What is the name of the hotel, sir ?”

“ Ah, that I don’t know, Luke. All I am aware of is, that there are hotels in that neighbourhood in plenty, and that you will be sure to come to one, and I tell you to take the first one on the right-hand, in order that I may know where to come to you.”

“ I quite understand, sir.”

“ Very good. Then remember, Luke, that I leave May in your care, and that I look to you to defend her.”

“ That I will do, sir; and you may be quite assured that, let what will happen, I will be by her side to screen her from all ill. I will not stir from this room, and so I shall be within call on the moment, should anything occur to require my aid.”

“ Be it so; and now good-by, Luke.”

“ Oh, sir, do not say good-by—it has a woful sound with it. Only say good-evening. That will be much better, because that sounds as if we were quite sure to meet again, sir.”

“ Very well—let it be good-evening, then, if you please.”

Duval shook hands with Luke, and then he at once left the room in order to keep his appointment with the Prince of Wales. Duval was not unmindful, though, of what he wanted to say to the landlady as he went out, and pausing in the passage of the house, he tapped at the door that happened to be the nearest to him.

“ Oh, sir, is that you?”

“ Yes,” said Duval; “ I merely wished to speak to you for a minute; but if you are busy, it don’t matter.”

“ Oh dear, no. Pray walk in, sir. Walk in—hem !”

The tone of voice in which she spoke, and the “ Hem !” with which she concluded, was quite enough to convince Duval that she was giving notice to somebody in the room to keep out of the way and hide themselves from him.

Duval did not wish, as he was, in a manner of speaking, forced to leave the place for a time, to let the landlady see that he had the least suspicion that everything was not quite right in her establishment, so he walked in with a deliberation that gave whoever was in the room ample time to escape from him, if they chose to do so; and then being very officiously offered a chair by the landlady, he took it, and said—

“ Madam, I am going to make some purchases in London to a very considerable amount, and I hope that everything I buy will be quite safe in your house, as I am informed that in London there are some of the most daring thieves that can be imagined.”

“ Oh, sir you might place sacks of gold in this house, and be quite sure that no thieves could get at them.”

“ Well, I am glad to hear that—very glad. The plan I am going to adopt is, to have the tradesmen come here with their goods for my inspection, and then I can choose what I like, and they can take away the remainder of them, you understand ?”

“ Perfectly, sir; and I can only say that all property will be quite safe. When do you intend bringing it here, sir ?”

“ To-morrow, I hope. I am going now to call upon some silversmiths to make an appointment with them to come here at particular times, and bring some of their goods with them to show me. I have not the money here to pay them, but my uncle has given me leave to give written orders upon his bankers for the amount of whatever I may purchase in this place.”

“ Oh, that is very convenient, indeed.”

Duval then rose, and after a remark or two concerning the weather, he politely took leave of his landlady, having, without a doubt, impressed her with the idea that he would bring a quantity of valuable property into the place in the course of the next day or two.

This was all that he wished to make her believe, for in that case if there were any sinister design against him or his friends in that house, it would, without a doubt, be put off until the time should come when so much more would be made by it than at present; and as he had taken good care to state that he had not money with him, he thought, and justly too, that he had provided against the contingency of their fancying they might have the cash in preference to the goods, which to thieves would, of course, be much more tempting.

"Now," he said, "for the prince.

The night had now got to be almost as dark as it would be ; for a heavy bank of clouds had come up from the south-west, and had stilled every breath of air, and obscured every particle of twilight that else would have remained.

Duval could hardly see the large trees in the park.

"How dark it is," he said. "This may be against or in favour of the enter-prise that the prince wants to send me upon, for aught I know ; but let it be what it may, I feel myself bound by the tie of gratitude to go upon it."

If Claude Duval had given the affair a little thought, he must have felt quite convinced that the prince was after no good when he required the services of such a one as he was. In the first place, if the enterprise had happened to be one that would have stood ultimately the trial of honourable inquiry, he, the Prince of Wales, would have found many ready to execute it for him, without the necessity of hvaing recourse to one of so questionable a character as Duval the highwayman.

If, however, it had struck Duval, that he was employed in the matter on the presumption that he was an unscrupulously bad character, he would have gone with very different feelings, indeed, to the appointment; but such an idea was not very likely to come across his mind.

In point of fact, as he now proceeded, his imagination was much more full of the strange sights and scenes at the lodging by Buckingham House than of the Prince of Wales and his probable affairs. Duval would have given anything to have been able to thoroughly convince himself that there was nothing at all to dread in what had taken place at the suspicious lodging, and, strange to say, he was much better pleased to think that it might really be supernatural, than as is if he had entertained exclusively the notion that there was danger in the matter.

Supernatural beings could but appear and terrify those to whom they for brief periods made themselves visible ; but if all that had taken place at the lodging were but a piece of trickery devised by mental means, then he might well feel some degree of apprehension for the safety of May.

"Well, well," he said, "Luke is with her, and I know well I can rely upon his fidelity to me, and I will myself get back as soon as I possibly can; for if I let my mind get too full of apprehension regarding her situation, I shall be anything but fit to do the service for the prince that he expects from me."

With these words upon his lips, Duval came to the wall of old St. James's Palace gardens, and he walked along for some time in the deep gloom of its shadow. Suddenly a man crossed his path.

Duval paused, and instantly laid his hand upon one of his pistols.

"I should not wonder," said the man, "if you are a friend."

"To whom?" said Duval.

The man approached close to him, and then said in a whisper—

"To a prince."

"I am ; and you?"

"Am the same. Pray follow me."

"I suppose it is all right; but I had hoped to meet his royal highness him-self about this spot."

"You shall, shortly," said the man. "Come on, if you are not afraid to do so."

"Afraid? That is an expression that, as regards my own feelings, I do not understand. Lead the way, and I will follow you, sir, be you whom you may."

"You will not regret it. When I said, afraid, I did not mean to impute the feeling of fear to you : I only meant that you might be apprehensive you were making a mistake, and following the wrong person."

" I accept the explanation," said Duval, "and I think you are the right person."

" Very good.   This way—this way."

The man, who was wrapped up in a cloth cloak, led the way for some little distance along the wall, and then he suddenly paused, and although the night was now much too dark for Duval to see that there was a door, yet, from the rattle of a key in a lock, he could deduce the fact that there was one in the wall.

" Come in," said the man.   " The door is open."

If Duval had had any suspicions before regarding the man being the right person for him to follow, they were dissipated now upon his finding that he had such easy access to the garden of the old palace, and, therefore, Duval followed him through a narrow doorway without the least hesitation.

" This is the palace garden ?" said Duval.

" Yes; but allow me to beg the favour of your being silent. We have a sentinel to pass, and it is as well that he should hear nothing but the pass-word, which will enable us to clear his post."

" Certainly—certainly."

The man walked on now with the rapidity of one well accustomed to the place, and took a short cut over a little plot of grass to reach the path that he wanted. It was only the larger vegetation that Duval could see in the garden, the darkness was so great ; and it was with difficulty he could even see a tree against the sky. It was only by the feel of the ground that he could tell if it were grass or gravel ; and, take it all together, so very black a night had scarcely ever loomed over London.

" Who goes there ?" said a voice, and at the same time there was the rattle of a firelock, as it was brought to the breast of the sentinel.

Duval's conductor immediately replied—

" The Prince at home !"

" Pass on," said the sentinel, and the butt of the musket rang upon the ground again. " Pass on !"

" I will recollect that pass-word for to-night," said Duval to himself, "for there is no knowing but it may be useful to me. ' The Prince at home.' That is it. I shall not certainly forget it."

The man hurried on now faster than before, but in Duval he had one who could have followed him at any speed ; and at length they reached the palace, and the man paused at a window that seemed to open right to the ground, close to a thick clump of brambles of some sort, which Duval could only see the black outline of against the house.

" Be still, now, for a few minutes, if you please," said Duval's conductor.

CHAPTER CXXXVII.

THE PRINCE SENDS DUVAL UPON A DOUBTFUL ERRAND.

The man tapped very cautiously at the window.

Duval would have had the greatest difficulty in seeing that it was a window at all that his unknown friend knocked at, if it had not been that a lamp a long way off happened to send a ray direct upon it, and so, with a very faint sparkle, lit it up.

Tap—tap ! the man went with his nails against the glass.

For a few moments there was no reply, and the man had just muttered something in a tone of surprise, when the window was hastily opend, and a voice said—

" It is you, Chalton ?"

" Yes, your royal highness."

"Oh, did he come ?"

"I am here, your royal highness," said Duval, "if you allude to me. I am here according to my orders. Nothing but death should have kept me from you, after receiving your commands."

"Oh, that is all right, then," said the prince. "Come on both of you. You know how to manage the window, Chalton ?"

"I do, your highness. Come on, Duval."

"Come on is very easily said," thought Duval, "but I wonder if it is all level within the window, otherwise one may have an ugly fall. Mr. Chalton," he said aloud, "is there any step or descent here ?"

"No—no; walk right on."

"That will do."

In another moment Duval was through the open window, and by the tread, he felt that he was upon a very soft carpet. It was like snow to his feet. The room, however, continued to be in total darkness.

The man named Chalton closed the window, and Duval heard it made fast, and then the prince spoke again.

"You are to your time, nearly, Duval," he said.

"I was in hopes, your highness, that I had been quite to it," said Duval.

"Yes—yes, perhaps I am wrong; but as the night was so particularly dark, I thought perhaps you would have been a little earlier, that is all. But there is time enough—quite time enough. Hem! Oh, quite."

It was evident that the prince had something to say that he did not very well like to say, but yet that he felt must be said.

"I trust, Duval," he said, "that as a man of gallantry, you think nothing of a little intrigue—eh ?"

"Nothing whatever, your royal highness, except that it is about one of the pleasantest pastimes going."

"That's right—that's quite right," said the prince, with more vivacity than he usually showed. "I like that. And so now I will tell you at once, Duval, that I must get you to carry off a young lady for me."

Duval was silent.

"She is quite willing herself," said Chalton, in a low tone, "and if his royal highness was not to carry her off, she would be grievously disappointed; only she prefers being taken to coming away herself, you see."

"That's it, Chalton, that's it," said the prince. "The fact is, Duval, that the girl, to save appearances and to give herself an opportunity of saying she could not help it afterwards, wants to be run away with, and to pretend all the time that it is against her will. Do you understand ?"

"Perfectly."

"Very well. Of course, I don't wish to show in the matter at all. The fact is, the stupid people she belongs to have a sort of suspicion, you see, that some one of rank is after her."

"But they have not the remotest idea that it is his royal highness," said Mr. Chalton, in his low, cringing kind of voice.

"Oh, no," added the prince, "not the least, nor would I have them think that for a thousand pounds. It would do me I don't know how much mischief just now, so that it will be a great care with you, Duval, not to mention me."

"I will be careful upon that head," said Duval.

"Very good. Of course, I tell you all this in perfect confidence; but the stupid people suspecting that some one was after her, packed her off to a school very quickly at a place called Hanger Hill."

"It is near Ealing ?" said Duval.

"Precisely. It was by the merest accident in the world that I found it out, for the affair was managed very well indeed; but there she is. It is not much of a school is it, Chalton ?"

"A finishing academy, your royal highness, for young ladies."

"Just so; and you understand, Duval, that what I want you to do is to get her away and to take her to Kew. Will you do it?"

"If I can."

"That is enough. Of course you can. I don't see what great difficulty there can be in the matter. Of course, I shall leave all the main details of the affair to you. By Jove, she is the most beautiful little creature I ever saw, or thought that there was in the world to see!"

"Is she so very beautiful?"

"She is beyond beautiful a long way. It is quite impossible that I can give you any idea of her. You couldn't describe her. Nobody could. And yet her friends are nobody."

"They are some low people in business somewhere," said Chalton, "but of no account; so that it is quite a delightful thing, that in this little transaction nobody's feelings can be hurt."

"Certainly not," said Duval. "Of course such people cannot have any feelings to hurt."

The tone of sarcasm in which Duval spoke these words, were too fine for the prince's apprehension, and he rapidly said—

"No—certainly. That is all right enough as you say. They have no feelings to hurt; and as for the girl, sweet little creature as she is, by Jove she! is worth a million of money down upon the nail, that she is! I would give every race-horse, and every diamond I ever saw for her, without grudging them."

"I have no doubt," said Duval, "but that she does credit to your royal highness's taste. She must be beautiful."

"She is—indeed, she is. Her name is Rosa——"

"Hem!" said Chalton.

"Oh, I think Duval ought to know her name," said the prince. "It is Rosa Bell."

"Rosa Bell!" repeated Duval.

"Yes, that is her name, bless her; but her name is of no consequence at all. It is herself that is all the consequence, and not her name, for there never was such a little beauty in form and face in all the world, I am quite certain. And now, Duval, I don't know any one who is more fitting than you are to conduct this enterprise. Of course you will have every assistance, and if you perform the matter to my satisfaction, you may count upon me not forgetting the service you will have rendered to me, and you will not ask of me anything in vain."

"I owe already," said Duval, "a heavy debt of gratitude to your royal highness, for favours already received. I am only too happy that I am able to be of any service to you. I understand, then, that the young lady is quite willing?"

"Oh, yes," said Chalton and the prince together; and then Chalton added—"I humbly beg your royal highness's pardon."

"Oh, no matter," said the prince. "You see, Duval, that for us to run away with her is just what she wants, although she thinks we are noblemen connected with the court merely; and in order that the schoolmistress shall not make a bad report of her, she will pretend not to like leaving the school at all, and will act all sorts of resistance and remonstrances; but you must look upon that as all show, and bring her away as if it were really by force."

Duval felt a little uneasy about the truth of the statement; but still as it might be as the prince stated, he did not feel himself at liberty to question it in any way, so he merely said—

"I shall obey your royal highness in all things. I shall require more minute information regarding the school, though."

"Oh, yes, you shall have every information. Chalton will be good enough to see to all that, and you will have him with you, and others to any number you think proper. A chariot will be at your disposal, and all I require of you is, to take the conduct of the expedition, and to plan it."

"Then, in fact," said Duval, "I am to find the means of taking a young girl by force or by fraud from a boarding-school?"

" Well, that's about it."

" And the only thing is, that as it is by her own consent, the transaction, of course, is not one of such iniquity as it otherwise would be ?"

" Exactly so ; but I warn you that she will resist you, or affect to resist you, and as all females from four years old to a hundred can command tears at pleasure, I am told she may cry, and all that sort of thing, at a great rate."

" So long as the young lady is only acting," said Duval, " I shall not object to her playing her part as well as she likes."

" Very good ; then that is all settled. I hope and expect that you will be successful, and I will, with such hope and expectation, be at Kew in the course of an hour or so at the outside. This will be a very good time to set about the business, and I leave it to you to execute.'

" Your royal highness must have some tolerable amount of confidence in what I can do in an hour," said Duval.

" Oh, yes. I have—I have. An hour is a long time."

" How many persons am I to have with me ?"

" As many as you like."

" If," said Chalton, " myself and two others will be sufficient, it would be safest to confine it to them. Will that do, Duval ?"

" Certainly. The fewer the better. I am quite ready to go at once upon the expedition ; but I beg to warn your royal highness that it may take a much longer time to carry out than I think, or than you may think ; and if you go to Kew in an hour's time, do not be impatient if I should not arrive with the young lady quite so soon. Of course you would not wish absolute violence to be used to females, and as it is a ladies' school, and kept by ladies, I would prefer stratagem to force."

" That will do. All's right. I leave it quite to you, Duval. You do the best you can, and so as you bring her to the palace at Kew, I shall not quarrel with you whether you are one hour or a dozen over the affair."

" I am quite satisfied, then."

" If you will follow me, Duval," said Chalton, " I will take you to those who will go with us, and to the chariot. This way, if you please."

" Good evening for the present," said the prince.

" I have the honour," said Duval, " of bidding your royal highness good evening, and the hope that I shall, sooner than I expect, be able to report to you the certain success of my undertaking."

Chalton laid his hand upon Duval's arm to lead him from the room, and Duval expected to be taken through the open window again ; but such was not the fact ; for Chalton opened a door in the wall opposite to the window, and led Duval into the interior of the palace.

This curious interview with the prince had taken place wholly in the dark, so that Claude Duval had not had the slightest opportunity of noticing the expression of his face. Perhaps his royal highness was not particularly anxious that he (Duval) should notice the expression he wore upon the occasion ; or there might be other and sufficient substantial reasons for conducting the interview in the dark.

After passing out of the room in the charge of Mr. Chalton, the darkness was quite as great, until, after traversing a long passage, a room door was opened, and Duval was ushered into it, where there was a table lamp burning and shedding a soft and pleasant light about it.

For the first time, then, Duval got a good look at Mr. Chalton.

That individual was rather below the middle height and of good figure. His form was exceedingly small, but there was an appearance of conceited cunning about it, if one may be allowed the expression, which Duval did not like at all.

After they both entered the room, they looked with mutual curiosity at each other for some few minutes, and then Chalton said—

" I think we shall know each other again, Duval."

"I shall certainly know you again," was Duval's reply." Pray, what situation are you supposed to fill about the palace ?"

"None."

"Humph ! You are then in the private service of his royal highness ?"

"Perhaps," said Chalton, "the best way is to ask no questions, and then you will not run the risk of having false statements made to you. I do not mean to speak offensively—nothing can be further from my intention ; but, if I do not very much mistake you, you are a man who likes plain dealing.'

"I do."

"So I thought, and, therefore, I speak to you in such a style. Now, here is plenty of refreshments of all kinds and descriptions upon the side table. Help yourself, and, as soon as you conveniently can, make up your mind as to what course you will adopt to carry out the wishes of the prince."

"My mind is already made up."

"Indeed ?"

"Yes ; I will go with you and the two persons you alluded to, and carry the young lady off at once, in despite of all opposition. I will ask to see her, and if once I do see her, she is booked for Kew Palace within the next hour."

"Well, you almost take my breath away !"

"Why so ?"

"Just because the affair would be an endless job to the people who before were in the confidence of his royal highness in these little matters. They would have planned, and plotted, and counter-plotted, and gone such a round-about way to work, that there would have been no end to their complications in the matter."

"The shortest way is the most direct to all objects."

"Not a doubt of it. But come, let us have a glass of wine to the success of our little expedition."

"One, and only one, then."

"As you please about that. You will find it of the right sort."

Chalton poured himself out a glass of wine, and then presented the decanter to Claude, who likewise helped himself.

"To the success of our enterprise !" said Chalton.

"Agreed," said Duval. "All's right."

They each drank the wine, and then Duval said, as if with a sudden thought,

"By-the-by, how old is Rosa Bell ?'

"How old ?"

"Yes, how old ?"

Chalton smiled.

"Perhaps, Duval, you have no objection to vary your question a little, and to say, ' How young ?' "

"Well. How young, then, is she ?"

"I should say about fourteen."

"Fourteen ? You cannot mean to tell me it is a child of fourteen that we are taking all this trouble about ?"

"Child, do you call her ? That all depends upon circumstances, I can tell you that. Although she has not reached her fifteenth year, I believe she is as fine a girl as ever I saw ; and the bloom of youth that is upon her cheeks, and its grace that is in every action, imparts to her an indescribable charm."

"Not a doubt—not a doubt; and yet——"

"Yet what ?"

"It appears so very odd to be enamoured of one so young."

"That is a matter of taste, certain'y. She will be well provided for, as a thing of course, and there are many who will envy her her good fortune. But now, if you are ready I am."

"Yes—oh, yes, I am quite ready. Come on, then."

Mr. Chalton led the way, and Duval followed him from the room. The more he, Duval, heard of the transaction, the less he liked it ; and yet, when he began to consider, he thought that he had seen many girls of about fifteen, who did look truly lovely and loveable, and that part of the affair he dismissed from his mind. The only doubt he had, was whether or not the affair was a regular abduction without the consent of the girl at all, or an intrigue to be managed in the way that the prince had thought proper to mention. That was a doubt,

CLAUDE ACCOSTED BY CHALTON NEAR TO THE PALACE.

however, which Duval made up his mind should be cleared up in the course of the affair.

Mr. Chalton led Duval to one of the smaller court-yards of the palace and after giving some whispered directions to a man who was there, he turned to Duval, saying—

" Our carriage and two assistants will meet us in St. James's Street, in the course of a few minutes from now."

" Where you please," said Duval. " It does not matter to me. You know the way to the school, I suppose ?"

" Oh, yes, I ought to know it, for I have already made two attempts to get speech of the young lady and failed. I don't mind telling you as much, for the authorities of the establishment, I assure you, are not a little vigilant."

" I thank you for the information."

They now left the palace by the old gate opening to St. James's Street, and as they sauntered up one side of that highly fashionable thoroughfare, Chalton informed Duval that the school was situated in a very retired spot, indeed, at Hanger Hill, but that the mistress of it was not a woman to be easily deceived, and that as she had received very special instructions with Rosa Bell, it was not likely she would yield to any ordinary application to see her.

All this was very proper for Duval to know, since he was going upon the expedition at all ; but it all tended to give him more and more uneasiness with regard to the real complexion of the affair.

Anything in reason, that only required courage and perseverance, that he could have done for the prince, Duval felt himself bound in common gratitude to do, since great favours had been conferred upon him ; but he certainly did not like the idea of being employed to seduce or to force young girls from boarding-schools. It was too late now, though, to made any objections of that character, and so with a resolution to be guided by circumstances as they should turn up, Duval accompanied Chalton right to the top of St. James's Street.

" Here is our vehicle," said Chalton.

A plain chariot stood there, with a pair of horses to it, in which two men were seated, who respectfully touched their hats to Chalton and Duval.

" They know nothing of me, of course ?" whispered Duval.

" Nothing whatever ; but they will expect you are some officer in the army, who is a boon companion with the prince, and they will be as obedient and respectful to you, as though you were the prince himself."

" You have already possessed them with that idea ?"

" Well, perhaps I have."

" That will do," said Duval. " Then drive to Hanger Hill at once, and we will see if we can't get this little adventure over at once."

" You are a wonderful man, Duval."

They got into the chariot after Chalton had given the direction to the driver, and in another moment off they went at as good a pace as a couple of the best horses of the royal stud could accomplish, and in a very short space of time indeed, considering the distance, they were in the immediate neighbourhood of the perfectly rural district of Hanger Hill.

CHAPTER CXXXVIII.

DUVAL FINDS SOME DIFFICULTIES IN HIS WAY.

DURING the journey to Hanger Hill, the thoughts of Duval more than once wandered to the lonely lodging in which he had left May and Luke, and at those moments he would have given anything to know what was going on there, and if all were safe with her to whom he was really greatly attached.

The heroic manner in which May had clung to him in all changes of his fortunes had had a sensible effect upon him.

The necessity of driving all other considerations from his mind now, except those that were essential to the purposes of his duty to the prince, was strongly apparent to the mind of Duval, and when the carriage stopped he awoke with a start from the reverie of his temporary trance into which he had fallen.

"Here we are," said Chalton.

"That will do, then. Let us alight."

"How silent you have been, Duval. I would not interrupt you, for I thought you were probably devising some plan of operations at the school."

"In good truth," said Duval, "I forgot that there was such a place as this school. My thoughts were in another direction entirely; but now I will give them entirely to the prince's affair."

"I beg of you to do so. If I had thought that your mind had been otherwise engaged, I should almost, I think, have taken the liberty of rousing you. But there is Hanger Hill, and a wild and desolate spot it is, too. What a mad riot he wind is making among the trees, to be sure."

"Do you call that a riot?'

"Indeed, I do."

"Well, then, my good sir, it is quite clear that you are town bred, and have seen very little of the country and its phenomena. Why, I have seen the wind tear up an oak by the roots, and play with it as though it were a rush.",

"Hem !" said Chalton.

Duval smiled to himself at the evident incredulity of Chalton, and then he ran up a bank of earth that was close at hand, and glanced around him. He had a general knowledge of that part of the country, and he wanted to try and see if he could recognise the exact spot where he was.

"All's right," he said. "Now I know where I am."

"Do you, Duval?"

"Yes; I have been all over these meadows, many a time. What establishment, by the bye, is that yonder? I have often seen it, but never knew whose it was."

"That is the school."

"Indeed, are we so near ?"

"We are, so that it behoves us to be as cautious as we possibly can. And now, if it's a fair question, what do you mean to do?"

"It is a fair question, and I will answer it frankly. I mean to go up to the mistress of the house and to demand admission in the usual way. The first person who comes to the door, I will seize and hand over to your keeping, and then I will walk into the house and find Rosa Bell and carry her out of it. I should say, rather, that our two friends can keep the door, and you and I had better go in together."

"Very well, they can but scratch us."

"Scratch us? What do you mean by that ?"

"Why, I believe, there is nobody in the house of a male description, and, therefore, the ladies may try to use their nails upon us. But we shall soon see ; I sincerely hope the attempt will be successful. The coach had better stay here with the driver, I suppose ?"

"Certainly. Now come on, if you please, Mr. Chalton."

Chalton beckoned to the two men to follow them, and the whole party strolled very leisurely down a narrow lane that led to the front gate of the school, which was a very large place indeed, and had at one time, no doubt, been a mansion of great importance.

The lane terminated in a broader road, and it was just at the juncture of the two that the iron gate enclosing the lawn that was before the front of the mansion was. A massive bell hung in the centre at the top of the gates, and a very slight examination convinced Duval that they were fast locked.

"Well, now," said Chalton, "here we are at a stand still."

"Not quite," said Claude. "We see the bell here, or what looks very like one, although, perhaps, it is an ornament merely."

"What shall we do, then ?"

"You will see. All we have to do is, by hook or by crook, to get hold of Rosa Bell and take her to Kew, where I do not by any means wish the prince to be kept waiting for his young lady love. I suppose the captivation of so young a girl was no difficult matter ?"

" Captivation ?" said Chalton.   " What do you mean by captivation ?"

" Why, has not the prince captivated her?   That is to say, made her fall in love with him ?"

" Oh—ah—hem !"

" Why do you say, Hem ?"

" 'Twas nothing at all, believe me; I was at the moment thinking of something that by no means concerned this affair at all.   But pray ring at the bell, Duval."

" I will."

Claude laid hold of the massive old iron bell-wire, and gave it such a pull that the bell set to tolling at a rate that was enough to alarm the whole neighbourhood, but, probably, the tone of the school-bell was pretty well known to all within ear-shot of it, and as the hour was not so late a one as to make it very surprising that a visitor should call at the establishment, it was thought not sufficiently alarming for any one to take special notice of it.

" That ought to bring them," said Duval.

" It will, too," said Chalton.

" Then let me request that you will keep out of sight while I speak to whoever may come in answer to the bell."

Upon this, Chalton and the two men retired on one side, and hid themselves in the deep shade of a tall tree that grew close at hand, and then Duval could hear footsteps approaching the gate, and could, in the darkness, see a dim-looking figure, carrying what seemed to be a lantern, that of all lanterns he had ever seen gave the worst possible light.

In a few minutes, this figure halted opposite to the gate, only that it took care to keep some yards from it.

"Who's there ?" said a sharp female voice, that betrayed that it had contracted much of the asperity of age.

" A visitor, if you please, madam," said Duval, in as soft and insinuating a tone as he could possibly assume.

" To whom ?" said the voice again.

" To the respected proprietress of this establishment, madam," said Duval.

" Oh, then, you can come again to-morrow."

" Dear me," he said, " that will be very inconvenient, indeed, for me, for I have come some distance to speak to the respected mistress of this school about placing a young lady under her care."

" Pray, what is your name, sir ?"

" Smith, madam.   Olianthus Probeck Olwerthy Smith, is my humble name, madam."

" Oh !" she said, and turned to walk away.

" This is very extraordinary conduct, permit me to say," added Duval.   " I thought, of course, that one of the first objects of a scholastic establishment was to get pupils, but here it seems not to be the case."

" Certainly not," said the lady, and she began to walk away.

' Stop—stop," said Duval.

" Well, what now ?"

" I can assure you that it was the flattering account I received of the school in the letter of a young lady who had been educated here, that induced me to come here to place my only daughter under your delightful care."

" What was the name of the young lady who wrote the flattering letter ?"

" Well, really, I forgot."

" Is she in the school now ?"

" Oh, yes—yes."

" It's a pity you don't recollect the name," added the female, with additional asperity of voice, " for if you had, the culprit would have been severely chastised in consequence."

"Chastised?"

"Yes, but now we cannot do it. It is against the rules of the establishment for any young lady to write a letter to any one. We will consider upon the propriety of whipping the whole school, until some one confesses."

"Confound it," thought Duval, "I have got them all into a pretty predicament, by saying a little too much."

Then he added aloud—

"I hope you will not think of adopting such a course, madam; and allow me to say, that it is decidedly contrary to the very spirit of the English law, which would rather allow the guilty to escape, than run the smallest risk of punishing the innocent."

"Oh, we don't care about the law here. If you call to-morrow you can see the principal."

"But not now?"

"Certainly not."

Upon this, the old lady trotted away, and although Duval called after her to say that he had forgotten something important that he had to add to what he had already said, she would not turn back again, but with the very inefficient lantern, quickly disappeared from his sight. Mr. Chalton, who had listened to the colloquy, now stepped forward, and rubbing his hands together, he said, with quite a grin of complacency—

"Ah, that's how they served me. They wouldn't let me within the gates. You may depend upon it, my good sir, that the people in this house are as jealous as dragons, and must be thoroughly upon their guard against any intruders."

"That was just what I wanted to find out," said Duval. "Our course is now quite clear and easy."

"Clear and easy?"

"Yes, to be sure. Now I know exactly the kind of humour the people of the house are in, I can adopt a course which will, of course, succeed. It would have been a pity, though, to throw away a decided chance of doing the job right off-hand at once, providing they would have been sufficiently confiding to have allowed me admittance into the house."

"And pray, then, what can you do now?"

"Get in without their leave."

"Oh, that is it, is it?"

"To be sure it is. I am at a loss to conceive now any other course can be adopted. If you must enter a house, and the people won't let you in, you must get in by some means without their leave, and that is the course I propose adopting, if you see no objection to it, Mr. Chalton. If you do, I shall listen with all the respect in the world to your suggestions upon the subject. Pray go on."

"Oh," said Chalton, as he made a mock bow of great apparent respect, "it is not for me to raise any objection. The conduct of this enterprise is entirely in your own hands, and for my own part, I feel that I have only to obey you, which, believe me, I shall do willingly, aiding you as effectually as it is in my power to do."

"That I believe you will, and, therefore, I tell you that we must make our way into the grounds of this house, and from the grounds we must make our way into the house itself, and by sheer force take away the girl we want. I do not think that we shall encounter much opposition. The very audacity of the affair will too much paralyse them with astonishment to enable them to effectually resist us."

"There is something in that, and I am perfectly willing that the plan should be tried, at all events. No doubt we shall be able to effect a retreat by the same way that we get into the premises, if we should see that it is absolutely necessary for us to do so."

"Not a doubt of that. But if I retreat it will be in the company, I hope, of Miss Rosa Bell."

"I hope so, too; but before we go, allow me to hope that you will not, from a foolish obstinacy in the affair, persevere against all hope."

"That I will not !"

The only fact now that Duval was anxious about, was to find out, if possible, the hour at which the whole establishment, scholars included, retired to rest for the night, as he did not wish to make the attempt to invade the premises until that event had taken place. It was only, however, by conjecturing upon the subject that any conclusion of that kind could be arrived at, as no positive information was by any means then available to be had. Duval thought that if he waited until it was half-past eleven o'clock, he ought to be able to conclude with perfect truth and safety that no one would be up in the school.

Mr. Chalton was of the same opinion in that particular.

"We have three quarters of an hour to wait," said Duval, "for now it wants but a quarter to eleven. The time will hang rather heavily upon our hands, no doubt, but that cannot be helped."

"And it will be cold, too," said Chalton, as he stamped upon the ground.

"That we can remedy," said Duval, "by exercise. I prefer a sharp walk up and down the lane, here."

Chalton assented to this, and during the period that they had to exist in each other's company, they entered freely into talk and got to be much better friends than they had been. Chalton was very guarded, though, as to what he said about the prince, and Duval did not think the less of him for being so, as he being in the confidence and employment of the prince, was bound above all others to keep his secrets, and to speak but little of him, while that little ought not to be anything disparaging.

At length the three quarters of an hour passed away, and Duval declared his intention of immediately commencing the enterprise. Chalton seemed to be a little nervous about it, though, as the time now came round to begin it.

During the walk down the lane, they had discovered a part of the high brick wall that enclosed the grounds of the school which was so much decayed, owing to being at an angle, and having caught all the worst of the winter storms for many years, that there could not be any great difficulty in climbing up it. Still, in order to afford greater facilities of descent, Duval procured from the man in charge of the carriage a spare trace, and a rope that they had with them.

"I dare say, Chalton," he said, "that you are not quite so good a climber as I am, so, if you please, I will go first, and fasten this trace to the bough of yon fig-tree that grows right over the wall at this point, and you will find it of material assistance to you as you climb up."

"I am more obliged to you than I can express," said Chalton, "for I must confess, as you surmise, that my climbing days are pretty nearly over, although that is a fact owing to the inactive life I lead in a palace and a prince's service, than of age."

Duval smiled to himself at the candid confession of Chalton ; and then, with great care, as he did not by any means wish that any little malapropos accident should mar the design at its commencement, he ascended the corner of the wall with the trace on his neck, so as to have it ready to fasten to the branch of the fig-tree the moment he should get high enough up to accomplish that desirable object.

There did not appear to be any one stirring in the garden, for Duval listened most attentively to catch the smallest sound that might arise from it, and heard nothing. He fastened the trace, by the aid of its buckle, to the tree, and found it of immense assistance to himself in getting over the wall.

CHAPTER CXXXIX.

DUVAL SUCCEEDS IN HIS ATTEMPT UPON THE PEACE OF THE SCHOOL.

"Is it all right ?" whispered Chalton from the lane.

"Hush ! Don't speak so loud," said Duval. "There is no one here. Let the men come up before or after you, as you think proper."

"Oh, I will come. They will follow. I suppose the trace is quite tight?"

"Yes—yes: it can't possibly give way. You may fully rely upon it. Have you got a good hold of it, now?"

"Capital!"

Duval stood upon the top of the wall, balancing himself by the branch of the tree, while Chalton ascended by the aid of the trace. Duval then tied one end of a stout bit of rope firmly to the branch of the tree, in that part of it that overhung the garden, and then he lightly swung himself down by it, and alighted in a flower-bed as softly and as comfortably as it was possible to do. He calculated, too, that that rope would be of immense assistance in leaving the premises, especially if they should chance to be rather hard pressed for time in doing so, which would be a very likely condition of their retreat, whenever they should think proper to make it, from the school, either with or without Miss Rosa Bell.

Dark as the night was, and fitfully rainy, there was yet the dim kind of perception of objects which any one whose eyes have got accustomed to the night air is sure to have after a time. A light, under such circumstances, would have been absolutely confusing, from the broad masses of shadow that it would have cast around it, so they did much better without one; and in that respect it was fortunate for them that their convenience and the secrecy of their enterprise jumped together.

In three or four minutes they were all over the wall in the garden; and then Duval began to make his depositions of his force.

"Let one of the men stay here," he said, "and let him be provided with the means of showing a light, if he hears any alarm."

"I can do that, sir," said one of the men. "We are provided with all those little matters. I will remain, if your honour chooses."

"Very well, do so, and recollect that you are not to move from the spot. You are to consider it as your post, and you are to hold it until I come to you again, or until you can hold it no longer."

"I understand, sir. It's all right."

"Very good. Then we will go now."

It would have been impossible for any one to see the three dark figures that were now moving along the garden with stealthy steps. Their forms were so mingled with the foliage of the tall trees, and the deep shadows that they cast about them, that they were completely hidden. The policy of preserving a strict silence for some time, was likewise too evident for any to avoid it, and on they went like three spectres, more than like three living men bent upon an errand concerning which Duval had his very serious doubts indeed.

By keeping a course of right angles with the inner face of the garden wall, Duval calculated upon soon coming upon some traces of the house, and he was right, for after passing through a complete belt of tall trees that shaded it from all observation from the road, he saw it quite plainly against the night sky.

Perhaps it was the undefined shape of the house by that dim night light which lent vastness to it; but certainly Duval thought it a place of great size even for the purpose to which it was devoted, that being a purpose which required great space and accommodation.

For some minutes he took a long and steady look at the house, and then Chalton, who was quite close to him, spoke in a whisper, saying—

"Well, what do you think of it?"

"Think of what?"

"The school-house, yonder. It was formerly the almost regal abode of one of the richest catholic noblemen of England, and they say that before it came into his hands as a secular residence, that it had been a nunnery of great repute and size."

"Size enough," said Duval, "there is, in all conscience. Do you see any light in any window?"

"Not the ghost of one."

"That's awkward ; but, perhaps, we are on the wrong side of the house to see. We will go round it."

"It will be as well to keep as far off it as possible while we do so. I would advise that we keep in the shadow of the trees."

"Be it so. It is good advice."

Slinking along as though they had come to rob the premises—and so they had in one sense—they all three now got round some straggling out-buildings to another face of the house, and then upon the upper floor Duval counted no less than five windows in a row, the whole of which were faintly illuminated by some light that was within. He stood gazing at the windows for a few minutes, and then Chalton said—

"What does that light mean ?"

"If I am not very much mistaken," said Duval, "I should pronounce those five windows to belong to the dormitory of the school."

"Oh, of course, of course. Not a doubt of it."

"Well, then, friend Chalton, it seems to me, that there is where we must get with as little delay as possible, and find among all the others the young lady who is to go to Kew with us. I suppose she will declare herself."

"Oh, yes, yes—that is, I don't know though."

"You don't ?"

"No ; for there is nothing that she is so anxious about as to preserve the idea in the school that she goes without her own consent, and that it is either power or fraud that takes her from beneath its roof ; so she may not be able to say anything regarding her own identity before the other girls ; but you will know her by her hair, which is of a beautiful golden tint—not yellow, nor the least touch of red— in fact, I don't know how to describe her hair, it is so very beautiful."

"I'll find her, then," said Duval, laughing, "if I have to pull the nightcaps off all the young ladies in the school."

"Well, now, the only difficulty is, I suppose, how to get into the house ?"

"It is—it is."

Duval remained for some minutes in silence looking up at the windows that he had no doubt were connected with the sleeping apartments of the school. There was a light balcony outside all these windows ; in fact, it ran along the whole length of that side of the house, and the height from the level of the garden was somewhere about twenty feet—rather a formidable height to get up without any aid.

"Oh, for a ladder !" said Duval.

"A ladder, sir ?" said the man who was with them. "I saw one lying along by the stumps of the trees yonder, and nearly broke my shins over it as I came after you just now."

"Did you, indeed ? That is the very thing we want. Go and get it at once, for a more fortunate discovery could not be. It will be everything for us to get at that room without the trouble, the toil, and the risk of going through the house."

"I'll soon bring it, your honour," said the man.

"Ah !" whispered Chalton, as he rubbed his hands together in rather a state of nervousness. "That ladder being seen by Jennings is quite providential— oh, quite. What a mercy it is that no one has interrupted us as yet !"

"It is a piece of good luck."

"Good gracious, what's that ?" said Chalton.

"Hush !—hush !"

A strange noise came upon their ears ; and then, just as Duval was beginning to be thoroughly posed as to what it could be, it deepened into the unmistakeable sounds of a battle between two cats, who fought, and spat, and swore at each other in a most diabolical manner, and finished by scampering over Chalton's feet, and terrifying him so that he fell down upon the grass and cried for mercy in much too audible a voice.

"Peace !" said Duval ; "do you want to ruin all ? How can you be such an idiot ?   One might surely have expected something like common discretion from you."

"Oh, dear!—oh, dear !"

"Silence !"

"Yes, I am—I will—that is to say, what two fiends they were, to be sure !"

CHALTON POINTS OUT TO DUVAL THE SCHOOL-HOUSE.

"Oh, stuff!   You are a pretty fellow to come here upon such an enterprise as this, and allow yourself to be frightened by a couple of cats."

"Were they cats ?"

"To the best of my belief, they were," laughed Duval.   "What did you take them to be if they were not cats ?"

"Devils, sir—devils !"

"Oh, nonsense! Come, now, get up. Here comes our friend Jennings, I think you named him, with the ladder, and I look forward to the speedy termination of our adventure now. Ah! that's the very thing."

"It's a deuce of a weight, your honour," said Jennings.

"Never mind that. I only hope your reward will be as heavy, in good current coin, too. Place it carefully up against the balcony. Now—now—I have a hold of it. Gently—that will do."

The ladder answered as well as if it had been made for the express purpose; and when it was fairly put up to the balcony, the passage to the upper floor of the house was as well established to any one as active as Claude Duval, as if it had been a well-trod'den highway.

"You are actually going to venture?" said Chalton.

"Yes, rather so."

"Oh, well, don't suppose that I hang back in any way—quite the reverse; only it is a risk."

"Well, then, Mr. Chalton, if you have the slightest objection to running that risk, my advice to you is to go home as quickly as you possibly can."

"Don't say that. I was only joking."

Chalton's teeth quite chattered again as he spoke; but Claude Duval was charitable enough to suppose that the cold might have something to do with that for the night was, to tell the truth, rather chilly.

"Now, Jennings," he said, "you will recollect that your foot is at the foot of the ladder, from which you are not to stir until you see me. If any one should interfere with you, of course you will adopt some mode of giving an alarm, and I shall be quite near at hand enough to hear you."

"I will, in truth, sir."

"Do so. That will answer the purpose very well, indeed."

"And what do you want me to do?" said Chalton.

"Nothing, but just come up to the balcony, and there wait for me, and assist me if there should arise any occasion to require such help."

"Very well. Oh, dear, yes. I will help you, and, of course, I fully expect that you will be so good as to inform the prince that I was as active and as eager and efficient as possible in the whole affair, from first to last."

"It would be a very hard thing," said Duval, with a laugh, "if we did not praise each other to the very echo—Come on."

Duval ascended the ladder lightly, and soon stood in the balcony. Chalton followed him; and now what they should have occasion to say to each other required to be said in the most cautious manner, lest they should give a premature alarm to any one in the room with the five windows.

"Stay here," whispered Duval to Chalton. "Keep a hold of the ladder, and then I shall be quite sure of where to find you."

"Yes, yes, I will."

The fact was, that Duval, from the evident fear that was beginning to show itself unmistakably about Chalton, saw that he would be more of a hinderance than an assistance, and he was glad to get rid of him. He now silently and cautiously approached one of the windows opening to the balcony. A glance through a little crevice by the side of the blind showed him that his supposition regarding the room being the dormitory of the school, was perfectly well founded.

The room into which Duval saw was a very extensive one, indeed, being lofty as well as spacious, and down each side of it he saw a row of little bedstead with dazzlingly white dimity curtains to each of them. Upon a bracket sufficiently high upon the wall, not to be reached by any of the scholars, was an oil lamp, from which came the faint light that shone through the window blinds, and which had, from the garden, induced Duval to think that that was the room of which he was in search, and which it turned out to be.

The profound stillness in the apartment was a pretty good evidence that the young ladies were asleep.

"It's a thousand pities," thought Duval, "to disturb all these young creatures now upon an errand of this sort ; but what can I do ? I am quite pledged to the prince to carry out this affair for him to the very utmost of my ability, and I must not now shrink from it, let the consequences be what they may."

The mode of getting into the room did not present itself as a very easy proposition. Indeed, there was only a hope regarding that point in the mind of Duval ; and that was that, as the room was on the upper floor of the mansion, and so apparently inaccessible, it was just possible the windows might not be made fast in any way.

"I can but try," he thought.

It was quite a ticklish affair that trying if the window that he was close to would open, for he knew that some windows would not open without uttering a scream in the process, that would be quite enough to awaken all the young ladies at once. He could only hope that that one went upon the silent system.

The frame-work of the window stuck a little, which at first made Duval think that it was really fast ; but as he increased the force that he used towards it, it suddenly gave way, and the window gave a slight kind of squeak.

"The deuce take it," said Duval, "they will be all up now."

He listened attentively to hear what effect the noise would have upon the young ladies in the domitory. He was not kept in doubt for very long, as a voice said, in low accents—

"Oh! what's that ?"

Duval felt very much tempted, indeed, at the instant to reply "Nothing; " but he restrained the impulse, and then another voice in the dormitory said—

"I am quite sure it was something."

"The horrid cats," said a third.

"Oh, you needn't say horrid cats," cried another ; "for if there's anything in all the world prettier than another, ain't it a nice little kitten ?"

"Oh, yes," cried some half-dozen of the young ladies all at once, but it is quite a shocking thing that they will grow to be cats in such a little time."

"You had better all be quiet and go to sleep," said one, now, from a remote corner of the room, "or you will awake Miss Garret, and then we shall all catch it."

"So we shall," said several.

"Oh, but we shall all say it is you," cried one, "and then if we stand by each other, and declare it's true, you will be whipped, and we shall all escape, and that will be such fun."

"Oh, be quiet, do."

Some of the young ladies laughed, but in a few moments a profound stillness reigned again in the school dormitory.

CHAPTER CXL.

DUVAL BEGINS NOT TO LIKE HIS MISSION.

THERE was something about the whole affair, now, of the abduction of the young girl from the shool, that began to jar upon the feelings of Claude Duval. Under ordinary circumstances, he was not, as the reader will be inclined to agree with us in opinion, very particular ; but there were some things upon which he felt rather strangely, and one of them was, that it was not very agreeable to be the agent of any one else's vices, even and although that other one might be a prince.

Duval often had said—"If I do an act which is not quite consistent with morality or virtue, let my own passions bear the blame, but I have never stooped to pander to those of another."

Upon this occasion he began to have rather a disagreeable suspicion that he was pandering to the vices of the heir-apparent.

"I will do nothing hastily," thought Duval, "but I will keep my eyes about me, and my ears open, and if I find I am being deceived in this business, I will adopt such a course as may be more consistent with my feelings probably, than with his royal highness's pleasure or gratification."

With this determination he awaited the course of events at the school.

The secretary who was with him, and who, although he arrogated to himself that title, was in all likelihood no higher in the social scale than a valet, had betrayed a kind of fear all along, which made him readily acquiesce in any proceeding that promised an issue to the enterprise, or that would accomplish it with the least possible trouble; so when Claude Duval whispered to him—"I think it will be only a prudent thing to wait a little while," he replied eagerly—"Oh, yes—yes, certainly let us wait."

The silence in the dormitory did not continue for very long. How could it be expected to do so, with such a number of young ladies in it? In the course of the next few minutes, one of them called out—

"I say?—I say?"

"Oh, what?" said another.

"What suppose it's thieves?"

"Oh, stuff!" said a third.

"Silks and satins," said a fourth.

There was a slight laugh at this, for it was one of the little stock jokes of the school to cry out when anybody said stuff, "Silks and satins," and being quite a comprehensible little joke, it was always successful.

"I declare now," said another, "that I will call out to Miss Garret, and tell of you all, if you don't be quiet."

"Oh, do," said several others in mocking tones. "Of course, if there's any tale-telling in the school, it's sure to come from Miss Robinson."

"No—no," said a calm, sweet voice. "Pray rest all of you, and don't tell any tales of each other."

The secretary pinched Duval's arm slightly, and then having thus directed his attention, he whispered in his ear, in defiance of grammar—

"That's her."

"Oh," said Duval; "then she is in the far corner by the fireplace."

"Is she?"

"Yes. I saw her head, as she spoke even now. How delighted she will be when she finds that we are here, won't she?"

"Oh, very—very, indeed. Her name is Emma."

"Yes, I know that; but, as I was saying, how impatient she must be for us, as the agents of the prince, to take her away from the school."

The secretary made a kind of humming noise, which almost degenerated into a cough, and no doubt would have done so, only that he felt the danger that would attend any such demonstrative sound.

If Duval had had any doubts before of the character of the enterprise upon which he now was, this conduct of the man who was associated with him in it would have dispelled them. From that moment he felt convinced that the whole affair was the genuine abduction of a girl from a boarding school; but still he felt that until he had such an assurance from the lips of the young lady herself, he had no right to assume positively such a state of things, and, therefore, he would not give up the enterprise; and, besides, he felt quite confident that if he did so, there would be found plenty of others who would be far from being so scrupulous; and so, if he really meant to save the young creature from the fate that was in store for her, it would be by remaining and seeming to execute the bad work that had been given to him to do, than by deserting it.

It was with such a feeling as this that Claude Duval persevered with his design, and seemed to be doing exactly as the prince wished him to do. The secretary had not the least suspicion that any one could have any kind of scruple at doing that which they were well paid for, and he thought from the first that it was quite a needless piece of delicacy upon the part of the prince to deceive Duval at all in the matter.

What his royal master had done, however, the secretary did not feel himself authorised to undo, so he kept up the delusion to a certain extent, although not so far as to prevent any one of an ordinary penetration from seeing through it.

Under such circumstances; Claude Duval, with all his tact and experience of the world and its affairs, was not likely to be deceived.

The good-tempered appeal that had been made by the young girl who was the object of the illicit passions of the Prince of Wales, seemed to have had its effect upon the rest of the inhabitants of the dormitory, for there was a general cry of "Good-night!—Good-night!" and then all was still again. It did seem now as if they all had addressed themselves to rest for the remainder of thenight and Claude Duval was exactly of that opinion.

"What do you think of it now?" interposed the secretary. "Is it time yet, think you?"

"It will be, soon. In a few more minutes I think we may venture to make a bold attempt."

"Which you will make?"

"If you please; but I thought that you would probably like to take the credit of having made it with the prince."

"Oh, dear, no."

"Very good; I promised to carry off the girl, and I will do it; but you must aid me by clearing the way for my retreat when I have once got her. That is all I shall require from you."

"That is just what I can do nicely; and, indeed, I think by the measures we have taken there can be no difficulty in that matter. We shall all come off with flying colours, I do believe."

"Not a doubt of it."

The stillness in the dormitory had now continued long enough to convince Duval that the young ladies must be all asleep; but yet even he—with all his courage and coolness in enterprises of all kinds and descriptions—felt a little daunted at the idea of showing himself, lest some one might be awake and raise a cry that would alarm all the others at once, in which case the completion of the affair might be attended with very many difficulties.

Duval waited another five minutes, and then, as the secretary was getting evidently very impatient, and hinted at a doubt if Claude liked the affair, he slowly opened the window of the large room.

No one moved or made any sound, so that he was now quite confirmed in his idea that they all slept soundly, and he got into the room with such extreme caution that he made no noise whatever. As he stood upon the floor of that sleeping chamber, the flush of shame was upon his cheek at the seeming unworthy part he was acting. To stop a man upon the highway and boldly demand his money, looked almost like a piece of rare courage, in comparison with what he was about now; but he calmed himself with the reflection that he had better motives in the affair than circumstances would seem to warrant.

"I come to save, not to destroy," he whispered to himself, and then he softly stole along the floor towards the bed upon which lay the young girl who was the object of the expedition.

The mode in which Claude Duval intended to proceed, was to wrap her up in the bed-clothes and carry her off at once to the window, and so down into the garden, and off the premises; which he hoped and expected to accomplish without any great difficulty, from the surprise and consternation which the boldness of the act would produce.

He had reached to within three or four paces of the bed, when one of the young ladies suddenly cried out—

"Oh, who is that?"

From that moment Claude Duval felt that any further secrecy was quite out of the question, and that the activity of his movements would alone be of any use in bringing the affair to a successful conclusion. With one bound he was by the bed-side of the young girl, and before she could open her eyes even, he had rolled the bed-clothes twice round her and had lifted her in his arms as though she were a mere doll, and was making his way towards the window with her.

This was done so quickly that it was all but accomplished before the others in the dormitory could gather breath to scream ; but when they did, the uproar was prodigious.

"Murder!—help!—Oh, murder!—murder!"

Such were the shouts, mingled with shrieks, indicating nothing but the very extremity of alarm, that came from some dozen or so throats at once. Claude felt staggered and alarmed at the noise ; but he was out at the window in a moment, nevertheless, and still holding the young girl in his arms, and got into the garden he hardly knew how, and ran along more by instinct than with any fixed purpose until he reached the wall.

The sound of screaming was now mingled with that of some immense bell ringing, and it was quite evident that if they did not get off the premises as quickly as possible, a general alarm would be given to the neighbourhood. How he got actually into the road, Claude Duval could hardly have told ; but he did so, and then in a loud voice he cried—

"The coach!—the coach!"

"Here, sir, this way," said one of the men. "This way, if you please, sir. This is the coach."

"Drive on—drive on!"

"But the secretary, sir?" said one of the men.

"D—n the secretary!" cried Claude. "Drive on at once, will you?"

"Yes, sir."

In another moment the horses were lashed to rather a perilous speed, and off they went towards town. Claude Duval had the young girl upon his lap, and what amazed him most was, that she neither spoke nor moved.

"Is it possible," he said, "that I am, after all, deceived, and that she is quite willing for the departure?"

It was a painful thought for him to think so, for by the glance he had caught of her in the dormitory, he could see that she was very young and very beautiful, and it shook his faith in the innocence and purity of human nature to think that she would be willing to go to the embraces of one who could not deceive her with any promises of a virtuous union with her.

The coach dashed on fiercely. Sometimes it met with rather a bad piece of road, and then the jolting was quite terrific, and then again for about a quarter or half a mile the road would be excellent ; but still the young girl neither spoke nor moved, and in the intense darkness of the night—for the suburbs of London were then rather worse lighted than they are now—he had no chance of seeing her face.

"I hope," he said at length, "that the abduction from your school is really with your own consent. That is to say, I do not exactly hope it, but I should ike to hear you say that it is so."

She made no reply.

"Let me beg that you will tell me," he added, "as your assurance, one way or the other, will guide me very much what to do."

Still no reply.

Claude Duval began to get a little alarmed, and for the first time it now struck him that it was just possible the young creature, through fear and amazement, had fallen into a swoon. This notion, when once it took possession of him, gathered strength each minute, and gave him much concern, for it entirely interfered with the course of action he had laid down for himself, inasmuch as it prevented him from discovering from her own lips whether or not she was a willing party to the intrigue.

The horses still tore on at a kind of half gallop, and it was quite evident that they were very rapidly approaching London. Claude Duval felt that he ought to moderate the speed, and he tapped upon the front glasses of the carriage, until he arrested the attention of the driver, who, therefore, with some difficulty, pulled up.

"Not so fast," said Claude.

"Any pace you please, sir."

"Go at a moderate one, then. There is no occasion for such speed now whatever."

"I am glad of it, sir; for it is not doing the cattle any good to set them to such a pace with a coach behind them."

"Very well, that will do."

The coach now proceeded with quiet moderation, so that Duval had time to think; but the more he thought, the more thoroughly perplexing did he find his situation become. If he took the young girl right to the palace at once, he would only be betraying her to the prince; and if he took her elsewhere, he would be placing himself in a great difficulty through not knowing whether or not she was really innocent or the reverse; and, besides, he felt what a peculiar situation he put himself in, by not acting with sincerity towards the Prince of Wales.

While he was in this state of conflicting thought, the young creature uttered a deep sigh.

"Thank God," said Claude, "she is recovering, and now there is a chance of my hearing from her own lips what she really thinks of this affair."

"Oh, what has happened ?" she said, faintly; "where am I now ?"

"Be assured," said Claude Duval, in the gentlest tone of voice he could assume, and in a low one, too, for he wished by all means that it should escape the attention of the driver. "Be assured that you are with one who will befriend you to any extent that you wish him. I am not your enemy, although circumstances may have made me appear so."

"Oh, God !—oh, God !"

This ejaculation, and the tone in which it was uttered, was all but convincing to Duval that his first suspicion was perfectly right, and that the young girl had no hand whatever in the atrocious plot that had been too successful in taking her from the school.

"Speak to me, now, I implore you," he said, "and let it be the truth that you speak, for upon what you say will hang your future fate. Did you, or did you not, wish and expect to be carried off from the school at Hanger Hill to-night ?"

"Oh, now I recollect," she said. "Oh, Heaven, have mercy upon me !"

"Answer my question. Was this abdication with your own connivance, or not ? Are you only acting a part by saying what you do, or shall I at once conclude that you are sought to be made the victim of the base passions of one who should be your protector instead of your destroyer ?"

"Oh, save me ! Save me, if you are human," she said. "Save me, if you have a hope of Heaven's blessing ! Save me, if you have one spark of feeling in your heart !"

CHAPTER CXLI.

DUVAL IS PLACED IN A VERY TROUBLESOME POSITION.

ALL Claude's doubts, if he could be said to have really had any up to this moment, now completely vanished, and he felt that what he had from the first suspected was the real truth, namely, that it was the beauty and the innocence of this young girl that had been her fatal attractions, and not any disposition upon her part to favour the passion of the prince.

"Don't speak so loud," he said, "and listen to me now."

"Oh, yes—yes. God give you the heart to aid me."

"Hush! I had it from the first. Now, attend to me. In the first place I make you a positive promise that I will save you."

"You will, indeed?"

"As I live, and if I live, I will."

"Who are you?"

"That I cannot at present tell you; but let it suffice, that I would not have taken you from the school, and so seemed to play the part of the vile agent of the man whom you have most to dread, if I had not felt, that if I did not do so, some one else, who would have too truly discharged their duty to him instead of to you and to human nature, would have taken my place."

"Yes—yes, I understand."

"But still further, let me tell you, that even I was to the last moment deceived into the belief that you waited with impatience for the seeming abduction from the school, and that it was your own wish that it should take place to save your character, but not your virtue."

"Oh, no—no! How shall I assure you of the falsehood of that?"

"You need not say one word upon that head. I am quite convinced already of it; so we will look upon that as settled. The only thing I am now anxious about is, that you should feel equally convinced of my wish to behave to you with good faith."

"I am—I am. I do not—I will not doubt you."

"That is well, but——"

"Why do you hesitate?"

"No—no, I don't hesitate—I will not hesitate for a moment. I tell you that the prince has it in his power to be to me a good friend or a bitter enemy. When he finds that I have played him false in this case, although it is in the cause of virtue, I shall experience his hatred."

"The prince, said you?"

"I did."

"Alas! then, the suspicion of my poor parents were but too true. They would have it that it was none other than the Prince of Wales who had cast his eyes upon me; but I could not think it."

"Does it make any difference to your feelings that you now know, without a doubt, the rank of your admirer?"

"None—none."

"I am glad to hear you say that; and now, let the consequences to myself be what they may, tell me where I shall take you to, and I will do it."

"Home—home! To my father's house!"

"Where is that?"

"In the Strand—I will show you the house; and, oh sir, if you will indeed take me home, I shall pray for you always as the best and truest friend I ever had, or can ever have in all the world."

"I will do it. Hilloa! driver."

"Yes, sir?" said the man.

"You will go direct to the Strand with us."

"The Strand, sir?"

"You rascal, do you hesitate?"

"Why, sir, I was to wait at Hyde Park Corner for the secretary, that is all, sir; but if you insist upon my going to the Strand, of course I shall obey you, sir, as you are the only one left of the party to give me any orders at all."

"Very well. Do as I bid you, then. Go to the Strand."

"All right, sir."

That this man was specially in the employment of the secretary, Duval now could not doubt; and as the vehicle went on towards the Strand, he tried to think of some plan of operation by which he might deceive him as to what was actually about to be done. Unfortunately, nothing occurred to Duval which would help him out of the dilemma, and he, therefore, resolved to trust to circumstances turning out right; but he would not allow the man to see where the young girl alighted, but ordered the coach to be stopped at a very dark corner, by Northumberland House.

"Is this," he whispered to the girl, "near your house?"

"Yes—oh, yes."

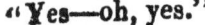

CLAUDE AND CHALTON ENTERING THE SCHOOL-HOUSE NEAR HANGER HILL.

"Very well, I will carry you to your father's door, for you cannot walk in the condition you are in, and then I must leave you to make you own explanation to him of what has occurred, and of the escape you have had."

"You will come in and listen to his gratitude?"

"Another time, perhaps, but not now. You need not get off your box, driver, I can manage without you."

Duval himself opened the coach door and sprang out. Then he took the young girl in his arms, still enveloped as she was in the bed-clothes, and ran along the Strand with her, until she stopped him at a hosier's shop, saying—

"Here is my home."

"Very well," he replied. "The place is all shut up, but I will soon knock them up. I see a light in one of the upper rooms."

"It is my mother's bed-room," sobbed the young girl, who seemed now upon the point of losing all her self-possession.

"Be calm. Hold up only for a little longer, and you will be in your mother's arms."

Claude knocked loudly at the door, and he had the satisfaction to see very soon the reflection of a light through the fanlight over the door. Another moment and the door was opened.

"Dear me," said a female voice, "who is this that's knocking so loud at this time of night?"

"Mother! Mother!" cried the girl, as she made a rush from the arms of Claude Duval into the passage; and in so doing, she left the counterpane of the bed in which she had been partially wrapped in his arms. He took it with him, as he cried—

"Good-night," and then, without waiting for a word from either mother or daughter, he ran along the Strand back to where the carriage was waiting.

"What a hurry you are in, my dear," said a female voice.

He glanced in the direction whence the voice came, and saw that it proceeded from one of the frail sisterhood who haunt that locality. The thought flashed across the brain of Claude Duval like lightning, that he might visit the prince with a just retribution.

"Step into the doorway," he said to the girl, "and let me look at you. Ah, you are young and good-looking."

"I am young," she replied, "and I am good-looking; but I am a wretch how—no—no—Good-night—good-night! This is one of my nights, when I feel as if I were going mad!"

"Stay," said Claude, "I pity you."

"You pity me? What do you mean?"

"Just what I say. That I pity you."

"Oh, no—no!"

The girl uttered that negative in so mournful a tone of voice, that Claude Duval was very much struck by it, indeed, and he said—

"Is pity so strange a sentiment that you cannot believe in its existence?"

'No; it may not be a strange sentiment; but no one ever pitied me before, that is all."

"I am very sorry to hear you say that; for surely the least feeling that any one could afford you would be pity."

"If I had been pitied long ago," added the girl, with a shudder, "I should not have been what I am now. But good-night; I don't want to have anything more to say to you. You make me sad, and I want to forget, not to think. If I were only to think for one half-hour, I should be lying calm and still at the bottom of the river the next. Do you understand that?"

"Alas! I do."

"Then leave me alone, and do not pity me, or any like me, again, I beg of you."

"Stop!" said Claude Duval, as she was turning from him. "I have something else to say to you, if you will listen to it."

"What is it?"

"Will you assist me if I promise you twenty pounds, and likewise tell you that you will do some good by following my directions—you will save another from falling to what you are?"

"I'll do that, then, without the twenty pounds."

"Come with me at once, then, and I will tell you, as we go along, all that I want you to do. Come, wrap yourself up closely in this counterpane. Nay, it is necessary to the affair that you should do so."

The girl hesitated for a moment or two, and then she said—

"As you please. I will trust you entirely. Take me where you will."

Upon this, Claude Duval wrapped the counterpane carefully around her, and lifting her in his arms, he ran towards the coach with her, and the driver did not entertain a doubt but that it was the same girl who had been so enveloped and carried away so recently by Claude Duval.

The coach-door was swinging open just as Duval had left it, so he had no difficulty in placing the girl within the vehicle at once. The driver had enough to do to manage the horses, for they had been rather put upon their metal by the gallop they had had so recently upon the Western Road, and wanted to be off again.

"Do you say that you were to meet the secretary at Hyde Park Corner?" said Claude Duval to him.

"Yes, sir, I was. He told me to do so, provided anything happened that he did not come away from Hanger Hill in the coach."

"Very good; go there, then."

"All right, sir."

The man was much better pleased at the idea of obeying the orders of the secretary, who he, no doubt, knew could do him a mischief, than those of Claude Duval, of whom he knew very little indeed, and merely thought to be some officer in the army, who had been picked up to assist the prince in the intrigue with the young girl from the boarding-school.

The coach went off at a rattling speed towards Hyde Park Corner, and then the girl who was to play the part of the young lady from the academy at Hanger Hill, turned to Claude and said—

"You promised to tell me what I was to do. Will you keep your word now, and let me know all?"

"I will, but you must let me preserve one little particle, which I feel bound by honour not to disclose, and that is the name of the person whom you will visit. I want you to act a part."

"What part is that?"

"It is the part of a virtuous young girl, who has been taken by force from her school a little way in the country. Can you play such a part, do you think, well?"

"I will try. Alas, it would have required no playing to show such a character in me only one short year ago. I am but eighteen now, and I became, a year and a few weeks since, the victim of a villain. He deserted me, and you can guess the rest."

"I can, indeed. And now understand me. What discoveries you make for yourself where you are going, I have nothing whatever to do with; but I tell you nothing but that you are to meet a gentleman who will very soon find out that you are not the person with whom he is enamoured; but in answer to all questions, all you have to say is that you were brought away from Miss Garret's school at Hanger Hill."

"I will—I will."

"Keep your face concealed as well as you can, and keep the counterpane around you, for the young lady is supposed to have been taken from her bed, and so not to be dressed, you understand."

"I will obey your directions in all things."

"Very good; and here are the twenty pounds that I promised to you. Nay, do not scruple to take them; and if you play your part well the parties that you will soon meet will be glad to give you as much more to silence you."

By the time all this was settled, the coach had reached to within a very little distance of Hyde Park, and the driver suddenly pulling up, cried out in a voice of surprise—

"Why, I declare, if there is not the secretary getting out of a common waggon!"

"Call to him, then," said Duval.

"Oh, he see us, sir; it's all right. Here he comes, as fast as he can. He knows the coach quite well, sir!"

The secretary reached the side of the coach, and cried out in a voice of alarm—

"Good gracious, what made you leave me behind? Oh, you don't know what I have gone through since you saw me. It was too bad to leave me behind. Why, I was chased for half a mile by a mad gardener with a pitchfork."

"Well—well," said Duval, "never mind. It is all right. I could have but one object, as you know, and that was to secure our prize."

"Ah, you have her, then?"

"I have; but she won't speak a word now."

"Never mind that. I can forget and forgive everything, since you have her all right. That is capital. The success, my good sir, of the enterprise amply compensates for all our troubles in the progress of it. I don't know, though, when I should have got home, if I had not come up to yonder waggon, which was coming from Wycombe."

The secretary now opened the coach-door and jumped in quite delighted with the idea that, after all, the wishes of the prince had been carried out, and that the young girl was fairly taken from the school. As well as he could, in the dubious night light, he took a glance at the figure wrapped up in the counterpane that was in the corner of the coach, and then rubbing his hands together, he said—

"I assure you, Miss, that you will have no sort of reason to complain of the events of the night, for all that is required of you is that you should be a good-tempered girl, and then, if you like, you may make your fortune."

The girl made no answer.

"Well—well," added the secretary, "you will, no doubt, find your tongue after a time. Of all things, the most difficult thing for a woman, old or young, to do, is to be silent, I rather suspect; so we shall hear quite enough of what you have to say in time, no doubt. Ha! ha!"

"Where are we going now?" said Duval in a whisper to the secretary.

"To Buckingham-house."

"Is it possible?"

"Yes, to be sure. There is no one living there but a few servants, who are all in the pay of his royal highness; so there he will be safer than anywhere else; and as we shall go in at a very quiet private entrance in an obscure street in Pimlico, no one will see us, and even this young creature will hardly be able to suspect that she is going into a royal palace."

"Very good," said Claude. "I give you felicitation upon the tact with which you manage such matters."

"Oh, yes, I have had a little experience. But does she suspect who it is that is at the bottom of the affair?"

"She don't seem to do so."

"That is all right. Confound it, what a trouble it has been to us all. Did I tell you that I was pursued by three countrymen, one of whom had a blunderbuss, and the other two pitchforks?"

"No. You spoke of one only."

"Oh, my dear sir, there were three, I assure you; and the only wonder is that I am here at all. It is quite a wonder, I assure you."

———

CHAPTER CLXII.

HIS ROYAL HIGHNESS IS DISAGREEABLY SURPRISED.

THIS little conversation between Claude Duval and the secretary was carried on in such a low tone of voice, that it was quite impossible the young girl who was in the corner of the coach could catch the least sound of it; and probably if she had heard just a word here and there, it would not have been sufficient to enable her to guess the whole truth of the affair, or to come to a clear understanding as to where she was going.

The coach took a round-about route by the back of old Buckingham House, and finally drew up at a very obscure doorway that did not look at all like the entrance to any royal residence.

"Is this the place?" said Duval.

"It is," said the secretary. "All's right, now. I will get out first, and you can bring the girl. I hope she will see the folly of making any resistance to what must be; so, there is no use in making a fuss about it."

The secretary said these words, so that they might reach the ears of the girl; but she took no sort of notice of them whatever, and Duval then alighting, helped her out of the coach, and the party passed through the obscure doorway, which the worthy secretary had opened with a key that he took from a secret pocket. He closed the door again, and all was darkness.

"Come straight on," he said. "There are no steps, and there is no turning, so that you cannot possibly miss your way, and there is nothing to fear. Come, on at once."

Upon this assurance, Claude Duval strode on, half supporting the girl as he went, for she was rather alarmed at the mystery that enveloped the whole transaction. Claude could feel her tremble, as he assisted her footsteps.

"Fear nothing," he said.

"I will be calm," she replied. "I do not think I ought to fear anything."

"What does she say?" said the secretary, eagerly.

"She would rather go home," replied Claude.

"Oh, pho! Nonsense!"

"That's just the sort of remark that I made to her."

"Come on. This is the way. All is right.—Home, indeed! I wonder where she would find a better home than this! Now wait a moment, and I will get a light, and then we shall see where we are."

Claude paused, and in a very few moments a light flashed upon the scene, and then he found that the secretary had led them into a pretty enough room upon the ground floor of the palace. A couple of folding doors divided this room from one that adjoined it.

"Permit me," said the secretary, with an odd mock-kind of respect, as he advanced to the young girl, who had covered her face now with one end of the counterpane. "Permit me to conduct you into the adjoining apartment, where you will be perfectly safe."

She made no remark or resistance, and he led her to one of the folding doors, which he opened, and then bowed, as she passed into the adjoining chamber in which there was a light. The secretary closed the door again.

"That's right," he said, as he rubbed his hands together. "I think that the prince cannot be otherwise than quite delighted at the promptitude and success with which we have settled the affair, and carried it out."

"I should never have got on without you," said Claude; "for you pointed out the young girl to me; but to my mind, there were some in the dormitory handsomer than she is."

"Oh, that is all a matter of taste. If his highness is pleased, of course that is everything; and we need not mind if she were as ugly as Satan, so long as he is satisfied with her, and satisfied with us."

"That is true, as you say; beauty is a mere matter of taste, in which scarcely any two people will agree."

"That is just it. And now if you will wait here and keep guard upon this little, piece of goods, I will go and apprise the prince that she is here, and waiting, for him."

The secretary left the room; but he had not been gone a moment, when the folding-doors opened, and the girl looked into the apartment Claude was in, saying—

"What is this that I have overheard? Did that man mention the word, prince, or am I mistaken?"

"You must draw your own conclusion," said Claude. "I can say nothing."

"But is it not much better to tell me?"

"Yes, I think it would be; but it is contrary to my honour to do so, and, therefore, I cannot. If you take care what you are about, this night's proceedings will be profitable enough to you, and possibly will enable you to leave the line of life you are in."

"Oh, if I thought that, I would bless you!"

"You can make the most of your opportunity—I can say no more. Hush! Retire at once—some one comes."

The sound of approaching footsteps was now quite plain. The young girl shut the door again, and Duval then faced the door of the apartment that opened into the long passage.

In another moment the secretary flung the door open, and the prince entered the room with a quick step. He had on a brocade dressing-gown and his face was a little flushed as though he had been drinking.

"Ah," he said, when he saw Claude. "My good friend, can it be possible that you have so well succeeded?"

"I have, your highness," said Duval.

"That is excellent. After all, there is nothing like giving these little affairs into the hands of really bold and enterprising people. You have been successful, too, in much less time than I could possibly have expected, and you are entitled to my warmest thanks for being so, ay, and you shall have something more substantial than thanks."

"I require nothing further," said Claude, "than your highness's approbation. Of course, upon reaching the school, I could have no idea which was the young lady who had been honoured by your highness's approbation; but my worthy and exemplary friend here, pointed her out to me, and from that moment I made up my mind to bring her here, or to perish in the attempt."

"Capital—capital! And is she really in the next apartment?"

"She is."

"Has she made much resistance—any screaming and all that sort of thing, eh? Any squabble with her?"

"No, your highness. She seems to be a very sensible girl, indeed, and to feel quite conscious of the honour conferred upon her."

"The deuce she does!"

"Exactly so. But still, if she had resisted ever so much, or had screamed ever so much, I would have brought her away with me, for when I undertake an enterprise, I carry it through, despite all obstacles."

"You are an admirable fellow; and now, just both of you wait here, while I go into the next room and speak to her, and try and reconcile her to her new situation. Is the wine and all that sort of thing there?"

"Yes, your highness," said the secretary.

"That will do. Don't let me be interrupted for the world."

"Certainly not, your highness."

With an alacrity that was quite at variance with his ordinary slow and lazy movements, the Prince of Wales entered the adjoining apartment. Claude Duval did not allow the least movement of the muscles of his face to indicate that he at all expected anything was amiss; and the secretary, as he inclined his head on one side to listen to what he might chance to hear from the inner-room, winked at Claude in a very knowing manner, indeed.

"His royal highness," said Duval, "is a great connoisseur in beauty?"

"Yes," said the secretary; "but he seldom cares for any quite so young as the one we have had the trouble to bring from Hanger Hill. 'Fat, fair, and forty,' is his royal highness's motto in such matters."

"Indeed?"

"Yes, you may stare; but it is a fact. Misses in teens he generally has rather a horror of."

"That is a strange taste for a young man," said Duval. "I never before heard of one who had such a piece of lunacy as regarded the fair sex."

"Lunacy do you call it?"

"Indeed I do. If I love at all, let it be a young, fresh, darling of a girl, with all the sparkling beauty of youth about her—with the laughing eye of early life —with the soft cheek of——"

"Murder!" cried the prince from the inner-room—"murder!" and then in a minute the folding-doors were thrown open, and he rushed frantically into the apartment where Claude Duval and the secetary had been so composedly settling the subject of taste. The countenance of his royal highness was in a state of the most ludicrous distortion from alarm. His royal eyes were wide open, and looked more stolid than usual, and the brocade dressing-gown streamed behind him like a great sail.

"Murder!" he cried again. "It's a dreadful mistake!"

"A mistake?" said Claude.

"A mistake?" groaned the secetary, as he dropped into a chair, quite forgetful at the moment that he was taking a great liberty by so doing in the presence of his royal master.

"Oh—oh—oh!" cried the prince, and then he too dropped into a chair, and looked the very semblance of ludicrous distress.

"May I have the honour," said Duval, "as well as take the great liberty of inquiring what is the matter?"

"The liberty be d——ned, and the honour too," said the prince. "Between you, you have brought me the wrong girl."

"The wrong girl, your highness?"

"The wrong female girl?" gasped the secetary.

"Yes, to be sure you have. I never saw the girl who is in the next room, and I don't like her at all. She is not the little creature that I wanted from the school at Hanger Hill. Oh—oh! You have done me an injury, both of you, instead of a benefit!"

"Do not say that, your royal highness," said Duval.

"But I do say it!"

"Nay, your highness, I had nothing to do with it."

"Nothing to do with it? D—n it, I thought you had everything to do with it! What do you mean by bringing me this wrong piece of goods, and then saying you had nothing to do with it?"

"I will explain that satisfactorily to your highness. It was this gentleman who chose the girl from a whole room full, and then I carried her off, as of course I had no knowledge of her myself, and was compelled to trust to his judgment."

"Oh, dear—oh, dear! Oh, you d——ned fool!"

The secetary fell to the floor at this cruel speech. He began to fear that his career of favour was at an end; and yet how the mistake could possibly have arose was far beyond his comprehension, for he felt certain that he had pointed out the right victim in the dormitory of the school, and he felt equally certain that Claude Duval had wrapped up that one, and brought her out of the house by the window.

"I shall go mad!" he said. "Quite mad!"

"And I am mad," said the prince.

"Well," said Claude Duval, "it is a good thing that there is one sane person among the three, at all events, although he is in a mist. But are you quite sure, your royal highness, that the young lady is not the right young lady? There is such a general sort of likeness among school girls, you know."

"Sure! Am I sure that this is my own head?"

Claude bowed respectfully, as he muttered to himself—

"And very little there is in it."

"Am I sure that I live and breathe?" added the prince, growing quite imaginative for once in the way. "Am I sure that I can eat and drink?"—that was a simile much more in his line—"Am I sure that I am sitting here?"

"After all those assurances, your royal highness can't possibly be mistaken," said Claude Duval, with another bow; "but if this young lady is not the young lady that this individual,"—Claude pointed to the prostrate secretary—"told me was the one your highness wanted, who is she?"

"Oh, I don't know," said the prince, "and I don't wish to know."

"But it is rather a dangerous thing," added Claude, "that she should be aware that such a little affair was in progress. Your royal highness had better sooth her as much as possible."

"Sooth her? Why she swears she is in love with me, and that she is quite delighted to be here, and I expected that the other one would have kicked dreadfully, which is what I admire very much. It is a virtuous girl, you understand, that I admire, and not a complying one. Oh, dear—oh, dear! I've half a mind to annihilate you, you blundering wretch!"

These last words were addressed to the secretary, and accompanied by a kick, as he lay upon the ground. How much further the royal anger would have gone it is hard to say, but the girl from the inner room at that moment made her appearance, and the prince cried out—

"Confound it! there she is."

"Oh, what is the meaning of all this?" she said, with a well-acted look of wonder. "Why am I brought here?"

"There appears to be some mistake," said Claude Duval; "but tell me, were you not sleeping at Mrs. Garret's school at Hanger Hill?"

"Oh, yes—yes."

"In a little bed at the right-hand corner of the dormitory, close to the fireplace?"

"Cetainly I was," said the girl, with the most unblushing assurance in all the world. "Of course I was."

"And did I not wrap you up in the bed-clothes and carry you off, and place you in a coach, and bring you eventually here?"

"You did certainly, and here I am."

"But she's dressed—she is dressed!" cried the secretary. "How comes she dressed? Do the young ladies at Mrs. Garret's school sleep in a puce-coloured silk dress? Ha! ha!"

"Ah!" said the prince. "There is something in that."

"I begin to smell a rat," said the secretary.

"Then you had better call the cat!" said Claude.

"Come, come," said the prince, "let us have no jokes. How does this girl appear now dressed in a silk frock when she was taken out of bed wrapped up in the bed-clothes to be brought here?"

"That is the question," said Claude.

"It is the question," said the secretary, as he rubbed his hands together; "and I at once, in the name of his royal highness, demand an answer to it."

"I can answer it easily," said the girl. "The fact is, my clothes were lying upon the bed, and when I was taken up, bedding and all, by this gentleman, he took my clothes wrapped up in the counterpane, and I put them on in the coach."

"Exactly so," said Claude.

"And he was good enough to hook-and-eye my dress for me."

"Oh!" said the secretary, and his countenance, which had begun to wear quite an expression of triumph, fell again. The prince looked from one to the other quite puzzled, to know what to make of it; but he could not positively say that it was not so, only he knew that it was a dreadful mistake to bring the wrong young lady to him.

"Well, well," he said, "I can't help it—I can't help it. Take her away at once. I don't want her here."

"You don't want me?" cried the girl. "Oh, how can you be so cruel when you know how I adore you ?"

"Be off, will you, madam? Pull her away. Help!"

She had flown at him, and got her arms round his neck, and was half smothering him by the energy of the embrace she gave him. Both Claude and the secretary had to interfere, and the former said to her—

"You had better go at once; you are not wanted here, you see, and I daresay this gentleman will give you a twenty-pound note to get rid of you."

"Oh, yes," said the prince, "with all the pleasure in life."

CHAPTER CXLIII.

DUVAL FINDS THINGS NOT AS THEY OUGHT TO BE IN THE LODGING.

THE girl naturally enough, after all that had happened, looked to Claude for advice and orders, and when she heard him make the proposal that she should take a twenty-pound note and go in peace, she at once acceded to it.

"It is a sad thing," she said. "I know I shall break my heart, for I do love some one, and hoped to be of great benefit to him."

"Benefit to me?" cried the prince.

"Ah, no!" she said, as she pointed to the trembling secretary. "That is the object of my affections, sir; and between us we thought we would make a good thing out of you; but, alas! I find that I am not agreeable to you, and, therefore, I must go now at once."

"Ah," said the prince, as he laid his finger by the side of his nose in a manner that he, no doubt, intended should look extremely sagacious, "I begin to see it now."

"Oh, no!" roared the secretary. "It is all a lie! I don't know her. I never saw her in my life before. It is all a fable. Oh, your royal highness, don't believe it."

"Now, what villany there is in this world!" said the prince to Duval, as if he were about one of the most virtuous of the inhabitants of the earth.

"There is, indeed," said Duval.

"Oh, it's a sad thing," added the prince, with all the air and manner of a martyr to his own innocence—"it is a sad thing that where most you put confidence, you are commonly the most deceived."

"It is, indeed," said Duval.

"But, oh, gracious, it isn't true!" cried the secretary, "I defy that dreadful female to say that she ever saw me in all her life before. I say, it is not true. I don't know anything of her. It is your highness's favour and countenance that I value above all things, and I know nothing of her, and have no compact with her."

"Oh, you dreadful wretch!" said the girl.

"I am afraid you are a bad fellow," said the prince.

"A very indifferent fellow," said Duval.

"Do you want to drive me mad among you?" cried the secretary, 'or is this all a dream—nothing in the world but a dream?"

"You will quit my service this moment," said the prince, "and you will take this female with you, who, bad as she is, yet possesses more candour than you do, for you do not even own your fault, but persist in trying to make your treachery and villany appear quite different to the last."

"But, your royal highness——"

"I will hear no more, sir. Go at once from this place."

"But, your royal——"

"Retire, sir, and take your female with you. Retire at once, I say."

"But, your——"

"Is this to be endured? Will you assist me, sir—(to Duval)—to turn this fellow out of the house?"

"With pleasure," said Duval; "but I think that it would be as well to give the girl the twenty pounds that we have mentioned," Duval appealed to the prince, and added in a whisper—"Give her the money, and you stop her tongue about this affair, which else will wag too freely about your highness's mode of spending your time."

"You are right—you are right. Give this to her. I am much obliged to you for the admirable manner in which you have acted in the whole affair, although I am, through the vile and criminal machinations of one whom I thought I could trust to any piece of rascality, both disappointed and deceived."

"But, your——"

"Silence, sir! Go at once."

Claude Duval placed the twenty-pound note that the prince gave him in the hands of the girl, just saying to her in a low tone—

"Leave at once."

"I will," she said. "I thank you."

"Hush! Go at once, without another word."

She walked to the door.

"I will relieve every one here of my presence," she said, "in a moment; but I am afraid I shall not find my way out of this place, as I was led into it in the dark."

"Take the light," said the prince to Duval, "and show them both out."

Duval took up the light, and pointing to the door, he said to the secretary—

"Now, if you please, you have heard his royal highness's orders. Am I to be under the disagreeable necessity of seconding them by force?"

"But I am innocent."

"Will you go?"

"But it is all wrong. I can prove that I don't know anything of her. I can show that I never saw her in this world before to-night. I can—Oh, oh! Murder! murder!"

Claude kicked him out of the room, and right down the narrow passage to the door, which he opened, and out they both went. Duval closed the door again, and shot a couple of bolts into their sockets.

Claude Duval was as fully alive as any one could possibly be to the great injustice that was done to the secretary in the affair; but he still considered it a kind of retribution to such a man, who played the part of an unprincipled pander to the prince, and whose whole career had been spent in deceiving others, and those others, in all probability, the most innocent and virtuous of the population.

"I imagine," he said to himself, as he slowly traversed the narrow passage back again to where the Prince of Wales was—"I imagine that I have not only saved that young girl, who was intended to be brought here, but I imagine as well that I have succeeded in getting that rascal turned off, whether justly or unjustly, for he richly deserves any species of punishment that can fall upon him."

When Duval reached the room again where he had left the Prince of Wales, he found that illustrious individual seated upon a couch, and looking about as miserable and as crest-fallen as he very well could.

"Now, isn't this a pretty state of things?" he said to Duval.

"Very, your highness; but what could I do?"

"Oh, nothing. I don't, you see, blame you in the least in the transaction. You were all right enough. It was all that rascal who I have discharged. It is a very difficult thing to deceive me."

"I should think it was."

"Oh, yes. Of course, I should have found him out, sooner or later; but this is a kind of transaction that is truly bad. Upon my word, it is dreadful to think of the want of common morality in the minds of some people. But he was always a very selfish fellow."

"So he appeared."

"Oh, yes; he thought of nothing, I do believe, but his own gratification from night till morning and morning till night again. Eating and drinking, and drinking and eating again. That was all he cared about; and, by-the-bye, talking of eating and drinking, that puts me in mind that I am hungry, for I have not had anything for these two hours; so I must give orders for something nice, or else I shall be quite famished, I declare."

"Eating and drinking are two good substitutes for anything that goes wrong in the world, your royal highness."

"I believe you, they are; and, indeed, I hardly know how I should get through the twenty-four hours if it were not for eating and drinking and sleeping. But I am detaining you, perhaps, and I can only say that 1 am very much obliged to you for what you have done, although it has been all marred by the intense selfishness of that rascal whom I have discharged ; but that, of course, you could not help."

" I wish it had been in my power," said Claude.

" Well, it is done now, so you may at any time depend upon my doing you a service, if I can ; and I strongly recommend you to take to some other line of life than the very dangerous one you practise."

Claude bowed.

" Good night, Duval; I daresay ycu can find your way out, and if you pull the door hard it will close at the end of the passage."

Claude Duval was not at all sorry to find himself thus dismissed from further attendance upon the prince; and, upon the whole, he considered that he had got out of a very difficult set of circumstances as well as it was at all possible to do.

" I humbly take my leave of your royal highness," he said; " and permit me to say, that at any time and at all times I shall be but too happy to be of service to you."

" Thank you—thank you. Good night."

" I have the honour of bidding your highness good night."

Claude Duval went out of the room and closed the door. The passage he was now in was most intensely dark, and he had to grope his way along the wall, so as to be sure that he was going right. As he thus went along, his hand came in contact with a cloak hanging upon the wall, and as he moved it, something fell to his feet.

" What is all this?" he said, as he felt about upon the floor to find what it was, and in a few minutes picked up a hat.

" A hat and a cloak," he muttered. " I wonder who they belong to ? The prince, no doubt. I will make free with them as remembrancers of this night's adventure. They may be useful to me in more ways than one."

With this feeling, Duval put on the cloak, and clasped it round the neck, and likewise placed the hat upon his head, and pulled it down a good way over his brows.

" All's right," he said, " I will now make what speed I can to that most mysterious lodging in which I left May and Luke, for my heart misgives me that during my long and enforced absence all has not been well with them. It is fortunate that I am so close to the spot."

Still feeling his way along the wall, Claude Duval at length came to the door at which he had expelled the secretary; and recollecting very well the position of the bolts, he drew them both and opened the door at once.

The cool night air that blew upon his face was very refreshing, and he had just pulled the door after him, and felt that it was closed by the latch portion of the lock, when a figure darted out from the shade of the shadows of some trees close at hand, and plumped down upon its knees at his feet.

" Oh, your royal highness," said the kneeling man, " now that you are alone I beg of you to hear me. I am innocent, I assure you, of all that is laid to my charge, and I am sure that the trick that has been played upon you to night is owing to the treachery of that man, Duval, whom your royal highness thought proper to associate with me in the enterprise."

From these words, in the voice of the discharged secretary, Claude Duval had no doubt but that in the dark he was mistaken for the Prince of Wales, and that that mistake arose from the assumption of the hat and cloak he had found in the passage, was but too probable.

Claude Duval was a pretty good mimic, and now he tried his hand at imitating the voice of the Prince of Wales, as he said—

" I don't want to have anything to say to you. Be off, or I will take measures to make you.   I advise you not to show yourself in London again.   I am quite hungry, now, and am going to get something to eat."

The delusion was perfect.

"Oh, your royal highness," added the man, "have mercy upon me!"

"Go away with you."

"Reinstate me in my situation, and you will soon find that I am the faithful servant that I have ever been, and that you ever thought me until to-night. There is nothing that I will not do, however despicable or wicked, if you will only take me back into your service.   If you see any girl that you admire, I will take her even from her mother's arms to bring her to you."

"I don't want you," said Duval.   "I don't want you, man.   I would rather not be troubled with you any more.   Get out of my way."

"Is the sentence irrevocable?   Will you not relent?"

"Certainly not."

"Then take that, for I am a desperate man!"

Bang went a pistol, and the bullet knocked the hat off Duval's head in a moment.

This assault from the discharged secretary was so totally unexpected, that it fairly staggered Claude for a moment, and he did not know whether he was murdered or not.   That the fellow might have the passion and the malevolence to think of such a piece of revenge, was likely enough; but yet one would hardly have thought that he would have had the courage to attempt it.

He fled the moment he could regain his feet, and by the time Duval had recovered his scattered senses sufficiently to take some measures consequent upon the dastardly attempt at assassination, the fellow was out of sight in the darkness around, and Duval did not know in what direction to pursue him, even if he had felt inclined to do so.

"Well," he said, "this is rather a puzzling state of affairs.   What ought I to do? Should I go back and tell the prince?   No.   In the first place, I have no key to the door in the wall, and in the second place my anxieties to reach the lodging where May and Luke are, exceed all other anxieties.   I will write to the prince in the morning, giving him an account of the attempted assassination, and cautioning him to be upon his guard.   I can do no more."

It is very unlikely if Claude had gone back, that he would have got any admittance to the presence of the prince, so it was just as well that he decided as he did, and went to attend to his own affairs, which he so strongly suspected required his instant presence.

Retaining the cloak and hat, for he picked up the latter again and put it on his head, he went at a quick pace towards the dingy street where the lodging was, and in which he had been so lately startled by the spectral appearance in the bedroom.   That appearance would have taken much stronger hold of Claude Duval's mind, and occupied much more of his thoughts than it had done, if he had not been since seeing it so intensely occupied in other and widely different affairs. Now, however, it came back to him with apparently redoubled mystery, and was more than ever provocative of anxiety.

Fixing, then, the hat — which without a doubt belonged to the Prince of Wales, since the secretary, who ought to know, had made a shot at it—firmly upon his head, Duval looked about him for a moment or two, to be quite certain of where he was, and then he was taken hold of by a mania which is very apt to possess people when they are in a desperate hurry.

That mania was the mania of taking a short cut to his destination, and we need not assert, since it is in the experience of every one, that the road you know is always the nearest.   Duval in a few minutes got completely lost in the intricacies of the then low district of Pimlico, a district that always was unhealthy and always will be, and that only the presence of the swarms of hangers-on of the court has made a little superficially clean.

The worst of it was, too, that Claude Duval had no sort of idea of the name of the street in which he had taken up the lodging that he was now so anxious to reach, so that he was now precluded from making any inquiry of any chance passengers or watchmen he might chance to meet.

There was no resource for it, but to ask his way to Buckingham House again, for when once there, he knew the route pretty well ; so he did so, and was duly directed.

The speed with which Duval went now, was such that he very soon reached the garden-wall of Buckingham House, and then turning his back to it once again, he, at a half run, proceeded toward the old building in which he hoped to find May and Luke quite safe, but dreaded to think that it might be otherwise with them.

Over and over again he cursed the prince and all his vices, and vowed in his own mind that let the consequences of a refusal be what they might, he would not again mix himself up in any of them.

CHAPTER CXLIV.

GIVES AN INSIGHT INTO WHAT HAPPENED AT THE LODGING WHILE CLAUDE WAS AWAY.

IT is hardly to be supposed that after the very strange and suspicious circumstances that had occurred in the mysterious lodging before Claude Duval left it to attend upon the Prince of Wales, everything should be quiet and in good order from that moment. We will, therefore, present to the reader now what took place after the departure of Duval upon that nefarious proceeding, which was marred by his better feeling to May, and to their faithful friend and attendant, Luke.

It seemed to May, when the door closed upon Duval, as though she was completely abandoned to some dreadful fate, the complexity and misery of which were only slowly developing, and yet she felt the necessity of his keeping his appointment with the prince.

" He is gone," she said, "and I feel very desolate, indeed ; but if he were at this moment to come back again, I feel that I ought to tell him to go."

By the advice of Duval, she had gone into the bed-chamber, with the hope that she would be able to sleep away the greater part of the time that he was absent, but nothing could very well be more utterly fallacious than that hope.

The state of dread and agitation that she was in effectually got the better of any feeling of fatigue that she felt, and she could only lie upon the bed and conjure up to herself all the frightful surmises of mischief to Duval and herself, which an active imagination in such a state of undue excitement is ever apt to do.

Luke remained in the outer room, resolved not to give way to sleep, but to keep a watch upon the safety of May, who had been so particularly committed to his charge by Claude Duval before his departure.

Luke acted with great judgment, for he considered that the special duty he had to perform was to protect May, and not to play the knight-errant as regarded any other proceedings, so he fastened the door of the outer room as firmly as he could, and having looked to his pistols, he made up his mind to sit up and wait until the return of Claude.

If Luke could only have guessed one half of the absolute terror that May was suffering in the adjoining apartment, he would have gone there and greatly relieved her from some of it by letting her hear the sound of a human voice, and that voice a friendly one.

From the stillness that was in that other room though, he, Luke, had every reason in the world to believe that May slept, and much pleased he was at the idea that she did so, for it made him think that the period of Duval's absence would seem light to her.

There could not have been a greater mistake, for May was perfectly wide awake.

May had a light in that inner room, and to all appearance it was one that ought to go on burning for some hours; but from the moment that she lay down upon the bed the light appeared to grow more and more dim, and to show evident symptoms of going out. Why it should do so defied all conjecture, as there was really plenty of candle left, and it was quite credulous that the light should deliberately expire of its own accord, which it seemed to be intent upon doing.

This, then, was the first singular circumstance that alarmed May, and she could do nothing but fix her eyes upon the light in surprise as the flame of it dwindled and dwindled each moment, until it got to be a mere little blue flickering light that seemed as if it would go out at the first moment that any adverse amount of air touched it.

"What can this mean?" said May to herself, in a whisper. "Is this house full of circumstances, and events, and existences, that are not of this world?"

It seemed to be that such was, indeed, the case, if one might judge from the singularity of the events that had already taken place within its walls.

After the light had got to such a miserable pass as that, and after it had ceased to give anything like illumination to the apartment, it went no lower; but, contrary to the expectations of May, who, to be sure, thought it was going completely out, it still preserved the little blue flame that it had changed to.

"What will happen next?" she said, in a tone of alarm, although it was not above a whisper.

A strange sound, something like a deep sigh, came upon her ears at that moment, and as she heard it, she thought that the whole current of her blood stopped in its accustomed channels with terror for a moment; and yet she knew not why she should be so alarmed at a mere sigh.

After that sigh, everything was so profoundly still that in a few moments the idea that it must have been merely a thing of imagination instantly suggested itself to May, and she recovered a little from the state of strange alarm into which she had been thrown.

One glance at the mysterious candle, however, threw her back again into the same condition, at all events, that she had been in before the sigh came upon her ears. And yet she tried hard to reason with herself, and to rise superior, if it were possible, to the many terrors with which she was surrounded.

"What have I to fear," she said, "from the supernatural world? I am guilty of no iniquity that should in any degree make me specially obnoxious to such beings; and if there really be such at all, which is not yet proved, it would be madness to suppose that they are not equally under the control of the Almighty along with all other created things; so why should I allow myself to be thus terrified?"

All this was very well. Thousands of people before the time of May, and thousands after, have reasoned in precisely the same way. But yet they have found it impossible to shake off the terrors connected with a subject that had nothing at all to do with reason, and which was all vague conjecture, appealing to the fancy rather than to the judgment.

We do not pretend here to give any opinion with regard to the long-disputed question of whether apparitions can exist as a part of the great scheme of creation; but it is a strange thing that all the world confesses with their fears to such a thing, even if they deny it with their judgment.

The candle now looked just like some little blue star in the darkness of the chamber; and certainly, if it gave any light at all, the rays were swallowed up in the darkness before they got twelve inches from their source; so that every object in the apartment was in the greatest state of gloom.

The terror of May was fading away a little, but only a little, when the deep sigh came again, and an an instant she was thrown back into the same state of alarm that she had been in before.

"It does mean something," she said, "and something will come of it. Oh, Heaven ! what is that ?   What do I see ?"

Her eyes were fixed upon the little blue light to which the flame of the candle had been reduced ; and then, just within the dim halo that it cast around, she saw the outline of a face !

There was nothing in that face of a particularly terrifying character—it was rather intense sorrow and anguish that were the feelings finding expression upon it ; but still it was terrible from the fact that no one who had looked upon it could for a moment believe that it belonged to this world.   That it was that gave the horror to what otherwise would have courted no other feeling than sympathy.

May tried to speak—she tried to scream, but it was all in vain.   She could not utter a word.   It seemed as if the sight of that face had exercised a spell over all her faculties, and prevented her from the exercise of any of them but such as were merely necessary to enable her to see and to appreciate the terror with which she was overwhelmed.

She could not have turned her eyes away from that face if the wealth of worlds had been offered her for doing so.   She continued to gaze at it with a fascination that would not be resisted ; and then, without movement, it seemed just within the faint sphere of the little light, evidently for the purpose that she should see it

What object could it have ?

How long a time elapsed, during which she could do nothing but gaze upon that face, May had no means of really knowing.   To her it appeared to be an age, although in reality it was only a few minutes ; and then it slowly faded away, and twice, as it did so, she heard the same deep sigh that had before disturbed her.

The candle burnt up again, slowly, to its usual yellow flame.

What with surprise and terror, May was unable to make any movement for some time, even now that she had so far recovered as to be free from the frightful fascination of that face ; but at length she did manage, in a faint voice, to say—

"Luke !—Luke !"

Amid the silence of the night generally, and the still more wrapt stillness of that room, Luke heard the voice calling to him.   To rise and rush into the chamber was the work of a moment.

" Did you call ?" he cried " What is it ?"

" Oh, help—help !"

Luke looked about him in astonishment.   He could see no foe to contend against, and May was sitting up in the bed, looking very much scared.

" What has alarmed you ?" he said. " I see no one."

" No, not now—not now !"

" Was there any one here ?"

" Alas ! I know not, but I have been frightfully alarmed, Luke.   Did you hear nothing ?"

" Nothing but your voice when you called me.   You said, ' Luke—Luke !' did you not ?"

" I did ; but it was as much as I could say.   Oh, Luke, believe me, this place is haunted.   Do not start—it is, indeed.   But whether it be so haunted by good or by evil spirits I cannot tell.   A further stay in it, though, would drive me mad.'

" Aas ! you must have been dreaming."

" No—no—no !"

" But what have you seen ?" added Luke, who, now that his first surprise was over, felt quite convinced that May must have gone to sleep, and let her imagination picture to her what was not real.   " What was it that you suppose you saw ?"

" Do not say, suppose, for I actually saw it."

" Tell me what it was, and where it was."

"Oh, Luke, you are a good and faithful friend of my husband's, and I beg of you for his sake to take me away from this dreadful place at once. I cannot stay here; I have seen the face of a being who is not of this world, glaring at me in this room."

CLAUDE BEARING AWAY ROSA BELL FROM THE SCHOOL NEAR HANGER HILL.

Luke felt very uneasy, and kept glancing around him as though he fancied that May's words might excite the reappearance of the spirit she talked of.

"It is gone," she said, "but I saw it as plainly as I can see you, and we must leave this place at once."

'Oh, reflect a little," said Luke, "before you come to that conclusion. How will Claude Duval know where to find us, if we go from here?"

That was a point of the question that had not occurred to May, and it rather stopped her in her desire to leave.

"But what can I do?" she said. "These rooms are full of horrors, and such appearances only come for two purposes——"

"Two purposes!" said Luke; "and pray what are they?" He was glad to get her into any conversation which was likely in any manner to divert her from her fears. "What two purposes are they that such beings make themselves visible to us for?"

"The one is to threaten, and the other is to warn."

Luke was silent.

"We have done nothing that we should be threatened for," she added, "and, therefore, I cannot believe that it is for anything but to warn us, that these appearances take place here. Oh, Luke, there is danger in this place. Danger to life. What shall we do?"

"In the first place," said Luke, composedly, "we will be quite calm and collected, otherwise, if there be danger, we shall fall an easy enough prey to it."

These words, spoken with calmness and courage, had a great effect upon May.

"Oh, yes," she said. "I agree with you there. We must be calm and collected, of course, Luke. That is evident."

"I am glad it is so evident to you," said Luke; "for now it will enable you to reason upon what has occurred to you. In the first place, you see, I am here, and well armed; and, in the second, if you go from here, we miss Duval; and in the third——"

Luke paused.

"Well, in the third—come, Luke, what then?"

"You will forgive me for saying that it is just possible, although I do not assert that such is the case, that you have dreamt all that you fancy you have seen."

"Oh, no—no!"

"Of course," added Luke, who would fain have pursuaded May that it was all a delusion, although he was far enough from having such an opinion of the matter himself. "Of course, I do not mean to say for one moment but that to you it appeared a reality; but it is always as well to mistrust ones own senses in affairs of this kind."

"Think you so?"

"I am sure of it. Your mind was prepossessed by superstitious feelings. You are very much overcome by fatigue. Your fears are all awakened for the safety of Duval; and in the midst of all that, you lie down to rest, and a light sleep comes over you, which steeps the judgment in repose and inaction, but which leaves the imagination wide awake and master of the brain; and then you see, or fancy you see, which is to you precisely the same thing, all sorts of strange appearances."

———

CHAPTER CXLV.

DETAILS FURTHER WHAT HAPPENED IN THE OLD LODGING HOUSE.

To say that May was at all convinced by what Luke said in the matter of the appearance that she had seen, would be to say a great deal too much; but his words had the effect of soothing her with a doubt of the reality of the seeming spectre.

Had Claude Duval only told her before he left the place what he had seen, she would triumphantly have answered to the fact, that such an appearance had come to her likewise as a proof of its correctness; but, as we are aware, he had, from consideration for her peace of mind, kept it from her knowledge that anything remarkable had occurred to him in the chamber.

"I hope," said Luke, "that you are now convinced there was no reality in what you thought you saw, and that you feel now at peace?"

"I can't gainsay your reasoning," said May. "Of course, it may be as you say, but I do not think it. Are all the doors fast?"

"They are."

"Have you examined the walls to see if there are any traces of secret modes of entering the rooms?"

"I have, and all seems to be quite secure."

"I will strive, then, to be content." She shuddered as she spoke, and looked around her in such a terrified manner, that it was quite evident it would be in vain trying to convince herself that what she had heard and saw was not real. "You will still watch over my safety, Luke?"

"With my life."

"I am satisfied. You will be within call?"

"The slightest sound shall bring me to you. When I have a duty to do, I am not one to shrink from it. I promised Claude Duval, who, from being his servant, now permits me to think myself his friend, that I would watch over your safety, and I will keep my word."

"Then leave me, Luke. I will not call to you if I can help it, unless there be occasion; but if I should do so, you will forgive me."

"Let me beg of you," said Luke, "to grant me one favour."

"What is it?"

"It is, that you will give an alarm at once, whether you are certain that there is any real danger or not. The trouble to me to come from the adjoining room to this is nothing; and if it causes you a moment's uneasiness, I beg that you will not hesitate to call me. I shall be only doing my duty by attending to you."

"You are very good and kind to me, Luke; and I will, indeed, call to you should anything occur."

Luke left the room, and half closed the door, as it had been before; but when he got right into the outer apartment, his countenance wonderfully changed, and he said, in low tones, the deep sincerity of which could not be mistaken—

"Oh, would that we were out of this place! Oh, would that Duval were back! I dread the progress of the next few hours. What may they not bring forth of terror to us?"

It was only wonderful that Luke had been able to put so bold a face upon the matter to May as he had done; for if there were any species of fear to which he was particularly obnoxious, they were those which had for their basis superstition.

Luke sat down in the same chair that he had before occupied; but now he shifted it along until he got the back of it right against the wall, so that he felt tolerably sure nothing could come behind him, and he was likewise in such a part of the room that he could command a good view of the whole of it.

"I shall be cold," he said; "but that is better than being terrified out of my life, and, perhaps, exposed to all sorts of danger. I will keep my eyes wide open, at all events."

With this resolve, poor Luke sat profoundly still, glaring at vacancy; and letting the fire go out just for want of a little common attention to it, and so cooling down the air of the apartment, which at that hour, as it was about half-past twelve o'clock, was not at all disposed to be in its most comfortable condition.

How still the house was, and how still the whole neighbourhood seemed to be! It was only now and then that, from afar off, Luke could hear the faint rumble of some hackney-coach or other vehicle while it passed the neighbourhood; and then all was still again as the very grave.

"Oh, Duval—Duval!" he half whispered to himself, "where are you now? Why do I not hear your welcome tap at the door?—why do I not see your face, and feel that all is well?"

Scarcely had Luke got to the end of this reflection, than he heard a faint noise as if some one were moving their hands over the wall in one part of the room. He glanced in that direction, but he could see nothing.

A terrible fear began to take possession of poor Luke.

Still the strange noise against the wall continued, and if Luke had not been so prepossessed with an idea that there were supernatural sights and sounds to be met with in that house, he would probably have come to the conclusion that it was just possible the sound he heard might come from the other side of the wall, instead of the side that met his eyes there and then by the dim light of the candle, the wick of which had grown to an amazing length for want of snuffing.

But such an idea did not just then strike Luke. He was prepared for a phantom, and he could not just yet turn his attention to what people of real flesh and blood and wickedness might be about to do in that old house.

The odd noise continued, and Luke began to fancy that the light had a strange blue tinge about it; but that was only fancy, and shows what the imagination can do when it is allowed full scope and power over the judgment and the senses. Perhaps if Luke had not, more by instinct than reflection, at once cast his gaze upon that part of the wall from which the singular sounds proceeded, he would have been in too great a state of derangement from his alarm to pitch upon it after a little time; but as it was, he never took his eyes off it, and it was well that he did not.

We must premise, now, that the walls of all the rooms upon that floor were of old wainscot paneling, as yellow as possible with age, and with abundance of dust collecting upon every available spot upon the mouldings where it could lodge itself, so that a hand passed over the wood-work might be expected to produce just the sort of sound that Luke heard.

It did not take long, now, to alter the state of affairs in those gloomy old rooms, and the alteration was rather astounding.

At first, when Luke saw that a portion of the old wainscot wall was moving aside, and leaving behind a black-looking chasm, long and narrow, he thought that surely he was dreaming; but when he saw the flash of light, he took quite a different view of the affair, and rising from the large, old, high-backed chair, upon which he was sitting, he noiselessly shrunk behind it, and crouching down there, was completely out of sight.

From that secure retreat he could observe well all that took place, and now it was strange what a complete revulsion of feeling took place in Luke. All his ideas that he was about to be subjected to the horrors of some supernatural appearance vanished on the moment, and he became possessed of the idea that it was a mortal and strictly human danger that was now at hand.

"Ghosts do not move panels in walls, nor carry lights," thought Luke; "and such being the case, I am armed against whatever may now happen."

It was quite evident now that some persons, who were a great deal better acquainted with the old house than either Luke or Duval was, were now coming into the room, through a secret door in the old panelled wall.

Wider and wider opened the tall, narrow slit, until it was about two feet from side to side, and then Luke saw an arm with a small lamp, and then a head. The head was not of the most prepossing appearance in the world.

The appearance was so anything but ghost-like, that if any remains of superstition had been in Luke's heart and brain concerning the sights and sounds that he had come across in the old house, they would surely now most completely vanish.

"Thieves," he thought to himself, "and in all probability murderers, have made this place the scene of their operations. We shall see what they will be at now."

The hand and the head remained for about half a minute at the opening in the wall, and retired abruptly, and in a manner that betrayed fright. Luke was quite at a loss to conceive what could have created the alarm; but after a little thought he decided in his own mind that it must be the light which was burning in the room, and which, no doubt, gave the depredators the idea that some one was sitting up.

It was quite a good thing that this little alarm had been given to the thieves, for it had the effect of giving Luke time to thoroughly recover himself, and make such arrangements as would best suffice to meet the danger.

Luke knew well that he could depend upon his pistols, and that they were loaded with care, so now he took them both from his pockets and prepared for action. The feeling of superstitious fear entirely faded away before this real danger that now beset him, and he did not feel the tremor of a single nerve as he waited the re-appearance of the man who had taken so stealthy a look into the room.

The only great dread that Luke might be said now to have was, that they should make noise enough to awaken May in the adjoining apartment, and that she, perchance, in her fright, rushing out, should create more danger than he, Luke, could save her from—but that, after all, was only a remote possibility.

It was a full minute before the head appeared again at the opening in the wall, and this time it was not accompanied by the hand nor by the light; the latter, no doubt, was considered to be superfluous, since a candle was burning in the room.

Luke strained his ears to catch the slightest sound that might be made, and he heard a low, rough, harsh voice, say—

"I think it's all right enough."

"Hush!" said another voice—"hush!"

"Oh, there's nobody here," said the first speaker. "I tell you it is all right enough. The room is empty. Come on, will you?"

Luke kept his eyes fixed upon the opening in the wall, and he saw a man attired in a dark overcoat step into the room. Immediately after him came a woman, carrying a light, and the first glance at this woman was sufficient to assure him (Luke) that she was no other than the landlady of the house.

All that had been before only suspicious, was now fully confirmed in a moment, and Luke felt convinced that he and his friends had taken up their abode in one of those houses of murder and rapine which it was believed abounded at that time, when the police force was by no means in the state even of partial efficiency that it is now, and when lawless deeds were far more common.

CHAPTER CXLVI.

LUKE AND MAY ARE BESIEGED IN THE OLD HOUSE.

LUKE kept his eyes firmly fixed upon the pair of worthies who had by such secret means entered the room. He had a fear that they might yet have further force at hand; but that fear soon dissipated, as no one else made an appearance in the apartment.

Even then Luke could with his pistols have taken both their lives; but he was far from being of a sanguinary disposition, and until he had further proofs of their murderous resolves, he could not bring himself to act violently against them in any way. In fair and open fight he would not even scruple to use such arms and means in the way; but to shoot any one from the covert behind the chair that he was in, looked so much like an assassination, that he dreaded to execute such justice even upon the those persons who, let their intentions be what they might, could not come to the room for good.

"Well," said the man, to the woman, "you see it's all right enough; don't you, now—eh?"

"Hush, I say!"

"Oh, I ain't speaking at all loud. Nobody will hear me, I'll be bound."

"But you don't know that."

"Yes, I do. Hold your row, will you? I don't want to be bothered. I don't feel quite well. I'm delicate."

"You always are."

"Well, I know I am. I ain't one of the strongest people in the world, you know. You ought to have let me have a drop more brandy."

"But you had a great quantity."

"No I didn't. Do you call half-a-pint a quantity? Oh, dear! I feel rather queer already."

"Come—come, you are all right enough. You know you have done many an odd piece of work in these rooms before to-night."

"Yes, I have; but somehow I feels rather queerish, on this 'ere occasion. But I suppose I must do it. Have you got the brandy bottle?"

"There—there—there! There it is; but don't take too much, for you know you are not very strong; and that if once you get drunk, you will be good for nothing at all."

"Oh, it's all right."

The landlady handed this delightful-looking gentleman a small flask botile, and he placed it to his lips, and evidently did not take it away again while anything remained in it.

"Ah!" he said, as he drew a long breath; "there wasn't much after all. Not much, by any manner of means."

"Quite enough; and now set to work, I beg of you; for although they may be asleep in the next room, we don't know a moment when they may wake up, and in that case, I know what you would do."

"What?"

"Run away, to be sure; for you are a coward at heart, you know you are. Oh, you needn't look at me so blustering-like. I know what you are well enough, and as you get your good and full share of the booty, I don't see that I need mind what I say to you."

"Now," said the fellow, "by all that's desperate, if a man had only said one half as much to me, I should have eaten him."

"Peace—peace; set about your work at once. You must cut all their throats, I tell you, or there will be no good done."

"Very good."

"It will never do to leave one alive to tell the tale of what has happened in this house."

"I know that. But do you think there's enough booty for the trouble?"

"I do. My opinion of the people is, that they are fugitives from somewhere, and under such circumstances, they are sure to have brought away with them property of value, which we may as well have as they."

"A great deal better."

"Very good—I quite agree with you there. Now set to work about the business. Come on, I will assist you, as usual. This way—this way. You see that there is no one here, so we will make our was to the sleeping room."

"But, stop; didn't you say there were three of them?"

"Yes, but I told you one of the men had gone out, and that, therefore, there is but one of them and the girl in the place, and surely you and I can manage them well enough."

"I should think we could. If there's only one man and a girl, and they both fast asleep, I don't mind trying what I can do in the matter, and I shouldn't at all wonder if I succeeded. Hem! come on. I'll cut the man's throat while you hold the girl, you know."

"Yes, yes."

"And then I'll cut hers."

"Will you, indeed!" thought Luke.

The murderous pair proceeded now at a very slow pace, and treading as stealthily as they possibly could towards the sleeping chamber; but before they got half way to the door of it, Luke rose up from behind the chair where he had been hidden, and cried in a clear, though not very loud voice, for he did not wish to alarm May—

"Hold!"

This exclamation, as might be expected, had about the same effect upon those wretches who were intent upon robbery and murder, as if a bomb-shell had suddenly lit between them and exploded. The woman uttered a scream of terror, and fell to the floor, while the cowardly ruffian of a man, making a wild kind of a rush to leave the room, stumbled over her, and fell sprawling.

It was not possible but that all this noise should have the effect of awakening May in the next room. She had dropped by that time into an uneasy slumber, and hearing the racket in the outer apartment, she at once sprang from the bed and listened intently. Luke made a rush towards his prostrate foes with the intent of taking them both prisoners, and then leaving the house, but, as bad luck would have it, he ran against the table upon which was the candle, and it being rather a rickty one, over it went, light and all.

In a moment the large apartment was in complete darkness.

Luke had every reason in the world to expect that some mischief would be attempted by the man and the woman during that darkness; but what most interested him, was to protect May from any assault upon their parts. He knew the direction in which he had fallen, and rising rapidly, he ran in the direction of the bed-room, and luckily finding the door, he made his way into it at once and closed it.

"Mercy! oh, help!" cried May.

"Hush. It it is only I," said Luke. "Where is your light?"

"Gone out, Luke. Is there danger?"

"There is—there is."

Luke placed his back against the door of the room, lest the murderer should come in in the dark, and try his power of mischief.

"We are beset in this place," said Luke, "by those whose object it is to take our lives, of that there cannot be a doubt now. Has there happened anything to alarm you since you have been in this room?"

"Oh, yes, much—much. Where is Claude?"

"Not yet returned, but we may minutely expect him. Let us listen if there are any sounds from the outer room."

They listened intently for the space of about three minutes, but all was profoundly still, and Luke was lost in wonder as to what had become of the woman and her hopeful associate in crime. He recollected that he had about him the means of getting a light, and he hastily, now, availed himself of the means, and shed a bright glow over the room by the little match that he lit.

"Did your candle burn out?" said Luke.

"No—no. It is here. I can't tell you how it went out, for it died away without apparent cause. Oh, Luke, this place is full of horrors and mysteries."

"It is —it is. But don't be alarmed."

"I cannot help it, Luke, I am truly terrified. I have seen a sight here that the boldest might shrink from."

"Indeed!"

"A being not of this world, Luke has been in this chamber."

"You do not mean that?"

"In good truth I do. I saw it as plainly as I now see you; I was lying upon the bed between sleeping and waking, and I saw it, Luke."

"You were, perhaps, more sleeping than waking."

"No—no. I know what you would intimate; you would try to persuade me that it is all a dream; but in truth and indeed it was not so, Luke. But hark! I think I hear something."

"And so do I. Hush!"

They both listened again, and then Luke felt quite sure that some one was upon the other side of the door, making a strong effort to open it. He had managed to shoot a small bolt into its socket that was upon the inside, so that the door was secure enough against anything but actual violence ; but the manner in which the bolt was strained showed that the pressure against it was very great.

"Light the candle," whispered Luke, "with this match, which is so fast going out, and then place it out of the way of the door. I will question the intruder."

May took the nearly expiring match from the hand of Luke, and lit the candle with it, while he called out, in a clear, distinct tone, to the person who was pushing against the door from the other side—

"Who is there ?—who is there ?"

There was no answer for a minute or two, and Luke thought that he heard a whispered conference going on.

"Who's there ?" he said again.

"Oh, it's all right," replied a voice. "I am your friend."

"What friend ?"

"Oh, your friend who left you a little while ago, to oe sure ; don't you know me ? Open the door."

"Confound your impudence," thought Luke, "I should like to get a pop at you, if I could ; but I suppose that is quite impossible. Preserve us from such friends, say I."

Luke was standing quite close to the side of the door where the hinges were situated, and owing to the wood being shook a good deal, there was a crevice between the door and the wall at that part of nearly a quarter of an inch, through which there came a current of cold air ; but in a few minutes, Luke found, to his cost, that something besides a current of cold air could get through that crevice for the long blade of a knife was suddenly thrust through, and gave him a slight wound in his side.

"This is a friend's trick, is it ?" said Luke.

A volley of the most terrible oaths was the only reply to this.

Luke did not hesitate a moment in what to do. He drew one of his pistols form his breast-pocket, and putting it fairly at the middle panel of the door, he fired it at once. With a crash, the bullet sped on its way through the panel.

CHAPTER CXLVII.

CLAUDE DUVAL ARRIVES RATHER OPPORTUNELY.

THE report of the pistol in the room was rather stunning ; but still it was not so loud as completely to drown every other noise, and Luke felt quite certain that along with its echoes he heard a cry of pain.

"I hit the rascal," he said.

"Come away, Luke, come away," said May. "They will fire again."

"Well thought of," said Luke, and he dropped to the floor in a moment, but yet not a moment too soon, for a bullet went directly over his head, and the stunning report of a gun or a pistol from the other room came upon their ears at the same instant.

Luke got in quick time out of the line of the door, and placed May in such a position that even a slant shot coming through the panels could not possibly hit her. She trembled very much, and was evidently in a great state of terror.

"Cheer up," said Luke. "I don't think we shall come to such an end as those wretches outside intend for us. Let us believe that we are born for something better than to be murdered by them."

"Heaven help us !"

Bang—crash ! came another shot into the room, and this one was fired within six inches of the floor, for it was, no doubt, shrewdly suspected that the other had gone too high to do any mischief.

"We are lost," said May.

"Not a bit of it," said Luke; " let them fire away. That will do us no harm, you see, now that they have sent two shots at us and done no sort of mischief, and I am quite sure that my first bullet did its duty. I will give them another on the chance of it."

Luke waited a few seconds before he fired again, for he thought it very likely

CLAUDE FINDS A SUBSTITUTE TO PERSONATE ROSA BELL TO THE PRINCE.

that whoever had sent the last shot into the bed-room would, immediately upon doing so, get out of the way, and he intended to give that individual, be he whom he might, time to gather confidence to come back again. After about half a minute, Luke thought that such an object was probably attained, and he fired through the middle panel of the door.

The yell that immediately rose from some one in the outer room was truly terrifying and May, placed her hands over her ears so that she might shut out the echoes of it. " This is, indeed, a dreadful night !"

" I think I had him there," said Luke.

" Oh, this is too terrible !" cried May. " When will Claude come home to us?"

" Fear nothing," said Luke. " The probability is, now, that our foes will leave us. I am certain I have hit one of them now. That cry could not be mistaken. It was the death-cry of some one."

" But how still they are now, Luke !"

" The stillness of death."

" Alas! alas! It is very dreadful to have to do such things."

" It is so ; but you will recollect that it is in self-defence that I do them now. We have the choice of defending ourselves as best we may, or of being murdered here, in this villanous place."

" Yes, Luke. Yes, I feel all that ; and far from blaming you, I know how much I am indebted to you. But for you, in all probability, I should now be no more."

" Do not speak in that strain, I beg of you. I am only doing my duty to you, and to Claude Duval ; and, at the same time, you should recollect than I am defending myself."

Luke and May were now silent, and they both listened most intently to hear if any words came from the outer room ; but, strange to say, after that one terrific yell, which had sufficiently plainly announced the fact that the pistol shot had taken effect upon somebody, all was profoundly still. Either death had taken place at once, or the person hit had had constancy of purpose sufficient to prevent him from making any other sound than the one they had heard.

This silence was more perplexing to Luke and May than anything else could have been, because it left their imaginations only in full play, and prevented them from taking any steps to rescue themselves from the awkward position in which they were. Indeed, after about five or six minutes, it became scarcely endurable, and Luke felt half inclined to open the door.

May, as she looked in his face by the dim light of the candle, which was now getting a long wick, seemed to discern what was passing in his mind, and she said—

" Do not run useless risks, Luke. We are in comparative security at present. Let us remain so."

" As you please," he said : " but I really begin to feel pretty well assured that our enemies have left the adjoining room."

" But we do not know that, Luke."

" Certainly not, and, therefore, I will be very careful, indeed ; and yet I should like much to ascertain the fact, and I think it may be done. In the first place, I can't imagine that we had more to contend with than the man and the woman."

" Think you not ?"

" That is my opinion ; and such being the case, you know, if I have shot the man, there is nothing particular to hinder me from going out of the room. But I will try a plan that will let me know if they are in ambush for me."

May was terrified at the idea of the door being opened at all ; but she did not like positively to stop Luke from doing what he was about, and she watched him with interest. Luke took off his coat and hat, and putting the latter on the top of a stick that he found in the room, and wrapping his coat round it, he held them both up to about the same height of himself, and he then very cautiously opened the door, and just a little way thrust out the hat and the coat upon the stick into the outer room.

No doubt. if his enemies had been there, so likely an opportunity of sending a bullet into his head would not have been let go past ; but all was profoundly still ; and from that circumstance, Luke felt that, to use military language, the siege of the bed-room was raised, and that he and May might sally forth in comparative safety.

"Do you see any one?" said May.

"Not a soul. You may depend we have routed them, and that we have the place to ourselves. Come out of that room. I can't help thinking that we shall be safer in this room, the windows of which look to the street. We can call for assistance easily."

"Yes," said May, " and when Claude comes here, we can warn him of the dangers that may await him below."

"We can bring the light, for I have a pistol ready charged in each hand. Hold it as high as you can."

May did so, but she and Luke had not advanced half-a-dozen paces into the room, when she uttered a cry of horror, and tottered into a seat. She had stepped into a pool of blood, and there, lying upon his face on the floor, was the ruffian who had accompanied the woman into the room upon their infamous expedition, that had been so signally defeated by Luke's bravery and alertness.

"Dead," said Luke, as he turned the body over with his foot. "Quite dead. That was my last shot."

"This is terrible," cried May. " I pray you take me away from this place at once. I can't remain here. The dreadful appearance of that body, and the awful scent of blood that is in the air, will drive me mad. Oh, take me away at once. We will wait in the street for Claude. I implore you, Luke, to take me away!"

"I will—I will. But pray be calm. You forget that there are others in the house, in all likelihood, as well as that woman, who, no doubt, would be glad enough to do you a mischief. Be calm, I pray you, and we'll leave this place, but not percipitately, by any means."

The tone of voice in which Luke spoke was greatly calculated to reassure May, and she was silent and still, although her feelings was deeply affected by the proximity of the dead body. Her reason might tell her over and over again, that the villain who now lay there so still, weltering in his blood, amply deserved the fate that had overtaken him, and that if he had not been killed, he might have condemned them to the same fate ; but reason has an up-hill fight ever with the feelings and the imagination, and May could not reconcile herself to remain in the same apartment with that dreadful witness of the result of crime before er

"If I were alone," said Luke to her, "I would march down to the street door with my weapons in my hands, but I dread to go with you!"

"Why do you dread to go with me, Luke?"

"Because I know not what mischief might be done to you in the event of an attack upon us. It looks cowardly to stay here, when, for all we know, there may be nobody but an old woman to interfere with us ; but yet, even she, before I could disarm her, or prevent her from being noxious to us, might rush upon you with a knife, or fire a pistol at you; and what, then, would be the use of my mastey over her and this wretch who lies here, if you were hurt or killed?"

"You speak the truth, Luke."

"How could I face Duval?"

"How, indeed! Say no more, Luke. I will abide by whatever decision you come to in this juncture."

"Very well. Then, I say, let us remain where we are, until Claude comes home. I will throw up the window and watch for him; or if I should see any one in the street who looks likely to be able to assist us, shall I call to him?"

"Oh, yes, yes!"

"But, remember, it is an important object with Duval to remain weeks in London. You are well aware upon what a thread, so to speak, his life hangs."

"Alas! alas! in the midst of my own trials and dangers, I had grown selfish, and, as you say, Luke, I had forgotten the dangers to which he was subject. We will wait for him as best we may."

"You have come to a right decision, I feel assured, and one that Claude will approve of when he comes back. I will now open the window and watch for him, for it is necessary that he should be put upon his guard, before he enters the house."

"I will watch for him," said May, "as well as you, because I think that will be the better arrangement, seeing that you can keep an eye upon the door of the room, in case of a surprise, as that the doing so will relieve me from looking at that dreadful corpse."

"As you please; but I will remove the corpse, for I like the look of it no more than you do."

As he spoke, Luke laid hold of the dead bravo by the feet, and dragging the body into the inner room, he closed the door upon it. To be sure, as it was dragged along it made a long smear of blood upon the floor, which was very horrible to see; but still, it was something to get rid of the corpse itself, and May did not see the blood, for she was looking out at the window, and watching the coming of the first dawn of day, and longing for Claude.

Suddenly she clapped her hands together with delight, as she cried—

"He is here! He is here!"

"Thank God for that," said Luke. "Call to him."

"I will. Claude!—Claude!—Claude!"

Duval had just come in sight of the house, when he heard May calling to him from the window in this way.

CHAPTER CXLVIII.

DETAILS HOW DUVAL ROBBED THE KING'S MESSENGER.

WE know that Duval had been exceedingly anxious to get back to the mysterious lodging-house, but that he had got so bewildered amid the intricacies of Hyde Park Corner and Pimlico as quite to lose his way, or he would have been there half an hour earlier than he was.

When, however, he got within sight of the house, and saw May at the window, and heard her call upon his name, he guessed that something was amiss, although it took off more than one half his anxiety to see that she was well and able to call him.

In a moment he was beneath the window.

"May—May! what would you say to me? I have come home as soon as it was possible for me to do so, I assure you."

"Oh, yes, Claude, I know that well," said May; "but I am here to warn you. There is murder in this house, Claude. Luke and I are prisoners in this room, and I am here to warn you."

"Prisoners?"

"Yes, Claude. Come to us, but be careful how you come, for there are foes in the shape of assassins in the lower part of the house. We had a narrow escape from them."

"We will soon see that," said Claude, and with one bound he flew at the street door, which, not being fast, opened against his weight, and let him down into the passage, so that if there had been any one there intent upon his destruction it might have been completed easy enough before he could recover from the surprise of his fall, and scramble, in the half-darkness, to his feet again.

To be sure, Claude Duval was not wanting in activity, and he, probably, got up rather sooner than most persons would have done; and then, with a pistol in his hand, he dashed into the passage.

Not a soul opposed the progress of Duval as he proceeded towards the staircase, and if they had, there is very little doubt but that, after what May had said, it would have fared but badly with them. He bounded up the stairs and reached the door of the room, which he flung open in a moment, and to the joy of May, held her in his arms the next instant.

"Good Heaven, Luke," he cried, "what is the meaning of all this?"

"The principal meaning," said Luke, "is, that I am quite delighted to see you. Did you meet no one below?"

"Not a soul."

"That is strange enough, for we dreaded to leave the room lest we should be exposed to some ambuscade-like attacks from some one whom it would be impossible to guard against. They must have forsaken the house."

"Oh, Claude, Claude!" said May, "what a joy it is to find you returned and quite safe. You have gone through all the prince wanted you to do, and are unhurt?"

"Completely so; and you?"

"Oh, Luke protected me, or I do not think that I should have lived to look upon your face again."

"My heart misgave me when I left you," said Claude, "that all was not well, and I have endured great anguish of spirit in thinking of you. But let us leave this place at once. We can easily get our horses and be off. London is not the sort of place for us. I hate it; and this house is a most ill-omened one. You have been threatened, I suppose?"

"A little more than threatened," said Luke. "I have been compelled to shoot one rascal. His body is in the adjoining room."

"Ah, indeed! Has it come to that?"

"Yes, Claude," said May, "it has, indeed. I thought that we were both lost, and that you and I would never meet again. But come away. There is a weight upon my spirits in this house. I cannot breathe in it. Oh, take me away at once Claude."

"Come, May, we will not remain, then, another minute. It is sufficient for me that you are both of you unhurt, and that you, Luke, have retaliated on one of your enemies, at least, with a proper retribution; so we will be off at once. This way. Come—come. Fear nothing, May, for upon my word I do not think there, is a soul in the house besides ourselves now."

"It is no doubt deserted by the hag of a woman, then," said Luke, "and after all, there were no more than herself and the man whom I shot to oppose me The midnight murderer does not want many accomplices to do his work of blood."

May leant upon the arm of Claude Duval, who, with his disengaged hand, held a pistol ready for immediate service, and Luke followed them closely, likewise with a pistol in his hand, and keeping a wary eye about him, lest suddenly, when they least expected it, they should be attacked by some one.

In this way they reached the street-door, and as they passed out of it without any interruption, they were only the more confirmed in their opinion that the woman had but that one man to assist her, and that when he fell, she had fled from the house.

A sleepy-looking watchman was at the corner of the street, and for a moment Claude thought of sending him to the house; but he abandoned the idea, as he considered it might get him into an altercation with the guardian of the night as to the propriety of going with him or not.

"I won't trouble the watch," said Claude to Luke, "but I will write to the magistrates about it as soon as convenient, so that it may not be supposed that a murder has been committed by any one in this house, which the appearance of the dead body might otherwise lead the police to think."

"They would be sure to think so," said Luke.

"Not a doubt of it. And now for our horses."

It was not above a ten minutes' job to get the horses, and when they were mounted, Claude Duval considered for a moment or two, and then he uttered the one word—"Hounslow."

May had often heard that that neighbourhood was one in which Claude had committed some of his most daring exploits, and her heart sunk when he thought of going there.

"Oh, Claude," she said, "will you be safe in such a neighbourhood?"

"As safe as I am anywhere, May."

"Do you think so, Luke?"

Luke did not say anything, but his glance at Claude showed that he wished entirely to defer to him in the matter.

"I tell you what, Luke," said Claude. "We will go to the old inn at the verge of the heath, called the Reindeer, and there we shall be safe enough, I promise you; but I have an idea in my head, which, after all, may take us to London again."

"What is that?"

"Why, you know that I have been always most successful in filling my pockets by mingling with the aristocracy; and I think if I can come out again at the west-end of the town, that there is still an opening for me. The season for all the principal entertainments of the nobility is close at hand. The royal gardens at Ranelagh will be open, and there will be some half-dozen masquerades at the Opera-house."

"Alas, alas!" said May.

"Why do you cry Alas?"

"Because I foresee much danger in all these."

"Oh, no; you are really much mistaken, May. These are the kind of scenes I assure you, in which I am able best to succeed; and if I have any talent at all, it is in mingling with the aristocracy of the city, who are mostly as ignorant and silly as possible, and aping their manners in such a way that they fully believe me to be one of themselves, and only find out the contrary when they have paid dearly for their information."

"You do not like the life on the road?" said Luke.

"Yes, I do at times. It is a delightful relief to me to be on a good horse on a cloudy night on the road. The freshness of the country brings a charm to my spirits after a little experience of the saloons of London, and then again I tire of that, and I long to get back again to a London life."

"But you said you hated London," said May.

"Ah, I was vexed when I said so. This infernal adventure that the prince sent me on, and the danger that I found you had passed through, combined to vex me. But come, here we are fairly on the road to Hounslow. How beautiful and fresh the country is at the evening hour. See how the mist is rising out of the little valley there by Acton."

"It is beautiful," said May.

"Very beautiful, indeed," added Luke. "Why, when the morning sun shines through it, it looks like a tissue of gold."

"It does—it does! And now it rolls off over the tops of the trees, and you can see the pale blue wreaths of smoke from the chimney-tops, where early fires are being lighted. Ah, I do think the country, when your heart and spirits happen to be in tune for it, beats the town hollow."

"Yes," said May, "the dear country for me. You will both laugh when I tell you, that the extent of my desire gets no higher than some pretty little cottage, with its flower garden, and its fruit trees, and perchance a little rivulet bubbling by it, and singing sweet murmuring sounds the whole day long—and then——"

"Somebody is coming," said Duval, "so we will hear all about love in a cottage another day. Hark! do you here anything, Luke?"

"Yes, the sound of a horse's feet."

"Let us go slow."

"Oh, Claude—Claude, for my sake——"

"Well, May, dear one, what can I do for your sake?"

"Nothing, Claude. It is that you should not do something that I pray you, and you understand me."

" I do ; you are afraid that I should stop this person ?"

" I am—I am."

" Then I promise you that I will not, and that, if I am not interfered with, I will let him pass me as if I were the sheriff of the county, and he an attorney Will that satisfy you ?"

" It will, Claude, and I thank you."

By the time this little rapid colloquy was over, a horseman, coming on at rather a dashing pace, was close at hand, and by the look that Duval gave to him he perceived that he was some half-pay officer of not very brilliant income. There was, however, a look of insolence about the fellow that was not very pleasing to Duval, who thought—and he was not deceived in that thought—that it had something about it like the insolence of office, for in England nothing can exceed the cool effrontery of official personages. Such people, by being the servants of the public, look upon themselves as having no masters at all, and knowing every one over whom they act have not the power of discharging them for insolence, they at last get up an idea in their own minds that they are the masters of the public, of which they are, after all, but the flunkies.

This country has not at all altered in that respect since the days of Claude Duval.

Well, as we were saying, there was in the look and manner of this man, as he rode up, that kind of sulky insolent style that is insulting of itself when even it is unaccompanied by any overt act, and Claude was rather savage at him accordingly.

CHAPTER CXLIX.

GIVES A GOOD LESSON TO JACKS IN OFFICE.

" HILLOA !" cried the man as he reached the party. " Hilloa ! Halt ! I say, halt !"

Claude drew up, and so did May and Luke. There was a slight—a very slight flush of colour upon the cheek of Duval, which both May and Luke knew brooded mischief ; but the man who had promoted it was by far too stupid to notice any such signs of the coming tempest.

" Come, sir," added the man. " Do you not see that my horse is lame ?"

" If you please, sir," said Claude with an air of affected humility, " I rather do. It is in the near fore-leg."

" Very well—I don't care which of you dismount, for you seem all pretty well mounted ; but I must trouble one of you to lend me your horse, and take mine, till I get to Guildford, where, probably, I shall leave it for you.

Luke looked at May, and May looked at Luke, in perfect amazement.

" Is there anything else, sir," said Claude, " in a small way, that you would be pleased to order, now that you are about it ?'

" Come, come—no insolence ! Dismount at once, one of you. You are in no hurry, I dare say, and I am ; and if you are, that makes no difference to me. Quick—quick !"

" We will consider, sir, just a little, if it is all the same to you," said Claude. " We hope you won't be violent, sir, if you please, as we are very simple, honest folk."

" Oh, no," said the fellow, stroking his whiskers. " There is no occasion for any violence, I dare say."

" We humbly thank you, sir."

" But, perhaps—ah—you—ah—don't know who I am ?"

It was quite clear that the fool was quite gratified at the respect and the humbleness of Duval's tone.

" Oh yes, sir, we do."

" Ah, indeed. Who am I ?"

Duval looked him right plainly in the face, as he said, in a clear tone of voice, and with the greatest deliberation—

" The d—dest idiot I ever met with in all my life without the shadow of an exception !"

If a thunderbolt had suddenly fallen at his feet the man could not have been more amazed than he was at this speech from the seemingly humble personage whom he thought he had completely cowed : He could do nothing but glare at Claude for some moments in silence, and so they continued looking at each other, and both Luke and May would have been amused, only that they dreaded what would be the result.

' Sir," said the stranger, " I begin to think you are a ruffian."

" Sir, I know you are an ass," said Claude.

" A what ?"

" An ass !"

" Oh, indeed ! Very good, sir. Then allow me to tell you that I am a king's messenger, and that, by virtue of my office, I am empowered to seize any man's horse for the service of the State. This, sir, is my badge of office—the silver hound. Perhaps you have heard of such a thing ?"

" It ought to have been a silver donkey !" said Claude, "and then it might have been mistaken for your portrait."

With a bound, then, of his horse, which sprang forward under the impulse that Claude gave it with the spurs, as though it were going to eat up the messenger and his steed, he was close to him, and dashing the muzzle of a pistol right into his mouth, to the great detriment of his front teeth, he cried—

" Your money or your life, sir ! I am a highwayman !"

The messenger fell off his horse, and lay at full length on the road, as if the very fright had killed him.

" Oh, Claude—Claude ! that is enough. Let us ride on, Claude, now. That is enough. Come on, I pray you."

" The rascal," said Duval, " to come with such insolence to me, upon the highway, too. Hold my horse a moment, Luke."

" Oh, Claude, you will not kill him ?"

" I kill him, May? O, dear no." Claude turned towards her with a smile upon his face. " Why what put that idea into your little head, eh ?"

' You are not angry then, now, Claude ?"

" Not a whit."

Luke held Claude's horse while he rapidly dismounted, and approached the prostrate king's messenger, who, when he saw him coming, managed to get up to his knees, and to whine out—

" Oh, dear, sir, spare my life !"

" Confound your life," said Claude, " if I were to take it, it is the most worthless article you are possessed of, I dare say. Where were you going?"

" To Guildford, sir, if you please. To the high-sheriff of the county, with a note from the Secretary of State."

" Give it to me."

" Oh, oh, then I shall be cashiered, I shall, indeed."

" Give it to me."

With reluctance, the messenger handed the letter to Claude, who put it in his pocket.

" Now give me the silver jackass—I mean the hound—that you have round your neck, and that ought to be either an ass or a goose."

" Oh dear, sir, spare me that; I can assure you that I——"

Claude took out his pistol again, and at the sight of it the terror of the messenger was so great that he gave up the little silver hound, which was the badge of his office, and a gold watch, and a well-filled purse, all in a moment.

"Now, what's your name, sir ?" said Claude.

"Captain Smith."

"A captain! Indeed, you are a pretty captain! Pray what were you before you became a captain ?"

"I was confidential valet to Lord Nhoodel, sir."

"Indeed! That is the way public offices are filled in this country, and the

THE PROMISING SON NERVING HIS COURAGE TO MURDER THE LODGERS.

army is disgraced. Farewell, captain. Your horse, I see, has comfortably bolted away through a gap in the hedge into the meadow, and if you value your neck, I advise you to take any road but the one you see us pursue. Do you hear ?"

"Yes, yes!"

The gallant captain fell flat on his back again, for he was afraid that at the last moment Claude Duval might think it safer to blow his brains out than to leave him to tell the story of how he had been robbed ; and then Duval left him and mounted his horse again.

"You have not hurt him, Claude ?" said May.

"Hurt him ? Certainly not. He is not worth the hurting. He is only frightened a little, and if you were to see him to-morrow by the time he has com, pletely recovered, I have no doubt you would find he was as great a man as ever, and in all probability he will tell how he was attacked upon the highway by a desperate gang of highwaymen, and his property and his despatch to the high-sheriff of the county taken from him."

"There is no doubt of that," said Luke. "But will you not see what th-dispatch is about ?"

"Yes, but it is rather prudent to have a gallop first, and so to place a little distance between us and that fellow, who may be much more cunning than he looks. Our horses are quite fresh, as they have had a long rest, and a gallop of a couple or three miles will do them more good than harm."

"It will," said Luke.

Upon this, they all three started off, and at capital speed passed a couple of mile-stones, and were close on to a third before Claude drew rein, and then, with a laughing face, he said—

"I do not think that our friend, the king's messenger, will catch us now. Shall we go on to the Reindeer ? Here is a lane to the right that leads to it."

"Why, if I might be so bold as to suggest such a thing," said Luke, "I should say that breakfast would not be the most disagreeable sight in the world just now."

"Ah, to be sure. A thousand thanks, Luke. Why, May, you must be half famished by this time."

"I must own," said May, "that I am not so romantic but that I can look with pleasure upon my breakfast."

"Come on, then, to the Reindeer ; it is only a short mile down this lane, and we shall soon be at the door of it, from which, too, we can have one of the finest views of the old heath that is to be got at all."

The mile of ground was soon passed over, and when Claude Duval drew rein at the door of the Reindeer, which was a well-known inn upon the border of the old heath at Hounslow, the landlord looked at him from an upper window, and cried out—

"Why, it's Du——Oh, I mean it's the colonel."

"That's right," said Claude, "caution is the word. When gentlemen travel they don't choose that their name should be blazed about, even to the morning air."

"To be sure not, colonel," cried the landlord, who knew Duval quite well, and had a heavy debt of gratitude to repay him, for Claude had once paid sixty pounds to save the house from being taken away from him, and all his goods sold. "To be sure, and there are few men who could draw rein at the door of the old Reindeer, who would be one-half so welcome as yourself."

"And my friends, I hope too," said Claude.

"Ay, and a hundred of them if you like."

"Very good. All I want, then, is that you forthwith place your friendship into the shape of a good breakfast."

"That I will do. Wait a minute."

The landlord was soon outside and close to the saddle of Claude's horse, and then he said to him—

"I hope nothing serious is amiss ?"

"Oh, no," said Claude, "only I should like our cattle put into a safe place."

"Yes, I know—where you can lay your hand on your horse's mane at any moment you please ?"

"Exactly so. I don't know that there will be any one here inquiring for me or anybody like me; but we will take possession of your most private apartment, if you please."

"So you shall."

"Is you daughter, Bessy, at home?"

"To be sure she is."

"Well, you see that young gentleman on the bay horse? Perhaps you will allow Bessy to attend to his comforts."

"Eh—what?"

Claude laughed.

"Pho, man, Bessy will not object, particularly when you tell her that that is my wife dressed *en cavelier* for the convenience of travelling."

"Ah, I see; that will do. And now for the breakfast.'

———

CHAPTER CL.

CLAUDE AND HIS FRIENDS DANCE AT THE SHERIFF'S BALL.

THE little adventure with the king's messenger seemed but to have added a zest to the capital breakfast which mine host of the Reindeer placed before Claude Duval, Luke, and May. They enjoyed a hearty laugh over it, and then Luke said—

"But, sir, you have not looked at the despatch that the fellow had to carry to the sheriff at Guild ord."

"By Jove, no! but I will look at it. What can it be all about, I wonder? We shall soon see; I am not very particular about the confidence of a Secretary of State."

"Considering," said Luke, "that Secretaries of State are not very particular about other folks' confidence. I don't seen why you should be.'

"Certainly not, Luke. This is the despatch—

"Downing Street.

"SIR—By this you will please to consider it a foremost duty to make every possible exertion for the apprehension of Claude Duval, the notorious highwayman, and some associates he has with him.—His Majesty's government desire that you spare no expense in the matter, and state that the Treasury will defray all such charges with great willingness. Let this note be a sufficient authority upon your part to call upon the military power to aid you in any emergency connected with the object herein mentioned.—I am, sir,

"Your's very truly,
"SAMUEL NORTH. P.S."

"What the deuce does he mean by P.S. at the end of his note?" said Luke. "It is rather strange."

"Oh, that is easily understood," replied Claude. "Sir Samuel North is the private secretary of the Secretary of State for the Home Department, and that is what the P.S. means. But the letter altogether has a more significant meaning. It means danger."

"Yes, Claude," said May. "They hunt you still."

"They do—they do, and it is a chase that I don't think, myself, they will ever tire of, May. Well—well, we must meet the exigencies of the moment as best, we may. What do you advise, Luke?"

"I hardly know what to say."

"And you, May?"

"Ah, Claude, you know that I have but one wish, and that is for your safety and that the only advice I could give you is too keep out of danger.'

"That is quite impossible. Danger is the very atmosphere that I breathe, and the only way I can get out of it is by going into my grave, so that is not to be thought of any longer. What say you to going on to Guildford at once—or at night, suppose we say? You look fatigued, May, so I would like you to rest till nightfall."

"By why to Guildford, Claude?"

Duval laughed.

"It would be a very unhandsome thing not to deliver the letter to the sheriff, don't you think? When so great a man as a Secretary of State writes to so great a man as a sheriff of a county, he likes him to get the epistle. Now what is to hinder us from going to Guildford and seeing what we can do there in the way of business?"

"Oh, Claude—Claude!"

"Oh, May—May, what do you fear?"

"Everything. You are so fond of running, as it were, into the lion's mouth. I should have thought, now, that Guildford would be the last place you would have thought of going to."

Luke shook his head as he said, in a low tone of voice—

"So should not I."

"There, you see," added Duval, with a smile, "Luke knows much better than you do, May. But in all sober seriousness, let me assure you, that I do not think there is any danger in going to Guildford with this letter of the king's messenger's. In the first place, I am confident Captain Smith will not go there. It will take him some days to recover from the fright he has been put into on the road, and as the Secretary of State has by this time dismissed the whole affair from his mind, there will be no inquiry made, and we shall be safe enough."

"But why go at all, Claude?"

"I owe this same sheriff a grudge, although he never saw me. Once when I was most defenceless, it could have done him no harm to let me go, he, on the contrary, took a delight in hunting me. I foiled him, but I made a resolve that he should hear of it."

"He will go," said Luke.

"Then he will not go alone," said May. "If it must be so, we will all go;— and yet, pardon me, Luke, for speaking so hastily for you."

"Luke is quite at liberty to go or stay," said Duval, "according to his own good pleasure—a fact concerning which, Luke is perfectly well aware, I rather think."

Luke looked hurt.

"Where you go I go," he said. "I thought that was quite sufficiently understood long ago, for it not to become a subject of discussion now."

"So it was, Luke; so it was," cried Claude, as he shook him by the hand. "So that is all settled quite comfortably, and we will go to Guildford as soon as the sun has set."

May felt that it would be as useless as it would be ungracious to attempt, now, to dissuade Claude Duval from his project; therefore, she abstained from any such attempt, and quietly retired to repose after the great fatigues she had undergone. The day soon slipped away, and the reader will be so good as to suppose that the sun has sunk for the space of about half an hour, and that the twilight is deepening into complete darkness—that the birds have gone to rest and the gentle flowers have closed their bosoms from the night air—that a soft wind, rather indicative of moisture in the air, is blowing, and that Claude Duval and those two faithful ones upon whose love and devotion to him he knew he could so well depend, are mounted and at the door of the inn.

Duval has made some alterations in his exterior, and he has sealed up the Secretary of State's letter again, so that it looks nearly as well as if it had never been meddled with. May still retains her masculine attire, and Luke has put on a very sober-looking cravat, indeed, intending to pass for a clerk in the Secretary of State's office.

"If we don't get something to put into the purse," said Duval, "we shall get some amusement; so come on. Good evening, landlord, and good fortune attend you always, and your fair daughter, Bessy."

"The same to you," cried the landlord; "you are a trump, I will say."

In another moment they were all three off, and making good speed on the shady side of the lane till they got into the highway, and then at a much more moderate pace they went towards Guildford.

"Now," said Duval, "I have no doubt in the world but that we shall get an invitation to the sheriff's house; and if so, I am determined to give him such a lesson as will, I hope, prevent him for the future joining in the hue-and-cry against any unfortunate individual who may become obnoxious to his authority. There is a wide difference between a man doing his duty and going out of his way to be a partizan in the matter."

We cannot exactly agree with Claude Duval here. Of course, though, he spoke in a prejudicial manner, for, after all, the duty of the sheriff, if it comes to that, was to spare no trouble in completing the objects he had in view. If one of them were the capture of Claude Duval, he could hardly be fairly blamed in the matter merely for showing too much zeal.

The air, probably from the fact that it was rather loaded with moisture, was exceedingly grateful and refreshing to the senses, and even May got rid of most of her fears, as she rode on by the side of Claude through the richly diversified piece of country that lay between their starting-post and Guildford. The distance they had to go was by no means great, and they soon came to the outskirts of the town. Several persons on horseback and on foot passed them, and at length a servant in livery, who was going in the same direction as themselves, was about to pass them at a canter, when Claude Duval called to him and he drew up.

"Don't let me interrupt you if you are at all hurried," said Claude, "but can you tell me if the sheriff of the county is at Guildford at the present time?"

"Oh, yes, sir. I am one of his servants. He is staying at his house in Guildford, sir, till Miss Forsyth is married."

"And who is she?"

"His youngest daughter, sir. She is to be married this morning, and then there is going to be a grand ball and a supper, sir, in honour of the event, and at midnight the bride and the bridegroom are going off to Paris for a little time, they say."

"Oh, indeed! I suppose the bridegroom is some young and handsome man?"

"Young and handsome, sir? Lor bless you! did you never hear of old Hunkers, the lawyer at Guildford?"

"Never."

"Why then, sir, that is the man. They do say—but I don't know how true that may be, so I shouldn't like to swear to it it—that he is worth some half a million of money."

"A good round sum, if he be worth half of it. He is older than the lady, then?"

"A little, sir. Miss Annie Forsyth is just seventeen, and old Hunkers is about sixty-eight. That's all the difference, sir. And he is as ugly as Satan, while she is as beautiful as an angel, poor young thing! Why, if she were a child of mine, though I am a poor fellow, she shouldn't be sold to old Hunkers—no! not if I had to beg bread from door to door."

"You are an honest fellow."

"Oh, sir, when I think of the whole affair, it makes my blood run cold first and then hot; I know I shall lose my place, for I can't help looking what I think, and I should not be at all surprised if I suddenly break out and say something that may astonish them all. But perhaps I have as good as done it now, for you may be friends of old Hunkers's."

"Certainly not."

"Well, I'm glad he hasn't a friend that looks so much like a gentleman.

But it's the sheriff you know there and that will settle my business all the quicker, I take it."

"No, my good fellow, we know none of the parties; my only business with the sheriff is to bring him a letter, that is all; and I never saw him in my life, and from what you say of the manner in which he is capable of sacrificing his own child for money, I don't want to cultivate his acquaintance. But still you are an imprudent man."

"I imprudent, sir?"

"Yes, so be sure. Here you open your heart to the first stranger you meet with upon the road, not knowing at all who he is."

"Ah, sir, when one's heart is full it will run over, sir. I and Mary, the under-housemaid, you see, sir, are going to make a match of it. We have made up our minds, as soon as we can, between us, see fifty pounds once ours, to take some country inn, with a little bit of a farm-yard, and a paddock or two at the back of it, and be as happy as the longest summer day is long; so, you see, sir, after all, I don't care much for the sheriff, nor for old Hunkers either."

"You are a frank, free-spirited fellow, and I hope we shall meet again. What is your name, my friend?"

"They call me Robert, sir, but my name is Robert Brown. Nobody thinks of calling me Brown, though. Good-day to you, gentlemen."

———

CHAPTER CLI.

CLAUDE DUVAL SEES AND PITIES THE YOUNG BRIDE.

CLAUDE and his friends looked at each other for some few moments in silence after Robert the groom had left them; and then it was May who broke the pause by saying—

"This is but too common a case, I fear, Claude."

"Common! It is common. But I hope that it will likewise be common enough for those who hear of such a piece of villany to do their best to thwart it. It is really and truly too bad."

"It is monstrous," said Luke.

"A young girl of seventeen cannot," added May, "but view an union with a man of sixty-eight as a serious sacrifice. What kind of idea can this sheriff have of the feelings of his child?"

"None at all," cried Claude Duval. "You may depend that he is one of those common-place, vulgar souls, who fancy that money is the end all, and the be all, of human life, and that so as you procure it in abundance, you have every-thing else. I grant that society, by the extravagantly undue influence it has given to mere wealth in this country, has done much to foster such an idea; but I cannot think it is very frequent that a man will sacrifice a young girl to his bloated cupidity."

"Alas, it is too frequent, Claude. But calm yourself; I know you feel strongly upon this question. But let me ask you one thing, and that is, what can you do in the affair?"

"Yes," said Luke, "that is the question."

"It is," said Claude, with a sigh, "indeed, and in truth it is. I feel that I can but make one reply, and that is, that I can do absolutely nothing in the matter."

"It is so."

"Well, well, let us go on to Guildford as quickly as we can, and banish from our minds the melancholy thought, for, in good truth, it is a melancholy one, that there are fathers in the world who will sell their daughters to the highest bidder. It is monstrous. And yet, I dare say now, the sheriff goes to church and pays for his pew, and turns up his eyes, and prays, and says,—'Oh, God, we have done those things that we ought not to have done, and we have left undone those things that we ought to have done;' and when some one comes before him in his magisterial capacity, for, no doubt, he is in the commission of the peace for the county, he will tell them to mind their oath, and that Heaven is looking down upon them, and all that sort of thing ; and then he sells his child to old Hunkers. Oh, it is monstrous !"

It was seldom that Claude Duval spoke at such length, for he commonly always endeavoured to put what he had to say into the shortest possible phrases. He was rather a man of action than of words, so May and Luke were both duly surprised to hear him discourse so.

The fact was, that nothing awakened the sympathy and the feelings of Claude Duval so much as any cruelty or injustice done to a young girl. There was some passion in this feeling, and some sentiment, for he was always prone to consider young girls as the most innocent and estimable of God's creatures, as well as the most lovely.

May looked at him rather in amazement, and she said with a smile as she laid her hand upon his arm—

"My dear Claude, there are many elderly poor women who are very much oppressed in this world, don't you think ?"

"Oh, ah—doubtless."

"And they will not have so many defenders as a young girl of seventeen ; so, if you are, indeed, to be a knight-errant, you know, Claude, let me commend the old women to your care."

"Thank you, you are very kind," laughed Claude. "Perhaps you are jealous of the sheriff's daughter ?"

"Yes, I am, and I shall be more so, if you get again into such heroics concerning her, Claude; so we will say no more about it, if you will ; but consider, as is the fact, that, after all, you cannot help it, and that it is no business of ours if we could."

Luke laughed to himself, for there was both jest and merriment in what May said ; but Duval made no answer at all to her just then, and as they had come to a very singularly dark bit of the wood, it was not possible for her to see his face and so detect from its expression what kind of feeling was at his heart.

How long the pause might have lasted between them it is hard to say; bu suddenly they were all three attracted by a sound that struck very painfully upon the ear amid the silence of the evening.

We should tell that the bit of road they were upon was bounded upon both sides by a tall hedge or embankment, upon the summit of which there grew brambles and other bushes in very great luxuriance indeed, and here and there a poplar shot up in the edge-row into the night sky, casting a dim, deepened shadow over the road-way. The sound that they heard evidently came from the other side of the hedge to their right hand, and it consisted of sobs from some one whose heart seemed bursting with the intensity of their grief.

"Who can that be ?" said Claude, as he drew up.

"Hush !" said May. "There it is again. I never heard utterance given to so much sorrow before."

The sound of their horses' feet did not seem to have had any effect upon the mourner, who was evidently in that extremity of woe that he—for it seemed to be a male voice—had thrown off all regard for the world, its thoughts and opinions, and given himself up wholly and entirely to the expression of his deep affliction.

"Oh, speak to him," said May, "speak to him, Claude. It it is terrible to hear any one so suffering—speak to him."

"It is horrible !—I will. Hold my horse, Luke, for a moment. I will get up the bank and see, if I can, who it is."

Claude sprung from his saddle in a moment and ran up the bank by the aid of some bushes of an alder-tree that grew close to the spot, and when he could look into the meadow beyond, he saw some dark object lying down, but the sobs and the moaning immediately ceased.

"Hilloa !" said Claude. "What is the matter ?"

"Nothing," said a faint voice, "nothing."

"Yes, but it is something "

"No—no. Go your way in peace, and leave me. That is all I ask of you. It is not much of a favour, surely."

"None at all, and it sounds very reasonable, indeed; only that as you are in great affliction and seem by your tones to be a very young man, I offer you frankly and freely such assistance as I can give you. If it be poverty that afflicts you in this way, here is gold."

"No—no—no!"

"If it be sickness, you shall mount my horse, and I will take you on to Guildford, and see that you are properly attended to. If it be sorrow, let me tell you that, at one time or another, such is the lot of all, and that it is a poor philosophy that falls down by the roadside to bewail it, for it will, in due time, pass away, and the sun will shine again. You do not answer me. Well, perhaps this is, after all, a very impertinent intrusion upon my part, and I apologise to you for it."

"Oh, no—no! Kindness can never be impertinent, sir. I thank you with all my heart and soul."

"That is well.—Come, now, get up."

"Oh, no—no! Let me lie here and die."

"Die, did you say?"

"Yes, it is my only hope, now.—What has life to give me in exchange for what I have lost?—I see nothing but despair in the future."

"Indeed?"

"It is so, sir.—Farewell."

"Shall I tell you why you see nothing but despair in the future?"

"How can you possibly know?"

"Yes, I do know. It is just because you cannot see far enough, that is all, my young friend. The future has too many changing hues to be all like despair. Pray, how far into futurity do you think you can see, now, if it be a fair question?"

"The reason is all upon your side, sir," said the young man in a calmer tone, "I am prone to admit that, but the feeling is all on mine."

"No—I feel for you; but my judgment is calm and clear, and yours is clouded by some calamity, or by some fancied calamity. Come, now, rouse yourself up, and speak to me like a man. I have two friends with me who will likewise advise with you. Despair, indeed! That is a word that no young man ought to use, except to wonder what it means. It is merely another term for cowardice."

"Do you think so?"

"I know so. There, now you are upon your feet, and you feel better, already. Now, what is the matter? Tell me at once, and frankly, like a man."

"Sir, I do not know what it is that induces me to tell you, but it seems as if something whispered to me to do so, and I will obey the admonition. In a word, sir, I am a clerk upon a small salary in the service of the sheriff of the county. My name is Harry Lucus, and from the moment I caught a glance of Annie Forsyth, his youngest daughter, I loved her with all my heart."

"Really?"

"Yes, sir, and once I met her when she was alone——"

"And you told her as much?"

"Well, I rather think I did hint at it; but she burst into tears, and told me never to think of her, for her father had, by a threat of committing suicide if she did not consent, forced her into acquiescence with a projected marriage with one whom she could never love,"

"The cowardly rascal!"

"It was cowardly, sir; and so when I heard that it was all arranged, and that this night my Annie, as I have been in the habit of fondly styling her, was about to be sacrificed, I felt maddened, and came here with a determination to put an end to my existence."

"Pho!—Stuff!"

"Stuff, sir, do you say ? Do you treat my sorrow with so much cold indifference?"

"Certainly not ; I treat only your despair in that way. Why, have you no spirit ? Have you no bravery about your love ? Were I you, I would snatch Annie Forsyth from old Hunkers and her father, even if she stood upon the very steps of the altar."

LUKE SHOOTS AT THE LANDLADY'S SON THROUGH THE DOOR.

"Hunkers! Gracious Heavens, then you know——"

"All about it. I know that the sheriff is about to sell his daughter to old Hunkers, and that the ceremony is to take place to-night at twelve."

"Yes—yes."

"And after that they are going to Paris."

"Oh, yes. It is so."

"And I know of a coward, who comes to a field and lies down under a hedge to cry, instead of acting like a man!"

"A man? I will act like a man! By Heaven! I'll blow up the whole of Guildford rather than Hunkers shall have her! I'll throttle Hunkers first. I'll take her away before them all, and woe be to him who stays me!"

CHAPTER CLII.

DETAILS WHAT HAPPENED AT THE WEDDING AT GUILDFORD.

WHEN young Harry Lucas spoke in this way, Claude burst into a peal of laughter, and then taking him by the hand, he said—

"That is it. That is the right spirit! Why didn't you think of all that before, eh?"

"I am ashamed of my folly."

"Nay, it was not folly. No natural feeling ought to be named folly; so don't think anything more about it, but come over the hedge and let us consult about what can best be done in this affair. Chance has made my two friends acquainted with the facts of the case, and as we sincerely sympathise with you and the young girl, we will do all we possibly can to aid you, whether that all should turn out to be much or little."

"I cannot thank you as I ought."

"Don't attempt it. Come this way at once."

The young clerk followed Claude Duval to the road, but there was no occasion to tell May and Luke what had taken place, for they had both ridden close to the hedge, and overheard every word that had been uttered both by Claude and the young clerk.

"In the first place, let me ask you a question," said Duval, "which you ought to have asked yourself some time ago."

"What is it, sir? I will fairly and truly answer it, I assure you, be it what it may."

"Then, have you the means—provided you were to marry her—of supporting the sheriff's daughter?"

"Yes."

"That is boldly and well answered. Now, what are those means?"

"Simply these. My mother is in independent circumstances; she resides on a pretty little farm of her own, not very far from here, and has a life investment in two thousand pounds, which at her death will come to me; and in the country she has offered me a home with Annie whenever I could prevail upon the dear girl to consent to be mine."

"Very good. That is quite sufficient. However, you will easily imagine that if you run off with her the sheriff is not likely to draw his purse-strings in your favour, either soon or late."

"The sheriff, sir, has not a farthing in his purse that he can call his own. He is a hopelessly condemned man, and it is with old Hunkers's money that he hopes to be able to hold up his head in the world."

"That makes his conduct all the worse, for if he were well to do himself, he might plead that it was his anxiety for his daughter's happiness, assuming happiness to mean plenty of money that makes him act as he does; but as it is, the whole affair centres in self."

"It does so, indeed."

"Well—will, Master Harry Lucas, never mind all that. We will do the best we can for you. Do you really think that Annie loves you?"

"Ah, yes; she whispered to me as much one day, while her head rested upon my breast, and her soft lips touched mine."

"Oh, that is quite enough. Why, you rascal, and yet you spoke of dying in yonder meadow after you had won the heart of a young girl? Stuff! Don't let me ever hear of such nonsense again. And now let me tell you that I am bound to the house of the sheriff with a letter from the Secretary of State, addressed to him, urging him to take immediate and active measures for the apprehension of Claude Duval the notorious highwayman."

"Indeed, sir ?"

"Yes, and you shall go with me."

"But I shall be known in a moment."

"Not so. We have the means of altering your appearance a little. Luke, I fancy that in the vallise you have ample means for transforming our young friend here into something rather different to what he is ?"

"Oh, yes, if we could only get a light, and I don't see why we should not arrange all that at the first cottage we come to. The people won't be able to tell but what it is merely some jest that we have on foot."

"Surely not. Let us push on at once. Jump up behind me, Mr. Lucas. My horse will carry double for a short distance without inconveniencing himself in the least, or giving it a thought."

"For Annie I will do anything," said the young man, as he actively sprang upon the horse's back. "You have given me a hope which, I trust, will only be crushed along with my existence. But will you pardon me for asking who you are ?"

"Permit me to keep that a secret for the present."

"Pardon me for asking you the question. I had no sort of right to do so. All I ought to think of doing is to thank you for your great kindness to me."

"I see a light," said Luke. "We are close upon some habitation."

"I know it well," said young Lucas. "It is the first of a few detached cottages, occupied by laundresses, at the commencement of the town. A little further on you will see the light in the High-street of Guildford."

"That will do, then," said Claude, as he dismounted and rapped at the cottage-door. The summons was answered by a woman, to whom Duval said—

"We want you to permit us the use of your fire-side for a few moments, if you please, ma'am, and for which we will pay you what you please. We re intent upon a little frolic, that is all. It is one that has no harm in it."

"Oh, certainly. Walk in, gentlemen."

"I will hold the horses," said May.

"Nay, bring them within the gate of the garden, and tie them by their bridles," said Claude. "They will not stray then.'

This was done, and the whole party entered the laundress's cottage. Luke brought with him the vallise that he always had strapped behind him over his horse, and to the astonishment of the woman, and also to the surprise of Harry Lucas, he took from it a complete change of clothing for the latter, and likewise a pair of false moustachoes and whisker, that, when they were put on, so completely altered the young man, that his most intimate associates would not have known him. In fact, when he was completely disguised by Luke, and took a glance at himself in the little glass on the laundress's chimney-piece he started back, as he exclaimed—

"This is truly wonderful!"

"I hope gentlemen," said the laundress, "that you are after no mischief."

"None in the least," said Duval. "I assure you again, that it is a harmless frolic, and contemplates doing good instead of evil."

As he spoke, he placed a guinea in her hand, which acted like a charm, for it banished all her scruples at once, and she did not stand upright again while they remained in the cottage, but kept up such a profusion of curtseys, that it was a relief to them all to get away.

Claude enjoined her to secrecy, and they left her swearing a vast number of extemporaneous oaths upon that portion of the subject, and calling down the most exemplary vengeance, and all sorts of judgments, if she ever said a word about the affair.

"Confound that woman," said Duval, "what a tongue she has, to be sure."

"She has, indeed," laughed May. "I can hear her yet."

They found the horses all right, and then as the distance to the town was so very short, Harry Lucas said he would rather walk it, and he was rather solicitous to know what plan of operation Claude Duval had concocted with regard to Annie Forsyth.

"Upon my word," said Duval, "you ask me a question that I confess puzzles me. We must be entirely guided by circumstances. All we know just now is, that it wants a good four hours to midnight, and, therefore, Annie is not married; and all I can see my way in is, that no doubt the sheriff will ask us to stay to the wedding, and that circumstances must be our guide as to what further proceedings we adopt in the matter."

"One thing," said May, who was considered by Harry Lucas to be quite a lad. "One thing will be very essential, and that is, that Mr. Lucas should, as soon as possible, procure an interview with Annie, so as to prepare her with the idea that something will be done."

"Oh yes, yes," said Harry Lucas, "I am sure that, by this time, her positive horror at the match must overcome every other feeling."

"It ought to do so."

"Well," said Claude, "we shall soon find out all that, when once we get the ear of the young lady. I will place the sheriff in such a situation that he cannot very well help inviting us, and then we shall see how the land lies."

With this understanding, then, which was by far too practical and sensible for any one to dispute, they rode into Guildford, and Claude, after a whispered consultation with Luke, stopped at the first inn on the London side of the town, and there proposed to put up their horses. They left the name of Smith with them, and let the ostler see them all four, so that he might know them again, and give up the steeds to any one of them who should come for them.

After this, Duval and Luke felt more at their ease in the matter, and they turned to Lucas and asked him to show the way to the sheriff's house.

"This way," said the young lover. "It is the largest house in the town, and he lives in it himself, as it is his own, because he cannot get any one to take it and keep the requisite establishment it would require. He is always groaning at the expense of it to him, which, to tell the truth, he can ill afford. This way, gentlemen, if you please, round this corner."

They turned a corner of a street rather abruptly, and came to the High-street, when there could not be any doubt as to which was the sheriff's house, where the wedding was to take place, for it was illuminated from the basement to the attic for the occasion.

A band of music in the roadway immediately facing the house was executing most horribly, out of all time and tune, some of what were called popular airs, and the whole town seemed to be quite in an uproar upon the occasion of the grand wedding.

"What a strange hour for the ceremony, twelve at night is," said May

"It is," replied Lucas, "but I was given to understand that such was the wish of the bride. What could have been her motives, except that she might avoid observation, I do not know."

"She should never have consented at all," added May; "she must be a very weak-minded girl."

"I beg your pardon," said Lucas, "I beg your pardon, young sir. She is not a weak-minded girl. She is as admirable in her mind, as she is beautiful in her person. Pardon me for contradicting you, but to my heart she is all goodness and all perfection."

"Believe me," said May, "I do not think the worse of you for this genuine and noble confidence in her whom you love. It is my prayer that you may ever feel towards her as you do now."

"Oh, I can know no change."

"You are a real lover, and deserve to be happy."

The young clerk was very much raised in the estimation of May by the manner in which he had defended Annie Forsyth, the sheriff's daughter, from even the shadow of blame, and she was now as willing as Claude could be to do all that was possible to save the young girl from the agony of a union with one so unsuited to her as old Hunkers.

"Hush!" said Lucas, as he tremblingly laid his hand upon the arm of Claude Duval. "Here we are at the door of the house. Dare I enter it?"

"To be sure. Follow me, and put a bold face upon the matter.''

CHAPTER CLIII.

CLAUDE DUVAL ASTONISHES THE OLD BRIDEGROOM.

A THRONG of servants filled the hall of the sheriff's house. Everything in and about the place had the appearance of wealth, and no wonder, for rich old Hunkers paid for all, and he had more money than even the exaggerated reports gave him credit for.

There is but one feeling that in such men will induce them to part with their money, and that is, their sinful passions, which at their age should surely be tame and dull upon the judgment. But the fact was, that old Hunkers, in imagination, gloated over the beauty of Annie Forsyth, and would have given double the price that he offered for her if the sheriff had only held out.

It is truly dreadful to think that such things take place here in what is called a Christian country; but how common they are, and how common it is to hear people talk about Turkey, where women are openly bought and sold, as if such were not done in England! Why, there are more young girls among the aristocracy of England bought and sold in a week, than there are in twelve months in Turkey.

Out upon such hypocrisy, for it is nothing else.

But to return to our tale. The hall of the sheriff's house was handsomely fitted up, and a number of guests were in the house. They were for the greater part his creditors, who, now that they fancied he was selling his child for gold to pay them, decided that he was a very nice man, and that they always thought so; and there were some even who went so far as to launch out in praise of old Hunkers himself.

Alas! what will people not do when there is plenty of money to gild over the follies and offences of others!

One of the servants, seeing that four strangers entered the hall, at once advanced to them, and said, politely—

"Will you favour me with your names, gentlemen? You are guests of the sheriff, I presume?"

"No," said Duval, "I am come upon business."

"Business, sir?"

The servant looked aghast at the idea of anybody coming on business at such a time as that, when certainly nothing but pleasure ought to be in the ascendant.

"Yes," added Duval; "you will be so good as to tell the sheriff that a gentleman from the secretary of state wishes to see him."

At these words the servant made a very elaborate bow, and said—

"Please, gentlemen, to step this way."

They were now led into a reception-room, that was blazing with wax-lights, and fitted up with great taste and luxury indeed. The bow windows were filled with choice plants, and, take the room for all in all, did great credit to the powers of some upholsterer of Guildford, who had had the putting it in order.

"I will tell my master, sir, that you are here," said the servant, and he then retired; but before the friends could make a single observation to each other, the door of the room opened, and there came in an old man, attired in a style that made his age look positively repulsive: he had on such a dress as some youth might have worn on his wedding day.

He stooped very much, and his form looked like an old parchment bag half stuffed out with rags. His teeth projected from his lips, and his eyes were half hidden beneath his shaggy brows. He looked more like a hideous old ape than a man, and the gaudy apparel that he wore was certainly, upon his part, a singular exhibition of bad taste and folly.

Tottering on his spindle-shanks into the middle of the room, this old being cried, or rather mumbled for he could not speak plain—

"Where is the sheriff? Where is the sheriff? I want the sheriff! I—I want him! Where is he?"

"Hunkers," whispered Harry Lucas in the ear of Claude Duval.

"I thought as much," said Claude.

"Eh? eh? What do you say?" cried old Hunkers. "Have you seen the sheriff?"

"Worthy sir, no," said Duval; "but allow me to congratulate you upon this auspicious occasion."

"Eh? Who are you—who are you?"

"A gentleman from London, sir. Nobody, I declare, would guess now, Mr. Hunkers, to look at you, that you were fifty years of age."

"Fifty, eh? Did you say fifty?"

"I did, sir."

Old Hunkers was quite delighted to have no less than eighteen years at once taken off his age, and then to be told that he looked younger even than that showed him to be. He grinned and mashed his old jaws together, and perked himself up, and strove to put on a gay air, as he said—

"Why, a—a—yes, eh?—I rather think I carry my age well."

"No one better, sir."

"Ah—eh?—you think so? Well, now, just looking at me with the advantages of dress, now, how old—eh?—how old should you say that I was, if you saw me for the first time, eh—eh?"

"Come a little more into the light, sir."

"Yes—yes—eh? Well, now?"

"Just turn round, sir, and let me get a good look at you, if you please. Round again, sir. That will do."

"Well—eh?—well, now, what do you think?"

"I should say at once, then, that you were about five or six-and-forty."

"Do you mean it?"

"I do, indeed, Mr. Hunkers. I have seen all conditions of men, and am generally considered, I assure you, to be rather a fair judge. But we will hear what my friends say. What do you think?"

"I differ from you a little," said May. "I think the gentleman scarcely look forty-two at the utmost."

"And," said Luke, "when you look at his back he don't look that. A fine figure never really looks old."

The old man was so delighted that he laughed and spun round upon his heels, until he gave himself such a fit of coughing that they all really thought it would be his death, and he was compelled to sink into a chair while Claude patted him on the back.

"I—I am better now. It was a something flew down my throat. Thank you

—very gentlemanly people, indeed—Creditors of the sheriff, no doubt, but very gentlemanly men. Oh—oh, dear, I am afraid the day will be too much for me. Oh, dear!"

At this moment a portly-looking personage entered the room. He had a great, fat, sensual-looking face, and indulgence and self were the obvious characteristics of his mind.

This was the sheriff. This was the man who wanted to sell his daughter to old Hunkers.

"Some gentleman wished to speak to me," said the sheriff, in so pompous a tone, that one would have thought that he was a very paragon of virtue, and felt that he deserved the respect of the world, the old sensuous rascal, and yet, there he was trafficking his daughter away to a baboon!

"I am that gentleman," said Claude, advancing. "I'm charged with a letter to you, sir, from the secretary of state."

"Oh, very good, sir, very good. Pray take a seat, sir, if you please. It gives me great pleasure to hear from my friend the secretary of state. Oh, Mr. Hunkers, pray pardon me, my dear sir, I did not see you. None of my lazy fellows told me you had come, my dear sir. I hope I see you well?"

"Pretty well, Mr. Sheriff, pretty well. I wonder my servants in the hall did not tell you their master was here—eh?—ah!"

It was quite clear from this little bit of badinage that old Hunkers felt a gratification in humbling the sheriff, whose great fat face took a different colour as the old man spoke.

"Ha! ha!" he laughed, "you are facetious, Mr. Hunkers."

"Oh, no, not at all, not at all. Never—never, I assure you. Only this affair costs me a trifle you know—eh!"

"Yes, my dear sir, yes—certainly, as you say. A good joke, truly. Will you permit me to read this letter, Mr. Hunkers?"

"Yes, oh yes ; you may sit down, too, upon one of my chairs, Mr. Sheriff, while I reach some wine for these gentlemen."

The sheriff looked as if it would have given him the greatest satisfaction to have rolled over old Hunkers, and so crushed him at once ; but he dissembled, as your great selfish hogs of people always can when their pockets and their appetites are concerned, and put on quite a smile as he read the letter which Claude Duval had taken from the unfortunate Captain Smith upon the highway.

"Why, Mr. Hunkers," said the sheriff, "this letter, from my friend the secretary of state, begs me to be so good as to do what I can to apprehend Claude Duval, the notorious highwayman."

"Indeed ?"

"Yes, sir ; and, of course, I shall write my friend a suitable reply."

"Oh, pho! stuff! Don't call him your friend ; he is no such thing. You know as well as I do that he don't know you from Adam, and that it is only an official letter, that's all ; and if he thought you were so poor as you are, he would remove you from the commission of the peace—ha!"

"How facetious you are to night," said the sheriff, biting his lips ; and then turning to Duval, he said—

"Gentlemen, I am very much obliged, and need not detain you. I will send one of my servants with a reply to the secretary of state."

"One of mine you mean," said Hunkers.

"As you please, sir. Damn it!" said the sheriff.

"Eh? What does he say?" cried Hunkers. "I didn't hear it."

"Cursed old thief," muttered the sheriff, as he walked to one of the windows to try and recover his temper again and then ; after a few minutes, he returned with a bland smile, and said—

"Good evening, gentlemen."

"Stop," said old Hunkers. "I know a gentleman when I see one, and it's quite a treat to have good company at one's wedding instead of a parcel of people who will come because somebody owes them money.   Gentlemen, will you do me the favour of staying to the ball and supper?"

"With pleasure," said Claude.

"Well—but—" interposed the sheriff, " I—I——"

"Yes, you are quite right," interrupted Hunkers; " you have nothing in the world to do with it.   I pay for all."

The sheriff bowed.

" And so, I rather think, I may be allowed the little privilege of inviting who I like.   Pray step up stairs, gentlemen.   You will find refreshments there in abundance, and my servants will attend upon you.   The sheriff is my guest like-wise, and a very nice man he is when you come to know him so well as I do, and how to manage him.   Ah—eh?"

The sheriff could not speak for anger, and Claude and his friends, highly amused, went up stairs to a handsome drawing-room on the first floor.

CHAPTER CLIV.

MR. HUNKERS AND THE SHERIFF HAVE A LITTLE DISAGREEMENT.

The moment the sheriff was alone with old Hunkers, he turned to him, and, half in anger half in entreaty, he said to him—

"Oh, Mr. Hunkers, how is it that you take a pleasure, in the presence of others, in talking of thi smatter, which, between you and me, ought to be kept perfectly private."

"Private—private? What do you mean, Mr. Sheriff?"

"I allude to our little money arrangements, Mr. Hunkers, and I cannot help saying that I think it is too bad—much too bad of you always to be teasing and twitting me with the fact that you are the richer man of the two."

"Richer? Oh, oh, oh!"

"What do you mean, sir?"

"Why, that anybody may be richer than you, and yet have nothing at all, Mr. Sheriff. You are five thousand pounds in debt, and that makes you, you know, five thousand pounds more than a beggar. Eh? don't it?"

"Sir, this is conduct—these are expressions—that—that——"

"You won't put up with. Very good, Mr. Sheriff: I can keep my money, and you can keep your daughter. There's plenty of other girls in Guildford, I can tell you, that will be glad enought to marry a man who can settle ten thousand pounds upon her. Ha—ha!"

"But, Mr. Hunkers——"

"Good-by—good evening, Mr. Sheriff. If you are not pleased with my way and my money, I can carry them elsewhere."

"Stop—stop, my dear sir. You misunderstand me—indeed you do. I beg of you only to be a little considerate. That is all, my good friend, Mr. Hunkers, and before strangers, too. That is all I ask of you."

"Yes; but ain't it true that you are a beggar?"

"Well—well."

"And ain't it a fact that I am supporting you? And ain't it a fact that you let me have Annie, because I have agreed to pay your debts, and to go on supporting you? Answer me all that."

"Well, we know, my dear sir—we know. The—the mutual attachment between you and my dear child, has induced me to consent to the union, and our little money matters should not be mixed up with that affair."

"Oh, indeed! Why, what a humbug you are, Mr. Sheriff."

"Sir!"

"Oh, you don't like that?—Very good; I'm off. Recollect, that you have not got my money yet, you know—I'm off."

"No—no. My dear Mr. Hunkers."

"Are you then, or are you not a humbug?"

"Well—well, anything you please, so that th happiness of my child may not be sacrificed, my dear sir. Of course she loves you, or she would never have

LUKE REMOVING THE DEAD BODY OF THE LANDLADY'S SON.

consented to the union, and nothing would be further from my character than in any way to force her inclination in the matter."

"Oh, dear—ah! Well, that will do. Let's say no more about it. But somebody told me there was a young clerk of yours that was making love to her. Is that true?"

No. 77.

" My dear sir, I suspected such a thing, and sent the vagabond away at once about his business."

" Oh, you did ? Well, that was right. I suppose he was poor, Mr. Sheriff, so you didn't feel inclined to lick his shoes, you humbug—eh ? Wasn't that it —eh ?"

" Really, Mr. Hunkers——"

" Oh, well, don't begin again. So as you know that you are a humbug, that is all that I have to say to you in the matter. Only when you thought of denying it, you know. I was forced to insist upon it ; so now I shall go up stairs and look for the bride."

" Do so, my dear, sir—do so ; and I hope that the same harmony that has ever reigned between us will ever continue."

" Stuff !"

Old Hunkers tottered up stairs, and as he went, he rubbed his old hands together, and muttered—

" Ah, I like to mortify the sheriff. I hate him—I detest him. He will live and get fatter and fatter upon my money now ; and if it were not for Annie, I would have him in jail in an hour, and there let him rot—rot !—that I would. But I like the girl—she is so young, and so nice, and round, and plump, and has such a beautiful skin. Ah ! I like the girl ; and she is not dear at any price. A nice plump young creature ! Just what I like. Ah ! let my money go—I can't lay it out better, I know."

The cogitations of the sheriff, when he was alone, were of much the same character, as regarded their gross selfishness.

" Curse that old rascal," he said. " If it wasn't that he is as rich as I don't know what, I would have kicked him out of the house at once ; but what can I do ? I would just ask any reasonable man what I can do. Here am I, having been used to good eating and drinking all my life, and now without any money. I cannot go about without a carriage. I ain't used to walking. I have never done anything but eat and drink, and enjoy myself, now for hard upon fifty years ; so what can I do but let old Hunkers have Annie ? It's quite a necessary sacrifice, for what would become of my comforts, I should like to know, if he didn't lend or give me money ?"

This was the way the worthy sheriff reasoned, as he called it, upon the infamous transaction ; and then, putting on as smiling a face as he could, he followed old Hunkers up stairs to the drawing-room, where our four friends were already arrived.

Poor Harry Lucas was in such a state of agitation for fear Annie should be in the drawing-room, that Duval was afraid he would betray himself, and whispered in his ear,—

" Remember, Mr. Lucas, that you have our incognito to see to as well as your own, and that if you are so imprudent as to let it be known who you are, we shall be under the necessity of leaving the house at once."

" I will be careful—indeed, I will."

" Be calm. Come in now."

Luckily for the nerves of Harry Lucas, Annie was not in the room. The fact is, the poor young thing was at that moment lying upon her bed in an agony of tears, and wishing herself dead rather than the bride of old Hunkers.

There were twelve or fourteen guests in the drawing-room, so that the entrance of Claude and his friends did not excite much attention ; and as people do in drawing-rooms, those who were there were cut up into little groups of twos and threes, talking together. This was a state of things which gave the confederates an opportunity of saying a few words to each other, and, accordingly, Claude said in a low voice to Lucas,—

" Now, you must take the first opportunity you can of getting a few minutes' private conversation with Annie."

" Oh, would that I could."

" You can, and must. If you determine upon doing so, you will find no great difficulty. It is quite essential you should ascertain her feelings with regard t the present arrangements, and whether she will aid us in anything we ma attempt."

"Yes—oh, yes. I understand. I will try it."

"Very good. You must follow her from the room boldly when she leaves it, after she has been here. In the crowd and confusion—for, you see, that the guests are each moment increasing in number—it will not be noticed whether you are going down stairs to the reception-room or not."

"Hush!" said May ; "here is Hunkers."

Rubbing his old withered hands together, Hunkers entered the room, and glanced around it to see if the bride were there. A darker shade came over the old man's face when he found that she was not, and turning to an old lady, he said, sharply,—

"Pray, ma'am, have you seen Miss Forsyth?"

"No, Mr. Hunkers, she has not come down stairs yet."

"Oh, very good. Dressing, I suppose?"

"Not a doubt of it, Mr. Hunkers. Dear me, sir, I have taken a peep into the supper-room, and I must say that it is laid out in the most charming manner that ever I saw anything."

"Oh, indeed, ma'am. Are you sure you have not been eating the raspberry tarts, ma'am?"

"Me eat the raspberry tarts? What a man you are, Mr. Hunkers, for your jokes, to be sure."

"Jokes, ma'am? It's no joke. I am quite sure you have been pitching into the pastry in the supper-room. But here's the delightful sheriff. Hilloa! Mr. Sheriff, where is the bride?"

"What, not here?" said the sheriff. "Really she ought to be. I will send for her at once, Mr. Hunkers. Will you be so good, Miss White, as to go to my daughter's room, and say that we shall be glad to see her here?"

———

CHAPTER CLV;

ANNIE FORSYTH IS RATHER OBSTINATE AND PREJUDICED.

Miss White was an elderly spinster, who had been invited to the wedding, and who was a sort of distant cousin of the sheriff's; so he could take the liberty of sending her upon any message he chose; and with many hideous contortions, which she intended for smiles, she left the room in search of Annie.

"She will come now," whispered Lucas to Claude.

"So much the better."

"Oh, yes—yes! But I am afraid that I shall never be able to preserve my composure. Oh, sir, you do not know how truly and fondly I love that girl."

"Yes I do; and it is upon that very account that you should act the part you have so prosperously begun as well as you can. Any failure upon your part will at once jeopardise our noble plan. Recollect that your disguise is perfect, if you yourself choose that it shall be so."

"Yes—yes! She comes."

"How do you know?"

"Oh, sir, my heart tells me as much. I am quite sure she is coming, now, and you will then see what a paragon of tenderness she is."

The agitation of the young lover was very great, and it was very natural too, for it must be recollected that his was a first love, and that he was very young, and that the dread of losing Annie had driven him to the verge of destruction, as the state in which Duval had found him sufficiently testified.

Under these circumstances, Claude kept himself back in the recess of one of the large bow-windows, so that he was quite sheltered from observation; and then, sure enough, as he had said, the door of the room was opened, and Miss White led in the bride.

Annie Forsyth was truly a beautiful girl. She looked, if anything, rather younger than she really was. She had the sweetest blue eye in all the world, and such a mass of dark glossy hair, that it was quite a sight to see it. Then her complexion was so delicately fair, and her mouth was so truly beautifully shaped, that at the first sight of her, Claude Duval no longer had any wonder at the infatuation of the young clerk.

"Oh, my Annie!" whispered Lucas.

"Hush!" said Claude. "Hush!"

"Yes—yes, I will be calm; but is she not all I said she was?"

"She is, and a thousand times more so. She is a most lovely girl."

"Ah! I knew you would say that."

"It would be impossible to say otherwise of her, with any regard to truth. But let us listen to what passes."

"My dear," said the sheriff, "we are glad to have you here among us upon this very suspicious—I mean, auspicious occasion."

Old Hunkers hobbled up to her, and looked in her face with such a hideous leer, that several of the company turned away in disgust. He seemed as though he would devour her with his greedy eyes.

"Well, my dear! Eh?" he said. "How are you? Quite well?"

Annie shuddered; but what reply she made was uttered in too low a tone to reach the ears of Duval.

"Did she speak?" said Lucas.

"Hush! Oh, hush!"

Old Hunkers took her hand, and leering in her face, and chuckling as he proceeded, he conducted her to a seat, and drew another close to her, and sat down by her side.

"Ah," said the sheriff, rubbing his great fat hands together. "There is nothing like love in this world, is there now?"

"And gold," said Hunkers. "And gold, eh?"

"Why, a—yes, that is to say—and gold."

It was in vain, now, that the sheriff tried to make the conversation of a general character, and to put people at their ease in that magnificent drawing-room. The fact was, that they could not feel easy while such an old satyr as Hunkers was looking into the face of such a nymph as Annie, and even Miss White looked ashamed.

Harry Lucas was in such a rage now, that he asked Claude Duval if he did not think the best plan would be for him, Harry, to throw old Hunkers at once out at one of the windows into the street, and so make an end of him and his disgusting pretensions at once?

"No," said Duval. "Come over to where they are sitting, and let us hear, if we can, what they say. You see that they are generally avoided. Luke, you, engage that Miss White in conversation, that she may not interrupt us, if you please."

"I will," said Luke.

Luke managed the part of the business that had been entrusted to him very adroitly; so that Miss White thought he was decidedly the best behaved man she had ever met with, and had the best taste, too, for did he not pay her some of the most elegant of compliments? and surely that was evidence.

Claude, and Lucas, and May, contrived, without exciting an attention, to place themselves so close to old Hunkers and Annie, that they with ease overheard all that they said. The old rascal was quite chuckling over the evident misery of the young girl.

Poor Annie was all but broken-hearted at the dismal prospect before her.

"Well, my dear, ain't you delighted to get married?"

"No, sir."

"Dear me—eh?—you surprise me! Most girls are, and I don't see why you should be an exception. He! he! he!"

"I am an exception, sir."

"But why are you, my beautiful little chit—why are you the exception, I should like to know? You will be the richest lady in all Guildford, or rather, I should say, you will have the richest husband, which comes to about the same thing, you know."

Annie was silent.

"Why don't you speak? What do you want? I'm sure I have been liberal enough to you; and the fact is, that if you will take the trouble to make yourself perfectly agreeable to me, and to please me, I don't mind how much money you cost me."

"Sir?"

"Well—well! Don't speak loud; only tell me what you want, and you shall have it, I assure you. You nice little plump thing, you know I adore you very much."

"I beg, sir, in the first place, that you will not make such remarks to me."

"What remarks?"

"Such as you were making. You understand me, sir, I am sure; and you know that I have only consented to this odious union for my father's sake."

"Odious union?"

"Yes. Oh, surely it is, and must ever be, odious in the sight of both God and man, sir. How can it be otherwise? You must know yourself that we are ill-matched. Oh, sir, do think a little."

"I have thought. I don't see why, because I am old, that I should not please myself. I like you. It is for my own pleasure that I marry you, and I have paid a good price."

"A good price?"

"Yes, to be sure. It's all very well to wrap the affair up in fine phrases, and all that sort of nonsense, but I have bought you. Your father would rot in prison, or perhaps cut his throat, but for my money."

"Alas!—alas!"

"Ah, my dear, you see what money does. Money—gold! You see it places in my arms the most blooming young virgin in all the country, whether she likes it or not. Ha! ha!"

"Oh, sir, if my death would satisfy you——"

"Your death? Pho! what do you mean by that? I don't like dead people. I don't like even to hear of them. What the deuce use would you be to me when you were dead? Your death, indeed! I should look upon it as a swindle, if you were to die after I have paid for you."

"Listen to me, Mr. Hunkers."

"Yes, my little duck, yes."

"I do not love you—I never can even like you or feel indifferent to you."

"Oh, nonsense—stuff!"

"I hate you!"

"Pho—pho!"

"Mr. Hunkers, I love another, and if you marry me it will be at your own risk, I warn you. Will not that move you?"

"Not a whit. I will run any risk, and trust to your virtue, my dear; and as for liking me, now, I dare say you will in the course of time; and it don't much matter whether you do or not—you will be mine, and that is about all that I look to."

"Oh, horror! horror! I cannot and will not make this frightful sacrifice."

"Then you destroy your father!"

"Mr. Hunkers, you are rich—very rich: no one knows, as I have heard you say yourself, the extent of your wealth; and you are old, too, and must now and then have thoughts of making your peace with Heaven. Oh, sir, could you not save the father and spare the child?"

"Yes, I could."

"And you will—you relent! Oh, tell me that you will!"

"If I do, may I be d——d!"

Annie shuddered and said no more. Old Hunkers's eyes flashed with passion, as, in a thick guttural voice close to her ear, he spluttered out—

"I tell you, girl, you shall be mine, I have made up my mind to it, or your father shall sleep even this night in prison. To provide against any drawback upon your part at the last moment, I have brought up a thousand pounds' worth of his debts, and I have got a bailiff in the house even now, who, at a word from me, will arrest him; and then if he likes to cut his throat he shall have every chance of so doing."

"Oh, no—no!"

"But I say, oh, yes—yes. It is so. Do you think I would be such a fool, old as I am, to trust to either you or your father in this matter? No—no. When I fairly get you as my wife out of this house, then I shall believe the affair is settled. And now you may do as you like."

"Heaven help me!"

"Pho! stuff! Heaven has something else to do than to interfere in such nonsense; so, my dear, you had better make up your mind to what is inevitable, and let us have no more grumbling about it."

The tears gushed to the eyes of Annie, and she rose and tottered towards the door of the room. Old Hunkers looked after her with a malignant glance, as he muttered—

"Wait till I get her alone—wait till then, that's all."

"Now follow her," whispered Claude to Harry Lucas; "you cannot have a better opportunity; and I will speak to Hunkers, and withdraw his observation from you."

"Yes," said Lucas, "I will first speak to Annie, and then I will throttle Hunkers."

With these words, he slipped out of the room; and when he got to the landing and looked up, he just saw the skirts of the white dress of Annie disappearing.

CHAPTER CLVI.

ANNIE PERPLEXES THE DESIGN OF THE CONFEDRATES.

ANNIE FORSYTH was making her way as rapidly as she could to her chamber after the painful interview she had had with old Hunkers, and it was fortunate that Harry Lucas was just in time to see where she went.

The fact was, that if he had only been another second later he would not have seen the skirts of her dress as she went up the staircase leading to the second floor of the house, and, consequently, he would not have known which way to go to follow her.

Luckily, there was no one in the way, so, with a bounding step, and taking three stairs at a time, Harry ascended to the second floor; but before he could reach the landing, Annie, little suspecting who was in the house, had reached her own room and closed the door.

To be sure, Harry Lucas had made hardly any noise in going up the stairs, but if he had, she was in such a state of mind that she would not have heard him. The poor young creature was, in truth, at that moment upon the very verge of insanity.

"Which is her room?" said Lucas to himself. "Ah, yes, I recollect. This must be the door, according to the plan of the house, or the room through the window of which I used to throw bonquets of flowers, that it cost me no little trouble to get."

He approached the door and listened. The sound of some one audibly sobbing within confirmed him.

"It is her room," he said, "and that is her voice. My Annie, I come to save you, I am here—I am here."

He placed his hand upon the lock as he spoke, and turned it. Annie had merely closed the door without locking it, so that he had no trouble in entering the chamber; and, in fact, he had got into the room and shut the door again behind him, before she had the least idea of the presence of any other person.

Nothing but the emergency of the circumstances could have induced Harry Lucas to thus trespass upon the bed-chamber of Annie; but certainly, if ever circumstances could excuse such an intrusion, those by which she was surrounded were such circumstances.

The young girl was kneeling on the floor, with her face resting upon her hands upon the seat of a large easy chair, that stood close to the bedside, and she was sobbing bitterly.

"Annie! My Annie!" cried Lucas.

With a cry of surprise and terror, she sprang to her feet.

"Annie! Dear, dear Annie!"

Poor Lucas quite forgot at that moment that he was capitally disguised, and that he wore a pair of mustachoes and false whiskers, which effectually altered his appearance, so that Annie, although the voice was familiar to her, could not suppose it to be him.

"Oh, heavens!" she said, "what is the meaning of this? Help!"

"Hush, Annie, hush. Do you not know me?"

"Know you? Oh, no—no!"

"Oh, God, not know Harry Lucas?'

"Harry Lucas?"

"Yes; oh, look at me, and satisfy yourself that I am indeed the **Harry Lucas** who loves you so well, and who, at least, thought that he would live in your remembrance."

"No. The more I look the more I am convinced that you are not Harry Lucas. You are a stranger, who can imitate his voice, but you are not Harry Lucas."

"This is madness!—Ah, no—now I recollect. These false whiskers and mustachoes, and an unnatural colour upon my cheeks—Oh, Annie, I am forced thus to disguise myself in order to approach you. Do you not know me now, my Annie?"

He smiled, and she knew the smile. With a cry of joy, she flung herself into his arms.

"Harry—Harry, you have come to save me?"

"I have—I have.'

"I thought that you had forsaken me, indeed I did. They said that you had gone from Guildford. Oh, what a world of agony I have suffered since last we met! Harry—Harry, you will not believe what I have suffered."

She clung to him frantically, and wept like a child upon his bosom. He was quite unnerved by her tears, and shook so that he could scarcely support her; and yet, in the midst of all his emotion, there was such a terrible anger fighting in his breast against Hunkers and her father, that he felt hot and cold by turns, and was ready to rush from her and annihilate them both.

"My darling," he said, "I have indeed come to save you. You shall not be made the victim of this detestable marriage."

"No—no, I cannot wed that vile man, I cannot—I cannot."

"You shall not."

"Hush! What is that? I hear footsteps."

"So do I."

"Some one comes, Harry—hide. No—I will make the door fast. It may be some one coming here."

She flew to the door and fastened it by a night-bolt, just as some one tapped at it. It was then with great difficulty that she could muster composure sufficient to say—

"Who is there?"

"It is only me, my dear," said Miss White.

"Well?"

"Open the door, love; I want to speak to you."

"I will soon return to the drawing-room, Miss White—very soon, and then I will seek you."

"But it's only me, my love. It is Cousin White; don't you hear, Annie? Miss White, my dear. Open the door."

"Not now, cousin."

"Why, what an odd girl you are. You don't suppose that the odious old wretch, Hunkres, is with me, do you?"

"Oh, no—no. But do not ask me to open the door now, Cousin White. Do not, I beg of you. I am quite sensible of your kind feelings towards me, and will come to you very soon."

"Very well, my dear. I take it as a little unkind of you not to open the door; but since you won't, I must tell you what I came to say, or my heart will burst with it."

"What is it, Cousin White?"

"Why, it is, that if I were you, I would die before I married that old ape—that abominable, vile, selfish old Hunkers; and I mean to tell your father that he is a disgrace to the name of man to let you make such a sacrifice of yourself. It is abominable, and I don't mean to stay in the house another hour. There, now! I have said my say, and I feel all the easier."

"Oh, dear, Cousin White, what shall I say to you?"

"Just what you like, Cousin Annie; so now I am off, as you don't feel inclined to open the door; and if you marry that horrid old sinner, never come near me, and I will never come near you again; no, not if you paid me a hundred pounds a visit."

With these words, the spinster bustled away from the door, and descended to the drawing-room in search of the sheriff.

Annie turned her pale, tearful face towards Harry Lucas, and he stepped up to her, and flung his arms around her, saying, as he did so,—

"You see, now, my Annie, what every one who dares to think at all, thinks of this dreadful union."

"Harry! Harry! what would you have me do?"

"Fly with me at once from this house. I will take you to my mother's house, and we shall be happy."

"And my father?"

"Well, your father?"

"What will become of him, Harry? Tell me that."

"Why, in a little time he will become inured to the match, as fathers always do who really love their daughters. He nor no man can say a word against my character; and so, when the first ebullition of anger has passed over, he will think as comfortably of the affair as possible, and you will be happy that you have consulted your heart instead of the purse of that frightful old scoundrel Hunkers."

"But—but—"

"Nay," Harry cried, "do not begin to doubt now, my darling Annie. You know that I love you with all my heart, and if you only think that you love me a little, we shall be happy. I happened, while below, to overhear all that passed between you and Hunkers a little while ago."

"You did?"

"Yes, I was sufficiently close to hear every word."

"Then, Harry, you heard his threats against my father—you heard how he had, with a diabolical ingenuity, arranged, that in the event of my refusing him my hand, he would this very night cast my father into jail—you heard how he had him in his power, and how he hinted even at the dreadful threat my father had already made of suicide if such a thing should happen?"

" Yes, I heard all that, Annie."

" Well, what can I do ?   What can you say to it ?"

" Simply, that I do not see that it constitutes a sufficient reason for you to commit worse than suicide."

" Me commit suicide ?"

" Yes; is it not a thousand times worse to go into a church, and there, in

MAY SCREENS CLAUDE FROM THE SEARCH OF THE POLICE-OFFICERS.

the presence of your Maker, vow that you love and honour Hunkers ?   Is it not worse than suicide to kill yourself with grief, and to kill your mind, at the same time, by an association with such a man ?   Oh, Annie, fancy yourself wedded to him, and his hands upon you—his face against yours, and his embraces forced upon you by a husband's right !"

"Oh, God!"

"The picture is too dreadful for you?"

"It is. I tell you, Harry, it should never come to that, for I would kill my self first. That I am resolved upon."

"And so, Annie, for fear that your father should carry out an idle threat, which he is the very last man in the world ever to think of seriously, you would actually commit self-murder?"

"Oh, Heaven direct me—Heaven direct me! What shall I do?—What shall I do?"

"Come away with me at once. I have friends here who are firm and true to me, and who will aid us. Only say the word, and, in open defiance of them all we will fly from this place."

"I dare not. About the power of Hunkers to throw my father into a jail there, can be no mistake. Such things are done every day."

"Yes; and how much less cruel, by a million times, would that circumstance be, than your sacrifice to Hunkers. Oh, Annie, what do you, in your innocent heart think of the fellow who would purchase his own ease and security at such a sacrifice? Answer me that."

"Leave me—leave me, Harry! I say, leave me. You will drive me mad! I must save my father! Say no more to me, if ever you loved me. Oh, God, help me! Leave me, Harry, I command you, or I shall hate you!"

Terrified at her manner, Harry Lucas hastily left the room.

CHAPTER CLVII.

DUVAL SHOWS THAT THERE ARE TWO WAYS TO STOP A MARRIAGE.

QUITE shocked and bewildered at the energy with which Annie, with the prospect of her father's danger before her, had dismissed him from her presence, poor Harry Lucas marched down the staircase to seek the advise of his friends in the drawing-room. Luckily, Claude was near the door, and saw the state of agitation he was in.

Stepping up to him at once, Duval placed his finger upon his lips, and shook his head, to indicate silence and caution, and then he took him by the arm and went out upon the landing with him.

The moment Luke and May saw this, they, likewise, with as quiet a manner as they could, went out of the drawing-room.

"What has happened?" said May.

"I will tell you—oh, I will tell you! There is no hope," said Lucas.

"Why, you are out of your mind, my friend," said Claude. "You are speaking too loud, too. Come out into the street, if you have anything to tell us. The servants will know us again when we return."

"It is of no use to return. I had better die at once. I will take poison to night, and there will be an end to all my sorrows at once."

"No, you must come down stairs, I tell you. Where are our hats, I wonder?"

"In the reception-room, below," said Luke. "This way. Be calm, Mr Lucas, whatever you do, for already some of the servants are looking at us with rather suspicious eyes."

"He is a madman," said Claude. "if he sacrifices all his hopes by any indis-cretion, now that we have gone so far."

"I have no hopes," said Lucas.

"Well, then, you have duties, and one of them is not to involve your friends in any disturbance upon your account."

This was a consideration that seemed to have some weight with Harry Lucas, for he strove to put on an aspect of tolerable calmness as he passed through the hall, and he succeeded so far as not to attract any very material notice. They all four sallied out into the street then, and after they had got some distance from the sheriff's house, they paused in rather a dark spot close to a garden wall, and under the spreading branches of a sycamore tree that was liberal of its foliage over the highway; and then Claude Duval said in a calm voice—

"Now, Mr. Lucas, collect yourself, and tell us what has happened to put you into such a fume as to make you take such a desponding view of your affairs?"

Confidence is to the full as contagious as fear, and the calm, assured tone in which Claude Duval spoke, had all its effects upon Harry Lucas. He began to get rather ashamed at the excess of emotion he had exhibited.

"Pardon me," he said, "I am giving you too much trouble."

"Not at all. Of that, pray, suffer us to be the judges. And, now, did you see Annie?"

"I did, and the reason of my despair is, that she can't make up her mind to fly with us from her father's house; and she feels certain that Hunkers will have him arrested in such an event, and she feels a dreadful doubt that he may carry out his threat of committing suicide."

"She is very wrong."

"Yes, but she is invincible upon that point, and her firmly-ex ressed intention is to wed Hunkers, and then to commit suicide herself."

"A pretty piece of business, truly."

"Is not that enough to drive me nearly mad, I ask you?"

"Yes, if it were really so; but we must stop her from carrying out any such mad-brained intentions, my friend. The marriage must not take place, by any means."

"But how can you stop it? She is evidently bent upon taking that course. She, no doubt, thinks that if Hunkers sees, without the idea of a doubt, that it is no fault of the sheriff's that she is not his, he will be merciful."

"In which she is much mistaken. Did you ever, or did anybody ever hear of a money-lender being honest, to say nothing at all of being merciful?"

"Alas, never—never; and the sacrifice will be in vain."

"You say 'will be,' my good friend, as if you were certain that it was going to take place. Now, I tell you, there shall be no such sacrifice. There are two ways of stopping a marriage."

"Two ways?"

"Yes. The one is by inducing the bride not to go to the church, and the other is by carrying the same idea out with regard to the bridegroom. Now, as Miss Annie is rather obstinate, we must try what we can do with our old friend Hunkers."

"Exactly," said Luke.

"Yes," said May, "that will be the way."

Poor Harry Lucas looked from one to the other of them, as well as he could see them in the darkness, with an expression of the most intense surprise.

"Why, you don't fancy for a moment," he said, "that he will listen to you? You are not so mad as to suppose that he is capable of being roused by remonstrances or alarmed by threats, into any course but the one he has laid down for himself in this dreadful affair?"

"We shall see, Master Lucas," said Claude. "All I have got to say is, that if old Hunkers weds Annie to-night, blame me for it."

"He will not wed her," said Luke.

"He will not?" cried Lucas.

"No," added Luke, as he pointed to Claude Duval. "He has said that he will not, and I will take his word in preference to the whole of the arrangements of the sheriff, and all the determinations of old Hunkers. You may depend upon it, Mr. Lucas, that now it is settled, and old Hunkers will not wed Annie Forsyth to-night."

"You amaze me! Are you a conjurer, sir? or what occult powers have you that enable you, in defiance of the intentions, apparently as fixed as fate, of other people, to say what shall be and what shall not?"

"No," said Claude, with a smile; "I am no conjurer, but I have an indomitable will, and a perseverance which nothing can subdue. I hold it as a principle that there are very few things indeed in the world that a man may not do, if he has the thorough will to do them, and makes up his mind that nothing shall deter or turn him from his purpose."

"You amaze me!"

"Well, I hope you will be pleased as well as amazed. What is the time?"

"Half past ten," said Luke.

"Very good, and the wedding is not to take place till twelve. We have loads of time to manage matters in. Where does Hunkers reside, Mr. Lucas? Is his dwelling in Guildford?"

"Oh, yes. He occupies a detached house nearly upon the outskirts of the town, where, they say, he carries on all his discounting business, and his money-lending by which he has made such a fortune."

"Good—that will do. Now let us go to Hunkers's house at once, for it is from there we will begin our operations."

Poor Harry Lucas looked thoroughly amazed. He could not imagine what they were to do at Hunkers's house; nevertheless, the manner in which Claude Duval had himself spoken, combined with the absolute confidence that those who were with him seemed to have in him, gave Lucas a gleam of hope.

"I will obey your directions," he said, "implicitly; and of one thing I feel assured, which is, if you cannot help me out of this difficulty and distress, no one can."

"Come on, then, at once," added Claude. "It is well to lose no time"

Of course, the town of Guildford was as well known to Harry Lucas as it could be, and he had no difficulty whatever in leading the friends to the house of the old bridegroom. It was a gloomy-looking place, surrounded on three sides by a rather unusually high brick wall, and on the forth it had a dwarf wall and a pair of iron gates, that, from their size, had evidently at one time belonged to a place of much larger pretensions than old Hunkers's cottage, for it was little more than a cottage.

"Now tell me," said Claude. "Does he keep many servant?"

"Many servants?—not he. An old woman and a boy are all his household, and he nearly starves them to death. No—no. Hunkers is not the sort of man to allow himself to be eaten up by servants."

"Well, so I should suppose. And now we will see who is at home."

With this, Claude, finding that the great gates were fast, rung rather a startling peal at a bell that hung there, and after about two or three minutes' waiting, there came an old woman, carrying a lantern, and hobbling along in such a manner, that she seemed almost more decrepit than her old master himself.

"What is it?" cried the old woman, stopping short six paces from the gate, as though she suspected some one might put his hand through the bars and catch hold of her. "What is it—eh?"

Claude thought that with this "eh?" she had very much the manner of old Hunkers himself. Probably she was a relation, or had caught his style of speaking by long residence with him.

"Mr. Hunkers, ma'm—I want to see Mr. Hunkers," said Claude in a hurried voice.

"Then he ain't at home."

"Well, but——"

"Oh, it's of no use bothering. I tell you he ain't at home, so you may as well jog on at once, for you won't be let in here. A likely thing, indeed, that I am going to open the gate to every jackanapes that comes and says he wants to see Hunkers."

"But, my good woman——"

"I ain't a good woman; so now you have got your answer, I hope."

"Very well, then, my bad woman——"

"You wretch! what do you mean?"

"Why, you denied being a good woman, so I suppose you are the other thing. But come—come, don't be foolish. I daresay Mr. Hunkers, as he is not quite a youth, has gone to bed by this time, for it is close on to eleven; bu if you will tell him that I have come to pay the three hundred pounds due on the bills, he will see me, no doubt."

"Three hundred pounds, do you say?"

"Yes, that is the amount; and if he don't take it to-night, there is a great probability that he will never have the chance again to do so."

"You don't mean that?—Stop."

"Oh, I can't stop to dispute with you about it. If you like to take the consequences of refusing to let me see him, why there's an end of it."

"No. But don't go. Three hundred pounds—what a sum of money! Stop. I assure you he is not here. The fact is, sir, the old fool has gone to get married to a little bit of a girl that might be his grandchild."

"You don't mean that, surely?"

"Yes, but I do, though. I'll lead her a pretty life, though, when she comes home here; I'll be bound she shan't be able to say her soul is her own, I'll warrant you. But come in, sir; I will send Dick for Hunkers, and if he were in the middle of the marriage ceremony he would come to the money, I know, the old villain."

With this the old woman opened the gate, but she was rather alarmed when so many people as four marched in.

"Don't be alarmed," said Claude. "It's all right; these are friends of mine."

CHAPTER CLVIII.

HUNKERS DOES NOT APPEAR AT THE WEDDING.

THE old dame was aaything but pleased now, for the fact was, that Claude only had stood forward and conversed with her at the gate, and she had no idea that there were three other persons besides. She shook so much with anger and alarm that she could hardly hold the lantern.

"You are distressing yourself about nothing, my good madam," said Claude. "In this gentleman with the mustache you see the young officer who borrowed the money. In me you see an attorney, who feels that it ought to be paid. In this young man—(turning to May)—you see my clerk; and in this gentleman—(turning to Luke)—you see a friend of the young officer's; so it is all right."

"I hope it is; but I can tell you that, if you were all the housebreakers and highwaymen in the world, you would get nothing here, for beyond two dozen of red herrings and the dregs of a cask of small beer, there's nothing in the house; and as for his money, Hunkers is too good a judge to leave that at home, I rather think."

"We neither want his herrings, nor his beer, nor his money. We came to pay him what he richly deserves, and then we will be off at once, for we have no desire to stay here, I can assure you, madam."

"Very well. I'll send Dick to the sheriff's house. You must know the old idiot is going to be married to little Miss Annie, the sheriff's daughter. Nothing would serve him but her dainty face with its white and red. Bah! I hate such folly."

"So do we."

"And the little slut is not above sixteen—a mere child, that ought to be kept in a nursery upon bread and butter, and well whipped always before going to bed."

"So she ought," said Claude. "Highly proper. That is precisely our opinion of the matter, madam. And now, if you will be so good as to send the Dick that you speak of, madam, to Mr. Hunkers, we shall be very much obliged to you, indeed."

By this time the old woman had led them to the house, and introduced them into one of the most miserable of all miserable parlours that the imagination can conceive. It was quite clear that the grate had not had a fire in it for years, and the few articles of furniture that were in the room were of the commonest and most wretched description.

The total value of everything in the apartment could not possibly exceed the sum of five shillings.

"This is the best parlour," said the old woman, "and, I suppose, this is where the bride thinks she will sit when she comes home : but she shan't. The things cost a deal of money, I assure you, and won't do to be used in common."

"So I should think," said Claude.

"Ah, you may say that. Don't put your feet on the rail of the chair, young man. What do you mean by it?"

"I won't," said May. "I forgot, at the moment, that I was in such a gorgeous place, I assure you, madam."

"Forget, indeed! I'm astonished at you. Why, that chair, only sixteen years ago, cost a matter of eightpence, and I do believe it was worth twopence more, as I am a Christian female. But I will send that rascal of a boy to Hunkers. Oh, gentlemen, you don't know what a hand I have with that boy. It's nothing with him but eat—eat—eat from morning till night, and he makes no more of a penny loaf than as if it cost nothing at all. Dick—Dick—Dick, I say!"

"Here you are!" said a voice.

"Come here, you vile, gormandizing wretch, you, and take the message that this gentleman will give you."

"Well, here I is," said the boy, "precious hungry, as usual. You haven't got such a thing as a pound of rumpsteaks and ingins about you, have you, Mrs. Cottle, and a pot of half-and-half, all for to wash it down with?"

"Oh, you wretch! Gentlemen, I do believe he would eat what he says just now, if he could only get it."

"Oh, wouldn't I!" said the boy. "I often wishes, Mrs. Cottle, as you was a nice fat young duck, wouldn't I make up a rousing fire, and do you brown in no time, and have a good feast for once in a way."

"You hannibal! You hannibal!" cried the old woman.

"Well, Dick," said Claude, who could hardly restrain his laughter, "here is half-a-crown for yourself, and we want you to go to the sheriff's house, and to tell your master, Mr. Hunkers, that a gentleman is waiting for him at home to pay him the three hundred pounds on the bills."

"Oh, won't I!"

"Half-a-crown!" shrieked Mrs. Cottle; "half a——Oh, give it to me, you vile boy! Give it to me to keep for you this moment."

"Don't you wish you may get it, old 'un?" said Dick. "Do you see anything particklar green in my face? No, rather not, I think."

"Oh, oh, oh!" murmured the old woman as Dick scampered off with the half-crown in his possession. "Oh, dear—oh, dear! Half-a-crown—a whole half! Oh, dear—oh, dear!"

"Madam," said Claude, "I feel that we have given you much trouble in this affair; so, if you will accept of half-a-guinea, we shall be happy to hand it to you; but we don't want to offend you by the offer in the least, if you take it as such."

"Offend me? Oh, gracious, no! Me offended?. Oh, gentlemen, I assure you I am the humblest person as is. Give me the money this moment. Thank you, gentlemen. I only hope you will come here again that's all. It's good, I suppose? —Hem! Thank you kindly, gentlemen. If it ain't good, I can pass it off on old Hunkers. I am very much obliged to you, sir, indeed; and shall be always glad to see you. It's quite a comfort to find real gentlemen coming to the old house at times. Of course, it's a sad trial to me to think that that little hussy of a sheriff's daughter is coming here, with her airs and graces, to eat us out of house and home; but I'll be even with her—I'll let her know what's what, I warrant—the odious little wretch! To think of marrying, at her age, too!"

Claude and his friends were very much amused at the violence of Mrs. Cottle's indignation at poor Annie, and they encouraged her to say such extraordinary things about her, that May was compelled to pull Claude by the arm to put him in mind that she was there.

While all this was going on at old Hunkers's house, the boy Dick, highly stimulated by the half-crown that Claude had given him, went at once to the sheriff's house, and much disturbed the mind of old Hunkers by delivering the message about the three hundred pounds.

"But what are the men?" said Hunkers.

"Don't know," said the boy; "but they have got lots of money."

"How do you know that?"

"Why, they gave me ever so much."

"They did? Then allow me, Dick, to take care of it for you."

"Oh, no, thank you, master, I can do that myself, easy. What shall I say to the gentlemen? That you won't come, sir?"

"Oh, no—no! don't say that. Run back and say, that I am coming as fast as I can. Dear me, what's o'clock? Oh, just upon eleven. That will do; I have plenty of time—plenty of time. I will just tell the sheriff that I shall be back in half an hour at the outside. No—the best way will be to say nothing at all. So that I am back in time to go to the church, it will be all right enough, of course."

With this, old Hunkers, with a mortal dread of losing the three hundred pounds, set off at a trot for his house.

Now, the old usurer was engaged in so many monetary transactions, that there was nothing at all out of the way in anybody coming to pay him such a sum as three hundred pounds, only he could not call to mind who it was that owed him such a sum at that precise time; but he had no doubt he should know the parties when he got home.

"It is not a sum to let go by one," he muttered, as he tried to run in the street, but was forced to stop owing to its bringing on his cough. "Dear me, the more haste the worst speed, as the proverb says, so I had better go slow and easy, after all. I wonder who it can possibly be?"

The distance was so short, however, that, notwithstanding all his trouble to get along, and his cough, and a stitch in the side, too, that he gave himself by the exertions he made, he soon stood at his own gate, and rang a lusty peal at the bell.

Old Mrs. Cottle answered him, and the first question he asked of her was—

"Who is it?—who is it?"

"Don't know!" was the short reply.

"You don't know? What do you mean by that, you old jade? Did they not leave their names?"

"No, stupid!"

"Curse you, what do you mean by this insolence? It would serve you right if I were to discharge you at once. I have put up with you and your impertinence too long—eh?"

"Oh, indeed, have you! My impertinence, indeed! I only wonder who you expect would live with you but me, you old ruffian? Perhaps you think that because you are going to bring home a young wife you can do without me; but I'll soon let you know——"

"Hold your tongue, will you?"

"No!"

"Then I'll kill you, you hag!"

" Hag! Do you call me a hag, you elderly vampire? How dare you call me a hag, I should like to know, you dreadful old wretch!"

How long this violent contention between old Hunkers and the amiable Mrs. Cottle would have lasted it is hard to say ; but the old man was in too great a state of anxiety to see the stranger who had to pay him the three hundred pounds to remain any longer contending with her, so, with a howl of passion, he rushed into the house and left her victorious.

A miserable rush-light was burning in the parlour, which had been placed by Mrs. Cottle for the convenience of the visitors, and by its feeble beams they had the pleasure of seeing old Hunkers make his appearance in the room.

Luke immediately went past him, and placed his back against the door, and Claude Duval advanced towards him, and looked him in the face.

" Well, sir," said Hunkers, " my money—money! Upon whose account do you come to pay me three hundred pounds? I beg that you will be quick, as I have some important business waiting for me to transact shortly,"

" Oh, there is no hurry, Mr. Hunkers."

" But there is, sir."

" But I say there is not. Really it's very uncivil to contradict a person in this kind of way, Mr. Hunkers."

" Pay me at once, sir. Whose bills are they you want to take up?"

" Oh, stuff, nobody's."

" Nobody's?"

" Certainly not. I only wonder how a man of your tact and experience could have been taken in by so flimsy a pretext. All we wanted was to get you here, that was all, Mr. Hunkers ; and as a bit of cheese tempts a rat, we thought that the mere mention of money would tempt you, and the event has quite justified our idea."

CHAPTER CLIX.

THE SHERIFF IS IN DESPAIR, AND ANNIE BEGINS TO HAVE BETTER HOPES.

AT these words uttered by Claude Duval, rage and fear struggled for mastery in the heart of old Hunkers, and he shook so fearfully that they all thought that moment of passion and alarm would be his last.

He recovered after a few moments, and with his very lips deathly pale, he gasped out—

" What is the meaning of this?—Who are you?—what are you?—what do you want? If it be robbery, there is not a sixpence in the house."

" It is not robbery."

" What then?—what then? What do you want with me?"

" To be quite plain with you, Mr. Hunkers, we do not intend to allow you to marry Annie Forsyth."

" Ah!"

" Oh, you may start and stamp your foot ; but, 'recollect, that you have not before you one who owes you anything. Such people as you are only powerful where you have lent your money, and the unhappy wretch to whom you have lent it cannot pay you. To such you may play the braggart, and the great man. To such, your wild, hideous passions may be terrible."

" You wretch! how dare you speak to me in such a way?"

" Hark you, Mr. Hunkers—if you were not a very old man you should not wag your tongue so insolently at us with impunity. We should ask you if you were tired of your life."

As he spoke, Claude took a pistol from his pocket, and placed the muzzle of it against the cheek of Hunkers, who, turning deadly blue and ashy-looking, sunk into a chair.

"Now, sir, you see we are in earnest with you."

"Oh!—oh!—oh! spare my life!"

"Your life? You ought to be thankful to any one who will take it. What is life to an old trembling wretch like you, that you set such store by it? Your life, indeed! Which, now, do you value most, your money or your life, Mr Hunkers?"

CLAUDE AND MAY FIND A WELCOME AT THE ROAD SIDE INN.

"Oh, my money—no I mean my life—that is, my money. Oh, spare me!

"You don't know which?"

"Alas!—Alas!"

"You may very well say alas; and as you had the vile criminality to dream of plunging that young creature, Annie Forsyth, into misery for life. Out upon you! That was truly a most rascally transaction."

"What is that to you?"

"Oh, you are not subdued yet, Mr. Hunkers?"

"No, I am not. But, of course, if four men attack one, what can the one do—eh?"

"Well, Mr. Hunkers, you have more boldness than I gave you credit for; but, after all, that may be more affected than real. The probability is, that you are cunning enough to see that we are not the likely sort of persons to do you any serious injury, and that if we accomplish our purpose of hindering you from marrying Annie Forsyth, that we shall be tolerably satisfied."

"I don't care."

"Oh, you don't care? Well, we shall see. Now, if you are anything of a judge of faces, Mr. Hunkers, and will look at mine, you will come to the conclusion that I am one of those persons who are exceedingly likely to keep their word."

"Well, what of that?"

"Just this, that you shall write a letter to the sheriff declining the hand of his daughter Annie, and suggesting that she should marry a young man named Harry Lucas, who, being young, and one whom she can really love, is a much more suitable match. Do you understand that?"

"Yes, but I won't do it!"

"You won't?"

"No, I won't."

"Very well. Then, Mr. Hunkers, we will hang you forthwith. Look round the room, my frends, and see if there be any nail strong enough to bear this old man's weight, and we will hang him out of hand in a moment, so that, at all events, the marriage will be effectually put a stop to at once and for ever."

"Here is one," said Luke, "and here is a strong piece of cord at the window which will carry double his weight."

"Be quick, then, about it."

Luke made a noose in the cord and put it round old Hunkers's neck, and then placed the table under the nail in the wall, to which he fastened the other end of the cord.

"He will hang capitally," said Luke, "as soon as we pull the table away from under him, and I will give him a good pull by the legs, which will finish the business for him."

Up to this point, with wonderful courage, the old man had preserved silence; but now, when he saw that one kick to the rickety table would leave him suspended, he quailed before the prospect of death, and shrieked out—

"My life!—My life! Oh, spare my life! I will write the letter. Anything so that you leave me my life."

"Very good," said Claude.

"Shall we let him down?" said Luke.

"Yes, it will be as well; but keep the noose round his neck."

"If you are going to take my life at any rate," said old Hunkers, "I don't see any good in doing your bidding."

"We are not going to take your life at any rate. What is your life to us? It is much easier for us to leave it to you than to take it. But you may take another obstinate determination which may make it necessary for us to string you up; and I swear, that if you give us any more trouble we will do so, despite all you can say to the contrary."

Hunkers was silent. He began to find that those with whom he had to deal were not exactly the sort of people to trifle with, and that if he really had any respect for his life, the best thing for him would be to do their bidding, without farther hesitation.

Old Mrs. Cottle, by this time, had got very curious to know what the rather long interview between Hunkers and the strangers in the parlour portended, and she hobbled from the kitchen and tried to listen, but the perceptions of Mrs. Cottle were not quite so acute as they had been forty years before, so that that good lady only heard a very indistinct murmur of voices, and feeling cold, she shrunk back again to consult Dick, who, notwithstanding his appetite and his aggravating ways, was a great oracle to Mrs. Cottle, who found that his knowledge of the world was something prodigious.

"Now, Mr. Hunkers," said Claude, "be quick, and write what we shall dictate to you."

"Well, well—what you like, now."

"Where are your writing materials? What you have to do must be done properly, and without any appearance of hurry or compulsion, or it will defeat our intentions."

"I will get them," said Hunkers, doggedly.

"Do so, and be quick."

The old man shuffled along to a cupboard that occupied one corner of the room, and which was of a triangular shape, so as to fit into the corner accurately as is frequently seen in old country houses. He opened the door of this cupboard, and seemed to be looking about in it.

Little did Duval or his friends think that old Hunkers would have the courage to attempt anything of a hostile character; but the fact was, that the old man had money in the house, and he could not divest himself of the idea that it was after that the strangers had come. Now, we know that a hen in defence of its chicks, will turn upon a dog, and so a miser, in defence of his money, gets desperate, and has a false show of valour in defence of it.

Such was the case with Hunkers.

Suddenly, then, turning round from the cupboard, he cried out in a croaking voice, that sounded like the last dying shriek of a turkey-cock—

"Now, you wretches, I will soon clear the house of you."

As he spoke, he presented a blunderbuss at the confederates, and to their surprise they found themselves confronted by a huge bell-mouthed brass barrel, that was wide enough to scatter shot to the destruction of them all, if it were well-directed.

"Confound him!" said Duval, as he made at once a dash forward to seize the weapon.

Click went the lock, but, fortunately, the blunderbuss missed fire, and in another moment Claude had hold of the barrel of it, and had turned the muzzle up to the ceiling. It was quite astonishing with what dexterity old Hunkers put the blunderbuss upon full-cock again, and pulled the trigger.

The second attempt sufficed. Off it went with a roar that shook the house; but the whole contents lodged in the ceiling, and by the recoil of the brute of a fire-arm, old Hunkers was sent, doubled up, right into the cupboard.

The candle was put out by the concussion of the air, and one half the panes of glass in the windows were broken at once.

If Mrs. Cottle had been ten times more deaf than she was, such a noise as this could not possibly have failed to rouse her up, and, accordingly, both she and Dick made a rush into the room. Dick carried the rushlight with him that they had been sitting by in the kitchen.

"Murder!" shouted Mrs. Cottle.

"Oh, what a lark," said Dick.

Old Hunkers now rolled out of the cupboard on to the floor, and looked as if he were at his last gasp.

"Silence!" cried Claude Duval, "nobody is hurt. It is of no consequence. Mr. Hunkers was only showing us his blunderbuss, when it went off accidentally, and the contents lodged in the ceiling."

"Oh, lor!" cried Dick, "and ain't bits of the old ceiling a-coming down like a rum 'un, too."

This was a fact that was, indeed, perfectly apparent by the parties in the room getting various thumps on the head with dabs of plaster, that kept detaching themselves from the ceiling.

"Dear me," said Mrs. Cottle, "what an old fool he must be to get, at his time of life, up to such tricks."

"Woman!" cried Hunkers, "you are a beast! Fetch the police!"

"Beast, in your teeth, Mr. Hunkers," shouted Mrs. Cottle, whose ire was so kindled at the opprobrious epithet, that she paid no attention at all to the conclusion of the sentence, and then she flounced out of the room.

"Dick," said Claude, "it is pen, ink, and paper that your master means. Do you know where to get them?"

"Oh, yes; in the kitchen. You know, he don't sit here. It's in the kitchen he does all his writing, and that sort of thing."

"Very well. Bring him the means of writing a letter, and there will be another half-crown at your service, Dick."

"Oh, won't I!"

"The moment Dick was gone from the room, Duval turned round to old Hunkers, and in a grave tone of voice, he said,—

"Now, sir, for this delicate attempt upon all our lives, we might, and most people in our situation would, take a bitter revenge; but considering that in some sort you were but defending yourself, we do not look upon your act as it might be looked upon. Do our bidding, and you will not find the consequences near so great as you might expect."

Old Hunkers expected nothing but death for the act he had just attempted; but these words of Duval's re-assured him a little.

"You intend, then, to spare my life?"

"Your life is in your own hands."

"How is that?—How can that be, when here I am quite helpless, and surrounded by four men, any one of whom might kill me?"

"Write what I shall dictate, and you live."

"I will—I will, fairly; only let it be quickly over, now, and go your way. I am weary of this dreadful evening."

"Here you are," said Dick, coming back with an old desk, and placing it upon the table. "Here you are, old Hunkers!"

"You rascal, how dare you to speak to me in that way? I'll discharge you, you vagabond, and you will have to go to the parish, and they will bind you apprentice to a sweep."

"Oh, will they. I thinks I seems 'em do it! No, old Hunkers, I means to stay with you till I'm big enough, and then I shall go for a soldier, into some regiment of Lancers, old chap!"

"Hold your vile tongue! Be off with you! I'm glad he is gone."

"Now Mr. Hunkers," said Claude, "write, if you please."

"Yes—yes, I will. Tell me what to write."

"To Mr. Forsyth.

"Sir,—I hereby beg to inform you, that I renounce all idea or intention of marrying your daughter Annie; and I think that Mr. Harry Lucas would be the best person you could bestow her upon.

"I am, sir, yours obediently,

"Jeremiah Hunkers."

The old man groaned as he wrote the above; but he did not make any opposition to so doing. All idea of resisting the commands of his persecutors was now past, and he duly folded up and addressed the letter to the sheriff at his house.

CHAPTER CLX.

SHOWS THAT A LITTLE CONFUSION TOOK PLACE AT THE CHURCH.

LUKE whispered to Claude Duval after he had got the letter,—

"You may depend that Hunkers will not be quiet after we leave him."

"I am thinking of that."

"He will yet baulk us. That old man has a devilish spirit and energy about him, that will not be easily subdued."

"You are right, Luke. I will take measures. Mr. Hunkers?"

"Well, what now?"

"Has the chimney in this room been swept lately?"

"What do you want to know that for, eh?"

"For a special reason."

"Well, then, it hasn't been touched since I have been in this house, and it won't be either, L can tell you. I'm not going to the expense of sweeps."

"Very good, Mr. Hunkers. Now, we will trouble you to get up that chimney as quickly as you can."

"What!"

"I have said it in plain language. We will trouble you to get up that chimney. Surely you understand that?"

"The devil!"

"You will look like one when you get down, I grant, Mr. Hunkers; but as you are a man of judgment, I will tell you the reason why we wish you to ascend the flue. We suspect, that when we are gone you will not be at rest until you have done something to baulk us in our intentions that are consequent upon the delivery of this note, you understand, to the sheriff. Now, when you are up the chimney, I shall fit a large pistol that I have here in such a manner in the grate, that by the aid of a cord it will go off in a moment, and the cord shall be so arranged, that if you attempt to come down, you shall not fail to touch it, and you will then infallibly be shot dead."

"Curses!"

"Oh, swear away as long as you like. We don't mind that a bit. To be sure, there is the top of the chimney for you to get out at, but we don't think you will try that; and if you call for aid from your servants, and they begin meddling with the pistol to try and relieve you, the charge is sure to go up the chimney, for it is one, the slightest touch at the trigger of which is sufficient to discharge it, and, unlike your blunderbuss, it never misses fire."

"But I won't get up the chimney, I'll be hanged if I do."

"You will be hanged if you don't."

"Oh, stuff! I won't come after you!"

"What's that by the side of the fire-place, Luke?"

"A toasting-fork."

"The very thing. Give it to me. Now, Mr. Hunkers, will you get up the chimney or will you not?"

"Murder! Don't be poking me with the three prongs of the toasting-fork! Murder! Oh, don't! Oh,—I will—don't—help! Oh, I can't stand that, you know. I'm going—oh, oh! He's doing it again! Murder! I'm getting up the chimney. Do you wish to kill me? There again! Oh, don't—don't—mercy! Have mercy upon me. You don't know what it—oh, oh! Try it only once on yourself, and you'll never poke a fellow creature with it again! I am half mad with it. Oh, murder—the devil!"

Claude continued poking old Hunkers with the toasting-fork with all the deliberation in the world, and as if he never so much as heard him make any objections to it, till, quite maddened by the agony it put him to every time it entered his skin, old Hunkers sprang to the fire-place as though he had been the youngest and most active sweep that ever was, and began scrambling up the chimney with quite an alarming alacrity.

The soot feel down in great lumps, and in blinding showers, and the old rascal's voice was still heard calling "Murder!" in the chimney, only that it sounded very faint and smothery, as Claude kept pegging away with the fork at his legs.

At last they too disappeared, and old Hunkers was fairly in the chimney, and out of sight.

"All right?"

A volley of smothered curses was the only reply.

"Ah, very good. Now, old Hunkers, as your wedding dress will be rather the worse for the little adventure, you had better hold on as well as you can, and hang the consequences."

More curses and soot came down the chimney.

"Now, Hunkers," called Claude again, "I am fixing the pistol so that we shall have the satisfaction of leaving your life entirely in your own hands, you know, and you can do just as you please."

Hunkers groaned, and Claude made a rattling about the bars of the grate to convey to him the notion that he was really carrying out his design of fixing the pistol in so dangerous a position, although, in realilty, he never brought any of his fire-arms near the grate, and had no intention of doing so for a moment.

Whether or not old Hunkers felt sure that there was such an amount of danger in descending, the mere doubt would be sufficient to keep him where he was long enough for Claude's purpose; so there he left him, and turning to his friends, he said—

"Now let us go to the sheriff's house, and at once."

"Hark!" said Luke.

"What is it? Is there any alarm?"

"No, but I hear a clock striking."

"Then it is twelve, by Heaven!" cried Harry Lucas, "and they will take Annie to the church."

"Well, my friend, you know that the bridegroom is not there, so you need not be in despair about it. It is twelve, and we have no time to lose. Let us, instead of going to the sheriff's house, go at once to the church, for, no doubt, there the wedding party will be, fully expecting the arrival of Hunkers. Come on—let us lose no time."

"It will be better, will it not," said Harry Lucas, "that I assume my own appearance?"

"That you can easily do. Take off the moustache and whiskers, and you are yourself again. Come on—come on."

"Good night, Hunkers," said Luke.

"Yes, good night," said Claude.

"And, Hunkers," called out Harry Lucas up the chimney, "don't you know me?"

"Go to the devil!" roared Hunkers.

"I am Harry Lucas, and I am going to marry Annie, in spite of you. How do you like that, old Hunkers?—The deuce take him!"

"What's the matter now?"

"Such a handful of soot in my eye."

"That won't improve your appearance," said May, "when you go into church. You had better get rid of it."

"I will—I will. There's a pump on our road, and that will soon cleanse me from it. Come on—I long to get to the church, for I think now that this note you take with you, my unknown friend, will suffice to induce Annie to fly with me to some place of security."

"It's a thousand pities that you cannot marry her," said Claude, as they left the house, and made their way to the garden gate.

"Why can he not?" said May.

"Because, you see, the clergy must have a license to marry him without the publication of banns, or their publication must be proved to his satisfaction; and neither of these conditions are in the power of our young friend Lucas to fulfil."

"Ah! true—true; I had not thought of that. It is so, indeed. Well, Mr. Lucas, your only honourable course; is to take her to your mother's house, and when once there, scandal will hardly reach her, and you can get a license as speedily as possible."

"Alas!" said Lucas, "I cannot get one at all. She is under age you see, and the only method by which our marriage can take place is by banns in some obscure church where no one will know us."

"Never mind, Lucas," cried Claude, "the time will soon slip away. The grand thing will be to get Annie to fly with you from her father. If she once does that, she is yours for ever."

"I think so, too, and nothing shall be wanting upon my part to make her happy; and even the sheriff, if he would have the courage to look his difficulties in the face, and take such assistance as his rich friends would give him, would be a thousand times better off than with any aid he could get from such a man as Hunkers, who is sure in the long run to deceive him."

"You could not say a truer thing than that, Lucas; and if you say as much to the sheriff, and he has one grain of sense left in him, he must see which is his true interest. Come on."

"Stop a moment only. Here is the pump."

Having soon cleansed his face from the soot that had fallen upon it, by giving it a liberal drenching with the pump-water, and then feeling much refreshed by the process, he ran on with his friends towards the church, where he knew the ceremony was to have been performed that would have consigned poor Annie to the arms of such a cold-blooded monster as old Hunkers, the usurer.

Upon turning a corner, they were within sight of the sacred edifice, and they saw at once that it was lighted up, and that there were several carriages at the door of it.

"She is there—she is there!" said Harry Lucas, in tones of emotion.

"Be calm, my friend, be calm," cried Claude. "Everything must be done now with judgment."

"Yes—oh yes. I will leave all to you, and what you direct shall be my law. I owe everything to you. Every hope of happiness that I have in the world now, you know that I owe to you."

"Say no more on that head, but come on at once."

With hasty steps they approached the portal of the church, which was quite blocked up by the carriages and servants that were in attendance. A portly beadle, with his wand of office, was there, but he did not think proper to obstruct Claude Duval and his friends, although he made a movement as if he meant to do so.

In another moment they entered the church.

The singular hour at which—in accordance with the wish of the bride—the ceremony had been appointed to take place, had occasioned a great deal of surmise and anxiety in Guildford. Heaven and her own heart only knew what were the motives of Anne in wishing such an arrangement.

If none had attended the marriage but those who were the absolutely invited guests, there would have been a tolerable throng of people; but the fact is, that there were many more.

Some of the inhabitants of the town, who had been not a little provoked by being overlooked when the invitations were issued, had determined, nevertheless, to be present, and it was impossible to prevent them from being so: therefore, the pews were pretty well occupied; and in the aisle nearest to the doors of the church, there was quite a concourse of people.

If any one now felt any great degree of dread for the result of all this affair, it was surely May; who, knowing the bold and adventurous character of Claude Duval, felt quite assured that now he had begun the business, he would go through with it, let the consequences be what they may. The young lover, too, trembled, but it was as much with hope as with any other feeling.

It had not, of course, been thought necessary to light up the whole of the church, just because a marriage was going to be celebrated at an unusual hour; so, with the exception of a couple of candles on the communion-table, and one chandelier that hung by a long chain from the roof just over the space in front of the railings that enclosed the communion-table, there was no light in the church.

The consequence of this arrangement was, that, although a tolerable glow was thrown upon those persons who happened to be quite close at hand to the railings of the communion-table, the rest of the sacred edifice, and every one in it, was thrown into a state of double gloom by the contrast with the light portion of it.

Such was the state of things when Claude and his friends entered the church, and made their way towards the group of persons about the spot over which hung the chandelier.

It is hard to say whether the fair young Annie repented or not of the kind of reply she had given to her lover a short time previously; but certainly nothing could exceed the amount of agony she endured at finding that the time was come when the awful sacrifice which her ideas of duty to her father induced must be made.

What a mockery of her heart that bridal dress was that she wore!—How little did she look in unison with the flowers that were in her hair, and the general appearance of festivity which her whole dress was made to wear upon that, to her, melancholy occasion! And yet there were, no doubt, many among the gazers upon that wedding who, knowing nothing of the sad circumstances under which it was sought to be brought about, envied the bride, and thought her a fortunate young female to wed with one so rich; for, after all, it is not who you are in this world, that is the first question asked, but how much have you.

CHAPTER CLXI.

SOME EXTRAORDINARY EVENTS TAKE PLACE IN THE CHURCH AT GUILDFORD.

THERE are few persons who would not have felt some little degree of hesitation at walking into a church upon such an errand as Claude Duval's was upon that occasion; but we have had amply sufficient opportunities of knowing that his nerves were tolerably steady.

As for poor Harry Lucas, May could see, even by the faint light in the church, that he was as pale as death itself.

"Courage—courage," she whispered to him.

"Yes—yes, I will nerve myself for anything."

"Recollect, that it is for Annie's sake all this is done"

"I will—I do! Her name is a spell that shall not leave me. I thank you for naming her to me."

Claude Duval quickened his pace, and reached the little throng of persons in front of the gilt railing to the communion-table; and as he did so, he heard the sheriff say, in a voice of vexation, not unmingled with dread that something was amiss—

"Dear me, what can keep our friend, Mr. Hunkers? It is past his time, now, nearly twenty minutes."

"And he so very punctual a man of business usually, too," said one of the guests in tones of irony.

"Particularly when a bill comes due," whispered another.

"Father, I will not remain here longer," said Annie. "Let us go."

"Ah," cried the sheriff, as he heard the footsteps of Claude and his friends speedily advancing up the aisle. "It is all right.—Here he is at last. Come, come, my friends, we won't say anything to vex the bridegroom, now that he has come; for nothing but some very important business could have detained him; and as such is the case, we need not vex him by reverting to it."

CLAUDE'S SURPRISE ON HEARING THE WAILINGS OF HARRY LUCAS.

Annie began to sob bitterly; and an old maid, of about forty-eight years of age, mistook the cause of her emotion completely, and tried to comfort her, saying—

"You know, my dear, this is what all us young girls expect, and are pretty sure to come to at last"

"Mr. Sheriff Forsyth," said Claude, in a clear voice.

"Sir!" cried the sheriff. "I—I—am in the church, and an arrest is not legal."

"I do not come to arrest you, sir, but on a message from Mr. Hunkers, if you please."

Annie, upon finding that it was not Hunkers himself, dried her sweet eyes, and looked up with some degree of interest and hope.

"A message, sir?" added the sheriff, looking very red in the face. A message, did you say, from Mr. Hunkers? Sir, we would rather see that gentleman himself than hear any message from him at such a time as this."

"Is the old man ill?" said one.

"Silence!" cried the sheriff. "I wonder at the indelicacy of anybody saying 'Is the old man ill?'"

"Is he dead?" said another.

"Oh!" cried the sheriff. "What indelicacy, upon the very moment of a man's marriage! I am shocked—I am quite shocked, and could hardly have thought it possible that any one could behave in such a way, in a church too. I suppose, sir,"—addressing Claude—"you come to tell me that the bridegroom will soon, be here to go through with the interesting ceremony?"

"No, sir."

"No, did you say? Do my ears hear aright?"

"Your ears do you justice, Mr. Sheriff. Here is a letter from Mr. Hunkers, to explain why it is he positively declines marrying Miss Annie Forsyth."

A shriek of joy burst from the lips of Annie, and all the ladies gathered round her, to console; but she burst through the throng, and making her way to Claude Duval, she said to him—

"Oh, sir, do not trifle with my feelings, but tell me truly. Is the purport of the letter you bring a renunciation of my hand upon the part of Mr. Hunkers?"

"It is."

"Never mind, my dear," said all the ladies in chorus. "Never mind. Take out your smelling salts, and never mind, my love."

"The men are all wretches!" said the old maid. "I was served in this way twenty-two years ago, come Michaelmas, exactly."

"Don't faint, my love, if you can help it," said another to Annie.

"Faint!" she cried. "Faint because I am not to be made such a sacrifice that death in any shape would have been infinitely preferable? On no, no!—God, what a happy release is this! I must be a special act of providence that has made the old man relent and not make me his victim. Oh, what a weight is lifted off my heart! I am happy once again."

While this little ebullition of feeling was taking place upon the part of Annie, the astounded sheriff had taken the letter from Claude Duval, and read it; and then crumpling it up in his hand, his great fat, sensual-looking face turned positively blue, and his eyes goggled so oddly, that he looked as though in another moment apoplexy would claim its victim.

But the sheriff's time had not yet come to shuffle off his mortal sheriffalty, and he recovered sufficiently to gasp out—

"Good gracious!"

"My dear sir," said one of the guests, "allow me to look at the letter."

"Go to the devil!" said the sheriff.

"Is it true, though?" cried everybody, now. "Is it true, Mr. Forsyth, that Mr. Hunkers won't be married?"

"Quite true—that is—I think—I don't know."

"An action will lie," said an attorney, shuffling up to his friend the sheriff, with an important air. "An action, my dear sir, and heavy damages. Breach of promise, you know."

"Be quiet."

"Yes, certainly. Mum is the word, my dear sir—mum is the word. We will trounce him. But advise the bride to be deeply affected. If she goes on in the way she is, we shall not win, my dear sir."

"Annie."

"Yes, father, I am here."

"Wretched girl!"

"Oh, don't say that, father! I am not a wretched girl at all. I never was so delighted in all my life. It is like a reprieve from death."

"She is light-headed," said the sheriff.

"Stick to that," whispered the attorney, "it's a good idea. Stick to it."

"I will. My poor, my unhappy child! What must be a father's feelings to see the effect of the deep disappointment upon you! Alas—alas—alas! that bright and—and beautiful intellect has received a jog, and is no more what it was. Oh—oh! Ah me, I am an unhappy father."

"Good," said the attorney, "that will do it."

"Father," said Annie, with a smile, and quite a provokingly sane look, "you are quite mistaken. It is the marriage that might have driven me mad, but not the breaking off of it. That latter circumstance has restored me to cheerfulness and joy, for you know that nothing could be more abhorrent to me than a union with Mr. Hunkers; and since he himself has put an end to all thought of it, he can blame no one, and I am happy once again."

"She will ruin all," whispered the attorney. "You will never recover a farthing if she goes on in that way, my dear sir."

Claude now saw that the sheriff had put the letter into his pocket, and had no sort of intention to let its precise contents ooze out, so he thought that it was rather time to interfere in the matter, and he said—

"But, Mr. Sheriff, I was present when that letter was written, and Mr. Hunkers intended, most probably, that it should be read to the bride."

"Indeed, sir?"

"Yes, Mr. Sheriff; and if you doubt that fact, here are other gentlemen who were present likewise, and who can confirm it."

"Yes, I can," said May, and Luke, and Harry Lucas, all in a breath.

The sheriff looked provoked.

"When one gentleman," he said, "addresses another, he has no right to dictate to whom he should show it."

"Oh, very well," said Claude; "then it will be my duty to state what is in it to all concerned; and if the sheriff does not show the letter itself to dispute the accuracy of my version of it, everybody will be able to take that as pretty good proof of my correctness."

"Hear him—hear him!" cried several. "What was in the letter, sir?"

"I will tell you."

"My dear sir," said the attorney, who had sidled round to Claude's elbow, "allow me to suggest that——"

"No, sir, I don't want any suggestions; so, for the good of all, I will state that in the first part of the letter Mr. Hunkers stated, that upon reflection he felt convinced that the disparity in the ages of himself and Miss Annie Forsyth was such that no happiness could be looked for from the union."

"How true," said several.

"I thank him at last," said Annie. "I did not think that he would take so just a thought, but I did him great injustice."

"There—there; very good, sir," said the sheriff, "we don't want to know any more; that is all that can be of any importance, my dear sir. That will do. Come home, Annie, my bereaved, heart-broken child; you are still most welcome to your father's arms."

"But I should like to hear what further was in the letter, sir," said Annie.

"You shall," added Claude. "It stated that as he knew a young and worthy man was sincerely attached to you, he hoped that you, with him, would know what real happiness was, and that his name was——"

"That will do—that will do," cried the sheriff.

"His name?" said Annie.

"Is Harry Lucas!" cried Lucas, springing forward and catching her in his arms, and kissing her twenty times before the astonished sheriff, with a roar of dismay, could come forward to stop him; and, somehow, Annie, although she might have done so, did not struggle so as to prevent Harry from kissing her, but put up with it in so resigned a manner, that the ladies, especially the old ones, were quite scandalised, and told each other how different girls were now to what they were some twenty years ago, and hinted what they would have done if any man had hugged them in such a manner, and taken to kissing them as if his life depended upon giving them a certain number in a certain space of time.

"Stop!" roared the sheriff.

"It is true," said Claude, speaking about an octave higher. "It is quite true, Mr. Sheriff. That was the name mentioned in Mr. Hunkers's note."

"It's false, and, besides, I don't approve of it, and so it is of no consequence whether it is true or not."

"But your daughter highly approves of it."

"She don't, sir. She is light-headed."

Young Harry Lucas turned full upon the sheriff, and in a voice that echoed through the church, as he held his arm round the waist of Annie, he cried out—

"That is false, Mr. Sheriff. You know well, sir, that the young maiden was all but dragged here to be offered up a sacrifice to the man who was to purchase her of you for gold. You know well that such was the fact, and, but that at the eleventh hour the hoary-headed sinner who offered you his ill-gotten wealth for this piece of rare perfection retracted, you would have allowed the sacrifice to be made. I say, sir, all this you know, and with truth you cannot deny it; and it is in vain that you now attempt to convert pure and holy joy at having escaped such pollution into evidence of light-headedness or want of thought."

"You infernal rascal!" cried the sheriff, "why, you are only a clerk, whose chief ability is that he can write a letter."

"Which you cannot."

"Come away from that villain, Annie. Come away from him, or I shall be tempted to strike you."

"If you do," said Harry Lucas, "were you ten times her father, I would annihilate you, even in the church here."

At this moment the clergyman stepped forward, for, hearing high voices, he had come out of the vestry to know what was the matter; and smoothing his ruffles and flourishing his white hands, he said—

"Allow me to suggest that somebody pay me my fees, and then that you all go somewhere else to quarrel, as the church is not exactly the proper place for such a proceeding."

"But, sir," said the sheriff, "my daughter, Annie——"

"Nay," cried Lucas, "you shall have your fees from me, and I only wish you would marry me to this young lady at once."

"I shall be very happy. Have you a licence?"

"Alas!—no."

"Claude!" whispered Luke in Duval's ear, "Claude, I say?"

"What is it, Luke?"

"Danger!"

"Ah! of what complexion is it, Luke?"

"Captain Smith, the king's messenger, is at the door of the church, with a half dozen constables, and, from what I heard them say, they are only waiting for a troop of light cavalry they have got the assistance of to arrive, and then a bold attempt will be made to arrest us all. How he came to know we were here puzzles me; but the fact is not to be disputed. What is to be done?"

CHAPTER CLXII.

AFFAIRS GET RATHER SERIOUS FOR CLAUDE AND HIS FRIENDS.

THE intelligence which Luke brought to Claude Duval was indeed of a serious character, and he pondered over it for a moment, and then he said—

"Luke, we must escape by some means. Do you think you could manage, at a signal from me, to put out the lights in the chandelier?"

"Yes, I think by throwing my hat at them that I could knock them all over easily enough."

"That will do, then; I want to see how this little affair of the young lovers can be brought to an end if we have time, and then we will see to our own safety. The lights on the communion-table, too, you must put out by some means."

"I will charge myself with all that," said Luke, "easily; and then there is one thing that is favourable, which is, that we cannot fail to hear the cavalry arrive at the door of the church."

"True. You keep a good look-out, Luke, while I attend to this matter of Lucas's, and see if I cannot do something more towards the happiness of Annie and her lover."

While this brief conversation took place between Luke and Duval, the clergyman was looking first to the sheriff and then to Harry Lucas, with the hope that one or the other of them would put his hand in his pocket and pay him his fees; but as they neither of them did so, he began to threaten them all with proceedings for breeding disturbances in the church.

Annie still clung to her lover. It was something for that young girl to have some one to cling to who loved her for herself alone, after being made such a thing of barter and sale by her father and old Hunkers; so she seemed to be in no hurry to quit his protecting arm.

"I will put an end to this," said the sheriff. "I command you to come home at once."

"Farewell," said Annie, to Lucas. "Farewell."

"Oh, no, no," whispered Lucas. "This is an opportunity that will not occur again. Let me take you at once to my mother's."

"Oh, if I dared!"

"There is no one to prevent you, Annie. You have heard sufficient of her to know you will be safe with her. This is a crisis both in your fate and mine, dear one, and if you will not now act with energy and be happy, the chance may never come again."

"But my father——"

"He will make up matters to-morrow morning with old Hunkers, and another day will be fixed for your wedding."

Annie shuddered.

"Oh, Harry! if, indeed, I thought that——"

"It is certain."

"I am yours, then—I am yours. Take me away."

"Oh, joy—joy!"

At this moment the clash of arms and the sound of horses' feet, came from the outside of the church quite plainly upon the ears of all present, and Claude Duval then knew that the foes he had most to dread were all but upon him.

A clashing noise, that reverberated through the church, at the next moment came upon his ears, and Duval called out in a loud voice—

"Luke—Luke! Where are you, now! Have you forgotten——"

"Not at all," said Luke, "I am fastening up the church door, and here is the key of it. Gentlemen, we are all besieged. Look to yourselves. There need be no alarm on the part of the ladies."

Luke took off his hat, and Claude, who knew well what he was going to do, cried out—

"Harry Lucas, keep by the side of Annie, and take care of her."

May clung to Claude's left arm, and in another moment Luke flung his hat and knocked over all the six candles that burnt in the chandelier. The ladies began to scream, and some of the gentlemen to swear. A sensation of great feat crept over the heart of the sheriff. Lucas called out—

"What is the meaning of this, my friend? Are you mad? Why place us all in the dark?—Hold—hold! Don't put out the lights on the communion-table."

Luke had vaulted over the gilt railings, and put out both the lights, and the church in a moment was in profound darkness. Just then there came a heavy hammering at the door, and voices cried out—

"Open—open! In the king's name, open the door! Open the door, or it will be broken open!"

The ladies screamed more lustily than before, and the gentlemen ran hither and thither, with the hope of effecting an escape. The parson got into a pew, and shut himself in, and crept under the seat. The old maid who in her way had been so compassionate to Annie, made a rush at the sheriff, and got hold of him round the neck in such a way, that he could not extricate himself ; and one old lady took refuge in the pulpit, where, likewise, the beadle made a rush for safety, and they both began thumping each other at the bottom of it.

May clung close to Claude, as he whispered her to do, and Annie was under the protection of Harry Lucas, who was rather bewildered at what was going on.

Bang! bang! bang! came blows upon the church door, now, again, and a loud voice, shouted—

"Open, in the king's name, or we shall be compelled to break down the door. Open for the officers of the police. We come to apprehend the notorious Claude Duval, and his associates. Open the door, some of you !"

"Claude Duval!" cried Harry. "Is it possible ?"

"It is possible," said Claude. "He who has befriended Harry Lucas, and he who has snatched Annie Forsyth from the horrors of a marriage with old Hunkers, is Claude Duval, the highwayman."

"Good God !" cried Harry Lucas.

"Farewell !" added Claude. "Henceforth, let us, if it so please you, be strangers."

"No—no! By Heaven, I will befriend you, if I can. You have done for me far more than any other human being would have done, and I will with my life defend you. She who is now hanging upon my arm approves the sentiment that actuates me, and we will both do for you and yours what we can."

"Somebody get a light, and let us seize the highwayman !" cried a voice. "Where is the sheriff ?"

"Nowhere," cried the sheriff. "An old hag has got hold of me."

"Oh you wretch !" cried the old maid, giving him a cuff on the nose, that made it bleed. "Take that, and mind you don't call a gentle and an interesting female a hag another time."

"Here's a lady says she is in an interesting situation," said a voice, and a roar of laughter from those who were the least frightened of all present at once ensued.

The laughter appeared to have the effect of wonderfully exciting the anger of those who were on the outside of the church, and the hammering away at the doors now assumed a really serious character.

"Duval—Claude Duval!" said a voice, in a whisper.

"I am here," said Duval. "Who speaks ?"

"A friend."

"If an enemy, let him be careful of himself."

"Don't you know my voice, Claude Duval? I am Harry Lucas."

"And I am Annie Forsyth," said a gentle voice.

"Ah, true—I know you both now," said Claude. "I wish you had been out of the church and fairly escaped, before this most untoward circumstance took place."

"Never mind," said Harry; "lay your hand upon my arm and follow me. I rather think I can take you to a place of safety."

"Do you really think so?"

"Yes; but speak low, for we don't know what listeners we may have in the dark here."

"True—true. Luke, where are you?"

"Here!" said Luke, so close to Claude's ear, that he could not help giving a start as he heard the sound.

"Follow us, then."

Young Harry Lucas led the way, now, carefully along one of the aisles of the church, followed by Claude, and May, and Luke. Annie still clung to the arm of her lover. Amide the noise and racket echoing through the church, in consequence of the violence of those who were trying to force an admission, not a word of what Harry Lucas had said had reached any other ears than those for which it was intended.

Claude was rather puzzled to think where Lucas could be leading him, so he said, in a low voice—

"Where are we going, Lucas?"

"I hope out of the church, but of that I do not feel certain. Close to a marble slab in the wall, there is, or there was, a small door that led into the burial ground. There was a talk about building it up, but I don't think it was ever done; and if not, I think we can force it open."

"I hope we may find it."

"I hope so, too. It is a chance, at all events, that I don't like to throw away. But is it really true that you are Claude Duval, the highwayman?"

"It is."

"Well, that don't matter to me a straw. You have shown yourself such a friend to me, that I feel I ought to do all in my power to aid you; and I am quite sure that Annie feels the same thing."

"I do, indeed," said Annie. "from my heart."

"We thank you both," said Claude; "and whether this adventure terminates ill or well, we shall not regret, I am certain, that we have put a stop to Hunker's nuptials, and prevented the sacrifice of so much beauty at the shrine of so much avarice and villany."

The blows at the church door suddenly ceased, and then a voice, in clear tones, spoke from without, dwelling upon each word so as to make it distinctly understood.

"Reluctant as we are," said the voice, "to break into a church, yet, under the circumstances, if the doors be not at once opened, we feel that we ought to do so, and the sin and sacrilege be upon the heads of those whose conduct enforces such a step."

The voice then paused, apparently to give some one within time to reply, but no one was in a position to do so with any effect but Luke. He certainly had the huge key of the church door in his hand, but he was not inclined to make use of it in the way suggested by those whose object was to take him and his friends into custody.

A single voice now from the middle of the church—it was from the beadle in the pulpit—cried out—

"Murder!"

This one startling cry seemed to awaken all the wedding-guests, and to induce them to join in one uproar of voices, and they shouted—

"Open the door! Break it down! Break it down! Murder—murder!"

Thus encouraged, the officers, who were without, thought that there was surely no cause for further hesitation, and they set about the task of breaking their way into the church at once.

The blows about the region of the lock became each instant more and more formidable, and the large door shook ominously. It was quite clear that it could not withstand such assaults for long.

By this time, though, Harry Lucas had got to the spot in the wall that he whished to reach, and found the door; but, by passing his hand up and down it, he discovered, to his chagrin, that it was in truth nailed up, by having a piece of planking fastened over it.

"Can you open it?" said Claude.

"Alas, no. It is too secure."

"Then that hope is lost?"

"I am afraid it is. What on earth will become of you?"

"The windows are low," said Annie, "and they can be easily broken through. The frame-work is but of sheet lead, as I have often noticed. Why not try to leave by one of them?"

"The only wonder," said Claude, "is that our foes have not yet attempted to enter the church by one of them."

As if his words had been prophetic, the moment he uttered them, crash came through into the aisle a great portion of one of the windows, and a rough voice cried out in true military style—

"Forward, my men, and make all prisoners that you find in the church. Forward!"

The night light was very dim, indeed, but still it was sufficient to let Claude and his friends see that soldiers were making their way into the church by the open window. He felt at that moment as though all were lost; but young Harry Lucas grasped him by the arm, and whispered—

"The vaults!"

"What do you mean?"

"I can conduct you to the vaults. It is the second chance that I spoke of, and the last. Follow me quickly."

"Anywhere," said Claude, "for we cannot fight a troop of cavalry."

The fugitives now, led by Lucas, returned a part of the way that they had come before. Carefully they reached the rails of the communion-table again, over which Harry Lucas, in whispers, explained that they must get. He assisted Annie, and the others were soon over.

"There is a square iron door behind the communion-table," whispered Harry, "that leads to the vaults, which have not been used now for half a century That door I know has no fastening. Will you descend?"

CHAPTER CLXIII.

MORE PERILS IN THE VAULTS OF THE OLD CHURCH.

B FORE Claude Duval could make any reply to this question that Harry Lucas had just put to him, there came such a clattering noise at the door of the church, that there could no longer be the shadow of a doubt but that it was fairly burst open.

"Lights—lights!" cried several voices. "Have you no lights here? Hilloa! We are not coming on without lights."

"The Lord have mercy upon our lights, and our livers, too," said the beadle from the pulpit.

The old lady who was there likewise tried to say "Amen," but she could not gather breath sufficient to do so.

"Lead us on anywhere," whispered Claude to Harry Lucas, "so that we get out of the church."

"Come this way, then We will go to the vaults. I don't think any one will be bold enough to follow us there."

"Nor I; but we have no foolish fears of such a place, so we will follow you at once."

"Anywhere," said May, "so that we escape. Where are you, Annie Forsyth?"

"I am here."

"Then you and I will keep together, as we ought to do."

"I beg your pardon," said Lucas.   "I can take care of Miss Forsyth, young sir, if you please."

THE FRIENDS DISGUISING THEMSELVES TO VISIT MR. HUNKERS.

"You mistake," said May. "I am the wife of Claude Duval.'

"The wife!   Then that alters the affair, indeed.   But here they are with a light from the vestry, and we have not another moment to lose."

Harry Lucas, as he spoke, stooped down nearly under the communion-table, and found the handle of a little iron trap-door which communicated with   the vaul.

He raised it without the least difficulty, and then, in a whisper, he said to his friends—

"Descend at once. There is, indeed, no time to lose. Descend, I pray you at once."

Luke began the descent, and Annie and May followed him closely. Harry Lucas would then have had Claude go, but the latter said—

"After you. Let me be the last. I will let the trap-door into its proper place, you may depend, Mr. Lucas."

"Be it so, then," said Lucas; "but I thought to have been the last, and so to have had the satisfaction of knowing that you were all in comparative safety."

The fact was, that Claude, with his eyes just over the edge of the communion-table, was watching what was taking place in the church, which was a sufficiently curious spectacle to arrest his attention, even at such a moment as that, when peril surrounded him on all sides.

The light that had been procured from the vestry shed but a faint glow over the large area of the church, but some of the officers were not slow to profit by its presence, and to light other candles that they found in different places, so that the sacred edifice was being gradually lit up; and as it was so, Claude Duval could see the situation of the various parties within it.

The panic-stricken guests had made their way, for the most part, into different pews for shelter; so that all that could be seen of them consisted of a few heads of the most venturous among them peeping over the mahogany divisions of the pews, and wondering what was going to happen next upon that extraordinary and alarming night.

The sheriff was nowhere to be seen, but the beadle's cocked hat projected over the pulpit, and his great sleepy-looking eyes, with just as little speculation in them as possible, was glaring upon the scene below.

Several of the ladies had fainted away, and lay in picturesque attitudes on the floor.

The lights, too, shone upon the arms and accoutrements of some dozen or so of dismounted cavalry, who were lancers, by their costume; and there was about half a score of constables, too, to aid the military force; so that it was tolerably evident they all thought they were on rather a hazardous and troublesome piece of duty.

Standing as close as he could get to the military, so as not absolutely to be in their way, was Captain Smith, the king's messenger, who, no doubt, had been the cause of bringing down upon Duval and his friends the force that now filled up the place.

"We are sure to have him, sir," said a police-officer to the lieutenant who had the command of the lancers, "if your men watch well the outside."

"Sentinels are placed, and, therefore, that part of the business is done," said the lieutenant, with a cold, uncomfortable tone of voice.

"Oh, very good, sir."

The lieutenant turned his back upon the officer of the police, and then said—

"I apprehend that all we have to do now is to aid you in case your force should not be sufficient. Take your prisoners, and we will escort you to the jail with them."

"That will do, sir, if you please," said the officer. "That will do. They are here, we are quite sure, and all we have to do is to ferret them out."

Upon this, Claude Duval thought that his most prudent course would be to get out of the way as quickly as possible, and he descended the staircase that was immediately below the little iron door in the floor, and cautiously let the door close above him.

What an intense darkness they were all in now; and what a strange, unearthly—so far as the daylight and open air of the earth were concerned—smell the place had that they were now in.

"Where are you all?" said Claude.

"Here," said Lucas. "Here, and all safe. What are they doing above?"

"They are just beginning a search. How many steps are there here ? I have come down six."

"Oh, there are three times that number. Come on; it is all fair ground at the foot of the stairs."

"Luke !"

"Yes, Duval, I am here. I think I know what you want: it is a light."

"It is."

"Ah, but," said Harry Lucus, "I fear that will be impossible to procure here."

"Not so," said Luke, "we always carry about with us the means of getting a light. We often owe our safety to such a wise provision. I will soon cast the illuminating focus of a wax taper, at all events, upon this place, if you think there is no danger in so doing ?"

"Danger there is none."

"Very good."

Upon this, Luke lit a phosphorus match, and speedily succeeded by its aid in igniting a wax taper which he had with him; and as it burnt slowly up into rather a sickly flame, for the air of the place was neither good for flame nor for animal life, they were able to see something of the gloomy region into which they had penetrated.

"Hold the light higher, Luke."

Luke did so, and then they had all a good view of the spot on which they were. They had all got to the foot of the stairs, which were somewhere about twenty in number, and they were standing upon a considerable thickness of sawdust, with which the ground was literally strewed. The space in which they were was about twelve feet square, and several passages branched off from it.

"This is a strange place," said Claude.

"It is so," replied Lucas, to whom the remark seemed to be more specially addressed. "I have heard that in Catholic times—for the church above and all these underground places belonged to the Catholics—there were strange doings in these vaults, and that in the dark days of persecution for religion's sake, they were often converted into dungeons."

"Not a doubt of it. Were you ever here yourself before, Lucas ?"

"Only once, and that was upon the occasion of a law suit regarding an estate in the immediate neighbourhood, when a search was made in these vaults to see if any coffin had a plate upon it bearing the name of one of the litigants. Then I and some others had a slight view of the place."

"Hush !"

A strange confused noise came from above, and it was quite evident that those who were in the church were pursuing the investigation they had resolved upon making with a vigour that was quite regardless of what noise or confusion it occasioned in the sacred edifice.

"They are looking for us," said Luke.

"But they will not find us," said Claude, "I think, for no one is likely to imagine but that we have found some mode of outlet from the church before now. This will not be a likely place to search."

"Far from it."

"Come on, then, as we are here, and let us see some of the wonders of these receptacles of the dead."

"You should say the terrors," remarked Annie Forsyth, with a shudder.

"Pardon me," added Claude. "I see that I was wrong now in asking you to advance beyond this spot. It is well to keep young minds free from the terrors that otherwise, in happier moments, might haunt them."

"Oh, listen !" said May, suddenly.

They were all as silent as the grave, and then they heard distinctly some blows given to the iron door at the top of the staircase.

"We are lost !" said Annie.

"Say, rather, found," whispered Lucas. "But yet there is a hope."

"Hush! hush!" said Claude. "They are coming now. Hush!"

With a wrench, the covering of the staircase leading to the vaults was opened, and at the same moment Luke extinguished his light, so that, with the exception of a very faint gleam of light that came down the stairs from the candles above, all was darkness again. It was evident, now, that several of their enemies were collected around the opening leading to the vaults, and every word that was said came plainly upon the ears of the anxious fugitives below.

"Yes, gentlemen," said some one—it was the beadle who spoke—"yes, gentlemen, these are the vaults; but, I assure you all, as they hasn't been opened no how for I don't know when; so it don't seem likely that they should have found out such a place."

"Indeed, it does not," said another.

"Well, but," cried a man in a cracked disputative voice, "we are hired to search everywhere, and you know upon that principle we should look here as well. If it comes to giving up looking in one place, because it ain't probable they are there, we may as well give up the search altogether, for I contend that people always do get into improbable places."

"Well—well, you go down," said another.

"Nay, why should I go alone? They might pop a bullet into me in a moment or two, and nice I should look then."

"Well—well, let's go down a little way, at all events."

"Come on, then. Hold the light, one of you. Bring two lights. That will do. Now look to your pistols, and come down. We won't have any one say that we did not look everywhere."

Upon this, Harry Lucas laid hold of Claude by the arm, and said in a whisper—

"Follow me, all of you. It is our only chance."

CHAPTER CLXIV.

DETAILS HOW THE FUGITIVES ESCAPED INTO THE MOONLIGHT.

THEY none of them knew very well where Harry Lucas proposed to lead them, but they followed him, hearing him speak of the chance yet of escape. He took a passage to the left of where they had been standing, and which was covered likewise with sawdust laid on some four or five inches in thickness, so that the sound of their footsteps was completely lost in it.

The roof and walls of this passage reeked with an unwholesome moisture, and they could all feel how very bad the air was to breathe by a feeling of oppression at the lungs, such as it would scarcely have been possible to endure for any length of time.

"Oh, Claude," whispered May, "this is some dreadful home of the dead."

"Courage—courage," said Claude.

"Yes, but where are we going? A thousand unknown fears oppress me, and I feel ready to sink to the earth."

"Let me support you, May. You will not sink, I am sure, while my arm is around you?"

"No—no, I shall not."

"Come now; courage—courage. Where are we, Mr. Lucas?"

"Stop," said Lucas. "Let us listen if our enemies are near at hand, or not. Do you hear anything?"

"Yes, the murmur of voices I hear," said Claude, "and that is all; but whether they come from the church above, or from persons in these vaults, I can't say."

"I will go on a little way towards the path we have trodden," said Luke, "and ascertain, if you like."

" Do so—do so. We will await your return, good Luke."

Before Luke had gone many paces, the sudden flash of a light came upon their eyes, and they could no longer doubt that the officers were determined upon making such an examination of the vaults as would thoroughly satisfy them.

Luke was back again in a moment.

"They come!"

"What are we to do, now?" said Claude, as he took his pistols from his pocket, and began to adjust them for use.

"Resistance will be madness," said Luke. "If we cannot hide from them we are taken. Recollect, Duval, that if we fire upon them, they will return the shots, and that in that case, May or Miss Forsyth might come to injury."

"That is true," said Duval, as he coolly replaced his pistols in his pockets. "Let them come now."

"It is all over," said May.

"No," said Harry Lucas, suddenly. "I have got open the door of one of the vaults here. Come in, all of you. We may yet elude them. They are only walking through the passages, as we have done. Recollect, they have not yet opened any of the chambers of the dead."

"True—true," said Claude.

"A light for one moment," whispered Harry Lucas. "One of the matches that you have got will do. Your enemies will not see it, having a light themselves; and I want to know where we are."

Luke quickly enough produced a light, and before it expired they all saw the open door that Lucas had in his hand. It was of iron, and led to a vaulted room. Above the door was rudely sculptured the arms of the family to whom the vault had originally belonged. There was no choice now but to remain in the passage, and be seen and captured by the officers, or to go into this open vault. They embraced the latter alternative, and at once crossed its threshold. Harry Lucas closed the door on the inside, and all was still.

"It is very strange," said Claude, in such a whisper that it was quite impossible it could get beyond the ears of his friends in the vault. "It is very strange that the air is purer shut up in this place than it is in the long passages on the outside."

"It is much purer," said May. "I can breathe here without difficulty."

"And so can I," said Annie.

"That is a circumstance I cannot account for," said Lucas. "I should like to see the place, though. Will you light another match, Mr. Luke, and let us look about us for a few brief seconds?"

"Willingly."

The match was lighted, and as Luke held it up, they saw around them, and a fearful sight it was.

Upon shelves all round the vault, with the exception of one part, which had very much the appearance of having been opened once and then built up again, were coffins; but the majority of them had rotted and broken, letting fall to the earth and sawdust below the skeleton remains of their occupants.

The side of one had fallen out, and the corpse, by some means, hung half-suspended between the shelf and the floor by some strong material that it had been wrapped up in, and which had resisted the decay of all else that was mortal about it. That was a strange and a hideous spectacle.

"Oh, this is dreadful," said Annie.

Out went the match, and all was intensely dark again, and then, before they could say another word, they heard the voices of their pursuers just outside the door; but Lucas was doing something to the door which puzzled Claude Duval, and he whispered—

"What are you about, Lucas? Are you trying to fasten the door?"

"I am not only trying, but I am fully succeeding in doing so."

"How do you mean? How is that possible?"

"Why, it seems odd to have fastenings on the inside of the door of a vault,

but while the match was alight, I saw that there were a couple of good stror
bolts to the door."

" You did ?"

" In good faith I did.   One at the top and another at the bottom, and they a
now in their sockets, so that I think our friends outside have no force sufficient t
break in here."

" This is most extraordinary," added Claude. " What possible motive coul
there be for putting fastenings upon the inner side of the door of a vault ?"

" It is inexplicable," said Lucas.

" Not so," whispered Luke, " I have an idea upon the subject which I wi
let you all know by and bye ; but at first let us consider that we have enough t
do to listen to what our enemies are about."

This was too self-evident a proposition to be denied, and they were all as sile
as the mouldering remains of the dead inhabitants of that apartment.   They coul
not detect any ray of light from the passage, which led them to think that th
door fitted into its framework so well that they might if they chose have a ligh
without incurring any danger.   Still they abstained from such an indulgence, fo
it was better to err upon the safe side.

" There is no one here," said a voice from the passage; " it is no use makin
onrselves sick with the pestiferous atmosphere of this place.   There is no one h
the passage."

" But the vaults themselves, the actual vaults, you know, we have not been i
any of them."

" No, nor are we going," said the first speaker.   " Here is a door, now."

" Yes, gentlemen," said the beadle, " that there door leads to the family vaul
of the family of the Fritles—a very great family in Guildford many years a gon
by, I assure you ; and them's their coats of arms over the door."

" And what's become of the family of the Fritles, now, Mr. Beadle ?"

" Dead and defunct, sir."

" What, all of them ?"

" Reether ! They is, in a manner of speaking, now, nothing in this here vassa
world, but ashes and dust."

" Well, it can't offend them, then, if we take a look into their vault. Open the
door, Mr. Beadle. What, is it fast ?"

" So it seems, sir, for it won't move no how.   Now, sir. they tells funny stories
about these Fritles."

" When they were alive, I suppose ?"

" Oh, dear, no, sir.   The funniness was all when they was dead, gentlemen.
They do say that whenever a Fritle was buried, or, rather, put on the shelf in the
family vault, and the door left just close, the dead Fritles got up and bolted it on
the inside till another of the family went dead."

" The deuce they did."

" Yes, gentleman ; and, would you believe it, once the Fritles gave leave to a
gentleman of the name of Podgers to put his wife in the vault, but when they
came with the coffin to this door it wasn't open !"

" You don't mean that ?"

" Yes, i does.   The dead Fritles in the inside wouldn't undo it to let in a
Podgers."

" Oh, I say, it's no use staying here.   Why, this vault of the Fritles is enough
of itself to make one's hair stand on end.   What, suppose all the dead Fritles
were to take it amiss our coming here now, and suddenly to pounce out upon us ?
I wouldn't be here if such a thing was to happen for a thousand pounds."

" Nor I," said another.

" Nor me !" cried the beadle ; " because, you see, gentlemen, me being the
beadle of the church, they would be sure to be down upon me."

Every word of this legend concerning the Fritles and their family vault was
heard distinctly by Claude Duval and his friends, and he thought it too good an
opportunity of alarming his pursuers to let slip ; so, watching his opportunity when

there was a lull in the conversation, and when it might be supposed that they were all looking at each other with terrified aspects, Claude tapped with his knuckles on the inside of the door, and made a strange moaning noise at the same time.

For a moment or two the seven or eight persons who were in the passage immediately outside the door of the Fritles' last home, were too much petrified by fright to move or speak ; but then, with one accord, they turned and fled.

It was truly ludicrous to hear their cries of alarm and shouts for succour as they ran along the passage towards the staircase that would lead them into the church. Some fell down and were run over by the others, and the beadle was the most afraid of the whole lot, and roared for mercy as if all the Fritles, each with a good cudgel, were at his heels.

"I think that has settled them," said Claude.

"Yes, for the time," said Luke ; "but it is doubtful if those who wait in the church the report of their exploring party, will take the same superstitious view of the matter."

"Well, Luke, you were saying that you had an idea connected with the bolts on the inner side of this door."

"I have, and that idea is, that the bolts would never have been there if there had not been some other mode of exit from the vault; and, what is more, the freshness of the air convinces me that such must be the case."

"A light, Luke," said Claude. "You are right."

Luke now lit one of his little bits of wax taper, and it soon gave sufficient light to enable them to take a thorough look all round the vault. It was then that, in the roof, at that part of the wall which seemed to have been built up, they found a narrow opening, about half the width of a brick, through which there came a current of cold air.

"We must pull down this bit of wall," said Luke, "and the sooner we set about it the better, for I am quite convinced that it will lead us to froodom by some route that will not be suspected. Come, Claude, you have a pistol with a spring bayonet to it, and that will work capitally. For myself, I will be content with my knife."

CHAPTER CLXV.

ANNIE FORSYTH GOES IN PEACE TO THE MOTHER OF HER LOVER.

THIS was one of those ideas and suggestions that bring conviction with them in a moment, and Claude commenced at once to act upon it. Luke placed the light upon the corner of a coffin, where it gave a very tolerable reflection over the whole vault, and then they both began to work upon the wall.

It did not take many moments to convince them that they would find no difficulty in getting a portion of it down. The bricks were but badly cemented together, or else the damp air of that region had had the effect of preventing the mortar from more thoroughly hardening.

Harry Lucas searched through the vault with the hope of finding something by the aid of which he could help his friends, but he was disappointed, and Claude, who guessed his intention, said—

"Come, Master Lucas, you can do quite as much good, if not more, by moving with your hands the bricks as we loosen them, than you could do if you were working away at the wall yourself."

"Can I, indeed ?"

"To be sure, so set about it at once."

Harry Lucas did set about it, with a good will, so that the united exertions of the three very soon succeeded in moving a portion of the wall that was quite large enough for a moderate sized person to pass through.

While this was going on, May and Annie were conversing together, and vow-ing to each other an eternal friendship, and Annie was bitterly lamenting the course of life that Claude Duval pursued.

The reader is well aware that she could not possibly lament that course of life more than May herself did, and the tears coursed down the cheeks of the latter as Annie hinted at what might be the dreadful termination of such a career as Claude Duval's.

"I know it all," she said. "I dream of it, and awaken to shudder at the awful visions of the night. Alas! alas! I am very wretched."

"Ah, now," said Annie, "I regret that I touched upon such a theme, since it is one upon which you feel so deeply."

"Could I feel otherwise than deeply?"

"But there are those who would not so feel. Pardon me, though, for making such a subject one of discussion between us."

"There needs no pardon. It is so natural a thought that those who feel kindly disposed towards me or him, cannot but speak of it."

"Now we shall get out of the vault," cried Lucas. "What is it that engages your joint attentions so deeply?"

"Nothing—nothing," said Annie.

"Are you successful?" said May.

"Yes—behold. There is a passage beyond this vault."

"And it leads to freedom," said Duvel, "for I can quite plainly feel the fresh air coming upon my face, and in that case we shall soon be out of this gloomy region entirely. Come on."

Claude took charge of May, and Lucas of Annie, while Luke carried the light, and so they all got through the opening in the wall that led from the vault of the Fritles.

The passage into which they emerged from the vault was very narrow, and they had not proceeded half-a-dozen paces along it, when a current of cold air blew out the light.

"Hilloa!" said Luke, "how is this? I can feel the open air raising the very hair upon my head. Where are we?"

"Behold!" said Claude. "There is the solution of the mystery. There is a grating over our heads."

When he pointed it out they all saw it, and by looking up, they could see the night sky and that the stars were shining. There could be no longer no w any doubt or perplexity about the mode in which the vault was constructed. The fact was, that there existed an entrance to it from a corner of the church-yard, and by the grating beneath which the adventurers now were.

Thus, then, was it that fastenings had been put in so apparently inscrutable a manner upon the inner side, as it seemed, of the door of the vault, for, no doubt, at one time the wall which our friends got through had been the mode by which the departed families had visited their last resting-place on earth.

The grating was not above four feet above their heads, so that Claude Duval could very easily reach it, and by the aid of Luke he did so, and one vigorous push opened it; for although it had a lock, rust and the effects of time had so eaten into it, that it could not withstand anything like violence.

"We are saved," said Claude. "I will get up, and then help you all out. That will do. Thank you, Luke."

By the aid of Luke, Claude drew himself through the opening, and in another moment stood in the old church-yard.

What a feeling of exquisite relief it was now to find that he was in the pure open air again. The wind was roaring monotonously amid the branches of the old yew-trees that were in the burial-ground, but the sky was clear, and millions of bright stars were peeping out from the blue vault of Heaven.

"This is truly beautiful," said Claude.

As he spoke, he heard a tramping sound outside the wall of the burial-ground. The wall was not above five feet high, so that there was no difficulty in his seeing over it. He shrunk down partially behind a grave-stone, and then he saw the whole troop of lancers ride past within six feet of him, and take the London road.

It was quite evident from that circumstance that the hunt for the fugitives was given up as unsuccessful, or the officers of police would never have been satisfied to let the soldiers go.

CLAUDE HAS A VISITOR TO HIS CELL IN NEWGATE.

It took some three or four minutes for them to pass, and not one cast a look into the old church-yard. No doubt, both officers and men were glad to be released from a duty which never comes with a pleasant idea to the military.

"Gone," said Claude, as he made his way back to the grating; and then, stooping over it, he added, "Did you all think I had forgotten you?"

"No, Claude," said Luke. "We heard the sound of horses' feet."

"Yes, it was that sound that detained me. The cavalry have all gone on, and we have nothing but the police to cope with, if, indeed, they now remain, which is doubtful."

"Then, we are saved, indeed."

"I hope so. May, where are you?"

"Here, Claude. Here."

May held up her arms to him, and Claude had no difficulty in drawing her up through the grating. He then did the same to Annie; and when they were both safe and seated upon an old tomb, he assisted Lucas and Luke to emerge from the region of the vaults, and then closed the grating, saying as he did so—

"Rest in peace, mouldering remains of the Fritles. It has not been with any wish to disturb you that we have this night trespassed upon your last resting-place; and can only hope never to have the necessity of cultivating your acquaintance again."

A feeling of joy came over them all, now that they stood in the open air. There is a something so delightful in the consciousness that there is nothing above us but the blue vault of Heaven, after going through some dreary and cavernous recess, that of itself becomes luxurious; and, although in reality no great change had taken place in his, Claude's, position or prospects, he felt as though such had been the case, so light of heart was he.

May clung to him, and, as well as the darkness would permit, looked tenderly up into his face; and Annie, as she was clasped to the heart of her lover, seemed to feel that all her trials were over, and that there was nothing now to come but a long sunny period of pure happiness.

"Well," said Luke, "I am glad to see you all so comfortable."

"My dear Luke," said Claude, with a smile, "you must fall in love and marry."

"Not I, Duval. I don't mean my words as any reproach to you, because if such another loving heart as you can call your own were to be offered to me, I should be only too happy to accept of it; but I don't think our life is exactly the sort of one to bring a young and tender girl to share."

Claude made no reply to this. Perhaps, notwithstanding the highly complimentary kind of accompaniment that Luke had given to the remark, it touched him a little too narrowly.

Harry Lucás advanced to Claude.

"What shall I say in the way of fervent thanks to you all," he said, and his voice shook as he spoke. "How is it possible that I shall ever be able to assure you of the deep sense of gratitude that pervades my heart?"

"And mine likewise?" said Annie.

"By your silence," said Claude. "Believe me, it is so sincere a pleasure to me that I am at times able to do such little kindnesses as I have done to you, that the joy of heart it brings me amply repays me for all trouble, toil, or danger in the process; and, besides, I fancy such actions to be some sort of set-off against the rather questionable mode of my life. But, now let us quit such a subject, and let me advise you, Lucas, to proceed to your mother's house as quickly as possible."

"I will, I will. There you will remain, my Annie, in safety and in honour beneath her roof."

"I know I shall, Harry."

"And it is better, too," added Claude, "that we should part as soon as possible, for your further association with us can do you no good. We will but see you a little on your way, and then you can forget that you ever encountered Claude Duval, upon whose head a price is set."

"Forget you?" said Annie. "Oh, never."

"Can you think so meanly of us?" said Harry Lucas.

"Enough! enough!" said Claude, with emotion. "Let us get on now. Oh, my friends, you do not know what sensations of bitterness and regret you awaken in my heart when I see that you are happy and virtuous, and at peace with that society which must ever regard me as an enemy."

May was sobbing while this little dialogue was proceeding, for it deeply affected her, inasmuch as it bore so directly upon that subject which was ever dear and present to her heart, namely, the possibility of Duval leaving his pursuits, and taking up some honest calling.

Fain would she have now put in a word or two to strengthen the feeling that she knew was at his heart, but she feared to procrastinate the time at such a moment, and, besides, she could tell by the tone of his voice that he felt keenly what had been said already, and she hardly knew how far he might be inclined to listen to more upon the subject.

"Come," said Claude, suddenly. "This is the way."

With these words, he walked so rapidly towards the gate of the little church-yard, that further conversation with him was then out of the question, unless it had been forced upon him in a voice that would not have been just or fair to him, seeing that he evidently wished to avoid it.

The little party followed him in silence, but the thoughts of all were engaged on the possible means of rescuing Duval from the consequences of a course of life which sooner or later was sure to be fatal to him.

CHAPTER CLXVI.

CLAUDE IS DEAF TO REMONSTRANCES, AND TAKES TO THE ROAD AGAIN.

THE route which Harry Lucas wished to take with Annie led past the house of old Hunkers, and they naturally enough rather hesitated about going that way.

"Never fear," said Claude. "I'll warrant he is still in the chimney."

"The chimney!" repeated Annie, with surprise.

"Yes, my dear," said Lucas. "We thought that such would be the most appropriate place for old Hunkers to pass his wedding night in." Harry then gave her a brief history of all that had taken place at old Hunkers's house, at which she could not help laughing, although she thought, she said, that they had been a little too severe upon the old man.

"Are you not going to let him down from his uncomfortable place of punishment?" she said.

"Not I."

"Nor I," said Claude: "if he should remain there till doomsday it will not matter to me. A more thoroughly selfish old rascal I think I never came across. But I wonder where our friends, the officers, are?"

"Don't speak of them," said May. "They may make an appearance when we least want them. Let us get out of the town as quickly as we can. I shall have a lively recollection of Guildford as long as I live."

"I shall always love the old town for Annie's sake," said Lucas. "It will, in my mind, ever be associated with her, and, therefore, it will have a claim upon me which it otherwise would want, no doubt."

"You are right," said May, "and I give you great credit for speaking so freely the true sentiments of your heart. You will be very happy, Annie Forsyth, as you deserve to be."

"I thank you," said Annie; "but——"

"Stop, all of you," said Claude. "Step into this gateway, and stoop low. There are some men coming. Do you not hear them?"

"Yes—yes."

"Then it will be just as well to escape a collision if they are foes, and the reverse observation if they are indifferent to us. They might recognise you, Annie."

"They might, indeed."

"And me, likewise," said Harry Lucas, "for I am pretty well known in Guildford; and now that I have not got any disguise upon me, there are few persons who would not be able to name me in the town."

"Capital reasons for caution," added Claude. "Let us keep out of the way."

The gateway which Duval had alluded to, seemed to lead into the yard of a builder; but it afforded them a good shelter, and they waited till the danger was past, for it was a danger.

About six or eight men, in a disorderly kind of throng, came on, and as they neared the spot, it was quite easy to hear what they were saying. A very few words of their conversation was sufficient to announce that it related to the fugitives, and before they had quite passed, Claude felt quite clear that they were the officers.

"I tell you," said one, "it's of no use now staying another moment in Guildford. He is off, and if once he has got fairly mounted and out of the town, he is out of our clutches by this time."

"Ah, and twenty miles off," said another, "though I don't know how the deuce we came to miss him. He was in the church."

"Oh, it's the unwillingness and carelessness of the soldiers. They pretended to have surrounded the church by sentinels, and we know that Duval was inside, and yet, lo and behold, off he goes! What are we to think of that, but just that the sentinels outside were too lazy to stop him, and that he and his friends with him got comfortably enough out at one of the old windows, and walked off without any difficulty."

"That's about it—that's about it."

"And then, you know, there's another thing——"

Here the distance that the officers had got past the builder's yard, where our friends were concealed, smothered their voices, and what the other thing was that one of the police was going to call attention to, was completely lost to them.

"A close touch that," said Luke.

"Very; but then, you know, Luke, a miss in these matters is as good as a mile; and as they have passed us, it is all the same to us as though they were at Jericho."

"So it is, Claude."

They thought it prudent, however, to wait a little time in the builder's yard, so that the officers should get some distance from the spot before they emerged on to the road again. At length Duval intimated that he thought they might venture with safety, and, accordingly, they sallied out.

Their route to where their horses had been left, took them exactly past old Hunkers's house, and they were not a little curious to discover whether or not he had had the courage to release himself from his rather painful situation in the chimney. Claude Duval could hardly think it possible, upon calm and cool reflection, that old Hunkers would remain in such a situation; but Luke would have it that there he was still, and argued that he was quite incapable of a sufficient amount of calm and cool reflection to enable him to leave the place.

"Well, we shall soon see," said Lucas.

In the course of the next three minute they were opposite Hunkers's house, and they paused on the opposite side of the road, which was flanked by a thick-set hedge.

A strange noise from the top of the house came upon their ears, and after looking up for a few moments, Claude said—

"Do you see anything particular about that stack of chimneys, Luke?"

"Yes, I do. I am tolerably long-sighted, and one of the particular things that I see is a dark object clinging to one of the chimney pots."

"Then that dark object must be our old and rather dark friend, Hunkers, I should say?"

"Not a doubt of it."

The odd lugubrious noise from the dark object on the house-top continued, and it was quite evident that old Hunkers was mingling his groans with the night wind, but had not the courage to call out loudly and energetically for help, lest the threat that Claude had held out to him of some one being on the watch to shoot him should turn out to be true.

"Surely," said Annie, "he is sufficiently punished now?"

"Do you think so?" said Lucas. "The old rascal, I should never think he was sufficiently punished for the suffering he made you endure."

"But the result of all that is, that I am yours, and so, you see, Lucas, how out of evil springeth good."

"Yes, I see that; and if I thought that old Hunkers repented of his rascalities, which I am tolerably sure he does not, I, too, could pity him."

"Let him down, Claude," said May, "oh, do let him down."

"You forget," said Duval, "that I can have but very little control over a man who is on the top of a house."

"But you can call to him that his charge is past."

"Yes," said Luke, "and alarm the neighbourhood."

"It must not be done," said Claude. "It does not now want but half an hour, if so much, to daylight, and when that comes, Hunkers will see that there is no one in his way, and that he can descend in safety. Come on!"

There was no resisting the reasoning of Claude in this affair, as it would have been quite absurd for them to endanger their own safety for the sake of sparing old Hunkers half an hour's uneasiness on the top of his house.

"Besides," Luke said, "it is a fine airy situation, and will do him good, no doubt; and if the wind should get up a little at sunrise, as it most possibly will, the soot will be blown off him, and he will come down quite cleansed from the impurities of the chimney."

They passed Hunkers's house, and made the best of their way now to the little, quiet inn, where they had left their horses. Everybody was in bed and asleep in that little hostel, but Claude Duval rang the ostler's bell several times loudly, and then a night-capped head popped out at one of the windows, and the voice belonging to the head called out—

"Hilloa! What's the matter? Is Guildford on fire?"

"No," said Claude. "I am sorry to disturb the house, but we want our horses that we left here early in the evening."

"Oh, it's all right—all right. Jem is getting up, I can hear him swearing, so he will soon attend to you."

"Thank you!"

"Good-night, or rather, good-morning, and a pleasant ride to you, gentlemen."

The landlord then popped in his head from the casement and closed it again, and in the course of a few minutes the ostler appeared, and let them into the stable-yard. He did not seem very well pleased at being disturbed, though, at such an hour.

"My friend," said Claude, "when I give any one extra trouble I give them extra pay, so take that guinea, and get us out our cattle as quickly as you can."

"Lor, sir! don't mention the trouble. I don't mind what I do for a real guinea—I mean a real gentleman, your honour. I'll get up any hour of the night to serve you, sir."

The ostler, who had really seemed to be half asleep before, now became so wide awake and active that it was quite wonderful to see him, and in a considerably short space of time the horses were at the door of the inn.

"Good-morning," said Claude, as they went off at a gentle trot, just to warm the blood of the animals before they resumed their pace.

"Now, Lucas," said Claude, "which is your route?"

"Straight on for half a mile or so, and then down the road to the right, which will take us to my mother's farm."

"Very well. Then we will bid you good-by at the corner of the road you speak of, and till then we can easily accommodate the pace of our cattle to your own, unless you don't mind Annie riding behind me for a little way, while I give May into your charge."

"If it will not be a trouble to you, I shall thank you."

"All's right. It's no trouble."

The arrangement did very well. Annie sat very comfortably behind Claude Duval, and held him firmly, while Lucas rode upon May's horse, and she sat behind him, and then they set off at a good canter, which was the easiest pace they could put the doubly-weighted horses to, although the addition of such light weights as Annie and May, to tell the truth, was not much.

The road which Harry Lucas was to take was soon gained, but Claude would not leave them there, but cantered down it until they came to a stile which would lead them across a couple of meadows to Mrs. Lucas's farm, and then he paused.

"Now, indeed, we part," said Claude, "and all I have to do is to bid you good morning, and to wish you all manner of happiness."

"That happiness," said Harry Lucas, as he wrung the hand of Claude in both of his own, "is entirely of your own making, and your name will be always remembered by us both with affection."

"It will, indeed," said Annie, who could not control her tears.

"Enough," said Claude. "Do not let us part with even the look of sorrow upon our faces. Farewell!"

May and Annie embraced each other tenderly, and then they parted. Claude put his horse to a gallop, and the others followed him, till turning round to Luke, he cried—

"Here we are on the road again. I will stop the first man I meet, for a highwayman I am and a highwayman I shall ever be."

CHAPTER CLXVII.

DUVAL DETERMINES TO PAY A SHORT VISIT TO PARIS.

THERE seemed to be a sort of desperation about the feelings and the manner of Claude Duval at this time which it would be difficult to account for. It is just possible that it was owing to the fact that he could not help observing the look of anguish that was upon the face of May at times.

Since she had commenced now saying much to him about the sort of life he led, she had evidently suffered much in silent reflection ; and he felt that the constant dread of something fatal occurring to him was the bane of her young existence. This was a feeling that in its turn had a depressing effect upon him, Claude, and it was under the impulse of it that he had just spoken.

May made no reply to him, but Luke glanced at him, as he said—

"Would it not be well first to find a home for——"

The significant inclination of Luke's head to May, filled up the sentence, and before Duval could reply, May spoke—

"No, Luke, oh, no! But when I say no, believe me that I appreciate your motives, and thank you for your good kindness to me. But it may not be : I have made up my mind now, that where he goes there will I go. His dangers shall be my dangers."

Luke merely slightly inclined his head, and then Duval, as he looked at May, said—

"And can you bring me into so much peril ?"

"I bring you into peril ?"

"Yes. Do you think that while you are with me I could attend to anything in all the world but to you? In seeing that you were not hurt, and in protecting you as far as possible from the likelihood of injury, I should come to destruction myself. Who is there in all the world that I have to love or to think of but you?"

"Claude," said May, and her voice shook as she spoke, "your last words put me in mind of a question that I have often thought to ask you. Have you no relations in the world?"

"Yes, May, I have; but do you think they would be glad to claim any connection or companionship with such as I am? No; they forget me and I forget them. And yet, there is one whom I should like to see. My father had a sister who was kind to me in my childhood: I know not where she is, but I should like to see her and shake her by the hand once again. That is a feeling I have often had."

"And where is she, Claude?"

"That I know not, or before this I should have made some attempt to see her. I don't mean to say, though, that I have been very active in trying to find her out, feeling that my acquaintance is not a good credit to any one."

"Hush!" said Luke. "A horseman comes."

"Get aside, then," said Claude, "for he belongs to me."

"Oh, Claude—Claude, you will not——"

"Will not what?"

"Stop this traveller who is approaching?"

"It is my business so to do, May. Luke, I entrust her to your care: but I am Claude Duval the highwayman, and, therefore, I must perform my mission. You had better ride on, you two, and then it will not be supposed that you are in any way connected with me."

The manner of Claude Duval was quite sufficient to let May see that any remonstrance with him would be quite fruitless; and, indeed, if she had talked for a month, what could she say but that he was a highwayman, and that she wished he was something else? She and Luke then trotted on, and Claude, turning his horse's head in the direction from whence the traveller was coming, met him at a walk.

The person whose destiny it was to be stopped upon that eventful occasion, was a big, burly-looking man, on a powerful black horse, and, indeed, take him altogether, he was a sort of person to look at that few persons would have felt inclined to stop on the highway alone.

"Stand!" cried Claude; "your money and your valuables, sir—if you please."

The man pulled up and looked amazed for a moment or two, and then he said—

"Why, you impudent rascal, do you think I am going to let myself be robbed on the highway by one man?"

"Yes."

"Well, then, you are mistaken. I am armed."

"So am I. What are your arms?"

"Fire-arms."

"Then, in the name of all that is abominable, why don't you produce them, and have it out? If you will have bloodshed over the fate of a few paltry guineas, begin it, and get it over as quickly as you can."

With these words, Claude produced a bright-barrelled pistol that had rather a serious look about it of mischief, and held it to the head of the horseman, who now turned rather pale, and in a much lower tone said—

"Well, you are right; I don't want to take the life of a fellow creature for the sake of a little money. There is my purse."

"How much is there?"

"About ten pounds."

"Go on, then. I believe you have more about you, but I never do things in such a shabby way as to search a gentleman. Go on, and think yourself well off that you listened to me in time.   What good on earth would it have done you to have had your brains blown out, and then your money taken from, your quivering corpse, eh ?"

"Oh, none—none," said the stranger, giving a shudder at the very idea. "None at all.   Have you any objection to tell me who you are ?"

Claude laughed. "They call me the Ladies' Highwayman," he said.

"Then, by Jove, you are Claude Duval ?"

"The same, sir, quite at your service whenever you bring another purse on the road."

The stranger did not wait to hear any more, but galloped off as hard as he could.   As he passed Luke and May he called out to them—

"I say, look after your pockets.   Claude Duval, the highwayman, is on the road.   You had better look sharp, or he will be down upon you before you know where you are."

"Thank you," said Luke.

The man then rode on, and May, who was very pale, turned her horse's head in the direction where Duval was now, and was about to ride towards him, when they heard the sound of wheels, and a gig, in which were two gentlemen, drew up.   This gig must have passed the flying horseman who had been robbed by Claude Duval, and that he had warned them.   This was evident by one of its occupants saying—

"Have you seen anything of a highwayman upon the road ?"

"No," said Luke.

"Well, there's a man on horseback just passed us who called out to us to look out for Claude Duval."

"It's not likely," said Luke; "but if you do meet him, the best way is to give in quiet, for he is a desperate fellow."

"Catch us at it ! We are going out shooting, and have plenty of arms with us. Are you riding our way ?"

"No, gentlemen.   I wish we were, because, of course, in union there is strength.   We are going in this direction.   Good-bye."

"They will kill him," said May, with a look of embarrassment at Luke.

"Not a bit of it.   He will stop them both.   They are as frightened as they can be.   Did you not see that by their looks, and did you not notice it in their wish that we should be going their way ?   You may depend when two men wish for further aid against a single highwayman, that there will be no great danger to apprehend from them."

"But this is terrible.   If he goes on stopping every one on the road that he meets, the result must be certain destruction at last."

"Oh, no—no.   Not at all.   Pray be composed.   We shall have him galloping after us all right in a little while."

The two men in the gig now drove on very carefully, and with rather scared looks.   They had a couple of guns slung in front of the vehicle, and in the lower part of it there was a kind of box for the reception of a pointer, who was snugly reposing upon some straw.

Duval saw them coming, and suddenly emerged from a lane that was by the side of the road, and which had rather hidden him.

"By Jove, there he is," said one of the shooting gentlemen.

"Oh, no," said the other, "that's no highwayman."

"Don't you think so ?   Oh, Lord, it's him.   Get out the guns."

"Yes, oh dear, yes.   You shoot him."

"Not for the world.   I wouldn't have his death at my door, poor devil.   Let's pity him, and give him a few pounds, and tell him to repent."

"But he won't, I'm afraid."

"Won't what ?"

"Repent, or take the few pounds, either.   Here's the gun.   You hold the barrel of it towards him, and I'll pull the trigger—Now for it.   Here he comes. Oh, Lord, if it should miss him !—Now—Are you ready ?"

"Yes."

Bang!

"Where is he?"

"All right, gentlemen," said Duval; "try the other barrel. It's my turn, though, now."

CLAUDE BECOMES THE PROTECTOR OF ANNIE FORSYTH FROM OLD HUNKERS.

Slap went one of Duval's pistols, but he purposely fired over their heads. Crack went another, a little nearer, and then the two sportsmen fell flat, one upon another, to the bottom of the gig, as though they had been both shot dead at once, and Claude rode up.

Now, May had heard the shots fired, and in spite of all that Luke could do to persuade her of the impolicy of the step, she rode back, calling out as she did so——

"Claude! Claude! Oh speak to me if you live! Claude—Claude!"

"All is right," said Duval. "Away with you. There is no harm done, and the battle is fought and won. For Heaven's sake away with you at once, for some one may come up."

Luke quite understood that what Claude intended was, that whatever happened upon the road he and May should not in any way seem to be connected with it, so he took the bridle of May's horse and turned it again, and went off in the direction from whence they had come.

"Now, gentlemen," said Claude, "my time is valuable if yours is not ; and you will be so good as to hand me your money as quickly as you can."

"I'm a dead man," said one.

"Heaven have mercy upon my sinful soul," said the other.

"Get up, will you ?" cried Duval, "or I shall be forced to make you."

"We are no more among the living," said the first one who had spoken. "We are now as those who have been."

"Yes," said the other ; "but who are not any more."

Duval saw that their fright was such that nothing but force would have any effect upon them ; so he stooped from his horse and seizing one of them by the collar he made him sit up, and then holding a pistol just to the lid of his eye, he said—

"Your money !"

"Money ! Cash do you mean ?"

"Yes."

"Oh, Lord, here it is! Take it all. There it is. It's all, but a few shillings, in that pocket-book in notes."

A glance at the pocket-book assured Claude that there were notes in it, and that satisfied him ; so he put it into his pocket at once, and letting that one go, he dragged up the other, and went through the same process with him ; but he was gone too far in fright to know what was wanted of him, yet he took his purse from his pocket, and deliberately handed it to Claude, saying as he did so—

"I beg to assure you, Mr. Highwayman, that he has no more money with him now ; you have it all."

"Very well, I will take your word for that ; and now drive on. I would advise you both to be very careful, though, how you proceed ; and if you meet any one upon the road who stops you, your answer will be 'Twenty-two.'"

"Twenty-two ?"

"That is a watchword, or signal, that will protect you, for I have quite taken possession of this road, and some of my men are in all sorts of disguises, so if you meet any of them, and, fancying they are strangers to me, say anything about being robbed, some hasty and heedless one may shoot you."

"Oh, dear—oh, dear! And ain't we shot, sir ?"

"You ought to know that. I fired twice at you, and purposely missed you. If I had fired again, your brains would have been scattered over this road. Farewell !"

Claude turned from the gig, but he had scarcely done so, when he heard quite a rush of wheels, and a cry of—"Clear the way! Hoi!—hoi!" and he saw a postchaise, with four horses, coming along at a dashing pace. He had just time to get to the side of the road as it whirled past, but one of the wheels caught the gig, and upset it and its occupants into a ditch in a moment.

This occurrence caused a slight detention of the postchaise, and a man looked out at the window next to Duval, with a pistol in his hand, and in a voice of passion, cried—

"What the devil is that ?"

Claude laughed, to which the passionate man replied, by at once discharging the pistol at his head, saying as he did so—

"Take that to stop your grinning. Drive on, postilion—drive on !"

The bullet passed so close to Claude's face, that for the moment he thought he was hit, and so staggered was he at this piece of brutal and reckless mischief, that the postchaise had got into motion before he could make up his mind what to do. He drew a pistol from his saddle, then, in a moment, and took aim, but a footman who was in the rumble behind, as he saw the movement, ducked his head, as he cried out—

"Oh, don't—don't fire. Mind the girl—you may hit the young girl."

These words caused Claude to pause, and he held the pistol in his hand while he advanced at a gallop after the coach, crying out as he did so—

"What girl?—What girl do you mean? I'll fire if you don't tell me."

The affrighted footman looked around, and pointed to the interior of the carriage, to signify that there was a girl there, and then, out came the head of the furious and irascible man again, with a roar of rage, as he shouted at Duval—

"What, ain't you dead? I thought I had shot you—you vagabond."

"Stop !" cried Claude. "Stop, I say."

The face had popped in again, but it was only for a moment, and then out it popped again, accompanied by a hand and a pistol. Claude was waiting for this, and he fired at the head directly, which disappeared the moment the report of his, Claude's pistol, was heard; and the footman in the rumble was so alarmed, that he scrambled up to the top of the coach, and from thence fell into the road.

Claude was going at speed, but the sudden appearance of the footman in the road bewildered and frightened the horse, which shied and stumbled, so that Claude was nearly unmounted, and as it was, he thought that if he secured the footman it would be the best thing he could do, as it would assure him who the carriage belonged to and who the bully that had fired at him was, as then he, Claude, could find him out.

May and Luke now came up, and Claude, while he soothed his horse, called out to Luke—

"Seize that man, Luke: don't let him go on any account. I shall have something to say to him."

"All 's right," said Luke. " I have him."

CHAPTER CLXVIII.

CLAUDE'S ADVENTURES ARE TENDING TO THE CONTINENT.

DUVAL'S horse was so disturbed by the firing and by the unexpected appearance of the footman in the middle of the road, that it was with the greatest difficulty his rider could pacify him. He who is well acquainted with the habits of the horse knows well how difficult it is to restore the eqanimity of that animal when once it has been disturbed. Still, if that was to be done at all, Claude Duval undoubtedly knew the way. By kindness he did more in three minutes than is attempted to be done frequently by some brutes in human shape by blows in an hour.

When the footman found himself in the custody of Luke, he gave up his life for lost, and getting upon his knees, he howled in such an awful manner that Luke was compelled to threaten him dreadfully before he would be quiet and attend to what Duval wanted to say to him.

"Oh, yes," he exclaimed at length. "Oh dear, yes, I will answer anything you like, indeed I will, if you will only spare my life. Oh dear, what good would it do you to kill a poor fellow like me? I assure you it would do you no good at all."

"Silence !" said Claude; "you are going the very way to make us think of knocking you on the head for the purpose of stopping that abominable clattering of yours. Silence, until you hear what I have to ask of you, and then make your replies short and distinct."

"Oh dear, yes, I will. I am a poor——"

Luke gave him an admonishing knock on the top of his head with the but-end of a holster pistol, and while he was rubbing the lump that was produced, Claude spoke to him—

"Whose carriage was that?"

"Major Brook's, gentlemen, and he——"

"Silence! What young lady was it you mentioned?"

"Why I'll tell you all, upon my life. We have been looking after her for a long time; but at last the major has got her, you see. He had been on the watch; and having the carriage all ready, she was caught up and popped into it before she knew where she was, and there she is, with a silk pocket handkerchief over her mouth so that she should not speak. Oh, gentlemen, I did take part in the affair, but I am as sorry as possible; and when I saw her pretty face, all tears and with such a look of despair upon it that it seemed as if her heart was broken, I felt that I could have throttled the major, only I wasn't strong enough."

"Who is she?"

"Why her name is Thornton, sir."

"Thornton?" said Claude. "Where does she live? Tell me that at once. Where did she come from?"

"Finchley, sir; but I don't know the exact house. They say, that is, the major's valet says—and he carried on all the affair—that she lived with her mother, a widow, and he says she is just sixteen years of age."

"But—but——"

Claude paused. "What am I to think," he then added, and for a moment or two he looked to the ground and seemed absorbed in reflection. Then looking up, he added—

"Where is this Major Brook going with the girl?"

"To Dover, sir. I don't mind telling all, for I shall not go back to his service again. Intrigues and vice among those who don't mind it, is one thing, but to lay hold of an innocent young girl, almost a child, is what I don't like, so I won't have anything more to do with it, no-how."

"I thank you for your information," said Claude Duval. "If you have anything else to tell, tell it now."

"Nothing, sir. But here's the letter that made the young girl meet the major on the high road, you see. I picked it up as it fell from her bosom in the struggle to put her into the coach, and I made up my mind that I would find out the person whose name is to it, and ask him if he wrote it; and if he didn't, ask him if he had a human heart in his bosom, and was going to put up with it."

Claude took the letter.

"This may enlighten me," he said; and he opened it, and cast his eyes over it. As he did so, he turned very white with passion; but he folded up the letter again and put it carefully in his pocket, and handing the footman a few guineas, he said—

"My good fellow, I thank you. Take this as an earnest of my good feeling towards you. Farewell."

"You didn't happen to want a fellow as footman?"

"No no, I can't take you. I am much beholden to you, my good man, and wish I could do you any service."

"Thank you, sir. I feel all the happier now that I have told some one of the wickedness of the major; but, oh, sir, don't let him injure her. If you had only seen that young creature's face as I saw it, you would feel all the blood in your body boiling."

"Silence!" cried Claude, in a voice that made them all start again. "Silence,

I say. My blood does boil, and by heaven I do feel it. Let him injure her? No, by all that is sacred I will not. Come on, Luke. May, come follow me."

Claude Duval put his horse to speed, and set off at a pace that it was rather difficult to follow, so that May had to call to him, and then he drew up, and when she reached his side he said—

"Finchley—Finchley! The nearest way to Finchley is what I want. Do you know it, May, or you, Luke?

"I do" said Luke, "and can show you."

"That is well; let us ride hard."

"Oh, Cluade! Claude!" cried May, laying her hand upon his arm, "what is the true meaning of all this? You terrify me. There is more in the affair than meets the eye, I feel assured. Oh, tell me what it is and what it all means before you go further. You know well that I am with you heart and soul, and that I will aid you in every possible way in what is right. All I ask of you is, that you should trust me."

"I will—I will. Luke, don't go away. I want you to know what I am about to explain."

Luke would have left May and Claude Duval to themselves, but now he rode up to them, and listened with interest to what Claude was going to say.

"Listen to me both of you," he said. "I feel that there are such things as foretokens in this world. You both heard me, and recollect, I daresay, that not an hour ago I was talking of my aunt?"

"Yes," said May.

"Well, her name is Thornton."

"Ah, now I see."

"Yes, you see some of it, but not all. I have reason to believe that this young girl who is in the coach is Lucy Thornton, my cousin, the youngest and the fairest of my aunt's family. I say, I believe that she is that person; and with that conviction, I will not rest till I have rescued her from the villain who has taken her from her home. My design is to go to Finchley first, and see my aunt, and then to start for Dover. What say you, May? Will you go with me?"

"With all my heart."

"And you, Luke?"

"To the end of the world, if you like."

"Be it so then. This young creature must and shall be rescued."

"But, Claude," said May, "are you quite sure that a similiarity of names merely does not lead you to this belief? Only think if that should not be your cousin Lucy—if the tale you have heard from the footman should not be true. I do not say that it is false; but you know, Claude, that there is room for doubt."

"No, there is none."

Claude Duval, as he said this, took from his breast-pocket the letter that the footman had given him as that which had been the inducement to the young girl to come alone and unprotected to the place where she was kidnapped.

"Read that," he said, "and read it aloud, so that Luke may hear it at the same time, and when you have done so, I think you will see that there is no room to doubt the fact of the young girl being my cousin, nor to doubt for one moment of the good faith and truthfulness of him who gave me the letter, and who sympathised with her."

May took the letter, and read from it as follows :—

"MY COUSIN LUCY,—You are but a young girl, but Heaven has by a strange chance given to you the power to serve me. It is true that since we were children you and I have never met; but yet you may remember your young playmate, who, by being some seven years or so older than yourself, was the partaker of your sports.

"Dear cousin Lucy, you know the life that I have led; report has come to your ears full of my deeds; but now I yearn towards a better life, and I will, if you will see me, explain to you how it is that you can aid me. If you will be at the place mentioned in the enclosed slip of paper, which you should take with you as your guide, as a rough place is close upon it, at the time there mentioned, I will meet you ; but if you tell anyone of this, all is lost.

" Oh, Lucy, will you come and save me from death and despair ?

" This is from your old playmate and loving cousin,

"CLAUDE DUVAL."

" Claude Duval ?" cried May.

" Claude Duval ?" cried Luke.

"Yes, you see that this letter purports to have come from me.   By some means or another, those who would betray the girl found out her relationship to me, and have practised upon her gentle, loving nature in my name to deceive her; but, oh, they shall rue the day they thought of such a plan."

" Alas !" said May, " I do now, indeed, see it all, and I admit that there is no room for doubt."

" It is most villanous," said Luke.

"And it shall be avenged," said Claude.   "No doubt this letter had all its effects upon her, and in her goodness she thought that she might have some power to do me good, and so she fell into the snare that was laid for her own destruction.   Poor—poor Lucy! I remember you well, a little smiling, blue-eyed child.   But this will drive me mad! I must be doing something. Let us be off now at once.   Oh, what fiend in human shape could have written that letter?"

" It is a woman's hand," said May.

" Is it so ?"

" Yes, and thus is it always that woman is the enemy and the arch-foe of woman. I do believe that never yet was there a deep plotting scheme contrived against a young girl, but a woman was at the bottom of it.   Be patient and considerate, Claude ; Luke and I will be with you heart and soul in this affair, and all may yet be well.'

" You have ample means, I hope ?" said Luke.

"Ah, I will see to that. What is in this pocket pook, Luke ?   Examine it for me."

Luke did so, and then said—

"Six hundred pounds in notes, Claude.   The Jews will give three hundred pounds for them upon the chance that the numbers may not all be known to the police within the next day or two,"

" That will do. I have gold beside.   Now I tell you that my idea is ; this Major Brown will take the girl to the continent.   It looks like it by his posting to Dover in such haste.   Have you any objection to following him abroad ?"

"None in the least," said both May and Luke—indeed tears of gratification rushed to the eyes of May, at the idea that by going out of England Claude would at all events be safe, and that it was possible she might prevail upon him to remain in some other country and live a different life from any that he had yet done in England.   It appeared to her as if out of the incident of that day there might arise abundance of good.

" Well, then," added Claude. " I feel that now I have got something to do. The first thing is to go to my aunt and satisfy her that not only I have no hand in this villanous affair, but that I will put it right if it be in the power of mortal man to do so, and then we will ride at speed to Dover.   If we find that such a person as Major Brown has been there and has crossed the channel, we will cross it after him, and woe be to him when we meet !   I have a little private account of my own, too, to settle with him, for he fired at me."

" Yes, and I think you wounded him," said Luke.

" Think you so ?"

" I do.   There was blood upon the road, and he popped his head in at the carriage window with marvellous quickness "

" I hope I did touch him. If I have, it may save Lucy for a time. There may be something providential even in that."

They now let Luke go first, as he knew the shortest route to Finchley Common, where it appeared, by the footman's statement, that Mrs. Thornton resided, and at the speed they went, they soon left a tract of country behind them, and finally emerged from a by-road on to the common.

The day was now near to its close, and they all three drew up at a little ale-house and inn, called the "Heifer," that was on the road-side. May looked very much fatigued, and as Duval lifted her from her horse, he said—

"You and Luke will stay here, dear May, while I go and look for my aunt. I will not be long."

CHAPTER CLXIX.

THE WIDOW'S HOUSE ON FINCHLEY COMMON.

MAY would fain have persuaded Claude to take some refreshment before he left the little inn, but one glass of wine and a crust of bread, was all he would eat or drink.

There was every accommodation at the little road-side inn, and May was fain to wait until the return of Claude. There was one thing, however, that enabled her to wait with some degree of patience, and that was, that she knew he was not going on any enterprise of danger, but one of mercy.

For a variety of reasons, May was well-pleased at the idea of leaving England. She hoped that Claude Duval would never return to it, but that he might be persuaded upon the continent to turn his abilities, for he unquestionably had abilities, to some better account than robbing on the highway.

The ideas of Claude himself flowed in a very different direction. He had but one thought now, and that was the rescue of his pretty little cousin, Lucy Thornton, from the hands of a villain. He consided that he was bound by every tie to so rescue her, and, moreover, it appeared to him as if by such an act he would seem to be making up to her family in some manner for the disgrace he brought upon them by his proceedings on the road, and which he felt conscious must produce considerable uneasiness among them.

The old common at Finchley, which is now scarcely to be called a common at all, was at the period of the existence of Claude Duval but thinly inhabited. A cottage here and there only appeared peeping up from the thick foliage of its little orchard and garden, while a large estate or two occupied the greater portion of the landscape.

It was with strange sensations that Claude Duval, on foot, for he had left his horse at the inn, approached his aunt's cottage. He had never expected to look any one, bound to him by the tie of relationship, in the face again, except by accident, and now it seemed to him as if the last few years of his life had been completely obliterated, and that he had only passed through some troubled dream.

"What will be the end of this career that I have shaped out for myself?" said Claude, as he came in sight of the cottage belonging to his aunt. "I have shaped it all out but the catastrophe; and that is hidden. Well, it has been half my choice, and half necessity, so I must pursue my destiny."

Before the cottage there were a couple of handsome lime trees, that made a pleasant rumbling in the soft air of the evening, and some hundreds of birds were going to rest in them and the neighbouring trees, and keeping up the chatter incidental to them at such a period. The last rays of the setting sun fell aslant the ruined wall of the old garden, and the place altogether had about it a pretty and gentle air of repose and beauty.

There was a small gate, and beyond it a little gravelled-path, and then an inner gate, at which hung a servant's bell, and through the latticed upper-half of that inner gate, Claude Duval could see the well kept little patch of garden ground, and a little fountain, and a summer-house at the farther end of it.

He rang the bell.

For about five minutes, then, he waited, but no one came near the gate, and Duval began to feel rather anxious about his aunt, and he rang again. Then a woman came and looked at him through the lattice-work of the door.

"What do you want?" she said.

Before Claude answered this woman he took a good look at her, and certainly a more unprepossessing looking personage it would have been impossible to conceive. She was above the ordinary height of women, and of a sharp, dark, frowning aspect. Her dress was what might be called serene, for it was composed of those colours and those fabrics which have a reputation for lasting; and the tone of her voice was anything but pleasant.

"Is this Mrs. Thornton's cottage?" said Claude.

"Well, what if it is?" said the woman.

"I asked a plain question," said Duval, "and I want a plain answer. Who are you that you thus domineer at the gate of a lady's house?"

"Hoity-toity!" cried the tall female, giving her head a toss that one might consider was about enough to jerk it off, "and who are you, I wonder, that comes here with your impudence?"

Claude controlled his rising anger, as he said—

"I want to see Mrs. Thornton."

"Then you can't."

"And why not, madam?"

"Because she is indisposed, and can only see her most intimate friends, so you had better go away at once."

Before Claude could reply to this insolent speech, a man's voice to his surprise called to the woman from the garden—

"Flora, my love, who is that?"

"Oh, I don't know, but he shan't come in; it's some man wanting Mrs. Thornton."

"Oh, well, of course he can't come in. Mrs. Thornton is very unwell, and we are at her urgent request taking care of her, that's all."

The man advanced now, and presented a portly, bloated appearance, and such a villanous expression upon his face, that Claude at once took up a very bad opinion of him. His attire, like his lady's, was serene, and there was a dash of the evangelical in the fold of his cravat, and in the cut of his clothing.

"So," he added, in a pompous way, "any business that you may have with Mrs. Thornton you will be so good as to communicate to me at once, and I will answer it. It is the will of the Lord that I and my wife should take care of her."

"The what?" said Claude.

"The will of the Lord, sir. I am a religious man, and I do the will of the Lord."

"Certainly," said the wife, "and we take care of the afflicted sinners."

"Very good," said Claude, "you forget that all this while you are keeping me outside the gate."

"No," said the woman, "we don't forget at all, and we beg to state that we mean to keep you there."

"Certainly," added the religious man, "as sure as my name is Jilky."

"Oh, that's your name, is it? Well, I have particular business with Mrs. Thornton, and I request you to allow me to speak to her. Go and tell her that a gentleman is here who has particular business with her."

"We decline," said Mr. Jilky, giving his head a slight shake, and looking contemptuously. "We decline, my good sir."

"Go away," said Mrs. Jilky; "it is easy to see that you are one of the ungodly. Go away, sir."

"Oh, very well," said Claude Duval, and then retreating a pace or two he lifted his foot, and made such a dash at the garden gate, that the lock of it flew off and hit Mr. Jilky such a rap on the side of the head, that he tottered and fell into a gooseberry bush, and the door flinging wide open, Claude walked deliberately into the garden.

Mrs. Jilky uttered a scream, but Duval merely said—

"Oh, scream away, ma'am, it don't make the least difference to me, I assure you. You can scream as much as you like."

CLAUDE DUVAL STOPS THE BULLYING FARMER.

"My dear," cried Mr. Jilky. "Oh, murder! I cannot get out of the bush. Yes, I have. Oh, dear—oh, dear! My love, don't scream, it's of no use. The neighbours do not like us, and they will not come. It is our painful lot, through our highly religious feelings, to be doubted and persecuted all over the neighbourhood."

"Hold your tongue! You are a fool, Mr. Jilky. I tell you, you are a fool to go on in that way. Now. sir, who are you?"

"I decline telling you," said Claude.

"Then out you go, sir. I am a weak woman, but I won't have you here. Out you go, sir, at once."

With this the weak woman flew at Claude like a tiger, but he saw her coming, and stooped so as to make a back for her, and over she went with such a certainty, that if they had planned it it could not have been done better.

"Now. madam," said Claude. "try it again."

Mrs. Jilky, however, had had enough of it, and she sat in one of the beds of the garden, looking the picture of discomfited rage. As for Mr. Jilky, he only rubbed his hands together, and said—

"Oh, dear!—Oh, dear!"

"Now I don't know what right either of you have here," said Claude Duval. "If Mrs. Thornton, however, chooses to have you, that is her business and not mine; but you have surely exceeded your position by denying her to any one who may call at the cottage. I told you I had business of importance with her."

"Oh, dear—oh, dear," said Mr. Jilky, again. "What shall we do?"

"Kill him, if you be a man," said Mrs. Jilky.

"Very religious that, madam," said Claude, "but it don't matter a bit: I am quite qualified to take care of myself, I assure you."

With this, Duval, paying no more attention to the highly religious couple than as if they had been a couple of plants in the garden, walked towards the cottage, and as he got to the door of it, he saw a young girl, of about fourteen or fifteen years of age, sitting on the step, crying.

"Who are you, pray?" said Claude.

"Oh. sir, I'm Mrs. Thornton's servant, sir, if you please."

"Well, what's the matter with you? You needn't shrink and tremble in such a way as that. What ails you?"

"Nothing ails me, sir; but—but ——"

"But what?"

"They have been ill-using me, sir. Mrs. Jilky beats me so, that I shall die if I stay here, and I don't like to leave Mrs. Thornton, for she is very good to me, and she is ill now. Oh, sir, what shall I do? Mr. Jilky, too, beats me, and they want to kill me between them, I do think."

Claude felt the flush of anger rising to his cheek, and then he said in a low tone, for he had a difficulty in controlling himself—

"Tell me, girl, who are these people, Jilky? What right have they here?"

"That I don't know, sir. They live in the neighbourhood, and as soon as they heard that Mrs. Thornton was ill, and laid up, they came and took possession of the house."

"But what excuse did they make for doing so?"

"They said it was in the name of the Lord, sir."

"Indeed! Now, of all the unparalleled piece of insolence that ever I heard of, this beats them. Does Mrs. Thornton like their company?"

"Oh, dear no, sir, she never could bear them. She never did like them at all, and nobody else in the neighbourhood does, sir; and if Mrs. Thornton had been well, they would never have got into the place. sir."

"Upon my word," said Claude, "this is about the coolest thing I ever heard of for a long time. And where is Mrs. Thornton?"

"Up stairs in her own room, sir. It's the loss of Miss Lucy, if you please, sir, that has all but killed her."

"Oh, no doubt—no doubt I will go to her at once."

Claude entered the cottage, and ascended the little staircase that led to the rooms above. He opened the door of one chamber. but no one was there, and then he heard from the adjoining room a faint voice say—

"Oh, who is there?—Who is there?   Because I am helpless, am I to be the prey of any one who chooses to come into the house?   Speak, who are you?"

Claude opened the door and walked into the room.   His aunt, looking much older than he thought to have found her, was partially dressed, and sitting in an easy chair by her bed-side.   Her eyes were red and swollen with weeping, and she looked at Claude with alarm, for she did not know him, and he for a few moments was too much affected to speak.

"Aunt," he said, at length, "I have come to see you."

The old lady uttered a cry of joy, and was nearly fainting; but Claude ran forward, and supported her in his arms, saying—

"Come now, don't be cast down; I have come to help you to recover Lucy, and with Heaven's aid I will do so."

"Oh, Claude—Claude—Claude!" was all she could say for some few minutes, and then she burst into tears, and wept bitterly.   Duval did not make any attempt to stop those tears.   He was confident that they would do her a world of good; and so they did, for the old lady was much more composed after they were over, and she was able to speak with greater ease.   "And so you are really my nephew, Claude?"

"I am, indeed, aunt.   Don't you feel sure that I am?"

"Let me look better at you.   Draw up the blind, Claude, and let me look well at your face and eyes."

Duval did so, and then, with a deep sigh, she said—

"Ah, yes, I do know you now, and I should know you among a thousand, Claude, you are so like your poor dear mother."

"Am I so?"

Claude felt a choking sensation, as he said this.

"Yes, you are; and she was so good, and so beautiful, and so true. But, oh, Claude, can it be really true that—that—"

"Go on, aunt."

"That you are the noted highwayman who they say terrifies everybody, and who will come to a bad end?   Can this be possible, Claude?"

"Aunt, you need not listen to one-half of what you hear in this world," said Claude; "and, I think, if you go that far, it is very liberal, indeed.   I don't believe half so much as that; so we will not talk just now of what I am; but I will tell you that anon.   Chance has brought me acquainted with the fact of the abduction of my cousin Lucy, and I have set for myself the task of saving her; so you may be certain that she is not entirely left to her fate.   I want you to tell me all you know of the affair."

At these words, Mrs. Thornton's tears flowed afresh, and for some time she was unable to speak to Claude; but again she recovered, and then she told him all she knew of the affair, which was, that a man, having the appearance of a gentleman, had haunted the place for some days, and finally called, and asked if a couple of rooms in the cottage would be let at any price, and upon being answered in the negative, he had politely gone away, and that on the next day she had observed that Lucy was frequently in tears, and that upon her disappearance, she, Mrs. Thornton, had been so much affected, that she had had to take to her bed, and was then very ill.

It was evident that Mrs. Thornton had no idea of who the villain was who had thus invaded her peaceful home, and Claude did not think fit just then to give her the name, lest she might mention it imprudently, and it should have the effect of paralysing his exertions to recover Lucy to her arms.

CHAPTER CLXX.

CLAUDE MAKES A LITTLE REVOLUTION IN HIS AUNT'S COTTAGE.

AT this juncture in his conversation with his aunt, Claude rose, and went to the landing-place at the head of the stairs, so as to be quite sure that no one was listening, and being satisfied of that fact, he came back again, and said to her in a serious tone—

"Aunt, let me be your nephew Robert, if you please. It will not do to call me Claude Duval."

"Oh, dear, no. Oh, my poor boy, why don't you turn a hatter, like your grandfather was, many years ago, in the Strand."

Claude laughed.

"I don't understand the business, aunt," he said; "but mind, now, I am your nephew Robert, and not Claude."

"Oh, yes, I will recollect."

"If you don't, the little affair is very likely to end by my being transferred to the Old Bailey, and all hopes then of the rescue of Lucy will be for ever at an end."

"Oh, you terrify me, Claude."

"Robert, if you please."

"Yes, Robert I mean. You terrify me, Cla—I mean, Robert."

"Oh, aunt—aunt, if, in the presence of others, you make so little account of uttering my name as you do to me, you will be my destruction, and Lucy's, likewise, poor girl; for who is there but myself in all the world who can and who will save her?"

"Oh, no one—no one. I will be careful, Robert. There, now, you see I am all right."

"Very well. Now tell me who are these people down stairs—Jilky they call themselves; but what do they do here, aunt? and why are they come?"

"They have forced themselves here. I cannot bear the sight of them; but as soon as they saw that I was ill, and unable to help myself, in they both came, and one stood on one side of my bed, and the other on the other, and they said that they thought it to be their duty as Christians to come and take possession of the house, and attend to me, and they meant to do it. Of course, they know I have some money, and they have made repeated efforts to get me to say where it is."

"But how have you money, aunt? You are poor rather."

"Oh, my brother left me one hundred pounds a-year."

"I am glad to hear it. I thought, and, indeed, I may say I knew, that you had enough to live upon, or I should have taken care that you should soon be provided with means; and having that sufficiency, aunt, I never offered you any of my ill-gotten gains."

"Ah, Claude—I mean, Robert—I am glad to hear you call them ill-gotten, for that gives me a hope that you will reform some of these days."

"Well, aunt, perhaps I may; but, to tell the honest truth, I find so many people so much worse than I am myself, that I don't know what to reform to. But you tell me, then, that these people, Jilky, have no right whatever to be here, and that their presence is an impertinent intrusion?"

"Just so. They thought I was dying, I do think."

"Ah! and if that had occurred, they would have taken possession of the place, and claimed everything as their own."

"No doubt, my dear, they would; and what could I have done in such a case? Just nothing, and that's the way, I suppose, that villanies take place in the world, that nobody hears anything about. They neven knew of any relations coming to see me; for excepting you and poor Lucy, you know, they are all dead now; but they little expected that you would turn up at such a juncture. Oh, my dear, restore that girl to me if you can, and I am sure then that Heaven will pardon you all that you have done."

Claude was very much affected at the simple earnestness of his aunt, and he made up his mind, although he did not say so much, to save his cousin Lucy, or to perish in the attempt.

"Now, aunt, I must leave you, for every hour is of importance. I will not leave you in the care of these people below. Is there any neighbour in whom you can depend?"

"Well, I don't know. There is Mr. Clarke, the lawyer. They say that he is a clever lawyer, and a very good man; but he has only come to live about here lately, and I don't know him a bit."

"Never mind; he will do. What is the name of your little servant girl whom I saw below?"

"Emily."

"Very well, I will call her."

Claude went to the top of the stairs and called to the girl; but the only answer he got was a cry for help; and then he heard a scuffle below, which at once convinced him something was going on in which he would like to have a hand. It did not take Claude half a minute to get to the hall, and then he saw Mr. Jilky holding the girl by the arms, while Mrs. Jilky applied a stick across her back with a vigour that was enough to kill the young creature.

Now, Claude was rather hasty in his temper, and he caught the stick from Mrs. Jilky, and placing his foot against the hind part of that lady's anatomy, he sent her through the open door into the garden with such awful velocity, that she went right into the middle of the duck-pond in a moment. As for Mr. Jilky, Claude just laid the stick over him with a speed and effect that was quite marvellous, and from the rapidity of the blows one would think that they were the produce of some ingenious machine made for the purpose of inflicting the greatest possible number in the least possible space of time upon the back of Mr. Jilky. He roared and stammered, and roared again, and fell down, and got up, and sat down, and still the stick descended; and, finally, he rolled out of the hall into the garden in such a condition, that it was quite impossible he could take any active part in anybody's affairs for some time to come.

" Now, Emily," said Claude, looking as cool as if nothing had happened. "you will put on your bonnet and go to Mr. Clarke, the lawyer, for me. I am Robert, the nephew of your mistress."

"Oh, sir, then you will save her from these people?"

" Yes, and you too. Why did you not go at once, before I came here, and bring in all the neighbours to turn them out?"

"I didn't know, sir, what to do. They said they had a right to be here in the name of the Lord, and when I didn't seem to like it, they beat me, as you happened to see them."

"Well, that's all over—they shan't beat you any more, Emily; so go off at once to the lawyer, if you please, and give Mrs. Thornton's compliments to him, and ask him to come here at once if he can."

"Yes, sir—oh, yes, sir, I will go at once. Anything to get rid of these dreadful people."

The little maid was so elated at the idea of getting rid of Mr. and Mrs. Jilky, that she ran off with great speed for the lawyer, and neither of the two highly religious people could stop her, for Mrs. Jilky was crawling out of the duck-pond rather slowly, and Mr. Jilky was lying upon his back among the cabbages.

Claude walked to and fro in the garden until the little servant came back to say that Mr. Clarke would be there in a few minutes, and then Mrs. Jilky called out in a garrulous tone—

"Mr. Jilky—Mr. Jilky, will you swear your life against this ma.

"Yes, oh, dear, yes, anything you please," groaned Jilky.

"You can swear what you like," said Claude, "both of you;" and then he walked into the house, where he met the little servant, who said—

"Oh, sir, if you please, I may as well tell you, but this morning I heard Mrs. Jilky say to Mr. Jilky that she supposed the major was far enough off by this time; and then they both laughed. I don't know what they meant, sir, but it's been on my mind all day that it might be something to do with poor Miss Lucy."

"You are quite right. Emily, in your supposition; it does concern Lucy, and you are a good girl for telling me of it, since it at once opens my eyes to the fact that these very people have been concerned in the taking away of your young mistress, Lucy. I shall now know what to do."

"Oh, thank you, sir; and if you can but bring her back it will be such a good thing, for she was very kind to me, that she was, sir."

"No doubt of it; I have hopes of bringing her back, at all events, Emily; and, in the meantime, you must stay and comfort your mistress as well as you can."

"I will, sir; and there's Mr. Clarke at the gate."

The attorney found no sort of difficulty in entering the garden, since Claude Duval had demolished the gate in the manner that he had, and Claude met him close to the door-step, and explained to him briefly how the Jilkys had taken possession of his aunt and her house in so strange a manner.

"Well," said Mr. Clarke "it is about as impudent an action as I ever heard of in all my life. What do they want?"

"Heaven only knows, sir; but, as my whole time and exertion will be rendered to discover my cousin Lucy, I hope you will in a faithful way take the care of my aunt in my absence, so far as to protect her from the return of these people."

"Oh, certainly; the police will at once put an end to that sort of thing. She must give them into custody if they come here again. I suppose they are gone now?"

"Not so, sir. There they are."

"Dear me, to be sure; yes."

It was truly ludicrous to see Mr. Jilky sitting up and looking about him in rather a wild way among the cabbages, and Mrs. Jilky sitting with her back against a tree trying to wring the wet out of her clothes, and looking as woeful as possible.

"If you will step up stairs for a moment, Mr. Clarke," added Claude, "my aunt will confirm all I have said, and give you her personal authority to act for her in my absence."

"Very good, sir. I will follow you."

"Well, aunt, here I am, your nephew Robert," said Claude, as he entered the room, for fear she should call him Claude from forgetfulness; "and here is Mr. Clarke. All he wants is, your authority."

"Oh, dear, yes," said Mrs. Thornton. "My dear Robert is quite right in all he says, Mr. Clarke; and he acts under my authority."

"Very good, madam. That is sufficient. Now, Mr. Rob—Rob——"

"Robert Thornton," said Claude.

"I beg your pardon. I had not the pleasure of knowing your name. Mr. Robert Thornton, you are justified in turning the people out of the premises, and in using sufficient force to make them go."

"I will."

"But mind me, in law you must not use more force than is necessary; although I admit, that when one kicks out an intruder from one's house, it is very difficult to give him only the requisite kick; and as in this case you will have no witnesses to the transaction, I think you need not be very particular, for I shall be looking at some of the plants in the garden, while you perform the operation."

There was a twinkle in the lawyer's eye, and a slight smile at the corners of his mouth, which showed how very much he should enjoy the kicking out of the Jilkys, so Claude marched down to the garden at once, and making a dart among the cabbages, he caught the pious Mr. Jilky by the collar, and led him towards the gate, bestowing upon him as he went such a succession of hearty kicks, that he roared and bellowed again for mercy; and when he got to the gate, and Claude let him go, he ran off as if he had not a moment to lose.

"A very nice little garden indeed," said Mr. Clarke. "A capital little garden, and beautiful flowers."

"Now, madam," said Claude to Mrs. Jilky.

"You beast!" cried the lady, "if you dare to lay hands upon me, I'll be the death of you! I'll have you all taken up, and hanged, and transported!"

"Now madam."

Mrs. Jilky moved towards the gate; but she was afraid to turn her back upon Claude, for she thought it just possible he might accelerate her progress by a kick or two, and so she went backwards all the way down the garden path, threatening vengeance as she went; and she would have got clear off in that way, but for a pig.

Yes, but for a pig, Mrs. Jilky would have escaped tolerably well; but as the garden gate was open, this pig, who was one of those troops of pigs who go about a parish picking up a living in a most disorderly and clandestine manner, made a rush to get into the premises, and just met the highly indignant lady as she was getting out of them.

The consequence of this state of things was a collision, which had the effect of rolling both pig and female in a ditch that was a short distance from the wall of the garden.

Claude Duval at a glance saw the state of affairs; and then he closed the garden gate, and took good care to fasten it.

A very short time, now, sufficed to make Claude's aunt and the attorney understand each other; and that gentleman promised her his most active professional protection. Claude's last words to his aunt were—

"Do not despair. I will bring Lucy back to you, aunt; and those who know me best say, that when I promise anything I am sure to do it."

CHAPTER CLXXI.

CLAUDE TAKES A HASTY RIDE TO DOVER, AND MISSES THE MAJOR.

No doubt Duval would gladly enough, under other circumstances, have lived for a short time beneath the roof of his aunt; but well he knew that each moment was precious, and by the time he got back to the inn at Finchley where he had left Luke and May, he was fretting at the delay that had already taken place in the pursuit of Major Brown and Lucy Thornton.

May was eagerly enough looking for him, and Luke had taken care that the horses were thoroughly refreshed, and ready again for the road. The slight rest they had had, and the rub down that Luke had taken care that they had, contributed not a little to freshen them.

"Is all right?" said Claude, as he entered the inn.

"Quite," replied Luke; "there has not been a soul here since you left a short time ago."

"No, sir," said the landlord, who was close at hand, "the more's the pity; but, somehow, we don't get the custom that we once did. Ah, times are not what they were."

Claude laughed. He well knew that that was the regular cry of all people in trades or professions of every kind or description, and he suspected that, let their circumstances be what they might, it would still continue to be the cry, and he was right enough there.

After liberally paying for what had been had, Claude sprang upon his horse, and May and Luke were soon by his side. The landlord was sorry to lose so liberal a customer, and stood looking after them as they went.

A man was coolly smoking his pipe by the stable door ; and taking it from his mouth, he pointed with the stem of it after Claude, and said, with all the delibe-ration in life—

" Do you know who that was, landlord ?"

" Dear me, no. How should I ?"

" Well, I do."

" Who was it then ?"

" Lor bless me, I thought, to be sure, you knew by the way you looked at him. Come now, you do know."

" Upon my word, I don't."

" Oh, well, I'm bound to believe you."

" Well, but who was it? Come now. Do tell."

" Certainly ; it's Claude Duval, the highwayman."

The landlord was so astonished at this information that, after staggering back a pace or two, he actually sat down upon his own door step, just in time for his wife to very nearly fall over him as she came to the door, hearing something going on.

" Dear me," she said. " What's the matter ?"

" Oh—oh—oh !" was all the landlord could say.

" Why, drat the man, what does he mean ? What is the matter with him, now ? Have you been to the old ale butt, John ?"

" Oh, dear no, wife; but what do you think? Oh, dear ! Oh, dear me, I have had such a chance!"

" A chance of what, idiot ?"

" Why, do you know, that tall fellow with the black hair, and the little mous-tache on his lip, was no other than Claude Duval the highwayman."

" Goodness gracious !"

" Yes, and if we had only laid hold of him, there would have been at least five hundred pounds reward. Think of that."

" Yes," said the man with the pipe, " that's about it; but as for laying hold of Claude Duval, that is quite another affair."

" Yes," said the landlady, " and if we had done so, and could have done it, I should have expected every guinea of the money to bring us nothing but bad luck. No, John, let us go on as well as we can ; and if we are poor we can't help it ; but never let it be said that we got money by selling the life of any one."

The man with the pipe walked slowly up to the landlady, and took her hand and gave it a shake.

" God bless you, missus," he said. " That Claude Duval saved my life once. God bless you, marm. You will do more good by saying what you have said than as if you had all the rewards that were ever offered for all the high-waymen that ever were."

" But, dear me," cried the landlord, " do only consider, five hundred pounds. Why we shall not make half as much as that in a whole year, I assure you."

" Hold your tongue," said the landlady, " and don't make a fool of yourself. Come in doors at once, do."

The man with the pipe strolled leisurely off, and the landlord, with deep regret that the five hundred pounds had escaped him after it had seemed to be thus, as it were, quite in his grasp, followed his wife into the house as an obedient hus-band should do.

Before this little colloquy at the door of the inn had come to an end, Claude Duval had got a couple of miles off, and there he and May and Luke had paused to consider what would be the most direct route to Dover, whither they did not entertain a doubt but that the major, with Lucy Thornton, had gone.

After some little pro and con upon the subject, Luke undertook to be their guide to the sea-port of Dover, as he happened to be tolerably well acquainted with the greater part of the way, so he rode on about twenty paces in advance, and May and Claude kept him in sight.

CLAUDE SEES THE INSIDE OF A PRISON.

The pace they now went at was not one that well suited conversation, so we will conclude that nothing very important transpired in the first stage, which they made a twenty-five-miles' one; and then as the horses, without showing positive distress, evidently were in need of a pause, they drew up at the first eligible spot they came to, and determined upon halting for one hour.

All along the road Claude had made inquiries regarding the appearance of such a carriage as that occupied by the major with his prisoner, for such in good truth Lucy was, and he obtained frequent assurances that such a vehicle had passed on only a few miles a-head of him, and yet, by some extraordinary means, he could not overtake it.

Of course, being mounted upon good horses, they might easily enough have come up with a vehicle of any sort, and it was not till they reached the inn at which they now stopped that they came to anything like a fair understanding of how it was that they missed the major's carriage. There they heard that there was what was called a lower road, as well as the high one which they had traversed, and that at once settled the difficulty, as, no doubt, the major had diverged to that lower road, thinking it better for his purpose, as it was less frequented than the other.

And now, were it not for the absolute necessity of resting the horses a little time, Claude, in his impatience, would have been off again at once; but any arrangement that was based upon humanity to animals, always met with a ready acquiescence from him, and he determined that he would not abridge the hour that the cattle absolutely required for rest and refreshment.

The major had an advantage over Claude and his friends which counterbalanced in a measure the difference in speed that they made. That advantage consisted in the fact that as he travelled fast with hack horses, he got a change directly he came up to a post-house, and was off again without the necessity of any delay, and, besides, it will be recollected that from the commencement of what may be fairly called the chase, he must have been one post, that is to say, about ten miles in advance of Claude, since time sufficient to accomplish that distance had been lost unavoidably by Claude at his aunt's house.

Sailors will tell you that a stern chase is a long chase, and, no doubt, it is, so that ten miles difference is a wonderful thing in a pursuit, however great the difference of speed may be between the parties.

The fact, however, and Claude in his own mind considered it as a fact, that the major was wounded, had a great effect upon him as regards soothing his mind, to think that there would be no great harm except the agony of mind that poor Lucy must suffer by the delay, and he waited the hour until the horses were again saddled and brought to the door of the inn.

In three minutes more they were all upon the road again, and to all appearance the horses seemed as though they were quite capable of doing another stage of twenty-five miles without any trouble to themselves. Perhaps they would do it better after the short rest they had had, than as if they had been indulged with a longer one, but certain it is they went on without any appearance of flagging in the least.

We need not pursue the journey to Dover in all its little incidents. Suffice it to say that after one other rest for the horses, and then a sharp trot, Claude and his friends reached their places of destination, and drawing up at one of the principal hotels, Claude flung himself from his horse, and eagerly said to the first person connected with the establishment he met with—

" I want to know if you have seen a gentleman who is wounded, and a young lady with him ? They came in a travelling carriage !"

" What, the mad young lady, sir ?" was the reply.

" Mad?" said Claude. " Oh, no, she is not mad. Quite a young lady, I mean. But not a mad person."

" Oh, dear, yes, sir: she is mad, sir. The gentleman said she was."

" The villain !" exclaimed Claude, for now it struck him at once that that was the excuse the major had made for the state of terror that Lucy would be sure to be in, and for the purpose of putting an end to all speculation concerning what she might say or do at the inn.

" Well," said Claude, smothering his feelings as best he could, " they are the people concering whom I inquire, I believe. Are they here ?"

" Oh, dear, no, sir."

"I am too late, then?"

"If you want to see them, sir, you are, indeed. The fact is, sir, they have gone off to Calais in the mail packet about two hours ago, sir. The young lady—poor thing!—had to be carried on board, for she took it into her head that her uncle was not her uncle."

"Indeed?"

"Yes, sir. You see, sir, her uncle who was with her had had quite a job in London to rescue her from a fellow who wanted to run away with her and seduce her; but the uncle was not going to stand that, you know, sir, so he flew like a shot after the guilty pair, and they fled from him like the forked lightning. The uncle found them out like one o'clock; but they packed up their things, and took to their heels like bricks. The uncle, however, sir, was after them like a greased arrow, and then the villain of a seducer shot him like winkings and then fled. The young lady went mad on the moment, and the uncle brought her here like a whirlwind, and paid his bill like the mild refulgence of a summer's day, and then cut his stick."

The waiter, for such he was, put himself into so many extraordinary attitude, while he delivered this harangue, that Claude strongly suspected his wits were a little deranged, and looked at him in amazement.

"Perhaps, sir," he said, as he wiped his brow with a rather ragged old handkerchief—"perhaps you think I am a little romantic?"

"Well, I do a little."

"Then you are right, sir, I am so; and I can assure you I have been in a wild fever ever since that mad young lady came here."

"Indeed?"

"Oh, yes—yes. I—I—Oh, Heaven! I don't mind telling you, sir, for you seem like a sympathetic gentleman—I say, I don't mind revealing my lacerated heart to you, sir, and so I tell you that—that—Oh, Heaven!"

"That what?"

"I love her!"

"You don't say so?"

"Yes, sir, I do say so. I love that mad young lady! From the first moment, sir, that I looked upon her face I said—'There is my fate!' I love her—how I love her! Oh, gracious! I keep dropping hot plates now, sir, every minute; and smash they go. I hear many bells a-ringing, and I take people things they didn't order, and I don't take them things they did, and I am a desperate waiter now, sir, I assure you, and my heart is broke into small bits."

"I am very sorry for you, indeed."

"Thank you, sir—oh, sir, thank you. The sympathy of a sympathetic individual is dear to a lacerated soul."

"You are quite welcome to all the sympathy that I can give to you. But you are sure the gentleman was wounded?"

"Oh, dear, yes, and he swore dreadfully."

"Well, now, can you tell me when I can cross the Channel?"

"To-morrow."

"To-morrow? Not before to-morrow?"

"No, sir, you can't. There's the mail packet as comes from Calais to-night will be going back again, and you can go back with her. Oh, would that I could go, and then, perhaps, I should look upon that face—that form—that ankle—those eyes—that chin—Oh—oh!"

Claude turned rather abruptly from the enthusiastic waiter, and spoke to May and Luke in a low tone of voice.

"We cannot do better," he said, "than put up here for the present. Do you two stay at this house while I go down to the water-side and see what can be done in the way of procuring a means of crossing the Channel. It is ridiculous to stay here till to-morrow with only some twenty miles of water to cross."

" Be careful, Claude," said May, " and look to your own safety.   Remember that you may find enemies everywhere."

."I will not be too heedless, you may depend," said Claude. " I have your safety as well as my own to look to. I leave you now with perfect confidence in the care of Luke."

Claude then left the house and proceeded on foot to the water side, where he eagerly inquired if by any means a boat or vessel of any kind could be got to enable him to cross the water to Calais.

" Why, yes, it's smooth water enough," said a rough-looking fellow, "and there's a nice little consarn riding at anchor there that would do it in a couple of hours in a lively fashion, if so be as the job paid her."

" What do you want ?"

" Well, perhaps a matter of five guineas."

" Say ten, and it is a bargain."

The man stared a moment or two at Claude, and then he said—

"To be sure it is a bargain.   We shall be ready in as many minutes as the guineas count up to, sir, if you are."

" That will do. I have a lady and gentleman at one of the inns to fetch, that is all.   There is no luggage, and we shall be here within the time you have just mentioned to me.   Be sure that you are ready."

———

CHAPTER CLXXII.

CLAUDE FINDS HIMSELF AND FRIENDS ON FRENCH GROUND.

DUVAL hurried back to the hotel where he had left Luke and May, and the horses, and found that everything was just as he had left. He hastily explained to them both that he had at once secured a passage to Calais, and then asking for the landlord, he told him that as he projected going over to France for perhaps a week or two, he wished to leave the horses in his care, and ordered the best attention should be given to them.

The landlord was all smiles and sweetness.   The value of the steeds was quite a sufficient guarantee that all would be right enough as regarded his bill for the meantime.

Duval, then, with Luke's assistance, packed all they thought they would want in the largest of the vallises, and Luke carried it easily down to the quay, closely followed by Duval and May.

When they reached the spot where Claude had made his bargain with the boatman, they found him and his mate waiting for them in a wherry, which they intended to pull off with to the little vessel that lay still at some distance.

"All ready?" said Claude.

" Ay—ay, sir, we are ready if you are."

"That will do."

They were in the boat in another moment, and a boy went with them to take the werry to shore again.   The sea was tolerably smooth, there being but a light breeze from the south-west, which, although it was not favourable exactly for them, yet would not materially interfere with so short a passage as that across the straits of Dover.

The little vessel, which resembled a pilot boat more than anything else, was soon reached, and the whole party stood upon her deck.   The boy went back with the wherry, and the two boatmen had up the anchor and a sails set in a very few minutes.   One took the helm and the other busied himself about the little craft.

" You have been the passage often, I suppose ?" said Duval.

" Lord bless you, sir, yes, time out of mind I've been it, and in this here little bit of a craft too. The tide is ebbing fast, and we shall soon get along with it. Keep her head well up to east, Jem."

"Ay—ay!"

" We shall get along, sir, somehow, and ten to one arter all but we shall beat that lubberly mail packet that went off some three hours gone by now, for she sails like a tub."

"I should like to land before she can place her passengers on shore, by all means," said Claude, "if it can be done."

"It's likely enough, sir. I'll take a long look a-head and see if I can catch a sight of her. I'll warrant she aint far off with the wind, any how."

The mail packet was not to be seen, though, notwithstanding the boatman's idea that his little craft could get in before she did, and Duval was soon convinced that the notion of such a thing was just one of those idle boasts which persons connected with the sea are so fond of indulging in respecting their own vessel to the desparagement of all others. Nevertheless, the little vessel did its duty well, and it was skilfully conducted by the two men, so that in a less time than he could have expected the outline of the coast of France was plainly perceptible.

"There," said Claude, as he pointed it out to May. "There is France. What do you think now of making a long stay there?"

"Oh, no—no, and yet why do I say so? Perhaps, Claude, you would be happier, and at least, you would be safer."

"No, May, I should not be happier, and I do not think that after a little time I should be very safe. I like old England, after all; and if I were to remain in France for long, I know I should be compelled to speak out and utter the real genuine feelings of contempt that I have for one of the most unstable nations upon the face of the earth. Perhaps it is nothing but prejudice, May; but a Frenchman to me is an animal that I could not endure for long."

"Nor I, sir," said Luke. "They are only fit for dancing-masters and cooks."

"Don't say cooks," said Duval. "The Lord preserve me from French cookery. Give me an English joint of meat, naturally cooked by the mere action of fire against it, in preference to all the wishy-washy compounds that tickle a French appetite, and that people in England, who ought to know better, pretend to like, because they think it is the fashion."

"Yes," said May, "as they pretend to be in raptures with the Italian Opera."

" Just so."

The little craft now was so near to the harbour at Calais, that her owners shortened sail, and were within ten minutes more right alongside the old jetty. Duval had paid them the ten guineas, and now he sprang ashore, and assisted May to do so, likewise, and Luke followed. The two Dover boatmen gave them a cheer at parting, and then were off again, and there stood our three friends on French ground.

A little man, with a face very much resembling an ape, but wearing a large cocked-hat and an odd-looking uniform, advanced to them with many grimaces and bows, and asked for the favour of their company.

Duval spoke French well, and he said with a smile—

" Where to, sir?"

"To the bureau of the commandant," replied the ape, " where you will be so good as to have your passports examined."

"Passports?" exclaimed Claude. "I had quite forgotten that. May and you, Luke, listen to me. We are in a pretty mess here. I quite forgot, before leaving England, that everybody in France must be ticketted and labelled and fully described by the police ; in fact, that they are all suspicious characters here, and that passports were necessary to know who and what we are, for fear we should take the country by storm."

The little ape-like officer, in the huge cocked-hat, stood grinning and smiling all this time, and then Claude turned to him and said in French—

" We have no passports."

This announcement seemed to strike the Frenchman with profound terror, and he whirled round several times so oddly that Claude thought he would inevitably fall on the quay into the water, and stretching out his hand to save him, he caught him by the collar, and firmly held him at arm's length off his legs. That he was going now at once to be sacrificed was evidently the idea of the French-man, and he set up such a screaming for the guard that Claude and his friends were nearly stunned.

" Why, what on earth," said Claude, " is the matter with you ? I don't want to hurt you, you contemptible animal."

" Murder !" roared the Frenchman. " Murder !—the English invasion ! Murder !—I'm a dead man. Murder! Guard ! Where is the guard—guard— guard ?"

The cries of the little Frenchman soon had the effect of bringing the guard to the spot, and in the course of a few minutes Claude and his friends found them-selves surrounded by about a dozen of the *gendarmerie*, looking as furious and as important as possible, and all talking at once, as it is the wont of Frenchmen to do.

The little officer, with such extraordinary gesticulations, that one would suppose a hot cinder was down his back, or that he was treading upon some-thing that gave him the most excrutiating agony to be still upon for a moment, explained to the guard the dreadful delinquency that Claude and his two com-panions had been guilty of.

" These wretched English," he said, " these perfidious John de Bulls have come here without a passport, on purpose to insult the grand nation."

" Yes—yes !" cried the guard, " that is it. They always try to insult the grand nation."

" They must be taken before the commandant," said the little officer.

" Of course. Yes—yes !" cried the guard. " March—march !"

" Really this is too ridiculous," said Claude, in English, to Luke. " I hardly know what to do. Of course, it would be easy enough to throw these fellows over the quay ; but that would not mend affairs, I am afraid."

" Not at all," said Luke.

" Don't think of violence, Claude," said May. " After all, they are only doing their duty, and I should think that when we come before any reasonable man, the motive of your visit to France will be quite sufficient to excuse the omission of a passport."

" Perhaps it may. I will speak to them."

Claude raised his voice and addressed the little officer and the gendarmes in a strain that met with the most ready attention from them; for no ears in all the world are so readily open to flattery as those of a Frenchman.

" Gentlemen," he said, " I am quite aware that France is the grandest nation on the face of the earth. The fact has long been familiar to me that a Frenchman inherits glory from the moment of his birth, and that in valour, wit, discretion, and modesty, no man can ever come near him."

" Exactly," said the gendarmes.

" Exactly," said the little officer.

" Just so," said the crowd of dirty-looking people, who began to collect upon the quay with the prospect of some amusement from the row that seemed to be on the *tapis.*

" Holding such opinions of France and Frenchmen," added Claude Duval, " and knowing that they are as gallant to the fair sex as they are terrible to their foes, I admit that I have come here without a passport, the reason of which I shall explain to the commandant, if this brave escort will do me and my friends the honour of conducting me to that functionary."

The little French officer was so enchanted at this address, that he first embraced

Claude, and then insisted upon his taking a pinch of snuff out of a huge gilt box that he took from his waistcoat pocket.

"When one brave man," he said, "meets another, he knows how to treat him. It is quite clear that monsieur is a hero, and I may say what I may seldom say of my own, not so fortunate as to be born here, that he is fit to be a Frenchman."

"He is," said the gendarmes.

"Perfectly," said the crowd.

"March!" cried the little officer, and so Claude Duval, and May, and Luke found themselves marched off as prisoners under an escort to the commandant of Calais. The manner in which Claude had spoken, though, had brought him and his party into such high favour, that the little officer and the gendarmes conducted themselves more as if they had been a guard of honour to their prisoners than anything else; and so, in great state, they all marched to the commandant's house.

By great good fortune that officer happened to be a reasonable man and a gentleman, and when Claude told him the errand that he came upon, he at once replied that he would do anything he possibly could to facilitate his views, and to promise him a special leave to hunt through France after the fugitives.

The English consul was sent for, who soon verified, from the account of Duval and his friends, that they were English, and when he heard the story, he had no hesitation in making himself responsible for the good behaviour of the parties, and so special passports were granted to Claude in the name of Thornton, and to his two companions, Luke in his proper name, and May in the name of Charles Thornton—for it will be recollected that May was in a very handsome suit of male attire, and Claude passed her off very well as his brother.

When this was all arranged, and they had left the bureau of the commandant, the English consul asked them to his house; but Claude shook his head, as he said—

"I thank you, sir, for this act of courtesy; but my great anxiety respecting my poor cousin, Lucy Thornton, will not permit me to accept of your kind offer. I have very little doubt but that the villain who has stolen her from her house has taken her over to Paris, and I do not wish to lose a moment in pursuing him."

"You are wrong," said the consul.

"Wrong, sir?"

"Yes. I can give you information which I did not wish to give you before the commandant. The fact is, if I could have seen him and you alone, I should have had no difficulty about the matter; for he is a gentleman and a man of honour; but you perceived how his secretary kept in the room all the time, and as the commandant himself did not order him to retire, it was no part of my business to take that liberty."

"I did see him. A dark, thin man?"

"Exactly; with gray moustache."

"Oh, yes. I noticed that he paid great attention to all I said to the commandant."

"Precisely. He did as you say, pay great attention to all you said to the commandant; and I have every reason to believe that he is well aware of the proceedings of the Major Brown, who has possessed himself, in so violent and daring a manner, of your young relation."

"Is it possible?"

"It is true."

"The villain! I will at once then return to the commandant's, and force the secret from him, if I have to half throttle him in the operation."

"You need not take that trouble. I can give you the information you require, sir."

" Even I; and now, as I give you so good a reason so to do, and as you may suppose that it is your best plan of operations, I hope you will be so good as to come to my house at once, and we will there consult about what is the best to be done in this matter. Recollect that you are not in England, where you would meet with ready assistance in this matter, and where every hand would be raised up for you, and where you could at once go to the nearest magistrate, and easily substantiate your complaint."

The idea of his going to a magistrate was not exactly the most pleasant one to Claude Duval, and he merely said—

" Well, sir, I can only say, that if you can and will assist me in the one sole object that has brought me to France, you will be laying me under a very great obligation, indeed, and I shall be truly grateful for so doing."

"Come along, then. Follow me; and as you do so, you can explain to your young brother here, and to your young friend, Mr. Luke, what I said."

The consul walked a few paces in advance, and Claude Duval took the opportunity thus afforded to him, and stated the effect of his conversation with the English consul, which had been carried on in too low a tone for them to hear it.

May was delighted at the idea that Claude had so soon found a friend who would be likely to assist him in the search for his cousin; and Luke was quite indignant at the commandant's secretary, whom he sincerely hoped he might meet some day upon English ground.

" Oh, if I could only encounter that fellow upon some such place now as Salisbury Plain," said Luke. " how delighted I should be to show him how an Englishman could use his fists."

" He would get the better of you, Luke," said Claude. " A Frenchman is full of kicks when he fights, and you never know what he is going to do. When you least expect it, you would find him down at your feet, and hold of both your ancles."

" Confound him," said Luke, " I'd smash him for all that."

CHAPTER CLXXIII.

CONDUCTS THE READER TO AN OLD CHATEAU NEAR CALAIS, AND SHOWS WHAT STRANGE EVENTS TOOK PLACE THERE.

THE consul did not wish to appear to be very intimate with his visitors, for he was quite aware that he was well watched by some of the emissaries of the secretary; and when a man in particular stopped the party, to beg them to purchase some fruit, the consul turned, and said—

" I will take good care that you have cattle that will speed you well *en route* to Paris; for here, I make no doubt, but you will find the fugitives; but you want a rest after your little voyage."

The look that the consul gave to the man who was offering the fruit for sale, convinced Claude and Luke that it was for his special edification he, the consul, said these words; and then they both concluded, which was the exact truth, that this pretended fruit-seller was nothing more nor less than one of the spies in the pay of the secretary of the commandant.

" Yes," replied Claude. " Paris will be our place."

" Not a doubt of that," said Luke, " and there you will find your cousin, Miss Thornton, and that rascally major."

" Buy some fruit, sirs," said the spy. " Pray buy some fruit of a poor man."

Claude was particularly anxious that this rascal of a spy should not get off quite scot-free, so as he walked along he pretended to tread upon a piece of orange-peel that was upon the ground, and to fall, and in his fall he caught hold of the spy by the ankle, and over he went on his back in a moment, with such a crash upon the stones, that they all thought he was killed.

"Quite an accident," said Claude.

"Oh, quite," said the consul. "Give the poor man a few coins. I dare say he is not hurt. Poor fellow."

"How sorry I am," said Claude. "But, you see, it was that treacherous piece of orange-peel that made me fall, and one is so apt, quite upon the impulse

of the moment, to catch hold of anything or anybody to save oneself, that I am afraid I really upset this poor, but, no doubt, very honest man."

The spy rose to a sitting posture, and as he held his head he uttered a string of the most horrible oaths in French that he could possibly recollect, and he flung the few pence that Claude placed in his basket from him with a rage that was quite ludicrous to see. It was quite as much as Claude and his friends could do to keep from laughing outright to see the look of rage and pain and doubt that was upon the face of the spy ; but they passed on, leaving him still sitting upon the ground in the centre of a little throng of people, which gathered round him to hear how his mishap had chanced.

The house inhabited by the consul was now close at hand, and when they all reached it, the consul cried out in a loud voice—

" Jacques—Jacques !"

" Yes, sir," replied a French servant.

" You will endeavour to have a caleche, with one pair of good horses, to take these gentlemen over to Paris, Jacques, and you will have it in readiness at the door in about an hour from now, Jacques ?"

" Certainly, sir."

The consul then led the way to a private apartment, and, when he had shut the door, he said,

" The only way to prevent the man you seek receiving information that there is danger, is to make it pretty well believed that you will soon be on the road to Paris, and that you have no suspicion the end of your journey is in the immediate neighbourhood of Calais."

" But is it so ?" cried Claude.

"Hush—speak low. I do not think that there is any danger of our being overheard, but, still, it is as well to be cautious. In answer to your question, I say, yes."

" You surprise me," added Claude. " But are you certain, sir, of what you state ? Is there no possibility of a mistake ?"

" I think none, and you will, yourself, be of the same opinion when you hear what I have to tell you. This Major Brown is very well known in Calais to some people, and when the packet came in a few hours ago, the commandant's secretary went on board at once and came ashore with him. They had a sedan chair brought right down to the quay, and a rumour was spread about that a young English lady, who had been driven mad by being first seduced and then abandoned by an officer in the army, prepared the minds of all parties for what was to follow. The young lady, with a handkerchief tied over her mouth, or, I should rather say, placed in it much in the same manner that you place a bit in the mouth of a horse, was brought out of the packet and placed in the sedan, and carried off to a lodging that the secretary of the commandant's has."

" And the major ?"

" He, with his shoulder bound up, and looking very pale, went with her and the secretary."

Claude sprang to his feet. " Is the lodging near at hand, sir ?"

" Stop a bit. It is ; but she is gone from there. I had a suspicion that all was not right, and I employed a servant of mine, upon whom I know I can rely, although he is a Frenchman, to watch these parties. He will be able to tell us all about them, and I expect they are at a chateau that belongs to the commandant, in Calais, and which that gentleman, who is too easy and good-tempered by half, permits his rascally secretary to have the care of, and never inquires about it. The fact is, that the commandant's wife died there, and as he was tenderly attached to her, he never has gone near the place since."

" Oh, sir, how can I thank you ?" said Claude. " I have a double interest in rescuing the poor girl from the villain who has stolen her, for it was by making use of my name that he got her to the unfrequented spot alone, from which he was able to kidnap her."

" Depend upon it," said the consul, " you shall have all the aid I can give to you in the matter, and I hope and trust we shall be successful."

" But," said Claude, " the commandant being the man he is, would it not be as well, and better too, to secure his aid ?"

" Yes, if it could be done with anything like safety," replied the consul; "but the onset of that visit, the spies of the secretary would take the alarm, and all our efforts would be frustrated. Everything depends upon it not being supposed that you have any idea of staying here at all, and upon the notice that you are posting to Paris."

"I can well perceive that there is good, sound sense in what you say, sir," said Claude Duval.

"You may depend that there is," added the consul. "Now, there are but two ways of communicating with the commandant; either I must go to him, or I must send and ask him to be so good as to come to me. It is quite impossible that either of those events could take place without the secretary being at once acquainted of it, and, coupling it with your presence here, of course, such a man would come to the instant conclusion that it concerned the hiding-place of the major, who, therefore, would receive intelligence within an hour that his position at the chateau was untenable, and the consequence would be, his flight in some direction that would leave us nothing but conjecture to go upon."

"I am quite bewildered," said May.

"And so am I," said Luke.

"Then allow me," added the consul, "to endeavour to get what information I can from the man I have mentioned."

As he spoke, the consul rang the bell, and a middle-aged man soon presented himself.

"Oh, Pierre," said the consul, "you are the very man I wanted. I was quite unhappy at the idea that you might not, yourself, have answered the bell, in which case I should really not have ventured upon asking for you. Monsieur Roche has so many spies about."

"Roche, then, is the name of the secretary?" said Claude.

"Just so," replied the consul. "Well, Pierre, what have you learnt?"

"The major and the mad young lady, are at Lannes."

"Ah, as I thought. That is the chateau, Mr. Thornton. And you have excited no suspicion, Pierre, that you were on the watch?"

"None in the least, sir, I will answer for that. But don't trust Jacques, sir; I know that he calls upon Roche."

"Confound the rascal! I know that, too, and I will not trust him half so far as I can see him. Do you think, Pierre, you could guide us to the chateau in the dark?"

"Oh, yes, easily, sir. I know every inch of the way."

"But what is to be done about this carriage that is ordered for Paris?" said Duval, with some uneasiness.

"That is easily managed. You must go off in it, and get on the road for about an hour or so, and then you must stay at some halting place till dark, after which, you must meet me and Pierre somewhere near to the outskirts of the town, here, and we will proceed to the chateau together. You can easily induce the driver of the carriage to wait for you, by saying you are going to make a call in the vicinity of the place you stop at, and all you have to do is, to very carefully observe your route, so that you will have no difficulty in walking back."

"Yes," said Pierre, "that is the only way to do it, so as to appear to be fairly off. Roche has so many spies about him, whom he only pays when they bring him any intelligence, and then pays liberally enough, that one cannot be too cautious."

"Let it be so, then," said Claude. "The carriage will not go very far in an hour, I suppose, and upon the roads about here?"

"Certainly not," said the consul. "Besides, you can stop it every now and then to look about you at the country, in which you can easily affect to be much interested, for recollect, it is time that is the object, not distance, and the sooner the night comes the better it will be."

"Where shall we meet the English gentleman?" said Pierre.

"At the ruined tower, I should say," replied the consul, and then turning to Claude, he said—"You will see, about one mile on the Paris road, from here, to the left of the road, a ruined tower, covered with ivy. There is a small gate leading from the main road up to it. At that gate, Pierre and I will be at the hour of midnight, as near as possible ; and should you be there much too soon, clamber over the gate, and stay in the tower. You will find no interruption there after sunset, I'll warrant."

"Not the least," said Pierre.

"Is there any special reason for that?" said Claude.

The consul smiled.

"It is haunted, that is all."

"Yes," said Pierre, "by fools."

"Well, we will not be scared from a place of refuge upon such a score as that," said Claude. "And now I think we all fully and clearly understand what we are to do in this affair, which, but for you, sir, would be quite unmanageable to us, I am afraid."

"Don't mention that," said the consul.

At this moment there was a tremendous rattling of wheels and cracking of a whip in the street, together with such a chattering of voices that one would have thought something very tremendous was about to happen, and that nothing near so simple as the arrival of a chaise and a pair of horses could have produced such an uproar and excitement ; but that was the real fact. The vehicle that the consul had ordered for Claude Duval and his friends had arrived at the door of the house.

"There is the chaise," said the consul, "and there, no doubt, is some spy of the secretary to see you safe off."

"Ah," said Pierre, "it will be a wonder if the driver himself is not in his pay, somehow or another."

The consul started rather at this alarming suggestion.

"Confound him," he said, "that may be true enough, and if so, I am afraid that our plans will be, after all, likely to miscarry, for if the rascal thinks you are all three coming back to Calais he will come likewise."

"But in that case," said Claude, "should we not see him on the road?"

"Of course you would."

"Very good, then, leave him to me. If he should attempt to pass us, I will adopt some means of convincing him that that will not be a judicial step. If that is all the danger of the scheme miscarrying, I will meet it."

"In that case, then, start at once," said the consul, "and good fortune attend you on your route. Remember the old tower covered with ivy."

There came a tap at the door of the room now, and then it was opened, and Jacques appeared at the entrance.

"The carriage is ready for Paris," he said.

"That will do," said Claude. "I will write to you, Mr. Consul, for the capital, and let you know how we get on. I will not fail, too, to call upon the two gentlemen you have so kindly given me notes of introduction to."

"They will assist you, I am sure," said the consul, who was glad to perceive that Claude adopted a style of talking that would tend to mystifying Jacques. "For my sake, I know they will do all they can for you, and you can stay with him who resides in the Rue St. Honore."

The postilion's whip, at the door, was cracking away all this time at quite a terrible rate.

The look of low cunning that was upon the face of Jacques was quite a sight to see, and Claude, if he had not been so really anxious about the actual result of the enterprise that he was upon, would have found no small amusement in the study of French character that was presented to him. As it was, he now hurried to the door to depart.

The carriage was just that sort of thing that never could have been produced in England at all, and if by any accident it had made an appearance there, it would have been as quickly as possible converted into fire-wood. A more miserable shaky concern Claude thought he had never seen. It was tied together by ropes in many places, and, in fact, it was upon a par with the two wretched animals who were, after the slovenly French fashion, harnessed to it, and they were dreadful to look at.

If Claude Duval had been really going to Paris instead of only a few miles away from Calais, he certainly would have made a stand against proceeding in any such vehicle, and with any such cattle; but as it was, it did not matter even if they did break down within a short time, a circumstance which he considered to be exceedingly probable.

It was amusing, too, to see the look of May and of Luke as they got into the vehicle, and Claude said to the consul—

"Is this the usual kind of conveyance here?"

"Not exactly," replied the consul with a smile, "but you must consider that they expect you to pay well, and, therefore, they have turned out their best carriage and horses."

"Their best?"

"Just so. There are maay equipages in this place much worse than this one, I assure you."

"Good gracious!" said Luke. "Then they must absolutely fall to pieces before they get a mile out of the town, for I thought it impossible anything could be worse than this."

CHAPTER CLXXIV.

CLAUDE DUVAL AND HIS FRIENDS REACH THE OLD CHATEAU DE LANNES.

THE postilion did not understand English, so he was not at all aware of the disparaging idea that the travellers had of his equipage; but he strutted to and fro, giving himself the airs of a field-marshal at the very least.

When Claude was seated, there came a couple of men, each of whom was bearing something that looked more like a gigantic churn than anything else, at a little distance, but as they came nearer, Claude said to May—

"Oh, they are boots. They are the sign, no doubt, to be fixed outside the house of some bootmaker, as we have seen them in London."

"Not at all," said the consul, " they are the postilion's boots."

"The postilion's boots? Impossible!"

"You will see. A French postillion would no more think of going on the road without his boots than without his head. You will soon see that I am right."

Claude and his friends did soon see that the consul understood these matters, for the two men with the boots advanced to one of the miserable horses and placed a boot on each side of him. Then they assisted the postilion on to his back, and his legs naturally fell into the huge boots.

The next thing was to get the boots into the stirrups, otherwise, of course, they would have fallen into the road the instant the vehicle went on. For this purpose some half dozen Frenchmen got on each side of the postilion, and hoisted him up by the boots, and so succeeded in fixing them in the stirrups; and there he was, looking as fierce as though he were the greatest man in all the world.

"Are the English ready?" said the postilion.

"Oh, yes, quite," said Claude.

With a sharp crack of his whip he put the wretched horses to a strange kind of trot, and then shouting, "For glory!—glory!" he managed to get round the next corner and the carriage was fairly started on the Paris road.

What glory there could be in driving a pair of miserable hacks that in England would be at once considered as too far gone for cats-meat, only a Frenchman could conceive; but when it is a positive fact that a Frenchman was once seen pulling perriwinkles out of their shells with a pin and muttering to himself that it was "for glory," we need not wonder at anything of that sort that the Grand Nation may do.

There was a pause at the gate of Calais for the purpose of examining the passports, but as everything was regular now, Claude and his party were allowed again to proceed, and they got into that dull, flat, terribly uninteresting tract of country that lies between Calais and Paris, and which is decidedly the most tiresome in the world.

To the left appeared in the distance a much more fertile and woody district, but to the right everything was as barren as possible, there appearing to be nothing but immense plains, scarcely relieved by a single tree ; and it was only now and then that the travellers saw a house, with its bit of garden attached, in some hollow.

The day was now rapidly sinking, and a dull glow was over the western sky as the sun, for that day, took its farewell of La Belle France.   Then there came some sombre clouds out of the south, and in a very few minutes they managed to sweep over the entire canopy of sky ; although, if you watched them ever so narrowly, they did not appear to be making any progress.

In another ten minutes it was night.

The wretched horses had gone indifferently well, and although the miserable vehicle cracked awfully, it did not absolutely break down, to the astonishment of both Claude and Luke, who fully expected it would have done so long before getting so far as it had.

The postilion made a horrible cracking noise with his whip, and now and then indulged himself by singing a highly national song, which, like the national songs of all Frenchmen, was about glory, and at the same time ardently intimated that the French nation was the first in the universe, and had always been such.

The vanity of a Frenchman is only to be equalled by that of an American ; but, then, the latter is certainly too degrading even to laugh at, while the Frenchman will always say or do something to excite your risibility.

"Claude," said May, "we must be looking out for the tower that the consul mentioned to us."

"Yes, I am keeping a wary watch."

"The postilion, I suppose," said Luke, "can't speak English."

"Oh, no, certainly not," replied Claude.   "It is not in any respect probable that he has been in the way of acquiring that language ; so, I think, we may converse with perfect freedom."

"Nothing has passed us on the road," said May, "and although I listen as acutely as I can, I do not hear any vehicle or horseman upon our track now."

"Oh, there is the tower," said Claude.   "Do you not see it covered with ivy, as the consul told us it was?   There, against the night sky."

They all three now saw the tower quite plainly, and they now did not care how soon they came to some house or village at which the carriage might be put up for a time, while they went back to meet the consul and Pierre at the old tower.

For some distance further, though, no available place to stop at presented itself to the travellers, and Claude was just thinking that their walk back would be too long a one to be pleasant, when the postilion, pointing with his whip forward, cried out—

"Behold, there is the post-house, and there, if messieurs the English please, we will rest these noble steeds."

Claude saw a light about a quarter of a mile ahead, and he replied,

"By all means.   I think the noble steeds and the glorious postilion both require rest and refreshment."

"You are right, sir—you are right, and, for an Englishman, tolerably considerate."

"I thank you for the compliment," said Claude.

"Duval," said Luke, "I have been looking on this side of the splendid vehicle at the wheels, and I find that the linch-pin of one of them is nothing but an old nail."

"Indeed?"

"That is all, and nothing would be easier than to get it out, so that when the glorious postilion had got a little futher on he would find his carriage broken down. What say you to that?"

"Just this, Luke, that there is one great advantage combined with the extreme simplicity of our travelling arrangements, which is, that no accident can possibly happen that may not be repaired again in quite as efficient a manner as the affair was before. Our glorious postilion will just find another nail for a linch-pin, and on we shall go."

"I did not think of that."

May laughed. "It won't do," she said. "Nothing but the positive death of the two horses will stop us."

"And it would be a mercy to help them from this world," said Claude.

"Stop a bit," cried Luke, "I have it. He can't make a wheel quite so easily as he can a linch-pin. I will wait till we are in a dark part of the road before I execute the manœuvre, and then I will try and throw the wheel away long before he can get out of those great boots of his."

"That is better," said Claude. "I think the loss of a wheel will pose him."

"Where shall I do it?"

"I think that you had better not meddle with the wheel at all till we get past the post-house at which he purposes to stop a little. Then, after we get about half a mile on the other side of it, nothing will be easier than the making of some excuse for him to stop. You can say you have lost your hat, and then you can get out and remove the linch-pin; and when we go down, and you get rid of the wheel, we can appear to go back to the post-house for help, and leave him alone on the road in his glory, while we make the best of our way to the old tower, and we shall meet our friend, the consul, and be off to this chateau he speaks of most likely before the postilion gets away to help him."

"Yes, I see; that will be the best plan."

"And here we are," said May, "close to the post-house."

The postilion was quite determined that the people at the post-house should have no reasonable excuse for not knowing that somebody of importance was coming, for he cracked his whip with such force, that it sounded like a sharp succession of pistol-shots, and he shouted at the same time with all his strength of lungs—

"Hilloa!—hilloa! House!—house! Mr. Lord Anglais and the brave postilion approaches!"

Such were the grand, eloquent tones in which the postilion thought proper to herald his approach to the post-house, and, no doubt, he well knew that they would have the desired effect; for, upon driving up with quite a dash to the door of quite a wretched-looking hovel, there were collected at the door of it the master, and the mistress, and the whole establishment.

The postilion was duly lifted out of his great boots ; and then he said something hastily to the landlord, which awakened the suspicions of Luke, who said to Claude Duval—

"Did you hear what he said just now? From his manner in saying it, I am afraid it was about us."

"You are quite right, Luke," replied Claude, with a smile. "It was about us; but it was nothing that we need care about. It was merely advising the man to charge us well for all that we had, for we were the cursed English, and had plenty of money."

"Confound his impudence!" said Luke.

"Yes, it is just what you may expect from such people. They will cringe and fawn to you before your face, and abuse you in the grossest terms the moment they think they can do so out of your hearing."

"We will see. It is just possible that I may find a means of repaying the postilion for his compliments to us before I part with him."

"Don't attempt it, Luke, I beg of you. Let him alone. I have but two desires, and they are just now to rescue Lucy Thornton, and then to get out of France."

They now alighted from the carriage, being all but embraced by the people of the house; but Claude put a damper upon their delightful feelings, by saying—

"Postilion, we have no time to spare upon the road, and expect you to be ready to start again in one quarter of an hour."

The postilion bowed, and grinned, and swore he was at their service to go to the farthest end of the world, if necessary, at that period of time; and then Claude and his friends entered the house.

Some refreshment was ordered, and when it came, they could touch nothing but the bread, which looked white and pure. There was something in a dish, which looked like pigs' ears stewed in rancid butter and flower, and there was a bottle of wine, which was so frightfully sour, that Luke would not be convinced that it was not a mistake, and that they had brought their stock of vinegar instead.

"No, Luke, it of no use to complain. This is French wine."

"Is it? Well, give me one half-pint of English porter before a hogshead of it. It is enough to give any one the stomach-ache to think of it."

"And have you any idea," said May to Claude, "of what this is that they have served us up in this dish?"

"Not the remotest. But I have quite made up my mind not to touch any of it."

"And I," said Luke.

May, too, shook her head at the mess of shiny-looking rubbish; so they contented themselves with the bread and some water.

The quarter of an hour soon expired, and they all sallied out to the door of the inn and post-house; and then Claude asked what was to pay, and the landlord, with a terrible grimace, said—"Ten francs."

This was a sum equivalent in English to about eight shillings and sixpence, and was a great deal more than should have been charged, but Claude held up his hands, and said in quite a tone of surprise—

"Only ten francs!"

"Y—e—s," said the innkeeper, doubtingly, for he had fully expected a row about the exorbitant nature of the demand.

"Well," added Claude, in a loud voice, "I am quite surprised that you should ask so little. There are the ten francs; but I was quite prepared to pay twenty-five at the very least, my friend."

Upon this, the innkeeper's wife was so enraged at the idea of what had escaped her cupidity, that she flew at the innkeeper, and began scratching and buffeting him at an awful rate, because he had not demanded more. The attack brought the innkeeper's sister to his aid, and she began to assault the wife, and the carriage with Claude and his friends drove off, leaving the whole family in a rolling, fighting, scratching, and kicking mass upon the ground in front of the house.

Luke clapped his hands with delight, and cried out—

"I only wish our friend the postilion were in the midst of that."

"It would serve him right," said Claude. "But we must now look to what we have to do. Luke, I rely upon your managing the wheel."

"I'll do it."

The night was so very dark that you could hardly have seen your hand held up within six inches of your eyes, and a cold wind, too, was sweeping over the flat, open country to the right of the road, and now and then it came in such a

CLAUDE FORCES IN THE GATE TO HIS AUNT'S GARDEN.

moaning blast, that Claude was inclined to dread a stormy night for the enterprise he was upon.

Such an idea would not have given him any concern, but that May was with
him, and he knew well that she was far from qualified to meet the evil influ-
ences of the weather. This consideration made him more anxious still that
they should, at least, get back to the tower as quickly as possible.

"Luke," he said, "this is a dreary bit of road. There seems to be nothing
but hedges on each side; suppose you do it now."

"Very good. Call to him to stop, and say that I have dropped my hat."

"Hillea! postilion!" shouted Claude.

"Ai—ai, monsieur?"

"Stop a minute. My friend has lost his hat in the road. Stop your horses."

There was no great difficulty in stopping the horses, who were, no doubt, glad enough of any temporary respite from their work, for which they were certainly in no proper condition; so the carriage was speedily enought at a stand-still.

"I am afraid, gentlemen," said the postilion, "that if I were to alight, these fine horses, having no longer the fear of my presence before their imaginations, would run away, and hurl you to destruction."

It was the dread of not being able to get into his boots again, that affected the postilion.

"Never mind," said Claude. "My friend will alight and get his hat himself. It is no trouble."

Luke sprang out of the carriage, and had the old nail out of the nave of the wheel in a moment.

"All's right," he said. "Hold on firmly to the near side."

Claude flung his arm round May's waist, to save her from the shock of the fall of the carriage, when the wheel should come off, for fall it assuredly would, upon the off-side in a few moments; and then he called out to the postilion—

"You can go on, my friend. It is all right, now. You can now make what speed you please."

CHAPTER CLXXV.

MAJOR BROWN FINDS HIS FOES RATHER TOO MANY FOR HIM.

CRACK! went the postilion's whip again, and off set the horses at a better trot that before. The wheel made about half a dozen turns upon its axle, and then off it went, and dropped the carriage upon that side, with a crash that bespoke the probability that the axle itself had given way with the sudden shock.

Our three friends being, as they were, prepared for the worst, did not sustain any damage whatever contingent upon it, but Claude thought it would be better to make an outcry, so he called out—

"Hilloa! hilloa! What's that?"

"The devil!" said the postilion, as he pulled up.

Luke jumped out of the carriage, and ran back till he found the wheel, which was a few paces off, and lifting it in his hand, he flung it right over the hedge by the side of a road, into a meadow. The state of perturbation in which the postilion was, prevented him from hearing the slight noise that the fall of the wheel upon the damp grass made, and, besides, Claude took care to keep calling out, so that his attention was distracted-

"What in the name of all that's abominable," cried Duval, "do you mean by putting us in a vehicle that falls to pieces before we have well begun our journey? It is abominable. What do you mean by it?"

"The devil—it's one of the wheels!" cried the postilion. "It's one of the wheels, that's all, and I'll soon put it to rights. I must dismount, sirs, and light a lantern, and then you will see how the glory of the French nation will be vindicted by putting on the wheel again."

"Confound you, and the French nation, too," said Claude. "I do believe that the whole concern has broken to pieces."

"Oh, no, sir—oh, no. Have patience and be tranquil. All will be well. Oh, *sacre*, where is my lantern, and where are my matches? Oh, here they are. Now, sirs, you will perceive how it is that the grand nation conquers all the world, and always means to continue to do so."

With some difficulty the postilion, from a square box that hung dangling from one of the shafts, procured the means of lighting a lantern, and then he set about examining the extent of the injury the carriage had received; but even his wish to make things out at the best could not prevent him from pulling a longer face e en than nature had given him, as he said—

" I cannot help perceiving, noble sirs, that the wheel has come off n consequence of the disarrangement of the admirable apparatus for keeping it on."

"Admirable apparatus?" said Claude. " Why, it was nothing but an old nail."

" Begging the pardon of so illustrious a person as Monsieur for differing with him in the least, I admit that it looked like an old nail, but that was the artifice of it, for it was in reality a wonderful piece of mechanism."

" And greatly to the glory of the French nation, no doubt?"

" Precisely so; but—but I can't see the wheel, and I am sorry to state that there is another little derangement."

" What is that?"

" Only a broken axle, that is all."

" And enough too, I think. I doubt, Master Postilion, if all the glory of the French nation is able to put us on our route again."

" Pardon me again, sir. I will find the wheel, and I will tie the axle with a piece of string, and then we shall go on again like the fiery-winged Pegasus."

" Oh, indeed. Very good."

The postilion looked for the wheel, but to find it was quite another thing, and they saw him peering about with his lantern and uttering curses at his non-success and the extraordinary disappearance of the wheel.

" What can the meaning of this be?" they heard him then mutter as he paused, and tried to think of some probable explanation of the really, to him, inexplicable phenomonen. " This is not glory, I am afraid."

" Have you found it?" said Claude.

" I am compelled to say, Monsieur, that hitherto I have not, but I soon shall, for, after all, nothing is impossible to the grand nation."

" Be quick about it, then."

" I shall—I shall."

The postilion now went over the ground still more carefully than before, but, of course, with a similar result, and then he came to the side of the carriage, and holding up his light, he looked in the face of Claude with a very woeful expression.

The wind appeared to have increased in force now, and it was quite evident that it bore upon its gusty wings particles of rain, so that the prognostications of Claude, regarding the night, seemed about to be truly fulfilled by the coming of wet, and most probably a squall.

" Well?" said Claude, after the postilion had shaken his head several times with a look of great wisdom.

" Alas! alas!"

" What is the matter now?"

" Nothing, now, gentlemen. Only, I cannot find the wheel, and such being the case, the glory of Europe is departed for ever."

" Indeed?"

" My impression," said Luke, " is, that you have swallowed it."

" Will you have the goodness to say that again, sir?" said the postilion.

" My impression is, that you have swallowed the wheel."

' Sir, I am a Frenchman, and a man of honour, and I shall expect——"

" What?" said Luke, preparing to get out of the carriage.

" Nothing," added the postilion, " but your most patient consideration, under the present painful circumstances. I cannot tell what has become of the wheel. I do not deny certainly that I am in despair, and that the glory of my life has faded away to leave not a trace behind.'

" I think," said Claude, " I can explain his singular occurrence."

" Oh, sir, if you can——"

" Well, at the moment that the wheel came off, something went through the air like a cannon-shot; I heard it go singing along at a tremendous rate; and I think the speed with which we were proceeding, combined with the revolution of the wheel on its own axle, and the composition of forces generally, made it fly from hence with a velocity that renders its destination very doubtful."

" I am much indebted to you, sir," said the postilion, "for so highly scientific and satisfactory an account of the affair ; but as it is difficult to get on upon three wheels I—that, is I——"

" Don't know exactly what to do ?"

" Exactly so, sir."

" Where will it be possible to get a new wheel ?"

" At the post-house which was honoured a little while ago by your noble presence, gentlemen. There, no doubt; another, although not a new wheel, can he got, and if you will all wait here with patience, I will go there and procure assistance"

" Not so," said Claude, " I feel cramped by sitting so long, and would much rather, for the sake of the exercise, go myself."

" So would I," said May.

"And so would I," said Luke.

"Then we will all go," added Claude, "and leave our friend the postilion here in charge of the chaise."

The postilion had to combat this arrangement as well as he could, for somehow he did not feel at all inclined to be left alone in the middle of the road with the carriage and horses. Soltiude is a Frenchman's bane; he can bear anything but that ; and but for the necessity there was of some one staying with the horses and carriage, no doubt the postilion would have insisted upon accompanying the party back to the post-house, but he dreaded the censure he should get for such a desertion of his employer's property, so with a sigh he saw that fate meant he should stay.

" Adieu !" he said. " Of course, Messieurs will be back as soon as possible?"

" Oh, of course," cried Claude.

They all three now set off to walk back upon the road they had come, and the last they saw of the postilion was his getting into the carriage, and placing the lantern upon the most prominent part of the roof of it to warn any other vehicle that might be upon the road not to run against him, as he had no means of getting out of the way quickly.

"Now," said Claude, " the thing will be to get past the post-house without observation. How is that to be done?"

"By going singly," said Luke, " I think, or you two can go together first, and I will follow in a few moments more. By keeping upon the opposite side of the road, too, there is very little likelihood indeed that we shall be seen by any one at the post house."

" And if dimly seen," said May, "in the dark, it will seem so utterly impossible that we should be the travellers who stopped there so short a time ago, that we shall escape inquiry."

" Be it so, then," said Claude, " I did think of taking to the fields."

" I am afraid," remarked Luke, " that in a totally unknown country that would be a hazardous proceeding."

"Perhaps so. We will try then to pass the post-house."

They walked with rapidity, for they were quite fresh, having not endured any fatigue of that character for so long, and the lights in the window of the post-house soon showed themselves a little in advance. They then separated, as Luke had suggested, and without the smallest difficulty they contrived to pass the post-house.

" We are of no importance now, you see," said Claude, "so we are not even looked at. If we had come back in the carriage, we should have been again much honoured guests."

"Not a doubt of it, Claude," said May, "but we are mu.. more obliged to them now for their neglect than for their homage"

"We are, indeed. Do not let me hurry you, May; but as fast as you can go with ease to yourself, we will keep up with adopting your pace."

These words were quite sufficient to let May know how anxious Claude was to get on with speed, and she went on at a pace that one would hardly have thought it possible she could have assumed; but May was of a hardier frame than any one would have thought to look at her; and, after all, when there is the will to encounter fatigue or danger, the physical powers generally surmount it.

From the point at which the carriage broke down to the tower covered with ivy, which was the place of rendezvous with the consul, was, as near as Claude and Luke could guess, about four miles, so that they considered if they did the distance in any space of time within the hour, they would be doing very well, indeed, considering that May was with them, who ought not to be expected to keep up any great speed.

Not a soul met them on the road, and it was strange that such should be the fact upon such a high road; but the probability was, that except the diligence to and from Paris, and any chance travellers who might be able and willing to go to the expense of a private conveyance, the road was but little used.

It was not so fashionable a thing as it is now to make a journey to Paris, and, besides, the state of France was just then anything but settled, and that circumstance, no doubt, had its effect in diminishing the number of tourists.

"This is the tower," said Luke, suddenly.

Claude looked in the direction where it was sure to be, if in sight, and there, sure enough, he saw rising blackly against the night sky the dark outline of the old building.

"It's a welcome sight," he said

"It is, indeed," said May.

The tone of voice in which May spoke made Claude think that the walk had been rather too much for her, and he said—

"You are fatigued, May. We should have made our break down of the carriage closer at hand, Luke."

"Oh, no—no!" said May. "It was not any sense of fatigue that made me speak, Claude, but an earnest desire that this adventure should be terminated to your satisfaction, that's all."

"You are kind and good to say so; but, after all, it has struck me several times that it would have been more generous of me to have left you somewhere in safety in England than brought you here."

"Can you think so?"

"Yes, May, whatever the self-denial might have cost me."

"Let me beg of you not to think so, then, and even to believe that the most generous course you can pursue towards me is to let me be ever with you."

Claude pressed her hand in silence, and they continued their route towards the old tower, which each moment was more plainly visible to them. Luke ran on same little distance in advance to be certain that there was no one there upon the watch who might turn out to be a foe, as well as to let the consul and Pierre know that they were coming, if they should chance to have arrived at the place of meeting. All, however, was profoundly still by the little gate which had been mentioned.

"We are in good time," said Luke, entering.

"Oh, yes," replied Claude; "it yet, I think, for I cannot see the hands of my watch, wants a good hour to midnight. We will have a light when we get under cover, and then see how the time goes. Lean upon my arm, May."

CLAUDE DUVAL,

"Nothing will convince you, then, that I am not equal to such a walk as this?" said May. "Is it not so?"

"Well, I admit it. But one's fears, you know, are so apt to outrun even one's reason, that you must excuse me."

"Excuse you? Ah! there wants no excuse for the fears that are engendered by affection."

When they reached the little gate which conducted through an old tangled garden, long since left to grow as nature pleased, they all three paused and listened attentively for the space of about three or four minutes, in order to assure themselves of the fact that no one was coming upon the road.

"We have it all to ourselves," said Claude.

"Assuredly so," said Luke.

"Open the gate, then, and let us seek the old tower."

Luke opened the gate, which made rather a harsh tone upon its hinges; and then May, in a low tone, said—

"Did they not say that this old place was haunted?"

"Yes, with owls."

"Nay, but, Claude, after our experience at that house by Old Pimlico, I have a dread of experiencing even certain disbelief in the fact of supernatural visitations."

"Well, I can't but admit, May, that we had all of us sufficient reason given us at that time to induce the belief that there was something of a strange and supernatural character going on there."

"We had, indeed."

"And yet, I still cling to the idea that even what we saw there was and is susceptible of some explanation."

"I hope so, Claude, for I would not willingly live under the impression that we, human beings, can in any way be open to the assaults of the supernatural world; and in our case all that we saw and heard appeared to be of a friendly character towards us, yet even that friendliness had its share of terrors, from which it was in vain to try to fly."

"Think no more of it, May. We shall not make a long stay in this place; and only see now, or rather feel, for see we scarcely can at all, what a strangely condensed spot of vegetation this is. We can hardly get along for the clinging of branches around our feet, and the trees quite meet overhead, forming an impenetrable roof of green. It, no doubt, is very beautiful in sunshine."

CHAPTER CLXXVI.

CONTAINS A STRANGE ADVENTURE IN THE TOWER ON THE ROAD SIDE.

CLAUDE DUVAL was right enough in speaking as he did of the luxuriant vegetation of that spot of earth. No doubt at one time it had been a well trained and admirably kept garden, and many plants, far from being indigenous to the soil, had been placed there; but for years past, scarcely, a human foot had trodden in the place, and it had become a little wood.

Garden plants that, kept within due limits and properly cultured, had been, no doubt, here very beautiful, had gone back to a completely wild state, growing out of all size, such as they ordinarily present, and clustering up the old trees and trailing along the ground in wanton freedom.

The low boughs, too, of many of the trees had so completely blocked up the pathways, that it was with the greatest difficulty, especially in the dark, and then only by stooping low, that they could be passed; but at length our friends reached a spot that was a little more open, close to the tower, and where there appeared to have been a well kept lawn.

The grass under foot at this part of the garden was short and thick, and of a very fine quality, and the tower, old, and covered with immense ivy leaves, rose up abruptly out of it, like a tall ship from the sea.

There they all three paused.

"Perhaps, after all," said Claude, " it would have been more prudent for us to have remained by the gate, since no one was there to disturb us."

"And yet," said May, " I had, and still have, a strange curiosity to see this old neglected tower, and, no doubt, the consul will conjecture we are here."

"But it is almost a pity to give him the job of fighting his way through such a tangled mass of vegetation ; and yet, as we are here, we will not fail to have a look at the old building. You have the means of precuring a light, of course, Luke ?"

"Oh, yes."

"Well, suppose then we venture upon our exploration of the place. I can see no entrance, although it don't seem so dark as it was."

"No," said Luke, "the change from the intense shadow of the vegetation to this open space makes us think it lighter, no doubt ; but I will soon have a small hand lantern, which I took care to provide myself with at Dover, while you were down at the quay, alight, and then we shall see where we are much better than we can now, for, as yet, I confess that there appears to be no entrance to the tower."

Luke lit one of his matches, and then soon had his lantern in good order, and through the powerful lens of it he cast a broad stream of light upon the old tower.

The stream of light moved up and down, exhibiting the ivy to great advantage, and disclosing about fifteen feet from the ground a small gothic window, but no doorway was at all visible.

" The entrance must be upon the other side," said Claude.

"No doubt," responded Luke, " and here, I see, are the remains of a path that winds, evidently, round the tower."

The path, which was nearly all overgrown with grass and weeds, they followed, and they found that it lead onward with a curve, and conducted them to a gothic old doorway that was in the side of the tower. The old oaken door was close shut, and they saw that it was studded with immense nails.

" If this be fast from within," said Claude, " I am afraid we shall have to satisfy our curiosity, as best we may, with a sight of the outside of the tower, May."

"We will try it," said Luke.

" You hold up the lantern, then," interposed Claude, "and I will see what I can do with the old door."

With all his force, Claude Duval made a rush against the door, and it flew open at once before him, and he fell right into the tower. May uttered a cry of alarm, and Luke sprang forward, but Claude called out—

"All's right—all's right. It really serves me right. The door was not fast at all and I don't know how I came to assume that it was. We might have opened it with a touch, you see."

" Yes, I see, now," said Luke. " But I should have done just as you did. The appearance of strength and solidity about the door would evidently lead to the idea that it was quite fast, and would require no ordinary force to open it."

" Just so," said Claude, laughing, and rubbing the dust off his clothes. " But here we are, at all events, within the haunted castle."

May laughed, likewise, at the little mishap, now that she saw that Claude was in no way injured by his tumble, and they entered the ground floor of the old tower

It was quite easy to see at a glance that the place had not been visited for a considerable time, for the dust lay so thickly upon the floor that their feet picked it up just as they would have done a light covering of snow upon a hard bit of road way.

The room, into which the door quite abruptly opened, was of an octagon shape, and there was but one window to it, which occupied one of the faces of the octagon. The roof was shaped dome fashion, and there was not an article of furniture of any sort or description in the place.

"Quite deserted," said Claude.

"Yes, and not very tempting," said Luke.

"Hush," said May, suddenly. "What is that?"

They all three listened, and they distinctly heard overhead a strange bumping noise, and then a peculiar cry, something between a groan and a shriek, such as in all their experiences, they had never heard yet.

For some few moments after these strange sounds had come upon their ears they all three remained motionless, listening to note if they would be repeated, but the most profound stillness then reigned in the old forsaken tower.

"What on earth," said Luke, "can that be?"

Claude shook his head.

"Is it human?" said May.

"Oh, yes—yes," said Luke. "We must not hastily conclude that it is aught else."

"Nor hastily conclude that it is not," added May, solemnly. "Claude, what is your real opinion regarding the noises?"

"I have no opinion, but I have a determination."

"What is it?"

"To get up to the room from whence they come, if it be at all possible so to do, May."

"Nay, but there may be danger."

"That I don't think will deter me. I hate to let anything make an impression upon my imagination without some attempt to remove it. There surely must be some door from this room to the upper part of the tower. Cast your light well about upon the walls, Luke, and if there be a door it can't escape us for long. It ought to be in one of these sides."

"Here it is," said Luke.

Both May and Claude hurried to the part of the room where Luke was, and there they saw that he had found a key-hole, although the door with which it was associated was so nicely fitted to the octagonal-side of the room that it would, no doubt, otherwise have escaped observation.

"Where there is a key-hole there is a lock," said Luke.

"And a door I should say, too," added Claude, "where the key-hole and the lock both happen to be, in such a position as this."

Claude rapped with his knuckles against the wainscot, and the hollow sound that was produced was quite conclusive upon the subject.

"It opens, most likely, this way," said Luke, "and, therefore, although locked, no doubt, that will be the only mode by which it is fastened. Suppose we try if a French-lock is as easily picked as an English one? I have seen you soon make one yield."

"I will try," said Claude.

Duval always had about with him a few tools that might be useful during the many dangers he encountered in his adventurous career, and among them were several picklocks of different sizes to suit different locks. Judging by the eye of the size he wanted, he now introduced one of the simply-shaped implements into the lock, and by a little skilful use of it he soon heard the click of the bolt back, and then a slight pull by the aid of the picklock at once opened the door.

Quite a volley of thick black dust came down upon Claude as the old door, that did not seem to have been opened for many a year, slowly creacked upon its rusted hinges.

"Be careful, Claude," said May.

"Yes, it is as well to be upon our guard," said Luke.

Claude drew back more on account of the dust than from the idea of their being any danger in the old place; but scarcely had he done so, than a strange

CLAUDE SQUARES ACCOUNTS WITH MR. JILKY FOR HIS AUNT.

moaning noise came from some distance on the other side of the door, and then they all thought that they heard a footstep.

"Ah," said Claude, "this is worth looking to. See to your arms, Luke. It is just possible enough that this old tower, after all, may be the haunt of banditti, and, in that case, we shall do a public service in France that ought to entitle us to the thanks of the government."

"Yes," said Luke, "and a frog-pie once a year. But listen—there is the same noise overhead that we heard some time ago."

"What can that be?" said Luke.

"I am as much puzzled as you are," replied Claude. "But do you think your lantern will keep its light for some time longer, Luke?"

"For hours, if necessary."

"Then come on. I propose that we put an end to all these doubts and surmises, by thoroughly exploring the tower."

"Oh, look!—look!" cried May, at this moment, as she pointed through the open doorway that they had succeeded in making available. "Look! Oh, Claude, what is that?"

Both Claude and Luke kept their hands upon their pistols as they each darted an eager glance in the direction indicated by May, and there, amid the gloom that lay beyond the door, they saw what could not be mistaken to be anything else than a pair of eyes glaring at them.

"Good Heavens!" cried Claude. "They are eyes."

"Not a doubt of it," added Luke.

"Are they human?" said May, as she shrunk close to Claude, and kept her eyes rivetted upon those eyes with a glare of fascination. If worlds had depended upon her doing so, she could not have withdrawn her steady gaze from them.

"Speak!" cried Duval. "Be you whom you may, speak, and proclaim yourself. We came here with no hostile intent towards you. Only speak and assure us that you here bear no ill will against us, and you are safe."

There was no reply; but there, amid the interse darkness, remained the two eyes glaring at the little party like coals of living fire.

"Oh, let us come away," said May. "This is too dreadful."

"No—no!" said Claude. "It would ill become us now to leave this place without making at least an effort to penetrate this mystery."

"Shall I fire?" said Luke.

"Oh, no—no!" said May. "We might regret that."

"Yes, I don't like the idea of a shot at random," said Claude. "Give me the light, Luke."

"But you will never go towards those eyes?" cried May. "Oh, think' Claude, that it is possible that you may be going into some terrible and unknown danger. Oh, do not—do not go!"

"Nay, May, I think that the only plan is to go. The eyes continue as they were, and so—"

"No—no! They do not continue as they were," cried May. "Look—oh, look at them!"

Suddenly the two great eyes now appeared to rise higher and higher through the darkness, until at last they disappeared altogether, leaving Claude and his friends quite bewildered to know what it could possibly all mean. For the space of about five minutes they remained quite motionless and silent; and then it was May who spoke.

"Come away at once," she said, in a low voice. "Oh, surely we have seen enough of the horrors of this place."

"Luke, what do you say?" inquired Claude.

"I am willing for anything you think proper."

"Well, my opinion, then, is, that if we were to go away now, and leave the mystery just as it is, that we should in broad daylight, when we came to talk it over, very much regret having done so. I never will willingly give way to the impression that what I see is supernatural, and, therefore, I again say, give me the lantern, Luke, and I will go forward and try to find out the meaning of all this."

May shuddered.

"After all," said Luke, and he intended it quite sincerly when he said it—"after all, Duval, it is only a French ghost, if it be such a thing at all, so there won't be much to fear from it."

Claude could not help smiling at the contemptuous idea that Luke had of the French ghosts, and he took the lantern, as he said—

"You two remain here, and if I want any assistance, I will call to you."

"No—no; that will not do," said May. "If you go, we will all go. I will follow you, Claude."

"I think," said Luke, "that will be the best way; so let us get on at once, and I hope we shall find out to whom the wonderful eyes belong to, after all."

Claude agreed to this proposition, for he could not help seeing that May was much too alarmed for his safety to let him go alone; so, holding the lantern as high as he conveniently could, so as to diffuse its light as much as possible, he crossed the threshold of the mysterious door.

A few steps were sufficient to take him to the foot of a flight of old black-looking steps, that, no doubt, led to the upper apartments of the tower, and they accounted for the odd manner in which the eyes had disappeared by ascending.

CHAPTER CLXXVII.

PURSUES THE ADVENTURES OF DUVAL AT THE TOWER AND THE CHATEAU.

"ONE of the mysteries is over," said Claude, "for the one of the eyes seeming to ascend was by their owner going backwards up these stairs."

"Oh, yes," said May, "that may be true; but—but——"

"But what, May?"

"There may be dangers as well as mysteries—dangers which we have to dread much more than anything the supernatural world may say or do regarding us."

"That is very true, May. But yet, you may depend, that the only way to make any danger decrease in importance is to look it boldly in the face; so come on, and don't be afraid. After all, we may find that there is nothing to excite our apprehension, and we shall only laugh at ourselves to-morrow if we were to suffer a pair of eyes to scare us from this place. Don't you think so, Luke?"

"Likely enough," said Luke; "but I am quite sure that it is for your sake May feels, and not for her own; so I propose that you both remain here where you are, while I ascend these stairs and ascertain where they lead to, and what there is to be seen at the top of them."

"And do you think, Luke, that I have no consideration for you?" said May. "Do you think that I forget your many acts of gallantry and discretion? No, I feel for you as well as for Claude, most sincerely. But as we are getting rather too sentimental over this business, I propose that we all go, and then we shall live or die together, at all events, which will be, I think, one great consolation."

"It will," said Luke.

"Yes, but I don't intend to do anything in the dying way," said Claude, laughing, "and so, May, we will not talk of that."

"Come on, then," she said, and before Claude or Luke could make the least effort to prevent her from so doing, she had passed them both and bounded up the dark staircase like a young fawn before them.

"Stop— stop!" cried Claude.

"Stop—stop!" shouted Luke. "There may, after all, be some unknown danger.

"Come on," cried May, " all is safe and clear. Follow me."

"Now, this is too bad," said Claude, as he dashed up the old rickety staircase, two stairs at a time. "Stop, May, if you love me. If you have no consideration for yourself, have some for those who would rather suffer a hundred deaths than that a hair of your head should be injured. Stop, I say. Where are you?"

"Here."

"But where is, here? I don't see you.   A light, Luke, a light."

" I am getting one," said Luke, "as fast as I can. I had a match alight, but the movement in the air blew it out.   Here is another; all's right, I hope."

"Oh, yes." said May, from the landing at the top of the stairs, "all is right. Here is a door, you see, or, rather, you will see when you both get up here, and I assure you there are no ghosts, unless the light should reveal a few to us."

"Oh, May," said Claude, as he reached the landing-place upon which she was standing, "you should not play me these tricks ; you did not know—you could not know but that there might have been danger."

"Ah, now," said May, with a smile, "now you see we have changed places, and it is you who talk of the unknown dangers that you made light of when you were below only a very few minutes since.   How is that ?"

" Do you not know how that is ?   Ah, you do."

" No, how should I know ?"

" Shall I tell you ?   It is because your safety instead of mine is now in question, or was, rather, before I reached this spot, for now I think Luke and I sufficient to protect you."

May answered this only by a look, but that look said much more to the heart of Claude Duval than the most eloquent rejoinder to his speech could have done. Luke reached the landing with a light, and then they all turned their attention to a door which appeared as though it were calculated to resist their further progress.

The door was of massive strength, and studded with iron nails, set very close to each other all over its surface. It was of a gothic shape, and to all appearance it was fast closed,

" Strong enough," said Luke, as he tapped at it with his knuckles.

The moment he did this, these arose from within the room at the other side of the door. a strange hoarse kind of cry, such as they had neither of them ever heard in their lives from the lips of man or beast, and they instinctively shrunk back with a feeling of dread even from a contact with the door.

May, notwithstanding she had braved so much in ascending the staircase alone, clung to Claude's arm, as she ejaculated—"Gracious Heaven what is that ?" and Luke held a pistol in his right hand pointed towards the door, while with his left he elevated the light as far as he could above his head.

"What on earth can it be?" he said.

Claude shook his head.

"It puzzles me. Luke, knock again."

Luke did not seem to like the job very well, but he did not refuse to do it. He knocked this time with the barrel of his pistol, and an impotent kind of shriek from some living thing in the room at once responded to the summons.

"I wonder if that means come in?" said Claude.

"Oh, Claude, can you jest at such a moment?" said May.   "Let us go now, surely we have had enough of the mysteries of this old tower."

" Not a bit of it," replied Claude, and advancing close to the door, he dealt it a vigorous kick with his toe, as he called out—

"Hilloa, there, anybody at home ? Hilloa!"

A scuffling of feet now was the only response to this bold inquiry, and Luke called out—

"The door is giving way, Duval—look out."

The door did give way about an inch, but in another moment, clap shut it went as it had been before.

"There is some one there," said May. "There can be no doubt of that, now."

"Not a shadow of doubt," said Claude. "No more doubt than that I will find out who it is.   Stand aside, May."

"What are you about to do?"

"Why, it strikes me that the door has no fastening within, and that it will be easier for us to force it open, than for anybody on the other side to hold it shut."

"Speak them fairly first," said Luke, "for as we really do not intend any injury to any one who attempts to do none to us, it is as well that whoever is there should not take up a mistaken notion concerning our motives."

"That is right, Luke," said Claude, and then, elevating his voice, he cried out— "Be you whoever you may who are in the tower, let me assure you that we are only travellers, and have no desire to injure, or even disturb you in any way. We feel, though, that we are bound to satisfy ourselves that you are human beings like ourselves, and then we will go our way. We are English, and can have neither interest in anything that may concern you, nor intention to harm you."

Not a syllable of reply was vouchsafed to this highly pacific speech from Claude Duval to the unknown inhabitants of the old tower.

"Well," said Claude, " they might have the civility to say something."

"I don't like this silence, much," said Luke.

"It is ominous," faltered May.

"Here goes, then," said Claude. "Mind the light is kept all safe, Luke."

"Oh, yes. I'll see to that."

Duval made a dash at the door with all his strength, and open it flew, and down he fell at full length in the room. In a moment, something of the most awful-looking description sprang over him, and darting between Luke and May, rushed down the stairs, making the most hideous cries. May screamed, and Claude Duval swore, while Luke had quite enough to do not to let darkness be added to the terrors and the uncertainties of the scene, by the failure of the light.

"What the deuce is it?" cried Duval, springing to his feet. "The light— the light! Here with it. Confound it, here are the two eyes glaring at me from a corner."

"Oh no—no," said May. "Impossible."

"True, though, for all that."

Both May and Luke rushed into the apartment, and the latter holding up the light, while May crouched down by the side of Claude and shook in every limb, they saw in one corner of the room the most gigantic owl they had ever beheld, or dreamt there was to behold.

The creature was winking at the light, and shivering, no doubt with fright at the presence of the strange intruders, and it is no exaggeration to say, that it stood a good three-feet from the floor. Its large flat face, and its brilliant eyes, with a circle of yellow at the outside of them, were immense ; and take it for all in all, it looked a most fearful bird.

" There's the mystry cleared up," said Claude.

"Why—a—yes," said Luke. "Confound it! why did we not think of that before?"

" And the consul told us there were owls here," said May.

"To be sure he did ; but who ever thought of seeing such a monster owl as that ? Why, what's that? Hilloa ! who are you?"

From behind the large owl there now emerged a small one, who, with a stately, curious kind of hop, step, and jump, approached Luke, and tried to bite his ankles.

"Curse you," cried Luke. " Get away, will you?"

Claude burst into a shout of laughter as the little owl now flew on to Luke's back, and would not go down upon any account for some time ; and it was not until the old owl in the corner uttered a peculiar sound, that the little one jumped off Luke's back, after giving him several digs about the neck, and hopped back to where it had come from.

" Well, this is truly ridiculous," said Claude.

"Oh, look—look!" cried May, as she pointed to the door. It was slowly pushed open, and the other old owl, which had made the rush over Claude down the staircase of the tower, made its appearance again, and glared defiance upon the intruders.

"Is he dangerous?" said May.

"Well, he may be; but if he tries any nonsense, I shall take the liberty of putting a bullet through him."

"But how can they live?" said Luke. "That is the mystery. I don't see any outlet for them, from this place, at all."

"Behold," said May, as she pointed to an old square opening in the wall of the tower. "Do you not see what has happened?"

Claude and Luke glanced at the spot, and there they saw that a large piece of stone, which had formed the upper portion of this opening in the wall, had got dislodged in some way, and had fallen so far down as quite to make it impossible for such great creatures as the owls to pass through, so that, as the outer door of the tower was shut, they were prisoners in it.

"Well," said Claude, "one never can tell when or how one can have an opportunity of doing a kind thing. It is quite clear that these creatures have not been very long in their present predicament, or they would have been starved to death, for they cannot get much food here."

"A few mice and spiders, I suppose," said Luke, "is about the extent of the game in this rather bare preserve."

"About it; but you hold the light, May, and we will see if we cannot clear this entrance for the owls of its obstruction."

The stone was rather securely wedged into the opening in the wall by its own weight, which was considerable, and it was not without great difficulty that the united exertions of Claude and Luke could succeed in moving it.

While they worked at it, it was quite a curious thing to see how deeply interested the pair of old owls were in what was going on. They flapped their immense wings, and made the most strange and uncouth noises that can be imagined, sometimes beginning with a cry like that of a child, and ending with a loud hoot, that would have been very alarming if one had not known from whence it proceeded.

One thing was quite clear, and that was, that the gigantic creatures knew what their visitors were about.

After considerable trouble they got the great square stone to move, and then by suddenly uniting their force, they succeeded in giving it a push that sent it through the window, thundering down the side of the tower.

The two owls set up shrieks of satisfaction, and one of them made a sudden swoop through the window into the night air.

"Gone!" said Luke.

"And come back again," said Claude, as the great creature dashed into the turret again with a hoot and a shrill shout.

"This is strange, indeed," said May. "These creatures now really seem grateful for the service you have rendered them."

"Well, I must say that they do."

"Yes," said Luke, "and you may depend upon it that these kind of creatures have much greater reflective powers than people are commonly inclined to give them credit for. One thing was quite evident, and that was, that they knew what we were about, and now——"

"Look out," said Claude, as he caught May round the waist, and hurried her from the room.

Luke had just time to follow them, and get the door shut, as the two old owls and all their family made a rush to attack them.

"That," said May, "is the owls gratitude, I suppose?"

Claude laughed immoderately.

"Oh, dear," he said, "I have no doubt in the world but that they thought we intended to take up our abode in the old tower, and that it was for our own convenience, and not for theirs, that we removed the great stone in the window, and so they were determined to fight for their lodgings."

"Hush!" said Luke, "what is that?"

A faint whistle from the outside of the tower fell upon their ears, and Claude at once ran down the stairs, and out into the open air.

" The consul ?" he said.

" Yes, the same. I am afraid we have kept you waiting."

" Don't mention it, sir. We have been agreeably entertained by the owls."

" Ah, by-the-by, I ought to have warned you against them, for they are considered to be most particularly furious creatures. They commit all sorts of ravages in the neighbourhood, and people are afraid to come to the tower after them. They have been fired at times out of number, but they seem to be shot-proof, for nobody has been able to hit them at all."

" Well, we have had rather an interesting interview with them, at all events, although I must confess that at last we retreated rather ignominiously before them, and left them masters of the field. But now, sir, if you can show us the way to the chateau, we shall be your debtors for a great service."

" I will. Come this way. I have no conveyance here, for if I had attempted to buy one large enough to take us all, it would have attracted notice, and possibly might have frustrated all our attempts at the rescue of the young lady. The distance is not very great, if you are ordinarily good pedestrians."

" Never fear us," said May, " we can walk."

" Very good, then, let us come on at once. I thought I heard a strange noise a little while ago as I approached the tower, as though some of it were falling to pieces. Was it so?"

" No," replied Claude Duval, " I can explain to you the cause of that noise as we go along."

" I shall be glad to hear it, for it frightened my mare, and rather induced me to think that the old tower had fallen at last."

Duval laughed, and then, in rather a humorous style, he recorded to the consul how he and Luke had thrown the block of stone from the window of the tower, and how great the joy of the owls seemed to be upon the occasion.

" They, and all the progeny," said the consul, " would soon have been starved to death. Why, you have established, no doubt, a high character among the owl race, and are entitled to their everlasting gratitude."

Duval smiled again, as he said—

" To tell the honest truth, sir, I think their is a great and striking similarity between owls and the human race."

" Indeed ! how so ?"

" Why, you will, I am sure, admit it when I tell you, that no sooner had the owls, by actual experiment, found out that egress from, and ingress to the tower were all right, than they commenced an attack upon us, their deliverers, and if we had not effected a speedy retreat, I don't know but we might have had our eyes pecked out in the conflict."

CHAPTER CLXXVIII.

DETAILS SOME OF THE PROCEEDINGS AT THE OLD FRENCH CHATEAU.

THE consul shook his head and laughed a little at this speech of Duval's, after which, he said—

" I can very easily perceive, sir, that you have suffered something from the ingratitude of your fellow-creatures, but I do not at all say that with any obtrusive curiosity concerning you, I assure you."

Claude Duval felt that this was a kind of hint to him, to say something about who and what he was, but he replied in rather a sad tone of voice—

" My mind is so full of the possible fate of Lucy Thornton, that I can think of nothing else for many minutes. Shall we soon reach the chateau ?"

" I hope so. Let us push on a little faster, if you have no objection ?"

" None in the least."

The party now increased its speed, and Claude Duval would have been glad to be able to help May on a little, but he feared to show her any marked attention, for fear the secret of her sex should become apparent, for as yet, dressed as she was, the consul only knew her as a young gentleman in the company of Mr. Thornton, as Claude Duval chose, upon that occasion, to call himself to every one.

The rain still continued, but the wind was nothing nearly so violent as it had been, and it was well for them all four that it was not, as they were traversing a very bleak and exposed bit of country.

The consul's servant had gone on in advance, he being well acquainted with the road, for the purpose of reconnoitring the environs of the old chateau, before the others should arrive, a proceeding which might have the effect of saving a good bit of time.

This open tract of country, however, soon disappeared, and they descended into a valley, which was well wooded, and at the bottom of which was a little stream. The consul shaded his eyes with his hands, and strove to penetrate the darkness, as he said—

"From this spot in daylight, the turrets of the old chateau are easily to be seen, but now I fear they are too much confounded with the night sky for anything of that sort."

"I can see nothing," said Claude, "but a very dark mass before us, but whether it consists of clouds or of trees I cannot say."

"It is the wood in which the old chateau is embedded," said the consul. "It is not a natural wood, but one created by art, and which in time has grown to be all but impervious."

"Ah!" said May, suddenly, "there is a light in the sky."

They all looked in the direction that May pointed, and they saw a strange light right above the tree tops. It did not take them many moments to come to the conclusion, though, that this light, which May had judged to be in the sky, was at the topmost apartment of one of the turrets of the old chateau.

"You now see," said the consul, "how high some part of the building is."

"I do, indeed," said Claude.

"It is quite clear to you, that that light shines through a loop-hole, or very narrow casement in a turret; you can see the shape of it."

Before they could speculate any further upon the little light, it was gone, and the sudden cessation of its brief radiance only served to make the darkness that now succeeded it all the more black and dreary.

"It is gone," said May, with a sigh.

"Yes," said the consul; "but let us hope that we shall soon see it yet closer. We are at the commencement of the wood, now, and we shall soon be close to the chateau; but let me warn you to be very cautious."

"That we will be," said Duval.

"And there is another thing," said the consul, "that I hope, for my sake, you will try do it."

"Name it," said Claude, "and you may depend that if it lies within our power at all, we will do it."

"It is this," continued the consul. "Situated as I was in an official position at Calais, it would do me great injury to be mixed up in any serious fracas; therefore, if in preference to force you could accomplish your object in visiting France by finesse, you would greatly oblige me."

"I have but one wish," said Claude, "and that is to rescue Lucy Thornton, and if that can be done quietly, I have no desire to make any disturbance; but you do not at all wish me to fail in such an enterprise for lack of courage to enforce the object of my visit?"

"Certainly not. If nothing but force will do, we must have recourse to it. Don't forget that I am an Englishman."

"I never can forget that," said Duval, "nor that you have in the most noble and disinterested way assisted us in this affair. Without all that you have done

CLAUDE DUVAL STOPS THE CARRIAGE IN WHICH IS MAJOR BROOK.

for us in it, I doubt, now, if it would have been at all possible to bring it to a successful issue, and I do not doubt but now we shall do so."

"Well, my good friend, we will do our best."

A low, chirping sound, like the call of some forest bird, came upon the night air at this moment, and the consul said—

"That is my man. He has something to say to us."

The consul then made a very similar noise, although it was not so well executed as that which his man made, and then through a thicket came the servant, moving with extreme caution.

"Well, how is the route to the chateau?"

"Guarded."

"Ah indeed? Can they have procured information?"

"No, sir, I think not. There is one man only on the watch, with one old carbine, and he is nearly asleep. He keeps his post by the front of the chateau; but you may depend upon it that nothing is at all suspected regarding our visit."

"That is good news, then."

"Yes," said Claude, "but if he chooses to fire the carbine, he gives an alarm, although we, of course, could easily enough conquer him."

"Oh, that is well thought of. Confound the carbine! And that, when one comes to think of it, is the sole reason why he is put upon guard. It is to give an alarm to the inhabitants of the chateau—not to fight."

"I should feel inclined to make a dash at the chateau," said Luke, "and carry it by storm, without any further trouble."

"In which case, long before we could break into it," said the consul drily, "the young lady would be placed in some hiding place, of which there are always plenty in such old buildings, and all search for her would be in vain. Mr. Thornton, I say again, we must proceed with the utmost caution in the matter."

"Of that I feel assured, and so does my friend here, upon reflection."

"Oh, yes, I am contented," said Luke.

The consul was evidently rather put out at the idea of the man with the carbine being on guard, but Claude Duval, after a little reflection, said gently—

"I can't see much difficulty in the matter. If I can only be brought near to him, I will engage to silence him."

"You would not kill him?"

"Oh, no—no. There is nothing that I so much dislike as the unnecessary effusion of blood; but I would manage to get his carbine from him, and we might then easily make a prisoner of him."

"That will do—that will do. You say that he is a sleepy-looking fellow?"

"He was yawning," said the scout.

"Come on, then. Come on. We can surely manage him."

They now crept along with redoubled caution, and any one to have seen them in the dim night stealthily creeping along through the trees, and bending low to escape the branches that grew sometimes within four feet or less of the ground, would have taken them for some party of Indians about to surprise an enemy.

If it had been daylight for them to see around them, no doubt Claude and his friends would have been very much entertained by the scenery that they passed, for, in good truth, it was a most charming spot, owing all that it could to art, while the sweet wildness of nature was still about to make it beautifully diversified, and full of rich straggling vegetables, such as seemed to have spontaneously sprung from the earth.

There is always something cheering and picturesque in a spot in which art has endeavoured to do much, and then neglected entirely to nature. There will be found that strange mixture of plants indigenous to many soils, but yet making a home together, although changing, perhaps, largely their natural characteristics; and there will be seen, likewise, some of the finest flowers of nature blooming in far greater beauty, unchecked and untrammelled by the hand of man, than as if attended to by the connoisseur in such matters, and believed to be the peculiar result of human care.

Night as it was, there would come upon the senses of the advancing party, the rich odour of some fair flower which they, unknowingly, trod down on their way; and, ever and anon, they could hear the trinkle of a little waterfall, which seemed to wind among the roots of the old trees in its passage to the stream in the valley.

Claude was now by the side of May, and, as he placed his arm around her waist in the darkness, with a perfect safety from being seen amid that leafy shadow, he whispered to her—

"You are weary, May—is it not so?"

"Oh, no—no."

"Are you quite sure?"

"Quite. How can I feel tired when I know that you are with me, Claude? Besides, is not this a just and noble expedition that you are going on? Ah, yes, Claude, it is thus that your chivalric spirit should find employment, and not in—in—"

Claude was silent. He well knew how she might have finished what she had to say, and he well appreciated the delicacy of thought and feeling that left it unfinished; but May was afraid she had offended him, and she said, after a pause—

"I am ever saying too much or too little."

"No, May, no—you cannot say too much, for I well know your motive, and fully and entirely appreciate it, and—"

"Hush!" said the consul. "Do you hear that?"

They were immediately still, and then there came the same low chirping sound from among the trees, as though some forest bird had been disturbed in its slumbers, that had before betokened the approach of the consul's man. In another moment he was with the little party, and, in a low voice, he said—

"We are just upon the verge of this cluster of trees, and shall in a few more moments emerge upon the plateau in front of the chateau. The man with the carbine is sitting down, half asleep."

"Show me to him," said Claude Duval, in the same low tone.

"This way, sir."

It was now so very dark that Claude Duval had to tread in the very footsteps of the guide, for fear he should lose him; but in the course of half a minute they both quite suddenly emerged from amid the deep shadow of the trees, and although the obscurity of rather an unusually dark night was upon all things, yet the change from the little wood to an open spot was very great, and Duval shrunk back with an idea, that any one looking that way must certainly see them.

"Where are we now?" he said.

"Speak low—all is safe. This is the piece of garden close to the chateau. The man is not far from us."

"Oh, I see him."

"Where?—where?"

"There, stretching out his hand. He is standing upon something."

"The saints be good to us! Monsieur, that is a statue of some heathen goddess, they say. There are many such in the garden, and you come upon them at odd times in the walks, and they make the blood freeze in your veins again. You should see them, as I have seen them once or twice, upon a moonlight night, when the broad patches of silver light, and the dark abrupt shadows, alter the whole aspect of the garden so that you would scarcely know it if you had been brought up in it. Then, indeed, you would start, and think that some of them meant to come off their pedestals and chase you till you went mad.'

"Well—well, don't excite yourself, my friend; but tell me where the sentinel is."

"That is true. I have been puzzled once or twice in the old garden, and once I ran madly into the fish pond. But follow me, monsieur—this is the way, and don't speak till I say something to you, and then don't let it be louder than as if you were about to whisper something in the ear of a ladybird."

The man now almost bent quite down to the earth as he crept slowly on, and Claude Duval followed him, imitating his movements as closely as he could. The rest of the party lingered by the verge of the trees, keeping just within their shadows, in case, by accident, they should be visible to eyes that they by no means wished to see them.

After proceeding in this way for some time, they rounded a clump of bushes, and came to a kind of artificial embankment. Then the guide laid his hand gently on Claude's arm, and placing his mouth close to his ear, he whispered in the lowest of all low tones—

" Here he is."

" Where ?" said Duval in the same tone.

" Just on the brow of this embankment. Look steadily, and you will see his back, and the top of his head. He is sitting down."

Claude did look steadily; and about a dozen paces from him, he saw, or he thought he saw, the dim outline of a dusky-looking figure. It was perfectly motionless.

" You are sure he has his carbine with him ?"

" Oh, yes monsieur ; and if you can only get hold of it, before he discharges it, all may be well; but if he takes the alarm, and has time to pull the trigger, why, then, we may as well go back to Calais for all the good we shall do here."

Duval felt now the full importance of preventing the man from giving the alarm, by firing his carbine ; and he wished to use every possible means he could command to prevent him from doing so.

Whispering to the guide to stay where he was, Claude slowly advanced.

CHAPTER CLXXIX.

MAJOR BROOK FINDS HIS AFFAIRS WEAR A CLOUDY ASPECT.

THE greatest difficulty that Claude Duval had to contend with in his advance towards where the sentinel with the carbine was placed, consisted in the fact that the ground was so saturated with moisture, that it was as slippery upon the surface of the short, fine grass as ice.

The moment he made an attempt to ascend the embankment, he felt quite convinced that he could not keep his feet, so he wisely abandoned the idea ; and dropping upon all fours, he crawled to the top of it.

If Duval had not adopted this course, he certainly never would have reached the man with the carbine; but a few moments, now, sufficed to bring him within arms-length of that worthy ; and then Duval heard him yawn in the most unmistakable manner, and utter three or four anything but formal oaths at the duty he was upon, and which it was quite clear he thought was an elaboration of caution not at all necessary under the circumstances of the case.

The great object of Claude was to get a sight of the carbine ; for if he could once find out the position in which the man held it, he could, with something like certainty, pounce upon it ; but if he were in the dark upon that point, any sudden attack upon the man, would, in all likelihood, only result in the immediate discharge of the fire-arm.

Time and patience conquers most difficulties ; and so Duval waited until the man stooped to rest his head upon his hands, and then he saw about six inches of the top part of the barrel of the carbine ; and he felt confident, by the position of it, that it was lying along his right arm. In such a position, a very slight touch indeed would, of course, be sufficient to discharge it ; and, therefore, it behoved Claude to do what he had to do with great judgment.

" Ah, dear me," said the man. " Wet through already. Well, I suppose one can't be more than wet through, that is one comfort ; because after that, the extra rain most naturally begins to pour out of one's clothes. I wonder, now, what put it into the stupid head of Brook to place me out here on the watch after nothing and nobody ? He's a coward, like all the English. Of course all the English are cowards; and it's a shocking reflection for them to think how dreadfully we treat them, both by sea and land always."

" Confound your national vanity !" thought Claude.

"Yes," added the sentinel, "I suppose some day we shall have to go and take possession of England, and make it a province of France."

Claude could have laughed at this, but that prudence required he should act otherwise; not that he was so much surprised at it as he might have been; for it was only a few days before he left England, that he had heard the same thing from an American, who said, he "guessed" some of these days they would have to take possession of old England.

Duval stretched out his hand slowly, till it was within an inch of the barrel of the carbine, and then, feeling sure that the right hand of the sentinel was not upon the trigger, he made a dart at it, and dragged it over his shoulder in a moment, and, with his left hand, he gave him a blow on the head that sent him rolling down the little declivity.

"Take the carbine," whispered Claude—"take it."

"I have it," said the consul's man. "All's right."

The moment Claude was released from the carbine, he rolled down the embankment after the sentinel, and caught him by the throat just as he was recovering from the shock he had sustained.

"Make the least resistance or noise," said Claude, "and I will stop your breath on the moment. Do you understand that?"

"Murder!"

"Silence!"

Claude tightened his grasp upon the fellow's throat, until he felt quite satisfied that he went to within an ace of strangulation, and then he relaxed his hold a little, and said—

"Do you understand me now?"

"Yes," gasped the Frenchman. "Have mercy upon me."

"Ah, that is quite another thing," said Claude. "Now attend to what I say. Nobody wishes to take your worthless life, if they are not compelled to do so. I have a strong force here, but I do not wish to make any alarm; so now, if you please to act with discretion, you may save your life; but if you attempt to escape or to give any alarm, you won't live another moment."

"I won't—oh, dear, indeed, I won't; only spare my wretched life."

"Come this way, then."

Claude still kept a hold of the fellow's collar, who followed him with whining supplications for his life, until he brought him to the verge of the little wood again, which was reached in a quarter of the time that it had taken Claude and the consul's servant to get to the spot where the sentinel had been sitting, because they had taken a round so as not to cross his line of possible vision, while, now, Duval boldly crossed the grass flat.

The consul's man arrived at the same moment with the carbine in his hand; so that the whole of the little party was together again, having made, at all events, one prisoner.

The consul, who, from prudential reasons connected with his official position, kept in the background, was very much delighted at the success with which the supposed Mr. Thornton had captured the man with the carbine, and he whispered to Luke—

"I daresay, your friend will go through a long life without again meeting with such an adventure as this."

"Such an adventure as this?" said Luke. "Why, it is nothing to us."

"Indeed!"

"No—that is to say, I am quite sure that in such a cause my friend Mr. Thornton thinks nothing of any danger or trouble that he may have to encounter."

"Oh, yes, I understand you."

Luke had very nearly gone too far in his surprise at the idea of the consul thinking that Claude Duval was not used to adventures; but he had his thoughts about him luckily in time, and got out of what might have been a scrape pretty well considering.

Duval now spoke in a tone of calm decision to the man whom he had made prisoner.

"Now, my friend, as I told you before, your life is in your own hands. If you are obedient to me, and truly answer the questions that I put to you, you will be safe enough, but if you choose to be obstinate and contumacious, I will blow your brains out rather than have any further trouble with you."

"Oh, dear—oh—oh!"

"Don't be making that noise."

"Well, but good Mr. Brigand, I assure you I have no money. I am only a poor fellow at the best of times; and just now, good Sir Robber, I am particularly poor, give me leave to assure you."

"You are mistaken in your ideas concerning us. We do not come here to rob, but to rescue the young lady who is with Major Brook now at the villa."

"What, Mademoiselle Lucy?"

"The same. You acknowledge, then, that she is there?"

"Yes, surely, and I don't mind, noble sir, if I help you. The major is a bully, and an ungrateful rascal. He expects brave men to risk their lives and to jeopardise their honour," here the sentinel laid his hand upon his heart in the true French style, "for little or nothing; but if you, sir, who, no doubt are some great English lord, will only take a poor fellow into your service, all will be well."

"I cannot take you into my service; but if you assist me in the recovery of the young lady, you shall be handsomely paid."

"Ah, sir, Major Brook only gives me five hundred francs a year, and he expects the greatest wonders of me."

"Well, that is about twenty pounds in English money. If you really assist us and are successful in placing in our hands the young lady, I will give you that sum, so that in the next hour it will be possible, you see, for you to earn an amount equal to one year's wages."

The sentinel, upon this, made a desperate effort to embrace Duval, but he got out of his way, and it was a failure.

"Permit me, noble-minded Anglois," he then said, "to assure you that my heart's blood is wholly and entirely yours."

"Remain here a moment or two, then, while I speak to my friends about you."

Claude then retired a few paces to where the consul was with Luke and May, and in a low tone he said—

"You have heard all that has passed between me and this fellow. Do you really think that I ought to trust him?"

"I think you may," replied the consul; "the offer you have made him has so completely dazzled him, that I am certain you may rely upon his very best exertions in your favour. He is but a hired slave of Major Brook's, and, no doubt, the only obligation between them is one of money."

"Very well; what think you, Luke?"

"Trust him, say I."

"And you?" said Claude to May. She made the same answer, and then Claude paid the compliment to the consul's man of asking him, and his reply was to the effect that for the sum Duval had named he had no doubt the man would have undertaken to cut Major Brook's throat.

"Very well, then," said Claude, with a laugh, "we are strong enough, I suppose, to take the chateau by storm?"

"Yes," said the consul; "but remember me."

"Pardon me; I had at the moment forgotten that by any rough mod of conducting this business we might be endangering your official position. We will proceed with all caution. Hilloa, you fellow, what is your name?"

"Roni, noble sir."

"Well, Monsieur Roni, have the goodness to explain to us the state of affairs in the chateau, and recollect that you are engaged, and that you will receive the sum we agreed upon without fail."

"A million thanks, noble sir. Permit me, then, to have the honour to inform you, that the household consists of four men, besides the owner and two women. The men are severe vagabonds and not like your humble servant, a highly respectable individual. The women, one of whom is old and ugly as Lucifer, are both devoted to the service of the major. They are not French, but I cannot well tell what country they come from ; however, this I know, that they have committed crimes which makes the seclusion of the chateau a very desirable place for them. The major has been confined to his own room by a wound, but he has drunk deeply and swore horribly the whole time he has been at the chateau. The young lady is, I have been told, imprisoned in a tower of the old place adjoining to the major's apartments, which occupy the left wing."

"Where, of course, you can guide us."

"With all the pleasure in life."

"Are there any other sentinels besides yourself in the grounds ?"

"Not one "

"Then there can be no hindrance to our proceeding at once," said Claude, "and I pray you to be so good, my friend, as to lead the way to this left wing of the chateau you talk of."

Upon this, they all followed their new guide, who took a course at first that looked as if it were directly away from the chateau, but they said nothing, and they soon found that they had no cause to be suspicious of him, for upon reaching a gate, which he opened with a key he had attached to several others about him, the course was altered, and they rapidly neared the old building.

The path they took was right across a small garden that showed more care in its general cultivation than any part of the grounds they had seen yet, so far as they could, at such an hour, observe it at all ; and then in a very short space of time, indeed, they passed round a cluster of trees, and found themselves directly in front of the chateau.

"There," whispered the guide. "Do you see a light shining from a window ?"

"Yes—yes," said Claude.

"That is the major's room. That one window is left without the shutters being closed, so that you see the reflection of the light through it ; but, in reality, there are no less than eight windows to the room in which he usually sits."

"And the tower where the young lady is imprisoned—where is that ?"

"There! Do you not see it? It is a square turret at yonder corner. There is but one room in it, and yonder is the window of it."

"I see nothing."

"Ah, then, some branch of a tree hides it from you. Come a little this way, and you will see it quite clearly."

Claude moved a few paces to the left, and then he clearly saw the turret, and a little gothic window in it, from which a pale light burned. That window was about twenty-five or thirty feet from the ground, so that there was no such thing as getting up to it from the outside.

"Well," said Claude, "here we are certainly, but still not much the forwarder, as it appears. It won't do to lose any more time, and I propose that we at once break into the house. There does not appear to be any force sufficient to oppose us, and if there was, I, for one, don't feel at all inclined to succumb to it."

"Nor I," said Luke.

"Nor I," said May.

"Oh, do be a little composed," said the man who was acting as their guide. "I assure you the major is a very desperate and resolved man, indeed, and surely it is better to avoid bloodshed if we possibly can."

"Yes," said the consul ; "but we don't know of what consequence even a few moments may be; therefore, i say, let us come on at once, and get into the house by some means."

––––––––––

CHAPTER LXXX.

MAJOR BROOK FIGHTS A DUEL AGAINST HIS WILL.

WHEN Major Brook's man saw that those with whom, it might be said, he had temporily taken service, were in so determined a state of mind, he no longer opposed the idea of at once making way into the house.

"I will take you," he said, "to the domestic offices, and then you will not find any difficulty in making your way into the old kitchen; but the woman you will find there is devoted to the major, so it won't do to trust to her any more than to Miss Devaux."

"And who is Miss Devaux?" said Claude Duval.

"Oh, she calls herself the housekeeper; but she lives at the chateau, and has been, no doubt, the mistress of the major; but now she assists him in the seduction of any young girl who, by force or fraud, can be got into the building."

"I understand; and who else shall we have to encounter?"

"I daresay there will be the secretary, as he is called, who calls Miss Devaux, sister; but as there is about twenty years difference in their ages the probability is that she is his mother. He is a mere lad of about eighteen years old, but as wicked and vicious as it is possible to suppose any human being to be. But I must assure you that the major, by bribing the French authorities at Calais, is protected by them in any iniquity."

"We happen to know that," said the consul.

"Yes," said Claude; "but we have taken such measures, I think, as will make that dignified protection of not much use to the rascal at present, so now that we understand everything, lead on to the kitchen you speak of, and we will commence by seeing the woman who is there, you say, on duty."

There can be no doubt but that Claude Duval alone, or at any rate along with Luke, would have been sufficient to carry out this adventure; but still he felt glad that he had got the consul and his servant with him, for it gave him far greater scope of action in the matter.

The man whom they had so fortunately picked up in the grounds of the chateau, now led the way round the front of that building, and across a marble kind of court-yard to the domestic offices. After they had proceeded for some distance they saw light shining from two windows, and the man pausing, said, in a cautious tone—

"That is the great kitchen."

"Oh, very well," said Claude. "I will soon be in it."

"Oh, monsieur, be careful of Suzanne—she is one of the most violent of women, and would think no more of running you through with a spit than of performing the same operation with a fowl."

"I will take care of myself you may depend. Indeed, I rather rejoice at the opportunity of letting this Madame Suzanne know that she has found one who can, and who will master her."

The man who had given the description of Suzanne, the servant at the chateau, was evidently in great fear of her, for now he took good care to get as far in the rear as he possibly could, so that her fury might be expended upon any one else, before it could possibly reach him.

"Follow me, Luke," said Duval. "Of course all we can do with this Sazanne is to tie her up in the kitchen, and prevent her from being mischievous or noisy, and it will entirely depend upon herself whether that operation is performed with ease and comfort to her, or in a manner quite the reverse."

THE ABDUCTION OF LUCY THORNTON BY MAJOR BROOK

"Precisely so," said Luke.

Claude then whispered to May to keep back, and by no means to allow the woman to make any attack upon her, as it would be impossible for her to resist it.

"I will take care of myself," said May, "you may depend.   I do think that yonder man has succeeded in impressing you all with a terrible idea of the prowess of this Suzanne, who, after all, I suppose, is nothing but some irritable cook."

"We shall soon see," said Dick.

The light that came from the two large windows of the old kitchen was quite sufficient to enable Claude and his friends to see an old fashioned doorway, with an overhanging portico, which, no doubt, led into that portion of the establishment.

In a whisper, now, Claude begged them all to pause on the door-step, while, he went in, alone, and confronted Suzanne. Luke was, however, close at hand in case he should be wanted.

Quite boldly and easily now, and without making any effort at concealment, Duval opened the door of the kitchen, and walked in. There was no passage, so that he was in the large apartment at once without any trouble.

A good fire of immense billets of wood was burning upon the ample hearth; and nearly in the middle of the room, too, there was a French stove, in which coal was burnt, and by the aid of which those messes in which our Gallic neighbours so much delight, and the compositions of which are so many mysteries to Englishmen, were cooked. From the ceiling hung by an iron chain a lamp, in which was burnt, after a sickly fashion, lumps of grease, the consumption of which imparted a rather uncomfortable odour to the whole atmosphere of the apartment.

At one glance Claude Duval took in all these particulars, and then he looked at the occupant of the room.

Sitting on a low wicker chair by the fire was a woman of about fifty years of age, with an enormous red face, and a Norman cap upon her head. She seemed to be nearly asleep, if one might judge by her attitude, and Duval had no difficulty in seeing that she was rather a large specimen of the fair sex.

Opposite to the door at which Duval had entered the kitchen he saw another, and as he, rightly enough, conjectured that it led to the other part of the chateau, he wisely took care to place himself between it and Madame Suzanne.

"Hilloa!" cried Claude, as he saw that no notice was taken of him. "Hilloa there!"

Suzanne sprang to her feet as though she were under the influence of an electric shock.

"Who is that?" she cried.

"Only me," said Claude.

"You—you? and who, pray, are you?"

"Well, that don't much matter, I suppose, so long as I am somebody. The fact is, I have come to see the major."

"Oh, have you?"

"Yes; and I will trouble you to tell me what part of the chateau he is in, as well as what part of it I shall find a young English girl in, who was brought here yesterday only. Come, be quick."

"Oh, yes, I will be quick," cried Suzanne; and turning to a corner of the kitchen she caught up a long roasting-spit, and made such a sudden attack at Claude Duval with it, that he really had some difficulty in darting out of the way in time to avoid the murderous intention; but he did manage to do so.

"So Madame Suzanne," he said, "that is the kind of reception you are inclined to give me, is it? Well, we shall soon see who will get the best of that matter.

With these words, Claude Duval dexterously passed the infuriated cook, and caught hold of her by the back of the neck, and the more she kicked and fought, the tighter he held her, and every time she tried to turn round, he turned with her, so that she could not come at him in any shape or way, although she waved the roasting-spit about, and made a great many well-enough intentioned thrusts at him with it.

"Well," said Duval, as at last she dropped to her knees, "are you tired of this?"

"Wretch! I will have your life."

"Oh, very good—go on. Have a little more of it."

She now fought with desperation, but Duval kept the hold he had of the back of her neck, until she was fairly exhausted, and then he said—

"Luke, my boy—where are you?"

"Here," said Luke, who had been holding the door ajar.

"Come on, then. We must tie this young lady's wrists together, and her ankles likewise, Luke, for I don't think she will be quiet long, and if you can find a cork, Luke, give it me.''

"Yes. All right. Here is plenty of cord hanging from a nail here in a corner."

"Very well ; now for her hands."

Suzanne, when she found she was about to be tied by the wrists, made such a desperate effort to get away, that it really was as much as both Luke and Claude could do to get the better of her without really injuring her, and that was what they neither of them liked to do, for, however unfeminine or wicked a woman she might be, still she was a woman, and that made them careful of actually raising a hand against her.

In a few minutes, though, Suzanne was fairly conquered, and tied hand and foot, and a cork put between her teeth, so that she could not even make a noise to warn the other inhabitants of the chateau of danger.

"Come in all of you," said Claude. "We have arranged matters with Suzanne, you perceive."

The consul could not help laughing at the plight of poor Suzanne, and the quondam servant of the major was delighted at the condition she was in, and went quite close to her, and with a piece of charred stick from the fire, he made upon her lip a great pair of moustachoes, and adorned the sides of her face with a great patch of black whiskers.

"Ah! Suzanne," he said, " you do now look something like a christian, but you never did before. I have the honour of bidding you be tranquil and happy, Suzanne. Ha—ha!"

These taunts made Susanne so frantic, that she rolled upon the kitchen floor in her rage ; but nobody cared for that, and Claude Duval, opening the door that led to the inner portion of the place, was about to pass through it, when he heard a sound as of voices not far off.

Holding up his hand to his friends as a sign to be cautious, he now listened to ascertain the precise direction from which the voices came, and he found that they seemed to go further off each moment, so that he came to the conclusion that two persons were conversing who were walking away to some other part of the old chateau.

Those two persons, if what the man had told him, Claude, could be relied upon, were the major and Miss Devaux.

After some few seconds given to deliberation, as to the best plan to pursue, now, Claude walked slowly on, followed by all the party, until he came to a door covered with red cloth, which, no doubt, had been established where it was for the purpose of shutting out all noise from the domestic portion of the house from reaching the other part of the building.

Duval pushed open this door, and found himself at once in the hall of the chateau, just within the principal entrance.

"Here we are," said Claude, in a low tone, "but I no longer hear the voices that a few moments ago were so apparent to us all."

"Permit me to suggest," said the major's man, "that Miss Devaux and the major have gone up stairs to the round tower where the young English girl is imprisoned."

"Ah ! think you so ?"

"Yes ; but——"

"Silence! I hear a footstep. Let us hide in this room."

From the hall where they were there ascended a flight of very handsome stairs, the balustrades of which were richly guilt, and the wall by the side of which was painted in allegorical subjects of great beauty.

It was down the staircase that Duval heard the sound of feet coming, and he and his friends had just time to take refuge in an apartment close at hand, when, through the narrow opening that he left in the door, he saw a tall, thin female coming down the stairs quickly.

There was a very handsome lamp hanging in the hall, suspended by a gilt chain, which, although very much the worse for the wear of some twenty years, still at places reflected the light, and had a rich and costly appearance.

The major's man touched Duval upon the arm, and whispered in his ear—

"That is Miss Devaux, and I do think, if anything, she is more violent than Suzanne the cook.

—

CHAPTER CLXXXI.

DUVAL TAKES AWAY LUCY THORNTON IN TRIUMPH.

The tone of terror in which the major's servant had spoken to Duval of Miss Devaux amused him rather; but he made no remark about it, for he was too intent upon watching the proceedings of that individual.

She seemed to be a woman of about forty-five years of age, and her face was evidently inflamed by drinking. A frown of severity was upon her brow, and a more forbidding countenance, take it for all in all, Claude really thought he had never seen. To his apprehension she looked worse than Suzanne.

She had got about half way down the stairs, when a voice from a man above called out to her—

"Devaux—Devaux!"

"Well, what now?" she said, pausing, and looking up.

"You had better tell Suzanne to fasten the kitchen door."

"Oh, nonsense. There is no one to interfere. I will bring up the wine, and if this little piece of English obstinacy don't like to drink it, we will resort to other means, that is all."

"Yes, oh, yes; of course we will."

"Will you go and speak to her at once? I will soon be with you. Perhaps you may frighten her before I come. Try it."

"I will—I will; don't be long."

"Oh, no—no. Go along, do."

The sharpness with which she spoke sufficiently showed that she had not much respect for the major, for it was he who maintained with her that little colloquy upon the staircase. That fact was intimated to Duval by the man, who now seemed to be nearly overcome by terror.

Miss Duvaux came down the stairs now very deliberately, and crossed the hall. It was quite evident, in a moment, that she was about to open the door of a room that was within a few paces of that now in the occupation of Claude Duval and his party; and when she did open the door, the reflection of a light from the room shone out into the passage.

Miss Devaux disappeared.

"Stay where you all are," said Claude. "I think, after settling the cook, I can surely manage this other one."

Stepping to the door of the apartment, which had lazily swung shut, Duval at once opened it, and entered the room.

"Good evening, Miss Devaux," he said.

The person thus addressed uttered a cry of surprise, and then turned and faced him, with rage depicted upon her countenance, saying, in a haughty tone—

"Who are you, sir?"

"No friend to you."

"But who are you, and what do you want here?"

"That you shall soon know."

"I suppose one word will suffice to describe you. You are a robber?"

"I have not come to rob, whatever I may be," said Claude, "and my advice to you, madam, or miss—whatever you like to call yourself—is, to be quiet and civil."

"Let me pass."

"Oh, no."

"Then take the reward of your folly in intruding into this house."

As she spoke, she suddenly drew from her breast, where she had it concealed among the folds of her clothing, a small, triangular-shaped dagger, and made a rush upon Claude with it; but she deceived herself very much if she thought that he was the sort of person to be taken by surprise by any one. He caught her by the wrist, and held her with a grasp of iron.

"Hold, madam," he said. "You are in the hands of one who is well able to take care of himself."

At the sound of the struggle, Luke made his appearance, and catching the lady round the waist, he dragged her back from Claude, saying, as he did so—

"Tie her as we did the delightful cook. I don't know really but that this one is the most vicious of the two."

"Tie me?" cried Miss Devaux. "If you do that you are stronger, both of you, than I think you."

With this, she commenced a struggle with Luke of the most desperate character, and it was with the greatest difficulty that Claude could get hold of her, and seat her upon what looked like a small ottoman in the middle of the room. He held her fast round the waist.

"Luke," he said, "have you any cord?"

"Yes—yes."

"Then tie her feet at once, and her wrists likewise, for she is still fighting like a devil."

"Murder!" said Miss Devaux. "Murder!"

"Stop her mouth, Luke."

"All right. I have quite a nice little gag that I have made on purpose for her, with a cork and a piece of string. There you are, ma'am. Now you may kick as long as you please."

Claude Duval still held her tightly round the waist from behind on to the ottoman, while Luke tied her ankles together, and then her wrists. But she still made all the exertion she possibly could to get away, and seemed to be half frantic.

"Can't you be quiet?" said Luke. "It is of no use knocking yourself about in that way."

"Luke," said Claude, "there is a strong smell of burning in the room. Don't you smell it?"

"Well, I thought I did; but as there is no fire, and the light is from that chandelier, how can it be? Why—why, Claude, her clothes are smouldering."

"Impossible."

"Yes. Oh, look! Oh dear, I shall die of laughing! We have placed her upon one of those stupid French charcoal stoves, and she don't feel at all comfortable!"

A smothered kind of howl from the abandoned creature at this moment testified to the amount of her sufferings, and then, as Claude let go of her, she rolled to the floor, and Luke was obliged to roll her up in a large table-cover and a hearth-rug, to put out the flames that were beginning to lay hold of her apparel.

"It serves you right," said Luke.

"It is something in the way of retribution for her wickedness," said Claude; "although I had no idea that she was put to the torture in such a manner."

The sweet Miss Devaux lay groaning, wrapped up in the cover of the table, and then Claude and Luke went into the hall again, and spoke to their friends, saying—

"I don't see anything of the lad they mentioned who was here, and my impression is, that now there is no one in the house but the major to contend with. Let me, therefore, beg that you will all remain where you are, and allow Luke and me to finish this adventure."

"Be careful," said May.

"I will—I will, you may depend.   Come, Luke, we will not lose another moment."

Luke was quite as desirous as Claude could possibly be to bring the affair to a speedy decision now, and they both ascended the grand staircase with speed, and found themselves in a long sort of corridor at the top of it, which was hung with many paintings in richly gilt frames.   At the farther end of the corridor they saw a door half open, and upon proceeding towards it they found that it connected with a flight of narrow stairs.

"This leads to the tower. you may depend," said Luke.

"Let us ascend, then.   Ah, did you hear that?"

"Yes—a girl's voice."

"Oh, have mercy upon me," said a low, wailing voice.   "What have I ever done to you that you should drag me thus from my home, and condemn me to such wretchedness?"

"Come on," whispered Claude, and with a bound or two he was up the narrow staircase.

"You are completely in my power in the chateau," said a rough voice.   "It is in vain that you appeal to any one.   There is not a soul here who is not devoted to me.   You may be comfortable enough if you like; but you will never see England again, I tell you, unless I get tired of your ill temper, and turn you out."

"Oh, no—no.   Surely Heaven will help me!"

"Ha! if you wait for that, my little beauty, you will wait long enough, I take it."

"To be deceived in so cruel a way, too, by my cousin, Claude," added the girl.   "Oh, God forgive him."

"Well," said the man, "I have no objection to tell you, if it is any consolation to you to know it, that your cousin, Claude Duval, had no more to do with the letter you received, and which brought you into my power, than the man in the moon."

"Is that possible?"

"It is true.   I tell you, I had it written.   The fact is, my young secretary, Andrew, wrote it, you see. and it anwered the purpose capitally, as the sequel has already shown.   As for the attack that was made upon me in England, it failed, you see, for I am quite well again."

"Alas!—alas!" sobbed Lucy; "and I have blamed my cousin, Claude, while he was innocent! Oh, sir, if he did but guess my situation, it is not the sea that would keep him from coming to my rescue."

"Indeed? Well, I can tell you that no doubt he is hanged by this time, in England, for some of his highway robberies."

"Oh, no—no!"

"But I say, oh, yes. Where, in the name of all that's diabolical, can that woman, Devaux, be all this time?   Drinking, as usual, I suppose.   I tell you what. girl—I will have submission, and not tears. Will you be still?"

"Mercy! Oh, Claude—Claude, my much injured cousin! where are you, now?"

"Here!" said Claude, as he dashed the door of the turret open, and strode into it.

"Oh, God," cried Lucy, "it is—yes, it is—my cousin, Claude! Oh, thank Heaven! The joy—the joy!"

She burst into tears, and rushed into Duval's arms.

"I am in time, dear Lucy," he said.

"Yes—yes, dear Claude."

The major's countenance assumed a perfectly purple tint with rage, and he bellowed out—

"Rascal, what do you do here? How came you here?"

"Oh, sir, I will explain all that."

"Explain be d——d, sir! Help—help! Where are you, Peter. Help here. Suzanne—Devaux, curses on you, where are you all? Andrew—Andrew!"

He would have rushed from the room, but Luke stood in the doorway, and gently stopped him, saying—

"Not yet, sir, if you please."

"Villain! I will knock you from top to bottom of the staircase."

"Try it," said Luke.

The major retreated, and caught up an iron bar; but at the moment that he did so, Luke closed upon him, and wrested it from him; but Claude Duval called out hastily—

"Don't hit him, Luke—don't hit him. I want him in as whole a condition as possible shortly."

"Very good," said Luke.

"Lucy calm yourself," added Claude Duval; "you are saved now. I and my friends have possession of the chateau, and you have nothing more to fear. I will not lose sight of you now until I place you in your mother's arms again."

"Oh, Claude—Claude, this seems like a dream. How came you to find out this dreadful place?"

"That, together with all other particulars, we shall have ample time to talk about; my business now is with this gentleman—Major Brook, I suppose you call yourself a gentleman?"

"Go to the d—l, sir!"

"I should be very sorry to go anywhere with such a certainty of meeting with you; but, as it is, I demand of you the satisfaction of a gentleman for the outrage and insult you have been guilty of towards this young lady. I have considered the matter, and although I should be quite justified in shooting you as one would a mad dog, I will prefer the milder and more gentlemanly course, and I tell you plainly that you must fight me."

CHAPTER CLXXXII.

CLAUDE AND HIS FRIENDS EMBARK FOR ENGLAND AGAIN.

When the major saw how resolved his enemy was, he shook as though all his vaunted courage were about to desert him. His countenance, too, was expressive of great consternation. It was in vain that he strove to hide these indications of fear. They grew upon him.

It was no doubt the fear of a guilty heart that weighed down the spirit of Major Brook at that moment.

Poor Lucy, too, was scarcely less terrified than he, for now she began to comprehend that her cousin, Claude, was not satisfied with rescuing her from the horrors of her situation, but that he intended, with so chivalrous a spirit, to give the major, perhaps, a chance of killing him. This was a state of things which, to the unsophisticated sense of the young girl, was most unreasonable.

"Claude," she said, "do you think that I could see you endanger your life against that of such a man?"

"Let me take my own course, Lucy."

"No—no; indeed, and in truth you must not, Claude. Come away with me at once from this dreadful house, the very air of which seems terrible to me to breathe. Oh, come, Claude, come."

"Soon, I hope and expect, Lucy; but I must and will settle affairs with this man first. Now, sir, your answer to what I have proposed."

The major made a desperate effort to recover his usual bullying tone and manner, and in a loud voice, he cried—

"Who are you, then, sir? It is, I suppose, not a very unreasonable thing for me to ask who it is who breaks into my house at this time of night, and coolly asks me to fight him on equal terms?"

"Let it suffice, sir, that I am this young lady's nearest male relation, and that gives me a title to be her defender. Lucy, oblige me by going down stairs, if you please. You will soon find kind friends who will welcome you."

"But, Claude——"

"Nay, will you not do so little for me, after all the trouble that I have taken in your behalf?"

"Anything in the world, Claude; but I cannot—I dare not leave you to the villany—the treachery of this man."

"My faithful friend, Luke, will stay with me."

"Must I go?"

"Yes, Lucy, and go quickly."

"Let the girl stay," said the major, his lips quivering with rage and fear. "Why do you send away a witness to your violence, sir? Let the girl stay."

"No, coward, the girl shall not stay. Go, Lucy."

Lucy reluctantly left the room; and then Claude made a sign to Luke to fasten the door, which he did.

"Now, major," he said, "I might, as I said before, shoot you like a mad dog, and be quite justified in so doing, for you already have fired at me with an intention, no doubt, to take my life if you could; but I will not do so. You shall have the chance for your life that I do not believe you would give to any one else."

"Do you wish to murder me?"

"Oh, dear, no."

"You do. You came here for the purpose of doing so. If you are the relation of the girl, I can tell you that she is as pure and innocent now as she was before she left her mother's house. That ought to satisfy you."

"I am satisfied upon that head, sir."

"Then be off with you, in the name of the devil, and take her along with you, and I only hope I may never look upon her or you again."

"That Lucy Thornton," said Claude, controlling the passion that was swelling in his bosom with no small difficulty, "is now pure and innocent, as when she left her mother's home on Finchley-common, may be, and I believe is a fact; but she owes none of that purity and that innocence to the forbearance of Major Brook. Her own courage and virtue are alone the safeguards, no doubt, that have hitherto sustained her, and your guilt is the same."

"Bah! Be off!"

"No, sir, you shall fight."

"Then, in a word, sir, I will not fight."

"You cannot mean that? Are you really an officer in the army?"

"Go to the devil, sir. I won't be bullied and cross-questioned by you, or by any man breathing."

"That's right, Major Brook; and so, you will fight?"

"I am wounded."

"That is no bar to the pulling the trigger of a pistol, major. Here are an excellent pair of weapons. This room is just about long enough for the purpose. Take one, and place yourself where you will, and my friend will give the word to us both to fire."

"I will," said Luke.

"I will meet you in England, sir. The laws of France are severe, and if either of us should fall, the survivor would be involved in much trouble. I say, sir, that I will meet you in England, where and when you will; but I will not fight a duel here, with no friend by me, and between four walls."

"Is that your determination, major?"

"It is."

at window."

"Yes—there it is," said Luke, as he flung open a small latticed-window, and looked out for a moment.

"Is it far down, Luke?"

"Well, I should say it is about sixty feet."

"That will do.   Now, major, as you will not fight, it becomes my painful

CLAUDE APOLOGISES TO THE SPY, AFTER HAVING PUSHED HIM DOWN.

duty to throw you out at this window, and leave you to take your chance of the result of that escapade."

"Out at this window? Why, it is certain death, and a horrible death too!"

"Then you will prefer fighting?"

"Give me a pistol: anything is better than that. If I must fight with a savage, why, the sooner it is over the better."

"Perfectly my idea, major. I thought we should understand each other in a little time. Choose which of the pistols you like, and take up your position."

"Are they both charged?"

"Yes, with ball, and primed carefully."

"Very well, sir. You force the duel upon me, recollect."

"Perfectly."

The major took one of the pistols from Claude and strode to the farther end of the room, pulling, as if accidentally, a table between him and his foe as he went; and then he turned sharply, and raising his pistol, cried—

"Take it, then, if you will have it!"

The sharp report of the pistol rang through the room in a moment, but, from the look of the major's eyes, Claude Duval had had his suspicions that some such a course might suggest itself to him, and he was ready to avoid the shot. The moment the major had turned, Claude ducked almost to the ground, and the bullet buried itself in the wainscot behind him.

"Villain!" shouted Luke.

"Oh!" added the major, who, through the smoke, could not tell what had been the effect of his shot, but who, hearing nothing, thought it was mortal to Claude. "Oh, I have a pistol of my own for you, my fine fellow, and so I will get rid of you both."

As he spoke, he fired at Luke, and hit him on the outside of the arm, only tearing his coat and making a gush of blood by the passage of the bullet just under the skin.

"Try it again, major," said Claude, coolly. "Have you any more shots to oblige us with?"

"By Heaven, I have missed him!"

"To be sure you have."

"And I am now defenceless."

"You don't say so?"

"You won't kill a man in cold blood? You are surely a gentleman, and not a murderer? Help—help!"

"Cold blood do you call it, major? Murder do you call it? Oh, very good, sir; you miscall things strangely. Who here would think of murdering you, I should like to know?"

"Then you will spare me?"

"Hark you, major. We are fighting a duel; you have had your shot—a little too soon, to be sure, but still you have had it—and, according to all rules, it is now my turn."

"No, no!"

"But I say, yes, yes. Stand firm now, major; you are an officer and a gentleman, and know what fair play is in these matters, of course."

The major shuddered up against the wall of the room as though by some means he could reduce himself to such a small space that it would be impossible to hit him?"

"Are you indeed a coward?" said Duval.

"No, confound you!"

"Take that, then."

Bang! went the pistol, and with a loud cry Major Brook fell to the ground. The report echoed through the mansion, and a volume of blue smoke whirled round the heads of the party.

"It is done,' said Claude, "and yet——"

"And yet what?" said Luke.

"I wish I had spared him."

"Well, Duval, it is too late for regrets now. Come away at once. I presume that your journey to France has now accomplished its object, and that you have no desire to stay here any longer?"

"None in the least."

Claude hastened to the door of the room, but a sudden thought seemed to come over him before he could leave it, and he turned back and approached the prostrate form of the major.

"It seems a hard thing to leave the poor devil there," he said. "He may be only wounded."

"You pity the man who would have inflicted an injury worse than death upon Lucy," said Luke, "and who would have assassinated you, notwithstanding you had the generosity to give him the fair chance that an honourable man, if you and he had fallen out, could but have expected."

"No—no. Let him lie."

"So say I. Come along, then, and, for the love of Heaven, let us get out of this abominable house as soon as we possibly can."

"I am quite as anxious to quit it as you can be, Luke. No doubt both May and Lucy are alarmed at the firing now, so we will go to them and relieve their fears."

Letting the door of the turret slam shut after them, which it had an inclination on its hinges to do, Duval and Luke now made their way at great speed down the staircase. They had not gone far when they heard the voice of May, crying—

"Claude—Claude, what has happened? Oh, speak to me! Are you safe? Speak, I charge you, Claude."

"All safe," said Duval.

In another moment he was in the arms of May.

"What an enthusiastic lad," said the consul, drily, "and how fearful he was that his brother would get into some mischief!"

These words, spoken as they were with a slight tone of sarcasm, were sufficient to let May know that her secret was suspected, if not discovered.

CHAPTER CLXXXIII.

THERE IS MORE DANGER AT THE CHATEAU, BUT THE ENGLISH PARTY ESCAPES.

It might be that the consul was a little vexed at finding he had not been treated quite so confidentially as, considering the great acts of friendship he had done for the party, he had rather a right to expect; and such a feeling may have given a little sarcasm to the tone in which he spoke when he made the remark concerning the great susceptibility of the pretended brother of Mr. Thornton, as Claude called himself.

If the consul had such a feeling, however, it quickly gave way before his better nature.

"Pardon me," he said to Claude, as he held out his hand. "I had no right to say what I did."

He saw that his words had attracted the attention both of Claude and the sham brother.

"Dont mention it," said Duval, with a smile, as he took the consul's offered hand. "I ought, in spite of the delicacy of a lady, to have confidentially told you what you suspect."

"No—no. I have no right and no desire to pry into your secrets at all."

"Nay, permit me. Step aside a moment, and I will tell you. That seeming youth is my cousin."

"Oh!"

"Yes; but as I could not persuade her to stay at home I made her assume the dress you see her in, as the one in which she was the least likely to come to any danger: and as one, too, which in appearance made our party look all the stronger. I pray you pardon this tardy confidence."

"I am excessively mortified with myself," said the consul, "that I have at all provoked it by a heedless remark."

"Tell me," said May, approaching Claude—"tell me what occasioned the shot that we heard just now."

"It was nothing. Let it suffice that we are all ready to leave the chateau, and that the sooner we get away from it the better. I shall be pleased, for one,"

"And I," said Luke.

"And I," said May.

"I think," sobbed Lucy, "I, too, may with truth say that."

"Come, then," added Claude. "Lean upon my arm, Lucy, and calm your agitation. You know that you are quite safe now; and as we go along, I will tell you how it was that I, of all people in the world, came to hear of your sad situation."

"And how you came to rescue me?"

"Nay, that latter proposition followed naturally enough upon the former one, Lucy. To know that you were in such peril was quite a natural course for such an effort."

"You are very kind and good to me, cousin Claude."

Claude passed her arm within his, and May was taken charge of by Luke. She was not at all jealous that Duval at that juncture paid the most attention to poor Lucy, who was evidently in a most deplorable state of nervous agitation.

And, indeed, when we come to consider what that young and lovely girl had had to go through, we need not feel any surprise at her state of mind, even if it had bordered upon insanity. Had she not been violently torn from her home, and forced into the society, during a journey of many miles, of a man whom she despised and loathed? And had she not been haunted with the apparent fact that she was far away from all succour? Had she not been even spared for so long upon that very ground, that she was a victim for whom there was no help— no redemption?

It was only something wonderful that a young girl of her age and little experience of the world had preserved her senses at all amid such a complication of evils.

Now she clung to Claude with such an intensity, that if he had been ever so much inclined to leave her even for a moment, he could not have done so without actual violence.

"You will, indeed, save me?" she said.   "You will take me with you now? You will not abandon me to that dreadful man?"

"Hush! hush! Lucy. I may tell you that it is impossible Major Brook can trouble you further in this world."

"In this world? What do you mean?"

"That he is dead."

"Dead!"

"Yes, Lucy; but in fair fight, so far as I was concerned, although most foul and dastardly fight, so far as he could make it. And now let me beg of you that you will dismiss him from your mind as though such a person never existed."

"Dead!"

"You do not regret it?"

"Regret it? Oh, no—no! I only wondered for what purpose Heaven could have created such a man, or having created him, could allow him to exist to the detriment of purer natures."

"Come—come, be calm. We will say no more of him."

They had now reached the front entrance to the chateau, at which the consul advised them to leave, as it cut off a considerable distance through the grounds, which, upon their arrival, they had traversed to get to the domestic portion of the establishment. Duval laid his hand upon the door, which was not fast, and swung it open.

"Fire!" cried a voice from the outside.

At the instant, Claude clasped Lucy in his arms, and dropped to the floor with her, as half-a-dozen bullets passed over his head, and went into the wainscoting at the farther end of the hall.

The rest of the party were not in the line of the shots at all, as the opening of the door shielded them completely, otherwise much mischief might have been done.

Indeed, if those who were without, be they whom they may, had not been so precipitate in their actions, the whole of Claude's party might then and there have perished. As it was, no mischief whatever was done, and Luke, seeing the immediate propriety of doing so, sprang forward and dashed the door shut, and put up a long bar against it.

All was confusion now for a few moments, for nobody could come to any precise opinion regarding the character or the meaning of this attack upon them from the outside.

Poor Lucy, overcome by the accumulated terrors she had passed through, now fainted away, and May held her in her arms, looking so bewildered herself that she was in all but as bad a condition as Lucy. Even Claude was so astounded by the sudden attack, that he stood for some moments irresolute.

It was Luke who roused him.

"Keep out of the line of the door!" he cried. "They may fire through the panels when they have loaded again."

Duval started like a man suddenly awakening from a dream, as he cried in a loud voice—

"What is the meaning of this? Can any one give me an explanation of this attack?"

"The brigands of Soissey," said the consul's servant.

"Brigands?"

"Yes. They are about this neighbourhood, but it is seldom that they have the daring to attack a chateau."

"Hark!" said Luke, "some one speaks from without."

They all listened intently.

"Surrender!" cried a loud voice. "Surrender, while you have life to do so, for we are determined to conquer you all, and it will be the worse for you if any of our brave band fall, or if any injury is done to the Chevalier Brook!"

"Ah," said the consul, "do you hear that? It throws a new light on the affair altogether"

"What new light?" said Duval.

"Why, it proves what I have suspected for some time past, namely, that this Major Brook, as he called himself, was in league with the brigands of Soissey."

"There's no doubt about it," said the consul's servant, "and they have come to avenge him, if too late to save him."

"But who could have warned them? I thought we had everybody safe here," said Claude. "Surely we had."

"No," said the consul, "there was a kind of youth here, forming a portion of the establishment, that we have not found. You may depend that he has had time to give some signal to the brigands. The wood in which it is reported they live is not far off."

"Let me explain this seeming mystery," said the man whom they had captured in the grounds of the chateau.

"Do so, if you can," said Claude.

"It is true that this Major Brook is an agent of the gang of banditti. They confine their depredations mostly to English travellers, and, consequently, as it is English coinage and English bank-notes that they get, they require an agent to dispose of them in England."

"And this Major Brook was that man?"

"He was. But is he really dead, sir?"

"I think so."

The man shook his head.

"Ah, gentlemen, you don't know him as I do. He has as many tricks and doubles as a fox. He is an old accomplished brigand, and unless you are quite sure he is dead, I will take the liberty to doubt it."

A strange grating noise at the door of the chateau at this moment sounded upon their ears, and they paused to listen.

"What does that mean?" said Luke.

"They are trying to open the door," said the consul; "but if they fail in that, they will soon find some other mode of getting into the chateau. This hall is spacious, and commands the upper story, which is from without not easily accessible. I recommend that we defend this hall as well as we can by closing and fastening all the doors leading to it or from it, and then try to discover the number of our foes."

This advice was too manifestly good for it not to be at once followed, and the consul, assisted by Luke and his own man, soon shut all the doors and locked them, and as they were very massive, it was pretty evident that the brigands could not advance upon the party in that way without giving effectual notice to the besieged of the fact.

"Gentlemen," said the man whom they had picked up in the grounds, and whose fidelity to them they had no reason to doubt, "I have a proposition to make to you, which, if you agree in, will, I think, save you all."

"Make it," said the consul.

"What is it?" said Claude.

"Just this—that I know how from the upper story to leave the chateau; and as the brigands know me to be one of the major's men, they will offer no opposition to me. I will, to them, exaggerate your force, so as to make them slow and cautious as to what they do, and then I will make my way into the stables and mount a swift horse, and ride to Calais for assistance."

"Do that, and I will give you a hundred pounds," said Claude.

"And I another," said the consul. "In the name of my government, I will promise such a sum to you."

"I will try my best, then, Messieurs."

"Hark you," said the consul. Go direct to the barracks of the fourteenth reigment of chasseurs, and ask for the colonel. "He is a friend of mine, and will hasten to the rescue."

CHAPTER CLXXXIV.

CLAUDE AND HIS FRIENDS DEFEND THEMSELVES MANFULLY IN THE CHATEAU.

HAVING then, received his instructions, the man started at once up the great staircase, waving his hand as he went, saying—

"Hold out for two hours, and all will be well."

"Two hours is a long time," said the consul, as he shook his head, "but we will do our best."

"There are some guns in a small recess on the staircase," said the consul's man. "I noticed them a little while ago."

"Get them, then, for Heaven's sake!" said Claude. "We are but insufficiently armed with pistols against these rascals without."

"I don't at all like the continuation of that noise at the door," said Luke. "Do you hear it still?"

"I do," said Claude. "I will creep forward, and find out what it is."

"No—no," said May, "You will be shot, perhaps. Oh, no, do not go!"

"Let me go," said Luke. "Stay where you are, and let me go."

Luke, without waiting for further argument about who was to go, at once advanced, crouching down quite low towards the door, and presently he returned, saying—

"They are only filing the bar in two."

" What, the bar behind the door ?"

"Yes ; but there are two bolts.   I have managed quietly to slip one into its socket ; but the other is high up."

" Here are five guns," said the consul's servant, approaching.

"Give me one," said Claude. "Ah! this will do."

He rapidly, from the little powder-flask he had with him, put a charge in the gun, and then rammed down, well wrapped in leather, a couple of pistol bullets.

"Now," he said, " I think I will give the gentleman with the file a little hint that we prefer the iron bar left alone."

"Claude, you will be killed !" said May.

"Cluade ?" said the consul. "Is that your name ?"

" Never mind, sir, just now.   Let us all fight like men, without reference to our names ; and when we get rid of the present danger, we can ask each other as particularly as we like who and what we are."

" You are right."

"Oh, do not—do not go !" said May.

"Hush !" said Claude. " It is not by avoiding danger that safety is best secured, but by meeting it with a determined front. Say no more to me. I will take good care of myself, you may depend."

May did not like to carry her remonstrances any further.   She knew quite enough of the daring character of Duval to be well aware how futile to him any reasoning that had for its basis personal danger would be to deter him from any act.

It was soon seen, though, that Duval was not inclined to give the enemy any advantage over him if he could at all help it ; for he made his advance towards the enemy with abundance of caution, and to see him one would have thought that he had been accomplished in the warfare of the Indians.

Throwing himself quite flat down upon the floor, he managed to get along to the door of the chateau, and when he was close to it, he heard the sound of the file at work upon the iron bar in as cool a manner as if the man who was using it had not the least idea that any one in the shape of an enemy was upon the other side.

The probability was, that these rascally brigands thought they had only to get face to face with those whom they intended to murder to achieve a victory at once.

It did not occur to them that the party was English, with the exception of the consul's servant.   If three Englishman were not a match for twenty French brigands, it would be a bad thing, indeed.

We shall soon see how the fight progressed.

When he got close to the door, Claude slowly rose up, and placed the muzzle of his gun within six inches of its panels, and just over the spot where the file was pursuing its operation.

That the well-rammed-down charge of the gun would go through the door Duval did not entertain a moment's doubt, and so he pulled the trigger.

The report, owing to the manner in which the gun had been loaded, was sharp and clear, and a yell from the other side, accompanied by the instant cessation of the work of the file, showed the effect of the shot.

In another moment some six or eight carbine shots came crashing through the door ; but they did no damage at all for directly he had discharged his gun, Claude had let himself drop flat upon the floor ; and as nobody else was at all in the line of the shots, they all flew over the hall as the others had done, only crashing a lamp and a statue in their progress.

" I don't think," said Claude, as he got back to his friends, " that we shall hear any more filing at the iron bar."

"You hit him ?" said Luke.

"I think so."

"Certainly so," said the consul. "1 never heard a clearer or sharper report from a gun."

"A small charge," said Claude, "well rammed down, will do wonders, with a good gun, as this undoubtedly is."

Dismal groans proceeded now from the other side of the door of the chateau, and then a voice was heard cursing and swearing at some one else for not being quiet.

"They don't like us to hear their wounded," said the consul. "Ha! they want a parley with us. Hush!"

"Hilloa!" said a voice from without, "open the door, now. It is all a mistake."

"Don't answer them," said the consul. "It is much better to leave them in doubt regarding us. Silence and mystery will terrify them more than anything else."

"Come—come, good friends," said the voice again from the outside. "We are willing to forget and forgive what is past, and to make good company with you all; or if your wish is to leave the chateau, I will withdraw my men, and you may do so in peace."

Not a word was spoken in reply.

"Are you deaf?" cried the voice in a tone of evident growing anger.

"That will do," said the consul; "that fellow will get into a passion in a moment or two, and then he will come out in his true character."

"Come now, Messieurs," added the voice. "This is a good joke, no doubt; but let it be considered over. You are men of honour, and so are we."

"Oh, dear!" said Luke.

"Hush! hush!"

"We fight for the glory of the French nation," added the voice, "but we are satisfied with what has been done, and we will no longer resist your departure from the chateau."

"That is cool," said Claude.

"Very," said Luke.

The captain or chief of the banditti now waited for a few moments to see how his pacific overture would be received; but as the same provoking silence was maintained, his patience forsook him, and he all at once burst out with a complete torrent of wrathful invectives.

"Curses on you all!" he said. "I swear to sacrifice every one of you to my just resentment. I will cut all your infernal throats myself with the most enthusiastic pleasure in life."

"For the glory of France, no doubt," said Claude.

The consul laughed.

"I will smash you all into pieces! Curses and maledictions light upon you," added the rascal. "Come, my brave band, fire again at the wretches—fire, I say!"

Another rattling discharge of fire-arms through the door now came to do as little injury as the former one had done; and then, when the echo of the stunning report was over, all was immediately still.

"What the deuce are they at now, I wonder?" said Luke. "They are trying on some nonsense or another, you may depend."

"And how still they are," said May.

"I don't like that stillness," said the consul. "Suffer me to go forward to the door with one of the guns."

"Why not go upstairs one of you," said May, "and reconnoitre the enemy from one of the windows of the upper story?"

"There now," said the consul, "we none of us thought of that before; but I am going too far, perhaps, by saying that. I should only say, that I did no think of it."

"Nor I," said Claude. ' The fact is, these fellows kept us so very busy here that we had no time to think of anything else. Will you go, Luke?"

"To be sure."

Luke hastened up the grand staircase, and then Claude said in anxious tones to May—

CLAUDE AND HIS FRIENDS ARRIVE IN SIGHT OF THE OLD TOWER.

"How is poor Lucy?"

"She is moving poor girl, but she has hardly spoken to me. A few nearly incoherent words are all I have been able to get from her, and those show that her mind is wandering."

"Poor girl!"

"Alas, Claude I fear that the repeated snocks her mind has sustained will have the effect of permanently affecting her."

" Let us hope not."

" Fire !"

Crash came half a dozen bullets right down upon the stone pavement of the hall from some opening a good height above the door of the chateau.

" Ha—ha !" laughed the captain of the banditti. "I had you there."

If the little party had not been all but within the shelter of a deep door-way of one of the principal rooms on the ground floor, there is very little doubt but that the discharge of the carbines of the banditti would have done some of them a serious injury ; but as it was, they all escaped, and the bullets were flattened against the stone-work of the hall.

" Don't speak," said the consul. "Don't say a word. It is only through a kind of fanlight that they have fired, and it is so narrow that they can see nothing through it."

" The rascals !" said Claude; " I will try a shot up at them."

" Claude ! Claude !" cried Luke from the staircase, in an earnest, but low voice—" Claude !"

" Yes, Luke?"

" Come this way."

" To greater peril," said May. "Oh, Luke ! how could you call him ?"

" You mistake," said Luke. "There is no danger ; this way. I have found a little window which commands a view of the outside, and from it you can see nearly every one of the brigands."

" Ah ! can you so ?"

" Yes. We may as well have a shot at them."

" Certainly. We will all go. Yet, no—Some one must stay with the ladies. Will you, Mr. Consul?"

" No," said May. "Leave us alone. You will not be far off, and I think we are tolerably safe where we now are."

" Quite safe ; and yet——"

" Go, then, Claude—go at once with your friends. I will take good care of Lucy, you may depend. Go, and strive to put an end to this dreadful contest."

CHAPTER CLXXXV.

THE CHASSEURS MAKE SHORT WORK WITH THE BRIGANDS OF SOISSEY.

THUS urged by May, and feeling that in real truth she was in as perfect safety for the time being without him as with him, Claude yielded to the impulse to accompany Luke to the upper story of the chateau.

The consul and the consul's man went likewise; so that May was left with the poor trembling Lucy in that besieged hall.

The spirit of the young creature did not quail at such a circumstance, for she called her reason to her aid, and told herself not only that there was no danger, but if there should any arise unexpectedly, she could raise her voice, so that Claude could hear her in a moment.

In the meantime, Luke led the way to the corridor on the floor above, and proceeded to a small window that was half hidden by foliage, but which looked right down upon the space in front of the chateau.

" I think," he said, " that the morning must be very close at hand, for there is a white kind of light in the air, by the aid of which you may see the rascals that are assembled to attack us."

" Capital !" said Claude. "Station me on the right spot, Luke."

" Here," said Luke; " a little more to the right. Can you see them now, Claude ? Ha ! you do?"

"I do."

"Is it not light, rather?"

"Yes, there is a white mist upon the ground, and the sky is rapidly getting lighter. I think with you Luke, that daybreak is near at hand; and now I see how these villains have made their way to the top of the door."

"Yes, a tree."

"Exactly. They have burnt down a young sapling, and tied it in some way, so that it makes quite a kind of rude platform to the top of the door; but they are none of them there now. Do you see, Luke?"

"Yes, with ease."

"And so do I," said the consul. "I have found a peep-hole here, through which I can easily reconnoitre the enemy. They are carefully reloading their carbines, are they not?"

"Yes," said Claude; "and they are short of bullets, for I can see them picking up small pebbles off the path, and putting them into the barrels of their carbines."

"Let's have a shot at them," said Luke.

"Stop a bit. We will see what they are going to be at next before we fire. We can do so at any moment. Count them, Luke, while I do the same, and we will see if our separate estimation agrees."

"I only make eleven of them," said Luke.

"And I twelve," said Claude.

"Yes, I now make twelve. There was one close to the door, whom I did not see. There are twelve."

"Besides the wounded," said the consul. "Long odds against us, rather, don't you think?—that is to say, if we were not in a fortress, which we have had the good luck to convert this chateau into."

"I don't know," said Claude. "I do think that three or four determined men might scatter them by making a rush among them."

"It would be hazardous," said Luke, "as they could afford losses that the three or four could not, you see, Claude."

"There is reason in that certainly. Mind you, I don't propose such a step, as we have those below whose safety is more dear to us than the glory of such a conquest; so I advise everything we do to be strictly on the defensive, and that we keep every advantage of position that we possibly can under the circumstances."

"That is good generalship," said the consul. "But watch them. What are they about now do you think?"

The brigands had duly loaded their carbines, and now they stood in a circle round their leader, who said something to them in a tone that did not reach Claude or his friends, but by his actions, he seemed to be pointing to a portion of the chateau at some distance from where they then were, and he was, no doubt, planning another mode of attack.

The little party at the window could see them plainly, and when the man who appeared to be the chief among them had explained what he meant, the others, by all the extravagant gestures of Frenchmen, showed how entirely they approved of the idea.

"They mean mischief," said Luke.

"Not a doubt of that," said the consul.

"Well," said Claude, "I dislike firing upon men who don't know that they are in danger; but our present position is an exceptional one, and these rascals deserve no consideration at our hands, inasmuch as they would, of course, take every advantage of us they possibly could; so I don't think we ought to let them walk off, to perpetrate the devil's own mischief, probably, at some part of the chateau which they know to be more assailable than this, without giving them a taste of our fire-arms."

"They are brigands," said the consul, "and there's a price upon every one of their heads. You ought to feel no compunctions at all about your mode of dealing with them, so that you repel them."

"Very well. When I give the word, you and Luke fire upon them."

"Agreed," said the consul.

"I am ready," said Luke.

From the elated manner of the brigands, and the ludicrous attitudes into which they threw themselves, it was quite evident that they were specially well pleased with the plan of their rascally chief, be it what it might.

As many Englishmen would have agreed to a proposition, and gone off to execute it at once, without any bother about it; but these Frenchmen could not go without putting themselves into such theatrical attitudes first, and stalking about, and twisting their moustachoes, and patting their breasts, as were quite amusing to see.

Perhaps, though, after all, that is the mode by which French courage is got up to the requisite point of enthusiasm to enable them to go through with any enterprise; for certain it is, that they make more noise over the most trifling affair, than the same number of Englishmen would make over the disruption of a kingdom.

"They are going now," said Claude.

"Yes—I see them," said Luke. "Give the word—give the word."

"Fire!" said Duval.

In an instant the three guns were discharged, and three of the brigands fell to the ground, for each had singled out his man. Claude had resolved to bring down the chief, and he succeeded in so doing, for that ruffian fell, and rolled over and over, and roared out in the most ludicrous manner imaginable, while the other two who were hit lay perfectly still.

Those two were killed upon the spot.

"Bravo!" said the consul. "Load again."

"Hilloa!" said Claude. "That fellow is up again."

The chief of the brigands rose to his feet, and the only indication he gave of having received any serious injury, was by shaking his head horribly, and grinning in the most diabolical manner. He yelled out some few words to his comrades, and they darted off through the bushes.

"You missed him, Claude," said Luke.

"Surely not."

"You may depend you did."

"I think so, too," said the consul.

"But he fell!"

"Yes, from fright, no doubt. The sudden and unexpected discharge of fire-arms had the effect of terrifying him, and he, no doubt, for the moment, thought himself a dead man; but you may depend he is not hit at all. He will pretend to his comrades that he is wounded, no doubt."

Claude looked very much disappointed, and swinging the gun in his hand, he said—

"This is an English gun, too. I can't imagine how I came to miss the rascal, for I put in a good charge, and rammed it down well."

"The fact is," said Luke, "we were forced to load with pistol bullets, and they, not filling the bore of a gun, are sure to fly stragglingly. I don't look upon your missing that fellow to be half so extraordinary as our hitting the two others, under the circumstances."

"Well, it may be so," laughed Claude. "At all events, I did miss him. And now we had better go down stairs to our friends below, who, no doubt, hearing these shots, will be somewhat anxious as to their cause."

"Of course they will," said Luke, "and we can do no more good here."

The party now left the window from which they had, at all events, done some execution, and proceeded to seek the spacious hall again, where they had left Lucy Thornton and May.

"All is well," said Claude, as he sprang down the great staircase. "We have done the rascals some damage—Hilloa !   Where are you ?   Speak, May, Lucy —Where are you both ?"

The tone of voice in which Claude Duval asked this question was quite sufficient to alarm Luke and the consul, and it did in truth do so.   They both sprang down the few remaining stairs that were between them and the hall, and cried out to Duval to tell them what was amiss.

" Good Heavens !" cried Luke, " where are the females ?"

" Our friends disappeared !" said the consul.

" Gone—gone !" said Duval.   "Oh! they are gone ! Help! help ! There is some terrible catastrophe impending, or some horrible one has happened.   Help! oh, help me !   They are lost !"

" Be more yourself," said Luke.   " You confuse us all by this raging passion. Oh, Claude, compose yourself."

" What ! in the face of a calamity like this ?   Can you ask me ?"

" It is necessary that you should do so," said the consul.   " We don't know yet but that, merely alarmed by the firing, they may be hiding somewhere.   Le us call to them at once, and all may yet be well."

" A blessed hope," said Claude Duval.   " A blessed hope.   Any words are now welcome to my ear that give me a hope, however weak."

With this, he raised his voice, and called aloud till the hall echoed again—

" May—May ! Lucy ! Speak ! Oh, speak ! Tis I, Claude, who calls to you now. Speak to me—speak to me !"

" Then," whispered the consul, " the brother, or I should say, the seeming brother, is a female ?"

" Yes," said Luke.   " His wife."

" I thought as much."

"No—no!" added Claude, " they cannot answer. They are dead—dead ! Oh, Heaven ! they are dead, and I am desolate !"

With these words, he in the most frantic manner flung himself to the ground, and lay apparently exhausted.

" Claude," said Luke, " I never, in all my acquaintance with you, saw you thus before.   It is with shame I see you now.   Oh, if you have a man's heart, let me beg of you to rise, and meet this misfortune like a man.   If it is to be encountered at all, it is not by sighs, and tears, and groans, but by courage and action."

" Yes," added the consul.   " A brave man only sees in misfortune a greater stimulus to exertion."

Claude Duval sprang to his feet.

" I will find them," he cried, " if they were hidden in the very bowels of the earth.   Who doubts but that I shall look for them and find them ?   Will any one here tell me that I shall not do so ?"

" Now," said Luke, " I know you again."

" And so do I," said the consul.   "Let us calmly and dispassionately try to find out how this has happened.   It is quite out of the question that they can be far from this spot."

" That is true," said Claude.

" The most strange thing is, that if danger threatened, they should have given no alarm."

" If they did," said Luke, " it might not have been heard amid the din that we ourselves occasioned by firing at the brigands a short time since."

" Help me, all of you !" cried Claude, as he set about a minute search of the hall.   " Help me to search for them.   We do not know what danger a minute may produce if we lose it."

Feeling the truth of that remark, the consul and Luke assisted most actively in searching the hall, but not the least trace of those whom they sought for could be found in any of the corners, or behind any of the statues.

" Some one of those doors must have been opened," said Claude.   " I will still cling to the hope that they themselves may have taken refuge in one of the rooms."

" Do so," said Luke. "Let us search them in regular order."

"Whatever you do, though," urged the consul, "I beg that you will not forget the assassins that are about the chateau. Be upon your guard, I beg of you, for you must recollect that the brigands had resolved upon some plan of action that we know not of."

" True—true," said Claude. " In good truth, I had forgotten them. But yet we will search the rooms. Come, Luke, I can count upon your aid."

CHAPTER CLXXXVI.

CLAUDE AND HIS FRIENDS ARE STILL BAFFLED BY THE MYSTERIOUS DISAPPEARANCE OF MAY AND LUCY.

THERE were some four or five doors opening from that hall, and they had been each securely fastened by Claude Duval and his party before the struggle with the brigands had proceeded far.

It was no easy job now to unfasten those doors again, for in some cases Luke had rather heedlessly thrown away the keys, and yet how poor a chance the opening of any of them presented of finding May and Lucy!

Was it at all likely that they could get any of those doors open? Was it at all likely that in the event of any alarm they would try to fly in any direction but that in which they knew well they might look for instant succour, namely, in the direction where Duval and his friends were to be found ?

It would have been up the grand staircase to the corridor that they would have rushed if they had had the power to do so.

Both Luke and the consul saw all these reasons plainly enough, but they saw likewise that Claude was in that state of mind that some immediate action was necessary in order to make him believe that he was doing something, or attempting something towards the finding of those whose disappearance in so very mysterious a manner had so maddened him.

It was for the purpose, then, of keeping him occupied more than for any hope they had of finding the last ones that they aided in opening the various doors leading from the hall.

The search was fruitless.

From room to room went Duval, until he had been in every apartment upon the ground-floor, but those whom he hoped to hear or see something of were neither to be heard nor seen.

It was in vain that he made the chateau resound with the name of May and Lucy. The echo of his own voice was the only response he met with.

Claude felt half maddened.

"Oh, my friends!" he cried. ' Tell me, in mercy, what I ought to do—tell me what it is possible for me to attempt?"

They were silent, and could only look at him with consternation in their countenances.

"I will have the chateau down," he said, "stone by stone, but I will find them. I will not leave one portion of the building standing upon another, but I will find them. They are hidden—only hidden. What say you, Luke ?"

" Just so,' said Luke.

"And you, sir ?"

" That is quite evident." said the consul.

" Tell me the truth, I beg of you. Conceal nothing from me. You—you do not think in your hearts that they are killed—murdered ?"

" No—no," said Luke, " that is not at all likely."

" Far from probable," added the consul. " But, hark ! I hear an unusual noise from yonder room that we were last in. A breaking of glass. Hark! there it is again."

"Yes, I hear it," said Luke.

"And I!" cried Duval, as, without a moment's consideration of the prudence or safety of the proceeding, he dashed into the room.

A loud shout from the brigands, who were making an entry into the chateau that way, by a window, come upon their ears, and half a dozen carbines were at once discharged at Claude.

He came staggering and bleeding out of the room.

"Hit, hit, at last!" he said. "Oh, Luke, I think they have hit me fairly this time, my friend."

"I hope to Heaven not. But we must barricade this door. Help me all of you who can."

In the hall there was a large table, the top of which was a marble slab of great weight, and this Luke at once laid hold of. The consul and his man saw what was his intention, and they assisted him with such good will, that in a moment the table was against the door, and the door itself locked.

Luke then piled upon the table a couple of heavy oaken chairs, and a marble statue and its pedestal.

"They won't break down all that in a hurry," said Luke; "and now, Claude, where are you?"

"Here," said Claude.

Luke turned to him and found him sitting on the staircase, and bleeding rather profusely from a wound at the side of his head. Sufficient light came into the hall now from the rapid approach of day to render every object clearly visible, and Luke quite staggered back to see the ghastly appearance which poor Claude presented at that moment.

"Alas!" he said, "they have killed you!"

"No," said Claude.

He spoke firmly, and Luke hastened to his side and held up the long hair that was matted with blood, and which hung over the side of his head that had been wounded.

"Why, Claude," he said, "it is not much."

"It is not. I am better."

"Ah! I see now how it was, quite well. A bullet hit you obliquely on the side of the head, and has given you an ugly scalp wound, and I daresay nearly stunned you for the time."

"It did. My impression was that I was shot right through the head; but, I suppose, it cannot be so bad as that, Luke?"

"Nothing like it. You seem calmer, though, and much more composed than you were. You have not forgotten the great loss that we have sustained?"

"No—no. I cannot forget that; but I think the liberal bleeding that those fellows gave me has had the effect of cooling my brain most wonderfully. I still feel as acutely the disappearance of May and Lucy; but my old coolness of judgment has come back to me."

"That Heaven, it has."

"Bind this handkerchief as tightly round my head as you can, Luke, and I shall be able to fight again."

Luke had just finished binding Claude Duval's wound, when a loud shout come from the brigands, who had made their way into the room, and a bullet came crashing through the upper panel of the door.

Claude sprang to his feet.

"Ah!" he said, "we are in the way of their fire. Clear to one side, friends. We will beat them yet."

"Of course we will," said Luke.

It was only just in time that Duval and his friends got out of the line of fire of the brigands: for in another moment a great discharge of fire-arms came through the door, and although some of the shots were intercepted by the articles piled upon the table, yet others of them passed clear of those obstacles, and rattled against the staircase and opposite wall.

"Keep close," said Claude. 'Let them fire away. It is of no use our wasting ammunition at random-shooting through a door."

The besieged party now kept close to the wall by the side of the door, so that it was quite impossible that any stray shot, whatever might be the eccentricity of its path through the door from the room, could hit any of them.

The brigands, after the volley they had fired, paused evidently to listen what effect it had had, and. no doubt, the stillness rather puzzled them, especially as they had placed one of their number on the watch at the front door to see that the besieged did not escape by that mode of retreat.

So still was the house, now, that Claude Duval and his friends could actually hear the murmured conversation of the brigands, and in the course of a few minutes more they made a determined effort to push the door open, and, no doubt, they were not a little surprised at the resistance they experienced.

The door fortunately opened outwards, and the weight that Luke, assisted by the consul and his man, had piled up against it was something very formidable, indeed.

Finding, then, that nothing was to be done in the way of breaking the door open, one of the brigands called out in a loud voice—

"If you do not at once surrender, we will at once burn the chateau down to the ground, and take good. care that if any of you try to escape the flames, you shall perish by our bullets; but if you quietly submit, we promise to spare your lives."

"Don't answer," said the consul.

"Perhaps you doubt our honour?" added the voice.

Both Claude and Luke would have laughed at this piece of impertinent assurance, if there had not been so many anxieties pressing upon their minds.

"We swear that if you submit, we will allow you to leave the chateau in perfect safety," said the voice again.

"They do not speak of May," said Claude, in a low tone, to Luke.

"No, Claude; but they may.'

"We swear it, on the honour of the grand nation!" added the voice.

"Was ever such insolence?" whispered the consul.

"If you won't answer, your fate be of your own seeking, and your dreadful doom be upon your own heads," added the brigand. "Fire!"

Another volley through the door rather manifested the rage of the brigands, than that they expected to accomplish any good by it.

"And no mention of May," sighed Claude. "Alas! I did hope that they would have spoken of her and of Lucy."

"I cannot understand it," said Luke. "It is very strange to me, I think, that the brigands know nothing about her."

"You may depend they do not." said the consul.

"What induced you to come to that conclusion?" said Claude, languidly, and in a state of great depression.

"This one fact," replied the consul. "If they had such hostages in their possession, do you not think they would make use of such an important means of thwarting us?"

"Oh, yes—yes."

"Then you may depend that they know nothing about our lost friends."

"It is too clear," said Claude, "and the mystery that hangs over their fate darkens more and more each moment like a thunder cloud. Alas! alas! what am I to think?"

"It is inexplicable," said Luke.

"What is that?" suddenly said the consul, rising to his feet, for they had all assumed a couching attitude close to the wall. "What strange cracking noise is that?"

"Ah!" said Luke, "the villains are as good as their word. I can smell the smoke of burning wood. They have, as they said they would, set fire to the chateau. In truth, I hardly thought that they would resort to such an extremity as that; but there is no mistaking it."

"We are lost," said the consul.

"No—no. You forget that the man **whom we had with us** has gone to Calais for help, and may yet bring it to us **in good time.**"

THE ALARM OF CLAUDE AND HIS FRIENDS BY THE OLD OWL.

'No—no, I had but little faith in him, and that little has now evaporated by his long absence. I fear that all is lost now.'

"And I am going mad!' said Claude.

"Oh, Claude! Hush! hush!" said Luke; "do not say that."

"It is the truth."

" No—no ; there is hope yet."

"Fire the chateau! Hurrah!" cried the brigands. "We will soon get rid of these detestable English now. Hurrah for the grand nation!"

"I am quite certain," said Luke, through his clenched teeth, "that there is one of the fellows close to the door, and I will have a shot at him, just to let him know that we are alive yet."

No one made any opposition to Luke trying a shot through the panel of the door now; so he rose, and taking a clear aim towards the spot where he felt certain one of the brigands was, from the sound of " Hurrah for the grand nation!" that he had heard him utter, he fired.

The stillness that had preceded this single shot that Luke sent into the camp of the enemy had been rather intense, so that it sounded clear and sharp, and a loud yell proclaimed that it had taken full effect.

Luke had the precaution to throw himself flat upon the floor the moment he had pulled the trigger of his gun, and it was well that he did so, for that one shot had the immediate effect of provoking a volley from the brigands; some one bullet of which might well have proved fatal to him.

As it was, he escaped unhurt.

"You hit your man," said the consul.

"Yes—as I fully expected."

"And still," said Claude, " the fire crackles—the hall is gradually filling with smoke, and I hear nothing, see nothing of May or of Lucy! This is truly maddening!"

CHAPTER CLXXXVII.

THE CHASSEURS FROM CALAIS ARRIVE TO THE RESCUE UNEXPECTEDLY AT THE CHATEAU.

EVEN as Claude spoke, a flame burst through one of the panels of the door of the room that had been most riddled by the bullets of the brigands, and it was quite evident that the dreadful and powerful agent, fire, that they had pressed into their service, would soon clear aside the obstructions between them and their foes.

There could be no doubt but that even now, despite all their losses, the brigands exceeded the numbers of the besieged English by, at least, four times, so that a hand to hand contest could not be doubtful; as a man can have but a poor chance surrounded by four enemies.

"Now, I suppose," said the consul, "they have us?"

"I won't think that yet," said Luke. "While we have any powder and bullets left we can still fight it out. Claude, rouse yourself. Recollect that before we commence a search for May and Lucy that may be successful, we must beat these fellows."

"That is true!" said Claude, with sudden vehemence. "That is true, and we will beat them!"

The contest now began to assume a very terrible character, for the brigands, perceiving that the fire had had an effect upon one of the panels of the door, commenced beating that panel completely open with the brass-bound buts of their carbines.

In the course of another moment there was a clear opening, and through the smoke, Claude and his friends could plainly see the ferocious countenances of the brigands.

"We will keep up a fire now," said Claude, " and they will be blinded by the smoke, which, you all see, blows from us to them. Now for it ! Give them a volley to begin with."

The brigands retired from the door upon this active demonstration from the besieged party, and taking up their positions at different parts of the room, they went on loading and firing as fast as they could, so that the din was truly terrific, and all the sound and appearance of a regular battle was heard in that chateau.

By stooping when they loaded, and by taking advantage of every little shelter that they could, the four persons in the hall managed to preserve themselves pretty well from the shots of the brigands, who, in consequence of their greater numbers, suffered rather severely from the constant firing of the little heroic band that was opposed to them.

It was in the midst of this contest that Luke said to Claude—

"Have you any powder?"

"Yes."

"Thank God for that, for my flask is empty."

"Then, Luke, we are as good as dead men, for when I say I have powder, I only allude to what is in the barrel of the gun, and there it goes. Now I am defenceless, save a pair of pistols."

Luke fired very carefully, and a brigand dropped.

"That's my last shot, too," he said.

"Powder! Give me some powder and bullets, if you please," said the consul, coming up to Claude at this moment. "I and my man have not another charge left."

Claude looked aghast! Here was an unexpected incident, which at once altered the whole aspect of affairs, and placed them all but at the mercy of the brigands.

If they made an attempt to leave the chateau by the front door they would have to traverse such an extent of garden ground that, knowing as they did that the brigands could not have failed to leave some of their number on the watch there, they felt it would be a running fight, which would be all but certain to terminate in their destruction.

Then again, even if by any means the chateau could have been left with safety, Claude Duval had the greatest objection to so leaving it, feeling that May and Lucy might still be in some one of its chambers.

The horror of, perhaps, leaving them to perish in the burning building, was so great to Claude, that at the mere thought of such a dire catastrophe, he made up his mind on the instant not to leave the place; but he spoke to the consul and to Luke with a generous abandonment of self, that showed that despair had taken possession of him completely upon the disappearance of Lucy and May.

"Go," he said to them. "Try to make your escape the best way you can, and leave me here. This is my place to live or to die in: I cannot go."

"Are you now indeed mad, Claude?" said Luke, in a voice of strong emotion.

"Perhaps I am, Luke. But do not question me. Go at once."

"Stoop," said the consul, "they are about to fire again."

The brigands sent another volley into the hall, and appeared rather surprised that no answering shots from the assailed replied to it; but Claude levelled his gun and so did the others, and then he cried out in a loud, clear voice—

"We will now give you a last opportunity of surrendering, and if you throw down your arms at once, I pledge myself that your lives shall be spared. If you continue further to resist, no mercy will be shown to you."

This cool demand from a party so inferior in numerical force, made the brigands look at each other with surprise, and at length one of them called out in jeering tones—

"It is we who promise to show no mercy."

"Ha! ha!" laughed the others as they loaded their carbines. "We will conquer these wretched English for the glory of France."

"We are done," said Luke.

"We must reserve our last fire," said Claude, who, in the exigency of the moment, appeared to have recovered his composure. "It won't do to let them know that we are in such a sad plight."

"Our best plan will be to retreat up the grand staircase," said the consul, "and to take possession of some of the upper rooms. Oh, for some succour now. But that man whom I sent to Calais has played us false."

"It seems so," said Claude. "But come, we will retreat up the staircase. At all events we secure by so doing the higher and the better position, and, thank Heaven, we have our pistols yet, if the struggle should come to a closer one than it is now."

The brigands suddenly raised a shout of gratification and triumph, and then the beleaguered party heard their leader cry out—

"They have no more ammunition. Follow me, my gallant comrades, and let us cover ourselves with glory."

How a party of thieves, numbering some sixteen or seventeen, were to cover themselves with glory by conquering four men who had no ammunition left, could only occur to the mind of a Frenchman; but the idea seemed to be perfectly satisfactory to the brigands, and they commenced operations at once.

With the butts of their carbines, now that they could see where to direct their blows, they commenced clearing away the obstructions that had been placed against the door.

Luke suddenly now laid his hand upon Claude's arm, and said—

"Listen!"

The sound of a bugle came faintly to their ears; but the brigands did not notice it, so actively engaged were they in moving the obstacles that stood between them and their prisoners.

Some of the villains now had drawn their knives, which they flourished in the air with mad delight at the idea of sheathing them in the hearts of those brave men who for so long had held them at bay. They did not take the trouble to fire at the besieged now, for they considered they had them in their hands, and could put them to any death they liked in the course of the next five minutes.

"What does that sound mean?" said Claude.

"It means hope," said Luke.

They both turned to the consul, who had his hand up in an attitude of listening. A smile came upon his face. Seizing Claude by the hand, he whispered to him—

"The chasseurs!"

"Ah! They come?"

"I heard their bugle. The front door must be unfastened now so admit them into the hall."

"In a moment."

Claude flew to the door and commenced moving the bolts and bars, at which the brigands raised a shout, and half-a-dozen shots rattled about him. With the last charge they had in their guns, the consul and his man returned the fire, and amid the smoke and noise, Claude flung the door of the chateau wide open.

At that moment there was a single carbine discharged in the garden, and before its echoes subsided there was another.

A crash in the hall betrayed the fact that the brigands had broken through the door.

"Follow me," said the consul, as he dashed out of the chateau into the garden.

Luke and Claude and the servant followed him closely, and the brigands, to the number now of fifteen men, pursued them with yells and shouts, making quite sure of their prey.

"Halt!" cried a loud voice.

At that instant, Claude and his party turned the angle of a row of tall dwarf trees, and came up to a party of dismounted cavalry soldiers, with carbines, and a couple of officers at their head.

"Surrender, or we fire!" cried the officer.

"Do you know me, captain?" cried the consul.

" Ah, these are friends."

" Yes, to be sure ; but the brigands are behind us."

" Good—Pass through our ranks, gentlemen. We will soon give you a good account of the rascals. Are they in force ?"

" Somewhere under twenty men."

" Indeed! Well, we are more than enough for them. Forward—March !"

The dismounted cavalry exactly consisted of twenty-five men and two officers. They had not now taken three steps in advance when the brigands, in hot pursuit of the party from the chateau, turned the corner of the trees and came in full front of them at a distance of about twenty feet.

" Make ready—present—Fire !" cried the commanding officer of the chasseurs, and in an instant the soldiers fired a volley.

There was an awful yell; and when the smoke cleared away, the brigands seemed to be lying in a confused mass upon the ground. Some three or four then struggled to their feet and tried to fly from the spot ; but the officer again, in the coolest manner in the world, cried out—

" Load, and fire, my men! We don't want prisoners whose only fate can be the guillotine."

Another rattling discharge from the carbines of those of the soldiery that had loaded again, quickly finished the business, and the few brigands who had escaped the first volley fell to rise no more.

" This is dreadful work," said Claude.

" They deserve it," said Luke.

" Oh, no doubt of that. I do not say they do not for a single moment."

The smoke rolled off over [the heads of the contrabandists, and then Claude, advancing to the officer, said—

" Gentlemen, we are indebted to you for our lives, but in the chateau there are yet two ladies who are concealed somewhere within its precincts. Let me implore you, as you are men and soldiers, to aid me in their recovery; they are both dear to me."

" You need not twice propose such a request to us, sir," said the officer. " It is a command. My men are at your service, and, you may be assured, that there is no nook or corner of the building that will escape their scrutiny. Forward, my men, forward !"

" I cannot thank you now," said Claude, " for my heart is too full."

———

CHAPTER CLXXXVIII.

CONTAINS SOME NEWS OF THE FATE OF MAY AND LUCY.

It appeared that the brigands had not in reality set fire to the chateau, as their only efforts in that line had been connected with the door of the room leading to the hall.

Probably such regard to the building was owing [to the fact that it belonged to their friend and leader, for such he was, Major Brook, of whose death they were by no means aware.

In the course of the next five minutes the consul made the officer fully acquainted with everything that had taken place at the chateau, so that he was better able to lend his aid towards discovering the place of retreat of the ladies than he otherwise would have been. He jumped to a conclusion at once that very much alarmed Claude Duval.

" You may depend upon it, gentlemen," he said, " that while you were absent from the vestibule of the chateau, which you tell me you were for a short time, some of the gang of rascals, the greater number of whom I hope lie dead on the lawn, found their way to the vestibule, and carried off the females. How they silenced them it is hard to say."

"They have murdered them !" said Claude.

"Oh, no, sir, far from it."

"How can you tell me that? Do you not know the blood-thirsty character of the men we have had to deal with? Do you not know that by the opposition we have given to them that we have awakened their worst passions ?"

"It is you, sir," said the officer, " who know them not. Unhappily, we of the neighbourhood are but too well acquainted with the rascals, and in the first place allow me to assure you that their worst passions need no awakening."

"That is surely true," said Luke.

"It is so ; and as regards the ladies, if they have fallen into the hands of the brigands, you may depend they will consider them by far too valuable as hostages to tamper with their lives in any way."

"Then there is hope ?"

"Certainly; every hope. If we do not find them quickly, I think we are very likely to hear of them from the brigands themselves soon. The only thing I would like to guard against is their being carried off and hidden somewhere at a distance from this spot."

"Ah, yes, that is a danger."

"Which I will guard against by placing sentinels at such points that they will command the surrounding country. So make yourself easy ; we are doing all we can."

The officer certainly spoke in a very business-like manner of the affair, but when he told Claude Duval to make himself easy, he said what it was far from being in the power of Claude to comply with.

It positively maddened him to think that coming there as he did for the purpose of saving his cousin Lucy, and succeeding as he had done in saving her, both she and his wife should be, as it were, spirited away from him at the very moment of his apparent triumph.

It was as much as Claude Duval could now do to preserve sufficient self-control to enable him to be of any use in the search that was taking place at all.

"Luke," he said, " while the others are doing all they can for me in this disastrous business, let you and I search the chateau thoroughly, and it is possible we may make some discoveries that may recompense us for the trouble of so doing."

"Agreed," said Luke.

"It is likely enough that some accident may give us a clue to the fate of those whom I seek."

"Yes, Duval, it is likely enough. Be of good cheer, I pray you. But we must tell our friends what we are about."

"Oh, yes—yes."

"We think," said Luke, then turning to the others, " of going over the chateau room by room, and making a minute search of it; but we will repair to this spot upon an agreed-upon signal being made that there is either information for us, or a requirement of our presence."

"The signal shall be a pistol-shot," said the officer.

"Be it so, sir."

"Do not run into any unnecessary danger," said the consul, " I beg of you. It is needless, now that the soldiers are here."

"We will not, my good sir," said Luke.

"No," said Claude Duval; " we have too much at stake to do that, and every moment is now too precious, sir, to allow me to utter a word of the gratitude to you for your assistance this night with which my heart is full."

"Say nothing of that. I only hope that the night will leave no regret, and that you will soon have in your arms those whom we all will seek for."

"With kind thoughts I leave you, sir," said Claude. "Come, Luke, now. Let us go upon our errand."

The soldiers were hastily engaged in searching the ground-floor and the gardens of the chateau, and one of the sub-officers was busy posting the sentinels that the officer in command had spoken of to Claude.

The consul and his man were engaged in an animated conversation regarding the disappearance of the two females, and the man seemed to be trying to impress his views of the case upon the consul.

In the midst of all this, then, Luke and Duval searched the chateau to look for those without whom it was not likely they would leave that spot.

Their first act in the hall was to look to the priming of their pistols, and so to satisfy themselves that they were ready for any sudden danger that might arise; and then they at once ascended the grand staircase to the upper part of the chateau.

"I think," said Luke, "I should like to take a look in that chamber where you left Major Brook."

"Very well. It is possible that we may make some discovery there."

Having been before quartered in that part of the building, they had no great difficulty now in going to it again, and they soon reached the little supplimentary flight of stairs that led to the apartment in which the strange duel had taken place.

Luke pushed open the door.

"Here we are," he said.

The morning light now streamed in at the long narrow window of that room, and one glance was sufficient to let Claude see that the body of his late adversary was not there.

"Ah!" he said, "where is the major?"

"Here he ought to be."

"But here he is not. How are we to account for that, Luke?"

Luke shook his head.

"I tell you what it is, Claude: I had a kind of feeling upon my mind, after you had accommodated that rascal by fighting a sort of duel with him, that we had been very imprudent to leave him here only under the supposition that he was dead."

"The supposition?"

"Yes. For you will recollect that we rather took that apparent fact for granted than actually satisfied ourselves of it."

"Yes—yes. We did."

"Well, then, you see, he is gone, and dead folks don't get up, and walk off in this sort of way."

"The living might carry off the dead."

"Not in this case, I think. It is a very unlikely circumstance, indeed, Duval, that, amid the hurry, the danger, and the excitement of having us to contend with, any one would take the trouble to lay a hand upon the dead body of a man whom none could love, however, for the sake of his pay, many might serve while living."

"That is all true."

"It is reasonable, Cláude, at all events."

"It comes across me, Luke, with the force of truth. It is the major and and some of his myrmidons who have been the cause of the absence of Lucy and May in this mysterious mansion."

"I shouldn't wonder. Hilloa! Hollow enough here, don't you think, Duval?"

Luke for the last few moments had been going round the walls of the room tapping the panels with the butt-end of one of his pistols, and he came to one that returned a most unmistakable sound of hollowness.

"A secret panel?" said Claude.

"Well, it may or it may not be."

They both looked up and down this panel very attentively; but they could find no means of opening it. There did not appear to be the smallest vestige of any point or spot in particular where one would suppose there was some hidden fastening.

" It is accidental, I fear," said Claude. "You may depend, Luke, it is only that the panel is a little further from the wall than the others."

" Well, we will see."

Luke glanced round him, and saw an iron bar that went across the lower part of the window, and which, from long use, had got to be very weak in its hold of the masonry at the sides—one vigorous pull got it away from one side, and then its own leverage was amply sufficient to release it altogether from the place.

The iron bar was of considerable weight, and when Luke brought it down with a smart blow upon the panel, it split it right up the centre with a loud crash.

The moment the panel was broken in this way it began to slide downwards to the great surprise of Claude and Luke, and, finally, it stopped at about a foot from the floor.

Immediately beyond this panel was a dark, cavernous-looking opening.

" I see how it acts now," said Luke. "If we had pressed upon it, we should have released a catch of some sort, and then, by its own weight, down it would have gone into a groove that receives it."

" But what is beyond?" said Claude.

" Be careful, Claude."

" I will. There is a staircase descending into absolute darkness, Luke," said Claude.

" Stop—stop."

" What for? I feel that if any discovery is to be made, it will be by descending this staircase."

" Yes; but there is no occasion to break our necks by descending in the dark. I have matches and tapers, as you well know it is an agreed-upon thing that I should never be without, when we come out upon any expedition."

" Oh, yes—yes. That will be better, Luke."

Luke, upon this, lit one of his tapers, and standing, then, quite close to the entrance to the black, cavernous-looking place, he held up the light till, burning steadily, it enabled them to look before them with some degree of ease.

" You see the staircase?" said Claude.

" I do,"

" How deep it looks."

" Yes. Our light will not penetrate its depths. But look, Claude. Do you not see that there are the marks of recent footsteps here upon the upper stairs?'

" I do—I do. I begin now, Luke, to subscribe to your opinion, and to think that, after all, this rascal, Major Brook, only shammed death, and that it is he, indeed, who is at the bottom of the mischief I deplore."

" I do not doubt it. Come on, Claude."

" Nay, let me go first. Your carrying the light will be better after me; and as you will be upon a higher stair than I, you can hold the light above my head, and I shall see any danger, and be quite prepared to meet it with my arms in my hands."

" That will do," said Luke.

In this manner, then, they both slowly commenced the descent of the mysterious little staircase.

CHAPTER CLXXXIX.

CLAUDE AND LUKE FIND OUT SOME OF THE SECRETS OF THE CHATEAU.

THERE was sufficient evidence upon the stairs by the disturbance of the dust, and the manifest marks of feet, to show that the place was in tolerably constant use; and they did not doubt but that it was the common thoroughfare by which Major Brook found his way to and from that room above.

"Where on earth," said Claude, "will this lead to?"

"No doubt, to some room on the ground-floor of the chateau, Claude. We have already descended half the height we came from the hall, I think."

THE SENTINEL NEAR MAJOR BROOK'S.

"Well, Luke, I suppose we have; and yet I cannot see the foot of the stairs."

"Let us look carefully at the walls as we go."

This they did; but they gained no information by the examination. The walls presented only an appearance of rough boarding, and by the nails that had been put in to secure it, it was pretty evident that there were no secret openings either to the right or to the left.

"No, Luke," said Claude, "I think this staircase, as a staircase, is quite intact, and that it has a fixed destination, which we shall soon find out."

"Likely enough. Keep a sharp eye before you, Claude."

"I will. Ah, I see the termination of it. Here we are, within half a dozen steps. Look, Luke—what are we to do now?"

They both paused, now, at the foot of the stairs, which terminated in a little square space not much larger than would just suffice to enable them both to stand in it.

"There does not seem to be any mode of exit from here," said Claude, "and yet, of course, there must be. Lend me the light, Luke."

Claude took the light, and slowly raised it up and down the walls, till at last he said—

"Here it is."

Luke regarded with curiosity a little spring bolt which Claude now pointed out to him, and which appeared fastened to the topmost portion of a long narrow panel.

"This is similar to the contrivance above stairs," said Claude, "and I have no doubt that sufficient pressure to release that bolt will open the panel at once."

Claude did not pause, now, in his operations; but releasing the bolt, he had the satisfaction of seeing the panel slowly descend, with a slight rumbling noise.

It was quite clear that the panel descended by the aid of a rope and a weight, which was sufficient to overcome its resistance, and cause its descent the moment it was released from the bolt that held it in its place.

Luke's light was blown out at once by the movement of the air contingent upon the rapid descent of the panel; but that was no evil, inasmuch as the opening in the wall led them, at once, into a handsome, though small apartment, through the stained glass-window of which there came a flood of morning light.

Neither Luke nor Claude spoke for a moment or two after they got into this room, they were both too much occupied in looking at it; but at length, Claude said—

"Can you take upon yourself now, Luke, to say where we are?"

"Indeed, I cannot."

"Well, a glance from the window may assist us, perhaps. I suppose we are upon the ground-floor of the chateau, though."

"No doubt of that."

It was not easy to get the glance from the window that Claude spoke of, for the stained glass being covered with a multitude of heraldic devices puzzled and perplexed the eye.

Duval, though, speedily put an end to that difficulty by breaking one of the diamond-shaped panes, and then he at once saw that they were nearly on the level of a part of the garden.

"It is as you say, Luke," he said. "We have come down to the ground-floor of the building; but I cannot, for the life of me, see any door to this room, except we may take upon ourselves to call that one at which we entered it."

"There must be some other mode of exit from it, Claude, and I cannot think it a very secret one, or else, why the window? That is, at once, a proclamation that there is a room here, and see, there is a chimney, too, and here is the door."

Luke pointed to a tall picture of a man on horseback, with a falcon upon his wrist, which was upon one of the walls, and which reached from the ceiling to the floor.

A rather close inspection of that picture was necessary to show that it constituted a door; but after that inspection, there could be no doubt about it.

"It is not intende d for secrecy," said Luke, "only, you see, when it is shut it has the effect of giving the room a regular appearance, with its panelled portraits, that otherwise would be quite lost."

"I see it. The doors spoil the look of all our houses in Eng'and, just for want of a little judgment in concealing them when shut, to look of a piece with the walls. But this is fast."

They both tried the door, but found that it would not even shake in the least; so that they almost began to have a doubt that, after all, it might be a delusion.

"I cannot brook this delay," said Claude, suddenly, and springing at the panel, he gave it such a dash with his foot that it was burst open the wrong way, for the hinges broke, and it fell outwards, whereas it ought to have opened inwards.

"Stand, or I fire !" cried a voice.

"Ah, look to your arms !" said Claude.

"Yes—yes," said Luke. "No—stop ! It's a soldier, Claude. Why—why, this is the hall!"

"Stand! who are you ?" cried the soldier. "Guard ! guard !"

A corporal and a couple of men came up, and at once recognised Claude and Luke, and they all stared at each other in anguish.

The appearance of Luke and Duval throug i the wall astonished the corporal and the soldiers, and the fact that they had reached the hall by such a means rather astonished them.

A little examination sufficed to show them the state of things.

There had been in the hall several large statues upon pedestals; but the firing of the brigands had destroyed most of them, and the door in the wall that led to the room from which Luke and Duval had come had been behind one of these statues. The statue was gone, so they had at once stepped into the hall.

"Gentlemen," said the corporal, "where have you come from ?"

"Well, I hardly know," said Claude; "but we found above-stairs a secret door and a staircase, and it has terminated here."

"In nothing satisfactory ?"

"Nothing at all," said Claude. "You have no news for me, I suppose ?"

"None, sir," said the corporal.

At this moment the consul entered the hall, and seeing Claude and Luke, he said—

"Oh. I was going over the chateau to seek you. The man who was in the kitchen has disappeared."

"And so has the major," said Claude.

The officer now came out of another room opening from the hall, and was talking hastily to one of his men; but the moment he saw Claude and Luke, he said—

"Oh, gentlemen, I have some news for you."

"Oh, tell us, sir, at once."

"Certainly. One of my men says, that he heard from somewhere, he thinks under ground, a stifled scream."

"A stifled scream ?"

"Yes. He thought that it was repeated, too, unless it was the echo of the faint cry that was still lingering in his ears. He will take you at once to the spot, if you wish it."

"Yes—oh, yes. I will follow you."

"This way, messieures," said the soldier. "I heard it plain enough, though it seemed to come out of the very bowels of the earth."

Much agitated at this information, Claude Duval followed the soldier and the officer, and Luke, too, kept close to them. The soldier led the way out of the chateau to a spot amid a little clump of trees about twenty paces from it, where there was a small kind of summer-house, with a conical roof to it. He paused at the door of that summer-house, saying—

"It was here I heard the sound."

"Here, upon the threshold of the summer-house?"

"Yes, I could not make up my mind whether it came from within or without. I waited hereabouts for some minutes, and then I considered it to be my duty to report the facts to my officer."

"Let us go in," said the officer.

They all entered the little summer-house together, and when there, they kept a profound stillness—so profound that the slightest whisper might have been heard, if it had been uttered at all.

This silence was too profound to be permitted to last long. The state of agitation that the feelings of Claude were in would not permit him to let it subsist beyond many minutes, and he broke it by saying in a voice of agony—

"There is nothing—oh, there is nothing. It was some delusion of the senses, surely."

"Hush!" said the consul.

They all listened attentively; and then, as if from somewhere under the ground at their feet, there came the feeble echo of a cry.

"Oh, heavens!" cried Claude, "that was a sound. Who else heard it but myself? Speak—oh, speak!"

"All—all," cried those present.

"Then it is no delusion."

"Hark! hark!"

Again there came the sound, and this time it seemed to die away into a long melancholy moan. Claude Duval staggered to a seat, of which there were several in the little pavillion, and he sat there looking more dead than alive for some minutes.

"Rouse yourself," said Luke—"rouse yourself. It is not by inaction that we shall come at the heart of this mystery."

Claude sprang to his feet.

"Show me what to do," he cried. "Show me the danger, and let me face it. Let me see what foes I have to encounter. Let the bright light of day fall upon me and those opposed to me, and I can dare all [and anything; but now with all this mystery and horror around me, I feel that I have nothing to combat with but my own despair."

"Listen to me," said Luke. "Claude, will you listen to me?"

"Say on, my friend. Say on."

It seems to me, then, that while May and Lucy were in the hall, they must have been suddenly surprised, and taken prisoners by some of the brigands, who found a way through some such secret door as that which led us to the spot."

"Yes—yes."

"Well, it is possible enough that there are passages and subterranean apartments connected with the chateau, and that we may be standing above one of them at this moment."

"If so," cried Claude, "I will dig to the centre of the earth but I will find them."

"Do not be precipitate. I recommend that a guard be left here, and that we go back to the hall, and try to find the regular passage or staircase through the wall, by which our dear friends have been hurried from us, for such they must have been. We may yet be in time to aid them, but any attempt from this spot would, long before we could be successful in it, be heard by our enemies and easily frustrated."

"All that is true," said Claude. "I will follow the advice of cooler heads than my own is just now, for I have so great a stake in the issue of this adventure, that my judgment is excited beyond its wont, and I cannot decide for myself."

"Follow me, then," said Luke, "and hope for the best."

"Alas! it is only a hope."

"Courage," said the officer, "all may yet be well, sir."

CHAPTER CXC.

LUKE FINDS THE WAY TO THE DUNGEON OF MAY AND OF LUCY.

WITH the view of carrying out at once this suggestion of Luke's, which certainly did seem the most likely mode of achieving the object they all had in view, the party proceeded to the chateau again. It seemed to suggest itself to every one, as highly probable that in the little room from which Claude and Luke had emerged to the hall, would be found some other secret door.

It was more than likely that it was through that room the captors of May and Lucy had made their way, and the only wonder was, how the affair had been conducted with such perfect silence as it had, or how it had been contrived so as to take place at a moment when the firing from the window upon the brigands had drowned every other sound.

Luke adopted the same course that he had done before, to find if any of the panelling of the room sounded hollow, namely, by tapping it with the butt-end of one of his pistols, and the effect was, that a long narrow panel, upon which appeared the painting of a lady going to a chase, sounded decidedly hollow, as the others had done which proved to be doors.

Claude would have flown at this panel, and broken it through by a blow with his foot as he had done the door leading into the hall, but the officer directed a soldier to knock it down with his carbine.

A couple of blows from the brass-bound stock of the fire-arm had the effect of smashing the panel to atoms.

Claude bounded forward.

"A light!—a light!"

"Here," said Luke. "Is their anything to be seen?"

"Yes, some stone steps. Something white lies upon them."

Claude dashed down the steps, and picked up a handkerchief, which he at once was able to rocognise as belonging to May.

"This is quite conclusive," he said, "of the fact, that we are on the track of our lost friends. The handkerchief the ruffians have heedlessly allowed to fall, and it is positive proof of the fact that they have passed this way."

"Very well," said the officer, "now we will take half a dozen of my men with us, and we will pursue this secret passage."

The men were soon brought to the spot, and the officer was about to head them himself, but Claude cried out—

"Sir, let me go first."

"Along with me, then, you can come," said the officer; "but it is my duty to lead my men upon any enterprise in which there may be danger."

Claude and Luke were forced to satisfy themselves by walking, then, immediately after the officer, and the soldiers followed them closely. The staircase that was immediately on the other side of the panel was only composed of eight steps, and terminated upon the earth, which seemed to have been beaten hard and flat, to make a kind of floor.

The passage at the foot of the steps was narrow, and arched at the top pointedly, by pieces of wood of that shape, being made to meet each other in the roof, and resting on rough hewn upright shafts of timber at the sides.

Altogether, there was much rudeness of construction about the passage, and it did not look as thought it were constructed with that regard to art and design which should make it strong.

Luke made the remark in a low tone, that a very little would bring it all down about their ears, and the soldiers looked up at the roof, where the displacement of a single one of the pieces of timber would lead to the displacement of several, with looks of suspicion.

Nobody liked to say anything of this source of insecurity of the passage, but all felt it.

After proceeding about thirty feet in this way, the passage branched off to the right, and the space that it occupied in its width was so trifling that it was quite out of the question for more than one person to walk at a time along it.

Claude now put the question quite at rest as to who was to take precedence in the passage, by darting forward into it; and as Luke had the only light which enabled the party to go on, they had to let him follow his friend, and the officer came next.

After proceeding nearly as far again as the first passage had extended, Claude came to a door, and he was just upon the point of saying something in a loud voice, when he heard the murmur of voies on the other side of it.

To turn to his friends, and hold up his hand as a signal for silence, was the work of a minute with Claude.

"Halt!" said the officer, in a low tone, and the soldiers immediately paused, and all was perfectly still.

"What did you hear?" said Luke, in a whisper.

"I hardly know; but we may hear it again, and then be better able to judge."

Then there was a confused kind of murmur, as of several voices at once; and as Luke laid his hand upon the door, it slowly yielded before his touch. The moment it was open a little way, they were quite startled by hearing a voice say, in clear accents—

"Do you think that the lives of my comrades are nothing? No—blood for blood is our motto!"

It took a minute to convince Claude that he was not actually in the presence of the speaker of those words, and then saw how it was that they had come so plainly to his ears.

At the distance of about five feet from the door, which had so very readily yielded to Luke's touch, there hung a piece of drapery in heavy folds from the ceiling to the floor of the narrow passage, and it was quite evident that upon the other side of it there were persons conversing, without the shadow of a suspicion that their foes were so near at hand to them as they were.

Oh, with what intense anxiety did Claude Duval now hope that he should be able to hear the sound of some voice that would assure him of the safety of those who were so dear to him!

In a moment or two another voice spoke.

"Don't be rash," it said. "It is easy to hang our prisoners at any moment we like."

"Yes, I know that," said the voice that had first sounded. "I know that; but a dozen of our best men lie dead in the garden, and we must have revenge! Where is the major?"

"Yonder," said the second voice.

"Yes," said Major Brook, for it was, indeed, that rascal who had escaped by same miracle the death that Claude Duval thought he had inflicted upon him. "Yes. I am here. As for the young spark yonder, I advise that you hang him up at once, and get rid of him. Lucy will still be in my power, and subject to my will."

"They live!" gasped Claude. "Ah, they both live. I am now sure of that! Did you hear, Luke?"

"Yes—Hush!"

"Spare me, I implore you!" said the voice of Lucy Thornton. "Spare me, and for the past all shall be forgiven."

"No," said May—and how the voice fell upon the heart of Claude!—"no—

all cannot be forgiven, Lucy. I here tell these men that if they so much as hurt a hair of your head, there will be a bitter retribution for it. They may entitle themselves to some mercy by at once releasing us; but that is their only course."

" You threaten, young spark," said the major.

" I do," said May.

" Well, you will be out of the way of danger soon. My men, listen to me. This young lad, for he is little better, is violent as well as dangerous. Hang him at once."

" Yes," said several voices. " He dies!"

" Oh, no—no!" shrieked Lucy. " No, I say. Oh, spare him! You do not know who and what——"

" Silence, Lucy," said May. " Would you be more cruel to me than these men? Oh, silence! Death is a pang; but there are worse ills than that."

" Heaven help me!" sobbed Lucy.

Claude Duval laid his hand gently upon the heavy curtain that was before him, and moved a portion of it on one side, so that he could just peep into the space beyond it.

He saw a circular room, about twelve feet in diameter, with a few rough articles of furniture in it. A dimly burning lamp was upon a table in the centre.

Lying half reclining on the floor were May and Lucy, both tied, hand and foot; and in the apartment, if apartment such a place could be called, there were six brigands. A little distance from the prisoners was Major Brook, looking pale and haggard, and with blood upon his face and hands.

"Do you see them?" whispered Luke.

" Yes—yes."

" Let me?"

"Look for a minute, Luke."

Luke did so, and then, drawing back, he looked to the priming of his pistols, and nodded significantly.

"Listen," said Claude to him.

"I do."

" When I say come, follow me. Touch none of the brigands, but fly to the rescue of May and Lucy. They lie upon the floor, both of them."

" I saw them."

" Gentlemen," whispered the officer, "if you will allow me to take the same survey of the proceedings that you have, I shall be able to decide upon my course of action."

They let the officer pass them with difficulty, and he, too, looked at the state of affairs within the brigands' den.

" Well, sir ?" whispered Claude.

"Nothing is more easy," whispered the officer, "than to settle this affair The brigands are all on their feet, the prisoners are lying on the ground; a volley from my men will pass over the latter and hit the former; and that is the course I shall take."

" But a stray bullet might do mischief ?"

" Oh, no. The walls are earth, and where a bullet hits it will lodge, so that your friends are perfectly safe."

" Well, sir, you have a right to have your own way here. Be it so."

The fact was, that Claude's judgment was convinced that by the course the officer suggested, no harm could possibly come to either Lucy or May.

The officer made the disposition of his men as well as he could in such a small space, so as to bring their carbines all to bear upon the men, and he spoke to each man, telling him not to fire low for fear of injuring the prisoners, who lay bound upon the floor.

" Now, sir," said the officer to Claude, " all I want you and your friend to do is, with suddenness, to pull down curtain when I give the word ' now.' "

" We will.'

" Are you all ready, men ?"

" Yes," whispered the men.

Claude and Luke got a good hold of the curtain.

" Now !" cried the officer.

With one sharp and sudden pull, the curtain was dragged in a heap to the ground, and then, before the brigands had a moment in which to recover from their surprise, the officer shouted—

" Fire !"

The volley from the carbines of the soldiers followed on the instant. By the concussion of the air, the light was at once extinguished, and one fearful yell arose from the discomfited thieves, who little expected such a fate was in store for them.

There arose, then, a scream from a female throat, and Claude Duval called out directly—

" May and Lucy, you are saved ! We are your friends. Do not stir from where you are, and all will be well."

"Will it ?" said a voice.

" Who was that ?" cried Claude.

" Help! help!" shrieked Lucy.

" A light," cried Claude Duval. " A light, Luke, if you love me."

" In a moment," said Luke.

The glimmer of a match then shone through the darkness, and Claude Duval saw the figure of a man close to where Lucy and May were, with an uplifted gun in his hands, apparently in the act of striking with the butt-end of it.

———

CHAPTER CXCI.

CLAUDE AND HIS FRIENDS REACH ENGLAND AGAIN IN SAFETY.

IF Claude Duval had been projected from a cannon he could not possibly have flown across the narrow apartment with greater speed than he now did. In another moment he and the man who had been in the act to strike at Lucy were rolling on the floor together ; but the fellow's spirit was cowed, while rage lent force to Duval, and he got him by the throat, and held him with a grasp of iron.

Luke quickly procured a good light, and then the scene of death and desolation which the fire of the soldiers had produced was quite apparent.

The brigands lay weltering in their blood, and Claude Duval, upon looking into the face of the man he had hold of, found that it was, indeed, no other than the infamous Major Brook.

". Villain !" cried Claude, " you alive still?"

" Yes ; but you choke me."

" I am glad to hear it. It will save the hangman some trouble, perhaps."

A voice now uttered Duval's name. It was the voice of May, and so Claude called out to Luke—

" Luke, take this fellow into your charge, my friend, and don't let him give us the slip a second time."

" I will take care he don't do that," said Luke.

In another moment May was in the arms of Claude Duval, and sobbing as though her heart would break.

" Cheer up," he said, " cheer up, all is well now. We have discomfited all the ruffians, and are masters of the place."

Lucy now took Claude's hand and pressed it to her lips.

" You have saved me, cousin," she said. " You have saved me from a fate ar worse than death."

" Come—come," said Claude, smiling, " we will say no more upon that head. You have to thank this gentleman and his brave soldiers."

The officer bowed, as he said—

"I did no more than my duty, but I certainly rejoice that in so doing I was able to perform a service which gives me so much pleasure."

The soldiers tied the hands of the only two brigands who were not mortally

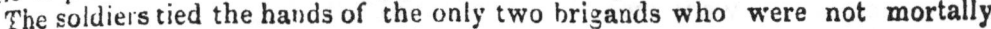

THE CONSUL STEALS UPON SUZANNF, THE COOK, UNAWARES.

wounded, and prepared to lead them from the cavernous place, but Luke said in a low tone to Claude—

"Here are two who can't move, but who are dying."

"I understand you, Luke. It would be a mercy to put an end to their sufferings, but it is repugnant to me to do it."

"And to me, likewise."

" Make yourselves at ease on that score," said the officer. "A couple of my men will linger behind a moment or two and despatch them. Now, ladies and gentlemen, I don't care how soon we get into daylight again, for the atmosphere of this place is not by any means very delightful."

Claude intimated that he was ready, and closely followed by May and Lucy he left the miserable abode. As they reached the daylight they heard the dull report of a couple of muskets.

" What is that ?" said May.

" Nothing to bespeak danger," said Claude. " Heed it not."

Duval well knew that it was the finish of the career of the two badly wounded brigands, but he did not like to shock May or Lucy with such information.

The party now soon got together in the garden of the chateau, and Claude turning to the officer, took him aside, saying—

" What can be done with Major Brook ? He is an English subject."

" He is the leader of a band of brigands," said the officer, " and he has shown that he is such without any doubt by the manner in which he has attacked the troops. Of course, he will be dealt with according to the law.'' ;

" But he has friends at Calais," said the consul.

"That is well thought of," replied the officer. "I will send a report of the whole transaction to the minister of police at Calais."

The day was now so bright that the chateau and its environs wore a wonderfully different aspect to any that it had yet done to the eye of its invaders, and as Claude Duval and his friends looked about them they were quite enchanted by the odd beauty of the time-worn place, and the rarity of the vegetation that surrounded it.

"Yes," said the consul, as he read this opinion in their looks. "It is a sweet place, but probably now it will remain unoccupied for many a long year, and will go quickly to decay."

" It is a pity," said Claude. " But, come, let us depart. Gentlemen, I am for England as soon as may be."

May sighed.

" You are unhappy," said Claude.

" Oh, no—no ; but I did hope——"

" What?"

" That in another country some new pursuit would, perhaps, present itself to you, Claude—some mode of life that would be free from the terrors and the risks of that which you lead in England."

Claude shook his head.

" No, May," he said, " not here. There is no such chance. We are too much in the centre of civilization for that. We should starve in this country, except——"

" Except what, Claude ?"

" I embraced the same mode of life as I pursued in England."

May shuddered.

" Better there than here," she said.

" So I think. But now I am quite sure that we all desire to know how it was that you and Lucy got into the hands of the brigands so quietly, and we, all the time, so close at hand to you?"

" I will tell you. At the moment that you fired from the window near the corridor at the brigands, there rushed into the hall four men. Two of them, before we could speak or think, enveloped our heads in cloths, and then we were at once lifted off our feet, and carried off with a celerity and ease that was truly surprising. The whole affair was over before the echo of the discharge of your guns had ceased in the chateau.

" And one of those men was the major ?"

" Oh, yes," said Lucy. " He threatened us with instant death if we ventured to make the least alarm ; and, in fact, we were so nearly suffocated by the time the clothes enveloping our heads were removed, that it was out of our power to raise a cry for aid."

"The rascals!" said Claude.

"They have met their deserts at last," said Luke.

"Not all!" cried a loud voice; and in another moment, to the surprise of Claude and his friends, the major passed them with a carbine in his hand, and at such a desperate pace, that it seemed to defy all pursuit. He was evidently making his way to a little clump of trees that was about a quarter of a mile from the line of march of the party.

"Escaped, by Heaven!" cried Claude.

"Not yet." shouted the officer. "After him, my men—after him! Shoot him down without mercy!"

The soldiers started in pursuit, and several carbines were discharged at the major, but without effect.

The mode by which he was enabled to attempt the audacious escape he meditated was simple enough. By some means he had contrived to sufficiently lossen the cord that bound his hands behind his back, so that at any moment he could slip them from off it, and then seeing that the soldiers held their carbines upon the hollow of their arms, the idea of seizing one of those weapons and trying the chance of flight, had occured to him.

Doubtless he knew that if he could reach the clump of trees, he would find a hiding-place, or he wodld have hardly chanced such a piece of desperation.

Suddenly he had dashed at one of the soldiers, and got possession of his carbine, and ran off in the extraordinary manner we have seen; and when a man flies for his life he certainly makes a speed that under any other less exciting circumstances would appear to him, as connected with his own powers of progression, to be perfectly fabulous.

Like a hunted hare, now, the major rushed onwards towards the little clump of trees, and as his foes kept firing after him they had to stop to do so with military precision, so that he gained upon them wonderfully, and finally it was quite evident that he would get to the shelter of the trees if he was not overtaken by one of the soldiers who had run on without stopping to fire, although he kept his carbine handily in his grasp.

It appeared that the major felt his danger from this one man and just partially under cover of the first tree of the clump which he had evidently wished to reach, he turned.

"Another step, and you are a dead man!" he cried to the soldier, whose only reply was to level his carbine and fire at him.

The major dropped, but half struggling to his feet, he took aim at the soldier and discharged his carbine.

The soldier fell backwards without a groan. The bullet had gone right through his brain.

Major Brook flung down the carbine and then disappeared among the trees.

It was about one minute's space of time before Claude and Luke and the others reached the spot. The officer was infuriated at the escape of his principal prisoner, and the other brigand prisoners looked their delight and grinned maliciously. It was only by an unusual paleness of his visage and by biting his lips that the officer exhibited how much he was put out of his way by what had happened.

"Halt!" he cried, with much his usual tone, and then glancing at the soldiers he added—"if we stay here a month I will not leave the spot without our prisoner, dead or alive."

The soldiers raised a shout in reply, and it was quite evident that the sight of their dead comrade had influenced all their passions against the man who had laid him low.

The officer now gave some rapid orders, and in the course of a few moments the wood, which was not above one hundred yards in diameter, was surrounded by sentinels, and still there was left a tolerably strong party to enter it on a voyage of discovery.

"Now, gentlemen," said the officer, to Claude Duval and his party, "you may dispose of yourselves how you like, or go on to Calais. My duty still lies here, as you perceive, and my men have orders to shoot the brigand as soon as they see him, for he deserves no mercy."

"We would rather stay here till the end," said Claude; "that is if—" he turned to May and Lucy, and the former said—

"With you we are willing to stay."

"I would not go for a hundred pounds," said Luke. "Claude, you stay and take care of the ladies, and permit me to accompany the captain with his men."

Claude bit his lip.

"I see how it is, Claude," said May, "you, too, wish to go, and I am sure this gentleman and his servant," turning to the consul and his man, "will give us the aid of their presence as a protection."

"I will leave a soldier, likewise," said the officer.

"No—no," said Claude. "I—that is—I ought——"

"Go!" said May—"go! It is my wish that you should do so. The gallant men are encountering dangers for our sakes, and much as I value your safety, I cannot counsel you to avoid your duty."

"Then I will go."

Claude Duval, to tell the truth, would have been specially unhappy if circumstances had not permitted him to accompany the officer and his soldiers into the little wood, and as the brigands were so completely destroyed, he felt that no possible danger could attack May and Lucy, with three men to defend them.

The cords that bound the other two prisoners were well looked to and tightened by the soldiers, so that they were anything but inclined to smile at the exploit of their leader, which, in its consequences, put them to no little pain, for the cords now quite dug into their flesh.

They uttered the most terrible imprecations against the soldiers, and against the major, who had been the cause of their varied sufferings. The first act of the daring exploit he had carried out flew to their minds, before the extra inconveniences it put them to.

"Now, gentlemen," said the officer to Claude and Luke, "if you are ready we will march at once."

CHAPTER CXCII.

THE MAJOR COMES TO A DREADFUL END, IN THE LITTLE WOOD.

CLAUDE and Luke wanted no urging to follow the officer and his men, and the party at once commenced their search for the brigand in the wood, which had, so opportunely for him, stood close enough to the line of march of his captors to afford him a shelter.

The only suspicion that Duval had concering the affair—which might have the effect of completely setting at naught all their efforts—was, that there might be some artificially contrived hiding-place in that wood, of which the major had the secret, and which they, his enemies, might hunt for in vain without the clue to it.

This was a supposition that was shared in by Luke.

"I do not like to say as much to the officer just yet," said Claude, "as it might have the effect of discouaging him; but to my mind it is highly probable."

"And to mine," said Luke, "it almost amounts to a fact, for we know well that real courage is not a characteristic of the man we seek, and I do not think he would have run the risk he did without some certainty of escape provided he could reach the place alive."

"Gentlemen," said the officer, approaching them, "as far as your observations went, do you think this rascal, whom we are now in search of, was wounded by the soldier whom he killed on the skirts of the wood?"

"I think he was," said Luke.

"I should not like to decide upon that point so hastily," said Claude. "He fell; but that is nothing. He fell before my fire some hours ago, and yet, after all, I found him alive, and apparently unhurt."

"I can't imagine how he escaped in the chateau," said Luke.

"And I disdainded to ask him," said Claude. "But I would not have you, captain, depend upon his being wounded."

"It makes no matter," said the officer, "except that if we thought he was so, I would set a couple of my men to search in the grass for any spots of blood."

"It will be as well to do so."

"Let that be my task then," said Luke.

A general order was given to the soldiers to spread themselves so as to go right through the wood, and leave no bush or brake of it unexplored, and they peered narrowly, too, into every tree, so that it was next thing to impossible for the major to escape, assuming that he was there, and above ground at all.

Luke, although he examined the grass with all the attention possible, could find no traces of blood, and after half an hour's most careful progress, the whole party arrived at their own sentinels, on the other side of the miniature wood, without having made any discovery.

In answer to the interrogation of their officer, the sentinels declared that no one had passed their post, and as the country beyond was very level and bare, and there was broad daylight to aid their observation, it did not seem possible that the fugitive could have left the wood.

A consultation now took place between the officer, Claude, and Luke, and the former was evidently completely puzzled to know what to be at.

"I don't know what to do," he said, "unless we burn down the wood; and I am not justified in that."

"Let us try over again a progress through it," said Claude. "Something may now strike us which failed to do so on our former progress."

"Be it so."

Luke now had a couple of the soldiers to assist him in his search for any track in the grass, whether of blood or footsteps; but for a time they were unsuccessful, until one of the soldiers cried out, in a loud voice—

"Here is something."

The officer, with Claude and Luke, hastened to the spot, and they saw a piece of blue woollen cloth caught by a prickly shrub, and fluttering in the wind.

"Don't touch it," said Luke. "It is the colour of the coat that the major had on, that I will swear to; and see, the twigs are all broken tnis way; so it is quite clear he has broken through this tangled piece of underwood towards the direction we are coming from."

"Then there is no use in our proceeding through the wood further," said the officer, "I take it."

"Stop a bit," said Luke. "Here it is."

"What—what?"

"A spot of blood upon this broad-leafed weed. Look; there can be no mistake about it."

"None whatever," said Claude. "He is wounded, then?"

"Yes," added Luke, "and hiding in the wood, that is certain. Now, it is just possible that there is some cavern in this wood; and if so, we may have some difficulty in unearthing him. My firm opinion is, that he came here with a specific purpose, and not with the mere vague idea of hiding among the trees."

"It must be so," said the officer; "but if nothing else will do, we will starve him out."

"That may be a long job," said Claude.

"Yes," added Luke, "and with this disadvantage attached to it—that we may never know when it is done."

"Then I must, in defiance of all obstruction, set fire to the wood."

"No—no. Here is blood, and we are aware now that he has struggled through this hedge. Let us look for another spot, if we can, so as to guide us in the direction he has taken."

They all now set to work upon this idea, and in the course of ten minutes Claude found another spot of blood upon the grass, which appeared to have been partially trampled out; but it might be some of their own footsteps that had done that.

Upon this discovery, the party proceeded onward till they came to the most open space in the wood, and which consisted of a pretty little spot, where there was a pool of water, and around which the grass took a more vivid green than it did at any other spot in the wood.

One gigantic tree, half decayed, and with some strips of its bark upon the point of falling from its aged trunk, stood close to the pool, and about the place there was an air of deep repose and quiet beauty that induced the party to pause, and take a glance around it in much admiration.

"A fine spot," said the officer.

"Yes," said Luke; "and I have a sort of presentiment that this is our destination. Look at yon tree."

They all gazed at the old denizen of the wood, and then Luke added—

"It seems to me that, lying among the old gnarled roots, there are some fresh leaves that appear as if they had been only pulled off lately; and, you see, that there is no bough bearing leaves at all within reach of any one on the ground."

"Then you conclude that our man is in that tree?"

"Hardly; and yet it is worth the trial. Lend me a carbine. I will try to frighten him out of it, if he be there. He will hardly allow himself to be shot down without a word. I will pretend to see him."

"Do so."

Luke took a carbine from one of the soldiers; and then pointing it up to the thickest part of the tree, he cried out in a very natural tone of voice, indeed, considering that he was only acting a part—

"Hold, all of you!—hold! I see him—I see him! I can hit him easily now. Keep quiet. I never miss when I see my mark! There he is! Ha! ha! Now for it!"

Luke took a deliberate aim with the carbine; but not the slightest sound came from any one in the tree, and he felt convinced that the experiment was unsuccessful. He lowered the carbine again, saying—

"He is not there, and it is of no use firing."

The officer looked puzzled.

"There is no saying," remarked Claude. "He might be cunning enough to chance the shot. I think it as well to fire. The report will not give any alarm to the sentinels, I suppose, captain?"

"None, whatever; beyond, perhaps, making them sharper on their posts."

"Blaze away, then, Luke."

"The rascal!" cried Luke, again. "I can only just see him; so here goes. One—two—three!"

Bang! went the carbine, and the leaves flew about the branch of the tree which Luke hit, but nothing further ensued from the shot.

Luke looked vexed.

"He is not there," he said, "and I own myself completely at fault."

"That tree is hollow," said one of the soldiers, "and if so, the inside of it is large enough to hold a file of men easily. If he be anywhere at all about it, that is where he is."

"A good thought, that," said the officer. "It sounds to me the most feasible idea of all. Fire a couple of shots into the trunk of the tree."

Two of the soldiers levelled their carbines and fired, and the officer then walked up to the trunk to examine it. He came back with a look of disappointment, as he said—

"The bullets are only in the bark. I thought, if the tree was very thin and hollow, they might go through; but it is not so, and what do you advise next, my friends?"

"Oh, for a sharp, long-handled, woodman's axe now," said Luke. "It is a weapon I know well how to use, and I would soon bring that old tree to the earth. But it is of no use wishing for what cannot be got, so there's an end of that. I must climb up, I see."

"Be careful, Luke."

"Oh, yes. Leave me alone for that. What I want to thoroughly ascertain is if there is a hollow in the trunk of the old tree or not."

"Very good," said the officer. That is an important point. Should anything happen we will support you; so you cannot be in much danger."

"Never mind the danger," said Luke.

Divesting himself, now, of his coat and hat, Luke cautiously approached the tree, and walked round it, looking for the best place to begin the ascent at. He saw that, after a little scramble, he could get hold of a short thick bush about eight feet from the ground, and placing his foot upon a portion of the roots, he made a spring at it, and was successful in getting a hold of it with his left hand.

After that, Luke's progress was tolerably easy, for that was a sort of work that, before he became acquainted with Claude Duval, he was rather an adapt at; and so he was soon in the first clump of vegetation that spread itself out from the old tree.

The others approached the trunk of the massive inhabitant of the little wood, and Claude observing Luke regarding very cautiously a fissure between two large arms of the tree, called out—

"What is it, Luke?"

"I hardly know yet."

"But is it hollow?"

"It is. There's no doubt about that. There seems to be some sort of bush growing in the hollow, or else there has been some branches thrust into it by some one."

"The latter, most likely, Luke."

"So I think; but I can see nothing but leaves, and the ends of branches in the hollow. I will fire a pistol shot down, and if any one is there it will be a hint to them at all events to say something."

"Mind you don't get a hurt in the same way from the rascal we are hunting," said Claude.

"Well, I must take my chance of that, I suppose; so here goes."

Luke had his pistols with him, so he had no difficulty in firing into the hollow of the tree.

The report ceased on the moment, and then they all listened with the most profound attention, but nothing ensued therefrom, and Luke was specially annoyed that all his trouble had been taken for nothing.

"It's of no use," he said. "I believe the fellow is the d—l himself. It's no use troubling about him any further, I do think."

"Plague take him," said Claude.

It was at this moment, and just as Luke was preparing to descend from the tree, that a pistol shot was heard, and a bullet whistled so close past the face of Claude, that there could be no reasonable doubt of the fact that it had been fired directly at him.

"That will do," said Duval.

"Where did the shot come from?" said the officer.

"The tree," cried all the soldiers at once.

"Then we have him," said Claude. "Come down, Luke, as quickly as you can. The enemy is here sure enough, and we have him safely."

CHAPTER CXCIII.

THE LITTLE WOOD IS DESTROYED BY FIRE.—THE MAJOR BIDS THE WORLD FAREWELL.

THERE could be now no rational doubt whatever of the fact that some one was hidden about the tree in some manner, for pistol shots do not usually make their appearance without human influence of some sort or another.

The only difficulty that remained was to find out how to attack the hidden foe.

Luke descended with rapidity when he saw that Claude Duval had been fired at, and he called out—

"You may take my word for it now that some one is in the hollow of the tree. What so easy as to drag some branches in after him? The brigand is there."

"Then out he shall come," said the officer, "dead or alive. I will summon him to surrender, though, first in the name of the law."

The officer felt that he was obliged to go through this formality before actually taking steps to destroy the chief of the robbers, and boldly advancing to the tree, he cried out—

"Major Brook, as you call yourself, I give you five minutes, in which to surrender and make your submission. If by the end of that time you do not do so, your life will be taken without further parley with you, as you will be considered to be out of the pale of the law, and as deserving of no quarter."

The only reply to this was in the shape of a pistol bullet, that gave the officer a flesh wound on the left arm.

"Very good," said the officer, with great coolness, as he brushed the blood from his sleeve. "As you will."

"You are hurt, sir," said Claude.

"A trifle only. Perhaps you will be so good as to bind this handkerchief round my arm. It is nothing, only a slight hurt deserves attention as well as a serious one."

"We had better keep out of range of the fellow's fire," said Luke. "Let us shift our ground a little. He may not have such a convenient loop-hole on the other side of the tree.

Bang! came another shot, and one of the soldiers fell. He was hit in the chest, and looked dying.

The officer bit his lip, as he cried out in a tone of intense excitement—

"Steady, my men, steady; you shall not be made targets of by that fellow for long. Collect dry brushwood in abundance, but don't take it to the tree till it can be taken all at once."

"You will smoke him out?" said Claude.

"Yes, smoke and flame must do it."

"It is a dreadful end for him, but, after all, I do not see that such a rascal deserves better treatment."

"Better treatment! He deserves worse. And yet I would not order this mode of operation if by any other plan I could succeed. I cannot remain here, though, and see my men shot down before my eyes by an invisible foe."

"Certainly not."

LUCY THORNTON APPEALING TO MAJOR BROOK'S HOUSEKEEPER.

Duval felt that he really could say nothing against the proceedings of the officer after what had taken place, and he watched the soldiers as they with avidity set about their task.

The manner in which two of their comrades had now fallen before the treacherous fire of the brigand had made them furious ; and while in regular battle with a military foe they would have looked upon the death of a comrade merely as one of the casualties of the profession, they now considered that the two who had fallen had been murdered.

In the depths of that little wood the rain had not been suffic iently heavyand prolonged to penetrate, and the soldiers soon had collected a considerabl e quantity of dry brushwood, and whole armfuls of crumbling decayed leaves, that the least touch of fire to would cause to burst into a fierce flame.

"Now, my men," said the officer, "advance all at once, and pile your combustibles round the tree. There is no wind; so I don't think we shall at all involve any other part of the wood in the destruction that we only intend for that one tree."

The soldiers made a dash forward, and in a few moments the dry foliage was piled breast-high round the old decayed trunk of the tree.

"I don't much like this," said Luke, "and yet I should be puzzled to suggest any other course. My opinion, though, is, that the whole wood will go, except the trees on the outskirts that are too moist to burn."

"Think you so ?"

"Yes. The underwood is dry, and there is an immense quantity of it. If it once catches, it will create an artificial draught, and then there will be no stopping it."

"That is true enough, Luke. Fire is a spirit which, when once evoked, is not so easy to lay again."

Neither Claude nor Luke, however, considered that they had any right to dictate to the French officer what he was or what he was not to do in what he might consider the discharge of his duty; so they contented themselves with the idea that they were but spectators of the scene that was about to take place.

Claude, however, knew that May and Lucy would be rather anxious at his prolonged absence; so he asked Luke to run back to where they had been left, and tell them that all was well as regarded him; but not to tell *them* what was about to be done for the purpose of unearthing the major from his hiding-place.

This was a message that Luke very quickly performed, for a great curiosity to know the result of affairs in the wood induced him to hurry back again with as much expedition as he well could.

By the time of Luke's return the preparations for firing the heap of brushwood round the tree were complete; and as the period had long since elapsed that the officer had offered to the brigand to make his submission in, there remained nothing to do but to proceed at once to extremities in the matter.

The soldiers looked on the preparations, which would enable them to revenge themselves upon the murderer of their comrades, with a sort of savage joy, and Claude and Luke stood apart, deeply interested, but by no means active spectators of the scene.

"Sergeant !" said the officer.

"Here," said the sergeant.

"Fire the brushwood."

"Yes, my officer."

The sergeant and a couple of men had already provided themselves with lights, and they approached the tree now at a steady pace to carry out their orders.

"Hold !" cried a stifled voice.

"Advance !" cried the officer.

The sergeant and the two men had for a moment only paused upon hearing the voice cry "Hold !" but at the sound of the order in their officer's tones, they walked steady on again.

There was then a bright flash and a report, and one of the men staggered as he exclaimed—

"I am hit !"

"Forward !" cried the sergeant, and in another moment the brushwood was alight.

The sergeant and the remaining soldier assisted their wounded comrade back, and laid him gently down at the officer's feet.

"That makes three," said the sergeant.

"They shall be avenged," said the officer. "Look!"

A dense cloud of white smoke, with here and there a bright blue streak among it, rose from the kindled brushwood, and so still and calm was the air, that in a thick dense column this smoke ascended quite to the top of the trees. It was then only that it met with a current of air that gently curled it over like an immense cloud to the eastward, and spread it over the little wood in that direction till there was nothing but a dim kind of twilight beneath it.

Not a sound was heard.

The smoke increased in vehemence. But now it changed its character, and more blue wreaths than white ones were visible.

In a few moments a crackling sound was audible.

"It has caught!" cried the sergeant. "It burns now."

A bright tongue of flame shot about twenty feet above the pile of brushwood, and the crackling noise became each moment more and more vehement.

"It is not a trifle that will put that out," said Luke.

"No, Luke," replied Claude; "and I am glad that the wind above the tree tops carries the smoke in a different direction to that in which May and Lucy are waiting for us."

"Yes, that is a mercy, for it is suffocating."

Luke coughed as he spoke, and the officer, they saw, was breathing through his handkerchief.

Now another flame of equal length to the other, but of greater breadth, burst up into the air, and the brushwood began to roar like an immense furnace. Some of the lower branches of the old tree took fire, and breaking off with a sullen crash, fell into the flames below. Once only Claude Duval thought he heard a cry from the midst of the flames, and he shuddered.

"Did you hear anything, Luke?"

"No, Claude."

"Then it was fancy, after all, or the crackling of the wood, or a flame forcing its way through a fissure in the old tree, I suppose; but I did think that I heard a cry."

The officer now approached.

"Don't you think it rather strange, gentleman, that we hear nothing of the brigand?"

"It is so."

"Perhaps he is suffocated," said Luke, "and it is possible enough that such may be his fate before he had time to cry out. We don't know how quickly the subtle smoke may have found its way into the hollow of the tree without our knowing it."

"True! true!"

"Hark!" said Claude.

There came a strange wailing cry, like a shriek from some one in mortal agony. The flames rose in all their majesty and might high above the tree, and the roaring was like the lashing of an angry sea upon a rocky coast.

"You heard that!" said Luke.

The officer nodded.

"It was shocking," said Claude.

"Let us hope," said the officer, "that it is his last cry,"

"Yes, on, yes; nothing human, surely, would utter such a cry, except in some horrible extremity."

It was at that moment that the old tree, with a loud crash, fell over to the eastward, shewing that even the very light wind that was aloft still had power sufficient to influence the direction which the charred and blazing trunk would fall.

Millions of sparks now shot upwards with all the beauty of some elaborately prepared firework intended to exhibit such an effect, and then for the space of a minute or so the smoke overpowered everything in the shape of flame.

This was a state of things, however, which did not last long. The pent-up, half-smothered flames soon found some opening, and then they burst with greater force than before, and the conflagration proceeded at a great rate, till the old tree wa evidently all but consumed.

" I think," said the officer, " that the rest of the wood will escape."

Luke shook his head, and pointed to a wreath of smoke rising from among the trees at some distance off.

" That shower of red-hot dust from the decayed tree has done it," he said. " Behold !"

Even as he spoke another volume of smoke mounted up a few feet from the first. The officer looked vexed, and Luke added—

" I rather think this wood will, in the next ten minutes, or, perhaps, less, be a little too hot to hold us."

" I didn't mean it," said the officer, " but it can't be helped now. If the wood will burn, why, it must, that's all."

———

CHAPTER CXCIV.

THE MAJOR IS AT LAST COMPELLED TO SHOW HIMSELF TO THE DAYLIGHT.

While they were looking at the wreaths of smoke that rose up among the trees in the direction the wind, such as there was of it, was blowing, a new danger suddenly threatened them.

It happened that about where they were standing there grew a peculiar kind of long light-coloured silky-looking grass, and a flame came bounding across it with great rapidity.

" This won't do," said Claude, " we shall get our feet scorched if we don't mind."

" Diable !" said the officer. " Which way can we go ?"

" Into the pool," said Luke, " I take it, will be the safest, unless the tree is sufficiently burnt to allow us to go near it, for all round it is charred and burnt to a cinder already, and we can stand there in safety from the burning grass."

This suggestion was at once attempted to be carried out, but the red-hot cinders of the tree sent out such a glow of heat that they found, turn which way they would, they could not bear it, and Luke first set the example of running to the pool, and standing knee deep in its water.

" This is capital," he said.

The soldiers and Claude quickly followed his example; but the officer did not seem to like it at all. Probably he thought it was rather a compromise of his dignity; but at last giving a slight toss to his head, and coughing, he cried out—

" Water before fire, any day, my good fellows ;" and he then took his place in the pool by the side of Claude.

They were not a moment too soon in the place of safety, for the bushy grass reached right to the edge of the pool, and they could feel the flash of the heat that it threw out upon their faces. It was quickly past, though; so that they had not to remain long in such an uncomfortable situation.

" And now," said the officer, " I suppose our work is done here ; but I shall not feel quite satisfied to leave this spot until I find some intimations of the fact that our enemy has perished in the flames."

The tree was rapidly cooling down now ; so they found they could approach it without much inconvenience, and every moment made it easier and easier still to bear the heat that it sent out.

The fire that had assaulted the rest of the wood had not made progress enough to give them any alarm; and so in the course of five minutes more the soldiers were, with the charred ends of some of the old branches of the tree, raking amongst the embers for some time for some trace of the body of the brigand major.

Both Luke and Claude watched this operation with a fearful kind of interest.

"He could not be wholly consumed," said the officer.

"Impossible," said Claude.

"Well, his bones will suffice."

"And they are not there," said Luke.

"Not there?"

"Certainly not; your men have turned the debris of the tree twice over; and if there be anything in the shape of a bone, I will eat it."

"This is still more extraordinary," said Claude. "Are we to be baffled, after all, in our chase of this man who seems to leave a charmed life? Is it impossible by bullet or by fire to slay him?"

"It seems so."

The soldiers commenced to rake away the charred rubbish, and looked at each other with vague astonishment, for they were quite unable to give the least guess regarding a solution of the mystery. Then Luke took up one of the stakes with which they had been raking the ground, and struck it against something among the embers, after which he looked at Claude and the officer, and beckoned them to step aside.

They eagerly followed him.

"What is it, Luke?"

"I have found the clue to the mystery."

"You have?"

"Yes, there is a trap-door among the roots of the old tree, and, no doubt, our friend, the major, is quietly ensconced in some cavern under our feet at the present moment."

"The d—l!" said Claude.

"Exactly so," said the officer. "I begin to think that he is no other than the veritable Diable himself. But how shall we get at him now?"

"By stratagem," said Luke.

"As you please. Stratagem is all right in war. What do you propose?"

"Just this. Let us appear to give up the affair as if satisfied that he must have perished in the ruins of the tree. March the soldiers away and let us talk loudly of going on to Calais. When we get a short distance off, you and I and my friend here and your sergeant can come back and keep a watch from behind this bush upon yonder spot where the old tree stood, and the likelihood is, I think, that our friend, the major, who cannot be comfortable where he is, will appear."

"Be it so," said the officer.

"That will do, I think," said Claude Duval.

The officer at once proceeded to carry out the plan. Advancing to the soldiers, he cried out, in a loud clear voice—

"My lads, I am satisfied that our work is done, and that the brigand chief is no more. We will, therefore, start for Calais at once. Fall in!"

The soldiers gathered themselves up.

"You will take your wounded comrades with you, and when we reach Calais, a carriage shall be despatched for the dead. Now, gentlemen, are you quite satisfied?"

"Quite," said Claude and Luke.

"March!"

The whole party left the little glade in which the old tree had been situated, and halted not until they reached the spot where May and Lucy were waiting for them.

"Now," said Luke, "back again."

"Yes," said Claude. "Come, sir," to the officer.

"I am ready. Sergeant, follow me with your carbine as lightly as foot can fall."

"Yes, my officer."

"What is all this?" said May. "Oh, Claude, are you returning to the wood again? It seems to be on fire. Tell me what is the meaning of all this?"

"Soon—soon," said Claude. "We have not now a moment to lose."

To the surprise, then, of May and Lucy, they all hurried into the wood again, leaving only the soldiers, who looked rather angered at the strange conduct of their officers and the English.

The officer and his sergeant went first, treading as lightly as they could, and yet notwithstanding with tolerable speed, through the wood, and Claude and Luke followed them. In two minutes more they were behind the bush that they had agreed to shelter themselves with, and they all stooped and tried to get as clear a sight as possible through the interstices of the natural screen which so effectually hid them.

"Shall we see him?" said the officer.

"Hush!" said Luke, "not a word yet."

They remained profoundly still for the space of ten minutes, during which it may safely be said that not one of them for an instant took his eyes off the spot that had been occupied by the gigantic tree, which was now such a heap of blackened ruin.

The officer was getting terribly impatient, and had given utterance to some rather stringent oaths between his teeth, when Luke suddenly said—

"Hist! Look!"

There was a visible commotion among the charred embers about the root of the old tree.

"Sacre!" said the officer.

"Hush—hush!" said Luke, "or all is lost."

The commotion about the root of the tree continued, and a heap of the still smouldering embers of the fire was suddenly threw aside as though some upheaving of something below there had taken place, and such indeed was the case.

In another moment a human head, blackened by smoke, with a handkerchief tied round, slowly rose up above the charred remains around it.

"It is he," said the officer.

"Hush! No—yes!"

Luke had said both no and yes, for although, in good truth, it was the major, he had suffered so much from the fire that at the moment no one could possibly have recognised him. His eyebrows and his moustache were scorched off; and from the manner in which the handkerchief enveloped his head, it seemed as if all his hair was singed off likewise.

They saw him raise his clenched hand, and they heard him speak in a howling voice of concentrated rage.

"If I live!" he cried, "and I will live, if for nothing else—if I live, I doom to death all who have this day molested me. Some horrible death I will devise for every one of them. They shall find poison in their food—an assassin in their chambers! Oh, I will be revenged, horribly revenged, yet! I—I will only live for vengeance!"

He fell down the trap-door again with a deep groan.

The officer looked at Claude and Luke, and they looked at the officer, and the sergeant looked at them all three.

"It was the man," said the officer.

"Oh, yes," said Claude.

"Not a doubt of it," said Luke, "and a nice, pleasant sort of person he seems, upon my word. He has sworn vengeance against us all."

"Yes," said Claude, "and he is just the sort of man, if I am any judge of human nature, to keep his word."

"We shall see," said the officer; "but let us advance, now, gentlemen, that we can secure the rascal in there."

"Wait a moment. Ah, look again."

Once more the horrible head projected above the trap-door, and the blood-shot glaring eyes were cast wildly around the spot.

"All gone—all gone," said the wretch—"all gone. They half burnt me to death before I could get the cursed trap open. I ought to have been in the cave from the first, and then all would have been well; but—but what with my wound, and what with the smoke, I could not open it, no—no, and it has nearly been my death. But I will live for revenge yet. Poison is sure and secret. Ha! —ha! I will kill them all yet! Kill—kill! and I will gloat over their agonies!"

Slowly and painfully the mangled wretch got half out of the cave, and he had his hands upon the edges of the trap-door, when the officer said something sharply to the sergeant which Claude did not catch.

"Eh?" he said.

"Move your head a trifle," said the sergeant.

Claude instantly did so, and in the next moment he was almost deafened by the discharge of the carbine close to his ear. The major uttered a yell, and sprang up into the air, and then fell headlong down the trap-door again, and all was still.

"I had him, then," said the sergeant.

"Good," said the officer. "Now, gentlemen, I rather think that the liberal promises of vengeance with which yon rascal regaled himself, are defeated; he has a bullet in his brain."

"He ought to have," said the sergeant.

"It is a dreadful, although I cannot say that it is not a deserving death," said Claude Duval, with a shudder.

"Hark you, gentlemen," said the officer. "If that wretch had been taken, death would have been his certain lot. It would have been a pity to give the Commune so much trouble; so, as a mercy to him and an obligation to others, I think he is well disposed of as it is."

"It is true," said Claude.

"Let us go and make sure," said Luke. "The fellow has got the better of us so often, that I can hardly persuade myself he is gone at last."

"I will forgive him, if he is not," said the sergeant, touching the butt of the carbine. "This don't fail, and I put the bullet in myself.

They all now sprung from their hiding place behind the bush, and made the best of their way to the tree, where they saw the trap-door open, and which, not-withstanding it was partially cased with iron, had suffered very much from the fire.

The opening in the ground looked of unfathomable depth; and at first they could see no mode of descent, but Luke in a few moments pointed out an iron chain connected with the rim of the excavation.

CHAPTER CXCV.

LUKE AND HIS FRIENDS RE-CROSS THE CHANNEL, AND LAND AT DOVER.

To tell the truth, Claude Duval would very gladly, now, after all that had happened, have left the place, for he was quite content with the retribution that had already come on the major, but he did not like to seem to desert those friends, who for so long had fought for him and for his.

It was that feeling alone that still kept him to the spot.

The cavernous place in the hollow roots of the old tree, that lay so blackened and charred at their feet, was certainly not one to tempt anybody to make the descent into, and the soldiers looked at the officer with an evident hope that they would not be ordered upon such an enterprise as that.

Luke seemed to be the only person who appeared to have anything like a serious idea of descending; and no doubt the soldiers devoutly hoped and desired that he would do so.

"What do you think of it, Claude?" whispered Luke.

"In what way?"

"I mean as to the going down."

"There can be but one opinion about that, Luke."

"And that is against it?"

"Rather so."

"Then, you won't go?"

"Certainly not, Luke; and allow me to hope that you will not, either, for I don't see the smallest necessity to risk your life in such a way as that. Nay, I should look upon it quite as an act of madness for you to go down that place. Who knows what you may encounter there?"

"It's not inviting, certainly; but yet, don't know—I feel as if I should not like that rascal to escape."

"No more should I; but I had rather he escaped than that you placed yourself in such peril."

"Surely," said the officer to Claude, "your friend does not think of descending this opening in the earth?"

"He did do so."

"Oh, no—no! That must not be thought of. The life of a brave and reputable man must not be sacrificed to that rascal who is now there."

"But what can be done?"

"Oh, we have a better plan than that comes to."

"If such be the case, then, of course, I and my friend will be only too happy to aid you."

The officer smiled.

"It don't need much aid," he said. "We mean to fill up this hole in the earth with sand and mould, so that it is quite impossible any one can get out, and then we shall be satisfied that the brigand is comfortably disposed of."

"But if he be alive?"

The officer shrugged his shoulders.

"Well, if he be so, it is his own fault, and I am sorry to say that I can't help it."

"This is dreadful!"

"Ah, my good friend, you don't know these brigands. The act that you call dreadful, in relation to this man, was a mere nothing in comparison with what he has done at different times."

"I do not doubt his wickedness, but still——"

"I understand you. You would say it behoves us not to follow his example. I respect you for the sentiment; and will yet make an effort to save the rascal from the doom, against which you seem to have an aversion. If he should refuse to save himself from it, then you can have no sort of objection to allowing him to choose for himself?"

"Certainly not."

"That is all I require, then," said the officer, and he went quite close to the edge of the deep hollow, and called out in a loud voice—

"Brigand, Major Brook—It is sufficient that you are below, and that you may be still in life. If so, you are recommended to come up and deliver yourself to the soldiery, to save yourself from the doom that awaits you, and which will consist of being built in with rock and earth, so that your escape from this place will be beyond the pale of all possibility."

There was no answer to this appeal.

"There, you see," said the officer. "He is obstinate or dead, and in either case I do not see that we can do any more than what we are now doing."

"I am perfectly satisfied," said Claude Duval.

"Now, soldiers," said the officer, in a loud tone of command, "let me make you fairly understand what you have to do."

The soldiers respectfully attended to him.

"You will set to work and fill up this cavernous opening in such a way that it

LUCY THORNTON.

shall be impossible for any person from below to free it from what you shall place within it.   Now to work."

The soldiers needed no further instructions of what they were to do, but with the greatest alacrity they set to work up the job that the officer suggested, and Claude and his friends looked on in silence.

The first quantity of earth that they brought to the mouth of the opening in the ground was rattled down, but hardly had it descended than a feeble voice from below called out, in accents of alarm—

"Hold—oh, hold!"

The officer nodded, and glanced at Claude Duval, as much as to say, "You see, sir, that this plan has fully answered my expectation," and then approaching the brink of the abyss, he cried down it—

"Ascend, or the work will go on."

"I am coming," said the voice; "but spare my life, I beg of you."

"You must surrender, unconditionally."

"Then if I am to be shot when I gain the surface, I may as well die here where I am."

"Well, I will promise that your life shall be spared if you surrender yourself, and make no attempt at escape."

"I promise."

The officer stepped aside, and then, with many moans and with such slow movements, that it was quite evident they were attended by the greatest pain, a figure slowly ascended from the deep opening in the earth, and appeared above the surface.

The head and face were blackened with smoke and gunpowder, and blood was streaming from several wounds.

It was the major; and the moment he got fairly upon the level ground, he fell flat upon the earth.

"He is dead," said the sergeant.

"No," said Luke. "Don't you fancy that, I beg. He is by no means dead yet, I assure you."

"But I shot him."

"Don't be too positive."

"He surely is no more," said the officer, as he stepped up to the prostrate figure, and touched it with the point of his sword. "Rise, brigand," he said, "if you can."

A low groan was the only answer.

"I knew I had hit him," said the sergeant.

"Major Brook," said Claude Duval, "all subterfuge is useless, now. You are a prisoner, and if you can rise it will be no worse for you, while any duplicity with regard to your real condition can but aggravate you captors."

Another groan was the only response to this appeal upon the part of Claude Duval.

"Turn him over," said the officer to the soldiers, "and let us have a look at him. We shall be better able to judge of his condition then."

The soldiers turned him with his face to the light, and propped him up against a portion of the half-consumed tree, and then one of them brought his cap full of water, and dashed it in the face of the really dying wretch, for the fact was, that such was his condition at that time.

The water had the effect of reviving Major Brook, and they saw him open his eyes and look wildly about him.

"I am dying," he said.

"It seems so," said the officer. "You will escape the scaffold."

The brigand nodded, and a faint smile passed over his blackened and blood-stained face.

"I am hit," he said.

"Where?"

He laid his hand upon his breast.

"I told you all so," said the sergeant. "My carbine did not fail me. I knew that I had hit him."

"It would be a mercy," said one of the soldiers, "to send a bullet through his skull, and put him out of his misery."

"No," said the officer. "Let him be. I promised him that he should not be shot, and I will keep my word to even such a man as he is. He cannot live long."

"He wishes to speak," said Luke.

"Speak, wretched criminal," said the officer, "if such is your desire. We will listen respectfully to the last words of even such a man as you are. Speak, I say."

The half-dead robber spoke in a low tone of voice.

"There is a young girl," he said—"a young English girl, whom I tore from her home and brought here. I—I would fain know if she is safe—safe. Oh, tell me!"

"She is," said Duval.

"Thank Heaven she is safe!"

"She is quite safe from you and your companions," added Duval. "I do not think but that you are the only survivor of the guilty band that held her in bondage."

"You only tell me that."

"What mean you? I tell you she is safe. Why should her deliverer falsify the fact in such a way?"

"I—I believe you now. Oh, God! I would fain die with the forgiveness of that girl!"

"She does forgive you."

"No—no. You only say that."

"That is true; but I so well know her gentle and kindly spirit that I am convinced when I say it I only say that which she would bear me out in."

"Oh, have mercy upon me!"

"What mercy can we show you, now? You are past all mercy, to my thinking. What can we do?"

"I want to hear from her own lips that she forgives me, that is all. I think it would soothe my last agony to hear so much from her."

"I am here," said Lucy, stepping to the side of Claude Duval—"I am here, and I do forgive you."

"Thank you—thank you!"

The hand of the wretched man was just within a fold of his apparel about his breast; and now he suddenly drew it, with a small pistol in it, and pulling the trigger right in the face of Lucy, he said—

"I do not die, after all, unrevenged! Ha! ha! Ah! foiled even at the last! Curses! curses!"

The pistol had missed fire, only faintly flashing in the pan; and as Major Brook flung it from him, he sank back on the earth behind him.

"Infamous wretch!" cried the officer, as he stepped aside. "You now die the death you deserve. Fire!"

A couple of the soldiers discharged their carbines at the head of Major Brook, and the brigand chief fell to rise no more in this world.

Lucy shuddered, as she clung to Claude Duval.

CHAPTER CXCVI.

BRINGS THE READER AGAIN TO ENGLISH GROUND.

WE will now beg the readers indulgence, while we rather hastily skim over the events of a day and a night.

After the tragical death of the major, the party which had so happily succeeded in dispersing one of the most dangerous bands of robbers that had ever infested the country about Calais, returned at once to that port.

Claude Duval and his friends accompanied them; and Claude, on his route, spoke to the consul about the best mode of getting to the coast of England again.

The reply of the consul was to the effect, that if he allowed himself to stay in France until the next day, he would find himself involved in so many vexatious inquiries of the police contingent upon a due explanation of the affair at the chateau, that he might be detained a month.

"That will never do," said Claude. "What would you advise me to do in such circumstances ?"

"Do you wish to go with all speed to England ?"

"Indeed, I do. I should like, if such a thing were possible, to start the moment we arrive at Calais."

"That cannot be done. All you have to do, though, is to come to my house, and there wait till nightfall, when we will find some fishing vessel that, for a few pounds, will take you over the channel to Dover. But you must say nothing of the intention to do so, or you will find yourself under the control of a couple of gendarmes."

"Trust me for keeping my own counsel," said Claude Duval.

Everything turned out as the consul had said. The officer in command of the military party told Duval that he would have to appear with all his party at the office of the *procureur de roi* on the morrow at twelve o'clock.

"I shall certainly be there," said Claude.

With that answer, the officer left him and his party in peace.

At about nine o'clock in the evening, while a misty rain was falling, and a rather blustering wind was blowing from the south, the consul accompanied Claude and his friends to the sea-side, where the consul's servant had hired a fishing vessel of excellent sailing qualities, and well manned, the crew of which had agreed to land them on the English coast for the sum of ten guineas.

After warmly thanking the consul for the great interest he had taken in their welfare, Claude and Luke, and May and Lucy, embarked in the fishing boat, and were soon at sea.

The wind was so favourable the whole way, that they very soon came running along the shore by Dover and Folkstone, looking for a landing-place, and, at one o'clock in the morning, Claude and his friends stood again upon English ground.

The reader will now be good enough to take for granted that no difficulties occurred in the route, and that they found their horses, and set off at an early hour, and just as the sun was rising, found themselves within twenty miles of London.

Their horses were rather tired, and they all drew up at a little road-side inn, where Claude thought it would be just as well if they rested some four or five hours, as well to rest their cattle as themselves.

Of course, Lucy was very anxious to get home; but still she could not but see the propriety of a rest for all parties, so she cheerfully acquiesced in it.

The inn had a very large and well-stocked garden attached to it, which was a great attraction to Duval and his friends, and they whiled away the hours there pleasantly enough, until they thought proper to start again.

Their mode of getting along attracted a little attention upon the road, for May was still in her male costume, and Lucy rode with her, clasping her round the waist to keep herself from falling ; so, as they neared London, a number of jokes were made of them as they jogged on.

"This won't do," said Duval. "We will hire a chaise for Lucy, and we can then all of us ride with it, as a sort of escort, which will look very much more respectable than the way we are getting on now, I think."

Luke approved of this suggestion, as it offered an easy mode of travelling to the metropolis, and so on, northwards of it, to the home of Lucy's mother, the aunt of Claude Duval.

When he had gone upon his continental expedition, Duval had taken good care to provide himself with a sufficient supply of cash; and as the affair had terminated so much sooner than he had expected. and had taken him and his party so short a distance from the coast of France, it had really cost him very little.

The aid and advice, too, of the consul at Calais had materially assisted in preventing Duval from incurring any heavy charges, so that he had his pockets pretty well supplied.

A post-chaise was easily procured. and Lucy occupied it along with May, while Luke led May's horse, and trotted along by the side of Claude Duval.

In this way they, in two stages of ten miles each, reached London, and after there refreshing themselves, they went on to the northern suburb of the metropolis, for Claude was anxious to get to Finchley-common with Lucy as soon as he possibly could do so.

While in the coach together, Lucy and May had some rather anxious conversation about Claude.

At first, Lucy hardly knew what to say to May, for she had a dread of uttering her real sentiments regarding the mode of life that her cousin was leading, and she was by far too truthful and single-hearted to say a word that she did not think.

May, however, soon relieved her from that embarrassment, by saying to her—

"Oh, Lucy, if you had but sufficient influence over your cousin, Claude, to induce him to exercise those abilities and talents with which Heaven has endowed him, in some other way than that dangerous and terrible one which he follows, how happy I should be."

" Ah, then." said Lucy, " you, too, mourn that he is what he is ?"

" With my whole heart and soul I do."

"And so do I. Alas ! it was with the hope that I might do something to rescue Claude from the dangerous and desperate course he goes upon, that I consented, as I thought, to meet him, and fell into the hands of that Major Brook, as he called himself."

"Yes—Claude has told me that much. But now, Lucy, there is an opportunity which, I think, may possibly never occur again, for making an attempt to nerve him to some better purpose than hitherto has actuated him. Will you second me?"

"I will, indeed. What is your thought upon such a deeply interesting subject ?"

" It is just this. I know that he loves you, and I need not say that I know that he loves me. He respects his aunt, too, your mother, very much ; and I have been thinking that if, when we reach your home, we were all to make an appeal to him, in the sacred name of our joint affection for him, it might be successful."

" It shall be done."

" You give me new life by saying that. What I want you to do is, to speak to your mother upon the subject, so that she, as well as you and I, may be prepared to take up every point of argument and entreaty that can be suggested."

" I will, you may be assured. But do you think that the man who is with him will not oppose such a project ?"

" Luke, you mean ?"

" Yes. It may not suit his views."

"Ah, you do not know Luke so well as I do; and how, indeed, should you ? But I can answer for him, that such will not be the case. Luke follows Duval from sheer affection, and anything in the world that can possibly be for his benefit, will be ever welcome to Luke."

"Then, in fact, he will join us in this matter?"

" Indeed, he will, with heart and hand."

May was deeply affected at even the dim prospect of being able to release

Claude Duval from the perils of his present mode of life; but the sagacious and thinking reader will not fail to perceive that there was one great hiatus in the plan of those two young persons.

That hiatus consisted in the fact that they provided no substitute for Claude Duval's present mode of getting a living. They were not able to say, "Leave the road, and all it's dangers and horrors, and do this and that instead." All they could say was, "Leave the road, and trust to fortune to put bread into your mouth."

Now, fortune does not put bread into people's mouths in that sort of way.

If they could but have been able to point out to Duval any alternative, he certainly would have found it very difficult, if not impossible, to have resisted solicitations that carried every principle of reason and justice with them; but, as it was, he had the ready answer of—

"Tell me what else to do, if I cease to be a highwayman, and leave the road for ever."

Sanguine natures, however, seldom thinks of everything, and so, for a little time, Lucy and May were all the happier for the thought that they might, when they arrived at Mrs. Thornton's, on Finchley Common, be the means, with her aid, of withdrawing Duval from the career which they both shuddered to contemplate the end of.

Duval had no idea that this little aimable plot was getting up against his highwayman propensities; and, as they neared the common, he rode to the side of the chaise, and said to Lucy—

"You will be soon at home, now, my dear Lucy; and I hope and expect you will find your mother perfectly well."

"I hope so, indeed," said Lucy. "But you must promise me one thing, Cousin Claude."

"What is it?"

"Nay, now, that is not right. I fully expected that you would have been so gallant as to promise me, without asking what it was."

"I will, then."

"Well, it is not much. It is only that you will stay for an hour or two at my mother's house, so that she and May may become in some measure acquainted with each other."

"I will do so, with pleasure."

"And then, Cousin Claude," said Lucy, as she leant a little from the window of the chaise, and looked earnestly in his face, "if ever May should want a temporary or a permanent refuge, here will be one for her, where, for your sake as well as for her own, she will meet with all the kindness that affection can suggest."

"Ah, Lucy, you are too good and kind."

"No—no. What do I not owe you?"

"And how richly am I repaid, by what you just now said. But there is your mother's house among the trees—I can just see it; and here we are on the common. I think we may dismiss the chaise and proceed on foot."

This was agreed to, and the chaise being dismissed, the little party proceeded on foot to the residence of old Mrs. Thornton.

Claude Duval, as he approached that house, could not help wondering to himself if the highly religious lady and gentleman had given any further trouble to his aunt since his absence; but he hardly thought that possible, when he considered the precaution he had taken to place a solicitor in a kind of guardianship over the place.

The feeling with which he looked upon that peaceful-looking abode, though, was rather of a painful character than otherwise.

CHAPTER CXCVII.

DUVAL IS DEAF TO THE SOLICITATIONS OF HIS AUNT AND COUSIN TO LEAVE.
THE ROAD.

WHEN Lucy saw that she was so near her mother's house that a few minutes-
more must take her into the well-known garden, and present to her the many
familiar objects which she had at one time, and that only a day or two since,
thought never to look upon again, her feelings almost overpowered her.

" Lucy, you are ill ?" said May.

" No—no."

" Yes, you are as pale as death."

" I feel a little faint. It is the flowing of my spirits, that is all, and the joy
of being so near my home again."

" Ah, that feeling will soon pass away, Lucy. Alas! I have no home to
go to."

" Oh, but you shall have one, for my home shall be your home, and if I could
only persuade Cousin Claude to let you stay, how happy I should be, with
the feeling that at least you were safe from the perils that environ his precarious.
existence."

" And do you think that I should be happy under such circumstances,
Lucy ?"

" Ah, no. How could I be so very forgetful! Your existence is bound up
in his, of course, and it is impossible that you can be happy with the continually
present thought upon your mind, that he may be in danger."

" That is true."

" You would rather, of course, be with him ?"

" Ah, yes. His danger I would have my danger—his safety my safety. But
we will hope, with the assistance of your mother, to wean him entirely from
this mode of life. Remember what we have talked of, and at least we will
make the effort."

" We will."

" You are better now, Lucy ?"

" Oh, much, much better. It was but a passing faintness. But the thought
that I had a duty to do, as regarded you and my cousin Claude, has quite
recovered me from it."

Claude stepped up to Lucy now, and told her in a few words in what condition he had found her mother upon his arrival, and how she was beleaguered by the
evangelical couple whom he had thought proper to turn out of the house upon
that occasion.

" Oh," said Lucy, " how could mother be so rash !"

" She was ill, Lucy, and that accounts for it; but I took care to alter all that
before I left."

" I owe you more than I thought I did, Cousin Claude," said Lucy, " for
you have been kind to my mother as well as to me."

They had now reached the garden gate, at which Claude Duval rang a hearty
peal, while poor Lucy began to tremble and turn pale again, with the apprehension of the possibility of her mother being no more by that time.

And yet, she had not been absent altogether a week from home; but what
an age had that week appeared to her, and what wondrous changes might not
have been effected during that small period of time.

Lucy might well tremble at the thought of what even one short week sometimes produces in the history of individuals.

Paul was rather surprised that no one answered the bell, and he rang again,
for he saw that the delay put poor Lucy upon the rack of agony and impatience.

" No one is here, surely," said Luke.

"Oh, yes—yes," said Claude. "Don't say that, Luke. Ah! I hear a footstep now."

"Thank Heaven!" said Lucy.

The little square panel in the middle of the garden door, through which it was the custom of the family to reconnoitre any visitor before opening the door wholly, as, at times, audacious mendicants visited the house, whom it was well worth while to keep outside, was now suddenly opened, and to the astonishment of Claude Duval, he saw the inflamed-looking face of the highly religious woman, whom he thought he had completely got rid of from the premises upon his last visit, at the opening.

"Who is there?" she said, in a snuffling sort of voice. "Who is there, now?"

"Open the door!" said Claude, sharply.

Clap shut went the little wicket, as the religious female uttered a scream of horror at the sight of him.

"Oh, what is the meaning of all this?" said Lucy. "My mother—my poor mother! Is she no more?"

"Hush!" said Claude. "There is no danger. Do you know that woman at all, Lucy?"

"Oh, no—no!"

"Well, then, I do. It is the very woman whom I sent out of the place upon my last visit, and to find her here amazes and annoys me ; for it shows me that the attorney I employed has completely and entirely neglected his trust."

"Here is some one," said Luke. "Perhaps we can inquire, and find out the state of affairs."

The person who was approaching was a tax-collector, and he rang rather sharply at the bell, but no one came.

"I cannot wait here all day," he said. "Do you know, sir," addressing Claude, "if any one is at home?"

"Oh, yes," said Claude; "but they don't seem inclined to open the door."

"I cannot wait, then. I must call again."

The tax-collector was going away, when Claude Duval asked him if the lawyer whom he named was still in the place.

"Oh, he is dead, poor man!" said the tax-collector. "He took ill, and died in two days."

"Dead?"

"Yes, sir. Are you a friend of his?"

"Yes, I am—I was, rather; but he looked, when I saw him about six or seven days ago, in the most perfect health."

"So he did, sir—so he did. Hem! He did, as you say. It isn't for me to say anything; but—ehm—hem!"

"In the name of Heaven, sir, what do you mean?"

"Oh, I mean nothing. I accuse nobody, but—but——"

"But what, sir? You say too little, or you say too much. There is some secret in this business that you dread to utter. Let me assure you, sir, that you may speak to me with the most perfect confidence, for I will not betray you. I have particular reasons for knowing all concerning that gentleman, as I left him in trust here of this very house for my aunt."

"Your aunt? Then, is Mrs. Thornton your aunt?"

"Precisely so."

"Then, sir, the lawyer, they say, poisoned himself; but—but——"

"Well?"

"It is just possible that somebody gave the poison to him ; and, sir, Mrs. Thornton is rather unwell in the same way."

Claude staggered back

The tax-gatherer nodded mysteriously, and then added—

"Don't say I told you. Good-day, sir."

CLAUDE AND LUKE SEEKING MAY AND LUCY IN THE CHATEU.

"But—stop, stop!   You don't mean to tell me that such things as this happen in the open day, in such a country as England, and that nobody interferes at all with the affair?"

"Well, sir, it comes to this, at last, you see.   People hear things, and think things ; but they are afraid, unless they can prove things, to say things.   We often hear that such a one is the greatest rogue existing, and yet if it came to the proof, how difficult it would be, partly from the fears and partly from the villanies of other people, to prove one act of roguery against him."

"True—most true."

"Why, sir, there was a man in London once, whom I knew, and he was about the most notorious scamp that ever lived : and I happened to say so publicly, and what was the consequence? He defied me to the proof, and, of course, everybody who could prove it shook their heads, and declared they knew nothing about it, and the affair ended in his getting a tea-service of silver presented to him, and delivering an essay on morality, while I was scouted by every one ; and yet that man had committed, and was committing at the time, almost every social enormity you can conceive a man to commit, while he cunningly kept just without the grasp of the law ! "

Claude shook hands with the tax-collector, for he acknowledged the truth of every word he uttered, and the man bustled away, quite in a heat with the recollection of his wrongs, and of the folly of society at large.

Lucy had not heard what passed ; but she could not fail to see, by the expression of Claude's countenance, that something rather serious was amiss, and she looked so imploringly at him, although she said nothing, that he said to her—

" Your mother lives, Lucy."

" Thank Heaven! But—but——"

" She is a little unwell ; but I have no doubt she is only suffering from anxiety at your absence, and the sight of you will put her all to rights again quickly enough."

" And in the meantime," said Luke, " here we are."

" Yes," said Claude, as he glanced around him ; " but we won't be here on the outside of the door long. Can you see anything, Luke, that will aid us in breaking open the door ?"

" Why, no—I cannot say that I do."

" What do you want? Evil-disposed and unrighteous people, what do you want here ?"

Claude glanced at the little square opening in the door, and he saw at it the face of the woman's husband whom he had dislodged so unceremoniously from the garden upon his former visit. There was a look of alarm, though, upon the face, which showed that the man was not at all at his ease.

CHAPTER CXCVIII.

A PLOT OF FEARFUL GUILT COMES TO THE LIGHT OF DAY.

" OPEN the door !" said Duval.

" I—I—that is——"

" Say you won't," cried the voice of the woman, who was prompting her husband, and whom he seemed to dread disobeying more than he did the vengeance of Claude Duval, for he said patly enough—

" I won't !"

" Very good," said Claude ; " then we will open it for ourselves."

" Thieves—thieves !" cried the woman.

" That's just my opinion," said Claude.

" Murder !" said the man.

" There may be," said Claude, " if you don't open the door at once, I can tell you, for I don't mean to be very particular."

" Here you are," said Luke at this moment, as he made his appearance with an immense block of stone in his hands of about sixty pounds in weight. " This will do, I think."

" Assuredly it will," said Claude. " Hit the lock, Luke, as hard as you can. Now for it."

Luke poised the stone in his hands for a few moments ; and then, with a tremendous force, he brought it down upon the lock of the door. With a crash, the lock was broken, and the door flew open.

"Come on," cried Claude ; "that's done !"

"Take that, then," said the woman, and she aimed a blow at Claude's head with a poker, the end of which was of a red heat—"take that, and much good may it do you."

The poker missed Duval's head, but fell upon his shoulder, where it would quickly enough have burnt a hole in his shoulder if he had not got hold of the other end of it, and wrenched it out of the woman's hand. Upon finding that she was disarmed, she ran shrieking up the garden path, pushing the man aside to get before him, while he was as anxious to keep her next to the enemy.

Claude Duval pursued them both with the poker ; and although he did not touch the female with it, she endured as much in terror of its contact with her as if he had liberally rubbed it upon her neck and shoulders, and burnt her to any extent.

Luke, with May and Lucy, followed Claude Duval.

Upon getting near to the house, the woman ran off by a side path, and Claude placed the hot end of the poker against the back of the man's neck, upon which he gave but one spring, and went right through a window into the house.

Claude now handed the poker to Luke, saying to him as he did so—

"You keep guard at the gate, Luke, and don't let them leave the place on any account, as yet. We can turn them out when we wish to do so easily ; and until I see what they have been about, I don't feel disposed to let them go."

"I'll take care of them," said Luke.

"Come, May, and you, Lucy, with me," said Claude. "Our first duty, now, is to seek your mother, Lucy."

"Yes—yes," said Lucy.

There was no difficulty, now, in getting into the house, as the door of it was only, as was customary, upon the latch. It was quite evident that for the security of the premises from any assault, the religious couple had wholly depended upon the strength of the garden door.

The impatience of Lucy was now so great, that she would have run on in advance of Claude; but he would not permit her to do that on any account, as he naturally enough thought that there might be danger in it, as her foes, and his foes, and the foes of her mother, and of all that was good and right, were in the house.

Well, too, did Claude Duval know that wickedness is never so great and so unscrupulous as when it assumes the cloak of religion with which to hide its baseness and its own hideous aspect ; and so he considered the man and woman who were in the house to be capable of any act of enormity.

"No, Lucy," he said. "Do not be precipitate."

"But my mother—my mother!"

"Hush ! We will all seek her together."

Seeing the state of mind that Lucy was in, and that she was really not to be trusted alone, Claude took care to keep fast hold of her hand as they proceeded along the hall of the house to the staircase conducting to the upper rooms.

Duval had a good recollection of the room in which he had left his aunt upon his former visit, and he now expected that she would be still there, as it was her bed-room, so he made his way at once to it; and as they did not encounter any one before reaching the door, Duval then said to Lucy—

"There is your mother's chamber. Enter ; and do you go with her, May."

They opened the door, and Lucy sprang into the room, crying out in shrieking accents—

"Mother—dear mother! I have come back to you. Oh, speak to me, and tell me that you are not dying !"

"What an indiscreet girl that is, to be sure," said Claude to himself, and popping his head in at the door of the room, he called out—

"Don't you be alarmed, aunt, I beg of you—all's right; and we have come to your assistance, and Lucy returns to you as she left you, only that she has been a little frightened, that's all."

Mrs. Thornton was now sitting up in her bed, and holding Lucy round the neck, while May was sobbing with emotion at the scene, and Lucy herself, after the first burst with which she had entered her mother's chamber, could say nothing.

Seeing the state of things, Claude Duval entered the room, and said in as cheerful a tone as he could—

"Aunt, how are you?"

"Dying—dying!"

"Oh, nonsense! There is no occasion to say that."

"Yes—oh, yes. And really within this last hour, do you know, a dreadful suspicion has come across my mind. It seemed as if a voice from another world had whispered to me to beware of those who are in the house."

"Indeed!"

"Yes—yes; and to say—'Poison—poison!'"

"Poison!" shrieked Lucy.

"Hush!" said Duval. "Lucy, you know not what mischief you may do to your mother, and to all of us, by this entire want of control you have over your feelings. Tell me, aunt, what makes you think you are subjected to such a criminal attempt?"

"I hardly know, except that I get worse and worse, and that they give me medicine which makes me so, I think. Oh, Claude, why did you leave them with me, and give them such a letter as you did, begging that I would have every confidence in them, for that they were friends of yours? Why did you do so, Claude?"

"I do so?"

"Yes, you."

"You amaze me, aunt. Before I left you, upon the last occasion that I was here, I kicked them both out of the place."

"Oh, no—no! The letter—the letter?"

"D—n the letter!" cried Claude. "I never wrote them any letter at all. Why, you must have been mad, aunt, to let a couple of villanous people like that deceive you in so flimsy a manner."

"Stop!" said a voice at the door of the room.

Claude started round, and then he saw the religious woman, who, with a slow step, advanced.

"Promise me that you will spare my life, and admit me as evidence against my husband, and I will tell all—I will confess all."

"Will you?" cried another voice, and in a moment the woman fell upon her face on the floor, with a loud yell of agony. A knife was sticking up to the hilt in her back.

They just saw the religious man then dart to the head of the staircase, and plunge down it at a frantic speed. He had been hiding on the landing, it would appear, and hearing his wife's offer to confess all if she were spared herself, had made up his mind to deprive her by death of the ability to do so, and he had executed his purpose horribly.

These terrible proceedings struck poor Lucy with so much terror, that she fainted, and fell by the side of her mother's bed; and May was in a state of great agitation.

As for poor Mrs. Thornton, they all expected that these dreadful acts would be the death of her, and Claude Duval—although he felt that the woman, who had expiated by her death some her of wickedness, amply deserved her fate—would fain have wished that the tragedy had taken place elsewhere.

They stood looking at each other in mute wonder, so that the desperate and evil-minded man had an opportunity of escaping into the garden before Claude could make up his mind to pursue him.

Luke, however, had command of the garden gate, so he felt quite certain that he could not leave the premises.

"Stop him, Luke—stop him!" shouted Claude.

"Hoi!" said Luke, from the garden. "Stop who? Oh, I see him—I see him."

"Good heavens! what is all this?" said May. "Claude—Claude, tell me what it all means!"

Duval could not answer her, but he ran down to the garden to see that the villain who had done so fearful a deed was properly secured; but the moment he got there, he saw Luke coming up the path in trepidation and haste.

"What is it, Luke?"

"Nothing particular. Only a party of police, well mounted, were passing the gate, and hearing the cries, they have made a halt, and are about to come into the garden. They are a few too many for us."

CHAPTER CXCIX.

DUVAL IS RECOGNISED BY THE CONSTABLES, AND HAS TO ESCAPE IN A HURRY.

CLAUDE DUVAL was rather staggered at this intelligence.

"Luke," he said, "are you certain?"

"Go and convince yourself. There they are, ringing away as hard as they can. I closed the door."

"Good. We must be off. I must leave Lucy to settle all her affairs here the best way she can, poor girl, and, indeed, I don't know that if we were all to stay we could do her any good; but certainly to stay to be apprehended would be to do her more harm than good."

May now clung to the arm of Claude Duval with affright in her looks, as she said—

"Oh, Claude, you are lost—you are lost!"

"Not at all."

"But what can save you? Hark! they are bursting in the door, and you stand here as calmly as though you had plenty of time before you. Rouse yourself, Claude, or all is lost."

"Hush, May. I was only looking to see which was the best route out of this place, and now I see it. I assure you no time is ever lost by a little judicious reflection. I know these premises pretty well, for they were quite familiar to me years ago, when I was a child. Follow me, both of you."

Claude Duval darted forward to a particular part of the garden, where it was only divided from one adjoining to it by a privet hedge, just as the gate began to yield to the efforts of the officers who were without.

To add to the confusion and danger, poor Lucy just at that moment appeared at the window of her mother's chamber, and screamed out to Duval with all her power.

"Claude—Claude, do not leave me now! They have murdered my mother. Help—oh, help!"

These cries only induced the officers to make greater exertions still to get into the garden, and the door gave way with a loud crash, just as Claude Duval and his party got through the privet hedge into the next garden, and began scrambling through a rather thick plantation of peas.

When the officers broke open the gate, the dastardly man who had committed such crimes, and who had been crouching down close to the wall after Luke had let go the hold he had at first taken of him, rose with a cry of fright, and fled in the direction that Duval and his friends had taken.

Not being able in his abject terror now to know which party he had the most to fear from, he ran towards the hedge and began struggling through it, calling out—

"Save me—save me! I have money. I will pay you well. I assure you it was all my wife's doings."

"That fellow will bring the officers at our heels," said Luke. "Confound him, he is born to be the death of us."

"Is he," said Duval, as he turned rapidly. "I will put a stop to all further trouble upon his account. It will save the hangman some trouble, that is all."

"Oh, Claude, don't!'" cried May.

She was too late, even if Claude had felt inclined to forego his intention at that moment, which is very doubtful, for his blood was up, and he felt that he was only ridding the world of a monster of iniquity by acting as he did. Drawing a pistol from the bosom of his apparel, he levelled it and fired at once at the fellow.

With a shriek, he fell backward into the garden again.

"Oh, this is dreadful!" said May.

"No more than he deserved," said Luke. "Come on, Claude. That shot has staggered the officers as well as our pious friend."

Claude was now followed closely by May and Luke, and sad havoc they certainly did make among the peas in the garden. A woman ran out of the cottage to which the garden belonged with a toasting-fork in her hand, which she brandished round her head, as she cried in furious and frantic accents upon seeing the damage done to her garden—

"My peas—my peas! You wretches, I will be the death of you all, that I will!"

"Out of the way," said Luke, as he gave the woman a push which sent her into a little duck-pond that was close at hand, and than Claude and his party ran through her house and were out at the front door of it long before she could scramble out again.

That cottage led them to the lane that was but a few paces from the corner, and Claude called out—

"To the inn—to the inn! We must get our cattle, and then we are all right again; but without them our lives are not worth a minute's purchase. Let me help you on, May."

"No—no, Claude. I am not tired at all. On—on!"

May proved herself to be more fleet of foot, for a little distance, than either of them, but she had not the power of continuance that they had, and before they reached the place at which they had left their horses she was compelled to stop, completely exhausted.

Claude now helped her on, although she urged him to go by himself and leave her, but that was a thing he was not at all likely to do, and, indeed, as there were no signs of pursuit, there was no such violent necessity for scampering on at such a rate.

"Keep a look out, Luke," said Claude. "Take your time, May, now. There is the inn. All is right, and it will be better to go quietly up to it than to appear flurried, as that might excite suspicion and delay."

"Yes—yes. We will look as calm and as cool as we can," said May.

Luckily, there was no suspicion or delay at the inn at all, so that the party got mounted and all ready for a start without the slightest difficulty. It was then that they heard the gallop of horses feet, and they saw a man come up to the inn-door at a gallop, and he cried out—

"Mr. Groves! Mr. Groves!"

"Who the deuce is he?" said Claude to Luke.

"Yes," said a man, coming to the door of the inn, with a glass of brandy-and-water in his hand. "Yes, what is it?"

"Mount, sir, and come with us. One of our men says that Claude Duval, the highwayman, is close at hand, and on foot."

"Duval?"

"Yes, Mr. Groves."

"My horse! My horse! Get me my horse! Oh, why did I stay here? My horse, I say."

This man was the head-officer in command of the party that had so inopportunely, for Claude and his friends, been passing the cottage of Lucy's mother; but before he could leave the door of the inn, Claude rode close up to him, and cried in a sharp, clear voice—

"Stop, Mr. Groves, don't trouble yourself, sir. You had much better remain where you are, and in the meantime I will drink your health."

As he spoke, Claude snatched the glass of brandy-and-water from his hand, and swallowed half the contents.

"You infernal rascal!" said the man, "what do you mean by that? Who the deuce are you, I should like to know?"

"Shall I tell you?"

"Ah, do."

"Claude Duval!"

Mr. Groves, the chief constable, staggered back a pace or two, and then caught a pistol from his pocket, but Duval, before he could bring it to a level, flung the glass that had contained the brandy-and-water right into his face, and with such good will, too, did he fling it, that the glass, albeit a thick one, was shivered to fragments, and the brandy getting into Mr. Groves's eyes made him dance again with agony, and he executed such a singular kind of polka, that everybody thought he was mad.

During these evolutions he fired the pistol that he had in his hand quite at random, and very nearly shot his own man who had come to give him the intelligence of Claude's being seen upon that spot.

"Come," said Duval, to Luke and May. "We have had enough of this. Off and away. We can do nobody any good by staying."

They put their horses to their mettle, and off they went at a pace that it would have taken a good steed and a good rider to follow, and which, after ten minutes had elapsed, had taken them so far from the inn that pursuit was quite out of the question.

Claude then slackened his pace a little.

"We are safe enough," he said, "or, rather, as safe as usual."

"Alas, yes," said May.

"Why do you say, alas?"

"No matter, now, Claude. I ought not to have said it—I ought only to feel too happy that you have escaped from your enemies. But what on earth do you purpose doing now? Here we are, with no very particular object in view, and with diminished resources. I fancy. Oh, Claude!"

"Go on, May."

"If now, at this juncture, something could be thought of by which you—you could——"

She stopped short.

"Could get an honest living, you mean?"

"Yes—oh, yes."

"No, it is out of the question—I am to well known, May. It cannot be helped now, but it is a fact, I assure you, for all that. No, Luke will tell you the same, notwithstanding all his wish, and I believe he has it, to snatch me from the perils of the road, haven't you, Luke?"

"I cannot say nay to that proposition," said Luke. "I wish from my heart that I could. Hem! what would you do, Claude, if you saw a couple of gentlemen on the road?"

"What would I do? Why, I should say, 'Stand and deliver!'"

"Well, here they are."

"The deuce they are !"

May shuddered as two horsemen suddenly appeared in sight—she knew not why; but, somehow, at the sight of them she felt such a pang of alarm, that she nearly fell from her horse.

"Yes, Claude," added Luke, "there they are."

Claude drew up, and patted the neck of his horse, which was rather inclined to be fretful from the gallop it had had so recently.

"Luke, what sort of folks do you think these are ?   Are they worth the stopping?"

"I doubt it."

"Oh, let them pass—let them pass for that doubt," said May.

"May," said Claude, "it is quite sufficient that you say let them pass to settle that point.   I am quite sure that when you see occasion to interfere, that you do so for some good reasons; so let them pass."

Now, poor May had no reason in the world why these two men of all others should be let pass without being stopped upon the highway by Claude Duval; so she took his words—although, in truth, he did not intend them for such—just as a piece of grave irony, and she was almost inclined to shed tears upon the occasion, and to make a resolve that she would never stop Claude in his professional pursuits again.

The conduct of the two men, though, now was so singular, that it soon attracted all May's attention, and it very much surprised both Claude Duval and his friend Luke.

We may say a word or two, though, as to the personal appearance of these two strangers who were upon the road.

In the first place, then, they were not gentlemen.   It did not require a conjurer to pronounce upon that fact.   They were smartly enough dressed; but it was that rakish kind of costume, which, allowing for the quaint sobriety and plainness of dress in the present day, has descended to the gent, as quite distinguished from the real gentleman.

They were, though, most capitally mounted.

Their horses were small, but of immense strength, and seemed capable of any work that was wanted, although, probably, at a leap they might have been altogether deficient.

These two strangers, then, paused and whispered together when they came within view of Claude and his party, and more than once they glanced behind them, as though they either expected or were apprehensive of some one coming upon the road after them.   They then nodded to each other, and began slowly to approach Claude and his friends.

"What, in the name of all that's wonderful, is the meaning of this?" said Claude.   "Can you make it out, Luke ?"

"Indeed I cannot."

"Let us turn and go away," said May.

"Oh, no—no—hardly.   Keep your pistols ready, Luke; and, May, if you leave us at all, you will ride to the side of the road, and take shelter among the trees."

"No, Claude, with you I will stay.   For the future, I am determined to share your perils as well as your joys."

"No—no !"

May would not hear him, and that was no moment in which to urge the matter; so Claude was compelled to let her remain where she was, and in the course of half a minute more the two men reached them ; and one, as he produced a pistol from his holster, said coolly—

"Gentlemen, no wish for violence exists upon our parts ; but we have just to say, ' Your money, or your lives !' and we don't stand any nonsense."

Claude looked at Luke, and Luke looked at Claude ; and then the latter said quite calmly—

"Pray, my good sir, who are you ?"

"It's no matter who I am.   What I am is sufficiently apparent.   I am a highwayman.   Now, sir, are you satisfied?   I will trouble you for your watch, too, as I see you have one in your fob."

"A highwayman, are you?" said Claude.   "You don't say so?"

DUVAL PURSUING HIS ROUTE AFTER HIS PARTY HAS BEEN AUGMENTED.

"Hark you, sir," said the man, sternly.   "I am not used to be trifled with. If you hold your life so cheap that you would as soon as not have a bullet in your brains, say so.   If not, give us what we demand, and we will leave you in peace."

CHAPTER CC.

CLAUDE AND HIS FRIENDS FALL INTO A TRAP LAID FOR THEIR DESTRUCTION.

CLAUDE DUVAL and his friends were as much astonished at this attack upon the highway as if by some particular right or patent he, Claude, was the only highwayman allowed in all England; and yet a moment's reflection ought to have given them a very different view of the matter.

As it was, he and Luke and May exchanged the most comical glances that can be imagined; and then the highwayman got impatient, and began to swear the most terrible oaths.

"Stop, sir," said Claude. "I beg to inform you that you are making a very serious mistake."

"As how, sir?"

"Why, the fact is, that, although according to the old proverb two of a trade never agree, there is no necessity why two of a trade should prey upon each other. Now, what would you say if I were to take a pistol from the holster of my saddle, as I do now, and clapping its muzzle, as I do now, at your head, cry to you 'Stand and deliver!' I ask you, what would you say to that?"

The man backed his horse a little way.

"Why, I should say that you were a knight of the road," he cried; "but it isn't possible, is it?"

"Possible enough. Why not?"

"Well, I don't know. I say, Will, come forward here. This gentleman says he is one of our own sort."

The other highwayman rode close up, and looked hard at Claude Duval, when he suddenly said, as he lifted his hat a little above his head for a moment—

"Good gracious, where were my eyes! This is Claude Duval."

"Claude Duval!" said the other. "The great, the celebrated Claude Duval—the dashing highwayman—the ladies' robber—the king of the road! Is that a fact?"

"I rather think it is," said Duval.

"A thousand pardons for this foolish mistake, Duval. Why, I would rather have lost the best booty I ever saw in all my life, than I would have pulled the trigger of this pistol against you."

"There was no danger," said Claude, "but to yourself. I saw that your pistol was at half-cock only, and if it had been otherwise, the probability is, that your brains would have been scattered upon the road."

The highwayman made a wry face.

"You would be sorry to serve one of your own profession in such a way, Duval."

"I should; but I am not used to have a pistol barrel quite so near my eyes as you placed yours, my friend."

"Well—well, pray let that pass, and say no more about it, I beg of you. Be so good as to introduce me to your friends."

"I don't know you."

"Oh, I am called Jumping Jemmy."

"Indeed! Then, Jumping Jemmy, I have the pleasure of bidding you a remarkably good-day."

"Stop, Duval, stop."

"Why should I?"

"Of course, I can't object to your declining my company, and that of my friend, but I don't like you to run into danger, if I can save you from it. I tell you, therefore, that if you ride on another mile, you will fall into such an ambuscade as you will find it difficult to escape from."

"What ambuscade?"

"Why, there is a magistrate of the county, named Lawson, who has got together a gang of fellows in the shape of special constables. They consist of gamekeepers and others who are well used to fire-aims, and the grand object of this is to catch you, and those who are with you. How they got any information that you were upon this road I don't know; but we very narrowly escaped them only half-an-hour ago."

"Luke," said Claude Duval, "do you know of any magistrate of the name of Lawson hereabouts?"

"Indeed, I do, Duval. He is one of the boldest and most active fellows ever I heard of, for his station in life."

Duval paused, and was silent for a few moments. He had no reason to doubt the truth of the information that was thus given to him by men who could surely have no object in deceiving him. He cast one glance at May, and the dread of leading her into any danger had the effect of at once admonishing him to be cautious, and to act upon the information of the highwaymen.

"I thank you for this news," he said.

"You are welcome, Duval; and I and my friend here will be well enough pleased if our telling you has the effect of saving you, and of thwarting the Philistines. Good-day."

"Stop!"

The two highwaymen paused.

"I beg that you will excuse me for being rather abrupt with you just now. The fact is, I—I—"

"Say nothing about it, Duval. If you don't want our company, we have no right to intrude it upon you, or to take any offence at your telling us as much. If it had been quite agreeable to you we would have ridden a few miles with you; and as we are well armed, and indifferently well mounted, as you see, we should, take us altogether, have made rather a strong party; but, as it is, of course you are the best judge."

"Nay, if I can make any reparation to you," said Claude Duval—who was struck by a certain gentlemanly bearing in the fellow who spoke to him—"for treating you with incivility, I would say, 'Have the goodness to ride a few miles with us, and we can be of mutual service, perhaps.'"

"With pleasure, Duval. What do you say, Will?"

"I am quite agreeable to go where you choose to lead me," said the other. "You are a gentleman, and I am but a poor fellow; that is to say, you were a gentleman before you took to the road. I can assure you, Duval, that his father is a general in the army, and he might have done well, but there was a certain young lady who jilted him, and there was a certain rival that she didn't jilt, so he shot him; but all in fair fight, though."

"Enough—enough!" said the other. "Duval don't want to be pestered with my history, I'm sure."

"Why, it's just upon all told," added Will; "so you may as well have it out. You see, Duval, all this preyed upon his spirits, and then he took to the glass, till spirits preyed upon him, you understand."

"Oh, stuff!"

"Come, now, let me tell all of it. After that he took to the bones."

"The bones!" said Luke. "What do you mean by taking to the bones?"

Will gave a peculiar shake to his elbow, and then Luke said—

"Oh, you mean the dice?"

"To be sure I do," said Will. "That didn't answer, you see."

"I never heard that it did," said Duval.

"Nor I. So then he took to the road, and here he is, and a nice little time he has had of it; but, as I always say, he has been a gentleman; so that's something, you know."

"Well—well," said the other, "I didn't want all those by-gone affairs brought forward by any one; but I know you think them all rather to my credit, Will, than otherwise."

"Indeed, I do; and the only thing I object to is your calling yourself Jumping Jemmy."

"Why so?"

"Because, you know, it sounds low."

"Ha—ha! That's good."

"I like your other name better."

"What is his other name?" said Claude Duval.

"His other name is Captain Smart."

"Well, I do think it is better, for Jumping Jemmy does sound low; therefore, with your permission, I will call you Captain Smart. And now let us be off at a good pace, for if these fellows with Lawson, the magistrate, are within a mile of us, that is much too near to be at all pleasant."

"It is," said Captain Smart, as we, in common with Claude Duval, rather prefer to call him—"it is; so come on. There is a cross-road close at hand to this one, and it leads alongside a plantation that this very Lawson, the magistrate, has had made for the preservation of his game, and if we are hard pushed, we may make our way there."

"Agreed," said Claude.

They all trotted on, not at a violent pace, but still at a good one; and after they had gone a little distance, Captain Smart, turning to Luke, said—

"You know this Lawson, then, by sight?"

"Not I."

"I was in hopes you did, and I thought you said you did."

"No, I only know him by reputation. I may have seen him, of course, but not to recognise him. I have heard him spoken of as a man who stops at no trifles in the pursuit of his objects; and if he has taken the field against us, I rather think we shall stand a chance of being hard pushed."

"Confound him!"

"So say I."

"It would be a good thing, if there should be an opportunity, just to pop off such a fellow as that with a pistol bullet, for he is more dangerous to gentlemen of our profession than a thousand of your ordinary officers, who are as great cowards, in the first place, as ever stepped, and in the next can always be bought off for a few pounds with the greatest ease."

"I can't say, Captain Smart," said Duval, "that I exactly coincide with you in the idea of popping off Mr. Lawson. If he should attack me, well and good, I will defend myself; but I always let my foes begin the battle. Then I look upon it that I act upon the defensive, and if any mischief comes of the affair, it is much more their doing than mine."

"That may be a very chivalric-like way of acting on the whole," said Captain Smart; "but I very much doubt if you would meet with anything like similar treatment on the part of others."

"Here we are at the cross-road," said Will.

"Very good, then," said Captain Smart, "just hold my horse, Will, and I will get over the hedge here and take a long look across the country, and see if I can get a sight of our doubtful friends the gamekeepers, and their leader, Mr. Lawson."

"Ah, do so," said Will.

Captain Smart, as he called himself, scrambled on to the top of a rather high bank, and from that he got up an alder tree, which took him a considerable height, and he took a long look in the direction the party had come.

"What do you see?" said Claude Duval.

"Nothing."

"Then they have not come this road, after all?"

"Ah, yes, stop—by George, here they are, one—two—three—No, they huddle so together that I can't count them; but there are twenty of them if there is one. Confound the rascals, they are coming exactly on the road that we have been over."

"Then the sooner we are off the better," said Will.

"Rather," said Captain Smart, as he rapidly descended from the alder tree and the bank, and mounted his horse. "This way, Duval—this way. I don't think we have much time to lose. Let us get down this cross-road, and they may pass right on ; and if they don't, why, there is the plantation of Squire Lawson to fall back upon at the last ; and if the whole five of us cannot make head against a rabble rout of rustics, it will be, I think, rather a hard case."

At a canter, as being the pace that made the least noise, the party now sped down the cross-road that had been recommended to then so warmly by Captain Smart.

CHAPTER CCI.

A GREAT MISFORTUNE HAPPENS TO CLAUDE DUVAL AND HIS FRIENDS.

IT was a singularly beautiful road that in which the party were now in, and had evidently been but recently made, from the state it was in on each side, where thousands of young tress had been planted in the most beautiful order.

The road way, too, was covered with gravel, and got up with great care and skill, so that their cattle travelled easily upon it and made good speed.

After a progress of about half a mile, Captain Smart pulled up, and called out to Duval, who passed him—

"Hilloa, Duval, stop!"

"What is it ?"

"What do you say to going into the plantation at once, and there waiting for an hour or so till we shall have a positive certainty that our foes have passed on ?"

"As you please—I don't mind it. It will give the horses a rest, too. But it won't do to go into the lion's den. You say that this plantation, through which the road winds, belongs to Lawson, the active magistrate, and we don't want to fall into his hands exactly."

"If you did," said Captain Smart, with a laugh, "I can assure you I don't, nor does Will ; but the fact is, he is on the road with all his men, and the plantations are as quiet, I'll be bound, to-day, as an original forest in some wilderness of nature."

"Let us to cover then. But the wood seems well fenced just hereabouts, and I don't think your cattle look of the jumping sort."

"They can do anything but leap."

"So I thought. How are we to get into the plantation, then ?"

"Well, that is a difficulty that did not strike me, just at first ; but let us ride on, perhaps we shall find some more accessible part than this that we are at."

They did ride on, and they were rewarded by so doing, for they came to a part of the road where the paling with which the plantation was being enclosed was not finished, and where they could easily ride into the thickest portion of the little wood.

"This will do," said Captain Smart, and he at once rode from the roadway among the trees. He was followed by Will ; and Claude Duval, although, to tell the truth, he felt a little hesitation about the matter, did not like to make any observation at that time, so he too rode into the wood.

So implicitly did May and Luke depend upon Duval's judgment, that they both followed him without a word. If Claude, though, had looked carefully in the face of May, he would have seen that there was an expression of anxiety upon it, of a deeper character than it usually wore, and much that followed might have been prevented.

Claude Duval did not look, though, at her particularly, and in a few minutes they were in a complete little wood, which was so dense, that there was quite a twilight about them.

"This is a secret place," said Captain Smart, "and when these trees grow a little more, it will be one of the finest covers for game in the whole country. I don't think that our friend Lawson, though, really contemplated that such sort of game as is now in it would find it a convenient cover."

"You may depend he didn't," said Will. "But what the deuce is that yonder, Captain Smart?"

"What?"

"Why, there sticking up among the trees."

They had all as good a look as they could get of the object that had attracted Will's curiosity, and Claude Duval, after raising himself in his stirrups and taking a long look, said at once, with a laugh—

"Oh, it's only the conical roof of some building in the plantation, that's all. Some deer-house, or keeper's lodge, or cottage, I fancy."

"It must be so," said Captain Smart; "but our best plan will be to keep away from it, for, after all, somebody may be there."

"Hush!" said Luke. "I hear the sound of horses' feet in the very cross-road that we have just emerged from."

"By Jove, then," said Captain Smart, "we have only just emerged from it in time. Who the deuce now would have thought they would have come down there? Bother take them!"

"I tell you what it is, sir," said Will. "You see, the cross-road winds right away round into the high-road again, and, as sure as eggs is eggs, that fellow, Lawson, has sent some of his men down it to have a look, and they will go on if they see nothing suspicious, and meet him again higher up. That's about it, you may depend, captain."

"Well, it may be so."

"It is more than probable," said Claude.

Captain Smart seemed to be in thought for a few moments, and then he said, as he dismounted—

"Hold my horse, Will, and I will creep on to that little building, the roof of which we see yonder, and ascertain what it is, and if there be any one there. It will be a place of rest to us, if it is only a house for the deer in bad weather, which it looks like."

Will held the captain's horse while Smart plunged among the trees in the direction of the little building. The sound of horses' footsteps in the cross-road still kept coming at intervals upon the ears of the fugitives, and the general impression was, that the party of officers there had seen the foot-prints of their horses' hoofs, and were cantering about to find which way they had gone. If such were the case, they ran the greatest possible risk of being yet followed into the wood.

"I'm sorry we came here," said Duval.

"So am I," said Luke; "and yet, if the party opposed be very strong, we did the best thing we could to get out of its way; though, perhaps, this was not the best way of doing that."

"No," added Claude. "I would rather not have been among these trees; our superiority in point of cattle is quite lost here."

"Claude?" said May.

She was about to say something rather earnestly to Duval, but at that moment Captain Smart came back from his expedition to the little building among the trees.

"I have seen it," he said.

"What is it?" said Claude Duval.

"Why, one of the safest places we can possibly get to, if we like, both for horse and man. It is a cottage, but unfinished, and it looks to me as if it had been, from some cause or another, quite abandoned, for it has evidently not been touched for some time; so, if we like to go there, there will be little enough likelihood of our being at all interrupted."

"Luke," said Claude, " what say you?"

" Just, that if we don't actually take possession of the place, it will be as well to be near it; for I can still hear horsemen in the cross-road."

"But, Claude?" said May.

" Well, what say you?"

" I know not what to say, but the dread of some calamity is upon my mind. I do not know what it is. But if I might counsel you, it would be to leave this place at once, and go out into the road, and endeavour to escape your enemies by speed."

" That might do," said Captain Smart; " but yet there are difficulties, if this Lawson has raised the country."

"Claude—Claude," said Luke, " I am positive there are people in the wood. I heard just now a voice."

" Then there is no time to be lost," said Captain Smart. " I tell you that, if needs be, we can make quite a little castle of the unfinished cottage, for all the walls are up, and the roof is on. Come this way."

May was again about to speak, but Claude looked at her with a smile, as he said—

" Come—come, May, I never saw you so nervous. I do not think that we have more, if so much, to fear now than we have had on many an occasion when you have shown a courage that would have been sufficient to impart spirit to any one. Come on."

" Yes, Claude, I will follow you."

"That is well. Be afraid of nothing. Only consider what a strong party we are now."

" I don't know that," said May, faintly.

At this time a strange and sudden darkness began to come over the place, and it was a darkness which could not be accounted for by any deep gloom of the little wood from the thickness of the trees, as, if there were any difference at all, the spot where they were was rather more cleared than any other. It was evident that some great change was taking place in the weather, and from a glance that Claude Duval took at the sky between the branches of two tall trees, he saw that it was rapidly darkening, and that some black and heavy clouds were slowly moving along, surcharged, no doubt, with rain.

" We shall have a storm," said Claude Duval.

May rode very close to him, and Captain Smart now paused, and looking up to the sky, nodded his head, as he said—

" You will all thank me for finding you shelter."

" Claude," said May, " never mind the storm."

" Well, I don't mind it, dear May."

" Well, but I don't mean that. I mean, don't go near the cottage. I feel as if—as if—"

" What on earth is the matter with you, May?"

" Claude, in a word, I don't like that man."

" Captain Smart?"

" Yes. I don't believe that he is what he pretends to be, Claude. I have observed him well, and I feel confident that he is playing a part. Oh, Claude, Claude, if there is anything that more than another you have specially to guard against, it is treachery."

" Treachery?"

" Yes, Claude; you are of a trusting nature."

" May, set your mind quite at ease upon that point. Captain Smart would need be a brave man, indeed, to attempt anything of the sort. It would be his sudden death. Come on, fear nothing."

They soon, now, reached the little unfinished cottage, and entered it. It was rather a long, irregular looking building, but quite secure from the rain, so it answered a good purpose. There was a bit of shed, too, at one side of it, in which they fastened their horses, at the suggestion of Will ; and then Luke said to Claude—

"You stay here, and I will go on first to reconnoitre, and thoroughly satisfy myself as to what is going on in the wood and the road."

"Do so, but don't be long gone."

"1 will not."

Luke left, and Claude picked up some loose pieces of timber, so as to make a seat for May, and looking to the priming of his pistols, he cast a wary eye around him. Captain Smart and his friend Will were near the door of the cottage, in attitudes of listening.

The rain continued to come down in fearful torrents, and the darkness was so great in the building, that it was only faintly the fugitives could distinguish each other's faces. The anxiety of Claude Duval for the return of Luke grew each moment stronger and stronger, and at last he strode to the door, saying—

"I am confident that something must have happened to my friend, or he would never have been so long gone."

"He has missed his way, perhaps, in the wood," said Captain Smart. "But the horses are all safe, that is a comfort."

"How do we know that?" said Duval, sharply.

"Don't you hear them ?"

"Not I, in faith. I hear nothing but the storm without. Ah! what cry was that? It was one of alarm !"

"Oh, stuff !"

"It is so. I will no longer remain here in this state of suspense. It is not fair and right to my friend that I should do so."

"Claude—Claude," said May, "do not leave me."

"But——"

Claude Duval turned to speak to May, when one of the mock highwaymen—for such, indeed, they were—flew at him, and clasped him round the waist, crying out, as he did so—

"The signal! Give the signal !"

His companion immediately fired a pistol, and before the echoes of the report were over, the cottage was full of armed officers, and Claude Duval was a prisoner.

With a shriek of anguish, May flung herself upon his breast.

———————

CHAPTER CCII.

THE FATE OF CLAUDE AND LUKE APPEARS TO BE INEVITABLE—BUT THEY DO NOT DESPAIR.

ALL this was done in a moment, so that Duval had not even an opportunity of resisting. provided he had chosen to do so to no less than sixteen or seventeen men, who were all determined to take him, dead or alive.

It was the treachery of the transaction that for the moment stunned him now, and made him look about him like a man scarcely awakened from some vivid dream.

"Claude—Claude," shrieked May, "I suspected this ! Oh, God ! I did suspect it, and yet I said it not !"

"Suspected !—you ! What is it ?"

"We are lost !"

"Lost ? Why, May, you do not mean to say that——"

"You are a prisoner, Claude Duval," said the mock gentleman highwayman,

MR. LAWRENCE, THE MAGISTRATE, AT THE WILLOW BRANCH INN.

advancing towards him.   "You will see, no doubt, that to be quite quiet, and tolerably civil, will be your best policy."

"Policy ?"

"Yes, I say so.   Escape is quite out of the question, and you will but pre-cipitate your fate by attempting it"

The only reply that Duval made to this was by a desperate effort to free himself from the grasp of the officers who held him ; but they had expected such an effort when he had sufficiently recovered from his first surprise, and they were quite prepared to resist it.

With all his strength, and all his energy, and, indeed, the kind of mad fury that came over him, it was quite impossible that he could successfully resist so many foes; and so the officers, after he had become exhausted by the struggle he had made, at last succeeded in tying his elbows together, and, likewise, in putting handcuffs on his wrists.

They dragged the shrieking May from him, and held her roughly, but the person, who had planned the whole affair, and who had some getlemanly feeling about him, said—

"Madam, I believe, notwithstanding your disguise, that you are the wife of Claude Duval. Is it so?"

"It is. Oh, yes, it is!" sobbed May.

"Then I will take upon myself to allow you to go free. You are at liberty to depart."

"Oh, no—no!"

"I decline taking you into custody, madam."

"Do you think for one moment that I would desert my husband, sir?"

"Madam, I cannot allow myself to think about it. I have a public duty to perform, and that is all that I want to think about just at present."

"May," said Claude Duval, "save yourself."

"By staying with you—yes: then I save myself from madness; but by leaving you I drive my very soul to despair. Oh, Claude—Claude, your word is law to me; but do not, I beg of you, do not send me from you!"

"This is the hardest trial of all."

"Don't say that," grinned one of the officers. "You'll have another trial soon, Claude Duval, that perhaps you may choose to think is just a little harder. Ha—ha!"

There was now a slight bustle at the door of the cottage, and four men entered, bringing with them a prisoner. That prisoner was Luke. He was very pale, and there was a streak of blood upon his face.

"Oh, Duval," he said, when he saw that Claude was in the hands of the officers, "I expected this. We are the victims of treachery."

"We are, Luke."

"Well, one of them has paid dearly for it."

"Indeed?"

"If you please, Mr. Lawson," said one of the men who had custody of Luke, "this man has shot Tomkins through the head, and he is quite dead, sir."

"A murder!"

"Not so," said Luke. "I was brutally attacked by no less than five men, and I defended myself as well as I could. In the contest, one of them fell. You may call that murder if you like, but I do not, sir."

"It is murder in the eye of the law."

"The law be—hem!" said Luke. "Well—well, it's no use putting ourselves out of the way about such matters. We are in for it now, and must abide the consequences."

"And so you are Mr. Lawson, the county magistrate, sir?" said Claude Duval, darting a keen glance at the man who had betrayed him.

"I am."

"Then, sir, I do not congratulate you upon the success with which you have played the part of a traitor, for to be treacherous is only to be more base."

"I have done my duty."

"And a little more, sir, which none but one with the mind and genius of a spy and a traitor would stoop to do."

"I am not to be deterred from the apprehension of a highwayman by the prospect of abuse. Look well to your pieces, my men. If they escape, I will take good care that the heaviest consequences shall fall upon you all. Convey them safely to Newgate, and you shall be well rewarded."

"The spy, too, ought to be well rewarded," said May. "The traitor, who, with the mask of friendship upon his face, led others, against whom he could have no cause of quarrel, to their ruin—ought not he to be well rewarded?"

"Perhaps I shall, madam," said Mr. Lawson, with an ironical bow to May.

"Be assured you shall," she said, "and I beg that you will take that as an earnest of your reward."

As she spoke, she drew from her pocket one of the little pistols with which Claude Duval had provided her, in case of any great emergency, and before any one could stop her, she had fired it right in the face of the magistrate.

With a groan, Mr. Lawson fell to the floor of the cottage, and May called out—

"Claude, at least you are avenged if you cannot be saved!"

A general scene of confusion now ensued. The officers were evidently in a great fright, and two of them seized May, and called out for help, as if they thought that she by her own unaided exertions might yet overcome the whole of the party. Claude Duval called out in a voice that reached above all others—

"Well done! A brave shot, May! We are indeed now avenged!"

"Oh, that our hands were free!" said Luke.

The smoke from the discharge of the pistol cleared away, and the officers began to recover from the panic into which they had been thrown, as they found there was no more danger to be apprehended. They lifted Mr. Lawson from the floor, and placed him on one of the chairs; and then one of the officers said to him—

"If you please, sir, are you dead?"

The others laughed at this, as though it were a capital joke; but Lawson only glared about him, and said—

"Who did it? Who did it?"

"The wife, sir."

"The wife—oh, the wife? Stop this blood."

"But ain't you shot through the head, sir?"

"No—no. Where's Harrison? He understands these kind of matters—He is as good at a wound as any surgeon that I ever meet with."

"He is keeping watch in the plantation, Mr. Lawson; but we will soon call him."

Harrison was called, and when he came and examined the wound of the magistrate, it was found that the small bullet from the pistol that May had fired had gone right through one of his cheeks into his mouth, and out at the other, without doing him the least further damage whatever.

"It's no great harm, sir," said Harrison. "You will feel it a little for a few weeks, and it will leave a couple of scars as long as you live; but it was a lucky shot. If it had been a little higher, or a little lower, or a little backward, it would have done you rather more harm, sir."

"Confound it!" muttered the magistrate, as Harrison bound his face up, and stopped the bleeding as well as he could. "Just see that the virago yonder has no more fire-arms."

"Take the pistols," said May. "These are all I have. One is still loaded."

She handed her pistols to the officers, and resigned herself to her fate as a prisoner; for now she felt quite certain that they would say no more to her about going away, and leaving Claude Duval in custody, without her.

"You have missed your intent," said Lawson. "I am scarcely to be said to be hurt at all."

"I am glad of it," said May.

"Permit me to doubt that."

"You may, sir, if you like; but the shot was one fired upon the impulse of a moment. I should regret even to have your life upon my hands to answer for."

"Ah, very likely, indeed. Put handcuffs upon her, and bring her along with the others."

"Surely, sir," said Duval, "that is a needless indignity. You and your men can prevent one weak woman from escaping without manacling her?"

"We don't know that. Some cats scratch. Put the handcuffs on her at once, my men.'

"We can't, sir."

"You can't? What do you mean by that?"

"Lor, sir, we haven't got a pair that's nigh small enough. She could shake off easily our smallest pair in a moment."

"Then tie her wrists together."

"Ah, that we can do."

They did tie poor May's wrists together; but although the piece of string which one of the officer's was officious enough to produce for the purpose hurt her very much, May declined to make any complaint to the men upon the subject. It was a great agony to Claude Duval to see her whom he loved so well treated in such a fashion.

"Are you men," he said, "that you can thus treat a female who has no means of making any further resistance?"

"Oh, it's all very fine," said one of the officers. "But the lady has shown already that she can do something; and so we are bound to take care of ourselves."

"I'm afraid, Mr. Lawson," said the man who was named Harrison, "that you won't be able to go to Newgate with us."

"I will go if I live," said Lawson.

"Very well, sir."

The rain still came down rather sharply; but so violently intent was the magistrate upon proceeding at once with his prisoners to Newgate, where he intended to lodge them, that he would not wait until the storm was over, notwithstanding it promised to be so in a very short time, indeed, but ordered the officers to bring their horses round to the cottage door, and so start at once.

It was with a pang that Claude now saw his own, and Luke's, and May's steeds brought to the cottage door, and saw them mounted by the officers, while the worst horses of the whole lot were devoted to the use of the prisoners.

Of course, it was but to be expected that the officers would act in this way; but still it was very provoking.

CHAPTER CCIII.

DETAILS SOME MISADVENTURES ON THE ROAD TO NEWGATE WITH THEIR PRISONERS.

THE only consolation that Claude Duval and May now had was that the officers did not make any resistance to their riding side by side. Luke, too, was permitted to ride with them.

The order of the march, then, consisted of two officers in advance, six on each side, and the remainder, with Mr. Lawson, the magistrate, behind the prisoners.

"Now, attend to me," said Lawson, speaking with difficulty, on account of the bandages that were about his face. "Upon the least attempt to escape, as I don't feel at all inclined to run after you with this wound of mine, I shall order these men who are with me to fire at you, and then you must fall, for there are pistols enough to sweep the road with bullets."

Claude and his friends made no answer whatever to this speech from the magistrate.

"Very good," added Lawson. "You need not speak; but I am quite satisfied that you heard me, and that is sufficient for me. Now, my men, move on."

They made their way through the rain out of the little wood into the cross-road again, and from thence they got into the high-road and turned their horses' heads towards London.

For some little time May could not speak to Claude for the tears that were gathering each moment in her eyes ; but at last she said to him, in a low voice—

"Claude—Claude, you do not look at me."

Duval had been in deep thought, but now he started, as he replied—

"Not look at you, May ? Oh, I was thinking of you and you only, dear one."

"Think not of me. It is of yourself that I would have you think, Claude. Oh, can you not project some plan of escape ? It is too terrible to think that you should continue as you are now."

"If I could only save you !"

"Oh, no—no, think not of me."

"I tell you what it is," said Luke ; "it is useless to contend in this way about who should think of escaping and who should not. If we are to do anything good at all, we shall all three get away ; but I must own that I don't see just now much chance of such an event."

"Alas, no !" said May.

"Nor I," said Claude.

"Please, Mr. Lawson," said one of the officers, "they are all of them consulting together, I know, about getting away."

"Shoot them if they attempt it," was the reply. "What is the use of all their consultations? They will be in Newgate in a couple of hours. I only wish I could ride faster, but if I attempt it the wounds in my face bleed afresh."

"They will not separate us yet," said May.

"No—no. They think us so utterly helpless."

"And yet," said Luke, speaking in the same low cautious tone that they all three now conversed in, "I am not without a hope that something may turn up yet to give us a chance of shaking off our present bondage."

Claude shook his head.

"You despond, Claude," said May.

"Call it not desponding, May," he replied, "but I really cannot flatter myself just now with any hopes of escape. Are we not here unarmed, and manacled besides ?"

"Yes, but——"

What May was about to say was interrupted by such a clap of thunder, that the horses one and all started and reared, and would scarcely be quieted, and then the sky rapidly darkened as if the night were coming suddenly, and hours before its time.

"Ah, this storm, that seemed as though it were over," said Luke, "had, in reality, only begun. I think we shall have the worst of it now. How dark it is."

"It is, indeed."

"Closer to your prisoners," cried Mr. Lawson ; "keep your pistols in youi hands, officers, and fire upon them if I give you the word to do so. We won't stand any nonsense because there is a little thunder in the air."

"All's right, sir. We had better push on."

"I cannot go quicker ; I am faint already with the loss of blood."

"Claude ?" whispered Luke.

"Yes, Luke ?"

"That Lawson will be done up soon. I have had my eye upon him. He can hardly keep his seat in his saddle now. The wound that May gave him has settled him for some time, although he don't like to own it."

The thunder roared and rattled again through the heavens, but it was rather surprising that they saw no lightning. The probability was that there we some low scudding clouds between the storm-clouds and the earth, which hid the lightning's flash.

"They will never go on through this," said Claude. "Do you know exactly where we are, Luke?"

"Yes, I do; we are close to the 'Willow Branch.'"

"What, the inn called such?"

"Yes, to be sure; and if we could only get them to stop there for an hour or so, I rather think Tom Oaks, who keeps it, would try what he could do in the way of outwitting the officers."

"I know he would."

"So do I. The fact is, he does a little in our line, and his brother, Jem Oaks, is a smuggler at the back of the Isle of Wight, and Tom gets rid of his goods for him."

"But you may depend the officers are aware of what sort of a house the Willow Branch is, and so they will not stop at it if they can by any possibility avoid it."

"We shall see."

"There is the rain," said May.

Some large spots of rain began to fall, and made a terrible pattering upon the leaves of the trees on the road-side. The small thick rain that had before been coming down rather smartly, had entirely ceased, and what was now reaching the earth was evidently the contents of a thunder-cloud. In fact, it was quite evident that the sort of weather that had begun would go on as long as the wind remained in its present quarter of the heavens. There might be breaks in the clouds, but that would be all.

The officers did not seem to relish the state of things, and at last one of them said—

"Mr. Lawson, it will be better to get shelter somewhere, sir, if it is all the same to you, till this spurt of a storm shall blow over, sir."

The magistrate made no answer to this.

"He won't reply to them," said Claude.

"He cannot," said Luke. "Only look at him now. He is rocking to and fro on his saddle. He can't speak, or else he would. Ah, he will be down directly, as sure as fate, and there he goes."

After reeling to and fro for a few moments, Mr. Lawson, who had held up so long against his wound, suddenly could do so no longer, but fainted, and fell from his horse to the roadway.

There was an instant halt among the officers, and one cried out—

"Hilloa, there he goes. I thought how it would be. He's down now, I say."

"Halt!" cried another. "Halt!"

"Look to the prisoners," cried a third. "It won't do to neglect them, I tell you."

"All's right—all's right."

Half a dozen of the officers rode up to the side of Claude Duval and his friends, and pointed their pistols towards them, one saying as they did so—

"Don't try any nonsense, Duval, for if you do, we must fire at you."

"Please yourselves," said Claude, with all the indifference in the world. "I am no way particular, I assure you."

Mr. Lawson was raised from the ground, and there was rather a discussion among the officers to know whether he was dead or not, till Harrison, the man who had some surgical skill, declared that he had only fainted.

"However," said Harrison, "we must get him to some house or another, for it won't do for him to go any further in this state. I told him he would not be able to go on, but there is no stopping him when once he takes a thing into his head, I know well enough."

The rain came down more quickly.

"There is a house a little further on," cried one of the foremost of the officers. "I can just see it."

"Push on, then, for it," said Harrison. "What is it? A public-house, or what?"

"Don't know yet, sir."

"Come on, though. Never mind what it is; we must get Mr. Lawson to bed. He will bleed to death if he is jolted much more. Carry him between you as well as you can."

The thunder roared again overhead, and this time they saw the lightning most vividly. The rain, too, was each moment on the increase, and now the party went on in much the same order as before, except that the officers who followed the prisoners closed rather more upon them, and kept their pistols actually pointed towards them, they were so afraid of some effort upon their parts to escape.

We can hardly wonder, after what we know of the history of Claude Duval, that the officers should be so full of precaution, for the many hair breadth escapes he had had, and the many daring tricks he had played the authorities from time to time, had had the effect of making them believe that they could hardly ever say they had him secure.

Luke did not like to say anything now, for fear the officers, who were so near at hand, would hear him; but he gave Claude an expressive look as a rounded part of the road being cleared brought them in sight of the Willow Branch Inn by the road-side.

"Why, it's the Willow Branch!" said one of the officers.

"No matter what they call it," said Harrison, "we must make some sort of a stop there."

"Yes," said the officer who had spoken; "but it's rather a kind of family house the Willow Branch is, and it is suspected it has afforded shelter to more than one knight of the road. I don't know of my own knowledge anything against it; but some of our men say that they mean to have an eye on it."

"Never mind; we must just stop there, for there is no other resource now. There are enough of you to take care of each other, and the prisoners, too, I rather think."

The whole party in a few moments drew up at the door of the Willow Branch Inn, and Mr. Lawson was carried in by two of the officers. In good truth, he did look much more dead than alive.

These had, however, with their burthen only got half way across the threshold, when a man met them, and cried out—

"God bless me! what is all this about?"

"Get out of the way," said Harrison. "This gentleman is wounded. It is Mr. Lawson, the magistrate. Who are you?"

"Why, I'm the landlord, gentlemen, if you please. But you really don't mean to say that anybody has been and done so very wrong a thing as to wound the great, and the active, and the respectable Mr. Lawson? Oh, dear— oh, dear! what will the world come to?"

CHAPTER CCIV.

SHOWS WHAT TOOK PLACE AT TOM OAKS'S, WILLOW BRANCH INN.

"THAT'S Tom Oaks, all over," said Claude Duval to May. "He will thoroughly confuse the officers."

"And save you?"

"I cannot say that. A man may have a good will to do a deed, but may not know how to set about it, you see, exactly. Still, this stop at this place is in our favour, May. Be of good heart."

"I am of all the better heart, Claude, that I see you are more cheerful than you were."

"The first shock is over."

"Thank Heaven that it is so. Oh, Claude! I would fain think and hope that all will yet be well."

"Come in—oh, dear me!—come in with poor, dear, respectable Mr. Lawson," cried Tom Oaks, the landlord. "Dear me—dear me! what a stormy day, too, Wife—wife! wife, I say! make up the best bed for the active, exemplary Mr. Lawson, the magistrate. Some awful wretch, without the fear of the law before his eyes, has given him a nob on his excellent head."

"No," said Harrison, "you are wrong there, for it is a pistol-bullet in his face."

"Wife, I am wrong. It is a pistol-bullet in his illustrious face. Oh, what a thing it is that such dreadful wretches should be in the world! This way, gents—this way. While my wife gets the bed ready, pray walk into the bar-parlour."

"Hark you, Mr. Oaks," said one of the officers, "you know me, I rather think."

"Eh? You, sir?"

"Yes—look at me."

"Well, I—really I don't know. Are you the tax-gatherer, sir? I thought I had seen your face once before."

"No, Mr. Oaks. My name is Jeffries. I am a Bow Street officer, and I once stopped here with a prisoner, and, somehow, the prisoner got away. Do you recollect that?"

"You don't say so?"

"Yes, I do."

"Did you nab him again, Mr. J.?"

"Curse your impudence! you know well enough that I did not! But recollect that there are rather too many of us to play any tricks to now. We have three prisoners, and we mean to keep them, Master Oaks; so, if you consult your own safety, you will keep yourself quiet upon this occasion."

"Oh, dear, sir, I'm one of the quietest men in the world, I rather think. I could get a certificate of respectability from the clergyman of the parish, and all the churchwardens. The idea that the Willow Branch should for one moment be supsected of being otherwise than a most delightfully respectable house!"

"Oh, gammon!"

"What did you say, sir?"

"Gammon."

"Oh, very good. I prefer the cushion of bacon to the gammon any day; but if there is a gammon in the house, you shall have it, you may depend."

The officer shook his head as Tom Oaks made a rush into the inn for the purpose, it appeared, of doing all he could for the comfort of Mr. Lawson; but the officers shrewdly suspected that his sympathies lay all the other way. It was then that Harrison and Jeffries came up to Claude Duval, and the latter said to him—

"Duval, we are only going to do our duty by taking care that you do not escape. It is a duty that we must not trifle with ; and so, upon my word as a man, I beg to assure you that, although I am quite willing to make you as comfortable as I can, I must and will shoot you if you try any tricks upon us."

"That is our determination," said Harrison.

"Gentlemen," said Duval, "your candour is very great, and very much to your credit ; but, in the meantime, we are getting wet through, for this rain is no trifle."

"Come in."

The officers led Duval, and May, and Luke into the bar-parlour of the public-house, and Tom Oaks pretended to lift up his hands in astonishment, as he said—

"Why, goodness gracious, you don't mean to say that these are suspicious characters?"

"Rather," said Jeffries.

CLAUDE AND LUKE ENTER THE SECRET PANEL IN THE OLD CHATEAU.

"Well, now, a poor, unsuspicious, hark-working man may be deceived. They really look to me so very respectable, that I declare to you gents, if they had come alone to this inn, I should have cheerfully trusted them to any amount within my means, that I should.   Oh, what a world we do live in, to be sure!"

" And what a humbug you are!" said Jeffries.

" Me, sir? Do you allude to me?"

" I do."

" Then, sir, I can assure you that I have not the remotest relationship to you or your family, so I don't very well see how I can be a very great humbug."

The other officers laughed at this, but Jeffries cried out—

" Pshaw! Stuff! Give us something to drink."

" Well," said Harrison, " you can drink what you like, as long as you look after the prisoners. I must go and see how Mr. Lawson is. I suppose they have put him to bed by this time."

Three chairs were placed side by side for the prisoners, and then Claude Duval said to Jeffries—

" You were kind enough to say that you would make me as comfortable as you could, consistent with your duty. If you really meant that, I ask you to take the cord off the wrists of Mrs. Duval here. It is not manly of you all to be so afraid of a woman that you are forced to tie her hands."

" Thank you, Claude," said Jeffries. " I beg to say that I prefer leaving things just as they are. When we get to Newgate there will, perhaps, be a different arrangement, but just now you must put up with a little inconvenience."

Claude bit his lips with vexation, but May said—

" Do not mind it, Claude. The cord don't hurt me now, I assure you."

" Then, perhaps," said Jeffries, " it is getting too loose."

As he spoke he stepped up to May; but Claude Duval was no longer able to control his passion, and rising on the moment, he raised both his hands, and brought them down together upon the head of Jeffries.

The corner of the handcuffs hit him, and down went the officer as if he had been felled by a mallet.

" Fire at him! Shoot him!" cried one.

" No—no," said another. " What's the use? It serves Jeffries right. Hold hard, all of you. Couldn't he let the young woman alone?"

" Well, but——"

" Oh, be quiet!"

" Jeffries is killed!"

" No, he isn't; and if he is, you know, you must take orders from me. I saw the whole affair. It was not an attempt to escape—far from it. I say, Claude Duval did what I would have done, and what you would have done, all of you, if you are men."

" Oh, Claude—Claude!" sobbed May.

" Peace, May—peace. I could not sit still and see you thus insulted."

" Oh, gracious providence," said Tom Oaks, " here is my excellent friend, Jeffries, I am afraid, rather stupider than usual."

Jeffries rose to a sitting posture, and as he rubbed his head, he made the most horrible faces, indicative of the pain that he was in, so that the other officers could not, for the life of them, keep from laughing, and but for the many anxieties that beset him, Claude Duval must have laughed likewise.

" D—n it!" said Jeffries. " What was that?"

" Something fell on your head," said Tom Oaks, pretending to look up at the ceiling with curious eyes.

" Did it?"

" Yes, my dear sir; and I'm afraid it has made a slight bump, do you know."

" A slight bump do you call it?" said Jeffries, rubbing his head, and making a few more dreadful faces.

The officers all burst into a roar, and Jeffries looked from one to the other with such an amazed look, that it was truly absurd to see him.

" What's all this?" said Harrison, making his appearance now in the bar-parlour. "What's the meaning of all this, I should like to know? Why, Jeffries, you seem fond of rather a low seat. What makes you choose the floor —eh?"

"Something came on my head, and I feel rather confused," said Jeffries, as he scrambled to his feet with some difficulty. "I don't know what it was; but it was something."

"A rusty nail, I rather think," said Tom Oaks, "or a dead fly, perhaps, gents."

The officers shook their heads and laughed; but as the knock on the head that Jeffries had got had evidently produced a complete oblivion for the time present, at all events, of the circumstances under which he got it, they did not think proper to give him any further information upon the subject.

"Well, it's a queer thing that anything should fall upon your head, Mr. Jeffries," said Harrison; "but Mr. Lawson is getting worse, I can tell you."

"And so is the storm," said one of the officers.

"Well, I want one of you to ride off to the nearest justice of the peace, and another to the nearest doctor, for I don't mean to take upon myself to do anything more in the case than I have done, or I may be blamed."

"Very good. Who is to go?"

"You, Jones, to the magistrate, and you, Wilkins, for the doctor."

The two men knew that they must obey orders; and as Harrison was a personal follower of Mr. Lawson's, and had acted the part of a highwayman with him, the officers did not dispute the command; but they turned to Oaks, and said—

"Where is there a justice?"

"And where is there a doctor?"

"Hem!" said Oaks; "a justice and a doctor? Well, it's a pleasing as well as a rather remarkable circumstance, that I am in a position to answer both those important inquiries at once, I may say at once. Wife!—wife!"

"Yes, Tom?"

"Bring a kettle of hot-water. The gents will take brandy-and-water, of course."

"Yes, Tom—I'm coming."

"Very good. Well, gents, sit down, and make yourselves as comfortable as you can. Lor! how it does rain, to be sure. Well, I never! It is coming down above a bit. And pray, gents, who is this individual that you, no doubt, very properly have in custody?"

Mr. Oaks pointed to Claude.

"Never you mind that," said Harrison. "What you are wanted to do is to direct these men to a justice, and to a surgeon."

"Oh, very good. Well, to find the justice, you go on to the right about half-a-mile, and then you turn off by Hobbs's turnip field, and after that you come to Nobbs's paddock, and you keep alongside of that till you come to Stubbs's well; but you needn't get down Stubbs's well, because he is a very particular man, and might not fancy the water afterwards, you see, and then there would be quite a disturbance in the parish."

"Hold your cursed tongue!" cried Harrison. "Go, my men, and inquire of the first person you meet. You will get no information from this fellow."

CHAPTER CCV.

AFFAIRS GROW RATHER CRITICAL AT THE WILLOW BRANCH.

THE anger of the chief officer against Tom Oaks was so great, that he would have knocked him down if he had dared do so; but the idea of creating another disturbance in the place did not present itself with any recommendatory features, so he thought it was as well to let him alone.

"Have we no chance ?" whispered Luke to Claude.

"Not yet."

" I'm afraid not at all."

"Oh, yes.   Trust to Tom Oaks."

At this moment Tom Oaks, as he passed May, just said in her ear—

"All's right."

The words were not much in themselves, but there was something so hopeful about them, that they cheered her up wonderfully.

"Claude ?" she said.

"Yes, May, dear ?"

"I seem now as if I had a presentiment that you would be yet saved, do you know, Claude."

"I hope it is a true one.   Speak low, May, whatever you do, for there are sharp ears about us."

"Yes—oh, yes."

"What makes you hopeful, then, of our condition ?"

"The landlord has just passed me, and he said—' All's right.' "

"If so, then you may depend that he has some plan of operation to try and rescue us.   Heaven send he may be successful in it.   He will do his best, I feel convinced."

"Wife !" cried Tom Oaks, "the hot-water.   Oh, here it is."

"Well, we will just take a glass, and then be off to London with our prisoners," said Harrison; "for we must not stay here.   How do you feel now, Jeffries ?"

"I hardly know.   Confound it, I can't think what it was that fell upon my head, just now.   But I suppose we mustn't go till a magistrate comes."

"Well, no.   I don't like to take the responsibility on myself of doing anything.   You see, while Mr. Lawson was up and about, it was all right, as he is in the commission of the peace; but now it's rather another thing, and I don't know whether to take the prisoners to Bow Street or to Newgate."

Claude, and Luke, and May heard this with satisfaction.   They knew there was no committal under the hand of a magistrate against them, although the personal attendance of Mr. Lawson at Newgate would have sufficed to get them incarcerated there at once; otherwise, the city prison was only for offenders committed for trial at the Old Bailey, and not for the detention of prisoners in the first instance.

"Claude," said Luke, "they won't find a magistrate in a hurry, I rather think."

" No ?"

"No, they won't.   The nearest to here, now that Squire Lawson, as he is called, is upset, is Colonel Bernley, and his place is nine miles off.   Then, too, he may be in town."

"So he may.   There is now hope."

At this moment one of the officers, who had been sent for a magistrate, came back, and entered the room, with the rain dripping from his clothes.

"Oh, Mr. Harrison," he said, "they tell me that there is no other magistrate for nine miles off but Mr. Lawson."

"The deuce there isn't.   Jeffries, what is to be done?   Is your head-piece sufficiently recovered to know what to be at for the best ?"

"Yes," said Jeffries, shaking his head.   "I say, come on to Newgate, and I don't doubt but that they will take care of our prisoners till to-morrow morning, at all events, and then it will be all right."

"But it's coming on to rain like the very devil !" said the officer who had been out in it.   "Look at me."

As he spoke, this officer turned round and round in the most comical manner in the world, and showed how saturated he was with rain. The others looked rather serious.

"Wife—wife!" cried the landlord.

"Yes, Tom?"

"Be sure you brown that leg of pork well, and take care that the turkey is properly boiled."

"Yes, Tom."

"Hem!" said Harrison, "Do you mean to say that you have now cooking a leg of pork and a boiled turkey?"

"Oh, yes, sir," said Tom. "The pork is being roasted, and is the finest leg you ever saw. The lean is like chicken, it is so sweet and so white, and there is only just fat enough to give it a rich creamy kind of flavour. It will be cooked to perfection, and nicely browned all over, and it will come up to table with hot plates, and you will hear it hissing and frizzling away even although taken up from the fire; and then when you put the knife in, out will gush the rich gravy, and the joint will gape open, and you will see how white and well done it is, too; and then you will see——"

"I'll stay to dinner—I'll stay to dinner," cried Harrison. "I do think it will be best to stay to dinner."

"So do I," said Jeffries. "My head is very much better, and I don't think the bump on it is so very large, after all; and if there is anything more than another that I think truly delightful, it is a hot roast leg of pork."

"Then the turkey," cried the landlord, "it weighed fourteen pounds before it was put into the saucepan to boil. It is as fat as fresh butter and as plump—ah, as plump as you can fancy it possible for a turkey to be; and it, too, will be done to a nicety, for my wife is one of the best cooks in all England; and when it comes up to table, then you will see it as white as milk, and just swaying to and fro on the dish like a barrel, it is so round and plump is that turkey; and upon my life, you may cut slices off it as you would off a round of beef and, by Jove, they will absolutely melt in your mouth, it is so tender."

"Have you got any baked potatoes?" cried one of the officers.

"Loads under the leg of pork. Delicious!"

"Is the pork stuffed?" said another.

"Crammed with rich stuffing."

"Can you let us have a slice of bacon with the turkey?" said a third.

"There is a Westphalia ham now cooking to eat with it. It weighs a matter of seventeen pounds if it weighs an ounce, I should say."

"We will dine here," cried all the officers in chorus.

"I feel quite queer," said Harrison, "for want of that leg of pork. I—I feel as if—oh, I could eat it all."

Bang—rattle and boom! came the thunder at this moment, and they all paused aghast at the dense darkness that swept over the face of nature.

"It's a good thing you are not on the road, gents," said the landlord, after rather a long pause. "This is not an evening to turn out a dog in."

"How dark it is!"

"Yes," said Jeffries, "but its nigh to sunset, recollect. Well, comrades, I propose that we all dine here, and that we then, if the storm has abated, start for London."

"Agreed—agreed."

"Landlord," said Harrison, after a whispered conference with Jeffries, "have you any room in the house where we could lock up the prisoners till it is time for us to go?"

"Why, a—well, I think I have."

"Very well. Now, look you, we are going to take such measures as will put an effectual stop to anything in the shape of an attempted escape, but we don't want while dining to be hampered with the care of Claude Duval and his friends."

"Certainly not. Step this way, and I will show you a room that I don't think it is at all possible they will be able to get out of, for the lock is good and the door is strong.”

“ We shall not wholly rely upon locks and doors, though, for all that,” said Jeffries.

While the other officers looked to the safety of the prisoners, the landlord conducted Harrison and Jeffries to a room on the first floor of the house, and said as he flung the door of it open—

“ This is the safest room I have, gents, if you think it will answer your purpose.”

“ Ah—ah,” said Harrison. “ What other rooms have you upon this floor, landlord? I suppose there are others?”

“ There’s one next to this that I don’t recommend so much as this, because, you see, the door is not as strong, and, indeed, I think you cannot do better than place them here.”

The two officers winked at each other, as much as to say—“ How green we should be to place our prisoners just where this man recommends us;” and then Jeffries said mildly—

“ Let us look at the next room.”

“ Well, of course, gents, I can show it to you,” said Tom Oaks, “ but I recommend this one, I assure you, for greater security.”

The other room was smaller, but if it had been larger, or if the door and its lock had been ten times worse than it was, the officers would have chosen it for the simple reason that Tom Oaks did not wish them to do so. At all events, they thought that he did not wish them to do so, which came to the same thing, so far as they were concerned.

The real fact was, that it did not matter to him one straw which room they took possession of, for he had his own mode of action connected as well with one as the other.

They at once, then, declared that their choice had fallen upon the smaller of the rooms, and Tom Oaks took care to put on a look of chagrin, as though their doing so had rather deranged some plans of his.

In the course of five minutes more Claude Duval, and Luke, and May, were placed in the room, and locked in ; but, as the officers had said, they did not by any means depend upon the security of the room for the retention of their prisoners, but they placed sentinels both within and without the house, that rendered escape next to impossible.

It was rather a sore trial to those who were placed upon duty as sentinels to know that the others were dining off the delicious leg of pork and the extraordinary turkey, but Harrison and Jeffries promised that they should be relieved every half hour, so that they had not long to wait.

One officer, then, was placed upon the landing outside the door of the room in which the prisoners were placed, and another was left at the outer door of the house, while it was made the special business of four others, well armed, to go round and round the house, two one way and two another, in order to render escape by any such mode of egress out of the question.

The landlord saw with some dismay these capital arrangements for the sure detention of the prisoners.

There was a slight suspicion in the minds of some of the officers that Mr. Tom Oaks had been rather romancing a little about the leg of pork and the turkey ; but such was not the fact. The only thing that he had drawn the long bow concerning was the Westphalia ham.

That ham certainly was doubtful, but when in talking in so very magnificent a style as Mr. Tom Oaks strove to talk in, surely he may be excused for such a trifling addition to the affair as a Westphalia ham may be considered.

The officers, however, were very well contented with what he could place before them without the ham at all. Indeed, they were rather surprised to find such fare as they did at all at such an out of the way rural little inn ; but then they did not know, whatever might be their suspicions, exactly what sort of customers dropped into that little roadside hostel.

CHAPTER CCVI.

THE OFFICERS FANCY THEY HAVE THEIR THREE PRISONERS SAFE IN A COACH.

THE situation of Claude and Luke and May in a now dark room, for night had come on very abruptly, at the Willow Branch Inn, was anything but delightful. They had ample time to reflect upon the circumstances that had led to their arrest, and upon the possible consequences that might result from it now that it had taken place.

.Perhaps Claude was more desponding than one would have supposed such a person as he would likely have been, considering all things; but the real fact was, that not one thought crossed his mind concerning his own fate.

The sole consideration that gave Duval uneasiness, and that uneasiness was of the highest possible character, consisted in the fact that by his want of caution and suspicion he had led May and Luke into this fresh and painful position.

It appeared to him, although the reader will certainly see that such was not in reality the case, that he, and he only, was to blame for all that had occurred. He was the leader of the party, and they did but follow him. He should have suspected the men who appeared to be upon such friendly terms with him and his. He should have rescued his attached follower, Luke, and his dear and much loved May, from the danger that had threatened them, and which had now burst over them like a thunder-cloud, and spread destruction in its progress.

Such were the thoughts and feelings of Claude Duval, however unjust they were to himself; and that they were unjust, the reader will agree with us in saying.

It was such a feeling, then, that imparted to the mind of Duval much despair, and it was to reason him from that, for she guessed well its cause, that May spoke to him.

"Claude," she said, "Claude, why is it that you look so depressed? for although this room is dark, and I can but dimly see here the outline of your face, yet I know well, by your manner and tone, that you do look depressed."

"Can you ask, May?"

"Yes, Claude, I do ask, and, I am sure, that Luke will join me in so asking; will you not, Luke?"

"Freely I will.'

"Then listen to me," said Claude Duval. "I feel—and nothing that you can say to the contrary in your wish to save me from the pangs of self-reproach will persuade me to the contrary—that it is I who have been the cause of this great misfortune that has happened to us."

"You, Claude?"

"Yes, May, it is I who am to blame. I should, in my large experience, have suspected—nay, I should have known that that man Lawson was a spy, and that there was danger in following him."

"And this depresses you?"

"It does."

"Well, Claude, I will not attempt to argue with you upon the subject, or to say whether you ought or ought not to have suspected that man who has betrayed us; but if you think that you have been unwise in any such way, it is clearly your duty, as it will, I am sure, be the first wish of your heart, to repair such an error."

"Repair it? I would do so with my life, if such a sacrifice would suffice to place you and Luke at liberty."

"Your dying, Claude, would serve us little; your living might serve us much. You must shake off this depression that has seized upon you, and which will prevent you from doing anything for us, Claude, and you must strive to free us from this place. Do you understand me?"

"I do—I do."

"And you will? for oh, Claude, in freeing us you will free yourself. Do you think that I would value liberty if deprived of you? No—no!"

"My darling, May, I now well understand that all you have been saying under the pretence that it is dictated by considerations for your own safety, is in reality upon my account. Do not deny it, it is so."

May had kept up very well till then, but the kind tone in which Duval spoke to her overcame her courage, and she burst into tears.

Luke retreated as far as he could to the end of the room, and amused himself in the execution of a very low-toned whistle, while Claude, as he pressed May to his heart, whispered to her—

"Too well—oh, much too well for your own peace and happiness do I know your devotion to me, May. But dry those tears; I will not give way to the depressing effects of the position in which we now are, but I will do all that may lie in the pale of man to rescue myself and you and Luke."

"But, Claude?"

"What would you say, dear one?"

"You need not do that at the expense of too much danger. Recollect, it is possible even to purchase liberty at too high a price."

"Nay, hardly."

"Oh, yes—yes, Claude! Recollect that without you I derive no liberty; and I will accept none."

"Well, well, we will go, or stay together."

"That is right, Claude. Luke, what say you?"

"To what?"

"Why, Claude and I have made a resolution—a sort of compact—that we will escape together, or not escape at all. Will you join us?"

"With all my heart. I am one who feels he has so little hold of life at all, unless he has that hold in the society he most prizes, that if you and Claude be not safe and free, I care not what they do to me."

"Hist!" said a voice at this moment. "Hist!"

"What is that?" said May.

"Hist!" said the voice again. "Duval!"

"I am here," said Duval. "Who are you who speak? I don't know where the voice comes from; and, as for seeing in this darkness, it is quite out of the question. Where are you?"

"Here. But don't speak so loud, whatever you do. Be quiet. I am Tom Oaks. Don't you know my voice?"

"I do now."

"Very good. I suppose you are hungry, to begin with, and thirsty in the second place? So, I have brought you something to eat, and something to drink, you see. Drink."

"Thank you. But where in the name of all that's odd are you?"

"Here, on top of the bedstead."

"How did you get there?"

"Oh, easily enough. Through the floor of the room above here. But, I say, Claude, it was rather queer of you to get taken in by Squire Lawson in the way you were, don't you think?"

"It was."

"Well, it's no use bothering you about that now. I rather think it will be some time before he feels much comfort again. I have been telling him that it is a sort of retribution for him since, and exhorting him to patience, till he is nearly mad with rage and impatience. Ha—ha! Now you can see me, I suppose, Claude?"